PENGUIN BOOKS

THE MIRROR OF BEAUTY

Acclaimed writer Shamsur Rahman Faruqi is also modern Urdu's most celebrated critic. He was editor and publisher of the highly regarded literary journal *Shabkhoon*, and is the author of a landmark four-volume study of the poet Mir Taqi Mir, and another four-volume work on Urdu's immense oral romance, *Dastan-e Amir Hamza*. He received the prestigious Saraswati Samman in 1996 for his contribution to Urdu literature. *The Mirror of Beauty*, originally published in Urdu to huge acclaim, is his first novel.

Praise for *The Mirror of Beauty*

'A true epic, *The Mirror of Beauty* is the Koh-i-Noor of Indian novels: majestic, glittering, mysterious. It will bring you a joy no book ever has.'
—Mohammed Hanif

'In every language there is a defining work of literature which absorbs all of its beauty, majesty, and powers of storytelling to create something in whose comparison future works will be judged. In *The Mirror of Beauty* Faruqi has created such a novel. His immaculate English translation takes that work further, and puts both Urdu language and world literature in his debt.'
—Musharraf Ali Farooqi

'A lovely and magical book. Shamsur Rahman Faruqi weaves history and illusion into one beautiful pattern. He clothes us richly in our past.'
—Nadeem Aslam

'An erudite, amazing historical novel, elegiac in tone and written with heartfelt attention to the details and the rituals of a lost culture.'
—Orhan Pamuk

'Poetry in slow motion.'
—*Financial Express*

'. . . a priceless portrait of a vanished time . . .'
—*Caravan*

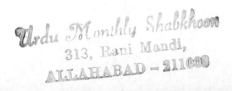

'A thing of beauty.'
—*The Hindu*

'Faruqi . . . has put together that pre-1857 Indo-Islamic world in such minute, painstaking detail that you actually see it unfold in your mind's eye: even the tiniest blade of grass by the roadside is vivid and alive.'
—*DNA*

'In the pages of this novel, an entire culture becomes whole again, salvaged from the wounds of history.'
—*Indian Express*

'*The Mirror of Beauty* is a paean to Indo-Islamic culture.'
—*Outlook*

'It's a book to be savoured . . . not to be gobbled up.'
—*Tribune*, New Delhi

'[Faruqi] brings alive our past in all its splendor and that is a magnificent achievement.'
—*Sunday Guardian*

'In *The Mirror of Beauty*, Shamsur Rahman Faruqi has packed the entire history of a fading era . . . All this makes for a cornucopia: the novel has layers stacked upon layers . . .'
—*Telegraph*

Praise for the Urdu and Hindi editions

'This novel creates in us the ability to rise above our cultural conflicts and uneasinesses.'
—Kedar Nath Singh in *Sakhi*

'Like stories of yore, which took away your sleep and which seemed endless, when this novel came to an end, I felt that I had nothing else to do in the world now.'
—Sadiqur Rahman Kidwai in *Urdu Adab*

'As the container of all the subtle truths about our history in the 18th and the 19th centuries, this novel is a must-read for anyone who seeks to know the history of the honour of our cultural past.'
—Vandana Rag in *Vasudha*

'You are in the presence of great poetic dignity . . . Events and characters become resident in the reader's heart and mind and become citizens of the land of the reader's own experience.'
—Vishwanath Tripathi in *Katha Des*

THE MIRROR OF BEAUTY

Being the tale of an extraordinary woman in nineteenth-century India who struggled all her life to choose for herself against all odds; narrated as a politico-historical romance

SHAMSUR RAHMAN FARUQI

PENGUIN BOOKS

PENGUIN BOOKS
Published by the Penguin Group
Penguin Books India Pvt. Ltd, 7th Floor, Infinity Tower C, DLF Cyber City, Gurgaon 122 002, Haryana, India
Penguin Group (USA) Inc., 375 Hudson Street, New York, New York 10014, USA
Penguin Group (Canada), 90 Eglinton Avenue East, Suite 700, Toronto, Ontario, M4P 2Y3, Canada
Penguin Books Ltd, 80 Strand, London WC2R 0RL, England
Penguin Ireland, 25 St Stephen's Green, Dublin 2, Ireland (a division of Penguin Books Ltd)
Penguin Group (Australia), 707 Collins Street, Melbourne, Victoria 3008, Australia
Penguin Group (NZ), 67 Apollo Drive, Rosedale, Auckland 0632, New Zealand
Penguin Books (South Africa) (Pty) Ltd, Block D, Rosebank Office Park, 181 Jan Smuts Avenue, Parktown North, Johannesburg 2193, South Africa

Penguin Books Ltd, Registered Offices: 80 Strand, London WC2R 0RL, England

First published in India in Urdu as ***Kai Chand The Sar-e Asman*** by Penguin-Yatra, New Delhi; and in Pakistan by Scheherazade, Karachi, 2006
First published in Hamish Hamilton by Penguin Books India 2013

Published in Penguin Books 2014

10 9 8 7 6 5 4 3 2

ISBN 9780143422730

Typeset in Dante MT by R. Ajith Kumar, New Delhi
Printed at Repro India Ltd, Navi Mumbai

A PENGUIN RANDOM HOUSE COMPANY

Dedicated to

29 C, Hastings Road, Allahabad, its
Lady of the House, and the two girls who are
the radiant roses of this garden and who
may perhaps be its keepers and gardeners in the future

Recorded at Allahabad, December 2005

*

Two years after

She, who for a long time—more than half a century in fact,
Made me happy with all her heart and body—
I must have done some wrong, for suddenly, she
Left our home and went to live where nothing lives.

You were my friend, my lover, safe home for my heart,
You breathed a fragrance, familiar, friendly, welcome;
During the day I may sometimes stray into a smile,
To fall asleep without weeping, such nights are rare now.

19 October 2007

CONTENTS

BOOK 5

BOOK 6

FAMILY TREES

The Ancestors of Wazir Khanam

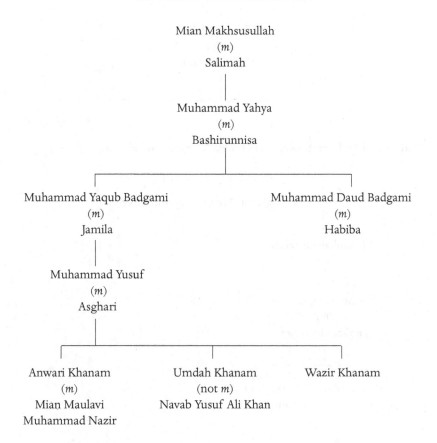

Mian Makhsusullah
(*m*)
Salimah

Muhammad Yahya
(*m*)
Bashirunnisa

Muhammad Yaqub Badgami
(*m*)
Jamila

Muhammad Daud Badgami
(*m*)
Habiba

Muhammad Yusuf
(*m*)
Asghari

Anwari Khanam
(*m*)
Mian Maulavi
Muhammad Nazir

Umdah Khanam
(not *m*)
Navab Yusuf Ali Khan

Wazir Khanam

Marston Blake and Wazir Khanam

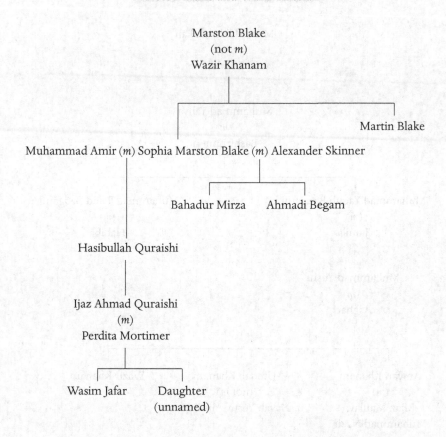

Marston Blake
(not *m*)
Wazir Khanam

Martin Blake

Muhammad Amir (*m*) Sophia Marston Blake (*m*) Alexander Skinner

Bahadur Mirza   Ahmadi Begam

Hasibullah Quraishi

Ijaz Ahmad Quraishi
(*m*)
Perdita Mortimer

Wasim Jafar   Daughter
(unnamed)

Navab Shamsuddin Ahmad Khan and Wazir Khanam

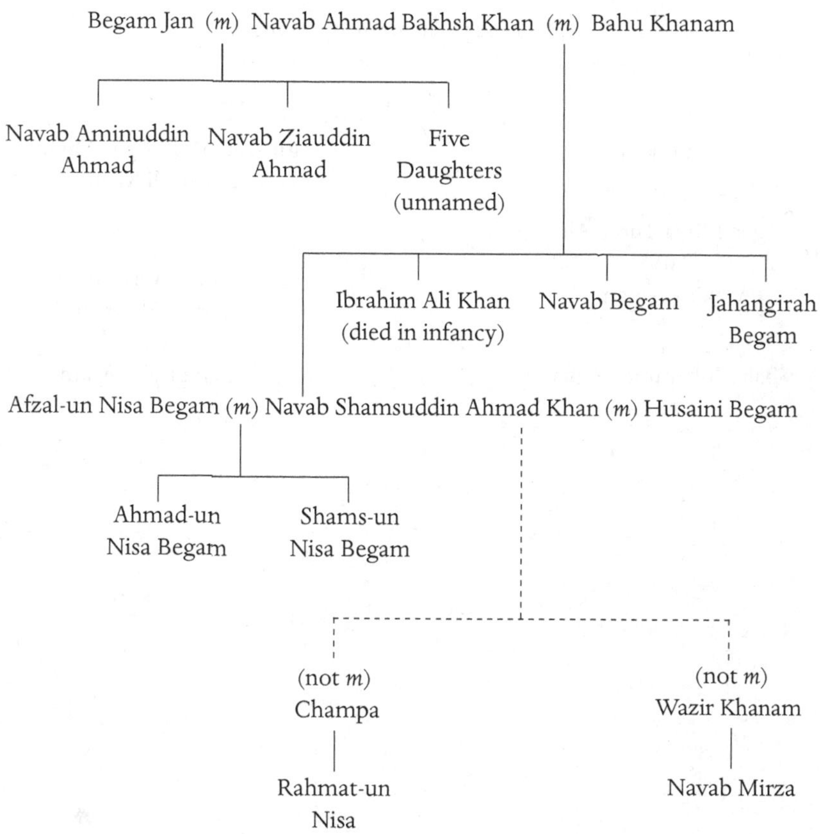

Agha Mirza Turab Ali and Wazir Khanam

Agha Mirza Muhammad Ahsan Ali

- Son (unnamed)
  - Agha Mirza Turab Ali (*m*) Wazir Khanam
    - Shah Muhammad Agha
- Itibar-ul Mulk Agha Mirza Amjad Ali Khan
  - Mirza Muhammad Azam Ali Khan (*m*) Jahangirah Begam

Mirza Fathul Mulk Bahadur and Wazir Khanam

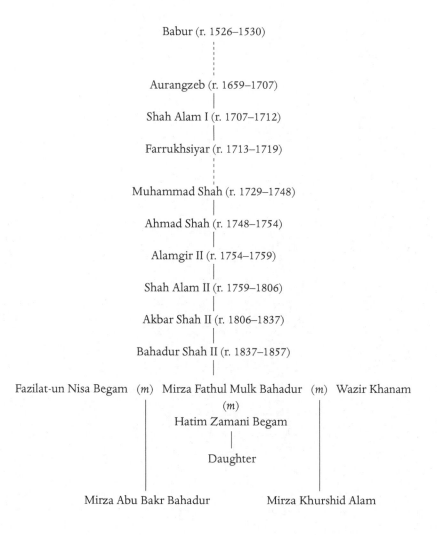

Babur (r. 1526–1530)

Aurangzeb (r. 1659–1707)

Shah Alam I (r. 1707–1712)

Farrukhsiyar (r. 1713–1719)

Muhammad Shah (r. 1729–1748)

Ahmad Shah (r. 1748–1754)

Alamgir II (r. 1754–1759)

Shah Alam II (r. 1759–1806)

Akbar Shah II (r. 1806–1837)

Bahadur Shah II (r. 1837–1857)

Fazilat-un Nisa Begam (*m*) Mirza Fathul Mulk Bahadur (*m*) Wazir Khanam

(*m*)

Hatim Zamani Begam

Daughter

Mirza Abu Bakr Bahadur

Mirza Khurshid Alam

CAST OF CHARACTERS

WAZIR KHANAM, also known as Chhoti Begam, daughter of Muhammad Yusuf Sadahkar and Asghari Begam

Her ancestors

MIAN MAKHSUSULLAH, a painter from Hindal Purwah in Rajputana

SALIMAH, his wife

MUHAMMAD YAHYA, son of Mian Makhsusullah and Salimah, a carpet designer from Badgam, Kashmir

BASHIRUNNISA, his wife

YAQUB BADGAMI and DAUD BADGAMI, twin sons of Muhammad Yahya and Bashirunnisa, musicians from Badgam, Kashmir

JAMILA and HABIBA, sisters, married to Yaqub and Daud respectively

MUHAMMAD YUSUF SADAHKAR, son of Yaqub and Jamila, maker of plain but delicate gold-and-silver ornaments in the city of Delhi

ASGHARI BEGAM, his wife, daughter of Akbari Bai

Her sisters

ANWARI KHANAM, also known as Bari Begam, eldest sister of Wazir Khanam

MIAN MAULAVI MUHAMMAD NAZIR RIFAI, her husband

AMAT-UL FATIMAH, also known as Fatimah and as Pari Bano, their daughter

UMDAH KHANAM, also known as Manjhli Begam, elder sister of Wazir Khanam

NAVAB YUSUF ALI KHAN BAHADUR, an aristocrat in a permanent relationship with Umdah Khanam, later the Navab of Rampur

The men in her life

CAPTAIN EDWARD MARSTON BLAKE, Assistant English Political Agent in Jaipur for the East India Company

SOPHIA BLAKE, also known as Masih Jan and as Badshah Begam, his daughter with Wazir Khanam

MARTIN BLAKE, also known as Amir Mirza, his son with Wazir Khanam

Dilawar-ul Mulk Navab Shamsuddin Ahmad Khan Bahadur, also known as Shamsuddin Ahmad Khan, ruler of Loharu and Firozepur Jhirka

Navab Mirza, also known as Bacche Mian and as Navab Mirza Khan Dagh, his son with Wazir Khanam, a poet

Agha Mirza Maulavi Turab Ali, also known as Agha Turab Ali, Manager of the Horse and Elephant Stable and Tent Equipment to the Navab of Rampur

Shah Muhammad Agha Mirza, also known as Shah Muhammad Agha, his son with Wazir Khanam

Mirza Muhammad Sultan Ghulam Fakhruddin Fathul Mulk Shah Bahadur, also known as Mirza Fathul Mulk Bahadur and as Sahib-e Alam wa Alamiyan and as Mirza Fakhru and as Ramz, the Third Heir Apparent to the Throne of Hindustan

Mirza Khurshid Alam, also known as Khurshid Mirza, his son with Wazir Khanam

In her establishment

Habib-un Nisa, also known as Habiba, Wazir Khanam's chief companion

Rahat Afza, her daughter

Others

Dr Khalil Asghar Farooqui, a retired ophthalmologist and amateur genealogist

Wasim Jafar, descendant of Sophia Blake, Assistant Keeper of Nineteenth-Century Mughal Paintings at the Victoria & Albert Museum, London

William Fraser, also known as Navab Resident Bahadur and as Navab Senior Sahib Bahadur, the Chief Resident of Delhi for the East India Company

Navab Mirza Asadullah Khan Bahadur Ghalib, also known as Mirza Naushah and as Mirza Ghalib, a poet

Karim Khan, Chief of the Hunt for Navab Shamsuddin Ahmad Khan

James Skinner, also known as Sikandar Sahib, Captain of the regiment known as Skinner's Horse

Abu Zafar Muhammad Sirajuddin Bahadur Shah II, the King Emperor of Hindustan and father of Mirza Fakhru

Navab Zinat Mahal, his favourite wife

Navab Ziauddin Ahmad Khan Bahadur, younger half-brother of Navab Shamsuddin Ahmad Khan

PRELUDE

Captain Edward Marston Blake, the Company sahib, rescues some travellers on the road to Delhi while returning from the Auspicious Fair at the Noble Village of Mehrauli

(From the notes and diaries of Dr Khalil Asghar Farooqui, Ophthalmologist)

WAZIR KHANAM, ALSO and perhaps better known as Chhoti Begam (Younger Lady), was born sometime around 1811. She was the third and youngest daughter of Muhammad Yusuf, maker of plain gold ornaments. She was born in Delhi, but Muhammad Yusuf was not native to Delhi. His ancestors were from Kashmir. How and when these people reached Delhi, and what befell them in Delhi is a very long story. Its details were never clear enough, and now, due to the passing of time and also due to some expediencies, have perhaps been entirely forgotten. Whatever could be known is narrated here, but it is not necessary that all of it should be historically accurate or true.

In the year 1245–1246 Hijri, which corresponds to 1829–1830 CE, Wazir Khanam had an arrangement by virtue of which she was 'attached' to Navab Shamsuddin Ahmad Khan, ruler of Firozepur Jhirka and Loharu. But before this, she had been similarly attached to Mr Edward Marston Blake, gent. During that time, she became the mother of Marston Blake's two children: a boy called Martin Blake, also known as Amir Mirza, and a girl called Sophia, also known as Masih Jan and Badshah Begam.

There's a strong likelihood that Marston Blake was the first man in Wazir's life and that they first met in Delhi. No verified or verifiable account of the occasion of their meeting is known. A Muslim girl living her life in seclusion behind closed doors and a veil, and who wasn't apparently a nautch girl or a courtesan: how did she come to be available to and appropriated by an Englishman? No written narrative or eyewitness account of events leading to this can be found. Whatever has been gleaned from parts of the narrative that was extant in the family a long time ago runs as follows.

Wise and knowing old women narrate that once, during the days of the Auspicious Fair at the Noble Village of Mehrauli around the sky-touching portal of the shrine of Khvajah Qutb sahib, Wazir Khanam and her father were on their way back to Delhi from the Fair. Evening had broken out in the sky. All those on the road were in a hurry to reach home. For, in those days, the ruins of the Hauz-e-Shamsi had been clandestinely adopted by some Pandari tribals as their hideout. Grabbing opportune moments, they preyed on the travellers of the night on that road. So everyone was trying their best to get quickly past the environs of the Hauz-e Shamsi and the Hauz-e Khas. An axle of the light two-bullock cart in which Wazir and her father were travelling was worn out to start with, and had deteriorated further over the journey. It was feared that the axle could break if the cart was driven faster. The bullock cart was moving at a gentle pace and had been overtaken by everyone else on the road: bullock carts, palanquins, tom johns. Those who rode elephants, dromedaries, buggies or horses had easily overtaken all others and had disappeared quickly from sight and sound.

It was the middle of Baisakh, the hottest month in Delhi. The westerly wind that blew regularly from Rewari and Loharu was hot, but it brought more dust and grit than heat. Four or five times a week, this dusty and gritty wind, having become drunk before sundown on the little moisture nestled in the jungles of Alwar and Ranthambhor, and dallying a little with the thorn and shrub and scrubland on the way, became a cloud-and-dust-storm by the time it kissed the skirts of Gurgaon. Stretching a light sheet of friendly and benign dust over everything and treating the city to gusts and even blasts of cool winds, the windstorm—gladdening the hearts of Delhi and its lands and pastures, and after play and frolic lasting two or two and a half watches of the evening—would pass on and lose itself in the lanes and alleys of Mathura; but not before it had cooled the hearts and courtyards of the rich and the poor, the commoner and the high born, the young and the old of the city of Delhi. But the dust storm became a trial for the lives of those who were far from their destination, or whose mounts were determined to fail them.

Suddenly, Wazir Khanam's bullock cart found itself choking in an invasion of sand and red grit. Alarm and pain forced shut the large eyes of the bullocks. Three of the cart's curtains flew off with a flapping noise, as if they were partridges surprised and frenzied by a fox. In the muddied light the grey-and-crimson curtains were suspended in air for a short time and then disappeared from view, having been flung far away or maybe snagged in a tree's branches. The sudden fluttering flight of the curtains, the shying of the bullocks and the displacement of the passengers within caused the cart to lose its balance and it tilted precariously on two wheels. The next blow of wind hurled the cart explosively against the earth. Simultaneously was heard the harsh, abominable sound of its axle breaking apart. It wasn't immediately clear if something had broken in the cart, or if it was a stout branch of a nearby tree being forced by the stormy wind to bite the dust. But in the twinkling of an eye the cart and one of its wheels separated; the cart barely escaped turning over. Only then did the luckless travellers realize the gravity of their estate.

Wazir Khanam's father resigned himself to his fate. He knew that night would be the last night of his and his daughter's lives. He had no hopes of encountering even a solitary straggler or two, far less a passing caravan. There were no rescuers abroad at that time of the night. All were safe in their havens. The passengers in the broken cart were destined to pass the night in the wilderness, and there was scant hope of their seeing the fair face of the morning. The girl would surely end up as a maidservant or in a brothel and the father's grave was to be nowhere else but in that wild and lonely place. The cart driver might just be spared.

Yet none can touch those whom God desires to save. A nimbus of dirty yellow light, like a patch of cloud shot through with the light of a dim sun, was descried moving along the road from the direction of Delhi. Then came the musical tinkle of the bells worn by dromedaries around their ankles. Then a horse-rider, before and behind whom were two lance-bearers, their faces covered against the dust and the wind, but putting each steady and firm foot with deliberate slowness. The horse too was highly trained so that the slaps of the gusting wind, or its roaring rush through the trees were quite unable to disrupt its concentration. To the right and left of the rider were two foot soldiers, one of them with a flambeau in hand, and the other carrying a badban. The flambeau was a middle-sized cup fitted to a stick, slightly smaller than that of a regular flame torch. Filled with inflammable materials like the thick residue of mustard oil or rags soaked in naphtha, the edge of the cup functioned like a windbreak for the flame and prevented the light from going out. A hand-held glass shade lighted from within and closed from all sides but with tiny holes all over to let in the air, was called a badban. The English lantern, called lalten in Hindi, was coming into common use, but was seldom used by Indian foot soldiers or torchbearers.

The dromedary rider, using his native sense, could discern from some distance through the fast-dimming environment that what he saw before him was a small bunch of travellers stranded due to some mishap; it could very well be thugs, but it was not the season for thugs to do their business, nor was the country within thug territory. And above all, there could be no women in a band of thugs. The dromedary rider and the lance-bearers continued up the road, but the rider stopped at some distance, flanked by his light-bearers.

The caste or community of the rider wasn't clear yet: it could be anybody. Occasionally on an evening, men in the employ of the Shadow of God His Majesty the King could be seen patrolling these areas. On some days one could even find the servants of the Honourable Company out and about in these places. On his part, the cart driver quickly determined that he and his travellers weren't confronted by dacoits or robbers, and succour could be sought from them.

The cart driver took a few tentative steps forward. The dromedary rider commanded his mount quickly to block the driver's progress. 'Who are you? And what are you doing here at this hour? Aren't you aware it is prohibited to saunter around after sundown unescorted by a caravan or a posse of soldiers?'

'Mai-baap, we know it well. We are returning from the Court of Bakhtiar Baba in the village of Khvajah sahib. The storm overtook us suddenly. Then our axle broke. We stood here lamenting, in fear of our lives. We have veiled lady passengers. Only Allah knows what would have befallen had not you and the Kaptan sahib . . . '

'Enough! No more of your mealy-mouthed elocution. Where is your master? Let him present himself before the Company sahib!'

'Present right here, your honour. Just let the women be placed behind a bit of cover so that they are not exposed to view.' Even in his abject state, the cart driver wasn't averse to hinting that the Firangee male had better be a mite distant from the female travellers.

Wazir Khanam's father came forward a bit, having extricated himself from the broken cart. The horse rider set his mount in motion and in a moment he and the travellers were face to face. In the meantime, the lance-bearer had lit a lantern too; the wind was freshening further and the flame of the lantern was smoking and spluttering. Suddenly, a strong gust, and the chador that Wazir Khanam had wrapped around her body fluttered free and her full face was revealed. Her face, full of fear and shame, felt dark and hot below her large brown-black eyes, like a deer's whose forehead had been burnt brown and black by a harsh sun. And the lantern's thrilling, trembling flame highlighted her body just a bit more. The Englishman stared, quite still. The importunate waves of youth, realizing the absorption of an attractive male in herself, became a little more impudent. Their eyes met for a split second. The cart driver, pulling out another chador quickly, veiled her body again.

The Englishman was Marston Blake, going to Arab Sarai to spend the night with his mistress. After a short discussion and some thought, it was decided that Marston Blake sahib would himself escort the travellers to Munir ka Bagh, a little past the Hauz-e- Shamsi. Reliable conveyance for Delhi could be arranged from that point. The ladies would somehow pack themselves in the narrow box on top of the dromedary; the rest were to walk beside the trotting horse. The travellers didn't have much luggage: some of it was loaded on the dromedary, the rest was somehow manhandled by the lance-bearers and the driver.

*

Marston Blake, using some pretext or the other, now began to wait upon Wazir Khanam's father every two or three days. He would talk entertainingly of excursions and diversions. Sometimes he would take Wazir out to Chandni Chowk to enjoy an evening walk on the banks of the canal. The mother, of course, had been dead for some time; the father would accompany them nolens volens, and always insisted on his daughter wrapping herself fully in a chador. Still, no one could know what relations developed quietly between Wazir and Blake and what promises and pacts were made.

Some months passed. One day, Marston Blake paid them a sort of farewell visit: he had been posted out to Jaipur as the Assistant English Political Agent. Nothing much transpired over that farewell visit, except formal expressions of regret from both sides and a promise by Marston Blake to keep relations alive with his Indian friends. A month or so later,

Marston Blake returned to report that he had now rented a suitable house and organized everything with servants and supplies as suited an English gentleman's household; he enjoyed a lavish salary, had an army of servants and didn't even need to rise to fetch himself a glass of water. 'I am very highly regarded and am welcome among all in Jeypore,' he said. 'It's just the Political Agent sahib, my chief, who outranks me there.'

Everyone fell silent upon hearing Marston Blake waxing eloquent about Jaipur. Then it was Marston Blake who took the first tentative step. Not saying anything, he looked at Wazir Khanam with meaningful, quizzing eyes. Judging that there was a responsive hint from the other side too, Blake and Yusuf drew quietly aside and conducted a whispered conversation.

A week after this, Marston Blake's Jaipur-bound caravan consisted also of a rath pulled by four bullocks bedecked with tinkling bells and with coloured beads hung around their necks. Bright with resplendent gold and silver ribbons, the rath was a fragrant zone scented with garlands of colourful flowers, looking for all the world like a young person flourishing verdant with vegetable, leaf and fruit. Clothed in the brilliant golds and yellows of a newly married bride, Wazir Khanam-Chhoti Begam rode in style inside that rath.

BOOK 1

1

The lives and destinies of Sophia's descendants, Salim Jafar and Shamim Jafar

(From the notes and diaries of Dr Khalil Asghar Farooqui, Ophthalmologist)

MARSTON BLAKE'S DEATH occurred in Jaipur in a local riot which suddenly erupted against the English officers there. The time was probably early 1830. The English, perhaps because of their lack of desire to act justly, or because of the extant English laws, had not recognized the conjugal relationship between Chhoti Begam and Marston Blake. Thus she could inherit nothing from the cash and other properties left by Marston Blake. Nor was she given a pension or subsistence grant by the Company.

As I mentioned earlier, Chhoti Begam had two children with Marston Blake: a son Martin and a daughter Sophia. These two were also to remain shut out from their father's inheritance but were brought up by relatives of their father, an uncle and aunt. Sophia was a celebrated beauty; her first husband was the famous Indo-Anglian officer Alexander Skinner, popularly known as 'Alec sahib' whose father James Skinner was more often called 'Sikandar sahib' by non-Europeans and the sepoys in his regiment, the widely acclaimed Skinner's Horse. Begam Skinner—that is to say Sophia, or Badshah Begam—came to be somewhat prominent among Urdu literary circles as the poetess Miss Blake Khafi, the latter being the name she used to refer to herself in her poems. She was counted among the more creative Urdu poets among her contemporaries.

Sophia Marston Blake bore two children with Alexander Skinner: a son Bahadur Mirza and a daughter Ahmadi Begam. Ahmadi was christened Charlotte but was known everywhere as Ahmadi Begam. In 1946, her progeny were living prosperous lives in Jaipur. Some say that the marriage of

Sophia and Alexander resulted in another son who was named Muhammad Amir, or Amir Mirza, or Amirullah. But that is not true. Amir Mirza was the nickname by which Martin, son of Marston Blake by Wazir Khanam, was known, especially among the natives.

It, however, is true that Sophia's other husband was known as Muhammad Amir, or Amirullah, and she had a son by him too. Nothing is known about him except that to this Amirullah was born a son named Hasibullah Quraishi. Hasibullah was born perhaps around 1890. It is possible that Amirullah was Sophia's first husband and she married Alec sahib after the first husband's death. It is also possible that Amirullah was the second husband or that he was not her husband even, but a lover with whom she lived as a concubine. Why did Hasibullah adopt the surname Quraishi and thus conceal his real lineage and parentage (that his mother was Sophia, daughter of Wazir Khanam and Marston Blake, and that his father was Amirullah) is a puzzle that has never been solved. It is quite possible that Amirullah came from a family whose surname was Quraishi, but the secrecy around Hasibullah's change of name suggests that Amirullah and Sophia were not really married and Hasibullah assumed the surname Quraishi to conceal the identity of his biological father Amirullah.

Anyway, it was this Hasibullah Quraishi who, as Salim Jafar, became moderately famous as a learned Urdu writer, critic and metrist. In 1951, Salim Jafar had an authoritative selection of the famous but little-read Urdu poet Nazir Akbarabadi (1735–1830) published from the Hindustani Academy, Allahabad. Called *Gulzar-e-Nazir* (Nazir's Garden), copies of the book are relatively rare now but not impossible to find. He also wrote on Ghalib and some other classical Urdu poets. In addition to Persian, he was well versed in Sanskrit and Hindi, and was of course perfectly bilingual in Urdu and English.

Salim Jafar died in Karachi. He held down a good civil service post in undivided India but failed to find in Pakistan a job appropriate or even somewhat approximate to his abilities. Perhaps this was because he had attained the age of superannuation (fifty-five years at that time) fixed by the British for their civil servants. He settled in Mirpur Khas, in Sind, and became a typist with Muhammad Latif Gandhi, a lawyer. He continued with his literary and authorial activities and he also put together an extensive dictionary of Urdu etymology. Called *Investigating the Language*, it listed the roots of all Urdu words borrowed from or derived from Sanskrit and

Persian. It is a pity that this dictionary is still waiting for a publisher. Salim Jafar's life in Mirpur Khas was saved from loneliness and boredom by his friendship and literary interactions with Adab Gulshanabadi and Professor Karrar Husain, two local luminaries of Urdu literature. Salim Jafar was persuaded by Karrar Husain to deliver a few lectures at the Shah Abdul Latif Bhitai College on comparative philology and similar scholarly subjects. These lectures went down very well, alike with the students and faculty of the college. Salim Jafar treated his students with great kindness, often helping them with their studies without any payment in return, though his own financial condition was not sound.

Salim Jafar's lone offspring was a son, Ijaz Ahmad Quraishi, with a taste for Urdu and Persian, and also a penchant for writing. He adopted Shamim Jafar as his nom de plume but left no finished work behind. Unlike his father, he regarded as worthwhile and valuable his family's connection, however distant, with the famous nineteenth-century Urdu poet Navab Mirza Khan Dagh (1831–1905). Shamim was assiduous at gleaning from oral or written sources details about Dagh's mother Wazir Khanam who was his great-grandmother.

Shamim Jafar married Perdita, daughter of an Indo-Anglian relative, Hermione Mortimer. At that time he was managing an extensive tea estate in East Pakistan (now Bangladesh). Once, when the workers at the tea estate went on strike, resentful of their supervisor's cruel treatment of a labourer, an angry crowd had gathered before Shamim Jafar's house by the time police arrived. Some of the strikers even inclined to violence, but confident of his popularity among the workers, Shamim confronted the mob with equanimity, ignoring the possibility of danger. He opened dialogue with their leaders with such good sense and sweetness of tone that the strike was withdrawn forthwith and the workers—intoxicated with the pleasure of success and the joy of the strike having ended so soon—raised Shamim Jafar on their shoulders and with jubilant cries of 'Long live our Manager sahib' proceeded back towards the tea garden. But the irony of fate and fortune made sure that Shamim Jafar's most refulgent moment as an officer of the tea estate became the reason for the darkening of his life and his family's small world.

It was the season of rains. The areas of the country where tea is grown receive rainfall much greater than the national average. Tea gardens are mostly planted on slopes of hilly terrain so that the plants receive precipitation and the rainwater does not stay, but drains away as soon as it falls. Drunk with a sense of gratitude and triumph, the labourers, bearing Jafar on their shoulders, tried to negotiate a rising slope more than usually sharp. As a labourer in the front lost his footing, the entire procession became a cascade dropping back into a deep gulch to the left. No life was lost, God be praised. But Shamim Jafar suffered severe injury in the head, resulting in complete loss of memory.

Prolonged treatment in Calcutta helped to a great extent restore his memory, but he became somewhat senile, for his brain regressed to a state much like childhood, obliging him finally to quit his job and go live with his father in Mirpur Khas. In his own mind, though, he remained the head of a big tea estate who counted among his friends important Englishmen and civil servants. Every evening, fully dressed in a natty suit, walking stick in one hand and a lighted cigar in the other, he would walk to the 'Club' at the 'Tea Estate'. There was, of course, no club and no scent of a single tea leaf to the farthest horizon. Still, Shamim Jafar, enjoying his reveries, smiling and talking to himself in English, would take his evening walk around the neighbourhood, returning at nightfall. His rigorous observance of a sahib's dress and manners caused the people, especially children, to ask him mockingly, 'Babu ji, what's the time like?' This happened often enough to earn him the half-mocking, half-jovial nickname of 'Time-Babu'.

Shamim Jafar's only son Wasim Jafar was about twelve at the time of his father's accidental fall and loss of memory. There was a daughter too, a couple of years older. She was mentally deficient and also had serious physical impairment. Shamim's wife Perdita and his father Salim Jafar looked after him as best they could, but his days seemed to have developed a mind of their own to turn from bad to worse. Salim Jafar suffered a fracture in the right hip in another accident. With his age and circumstances against him, even an improvement in his state, far less recovery, was nearly impossible. His daughter-in-law was caregiver not only for him, but also for her mentally incapacitated husband and her doubly handicapped daughter. Salim Jafar developed bedsores and foul-smelling blisters all over his body, which soon became septic. Seeing the once-fastidious and -sophisticated Salim Jafar falling into such a circumstance saddened and frightened all those who knew him; how the invalid felt and how much he suffered was obviously beyond imagination. Ultimately, even more incapacitated than ever, he was transported to Karachi where he had a distantly related uncle.

But now, more than any therapeutic process, his condition begged for prayer that he may be finally released from this world, the House of Pain. He suffered for many more months before he could submit his life to the Giver of Life. According to some reports, the year was 1959.

Salim Jafar left a will, providing as much as he could for his son; he left the papers in the custody of Muhammad Latif Gandhi, the attorney with whom he had long been a typist. Perdita planned to move to England with her mentally deranged husband and the two children. But the call came also to Shamim just a few months after his father. After his funeral, the mother and the children emigrated to England through a relative from the mother's side who sponsored their visa.

Quite contrary to the mother's hopes and expectations, Wasim Jafar loved to saturate himself with the cultural and literary past of his grandfather. As much as Wasim Jafar could, he consciously took for his own the fields in which Salim Jafar was learned: the way of life, the letters and science that he had come to see as Salim Jafar's legacy to him. Wasim studied at London's School of Oriental and African Studies for many years, acquiring a sound knowledge of Urdu and Persian. Always having spoken Urdu with his father, he spoke idiomatic Urdu fluently enough; with his mother, he spoke a conscious mixture of English and Urdu. Now having thoroughly acquired the latter language at the School, he became quite competent at speaking and writing literary Urdu as well.

He had learnt a little about Wazir Khanam from the stories that his grandfather told him and a bit more from stray conversations between his father and grandfather before his father lost his mind. Apart from Urdu and Persian, painting was his other great love and he learnt its techniques by attending evening classes at London's celebrated Slade School of Art. Realizing that his true avocation was Mughal painting, he acquired its knowledge and learnt its history, spending a great deal of time and effort over it. He was eventually appointed Assistant Keeper of Nineteenth-century Mughal (and Company School) paintings at London's Victoria and Albert Museum. He spent much of his spare time in the India Office Library and Records, poring over manuscripts and publications of eighteenth- and nineteenth-century India. (The Library has now become part of the British Library, but old-fashioned persons still call it India Office Library and Records.)

For many years now, Wasim Jafar had been researching some of the

Indian families of the eighteenth and nineteenth centuries: families that had been extremely notable in their time but had now been buried in the dunghill of unread pages. Their names, if known at all, were known only to some specialist historians. Some of them prospered and foliated under British patronage but fell into ignominy or ruin because of their progeny's unworthiness; and there were those that were put on the scales of tyrannous English swords or the fairness-feigning English justice system before or after 1857 and were found deficient. He aspired to write their story someday.

⋆

We can freely grant that today it is barely a handful of specialist historians who are acquainted with the names of those families, but in their own day they were the cradle and breeding ground for the arts and knowledge, especially poetry, music and painting. If the family papers and manuscripts of those houses were to be studied, they would yield information about countless rare gems of the Indo-Islamic culture dormant in those pages, waiting for their inevitable death. There were some names which were of particular interest to Wasim Jafar, and he was researching them or looking for material about them: Raja Ratan Singh Zakhmi of Bareilly, Rai Balmukund Shahud of Kara Manakpur, Sahib Ram Khamosh of Benaras (later Banaras and now Varanasi), Ali Bahadur Khan of Banda, Tajammul Husain Khan of Farrukhabad, Shamsuddin Ahmad Khan of Firozepur Jhirka, Colonel Gardner of Cossganj (now Khasganj) and his Begam who was a daughter of the Navab of Khambayat, and the Colonel's daughter-in-law who was a daughter of Emperor Shah Alam Bahadur Shah the Second who Abides in Paradise. The Princess, full of hatred and rebellion against the 'gentle' treatment meted out to her by her first husband and his father the King of Avadh, had finally eloped with Colonel Gardner's son. Navab Husamuddin Haydar and Divan Fazlullah Khan of Delhi . . . and many more such whose stories cried out to be written someday.

Wasim Jafar often asked himself: Was the decline and decay of those houses inevitable, absent the political pressure and military conflicts of those times? How do they look now, dimly descried from this distance of time? What is it that veils their images now? Is it the sooty dark of the past, or the pink haze of nostalgia and longing? How did these people regard themselves? What value did they put on their own selves? What kind of light coloured their self-perception? Did they apprehend or even imagine that the glorious sheathing that was their culture was soon to be rent asunder so that their value systems would mutate into the impenetrable smoke of a country in conflagration, with the smoke destined to dissolve itself into the ocean of the new age, and that the discontinuity wrought by this dissolution would be a gulf whose depth no one could sound and into which men's power to recall the past would weaken and dissolve, and their memories would lose their way forever?

Wasim Jafar was not sure that he would ever have his answers, but he also rejected the notion that the past is a foreign country and strangers who visit there cannot comprehend its language. He used to say that old words can be re-narrated in new words: all that was needed was empathy, a power and ability to embrace and to feel the warmth of the embrace.

2

Dr Farooqui, retired ophthalmologist and amateur genealogist, meets Wasim Jafar in London and learns of his extraordinary discovery

(From the notes and diaries of Dr Khalil Asghar Farooqui, Ophthalmologist)

AS NARRATED ABOVE, Wasim Jafar lived in London. He was not my relative and in fact I did not even know him, or about him, before we came to meet in rather unexpected circumstances. Nor do I live in London myself. Some time ago I did read with great interest an account of the family history of Wasim's grandfather Salim Jafar in the correspondence of the well-known academic and Sufi Maulana Hamid Hasan Qadiri, published recently by his son Khalid Hasan Qadiri of the London School of Oriental and African Studies. I was familiar with Salim Jafar's writings and had believed him to be from some sophisticated Urdu-speaking family from Hyderabad or Lucknow or Delhi.

I knew nothing about Salim Jafar's offspring; nor had I any interest to know where, if at all, they were living. I just assumed that he was a much older person than I and would by now be dead and gone and buried somewhere like myriad other authors whose works I was familiar with but the details of whose lives and circumstances were obscure.

In the ordinary course of things, following the bent of my mind, I would have been curious to know more not about Salim Jafar but rather about Wazir Khanam, the poet Navab Mirza Khan Dagh's mother, the unusual vicissitudes of her life, and in what way Salim Jafar was connected with her; I would have tried to trace Salim Jafar's descendants in order to learn more, if possible, about Wazir Khanam rather than Salim Jafar.

In those days I had quite another bee in my bonnet (please excuse this archaic phrase). I had occasion, last year, to go to London for a wedding.

I do feel a little diffident recording anything here about my own self. And the narrative that follows does not really concern me personally. Suffice it to say that vocationally I am an eye surgeon of some repute but have a sort of informed outsider's interest in poets and poetry, and write poems occasionally. But my real hobby is genealogy. Had I been born in the middle ages, I would have been called a nassab, that is, someone who knows by heart the names of the ancestors and the seed and progeny of individual members of his tribe and also those of all neighbouring tribes. I am keenly interested in finding out about family histories, drawing up family trees, and discovering links connecting members of families distant and disparate from one another. Though I am not yet of retiring age, I have given up the practice of medicine and closed down my surgery, devoting much of my time to family histories and genealogies.

I spoke above of an avid pursuit. But it would not be wrong if I said two pursuits, instead of one. At the time that I was reading Hamid Hasan Qadiri's letters, it had occurred to me, for no perceivable reason, to search for and write about the family tree of Bomanji Khudaiji, a Parsee merchant family of Gorakhpur. It was said that their ancestor Jamshed Aryanpur was the person whom the English traveller Tom Coryat had hired as guide to take him through western India to Gorakhpur, far in the east and the north. It was the time of the Mughal Emperor Nuruddin Jahangir. Coryat had travelled thousands of miles on foot through Europe and Asia and, finally, travelling with Jahangir's Court as camp follower, he went to Ajmer from Agra and through Sind to Turkestan and China.

Coryat got nothing much from Jahangir, but something about Jamshed Aryanpur pleased the Emperor so much that he was awarded from the Royal Seat of the Khaqan of India the licence to conduct trade in wines and some jungle products like honey and the manna of the bamboo in the area which now forms part of eastern Uttar Pradesh and was then the north-eastern territory of the province of Avadh. The present-day wine merchant Bomanji Khudaiji of Gorakhpur was reputedly descended from the aforesaid Jamshed Aryanpur.

The other thing that engaged my curiosity was about my own people. Many people know that the Sayyids have predominated historically among the Sufis and Muslim saints of India. What many do not know is that after the children of Abdul Muttalib (that is, the family of the Prophet), the predominant clan among the Sufis and saints are the children of

Khattab (that is, the father of Omar-e Faruq, the second Caliph of Islam). Similarly, only professional historians now know that India has had scores of rulers from among the Sayyids, the Turks and the Pathans, but there has been only one Farooqui—variously spelt in India as Faruqui, Farooqui, Farooqee, Farooquee, Faruqi, even Faruki or Farooki (I prefer Farooqui, though purists approve of Faruqi)—House to have ruled anywhere in the subcontinent. The Farooqui kingdom of Burhanpur in south and central India was established in 1397 by one Malik Raja Farooqui. They ruled over their kingdom for more than two centuries, until the blasts of the advancing winds of the Mughal Emperor Jalaluddin Muhammad Akbar's daystar extinguished the light of the Farooquis of Burhanpur in the year 1601.

After the tearing up of the kingdom, the name Farooqui was somehow effectually washed off the pages of history as if, with the dissolution of the soot and dust of battle, the epithet 'Farooqui' also went up in smoke and dissolved forever in the stratosphere.

Quite by chance, I found out about the Farooquis of Burhanpur; ever since then I have had the obsession or ridiculous notion to discover what befell the Farooquis of Burhanpur after the fall of the kingdom. Family legend has it that we, the Farooquis of Azamgarh, settled in our ancestral village a little before the death of Firoze Tughlaq in 1388, well before Malik Raja founded his kingdom in Burhanpur. Yet who knows, some of our forebears may have been connected with the Farooquis of Burhanpur; or perhaps such a connection could have been born during Akbar's long reign?

I had had no success in any of my projects; nor did I see any real possibility of my obtaining even partial success in my endeavours. Actually, I made the wedding an occasion for my trip to London in the vain hope that I might thus extend my area of search. Therefore, the very next day after the conclusion of the wedding ceremonies and the following dinner, I organized the necessary permission and facilities for making use of the India Office Library and Records so as to go to its reading room for several hours every day and consult the catalogues, bibliographies, family papers and documents of important British civil servants of the nineteenth century. A corner workstation, a computer terminal and a small shelf for storing papers and documents in use were provided to me on the ground floor of the Library, thus enabling me to avail of all the necessary facilities there.

Though I suppose it is common to all research libraries, there is a prolonged wait before anything can be made available. Often the search for old family papers and legal instruments which are not in the best of shape to begin with, has to be handled with extra care and they take even longer to search for and be produced for study.

I hired rooms in one of the mews in Great West Russell Street. As those who have lived in London know, the mews in Central London are extremely popular, highly regarded and expensive. It was just my good luck to have found a comfortable set of rooms at what seemed to me to be reasonable rent. The British Library was barely twenty minutes away on foot. Eating places and teashops were everywhere around. There weren't many Indian restaurants, but the Goanese dish chicken vindaloo, the Punjabi dish dam alu, and the Mughlai grilled chicken tikka were served in most restaurants. I recently read the modern English novelist and critic Peter Ackroyd saying in one of his books that chicken vindaloo had now effectively replaced fish and chips as the British national food.

It had been just a few days since I had been going to the Library that I noticed an Indian gentleman who was said to be the Assistant Keeper of Nineteenth-century Mughal (and Company School) paintings at the V&A Museum. As for me, I just saw him as a somewhat worried-looking, tall and thin gentleman, his complexion very fair but darkening somewhat due to age, his white hair unfashionably long and his moustaches comparatively thin, who kept his head covered with a woollen cap in all weathers, going quickly up the stairs, lost in his thoughts, with a briefcase in each hand. As I learnt later, one of the briefcases invariably contained papers, pens and pencils, a diary, post-it memoranda, a book or two, a chequebook, credit cards, and similar odds and ends. No one could discover what the other briefcase contained; maybe he carried some food in it. But he lunched always at the Central Restaurant near the British Museum. I conjectured that the other briefcase had medications, for he always looked somewhat sickly to me.

When I saw him for the first time, I imagined him to be a relic of the Indian-British times, an expert at deciphering manuscripts, something of an Englishman's 'moonshie' type who did not return home even after Independence, for he had no one to welcome him back. He always wore a loose-fitting, rumpled suit or sherwani whose colour seemed to be somehow faded to a dull grey.

His shoes, hat, stick, umbrella, all were quite expensive and in the fashion of the day. His clothes were always of good quality, but worn carelessly; it was clear that their wearer was not too particular about their being free of wrinkles or being carefully brushed free of dust and dirt. He would alight from the bus at a bus stop on Great West Russell Street that was just before the Library, buy the day's copy of the *International Herald Tribune* from the newsboy (funny how everybody said 'newsboy' even if the person was old), then rolling it tight and sticking it under his arm, he would walk to the Library.

Quite by chance once he and I came together in the lift. I said, 'Salam alaikum', greeting him in the Indo-Muslim way. He responded with some warmth, though I had not really expected any great warmth from him, given his age and general deportment. That day, looking at him from close quarters, I realized that his badly fitting suit was not because of his tailor's slipshod work, or his own lack of careful maintenance of his wardrobe, or because the suit was made when he was younger and heavier and that was the reason why it now hung so loose on him. He was, in fact, very thin. His skin hung slack and dry on his neck, hands and face, as if the flesh inside had wasted away and the external skin had been somehow pasted onto the bones and if I were to touch it, it would scrape against my fingers like crinkled paper. The wrist on which his stick hung seemed like that of a small boy. It called to mind a verse of the eighteenth-century Urdu poet Mir:

It's just your imagining that
There's a feeble body inside my clothes;
In fact, there is nothing there
But a mere idea of myself.

I was still lost in these thoughts when we exited the lift. The secretaries passing by greeted him with open, smiling faces. Their words, 'Good morning, Doctor' or 'Good morning, Wasim', indicated that he was very well known here. His name was Wasim; his full name would therefore be Wasim Ahmad or Wasim Akhtar or some such routine Indo-Muslim name. On the landing, he said to me with a brief smile, 'Salam alaikum, we'll meet again, God willing,' and turned into the corridor on the right.

I reached my workstation and was pleasantly, indeed joyfully, surprised to find that the books and papers I had indented for the previous evening had been placed neatly on the shelf of my desk. The legal papers were mostly from after 1661 when the Portuguese transferred the seven islands—called

Bom Bahia or even Bombaim (both meaning 'Good Bay') by them, and Mambai by many of the native inhabitants (the city is now again known by that name—Mumbai)—to the English as dowry when the Portuguese Princess Catharine was married to King Charles. Among the British, the Portuguese Bom Bahia / Bombaim evolved to Mumbay, then to Bombay over the years. At that time, many Parsees and Jews had been living there for decades and some information about them was available in the papers of Buddhist monks and educational establishments of those times, but the information was sporadic and discontinuous. Towards the end of the century, the English set up a municipality there and legal papers and documents since that date were extant and more or less continuous, stored safely in cloth bundles or boxes.

I busied myself with the papers. As I was not in the habit of eating lunch, I got some sense of the passing of time only when my neighbouring workstations began emptying slowly. I too rose and it occurred to me that Mr Wasim might still be around and it might be enjoyable to spend time with him. But I decided to meet him some other time, for he might have left the V&A earlier or he might still be working. It was Sunday the next day. A big used-books market would spring up as usual in the open spaces on the bank of the Thames in front of the theatre district. I planned to go there in the very first hour and spend a pleasant day among the books; maybe I would find something of interest to me.

The market that Sunday had a few stalls showing old maps and old paintings too. Obviously it was impossible to light upon something rare, or of real quality. Most of the paper wares on show consisted of printed copies of old pictures, but discrete illustrated pages of eighteenth-century English magazines were aplenty, and at very reasonable prices. At one stall I acquired an illustrated page of the *Gentleman's Magazine* of January 1772 for just ten pounds. The page clearly showed the date and the name of the magazine; two black-and-white animal drawings were displayed on it. One was described as a 'Giraffe' and the other as 'Chinese Antelope'. Although the drawings were far from accurate, their ink was still quite bright and the page was just slightly water stained. I looked around for an empty cardboard tube into which I could insert my precious page safely. There was an old gentleman nearby with a heap of old maps. I turned to his stall to find a familiar face: It was Mr Wasim, examining a small map from various angles, occasionally holding it against the light.

'Salam alaikum, sir,' I approached him and said with some delight, 'well met, indeed!'

He looked hard at me from behind his glasses, his brow slightly knotted. Perhaps he did not like my interrupting him in his examination of the map. Later I found out that he could not place me at first sight.

'Oh, so it's you! How did you chance to be here? But pardon me, we haven't been properly introduced yet though I did see you yesterday at the Library.'

His voice was hoarse, almost strangled, as if he had a quantity of phlegm blocking his voice box. His breath was also shallow; it seemed to me that he was not able to inhale enough oxygen for some reason.

'I am sorry, it's my fault. I know your honourable name is Wasim and at the V&A you are . . .'

'Yes, sir, I'm known by that name, Wasim Jafar, to be precise. But the V&A is nothing very important. Let it take care of itself. Tell me about yourself.'

'Well, dear sir, my name is Khalil Asghar Farooqui. I practised as an ophthalmologist. Now I'm retired and pursue my hobby.'

'Very nice,' he said in between short, dry coughs. 'There isn't anything better for one than to be solely pursuing a hobby. Freedom from want, a quiet corner of a pleasant home, and a hobby. How extremely agreeable! Only God is untouched by blemish!' he exclaimed, using the phrase universally employed by the Indo-Muslims to express admiration and praise, and also to declare with humility that however perfect a person or thing may be, it can never attain anything like God's eternal perfection.

Wasim Jafar? It suddenly struck me that the great-grandson of the poet Navab Mirza Khan Dagh was called Salim Jafar. Was there a connection there? I had an urge to ask him, but thought better of it. Clearly, Salim Jafar had liked to keep obscure his relationship with Dagh, or why else should he have changed his name? But the change of name could also be in accordance with the well-known practice of poets in our culture to assume a 'literary' name in their writings.

Seeing me lost in thought, Wasim Jafar smiled and said, 'What happened to make you so quiet? Did my words call to your mind Omar Khayyam's poem of a flask of wine and a book of verse beneath the bough? Oh, but I haven't yet got to know your hobby. One hopes you are not an enemy of property and home, and that's why you are in a strange land? Where do you come from? Or are you permanently settled here?'

'My hobby . . . well, you can call me a nassab. I am interested in old genealogies—'

Without letting me finish my sentence, he cut me short eagerly. 'How interesting! A modern genealogist! You must be accounted as a rarity, a prize. Have you written something, too?'

'I do plead guilty to that, but I am by no means a prized individual.' Now I was certain that the old gentleman was a son or nephew of Salim Jafar. Where else could this sophisticated speech, laden with literary allusions, come from? 'And it's people like you who are the prize of the age. I am well acquainted with the name and works of Salim Jafar sahib.'

'So you're familiar with the writings of my grandfather! Only God is untouched by blemish! Then you are just the fellow after my heart. Indeed, I am not a patch on him; it's just the training and nurture of my parents and grandparents that I became somewhat literate and gained a little familiarity with drawings and paintings.' With a sigh of regret he said, 'How wonderful were those people! God's name is forever.'

I picked up courage to ask, 'And what do you think of the lady, Wazir Khanam . . .?

'Only God is untouched by blemish!' he exclaimed and repeated the phrase. 'A lady of such grace, such gravitas, such elegance and dignity! And actually, I am looking for some things that had to do with her.'

'That's very good indeed. But sir, what's that map in your hands?'

'Map?' He laughed delightedly, but his laughter turned into a cough. The long bout of coughing made his face turn alarmingly florid. Helpless, I looked on. He pulled a small metallic tube from his pocket and trying to suck in a deep breath, sprayed medicine into his throat. He held his breath for a few precarious seconds and then expelled it. Presently, when he felt and looked somewhat better, he said, 'Well, dear sir, this is a map of Mumbai, dated 1694. Obviously the city has travelled quite far since then.'

'Yes indeed,' I said. 'But it's obvious that the map has great value as a historical and legal document. And by a happy chance I am interested in something at present which has a Mumbai connection.'

'Is that so?' He smiled. 'Okay, then let's buy the map right away. We can talk about other things later.' He promptly purchased the map for its asking price of £160.

Chatting amiably, we walked towards the district of Pimlico where he was meeting with someone. As we conversed, we learnt more about each other. As a genealogist of old families, I was also interested in antiquarian books and old legal deeds and documents. He was a decipherer of manuscripts, an antiquarian and an expert at judging premodern Indo-Muslim paintings. Old pictures, books, documents, manuscripts were thus milk and bread to him. He knew a lot of poetry by heart but had not read any Urdu poet after Muhammad Iqbal (1877–1938). He had no taste for fiction, but had read Qurratulain Hyder's (1926–2007) long narratives, especially her *Kar-e Jahan Daraz Hai* (The Business of the World Is Too Long), and held them to be useful for him as a professional antiquary.

After we arrived at a convenient point, he extended both his hands to me for the traditional Indo-Muslim handshake, and said, 'Don't trouble yourself any farther. I'll turn left here in the adjoining lane and reach my friend's house without difficulty. We'll meet again tomorrow.'

I was worried lest his cough trouble him again, but he scoffed at the thought and said, 'Well, sir, you are a real one! To be worried about a simple cough! Goodbye.'

He turned towards the lane on the left. Suddenly, he paused and said, 'Do you know the Arabic for "cough"?'

'No, sorry. I've but a smattering of Arabic.'

'Streetwalker,' he smiled.

I was puzzled. Was he indicating that I look at some passing woman? 'Sorry, I don't follow.'

He tried to laugh a good-humoured laugh, but began to cough yet again. He coughed for some considerable time even though this time he had kept both hands pressed to his chest. When the cough let up a little, he smiled again and said, 'Actually, it was this damn cough that made me think of it. In old Arabia, streetwalkers would try to attract the attention of a prospective client by gently coughing and clearing their throat. Since this action is called qahabah in Arabic, the word also came to mean a streetwalker.'

'What an interesting bit of information!' I laughed in amusement. 'Language is indeed a wonderful phenomenon. In American English one of the words for "streetwalker" is "hooker". That word too must have some historic origin, I think. But, my dear sir, you must have your cough treated quickly. It's not good at all at your age to be neglectful of such things.'

A strange kind of cloud passed over his face. 'Treatment? Ye . . . yes, I do get treatment.' He smiled wanly. 'But why would a streetwalker quit her beat? Goodbye, again.' He turned into the lane and quickly disappeared from sight.

The next day he took the trouble to look for me and take me out to lunch at his favourite Court Restaurant.

'Did you know that Virginia Woolf used to eat lunch here during the days that she worked at the British Museum?' he said, and added, 'She has mentioned this in her little book, *A Room of One's Own.*'

Wasim Jafar's mind was like the storerooms of the bigger museums where items are kept that are not on display for some reason. Such rooms are full of the most unexpected, strange and rare objects.

The redoubtable Wasim Jafar was also a repository of strange titbits of information. He regarded me as a shy, retiring person, one who was not too keen to show his face in society. Once, as we passed in front of the Royal Society, he stated to me that extreme shyness and the urge to keep oneself in privacy and retirement could ensure high literary or scientific achievement. He told me of Henry Cavendish who was shy almost to a pathological degree: he was unable to engage in the most casual of conversations even with his domestic help. He and his housekeeper exchanged numerous notes during the day to enable her to run the house. He usually answered the housekeeper's queries in laconic monosyllables like 'Yes', 'No', 'Let it pass'. And yet, Cavendish made many scientific discoveries which were centuries ahead of his times. Closeted at home, and armed with a crude machine, some primitive instruments and pen and paper, Cavendish calculated so accurately the earth's weight that his result was off the mark by less than one per cent of the weight arrived at in the modern laboratories with the aid of the most delicate and subtle instruments.

'So, my dear Khalil, it wasn't a wise saw devised by our elders to the effect that one who is shy loses all good fortune,' he said. 'The real necessity is to continue to feel ashamed of one's own deeds.' He changed the subject suddenly. 'Only recently, I was looking into the papers and the correspondence between Lord Lake and Maharaval Bakhtawar Singh. The Maharaval employed some fine painters. I'm looking for the paintings made by them.'

A violent bout of coughing overtook him. It shook his frail frame and he was obliged to shrink within himself and sit down at the lower step of a shop by the roadside.

Persistent coughing and hoarseness of voice of this kind combined with shallow breathing did not augur well for him at all. Trying to change the subject and turn his attention away from the distress caused by the cough, I said, 'But sir, weren't you looking for certain things related to Navab Ahmad Bakhsh Khan and Wazir Khanam? And didn't Ghalib say that to feel shy of one's own self was also a way of coquetry? Wazir Khanam would have been a proper subject for your advice, wouldn't she?'

The cough attacked him again, but less violently. He wiped his mouth with a linen handkerchief, paused for a second, and said, 'Yes, my dear young gentleman, how could people like us who are brought up on the culture of the tube and the internet understand delicate and subtle matters like the styles and ways of coquetry? But young sir, I meant that we really needed to develop some sense, some understanding about our *kukaram*, our evil deeds . . .'

I noted that in Bengali, and in some north Indian languages like Bhojpuri, *kukur* means 'dog'. I very nearly burst out laughing. 'Kukaram, what a wonderful word to use! How did you think of it? It would make a normal and fully fledged human being think he was a dog.'

'Well, that is the beauty of this word,' he said, smiling. 'Was it not Auden who wrote a play entitled *The Dog Beneath the Skin*? So wasn't it quite proper?'

'Yes, the late Ameeq Hanfi, a famous modern Urdu poet, also wrote in one of his poems, "Let someone restrain the dog that barks inside me".'

'I don't know who this Mr Ameeq Hanfi might have been, but he got it quite right. So look, how useful this word is. But my dear sir, I tell you the truth: *Were we to become conscious of our own faults—*'

'*Then there would be none to blame in our eyes*.' I quoted part of a well-known verse by Bahadur Shah Zafar, Delhi's last Emperor.

'No, no, never. Not at all. Bad we all are, but some of us regard our wickedness as goodness. Just take William Fraser, he strutted around looking like an Indian to all intents. Yet he couldn't forbear Navab Shamsuddin Ahmad Khan's affair with Wazir Khanam. And the Navab, his heart swelling with hatred, never forgave his siblings because their mother didn't treat his own mother well.'

'And Wazir Khanam, your ancestress?'

'Oh, she was a very complex person, and brave too. I'm really madly in pursuit of her portrait. I might understand her better if I could see what she looked like.'

We now began to meet frequently over tea or lunch. He knew quite a few obscure facts about Wazir Khanam, Marston Blake, Navab Ahmad Bakhsh Khan, Bahadur Shah's last recognized heir Mirza Fathul Mulk Bahadur and many others of those perilous times. He narrated to me in full detail the circumstances of Marston Blake's death.

When I expressed surprise that such 'treasonous' acts and events could happen against the iron rule of the English in the early nineteenth century, he removed my misunderstanding by telling me that between 1800 and 1857 there were several occasions when Indians had resorted to armed action against their Firangee masters and each time inflicted substantial loss of life and property on them. He made particular mention of the events at Bareilly and Benares. In Benares, there was Jahandar Shah, the exiled son of Shah Alam II, and one with abundant promise and talent. He had in fact fired at and seriously injured an English officer. Yet another Mughal Prince, Jahangir Bakht, also fired a shot in anger at an English officer who had misbehaved with him, and was banished to Allahabad as a retributive measure.

'There was some truth in Syed Ahmad Khan's assertion in his pamphlet about the 1857 rebellion in Bijnor,' Wasim Jafar said. 'Syed Ahmad Khan said that there was much anger and resentment in Indian hearts because far from treating the Indians as their equals, the English didn't even treat them as humans. This was tellingly stated in an astonishing and unexpected way by his son Syed Mahmud in a banquet speech in Benares much later. He rejected the English notion of Indians being subjects to the English ruler; on the contrary, the Indian and the English, he said, as subjects to the same sovereign, the Queen, were all equal, and our rights and duties are the same.'

'Well, that was certainly a bold and marvellous thing to say in those times,' I said. 'Rather, Syed Mahmud's idea was an extremely novel one. So how did the English react to it?'

'My boy, the British are a uniquely canny people. The occasion was a banquet hosted by Syed Ahmad Khan to honour Mr Shakespear, his former District Magistrate in Bijnor and now his Commissioner in Benares. All the elites of the town were present. Syed Mahmud's speech was brushed aside as a light-hearted after-dinner speech. Also, what could the poor Commissioner do? Syed Mahmud could never have presented his claims before the Government. If he had, he would have been dismissed from service.'

He laughed his usual raspy laugh, which quickly deteriorated into yet another spell of coughing.

*

Finally, Wasim Jafar invited me to dinner at his flat in Portobello Road. It was not a very fashionable neighbourhood, and his flat was on the third floor of a rather ancient building which did not boast of a lift. The flat was reached by a set of narrow stairs of the old style. I wondered how Wasim negotiated them many times a day, day after day.

As I entered, I realized at once that he lived in that unfashionable neighbourhood in a comparatively comfortless flat because he could not afford a better one, and the reason for it was not poverty, but his collector's zeal or rather obsession. His two-room flat was bursting with antiquarian collectibles: maps, paintings, books, manuscripts, glassware . . . you name it. And here was another reason for his living in Portobello Road: the moderately priced antique shops that abounded there. So it provided in ample measure articles to meet his craving. Anything that I picked up in the flat, I found it unique or certainly a rarity of its class.

He smiled faintly at my fascination and wonderment at the contents of his flat, and said, 'I've troubled you here for a special reason.'

'Oh, so you aren't going to feed me?' I said, attempting a feeble joke.

'We'll dine; we'll surely dine, dear sir. But just tell me, have you read the collection of Muhammad Ibrahim Zauq's (1788–1854) poetry, as edited by his disciple Muhammad Husain Azad (1831–1910)?'

'No, I don't think so,' I replied after some thought. 'I've certainly read Zauq from here and there, but the *Collected Works* edited by Maulana Muhammad Husain Azad? No, I think I haven't even cast an eye on it; it must be pretty rare now. The collection edited by T.A. Alavi is of course available freely.'

'You did well if you didn't cast an eye on it.' Suddenly, his face flashed red and hot with displeasure, as if flushed with a fever.

I had always found him cool tempered, not reacting strongly to things he found unpleasant. I felt uneasy at this sudden and apparently unprovoked rush of rage. I tried to laugh the matter away. 'Okay, then we can let the matter pass. I was worried that you would punish me by not giving me food, had I not read that book.'

He made an obvious effort to control his fury. 'No, it's nothing like that. Nothing that would result in one being deprived of dinner. . . . But the person who wrote this didn't pay the scantest regard to honesty and justice.'

I was a little mystified. Seeing me speechless, Wasim Jafar's ire cooled a little. 'Just see,' he said, 'here, on this page, Muhammad Husain Azad has been guilty of such hurtful prejudice and injustice.'

'Well . . . I haven't read the book, but I don't imagine Azad, who practically idolized Zauq, would have said something bad or hurtful about him.'

'Yes, he did love Zauq just this side of idolatry,' he said heatedly, 'but I'm not talking about Azad on Zauq. Azad had no love for the King, nor for Mirza Fathul Mulk, nor for Shaukat Mahal!'

His face was flushed again, his breath became quick and short. I was at a loss to know what I should say or do. Who this Shaukat Mahal, apparently a woman, could be, I had not the faintest idea. Nor did I know if Wasim Jafar was frequently subject to such fits, or if it was only today that the attack had happened. Nor had I any idea of where his doctor or his National Health Service hospital could be found. Was it at all wise to call in a doctor at this time? I began to lose my nerve. I knew nothing about the state of Wasim Jafar's health, and I did not want him to die on my hands. He certainly looked ill, but as a retired ophthalmologist I did not know how to measure his blood pressure even. Flustered and confused, I took out a bottle of water from the refrigerator and offered him a glass.

'Come, have some water first. Let your breath become even before we talk further,' I said to him gently and soothingly.

He thanked me in a choked voice. Having taken a sip or two of water, he seemed to calm down a little. He sat quiet and unmoving for a few minutes, though the expression on his face said that he was still far from normal: he looked wild and distracted.

A few minutes passed; both of us were silent. Then he drew a deep breath, and rubbed his face and eyes vigorously with his hands as if he had just woken up. Then he drank the rest of the water in one long draught and spoke in his normal voice: 'Khalil Asghar, what is your opinion on thieving?'

I did not know what to say, and would have said something untoward in my confusion. Fortunately, he went on in the same normal voice, 'I mean, what is your moral and legal view about stealing?'

I felt harassed and put upon. What the hell should I say to this? I was his dinner guest, but he was subjecting me to all sorts of ridiculous talk. I tried to laugh the question off and said light-heartedly, 'Well, sir, stealing is one of the five deadly sins, or seven deadly sins. But are you going to publish some juridical opinion on this, or have you had something stolen from you?'

His face clouded over with vexation and annoyance, as if he did not approve of my frivolous way of dealing with what was perhaps important for him. Or was there something which he wanted to reveal to me, but it was extremely upsetting for him and yet he had no option but to disclose it to me?

'Look,' his tone was that of a pedagogue explaining something to a child or a feeble-minded person, 'let's suppose there's something of yours stolen by someone, do you follow, wouldn't you have the right to take your property back?'

'Well, is that not an im . . . imaginary issue?' Suddenly, I was almost stammering, at a loss for words. 'I . . . I mean that, er . . . what in English is described as hypothetical . . .'

I dreaded evading or declining to engage with his question. It might, I feared, bring back his rage or his cough, or both. But his question was ambiguous, if not entirely vague. I could not determine what my best response could be, such that it should not seem patronizing or evasive.

He fell silent again. Then he spoke firmly, as if he had arrived at a decision. 'Tell me, doesn't a huge part of the inventories held by the British Library or the V&A, belong by rights to India or what's now called South Asia?'

'Doubtless. Not necessarily of a given individual, but it certainly belongs to the people of India or South Asia.'

'Good,' he said, 'and the same is the status of other similar properties in different museums, private homes and also in the Buckingham Palace?'

'Yes, undoubtedly. But some of the property must also have been presented as gifts to the current owners.'

'Undoubtedly,' he echoed my words but there was no sarcasm in his voice. 'I am quite willing to voluntarily give up all that was given as gift, and under no pressure. But how would you adjudicate about valuable things given by way of bribe, or to gain favour, or plundered, or confiscated under some tyrannous regulation?'

I could vaguely see the course that the discussion was taking. But what was the purpose of it all? I spoke slowly, after a great deal of thought. 'Should a legally correct and legitimate heir to that property appear on the scene, I . . . I suppose he can sue for the return of such property.'

'But if there wasn't any hope at all for the suit to succeed?'

'Well . . . isn't recourse to the law the only course open to a litigant?'

'Why? Why isn't another course available?'

'Well, what else is there? Should the claimant go and take it away by force? And taking by force, is that at all in his power?'

'No, it's not a matter of taking by force.'

'Mr Wasim Jafar, sir, please don't speak in riddles. I feel stifled and put upon already.' I said this with some asperity and in a plaintive show of heat, though I apprehended that Wasim Jafar would be upset again.

But he again fell silent for a little while, and then said, 'You know that Wazir Khanam was my great-grandmother and I am researching the circumstances of her life?'

'Yes. And you are particularly seeking her portrait, if there's any.'

'Muhammad Husain Azad speaks of a portrait, in that same *Collected Works* of Zauq that I just spoke to you about.'

'Oh, how nice! I didn't know that.'

'I've found that portrait,' he spoke in a low, almost subdued voice.

'Oh my God! Is that so?' I almost leapt up from my chair. 'Then it must be worth a fortune from the point of view of both history and literature! I must admire your success. It's a marvellous coup, really!'

'As the sole surviving male heir of Wazir Khanam, I am the legal proprietor of that portrait.' His voice now sounded even more hoarse.

'But where is that portrait? Will its present owner sell it to you?'

'Why in the world would he? Did the British Government return Abdul Hamid Lahori's *Padshah Namah*?'

I knew that the *Padshah Namah* was the famous history of the Mughal Emperor Shahjahan (r. 1627–1658), one of the most sumptuously illuminated manuscripts in the world, finished by one of Lahori's pupils after his death in 1654. It was presented to an official of the East India Company by a ruler of Avadh.

He interrupted my thoughts, almost shouting angrily: 'Did they return the Koh-i Nur diamond?'

'But those things are worth tens of millions, in pound sterling, not rupees. This, sir, is a mere portrait, and that too not of a queen or princess.

Its current owner will give it away to you, or at worst will charge you a hefty sum for it. Am I wrong?'

'I grant that it's not a treasure that we are talking about. But this nation is not the kind to let up on such things.'

'Do I understand you to mean that the portrait is in the possession of the British Government and you're not in a position or inclined to ask for it?'

'Well, both, actually.'

I almost lost my temper. 'Pardon me, but why are you speaking in bits and driblets? Why shouldn't you be candid if you want my advice?'

'You can't do a thing.' He spoke with cool deliberation. 'But listen, anyway. You know I keep looking for things in the British Library. Once, quite by chance I happened upon information about a diary of Lord Roberts—the very Lord Roberts who wrote *Forty-one Years in India* and who on one occasion was intolerably presumptuous about Zeenat Mahal, Bahadur Shah's queen. He had drawn upon his diary extensively in writing his book. I came to know that the diary in question is held by the library of the University of Aberdeen in its rare manuscripts section. Using my old network, I gained access to the diary. In it I found many things which he had not written about in his book.'

'That is, events of rapine and plunder?'

'Those too, but it also mentioned some private papers of the King and Fathul Mulk Bahadur that were found by Company soldiers during the sack of the Red Fort and its Chancery. For instance, the diary mentioned an ephemeris of the doings at Fathul Mulk's Court. Before this, I hadn't heard about the journal of an even insignificant prince, far less the last heir apparent. Roberts wrote that he had those papers deposited in the India Office Library and Records.'

'I'm truly astonished that no one else ever thought of it! Your discovery is surely of substantive importance, but why Aberdeen?'

'Oh well, because his mother was Scottish. Then I looked everywhere in the British Library. I went over all possible catalogues, handlists and annual reports, but drew a blank everywhere. I'd lost all hope, but I again lit upon an unlikely source. It was a retired employee, a venerable old gentleman who retired from the Library about thirty years ago. We fell to talking about the old times, and when I asked him about Roberts' papers, he promptly told me that a huge cache of papers concerning 1857 had not even been catalogued, for they were determined to be of little or no immediate importance. Those papers, he told me, were stored in boxes in the basement.'

'Indeed!'

'Yes, the idea was that in due course they'd be catalogued for access when more important papers of that time had been dealt with. That occasion never arose.'

'How interesting! It really becomes more and more curious, like a forgotten bit of family history.'

'Yes. But let me skip the minor details and tell you just the kernel of my story. I did get to those boxes, or footlockers, after a lot of search and bureaucratic hassle. There were seven in all. The contents of each box were inventoried neatly on top of the papers it contained. One of the footlockers had some legal papers and miscellaneous documents . . . ,' he paused, and then continued, 'and also the ephemeris of Fathul Mulk Bahadur. . . . There was something else, too.'

Again, he fell silent, as if unwilling to go on. My curiosity was aroused now. What could it be? The last will and testament of the King, some new facts about the treasonous conduct of Mirza Ilahi Bakhsh, or yes, some hard information about the tunnel rumoured to connect the two Red Forts of Delhi and Agra? Clues about some buried treasure? What could it be, after all?

'May I know what it was, that something else?' I spoke slowly, with adequate pauses, so as not to spook him.

'Know? Why should you just "know" about it? I'll show it to you.'

He rose, and opening his briefcase, extracted from it a stout, cloth-backed buff envelope as was commonly used in British India to secure important documents, and extended it towards me. I noticed that there was a distinct tremor in his hand. The envelope was not sealed, so I pulled open the flap and drew out a stiff piece of paper, about six inches by five.

It was a portrait of an extremely beautiful woman. She was in her mid-twenties, or maybe even less. Very light brown of colour—such as would be described as 'light brown' in Europe and America—and the face so radiant, so glowingly fresh, as if it was painted not in watercolour but with the freshly expressed juice of iris blooms. Her nose was straight and delicate, with the nostrils flared just a tiny bit, as if she was enjoying some subtle joke or was about to utter some subtlety. It was a full-face portrait—what was called a 'two-eyed portrait' by the later Mughal and other Indian painters—more than a century and a half, maybe two centuries, old. Quite contrary to the portraiture of those times, the sitter was shown as being quite aware, not only of the painter but also of the onlooker who would be looking at her when the painting was finished. Her eyes were full of such vibrant consciousness of youth and sex appeal that my heartbeat quickened. It seemed that the person in the painting was about to say something to me with her eyes or with a faint lift of her eyebrow. But there was not a vestige of vulgarity, absolutely just no hint of come-hitherness anywhere in her face. The gesture, when it came, would be a challenge of some sort, as if to say: Are you capable of dealing with such mischief-filled eyes? This seductive, tormenting face?

A perfectly sculpted face, adorned with exceptionally big eyes, the long eyelashes not inclining downwards like a curtain, but raised slightly, rather like delicately latticed bamboo curtains. The eyes dark brown with a hint of very light leaf-green with golden flecks, like the cool drink made of the juice of hibiscus flowers sweetened with raw Indian sugar. The technical name of this eye colour among traditional Indian beauticians is sharbati, from which the English word 'sherbet' derives. The whites of the eyes were clear and cool, just like a freshly blossomed eglantine. The neck, long and delicate, fawn-like, was adorned with a nine-stringed necklace of glowing light green emeralds, all exactly alike in cut and shape. There was nothing but emeralds the size of half a chickpea from the neck to the delicately hinted cleft below it. Their green hue was a luxurious sight that went deep into the eyes, absorbing them, like the colour of a freshly sprouted meadow. The head was not covered with the traditional light scarf for head and breasts, known as the dupatta. It was quite clear that the sitter was perfectly conscious of her bareheadedness. The sky-blue dupatta of an extremely light fabric, shot through with delicate golden thread, carelessly flung over the breasts and around the shoulders, was casually concealing, and also revealing, of the torso. The hair, densely black, was in just one thick and long braid which broke into two at the end, one large grey pearl loosely strung in each braid as if they had just wandered in there.

But, what a pity, the portrait was incomplete; not because the painter had left it unfinished, but because its lower half had been torn off brutally, so that nearly a third of the painting was lost.

I spoke again, haltingly, measuring each word carefully: 'This . . . this portrait, is it Wazir Khanam? Who tore it up?' In my anxiety in trying to keep myself calm, I did not realize the stupidity of my second question.

Wasim Jafar said, 'Read the inscription on the back.' His face was an unusual colour now, dark and hot, as if he were ill or in pain, and his voice tremulous.

I turned the paper over. There was a short inscription in the Persian script called Shikastah, (meaning, full of curls), the almost undecipherable style of writing used in Mughal chanceries. The words showed a slight rubbing, as if someone had tried to wash them off. Though the writing was quite small, I could read it with a little effort, thanks to my familiarity with old family trees and documents. 'True likeness of Wazir Khanam sahib, also known as Chhoti Begam, May God preserve her.' A date followed, but I was unable to decipher it.

'Congratulations, Mr Wasim Jafar, sir. You succeeded in your quest,' I said, my voice warm with enthusiasm. 'But . . . but did you find the portrait in one of those boxes? If it's so, then . . . then how . . . how could you get it out of the Library?'

'Yes!' he said with some force and heat. 'I did get it out. Now it's mine!' There was a challenge of sorts implied in his tone, as if he were saying: 'So I got it out. And what are you going to do about it? Will you report it to the Library and make me lose my find?'

'But . . . how was that made possible?' I asked meekly. I did not at all want to annoy him, and anyway I had no desire to conduct myself as a censor of morals in this matter. Whatever its legal status, the portrait belonged by right to Wasim Jafar.

'Well, my dear Khalil Asghar,' he was conspiratorial, friendly, 'the fact of the matter is, there is no record, no accession list, of this portrait. The contents of those footlockers haven't been catalogued. There's just a first draft of a handwritten list of its contents deposited with each box; this portrait doesn't find place in those rough catalogue lists. A copy of each of the lists is held in safe deposit at the Director's office. But I am certain that this portrait is not listed there.'

He paused, perhaps trying to find a suitable way to transit to the next part of his story. I did not say a word; fearful of saying something that may not go down well with the old gentleman, I held my tongue. He resumed after a minute or two, his speech even slower than before, and his voice still lower.

'Actually, the portrait was held between two loose leaves of the journal of

Mirza Fakhru's Court, its condition just as you see it now . . . I am perhaps the first person ever to have turned over each and every page of that journal and examined it carefully. It was like a stroke of lightning, when my eye first fell on that portrait. Who else could it be, if not Wazir Khanam? My God, to have such a stroke of luck! I could never be so lucky.'

Slightly short of breath, he stopped again. I did not know what to say, he was in such a state, it was almost like an epiphany.

'For a long time I couldn't gather the courage to turn the portrait over and try to identify its sitter. Maybe it wasn't Wazir Khanam, maybe it was somebody, anybody . . . who could know? Then, squeezing my eyes shut, I turned the portrait over and over, a number of times. Then I opened my eyes . . . well, you already read that little text on the back of the portrait . . .

'Now what more can I say? Acting on a sudden impulse, I inserted the portrait in the inside pocket of my jacket. You know it's prohibited to bring anything into the Library: no briefcase, no handbag and no packets. Winter overcoats are to be invariably deposited in the coatroom. But it was just a plain jacket that I had on, and it was a small picture anyway, utterly unknown and no one would suspect me. The only departure from routine that I made that day was to cease work immediately. Collecting whatever else had been issued to me and putting those back neatly on the shelf, I walked out with quiet, sedate steps, hands in the front pockets of my jacket.'

'The rightful claimant got his claim!' I uttered an extremely famous Persian saying, also popular in Urdu.

He looked hard at me, as if trying to determine if I was being sarcastic. 'Is that so?' he said sharply. 'Do you really think so?'

Since I was quite clear in my mind that he was morally the rightful owner of the painting, I spoke earnestly, 'Yes. I am quite, quite sure.' I followed it up with an equally earnest word of prayer, often used on happy occasions, 'May God make it auspicious for you!'

Again, he looked hard at me—in fact, he almost glared. It seemed as if he were cautioning me to understand that he did not at all care what I did or did not believe. The painting was his property, and would always remain so.

'Now cast a look on Zauq's *Collected Works* as edited by Muhammad Husain Azad,' he said, passing a somewhat foxed, medium-sized volume to me.

I was ravenous by then, and my mind was also in such a whirl that I could not comprehend what I was required to do with it. I looked open-mouthed at him like a rattle-brain. Then the penny dropped, I recalled that some while ago he had talked about Zauq's *Collected Works* and something written there that he did not approve of. As I put forth my hand to take the book from him, he directed me to page 41.

'I've placed a bookmark there,' he said.

I opened the page and read, with rising disgust, revulsion and astonishment, the following words:

> There was, in the city, a ravishing beauty called Chhoti Begam, fully a mistress of her arts. The brilliant midday sun of her life was in sinkage. She had already slain and ingested an uncounted number of Delhi's nobility and yet she still pretended to be picking the florets of early youth. Mirza Fakhru [Mirza Ghulam Fakhruddin Fathul Mulk Bahadur] was just around twenty-four or twenty-five at that time. He hired a whore and himself ended up her slave. The Mirza drew out a picture from his private strongbox, looked at it, and said, 'Maestro [the poet Zauq], just take a look.' The maestro at once knew it to be a portrait of that one. Glancing at it, he said, 'Very nice.' But this would not do for the Mirza. Again, he said, 'Do take a look. If there were to be a sweetheart, shouldn't she be like this one?' The maestro now understood: his heart has gone and walked off to the woman and he wants me too to admire the hag. Still, he said, 'Nice, very nice!' But the Mirza was not to be content with such faint praise. For a third time, he put the portrait in the maestro's hands and said, 'Well, maestro, just look. Do you see any imperfection here?' The maestro took a proper look and observed, 'The breasts are slightly droopy.' The maestro used to say that he would never have uttered such words, but his heart importuned: he's a mere boy, caught in a harlot's trap. Do say what you should; maybe he will take a hint.

I felt like tearing out the page, shredding it and flushing it down the toilet. But I knew that would be silly, and in bad taste.

'I am not prepared to accept this account. A Mughal prince, and an heir apparent at that, would never behave in this way even if his estate had declined a thousand times,' I cried hotly. 'Kings had their protocol and their sense of honour. They would never permit an outsider's gaze to fall on their women, even if he were a prince, far less a petty employee, though he be a formal mentor in poetry. Then,' I slowed down a little, 'aren't gravitas and a sense of dignity something in their own right? It seems to me that Muhammad Husain Azad harboured some grudge against Mirza Fakhru and his stepson Dagh.'

'I wouldn't rule it out, particularly when we see that this account, or anecdote, has been inserted here entirely out of context and with no occasion to warrant it. Then, even if the heir apparent was coarse enough to show his sweetheart's portrait to his mentor, Zauq couldn't have ever dared to reply with such indecency.'

'But then, why would the venerable Azad be so spiteful? There must be some reason, surely.'

'I really don't know,' Wasim Jafar replied in a dejected tone of voice. 'But you might perhaps have noticed that Azad has been malicious against the King and the princes of the Red Fort elsewhere too, and on numerous occasions, in fact. Perhaps that was the mode of the historiography then. Or maybe he was hinting that those who lived in the Fort were indeed so decadent and bereft of a sense of honour that they were best put to the sword and laid waste.'

'Yes, after him it became a fashion veritably to vilify them. As if Niaz Fat'hpuri weren't malicious enough, even Mirza Farhatullah Beg, a true citizen of Delhi, didn't do much justice to the princes of the Fort.'

'Oh well, Beg was in fact quite restrained in comparison to Azad. Just see, Azad describes Mirza Fakhru as a 'mere boy' of twenty-four or twenty-five, and adds that Wazir Khanam was a 'hag'. The fact is that both the Mirza and Wazir Khanam were about the same age. The Prince was born in 1811, and Wazir Khanam was also born around that time. In fact she might have been a little younger.'

'Anyway, let it pass. The portrait is now in your possession and that's great success indeed. Pity you can't write about these matters.'

'Why can't I? You wait and see. I'll write about these matters someday.'

*

I returned to India a short while after that conversation. Unlike Wasim Jafar, I had had no success at all in my purposes. Both the Farooquis of Burhanpur and the Khudaijis of Gorakhpur stubbornly avoided revealing themselves to me. I got over those disappointments, more or less, but I could never forget Wazir Khanam. My regret was that I was neither a historian nor a fiction writer, or I would surely have narrated her tale.

About three or four months after my return, I received a letter from Mr Douglas Abernethy, partner in a law firm in London called Martin and Martin. Accompanying the letter were a sealed envelope and a packet of papers. Here is what the letter said:

> We are sorry to inform you that an old and valued client, Dr Wasim Jafar, Ph.D., F.R.H.S., etc, resident of 14/42 Portobello Road, London, breathed his last on 19 September in London. He had cancer of the lungs. Until the very last moment he battled against the disease with great fortitude. But the cancer had slowly metastasized to many of his organs. In his will, Dr. Jafar had instructed that the enclosed papers and the sealed envelope be despatched to you after his decease. The deceased also desired that should you like to put together a historical narrative based on the enclosed, a sum of £1000 sterling be made available to you towards research and ancillary expenses. Furthermore, all the papers of Dr. Jafar are deposited in the British Library. According to his will, should you, for the purposes of your opus, feel the need for the copy of a document or book in his collection, the same will be made available to you at the expense of his estate.
>
> We would be grateful for you to confirm the receipt of this letter and the enclosed.
>
> We remain, dear sir,
> Yours truly,
> For Martin and Martin,
> Douglas Abernethy, Junior Partner.

Putting aside the papers, I opened the envelope. It contained the portrait of Wazir Khanam. In a corner on the back of it, Wasim Jafar had inscribed his dated signature in his fine and clear handwriting.

3

A mysterious book appears, and also an unnamed spirit, enchanting Wasim Jafar

(From the notes and memoranda of Dr Wasim Jafar)

IT WAS NOT big, in fact it was quite like the first and only edition of Safir Bilgrami's (1834–1890) *Rashhat-e-Safir*.

But what was this book and whose was it? Who brought it and left it here on my bed as I slept? It felt somewhat warm to my touch, as if someone had just picked it up from near a fire or from somewhere in the sun. I tried to open it, but felt some obstruction, as if the pages under the pasteboard were stuck to the flyleaf and also to each other.

The leather binding bore no name or title, nor did the spine, which was cracked in many places; but it was clear that there had never been a title at all, nor did it ever bear any information about the author or the publisher. Was it a manuscript, or was it a printed book? It did not seem all that ancient to me; it could not have been older than a century or a century and a half. But a book of even so little antiquity could be extremely valuable. Could it be something entirely rare, something unique like, say, the letters of the great eighteenth-century Urdu poet Muhammad Taqi Mir, or a collection of the last Mughal Emperor Bahadur Shah Zafar's poems written in his own hand?

I felt a sudden tremor run through my body. But should I force the book open even though the pages were stuck together? In that case I might permanently damage it. So then, what? I said to myself with some irritation and impatience. Damage the whole thing? Let the damn thing be damaged entirely—it is of no use to me even now, in its present state. If it cannot be opened, it will remain shut forever.

Now I struck my palm on the book a little more forcibly. It still seemed to have low-grade temperature, as before. Temperature? That was a word that we normally use for human beings. 'He's running a little temperature,' for example. How could a book be running a temperature? And even if it came piping hot from somewhere . . . piping hot from somewhere . . . ? What does that mean? Is it a hot shish kebab fresh from a skewer above a fire? And even if it did come piping hot, it should have cooled by this time. Lines from the poet Iqbal occurred to me suddenly, of their own accord:

Here, there were fires, now quenched,
There, a few pieces of tent-ropes, broken: How many
Caravans passed by here? Who knows?

Yes, who knows how many hands it has passed through between here and now, and then, when it was made? How many have been the hands that touched it, opened it; how many the eyes that read it? And why suppose that it must be a book written in Urdu? Persian, Arabic, Hebrew . . . there are numerous possibilities. But yes, it could not be in Sanskrit or English, for then it would open from the left and not from the right. But how do I know which side it should open from? Unless it is open, how can I know which is the right side to open?

I mustered up my courage and tried to open the book from somewhere in the middle, though not without some trepidation. The pages felt a little thicker and heavier than usual, but they were not stuck together. Rather, it seemed as though they had dried slowly in the shade after a long immersion in water. The great modern Indian painter Abdur Rahman Chaghatai used to give some similar treatment to the paper on which he painted his watercolours. But that paper was of a special quality and he also treated it with egg white and some arcane spices and a light coat of aniseed oil. He would then expose the treated paper to water, or in fact on certain occasions, to rain. So was this book calligraphed on some such paper? It wouldn't be much of an antique then . . .

But now it seemed to me that the book's pages were somewhat thickened because some mischance had caused them to be affected by water for some considerable time. Maybe some irascible nobleman, irritated by something in the book, or being just bored, threw it down into the ornamental pond in his mansion, and then, repentant some time later, had it recovered and dried out? (I recalled the anecdote that an aristocratic rival of the seventeenth-century Urdu poet Vali was so piqued with the excellence of Vali's poems that he suddenly hurled the book into the river on the bank of which he was being regaled with Vali's poems by a courtier.)

And was it not the pages of the poet Mir Soz that Muhammad Taqi Mir had snatched from the hands of the hapless Soz and dunked it in the ornamental pool right in front of Navab Asifuddaulah, who was the patron of both? My heart leapt up. If not Vali, let it be Mir Soz. Maybe Soz had later surreptitiously, away from Muhammad Taqi Mir's eyes, recovered those pages and had them bound? What a marvellous find that would be! But I knew that both the stories were equally apocryphal.

Let the stories be apocryphal, but there was nothing apocryphal about the pages of this book being water-drenched once or twice, and for quite some length of time.

Gingerly, I now lifted the hard cover, hoping that it may have dried out now and the endpaper could perhaps be observed. The hard cover opened easily, almost gently. I forgot that a moment ago I had been torn between conflicting imaginings, anxieties and perplexities about the state of the pages inside the book. I forgot my fear that all the pages and the flyleaf may have coalesced due to moisture and formed one solid tablet.

I opened the hard cover to find a tiny silverfish between the fold of the spine and the endpaper. Oh, oh, the poor little thing that was supposed to be this small garden's guardian was itself overtaken by death! Yet, touched by the air, it seemed to move a tiny bit (. . . touched by the air? For all that I knew, silverfish could not survive and would die quickly if a book was aired frequently.). And then, sliding ever so slowly, the silverfish disappeared behind the spine.

The endpaper was heavy, dark brown and yellow of hue, the wavy design upon it suggesting snakeskin. This type of endpaper was popular over a century ago. It had been popularized by the English bookbinders in Calcutta who imported it from England. The colour of the design was so dark, and the design so dense, that no writing would be visible on the paper, even if something had been written on it. Besides, the paper was now brittle and broken in many places. That, in fact, was a manufacturing defect: the paper was hard, lacking in suppleness, and therefore broke easily when folded. The pressure exerted by the seam, and its natural brittleness had been too much for it. (The silverfish had hidden under the page, taking advantage of one of the many cracks in the endpaper. No, it couldn't have gone into hiding, it must have slipped through, for how could a dead insect move of its own accord?)

The seam appeared undamaged, but the inner lining of the spine was peeling away from the signatures. Glue, not gum or paste, had been used to fasten the spine to the signatures. The glue had lost its odour ages ago, but its layers, hard and brittle like dirty yellow glass, stuck to the signatures and the inner surface of the spine in many places. Thank God for small mercies, the stitching was not broken; the signatures could be seen clearly. An expert bookbinder would be able to rip the spine off and safely open the signatures even if the book could not be opened from the top by a reader.

I turned the endpaper over. The overleaf of this kind of endpaper was always blank and writeable. That is to say, it was buff or biscuit coloured and quite easy to write on; you only needed a broad pen and bright ink. In this book, the page was quite blank, so was the next page, the verso, which was the first page of the book. What the hell does this mean? If it was a proper book, the owner or at least someone else would have inscribed something there: name, signature, date, logo, stamp. It should have at least been 'There are a hundred forms of desolation here; still, something is left standing,' as Mir said. I should then have something extant for me on the page.

As for me, I always inscribe, as far as possible, my name on every book that I acquire. And if the book is of antique character, I also put down brief notes about it. Greatly disappointed, and apprehensive that the whole book might consist of just blank pages, I said to myself, okay, let's quit now. We'll look into this tomorrow.

I was just about to close and push the book under my pillow when I felt the fine hairs on my neck prickle and rise as if stirred by some breeze. As if there was someone behind me, bending over my shoulder and trying to read or identify the book, and his breath was upon and around my neck. There was no one else in this house but me, so who . . . ? I didn't feel plucky enough to turn my head and look, and I suffer from a permanently stiff neck anyway, the gift of chronic spondylosis. As always, I recalled spontaneously and quite out of context a punning line from Mir whose point turns on the stiff neck: a stiff-necked person is supposed to be proud and arrogant. And equally unexpectedly and out of context I recalled yet another line from Mir where he says, 'I don't bend my neck to anyone at all. What a pity, I am God's slave, not God himself.'

Well, that is how nature and language have their fun with us. Still, I could have turned my head slowly, not without some considerable pain, if I could have gathered my courage, which seemed to be quite shattered. I could hear the soft sound of breathing behind me. The book was open, as before.

Suddenly, with a faint sound, the book closed of its own accord. I had not quite registered and responded to the event when the book opened again, and someone spoke in a whisper, enunciating every syllable clearly, but I could not determine the language. It did sound somewhat like Urdu . . . or Turkish . . . or Pushto, but I could not make any sense of it. I tried to gather my courage again: let me see at least what is happening behind me, or am I dreaming?

An orange-vermilion wave seemed to ripple through and pass over the open page. No, wait a minute, perhaps I forget. The wave did not just ripple; it behaved as if it was sentient. It twisted and turned like a ray directed from a burning ball. But the page was still blank . . . No, it now seemed that it did have something written on it; some heartless person had rubbed the writing off with deliberate, slow thoroughness. I said to myself, let me just grab my magnifying glass, it's right here in this drawer. But no, that wretched desk isn't here, I am in my bed.

I closed my left fist tightly, leaving a tiny hole at the end, as I often used to do when I was small. While I read quietly at night I sometimes played the game of 'microscope', that is, I would imagine that my closed fist with a small aperture at the end was a microscope. Then, closing my right eye, I would place my left eye on the bigger end of the fist—my imagined eyepiece of the imagined microscope. An infinitely small ray of light, I supposed, passed from my eye through the eyepiece along the focal length made by my little fist, and would fall on the page. The word or two that the aperture at the end of the fist enabled me to see, would always seem brighter than before, if not actually enlarged.

But now I know all about the reality of the eye and its rays. I know that the rays are just an illusion, or useless supposition. There is no ray of light, however thin and subtle, passing from the eye to the object that is being seen by the eye. No light emanates from the eye: we see only when external light falls on an object. The Egyptian Arab Alhazen told us about it more than a thousand years ago but we were persuaded only when we found it in books written by the Europeans.

Recently, I had my eyes examined by my ophthalmologist. He placed on my eyes a black disc, which had an extremely narrow hole at the centre. When he placed the disc even on my weak eye, I could see those letters on the board, which had otherwise been impossible for me to decipher. I was delighted that even my half-blind eye was getting better. But the doctor dashed my hopes with a brief smile, saying that what I had experienced was interesting, but it meant nothing really. It was just what he called the pinhole effect. So why shouldn't I take advantage of the pinhole effect when I did not have access to a magnifying glass?

But my hands were shaking, making it impossible to close them in a fist. In fact, even my body was lightly aflutter. There was someone behind me, a half-smile on his face . . . From somewhere, someone whispered to me a description of the poet Dagh in early youth—his face was wonderfully soft—the countenance aglow with delight, like a newly opened bloom.

Terror-stricken as I was, had I also lost my mind? I did not look behind; nor could I have done so with my pathologically stiff neck. Nor was there really a face or a being looking over my shoulder, trying to read the book—or my book. And there was no one, indeed no one was visible, and yet, someone was there with a face that bloomed like a bed of roses in summer. Someone whispering, someone's breath, warm and pleasant on my neck and shoulders, the house, empty but for my presence. Whom should I call out to? For God's sake, save me from this!

Was it a book or was it a tablet to open up some magic land? But a magic land's tablet has some writing upon it, which can be deciphered only by him whose destiny it is to open up the magic land. A drop of sweat slithered down from my forehead into my right eye. My left is very feeble; I do all my reading of fine print or examining a manuscript with my right eye alone. Involuntarily, my hand rose up to dry the drop of perspiration. 'It will open,' someone said. My nerves were so shot by now that the voice was like a pulley over which my involuntarily closed fist was swung up to hit my eye with force, as if it was a hammer striking at my eyebrow and eye.

At the end of the tiny hole, small like a true pinhole, something dazzled like a minuscule topaz crystal, and on the first page of the book, in the margin—had there been a margin there—something was written in that same golden topaz-coloured ink, but erased, though not fully so. I shut one eye extremely tight and put the other one on the aperture made by the open end of my fist, trying to fix the eye on it as hard as I could.

'You shall hear when the book opens,' someone said. To my ragged senses, it seemed that the voice fell not on my ear but penetrated my spine. Minute drops of perspiration, flowing from my forehead and into my eye, as if tears had slowly sprung forth, were now wetting my fist. There was no way that I could see anything.

A little angered and not a little flustered and unnerved, I tried to push the book away . . . but no, it would not move, having become a block of stone. I was just about to dare and apply a little more force, I hadn't even stretched my hand towards it . . . look here, the book opened yet again as if a light gust of wind, not felt by me at all, had done the job. There was some writing, Persian or Urdu, I could not determine. The entire page on both sides had small holes where the termites had been at work. Hardly a line was free from those holes. Frustration, disappointment and fury almost drove me to tears. No! There are no tears in my eyes, just the mistiness of water. Where did the water come from? From where else, but the moisture contained in the stained pages of the book. That first page opened slowly, under its own power, turned over by its own force; perhaps the book was about to open. On the next leaf, near the top right-hand side, some words could be descried.

It was perhaps a line or two of verse, but most of the letters had been eaten away by the termites. I tried my best, first trying to peer through the pinhole made by my fist, then bringing the page as close to my eye as I could. It was something like: . . . y wak . . . ful . . . ness in this nig . . . t of separatio . . . knocks at . . . the door . . . death . . . it's not a nig . . . that can pas . . . in story . . .

Whose verse was it? I remember having read it and recited it to myself hundreds of times in my heart, and been driven to frenzied appreciation at its mood of anguish and mystery. It was a Persian poet called Baba . . . Baba Tahir Uryan? No, the language is not his. Baba . . . Baba . . . Fughani Gilani? No, there is no such poet. Nasiri Gilani? Yes, that was it. Baba Nasiri Gilani, and then I could read the whole verse, or I recalled it and believed that I had deciphered the mutilated words:

It is a night of separation. I cannot sleep.
My restlessness knocks at the door of death.
It is not a night that can pass
In telling stories.

The writing was in the same topaz-golden ink that I had noticed through my pinhole, slightly rubbed, but the letters seemed to burst forth into a daffodil-yellow light. What excellence in calligraphy, how attractive the slightly lengthened lines and how firm the ligatures! Just a couple of almost perfect three-quarter circles with the appropriate sharpness and thickness, and numerous elongations. Each of the Persian words—especially those which I translate as 'my restlessness', 'death', 'night', 'is not'—were so attractively crafted, almost like careful drawings. And the long, upstanding letter alif, occurring many times, confident and erect, as standards.

It is not a night that can pass
In telling stories.

How mysterious was that message, and coming as it did, it seemed even more pregnant with hints and suggestions. It was not a night that could come to an end, like a story, or which could be brought to conclusion by telling stories; but who was offering to tell stories, and to whom?

'I can tell, if you listen.' Again someone speaking, whispering. What was it then, a genie, or a hidden genius? The jungle of my body and soul thrilled to the sound. I remembered the long-forgotten lines of a poem:

Who was it that passed, with long steps
Over the silent and grave surface of the night?

Who would tell, if I listened? And what would he tell? Surely, there was someone, some living being that just admonished me, 'I can tell, if you listen.' What should I listen to, and why should I listen? Ghalib's line came to mind: 'An excess of naiveté chokes the ears of good sense with the meaningless foam of noise.'

The book shut with a little snap. I had no control over my hands, and not only my hands, but also my body, my being. However much I desired to stay stout of heart, I squeezed my eyes tightly shut, and kept them shut for some time. And then, I looked most stealthily out of the corner of my eye to see if the book was still there, if the man (or woman) at my shoulder was still breathing soft breeze over the scattered down on my neck.

Open your eyes, oh, do open them and look
What times, what scenes are passing!

A verse from Mir, my favourite poet, who now peeped out through the window, or no, he did not, for there was no window there, just a wall made of very fine glazing on which was inscribed the manuscript. Also there was inscribed in the manuscript the entire scene beyond the manuscript-glass, and where there was some open space, the morning breeze came in like a beloved or a line of verse which was to provide the theme and motif for other verses that were to come. Is this a book, or is it a scene composed haphazardly with all sorts of irrelevant, found objects?

But my eyes are still shut, I said to myself. Perhaps my eyes were shut because of my terror. But it was not the book that terrorized me. I stood in terror of myself . . . There was some inscription too under the verse, its ink the same vermilionesque, with a hint of gold dust. Or perhaps the ink was made from lapis lazuli, but how could the blue-green of lapis lazuli be mistaken for the reddish orange of vermilion?

I had handled hundreds, not to say thousands of antique Urdu and Persian books, and in my own library I had quite a few of them. I had never seen such yellow-blue and ochre. Traditional painters and calligraphers in Delhi had four special colours: white, gold, lapis lazuli and vermilion. These colours were always prepared within the four walls of the painter's lodgings and in great secrecy. There was just no question of the prescription being passed from one house to another. So maybe this orange-blue was the secret special ink of some atelier?

The first decipherable word of the inscription was Mirza, with one or two words preceding it. Was it the great eighteenth-century poet Mirza Sauda, or the more famous one of the nineteenth century, Mirza Ghalib? I could barely discern something like 'nau', so should I understand it to be Mirza Naushah, the appellative that was often used affectionately for Ghalib? Was I looking at an autograph of Mirza Ghalib? My heart missed a beat. But no, Ghalib never signed as Mirza Naushah—others used to describe him thus. Then Naushah . . . Navab . . . was it Ghalib's name, but in someone else's hand?

It suddenly occurred to me that it was Navab Mirza, and not Mirza Naushah, and in fact the whole inscription, or autograph, was Navab Mirza Khan Dagh, the famous poet and Wazir Khanam's son . . .

The book closed, all of a sudden, before I could even realize that it was closing. I looked at it, slightly bewildered. But then, almost at once there was a faint click and another page opened at another place. There was some writing in English. I could not decide if it was calligraphy or cast-iron type. It must have been a master calligrapher, to write such an elegant, cursive and decorative copperplate in black. I could read:

Lord Roberts

Then I could clearly see, near the bottom of the page and in the same hand:

Meerza Futhoolmoolk Bahadoor Ghoolam Fukhrooddin Rumz, 1849

Now I found that I could touch the book and turn the page over. There was nothing written overleaf. The next page, recto, had some writing on it but I could not make out if it was Persian or Urdu. I felt perplexed and aggravated. So what kind of book was this? Was it handwritten or printed? Had it been printed, it should not have so many pages that were blank or sparse in text, with some others so densely composed as to be unreadable. There was English in places and then some other language elsewhere. More a genie than a book. I decided to stow it safely away under my pillow and to deal with it the next day. But it was quite early in the evening yet, not at all the time for me to retire for the night.

Surely, it was not a book in the normal sense of the word. It was some sort of an enchantment. It talked; it fell silent; it opened by itself, shut by itself. By turns, it both terrified and seduced. Arthur Koestler named his book *The Ghost in the Machine*. So should I call my book *The Ghost in the Book*? But Koestler, in naming his book thus, was alluding to the Cartesian formulation that the human body is a container, and the soul or the mind or the power of thought, its content. Thus mind or spirit and matter were two separate entities. Koestler apprehended that Science, if it went forward furiously as it seemed to be doing then, would one day insinuate or discover an organicity in the machine too. And I, well, I was trying to locate lost things (for, we are the birds that are from places which are now lost, as some Urdu poet said). Things that we boxed off in books, books that were wrapped in blue or black cloth and thrown away in the bushes and shrubs across the river, for our shoulder straps were loose, our backs bent, and the burden too great for us to bear. And when on the black and grey sandbanks of the river we looked for boats, stumbling and falling in the half-dark, those bundles kept slipping from our backs but we did not think much about them, busy as we were in trying to save ourselves.

You, oh you conjurer up of the fairies,
This is no conjuring up of fairies.

It seemed this was a night for me to conjure up half-forgotten Persian or Urdu verses. There was a sound, a voice, emanating from that book, as if someone were humming a tune, like water trickling down and gathering in a carafe; as if there was a peri, busy in perfecting and balancing the drone on a very small, very delicate, stringed instrument. A heart-ravishing, soul-seducing reverberation. Soft but deep.

Melody falls, drop by drop, and yet
It raises reverberations so deep;
Thought rises like dust and flies in the brain.

Then, suddenly the page of the book became illuminated like a small cinema screen and the pictures were in full colour.

Delhi's Red Fort, its Lahori Gate . . . known images, but wasn't the stir and bustle of a different type? I did not see men in pants or blue jeans and bush shirts or T-shirts, their bodies disproportionately bulging at the waist or abdomen, eating slices of bananas sprinkled with salt and pepper; I did not see women with sullen faces and pouting, prominent lips heavily painted; there were no women around looking somewhat bored and somewhat unhappy with everything; no din and rattle and growl of scores of ancient buses, aggressively driven cars and nimble three-wheeler scooters passing every minute in front of me on a road loaded with pedestrians and pushcarts; there was nothing of the grubby kiosks and wheelbarrows, a plethora of polythene in ugly, sickly colours, stalls selling sharp-smelling and sharp-tasting savouries which were served in plastic cups or wrapped in newspaper cones.

No, not at all, there was nothing at all of those things. I could see the mosque of Shahjahan clearly behind me. I heard someone say: 'Today the Chowk of Sadullah Khan wears wonderful lineaments and has an out-of-the-world look to it. The True Presence, the Master and Mentor of Divine Authority, Shadow of God on Earth, Dispenser of Destinies, will betake himself to the Mina Bazaar.' And then from somewhere arise the introductory notes of some raga in bass.

pa . . . ni . . . sa . . . rè . . . rè . . .

Oh, oh! This is the Tilak Kamoda. The introductory notes have a slight touch of two other modes, but the bass is in full power. The sound overflows, reverberates, so deep that it does not sound like the sitar; it has the tones of the sarod. Who can say how much power, how much strength would have been needed to pluck the strings, and how powerful would the plectrum need to be, to permit such pulling. The notes themselves had such a wonderful range, such depth and such gravitas. The introductory notes came to a conclusion.

pa . . . ma . . . pa . . . ni . . . sa . . .

And then the raga, fully fledged.

sa . . . ni . . . dhi . . . pa . . . ma . . . ga. . . rè . . . gi . . . sa. . .

And then the full configuration.

sa . . . ni . . . sa . . . rè . . . rè . . . pa . . . ma . . . gi . . .

Neither the player, nor the accompanists were anywhere to be seen, but the elegance and the lustre at the Lahori Gate was even more prominent than before. Yet there were some in the buzz and bustle who were noticeable because of their slow, almost sad and sluggish gait. The Tilak Kamoda is a raga for the second watch of the night. It is very similar to the ragas

Sauratha and Desa, and only the expert singer or player can render it so as to keep the distinctions.

This raga expresses the pain of the night that is passing, and the ache of lost moments and the dread of the coming morning when the candles will be extinguished, when the flames of the torches will be decapitated.

BOOK 2

4

Mian Makhsusullah's portrait causes a furore

MY NAME IS Muhammad Yusuf. I am a sadahkar, that is, a maker of delicate gold or silver ornaments with no gemstones. I am originally from Kashmir, but the matter of my origins is not so simple really. If I were to narrate it from the beginning, it has bewildering complications, twists and turns which will turn out to be confusing, if not tiring. But if I do not begin at the beginning, its fine and complex details will elude most listeners.

I am at that stage of my life (forty-seven years old in 1840, according to the English calendar) where one tends to look back and determine if all that had happened was destined to be that way, or if there had been any other possibilities. And above all, at this time of life one wants to examine the stages and the hurdles that had to be negotiated before Time's Great Designer could present to the world the aspects and forms with which a man and his progeny ended up finally. The great poet Mir, respected by all of us, said, 'A thousand shapes were unshaped before these figures were made.' This seems to be true for us in more senses than one.

There is something else: at a time of life when women seek comfort and sisterhood with those of their own blood, and a man sees a comrade and friend in the woman of his home, I am alone from all sides. My wife of sweet nature and good fortune was called to God suddenly and quietly, like a dewdrop lifted up by the world-illuminating sun from the point of a thorn. All three of my daughters are living separately from me in their own homes and I have now nothing more to do here. Happy would be the day when I go away from this desolate home, as the poet said. And there is another good to be had from this loneliness and this hope and longing for death: Whatever I narrate will be true, and I will not hide anything, for I have no expectations from anyone, or fears.

The making of plain gold ornaments is not our ancestral craft. My father Muhammad Daud Badgami and his younger brother Muhammad Yaqub Badgami had been living in Kashmir for a very long time; in fact, they were born there, but they were not true Kashmiris. Their grandfather was Mian Makhsusullah, the painter. This Mian sahib was an inhabitant of a small village called Hindal Vali ka Purwah in Kishangarh, Rajputana. It was during the auspicious, fortunate and Paradise-certified reign of the Presence, King of the World and of all those who dwelt in it, He whose emblem was the sign of advancement, whose world was the world of Fortune, Muhammad Raushan Akhtar Padishah, Fighter in the cause of Islam, who now rests in Paradise.

Perhaps I do not need to state or emphasize that especially throughout Rajputana, and generally all over the land of Hind, the Presence, the Sun of the firmament of Friendship with God, the firmament for the Sun of generosity and excellence, the Great Master, Benefactor of the poor, Creator of kingships, the Saint of all Saints, Bestower of the crown to kings, Protector of those who have none, our Lover and Beloved, Babu Muinuddin Sahib Chishti, Beloved of God, is lovingly called by the title Hind-al Vali.

Previously, there was only one village in Rajputana called by the illustrious name Hindal Vali ka Purwah; it was situated somewhere near the small settlement known as Khvajah Sahib ka Chillah. In fullness of time, the names of many villages came to include the auspicious prefix Hindal Vali.

Due to frequent usage, the name of our village contracted to Hindal Purwah. The village proper had just three Muslim homes. There were one or two Brahmin and about five or seven Rajput homes, and the rest were all artisans. They all depended on painting for earning their daily bread. All the beauty and all the grace of the school of painting of Kishangarh Qalam was owed to the expertise of those good-natured, law-abiding and indigent village craftsmen, their inventiveness in creating colours, and their creativity in treating paper for painting. As for the city of Kishangarh, it was inhabited only by greenhorns and the middlemen through whom the painters' produce was brought to the market. The actual work was done by us, unknown villagers, and the name and fame went to Kishangarh Qalam. Occasionally, buyers approached us directly and paid without demur the price a painter charged for a portrait. These portraits were mostly imaginary; in fact, painting portraits from life was regarded with distaste.

I do not know the real name of Mian Makhsusullah, nor can I give a fair estimate of his age at the time this story begins. The village Hindal Purwah no longer exists on the face of the earth. Thus there is none from whom the Mian's age could now be possibly ascertained. All that I know for certain, I have already submitted to my dear readers; it is probable that he was not a Muslim originally, and had a different name. He must not have been more than thirty or thirty-five years of age at that time, but by virtue of spending much of his time in seclusion, away from the village, and also due to his not being mindful at all of his food or dress, he looked much older. Everyone in the village called him 'Mian' or 'Baba'.

The population of the village was not in excess of 150 or 175 souls; most of them, as I narrated above, depended on the craft of painting for eking out a living. A little away from the traditional village boundary, there were a few homes of Muslim and Hindu shepherds and camel drivers. There were also a couple of hereditary but petty farmers. There had been a long-standing suspicion about them that they were thugs and it was their creed to commit murder without actually shedding blood, plundering the body and then burying it so deep that it could forever remain undiscovered. But this rumour had never been established to be true in or around the village. Let alone being established as truth, no one ever had reason to hold even the slightest presumption of such a crime against them.

There were some Muslims among those putative thugs; the rest were of different castes and one was even reputed to be a Brahmin. The Muslims regularly said their five daily prayers and fasted in the month of Ramadan; the Hindus worshipped their gods and goddesses, each according to their family tradition. It was reported that Hindu or Muslim, the true god of the thugs was Durga, or Mother Kali, whom they worshipped as Bhawani.

The main source of the prosperity of our village was the income generated by the painters. The painters of Hindal Purwah had inherited techniques and methods of making or extracting colour from herbs, leaves, barks, flowers, fruits and some insects. These colours had absolutely no element of oil, except the oil that was originally contained in the vegetable or animal source. The colours were first formed as a dry, somewhat loose mass or lump. Then a piece of very fine muslin was placed above and below the lump, which was then gently beaten with soft, smooth soapstone. The process of beating and grinding was so gentle that nothing could be heard even by anyone nearby. If, by any chance, the muslin tore or developed holes, it was changed immediately.

This process of beating and grinding would take a few months by which time the lump of colour became extremely fine and powdery so that it would float in the air of its own accord. Then, in order to make sure that no impurity remained, it was filtered through another piece of fine muslin and was only then made into a thick paste. The colours of Kishangarh were prepared only as needed. At other times the powder-colours were kept sealed in small zinc jars.

For their brush, the painters used the gently pulled inner down of a baby camel's tail, or the ultra soft down from the ears of newborn wild asses of Kutch. The water which was used to make the paste was special too: it was drawn only from an underwater pool at the western end of the ancient lake in Kishangarh. An unusual kind of waterweed grew here. (It was reputed to have been watered by the urine of the crocodiles that lived in the lake; they were reputed to be descended from the crocodile gods of Lake Pushkar, a hundred miles away.)

This waterweed did not have the hard, dense, sharp-edged leaves of sivar, *Amaranthus sanguinus*, nor was it long, thin, twisted and clammy like the fish weed. This weed consisted of thick, almost leafless and very nearly fibreless stalks, and it grew in such odd, bent and convoluted shapes that it looked more like some twisted sculpture than an organic weed. Some of it looked as if a sharp-toothed animal had been nibbling at it; and thus shorn of leaves and scraped and cut in many places, the intertwined weed seemed to be carved from stone, rather than vegetative material. In fact, it seemed more like the complicated inlay work on the walls of the Red Fort, or the big fort at Ambèr near Jaipur.

The shrub and the weed would always remain submerged in water. Sometimes at the peak of the hot months, the water level sank a little below the stalks of the weed and there was a danger of the incandescent sun touching them; the stalks themselves would ooze and sweat, in fact almost extrude moisture drop by drop, until the entire plant above water became wet and secure from the effect of the sun.

The water from Kishangarh's ancient lake was first cooled in small earthen pitchers before being used for mixing colours. Sometimes, small lumps of lapis lazuli or jasper and chrysoberyl were immersed in the same water pitchers for months. When they were needed, the pitchers were unsealed but not without consulting the astrological ephemeris, and taking into account the colour of the sky, and the advice of the local Brahmin.

*

Makhsusullah (or whatever may have been his name at that time; so it is perhaps better to just call him 'Mian') never painted animals or scenes of hunting, nor yet scenes of battle. Most of his pictures showed an ancient, tall, desolate or dilapidated minaret for a background, with a young girl in the foreground sitting on or leaning against a broken, browned and mossy stone or a low but verdant rise in the earth, and somehow the poise and posture of her body never failed to suggest that, moments ago, there had been someone there looking at her and the girl was also conscious of the gazer's presence, but now something to her left had caught her eye and she had turned her head slightly in that direction, thus presenting only her profile to the person who now gazed at the painting. Her breasts are just a little prominent because of the slight turn of the neck and the gentle tension in the muscles of her shoulder. There is a charming, subtle tension in the fair, slender neck too. The skin from the delicate chin to the eye gives the effect of just a hint of tightness, just an extremely tiny sense of stretching, as if there was a smile on her lips just a couple of seconds ago, but now the wave of the smile has played itself out, leaving the ambiguity of signs on her face. More than half of the forehead is covered by part of her orhni (a light wrap or mantle for the upper body, lighter than the more formal dupatta), but the fine lace of the orhni's border is transparent enough to permit a view of the combed and coiffured hair, decorated with blooms of gul-e-dupaharia (the Marvel of Peru, a flower that blooms after the sun is well up and closes just after midday). Because the portrait was in profile, the bright hint of the braid of her hair, the neck and the shoulders exuded a sense of the ravishing tide of spring.

Who the girl was, and in what way she was related to Mian, were questions to which no one knew the answers, and no one dared ask him. He barely enunciated a dozen or so words in monosyllables during the day. Many a night he would go off to the forest, lying mute in the moonlit night under the shade of a sand dune. Did he lie mute, or did he pray and worship? No one knew. Sometimes, he would pack a cloth bag with millet bread, chutney, some powder-colour carefully wrapped in small packets, some blank sheets of paper and a small goatskin of water, and disappear for two or three days on end.

Our village was situated about twenty miles from Kishangarh town in the north-east on the Barmer–Jaisalmer trail. Centuries of footprints and marks made by camel, bullock cart, horse, the occasional rath and frequent pedestrians had created a narrow bridle path. There was no rain, except the occasional shower once in three or four years. Thus there was no real possibility of cart or mount getting mired in mud, but there were deep potholes and even pits in the path, covered by innocuous-looking sand, and the slightest bit of carelessness by the driver or a false-footed step by the pedestrian could lead a wheel or leg to be trapped in a pit, and that could result in a broken limb or other harm. In those days, the great Indian bustard, tughdar, was extremely common in the environs of our village. It dined avidly on small snakes and rodents, locusts and other large insects. Above all, it had a great liking for the phoorsa, the deadliest of snakes in our part of the world. Hardly about two or two and a half hands long, thin and brownish with black spots, its venom was so powerful that its bite was almost always fatal to man or beast. It was extremely fast and aggressive, and had a very loud, distinct hiss which gave it the name phoorsa ('hisser'), and it rarely missed its target, rising up to almost half its length to attack. It was fond of sleeping quietly in the shade afforded by the indentation made by the wheels of heavy vehicles like the bullock cart, or by the bullock's footprints. If a pedestrian was unfortunate enough to put his foot in the little pit where the phoorsa slept, there was truly nothing that could then be done for him; the phoorsa, with its loud, menacing hiss, would rise and strike at the opponent's thigh or stomach. The bite led to a few hours' of coma and almost inevitable death. It was the intrepid tughdar that was the nemesis and undoing of the phoorsa. We loved and valued the tughdar for its courage and speed in freely killing the hated snake. We would always exhort Makhsusullah Mian to direct his steps towards where the tughdar abounded.

*

Maharaval Gajendrapati Singh, among whose properties our village was counted, was actually descended from the House of Bundi, but marriage and thereafter an informal status of resident son-in-law had led to his permanent habitation in Kishangarh. Except for festive days, the Maharaval rarely, if ever, graced our village with a visit. He would arrive, if with some delay, late in the morning of the day of the festival, accept presents without dismounting, scatter flowers made of gold lace and thin gold and silver tape, deign to distribute clothes or jewellery to some select few, and then depart. The revenue that accrued to him from the village did not come from agriculture. So he was not interested in matters relating to seeds, irrigation or crops.

News went round suddenly one day that the Maharaval intended to visit the village on an excursion. Now this was something quite strange, in fact, unheard of. Let alone the Maharaval, even his agent never came to the village for excursion or entertainment. Everyone spruced up the facades of their houses and doorways; water was sprinkled in front of each house. Pictures were quickly painted on the walls facing the sole village street, and colourful, floral and abstract drawings called rangoli were drawn in front of the door sills. There was no dearth of peacocks in the area, so colourful peacock-feather fans were hung up at appropriate places. Within minutes, the village looked like a bazaar on a festival day.

Makhsusullah Mian was away on one of his usual outings, but he had completed a new painting just a few days before. Taking a light but strong piece of white silk, he had first dyed it lightly and then had painted the portrait on it. Was it a painting, or was it a peri charmed and confined in a mirror? It was Mian's special subject at its best.

A girl, fourteen or fifteen years of age, sitting on a small, somewhat dilapidated platform of black marble: She sat with supreme self-confidence as if saying that once she rose up, she would arise a full woman. The spirit of youth, rising up and brimming over, seemed to knock at every visible part of her body. Her skirt was a little longer and looser than usual; her ankles, more delicate than a rose bloom, and her feet, slightly restless, softer, more alive, more subtle in colour than a rose petal, could be seen peeping from under the flared skirt. A very slight stain on the sole of one foot: maybe a beauty spot or perhaps a rose petal had sacrificed itself underneath her foot? The neck and head slightly turned to one side, presenting the profile, as in Mian's earlier paintings; her dress not at all gorgeous or coquettish, but white and saffron and pink: the three colours so appropriate, so full of élan that the painting seemed to be vibrant and alive. She had a light wrap for her upper body, picked at the edges with fine gold lace, some of it straight and some of it twisted, and still, the whole seemed to suggest that the wrap was just about to slide down, revealing the full face. You might think that you could just stretch your hand and pinch the fabric with thumb and forefinger, but once you let go, the orhni would fall back on the forehead and be just as before. The nose straight and well formed, the gracile neck rising proud, a very long, somewhat slanting large eyes, like slices of the star fruit, green and golden, tapering at both ends. The pupil of the eyes fully black, and the white fully white, but with a slight hint of ruby red, as if invisible pink rays ran underneath, giving extra liveliness to them.

All of this was typical of the Kishangarh school, but not the lightness of jewellery and ornamentation. She wore just one plain gold necklace with a large star ruby, cut cabochon, for a pendant. On her wrists she had just a pair of gold bangles whose ends were fashioned long, like the head of a crocodile. The master had so organized lights and masses that some light fell on the star ruby so that all six points of the star were illumined. The eyes, cool and deep like a mountain lake, revealed a combination of sweetness of nature, playfulness and haughtiness. The lips were devoid of a clear smile, but she sat there with quiet dignity and perfect self-confidence, free from all worldly fear.

The portrait hung in an alcove of Mian's hut. People came from all around to look and admire. Yet within just a day or two of its being exhibited, whispers had begun to go round that there was something wrong with the picture. Wrong? What kind of wrong? Do we not all know that all portraits of ladies are imaginary?

'No,' an infantryman of the Maharaval who stood nearby, spoke in a whisper, his voice full of anxiety. 'It is real.' Then he shut up quickly, his hands on his ears, his mouth tightly shut.

Evening light had begun to flourish in the sky, but unlike other evenings, it did not have the glimmering effect of light falling on minute grains of sand. Dark lines, black, like extremely thick and heavy cord, slowly shuffled across the horizon. Even in the normal course of things, evening overtook our sky and environs with extreme quickness, like a leopard suddenly bursting into speed to pounce on its prey. It was light one moment and dark the next. And on that day, there were also clouds across the sky, full of dust and water vapour, twisting and writhing like serpents.

'What's that? What do you mean by "real"?' someone spoke up sharply and harshly. 'These girls are not the females of just anyone's family. These are apsaras, fairies at the Court of Indra, the King of all gods. Did anyone ever see banithani? Did anyone ever have a sight of her even in a dream? We do not paint real women. We are painters, we paint suns and moons.'

They were shocked. They all knew that 'The Bedecked One'—the strikingly beautiful portrait of the queen of a seventeenth-century ruler of Kishangarh—was called banithani. Some people also described it as 'The Radha of Kishangarh', meaning the beloved of God Krishna. Copies of the original painting are made everywhere in modern-day Rajasthan. They are still described as banithani but are assumed to be portraits of Radha.

'Hush! Be silent!' Someone whose face was half hidden behind a thick scarf and who had been standing a little apart from the onlookers now drew near and issued the warning.

'There is no time for arguments. Remove this picture at once! Bury it in the sand! Throw it away!' His agitation had risen many degrees and he was almost in a frenzy now. He pulled deeply on his short pipe, and thick, dirty yellow smoke curled and twisted through and over his dense beard, spreading around him. The heavy, sickly sweet smell of cannabis hung in the air.

'Why? Why should we throw the picture away?' someone inquired, his lips and nose curled in disgust and contempt. 'We do not even have Mian here whose consent needs to be taken. Who knows, it might already be sold . . .'

Another bystander, cutting him short, addressed the cannabis fancier: 'You, you son of a gun! What kind of opium-den gossip is this? Real? Imaginary? What nonsense is that? Plainly and simply, it is banithani, The Bedecked One of great renown.'

'Hush! Hush!' The cannabis smoker hissed like a snake. 'This village will be sacked and plundered. This village will be destroyed, laid to waste. Do you not hear the thump of the feet of tall dromedaries ridden by soldiers, and the whack of the hoofs of mountainous, heavy chargers rushing up here like the wind? On! Come on! It's all over now. The Mian has had us all hung on the gibbets. Your fortunes have now been shaken off their firm stations.'

His eyes were welling up with tears of terror, and his knees were knocking against each other like pieces of dry wood.

'Have you lost it, you wretched smoker and drinker of all kinds of foul things? Make tracks, begone this minute! Or your neck will be wrung in no time.'

Someone shoved him so that he lost his footing. He shouted as he fell: 'It's not The Bedecked One; it . . . is . . . not . . . The Bedecked One!' He spoke in an emphatic tone, pausing on every word, as if hailing somebody from far. Decades of cannabis smoking had thickened his tongue, but at that moment there was not the least shadow of slurring or imperfect enunciation in his voice.

'It . . . is . . . Man . . . Mohini,' he shouted.

5

The master of Hindal Purwah is enraged by the threat to his honour

SILENCE STRUCK EVERYONE like thunder. Man Mohini? Man Mohini? But was she not the Maharaval's younger daughter? Just about fifteen years old, her beauty was proverbial everywhere in and around Kishangarh. But no one had ever seen her. She was kept hidden behind seventy curtains. No one, but no one, except her special toilette maid, could dare see her hands and feet; and as for viewing her face or body, it was as impossible as going to the moon. Then how could the portrait be hers? Suppose someone had in fact dared make an imaginary picture of her, but how could it conform to her real appearance in any meaningful way? How could anyone, anywhere, make her portrait when the proportions of her face, her bone structure, were unknown to them?

'No, no! This is false; this is absurd!' someone cried out. 'If anybody tries to calumniate our Princess, he will have his tongue torn out!'

'But why should anyone try to malign her at all?' an old woman asked. 'What use will it be to anyone to slather cattle dung on pure cream? Please, try to reach to the depth of this matter,' she pleaded. 'This is not the time for yelling at each other and losing your temper. What use is it for one to catch hold of another by the neck?'

'Maybe it's a conspiracy to bring a bad name to the Maharaval,' someone speculated, scratching his head. 'But . . . '

Before he could complete his sentence, one could hear the growl of hoofs at the outer limits of our village. A torrent of dust arose and in the twinkling of an eye, spread over the whole village.

'Where is the Mian? Where is the Mian? . . . Where is the Mian?'

Voices piercing the hazy grey of the dust; sparks flying from the horses' hoofs as they struck stones on their way; stones scattering, raining down as they flew from under the speeding hoofs; the earth trembling like a frightened child as the booming waves of the speeding horses hit the village like a shock.

'Mian is not here, Mian is not here, Mian is not here. There is no one here!'

'None of us here bear arms! Your Excellency, Your Command, we are totally blameless!' an intrepid villager cried out. Then there were many other voices, saying the same thing in their own words. Yet no one could really hear or understand anything because of the tumult.

The painting in the alcove of Mian's cottage was fluttering, as if an earthquake was about to hit, razing everything, forcing all to kiss the earth. The entire village had been surrounded. It was a tiny collection of hutments, after all. It did not even boast of a marketplace. Now the force of the noise abated somewhat. Old women and children were on their knees, eyes downcast, with a rag or wrap covering their heads. They knew that the gesture of submission would not save their lives, but they would at least be spared the sight of the massacre that would stab their eyes like a dagger.

At times silence fell everywhere; at times a powerful buzzing sound waxed and waned throughout the village. Most people had their eyes on the ground, or on their door sill. There was rarely an eye that rose above the level of the forehead of the person in front. Some few, the bravest of them all, gazed at the point of the dromedary riders' lances. And each lance was trained at some door, some breast, some child, some woman. Tall spears finely balanced in their hands, the lancers rode high and strong, their faces devoid of all expression: neither harshness, nor displeasure, nor the passion for shedding blood. Their lances were a hand, or a hand and a half, more than man size, their blades just a little shy of half the length of the lances. Their points were long and sharp but without the delicacy and suppleness of the backscratchers that were wrought in ivory. Here, it seemed a warthog's tusks had been scraped and then straightened and fitted on to the end of the spear which was then strengthened by wrapping the joint in silver sheeting. The riders' seat on their mounts, and the balance of the spear in their hand, shoulder or arms was so harmonious that they had become practically indistinguishable. The lancer was the lance.

A bit of a commotion near the boundary hedges of the village; the ranks of soldiers broke and divided into many companies. The Maharaval, on his Arabian, was in front of them, but without headgear. The Maharaval, bareheaded? Bareheaded, the Maharaval? The sight had perhaps not been seen even by the eye of heaven, not to mention the villagers here or villagers anywhere else. What was happening? It was a sight to make the world tremble as if it was struck with ague. Scented perspiration, trickling down from his hair to the forehead and face, gave an odd glow to his visage. The dense locks of hair that came down the sides of the head to his ears and touched the moustaches seemed a little disarranged and out of true. And behind the Maharaval: an open palanquin. A lady's palanquin, and open? What kind of wonder was that? The bolder ones saw from the corners of their eyes, squeezed their eyes shut, opened them and looked again.

They rubbed their eyes, and looked again. The palanquin had no curtains, and Man Mohini was in it, her body without the chador, her feet shoeless. Her nose, hands and feet bereft of jewellery, there was not the least hint of the pink of pride and health in her face, but her head was erect. The slender neck had the familiar tension of arrogance, as if she had been married just a few months ago, and queen-like, was visiting her prince's palace, full of the pride of her station, and had made rubies and topaz grow in her lover's city, and was now haughty with the weight of pregnancy. The fourteen-year-old Princess had never seen even the threshold of the main palace door, and here she was, in the painting exhibited in the alcove of Mian Makhsusullah's humble hut. And if it was not she, it was somebody in her true image, one who looked as she was in real life, looked real in every apparent detail. And if it was painted, there must have been a painter too.

With no command or gesture from anyone, Man Mohini's palanquin stopped precisely opposite Makhsusullah's hut, as if it knew that she had arrived at her destination. She stretched her legs, as if trying to get down, and all those present there saw to their horror that her legs were in irons, and her lily-like delicate feet had no ornaments either. Like one paralysed, she dragged herself out with the support of her shoulders and elbows and stood erect by the door of the palanquin.

'Man Mohini . . .' The tone of the speaker was charged with a strange heart-rending pain, a tone that had strains of entreaty, terror and the pain of an anger which was like the anger expressed in the infinite chopping and mincing power of the saw-toothed blade of the dagger worn by a hunter close upon his body. But the anger had trailed off into a suppressed sigh.

'Man Mohini . . . , look at me, Man Mohini!'

The girl raised her head, but her eyes were unable to reach the father's face. Her eyes were intent on the star ruby—red as the pigeon's blood—

pendant on her chest. Rays of light from near and distant torches touched the ruby as the breeze rose or died, making the stone coruscate through all the six sides of its star, as if determined to pierce Man Mohini's heart.

'You are my daughter, Man Mohini, and I, Valajah Gajendrapati Mirza, your father. I didn't give you life so that you should dishonour me and dishonour yourself! How did your portrait happen to be here? Who looked at you, and who accorded to him the audacity to make your portrait which is a profound wound in my side, so that your name may be taken in the streets and lanes so loudly that it should become free entertainment on the earth and in the sky, like a shooting star?'

Man Mohini said nothing. Her head remained bent, as before. Stones and gravel on the harsh sandy ground must have hurt her bare feet, but her body betrayed no tremor, no discomfort.

'Mohini,' said her father in tones of abject plea, 'please turn, and look. Whose portrait is it? How does it come to be here? How are you here? Who is he? The painter who made this picture, who is he? Speak! Who wrote the colours of soot on your face?'

The girl turned gently to look behind her shoulder. There was the portrait, like a lamp lighting the dark of the evening, its body language just the same as that of the real girl. The same dark natural grey-green orhni with tiny white flowers scattered lightly across it, the orhni slipping a bit, a moderate effect of light falling from behind and brightening her hair whose colour seemed in some places to have become almost one with the orhni that it was difficult to distinguish one from the other, so much so that the hair seemed to give the effect of a background against which the face was painted. Large eyes, black like the jamun fruit, the corners inclined to one side, as if on hearing the sound of approaching footsteps, she was turning her attention to whoever it was who was coming.

'Turn your face towards me. Look at me.' This time, her father's tone was devoid of appeal, terror, pain. There was nothing but plain command there. Slowly, she turned, and her full face was before everyone. Gajendrapati Mirza now spurred his roan Arabian back, so much that it stopped some two hundred steps away from the girl. Placing his lance parallel to the horse's back and shanks, he transferred it to his left hand thus that the lance's point now rested dead centre between the horse's ears. Then he drew his sword from its sheath, and balancing it firmly in his right fist, he spread out his hand. It seemed to those who looked that a skyey eagle's powerful wing had grown out from the Maharaval's fist. A light spur to the horse, the sword and the arm stiff and unmoving, pressing his thighs to the sides of his wind-rushing mount, the Maharaval gave some subtle command to it, and the horse took a short leap. After that, no one could determine when the horse and rider covered the space of two hundred steps overtopping Mohini's slight body, when the sword's edge, sharper and finer than a hair, drew a bloody line across Mohini's neck from end to end.

Master rider and his mount went on ahead, without pausing. For a few heartbeats' length of time, Mohini's head remained on her shoulders. Then, just as the shock of the mountain-bodied stallion's pounding hoofs travelled upwards and reached her dead body, the girl's head rolled off and came to rest a few yards away on the rough, grey, unfeeling earth. But a few more moments were needed for the verdant tree that was Mohini's body to kiss the earth. Blood covered her sides and bosom like a veil, her tall frame swayed as if in a dance. Then the body, nurtured on the softest of beds, was in the embrace of the hot, harsh dust of the village which was named after one of the most benign and universally loved saints in the land of Hindustan.

In a fluid movement, the rider turned easily like a wave, as if he were not going anywhere forward but just showing off the style and step in dressage, and the sword, moving with the same feline, rippling motion went back in its sheath. Now the lance was back in his hand. He did not even cast an eye on the headless houri whose body lay at Mian's doorstep. He just straightened his arm, which had the lance, and reached its point to the alcove in Mian's hut. In a practised movement, the lance pierced the painting and pulled it out smoothly like a master fisherman pushing his spear under water and piercing the unsuspecting fish. A jerk, and the painting was free of the lance's point, lying on the dirt path. Then a gesture to the horse, and his heavy hoof had crushed the painting.

'Let these people vacate the village before the morning,' he turned slightly and told someone. 'I would not answer for their lives and property beyond the morning.' Then he placed the lance straight between the night-coloured ears of his steed and passed unhindered through the assemblage.

6

Mian Makhsusullah flees to the cold north of Hindustan

A LONG SIGH rose and was lost like an eagle in the sky. It rose from somebody's throat, somebody's breast, somebody's whole being, but there was no increase in the darkness of the air. Children wailing for their mothers, mothers calling out to their sons, young men hastening to cover old men, wives or beloveds under the flimsy security of a chador . . . How many people were there in that hamlet, after all? Three miles away from his village, Mian found the stragglers among the exiles. His cloth bag—containing feathers of the great bustard, the black-headed golden oriole and the peacock—balanced carefully on his frail shoulder, the tired painter asked a few questions, understood many things without asking, and quietly joined the tail of the walking caravan.

The morning was hot and bright in the sky before they reached the high road from Delhi which passed through Merath, Bayana, Rewari, and then, touching Kotah, turned to the right, going north to Lahore. Then it turned south-west, and passing through Gujranwalah, Wazirabad, Jhelam, it reached Rawalpindi. From there, it turned north-east and went on to Srinagar, finally ending at Barahmulah. The elders made their arcane calculations and decided that the north-west direction was better than the south-east, even if the region's climate, tongue, manners and rituals were all entirely alien. Now they stopped at the highway, looking to the coming of some large and reliable caravan headed to the north-west so that they could join it.

They had to wait three days before they could find a caravan that suited them. Then, stopping at many places, halting for a few nights at different stations, packing and unpacking their meagre bags and bundles, they went farther and farther from their origins, drawing nearer to a new origin.

Many members of the caravan, tired and wan with care, dropped out at each halting place.

Having suffered the hurly-burly and the distress of a very long journey done mostly on foot, the travellers from Hindal Purwah took five months to reach Barahmulah. By then, their numbers had dwindled substantially.

Mian the Painter was the most prominent of those who had remained till the end. Those who knew him also knew that the rainbow was in his hands, and that his fingers commanded the lights of the morning and of the moonlit night, and the shadows of the clouds and the dark of the evening. Give him a dry leaf of the mighty chinar, a cup of water and a few lumps of apparently grubby colour, and he could revive not the entire tree, but at least that shrivelled leaf. This was why every traveller with the caravan took care of him as best they could, treated him with reverence and gave him all possible protection against enemies, predatory animals and the journey's hardships, and kept him bundled up to the extent possible against the enchanting and stunning sights of the twists and turns of the road as it rose towards the mountains.

Mian the Painter had forgotten much of his Rajputani tongue by the time the caravan arrived in Barahmulah. It was only a few more months before he ceased to remember the art of making the colours for his Kishangarh style of painting.

And how could he not lose the memory of those things? There was nothing around to remind him of home: not those herbs and shrubs that yielded colour from their roots and leaves; not those rocks and the legendary water of the lake at Kishangarh; not those hue-giving insects that swarmed at different times of the year. Above all, the new land did not have those goddess-like girls, tall and slim, whose copper-hued bodies, hard and bright like the garnet, made the very air colourful when they passed; girls so dextrous that with one stroke of the mallet they could break into three a dirt-coloured lump of lapis lazuli or jasper. Then, taking the bigger lump in hand first, they would rub it and chafe it in a bowl of water, so much and so long that the defective and dull part of the stone would be abraded, and its true colour, blue like an Egyptian scarab or reddish blue like the jasmine, would emerge.

The delicate fingers and the supple wrists of Kashmiri girls had neither those skills nor that muscular heft. Nor had their fair, tiny hands the brute force to wield and apply the Rajputani girls' wooden mallets that looked deceptively light and slim, but were in fact hard enough that they could, if applied from the proper angle, easily do their job on the gemstone lode.

Mian began his new life learning to paint flower and foliage patterns and geometrical designs on wood. The fact of the matter is that he soon became quite adept at his new craft. Kashmiri painting did not have the delicate effect that only fine drawing could produce. Kashmiris drew on thin wooden boards with soft charcoal. The board was first treated by immersion in pine oil until it was fully saturated in the oil and became strong like double- or triple-distilled spirit. Now the board was supple and could be rolled like a sheet of paper, but it was also easy to break. So it was primed with light coats of shellac, giving ample time for each coat to dry. Thus the board became strong inside and glistened on the outside, giving the effect of lamination. The drying was done in the shade to produce uniformity and prevent cracking or caking. The wooden board was considered ready to paint when it felt like pasteboard. It was then fit to be sold at a good price to a painter.

That was all very well. But there was no banithani here. And again, where were those golden-haired dromedaries whose pelage hung from their bodies like tassels? And where were those she-camels whose eyes were large like those of the gazelle, but deeper and more intense than those of the charging horse? None of them measured less than ten, twelve hands in height but their feet fell with such softness on the sands of the desert that one could not tell the steps of a she-camel which had already foaled from those of one which had not. Where were the leopards and panthers, as much as eight hands in length, that could crawl, python-like at night into a villager's hut through a narrow aperture high in the wall when the door had been fastened, and half kill their human prey with such speed that the victim would breathe not a sigh or a sob? Having made the prey helpless, the man-eating predator could spring and drag him away through the sliver of a gap in the wall with such stealth and quietness that the victim's passing could become known only when the clay tobacco pipe dropped from his hands, scattering live embers of charcoal and tobacco on the dirt floor like the blossoms of the moon flower.

Here, instead, were cypresses and oaks that seemed to kiss the heavens with their high branches, their heads rising proud, arrogant, dark and mysterious. Heavy and imposing, straight and stiff-backed, thickening, spiralling, coiling and winding into their own selves, it seemed no bird would ever make its home in their denseness. And they, too, would never speak to animal or bird, not even shake their head in recognition. When the icicles and snow crystals sprouted on their branches and then on each and every one of their leaves, even then they would not say a word to anyone at all. Perhaps they would incline just a tiny bit towards the earth from which they had sprung. Or maybe sometimes, eloquent in their silence, they could be saying that we come from nowhere else but here, this cold land. The Lord has raised our heads high, so what is wrong if He sometimes lets these stony needles enter every nerve and thread of our bodies so as to give us a foretaste of the cold of death?

Those black pines, rising menacingly into the sky, dark and damp, Mian could never bring himself to like them. As for the flowers that somehow or the other managed to bloom all the year round in Barahmulah on the banks of the river Jhelam, except during the days of the snow, he liked them, but their petals were light and their veins so thin and subtle that Mian had no use for them. He liked to draw the large leaves of the chinar or the plane—each and every filament clearly visible, each dry vein spreading out in a precise geometrical manner, creating a fine net as if of the finest muslin, and the whole leaf soft and supple as if made of silk.

Overcoming his reservations, Mian finally learnt and then mastered the art and craft of painting on thick paper and wooden boards. He also became proficient in lacquer work. Within a mere couple of years he began to be regarded as a master of Kashmiri art. Viewers and connoisseurs, when exposed to his work, would inevitably regard him as a son of Kashmir and did not even notice his alien accent or his non-Kashmiri looks and deportment.

A few more years passed. Mian the Painter was now Makhsusullah the Picture Craftsman. He married Salimah, a girl from Kupwarah, a small town a few miles to the north of Baramulah, and made his home there. His atelier prospered, but he still sought to find inventive modes, and was always thinking about new ways of doing things. There was no tradition of making ivory miniatures in Kishangarh, and whatever was extant of the Kangra style in Kashmir could not manage to achieve the fineness and delicacy of drawing which was needed for painting a miniature on ivory. Nor could the Kashmiri style afford to organize the large painting surfaces that were needed for the Kishangarh style. Still, using some mysterious skill,

Makhsusullah managed to paint a miniature of banithani on ivory, mixing something of Kishangarh and something of Kashmir in it. This painting he hung in an alcove in his atelier. When anyone tried to find out about Kishangarh, or about that strange ivory portrait in miniature, he did not furnish any kind of answer and quickly changed the subject. Sometimes he even acted a little peevish, sending out clear signals that he did not like anyone, or himself even, to broach the subject.

A lamp burnt all night in the alcove which was adorned by banithani's portrait. None dared ask him why, but perhaps because Makhsusullah would oftentimes gaze at it every day for long periods of time, and also, as Salimah suspected, keep awake at night and gaze at the painting the whole night through, Makhsusullah's temper developed a kind of derangement, some unknowable disorder that kept him away from work for days on end. Sometimes he spoke nothing, ate nothing or very little over two or three days. Sometimes he would count the sprigs sprouting on the almond or apricot trees in his courtyard, and bet with the neighbours' children about which of them would bloom first and then become a fruit.

Then one day, Makhsusullah declared that the water-and-oil style of painting did not at all please his heart. He put the banithani portrait in his pocket, tightened his turban on his head, and announced that he was now on his way.

Salimah struck her forehead, half in grief and half in protest, and said, using the familiar tum, 'So what will you eat? And what will you feed us with? You're long past the age to learn some new craft. Illiterate as you are, you cannot be employed as a writer at Court or in some office. You're thin and light of frame, so you are unfit to be a soldier or horseman. Boatmanship is not your ancestral calling . . . '

'Keep quiet, woman. He who created the mouth will also fill it for sure. So why should we worry?'

Salimah was about to say something in reply, but suddenly, Makhsusullah flew into a rage. Pulling the mouthpiece of his hookah from his lips and casting it aside, he roared, using the tu of disdain, instead of the familiar, if not quite friendly, tum, 'I am not one of your Kashmiri starvelings. I am the Painter of Kishangarh. I just need to raise my hand and I will become that painter again. Your fair colour, your soft white skin, of what use can these be to me? Had you come from my people, I would thrust an axe in your hand and put on your head a thick wicker basket with a ten-yard-long stout rope in it. A couple of snakes or scorpions might sting you during the day's labour, but you would at least have collected a whole week's kindling for the house. How can you at all cut the branches from trees that grow here on these cold, wet, slippery mountains? You aren't even fit to help light up the stove! This land is bereft even of the wild jujube, the thorn bush, the fragrant maulsari or even the henna that women use to beautify themselves.'

A bout of coughing overtook him. He fell silent. Perhaps he felt that he should not push the matter too far. He was now feeling around in his heart for some decent way of ending his tirade. But suddenly, he was fired up again by an outrage of passion: 'Your unfriendly weathers, so full of snow, have yellowed my dark colour. And your rain-filled winds have thinned my blood, hollowed out my bones . . .' He paused, then spoke in still angry but pleading tones, 'If you can do nothing else, at least make me a baby, I'll bring it up my way.'

Saying this, Mian the Painter covered his head with his shawl-like kerchief, lay himself down on a charpoy in the sun, and he stayed there, not moving or talking, for three days.

Salimah had his bed moved inside when it was evening. Still, Makhsusullah's body warmth seemed unchanged; he was neither too warm nor too cold. His heartbeat was also quite clear and loud, like that of a normal person; yet he did not respond even when they shook him by the shoulder or called out to him. Salimah blew prayers on fragrant joss sticks, lit them and placed them everywhere in the house. She fetched from the nearby mosque a jug of water on which the mullah had said prayers and into which he had blown his breath. The water was sprinkled in every nook and cranny of the house so as to drive away the effects of evil spirits or genies. She also forced open Makhsusullah's jaw and wet his tongue and throat with a few drops of the sacred water. A physician was brought from a village a few miles away. He suspected grand mal and prescribed cupping the patient; but cupping brought no benefit to him. Nothing availed. Makhsusullah remained dead to the world for three days and nights.

On the fourth morning, Makhsusullah rose up by himself. The calls to the predawn prayers had not been sounded yet, but he was not particular about prayers. He did, on occasion, sing a song in praise of Shaikhul Alam Shaikh Nuruddin Vali whose shrine was at a place called Chirar Sharif, many miles away from Kupwarah. Sometimes the song, which had many verses in the style of a formal panegyric, would, almost without his intending to do so, become directed towards Hindal Vali whom he had left such a long time ago in faraway Rajputana. Sometimes, overcome by some mysterious mood or emotion, his eyes would begin to tear and overflow; and in his half-childish voice in which Kashmiri and Rajputani languages were commingled, he would call out to Shaikhul Alam, and talk to him as if he was in the Shaikh's presence, and the Shaikh was attentive to whatever he was babbling away.

Salimah, who had scarcely slept the night, woke up from her uneasy slumber as if someone had rudely shaken her awake. She was stunned. Her house seemed to glimmer in a soft blue-green light, such as she had never seen on any mountain. Makhsusullah, fully awake, was on his prayer mat pouring his heart and soul out to Shaikhul Alam. She was not sure how to interpret the phenomenon or the omen, when Makhsusullah, having heard or rather felt her footfall, raised his eyes to her. There was total silence for a heartbeat. Then Makhsusullah rose from the prayer mat, dried his eyes, and gestured for the cup of milk that had been his breakfast for many years now.

Having drunk the milk, Makhsusullah untied a knot in his cotton sash, brought out three gold mohurs minted in the time of Emperor Farrukh Siyar and put them in his wife's hands.

'Well, I now go away to learn a new craft. I already told you that your people's water-and-oil painting cannot by any means be my line of work now.'

'Please. What new craft can you learn at this time of your life? And what worth can you attain in it? You are really out of your mind.'

'Hush, woman. Be quiet. Women don't talk back to their men.' His tone of voice was apparently that of affectionate admonition, but deep within, there was the thorny prick of pessimism and failure.

'I was born to imbibe in my heart and breast the light, sharp grains of sand that the hot winds would blow into me. But now that your country's breezes, white as snow and pointed like the scorpion's tail, and the frozen spicules of snow that ride on them have become my lot, I will keep faith with them, too.'

'But where are you bound for? Why don't you want to take me with you?'

'Where else but Chirar Sharif? I shall do forty days' penance and meditation there. Then, what will be, will be.'

'So what new craft can you learn at the shrine? What kind of talk is this? You seem not in your senses.'

'Salimah, this is just the difference between you and me. For me, the same warmth seems to bubble forth at the saint's Court in Chirar Sharif which, in its turn, becomes the cool waters of Verinag from where the Jhelam springs and goes on to irrigate the whole of the Kashmir Valley. The King at Chirar Sharif will grow the seeds that I will sow. He will ripen the grain, he will keep it warm and will fill your and my belly with it.'

'Ya Shaikhul Alam!' Hailing the Shaikh of Chirar, Makhsusullah the Picture Craftsman walked out of the door and did not look back. Within a couple of moments, he had disappeared, as if he was not a human being made of flesh and blood like us, but a puff of dust, and it was not an alley but a cave into which he had ventured.

'Where will you stay, when will you come back?' Salimah kept calling out after him, but Makhsusullah heard nothing, recked nothing. It seemed as if some hidden power was pulling him away.

He did not know the way to Chirar Sharif, nor did he have any idea of its location, whether it was on a mountaintop or in a valley, north or south. All he knew was that if the sunset on Lake Manas Bal commanded hundreds of hues of such subtle difference in shade that his brush could never aspire to state them in a painting; if the village of Yus Marg, grown and nurtured by the moist breezes at the top of a high hill, surrounded by the sky-touching wall of black pines so dense that bright sunlight appears greenish beneath them, as if the whole village were shimmering under water; if, beyond Barahmulah, one were to see the Jhelam descend from the heights, and see green and blue and orange playing the game of hide and seek in its spraying waters; and if the fountains at Achhabal spout water as white as glass crystals, then his world, his Kashmir (yes, now it was his Kashmir) . . . The sun of Kashmir is not the cruel sun of Kishangarh whose dazzling heat turns brown to black, and black to blue and green to red; where the darkness puts to shame the dark that surrounds the Water of Life; where the noontide of the cool, pink months paints the faces of young girls with heavenly rouge . . . So now shall I observe those colours which are the colours of my Kashmir? Then I will let those colours seep into my heart and I will enter the heart of those colours.

7

Mian Makhsusullah, the Portrait Painter, learns the mysterious art of talim

HE DID NOT know for how many days he had travelled, but Chirar Sharif was still quite far. He found himself in front of the big Friday mosque of Badgam. He entered the ablution chamber of the mosque, passed water at the urinal there, and then performed the ritual cleansing necessary before prayer. He recited the first verse of the Quran and stepped into the coolness of the courtyard.

The evening prayer assembled; some people left after the prayer, some came in later. There were some who read from the Quran, some others hummed poems in praise of the Prophet. Many newcomers laid themselves down to sleep near the heating stove with their knees to the stomach, the head resting upon the knees, intending to wake up only when the night-time prayer was called.

The night-time prayer was eventually called and assembled. Makhsusullah did not leave or even rise from his place after the prayers had been said. He was now shivering from the cold, and hunger was waxing in him like the light of the stars late on a clear night.

'Are you a traveller from somewhere?' someone asked him in an extremely gentle, honey-sweet voice.

'Yes . . . No . . . Yes, sir. You can describe me as a traveller. I'm a stranger in these parts.'

'Where is it that you want to go?' The inquirer's tone of voice had the music, the douceur of the speech of the tribesmen of the valley of Laulab. It was reputed that their singing, when heard from far, sounded like a Bedouin reciting the Quran in his pure Arabic timbre. Whereas Mian Makhsusullah's speech still had powerful remnants of the strong, harsh, brick-red colour of the Rajputani.

'I do not now know where I am headed. It was a restlessness of spirit that forced me away from hearth and home. Perhaps Shaikhul Alam . . .'

'You will surely reach your destination if Shaikhul Alam has summoned you. But what do you have by way of travel provision, and where have you put it for safety's sake?' The stranger's body was almost fully covered by the poncho-like upper garment worn by both men and women in Kashmir. And his turban was tied so low that his face was only partially visible. Makhsusullah was unable to determine the status of the stranger, except that he had a rosary in his right hand and he constantly but inaudibly counted its beads. This fact placed him among ordinary human beings: there was nothing unusual, except that his face was partially hidden. Makhsusullah noticed the stranger's fingers, they were soft and pointed like unopened almond blossoms.

'Provision?' Makhsusullah spoke, as if to himself. 'I have no achievements to show. I'm devoid of learning too. I have nothing but an impatience, a distraction of the mind, or a compulsion that seems to have dragged me here to be at your feet. But who . . . ?'

He had plucked up the courage to put the question to the stranger but was now inwardly reproaching himself for what he thought was his dire impertinence: his own life was in question here; he had no right to ask about others.

'When did you eat last?' The question was asked in the same honey-sweet voice, but it was pointedly ignored.

'I left home without eating. When I left, the clouds were massing in the sky at Gandra Bal. The weeping willow's eyes were wet on the banks of the Jhelam. I do not remember how many days ago.'

'So let's go eat first.'

Without further ado, Makhsusullah went out with the stranger. Quitting the lane where the mosque was situated, they found themselves in front of a large, formal building that seemed more like a monastery or a lightly fortified workshop. It seemed to be everything at once. They entered a large hall-like room whose wooden floor was almost entirely covered with expensive carpets. The air had a slight scent of the attar of saffron. On the walls and in the alcoves there were no candles but the resinous branches of the pine and the eucalyptus had been given the shape of candles and lit up. The fragrance of pine and eucalyptus, mingling with the whiff of saffron, made for a strangely mellow and pleasant environment.

The scent of the wooden candles and flambeaux which gave out a light smoke; the subdued snap and crackle of the wood as it burnt; the hall filled with soothing music made by unseen instruments; the light, silken sound waves of conversation among groups of ten, twelve people as they sat on the carpeted floor—all this made for a mood that pervaded the environment of the room like an invisible but unmistakable penumbra of felicity.

In front of every group was a long, low oak wood table, about a hand in height and about eight or ten hands in length. There was no tablecloth, but each table had a whole sheep on a large tray, roasted, surrounded by heaps of bread. Some were eating quietly, some spoke briefly, in low tones, between each mouthful. Everyone became attentive and respectful when Makhsusullah and the old man entered, but none spoke. Both took their seat at one of the long dining tables in a corner. Barring that small, silent gesture of silence, there was nothing else to indicate the special status of the old man or his guest.

It took some time for Makhsusullah's palate to become acquainted with the taste of this unusual food. Similarly, it took some time before his ears could become attuned to the rhythms of the conversation going on in that large room, and before his senses could take in all that was going on there. He noticed, with not a little wonder, that the diners' language was indeed Kashmiri, but it contained many words that were entirely unfamiliar to him, and their speech was delivered at a much faster pace than he had been accustomed to in Kupwarah, which was apparently to the north-west of where he was now. He lent his ears more intently and heard that their conversation went something like this:

'Here you will apply the fortieth of one thread's thickness; here, a fourth of three threads' thickness. Then here is how the drawing will be like.' The speaker showed to his interlocutor a piece of khaki paper with some strange notations marked upon it in saffron ink. Then he exhibited another, similar piece of paper on which was the coloured design of a part of a carpet.

'Join this cochineal with eucalyptus green, and when the resulting green is joined with the golden green of the weeping willow, this will be the effect.' But instead of a fabric of that colour, the speaker exhibited a corner of a small piece of khaki paper with a drawing in a strange ochre-green tint. The speaker's voice had the self-confidence of a king, or the captivating power of the discourse of a True Friend of God.

In the meantime, a young man of eighteen or nineteen approached the old man and spoke with some exasperation, but his tone also held the assurance of a loved one: 'Maestro, I for one cannot get this design right.' He showed the old man a longish slip of khaki paper, which bore the same apparently meaningless notations in saffron ink. 'It's just beyond me, reading off so many threads and so many strands. If there was someone to read out aloud to me . . .'

'Well, that too can be organized,' the old man said. 'But you want to learn how to write the talim, so you must begin by learning to read it.'

Then the old man took the somewhat worn-out piece of paper from the young man and showed it to Makhsusullah. 'This is called talim. This paper contains the entire design of a carpet, six yards long and three and a half yards wide. Each colour, each thread, is represented by these symbols. Reading these is very difficult, not to speak of inventing such a design or such a talim. Readers of these papers do not study the poems of Sadi, long popular for teaching Persian to young people. Nor do the readers of these documents know mathematics or mensuration. It is a science, but of a different kind. Experts of this science can create these little, apparently meaningless notations by using imagination, creativity and originality. Yet they hardly ever sign their name to the design created by them.'

His mouth wide open, Makhsusullah gazed at the old man as he spoke. So this was something like a secret language, he thought. One needed to know many disciplines, like mathematics, painting and dyeing, before one could begin to master this science. And, of course, possess an extraordinary power of memory; and something else for which Makhsusullah could not find a name, but it was some power which enabled the talim maker to visualize in an almost physical way how a given pattern of inert lines and colours would look when translated on to an actual carpet.

The old man held Makhsusullah by the elbow and led him into another room. Many weavers were engaged in the task of weaving carpets. A venerable-looking man sat on a slightly elevated seat and spoke some words aloud, as if dictating a text.

'Each fragment of the talim is called ultsh,' his host told him. 'And each line is called var. Attend carefully; hear what the maestro is saying.'

The maestro called out:

'One white sugar,

'One deep yellow,

'Nine white sugar,

'Three cream,

'One almond light brown,
'One pomegranate red,
'One white sugar,
'One simple pink,
'Did you fellows do it?'

Now all the weavers who were weaving to the maestro's dictation or direction spoke in one voice: 'Yes, Master, we did. Please go on, brothers.'

Makhsusullah stepped forward and looked carefully at the talim paper. There was nothing but symbols on it, somewhat as follows:

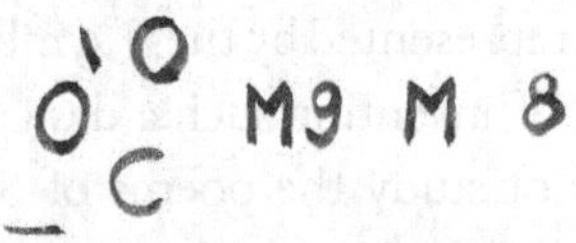

(It must be noted here that the actual notational symbols in the talim have nothing to do with Roman letters or Arabic numerals. The resemblance is quite by chance, and of course on an actual talim paper, they look very different.)

Makhsusullah looked at his host with eyes that were full of anxiety and confusion. He smiled and said, 'Have no fears, everything becomes easy once you have learnt it. The first symbol is "one white sugar", that is to say, the thread the colour of white sugar to be used once, and so on. Thus each symbol describes the colour of the thread and the number of times the thread is to be used. Having finished one line, the maestro asks, "Did you fellows do it?", that is, have you done exactly as I directed? Then the weavers answer, "Yes, ustad, we did", and then signal their readiness for the next line by calling out, "Please go on, brothers". Sometimes they say, "Go ahead, ustad, go ahead".'

'Only God is untouched by blemish!' Makhsusullah exclaimed. 'Understanding a talim is only a little less hard than creating one.'

The old man continued, but this time he spoke somewhat hortatively, as if trying to bring Makhsusullah round to what he was asking him to do. 'You are a lover of colours, but the objects of your desire are colours that are sharp and bright, smooth like pine oil, transparent like the soap bubble, colours that shimmer and slip from the beholder's hand, colours that are hot and bright, that clash with each other, but are on some level harmonious while they still retain their existential reality. You wish to plant a garden on a sheet of paper, a garden where there are sparkling fountains and colourful birds, and herds of the Kashmiri deer.

'You wish to paint the mountains which are dappled with the shades of trees, where the clouded leopard walks with his stately, carefree gait, whose body is supple like the grass that grows on the banks of Lake Wular. The leopard disappears when his colour mingles with the shadow of the black pine where the earth is covered with snow. And when the snow leopard is seen in the background of white snow, its pelage emits a dazzling light of its own, such that the snow wraps itself around the leopard, making it invisible. The snow transforms the leopard into a coded missive, to be read only by those who can crack the code.'

The old man fell silent, his eyes intent upon some faraway scene, as if the snowscape, the leopard, the black pines in whose environs the kalij pheasant forages for food all the livelong day, all were right there, in front of his eyes, and Makhsusullah had been left somewhere far behind. He, Makhsusullah, could not of course dare interrupt or ask a question.

After a moment's silence, his host resumed: 'You want to see a two-yard-long bear sleeping in the shade of the twenty-and-more-yards-high black pine, so that from one side the black bear and the black pine seem one, and from another angle they seem separate. You want to bring together the soft green of the Sanctuary of God and the deep green of the Sanctuary of the Prophet of God. You also want to somehow learn the secret of the sky blue, and the peacock blue, and the orange-red used by the Ladakhi women carpet weavers. So learn that this whole world—in fact, the Universe in its totality—is nothing but twisting and intertwining waves of colour, and above it all is the Colour of which there is no hue.'

Mian Makhsusullah stared at his host in astonished wonder, unable to properly follow anything at all of the old man's discourse. Is this august personage making fun of me, or can he really know my deepest thoughts? Does he truly possess knowledge of what I must do, and also how my task can be fulfilled?

The old man had closed his eyes as he spoke. Now, he opened them suddenly and holding Makhsusullah powerfully by the hand, he said, 'Come with me. I will teach you the mysteries of the talim. Carpet weaving is also a kind of painting, and the talim contains those secret letters in which are hidden the ethereal archetypes which will become actual carpets. By the power of his imagination, the creator of the talim spreads the carpet of the future in the air, in front of his eyes. Then, with the eyes of thought, he looks at it from all possible angles and sides. How does it look from above? How does it look from the right? What will be the effect if the carpet were hung on a wall, in front of a mirror? What effect will be generated if the carpet was spread from wall to wall; and if it were spread so that light fell upon it from outside too? There are numerous subtle points like these which the talim writer has to visualize and then make his decision. The painter sees what he's doing.'

He fell silent for a moment, as if contemplating his own forbidding words.

Makhsusullah found in himself the courage to stammer: 'I . . . I know to m . . . make only p . . . pictures. But I can take account of all such matters while I'm putting the picture down on the paper.'

'Our elders and forebears learnt patterns and designs in the days long past from Iran and Kashan and Aksai Chin. They learnt techniques and styles, and new methods, too, of designing and making carpets. Do you think all those have remained with us unchanged all these years? At a casual glance, our work will seem to have remained the same over the centuries. But if you look closely, you will find that talim writers of each age, in fact, each generation, have grafted newer and yet newer cuttings on the old branches, and have grown flowers on them brimming with fresh inventiveness. Every new talim is brighter and more colourful, with new borders, new clusters and new lengths of leaf and flower. A talim writer has to be poet, painter, dancer, musician, all rolled into one.'

Mian Makhsusullah had barely opened his mouth to say something when the old man spoke in an unusually deep, resounding, authoritative voice: 'You will learn talim.' His utterance was neither question nor prediction. It seemed to imply that Makhsusullah had been fated to be a maestro at talim from the very dawn of creation.

'Do you . . . do you mean . . . do you mean me?' He fumbled for words. 'Yes, maestro, I should count myself honoured if I was considered . . .' Suddenly, his back straightened, his neck became erect. 'Perhaps the Presence is not aware of the name and fame that I commanded as a painter of portraits in Kishangarh. I made imaginary pictures . . .'

'I do not want to go into all that.' The old master's tone now had a sudden finality, as if he was pronouncing a judgement. 'I know. If the painter is of true seed, every portrait, however imaginary, is real for him. But I am talking about the art of talim. Are you willing to become an adept at our art?'

Quite involuntarily, Makhsusullah said, 'With all my heart and soul!' Overcome by some inner, mysterious state, he bent his head. And then his head bent so low that it almost touched the feet of the old man.

*

For eight years, Makhsusullah toiled hard, as hard as if his life depended on it. The art of talim was not in his history, but it was in his soul. The venerable master at whose feet he learned the talim would narrate a tale every now and then, which all his pupils came to know by heart.

'Do you hear, you uncouth desert dweller from Rajputana?' He used the familiar tu almost contemptuously.

'Yes, Ustad, I do hear.'

'In ancient times, there was a rajah. Do you hear?'

'Yes, I hear, my master.'

'The Rajah was a cretin like you. But his Vizier was extremely wise. Are you listening?'

'Yes, Master, the Vizier was extremely sagacious and full of understanding.'

'Did I say extremely sagacious and full of understanding? I said he was extremely wise.'

'Master, I beg your pardon. The Vizier was extremely wise.'

'I say something and you hear something else. Then how on earth will you learn the talim? It is not an art that can be learnt by drinkers of the sap of cactus and eaters of the flesh of the pangolin. Do you get me, you bumpkin from Rajputana?' Then the master would address the entire class, 'Listen, you asinine children of the Kashmir stag! There was, in ancient times, a rajah. He was a fool, but he loved the arts. And his Vizier was extremely wise. Do you hear, you memorials of Buddhist Tibetan females?'

Everyone had heard the tales dozens of times, yet all spoke in one voice, 'Yes Master, we hear.'

'So the Rajah commanded his Vizier, "Teach me calligraphy." The Vizier said, "Refuge of the world, in order to be a calligrapher, one must first be a dancer." "All right, come then, teach me how to dance," commanded the Rajah. The Vizier answered . . . Do you know what the Vizier said?'

All knew the answer to this, but they held their tongues. 'The Vizier said,' the master spoke, stressing every word, '"Protector of the world, it is necessary for a dancer to be a painter first." "Fine, let's then learn painting," the Rajah commanded. But then, the Vizier submitted, "Shadow of God, only that person can be a painter who is an architect." The Rajah was annoyed, but controlling his displeasure, he commanded: "So be it. As from today, I will be a student of architecture." The Vizier was silent for a while, and then he said . . . Do you know what the Vizier will now say?'

Clearly, everyone present knew the answer, but everyone kept it to himself. The master spoke triumphantly: 'The Vizier submitted, "Our Home and Refuge, oh Excellency, only he can be an architect who is an engineer." The Rajah laughed indulgently, and said, "Well, one does have to start somewhere. I am willing to be trained as an engineer!"'

The master fell silent, as if creating suspense. Then he spoke slowly, with a small pause between each word. 'But the Vizier answered, "Shadow of God, it is necessary to be a dancer in order to be an engineer." And only a calligrapher can learn how to dance,' the master almost mumbled, as if reminding himself. He seemed to hold his breath for a long moment; then he drew a deep sigh and spoke: 'Man's being is indivisible. Can you know where the body ends and the soul begins? Do you know that one who cannot hear can see much better than his peers? But he who cannot hear cannot speak either, and he who cannot speak, cannot sing, and yet he can dance. There is no wall dividing the seven notes from each other. All the seven can commingle to become one, but each can also be heard separate from the other. All these noble arts are the being of man, and the exemplars of man's being are the seven notes, seventy colours and seven hundred angles.'

Makhsusullah felt as if something was obstructing his windpipe, as if his breathing had come to a stop. He said to himself, if I understood all this, I could pour the whole of creation into one talim.

The master said, 'Learn to see. But you will learn to see only when you are able to hear the symphony of colours. Makhsusullah, tell me how many kinds of green are there?'

The master's eye was intent upon Makhsusullah, as if the sharp point of a dagger was resting at his breast.

'Green? Do you . . . ? Master, do you mean the shades of green? Well, there must be . . . must be . . . fifteen? Maybe sixteen?'

The master glared at him. The needle-sharp point of the dagger pierced the breast to a very tiny depth.

'What a dummy, what a wastrel of a dummy he is! My fool of a boy, I could show you sixty, sixty-two shades of green here, right here! One just needs the discerning eye. Come now, think in the context of the seasons, in the context of a given moment of time.'

'Yes, Master, I do think . . . ' Makhsusullah blurted out, unthinkingly.

'No, you have not given thought at all, my little one.' The maestro spoke with a caress in his voice, as if he was talking to a child. 'My dear young fellow, just imagine summer, the sun sinking behind Lake Manas Bal, the green hue of the newly sprouted leaves of the chinar, the greenness of unripe apples. Look at the black pine when its new, tender shoots start coming out after the rainy season is over, how green, and what kind of green are those new tendrils? Imagine the green of the lump of emerald newly cut out from the living rock; in the middle of the lump is a little gemstone, but around that nugget is the green that is earth-brown and green, and yet not truly green, not fully formed to gemstone grade. It cradles the gem, but is of a different hue. Imagine how one is different from the other. And then, when the summers are winding down, look at the golden yellow-green of the tender leaves of the rice plants growing tall in the valley of Lake Wular. Look at the still water in the furrows in which the growing plants are reflected, and note how different that green is. Imagine how green would the water be when the blue of the sky is reflected in it. Visualize the green waving length of the lithe water snake gliding through the water . . . What are these, ultimately? Are they not the same green hue? Listen to their music, pay heed to the scales as they ascend and descend. See and hear all this, only then you will know, my child, if the talim is the cosmic web of maya or if it is a web of plain, human deception.'

Makhsusullah felt as if his head was in a whirl. Even an ant could not see with such acuity, he said to himself.

The master would fall silent after such perorations. All the pupils would then go back to doing what they had been doing. Those who could not do much would examine old talims, or ravel and unravel skeins of wool or silk, or sort and scramble sheets of the almond-brown paper used to write the talim.

*

Eight years passed. By the end of that time, Makhsusullah became the greatest living talim writer in Kashmir. His unorthodox creativity, his sharpness and fecundity of vision, and the subtlety of his drawing were such as had never been seen or heard of in the elite community of carpet designers from Kashmir to Central Asia. He returned to Kupwarah a famous artist whose creations were known in Hindustan, the Deccan, and Iran and Kashan.

It was the fifth year of Emperor Ahmad Shah's ascension to the Royal Seat in Delhi when the Almighty vouchsafed a son to Makhsusullah. It was as if the Dispenser of Destinies had now placed the seal of approval and verification on the scroll of Makhsusullah's success and good fortune. Makhsusullah named the child Yahya, which is the name of a prophet and which is Arabic for 'he lives'. For, Makhsusullah believed that the child's inner self had the potential of fulfilling his hope and desire for his creativity and art to live a new life.

Yahya's birth and Makhsusullah's death occurred almost at the same time. But no one could know the manner of his passing, nor could anyone know why he let himself be gathered by death. He was busy in his workroom when Salimah went into labour. He worked in a special room in the outer part of the house: none could enter it without his permission. He had recently invented a new talim, which he believed was so complex that none but he could understand it, far less put it into effect as a real carpet. Another point of concern was that Makhsusullah had used certain colours like orange-gold and black, which he feared would be considered outré by conventional buyers and critics who would fail to grasp the true meaning of those colours.

When he was given the news of Salimah's labour, Makhsusullah promptly locked his workroom and came and sat on a prayer mat near the labour room. He spoke to no one, nor did anyone speak to him; all were anxious and busy attending to the woman in her distress.

He seemed to be in a different world then. It was as if he was explaining to a young carpet weaver the intricacies of a new design with the greatest possible attention to detail and concentration on the exquisiteness of the colours, making the young weaver aware of every thread and every knot. It was as if he was taking a little child by the hand to help him go up and down the turns and twists and slopes and gradients of a narrow path until he brought them both safely home. This was just what he was doing, except that sitting on the prayer mat, he spoke to his ancestors, to his spiritual masters, especially the Shaikhul Alam, and to Khvajah Khizr, the Evergreen Guide and Solver of Problems, and then to his own Prophet. He took their names as if he was in their presence and petitioned them to make easy his wife's passage through hard labour to the birth. The path is new and untrodden for my baby, hold it by the hand, look at it with love and compassion, let it be good-looking, well made in every way, not deformed in body or deficient in the brain. Will the child be male or female? He did not consciously think of this at all. He imagined the unborn as a 'baby', but the words he used for it were of the masculine gender. However, he hadn't determined, in practical or intellectual terms, if it would be a boy or a girl.

8

A much-awaited birth is followed by an unexpected and inexplicable death

IT HAD BEEN an extremely cold winter night. Snow had fallen so profusely during the day that the wooden stairs that led from Makhsusullah's veranda to the labour room upstairs had been unable to stand the weight of the additional snowfall over the frozen snow, and crashed to the earth with a loud noise before the light of the morning could properly, if hesitantly, make things clear. Makhsusullah remained seated on his prayer mat; the noise had not affected his concentration and the urgency of his entreaties to his holy masters. The night's snowfall and the debris of the crashed staircase had blocked any possibility of carving out a quick way of entering the labour room. Even a temporary ladder would need the snow to be shovelled off before it could be hooked up to the room above. Efforts were being made to rig a light makeshift ladder when the crying of the newborn was heard, followed by the voice of the midwife: 'Oh really, Salimah ma'am! A baby so healthy and so stout, and yet so dark! Is it a baby or a black rose from the Royal Gardens at Nishat Bagh! Praised be God, for only He is free from all blemish.'

Then the loud voices of women, singing congratulatory songs and playing on the light Kashmiri drum, rose from every part of the house. After a long interval of the noise of songs and felicitations all around, an old woman came to the door of the labour room and called out, 'Please take the baby!'

But how can I take the baby? Makhsusullah said to himself: there is no way up. The woman's voice came again, somewhat louder this time: 'Please take the baby. The call to prayer has to be said in its ears.'

Makhsusullah looked up to see the midwife standing at the door upstairs, holding the baby like a bundle, fully secured from the cold, wrapped in a heavy white sheet of homespun wool.

'Please come here, right close to me, just below the door, and spread your arms. It is not much of a height, and it is such a small baby. Spread a double-sized shawl on your arms and catch the baby as I bend and let it down. It is better not to delay the saying of the call to prayer in its ears. That is the first thing that it should hear.'

How can I let the little thing be brought down in this fashion? Makhsusullah said to himself. The shock of the fall and the passage through air might do it some harm.

'No, that is not the way to do it,' he called out. 'Let me organize a basket and rope and let the baby be set down in the basket. Just wait a while.'

A basket with makeshift rope handles with longer ropes secured to them was sent up for the baby. It was not a proper rope even, just strips torn from bedsheets and wound like twine; the basket was also just an old fruit basket strengthened with a shawl wrapped around it. It had not been possible to find anything better in the snowbound morning with the snow still falling.

'Let it come down! Let it come down!' Makhsusullah cried. 'You will see how carefully I receive the basket in my arms! There won't even be a jolt, let alone a shock to the little one.'

The basket and its valuable cargo were made to descend as slowly as could be. Makhsusullah walked through the courtyard in almost knee high snow and let the basket come into his arms, carefully balanced. He kissed the baby on the forehead and said, 'I name this child Muhammad Yahya. God willing, this little one will have a long life. My boy will instil new life in the arts of carpet designing and carpet making. Then the two of us together will take the land of Hindustan.'

His voice became hoarse with emotion. Surreptitiously, he wiped his eyes with his long sleeve and said the call to prayer in the baby's right ear. He pronounced the ritual phrase of Affirmation of the Unity of God and of Muhammad being his Prophet, and blew into its left ear. He then put his right index finger in its mouth to suck, and asked the midwife, 'Is his mother all right in every way? Does she have milk yet?'

'Mian, everything is just right, everything. It's only that her milking is hurting a little, but my little one has been sucking away like mad. You both are indeed extremely fortunate. You must give alms, and give to charities in the name of God, and should also reward us!'

'Yes, yes. All that and more will be done. Just let the sun go up and let the dear one's limbs gain some strength. Then you will see.'

Saying this, he placed his firstborn in the arms of Salimah's brother who was standing next to him. Then he went out of the house and did not return.

At first, no one missed him. What with the singing of songs, the visitors' loud conversation and exchange of congratulations, the coming and going of guests, and the happy bustle of a newly blessed house, Makhsusullah slipped everyone's mind. But when the sun went far up in the sky, they began to look for him. Their casual search became quickly charged with urgency and anxiety. By the next morning, people had begun to hope, wishfully, that Mian would surely come back sooner or later. After all, it was not the first time that he had disappeared. Urgent word was sent to Badgam, but none had seen him there either.

Salimah was able to go out of the house after her ritual bath on the sixth day, and she went to the saints' mausoleums to pray for her husband's quick and safe return. She fasted for many days, hoping that her prayers would be better heard while she was fasting in the name of God. She obtained talismans from holy men and buried or pressed the talismans under stones, but nothing availed. Then news came one day that a stranger's body had been found deep in the forest of Dachigam.

It was still snowing hard when Salimah's brother left for Dachigam to investigate. The forest guard reported to him that the stranger's body had not yet been identified and it lay, unclaimed and unguarded, a few miles away. Trying to somehow keep their staggering steps steady in the soft snow, wrapping their heads and necks firmly against the cold and keeping the kangri steadily burning near the chest under their loose robes, and braving the fierce winds, they took several hours to reach the spot.

It was none other than Makhsusullah. Reclining against the trunk of a powerful oak tree, his body fully covered, he seemed more asleep than dead. His lower body was buried in the snow and his face was peaceful, as if he was quite content with what was happening to him. It seemed as if the Angel of Death had taken him as he slept, oblivious to everything. In the extreme cold of intense snowfall, the body quickly begins to lose heat, then its energy diminishes fast. The circulation of blood slows down. The heart strives to pump blood faster and yet faster to make up for the slow circulation. Yet, the blood, thickening due to the continuing onslaught of the cold, and the narrowing arteries obstructing the natural flow and rhythm of blood at normal temperature, becomes sluggish and more sluggish still. Thus the heart is subjected to an ever-escalating demand for supply of blood to the muscles, the nerves, the arteries. It tries to beat faster, but ceaselessly resisting and fighting against the thickening of the blood and the narrowing of the blood-carrying canals, it begins to tire. The extremities, and then other body parts that are far from the heart, are the first to start going numb. This in fact is a defence mechanism of sorts, for the alternative to loss of sensation is unbearable, almost death-bringing pain. Thinner than the thinnest strand of hair, the capillaries of the eyes then begin to fade into inactivity for want of blood. The vision grows obscure, clouded, blurred.

At first the brain commands the muscles to shake and shiver, so as to generate heat. For heat is the energy that sustains life. But soon enough the investment of the energy in making the body shiver, brings less and less return. For there is a steady deficit in the heat-energy produced by the shaking of the body and the heat-energy expended in that activity. As the feeling of cold grows, the brain grows frantic and yet more frantic in ordering the body to shiver. The deficit of energy thus grows apace, bringing on a state when the body stops shivering, unable to carry out the brain's commands. Drowsiness supervenes. The body, almost totally disconnected from the brain, feels an almost heavenly pleasure in lying quiet, unmoving. The slumber generates a peace, which seems spiritual. Were someone to try to shake the cold body back to sensibility and even put a hot cup of qahva to the blue lips, the slumberer feels an almost murderous rage at the rude awakener.

A long sleep. The body then loses all motion, even the tiniest of nerves lose their urge to act. Then the lights of the brain start going out in quick succession.

Some such event must have happened to Makhsusullah. When they lifted him from his bed of snow and unwrapped the shawl from his inert body, the tightly closed fist of his right hand was seen to be clutching a scrap of stiff paper. It was the colour of ivory, and brittle from the cold. Extracted with great difficulty from the clutch of the dead fist and gingerly straightened out so as to prevent it from breaking like old, worn-wood shaving, it was seen to be something which was not paper; they did not know about ivory, and understood it to be some kind of animal's bone. On that bone, there was a portrait of an extremely unfamiliar but extremely beautiful girl. It was banithani. But how could the people of faraway Kashmir know her? They buried the portrait in the snow, side by side with the grave of the painter who had made it.

9

Mian Makhsusullah's son and grandsons prosper and flourish

FOR FORTY DAYS, Salimah wore black for her husband. As the days and weeks passed, she started feeling that she had not understood her husband fully, and perhaps she had never made a serious effort to do so. But it was a puzzle for her that she should now have begun to have this feeling of failure to understand her husband, and that her husband had deserved somewhat more than just being looked upon by her as her god on earth in the metaphorical, conventional sense; that she ought have regarded him as a human being too, one whose feelings and anxieties could be different from those of the traditional kinds of husbands in her culture. That is to say, she should have been intimately familiar both with the open surfaces and the hidden nooks and crevasses of his personality: what showed above and what subsisted deep inside.

It was a novel notion for her: to 'understand' her husband. It was a notion wholly alien to her being and upbringing, a notion that was entirely out of her world. Everything that she had learnt at her parents' home, in her extended family, in her cultural environment, was silent on this matter. The husband for her was as a prayer, or an amulet, which did not need to be understood for its efficacy to be ensured. In fact, it was generally forbidden for an amulet to be opened to see what was inscribed on it. And the words of a prayer were almost always in Arabic, which would perhaps be not understood even by the mullah at the mosque. It was enough, and in fact quite desirable, to wear the amulet round your neck, or recite the prayer in the prescribed manner. The function of the amulet or the prayer was to protect one from calamity, to convert sickness into health, to enable the women to bear boys rather than girls, to keep the even rhythm of domestic life flowing without obstruction. And this was exactly what a husband was needed for. Just as one genuinely hoped for the amulet or the prayer to work, and went on hoping even if it was ineffectual, quite in the same way, one hoped for the husband to do his work as provider and master, as the begetter and protector for his woman and her children, and one must continue to be patient, praying and hoping for improvement and change if things did not work out quite that way. To look at her husband ever thus was a woman's true vocation and purpose in life.

Possibly there had always been a quiet misgiving, a tiny prick of doubt in Salimah's mind that she and her husband did not come from the same inner stock: his feelings and reactions to things could be different from those of her own people. The eye with which he saw the world was dissimilar to the eye that we have. Above all, he was a painter, and his painting too was not at all similar to our painting. Perhaps he could not be made happy with the strategies that other women among her own people adopted, though they were quite sufficient for them and their husbands to be kept in good humour.

But then, what could she do, even if she desired to do something? Her life would end and marital matters, day-to-day questions or big affairs, would still remain tied like a knot in her shawl, or like things saved and tied up in a corner of her dress for some unknown moment in the future. There was none to advise her, and even if there were one, she would be just another Kashmiri; what knowledge, what insight could she have into the psyche of a middle-aged man from Rajputana?

Salimah went through her life with the niggling thought that there had been some want in the inner being of her husband: a want that only she, his wedded wife, could have satisfied. But she could not ever decide if Makhsusullah had been conscious of that want. The way their life was spent, they rarely talked in private, in confidential or intimate ways. And it was not just with Salimah; Makhsusullah never let himself out before anyone, except when he played with the children of his neighbours or his wife's relatives. Now, when he was gone forever, Salimah felt like chewing her heart out; she ardently longed to do something, something for her husband that she thought she did not do when she was with him. It was precisely this feeling of nostalgia, of things left undone, that revealed to her the fact that a husband is not just the rampart of the castle of a woman's life: he also lives in it.

Through forty days of intense public mourning and the frozen silence of her inner being, she gradually realized the truth about her marriage: He who had gone away from her had never truly stayed; and if he had never truly stayed, he would remain an unfamiliar traveller for her even if he did stay a thousand physical years.

In spite of this knowledge, Salimah decided that at least now she must do everything in her power to bring her husband close to her; she should attempt to perform the task which she had so lamentably failed to do when her husband had been physically there with her.

Salimah vowed in her heart to do everything possible to bring her dead husband nearer to her: the husband who had been unable to or had been prevented from coming close to her in life. So the first thing she did at the end of the statutory Islamic mandate for a widow not to leave her house was to leave Kupwarah and choose a suitable home for herself in Badgam. Although she was past the age to start studying talim, nor were women then regarded as suitable for such professions, she struck up acquaintance with the women and wives of talim masters, began to visit them off and on, observing and trying to understand at least a little of their way of life, their attitude to things, the mindset and the moods of the masters, their idiosyncrasies, their aversions.

Muhammad Yahya was initiated in the art of reading when he reached the prescribed age of four years and four months, the age which was considered both suitable and auspicious for a child to begin learning the mysteries of the alphabet. First, he was made to recite after his tutor the basmalah in full. When the first verse of the Quran is recited, the act is called basmalah and it means, 'to do, or pronounce, the first verse of the Quran'. And it is recited in full when something is begun, especially something formal. By the time he was five, Salimah began to narrate to him the life and circumstances of his father in the form of stories. One day, during her normal conversations with the child, she asked him casually, though with some purpose hidden somewhere in her mind, 'My son, does your heart ever hanker after your father's land, so that you may go and visit it?'

'Where else shall I go, Mother? My father's land is right here, is that not the fact?'

'Well, what I meant was, your father was originally not from here. You see, he came from far, from the land of Hindustan actually.'

'But Mother, you are of this place. Didn't my father accept you and this land for his own? No, I am not going anywhere else.'

Tears overflowed from Salimah's eyes, falling like the gentle rain of early summer, wetting the light upper mantle on her body. With eyes dimmed by the flood, she tried to descry the lineages of the father on the son's face. There was nothing apparent there of Makhsusullah except his dark ebonite colour.

'All right, someday I'll take you to the place where my own people live.'

On many dark and silent nights, Salimah would sit quietly on her prayer mat and pray to God for her son never to leave her. Let him have daughters born to his bride here, delicate and pale white like the first little narcissi that germinated after the first snow and were the first to peep out from under the snow as it started to dwindle; delicate and fair as the rose in the summer, but also hardy and full of the strength to survive. Let their aspect and lineaments be free from the shadow even of the colours of distant lands; let no outsider carry them away. Let the lives of his sons flourish and prosper like the ears of rice paddy rising and swaying in the cool breezes of the valley of Kashmir; and let them grow tall and strong and prosperous in the air of these hills and vales and no other.

*

Muhammad Yahya soon earned a reputation as a fine artist of talim. He also studied Persian, and picked up a smattering of Arabic and some fundamentals of the science of numbers. Thus he became known among his peers as both Artist and Mullah. He had the strong presence of a fully grown-up person by the time he was fifteen, and in looks he turned out to have been made in the exact image of his father. Whereas there had been, in Makhsusullah's visage, a kind of crazed absorption, a fierce concentration, Yahya's mien reflected an inner peace, as if a quivering ray of inner light always emanated from the quiet depths of his soul and played upon his face like the delicate pink light of the false dawn on the waters of the sparkling cataracts of the valley of Laulab.

By the time he was eighteen, marriage proposals began to abound for Muhammad Yahya. After full thought and careful search, Salimah got him married to a quiet, homey and pretty girl called Bashirunnisa from her home town of Kupwarah. A few weeks short of a couple of years of marriage, Yahya's wife was delivered of twins with only an hour's gap between the siblings. The babies bore a clear resemblance to the mother, but their complexion was swarthy and deep brown like their father's. The elder one was named Muhammad Yaqub; the younger one, Muhammad Daud. They grew up to become distinguished merchants in silk, saffron and honey. By virtue of having been born and brought up in Badgam, they became known as Yaqub Badgami and Daud Badgami.

In spite of their father's close connection to Badgam, and Badgam being the place from which they derived part of their identity, neither Yaqub nor Daud inherited their father's talent for the visual arts. They had no interest in talim or wood carving or carpet weaving. Yet they did have beautiful singing voices and a flair for music. They sang the Kashmiri poems of the woman saint Lall Ded and the ghazals of the seventeenth-century Kashmiri Persian poet Mullah Tahir Ghani with equal felicity and proficiency. Gradually, the brother-singer duo became known all over Kashmir. Sometimes their business and at other times their virtuosity at music took them to different places, not only around Badgam, but also to the far corners of the valley. There were times when father and sons did not really get to be together for weeks and months. As their reputation grew, they could be found travelling as far as Balkh in the west and Lahore in the east.

Salimah died at a ripe age, that is, at fifty-five, but died with her longing to have granddaughters unfulfilled. She was buried according to her wish in the forest of Dachigam at the foot of Mian Makhsusullah's grave. Muhammad Yahya was greatly disappointed with his sons, and this disappointment always hung heavy on his spirits. He had had hopes for them to keep and grow the artistic legacy of their father and grandfather, rather than wander through hills and forests and villages like journeymen hawkers, burdened with bottles of honey and bales of silk and pouches full of saffron. Worse still was their propensity for singing and playing the traditional Kashmiri string instrument called the santur. He considered such things much below his station, worthy only of crude, illiterate bards and rhymesters. Salimah would plead for them before her son all the time, but Yahya's heart would not be consoled. As for Salimah, she could not love her son more, but her heart always felt the niggling throb of a tiny thorn for not having been given granddaughters and for the grandsons not having turned out worthy. Perhaps Mian's soul too was not entirely at peace in Paradise.

INTERLUDE

Sindhia achieves the unachievable elevation and issues orders for celebratory fairs to be held throughout the realm

UNLIKE DAUD AND Yaqub, whose spirit was that of truly hardened tourists and travellers, Muhammad Yahya left his home just once in his life. There is a fascinating story about why this journey happened. I might well narrate it here, for the people of today are developing the habit of forgetting. The dust and smoke of modern life are busy obliterating, or at least dimming, many such events hidden in the mazes of family stories and even the histories of nations.

The year was 1207 of the Hegira, concordant with the English year 1792–1793. It had been nearly five years since the execution of Ghulam Qadir Ruhela and the total rout of the Ruhela Pathans; God's Shadow on Earth, Emperor Ali Gauhar Muhammad Abdullah Shah Alam the Second, Fighter of Holy Battles, had been reinstated on the Royal Throne in the Red Fort. During these five years, with the support and backing of the Maratha, the light of the crimson chandeliers of the Mughal Empire, though quite dim and hazy, was still bright enough to dazzle the observers close by. Madhava Rao Sindhia, whose popular appellative was Mahada ji, had been ennobled and elevated by the Emperor with the titles of Beloved Son, Absolute Plenipotentiary, Minister in Chief, Exalted in Fortune, Madhava Rao ji Sindhia Bahadur. Very nearly the whole of Hindustan, barring the territories of Nizamul Mulk and Tipu Sultan, and more than half the land of the Deccan paid fealty to the Sindhia. Some of the country he ruled directly on behalf of the Maratha chief, designated as Peshwa, some in the name of Shah Alam, and a few smaller areas on behalf of sundry Maratha warlords and potentates. True, the Company Bahadur ruled very large tracts of Shah Alam's empire, but the people of India did not yet, in their hearts, accord it the legitimacy to reign and be entitled to tribute and land revenue. The Company may have been ruling, but it did not reign.

It was a hot midday of 21 Ziqadah, 1207 Hegira, corresponding to 11

June 1792, when Madhava Rao Sindhia entered the environs of Poona, accompanied by a small but magnificent retinue; breezes, lightly hinting at the coming rains, preceded him like a happy vanguard. His namesake, the nineteen-year-old Peshwa Madhava Rao II, awaited him, but Sindhia had his camp and tents set up in the big maidan opposite the English Residency. He presented himself at the Court of Chhatrapati Shivaji's Vicegerent, the Peshwa of the Council of Eight or the Maratha Oligarchy, the Leader of Exalted Fortune, he whose Camp was the sky and whose Station and Abode was Mars the Planet of War, namely, Madhava Rao Bahadur the Second.

Madhava Rao Sindhia alighted from his elephant when he was a mile away from the Auspicious Fort, and walked the rest of the distance in spite of his game leg. He discarded even the golden canopy that was always carried above his head. He covered the distance in a little less than half an hour without mopping his sweating face or stopping even for a minute, braving the brilliant sun whose rays were glaring back against the stunted, dark rocks of the Sat Pura range, billions of years old.

Arriving at the principal portal of the Auspicious Fort, Sindhia removed his weapons, slipped out of his shoes, and, spreading his wide sash on the bare floor in front of the Hall of Public Audience where everyone deposited their shoes before entering upon the Presence, he sat down, surrounded not by soldiers and gallants, but by shoes and sandals. In his right hand he had a parcel wrapped in gold-embroidered cloth. He had already surrendered all his weaponry to his personal bodyguard; so what could that box-like package contain, was a question that none dared ask him.

The black velvet curtain that hung at the far end of the huge hall was pulled open the moment Sindhia sat down with his golden parcel. Once the curtain had been drawn back to its full extent, a platform could be seen; it was about two hands in height, twenty hands in length and fourteen in width, and was covered with a golden-yellow silk carpet from Yemen. Skins of tigers and cheetahs, thrown about with apparent casualness but in reality with considerable care and design, adorned the elevated space.

Peshwa Madhava Rao the Second could now be seen seated on a large and wide ebony chair. But for his straight-backed posture and stance, erect and proud neck, and eyes full of total self-confidence, his slight, teenager's body and somewhat pinched face—which already bore signs of near alcoholism—would have seemed small and inappropriate for the vast chair which he occupied with perfect ease. At this moment, that wide and heavy chair somehow seemed small for him.

The Peshwa rose from his chair when he noticed Mahada ji sitting on the floor at the entrance to the Hall, but he was still negotiating the second step down from his elevated platform when Mahada ji stepped up to him and bending three times to touch the earth with his right hand and then bringing it to his forehead, he made the formal gesture of submission to his master. Unwrapping his gold-braided parcel, he produced a pair of sandals of the formal Maratha style, and spoke in chaste Persian: 'My ancestors always regarded this honour as the source of their greatest pride. Please, grant me your gracious permission that I attain the auspicious fortune of putting these on your sacred feet.'

Madhava Rao smiled and stopped where he was, placing his right hand to his breast. Mahada ji stepped up and put the sandals on the Peshwa's feet. The old sandals he enfolded in his golden cloth and put the bundle under his right arm, to be placed on the chair which would be offered to him further in the proceedings. It was a tall wooden chair, worked out in gold, just below the Peshwa's platform, and covered with a heavy crimson and blue saddlecloth. A huge Ethiopian who stood bearing a mace behind and slightly to the left of the Peshwa quickly stepped forward and removed the saddlecloth and just as quickly regained his station behind his master. With the tiniest of gestures of his neck and eye, the Peshwa granted Mahada ji permission to be seated.

A brief welcome song in the raga Bahar was now sung in the ancient Indian classical style called dhrupad. This signalled the conclusion of the proceedings because the Court had assembled at that time just to welcome Mahada ji and grant him audience.

The next day, the Court assembled not in the Hall of Public Audience, but in a large and open space. A forest of tents of all descriptions—quadrangular but ropeless tents, large, open tents, huge, pillared canopies with convex, painted and decorated ceilings, Court pavilions with proper arched and decorated doors with private apartments, and high, painted canvas walls supported by covered bamboo pillars at the back—grew up overnight to accommodate the attendees. All the tents intended for the guest and his main companions were covered in red-and-blue cloths of gold.

The tents of Peshwa Madhava Rao's nobles were no less lavishly provided. The spires of some of the tallest ones could be seen bright and resplendent from some distance. In order to temper the heat inside, extremely light sprays of rose water were sprinkled everywhere all the time; the air was circulated with long, heavy cloth fans hung on wooden beams pulled by stout ropes; there being two to six men pulling six or eight fans together. Apart from the elephants with golden, even bejewelled, caparisons, powerful horses wearing colourful leather saddles, bejewelled egrets, and tails bedecked with gold-and-silver-filigreed cloth, there was something else here which was never seen at the Mughal courts, whether held inside or in the open: two thousand or more heavily armed soldiers surrounded the entire meadow which housed the tents and the equipage.

Exactly in the centre of this huge camp was the Royal Pavilion containing a brilliantly worked empty throne: empty because it symbolized the Prosperity Assuring Feet and the Auspicious Presence of Shah Alam the Second, the Shadow of God on Earth, King of the World and of All that there Is in it. Peshwa Madhava Rao the Second, barefooted but in full court dress, approached the Royal Pavilion and waited at the door. The Steward of the Pavilion called out in Persian: 'The Peshwa of the Maratha Court of the City of Satara is here to submit his offering to the August Presence, Shadow of God on Earth, Protector of the World whose Pavilion is upon the High, Emperor of Hindustan and the Deccan.'

The entire Court rose, and Madhava Rao II entered the Pavilion, bowing seven times and as many times putting his right hand on his forehead; Mahada ji followed closely. Approaching as close to the throne as was needed to let his hand touch it, Madhava Rao II bent his head, went down on his knees and placed a gold-embroidered and tasselled pouch containing one hundred and one Shah Alami gold mohurs on the throne. A loud babble of congratulations and compliments arose.

Now, walking backwards, the Peshwa and Mahada ji approached a heavy golden curtain to the left and behind the throne. Still walking backwards, they entered a door behind the curtain. The curtain was now fully drawn back, revealing a heavily ornamented chamber. Here, both stood so as to be in full view, and the Peshwa draped around Mahada ji's shoulders and lower body a Robe of Honour sent for him by the King. The Robe consisted of five priceless gems and nine separate items of apparel. Then he placed a bejewelled sword in Mahada ji's left hand; in his right hand, the Peshwa placed an ebony inkstand and the Royal Seal.

Quitting the chamber of investiture, Mahada ji first kissed the foot of the throne, then he kissed the Peshwa's right hand. The Court Proclaimer spoke in his stentorian voice: 'The Protector of the Caliphate, Shadow of God on Earth, Pride of the House of Babur, Most Superior among the Offspring of Timur, Sovereign Son of Sovereign, Sultan Son of Sultan, the Presence, Ali Gauhar, Shah Alam Bahadur Secundus, May God Perpetuate His Rule and Preserve His Power Forever, has, in addition to the Sword and Pen, vouchsafed a peacock-feather fan, a golden chair, six elephants with howdahs and ensign, and a warhorse to his Beloved Son, Royal Plenipotentiary, Exalted in Fortune, Madhava Rao Sindhia Bahadur.'

The clamour and din of rejoicing and acclaim rose again, louder this time. Drums were sounded. Rose water, attenuated solutions of attar and ambergris were sprayed upon those present. Then Sindhia made a small gesture to a secretary who stood near. He bore on his head a heavy copper tray covered with a blue velvet cloth picked with gold. On the velvet were two Royal Edicts. Again, Sindhia bending three times and touching his right hand to his head, put out his right hand and removed the two scrolls, kissed them, then touched them to his eyes and put them on his head. The secretary now advanced and unrolled the scrolls one by one and presented them to Sindhia.

With proper pauses, and in a grave voice, Sindhia read out the contents before the Court. The purport of the first was that the Heaven Blessed Navab, Peshwa of the Maratha Court, Madhava Rao II, is hereby appointed to the Office of Imperial Vicegerent. He is permitted to use the Exalted Insignia of the Fish in his formal processions, and the privilege of placing a pearl necklace around the turban ornament on his head.

Celebratory noises of jubilation and congratulations reverberated through the Court and even outside it. Cannons were fired in the maidan, huge firework wheels were fired in the sky, and celebratory music was played on fifes and hautboys. When the noise abated, and before the second Edict could be read out, the Peshwa advanced into the assembly and announced in his thin but clear voice: 'I appoint my brother and chieftain of the Court at Satara, Madhava Rao Sindhia, Vicegerent to the Imperial Vicegerent.'

Sindhia bowed and touched the Peshwa's feet. Then, he read out the second Edict according to which Madhava Rao Sindhia, Exalted in Fortune, Minister in Chief, Absolute Plenipotentiary, was granted the power to choose his own successor as Absolute Plenipotentiary.

Stunned, the assembly heard the unbelievable announcement in silence. Such an honour had never been granted to anyone in the long history of Mughal supremacy in India. But when the Peshwa himself stepped up to embrace Sindhia and murmur his congratulations, the assemblage realized the magnitude of the moment and erupted into a tumult of praise and felicitation. Sindhia moved a step further into the Court and bowed in acknowledgement. He then rose, and read out the last proclamation in a loud voice that seemed to overflow the Court:

> **As from this day, we prohibit, throughout**
> **the length and breadth of our Empire,**
> **the slaughter of horned animals.**

Everyone knew that this was a mere token concession, empty of content. But Sindhia's supporters immediately realized it to be more than a victory for the Hindu faith; it was a major victory within the intricacies of Maratha politics. What it meant was that a shoe-bearer of the Peshwas, one from the lowly caste of the Patels, had achieved what had been unachievable for the Brahmin Peshwas and their great minister, the wily Nana Farnavis. This was the most precious moment of Mahada ji's eventful and colourful life.

After he returned from Court, Mahada ji issued orders for celebrations to be held throughout the empire, with carnivals and women's exclusive bazaars (called Mina Bazaar, where only women of the nobility could establish their shops and only men of the nobility could enter them for shopping, with more than usual haggling and not a little banter). He also ordered fairs to be organized where artisans, craftsmen and artists were to be invited from faraway places. It was ordered that practitioners of the arts should assemble in every big city from far and near and put on sale and display examples of their mastery and the quality of their work. One of the purposes behind this order was to disseminate the news of the interdict on the slaughter of animals, and to spread the word about Mahada ji's own honour and elevation throughout the realm.

Thus it came to pass that in Lahore a Mina Bazaar and Crafts Fair was held for two weeks, from 11 Zilhijja 1207 (30 June 1792), and Muhammad Yahya Badgami was specially invited to bring his wares from Kashmir.

10

Yahya witnesses a lamentation of extraordinary power and beauty, and meets painters and singers from Rajputana

IT SEEMED AS if the hot days would never cease. The season of the rains was like an experienced seductress of the bazaars who promised a glimpse of her riches and would then suddenly disappear. Those were burning, broiling days whose combustive heat obliged even the kites to leave their eggs untended and the hill chameleon's liver burnt like a kebab with thirst; with the hot gusts whispering even more heat in the burning heart of simmering nights. The winds that rose during the day in the desert of Bikaner, trampled Jodhpur and Multan underfoot, filled or covered everything with dust in their wake—tree and shrub, stone and grass, man and woman— and arrived in Lahore at high noon, rustling and susurrating and wreaking havoc through the deserted bazaars and alleys of the city.

What wetness could a tiny spray of rain bring down to moisten the parched lips of Lahore's soil, brittle and black like bread burnt in a clay oven? The drop or two of rain that fell infrequently would sizzle and disappear like a droplet of milk on a red-hot iron pan. The hot nights, quiet because everyone was indoors, seemed to have frozen over the city. The world, in Lahore, seemed to be devoid of life.

Poor Yahya Badgami! Never in his life had he imagined, far less seen, such a summer. Every day, in fact every hour of the day and every watch of the night, was like hell for him. True, his art was the talk of the town: his showroom was ever crowded until late at night with buyers and connoisseurs of fine carpets. And he was paid without hassle or bargaining; he commanded his own price. Where else could he gain such honour, such approbation? Certainly not in Kashmir. Here in Lahore there were artists and buyers from Badakhshan, Transoxiana, Sistan, Iran, Azerbaijan, even Turkey; they marvelled at Yahya's art and did not tire of praising it. The craftsmen of Lahore, old and young, and, in fact, even some women, came to see him at work and tried directly or indirectly to learn from him, to imitate him and to adopt his innovative designs. But Yahya's heart bled for Kashmir. He looked forward impatiently to the time when the fair would be rolled up and concluded, and he would be allowed to go back home. This was scheduled to be before the moon of Muharram, the month of mourning, was sighted.

He recited to himself all the time the rubai of Mullah Tahir Ghani, the great Kashmiri Persian poet:

The winds of Hind have constricted my heart,
Oh breezes, wing me to the garden of Kashmir!
The fiery state of being a stranger here has made me faint,
Give to me the cool manna of morning in my land.

Fate had, however, something else in store for him. There were a few more days to go before the month of Muharram could commence with the sighting of its moon. Yet arrangements for the rituals of Muharram—mourning and special assemblies to narrate the sorrows and the Passion of Husain, the grandson of the Prophet of Islam who is almost universally called Imam (the Leader)—had already begun in Lahore, thanks to the convention established by the Presence, who now has his abode in Paradise, Bahadur Shah I, during his reign from 1707 to 1712. Preparations for various functions and ceremonies were greater and more intensive than before. The winds of mourning seemed to begin blowing over the city right from the 22nd day Zilhijja, that is, six or seven days before Muharram's moon could be sighted.

The Mina Bazaar concluded the next day, and preparations for Muharram became more frenzied. Everybody began to look for black dresses, black sashes and light black wraps for the upper body. Along with the search in the shops for black velvet sandals, people who wore arms at all times began to look for scabbards and sheaths covered in black. Houses dedicated to mourning assemblies began to be cleaned, whitewashed and generally spruced up. Children, youth, old people, women, men—without distinction of faith or creed—began to dust off the previous year's anthologies of special mourning poems for Muharram. Poems learnt or committed to memory were refreshed through quiet practice. There were many genres, the most popular being the marsiyah (or elegy upon Husain), the nauha (poem of lament, generally performed to a simple tune without music), and the soz (a short poem of greater literary import than the nauha, performed in a raga from classical music, but without the support of any instrument at all). This last was obviously the most difficult and was often presented by professionals.

During those days the tunes heard even from the 'women of the upper storey', the dancing and singing girls of Hira Mandi, were mournful and charged with the emotions of pain and parting.

Yahya Badgami was not particularly enamoured of ceremonies of mourning during Muharram and of attending assemblies where accounts of the Passion and suffering of Husain and his companions were narrated, but he was second to none in his respect and love for the Prophet's beloved grandson and those who were martyred with him at Karbala on the tenth of Muharram in the year 61 of the Hegira (corresponding to 10 October 680 of the English calendar). So he decided that he should now begin to organize suitable mounts, pack animals, guards and guides for his return journey. Should he succeed in getting all this done quickly, and even maybe find a small caravan bound for Kashmir on the planned day, he would be able to depart Lahore very early on the 3rd of Muharram and reach Srinagar on the evening of the 10th of Muharram, the chief of all mourning days. He would then immediately go to the Mosque of Shah-e Hamadan in Zaina Kadal on the left bank of the river Jhelam and listen in the mosque, or in the attached hospice, to professionally qualified men of learning extol the goodness and holiness of Husain and his companions, and then going on to narrate the tragic tale of their death at Karbala.

Muhammad Yahya settled his business accounts on the 1st of Muharram, hired a palanquin and proceeded to Gariban Tola, the part of the city where cart and camel drivers, guides and other people generally connected with long travels lived. His main objective was to find and clinch a deal with the family of drivers and guides recommended to him by a well-wisher. Adjacent to the building where that family was to be found, there was a large caravanserai, perhaps as old as the Lahore Fort. Among the guests at that inn were a miscellaneous group of leather-and-brocade shoemakers from Ajmer, painters from Kishangarh and gold enamel craftsmen from Jaipur.

Obviously, these people had come to take part in the Crafts Fair, but did not seem to be in a hurry to return home. The reasons for their staying on were many: the weather on the roads to their homes in Rajputana, and also in the towns and villages where they actually lived, was much harsher than the present weather at Lahore. Further, if the rainy season started while they were still en route, their journey could cause them greater hardship and grief than a trip to hell. But the main reason for their not starting for home immediately was that it was traditionally regarded by them as wrong and unpropitious to travel during the first ten days of Muharram.

Muhammad Yahya's palanquin was now opposite the caravanserai's tall and massive gate. He observed the wide expansiveness of the courtyard, and then noticed a group of women assembling there. They were clad in solid black; nothing was to be seen of their bodies, except that their faces were uncovered and their hair was open and undone. There were some men, too, behind the women, but dressed in a similar way: they had no cummerbund or sash or dupatta around their waists; the few who had them, had let their ends hang loose. They all wore light, black cotton tunics and white pyjamas. Some wore an outer garment, but here again, the strings and buttons were undone, revealing much of the chest. All were barefoot. Muhammad Yahya could not even begin to guess at their religion or creed, except that some were clearly not Muslim; some, with shaven chins but fairly prominent moustaches, bore no signs to distinguish Muslim from non-Muslim.

It was anyway clear that all were mourners for the Martyred Imam. He got down from his palanquin in deference to them and walking slowly, he approached the guardhouse of the caravanserai. He stood silently with his eyes fixed on the ground, so as to alleviate any suspicion of his having stopped there to look at the women.

A few minutes passed. Almost by itself, a pattern emerged among the mourners: the throng organized so that the women were at the core, and the men were around them. The women's faces, tanned like old copper, were even more dark now because of grieving, their eyes totally downcast. The men's faces apparently bore no expression.

Suddenly, from somewhere inside, a loud cry arose: *Wa Husaina! Wa Husaina!* It seemed to Yahya that a procession of mourners was about to appear, but none came. Perhaps it was some unfortunate person, physically disadvantaged due to disease or injury, and unable to come out with the mourners. A minute later, a venerable old gentleman did come out, moving with very slow, measured steps but he could not have been the one who had cried out. Everything about him was different from the congregation that he now joined: his gait, the bone structure of his face, his style of dress. His turban was black and his shoulders were draped in a wide, soft, black shawl.

Not looking to the right or left, the old man, facing his audience and standing to their right, recited a rubai in Persian. His voice had a strange tone, something of the rustle of leaves in a gentle breeze, something of a sob, something of a cry of pain. It seemed as if there was an effort to suppress a sob, but the cry of pain was trying to prevail over the sob, as if the cry wanted to bury the sob in the throat and the breast, and come pouring out and flying away to the high heavens, transcending the human limits of the earth:

Husain, son of Ali, beloved little one of the Prophet,
Newly ripened fruit of the Prophet's Garden, his favourite Prince,
Woe, woe! With cruelty's axe and maleficent dagger
The villainous gang cut down that Fruit, that Prince.

Having finishing reciting the whole rubai, he recited the last line again. Then, he enunciated the first word of the line (*darda* in Persian) in a different tone, such that the first note of the mournful raga called Des could be discerned clearly. Now the women took up the sound and in a style that generally followed the raga, they began to perform the nauha:

Someone, on the way to Kufah . . .
Someone, on the way to Kufah, brought to the Sovereign Lord the news
That they have been murdered,
That they have been murdered: Muslim and both his sons;
If you didn't go to Kufah . . .
If you didn't go to Kufah, it would be better.
He heard, and began to say . . .
He heard, and he began to say, that Imam of Genies
and of Men . . .

All the performers fell silent, as if none had the strength to repeat what the Imam of the worlds had said; as if too, none had the fortitude to hear those words. The hiraman parakeets, yellow of beak and pink of head, their neck ringed with black; large Indian parakeets with sharp red beaks and of darker green hue; Lahori waxbills, tiny, extremely dark red with little white spots on their tiny wings; brown waxbills with numerous little dots on their chests; noisy flocks of pesky sparrows whose chirping always kept the environment warm and ardent; and all other birds returning home to the mammoth banyan tree that stood opposite the caravanserai: all of these too seemed to have fallen silent. The sounds of the bazaar seemed to have dimmed and become feeble. Then, for a moment, it seemed that everything had become static. Pedestrians, horse riders, camel riders, palanquins, raths, all stopped where they were; buyers and sellers postponed their transactions: the whole world seemed to have bent its head, as if in supplication.

From among the women in the middle of the circle someone now began to pronounce somewhat unfamiliar words. In the sharpest and most intense note permissible in the raga Des, she started to recite two lines in Persian, but the enunciation was of such razor-sharp height in pitch that both lines seemed as if they had been uttered almost continuously; but the note slowed down considerably towards the end, as if the raga and its performer both had reached the limit of their power:

Pulled and led by death-destiny, I walk towards pain and affliction,
trial and calamity:
The bell has tolled for Muslim, now it will toll for me.

When the woman reached the word 'me' (*ma* in Persian), the old man again repeated the call in Persian in the same raga, but in a deeper note. And the women began again:

Someone, on the way to Kufah . . .
Someone, on the way to Kufah, brought to the Sovereign Lord the news . . .

After the entire nauha had been repeated in the same manner as before, small children came out from the rooms in a brief procession. They were bareheaded and barefoot; striking their hands on their breasts, they chanted, 'Hasan, Husain! Hasan, Husain! Hasan, Husain!' These children represented those of the same age whom Husain was supposed to have employed in his battle at Karbala as runners. The women took the children in their midst and caressing their heads, they began to call in Persian:

Husain is slain . . . Woe, woe,
Husain is slain!

The men also began to beat their breasts when the children began their mourning. Gradually, their voices became muted; eventually, they fell silent and started slowly to go back inside.

Yahya had never experienced such pain-filled lamentation, such an accomplished performance of the nauha, so full of the feeling of love and empathic suffering. The prickling of the hurt flowing from the voices of the mourning crowd throbbed in his blood like heartbeat. Quite forgetting his original purpose for being in that place, he made to follow the procession inside. Nevertheless, he hesitated; there was no one in the caravanserai with whom he was acquainted; whom should he ask, and what should he say to them? In any case, he was never so active in the lamentations of Muharram, he thought. And he needed immediately to organize the pack animals and guides and mounts so that he could return home.

He said to himself: I have nothing to do with them really, nor do I know anything of their manners and etiquette. Suppose I blurted out something that does not go down well with them? They might just laugh it off, but I could run the risk of annoying the Spirit of the Imam! But really, how utterly exquisite were the voices, how artless and chaste the way they organized the dirge, how heart-rending their pain! Praised and saluted be the Prophet for such things!

He tried to shake off his feelings and turn towards his palanquin so as to resume his purpose. A dark and tall young man, whose whiskers were just sprouting, came out of the caravanserai and approached him. His large and expressive eyes, which would have been bright normally, seemed a little dulled and tired, perhaps with mourning. He wore a long shirt and loose trousers in the Afghan style, of such dark green that it was almost black. He had on his head a short cotton turban, scarlet and black, and his feet were shod in sandals whose toes were upturned and pointed. Muhammad Yahya later found out that such shoes were the speciality of the shoemakers of a city called Jodhpur in Rajputana.

The young man respectfully gestured to Yahya that he wait for him. Yahya did not quite understand, but thought it polite not to ignore the apparently friendly gesture. The young man came up to Yahya, greeted him by bending a bit and putting his right hand to his forehead. 'Sir, your share of the consecrated gift awaits you,' he said. 'Our Venerable Public Orator says for you to accept your share before you go.'

'Share? What kind of share? Sorry, I do not follow.'

'On this day in our village we have prayers recited over some food and fruits, and we consecrate it to the Holy Imams. This food is then distributed among the poor and among those present,' he explained. 'Our Venerable says that since you were present at the time when the nauha was performed, you too should have a bit of the benediction.'

'But . . . but young man, this is not your village. You are now in . . .'

The youth smiled a genial smile. 'Undoubtedly, this is Lahore,' he said. 'We are from Rajputana, from a placed called Kishangarh, actually. We observe the rituals of all the important days: Baisakhi, the first and the tenth days of Muharram, and all the rest of it. For Muharram, we specially invite our Venerable Orator from Ajmer. Our nauhas and the makers of the replicas of the Imam's tombs and other sacred things, they too come from Ajmer.'

They entered the inn through its massive gate. 'So your people are not Muslim?' Yahya asked.

'No. Some of us are painters; some are singers. The painters make pictures of men and women; the singers sing ancient tales extolling the exploits of Raja Gopichand of Bengal and Raja Bharthari of Ujjain.'

'Yes, indeed. But who exactly are those rajas and maharajas? And are your songs in Hindi or in Rajputani?'

'Raja Gopichand and Raja Bharthari are from thousands, in fact hundreds of thousands, of years ago. They are like the immortal gods. We who sing their stories and their hallowed legends are called Nath, the Naths of village Ghatiali, in fact. Our village is not far from Ajmer. Are you familiar with the noble city of Ajmer?'

'Yes, indeed. In our land there are numerous devotees of the Khvajah of Ajmer, Friend of the strangers and the poor.'

Having walked past the vast courtyard and the little water channel that flowed through it, they were now stepping into the wide, twelve-arched, double veranda.

'Let's stay right here,' the young singer said. 'There may be some ladies there in purdah. Our Venerable Orator should be here any time now.'

'Yes. But you were telling me about your tongue?'

'Sir, we speak the Marwari language in our homes. Among ourselves, we almost never use Hindi. There is no language called Rajputani, but our Rajputana has many languages: Bhili, Mewari, Bikaneri and Dhundhari. In fact, there are many more. The speech of our village and its environs is Marwari.'

There was a slight commotion at one end of the long veranda. A curtain was moved aside. The old gentleman, who had led the nauha performance, came out accompanied by a small group of middle-aged men. The Orator extended his hand deferentially and shaking Yahya by the hand, he said, 'I present my humble compliments. My name is Taqiuddin Haidar Ruknabadi. The firmness of love and respect that you evinced, and my feeling that you were not a stranger but an actual participant at the nauha, obliged me to trouble you and invite you here among us.'

Muhammad Yahya Badgami inclined his head low in greeting, bringing his hand up to touch his forehead. As he raised his head, he tried to steal a look at the Orator's face: his beard was of the Iranian style, light and not long; very fair in colour, his face was slightly long but delicately boned; he was tall, but slightly bent, as if the weight of learning, or excessive weeping and mourning for the dead of Karbala, had aged him before his time.

'I beg to submit my greetings, honoured sir,' said Yahya. 'This servant is known by the name of Muhammad Yahya. It is no trouble at all; meeting and clasping the hand of a holy man of God like you is in fact my good fortune and an auspicious occasion for me.'

'I live in Ajmer,' Taqiuddin said. 'Some of my people there are servitors at the exalted Porte of Khvajah Sahib the Magnificent. Some are engaged in narrating the merits and the goodness and the sufferings and Passion of the Prophet's kindred; may there be greetings and salutations to them all.'

Muhammad Yahya listened to the mellifluous voice with rapt attention. Taqiuddin went on: 'This useless one is one of those narrators. My companions here are mostly of the Hindu faith. They have been, for a long time now, organizing mourning assemblies in their villages and hamlets through the month of Muharram. They are so ardent of faith that since they were obliged to be in Lahore this month of Muharram, they summoned me here all the way from the radiant place of Khvajah Sahib the Magnificent. For, as you might know, dear sir, Ajmer is countless miles away from Lahore.'

Taqiuddin Haidar made his narrative with pauses, with no hint of oration, but rather an air of sophisticated conversation. His accent did not have the solid, hard, ringing tone of the Lahori or the Kashmiri. It sounded extremely dulcet. Muhammad Yahya imagined it to be of Delhi, or maybe Iran. But the fact of the matter was that just a few miles east of Ajmer began the territory of the Dhundhari speech; and the territory of the Braj Bhasha, sweetest among the tongues of Hindustan, was contiguous to the land of those who spoke Dhundhari. Thus the accents of Taqiuddin owed their softness not to the Hindi of Delhi, but to the Braj Bhasha of Agra.

Muhammad Yahya, of course, had no idea of these subtleties. Like most Kashmiris, he had adequate Hindi; but he liked the Orator's refined accents so much that he felt he could go on listening endlessly.

'It is the bounty of the Master,' he spoke with his head bent. He had used the word 'Maula' for 'Master' which was used for God, but those of Taqiuddin's faith also used it for Ali, the Prophet's son-in-law and Husain's father. 'Your coming here gave me the occasion to see you. It is so meritorious, it is like a pilgrimage.'

'Honourable sir, perhaps you are from Kashmir, the land that God modelled on Paradise? May I know what keeps you occupied there?'

'Sir, I design carpets. My father, may God's mercy be upon him, was also a designer of carpets, but he had been a painter as well.'

The word 'painter' created a ripple of interest among Taqiuddin Haidar's companions. Everybody's eyes and ears were now on Muhammad Yahya.

'I also understand,' Yahya now addressed the persons gathered there, 'that my late father, may God grant him Paradise, actually came from somewhere that is in your part of the world.'

'Excellent! How nice indeed!' said one of the older men among those present. 'It is God's indulgence towards us; by the Master's grace we are united with a compatriot thousands of miles from home!' He used the Hindu word for 'God' and the Muslim term for 'Master'.

'Yes, dear sir. I too feel extremely at home here among you.'

Taqiuddin Haidar said, 'Sir, you are from a land where the trees are never sere, where the leaves never have to go away from the branch which gave them life. Our country is also called Marudhar, which in the tongue of the Brahmin means Region of Death. Yet it has its own living beings; the eternal motion of life and its benedictions are there too.'

'Doubtless, my dear sir; everywhere the waves of life's oceans bear their pearls; and also everywhere are the excellent makers of images who can capture the pearls of the greatest water and enclose them in their hands.'

'Very well put, dear sir,' said Taqiuddin, 'and why not, you are yourself a maker of images. A branch of one of the families of my companions here was ennobled by Islam in the days of the Presence, Emperor Shihabuddin Shah Jahan, whose abode now is the highest level of Paradise. Even to this day, they are Muslim but they also practise, to this day, their ancient craft of painting images. They paint pictures of Shri Radha.'

This account perhaps gave some indication about the old man who had spoken earlier. He said, 'I am sure your honour would also have some interest in making pictures. May I have your permission to show you some that I have made?'

'Certainly sir, I would deem it an honour.'

On a brief gesture from his father, the young man who had borne Taqiuddin's invitation to Yahya, quickly went inside; within minutes, he brought back a parcel wrapped in thick, waterproof cloth. He dusted off a large, low wooden platform used for communal seating or eating, shook out the white sheet that covered it and placed it again neatly on the platform. The old man thumped the packet gently to make sure that there was no dust or dirt on it.

Now that all preparations had been made, the old man gingerly untied the knots on the packet and opened it. The first painting was that of a woman . . .

11

Yahya is captivated by the portrait of a beautiful woman

SHE WORE A sari of a light reddish-violet colour, much worked in gold. The sari's edge and border covered her head, but the fabric was so fine as to be almost transparent; thus her full head of dark hair, the light dusting of gold in the white centre parting, and the rubies, diamonds, garnets and yellow-red transparent zircons with which her forehead ornament was encrusted, were clearly visible. Her colour was light, such that it would be considered fair and not dark among Indians. A slight smile adorned her lips like the faint red-gold of the last of sunset. And the painter was so dexterous that he could depict even the faint blush and the stretching of the ear lobe. Large eyes, dark violet, almost black, tapering like a sword and pointing slightly up towards the temple; the nose slim and straight and fully in proportion to the eyes, though at first glance it gave the impression of being a touch long to be called perfect. A large, gold circlet with a dark grey pearl worked in it, decorated the nose; the neck, high and delicate and erect, was the picture of self-confidence and pride but without even a hint of arrogance. Around the neck was a necklace of large, round amethysts among which were interspersed pear-shaped beads of a yellowish-pink stone which Yahya did not recognize. (He learnt later that it was a semi-precious stone called katahla, found only in Rajputana, especially Jaipur.) In the present instance, the pear-shaped cut of the stones had enhanced their value. On her delicate chin, a beauty spot, as if winking at the brightness of the dark eyes. It was difficult to determine if the sari was silk or cotton; it was almost transparent, but the painter's perfect mastery in drawing the body had let absolutely no hint of coquetry or erotic posture sneak into the painting. The girl held one end of the sari in one hand, so that the hennaed palm of the hand could be glimpsed; just one light bar of henna had been drawn on the distances between each joint of the delicate, pointed fingers. She wore but one ring—the stone was a large, red ruby surrounded by tiny diamonds. The one shapely wrist that was visible had a mirror bracelet on it; the fingers of that hand, soft and sweet like milk, held a tall, purple-blue lotus blossom. Only the upper arm of the other hand could be seen, but it was clear that the hand rested demurely in her lap.

Above all, the girl's face had a gravitas that gave her angelic grace and charm. The Master Painter had conveyed this not just through the magic of the drawing and the colours, but also through the delicate but firm manner in which the neck and chin were raised, and the angle from which she seemed to be looking not at the viewer, nor at any particular object—somehow her gaze seemed to be turned inward. Had she not been depicted with that slight smile, all this would perhaps give the effect of hauteur, of beauty's awful majesty; now the face had the dignity that came from her self-realization in the consciousness of her own irresistible pulchritude. As it was, the painting seemed to portray a peri, installed like a queen on a throne that was the viewer's heart, issuing commands throughout the realm of all beautiful women. A mood of complete stability and inner peace seemed to pervade the painting.

A fairy from the far mount of Caucasus has come down, of her own volition, into a mirror; and the mirror sleeps, still and wonderstruck, with her in its arms. Muhammad Yahya said to himself in the words of a Persian poet:

Like a difficult text in front of a dull scholar:
When you look into the mirror, your beauty
Sends the mirror to sleep.

Muhammad Yahya knew perfectly well that the portrait was not real: there was no such person. It was Shri Radha of Rajputana, or more properly, of Kishangarh. The esoteric meaning of the bluish-purple lotus blossom in her hand was just this: the blossom symbolized the heart, and Shri Krishna is always painted blue, to suggest his dark complexion. And there had never been a model for the girl; the painters of Kishangarh had for centuries been painting Shri Radha in that way, and she was affectionately known as banithani, 'The Bedecked One'.

It seemed to Yahya that his heart had been torn out from his breast, like a fish pulled out of water with a powerful harpoon. His complexion, naturally dark, became swarthier; light tremors ran through his body. Yet, in spite of this apparent loss of control, Yahya was quite aware that there was not a speck of lust in his feelings. It was only now that he realized the meaning of words such as 'adore', 'worship', 'prostrate', 'treat as idol or god' that poets used when they spoke of a beloved. It was only now that he understood how it was possible for someone to love a human being in the way people love flocks of birds as they go back to their nests on an evening bathed in the orange light scattered on a river's bank; the way people can love the raga Bhairavi being played on the santur in the last watch of the night; the way people can love the sound of a cataract in the background of snow-clad peaks when the dark night's collar is sundered by the first rays of morning; the way people love their doorstep when they return home from a long journey; the way people love beautiful carpets, heart-ravishing paintings: they want to just go on looking, watching, hearing, with no desire to possess, no expectation of a result, no experience of time passing, no illusion of something achieved.

Yahya Badgami felt his heart urging him to clasp the picture to his breast, to fill his heart with it, and go to sleep, never to awake. Noticing Yahya's absorption, Taqiuddin Haidar said: 'It is an imaginary portrait, my dear sir. It seems you like it. If so, please be good enough to accept . . .'

'Accept? Did you say "accept", honoured sir?' Yahya's voice and heart were both full of confusion. 'How can I . . . ? Your gift is an honour, I would put it on my head and kiss it with my eyes . . . but . . . but how in the name of heaven can I accept it? Granted that this is an imaginary representation, still, how could I take such a priceless gift?'

Yahya almost added 'from a stranger like you', but checked himself in time. He was hating himself in his heart for having so lost himself as to betray his deepest feelings so easily. A Persian verse of Baqar of Transoxiana came to his mind as he berated himself for his face betraying what his eyes must have spoken wordlessly. He pursed his lips tightly shut, but it was too late.

Love said to Mansur: Oh you, full of the thirst of love—
Let there be no other like you in self-betrayal.

'Kind sir, please give no thought to the price,' said Taqiuddin Haidar in the dulcet tone which was so specially his own, and he looked at the painter, as if in confirmation. 'The price of an object is in the viewer's eye. If a painting meets the approval of discerning eyes, its price is paid. If not, it is nothing more than a paltry piece of paper.'

Muhammad Yahya was still perplexed, undecided. Then the painter, who was a Hindu called Girdhar Nath, spoke up: 'Honourable maestro, Khan ji dear, please do not derange yourself about such an insignificant matter. First, these things are our domestic property, produced at home. By no means can they be considered saleable, far less at great price. We are taught to paint, for practice, this kind of portrait of Shri Radha, from our boyhood. We call it banithani. Respected Maulavi Yahya, you too must have heard of Shri Radha. Believe me, we will feel hurt if you avoid accepting what our Orator has offered to you.'

'Sir, it is not at all the question of avoiding something,' Yahya spoke with such humbleness that there was not the least vestige of arrogance or self-regard in his tone. 'The truth is, I know nothing of the complexities and subtleties of this art; I just know that such portraits should be the wonder of the age. They are not at all to be owned by one who knows not their true merits. And . . . it is beyond my humble station to construct a chamber or alcove suited to the queen Shri Radha ji.'

'Muhammad Yahya, my dear sir, your absorption told a different tale,' Taqiuddin Haidar smiled a good-natured smile. 'Your Honour is after all the fruit-bearing tree of the seed of a painter and carpet designer of high renown. And it is a mere picture. Believe me, it has nothing at all to do with idol worship or with matters of another faith.'

'Doubtless, the words of the Honourable Presence are perfectly true. But please, my admiration was that of just an ignorant lout: it was nothing more than what the Sufis term the "despicable wonder of an ignoramus". It is true, from the time that I gained the age of discernment to the time of intellectual appreciation, and then from that time to this, I have been in the company of perfectionist masters of all arts and crafts. I've heard their conversations, yet . . .'

Meanwhile, Girdhar Nath, who had been rummaging into the bundle of paintings, produced another example of his art, and hurried to say: 'Well, sir, here is another portrait; it is the same as the first one but is half its size and is on ordinary thick paper, not silk. Please accept this portrait; it is of no value at all.'

Muhammad Yahya now had no excuse; he accepted the portrait with as much good grace as possible and took his leave shortly after. He rolled up the portrait with care and wrapped it in cloth, for further safety's sake. On the way back, he had no thoughts but about the painting. His heart was heavy with unspoken and unutterable fears and anxieties. The arrival of the portrait called banithani all the way from Rajputana, rending asunder the upper, apparently safe layers, of his being; its creating such tumult in the profundities of his existence which had so far been so practical, so wise and so much aware of the peaks and troughs of life—all this seemed to presage some cataclysmic change in the quiet and complacent tenor of his being.

Yes, he knew; he very well knew that there was no real person of whom banithani was the portrait . . . (But, didn't people lose their hearts and lives for imaginary portraits too? At least this was what was told in many stories; stories that he had heard professional storytellers narrate in the marketplaces.)

It could not be without an original somewhere: beauty that combined pride and submission; a soul that was at peace with itself, and yet was capable of destroying people and their homes; beauty whose placidity was like the apparently unfathomable silences of the lakes of Kashmir—the Wular, the Dal, the Nagin—and yet seemed to command on its little finger the untameable, intractable strong-mindedness of the speed and the clamour of the river Leddor's waters at Pahalgam.

Surely, there must have been a woman who would have sat for the portrait? The first portrait, at least? True, there was nothing that he would ever have opted to give up—his home, his wife and sons, his art—he could never, never part with any of them in any meaningful sense, or take them away from his heart even for a moment. Leaving them was out of the question . . .

Yet . . . yet what can I do? He asked his heart and his heart asked him. That face, that image, have pierced my being like an ice pick struck into my side with the fullest force. What I truly want is . . . that I should not return home, that I should surrender to the ignominy of a middle-aged man falling in love with a picture. I will gain a sort of fame, will I not? How well the Persian poet spoke:

Even if ignominy in love avails nothing,
There is the fieriness of contest, there is the crowd
Of onlookers in the marketplace!

But what do I want name and fame for? Do I not command enough renown of my own? The whole of Kashmir knows me. And now people have begun to know me outside Kashmir, and in Hind too. Am I now of the age for such escapades and peccadilloes? Is this the time for me to play at the game of love, or any stupid game at that? But who calls it a stupid game? No, it is an earthquake; do I not know that a seismic event of this magnitude turns everything upside down? Don't people rush blindly out of their homes when there is an earthquake?

. . . But then, but then, has my reason too rushed out from its home, and am I now alone here to face the risks and threats of unknown paths? Have I taken off my heart from everything? Do I have no home and no relatives? . . . What is this garbage that I spout? Have I really lost my mind?

Muhammad Yahya was well aware that there was no such person. Life deceives us in many different ways. Age lays new traps for us, preys upon us in new ways. Sometimes an old man experiences the illusion that he is young, that he can conquer the world; sometimes a young man sees the whole of this world as old, and all of that old age seems in his eyes to be the servant of youth. Sometimes we are deceived into believing another's fire to be our own light; sometimes our own shallowness appears to us as an ocean in tumult.

I am not going anywhere; I have reached my level. I have found my illumination . . . But then, there must be some great sign in it for me: the portrait coming to hand in this place and in such circumstances. But why should it mean anything? The portrait did not say anything to me. It occurred to him that he should ask the palanquin-bearers to stop somewhere in the open, like a garden, and sitting in a quiet corner, he should look at the portrait again in strong light. Maybe it would say something to him then?

No, it would be quite meaningless certainly, hoping that a portrait could talk. Has such a thing ever happened? Do portraits talk, and talk to strangers at that? I am a total stranger to these people, not just any old stranger. I have no connection with them or theirs, nor they with me. So there would not even be any commonality of thought or subject. Why should one of them speak to me, and if they did, what would they say to me?

Yes, all these considerations were valid; but Yahya's heart longed to put them aside. Again and again, he asked himself: What does it mean, why was the portrait given to me now, and in this way? Granted that I am a universally acknowledged master at the creation of talim, Kashmir's greatest in the art and craft of carpet making; I am a connoisseur of Persian poetry, I love Ghani Kashmiri as my very own special poet. The pages of the springtimes in my life are bound by the thread of the pure, unpolluted scent of almond blossoms; the orange-yellow of the fields of saffron in the valley of Qazi Gund as the plants start to grow and beam with the first buds; the delicate, green rice fields around Lake Wular as they ascend or descend with the surrounding hills, bathed in the ruby-coloured light of the setting sun. Why should I surrender them? And surrender them for what? My home, my wife, the very picture of fidelity, my friend and comrade in happiness and in grief . . . But no, I am not from Kashmir. I am of that faraway land, dull and grey and dry, where the dust is of the colour of the scorpion, where death dances night and day, clad in a black, leaden mantle, spurred on by the slapping blasts of the desert wind, where no rain falls for as long as two or three years on end.

12

Yahya reaffirms his love for the Garden that is Kashmir. He also sees, for the very first time, his sons perform

MANY YEARS AGO, I do not remember how long ago it was, I ride a pony with my mother; or rather, my mother rides a mountain palanquin, which is open on all sides, and I am behind her. Clinging to the pony's back and tied to it with a long sash, I almost hang down from it. Occasionally a gust of wind catches my mother's chador and it flows towards me and I try to get hold of it. The palanquin-bearers call out, 'Beware! Beware!' and I, imagining that they are chastising me, pull back my hand fearfully. Much later, I come to know that the palanquin-bearers make these calls often as they negotiate the tortuous ups and downs of the hilly trail that goes by the grand name of a road in that part of the world.

The rains have not yet arrived, but the sky is filling up with clouds on both banks of the river Jhelam. Until yesterday, it seems to me, there was a delicate chill in the air. Now, the vibrant colours of the lilies and violets have begun to rule the air—all laid out in turves ready to be sold in sizes as ordered—green, light grey, lead grey, violet—all loaded on to the flower-sellers' budgerows. On the riverbanks, the golden-yellow fragrance of ripening apricots sways and flows like the rippling, drunken waves of a river. The atmosphere is cold and gets colder as we climb.

Our tiny caravan is bound for Sona Marg. I have no clear idea of the purpose: maybe it is a fair, maybe a relative's marriage. It is an occasion for rejoicing, but I am full of joy for my own self in the expectation of finding or looking at numerous novelties: new people, new birds, new flowers. I will learn and sing new songs.

In the morning, when we set off again on our journey after a night's halt, there is an expanse of water before us as far as the eye could see. We are at some elevation, and from the distance the water appears to be light blue, somewhat like jasper; sometimes, when the sun's rays seem to wish to come up for air after immersion in the water, the waves become little spears of blue sapphire or diamond. Tiny chains of wavelets glint on the dark-blue surface.

The lakeshore seems still quite far when we descend. There are fields all around the lake but the plants have not fully opened their eyes yet. The fields are waterlogged and the little tips of the plants can barely be seen above the water.

'This is Lake Wular,' someone said. 'And around it everywhere are rice fields.'

Very soon, we are past the lower valleys and are climbing again, negotiating the twists and turns of the steep upward slopes. The rice fields accompany us for some distance. Little furrows, full of water, like miniature pools, and rice plants raising their heads from them to meet the sun: narrow or somewhat less narrow strips of earth where the rains and winds have licked away the hard rock and created soft, arable land. I keep looking back towards the fields for as long as I can see them.

Soon, we are farther along and higher up: now I can see the rice fields like a huge green circle around the lake, like some heavenly being's ring. I get an occasional glimpse of the bright water of the lake, but the fields around it are like thin green lines, and then, not even that much—we have left everything behind. The tall chinars with their funny-looking large and five-pointed leaves, and the sweet, slightly resin-smelling bright-green pine trees have long deserted us, to be replaced by big oaks with their long branches growing almost down to their trunks. Then the oaks too disappear from the moisture-laden heights; black pines take their place. Their darkness, that seems almost to darken the sky itself, holds nameless terrors for me.

Rills and streams of sweet water trilling away everywhere; they never left us: there was never a time when the glint, or the soft burble, or the loud humming of water was not with us, like outriders. Then, on the third day, we touch heights where even the black pines desert us, exhausted by the lack of air. Water is with us still. He says to himself: 'It seems these mountains were founded on water. Some of the water rose up to here, and a great lot of it flowed down into the lake at Wular and into the valley of Watlab and its streams.'

But the wonder of wonders is that while Sona Marg is full of snow, and it has a river too, there is very little greenery. 'Why is it so?' I ask my mother.

'It is very cold here,' my mother tells me. 'The cold has burnt away the greenery.'

So even the cold can burn things out? I ask myself in wonder.

Having made merry in the bracing cold of the snowbound fields and valleys, and even venturing out on an apparently stout snow bridge that spans the river, we return home after a month or a month and a half.

Was there a fair held there? No, I do not remember the fair. A sister of my mother lived in Sona Marg. We had stayed with her and she pampered me even more than I was pampered by my mother at home. I gained quite a bit of weight and looked taller as well.

Quite a different map seems to have been drawn above and around Lake Wular now. Or rather, new flowers have sprung up to draw a new map. The rice plants have grown taller. It seems as if someone had raised them and settled them at a newer elevation. The plants have their heads raised, as if they are looking at the new scene. The way the plants sway and rise and bend with the breeze seems to tell him that they too are enjoying themselves. There is no water in the fields now; the roots of the plants are hidden in the damp, drenched blackish-brown earth, and the plants look dark green, almost swarthy, as if blood were coursing fast in their bodies.

It was a transformation that Muhammad Yahya had never imagined possible, far less experienced with his own eyes. Within a few weeks, water and earth and air had stripped the old surface and spread new carpets there with high piles.

. . . Marudhar . . . people go there to die . . .

In Kashmir the leaves are never sere, trees are never starved of water.

The anguished soul, burnt out with pain,
Even if it were a bird, roasted to a kebab
If it went to Kashmir, its wings and feathers
Would be renewed; let there be no doubt about it.

Thus said Urfi, the poet of the Great Mughal. But do not life's springs call even from the Black Ocean or the Assembly of the Cosmos?

The face on which an angelic tranquillity plays so alluringly,
The neck and its light hint of a tiny turn towards . . . whom?

The slight bend of the neck brimming with self-confidence and dignity . . .
What are those eyes looking at? None can stand and stare. But the eyes are not downcast either
Kashmir's wealth will not diminish, even if I were to go away
But why should I . . .
Rocks cracking up under the fierce noonday sun, scorpions, black, grey, thirsty, lurking under the stones, trying
to escape the killing heat.
Fields of saffron, the snow leopards or the clouded
leopards, flocks and flocks of heavy-horned Kashmiri deer
Orchards with trees loaded with apple and apricot and almond
The royal gardens: Chashma-e-Shahi, the Shalimar, woven on the carpets
I need to go home
Oh my destiny, transport me to the Garden of Kashmir . . .

The next day, Muhammad Yahya hired a rider and a mace-bearer. He sent with them gifts of a bag of almonds, another of dried apricots and a leather bottle of honey for Taqiuddin Haidar, and a small elegant carpet of his own design for Girdhar Nath, the old painter from Kishangarh, with submissions of friendship and humility, and to regretfully say that he had had to return home quickly and was thus unable to present himself in person to make his respectful salutations to their Presence.

The carpet that Yahya sent to Girdhar Nath had the unusual merit of the use of Chinese-style yellow and lapis lazuli. These colours were not found in Kashmiri or Iranian carpets.

He left Lahore that very evening and spent the night in a small caravanserai close to Empress Nur Jahan's tomb. The departure for Kashmir took place early next day. For a long while he had been unable to fathom why he left Lahore in the evening when the journey proper was to commence the next morning. Many days later, when his caravan arrived at Kotli, the first important stage on the long road to Srinagar, and many stages beyond the river Jhelam, he stayed there for a couple of nights, though he did not sleep very well on either night. He spent those nights in the arms of a strange kind of exultation, drunk on a joy that he had not often known. Yet the joy was tinged with a nameless melancholy. Only now he understood why that last night in Lahore had loomed so heavy before him. He was not running away from Lahore: he was running away from banithani. Now that there were pine trees all around, and the mischievous and smart-looking mountain bulbuls were twittering away on those trees, and he could see a few poplars too here and there, and the air was scented with pine needles, he could be sure that he was finally released from the sorcery that the portrait had worked upon him.

*

Having descended the heights and entered the Pir Panjal Valley through its rather difficult pass, the turmoil in Yahya's spirit seemed to have finally settled. A mantle of peace descended on his heart and soul. Today, he could clearly see the faces of his sons and his wife. The eye of his mind saw them in their home, the home that was his home too. A new concentration of mind and a new feeling of presence seemed to have overtaken him; it pulled his mind away to his very first home, the home where the walls and doors were familiar like childhood memories. Yet there was a sort of dimness or opacity around those images, which made them difficult to be identified and separated from one another. He did remember vividly, however, telling his mother at one time as a child that it did not matter if his father was a foreigner: he had made you his own and you had made him your own; so I am not going anywhere. And the truth is that Kashmir had made Muhammad Yahya one of its own. He owed everything of his life and personality to Kashmir.

Still, sometimes in the dreams that he dreamt at home, he saw such scenes and places too as he had never been able to identify. For instance, one dream went like this: Far away, almost at the very limit of the power of the eye to see, there are trains of huge, gangling animals passing silently. Somewhere, nearby, water glints and beckons. But when I go near it, I see it disappear before my very eyes. I turn and look back and see the high road that goes to the Shalimar Garden from Srinagar, and on one side of it, I can see the glimmer of the turquoise waters of Lake Nagin.

He wakes up; turning in his bed as sleep eludes him now, trying to grasp the meaning and purpose of the dream. He wonders if there was a sign in it for him.

Well, if there was a sign, its meaning always eluded him. But there was one thing that always happened to him on the morning after the dream. He would have an uneasy feeling that he needed to go on a journey, but he does not remember where actually he needed to go, and why he needed to go there. He also had premonitions that this forgetting did not augur well for him. And today, when he was returning home from a real journey, love for home bubbled up in his heart like a powerful torrent. Today, his heart did not harbour even that tiny unhappiness with his sons' choice of profession: that they had become tradesmen and minstrels rather than real artists. Those essences and qualities, love of art and learning, which the Eternal Giver had bestowed upon him, did not fall to the share of his children. But that was all right, really: they were still in their days of fun and play and enjoyment. They will surely sober up when they reach my age. My house is full of things that God gives to his slaves, and by His grace, the boys too are second to none in earning and spending money.

As distances go, Badgam was not too far away from Srinagar—it was just about twenty miles to the south. But the road passed through dangerous chasms, which had become full of mud and slush because of the recent rains. Thus the short distance of twenty miles could now consume three or even four days. Muhammad Yahya was looking for suitable companions for the journey when he suddenly got the news that Habibullah Bhatt, a famous and prosperous merchant, was hosting a musical soirée, to be followed by the sumptuous formal dinner called wazwan. He was also told that the two chief singers would be Yaqub and Daud. He felt a small pang of hurt that his children should be counted among professional vocalists for hire; then he consoled himself with his usual argument: they are children, after all. There was no harm in them following their predilection. Vocal music was after all something that was favoured by many important Sufi saints.

He was lost in these thoughts when the innkeeper came to inform him that Habibullah Bhatt was on his way to pay his compliments to him. He was a bit surprised, for they had no previous acquaintanceship. Anyway, Habibullah Bhatt, an elderly and jovial-looking man, appeared soon after and making the formal salutation 'salam alaikum', he added, 'Your Presence, sir'—an additional address of respect. Muhammad Yahya rose to embrace him and made him sit next to him on his couch. Habibullah Bhatt presented two gold mohurs and a small box expertly carved from walnut wood and containing two packets of saffron to Yahya, and then he said, 'Honoured Maestro, I apologize for barging in without an introduction, but it was my ardent desire to welcome you back to Kashmir by having you share my pleasure in listening to the singing of your talented sons. We are aware that you return from the lands of Hind after plundering from there a great lot of praise and success, and honour. You brighten Kashmir's name. Praised be God, All is as Allah wills.' Then he recited a famous line of a Persian verse:

You performed this tremendous job, and that is
How true men give account of themselves.

Muhammad Yahya felt a sudden stab of pain in his heart. The image that he had buried under sevenfold heavy curtains in his soul suddenly acquired the power to smile, and to speak: 'You have left something behind in the land of Hind. You have plundered nothing. You have perhaps let yourself be plundered of something.'

'No. No. That is not right. Whatever I gained or lost, I left it behind me, in Nur Jahan's mausoleum.'

Observing Yahya's silence, Habibullah Bhatt feared that he had said or done something to annoy the great man. Folding his hands in front of his chest, he spoke with humility, lowering his eyes: 'Sir, I was guilty of impertinence in having dared gain access to your honoured doorstep without introduction. I give you my word in the name of God: I have no desire to upset or annoy. The whole city is ringing with your name, so it was natural for me to give in to my desire to kiss your feet. And above all, the dear ones of the one upon whom I wait now will also be the enhancers of the elegance and grace of the assembly. All this helped me make bold . . .'

'No, my dear and honoured sir,' Muhammad Yahya hastened to reply, 'there is no question of my being upset or annoyed. It is just that I was rather in a hurry to reach home. But yes, if you insist; and also, what better occasion for me to visit you than when Yaqub and Daud are your guests?'

*

Each brother held a taus in their hands, the traditional instrument for providing the drone. To their right, they had a santur player, and to the left, a daf player. The daf is a small percussion instrument, typical of the Arabs and made much popular by the Iranians. Behind the santur player, there was another santur player, and a very old musician who played a brass flute. Behind this group were three young men, each holding a sih tar, a three-stringed instrument much loved in the part of Greater Iran which is now Uzbekistan and Tajikistan. The strings of the taus and sih tar were being plucked gently, to bring them fully in tune with each other. But for the very occasional trill from the flute, everything else was silent.

The guests numbered about twenty or twenty-five, all seated on expensive carpets—lotus fashion or with their feet tucked in underneath their thighs; the latter posture was difficult to maintain beyond an hour or so, but poets, musicians and their informed audience were well trained to sit unmoving in that posture for many hours, sometimes a whole night. Apart from the sih tar players, the musicians were seated in the centre of the chamber, so that the audience made a circle around them. The chamber was not brightly lit; the dense fragrance of the attar of sandalwood, attenuated by the mixture of some other much lighter perfume, pervaded the air through occasional sprays delivered by the servants who stood quietly and unobtrusively around the chamber. There were four incense burners in alcoves at four corners of the chamber; some special additive must have made them burn slowly but not heavily. Their smoke, very light and thin, rose lazily in the closed air of the chamber; it had a hint of ambergris and aloes wood.

The moment Muhammad Yahya entered, both his sons stepped up quickly and touched his feet briefly, then they kissed the hem of his outer garment and hands and cried: 'Baba, Baba! Why did you take the trouble? We would have gladly and immediately presented ourselves. We had no idea that you are back from Hindustan. It is our great good fortune that we could see your Blessed Presence here!'

Yahya's eyes welled over, though he could not say why. He took out his handkerchief and passed it over his face quickly so as to hide the fact that he was wiping his tears. He said, with a half-hearted attempt at levity, 'Indeed, how could I pass up the opportunity to hear the mellifluous songs of David and the burning, heartfelt tunes of Jacob!'

Warmly, he hugged his sons one by one, slapped them on the back affectionately, kissed them on the forehead, and then inquired smilingly: 'All right, let's now know when the Princes of Music left home and how their mother is doing.'

'Yes, sir. By the will of God, she's quite well. We arrived here just yesterday from Badgam.'

'Very nice, very nice indeed,' said Yahya and accompanied his sons to the seat meant for them, and saying, 'Salam alaikum, gentlemen,' he sat down.

Folding his hands as if in prayer, Habibullah Bhatt asked Yahya: 'We will await your command to start.'

'Of course, let's start,' Yahya said, 'Bismillah-i al-Rahman wa al-Rahim.'

During this time, the three santurs had begun to play, in low tones. The sons applied themselves again to tuning their taus. When all the instruments fell fully in tune, the brothers rose and having greeted the audience with a formal salaam, paid obeisance to their father with bent head and folded hands, and said, 'Elevated Presences, this is a first occasion for us to enunciate some broken, stuttering words before an audience of such splendour and such qualities of discrimination while our most revered father is present too. We pray that our shortcomings do not displease you and that you listen with the intent to correct our errors.'

'Before Heaven, dear and respected young men, please begin. We are all ears,' an extremely old man said.

'Doubtless, we don't now have the strength to wait,' someone else called. 'Bismillah!'

By now the sharper sound of the sih tars was rising, though in tune with the softer humming of the santurs. Muhammad Daud started the initial notes of the raga Chandni Kedara, an evening raga, expressive of the softness and tenderness of love and of total devotion. Muhammad Yaqub said, 'Honoured gentlemen, it is a rubai from Sultan Abu Said Abi al Khair. Please listen with your ears and your hearts. As you must know, he is called "Sultan" not because he ruled a country, but because he was regarded in his times as the greatest of Sufis.'

Everyone among the audience settled themselves better to pay full attention to the singer.

Yaqub began to sing:

The heart never takes a step except in the path of your love;
And never reveals your secrets, ever;
Your love changed the vast plain of my heart into a salt marsh,
So that another's love may not grow in it, ever.

Having sung the first line, Yaqub paused a bit. Muhammad Daud then picked up the initial raga, taking it to a higher pitch, but then he sang the second line softly. As a rule, one of the two among those who usually sing as a pair has a low, heavy voice; the voice of the other is then high, somewhat piping.

But this was not the case with Yaqub and Daud. The voices of both were equally balanced and matched. Neither one was high, and both seemed so similar, and their practice so perfect, that unless one paid attention, one was likely to miss who sang the introductory notes, who went on to the middle ones, and so on. Their voices were so polished and so ripe that they had no need to take the support of trick turns of voice or of excessive ornamentation. The listener sometimes felt that in a lonely snowbound night somewhere in Ladakh, two Gujar tribesmen were conversing with each other through the raga. Sometimes it was like the sound of copper bells, ringing somewhere faraway in a Buddhist temple. Their voices were like a beloved's long tresses, combed and set by the hairdresser with such incomparable mastery and scrupulous care that not one hair was out of place, nor above or below its prescribed place to the smallest degree. The last line was rendered with a flow and power that seemed to outdo the mountain streams in the Laulab Valley.

Muhammad Yahya had no interest in music; he considered the profession to be inferior to that of a true artist. Yet it was not the case that he was a stranger to the effect and the power of the ragas. It had often happened that hearing the distant sound of an expert singer or an instrument, his heart became so moved and restless as if it were a prisoner in his breast, struggling and straining to become free. Sometimes music affected him so much that he felt like hurling to the ground his turban and cloak of respectability and running off to some distant forest, to wander and listen to the music of the wild tribesmen.

Those nights, especially, when he woke up suddenly before the true dawn to the strains of flutes being played on the hill behind his house by the gypsies of Kargil or Gilgit who occasionally visited Badgam during summer, those were the nights of maximum torment for him. With great difficulty and self-control, he resisted his urge to leave his bedroom and go join the gypsies at their song. Here, at Habibullah's house, as he heard the rubai sung by his sons, the image of Shri Radha, or banithani—or whoever that person was; it was not clear in his mind yet if he was a prisoner of an enchantment wrought upon him by a real being or if he was dying away in his heart for something unreal and imaginary—flashed before his mind's eye, clear and bright; it could not have been clearer if she was a real person. He suddenly felt his chest to be choking due to some kind of smoke that swirled and roiled, swirled and roiled, making his heart an unwilling captive and forcing it to forget its normal rhythms.

Words of praise, and cries of 'Excellent!' uttered by the audience awakened Muhammad Yahya to his immediate surroundings. From the corner of his eye, he could see the audience, raptly swaying to the music that was still ringing in their hearts. He wanted to rise and go to his sons to give them accolades and pat them on their backs. But this seemed to be too much like displaying his own merit before the assembly, or smelling the flowers of his own garden and gleefully telling the world how excellently scented his roses were.

In spite of these thoughts, he had almost persuaded himself to go up to the sons, when the matter was taken out of his hands. Yaqub and Daud rose to half their height, bent low and raised their hands to their head and thanked the audience for their encouragement. Then pausing a moment, Yaqub announced in a voice full of respect, almost awe: 'Now, I take my courage in my hands and inform this august house that we will perform some miracle-like verses of Kashmir's unrivalled maestro, the object of the admiration of such Iranian masters as Saib of Tabriz and Kalim of Hamadan; that is, of none other than the High Presence, the Mullah Muhammad Tahir Ghani, may God illumine his grave and elevate his status. Please, hear.'

The entire assembly echoed with the sounds of 'Oh!', 'Ah!', 'Bravo!' and 'How extremely appropriate!' while the brothers retuned their taus, and the wooden sticks struck the santurs a little louder. Both singers began the initial notes of the raga called Pilu, a love raga suited to melancholy and loneliness. They began to sing:

My walking cypress—in whose arms does she rest now?
Her benign hand—on whose shoulder does it rest now?

Muhammad Yahya felt as if it was his tongue that was uttering those words. A thrill, a wave ran through each and every nerve in his body. The sons, utterly unaware of the effect upon their father, continued:

My eyesight, like a thread, is beaded with tears:
Yearning for whose earlobes do my eyes make these pearls?

Muhammad Yahya had the same old feeling of a weaving, spiralling, whitish-grey smoke rising in his chest menacingly. After a few seconds, he realized that there was some sort of vague pain, radiating from near his sternum to the upper chest and then to his left shoulder. He had some difficulty breathing; but in the meantime the boys presented the next verse:

Missing her all the time, my body is frail now like a thread, suited to tie a bunch of flowers:
My bunch of flowers, in whose hands does she rest now?

The entire assembly was lost in the mood of the poem and the quality of the singing. The last verse, though it was just a conventional boast of a great poet, produced even greater pleasure because it was so appropriate:

My verse does not wait on anyone's ears: fellow poet or rival;
My delectable tray of poems, it needs no one's lid to keep it covered.

With each one among the audience barely looking at the other, there was none who could know about Yahya's state of body or mind. The pain in his chest grew, and then it subsided, but left him limp. When the clamour of the pain diminished a bit, he thought of getting up and seeking permission to go. But there seemed no power in his heart, no vitality in his liver. He placed his hands on the carpet and tried to gain leverage to rise, but he sat where he was, quite unable to exert the needed force.

Yahya's sons had so far attributed their father's loss of colour to the effect of the music; now they had the leisure to stop and observe that his face was much more drawn and pale than usual, with beads of perspiration on his forehead, and his brow was knitted with discomfort. They immediately realized that something was wrong and beckoned their host to come to their aid.

The sudden, unexpected attention from all present caused Yahya much distress, but he could only utter feebly that he needed no assistance, that he was quite well. There was a physician present who felt the patient's pulse. He was unfortunately unable to reach the correct conclusion, and diagnosed that there was a build-up of gas in the upper stomach because of the warmth and excitement; the gas had risen and exerted pressure on the diaphragm. It was the pressure of the gas writhing in a small space that was causing the heaviness in the heart and giddiness in the head. He prescribed the standard medication for reduction of tension and high blood pressure (fermentation of the plant ox tongue's flowers with additives of honey, ambergris and gemstones): one dose to be taken at once with the juice of the musk-willow, then repeated after one hour. Given full bed rest and the medication, the patient was sure to gain full recovery, God willing. If he had difficulty sleeping, almond oil should be gently rubbed for some time on the soles of his feet.

Muhammad Yahya's sons accompanied him to the caravanserai. They arranged for the medicines to be procured and administered. They stayed by his bed throughout the night. The patient felt much improved in the morning, and ordered that preparations be made for a quick departure for home. His sons secretly thought that the old man should rest for a few days, but not wanting to oppose him, they cancelled their engagements and left for Badgam the same day with their father travelling in a comfortable palanquin.

13

Daud and Yaqub take stock of their inheritance and make a life-changing decision

THE JOURNEY BACK home ended in security and comfort. Bashirunnisa's eyes, red with waiting and waking, now felt cool and fulfilled at the sight of her husband and the two sons, the true light of her eyes. This was Yahya's first really long journey and such a successful one at that, too. Bashirunnisa was hoping for her husband to recount some stories of his success and the details of the places he had visited. But Yahya seemed introspective and uncommunicative. It must be the fatigue of travel, Bashirunnisa told herself. No one could imagine that Yahya's short illness in Srinagar could be serious, or even life threatening.

Yahya's colour was now pale, turning blue, as if cyanotic. He seemed not to have anything to say to anyone, nor to have his ears assailed by anyone's voice. He rose late in the morning, feeling detached from things somehow, and wishing to go away somewhere far from home, untroubled by the affairs of the day. In the days that followed, when he did persuade himself to put on proper clothes and come down from his room to face the world, more often than not, he felt that he lacked not only the physical strength but also the fortitude of mind for the task. And when, on the rare occasion that he did come down and attend to the business of the day, climbing the stairs back to his bedroom seemed like climbing the Nanga Parbat, the most difficult peak in the Himalayan range. The climb always caused him mild pain in the chest, dryness in the throat and heaviness in the left shoulder.

Given all this, still no one thought of consulting a physician. As for Yahya, he seemed to have no interest in the matter. He did not seem to care if he was unwell, or could at all be unwell. The moment he felt unharried by the pain, or by the business of life, the eye of his mind seemed to create images of things unimagined or unseen by him in the past: objects that were covered with one or more layers of fine, yellow-grey dust; tall saddles for camels, full equipage for horses; huge jars made of baked and sun-hardened clay, or maybe made of stone, but there was no water in the jars; a wilderness extending to the farthest horizon, but the light over it was dim or misty—a thin sheet of snow covered the whole wilderness, but the snow was so light that it seemed like sand; heavy bells hanging by the heavy chain-collars of the camels; maidens of the Kashmiri Gujar tribe singing in the night; broken wheels of ancient chariots; pink and orange borders of young girls' garments rippling in a gentle breeze; a screen made of some almost transparent cotton fabric, very light, very thin, and behind it: large, luminous eyes, radiant forehead, long tresses, the face glowing with self-confidence, but indifferent to me like the light-blue rays of the sun at high noon . . . No, the eyes are looking at me, are aware of me . . . No. No. That is not true. She seems to be aware of me but is actually quite insouciant, quite carefree . . .

Muhammad Yahya is dreaming; it is very late in the night, or maybe very early in the morning. He does not know what time it is, because his eyes are shut. His chest is hurting. Yet the pain neither intensifies nor abates. It is like a vague echo, just like the muted sound of the artificial waterfalls at the Mughal Garden called the Royal Spring. The sound is continuous, but it is neither a boom nor a whisper. It keeps on colliding with my ears, as if it wants to enter my head, and the pain . . . the pain is not just in my chest or shoulder. Something has made my throat its home; it has occupied my throat by force. Signals are going from there to my brain that something is jammed here, there is pain here, and my breath is not able to find a way out or in.

Still asleep, Yahya threw off the blanket that covered him; he wanted to get up but found that his legs seemed to be locked at the knees and refused to move. He turned from one side to the other a couple of times and went back to sleep. Or rather, he began to dream again.

The wave of pain is continuous, like the drone of water falling nearby; but now the waterfall seems to be taller and stronger, and the spot where the water falls is somewhat hot so that the tiny droplets of water have turned into smoke and are creating a kind of mist around my heart. He feels the moisture of the droplets on his chest and neck, but he cannot raise his hands to wipe away the moisture. Then someone says to him: It is not smoke, really. It is just the fine, needle-like spray scattering at great speed. But, he says to himself, how did the curls of smoke enter my breast, and from where? And now even his chest seems to be damp, moist in fact.

The pain suddenly stabbed his heart, sharp and acute, as if a surgeon's hand had slipped, sending the lancet into the patient's side where it did not belong. An audible sob escaped his lips, prompted by the pain; his eyes opened. The dream, if it was a dream, was over. But no, it was by no means a dream. Pain was coursing through his chest, his jaws, shoulders and arms. Even his forearms seemed to be hurting as never before. Breathing became harder by the moment. He called out to Bashirunnisa with all his might, but he could not hear his own voice. He groped towards the side table, looking for the water carafe to take a sip and moisten his throat. Then he saw that his eyes were shut, but also open, somehow. He knew that he was not dreaming; someone, something had forcibly shut his eyes. He recalled that when, as a small child, he hurt himself and the pain seemed unbearable, he would squeeze his eyes shut, as if his closed eyes would deter the pain from being felt. He did not realize that whereas closed eyes would keep the pain from coming in, they could also prevent the pain that was already there from going out.

He called out to Bashirunnisa again, with the fullest lung-power at his command but he still could not hear himself. So I'm dead, perhaps? He said to himself with great tranquillity of heart and mind. But no, the pain was still stumbling and rumbling through his chest, and there was also a sound like a mild breeze rustling, whispering into his ears.

With no conscious effort, an entirely new design for a carpet glimmered before him, glimmered and disappeared and reappeared. He could see it clearly: the colours so shocking that even the most inventive of designers in Tibet and Kashan could not have imagined them. Luminous blue, like the sky after the rain clears up on the heights of Yus Marg. Around the blue, some sort of yellowish white, like the almond's kernel, then the green of unripe apricots, then deep blue, very deep blue; could even the waters of Lake Manas Bal be so deep? The depth of the hue made him blink, as if he could not face it. So it is I who designed this carpet? No, no. It has been spread for me. But where? Where am I? It is snowing. Oh yes, but there is a mansion in front of me, so tall that the arch of its main entrance seems to be lost in the clouds. And that carpet is spread for me; it spreads from under my feet to the main entrance, and I am to go there. So, let me go forward, but . . . there is something written there at the wide portal. Let me read it first, maybe it is something of import.

But I can see nothing at all. Someone has painted a huge quantity of lampblack on my walls and doors and ceilings. Or am I imprisoned in some kind of a tunnel? Good, my Lord, to feel like a stranger in my own home! The moment this thought came to him, he had another: I will now forever be a stranger to this home, to the world. The doors of my house will never open for me.

A unique sense of success possessed him. Only God is untouched by blemish! I should give thanks to Him! The sacred words of the Prophet of God flashed upon his inward eye: So should I not be a slave who thanks his Lord always? He raised his right index finger and pronounced the words of the Quran universally uttered by Muslims to thank God: All praise is due to Allah. Then he recited the essential Affirmation of Faith, looked at Bashirunnisa lovingly with his closed eyes, concentrated for a passing moment on his sons, and then he called out 'Ya Shaikhul Alam' and went to sleep, with the Green Dome of the Prophet's mausoleum clasped to his breast.

*

Bashirunnisa took to her bed after the fortieth-day mourning ceremonies were over. In fact, she was quite well apparently up until that day. A few days earlier, she even had a pleasant, almost light-hearted conversation with her sons about their possible marriage. But the departure of the last guest seemed to signal the departure of her resistance of body and endurance of spirit. She almost gave up eating and a silence of both body and mind seemed to overtake her gradually. She was not literate, but knew a few verses of the Quran, sufficient to say her daily prayers. She also knew by heart many prayers in Arabic known and recommended since antiquity for their merit and efficacy. Lying in bed, she would say her five prayers and then recite remembered verses from the Quran and other prayers when her strength permitted. After every such occasion, she would pray to God that any merit accrued to her for the prayers and the Quranic recitations may be counted among her husband's good deeds.

It was the beginning of the third month since Muhammad Yahya's death when Bashirunnisa summoned her sons after the predawn prayer, and looking at them with eyes full of hope about some things and with regret for that which would now not happen for her, she instructed them in her frail voice: 'Turn my bed so that my face is towards the Kabah.'

The sons could not make bold to ask the reason why, but they understood well enough in their hearts. With tears flowing down their faces, they shifted the bed towards the desired direction, begged their mother to forgive their transgressions, and supplicated to her to forgo the debt that they owed to her for having expended her blood in breastfeeding them. They then recited the Quranic chapter Ya-Sin, which is believed to ease the pangs of death. Suddenly, she cried out in a voice much louder than usual: 'Allah! My heart and liver do ache so much!'

The sons stopped their recitation and bent over their mother's breast. With great difficulty, she tried to clutch their much bigger right hands with her emaciated, white, right hand, attempted a smile, and said, 'You two will bear witness, will you not?'

The sons' throats were choked; no words came out but they affirmed strongly, over and over again, by assenting with their heads. They recited the essential Affirmation of Faith, blew on their hands and passed the hands over that beloved face. She whispered, 'Please bury me next to him,' and then recited the Affirmation as best she could and closed her eyes.

For how long can you go on asking
About life, about death?
The sun entered through a crack in the wall, and went away.

*

However large or great a house, its life resides in just one being. It may be a mansion of a navab or a rajah, or a sky-kissing palace of a king, but it loses its life when that crucial being ceases to exist. If one went by the papers, or the common practice and belief, it was Muhammad Yahya who was the owner, but the spirit of the house lodged in Bashirunnisa, not just in the sense of her good management, her sense of the appropriate, the aesthetic and the useful, not just even in the sweetness of her temperament; indeed, it seemed not a dwelling, but a harvest of fragrant apples on which rained blossoms of almond and violet. No, the real reason was that her personality had such a welcome shade of cool comfort, her treatment of all things so large hearted, so salubrious and redolent with sweetness, that it reminded everyone of the deep spring of Vernak, the source of the river Jhelam.

The source spring of the Jhelam was like a huge well, full of water right up to the brim. The Emperor Jahangir's engineers had sounded its depth to be fourteen yards. The water was bluish and had always teemed with large, black mahasher fish and orange-red trout. Jahangir had had their snouts bored and strung with gold nose rings. Bashirunnisa's temperament called to everyone's mind the sweetness, the teeming wealth and the depth of Vernak. The spring's majestic width and flow, and the miraculous agreeableness of its air were also not far behind in the minds of those who had anything to do with her.

The house seemed suddenly fearsome, desolate and untended after Bashirunnisa's death. Yaqub and Daud found themselves, in their hearts, on the verge of quitting the house and leaving at once. But the rules and the rites of the world were as important for the dead as for the living. There was also the problem of disposing of or giving away the goods and appurtenances; the house seemed to be overflowing with them. There were numerous carpets, old and new. Of much greater value to the boys were the new designs of carpets on which Muhammad Yahya was at work at the time of his death.

Apart from these, there were utensils made of oak or walnut wood; then chairs, chaises longues, some of which were of antique value. The storerooms abounded with old silver carafes, cups and plates; painted or engraved wooden or china cups from the Central Asian cities of Khallukh and Khotan and many others; rosaries of agate and turquoise from Tibet and Ladakh; silk curtains and fabrics from Kashan and Kashghar in Chinese Turkestan; pottery and silverware from Samarqand and Bukhara; woollen shawls and cloaks from Kirghizistan, leather water bottles and tambourines from Khazakhstan; pelts of snow leopards; heads and horns of the hangul, the largest of Kashmiri stags; leathern vials for musk; oilskin packets of saffron—everything and more that one could expect in an affluent and well-established Kashmiri mansion.

Yaqub and Daud found it stifling, this huge cornucopia assembled over two or more generations. But they could not, obviously, throw it away. And while there were no close relatives, there certainly were many distant relatives who would appreciate such things as gifts, and might in fact be entitled to small inheritances from Yahya or Bashirunnisa.

They arranged to observe the fortieth-day ceremonies on the eleventh day. When all the ceremonies—prayers, distribution of food to the poor, feast for the guests—were over, they took their musical instruments to their mother's room. They first tried to console their hearts by singing poems in praise of God and his Prophet, and poems of Sufi character. In the end, they recited the Quranic prayer for the peace of her soul.

They began, in the raga Darbari, one of the most formal and grave of the ragas, with some verses of the great thirteenth-century Indian Persian poet Khusrau's, addressed to God:

Oh You who are beyond our imagining, how could
Thought ever come close to You?
How can the intellect boast of the capability to describe
Your attributes?
If all humans, all angels, ground themselves to dust at your doorstep,
Could ever the dust of decrescence touch even the fringe of the garment of
Your power, Your glory?
Hundreds, like Husain of Karbala, prostrate
Dying of thirst by the wayside of Your
Supreme Indifference; could any ever reach
The spring of pure water?
From the garden, where the angel Gabriel does not
Deserve to serve as nightingale,
How could even a whiff of Union
Reach the dwellers of the dust heap?

Up until now, the poem's mood of sorrow, the sorrow of unreaching, of man being rent asunder, and their own heartache, had coalesced and dominated their low, deep tones. The bass seemed to be about to boil over with the expression of pure pain. It seemed as if it was just a matter of a moment for the two to stop singing and start sobbing their hearts out. Suddenly, Daud's voice rose to a very high pitch and restated the opening notes of the raga, and Yaqub's voice became filled with the intoxication of beatitude, as if they had just had some revelation about their dear mother's journey: the novice, travelling alone on her path of fear had attained her destination, safe and unscathed.

It suits the heads and faces of those like me
For the brightness of love's light to shine on us;
The chaste traveller has no fear
Of defilement with bane and distress.

They had no clear idea why they sang those of Khusrau's verses which were comparatively unfamiliar in their day; but they were somehow sure that their mother's soul had ascended to the transcendental space where the Soul of all Souls resides according to the Sufi belief, and their mother had thus rejoined her origins. They could almost see the golden-blue flashes of the blissful Regard of the Eye of the Absolute Being, presaging the cool precipitation of spring on their mother's spirit on its journey to the higher regions. Inspired by this vision, they went on uttering the last verse over and over again, in a rare exhibition of the variety and virtuosity of presentation that would have amazed and overwhelmed a knowledgeable audience, had such a one been present.

Daud fell silent. Yaqub now switched to another raga, the Malkaus, another grave raga, suited to the deepening of the night's shadows and the mystery of being. He began with the taranah mode, which represents the purest form of a raga because it consists of short syllables devoid of meaning, only symbolizing the pristine purity of sound. Consciously, or perhaps unconsciously, he chose a rubai of Sarmad, the seventeenth-century Sufi poet, celebrating the Prophet's Ascension:

The one who firmly believed in His Truth,
He became larger, and vaster than the
Skies that spread everywhere.
The Mullah said: Ahmad was in the skies;
Sarmad said: The skies were in Ahmad.

They sang for a long time, at a speed quicker than usual, completely absorbed in the power of the poem and their own interpretation of it. They stopped suddenly as they reached the quickest speed of their rendering; for, both broke into uncontrollable sobs. Gently, Daud put away his drone instrument, bent his head on the frame of their mother's empty bed, and began to cry like a child. Yaqub raised his brother's head, put it on his own shoulder; he patted him lovingly on the back and said, 'Do remember what

Amir Khusrau said, "The chaste traveller has no fear." I have no doubt, she must be in Paradise, and must be praying for us there too. Do not lacerate your liver so. She is in a very good place.'

Then he recited a rubai of the sixteenth-century Persian poet Sahabi. His voice hovered between a whisper to himself and a plain tone of conversation:

Through whatever attribute one may incline
To the Being, it is sweet, and beautiful;
The song, to whichever tune it is sung
Is sweet, and beautiful,
No action taken for the sake of God is wasted:
By whichever door one may enter Paradise
It is sweet, and beautiful.

By the time he ended, he too could not check his tears. He pushed aside his little drum, approached his mother's bed, and said, 'Dear Mother, now that you are not here, there is no one before whom we would most love to sing. You placated Baba in so many ways when our music annoyed him. At last, God granted us the occasion that he heard us sing in open assembly, and I dare to think that he was not displeased. Now that you both are not, our music too will not be.'

Up until now, it was not clear to them what they should do with their life. It seemed to be glowering at them, vast and cold like a snow desert. Where and how would it be for them when they had relinquished their music? They were quite clear that they would no longer live in Badgam; they would do no music or trade, whether for pleasure or profit. It was also clear that the first thing for them to do was to make the necessary arrangements for their house and properties.

The pink of dawn was spreading slowly in the sky when they firmed up their resolve: they began to sort out the goods in the house. Before anything else, they opened the boxes that their father had brought back from his journey to Hind; they had not even been opened since his return.

With trembling hands they picked up and placed everything in its appropriate place, as if they were handling the sacred and holy relics of the great saints. In the last box was a thick, heavy piece of paper wrapped in silk. With some curiosity, they opened the packet, assuming it to be the sale or purchase deed of some property or some agreement for trading in Lahore. They were shocked and saddened to find that it was the portrait of a woman.

A strange woman's portrait? How and why should such a thing find a place in their father's effects? As far as they knew, their father had had no interest in women or in carnal affairs of any kind. Doubtless, they stood in awe of their father, and also believed that they understood him well enough. They were quite certain that their father had absolutely no predilection for vulgarities, women of the profession, or enjoying the sights and sounds of fairs and bazaars. Then who was this young woman? Clearly, she had great style, a marvellous panache. Did our father contemplate a second marriage? Or was she a secret mistress of his, or perhaps a nautch girl of Lahore whom he desired as a second woman in his life, to be kept in Lahore?

They had heard that major changes take place in men's character and temperament when they start to grow old. The twins' hearts began to heave and swell with regret and revulsion. Better rend to little pieces this unfortunate paper and fling it into a stream to be carried off to extinction. Their father's secret will thus be buried in water, forever.

Yaqub snatched the accursed paper from Daud's hand, intending to rip and shred it, but he stopped short on some impulse. He paused to consider: The facts won't change by our destroying the evidence. All that will happen is that the physical proof may cease to exist; but whatever has passed before our very eyes, there is no way to make it unpass: it has already happened. And one has no real option but to bear the burden of reality; it is a load that cannot be shaken off our heads. And who knows what is the reality of all this? It is, of course, obvious that this portrait was not brought back by Baba as a possible bride for one of us. He said, 'Brother, stay a little. Let us give it some more thought. It seems to me that there might be complications here . . .'

'Complications? What complications?' Daud said with sudden asperity. 'Regret there is, undoubtedly. But how could there be anything else here to consider?'

'No. Let us please apply our minds. This woman is not a Muslim, that much is clear. But equally clearly, she's not of the profession. Such splendour, such dignity, such self-confidence . . . these are rare qualities. And her forehead, it is radiant with power . . .'

'Brother, what is it that I hear you say? Could she at all be anything other than . . . ?'

'Let us not decide in haste, dear Brother. Her body has been drawn with rare proportion, the waist is so narrow against her upper torso which still does not seem to carry much bulk. Truly, it is a heavenly face. There could be some other mystery here. Our father was never of the sort to go after other women. To me, she looks like the queen of some distant land. Maybe she was pleased with Baba for some reason—his art, maybe—and awarded him this portrait as a memento and a prize? She certainly is not from our parts, or even from the Panjab.'

Now Daud regarded the portrait with some care. A tremor seemed to run through his heart, and soon the tremor shifted to his hands. The woman's smile had a hint of archness, but of sarcasm, not flirtation. It seemed that the sitter was somehow aware of his opinion of her and was laughing at him in her heart: Indeed, how well you understood the mystery! Everyone thinks only as far as one dares. I am too distant, too far from your mere human considerations.

Daud looked at the portrait again, more intently. The sitter's lips were lustrous with the redness of a faint smile. Incandescence seemed to sparkle from behind her fair complexion, which yet did not have the fairness of Kashmiri women. The painting was just a portrait a moment ago, but how is it that now it seems to have acquired the aspect of a living body? He tried to regain control over his senses. Foolish young man, he said to himself, this is not some elementary note in a piece of music that you may master it in a moment. The self-confidence in her countenance is effulgent with abhuman light. What energy, what iconic form . . . !

He pulled himself short. Energy? Iconic form? He had never heard those words before, far less ever used them in regard to a woman's face. Who taught me such words . . . ? And how utterly suitable they are for the person in the portrait! It must be some goddess of the Hindus, speaking to me in my imagination. She must be a goddess. No human face can have such refulgence.

Yaqub's voice saved him from losing himself in utter confusion.

'Let us turn the page over,' he said, 'and look at the back carefully. Perhaps there will be some clue there. This woman is certainly not some honourless strumpet of easy virtue.'

On turning the page over, he felt that there was some kind of backing or lining attaching to it. Perhaps it was intended to strengthen the paper on which the portrait was painted, or the idea was to protect it from oil or damp. Gingerly, Daud inserted the point of a thin-bladed paper knife between the backing and the portrait, and taking care not to damage the painting, he finally succeeded in separating the two.

He could now see, on the back of the picture, some Persian writing in the dead centre; the script was stylish, but in the manner of Shikastah, as in informal Mughal documents. This is what the inscription said:

> Portrait, imaginary, of Shri Radha ji, famed as banithani:
> Brotherly and loving gift, tendered to the Presence, most eminent maestro and inimitable craftsman Muhammad Yahya Badgami Kashmiri, May God grant him a long life and gild his craftsmanship yet more; From Girdhar Nath painter, the lowliest of the lowly, resident of Ghatiali, and Most inferior subject of Rajah of Rajahs, Maharajah of Kishangarh, of the province of Ajmer in Rajputana.

So the mystery of the portrait was now solved. They were not unfamiliar with the loving sportiveness, the phenomenon of the gamesome godhood of Shri Krishna and his consort Radha. They did not understand the meaning or significance of banithani, but it was now quite clear that it was all subjective and faith related: the devotion, the enchantment, the supreme beauty. They had no reason to worry about or harbour any guilt or shame for their father.

They could not, of course, know about the devastation caused by the portrait to their father who had been a rational being all his life and who had had control over his emotions. But even then, the brothers could feel the fire of her beauty coursing through their veins and sinews, like the moisture of the early morning breeze touching the petals of the violet flower and giving it a new lease of life. They looked at each other and then returned their gaze to banithani. Being twins, each could easily read or even anticipate the other's emotions or intentions. It often was the case that one brother would utter those very words that the other was about to say. Or if one brother was thinking of visiting some place, the other would begin praising that place, regardless of the context. If one brother was annoyed with someone, or he did not feel like having to do something with someone, the other brother would immediately have the same feelings about that person. And this was why, very often, as the two sang together, those who heard them from some distance believed that there was only one singer. This was one of the reasons why they were considered entirely unique as singers.

Simultaneously, both of them raised their eyes from the painting. Daud said, 'Kishangarh . . . '

'Our grandfather came from there,' Yaqub said.

'I had heard someone say that Grandmother once asked Baba if his heart ever hankered after Kishangarh.'

'Yes, and Baba was just a child at that time. Even so, he said to Grandmother that there was no one there whom he could call his own. He added that his father had made her his, and likewise she had made him her own. So he did not need go anywhere else.'

Their eyes welled up with copious tears. 'But we have none here now to call our own.'

'Why did Baba take so much care to save and protect the picture? It occurs to me that he had some good cause in view, or some expediency.'

'What good cause and what expediency?' Daud was a little upset at the implications of his brother's observation. 'They were artists from a faraway place; in fact, they were like foreigners. It was a present from them. That is all there is to it.'

'But I seem to see some augury . . . something shown to us with a suggestion hidden in the showing . . . And, Brother, have we not decided not to stay here . . . ?'

'A strange land, strange people; we don't know their language, nor do they know ours. We are ignorant of their religion, their creed; they are ignorant of ours. Just pause to think. What are you suggesting?'

'We have wandered through cities and towns for our musical performances and for buying and selling our goods. It is no matter that we have not been to Ajmer or Delhi. Certainly, Lahore has been our destination on numerous occasions.'

'But, Brother, is this portrait not entirely imaginary?'

'No doors can remain closed for the accomplished ones. We will transform thought into reality.'

*

They had no further discussions on this matter. They were clear in their minds that they must go to Kishangarh. What they would do there was not clear and did not seem important, at least then. Similarly, the question whether they would settle in Kishangarh or would merely visit had not merited any examination.

They began to empty the house. They immediately gave away in charity almost everything of daily domestic use. There were no debts to pay, and no close relatives to inherit any substantial cash or property. So they freely distributed among poor relations and other needy ones all that was valuable in the house. They saved just a few items and the greatest part of the cash for their use. Whatever still remained, they sent off to a school in the neighbourhood. They did, however, keep the house, and appointed a steward to look after it, establishing an endowment to pay for his salary. There was a patch of hard, stony earth in front of their main door. They had it dug up at considerable labour and expense and had all their musical instruments and appurtenances buried deep in it.

They buried their mother by the side of their father and had a simple epigraph carved on a marble headstone:

Dweller of Paradise, Bashirunnisa Begam

The blood that your love turned to milk and on which you suckled us
Now turns to blood again and flows from our eyes.

Daud and Yaqub, Her Sons & Mourners

—1207th Year of the Hegira

Soon thereafter, they left Badgam for Lahore. From Lahore they went to Rewari, their route taking them through Qasur, Firozepur, Malerkotla and Hisar. Rewari was the point where the road built by the Afghan King Sher Shah in the early sixteenth century turned further east and south towards Delhi. Delhi was not too far from there, but the tune to which their hearts were singing was that of the sand-and-gravel land of Rajputana; Rajputana fired their imagination and was their most ardent passion. So what business could they have had with Delhi? They said in their hearts the famous verse of Khusrau in praise of Delhi and turned their face to Loharu and beyond it to Alwar:

Delhi is the Presence, preserver and protector
of Justice and of the Path;
Paradise of rectitude, may it continue to prosper.

A number of high roads joined and separated at Alwar. One of them went back to Emperor Akbar's time, joining Agra to Ajmer through Bandikui. It was the famous road which Akbar walked three times all the way from Agra to Ajmer to pay obeisance to Shaikh Muinuddin Chishti at his mausoleum. Prince Khurram (later known as Emperor Shah Jahan) had, during his Mewar campaign, joined Alwar directly to Jaipur, Bandikui and then on to Ajmer with a wide road. Kishangarh was situated about halfway through on this high road between Jaipur and Ajmer.

The brothers were so eager to reach Kishangarh that they did not stop an extra day even to visit the famous observatory built just a few decades ago by Sawai Raja Jai Singh of Jaipur. The title Sawai Raja means 'a Raja and a quarter' and was bestowed by the Mughal Emperor Aurangzeb upon Jai Singh I, his brilliant general and courtier, to signify Jai Singh's elevated position among all other generals and nobles of the Empire. The observatory attracted visitors from everywhere, but the brothers had no eyes for it.

The caravan had many travellers of substance from Alwar to Jaipur. Most of them were jewellers, dealing in gemstones. Some were importers of valuable cotton and silk fabrics. Since it was Jaipur that they were ultimately bound for and they had much business to transact there, most of the caravan changed status from traveller to resident at Jaipur. Daud and Yaqub preferred not to wait for another caravan to assemble; it was, after all, only about three days' journey to Kishangarh. They bought four fine horses, hired a groom who would double as guide, and left for Kishangarh just before dawn the day after they reached Jaipur.

14

Yaqub and Daud travel through the harsh desert of Rajputana on their way to Kishangarh

THEY WERE JUST a few miles out of Jaipur when the world changed drastically before their very eyes. True, changes in the flora and fauna and the topography of the land had become apparent even before they had entered the city of Lahore. As they travelled beyond Qasur, the squat, hot, grey and black hills of the Iravali range confronted them. Most of them looked like huge boulders, haphazardly collected and then thrown about the landscape by a giant. Thus their journey after Jaipur did not seem totally strange. Certainly, it was very hot. But it was the time of hot weather in Kashmir as well, so the weather's tyranny was well within their power of endurance. Forests they knew very well, but the lack of water in these regions of Hind always astonished them.

In the past, they did have occasion once to travel up to Multan, an arid region to the south and west of Lahore. But even there, the dryness and the abundance of thorny shrubs was nothing compared to what they now experienced on the high road to Kishangarh. Dense and far spread, the tall, grey and brown thorny shrubs on both sides of the road looked menacing and induced moods of melancholy and depression. Their names too sounded inhospitable and irascible: bhatkataiya, jhar beri, gokhru, kubabul, karail, thuhar, nag-phani. The nag-phani was a wondrous thing: its name meant 'cobra's hood' and the plant was even more frightful than its name.

Some of the cobra-hood plants (if plants they really were) grew in clusters, to a height of two and a half or three yards, if not more. Their leaves—most of which did resemble the expanded hood of a large snake—were thick, fat and dark green, in fact, almost grey. Many of the nag-phanis had hardly any trunk or stem, and some were nothing but tall trunks. Trunk, stem or leaf, everything was covered with thorns. Some had branches so thick that they resembled long, flabby breads specially baked for elephants. But there was nothing bread-like about them. The leaves and branches came in many sizes, but they all seemed to be like the ears of a gigantic carnivorous hare or wild ass. No roots visible above the earth, growing straight up from the desert floor, and so powerfully intertwined that no beast, far less a human, could pass through. Their evil bodies seemed to ooze the frightful aura of a cancer or carbuncle.

Their first two days on the road were uneventful. The third day's reveille and departure were before dawn as usual. But not many hours had passed when a dust storm overtook them. Their groom was in fact familiar only with straight roads, where mile-towers marking the distance could be seen from far, roads on which there were caravanserais, large or small, at every ten or fourteen miles. Sometimes one could even encounter small villages or one or two of their inhabitants who could put them wise about the road ahead.

On this road, the gusting winds first blew away their awareness of the direction in which they were expected to travel. As far as they could discern, there was no shady tree, no thatched roof, no yogi's tiny hermitage. And how could they, in fact, descry anything at all? There was such a quantity of gritty dust flying around that visibility had been reduced to a bare two or three yards. The horses found it difficult to recover from repeated stumbles, raising the fear that they might fall or injure themselves. To stop and start every few minutes seemed to be the best option. But after some time they lost their sense of direction. For all they knew, they might have been going round in tighter and tighter circles. Or very possibly, with every new circle, the centre of the circle changed without their being aware of the fact: the path, the direction, all seemed to have been in bonded slavery to the sands. They did not know when they left the road and entered the wilderness . . .

> It was a wilderness where there was not the smallest hint or sign of shade. Water could be found nowhere at all: for miles and miles, there was a famine of moisture. No spring, no well, no pond, no stream, an empty vastness. It was just like how someone had said: The field was plain and barren, like the palm of a hand; and, oh! There was nothing there but the Hand of God. As the sun moves higher in the sky, the throbbing heat and the agitation move higher in proportionate degree; the sunlight becomes hotter and harsher. The hot sun reduced them to

a state where their thirst overcame every other feeling. And since the wilderness had no trees or shrubs, they could not get to a fruit or leaf or even wild vegetation to assuage their hunger. What a wilderness it was, such that even prophets like Elijah and Khizr would have wandered helplessly, their brains vertiginous. Even great champions would fear to traverse such a vast emptiness; they would strike their heads on the ground and give up the ghost for total want of water. They had gone just three or four miles when the sun rode high in the sky, and the sun's rays were so powerful that they began to feel as if they were about to faint. Somehow, they regained their wits, remounted their horses, and went ahead. Now, hunger and thirst were harassing them, so much so that they could not remain in the saddle. And the poor horses! They were in a truly dire state: the tongue hanging out due to thirst, the legs refusing to move, and on top of all this, the rider on the back. What a desert to beat all deserts! There was nothing visible but sand. And if they sighted some tree-like object, and hurried towards it in the hope that they might enjoy a breather in its shade for a breath or two and stay there a while, when they approached near, they found that even that tree was burnt away for lack of water: no leaves, no fruits on it. Just the bare trunk, and that too entirely devoid of moisture. If they espied a stream or a spring from afar, they made haste towards it, hoping for water. When they came near, they found no water, in the first place. And if they did find some water, it was so noisome that at the sight of it, they felt like throwing up. They saw serpents and pythons writhing and roiling in the stream, and vomiting away their venom into the water because of the violence of the heat. Seeing this, they would leave that spot quickly and go forward. Now the wind began to blow strongly, so that particles of dust and grit struck their bodies with force, and the particles felt hot on their bodies like live coals. And the horses were now all but dead of the thirst. Seeing their horses' straits, they dismounted and tried to go forward leading them by the bridle. But the earth was burning so that it seemed as if a steel plate had been heated up and thrown under their feet. Blisters sprang up on the soles if their feet touched the ground. That empty plain was like the Doomsday plain where the sun, it is said, will glare down on earth from the distance of only a lance and a quarter. The heat made it impossible to go forward; flames seemed to be shooting forth from the ground and the sky raining

> down fire. The air was so heated that a single blast seemed as though it could burn the body right up to the bones. Somehow, the sun travelled down, below the high point of noon; the heat and the power of the sun diminished a bit; the wind also began to die down. But hunger and thirst prevented their putting one foot after the other; and the horses, poor beasts, it seemed that they were only a moment more for the world. How could the barren and empty vastness support grass or grain? Not to speak of humans, even birds and ungulates were utterly missing. If, by any chance, some unfortunate beast like the kite or vulture strayed there, its feathers and wings burnt to ashes, and the poor bird became roasted like a kebab. If somehow one of them did escape, it didn't go far: its bones could be seen littering the sandy earth just a few yards further. Clearly, it was unequal to the act of flying off. Bones, human bones, were lying around; perhaps some intrepid traveller had come up to this place, only to die of thirst and hunger. There were bones even of some carnivores; there were deep holes inhabited by the pythons. In some places they could see black caves; obviously the caves were home to ghouls. None else but a ghoul could have survived there. At long last the sun, pale of face, and trembling all over, took refuge in its western retreat.*

But Yaqub and Daud were quite clear in their minds that going forward or backward meant nothing more than a guarantee for straying even farther from their objective. They wrapped their bodies tightly with sheets, covering even their noses and eyes. They got down from their horses and lay themselves down in the imagined shade of the quadrupeds' bodies. The wind slowed down as the day began to decline. Dust settled slowly on the stunted shrubs and thorny plants. Now everything was visible, but there was nothing to see. In that vast, alien desert, home to anguish and affliction, they could see no path; or the path was like light from a painted eye. They knew at least the direction that they must take: it was south-west, or south-south-west. The setting sun was before their eyes, so they judged their route as best they could; it was imperative to regain the road. Even more important was to find anything—a hutment, a small village,

---

* Translated from the Urdu oral Romance *Aftab-e-Shuja'at* (vol. 1), narrated by Shaikh Tasadduq Husain. Lucknow: Naval Kishor Press. p. 153–54. 1893

an inn—where they could spend the night under some sort of a roof, free from the fears that lurked in open spaces.

Yaqub and Daud were in luck. Or perhaps the being which had dragged them away from their verdant home to the sandy, thorny desert, was watching over them in some way. Whatever might have been the case, but an hour's journey brought them within sight of the dim, grey outline of an inhabited space. Then small flocks of sheep and a herd or two of cows could be seen, placidly shaking their heads and walking back home. The music of their tinkling bells seemed to instil welcome moisture in the air. Even farther away, gigantic outlines of camels were sedately moving towards them in single file.

These scenes affected their senses as if they were dreaming and once they woke up, there would be nothing else but the same inimical, immense, untraversable sand, with their helplessness as their sole guide and companion. Their human guide was both laughing and crying. He was much more aware of the hazards of the journey than the newcomers.

15

Yaqub and Daud lose their hearts to two houris of the desert

THEY REACHED THE village soon enough; not a village really, it was more like a tiny hamlet. Fifty or sixty homes, a few trees, some herds of cattle which seemed to be underfed, a temple, a well: these were all that made up the village. The sun was just about to set when they arrived at the well. Women of all descriptions and ages: young nubile girls, middle-aged and young widows, mothers of children with the children clinging to the low skirt-like garment that covered their lower limbs, loose and flapping. At best, their clothes would be described as shabby. There was on their faces, without exception, a tiredness tinged with the dim, grey reflection of an obscure light: the visitors realized with dismay that the light was of melancholy; these women lived under the shadow of sadness. Their eyes were devoid of even a hint of the moon-glow which is the surpassing wealth of contentment: the true endowment of married women, or of mothers living lives that were full of hope. Instead of the moon-glow, their faces seemed to be hidden under a fine veil of dust, representing their past days and presaging the days to come. They were talking among themselves, but not like parakeets that chatter happily among themselves, competing to outdo their companions in a glittering contest of sound at the time of the evening when they returned home.

The visitors observed the scene a little more closely. They then saw that the middle-aged women were not really middle-aged. None of them would be older than thirty or thirty-five, at most. But youth had departed their faces at some uncertain time in the past. Becoming pregnant with monotonous and distressing regularity, then bearing the burden of bringing up the children, and the daily workload of their numerous domestic duties; being subjected to scolding, even beatings at the husband's home instead of their parents' love and overindulgence, and an indifferent husband; above all, the unsympathetic land, incognizant of the notion of treating its children with friendly hospitality, and the unrelenting routine of bearing with the hardship of its murderously extreme climate had broken their spirits and their bodies too. True, they were narrow-waisted even now, but their breasts and hips lacked the proud tightness of the burgeoning of youth. Each of them had a heavy brass pitcher of water on her head or hip; some even had two, one on the hip and one on the head.

There was not a single male or a hired labourer among those drawing water. The metallic pail used for it was rather ancient, quite large, with a wide mouth and only a slightly narrower bottom. It had developed many small holes over the years. It was big in size such that a woman could not draw it when full; they pulled it up when it was not quite full, with water leaking or even spraying off from it all the time. Thus, one draught of its water sufficed for only one pitcher. Each woman at the well rested between the pulls, another replacing her quickly; even so, the group of women around the well was taking time in thinning out.

The newcomers watched from a respectable distance; an hour passed, or somewhat less. They looked forward avidly for a suitable moment to enable them to go nearer, enjoy a long pull of cool, fresh water, and also inquire about a place to pass the night in comfort. But they lacked the temerity needed to thrust themselves upon a group of women to whom they were utter strangers. They stood, pretending aloofness, their horses tightly reined.

They held their patience some more, and dared to advance only when there was just a small number of women left. Their horses too, having smelt fresh water for so long, were now whinnying and striking their hoofs on the ground. They let the horses go forward and looked somewhat closely at the women. Among those who were very nearly the last were two girls. Around fifteen or sixteen years of age, each of them bore two pitchers on her head. The pitchers were empty; still, their heft was enough to bend their backs a little. They had the light wrap of their orhni tightly wound around their torsos. This, and their slightly bent backs, made their young breasts prominent, but they did not have the arch playfulness which girls of their age develop as they begin to gain fuller awareness of their passage from girlhood to womanhood. But their slim necks, raised like a deer's, and the alertness of their eyes somehow seemed full of some kind of a promise to the visitors.

They stood separate from the rest. Perhaps they were on their own and had no relatives among the women. They were talking to each other in undertones. Both the brothers felt that the visions and fancies of their consciousness of being lovable and desirable had not faded from their eyes, even though they seemed to have made conscious efforts in that direction.

Both girls had on wide skirts of a coarse cotton fabric, with orange and pink stripes and patterns of small flowers on the border. Their tunics, light green and pale yellow, were again of inexpensive cotton, but slightly fancier than the skirts. Their bright red-and-yellow orhnis, actually chunri in Rajputana, were from Churu, a small town known for its tie-and-dye light cotton fabrics. Taller than the average girls of their part of the world, they were slender and willowy of body; their faces oval, their eyes very dark brown, with a hint of thin red streaks which created the illusion of their having drunk a tiny draught of some mild inebriant. Their hair was thick and dense but not too long. A lock or two of their bright-black tresses framed their faces and fluttered lightly in the breeze. Both wore a black thread around the neck; heavy ivory bangles almost clung to the rounded, well-formed wrists; plain gold pins adorned their nose and each had very thin gold circlets in the ears. The skirts were not too low, so a good bit of the legs from the ankles to the knees were delectably visible. They wore simple silver anklets but were barefoot. The surprising thing was that their toes were not ugly and splayed as happens ordinarily with people who walk barefoot.

The girls would occasionally raise their eyes towards the young travellers, but the action always seemed involuntary and accidental. Still, the eyes wouldn't lower immediately, as if two people's fingers should touch accidentally in some assembly, but not disengage quickly enough.

Darkness was vaulting down from the sky; the brothers saw that they must act then and there, for it would not take much longer to be fully dark, and for the two mermaids to disappear in it. They brought their horses nearer. The two girls were still trying to draw the heavy pail up from the well, but were not able to bring up enough water in it.

'Please. You can come away from the well. We will draw the water for you,' Yaqub said to no one in particular.

The girls raised their doe-like eyes; they looked at the two who were now so close, then looked behind them. The line of the water drawers had not gone too far yet. Their closeness was a kind of warrant for the girls' security. With a brief smile, they withdrew from the well. Although the smiles were impersonal enough, the two visitors believed that it was they who were the intended recipients of the favour.

'We are almost dying of thirst,' Daud said as he let the pail down into the well. 'If permission were granted, we would drink some water too and water our animals.'

Again that brief smile, but it was accompanied this time with a tiny nod of the head. Now the girls' bodies, the rhythm of their gait, revealed no tension, as if that brief wordless exchange had been sufficient to allay their fears. Both sat comfortably on the wide stone rim of the well. In no time, the young travellers had filled up the girls' four pitchers. Before they could bend to lift up their pitchers, the travellers produced four heavy, engraved copper cups from their luggage; then they took out handfuls of almond, walnut and dried apricot from a bag that hung by the saddle of one of the horses. They put the fruits in another cup and offered it with water to the girls.

'Please. Give us company,' one of the brothers smiled.

'Yes, indeed,' said the other. 'You must be thirsty, too.'

The girls stared for a moment, and then they looked towards the guide who stood at some distance and was organizing water for the horses to drink.

'Who are these people and what are they giving us to eat?' The older girl spoke to him in Marwari. Her voice was a heart-enticing mixture of maturity and girlhood. It was a voice where adolescence was embracing full puberty, but it also notified to the interlocutor that she was not to be taken for a simpleton: she knew not a little about the world and the people in it.

The guide did not quite know what to say. He had clearly felt some alchemy, some electrical impulse occurring here, but had not yet figured out its meaning or significance. It was clear in his mind that he should speak the truth, but was not sure if his employers expected him to tell the truth.

'These people are from Kashmir,' he began cautiously. 'I know nothing about their caste or creed, except that they are Turks, and they're well mannered. Their cup contains fruits from Kashmir. These are eaten dry.'

Daud and Yaqub could very well understand the words 'Turks' and 'Kashmir'. They knew no Marwari, but had been able so far to manage pretty adequately with their limited Hindi. They could now make out the general sense of the guide's words.

Yaqub advanced a little and said, 'These fruits have nothing against your ways or your creed. We practise the Prophet's essential Affirmation of Faith and are particular about ritual cleanliness and religious permissibility in matters of food.'

Yaqub's words were designedly such that they would not offend a Hindu and would satisfy a Muslim. A faint smile appeared on the lips of the older of the girls. She put her hand on the black thread on her throat and pulled a part of it out to reveal that there was nothing Hindu about it. A thin, silver amulet was strung on the thread, and the word Allah engraved in the Arabic script was clearly visible upon it. Even that little movement of her body had something, not exactly coy, but a flow and subtleness of rhythm, which no amount of practice at the art of seduction could have effected.

Looking at the amulet and the glow on its wearer's face, Daud made bold to strike a personal note: 'Please look upon us as your well-wishers and friends. I am Daud, of Kashmir, and this is my twin brother, Yaqub. We are merchants but have also a taste for music and song. Our grandfather was a painter. He was originally from this very place, from Kishangarh . . .'

He paused for a moment, but Yaqub took up the thread, '. . . and he died long ago.' He added, 'We have neither father nor mother. We forsook our hilly terrain for your hard-hearted land, hoping to find a place where we could put a roof over our heads.'

He spoke in a sombre voice and suddenly his own words affected him so much that his eyes became wet. He had heard that if someone wept suddenly without cause on an evening, a flight of angels might have passed over their head, to be lost in the half-light of the westering sun.

The striking good looks and the sophisticated speech of these unexpected guests did not have so much effect on the girls as the welling up of Yaqub's eyes. Acting on a sudden impulse, the younger one was about to rise and go to Yaqub to commiserate with him, but the older girl gestured her to stop although she was a little moved and disturbed in her heart to notice that the other brother's eyes too had the dim glimmer of tears.

Love's sun, before it rises, softens the earthlings' hard hearts by its warmth; it heats up the dry dirt and makes life's kindling ready to burn. Warn the young and the old: Love is fire. The girls could not decide upon a course of action, except to reply to the brothers' confidences with their own and thus reduce the tension in the travellers' hearts.

'Sir, my name is Habiba,' she said with downcast eyes. 'And . . . and this is my younger sister, Jamila . . . two years younger . . .'

'. . . and we are orphans too,' Jamila spoke quickly. 'We are alone in this world.'

The Hindi of both the girls had a tincture of the mellifluent Braj in the flinty accents of the Marwari spoken in their area. The travellers, of course, could have not the least notion of these intricacies. For them, the girls' voices, clear as a bell, and the sweet syllables as they fell from their lips were enough to enchant them.

'Quiet!' Habiba glared at her. 'We have our Babu, do we not?' She softened her tone. 'No more loose talk. Let's go back home now. I do not know what meanings people will put on our tarrying here.'

'No, please!' Daud said. 'Do stay a little longer! Drawing and carrying water must be such a hardship for you. You don't have domestic help?'

'Domestic help?' Jamila repeated in a low voice. 'Do you mean servants? No. We have no domestic help. Women do all the work.' Saying this, she opened and spread the palms of her hand. Deep brown calluses were clearly visible on them, even though the light was failing fast.

'How sad! All right, then you must employ us as your servants. We will thus have a roof on our head.'

'Indeed, dear Kashmiri gentlemen! What ideas do you harbour in your pretty heads!' Jamila smiled a pert smile. The gentleness of the travellers of the desert and the sweetness of their speech had emboldened her.

'Hush, you stupid witch!' Habiba scolded her in right earnest. 'Have you lost your mind?'

Jamila ignored her and continued to twit Daud. 'Go jump in a lake. Serving us is not like dawdling in your dear auntie's house, do you hear?'

These words were charged with meaning, and neither Daud nor Yaqub was loath to interpret them, yet both were hesitant. They did not want to be too quick to cross the stages of intimacy. Daud held out the fruit bowl, went down on his knees, sat near Jamila and spoke as if there had been no other conversation in between. He said, 'Here, please eat just a little. Do stay a little longer.'

With extreme diffidence, Habiba took a small sip of the water. Although a Muslim, she had the Hindu's horror of touching any strange person, woman or man, or eating from their pots and plates for fear of ritual pollution. Still, the strangers' deportment and their conversation had a rare magnetism; she did not have the heart to turn down their plea. Following Habiba's example, Jamila went one step ahead. She picked a couple of almonds from the bowl and began to munch.

'Who cooks for you at home?' Since the things that were worth saying could not be said easily, Yaqub used a weak conversational gambit just to keep them from going away.

'We employ the chief cook from Shah Alam Badshah Ghazi's special kitchen,' said Jamila. Her tone of voice was flat, matter of fact.

Habiba scolded her again, using the familiar 'tu': 'Keep quiet, you! I do not at all approve of such chaff and banter.'

Then she addressed the newcomers. 'Mister, I understand not your talk. Where are you from? Are we not capable of cooking for ourselves? And how much do we eat? We thank the Master if He gives us a dry crust and a bowl of lentils. Sometimes we do not get even that.'

'We would like you to share our food. Will you eat with us?'

'I beg your pardon!' Habiba said, with a touch of pique and an arch gesture. 'As children we were told that some people force themselves upon the host even if they are unwanted and unwelcome. But your river is flowing against the slope!'

Daud smiled. 'Please do not regard us as guests and outsiders. Treat us as the men of your own house.'

The double entendre was intended, and its import was clear to the girls. Their ear lobes reddened.

'No. We should be going now,' Habiba said. 'Babu must be wondering where we have gone to. Are you finished drinking the water?'

'Well . . . we did drink, but our thirst did not go away.'

'In fact, we drank the water, but no one asked about our caste and creed!'

Jamila said a little tartly, 'All right, dear sir, drink your fill but please do not make a sport of us, do you hear? Are you really thirsty or are you having us on?'

'No, I truly swear upon my life, we are very thirsty. Come, let me drink from the hollow of my hands.' Saying this, Daud handed the water cup back to Jamila and sat himself down before her with his legs under him, as suppliants do. With his palms outstretched, he seemed to be begging, if not praying.

The two sisters had so far been distancing themselves as much as they could, correctly treating the brothers as newcomers and strangers. Now

Jamila, stepping with small, measured steps like a pigeon alighted on an unfamiliar courtyard by mistake, approached close to Daud and began to pour the water from the cup into the hollow of his open palms. Her eyes were not on Daud's hands, but on his bent head. She did not realize that Daud was gazing at her from under his eyelashes and was not drinking the water, which flowed on to the earth, unbeknownst to her, until the cup emptied. Now Jamila realized what had been happening. A little abashed and not a little piqued, she flung the cup away and cried, 'May good fortune visit you, Maharaj! You pretended to be dying of thirst and here you wasted a whole cupful of water! Are you not ashamed?'

Habiba's eyes, meanwhile, had been on Yaqub whose eyes seemed to have a subtle message for her. It was quite late now, dusk had fallen all around with its usual quickness. The desert-born girls, delicate-boned and timid, like Chinese figurines, could not muster the nerve to stay. Helped by the groom, they hauled up the two pitchers each on their head and hip, and casting a seemingly casual glance at the brothers, got down from the well's rim and stepped out purposefully on to the darkening alley. The brothers called out, 'Please, please listen . . .' repeatedly, but they paid no attention.

The environment was darkening by the minute. The girls quickly disappeared from view.

Daud and Yaqub thought it best to remain at the well, and send out the groom to inquire about lodgings in or near the village. The idea that had settled firmly in the heart of both brothers was that they were not going anywhere now. It was like the way it had always been in the past: the idea came to them involuntarily and at the same time; there was no articulation needed. They knew intuitively that they would arrive nowhere even if they went away. It was one destination everywhere and the same road to the destination. As the Persian poet said:

As much as we walk, we arrive nowhere:
The sand may go on shifting,
But it can never find a way out of the desert.

In about half an hour, the guide returned with news of a caravanserai of Shah Jahan's times. It was about five miles from the village, and though not quite along the road, it was not too far from it either. They took the south-westerly direction and reached the caravanserai in about three quarters of an hour. The high road was another twenty minutes away.

The twins hardly slept that night. All night long they imagined the well, the water, the big, dark-brown eyes; they sank and swam in those big eyes; there was the same flirtatious talk, the same open-heartedness from their side, the same tiny welcoming signs from the girls'. On the one hand, their imaginings fluctuated so quickly and were so diverse that in spite of their best efforts they could not truly recapture the girls' persons, the melody of their accents, the sweet harmony of their loving words—for, they did believe that love lurked somewhere under those plain syllables. Sometimes they could get hold of a gesture, a word of their body's gestures; many more times, many things would display a distant glimmer like the ignis fatuus, beckoning them to follow, and disappear at the next bend in their thoughts.

Yet, on the other hand, it seemed to them that all the time their souls—and not just their souls, their bodies too—were lit by a cool green-blue light whose source was a being whom they did not know or recognize. Their bodies seemed tremulous with the effect of delicate waves running through them. Who could know what is to happen tomorrow? But one thing was certain: the love of the two houris of the desert was now so entrenched in their hearts that it seemed impossible for them to go away somewhere else, or go on to Kishangarh, as they had planned:

Though your playful, mocking beauty
Does not let you rest in one place,
You never go out from a heart
Which you made your home.

Without any mutual consultation or discussion of their claim, the twins had decided that Jamila was the home for the hopes of Yaqub, while Habiba held the desire of the heart of Daud. How would their campaigns be won? They had no idea. And if they did not succeed, what then? Should the girls be taken by force? God forbid! What vile thoughts . . .

*

It was not even the false dawn when the twins rose from their restless beds. Contrary to custom, they had long baths, oiled their hair lightly with the oil of aloes wood; equally lightly, they scented their beards and necks with the delicate attar extracted from sandalwood. Each put a gold amulet around his neck encrusted with a large, oval, grey topaz. Their dresses were identical too. They wore a long, loose shirt of a flowery striped fabric; a small component of Ladakhi wool gave it body, preventing it from flapping. Their pants, called shalwar, were equally copious. As top dress, they wore waistcoats made of light-blue velvet from Bukhara; their necks were wide in the Turkish style, but had three buttons made of white sapphire at the bottom. They wore wide sashes of red-and-green silk made in Benares, tied tightly like a scarf around the waist, below the waistcoat. On the left, they hung a very long and thin dagger, delicate like a penknife. The dagger was placed inside an ebony sheath, engraved and inlaid with silver, an arrangement that went very well with the sash and the waistcoat.

On their heads, they tied formal turbans of ultra soft and smooth chintz, but the turbans were tied rather loose and rakish, after the fashion of the day. They were shod in Mughal-style sandals made of white deerskin; long in the uppers and open at the back, they tested the rider's skill in staying firmly on the feet, especially when riding at full tilt. Although English-style boots with laces were not entirely unfamiliar by then, their use was looked down upon in upper-class Indian social circles. And in any case, the common view was that he was no rider whose shoes did not go firmly with his feet, and whose shoes were not attached fast to his stirrups.

They instructed the mistress of the caravanserai to look after and feed their guide well, and to convey to him to wait up for them, for they were going out on an excursion. They spurred their horses to speed and quickly disappeared into the changing light of the false dawn. By the time they arrived at the well, true dawn had spread its wings everywhere. They took position behind the sand dunes not too near the well and viewed the scene. The water drawers, all of them women, naturally, had begun to arrive but there was no sign yet of Jamila or Habiba.

The crowd grew slowly, then it diminished slowly. The two sisters were then sighted. Each carried a pitcher on her head and hip, as they had yesterday. Their steps seemed sluggish for some reason, as if they were in a quandary about going to the well. Uncertain or not, water they must draw, and that meant going up to the well, which they did, and then seemed not too keen to leave quickly. Their eyes were apparently searching the environment stealthily. They could have seen nothing from the well;

perhaps their intuition told them that the brothers were somewhere near.

The crowd thinned to a very few women. The sisters still showed no inclination to leave, or to advance into the open, beyond the well.

The brothers, their eyes intently examining the well and its surrounds, decided that now was the time to advance. They quietly went on ahead for some distance, returning at a gallop as if they had come from somewhere far. Seeing them come, a woman nudged an elbow in Habiba's side and whispered, 'Lo and behold, your thirsty travellers!'

'I do beg your pardon, elder Sister! What kind of talk is this? Why should they be "our thirsty travellers"? I, for one, would not employ them to fetch and carry water for my ablutions!'

'Honourable ladies, I beg to make my submissions,' Yaqub, approaching nearer, said with false modesty. 'Returning as we are from the hunt, we are very thirsty. Please, could we have some water to drink?'

The remaining women, collecting their full pitchers and jars, made for their homes, but not before giving a meaningful smile, to no one in particular. They evinced no haste to leave, or intent to tarry longer, nor did they say anything to anyone, but the two sisters' faces turned a rosy hue.

'Well, mistress, is there no water here to drink?' Daud now became bolder as the other women prepared to leave. He smiled, 'The custom at the wells is not the waterless Karbala, but free water for all comers.'

Now Jamila spoke in caustic tones: 'Produce a cup or a utensil if you have one. You seem not to have learnt even to drink from the hollow of your hands.'

'There are many more ways of drinking and making others drunk, and there are many more things to drink from than a mere cup.'

Jamila turned her face away. 'I am not having any more of your false turns of phrase. We are getting late, as it is.'

By now the group of women had dispersed from the well. They had not gone far, and could still be seen. Habiba looked back at the women briefly and spoke in a low voice, 'It is not good, not at all. And such goings and comings do not fit your rank and position. Just think, what will people say?'

'We are not jobless profligates; please do not imagine us to be like others. There are men and men; some are diamonds, some are mere rocks.'

Jamila looked askance at them, but spoke with the hint of an amused smile, 'So which of you is the diamond and which the mere rock?'

Daud said, 'The one who is trampled to dust under your foot is the diamond, and the one whom you kick out of your path is the mere rock.'

'Mian sahib knows to do poetry a great lot, but is perhaps not aware that sweet and well ordered as poetry is, real life is hard and bitter.' There was an unexpected coldness and acidity of contempt in Habiba's words.

'If spent alone, life is certainly bitter and hard. But if one found a compatible lover, then the pleasure of life and the joy of love are something else.'

'So you came here searching for something? Mind how you go. You may be misled.'

'We had none there to call our own. Our origin is from here. To be deceived by one's own has its own pleasure,' Yaqub spoke gravely, but with a hint of flirtation.

Daud carried the tune further: 'We had lost our minds and hearts to banithani. We came here, wandering, looking for her with our hair dishevelled and our hearts on fire. It so happened that two houris transported us to some other universe.'

Yaqub was losing patience. He felt it was no use exchanging fine sentences and indulging in apparently light-hearted twitter any longer—let us now come down to business. He said, 'So, that person whom you call Babu, how is he related to you? Can we meet him?'

Both the girls' faces paled into swarthiness. Jamila's liveliness disappeared like the morning mist under a hot sun. Habiba, scratching the earth with her big toe, said in a low voice, 'He is our other father.'

Jamila's voice, bright with transparency for so long, suddenly became misty and dull. 'Did we not tell you that we have no father and no mother?'

The twins were shocked into silence for a moment.

'But there must be some others, some elders in the family who are the decision-makers?' Yaqub inquired somewhat uncertainly.

'We have no one, no one in this whole world. Our father died after he was bitten by a phoorsa in the desert. Our brother was a suckling baby at that time. There was no other relative. Our mother was not from this village. Her people abandoned her to her fate. Mother withstood the hardship as best she could, but not for long . . .'

'. . . but there was no support, nor the hope of one,' Habiba continued the story. 'A woman alone in a village which was not her own. So she remarried. Not many days had passed when our brother was taken off by Mother Sitala.'

'Mother Sitala . . . ?' Yaqub asked in astonishment.

'Hush!' Daud whispered urgently. 'Smallpox. These people don't take its name.'

'My poor little brother's body seemed on fire, the fever was so hot . . . and the pustules this big,' Habiba gestured with forefinger and thumb. 'Mother not only kept suckling him; she slept with him by her side always. Fever invaded her body just after they buried our little brother . . .'

'. . . and our mother passed away just four days later.'

Both the girls were now weeping and wailing openly. 'Babu looks at us with pernicious eyes. Sometimes he shouts in his rage that he will take us to Jaipur and sell us there.'

Neither Yaqub nor Daud had ever faced a situation like this. They did not know what to do or what to say in reply. One of them quickly stepped up to the well, drew water in the pail and gingerly laved the sisters' faces with his wet palms and fingers. It was thrilling to pass his hands on the lips and face of the one for whose sight and voice he had lain on hot coals through the night; but this was not the time to savour that moment. The important thing to do was to dry their tears and console them.

The girls took small sips of water after much cajoling. They dried their tears with the hem of their light wrap. Making an unsuccessful attempt at a smile, Habiba said, 'Please forgive us. You would be thinking that these pitiable ones are good for nothing, they can only lament upon their own pain; but this is the thirteenth century Hijri. Anything can happen at any moment. We prostrate ourselves in our hearts at the Great Khvajah ji's doorstep that the honour of our maidenhood may remain secure.' Her eyes began to overflow again with tears.

'Do not distress yourself, nor should you lose your will to resist; for, He is the greatest Doer of deeds and Solver of difficulties . . . But say, did you ever give thought to what you should be doing for your future?'

'What thought could we give, and relying on whom?' Jamila spoke in a voice dulled with pain.

'Dear and honourable ladies, everyone is helpless against the adverse moves of the heavens. But is He who makes the heavens move also helpless?' Yaqub said.

Habiba spoke up, 'Our lives have been lived so long upon the faith of this very hope; but now every day of our lives is worse than death. How I wish I could find some poison and swallow it and sleep. This country is known as the place of death. I wish I could hide somewhere in it so that even crows and kites could never find us.'

'Hush! One must not bring such words to the lips. Is there anything difficult for the Almighty? He can create a path through impenetrable mountains in no time.'

'Well, your path is open before you. Come tomorrow, you will be in someplace else.'

Yaqub spoke gently, his eyes on his feet: 'But you have blocked all our paths.'

Habiba gazed at him in silent unbelief. After a long minute of silence, Yaqub spoke with the greatest possible confidence, 'We are not going anywhere now.' Then Daud added with equal force, 'To lie as beggars at your door is greater for us than being king elsewhere.'

'What is it that you say? You take this matter also as a business transaction? And what is it about our door and our alley? All we know is that a snake and a woman are best under the earth.'

'I curse those who say so, and woe is to a world that obliges you two, the true glory of the garden of beauty and nightingales of loveliness . . .'

Jamila interrupted him with a short, sardonic laugh. 'Maulavi ji, don't talk to us in your convoluted Persian, we do not ken even Hindi properly.'

'The sun is riding up fast in the sky,' Daud said. 'Just think, you see a route bright and open before you. If not, this day will also turn into night.'

Yaqub spoke in a voice charged with humble entreaty: 'There will be people everywhere around in a few moments. We must leave now; we will return in the evening if you want us, or else we may have to . . .'

Habiba spoke firmly: 'No. You will find us here in the evening, at this very spot.'

What meaning did those words have? Was there some hint there, or was it just a conventional way of concluding a casual conversation? The girls' eyes, so eloquent at other times, held no sign or message; their tone of voice was neutral. Their faces bore no frown of displeasure, their brows had no wrinkle indicating constriction of the spirit. It was for the twins to extract meaning from the utterance; but did the person who made the utterance put any meaning there at all? The gold of meaning is extractable by all, but to each according to their capacity or divine grace. None are deprived of their just share from the Universal Wine House. But who is to say which is the actual tavern where we are fated to go?

Notoriety came to the devout through the mosque;
Mine came from the tavern: the secrets of each
Are laid bare in one place or another.

Granted that they were not certain, but both were determined to test their luck to the uttermost. They had no intention to quit if they failed that evening. And if, God willing, they got their hearts' desire, they had planned out a course for their future too.

Returning to the inn, they dismissed their groom with a substantial remuneration and generous reward. They told him that they knew the way from there to Akbarabad, which was their ultimate destination. Their next halt would be at Bandikui, they said. Having dismissed the groom, they travelled the Bandikui road on their own and booked their rooms in a caravanserai about sixteen miles from the village. It was almost evening by the time they returned. They packed their luggage, settled with the innkeeper, adding a substantial tip. They left ostensibly for Bandikui, but halted at a suitable place a few miles on, refreshed the four horses and rode again to the hamlet with the well. This time, they had a sword hung by their neck in addition to the thin dagger at their waist.

It was not quite dark when they came to the well. For some reason, or by a happy coincidence, there was no other person there but the two girls. They approached fast and fearlessly, but were surprised, more thrilled and exultant than surprised, to see each of the girls carrying a small bundle which apparently contained their clothes.

'Honoured ladies, we make our submissions. We are present here, as we promised.'

Habiba spoke with a bashful smile. 'We are here, too. Let our fate take us where it will,' she said, shyly pointing to their bundles. 'But our homes will go with us.'

Daud spoke with a tremor in his voice: 'Only God is untouched by blemish! What great good luck, and how wonderful our fortune! Please step forward, your mounts await you.'

Both Daud and Yaqub had just sprung forward with their arms

outstretched when both the girls, terror-struck, stopped in their tracks. They heard a loud voice, deep as a roar.

'Stop! You whores! I will reduce you to a state where the kites and crows will pity you. You loose, shameless ones, you lust for your wretched paramours and show it when the whole village is looking! You little chits of sex-crazed girls, you dare this . . .'

'Babu is here!' Habiba said between sobs. 'Ya Allah! What is going to happen to us now?'

A man, somewhat past middle age, appeared. He wore a cotton wrap on his lower body in the village style, common to all communities there. His tunic was thick and of some coarse cotton fabric. He had a black thread and amulet round his neck, and a long Rajputi spear in his hands. He trudged forward with strong, decisive steps. His small, yellowish eyes seemed ablaze like a hyena's at night.

He entered what could be called the attack zone for the long spear, but did not look at the travellers at all. He made as if to spring upon the girls. Daud extended a long leg and tripped him neatly. As he struggled to get up, Yaqub drew his sword and cried: 'You have no authority over these girls. According to Islamic law, they are adult and mistress of their own fate. You want to make them victims of your lust and then sell them off in a brothel. We will not let that happen.'

Babu tried to regain his balance with the support of his spear, and shouted, 'Who are you? You motherfuckers, you cannot tell me what is and what is not!'

Yaqub pricked Babu's foot with the point of his sword and said coldly, using the 'tu' of contempt, 'Rise, and go back without saying a word. These girls will be taken by us as wives according to the laws of Islam. You can have nothing to do with them. They owe you nothing. Still, if you imagined that something was due from them to you, take this!'

Unwinding his belt, Yaqub took out and threw down two stout cotton bags, each full of hundred-rupee coins, but he threw them with such cunning that one of the bags opened as it fell, scattering the bright, clinking coins over Babu's head and face. Instinctively, he turned to gather the shower of the coins and the twins put the girls behind them on their mounts, one each on his horse. They dug the spurs into their horses' sides and disappeared from view within the blink of an eye. The spare horses ran on behind them with equal speed.

16

Yaqub and Daud learn new trades, and a son is born to the former

THEY DID NOT make a night halt at the first stage of their journey. Four horsemen, who were waiting for them, joined them as guards for the onward journey. The brothers had made this arrangement beforehand. Two of the horsemen had rifles of French design; the other two had Indian double-barrelled shotguns. The rifles were superior in terms of accuracy and distance shooting; for closer situations, especially for dispersing a hostile crowd, the Indian guns scored over all else. These guns could use both birdshot and grapeshot. The four guards were also equipped with sel: short spears, smaller than a lance and lighter than a bayonet, they could be thrown easily to a good distance and were also suitable for hand-to-hand combat. Each of the four had also a badban, which they kept lit throughout the nocturnal journey while the travellers' mounts always stayed behind, covered by the dark. Two riders rode in front, about fifty paces ahead, while the other two rode behind.

The spare horses enabled them to ride through the night. They would stop every hour for a short while, change and refresh the horses, and go on. It was nearly morning when they arrived in Bandikui. They halted in the caravanserai and presented themselves later at the Court in Bandikui with the story that the girls had been bought by them in a village and they wanted to marry these girls. The Judge ordered that the girls be first given letters of manumission. Having the letters sealed, signed and delivered, the Judge asked the girls some routine questions, and married Yaqub to Jamila and Daud to Habiba, at his own cognizance as the legal guardian of the manumitted slave girls. The four horsemen appeared as witnesses.

*

Eleven months after the events narrated above, my father of exalted presence, my dear father Yaqub Badgami, may God have mercy upon him, and my dear mother Bibi Jamila, may God have mercy upon her soul, were given a son. In keeping with the family tradition of naming the male children after the Prophets' names, my dear father named me Muhammad Yusuf. The year, according to the English calendar, was 1793. My revered uncle remained without issue. The two brothers retained their old spiritual affinity and mutual affiliations of the heart which, with the passing of time, went beyond the brotherhood based on nativity as fraternal twins and attained the nature of mutual dependency, like that of identical twins. The shortages at one's house were replenished by the other; the problems of one were solved by the other; even the pain of one was shared by the other.

They left Bandikui just two days after the registration of the marriages and the twin marriage feasts. As a measure of caution, they had decided to settle in Farrukhabad, a prosperous city far enough from Jaipur and Mewar. They reached Akbarabad comfortably in eight days, their route taking them through Gangapur, Bayana and Fatehpur Sikri. Halting there for a few days, they travelled to Farrukhabad, touching Firozabad, Mainpuri and Beawar, and avoiding the English cantonment at nearby Fatehgarh.

The most important reason for settling in Farrukhabad was that the Maratha power had been much weakened there, if not entirely cancelled out. Four decades ago (1750), Navab Ahmad Khan Bangash had resisted and repelled the combined attack of Safdar Jang and Raja Naval Rai. Since then, and especially after the succession (in 1771) of the current Navab, Diler Himmat Khan Muzaffar Husain Bangash, life in Farrukhabad had been enjoyable and peaceful. The High Presence of Delhi was also favourably inclined towards him. The Firangee was, doubtless, extending his influence and had established a cantonment in Fatehgarh, stationing a platoon of the Bengal Native Infantry there.

Looking at matters from one point of view, it could be said that the country, though governed by the Navab and technically part of the Mughal State, was also supported, if not directly protected, by the Firangee. Wealth and prosperity abounded there like the rains in the month of Shravan. There was not much scope in Farrukhabad for trading in Kashmiri carpets or dry fruits. Thus, following their artistic bent of mind, and also because the industry and trade in gold and silver ornaments were extremely popular there, the twins preferred to become sadahkar, designers and makers of plain but delicate ornaments. Following the same artistic propensity, they also turned their interest to the ancient local craft of Farrukhabad: designing and printing flowered chintz and calico, called qalamkari in Hindi. Very soon, the twins were in demand everywhere for their excellence at the two arts.

The profession of qalamkari was entirely practised by a closed group of Muslims who by profession were known as chapera, but their community was known as Sadh. These are the names by which they are known even today. They were extremely secretive about the techniques and intricacies of their art and craft, not to speak of permitting any outsider to enter their professional territory. But my father and uncle were so charismatic in dealing with them that the Sadh became almost their disciples and followers. As sadahkar, too, they earned a good reputation far and wide, and commanded very good prices. Some of the Firangee women admired their work so much that they would, without demur, deposit Shah Alami gold mohurs or English guineas as advance payment against orders to be delivered in the brothers' own good time. As for the rupee coins of Farrukhabad, there was almost no end to the customers who came with them to buy their services.

There was one great advantage in establishing and keeping up friendly relations with the chaperas: although they were Muslim, many of their customs and rituals were very close to those of the Hindus. My mother and aunt were of the Marwari Jat community and many of their practices and superstitions were Hindu influenced. Thus they found a natural rapport with them, which helped in lightening from their hearts the scar of the loss of their native land.

*

A decade passed, a decade of comfort and content. The Company Bahadur's influence and ascendancy grew apace. By the end of the decade, the state of affairs was that the Exalted Presence, our Navab, became an almost ineffectual limb of governance in his own land. On the other side, in Delhi, the city of great fortune on whose land the legs of the Royal Throne rested, came to be more and more burdened with the influence of the Marathas. Even the advance of the flood waters of the Ganga could bear no realistic comparison to the advancing flood of the Maratha power on that city of fortunate foundation on the bank of the river Jamna. In Farrukhabad, and below it, there was the Firangee everywhere; in Delhi, and around it, the rise of the Maratha power was adequate reason and ground for competition and rivalry between the two.

A couple of decades or a little more had passed since the King, whose glory rivals that of the legendary Jamshed, the Presence, Ali Gauhar, the people's Sustainer, the Centre of the Universe, Emperor Shah Alam II, had severed his connection with the English, and had put his seal of affirmation of friendship with Mahada ji Sindhia, the Maratha potentate. Leaving Allahabad, the Emperor had moved to the Red Fort in Delhi.

Clearly, a people as malicious and vengeful as the English could never forget being slighted thus at the hands of the King. They continued to scheme and plot, extending their influence. Aiding and abetting Shuja'uddaulah of Avadh to fight and kill Hafiz-ul Mulk Hafiz Rahmat Khan, the Ruhela chieftain, in battle, they broke the back of the Ruhelas of Baraich extraction. Once the Hafiz had been defeated and killed, it was only the Muhammad Khani Bangash Ruhelas who could pose a challenge or an obstruction to them on their way to Delhi.

The English had already stationed at Fatehgarh a part of their forces from Cawnpore. Now, a 'Grand Army' began to be assembled under the command and supervision of Lord Lake Sahib Bahadur. The English pressure depressed the morale of the Navab to an unbearable extent, obliging him to sign a treaty with the English in 1217 Hegira (1802 of the English calendar), making over the administration of his lands to them against an annual payment of 125,000 rupees. The Company Bahadur was now master of the entire Bangash territory.

17

The Firangee fights the Maratha in a terrible battle that leaves Muhammad Yusuf orphaned

WITH FARRUKHABAD SAFELY behind their back, it was now easy for the English to attack Delhi and 'emancipate' the King whose Court Pavilion is the sky, and around whom rotate the sun and the moon, the Presence, Shah Alam II, from the 'durance vile' of the Marathas. Thus, one wing of the ocean-swell of the English army rose out of Cawnpore, flowing like a river in spate. The date according to the English calendar was 8 August 1803. The branch of the army that was cantoned in Fatehgarh joined the Cawnpore forces on 20 August 1803.

Our entire family was there with the Fatehgarh force as camp followers. This misfortune—in fact, calamity—had befallen us because of the gratuitous kindness and persuasion of some of our sadahkar friends. They spoke in glowing terms of the wealth and the opportunity to earn it in the English army, and seduced my father and uncle to become camp followers. Not to speak of the commandants, they said, even the women of inferior sepoys in that army are inordinately fond of gold. Further, there is no dearth of gold in the booty or bounty that they earn when a battle is won. If the Lord Lake sahib wins in Delhi, we are in clover; and if the battle goes the other way, we still lose nothing, in fact our business prospers even more, they said.

May God bestow cool comfort on the graves of my progenitors—I do not even know where they are buried—but this adventure was the first and the last mistake of their lives.

The Lord Sahib's 'Grand Army' arrived in the Delhi area on 10 September 1803, and camped near the river Hindan, at a little distance from the bank of the river Jamna. How can one like me whose speech is mere jargon, and that too, impeded with stutter, summon the power of expression to describe the glory and grandeur of the great Lord Sahib's army whose status was high like the sky? Imagine a huge rectangular courtyard, covering many square miles; imagine it moving. On the right-hand side, the right wing, comprising foot soldiers and musketeers; on the left, the left wing, comprising the cavalry. A strong vanguard, then the runners and more foot soldiers, followed by the rearguard. Guns, cannons, batteries and gunpowder stores surrounded and followed the rearguard; the vanguard was equipped with light cannon and battery.

As for personal weapons, all cavalry and detachments were heavily armed: sword, spear, carbine or rifle, with a short dagger hung at the midriff; English commandants had a pistol instead of the dagger.

It was impossible to count the number of horses, elephants, camels, bullock carts, oxen, ponies and donkeys. Each horseman had two servitors: a groom and a grass cutter. Each elephant had a mahout; there was a cameleer or cart driver for every three camels or oxen. Each Firangee commandant had his own tent; each tent had a number of attendants called lascars for pitching and unpitching it. Above all this, each English officer had a permanent provision of sheep, goats, chickens, eggs, and a small portable stove for boiling water and eggs, and making tea in emergencies. These stoves used an alcohol-like or actually alcohol fuel.

The Firangee commandants were served by a crowd of servants. Each Lieutenant had a minimum of ten attendants called orderlies; a Captain had at least twenty such, and above him, the commandant of the battalion had thirty or more orderlies. As for the numerical strength of the men serving the General sahibs, and the Lord Lake sahib himself, it was beyond counting. Then, some of the Firangee sahibs were accompanied by their ladies too. They had a separate establishment of maids and waiting women.

The rearguard was accompanied by the grain merchants. Called banjaras, they walked the ants' walk, with ten thousand or more light bullock carts carrying their goods. Perforce, the army had to keep pace with them. The total number of persons in that army would easily top a hundred and fifty thousand.

Once the army halted to camp, tents would be erected in the twinkling of an eye. Within half an hour, there would be a bazaar bustling and doing business. There would be all kinds of tents and marquees and screens: ropeless tents, wide and quadrangular tents, and the tents of grander officers that had flying pennants and scintillating spires. Such tents were set up like pavilions, with front rooms and waiting areas. If there were ladies accompanying, there was always a security zone, closed to the common gaze.

The army camp was organized like the city: each profession, each kind of merchant, had separate areas or even bazaars allotted to them. There were always grain merchants, butchers, and other food sellers, especially those who cooked on the spot and sold heavily fried, thick pancake-like breads and kebabs. In addition, there would be at least one eating house, complete with cooks and special breadmakers.

There were English merchants too; they were called 'saudagar', a term somewhat grander than a shopkeeper or a petty merchant. The saudagars only dealt in wines, spirits, and delicacies like cakes and pastries. Among the native tradesmen, the most prominent were moneylenders, jewellers, plain gold ornament makers and sellers, Kashmiri shawl sellers, and dealers in the famous muslin of Dhaka in Bengal. But even above them in fame were the nautch girls, providers of carnal gratification, and established courtesans who occupied such an exalted position that they did not visit anywhere and entertained only in their own tents. The inferior ones had what were just called 'beds', while the others had tents or streetwalking areas; all this was confined to a specialized part of the camp.

Once you went into the markets, you could hear Hindi, Bhasha, Marwari, Telangi, Bengali, Kashmiri, Pushto, Persian, even Arabic and of course English being spoken around you; as many languages, as many were the dresses and equipment and styles of the speakers. And then there were the horses with golden saddlery, camels and elephants with costly sheets called 'jhul', silver howdahs and coverlets. The horses and the camels had crested ornaments of colourful feathers. The elephants had brightly painted foreheads and trunks, with golden rings mounted on their tusks. Mellifluous bells hung from the necks of the bullocks and the elephants; and the most enjoyable part of it was that the two bells, though equally sweet sounding, were quite distinct. One could tell one bell from the other from far. The camels had ankle bells, which had a low, musical sound.

Imagine now the colourful uniforms of the sepoys of different regiments, and the garish but brilliant dresses of the guards and doorkeepers of some of the fabulously rich courtesans; the memsahibs, bejewelled and richly dressed, arrogant as such beauties must be; and the colourful entourages of the General sahibs, and the pomp and splendour of the great Lord Sahib.

Would you think that a scene from the *Arabian Nights* could exceed this one in grandeur and ostentation?

Alas! In a very short while all this was to become, for me, a scene from hell. It was not quite false dawn yet; perhaps it was about three o'clock when Lord Lake sahib ordered a general attack on the Maratha forces. It was just short of true dawn when they sighted the Marathas. Visibility was rather poor; and on both sides of the river there was, as far as could be descried, a dense jungle of thorn bush, wild filbert, dwarf jujube, acacia and henna. We could sometimes see the river flash like weak lightning.

The Marathas had their first fortified lines on a low but safe hill and the sun was behind them in the south-west. The Royal troops were not to be seen anywhere. As the assault began, the dim light of the morning favoured the English, because they could discern the Maratha lines from a distance, even if hazily. As the sun rose higher, the Lord sahib's soldiers were constantly dazzled by the hot, bright sun, seriously reducing their power of sight. The Lord sahib's artillery had not yet begun fire, but the foot soldiers, trying to break into the enemy lines, started their charge immediately as the musketry and then the cavalry opened fire. It was difficult to pass through the dense thorny trees and bushes; a real charge was in fact impossible. The foot sepoys of the Bengal regiment, muskets on their shoulders and axes in their hands, slowly hacked a path through which the cavalry advanced, raining down heavy rifle fire.

All the camp followers of the English army were placed at the very end; they had only the rearguard to protect them. The howitzers, followed by the heavier field pieces, advanced much further and were now marching parallel to the cavalry; they opened fire just as they cleared the cavalry lines. But the English forces too were now within the range of the Maratha gunnery. They laid down an extremely heavy fire on the English army, which had cut off its own retreat by advancing beyond the cavalry.

It took just about an hour for the Maratha to put the Firangee to flight. Having suffered heavy casualties, the infantry and the cavalry, as well as the light batteries, were in disarray. In the confusion of the retreat, vanguard and rearguard became undistinguishable. Had they been forced to a disorderly withdrawal across the river Hindan, it would have been a stampede, not a retreat.

It was the luck, or the ascendant fortune of the Lord Lake sahib and his Firangee generals, that the best part of their musketry safely went over. The

Maratha General, observing the Firangee in retreat with the river behind him, believed that the enemy had no escape and brought down from the high ground his heavy field pieces, numbering more than one hundred. The Maratha cannon fire now very nearly put the English to rout.

Finding no way to retreat in good order, the Lord Sahib, acting with exemplary tactical wisdom, ordered his troops to scatter in the jungle so as to give a false impression of an army running away without a plan. On the other hand, the Lord Sahib sent urgent messages through his runners to the cavalry not to advance, and to return with due stealth and all possible speed.

The Maratha General was deceived by the English army's apparent dispersal, and came out in hot pursuit. The Marathas advanced quickly, with their heavy field guns firing incessantly, until the gap between the opposing armies was further reduced, bringing the English within the range of the light artillery. The Maratha force laid down an extremely heavy fire with their muskets and carbines.

It was nearly noon. Lord Lake sahib was creeping up on the Marathas slowly, but his right wing and vanguard which had apparently dispersed, and his entire encampment and the camp followers were now within range of the enemy's light batteries. Surrounded as we were by dense thorn bush and wild jujube, we could not properly see who exactly was disposed in what place. All that we could know about the fighting were the frightening noises: of guns, animals, humans; the jungle reverberated with the heavy steps of soldiers running away or ahead. The clamour was so great that it was impossible for us to talk and discuss our plan of action. We were anxious to find some safe place to make camp and perhaps eat something and rest until the clamour died down.

Among our fellow travellers was the household of a famous courtesan of Farrukhabad. Akbari Bai was extremely rich, highly popular, and counted many members of the nobility among her admirers. She had female singers, musicians, music masters, armed guards and outriders: a whole range of attendants and dependants travelling with her. During the long journey from Fatehgarh, they and our people had become friends. Akbari Bai's Gurkha musketeers found a reasonable clearing and began to set up tents for all of us.

Suddenly, it seemed as if the sun had crashed among us. The Marathas were not at such a distance from us as we had imagined. And the noises made it impossible to hear their advance or to distinguish friend from foe.

We were just about to leave our bullock carts to enter our tent when we were struck by a cannonade of dozens of shells. We took a direct hit from explosive shells packed with sulphur, saltpetre and pitch. Many more of the exploding shells were full of iron bolts, chains and grapnel. It took less time than it has taken me to narrate our ruination. Tents, animals, men, women perished. They included my dearest parents, my uncle and aunt, our servants, in fact everything that we had possessed.

It was only your unfortunate narrator who was saved in our doomed family. Akbari Bai's own tent escaped destruction because it had not yet been erected. Akbari Bai, her little daughter Asghari, a couple of maids and the girl's nursemaids were saved. They were lightly seared by the fire, having been inside their bullock cart just out of the circle of fire.

I was ten years old at that time and well understood my state and what fate would now be mine. I knew that if I lived even a little more, it would be a life worse than what that day's disaster had wrought upon me. I began to run blindly for the river, hoping to drown, or perhaps that a bullet or shell would find me. One of Akbari Bai's braver maids caught hold of me quickly, or rather pinioned my arms and legs. Cry or scratch and bite however much I could, she did not let go of me until I fell into an exhausted sleep.

Evening was upon us when I opened my eyes and found myself in the bullock cart with Akbari Bai sahib. The battle's boom and din had fallen silent. None of the pursuers or the pursued could be seen anywhere. It took me quite a while to realize that it was the day after the conflict; the moment of destiny had come to pass. Executing the Lord Lake sahib's tactics, his cavalry had appeared suddenly, and surrounding the Marathas, had turned the tables on them. Countless numbers drowned in the Hindan, but a substantial part of the Maratha soldiery sold their lives dearly. Many hundreds of the Firangee army were also killed. A few of the English commandants also drank the draught of death. Among the native sepoys, five to seven hundred of them were wounded; an equal number were missing. No account was kept of the loss of life and property among the camp followers and non-combatants.

18

Muhammad Yusuf and Asghari have three beautiful daughters of differing temperaments

BY THE TIME I regained consciousness, the armies of the Lord Lake sahib were entering the city of Delhi, flying the standard of victory. Such of the camp followers as had escaped death or devastation followed immediately behind. We, the broken-hearted and broken-bodied remnants of the non-combatants, were about to cross the river Jamna. Having negotiated the crossing safely, we reached the outskirts of the city only to find none of the usual colourful crowd of strollers, buyers and sellers. The entire citizenry of Delhi seemed to have barricaded themselves behind the safety of their doors, not knowing what kind of devastation and booty hunting the Firangee army was planning to visit upon them. Fortunately God's mercy was upon them: the moment of peril passed safely.

We heard that the Heir Apparent Bahadur was to come out of the Red Fort to welcome the Lord sahib and escort him to the Court of the Presence, the Shadow of God on Earth. But he took a long time to appear. Perforce, the Lord sahib had to wait for him. He used the time to deploy his forces away from the city wall, even beyond Kashmiri Gate, in and upon the hills and the jungle. They were ordered to untie their belts and retire, to cook, eat and rest.

Akbari Bai stayed with her entourage as house guests of a cousin sister of hers in Chowri Bazaar. She had originally thought to stay for a few days until the shock and grief of her ill fortune and the journey's fatigue abated a little, so that she could return to Farrukhabad somewhat healed in body and mind. But her cousin said to her, 'Darling Sister, we have been one of a twosome for a long time. And now that you are here, you should stay on. And where will you go back, after all? We have none left back there in godforsaken Farrukhabad. Surely, God and Maula Ali will provide here as elsewhere.'

Her repeated entreaties finally softened Akbari Bai's heart. Having decided to settle in Delhi, she began to look for and soon found a good residence in Chowri Bazaar, just where the street turned left into Kucha Pandit. The whole neighbourhood consisted of grand houses of the nautch girls and courtesans of quality. Akbari Bai's establishment soon attracted visitors and admirers from the elites of the city. Her establishment and her house came to be known everywhere for its refinement and élan.

I can never forget Akbari Bai's kindness to me. It was entirely compassionate and gratuitous. She brought me up as if I was her own child. She sent me to school at the madrasa of Ghazi-ud Din Khan in Ajmeri Gate. There I acquired considerable knowledge of Arabic and Persian. At home, she had me educated in the elements of music and I gained some skill in playing one or two instruments as well. I did not need to go to a madrasa for education in Hindi. In fact, Hindi was not taught at any school at that time. Very soon, I became acquainted with the names and works of Delhi's greats in Persian literature like Mian Nasir Ali, Mian Nurul Ain Vaqif, Rai Anand Ram Mukhlis, Kishan Chand Ikhlas, Sukhraj Sabqat, and the Presence, the Master among them all, Mirza Abdul Qadir Bedil. In Hindi, I got to know and read the works of its chiefest master Shah Hatim and his disciple Mirza Muhammad Rafi Sauda, who perhaps was even greater than his teacher; I also got to know the works of Mir Muhammad Taqi Sahib, known among all as just Mir, the honourable Khvajah Mir Dard, and his equally distinguished brother Mir Asar, Rai Sarb Sukh Divanah, apart from those of many others of renown and fame.

All that was very well, but there could be no greater testament to the goodness and kindness that Akbari Bai sahib showered on me than the fact that when I turned fifteen, and her own daughter Asghari turned thirteen, she tied us together in the wedding knot. She would have liked to have us stay on as part of her household, but I preferred that we live on our own and I become, like my blessed father, a sadahkar. She agreed most good-naturedly, and she did not just grant us permission: she also bought for us a suitable house in Kucha Rai Man.

My business picked up quickly, and our days passed in reasonable prosperity. Asghari would often go visiting with her mother and I too went there, though less frequently. A daughter was born to us in the second year of our marriage. Rather fair and pink, like her maternal grandmother, she had delicate features and limbs and an extremely good, dense and curly head of hair even at birth, that it seemed as if some heavenly hairdresser had set it even before she was born. We called her Anwari Khanam, and also Bari Begam (Senior Lady). After her, two more girls were given to us consecutively, year to year. Both extremely good-looking, but swarthy or rather light brown of complexion taking after their father and grandfather. If Bari Begam had the features and bone structure of the girls of Hindustan, the other two looked exactly like Kashmiri girls, except for their colour. The second daughter was called Umdah Khanam or Manjhli Begam (Middle Lady). The last one we called Wazir Khanam or Chhoti Begam (Junior Lady). These two, when they grew up, even walked like the beauties of Kashmir, or so said Akbari Bai sahib. It was just like the old saying: The mother's womb or the potter's kiln, some are fair, some are dark.

Even as a little child, Bari Begam was much given to praying—the love of God and His Prophet was the mainstay of her young life. She had not missed any of the five mandatory prayers ever since she was seven, and had fasted all through the month of Ramadan since the age of nine. She quickly learnt by heart many of the smaller Quranic chapters, some prayers and sayings of the Prophet of God, and pages from *Stories of the Prophets*. Without being told to do so, she observed the purdah most strictly. She had no propensity for playing with dolls or any kind of games; she never went to any fairs, not even to Delhi's most famous one—the festivities of Basant celebrated just after the end of winter. During the mourning month of Muharram, women from everywhere, young and old, would foregather on the upper storeys, balconies, terraces of the houses of the rich—Hindu or Muslim—and watch the Muharram processions, especially the replicas, called taziah, of the tombs of the martyrs. Women came from Khanam ka Bazaar, Chowri Bazaar and Kucha Chelan, to watch, and, if possible, take part in the proceedings. But not my firstborn: she had no interest in these things.

Bari Begam would occasionally go to hear the speeches or sermons of Shah Abdul Aziz, Delhi's greatest Muslim saint and scholar, when he spoke at the nearby Jami Masjid of Fatehpuri. Her conduct was angelic just as her looks were those of a houri. Thus she was barely ten when we began to get messages and proposals of marriage for her. We gave serious thought to the matter, and choosing the best of the homes from among the marriage seekers, I married her off when she was twelve. They were a prosperous family, but not too rich, and from the Shaikh community. Their manners and domestic culture were superior and pious; in short, they were

Mirza by deportment and Sufi by persuasion; thus they enjoyed a generous share of the religious as well as the mundane. Her family by marriage was settled in Phatak Habash Khan, adjacent to the huge pile known as Haveli Husamuddin Haidar. Her husband, Mian Maulavi Muhammad Nazir, was connected to a Sufi silsilah, or line, and was a man of some means. By the Almighty's grace, our daughter was happy in her marriage. Praise is to God for His kindness and goodness to us.

Manjhli Begam was also of a grave temperament, but she liked her maternal grandmother and her house above all things and would fain have moved in there if she had her way. The company of Akbari Bai sahib and her professional attendants inculcated in her all the heart-ravishing sophistications that suited a begam of quality. She spoke in refined accents, was adept at repartee and the exchange of lively and light-hearted dialogue, and knew hundreds of Urdu and Persian verses, which she often used in her conversation intelligently and appropriately. She was poetically inclined with a good ear for the rhythm of poetry, and composed an occasional verse or two. She was also well acquainted with the new style of singing, the khiyal, which came into vogue during the times of Muhammad Raushan Akhtar Muhammad Shah Padshah, who now rests in Paradise. She learnt the musical arts not as a professional matter, but merely in order to indulge her taste for such things.

Navab Syed Yusuf Ali Khan Bahadur, scion of Navab Syed Muhammad Said Khan Bahadur, was at that time an ornament to the city of Delhi, having moved there from the exhilarating city of Rampur, before he was appointed Heir Apparent to the State of Rampur. He had come to Delhi to study Islamic and philosophical subjects with the Sadr-us Sudur, equal of Jalaluddin Davvani and Taftazani, Maulana Sadruddin Khan sahib Azurdah, and the Aristotle of the age, Avicenna of the times, the envy of Nasiruddin Tusi, the pride of Rhazes, the Presence, Maulana Fazl-e-Haq Khairabadi; the Navab was one of their most well-instructed pupils. When free from his lessons, the Navab would trouble his steps to visit the house of Akbari Bai sahib for relaxation. Here, his eye fell upon Manjhli Begam and he viewed her with favour.

Treating this connection as the advent of good fortune and prosperity, Akbari Bai sahib supported it with all her heart and soul. As a result, despite serious resistance from me and her mother, Manjhli Begam became attached to the establishment of that elegant and gracious Navab.

How much could I complain or fret and weep for Manjhli when Chhoti began to fly higher and wilder when she was only a fledgling? Even as a child, she exuded a sort of maturity, and her behaviour and manner of dealing with others had a sort of conscious coquetry, such that as I watched her grow up, I despaired for her, fearing to imagine the kind of devastation she would wreak upon men when she became a woman. Her mother's admonitions, the love and the role model of her oldest sister, all these were cast aside against the wilful pranks of the beloved grandchild of her maternal grandmother. Once she was ten years old, she spent most of her time in the luxurious environment of Akbari Bai sahib's boudoir. True, she acquired a little bit of singing and music from that place, but her real education from there was in those arts and mysteries whose mastery enables a woman to command the will and passion of a man. In fact, even when she was just seven or eight, she was aware of her beauty, and even more aware of her beauty's power, and her own unique ability to use that power.

She could make serving girls, hawkers, tinkers, water carriers, flower sellers, cart drivers, petty traders, and even her parents, dance to her tune, leading them as she wished. She took whatever she wanted and she extracted consent from whomever for whatever purpose she desired. If offended, she took to sulking in such a way as to tug and tear the hearts of those who saw her in that mode. Who could have been cruel to this delicate, flower-like soul? they would wonder sadly. If she burst out laughing, it was as if a bulbul were trilling away in a garden of Shiraz, a rose petal held in her tiny beak. Put whatever dress on her, you would feel that the Tailor of Eternity had cut all dresses for her and her alone.

As was quite proper, Anwari spent almost all of her time with her husband, at his parents'. She would visit us at least once a month, and would always send gifts on festive occasions. She was, practically, not on speaking terms with Manjhli. As for Chhoti, she had hardly any time for others, absorbed as she was in her own self. By the time she was eleven, she became celebrated as a budding beauty not only in Kucha Rai Man, but also in the neighbouring streets and bylanes and houses, so that visitors came with excuses or pretences simply to look at her. They would show up as cloth merchants, sellers of savouries or as sorbet vendors, yet others came as flower sellers. If no other excuse occurred to a visitor, he would wander into our street as one who had lost his way.

Of course, Chhoti would never open the door to the full, far less come out into the street. She would dismiss them with a word or two from behind the door, or from behind a half-open window in the balcony. Sometimes it would happen that the more brash among the adolescents from upper-class homes who frequented the bazaars and coffee houses appeared with a gemstone merchant or a dealer in jewelled ornaments, claiming that they were informed that such a tradesman was needed here, so they had brought him along to our doorstep. Please order or buy whatever you like from his wares, they pleaded, and not to worry about the payment, we will make sure that the merchant gets his money.

Jewellery in the newest designs, dresses in the styles that had just come into vogue, fabrics and dresses from faraway lands and of unusual cut or colour, shoes and sandals of the newest models and styles: Chhoti was crazy about such things. She knew the names of all the ornaments, however arcane, and she had an excellent notion of the various kinds of fabrics and their prices. She was well aware of what fashionable women of the upper classes were wearing in Calcutta, Hyderabad and Lucknow. I never could find out whom she asked and where she inquired, but she had unerring information on all this.

There were occasions when wealthy brats would find excuses to send her novelties and collectibles and fine gifts from distant climes; sometimes they even used the services of women who were more or less professional go-betweens for exchange of messages and conveyance of proposals for marriage, to send to Chhoti, at Akbari Bai's house. I and Asghari always protested and refused such uncalled-for gratuities. Chhoti's admirers would stop for some time, and then renew their unwelcome importunities with redoubled vigour.

Formal proposals for her hand began to arrive as Wazir entered her thirteenth year. Some of these were from good houses, or even minor nobility. Some suggested that Wazir could even stay at her own home, but as a concubine fully committed to a single person, namely, the proposer. But word of marrying someone or setting up a domestic arrangement with someone would inflame her as if she had been lit by some inner fire. Her face flushed with displeasure, her brow knit in disapproval, she would say with the arrogance of a princess that she was not interested in imbibing the disease of domesticity.

By that time, her other qualities had become apparent too, or had become more noticeable. She had always had a good singing voice and though she did not have the head or heart for the hard practice and labour needed to master our ragas and musical modes, she learnt many ragas and sub-ragas by just listening to them at her grandmother's. For instance, she knew Basant, Yaman, Bahar and Bagesari among the ragas, and also some of the more popular modes likes the Dadra; further, she knew some of the well-known tunes like the Chaiti, much favoured by shepherds, and the Benarasi Thumri, a recent import from Avadh; and she could sing long excerpts from Afzal Gopal's Bikat Kahani in the manner of the Hindu trading men's wives in such a soulful voice as to melt the hearts of her listeners into profuse tears.

As I said above, she had a good ear for the rhythm of Hindi poetry and in due course she became a disciple of the famous maestro Mian Shah Nasir in the art and craft of the ghazal. She found access to Shah sahib through Muzaffar-ud Daulah Nasirul Mulk Mirza Saifuddin Haidar Khan Saif Jang, second son of Navab Husamuddin Haidar Khan Bahadur. As I said earlier, Bari Begam's husband and family lived close to Husamuddin Haidar Khan's mansion, so there was some acquaintance between them, and maybe Husamuddin Haidar Khan was familiar with Wazir's name as well. Anyway, Husamuddin Haidar Khan occasionally visited the house of Akbari Bai sahib, and it was there that Chhoti Begam obtained the honour and distinction of a personal introduction and exchange of greetings—respectful on her side, kind and gentle on his—with the Navab.

Shah Nasir Sahib was a kind mentor. He himself suggested Zuhrah—Venus in the speech of the Firangee—as Chhoti's nom de plume. It was rarely that he did not mark at least one verse with special approval when he returned his bright pupil's ghazal after correction. Occasionally, she would send some small offering with her ghazal which the mentor would accept graciously, but always with some remark—always in Persian—like, 'That dear person has fresh and blooming lines of poetry, and invents fine phrases. May God enhance and yet enhance these. There is no need for other offerings. Faquir, Shah Nasir.'

As for having a temperament suited to poetry, Manjhli was no less. She became a disciple of Hafiz Abdur Rahman Khan Ihsan through the good offices of Navab Yusuf Ali Khan, and it was the Navab who suggested Mah ('Moon') for her nom de plume, but poetry was not her true avocation. She was more interested in calligraphy and embroidery work. Now that she often travelled to and from Rampur, she had little time for the strenuous mental discipline needed for poetry. Had Wazir worked hard enough and applied her mind to poetry, she would not have been a lesser poet than the famous songstress and poet Mah Laqa Bai Chanda of Hyderabad. But she regarded the writing of poetry as nothing more than a pastime to claim equality with the menfolk, and as a means of capturing and taking away their hearts. To that extent, she was a true master in the art of composing poems; the rest was not germane. I have preserved a ghazal that she composed before she went off to Jaipur. It also bears the corrections made by her revered master. The ghazal was written in the metre and rhyme of a line prescribed beforehand. The line in question was:

None give countenance and caresses to a beggar;

Wazir completed the verse with a first line of her own:

Zuhrah, she is not going to give you a kiss:
None give countenance or caresses to a beggar.

Her mentor had put the sign of approval against the verse. I give below the whole ghazal, and also the corrections made by the maestro:

Come, let me throw this heart of mine down a well
somewhere
And thus solve all my problems.

Waves of pain, rising from the heart,
These waves break against and erode the riverbank.

~~*Roiling in his own blood, lying in her path:*~~
The hunter went, leaving the victim wounded:
Would that somebody picked up the wounded lover!

It was not often that Shah Sahib explained or adduced a reason for a given correction, but he scored through the first line and inserted a line of his own instead. In the margin, he wrote, again in Persian, 'Only God is untouched by blemish! In whose path, and why roiling in blood? The two lines lack connection.'

~~Oh! how tedious, the long winded Preacher!~~
Better hear out the Counsellor and say nothing,
I for sure am not going to answer him, he is so foolish.

Here too, the first line was replaced by a new one composed by Shah Sahib himself. He gave no reason for it, but the matter should be obvious: the correction made the verses more in line with sophisticated idiom and, further, the occasion for answering is more suited to a counsellor than a pulpit speaker.

~~Is the hunter-catcher back in the flower garden?~~
Is the hunter-catcher roaming the flower garden?
~~What happened? Why fallen silent are the bulbuls?~~
Why are the bulbuls silent? What happened?

No reason was given for the correction in either of the two lines, but it seems clear enough. The first line, as corrected, gains in flow and appropriateness of idiom, the second line follows the grammar and syntax better, although the words are the same, but for one omission.

Lailah's fragrance pervades desert and hill,
Poor camel driver, he watches over her camel's litter!

The gracious ustad put his sign of approval over this verse too. And now the final verse:

Zuhrah, she is not going to give you a kiss:
None give countenance or caresses to a beggar.

It may not seem my place to say this, but the fact is that all the verses show intellectual vigour and the prowess for creating new themes. Rather than the creation of a fourteen-year-old unmarried and purdah-observing girl, the ghazal gives the impression of being the work of a mature poet who has had experience of the company of master poets.

*

Wazir was in her fifteenth year when the heavens fell on us, most unexpectedly. Asghari fell ill and breathed her last in no time at all, in just four days, in fact. One often hears the proverb that daily bread needs finesse, and death, just any excuse, but Delhi in those days was singularly devoid of things that are considered to bring death: no epidemic, no flooding of the river, no earthquake, nor yet the advent of any marauders, Marathas or Durranis. There was no excuse for the powers that determine fate and dole out destinies to darken the brightest arch of my house in this fashion.

Winter was on the wane. My sweet and loving lady had a bit of a cold and cough and catarrh over a brief few days, nothing serious, just the usual kind of complaint that arises when two seasons come together. Everyone among us believed that the cold would run its course in a week or ten days: that the congestion in the nose and throat would dissolve and flow down the sinuses, bringing relief. No medication was considered necessary, except the medicinal infusion normally prescribed for such colds. I used to procure it regularly from the clinic of Hakim Mahmud Khan sahib, which was not far from where we lived.

Asghari felt better on the fifth day. She thought to take a thorough bath with cold water, for she felt stale and grubby, not having taken a bath or changed her clothes all those four days. Well, that bath turned out to be no ordinary bath: it was an invitation to death. Almost at once after the bath, her body began to burn with high fever. She wrapped herself tightly in a shawl and fell onto the bed, barely conscious of what she was doing. I was not in the house at that time, for I had gone out for a short while to deliver some ornaments to a client. Returning home and finding her in bed, I believed her to be fast asleep, relaxed by her bath. Quite by chance I felt her wrist and instantly withdrew my hand in shock. She was not asleep: she was practically unconscious and a blazing fever was raging through her slight frame.

As for Chhoti, she was upstairs, indulging her individualistic fancies, absorbed in her usual self-regard. She had no idea of the state of her mother and the soul-searing scene downstairs. Urgently calling her to come down, I ran out to Hakim Mahmud Khan sahib's mansion only to find to my shock and misfortune that he was not available. In a frenzy of anxiety I narrated the case to an assistant, had him fill in his prescription as quickly as possible, and dashed back home; but Asghari was still unconscious.

We passed the day hovering about her bed, hoping to see her open her eyes. It was nearly evening when we were informed that Hakim Mahmud Khan was still unavailable but he had deputed Hakim Bhure Khan sahib, his best assistant and disciple, to examine the patient and prescribe. In those days Hakim Bhure Khan was fast establishing a formidable reputation. He rode to our house in his open palanquin. His face became sombre as he felt the patient's pulse. In a low voice he commanded: 'There is acute inflammation of the lungs, affecting the pleurae, and in her weak condition the patient is unable to express the mucus. Should the mucus advance and block the trachea . . .'

'Hakim sahib, please do something for the discharge of the mucus . . . I will go immediately and procure by any means whatever you prescribe, and . . . perhaps it would be a good idea to consult with Hakim Mahmud Khan sahib as well?'

'Certainly, I will consult with him. But right now, the mucus is accumulating fast.' He wrote out something on a piece of paper in the physicians' illegible scrawl. 'Here, take this prescription for a poultice. Go just now to Lal Kuan and have it made by the apothecary Abdul Majid without any delay. Warm the poultice moderately, spread it on the bandages, and apply to the affected parts. Do this every three quarters of an hour. God is the Lord of us all.'

'Hakim sahib, what about the fever?' I made bold to ask.

'We will take care of it in due course, certainly. At present the compacted mucus and the interior inflammation make it impossible for any medication to go down the patient's throat.'

I left at the same time as the hakim and ran to the apothecary's at Lal Kuan. Asking him to prepare and keep the medicine ready for me, I dashed off to inform Akbari Bai sahib in Kucha Pandit and immediately retraced my steps to the apothecary's, and back home.

By the time I returned, Akbari Bai, followed by Manjhli and Bari had ridden fast to their mother's home. The girls and I spent that whole long night clinging to Asghari's bedside, watching the breath of life heaving to and fro in her fever-racked body. Had the urgent supplications and tearful lamentations of the caregivers carried any value at all, not one but even a hundred Angels of Death could not have taken away my dear wife. It was past midnight when her breathing became irregular. There was no strength in her to cough out even a little of the mucus that was squeezing her lungs. Her throat was now choked to the uttermost, her breath a huge rasping wheeze, as if a saw were working on her ribs. The only speech that she could manage was an occasional gasp followed by 'Allah, Allah', nothing more.

As the new day was dawning, the women began to recite the Quranic chapter Ya-Sin which eases the throes of death. Just before the muezzins began to call the world to the morning prayer, Asghari's neck drooped to one side, her immortal soul left its mortal coils. Without doubt we belong to God and without doubt, we are to return to Him.

It may have been morning outside everywhere; my home was shrouded by night.

*

Both my daughters, Bari Begam and Manjhli Begam, stayed on with me until the fortieth-day mourning ceremonies. Before going back to her husband's, Bari said to me, with some considerable hesitation, 'May I say something, Father?'

'You do not need to ask. Speak freely.'

'You are quite alone now,' she said with her eyes on the floor. 'None can say anything about Umdah Khanam's future, her ways are strange and alien anyway. But my real source of anxiety is the little one. It is best that she live here and take care of you in your lonely old age. But her flightiness makes me fearful, lest something . . . something out of line happens. She was restrained somewhat by Mother's presence, now she is gone. I think you shouldn't delay. Find her a suitable husband . . .'

'It is certainly my own heart's desire,' I said. 'And your mother, may God grant her Paradise, had the same thought too, but Wazir does not and will not listen to anyone. I am wan with care, for how can I keep her under my power on my own, without your mother's support? And how can I try to cope with our loss while I have constantly to worry about her? Truly, I am in torment . . . and it would be still worse if I asked her grandmother to take charge of her.'

'No. Please do not send her there. I shall talk to her. Perhaps some way could be found.'

The conversation between the two sisters had the same result, the one that I had feared. There was no way to find a way past her recalcitrance. A way could be found for those who wished for a way to be found. As the poet said, *Can anyone make me understand, if I do not want to?*

'Chhoti, I speak with only your good at heart,' Anwari said, using the familiar 'tu' in an affectionate tone. 'To heed advice is to sow the seed for prosperity. Just think about yourself, what is going to happen to you in the future?'

'Why should anything happen to me? Do I have some kind of illness? There is not even a speck of dirt on our mother's shroud and you've begun shooting your barbs at me!'

'What barbs? There are no barbs. All that I am saying is . . .'

'. . . that my virtue and my prosperity lie in my getting married. But why? Is there a defect in my character, a fault that marriage will rectify?'

'My dear child, with our mother gone, our home is without a mistress to regulate it. To expect our father to guard you, run the house and feed you single-handedly . . . how could that be?'

'Why should he guard me? Am I a little baby that someone will make off with me? Please listen carefully, I fear no one and I shall be cowed by no one.'

'So you will remain unmarried all your life? And what about those scores of proposals and suggestions that keep coming for you?'

'Baji,' she spoke mildly, but in a reasoning tone, as if she was the older sibling, 'stones must fall in a home that has a jujube tree. There is nothing to worry about. All things will happen at the appointed time.'

'Is that true? So should I tell Father . . . ?'

Wazir laughed. 'There is nothing to tell Father. All I am saying is that you should wait and watch. Everything will happen, when the time for it arrives.'

'What is it that you keep saying about "appointed time"? I just don't understand your parroting about it. What is it that you want us to do? Should we look for a suitable match for you, or no?' Bari felt defeated and tired of arguing.

'So listen,' Wazir said in a patronizing tone, 'I am not the marrying type. I am not marrying anyone.'

'Why? Why will you not marry? And what will you do if you don't marry? Girls are born so that they should be married, they should have a home, and . . .'

'. . . bear children, be battered by husband and mother-in-law, be ground and scorched in millstone and oven, and grow old before their time. Is that it?' Wazir mocked her eldest sister.

'What else? Should girls go settle with some madams in a bordello? Ruin themselves in both this world and the hereafter? Blacken and heap obloquy on their parents' fair name?'

'Baji,' Chhoti again spoke in a tone of reasoning and conciliation, 'do girls have just these two choices? Is this all that God's bounty and justice gives them?'

'I know nothing of bounty or justice. Let God attend to God's affairs. But ever since there has been a world, women have been deployed in these things alone: there is the way of the good and the noble, and there is the way of the lowly and the mean.'

'Stop, please stop uttering these words about the noble and the mean. Let men do what they will, no blame will ever attach to them. And let us, the women, speak just a little above a whisper: we will at once be condemned as loud-mouthed harlots and hussies. Oh God, is that justice?'

'Well, that is the custom, and the custom is based upon nothing but justice. God has created woman as the very image of modesty, bashfulness, motherly love, pity and self-sacrifice.'

'I don't want to be the image or caricature of anything or anyone. I am good-looking, I have a sharp mind, and I have no member that is broken or paralysed. Show me a man to whom I could be inferior. Would the God Who put together so much in me, suffer me to lodge my talents useless in me? Would He approve my being sacrificed on the false altar of men's carnal lust?'

'Little one, who dare sacrifice you for someone's lust? Your husband will take you to your new home riding on a pacing steed. He will keep you in comfort; he will bend himself to your will.'

'Yes, and then kick me out when he feels like it. Or, he will lock me up in a black cell, and will brazenly do what he likes, go where he lists, make eyes or worse at whomever he desires.'

'Who can argue with you, dear girl? You want excuses to quarrel, to score points, as in a debate.'

'Look, Baji darling, why should I put myself in a trap all through my life by marrying? Those attachments are best which can be broken.'

'Oh my God! Chhoti, what is it that you utter! It is clear infidelity, a rejection of Islam and its laws!'

'Maybe. But I will surely ask God about the infidelity that I was guilty of by being born a woman. Was it a sin so heinous that I should be thrust into hell here in this very world? It was You Who made me a woman; I did not become a woman by my own choice.'

'Man is integrally necessary for woman. Woman is man's grace and dignity, honour and esteem. Man is woman's protector, lord and master.'

'All right, let him be all that, but is marriage necessary too?'

'So you will commit that which is most illegitimate? Dear girl, do fear God!'

'Do you really believe that the illegitimate became lawful by pronouncing just a couple of words of mumbo jumbo? And your sister, is she a cow whose sacrifice becomes lawful because a few words are uttered before the knife is taken to her? Baji darling, listen, and remember. I will not marry. And even if I did, I am certainly not going to choose a husband from among tawdry sellers of food on portable trays or petty morsel-begging, illiterate mullahs or pauperish, pension-begging so-called high-born hypocrites!'

'And do you think a navab or a prince will come begging for your hand? Dear girl, one must not be so proud. The good God does not approve of pride.'

'If a prince is writ in my destiny, he will come, surely. If not, no matter. I will first taste the man who wants me. I will let him stay if I like him, if not, I'll show him the door.'

'Oh God, oh God! Instruct this young woman in the path of righteousness, make her see reason,' Bari said, wiping her tears. 'Her brain is ruined.'

BOOK 3

19

Chhoti Begam sets aside questions of love and learns to be a bibi in the house of a sahib

MARSTON BLAKE WAS a slim, tall young man with an athletic body. Around twenty-eight years of age, he was not particularly good-looking. He was very fair and brown-haired, and his eyes were small and light brown. One does not know about his English—it was his mother tongue anyway—but he was fairly fluent in Hindi, and had some skill in what was known among the English as 'the Persian of the Moonshies'. A sense of humour and a ready sociability were his best qualities.

He was extremely fond of Wazir Khanam, but it is difficult to say that he was willing to make her his wife and give her the status that he would give to an English wife. The English, of course, have no distinctions of caste or notion of inherent quality based upon birth, but they did show extreme regard and respect to those who were born to ancient families in their own country. Wealth counted for a great deal, doubtless, and the moneyed classes wielded great influence. If wealth combined with what they called noble birth, then it was an unbeatable combination.

A white skin was, in their eyes, the most important thing for a man. Certainly, there were sahibs in whose blood some 'native' element had entered some generations ago. The 'pure' English sahibs looked upon them with a superior eye, though they were given regular promotion or preferment if they proved their ability and performed well in the service of the Company Bahadur. Still, outside of the offices or the courts, the 'true' Englishmen did not mix much with those other kinds of sahibs.

White-skinned women were mostly unattractive—phika, or tasteless, little sugar and much water, was how their complexion was often described—arrogant, and not very intelligent. The way they made up their faces, and their airs and graces lacked warmth and pleasurability. This was the reason why every Englishman invariably kept Indian bibis: not just one, in fact four or even more. Temporary dalliances with prostitutes or nautch girls, and an occasional visit to dosshouses were an extra treat.

Whatever Wazir Khanam had gleaned about the family and circumstances through casual and discreet inquiries or through her own inferences, never directly from Marston Blake, indicated that he did not come from a prominent or rich English family. But he was of 'unmixed' blood, so his paths to advancement were wide and long, provided he had ability, and was assiduous in the performance of his duties. In those days, the following appointments were the highest regarded for an Englishman in the administration of the Glorious Sahibs: Resident / Political Agent, Officer in the armed forces, and Revenue Officer, which included in its purview land revenue, taxes, customs and excise duties. All the rest were of lower account even if they were held by the English. Nine out of ten stations of Resident or Political Agent were filled from selected military officers, while the rest came from the revenue arm of the service. Limited to their own districts, officers who collected the revenue and settled cases relating to land and its revenues and who were also in charge of Faujdari (minor criminal matters) were first in order of precedence.

These officers were named Collector or Deputy Commissioner and the first item in their job description was round-the-clock availability and readiness to work and shoulder responsibility on their own. They must use their discretion all the time, promptly deal with day-to-day issues and problems and maintain the authority, dignity and awful majesty of the Company without compromise. These jobs were difficult and were often discharged by the Collector with no support from another Englishman. Barring one or two junior colleagues, if at all, the Englishman in charge of a district—District Officer in the English idiom of the day—had none to support or overrule him.

Political importance, prominence over a large area, and near equality with the ruler or even the King in whose Court the Resident was stationed, and, most importantly, his being fully au fait with the affairs of the State and having personal influence over the ruler gave an unmatchable cachet and weight to the Resident or Political Agent above all other employees of the Company.

In Wazir Khanam's eyes, Marston Blake's greatest merit was his having attained the rank of Captain at the young age of twenty-eight, and that he was now Assistant Political Agent. She could dream of the days to come when he, like General Ochterlony (popularly known among the natives as Akhtarloni sahib), would be a general in the English army and stationed as Resident to the Court at Red Fort, popularly and plainly called Haveli (Mansion) or at best Lal Haveli (Red Mansion) by Delhiwallas as a mark of affection or reverse snobbery. Marston Blake's other desirable quality—rare among the Firangee of his class—was that, after establishing his liaison with Wazir Khanam, he had not cast as much as a casual eye on any other Indian or Firangee woman. Thus while she could see with the eye of her mind Marston Blake firmly lodged on Ochterlony's throne-like chair, she did not visualize herself as one of the many bibis of Ochterlony who rode behind him—eleven or (according to some) thirteen in number—in a procession of elephants when Akhtarloni sahib came out on the streets of Delhi of an evening to take the air.

Wazir Khanam's world suffered a sea change in Jaipur. So far, she had been a girl in an average Muslim home, used to the restriction of purdah, and to doing most of her work with her own hands. In Delhi, there was an old maid in the house and a middle-aged servant for outdoor work—such servants were often sepoys who had been obliged to leave their regiment to settle in Delhi. That was all there was to it by the name of domestic establishment. Wazir's people were on visiting terms with a few of the city's families of their own station, and there was of course the house of Anwari Begam's husband. Many of the better-born families became distant and cold towards Wazir's people once Manjhli was set up in Navab Yusuf Ali Khan's house. Still, Wazir's parents were not entirely ignored or debarred from all good homes. Then it so happened that the Navab connection produced its own network of important or unimportant acquaintances among the families which were dependent, one way or another, on Navab Yusuf Ali Khan or his father.

There had been no bar on Wazir Khanam's going out on family excursions, or enjoying the lights and bustle and conglomeration of the numerous tradesmen, players, acrobats and singers who thronged Delhi's numerous fairs. Similarly, she could freely, from her home or in open bazaar, inspect, assess, haggle, bargain for and buy, subject to her purchasing ability, the merchandise that interested her. Anyway, Wazir had had no scarcity of admirers who kept pestering her with presents and delicacies, urging her to come to the bazaar or a fair with them. If nothing else, they insisted on composing Hindi poems in praise of her largely unseen good looks. Thus Wazir had never felt cribbed or confined at home, away from the bigger and colourful world of the capital.

Yet the world in Jaipur was curious in many ways. There was a whole throng and crush of domestic help, and then there were those thousands of little chores necessary to run a household which had so far been attended to by her parents; above all else, the household affairs and the nature of the house were quite unusual for her. There was a string of visitors every day of the week, and apparently no restriction on expenditure and no lack of money. An extremely important or perhaps the most important point of difference was, however, something for which she had not prepared herself. She found that in Jaipur she was not part of the social zone of the well born as she had been among Delhi's Muslims and Hindus, nor was she a denizen of the world of the Glorious Sahibs.

True, there was more social life than before, but none of those who came to call, even on festival days, were from the well born, Hindu or Muslim. In Delhi, she had, at least for form's sake, many among her circle of acquaintances who were from high-born or middle-level well-born circles; the encouragement and patronage of Mian Shah Nasir had brought some men and women poets within the ambit of her confrères. She had hoped, if only dimly, that while she might not have access to the Maharajah's Palace in Amber, she could at least count among her social circle those who occupied the courtiers' mansions.

She was disabused of all such notions within a few weeks of her life in Jaipur. She found that no Indian, none at all, except the domestic help, could ever be counted among those who knew her. There was, of course, no question of mixing with the English, women or men. If on rare occasions an Englishman visited Marston Blake out of boredom or for some official work, she would certainly organize hospitality for him, but she was never asked into the drawing room (she knew that the English women invariably did get so asked), nor would the English visitor ever say or even hint that he would be happy to receive the bibi at his home.

Hospitality always included wines or spirits, and this was repulsive to her in the extreme. Many English sahibs did not drink much, but they readily drank something effervescent—which they called 'soda water'—with a liberal dash of fresh lime juice and ice, especially in the summers. This drink was gradually acquiring the generic name of nimbu pani ('lime and water') and every English household had plenty of supply of fresh lime and ice in the summers, and bottles of 'soda water'. For a long time, Wazir refused to touch the 'soda water', believing it to be a kind of wine. Marston Blake had his work cut out to convince her that it was just aerated water.

Similarly, Wazir was certain that pork must have been eaten regularly in Marston Blake's house before her advent. So, without asking him, Wazir had all the crockery, cutlery and pots scrubbed and then 'purified' with the water of Zamzam, the sacred well at Mecca. In fact, anticipating that state of affairs, she had brought with her a leathern vial full of the water. She declared to Marston Blake that she would swallow poison if even the name of that death-deserving unclean beast was ever taken in the house.

Marston Blake put his arm around her shoulder, almost pulling her tight in a close embrace, and said, 'Wazir, you're not just vizier [English for Wazir], you are the queen of this house. Whatever you say will be done.'

Saying this, he kissed her a number of times on the mouth. Wazir extricated herself with some difficulty and ran into her bedroom, saying, 'Please let go of me. No more of this. All conversations have their time and place.'

'I know,' he smiled. 'And I also know what "conversation" means in your language.'

Marston Blake was savvy enough in Hindi to know that the Hindi word 'bat' ('conversation') could also mean 'sexual intercourse', in women's speech, just as 'conversation' also meant the same in English in the sixteenth century.

His accent and intonation were like those of other Englishmen: not very fluent, and a little guttural. He could pronounce the soft t's and d's, and his voice was deep, which was described in those days as typically male. On account of his little hesitancies as he searched for the proper word, hearing his Hindi was pleasurable but surprising, as if a child were trying to talk like a grown-up. But his voice had no flexibility, no sense of harmony or music. She called to mind Shah Nasir sahib's accents, so musical, so mellifluous. He pronounced each letter with equal care and deliberation, but not like a mullah whose voice, though clearly enunciated, had a rigidity, a stiffness, as if he were trying to clear his throat. When Shah sahib spoke, it was like gentle rain on a vine trellis, heavy with leaf and fruit.

Wazir felt panicky for a second; now she had to spend her life in the company of Marston Blake's voice. But she set aside the thought deliberately, and answered in cool tones, 'So all right, I well know what is that which is called conversation. The essence of man's spirit is in speech. You have come home quite tired. Now off you go, please, freshen up, take a bath . . .'

'Should we not take a bath after . . . ? I believed you were a devout Muslim, but now you want that I should bathe before . . .'

Wazir reddened. She bunched a corner of her orhni, and pushing it into her mouth to prevent herself from laughing out loud, said, 'Go, please go. I won't talk to you. Have you no shame? These troops of servants stand open-mouthed before us and you . . .'

He laughed. 'Wazir Begam, this is an Englishman's house. There is no deliverance from them even in death. They are your subjects and you are their lawful mistress. Nothing can be kept hidden from them.'

And it was a fact, too. She had not seen so many servants in even Yusuf Ali Khan Bahadur's palatial mansion. The Navab lived in great style, but his battery of servants consisted mainly of horsemen, foot soldiers, gun-wielding sepoys, lance-bearers, and others of that sort. There were four or five maids as Manjhli's personal attendants, that was all. Here, there was a veritable army of serving persons, and the duties of many of them were strange, to say the least.

While the horde of servants did give her a sense of power, a light intoxication, it also told her in no uncertain terms that in her new realm there would be none of the whispers, the silences, the intimate conversations, the exchange of quick, friendly phrases, the faces showing through narrow windows at the back that provided safe communication between homes, the phrases sweet and musical like the trill of the harmonicon—a small little interior hutch of one's own heart in spite of lives lived together in narrow houses. All that was Delhi, and all that was behind her now.

Once she had determined, albeit gradually, to give her hand in Marston Blake's hand, she had a vague hope, a faint notion rather, that her momentous step, besides giving her rank and power, would also pave the way for her becoming acquainted on equal if not friendly terms with the women of the well born and the nobility among the Indians at least, if not among the memsahibs of the English homes. But the facts had turned out to be quite different.

She found out that there was a world of the well-born Indian families, a world that was becoming powerless—bloodless against the full-blooded advance of the English force—but it was a world which still had its sense of self-worth, and of the rules and conventions that governed it. Then, there was a world of the English, a world in which the Indian had no entry. And there was yet another world: the world of the bibis, their servants and hangers-on. Only servants from the bibis' world could have access to the other two worlds, and that too rarely. Otherwise, the English world was a world sealed to the ordinary person, self-existing and mysterious.

She also found out that all bibis were just that: bibis. There was no distinction or restriction of Hindu or Muslim, high-born or low-born, educated or from among the artisan community, nor was there any limit to the numbers; and also, all bibis were not ranked equal, their importance being determined by the rank of their sahibs—the bigger or higher the sahib, the more substance commanded by the bibi. Thus the highest-ranked bibi in Jaipur was the Resident's, then came Wazir Khanam, and then the army officers' bibis, according to rank.

Wazir's greatest satisfaction was that she was the lone bibi and Marston Blake described her as his wedded wife, at least in private conversations. The common practice was that a Firangee almost never went through a marriage ceremony, Islamic, Hindu or Christian, with his bibi. The best that could happen was that the sahib, immediately before or after taking a bibi, would report the fact to his superior; the report could be in writing but in actual fact it was mostly oral, and this too was limited to the middle-grade sahibs. The Great Sahibs—members of the Governor General's Council, Governors, Residents or Political Agents to the larger native states, senior military commanders—did not consider themselves bound to make any report about their bibis. Some, in fact, kept the existence of their bibi hidden. Similarly, while some of the Sahib Bahadurs, when leaving India, or making their wills, left some money or bequest to the bibi, many did not refer to them at all, leaving them to their own devices.

It also happened oftentimes that the sahib would abandon a low-born bibi in favour of a well-born or a high-born one, firmly turning his back upon the former, his own offspring by her and any others that she may have had from before. Should an Englishman make an announcement in a bibi's favour that he had taken her as his wedded wife, the English law and the rules of the Company Bahadur would not take cognizance of the marriage until it was solemnized in a proper church or had been contracted before a court recognized by the Company.

Even a Firangee's married wife, were she Indian, had no moral or legal right over the children she bore him. All that was allowed by stretching matters to the uttermost was that such offspring had two names, one Christian, the other Indian. Much of the regime and curriculum of the children's education and training were organized on English principles. Very often, the child—boy or girl—was taken away from the mother at about seven or eight years of age and sent off 'home', to England; sometimes the mother consented, sometimes her own wishes counted for nothing. In such cases, if the child returned to India and the mother's relationship with the sahib remained intact, or if the sahib himself had quit India or the life, but the child knew something about the mother's identity, he or she could find the mother, or maybe not. Their two spheres remained separate, regardless of whether or not the black waters of the ocean separated them.

Wazir Khanam was dimly conscious of these matters, but truth to tell, she did not feel much concerned. She knew, or imagined, that however much the sahibs might practise chicanery in their dealings with Indians as adversaries, they were scrupulously fair with the people whom they called their own: they kept their promises to them and they had a strong sense of personal honour. Thus, Marston Blake might not love her truly, but he would not break his word if he gave it to her. This was the reason why, she believed, he always addressed or described her as 'begam' in front of the servants and led everyone to assume that they had undergone an 'official' marriage or a nikah according to the Islamic law. This filled her with a measure of pride. She also led herself to assume that having orally affirmed the fact, there was no real hurry for Marston Blake to get the paperwork done and have witnesses to put their signatures on the document.

She did, once or twice, ask Marston Blake in guarded terms about a marriage contract and he always asserted that he had had both their names registered at the Residency as Sahib and Bibi and that she should regard this as no less than nikah. About their offspring, their rights and upbringing, Wazir believed that it was too early to ponder over those matters. She had no particular desire for motherhood and, in fact, often thought that over her next trip to Delhi she should consult Manjhli about birth control. It was only Manjhli who had some idea of Chhoti's state of mind, of the immense attraction that her body and her inner being as reflected in her external presence wielded over men of all types, and who knew that Wazir regarded her beauty and charisma as her only and entire possession and that she was determined to map out a new life for herself solely on the strength of her beauty and the power of her personality.

*

It took less than six months for Wazir to realize that though she was the mistress of the teeming, prosperous establishment of Marston Blake, her real position was that of a warm, attractive body in his bed. She came finally to appreciate the reality: it was pointless to expect that Marston Blake would have her in his house as his wedded wife and give her at least those rights which the Firangee sahibs suffered to bestow upon the Indian begams to whom they were officially married. Not too many weeks after her coming to Jaipur she heard about the circumstances of the celebrated General Palmer of the Deccan and Colonel Gardner of Avadh which encouraged her to dimly hope that a day would come when she and Marston Blake could spend their life as a respectable married couple, like those of other well-born families. She would adhere to her religion and her cultural practices, Marston Blake would follow his own creed, but inside the zenana, the real power would be in Wazir's hands; their children would grow up and stay in India and would rightfully be counted among the well-born Muslims.

As she constructed these elaborate castles of hope in her mind, she did not take account of the fact that Colonel Gardner's begam was high-born and that her people were not part of the plebeian class. She owned property in her own right, and was a daughter of the Navab of Khambayat. As for General Palmer's begam, indeed she was an adoptive daughter to the Emperor Shah Alam Bahadur Shah who now rested in Paradise. Where would Wazir stand in comparison to such eminence? It was like the lowly earth in contrast to the Higher Sphere where only spirits can dwell. Above all, both the General and the Colonel had given up their native country for good and adopted India as their home. Clearly, Marston Blake had no such intent at the present time, nor had he even hinted at doing so in the future.

Certainly, Wazir knew that even if the sahibs did not believe in caste or integral quality in birth, they were no less than Indians in the observance of rank and protocol and the regard that a person deserved by virtue of birth. On the contrary, the Indians had no problem with the women whom their own Indian masters married or with whom they had relations. They were quite willing to accept such a woman as queen or mistress or consort to the ruler. Yet they were strongly prejudiced against, and in fact, almost abhorred, the women possessed by the Firangee sahibs.

General Ochterlony had a low-caste Maratha maidservant convert to Islam and then he entered into a legal marriage with her. He remembered her in his will as 'Bibi Muhtaram Mubarakunnisa Begam, popularly called Begam Ochterlony', that is, 'The Honourable Bibi Mubarakunnisa Begam, also known as Begam Ochterlony'. He left her much money and property. Yet the Indians obstinately refused to honour her Islamic identity, far less her Navabi status. Her mansion, called the Haveli of Mubarakunnisa Begam, existed for many decades with no one living in it, and as narrated by the modern Urdu writer Mirza Farhatullah Beg, it was ultimately purchased to house a printing press, by one Maulavi Karimuddin, known to later generations as Fallon's collaborator on his *A New Hindustani English Dictionary* (1879). The mosque that she built in Hauz Qazi near her mansion still stands, but none go there to pray and people have named it 'Harlot's Mosque'.

Given these circumstances, could Wazir Khanam hope for any better treatment at the hands of her beloved compatriots? Was she willing to exist as a mere entertainment doll for an Englishman who not only professed a different religion but was also of a different social order, as well as one who led an alien way of life? Granted that she did not want for comforts, and that Indians of the low castes stinted nothing in giving her honour and respect. On her outings she travelled in a nalki. A closed, hard-roofed palanquin with a door and sunshade or a balcony at the front, a nalki was permitted only to the rich and powerful. But how long was all this going to last?

Wazir believed that she knew something above love, and even about 'ishq', a word that has so many meanings and is of such intensity that 'love' is perhaps the most banal translation of it. Did she have ishq for Marston Blake? She knew most of the famous lines of poems about love: someone seems to penetrate my heart without my knowing or asking; a fire seems to be raging in my breast. But what did the words really mean? Where did their truest meaning lie: the meaning that the heart should seize as the final, ineluctable truth? Did her heart always wish, always want that she should have her sahib in front of her always? He may be cold towards her or passionate, malicious or generous and loving, but she should have nothing in her heart but boundless attraction, constant susceptibility and unfathomable desire for Marston Blake. Did she have such feelings for him?

She recalled some verses of the Persian poet Jami (d. 1492) in his long poem *Yusuf Zulaikha*. Driven to the frenzy of total madness in her love for the Prophet Yusuf, Zulaikha had renounced the world and become a wandering mendicant. Many years later, when Yusuf encountered Zulaikha, it was not the imperious, uniquely beautiful Zulaikha, none of whose companions and ladies and maids could even begin to compete with her in beauty, whose proud, remote behaviour sent shivers down the spine of even the King of Egypt. Zulaikha's face was drawn, her beauty's harvest was laid waste, her back was bent and her steps unfirm, stumbling. Her eyes no longer glittered like diamonds; instead of gold-embroidered brilliantly designed dresses and gem-encrusted ornaments, rags covered her cachectic body.

Jami had described that poignant moment in the form of a question-and-answer dialogue between Yusuf and Zulaikha. A well-known conceit of Persian poetry, called saval-o-javab, the great poet had turned it into a tour de force of lyric and tragedy.

He said:
Where is your youth, where your beauty?
She said:
Far away from your union, I lost them on the way.
He said:
Why are your eyes so dull, so devoid of lustre?
She said:
Immersed in blood, lacking the sight of you.
He said:
How did your proud cypress-body become bent?
She said:
Because of the soul-searing weight of your absence.
He said:
Where are the gold, and the silver, that you had?
Where is your crown, where your jewelled diadem?
She said:
Everyone praised your beauty, everyone
Scattered pearls of your praise on my head
I bent my head, strewed my gold at their feet
And thus did I recompense them for the pearls they sprinkled
on me.

Chhoti Begam vividly remembered the emotion and the grief which overtook her when she first read those lines. She sobbed uncontrollably and barely managed a few hours' interrupted sleep that night. Turning over and over in her restless bed, she was overrun with the hope and the desire that she too may be lucky someday to know someone for whom her life and circumstances would change as they had for Zulaikha. So, did she have the same kind of resolve to cancel and negate her own being for the sake of Marston Blake? Oh, please be your age, Chhoti Begam! Poetry is just that, poetry, nothing more. But then, why did you cry so copiously when you read those lines? What were the tents of hope that you had erected in your heart: perhaps you too could love someone in the same way? Poetry sometimes assumes the degree of truth which people generally save for their faith.

Maybe, but what am I to do with that English scoundrel? When he looks at me meaningfully with his lips reddened with betel juice, I do want ardently that he take me in his arms . . .

If nothing else, Marston Blake was certainly very skilled in matters of love and making love. Experienced, possessed of unerring intuition, knowledgeable about women, he could understand, if not always anticipate, Wazir's every mood, every desire and every need, and he was fully able to satisfy her according to her mood of the moment. He never pursued her with such importunity as to make her feel tired; he never put her out of humour, or caused her to turn her face away. Nor did he ever behave so distantly that she would fret for his attention, wondering when it would be that he would look at her again and when would the dense scent of desire escape from his body and come flying to hers.

Marston Blake had a curious knack for knowing how to behave with Wazir in bed. He knew almost before Wazir herself what she wanted from him: when it was just a routine coupling, and when it was something more. When both were truly in the mood and their mutual responsiveness did not abate, then it would be that she did not feel put upon or he slow down for almost all night long.

As would be obvious, Wazir was a total stranger to the eroticism of sex and the manners and levels of lovemaking. She had made up for the deficiency—to a small extent certainly—by imagination, visualization and intimate girl talk with friends. But she learnt most from her own inner development and the changing climate of her body. Still, Marston

Blake would wing her along into worlds about which she could not have known in her hottest dreams and highest leaps and levels of imagination. For instance, she had been told that men knew nothing except fulfilment of their carnal desire. Many did not even know that a woman too could have demands of her own. And those who did know, could not care less. She often heard from her friends that so-and-so became pregnant quite by chance; her man might have taken some part in it, but she had had no idea at all—she had contributed nothing.

Men, she knew, wanted what they wanted and did what they did. They spared no thought for the woman's weariness, her not being in the mood, or not deriving any pleasure from the act. They had no idea about the woman's satisfaction: in fact, they could hardly imagine such a thing. Such was not the case with Marston Blake.

But did he love her? Did he feel ishq for her, by any chance? Or was it that rare stage after ishq, the state of fully knowing and being happy with someone? The Sufi calls it 'uns'. It happens when the frenzy of desire slackens, giving place to the calm of mind when desire, while not being irrelevant, is no longer the overmastering emotion. I do not know if these words have any real meaning at all. The signs and symptoms of love as described in books and by the poets, none of them seem of any consequence here.

Mir, a great poet of the eighteenth century, affectionately called Mir sahib, had such a neat verse about the symptoms of love. Wazir liked it so much that she often used to hum it when alone back in Delhi. Sometimes she even plucked up her courage and recited it to those who insisted on giving her presents as a token of their regard:

Everybody has claims to being a true lover
But how can I accept when there is nothing to show?
A tinge of blood in the tears, pallor on the face,
There should at least be some indicator of love.

Truth to tell, Marston Blake's face would bloom at the sight of her. His every gesture, all his body's gestures and his affectionate deportment revealed more than mere words that he delighted in her company and would always want to be around her. But then . . . ? Marital bond, formal ceremonies of pairing, these were too far yet. There was not even an informal paper between them. Still she felt confident that Marston Blake sahib would not be treacherous. And when a whole life stretched in front of them, it seemed inauspicious to talk about paper and signature and seal so early in the proceedings.

But does he love me true? And if he does, then what do I feel for him? There indeed was a small niggle in her heart somewhere. I know that I always look forward to his returning home. Granted that I worry about him when he is late. Agreed that over many nights we . . . Is this also called love? And if it is not love, why did I forsake my home, my father's door, my siblings' love, my religion, my caste and birth, and come here? There is an old saying: Keep your honour, then let others give you honour. I came here, leaving my honour back in Shahjahanabad. Will there be anyone whom I can call mine should he let go of my hand? Would I not be entirely without a home were I to leave him?

Let the future hold whatever it will. Now my life is without worries or discomfort. If wealth does not flow profusely, there is no want of it either. I command no respect among my equals of birth and family, but I do command the awe of outsiders and the low-born. I have forty or fifty servants all ready and alert to carry out my slightest wish. I am not just a Firangee's bibi, I am among the prominent figures of the city of Jaipur and am distinguished among all the bibis by virtue of my looks and good management of my home. My Sahib desires me greatly, all the serving men and women are happy under my regimen, and the tradesmen and moneylenders have respect for me. I am known as 'the begam from Delhi'. So what else should one need?

In fact, I am better off than that miss: Umdah Khanam. Could one ever put one's faith in the affection of these Navab types? They always keep their true emotions under wraps. Who is the true object of their desire? With whom are they really involved or will soon become involved? None can say. And then his is not the real Navabi yet. He is yet to occupy the Chair: who knows what will happen tomorrow? Anything may befall him, and he has no wealth of his own and is only a pensioner of the ruling Navab. His pension is certainly sumptuous, but the mansion, the appointments of the mansion, furniture, carpets—he owns nothing of those. All right, he has some servants of his own, but the rest are paid for by the State of Rampur and are not truly answerable to him.

Just let Manjhli look at me. This whole crowd of domestics and flunkeys are entirely under my thumb. I can fire whomever I want to and hire whomever I want. Before I came here, the Sahib had a maidservant, she was young, from somewhere in the east. She was always well turned out and bore herself with an air. She was ostensibly employed for gently kneading and pressing the Sahib's body so as to relax him when he was tired . . . and maybe something more . . . Well, I dismissed her out of hand, saying that if any such duties were needed, I was quite capable of performing them. The sahib did not dare utter a word.

And our eldest sister? Well, who can even begin competing with her? Chaste and pure and sweet like a houri from Paradise. But is her life at all worth being called a life? The business of bringing up the children, meeting all their needs by day or night, doing the husband's bidding and being at his beck and call at all times, living one's life in the thrall of the parents-in-law: can this be called living? At least, thus far I have not had to chafe under the airs and whims of my Sahib; on the contrary, it is he who has been deferring to me in all things. How sweet, how fresh were Bari's face and complexion, just like an Armenian doll, and now she is so dried out, so shrunk. Why should only women gather all the world's pain? Why should they bear all the load, I say! Is there not a proverb 'Call the handmaid a handmaid, she will weep in displeasure; call the wife a handmaid, she will smile at the joke'? That is just the reason why they say: Pronounce two words from the book and make her do whatever service you want. She will laugh it off even if you demean her. She will pretend it was a joke. Of what use is one's title of Begam sahib if that is where one ends up as a begam?

Well, I certainly am better than those 'ladies'. As they say: A live cat is better than a dead tiger. To hell with it if I am not a begam. But I am certainly not a maid or a nanny.

*

Gradually, Wazir taught herself to live as a bibi, and then, to be happy as a bibi. For this, she had to not only abandon her interior conflicts and questions about the world of love, but also make compromises, just as Marston Blake was obliged to make them. It must be granted here that Marston Blake did not stint the smallest bit in making the compromises and allowed Wazir to organize and run their house on lines that were desirable or at least acceptable to her.

The kind of homes that Wazir was familiar with always had a separate room for storing water. The water room had somewhat tall, wooden stands on which stood earthen pitchers and metal dippers. Well-to-do homes had also bottles of soft drinks made from the extract of keora, a plant that bears a uniquely scented flower, from mango pulp, and from thickened juice of pomegranate. A large, wooden tub for storing ice during the summer, with the ice coated with sawdust and covered with hessian, was an important fixture. There was a small platform, wooden or masonry, about nine to twelve inches high, at the distant end of the water room, away from the door. This platform had one or two large-mouthed earthen pitchers for storing water meant for a bath. The platform and the alcove nearby had also packets, boxes and leathern bottles containing oils, henna and chickpea flour treated with herbs (used as shampoo or soap), and bottles of fragrant water.

If the water room had space enough, a corner of it was used as a urinal in the winter and, in fact, in all weathers, if the room was large enough. It was directly connected to a water outlet and the user was expected to wash it down with sufficient water after every use so as to drive away the smell. The lavatory used to be quite separate, in a far corner of the home.

Wazir was annoyed no end to see that Marston Blake was using the water room as a lumber room. He told her that very little water was drunk in English homes, and a china or enamel bowl was used in the bedroom for passing water. It stood on a small stool, or sometimes under the bed. Wazir had never seen a pisspot before and was horrified when Marston Blake pointed it out to her in his bedroom. She learnt that women and men used their own pots; no regard was paid to cleaning up after using the pot, nor was the sharp alkaline smell considered a problem in the bedroom. A scavenging woman reported every morning and evening to empty and, if necessary, rinse the pot. And bathing? Well, one thorough bath every four or five weeks was considered quite hygienic, and that was it. Scrubbing the face and body vigorously and then applying a very fine dust all over was seen as sufficient. This dust, fragrant like soap, and white and far finer than the finest flour, often stuck to the hands or the face and body. It was something like rouge, used in superabundance, and could have been called an unguent if it were not dry and fine like soapstone dust. Its generic name was 'powder', but Wazir never learnt to pronounce it correctly so as to rhyme with 'louder'. She always pronounced it to sound somewhat like 'pauder'.

This pauder, God help her, was used many times a day by Marston Blake, but could not really take away his body odour. English menfolk never used any attar or any kind of perfume. Marston Blake always said that women may scent themselves as much as they want, but the scent of tobacco was the best kind of perfume there was for a man.

20

Marston Blake asks an unexpected question of Wazir Khanam, now the mother of his two children

WAZIR SET UP the water room once again, gave away the hated pisspots to the scavenging woman and established the routine of daily baths in the morning. These were obligatory on Marston Blake too. After this first major change, her second step was to send the woman packing who had been employed at the job of kneading and gently pressing Marston Blake's tired limbs. The next major change she instituted in culinary matters. She knew that in the Christian religion, no foods were forbidden, practically nothing was taboo. Pork she had already declared out of bounds for her house. About wines and spirits she conceded that they could be consumed in the drawing room, but nowhere else. The most surprising thing that she found about foods was that the English had no concept of fresh or stale in regard to meat. Other than pork, they were, of course obliged to eat the meat called zabiha, that is, meat of animals slaughtered in accordance with the formalities prescribed by the Islamic law: the shariah. This was because non-zabiha meat was not sold anywhere in the city. But the English were not very particular about stale or smelly meat. The trick was to kill the smell by the liberal use of strong spices.

In regard to milk, the English favoured goat's milk above all others; they did not mind, or were unable to feel, its strong smell. Wazir prohibited goat's milk and stale meat. In order that there would be a continuous supply of fresh meat and eggs, she set up a virtual aviary of chickens, partridges, quails, ducks, peafowls and pigeons. Marston Blake wanted to keep rabbits too, but Wazir refused. She knew that rabbit's meat was not forbidden, but it was not among the favoured Muslim foods. Two cows and one water buffalo were acquired to ensure continuous supply of fresh milk. Additional staff was appointed to take care of the birds and animals.

There was a department of the hunt, which had dogs and their specialized caretakers, called doria. Surplus game meat, fowl or ungulate, was never kept overnight. It was given away to the servants and favoured neighbours.

Yet there was one matter in which Marston Blake just did not consent to Wazir's wish. In the homes of well-born Indians, women ate after the men and in strict seclusion. Even the husband or male siblings were not permitted to enter the zenana when women were eating. Marston Blake insisted that if not breakfast, Wazir must sit with him at the table for lunch and dinner. She must use knives and forks as well. Chhoti Begam declared that she would much rather take poison than commit the shameless act of eating in his company. After a prolonged argument it was decided that the Sahib and the bibi would eat dinner together at the table, but if there was another male guest for dinner, Wazir would join them only if the guest was a really special person. She was not obligated to go beyond that in the service of the Sahib. Eating with him at the table or even on the floor around a tablecloth was like an onerous service to her. When Marston Blake began to educate her in the use of different knives and forks, he was surprised and delighted that his lovely pupil picked up the distinctions between different knives and forks in just one or two lessons.

Wazir's conversations with Marston Blake did not normally go beyond household matters or a cursory exchange of news. Her Sahib regularly received the post from Vilayat ('The Country', meaning England), but Wazir was never made privy to their contents. Did Marston Blake have a family, or sisters and brothers in The Country? Were his parents alive and if so where were they and what was their state of affairs? He never shared information with her on these matters.

Wazir knew, or had heard people say, that many sahibs acquired bibis in India while they had a wife or a girl to whom they were formally engaged to be married back in Vilayat. It was but certain that they would go back to them whenever the occasion arose. No bibi could resist or obstruct them in this matter. Since she had no idea of her Sahib's parents, there was little chance of her getting to know about the existence of a Firangee wife or a betrothed in the far country.

There was much that she did not approve of in the Firangees', and even Marston Blake's, attitude to and opinion about Indians. There were occasions when her disagreement would result in a quarrel. Marston Blake believed that Indians were, by and large, primitive and lacked culture. He scoffed at their excessive preoccupation with elaborate ceremonies at every possible occasion of their lives. He would often say to Wazir that her people had found a nice way of losing both money and honour. Well, so far Wazir perhaps could agree with him, at least partially, but the English placed no value on the beliefs of Indians, their ways of life, their professions, their faiths. Worse still, two things were clear not merely through their words or even veiled remarks, but in their way of spending time in India, and their strategies and tactics for enhancing their personal wealth. First, they were here to exact and extract wealth; and second, if on their way to exacting wealth they were obliged to rule, they were not above practising deception, conspiracy, bribery or war. In fact, they were always prepared to do so. She remembered the verse of Mushafi:

How well are the Nazarenes versed in scheming
to join or break off!
First thing they do in battle is to induce
the enemy commander to break away.

Wazir observed a curious thing in Marston Blake's house: petty thefts were endemic. It was a rare servant who was not a petty thief by habit or was averse to fudging the household accounts by small amounts. These petty dishonesties did not cause much damage to the house finances, but they irked Marston Blake no end; he always fretted and fumed when such things happened and the truth was he did have the right on his side. Yet there came occasions, though very rarely, when he lost his temper and stormed at Indians in general and declared them dishonest by nature.

Wazir would then cry angrily that there was something wrong in the home arrangement or even the character of the English sahibs—may their heads be cut off—for, servants in our homes never, never committed the smallest theft of cash or goods.

'So you mean to say that we taught them to steal?' Marston Blake would retort angrily.

'You may not have taught them,' she would cry out, 'but God will be our witness to say that our servants are not thieves. True, you did not teach them to steal. But did you ever stop to think from whom they contracted this vicious habit?'

'There is nothing to think about. All bastards, these Indians. They are all the same.'

'It is you, the English, who don't believe in marriage or legal wedding, and you describe my people as bastards! Don't let such words ever pass your lips again, or I . . .'

She was panting a little because of fury and the heat of emotion. Marston Blake also realized that he had, for no reason, let the matter deteriorate into a quarrel. He fetched a bottle of pomegranate juice from the water room, and said to her humbly, trying to placate her: 'Here, drink a couple of spoonfuls of this. It will soothe your nerves. Come, put an end to all this. I am sorry.'

Wazir wiped her eyes with the hem of her light wrap; a tiny smile illumined her lips. The Sahib's habit of apologizing always seemed strange and also pleasing and heart-warming to her. He never hesitated to say 'I'm sorry'. She always heard it as 'Am sorrrray' and loved to hear it. She knew that men, as a rule, never apologized. Sometimes she would deliberately play a little harmless mischief, starting an argument, which would end with the Sahib's 'Am sorrrray'.

On the other side, the Sahib also loved his bibi's mutilation of simple English words, which she somehow could never learn to pronounce with a modicum of accuracy. In her argot, 'Christmas' was 'kismis', 'champagne' was 'sampan', 'parsley' was 'petersly'. To be sure, her Sahib was no less in making mincemeat of simple Hindi words, some of which, she learnt much later, had passed into the English language of the day. When he talked to Wazir, Marston Blake always pronounced those and other Hindi words with reasonable correctness, but his tone and pronunciation changed when he spoke to the servants or other Englishmen. Then, pikdan (spittoon) would become pigdane; pikdani (small spittoon) would be pigdanny; chhint (cotton cloth with small floral patterns) became chintz; chitthi (a note, a letter) changed shape as chit; champi (rubdown) became shampoo; a sipahi was turned into a sepoy, and the extremely simple food cooked with plain rice and lentil was transformed from khhichri to kedgeree, a dish somewhat superior to the poor khhichri.

All this was child's play for the Sahib. Their life did not lack for moments of levity and good humour, and the mangling of Hindi words provided yet another such occasion. But there was always a little bit of discomposure in her heart about those domestic thefts, as if there was some business which she had left unfinished. She wanted to tell the Sahib that in our heart we Indians regard you Firangees as usurpers and interlopers and that is the reason why some of our people have no hesitation or scruple about stealing from you. Then, she had wanted to go on and say, you have no respect for us as a people. You came here to do trade, but your inequities have exceeded even that low-born water carrier's who was said to have become King of Kabul for two and a half days. Your people have assumed the airs and styles of kings and rulers. You converted into a kitchen the Divan-e Khas of our King's Fort in Agra. The Fort had already suffered much from the depredations of the Afghans and the Jats and the Marathas, now your men are intent upon making a little quick money by selling off its yet extant beauties. Yes, I grant that you as a person are very good to me, but God's land is much wider than this little house here in Jaipur.

There was this, and much more, which she never could articulate. Her greatest dilemma was that Marston Blake pleased her no end; she wanted him, and yet if she did not hate the English and their ways, she was certainly repelled by many things they did. In regard to personal hygiene and ritual cleanliness, she had already converted the Sahib to her belief and practice. She had, of course, given her firm verdict about the pig, that black-faced unclean beast on the very first day; and she had her own water room and water man because in English homes the water man also served wines and spirits, so the Sahib's water man was an untouchable for her.

All that was very well, but it seemed certain to her that in matters of state, the Firangees had plans to eventually rule her land, enforce their laws and customs everywhere, and make Indians their subjects just as she was her sahib's subject. She was also now convinced that the Sahib, like all other Firangees, did not in the least bit like anything of India or Indians. She could now appreciate how difficult it was to live with people with myriad complexities and unpredictabilities built into the situation.

With whom could she share such confidences, and if she did have such a confidante, how and from where could she find the words to say the unsayable and the intangible? She knew very well that the relationship between her and her Sahib was primarily based on matters and transactions of the bedroom; matters of state and politics did not intrude there. Whom should she look to were the Sahib to leave her? She would have to restart her struggle to meliorate her affairs and use her beauty as her capital.

The times were such that whether it be the capital in Delhi, or the whole of the land of Hindustan, all were absorbed in their own affairs and in the making or unmaking of their own lives. It was each one to himself. And so, if Chhoti Begam too was looking to manage and improve her own lot, who could blame her?

The Red Haveli in Delhi, subjected to repeated acts of vandalism and war, was still home to those who ruled her land, and it was a formidable memorial to their forebears. It would now seem that unless razed to the ground by the English cannonade, the time would come soon enough when the Firangee flag would be flying from its ramparts. Ruler and Emperor, both roles would be assigned to or seized by the Kristans. Small wonder if thousands of girls like Wazir were trampled underfoot or ground to paste in the race for self-aggrandizement and the mad pursuit of self-interest that was bound to take place among the warring parties.

Today, she at least had a haven, but what of that? I should have been running a state or a court, or been the chief ornament of a royal bedroom, rather than having to earn my keep by doing domestic drudgery for a white-skinned buffoon, living as a queen in name and a slave in effect.

But . . . it is also a fact that my Sahib desires me immensely and I too love to be with him in the privacy of . . .

*

It took a great deal of argument before Wazir could persuade Marston Blake to approve the name Badshah Begam for their first daughter. He refused to consider any other name than Sophia, a name that identified her as a Christian. After a great amount of discussion in the first instance, he agreed to Masih Jan, a name that was vaguely Muslim and could also be taken as Christian, but the baby was to be baptized only as Sophia. When, in the labour room, Chhoti Begam turned her face away from everyone present and swore an oath that she did not mind the baby being taken away from her, but she would not ever look at her if she was to be named just Sophia, Marston Blake softened a little. But there was more disputation and contestation before it was agreed that 'Badshah Begam' too would be one of the infant's names, but she must be baptized as Sophia, though the mullah would utter the ritual call to prayer in the baby's ear with Badshah Begam as her name.

So the dispute was somehow resolved, but during those days Wazir was introduced to some of Marston Blake's relatives: William Cotterill Tyndale, a cousin from his mother's side, and his sister Abigail Tyndale. William had been in Mysore and was engaged in the trade of making supplies to the English troops. The regiment to which he was attached had now moved to Jaipur and the Tyndales had followed in due course.

William was unmarried yet and his sister, though older by many years, was a spinster still. Many years ago she had left the mother country to join her little brother and had since been living with him as housekeeper and virtual owner of William's establishment. She was quite short of stature, with small blue eyes and brown hair shot with grey, and she had a pleasing though high voice. She was a strong churchgoer and extremely pious.

Very soon Abigail became 'Aby memsahib' to everyone in Marston Blake's house, including Chhoti Begam. William and Aby had set up their own house but the latter spent quite a bit of her time at Marston Blake's, and unofficially assumed the role of governess and caregiver to Sophia. It was therefore natural that Sophia's upbringing imbibed a strong colour of Protestant Christianity. Aby memsahib talked to Sophia in English. Sophia's mother and sundry maids in the house had of course no English, so they talked to her in Hindi. Thus Sophia, by the age of two or a little less, became perfectly bilingual in Hindi and English.

It was an irony of sorts that in spite of having been taught by a native speaker to speak English, the 'true' English sahibs and memsahibs believed that Sophia's English accent had a heavy overlay of Hindustani speech. Many years later, when Lady Emily Bayley, daughter of Sir Thomas Metcalfe, Agent to the Governor General Bahadur and Resident at the Court of Delhi, had occasion to meet Sophia Marston Blake socially, she recorded scornfully in her diary that Sophia sang an English song, but her accent was so heavily plebeian and Hindustani that she, Emily Bayley, could not understand a word of what she sang.

As recorded above, the Tyndale brother and sister were staunch Protestants, and even more than that, they were Calvinists. Thus, while they accorded high value to 'service', 'patriotism', 'industry' and 'thrift', they were also self-righteous and regarded all other sects, whether Christian or not, as benighted. They looked upon poverty and the poor with undisguised suspicion and hostility because they had been led to believe that God must have had very good reasons to make someone poor. They had no sense of humour and lacked the taste for all non-religious poetry and music.

William was a man of few words, but Aby's tongue worked like a pair of sharp scissors in expert hands. She missed no opportunity to assert or declare that Indians were black not only from the outside, but also that there was no difference between blackness of skin and the absolute colour of blackness; and as blackness meant depravity and poverty in reasoning power, there could be no salvation for Indians. Wazir's colour, which Indians regarded as light brown and desirably salty, was nothing but 'dark brown' in her eyes. She plotted and planned in her heart to liberate her cousin from the clutches of his dark woman and marry him off to some suitable, white, soft-spoken, good Christian girl. Since that consummation was not on the immediate horizon, she devoted all her energy to the upbringing and moral education of Sophia so that she could save at least one soul from perdition.

Chhoti Begam found the Tyndales different from Marston Blake in many ways. She now realized that all Firangees were not similar in character and temperament, but arrogance, pomposity and the sense of being members of the ruling elite were traits common to all of them. Marston Blake and the Tyndales were dissimilar, but also similar in many ways. For instance, Aby was even less meticulous than Marston Blake in personal hygiene. She did not clip her fingernails regularly and very often the undersides of her nails were encrusted and discoloured with dirt. Still, Aby had no hesitation in pushing her finger into the mouths of Wazir's children, encouraging them to suck. Wazir felt revolted but could do nothing except wait for an opportune moment to disengage the offending finger; complaining to Marston Blake would have been of no avail. A dirty fingernail or two in the mouth of his baby mattered little to him.

Quite unlike his sister, William Tyndale was almost obsessive about personal hygiene. And he was soft-spoken and said little, while Aby was quick to take offence. In matters of money they were similar: both brother and sister were pretty close with it. Neither was particular about food though, unlike their cousin who had a gourmet's taste for good food. However, no matter their unattractive qualities, the Tyndales had conferred a great advantage on Wazir: Now she could proudly and truthfully say that she had social relations with the Firangees too. She did not look upon herself any more as one who lagged behind in the social field, as had been the case when she first arrived in Jaipur and the English would not deign to give her even a casual glance.

Sometimes, Chhoti Begam sensed that Aby was jealous of her because she was pretty and generally attractive in spite of her complexion. She suspected that Aby expended so much attention and affection on her children because Aby saw it as a strategy to wean away Marston Blake's children from their mother's influence. Chhoti disliked this cordially, but she suffered Aby's attention to the children because, in the first place, she did not feel much inclined to go the hard way in bringing up and nurturing her children, and in the second place, she was really too young to be a fully attentive mother. She believed that suckling the babies for too long and keeping awake at night to change their diapers, put them on her shoulder, burp them and lull them to sleep, would cause her body to lose its youthful tightness and proportionate shapeliness, and the fresh bloom of her face would give place to sickly pallor. True, she loved to have babies, but to undergo the hardship of bringing them up . . . May God and the Prophet forgive me, I cannot do it. Not everyone has the stamina of Bari Baji.

These were the reasons why Chhoti was content to delegate most, if not all, the duties of her children to the maids and to Aby memsahib. At the time of Badshah Begam's birth, Martin Blake, also named Amir Mirza, was about two years old (b. 1827). There was an in-house ayah for the two children, while for outdoor care and supervision, there was a maid called 'dai khilai' ('maid-for-play'). There was also a suckling maid for Sophia, and there had been one for Amir Mirza when he was small. Wazir had been careful in her choice of suckling maids. They were Muslim, and not low-born. Marston Blake was quite content with the arrangement about suckling the babies, for this made for easy availability of Wazir's services in bed and general erotic play. He was not too fond of young babies anyway, but was certainly generous in bringing them gifts, sweets and toys.

*

The weather was very cold; there were a few weeks to the Christmas—called Bara Din (Great Day) by Indians—of 1829, but preparations for it had had commenced already. Animals were being fatted, cases of champagne and Portuguese and English wines were being procured from Calcutta. Christmas gifts were being organized for near and distant relatives, children, hangers-on, servants. The servants too were much taken by the task of having to find suitable presents, called 'dali' (basket), for their masters.

The convention for the dali was that the gift-giver had to be presented with a gift of the same value or somewhat greater than the original one. The servants at Jaipur brought, instead of the popular gifts of sweets or fruits, items of local craftsmanship, some of which could be used in the house, and some that were merely decorative pieces of no particular use. Still, their price was assessed and a return gift of a suitable value given. Wealthy Indians and some of the English imported, at good prices, well in advance of the great day, costly goods for the purpose of giving presents to the high and mighty: silk fabrics with gold-works from Benaras, gold lace thread from Delhi and Agra, stylish shoes from Ajmer, jewellery with enamel on gold from Udaipur, silk, woollen shawls and bales for dresses from Kashmir. These and similar objects were much in demand. Sophia was eighteen months old at that time, and Martin was just above three. Maids-to-play and other ayahs were in place for them. Aby memsahib had forced the removal of Sophia's suckling maid, to no great objection from Wazir, so as to inculcate self-confidence in the child.

As preparations for Bara Din were going on, one day, both children were out playing under the watchful eyes of their maids. Marston Blake was a little under the weather and had taken the day off. Lying face down on his huge bed, he was trying to get some sleep. Wazir was gently pressing his back.

'Stop all this,' he smiled. 'Or I'll have to shut the door.'

'May the good God forgive us,' she retorted. 'All the time you have no thought but this. Look at these servants, sneaking everywhere like thieves to see how the land lies. What will they say?' The plethora of servants made it difficult for conversations to be carried out with any degree of privacy.

'What could they say? Do such things not happen in their homes?'

'I beg God's forgiveness! I will go away now and leave you alone!' Wazir was about to rise but Marston Blake held her firmly by the forearm, sat up on the bed, and said, 'All right. But tell me, are you happy with me?' He held her chin and raised her head so that he could look into those eyes, dark brown with a hint of leaf green and flashes of gold. 'Have no fear. Tell me boldly.'

Wazir lowered her large eloquent eyes, as if she were thinking, weighing her words before she spoke. And fallen in serious thought she really was. Why was Sahib asking this question at this time? Nothing had been discussed of late, for example, about the children's future, or about her desire to go back home, even if briefly, and visit with her father and sisters. One of the things that she greatly liked about Marston Blake was his frankness and refusal to beat about the bush. Unlike Indians, who always took their time and used devious paths to arrive at a point, and even then preferred to state their purpose through vague hints, Marston Blake came to the point without demur and stated his purpose quite unambiguously. Indians were reticent with everyone, husband with wife, son with father, and so on, but her Sahib had no time for such reticence. He spoke plain and fair, and Wazir too adopted this way to a large extent. Still, she found herself diffident and nearly tongue-tied when she needed to speak her mind freely, and her Sahib was such a dolt (such persons must be called by no other name) that he would never take a hint, or was never prepared to take the hint.

She had a sudden impulse to say, 'All else is well, but there is no paper, no covenant between us. Have you given any thought at all to my future?' But she could not have said such words, even on pain of death. She raised her eyes, smiled briefly, and said, 'Yes, happy I am. Very happy, but . . .' She lowered her head again.

'Go on, go on. But what? What is it that you lack? Tell me, I'll provide it at once. Don't be scared. Speak freely.'

'No. Not at all. I do not lack anything,' she said, giving an unconscious or conscious stress on 'thing'. 'Don't I have all that I need? But why do you ask this today? I know; you aren't well today, so it has occurred to you to make a little fun of me for you have nothing else to do.'

'No. Fun has got nothing to do with what I am asking. In fact, the thought just crossed my mind that you're here far away from your own for my sake.'

'I am here for no other reason. You know it well. And this is precisely my answer.'

'Bravo! My dear one!' Marston Blake said. Both were, of course, speaking in Hindi. On occasions such as this, the Sahib's accent unconsciously assumed the intonations of the English when they mispronounced or mutilated Hindi words out of ignorance or out of the desire to maintain distance and superiority. Wazir Khanam did not like it at all but always succeeded in suppressing her distaste. 'I am very, very pleased with you.' He continued in the same patronizing tone. 'I'm proud of you.'

Wazir disliked the patronizing tone even more than the artificial Hindi accent, but again, she pretended that she too was 'very, very' pleased.

'Sahib, what is there indeed for you to be proud about? Is there anyone anywhere who would not like to live in your benevolent shade?'

'No, you are different, different altogether. Just what was that verse of Khusrau, your Persian poet of Delhi? What a delightful verse! I cannot exactly recall the words, please just give me a clue.'

'I do not know which verse you're referring to.'

'Oh, please do try to recall it . . . something like this: "You are different . . ." Do you recall now?'

Now Wazir Khanam had no choice but to recite the verse in question. 'Yes, I do remember now,' she said.

I have roamed the universe, have assessed the loves of all beauties,
I have seen many lovely ones, but . . .

Marston Blank promptly supplied the remaining words:

. . . you are something different!

'Great! How true indeed!' he added.

'That may be,' Wazir replied. 'Those were other people, other times—'

But Marston Blake interrupted her again. 'All right, everything is understood. But do please tell me if you're happy living with me, or not.'

She laughed. 'Look at the poor man! He heard the whole of the Ramayana and now he wants to know who is Sita! Did I not say that it is for your sake that I live here? Your doorstep is the threshold of my joys. There, are you content? You now know the full account of my heart.'

Marston Blake made no reply this time. Perhaps he wanted something more from Chhoti Begam. Perhaps he hoped for her to be more passionate in her declarations, talk about everlasting gratitude, and about the pleasures of the body that were hers because of him. She remained silent for a moment, and then spoke, 'This huge, magnificent home, full of people and things, the power, the honour, and you . . .'

She wanted to say, 'Your love, your ways of enticing and ravishing my heart', but something, perhaps modesty, had descended from somewhere upon her tongue and stopped it. Her desired words remained buried in the depths of her heart. Marston Blake smiled enigmatically.

'And those two babies, like the sun and the moon,' he said, 'and I, who would give up my life for your beauty's sake . . .'

'Certainly, where else could I have found these things? And not only me, none in the world could have ever found such blessings. It is God's own special grace on me.'

She did say the words sincerely enough, but had also thought to ask somehow, in some way or the other: If you really are so keen and ready to give up your very life for me, would it not be proper for you to make me at least your official bibi, if not your legally wedded wife? But the Sahib was looking at her in that special way of his, his eyes full of heartfelt desire and pride, and a sense of both belonging and ownership. Wazir felt she was melting inside.

'May I say something?' Marston Blake asked suddenly.

'Yes, surely. You do not need to ask me.'

'So then listen. At the beginning of the New Year 1830, I will petition you for your hand in marriage. I'll get a pay raise next year, and maybe later a raise in rank as well. Then we could perhaps move back to Delhi.'

Wazir was struck dumb to the core of her being. Delhi? As the legally married wife of a sahib like Blak sahib? Does a blind man need eyes! A tremor ran through her body, almost unendingly. She somehow rose and grasped Marston Blake's hand firmly as if she were tying the marriage knot right at that moment.

'So? Do you accept? Are you happy now?'

'Very happy! I was happy before too. But now you promise me Paradise even as I live. May God enhance your fortunes even more.'

Marston Blake caught her in his arms and began to shower kisses on her hands, lips, hair, neck and forehead. She kept trying to ward him off, saying, 'Please. Let me be, leave me. The servants will see us!'

*

A little while later, Marston Blake lay back on the bed and turning so as to face Wazir, fell asleep almost immediately. Perhaps his heart was now lightened after disclosing his proposal for marriage. The tremor in Wazir's heart was now diminished, but only to be replaced by worry, and something like perplexity.

She had been free so far, at least this was what she believed. If disagreements happened between her and the Sahib, or if the Sahib himself became bored with her, the possibility existed of her throwing a handful of dust at the past and beginning anew. But marriage? She would then become just another bonded labourer, or at best yet another maidservant. The Sahib could divorce her at will, and if that happened, it would be like having her hands and legs broken. A mere maidservant you already are, don't delude yourself. Can you live without your children? But are the children really mine? True, they're fluent in Hindi; if they grow up and live long enough I'll teach them ghazal, masnavi and other forms of Hindi poetry. I'll have them read Persian, and Arabic too. I'll have them trained in calligraphy, in horsemanship. I will make them Mirzas, people of culture and quality. But let them first be with me, grow up alongside me, only then can these things be. The Sahib has not expressed any intent to me about the children one way or another. But Aby memsahib's schemes are quite clear to me. She's determined to make them not only Christian, but properly English too and will not rest until they're taken away from me. They say the English never let go of one of their own blood, even if he has Muslim blood too. In fact, that was why Akhtarloni sahib converted his Maratha maid to Islam, named her Mubarakunnisa, and gave her the title of Begam. Blak sahib will also take away my babies eventually . . . I was made to live my life on my own, surely. These times are not ordinary times, they're like the upheaval and the tumult of Doomsday, it is each one to himself, no one is ever going to stop and look to the other. I and Blak sahib . . . the servants say we make a nice couple . . . but he's Kristan and English, I am Indian and Muslim to boot. His people dream of ruling us someday soon. Can such a man ever be mine and remain mine? And I too need some room, a place of my own to breathe freely. Why should I live as someone's subject, even if that someone was a Firangee sahib? Should I reject his proposal to marry? Indeed, Blak sahib seems to think that he's doing me a world of good, and asking nothing new in return. But I have already given away my honour to him. Now he may do gratuitous good to me or deliver a kick on my back. I have drawn the map of my life. There is a great deal of Blak sahib in it, but then . . .? If I refuse to marry him, will he still keep me or will he ask me to leave? Truth to tell, leaving does not seem to be a bad prospect, but where do I go, what should I take with me? What should I leave behind? My soul may be in my body or may leave it, but Blak sahib's love is ensconced in it. I should undergo a Muslim marriage with him and also have the paper ratified in the Firangee's Court. But then I will become more bound and yet more bound. Think, how calamitous and frightening are these times. There is nothing to be relied upon, neither life nor promise nor covenant. Blak sahib is an officer in the army. One day, he will certainly be sent to the active front. Then . . . I hope the devil is not listening! Who knows what may befall him? If nothing much, he might still be wounded and lose his limbs. Who will then look after him, feed him, change his clothes? And suppose—far be it from the reality—he loses his life there, who will hold the hand of poor, unlucky me in my disaster? Granted that these are remote possibilities; nothing of the sort will happen. But if Blak sahib decides to return to The Country? True, he does say that he will live here and die here, but can anyone ever place her trust in a male, and on top of that, a Nazarene Firangee one? I would say even an atheist is better. Who knows when his people in The Country, or if no one else, this Aby memsahib and her brother, may conspire against me? Blak sahib may lose his heart someday to a woman of white skin. In fact, I should first take care of my own self. But there is no doubt about it: Blak sahib has some strange power to attract, like the effect of the magic mantra called mohini. It is said that one who knows it can make any woman fall in love with him. He must possess something of that sort. That terrible night, on our way back from Khvajah Sahib, overtaken by the dust storm, how my heart leapt up when I first looked at him! Had he not held our hand, it would have been curtains for all of us there. Dacoits would have grabbed me, or who knows a genie might have carried me off. He did not lack for women to service him or love him. But am I not one in a thousand myself? Could he ever find a wife so accomplished, meritorious and pretty as me? Maybe his relatives and friends do not approve, but he took me by the hand and is now talking of marriage. Should I look at things from his point of view? Did God give me a heart so that it should ache at everyone's loss and pain? If Blak sahib loves me true, I too have given up all for him. I too have lost so much to get him. Are there great sacrifices on his side alone and on my side only carnal joys and living expensively with not a care in the world? The reality is quite different. But are there any to see with the eye of justice?

Sleep overtook her, she did not know when. She awoke to the happy noise of the children when they came back from play. With her head and shoulder on the bed frame, she had been sleeping in a singularly uncomfortable posture. Her body ached from head to toe, but what surprised her was the wetness of her dupatta. It could not have been perspiration alone.

21

Marston Blake faces danger as intrigue smoulders in the Jaipur Palace

GREAT DAY CAME, with celebration and rejoicing everywhere. Christmas bells were tolled in the churches, services were held; there were visits and return visits. Heaps of sweets and other presents filled Wazir's house. Even the Maharajah sent some choice goods, including a rath made of ivory: about one and a half feet in length and a little less than a foot high, it had two bullocks saddled to it, the rath driver on his box, and inside the rath, a newly married young couple in full court dress. From the designs on the foreheads of the bullocks to the dresses and ornaments of the young couple, everything was so neatly and accurately carved, and painted in such appropriate colours that it seemed they had been carved from life and represented the real people of some country where everything was small. Wazir was transported at the beautiful and obviously costly gift. She spent a whole day considering, experimenting, placing and replacing the rath in various parts of the house so as to gain the maximum effect of the magnificent objet d'art.

The New Year arrived almost in continuation of Great Day and was celebrated with its wonted pomp and enthusiasm. Immediately after the New Year's Day, Colonel Alves Sahib, the Political Agent for Rajputana, proceeded to Calcutta on six weeks' holiday, appointing Marston Blake to function as his Deputy and be in charge of the Residency. This was an even happier day for Wazir, for, according to her understanding, this should be the first, even if tentative, step towards her Sahib's preferment. Her impression became stronger when, apart from the domestic staff, even the Tyndales congratulated her and Marston Blake at the event.

As the Hindi poet says: *Those whose rank is higher, their problems too are greater*. With the increase in Marston Blake's power and responsibility came more work and cause for anxiety. According to the Company Bahadur's method of working, the Political Agent's duties included those of the Chief of Police and Judge for areas directly controlled by it. Every day, there was a cause list to be attended to, and small or large matters to be adjudicated. Sometimes the Maharajah's Court referred complaints or controversial issues to the Political Agent for immediate advice or direction, if the issue had some political significance. General political matters, the mail from Calcutta and from Residents of nearby states: these needed to be tackled on an immediate basis. All this made Marston Blake's usually sunny temperament somewhat irascible; moreover, he had to bear the hardship of having to attend to papers at home too—a bundle of important documents always followed him home.

The internal, local politics of the native states, the rivalries between the ranis competing for the Rajah's favour, military expenditure, training and instruction of incompetent or inefficient rulers or their progeny, reports about unrest or the state of peace and prosperity among the Maharajah's subjects, these matters needed daily monitoring by the Political Agent. It was not irregular for some Residents to spend most of their time in secretly acquiring information from their spies and communicating with their informers at the Court.

About two weeks had passed since Colonel Alves's departure for Calcutta when Chand Khan the cook, returning from important purchases for the kitchen, stood at Marston Blake's camp office door at home. Marston Blake was busy with the mail from Calcutta and took no notice of the cook. After waiting some time, Chand Khan cleared his throat to signal his presence. Entering the camp office without permission was forbidden, and Blake's inattention to Chand Khan's presence signalled his unwillingness to let anyone interrupt him at his work at that moment. Gathering up his courage, Chand Khan again cleared his throat, louder this time. Marston Blake looked up and asked somewhat unpleasantly, 'Yes? What is it? I'm busy.'

'With Your Honour's permission, I have to say something . . . May I come in?'

Observing the tension and anxiety on Chand Khan's face, Marston Blake said grudgingly, 'All right. Be quick about what you have to say. What is it, is there a crisis of some sort?'

'Yes, Your Honour . . . our Sawai Maharajah Jai Singh Sahib Bahadur . . . Your Honour knows he has been unwell for some time.'

Marston Blake did not at all like the phrase 'our Maharajah', but he let it pass and spoke reprovingly with knitted brow, 'Yes, so what? How are you concerned? You are our servant, aren't you?'

'Yes, Your Honour, but . . . but the matter is that . . .'

'Out with whatever the hell you wish to say! Stop this stupid repetition of buts and ifs, man!'

'Yes, Your Command, the matter is that . . . rumours are rife in the bazaar that there is a conspiracy . . . to poison the Maharajah.'

At this Marston Blake sat up, putting back his papers in their cloth portfolio; he straightened the wrinkles in his tunic and rearranged on his desk various items like inkstand and paperweights, thus gaining some time to collect his thoughts. The Maharajah did not lack enemies. Such rumours were routine anyway. But then, at the present juncture, this rumour had quite another meaning. He said, with apparent unconcern, 'This must have originated in some opium den. Where did you get to hear it, man?'

'Your Command, I had gone to the Hawa Mahal to visit with my brother. The Maharajah's army is stationed there. Your Command is aware that my brother is also in that army.'

Marston Blake made no reply. He knew about the cook's brother. It was his business to know such things. He waited for the cook to go on.

'There was a whisper circulating there among the sepoys that Lala Jhunta Ram, the Maharajah's Attorney General, is of the view that the ailing Maharajah should be removed and the way cleared for himself to become the Regent of the Infant Maharajah and rule in his name. But the people do not at all like Jhunta Ram.'

'That is, should it happen, the people will be up in arms against the Attorney General?'

'It is strongly possible, Your Presence.'

What was more significant from the Company's point of view was that Jhunta Ram was on good terms with the neighbouring rajahs of Ajmer, Marwar and Alwar. The business of moneylending had been in his family over centuries, and all the rajahs of Rajputana, especially the neighbouring ones, had or had had dealings with him. Now if Jhunta Ram seized the Regency, he could conceivably establish a united front or a chain of influence, which could be detrimental to the Company's interests. Whether Sawai Rajah Jai Singh died a natural death or was murdered as a result of a conspiracy was not of much importance at the present moment. The important thing was that the person who became the guardian of the

Infant Maharajah and ruled as Regent should be amenable to the Company. As the Company Bahadur's representative on the spot, it was for Marston Blake to find a way to block Lala Jhunta Ram's bid for power.

'The Sawai Rajah sahib is not all that sick. I have just been informed of this by my news reporters.'

'Yes, Your Command, but the real truth is known to the Maharajah's physician alone. It is said that he was heard instructing the Honourable Palace that the Maharajah was not going to recover. He should be watched day and night so as to ensure his maximum comfort.'

'I see. So that is why Jhunta Ram is in such a hurry. Did anyone report the situation to the Chief Treasurer, Seth Rawal Ram?'

'Presence, he is getting reports from moment to moment, but his hands are tied. Access to Sawai Maharajah Jai Singh Sahib Bahadur has been denied to him.'

Rawal Seth's relations with the English, particularly the Political Agent, were extremely cordial. Were the Sawai Maharajah to die, and should his infant son be placed under a Regent, the Seth was the right person for the job.

Marston Blake dismissed Chand Khan with a gesture and fell into a deep reverie. He wished it had been Colonel Alves at the helm of affairs. To weaken or destroy Jhunta Ram's power and place Rawal Ram in his stead would have been simple for the wily Colonel, but it seems beyond my power. So is it in my power to prevent the Sawai Maharajah from falling prey to Jhunta Ram's conspiracy? Should I summon Jhunta Ram to the Residency and put him under arrest? But on what charge? And his company of bodyguards comprises hard-boiled, loyal Rajputs and Farmuli Pathans. The Farmulis, he knew, were originally Rajputs and had converted to Islam during the reign of Sher Shah in the early sixteenth century and had been inducted in the King's army as Pathans. It was very hard to get the better of them, and Seth Jhunta Ram never went out unaccompanied by his guards. In fact, he never left the Palace for fear that he might be surprised somewhere.

Should I issue a proclamation on behalf of the Political Agent, deposing the Sawai Maharajah Jai Singh on account of his being incapacitated, and simultaneously announce the succession of the Infant Sawai Maharajah Ram Singh, appointing Seth Rawal Ram the Regent for the interim? But what if the proclamation was not acted upon? I'll suffer a huge loss of face and while I would in any case have to leave Jaipur, the Company's honour too would be ground to dust. How I wish for the Colonel to be here!

A recent dispatch from Calcutta had reported that the Colonel had left for Jaipur, but might be delayed on the way because he had chosen to travel part of the distance by water. The first thing that he should do now is to send expert dromedary riders to Delhi to ascertain the present location of Colonel Alves. He should also send a full report, with those very riders, to the Secretary to the Governor General, Lord William Bentinck, for onward transmission to Calcutta from Delhi by the quickest post. Here, at my end, I should station the Company physician in the Palace, or rather at the sickbed of the Maharajah. Now if there was some opposition from the Palace—that is to say, from the Attorney General—to this posting, the opposition will have to be crushed ruthlessly. We will then see what turn the events take.

Having made these decisions, Marston Blake took steps to implement them without delay. He summoned Major Theobald MacDonald, the Company doctor, to the Residency and briefing him on the situation, he wrote a laisser passer to him for the Palace at Amber, dispatching him with full instructions, along with a small contingent of two English sergeants and six native—but not local—sepoys. Judging by his rank in the army, Theobald MacDonald obviously outranked Marston Blake, but according to the administration protocol, the physician was subordinate to the Acting Political Agent.

Before it was quite evening, the Residency's spies reported to Marston Blake that the Maharajah now seemed to be on his last legs, and Seth Jhunta Ram had troops stationed all around the Palace, preventing entry or exit. No report was filed about the rumour that the Maharajah was to be poisoned to death. Marston Blake himself interviewed the spies but they denied the existence or even knowledge of any conspiracy. Still, Marston Blake felt uneasy, especially because the spies had no answer to his query about why all entrances and exits to the Palace were placed under armed pickets. He instructed the spies to return post-haste and investigate the matter more closely.

The next day, at midday, the spies reported a scarcity of essential commodities in the bazaars and consequent rise in prices. In fact, spies were not needed for this information because Marston Blake's own servants and those of the Tyndales had already reported this early enough in the day, and the news had reached the ears of Wazir Khanam who had instantly conveyed it to her Sahib. Yet he was foolish enough not to give any credence to the information, attributing it to bazaar gossip or the natural dishonesty of Indian servants who wanted just to make a little extra money on this pretext. But this information, when purveyed by his own spies, gave quite another colour to the phenomenon. Marston Blake was now forced to conclude that the unusual situation obtaining at the Palace and the uncertainty about the succession had caused the scarcity and driven the prices upwards.

At teatime, the spies finally reported that the positioning of armed pickets everywhere around the Palace was most probably on account of the Maharajah's soul having left for its heavenly abode; and Seth Jhunta Ram did not want the news to be made known to the people because he was waiting for something or someone. Marston Blake immediately realized that the wait would certainly not be for the Political Agent; the reason must be much more ominous, perhaps a conspiracy was being hatched, larger than even the one that was rumoured. He inquired about the Company's physician and his contingent, and was informed that they were in preventive custody, but unharmed.

That same evening, Marston Blake left his own home and moved into the Residency. He left Wazir and the children at the Tyndales', requesting his cousins to take care of them for the few days that he was likely to be at the Residency. He did not consider any aggressive gestures or actions necessary at that time, except to fortify the Residency with armed guards at all strategic points. There had been no announcement or proclamation about the Maharajah from the Palace, nor had he yet received a reply to the written rogatory that he had sent to the Palace inquiring about the Company doctor and his contingent. He also requested that they be sent back if there was no longer any need for them.

The next morning brought in a new rumour, which spread throughout the city like the breeze. People were talking about an army which had left Ajmer for Jaipur a few days ago. It broke camp the previous night at Kishangarh and was expected to enter the city of Jaipur by the evening of the day after. None could say whose army it was, but everybody, commoner or spy, understood its objective to be to support and aid Seth Jhunta Ram. Marston Blake again sent for information about Major MacDonald and his men, and this time he was informed by the Palace that they were attending the sick Maharajah and their return was not possible yet. Since the reply was plausible enough, Marston Blake gritted his teeth and kept his own counsel. He was, however, sure that even if under detention, the doctor and his party would come to no harm at all, thanks to the ascendant fortunes of the Company Bahadur.

On the fifth day since the departure of the dromedary riders for Delhi, the spies reported that according to the bazaar gossip, the dromedary runners had reached Delhi; not only this, but also that the Political Agent Bahadur, after reaching Delhi, had immediately started for Jaipur by the Dawk Service, namely, the Post Coach, which travelled faster as its horses were changed frequently. Thus it was most probable that he would be in Jaipur on the fourth day from when he set out. The other side of the picture was not so bright: the army from Ajmer was not far from Jaipur now.

There had been no official information on any of these matters yet, but Marston Blake knew that news, often accurate, travelled very fast in India and certainly faster than the official postal service. No runners, no messengers, no spies ever seemed to be in action, yet the news always arrived and was disseminated through some mysterious system and often it took a week before its official confirmation was forthcoming.

Marston Blake figured that the news of the expected arrival of Colonel Alves within a very few days had lent strength and a bit of daring to the faction that was opposed to Lala Jhunta Ram. It occurred to him that he might take advantage of the situation and remove Jhunta Ram from his post. He acted immediately, little appreciating the fact that it was inexperience, and not sagacity that had suggested this course of action to him. He paid for his life by acting as he did. The first flaw in his decision was that it necessitated deployment of a company of twelve Telanga guards to the Palace at Amber under the command of Lieutenant Marcus Inchbold, thus reducing the level of security at the Residency. Worse still, rumours spread, or were caused to be spread, like lightning throughout the city, that the Company intended to place the Infant Successor Maharajah Ram Singh in detention, and maybe even murder him and put a maharajah of its own choice in place. And that the actual purpose of deploying the company of armed Telangas headed by an English officer was to install a puppet Maharajah even without waiting for the demise of the ailing Maharajah, and, if possible, his life too might be extinguished before his appointed time came.

Now, when Lieutenant Inchbold arrived with the Political Agent's fiat for the removal of Seth Jhunta Ram, the officers and soldiers of the

Maharajah's guard and Jhunta Ram's armed guards had already taken position to defend the Palace and resist the Company's force; they did not waste time in examining and disputing the legality of the removal order. Inchbold had just alighted from his elephant when he was put under arrest and made to cool his heels in a basement.

The proper thing to do should have been to gain the approval of all of the Maharajah's subjects for the bold step taken by the Political Agent, and they would have supported him. But what actually transpired were abuses being hurled at the Political Agent, blaming him for plotting the Infant Maharajah's murder. However, Marston Blake's informers and spies did not let him get a whiff of this development. Marston Blake remained under the delusion that the people were in his favour. He did not rethink his position even after it was reported to him that Inchbold and his company of soldiers had been placed under arrest. He figured that there was no cause for worry, that in only a matter of days Colonel Alves would be in the city and everything would pan out the way they wanted it to. In the meanwhile, nothing untoward could happen in the presence, even if restricted, of the English officers inside the Palace.

Marston Blake was right at least in his hopeful presumption about Colonel Alves. The very next day saw the entry of the Colonel into the city, accompanied by the famous company of Sikandar sahib—Skinner's Horse—armed to the very teeth. The Colonel ordered the Residency's remaining platoons and Skinner's Horse to accompany him to the Palace. Before starting, he had a Proclamation prepared on the Company's paper recognizing the Infant Ram Singh as the legal successor to the Sawai Maharajah Jai Singh, and describing him as the Sawai Maharajah Ram Singh. Then he wrote in his own hand a Decree of the State, declaring Seth Rawal Ram Regent until the Maharajah came of age, and ordering life imprisonment for Seth Jhunta Ram. Ram Singh was barely eighteen months old at that time, but the Colonel's scheme was to obtain the signatures of the Queen Mother on Ram Singh's succession and in due course have it ratified by the Governor General in Council at Calcutta.

Colonel Alves was well aware of the state of Major MacDonald and Lieutenant Inchbold, and he forestalled any adverse reactions or misunderstanding by dispatching a procession of nautch girls, dancers, singers and ordinary men and women to the Palace at Amber; they went there singing tunes and songs of congratulations, celebrating the succession of the Infant Maharajah. He thus intended to prevent any trigger-happy reaction from the Palace guards and warn Jhunta Ram too of the possible consequences of resistance. The position of Jhunta Ram was weakened anyway by the failure of the army from Ajmer to arrive.

By sunup, a whole multitude of the Maharajah's subjects had gathered in front of and around the Amber Palace. Armour-plated elephants, armed with elephant cannon and ridden by Jhunta Ram's guards with loaded carbines, swayed gently at the huge main gate of the Palace, which had to be approached through a steep road, for the Palace was built upon a high hill. The advance party of the Residency's armed battalions had been, however, as a diplomatic measure, allowed to pass through the gate. Some of them waited for the Colonel in front of the Hall of Public Audience, while some had gathered at the gate to the Hall of Private Audience. The Infant Maharajah Ram Singh was inside the Hall of Private Audience. He was in full regalia, supported by the arms of two stalwart Rajput soldiers, and surrounded by numerous women servants, attendants and bodyguards. Jhunta Ram stood before the Maharajah, his hands folded on his chest in the traditional gesture of submission.

There was no reaction from Jhunta Ram at the entry of the Political Agent in the Hall of Private Audience. This was his cardinal mistake. Had he indicated to his armed men by secret sign or gesture to deal with the Colonel, rivers of blood would have flowed and Jhunta Ram's position would have been the stronger of the two, for the English would have had to withdraw after a bloody hand-to-hand battle. Perhaps Jhunta Ram still hoped that by playing it safe, he could win the Company's favour in the near future. He even had a large quantity of coin and bullion stashed away for just this purpose. However, he lost sight of the simple fact that after making the Company lose face, even if in a small way, by detaining its English officers, he had irretrievably lost his game.

Major Craddock, adjutant to Colonel Alves, put his right hand on the pistol in his belt and placing his left hand on Jhunta Ram's shoulder, spoke in a stern voice, 'Come with me. You are under arrest.'

Two sepoys stepped forward smartly and bound Jhunta Ram's hands behind his back, and immobilized him by putting leg irons on him. Seeing their master so humiliated, Jhunta Ram's bodyguards drew their swords. A strong blow from one of the guards struck Colonel Alves deep on the shoulder and his arm hung useless, joined to the body only by a few tendons.

Captain Marston Blake, who was right next to the Colonel, pulled out his sword with lightning speed and ran it through the Colonel's assailant who fell dead; the Captain's white uniform was bespattered with his victim's blood.

The Company's force decided upon close combat with pistols, daggers and bayonets. With women, children and other non-fighting bodies packed in the narrow space, it became a melee rather than a combat. The Infant Maharajah's soldiers, instead of fighting freely, were practically paralysed by the fear of the Infant getting hurt by their own hands. The pistols of the Company's force and the daggers of Sikandar sahib's Horse made short work of the opposition, with the confrontation lasting less than half an hour. Jhunta Ram, bound and manacled, was thrown into a dungeon. The general forces of the Maharajah present in the Palace were amnestied, but the survivors of the combat who had inflicted a wound on any of the Company's soldiers were shot dead on the spot.

On behalf of the Company, Colonel Alves tied a jigha around the formal turban already worn by Ram Singh. The jigha, recognized as a token of sovereignty since early Mughal times, was a velvet band about two inches broad. The band, profusely and beautifully embroidered in gold, had a gold plate of suitable length in which was set a large emerald surrounded by other gemstones. The Colonel also fixed a plume of white feathers in the turban and tied to the Infant's waist a dagger in a jewelled sheath, both the sheath and the handle of the dagger heavily worked in gold. The Political Agent then made a formal announcement of the Regency of Seth Rawal Ram. The pandits performed the necessary rites and pronounced auspicious mantras. Congratulatory music was played during a short, formal banquet. It was decided that the ascension would take place after consulting the almanacs and other documents, so as to ensure the favourability of the positions of the stars.

Colonel Alves was in a bad shape by then, his wound was bleeding still and he was fast losing his strength in spite of MacDonald's ministrations. Semi-conscious, he was put in a palanquin and the Company's physician supervised his return to the city. English officers and the Company's soldiers followed suit. Keen to give Wazir the good news about his success and his safety, Marston Blake decided to take a different route into the city that would take him past the Tyndale residence before he approached the Residency.

As the Company's officers and men took the main road into the city, Marston Blake and his three personal attendants turned into a narrow, less-frequented road. He was the only Firangee on the road at that time; the air was full of festivity everywhere. People were out on the street, waving banners, dancing and singing. The happiest and most prosperous among the new Regent's supporters had set up stalls where sweets, flower garlands, fruits, and even garments like saris for the women and dhotis for the men were distributed to all comers. With so much colourful merrymaking, the crossroads presented the look of a fair or a festival. Marston Blake felt quite safe, unaware of the storm that was brewing right in his path home.

Rumours had been circulated in the city that Marston Blake had been plotting to put to death both the ailing Maharajah and the Infant Maharajah, and install Seth Jhunta Ram as temporary ruler pending the conclusion of the complicated formalities of the selection of a maharajah of royal lineage. When he was seen coming out of the Palace at Amber with his bloodied clothes, and then being left alone to go off unaccompanied by the Company's pomp and splendid entourage, the rumour preceded him that he did actually kill the Infant and would install a new Maharajah as soon as the army from Ajmer arrived to support Jhunta Ram's faction.

By the time Marston Blake entered the city proper, this rumour had gained so much strength that at many places the celebration and festivities at the installation of the Infant as Maharajah had been cancelled, and the rejoicing crowd had been replaced by sullen groups of people talking to each other quietly and using foul, abusive language against the Company and the 'criminal' Captain. When Marston Blake was found travelling alone with just three attendants, a group assembled on the road and attempted to block his progress. A few slogans were shouted too. Marston Blake did not get their import but his lance-bearer tried to hide under the jutting counter of a closed shop, calling out that His Honour's life was in danger because these people believed that he had killed the Infant Maharajah.

The identity of this group was never ascertained. It was said that they were supporters or mercenaries of Jhunta Ram who wanted to avenge the capture and arrest of their master and patron. But Jhunta Ram had no real power left; his supporters had cooled off like the winter sun. Some expressed the view that since Marston Blake's treatment of Indians, especially of those who were employees of the Maharajah, was of an extremely harsh and disdainful nature, if not plain insolent, he had earned the malice of many in the local population, some of whom were also habitual criminals. It was they who took advantage of the rumours against him when they found him alone. They did not necessarily want to kill him, but the small horde of people soon began to evince signs of turning violent. When the lance-bearer found no protection under the counter and some of the mob turned towards him, he ran off and disappeared in a narrow lane, calling out to Marston Blake to defend himself as best he could while he rushed off to the Residency to summon soldiers for help.

Marston Blake now had just two mace-bearers, both unarmed. He took them to his right and left, and pulling his pistol from the holster fired a few quick shots in the air to scare the crowd so as to clear a path for his progress. Having fired high above the mass of the people, he could not have hit anyone, but suddenly a man threw himself on the ground and began to writhe and cry as if in great pain, 'Oh! Oh! I am hit! I am killed! Please save me, please save me!'

His cries were like oil on flames. The throng was much too inflamed now and began to shout slogans and abuses in unison:

'Kill, kill the Firangee!'

'Kill the Maharajah's murderer!'

'Don't let him get away, the motherfucker, fell him to the ground right here!'

'Come on, step up to the bastard and cut him down . . . bastard son of a fornicating mother!'

'The sister-fucking dog cannot escape, must not escape!'

Very soon the shouts of the multitude changed into growls and snarls. Within minutes the rabble, which initially consisted of barely twenty or twenty-five out-of-work and ne'er-do-well loafers, was transformed into a mob of three to four hundred, collectively bent upon mischief. Marston Blake, finding no room to stay and none to go forward, decided to force his way to the next crossroads which was not very far and where he could perhaps find a police post to take refuge. He handed over his other pistol to one of the mace-bearers, and firing his own pistol, shouted to him, 'What are you looking for now, you fool! Fire, and try to get clear. There is no other way to save our lives now!'

With both the pistols firing together, the mob showed signs of being routed, at least enough to let them pass, and Marston Blake spurred his horse forward into the multitude. The mace-bearer was firing from behind the horse, in comparative shelter. But his pistol was of an older model, nor did he have any real experience of shooting with a pistol, and that too at human beings. So his rate of fire was slow and erratic. The other mace-bearer stumbled and was caught under the crush, breaking every last bone in his body. Marston Blake had a modern pistol with a five-shot magazine, so he was firing quicker and placing his shots better. His Arabian was also extremely stout-hearted and highly trained. It instantly obeyed its rider's slightest gesture or command; it went on steadily, not caring if something came underfoot.

When Marston Blake got out of the narrow alley, he was disappointed to find no crossroads there, nor a police post. He was facing a small clearing at the end of which was a temple. There were roads running on both sides of the temple outside the clearing, but Marston Blake had no idea of where the roads led. He turned and looked inquiringly at the pistol-wielding mace-bearer. The mace-bearer shook his head in a negative gesture and pointed towards the temple as a possible sanctuary.

Having made one mistake about the route and the end of the alley, Marston Blake was thoroughly rattled. Without giving thought to the possible consequences of his instantaneous decision, he vaulted forward at the best speed that his Arabian could muster. Having made it safely to the temple door, he noticed that the pursuing mob was fifty or more yards behind, but their clamour had attracted more loafers and vagabonds from the opposite side and he was within their reach. And if his horse had the advantage of the open field to put up a burst of speed, his pursuers could also fan out comfortably, not being constricted by the narrow walls of the alley.

He dismounted and went boldly into the temple. His mace-bearer had exhausted his magazines, so the mob brought him down in one swoop and cut him to pieces. Marston Blake thought himself safe, at least for the moment, because as a Christian he looked upon a church, any church, as a sanctuary and mistakenly believed a temple to be sacrosanct in the same way. But Marston Blake was ignorant of two important points.

First, the temple was dedicated to the Goddess Kali and thus had been the site of blood sacrifices and sanguinary activities for centuries. Second, the pandit who officiated at that temple was the traditional priest of the family of the Maharajah of Alwar who had business dealings with Seth Jhunta Ram. When he found out that the person seeking sanctuary in his temple was Marston Blake whom the mob described as Seth Jhunta Ram's enemy, he not only kept the temple door open, offering no resistance to the blood-hungry mob, but also permitted them to surround and storm the shrine.

No eyewitness could give any kind of account of what followed. Later, when the Company Bahadur appointed a military Judge-Advocate to inquire into the matter, the pandit of the temple and everyone else averred on oath that they had not seen who had raised the first hand on Blak sahib, and once a hand had been raised, who could have the manliness to stop the others?

It took less than half an hour for Marston Blake's body to have swords run through it from head to foot. Then his murderers put his mortal remains on his steed and turned it out of the clearing, to stand on the road. By the time the English army officers and their force arrived, armed to the teeth, on galloping horses amidst the trumpet of bugles and shouts of 'Give Way!' and 'Clear the Road!', they found the Arabian of Captain Edward Marston Blake bearing the body of his master on its sad and bent back, its noble head lowered, on a three-way road junction, as if undecided which way to go. All the valuable and useful things of the horse's equipment had been taken; as also everything on the Captain's body that could be put to any kind of use. But the mob had had the decency at least of not stripping the body of its uniform and had not dishonoured or mutilated it. The temple's priest was nowhere to be seen, and the riotous mob did not seem to have existed. Even the ground everywhere around the temple had been swept to make the finding of foot or hoof marks of man or beast utterly impossible.

22

Wazir Khanam negotiates a deal with the Tyndales

IT SEEMED TO Wazir that someone had gashed her side and, having torn out her liver and spleen by main force, had drained off all the blood in her body. It seemed there was nothing now in her body that was her own. She had last seen Marston Blake when, leaving her and the children in the care of the Tyndales, he had assured her that he would be perfectly safe in the Residency and she should not worry at all; that he would return soon, very soon, and they would re-people their home anew.

Verses of Hafiz came to her mind again and again, and she would say them to herself and weep:

Let someone go and tell my unkind moon:
Please return, for your lovers are dead with the agony of waiting;
I gave you my heart and bought your love with my life,
Now do not perpetrate upon me the tyranny of being separated from you.

She mourned her Sahib for twenty-one days. His funeral rites were performed according to the Christian way, and services were held at the church in the prescribed manner. But on her own too, Wazir organized recitations from the Quran in the mosques for the peace and extra merit of the departed soul, and had the students in the nearby madrasa fed in his name for three days. She herself said the prescribed five prayers a day and special prayers for the mercy of God to be available to her Sahib.

As her pain abated somewhat, another worry began to eat into her soul like a worm: she looked around and wondered if at all she would survive her loss, and if she did, what would be her means to live a life without support or succour? She recalled another verse from the same ghazal of Hafiz—not for nothing was he known and loved as the Tongue of the Unseen:

Oh heart! Make peace with your grief and be patient,
Oh eyes! Do not weep blood more than this much in separation.

But living a life needed much more and much else than mere patience. How should I bring up and nurture two children, live here on whose support, rely upon whom in a strange land? How can I live like a serving maid and an abject dependent in a house where I had once ruled like a queen?

Marston Blake had died intestate, and there was no record of Wazir Khanam as his bibi in the Company's papers. The day after her cousin brother's funeral, Aby memsahib had clearly informed Wazir that there was nothing there that belonged to her, except her clothes. Wazir made no response at that time, but later, after the storm of grief had passed and her heart was somewhat more stable, she broached the matter again and had a clear and frank discussion with the Tyndales. True, she had not come with anything like a sumptuous dowry, but she certainly had claim to the presents that Marston Blake had given her. The moneys deposited by him in her name in the bank of General Palmer sahib were also hers, both capital and interest. Articles of daily use which had been in her possession all these years must also be considered her property.

The conversation seemed to be veering towards heat and bitterness. William Tyndale said something to his sister in English. Aby fell silent for a minute, as if she was a little hesitant, or even reluctant to bring herself to repeat what her brother had been saying. After a little while, she said, 'And the children, Martin and Sophia, what have you thought about them?'

'What is there to think?' Wazir replied promptly. 'They are my children, I will bring them up.'

'What means do you possess to enable you to do so? And on top of it, you will live alone. But if you get to hold someone else's hand . . . ?'

'Aby memsahib, pray do not worry your head about matters that are not your concern. Didn't I say that they are my babies? I'll survive on one meal if need be, but I will take good care of them. What does this have to do with you?'

'The children are ours too!' William Tyndale spoke up suddenly. 'Edward had their births registered by putting down his name as their father.'

This was something that Chhoti Begam had not known. She was unable also to assess the actual or potential legal mischief that Marston Blake's owning his fatherhood without reporting the mother's name could have on her chances to claim the children as exclusively her own. She was unable to make a coherent reply immediately and kept her counsel. Aby said, 'Now listen. I've a proposal for you and I think in its acceptance lies your good.'

For a brief moment, Aby considered exactly how she should frame her proposal. All three were quiet, and then Wazir said, not without letting a bit of sarcasm creep into her voice, 'Please command, I'm listening.'

'All right, listen,' Aby was slightly nettled. 'You make the children over to us—'

'What is that supposed to mean?' Wazir interrupted somewhat harshly. 'You will rip them off from me, Christianize them, remove them from my life? You forget that they are my children too.'

'Yes, they're your children too. But you're nothing now. Brought up in pomp and luxury, cared for by an army of servitors, used to everything in abundance and the sense of power that an English home gave them: can you offer them these, ever at all?'

'And what about their faith, their way of life?'

'Don't talk to me anything about their faith. They have been baptized as Christians. I know it for certain. Don't even dream of making Mussulmans of them.'

'Why should I? They will become what they will. But you have no right to thrust your Firangee creed down their throats.'

'Behold this little woman, saying what she does!' Aby laughed out aloud. 'Why ever should we push anything down anybody's gullet? They were born Christian and Christian they will remain.'

'Why should they "remain" Christian?' Wazir retorted. 'Let them be told about the essentials of Islam and then let them choose.'

'Well, that is something unheard of!'

'You may not have heard of such things. But my Sahib too had the same thought. Why else should he have given them two names?'

'So what do you desire for the children? Don't you see, they must live with us. You have no money, no honour . . .'

'Who gave you the authority to measure my honour, Aby memsahib? Forgive my plain speaking, but you should not jump your limits. I too have my people, my family. I know that my Sahib's martyrdom has made me homeless, but I have not lost my honour. State whatever proposal you have, but don't slight my family.'

'Well, what I have to say is just this: the children to remain with us;

the essential goods of the house to be yours; whatever you got from our brother, you keep. You may live here in Jaipur or elsewhere, you can pay occasional visits to the children, but they won't ever visit you anywhere.'

Wazir did not fail to notice that the word 'you' had been enunciated with barely concealed contempt. She wanted to interrupt, but Aby raised her hand to stop her and continued, 'You need not spend anything on the upkeep of the children.'

'And their marriage, their education, their upbringing?'

'Obviously, they will grow up with us and be like us. They can marry according to their choice, but with our approval. They will be educated and brought up as the children of an Englishman.'

Wazir Khanam stood up. She cried harshly, 'Your proposals are entirely unacceptable to me and—'

But before she could complete her sentence, William again said something to his sister in English. She nodded vigorously and said, 'Young woman, sit down. Listen, you can establish no claim on the children. We can, in no time, get a decree against you from the Company Bahadur's Court, and if need be, from the Maharajah's Court as well.'

Wazir, who was about to flounce out with her nose in the air, shrank and stopped short, then slowly, she regained her seat.

'Our proposal takes account of your situation,' said Aby, 'and is the kindest possible under the circumstances. We can negotiate other matters, but do not even imagine anything about the children, other than the fact that they are ours and will always remain ours.'

Wazir Khanam well appreciated the fact that any transaction of this sort could not be one-sided: the Tyndales had also their own axe to grind. Hence, their willingness to negotiate and compromise. They had the power, doubtless, but they did not want the matter to drag on and assume contentious proportions; whereas her problem was that bringing up and caring for the children as behoved her and them was extremely difficult for her on her own resources.

She gave as much consideration to the matter as was possible at that moment, and said, 'All right, the first thing you should bear in mind is that a decree from the courts at Jaipur will not close the issue. There is the Lord Governor General Sahib, and his Court in Calcutta. I am quite prepared to go up to the Lord Governor General Bahadur in appeal. But such contentions and disputes are unbecoming of good families. So I have some proposals of my own.'

'So, let it be as you say. State your proposals,' Aby spoke airily, as if Wazir could not really have anything to say which she could not reject out of hand.

'I will bear all expenses to be incurred upon my children for their upkeep, and for everything else.'

Brother and sister both started and exclaimed, 'Oh!'

'Do not be surprised. As of now, I'll pay twenty rupees per month for each of the children and will raise the amount when they grow up. Where this money comes from should be of no interest to you. It is my own concern entirely.'

'And what else?'

'They will be educated in Hindi and Persian. English they may read as much as you or they desire, I have nothing to say about it. They must be allowed to dress both like us and like you. I will not agree to their wearing English dress alone.'

'Well, this too can be considered. Anything else?' Aby could not keep the sarcasm out of her voice.

'I should have the freedom to visit them when I like. I should be consulted in matters relating to their marriage.'

'We will see. Is that all?'

Wazir took a deep breath and spoke in measured tones, enunciating every word clearly, 'In return for my sacrifices, I will be the sole owner of everything in this house: furniture, carpets, glass, metal utensils, chandeliers, all should be mine.'

The Tyndales were mildly shocked. In taking custody of the children, they had planned to gain religious merit as also some worldly benefit. Thus they were hoping to inherit most, if not all, of the appurtenances of Marston Blake's house. They were silent for a minute or two, and then conferred in English. Finally, they said, 'We agree.'

'Very well, I am grateful to you.' Saying this, her eyes welled up suddenly, but she extended her hand firmly to shake hands on the agreement.

The Tyndales had not expected an Indian woman to negotiate with so much skill and then shake hands on the deal like a man. They shook hands with the best grace that they could muster and promised that all papers would be made ready within four days. In the meantime, should Wazir so desire, she could have a full inventory made of the household effects that she proposed to take with her. It was understood without it being mentioned that she would go back to Delhi, leaving Jaipur for good.

On the eighth day after the conversation reported above, Wazir had her effects loaded on camel carts and appointed a reliable caravan leader; she organized her return to Delhi by the Dawk. In the presence of the two children, she entrusted five bags of one hundred rupees each to Aby, saying that it was for the expenses of the little ones for one year. She wept and embraced and hugged the children, kissing them over and over again, promising that she would soon have them back with her, or would come visit them. She could not have thought even in her worst nightmares that she would never set her eyes on them again. This much, however, was obvious to all: that a phase of Wazir Khanam's life was irrevocably over, and over too soon. Perhaps the next phase would last longer. She thought of the words of Hafiz:

I thought of asking her how goes it with the ball they call the sky,
She said: I will pull and rotate it in the curve of my polo bat such that there will be nothing left to ask about.

BOOK 4

23

Wazir Khanam makes herself at home in the glorious city of Delhi

SHE REACHED DELHI on the evening of the fifth day, but did not go to her father's house. She had fixed up a suitable house on rent in Sirki Walan through the good offices of Manjhli. On the sixth day of her arrival, her personal effects reached Delhi, loaded on seven camel carts. She also brought back her cash and jewellery. At that time, Wazir Khanam was nineteen years and a few days' old. Two childbirths, the shock and grief of her Sahib's death, and the separation from her children: in spite of all this, her beauty was such that one gazed and gazed and would swear by her beauty to gaze again.

It was the month of March, and the year was 1830. Two problems faced Chhoti Begam: loneliness and livelihood. Granted that the valuables inherited by her from Sahib and her own savings—collected by virtue of good management over the last five years—were quite substantial; but if one's possessions did not increase and one's cash outgo was constant, even the wealth of Croesus would not suffice for too long.

Of course, it was impossible to afford a mansion-like house that she had had in Jaipur, with its battalion of servitors, the palanquin, the nalki, the buggy, the horses, the cattle, the dogs and other animals, and the throng of hangers-on. She could not even dream of these things. She was quite reconciled to the idea of living in a style much reduced from what she had been used to. But reconciled to what, and to what extent, was the question. She needed a regular, fixed amount for minimum domestic expenses. Security personnel and a servant for outdoor duties like shopping were essential above the expenditure on food and other disbursements. She would not, of course, be a reckless spender or squander money on accumulating comforts, far less luxuries, but she did need to live decently, and also keep up appearances, including her personal appearance.

She was not without some skill in singing and dancing, but she had no interest in such things. To break into spontaneous song or do a bit of dancing among women friends or in assemblies of women during a marriage, for example, was something else. She had no desire to dance or sing for her livelihood. This question did not figure in her concept of living, or her self-image: she would not sell her skills or her body to acquire a modicum of subsistence or to carve out a style of life comfortable for her. She was prepared to deal with men, but on her own terms. If she did not succeed in getting all her conditions accepted, she would at least need full acceptance of her most important stipulations before she could agree to establish relations with someone, not to speak of entering his harem.

The murder of the English Assistant Political Agent at Jaipur was not an event whose echoes would not be heard widely in Delhi. And those who were interested in matters of pleasure and enjoyment of the physical aspects of living were not unaware that Wazir Khanam was in Delhi, that her children were not with her, and that she had not yet been introduced in Society, much less entered into any kind of understanding with someone.

No one was sure for how long she would be in mourning for her Sahib. Nor did anyone have an inkling of her plans once she took off her black. It was obvious that a glamorous woman like Wazir Khanam, endowed generously with beauty's gold, and reasonably wealthy in her own right, would not ever lack for men who desired her. What she herself desired was not open to conjecture. Then, it was also a fact of her life that in Delhi's social circles she was regarded, especially after the example of Manjhli Begam, as one whose favours could be won, given the right conditions.

Yet, speculate about her whatever they might in Delhi's Society, Wazir Khanam did not consider herself in any way less than a begam. Now it was another matter that she was a begam whose every part, every gesture, every grace, every utterance exuded an erotic challenge which no man could resist. As for eminence in courage to give up some valuable worldly goods, or accept something like adversity of fortune, and firmness of will, no princess, no queen could ever begin to exceed her in these qualities. And it was the Presence, Delhi, and nowhere else, where she was to be found.

True, Delhi's glory was on the wane in those times, but remember, an elephant, however much reduced in body weight, would still turn the scales at more than ten thousand pounds. In every alley, at every door, one would find the brilliant lights of the pious, the learned, the Sufi, the poet, the lover of beauty, the dandy, the flâneur, the musician, the master chess player, the unerring marksman, the most eminent of fencers and swordsmen, the inspired fortune teller, the astrologer. Then how was it possible that people did not know that a beauty like Wazir Khanam was enhancing the tone of Delhi's population by settling there? It was not possible not to know that that half-open blossom, now the springtime of a thousand flowers and the flower of a thousand springs, had come from the thorn lands of Rajputana to spread its fragrance again in Delhi's bedchambers of joy and to rekindle the flame of distance in its fiery lands of separation.

Within a week or ten days of Wazir's arrival in Delhi, hints and suggestions began coming to her through various sources. Women expert at the profession of arranging marriages or liaisons began to seek permission to enter her door; and the easiest excuse was, of course, Manjhli Begam. Whoever visited her, invariably found some occasion to ask about Chhoti. Chhoti, too, would now sometimes hold a dialogue with herself: For how long will you go on wearing a widow's weeds? You have to live, after all, and have two more souls to provide for. You must not demean yourself but yet must find ways to improve your present state.

Through the medium of Umdah Khanam, she had access to Navab Yusuf Ali Khan, but her visits there were purely domestic, sisterly affairs. She did not raise questions of establishing connections or going away somewhere, nor did the Navab give out any such hints. All that occurred between them was if the Navab was in the mansion while she was visiting with Manjhli, she would present herself before him to pay obeisance. There was not much conversation, but in her position as the younger sister, she would be welcomed with kind words of blessing, treated with some gift of fruits or money and the usual hospitalities.

Several months passed in this fashion, but one day, as she turned to go back after paying her usual respects, the Navab commanded in his miracle-working words, 'Chhoti Begam, you aren't in a hurry, are you? Please stay awhile.'

'Sir, your servant girl is at your service here, with her heart and soul,' she said and sat down on the carpet with her feet tucked under her thighs.

It was the first time that Navab Yusuf Ali Khan had looked Wazir full in the face, from hard by. During earlier meetings he had always kept his eyes lowered and spoken just a few words, observing formal decorum. At this time, she was wearing loose, somewhat baggy trousers put together with multi-hued strips of the light silk fabric called gulbadan, made in Benaras. The trousers were narrow above, but increased in fullness as the dress descended her body. The colours of the strips—peacock-green, gold and azure—were very suitable for the weather. Baggy pants are usually worn to conceal the contours of the body, but Wazir, following the dictates of modesty, sat with her body gathered in such a way that the angles of her thighs could be discerned dimly. Her bodice, made of fine netting of cream-coloured silk known as tash, was a good fit, not tight but appropriate. The sleeves of the bodice were short, barely concealing the upper part of the arms, and heavy with elaborately worked gold lace. The neckline was low, but not so as to compromise modesty. The cups of the bodice were more or less plain but with tiny stars of very thin gold thread worked over them, though not heavily. The front and the back of the bodice were wide, but the attentive gazer might have an occasional glimpse of the stomach and the back. On top of the bodice, she had on a sleeveless tunic, rather low and loose fitting. The fabric was white cotton of the finest quality called shabnam, worked over lightly in gold, while its front and back hem were heavy with delicate gold filigree.

The bodice and the tunic combined to reveal and conceal her upper body, creating the delightful situation of arousing curiosity and leaving it unsatisfied. The tunic was made from such a light and delicate fabric that the bodice's colours could be descried clearly, but still the art of concealment had been used to such effect that below the neckline, there were only hints and suggestions, nothing in plain language.

Her head was properly covered with a dupatta, and this wrap had also the same effect of hints and promises. Full six yards of extremely delicate netting in sky-blue cotton, the fabric was known as sharbati: it was cotton just in name, for its edges on all four sides had pure gold work and tassels of gold thread. Tiny gold stars had been worked all over it; thus that lightest of cotton nettings had become heavy and sumptuous.

It was not a dupatta on Wazir Khanam's body, it was a bluish golden cloud behind which gleamed the light brown skin of her forehead, face and chin, pleasurable like lightly salted condiment. Behind the cloud could also be discerned the scintilla, the spangle of the ups and downs of her body, tight as a bow, and her nine-gemmed necklace, dominated by lapis lazuli. A small mirror ornament surrounded by blue sapphires worked in gold hung in a fine silk and gold thread just above her cleavage; gold earrings made like circlets with a small ruby strung in each; jewel-encrusted wide bangles with tiger-jaws fashioned where the two ends met, and light-green glass bangles between the two jewelled bangles on each wrist; diamond and cat's eye-rings on the index finger and the little finger of each hand; a nose ring with emeralds set in it: all this coruscated like lightning in the bright illumination given off by globe lamps set on the floor.

The sky-blue dupatta, the cream-coloured bodice and the pure white tunic, Wazir's complexion, her black eyes, long, slanting, like the starfruit, with a very light, thin line of potent black kajal against the lower eyelids, the well-formed neck rising from the neckline: the combination of all these colours so proportionate, mixing and matching harmoniously without any suggestion of overstatement stunned even such an experienced connoisseur of female beauty as the Navab. Moments passed, but he could not take his eyes away, yet he also had an almost mystic experience of hot waves emanating from Wazir's body, as if she was running a high temperature and the ripples of the fevered heat were surging about his body. Abashed, he lowered his eyes, cleared his throat, and said, 'Chhoti Begam, you're doing all right, are you not? You aren't in need of anything?'

'Thanks to the noble Navab's generosity and the Almighty's bountifulness, everything has been all right, at least thus far.'

The Navab smiled. 'Thus far? Why only thus far, and not further?'

Wazir smiled a thin, pallid smile and said, 'The miracle-like verse of the Shadow of God on Earth, who now reposes in Paradise, must be within the auspicious power of the Honourable Navab's recall?'

The Navab instantly recited the famous verse of Emperor Shah Alam II:

God should have knowledge of hereafter,
As of now, it passes in comfort.

'Everything is clear like a mirror before the Honourable Sir. I am sure there must have been something inspired upon the heart of the Shadow of God on Earth from the Voice of the Unseen. He might not have been aware of it, but the hint was present: 'hereafter' surely meant the future in this very world when he would be 'plundered', if not of the treasure of life, but certainly of the treasure of sight. In my case too . . .'

'Take the name of God, young lady! God forbid, why should you be subjected to such catastrophes?'

'God will also be kind so long as the Honourable Navab's shadow is over my head.'

'Oh, well. God is the Protector and Preserver of all. But say something about yourself. Does everything go well with you?'

Finally, the Navab's purpose dawned upon Chhoti. A slight wave of rosy bashfulness came and went quickly from her face. She bent her head and almost whispered, 'The Noble Navab knows that I am quite alone. I cool my heart with the sight of Manjhli and your benevolent face. I have no one else.'

This was not quite true, but was based on the realities of Wazir's life. Her father had sent her a formal message of condolence when the news of Marston Blake's murder reached him, but he had not asked her to return home. Wazir's elder sister, Anwari Khanam, had been a true consoler and sharer of her sorrow and had visited a number of times since her return to Delhi. But her solution to Wazir's real problems was that she go back to their father. She said, 'I promise I will look for a suitable widower for you and will have you married to him within the next twelve months or even less.'

But this was entirely unacceptable to Wazir. She wanted to be the arbiter of her own fate. Having no choice, Bari gradually reduced her contacts with Chhoti, and now Manjhli was the only one with whom she had friendly relations.

Obviously, the Navab had kept himself informed of these developments. His main aim was to ascertain if Wazir had any specific plans about her future existence, and if so, the nature of those plans.

'So you've given up seeing people. You have no social life?'

'Please, Navab Sahib, a woman's chastity is tested when she's without a covering. Do I see anyone here worth meeting and knowing?'

'Well, that is what I wanted to say. There are some people here who are keen to know you.'

Wazir was confused. Did the Navab plan to have her join her sister . . . ?

Yusuf Ali Khan immediately understood that his words were open to misinterpretation. He hastened to elucidate, 'There are some members of the nobility and the elite of Delhi of my acquaintance who have heard favourably of you. They're extremely desirous of getting to know you personally.'

Wazir breathed a secret sigh of relief. She paused a moment and then answered, 'I am your servitor. I cannot transgress your command.'

'Good. Very good. May God grant happiness to you always,' saying this, the Navab gestured briefly with his hand. Wazir had been unable to spot the movement, but the Navab's usher who stood behind indicated with a side glance that the audience was now over. Wazir rose, made three salaams and walking backward, exited the divan khanah, the meeting chamber, and re-entered the zenana.

24

Wazir Khanam is invited to Fraser sahib's stately and sumptuous mansion on the Hill

ABOUT EIGHT OR ten days later, a staff-bearer and a mace-bearer, dispatched by Navab Yusuf Ali Khan, appeared at Wazir's door, bearing the Navab's missive and ten bags of money, each containing a hundred rupees. The gracious Navab had written in his own hand in Persian to say that may it please Wazir Khanam, may she be always secure, after our prayers for enhancement of her beauty's riches and permanence of her good fortunes, to peruse that, on the evening of coming Thursday, after the prayers prescribed to be offered immediately after sundown, an assembly of poetry and conversation will be held in the elevated Hall, located on the Hill in Delhi, of Navab William Fraser Sahib, Resident to the State of the Company Bahadur, may His shadow be perpetual and may His bounties increase and spread. Navab Mirza Asadullah Khan sahib, whose nom de plume is Ghalib and whose honorific is Mirza Naushah, will ennoble the assembly with a recital of his latest poetry. Selected noblemen and elites of the Presence, Delhi, will also enhance the company's elegance. It will be truly a cause of happiness, should that dear and honoured one bestow the trouble of movement to her feet which are known to usher in good fortune and happiness, and betake herself there.

Let it be noted here that the hilly, semi-forested zone that lies in the north-west of modern Delhi, beyond Kashmiri Darwazah and Paharganj, now known as the Ridge, was called Pahari (Hill) in those days. The Rai Sina Hill and the semi-forested hilly tract in the south-west that is now considered the heart of New Delhi, was far away from the city of Shahjahanabad and almost did not exist for citizens of Delhi in the early nineteenth century.

Liberally rewarding the servants, Wazir immediately sent them back with her note of acceptance, but the name of William Fraser had set her heart beating wildly. Was there anyone in Delhi not familiar with Fraser's name? She had once heard from her Sahib that after General Akhtarloni's death (in 1825), Edward Colebrooke sahib who was appointed Resident at Delhi, was implicated in sundry instances of corruption. He was suspended and William Fraser was made Acting Resident. In fact, the hopes of her own Mattan Blak sahib had resided in the possibility, eventually, of Fraser sahib's promotion on a long-term basis and of him being asked to fill the station vacated by Fraser sahib. But now, it was the case of, as the Persian poet said: *That wine cup broke, that cup-bearer did not remain*. The position was, however, vacant even now. Fraser sahib, to be sure, was lording it over in Delhi as Acting Resident.

There were rumours in abundance about Fraser. One of them was that he had converted to Islam. This might not have been true but it was quite certain that like General Akhtarloni, Fraser had fully adapted to Indian ways. He did not eat beef or pork, and was extremely fond of betels, hookah and Indian attars. He was not so fond of Indian wines, but consumed French wines in copious quantities. He was fully fluent in Persian and was also interested in Hindi poetry, what was then also called Rekhta.

That said, Fraser sahib had a murky reputation for tyranny as well. He was so severe with the peasants in fixing land-revenue rates and their recovery that many villages in and around Delhi had become desolate and were laid waste, because the peasants, unable to meet his demands, had run off to the hills or to other districts. It was said that his lifestyle, dress and deportment were exactly like those of the Indian nobility. His drawing room was not equipped with European furniture such as sofas, frog chairs, chaises longues. Rather, it was adorned with carpets, soft, quilted coverings on the floors where there were no carpets, or often under the carpets, and Turkish-style divans. He entered his zenana and his kitchen barefooted, following the Hindu custom.

His tyrannical ways of tax collection apart, there were aspects to Fraser's lifestyle which were not looked upon with favour by the people of Delhi. He had six or seven bibis and also a number of boys as his lovers. Although 'boy love' was nothing unheard of in Delhi, he also had a reputation for high-handedness and was not above trying to seduce or ravish those who were attached to his friends or acquaintances.

An uncomfortable feeling, something like a thrill, rose in Wazir's body. If Fraser sahib wants me . . . But will it be acceptable to me to be one of his servants? Mattan Blak sahib's home was a different matter. There, I was the sole woman. And here . . . I beg God's forgiveness . . . Oh, how I hate the catamites and eunuchs . . . and on top of that, there are many bibis already there. I am not prepared to live where I would be under anyone's senior or superior presence. And I will never tolerate living with others in the same house or in a big mansion even.

So should I not go to that place? But it is not a given that Fraser sahib will be interested in me. Possibly he has invited me as just one among other invitees. Navab sahib actually told me that there are many desirous of getting to know me personally. What interest could Fraser sahib have in me? He has countless lovers ready to give up their life for him, and I shouldn't be surprised if there are many among them who are better looking than me. Really, I'm putting too high a value on myself; I'm building castles in the air when there is no real occasion for all that.

And what face will I show to Navab sahib if I don't go? I've sent word to him that I, his servant girl, will undoubtedly be there. And those thousand rupees that he sent me to prepare for the visit? Should I repay such open-hearted generosity with doltish indifference?

Yet, yet, if Fraser sahib . . . suppose he does end up giving a hint or even making a suggestion? What reply will I make then? Reply? No reply at all. Not answering is reply enough from us. And if he's displeased or annoyed? So what? Let him be displeased, I could not care less. I would put men like him at the end of the toe of my shoes, what harm can he do to me? Navab sahib might become unhappy, but I'll mollify him. If I cannot, then Manjhli Baji is there, is she not? Navab sahib is just like wax in her hands. I'll have her intercede. I am not going to rot in the harem of a muscle-bound, lustful Englishman—let death take him—even if he speaks Persian.

I have to map out my life now in such a way that my life's game, which stood stalemated with Blak sahib's untimely and occasionless passing, should find ways to flow again and my honour should also be intact. Let them not imagine that I am one of those who are to be found in the bazaars, seated on a rickety reed-stool, soliciting clients, totally void of shame. There might be others, sightless and shameless, who sell their honour for two square meals. Well, I am not like them.

*

She borrowed a rath from Manjhli Begam's stable, hired two staff-bearers and left for the Hill with half an hour's sunlight left. She was worried about having to return alone after nightfall. Then she realized that there would be many others returning; the Navab Yusuf Ali Khan Sahib Bahadur would also be there, he would have me escorted safely back.

The rath was drawn by two bullocks, one jet black and the other milk white. Their horns had silver and gold foil wrapped around the tips. Their bodies were covered with heavy silk sheets with pearls worked into the tassels, their feet adorned with brass bells. The rath was a high carriage about three feet from the ground, and wide and high enough inside to permit women or children to stand more or less erect. Made of superior quality seasoned Indian rosewood or teak, this box-like carriage was closed on all sides, and its ceiling was made with strong splinters of teak or sal wood which could be made light or heavy with felt or thatching or extra awning, according to the dictates of the weather.

The wheels of Navab Yusuf Ali Khan's rath were adorned with brass flowers and the upper half of each had thick canvas curtains or covers to prevent mud or water splashing inside. There were velvet curtains on the sides and the back, with gold tassels used liberally, and the small windows on both sides enabled light and air to enter, though in cold weather a brocade curtain was hung on the windows under the velvet. In the same style, covered with the outer velvet and the inner brocade curtains, there were two doors for ingress and egress. For entering or coming out of the rath, wide wooden steps were used which were kept with the driver when not in use.

Inside, the floor was covered with soft carpets upon which were two low, padded chairs for the travellers. On the opposite side a box doubled as a servant's seat and store for additional curtains, padded quilts, dry fruits and similar eatables. Drinks and water carafes were kept outside with the driver in his box.

Passing by the open-air Id Gah at Paharganj, and then the shrine of the seventeenth-century Muslim saint Khvajah Baqi bi-Allah, Wazir Khanam's rath negotiated the gentle upward ascent of the Hill quite comfortably. The road then took a turn from behind the ancient caravanserai, from where began the true range of the Aravali mountains of which Delhi's Hill was a small part. The ascent was harder now. On both sides of the narrow road—a path really—were dense, thorny shrubs of wild jujube, big-leaved wild palash, acacia, the flowering malti and many others of a similar type.

The rainy season was almost at its end. Its air, wet but not heavy, conducive to wild and natural growths, had loaded and enriched with greenery even ageing shrubs and trees. Bushes which normally are melancholy with their heads lowered towards extinction were spreading out to occupy nearby empty spaces. The lights of the caravanserai, now distant, had dimmed and then disappeared, but as they neared the Navab Resident's mansion, it seemed like the festival of lights. Much before the palatial house could be approached, there were lights on both sides of the road and the main gate was brilliant with globes, English lanterns and drum-shaped glass chandeliers. The bayonets and crests of the sepoys glinted everywhere. Wazir Khanam's carriage was allowed to pass through after some routine questioning.

The path inside the gate was long and after meandering a little, it turned to the right from where the rath needed to negotiate a somewhat sharper gradient before the Resident Bahadur's mansion came into view. A tall, large, white structure built on a high plinth, with a wide veranda in front, and circular and thick stone pillars supporting the western-style arches on which rested the white roof of the veranda, could be seen from some distance. From each of the arches hung a chandelier, and the arches themselves bore designs and mouldings in stucco. Sheltered all around by the overgrown jungle of shrub and scrub, the huge, white and well-lit mansion seemed like some English cake, made of butter and cream.

The house's outward facade hid behind it a strong, fortress-like structure. Some idea of its fortified character could be had when the mansion was viewed in daylight. Fraser, writing to his father in AH 1235 (1819–1820) after the completion of its construction, said that he had built 'a large white house on top of a hill from the top of which I am getting a large view of Dehlee'. It was said the house was built on the spot where, five centuries ago, Timur the Lame had set up first camp before launching his attack on Delhi. Someone even wrote a poem in Hindi about Fraser's house which gained quite a bit of currency in the early 1820s.

There was an open portico in front of the twelve- or fourteen-foot-wide veranda. The rath stopped there. Many syces could be seen holding the reins of horses. On the far side, a couple of raths and palanquins, an English-style carriage called a charet, and a closed buggy stood, their drivers or bearers keeping watch on them. Most of the attendants were smoking the primitive kind of hookah called naryal, while some were enjoying a bottle. The veranda opened on to a large, high-ceilinged room whose three double doors, themselves quite high, were draped with heavy curtains. Sounds of convivial conversation could be heard from behind the doors.

The liveried servant who was stationed at the portico went forward quickly and lifted the curtain of Wazir Khanam's rath, bent low in salaam, and said in a soft and respectful voice: 'Be pleased to alight. Bismillah.'

Wazir alighted, taking care of her wide dupatta. Another doorman moved aside a part of the curtain on the middle door and announced: 'The Honourable Wazir Khanam sahib has come.'

As the announcement concluded, Wazir alighted on the first step of the veranda and at the same instant William Fraser Navab Resident Bahadur himself troubled his feet to come out. Extending both hands in welcome, he smilingly spoke in Persian: 'Welcome! And welcome again! Indeed your coming is cause of happiness to my heart.'

He had used a set phrase of Arabic and a famous line of a Persian verse; he spoke clearly and fluently, but not like a native speaker, Persian or Indian. His voice was heavy, with a hint of a growl in it, as was the case with all Firangees when they spoke Hindi or Persian. Wazir Khanam bent low in salaam, and without giving any hint of pleasure or obsequiousness, answered in Persian: 'Your Presence, Senior Sahib Bahadur, I am your poor serving maid and I will ever pray for your prosperity.'

Fraser switched to Hindi. 'The eyes and the heart are spread for you like carpets. Please come inside,' Fraser said gravely, to suggest that the set phrases that he was using were not just formulas of welcome.

He gestured to Wazir to enter through the open door and turned towards it, providing the lead to his cherished guest. Wazir Khanam was now behind him. She noticed that Fraser walked with a little limp. She had heard about Fraser's participation in many battles but had not known of any wound that he had suffered.

This was Wazir's first sight of him. He should certainly have been on the wrong side of fifty, but he was in good health and had a naturally strong constitution and athletic build, so he looked not more than forty-five. Even so, to Wazir he seemed quite advanced in years. She was also a bit surprised to find that he was not tall, even by Indian standards, for an average Indian was shorter than an average Englishman. Yet Fraser sahib's height appeared to be even less than an average Indian's. His moustaches were reddish brown and thick, with hints of both Mussulmani and Rajputi styles. Thick mutton-chop whiskers became a brown beard as they touched his chin. The beard had been parted in the middle, in the Rajputi style, and had been combed upwards to show a clear parting line on the chin. But the chin did not evince the strength which is generally regarded as an indication of a firm, determined type of mind, and the dense whiskers did not succeed in camouflaging the weakness of the chin.

Fraser had large, expressive eyes, a well-formed straight nose, and lips a little thicker than usual but attractive with the redness of betel leaves. His smiling visage hinted at a sense of humour and capacity to enjoy banter, but his eyes revealed a wild glimmer; heavy drinking had made his face slightly puffy which sat somewhat discordantly with his florid mien. His dress was fully Indian: narrow trousers of the famous cotton fabric himru which was produced only in Aurangabad in the far south-west of Delhi, and a long tunic, or kurta, of a fine cotton fabric called tanzeb. This fabric was always dazzlingly white and so tightly woven that it felt like paper when you ran your fingers on it. On top of the kurta, he wore in black velvet an expensive nima—a long-sleeved but short upper garment with its sleeves cut away from below, leaving them hanging free. Above it, he wore a vaguely English-looking indoor cloak; it had buttons, but none of them was fastened and its sleeves were very short, so as to reveal the cutaway sleeves of the nima. He had expensive rings on eight of the ten fingers of his hands and a long necklace of white pearls hung from his well-formed neck. He wore Jodhpuri shoes of raised and pointed toes, worked all over in gold filigree. On his head was a short turban of red, twisted silk with small, black flowers printed on it.

In short, William Fraser looked every inch a wealthy nobleman of Delhi.

25

Fanny Parkes provides an animated account of life in Allahabad

THEY ENTERED THE room like a small procession: Fraser, walking somewhat fast, followed by Wazir Khanam, as if she were a princess and Fraser her herald. Inside, she found that the room was very large, so big in fact that in spite of the bright lights, she was unable to see the far end at a glance. Chhoti Begam was a little nervous; in spite of the cool air, she apprehended that she might break into perspiration. Her steps fell uncertainly for a brief moment, but then she checked herself and resumed her usual easy, rhythmic walk.

The guests included Indians and Englishmen in almost equal proportions. There were only a few women, and all of them were English. In spite of the somewhat moist coolth of the departing season of rains, the environment in the room was comfortably warm, with the scent of good quality khamira tobacco—a deft mixture of fermented apple or pineapple juice allowed to leaven the tobacco paste, and then the tobacco smoked in hookahs with great sophistication—mixing agreeably with the mellow fragrance of English wines.

As Wazir entered the room, which was bubbling over with friendly, easy conversation, everything seemed to slow down a little. Women, men, everybody's attention was caught by her entry, preceded by no less a person than Fraser himself. Wazir, apparently unmindful of the attention, put each foot firmly forward with dignity and without haste. She was wearing light yellow trousers, made from a silk fabric called bulbul chashm (bulbul's eyes), for the print on it was supposed to look like the round, somewhat pert-looking eyes of the bird bulbul. The print on the trousers that she wore was peacock blue and gold. Contrary to custom, her trousers were rather narrow, especially from a little below the thighs, descending on to the calves right up to her ankles. The trousers were slightly revealing, but entirely free from the least hint of lack of taste or sophistication. The technical name for such pants was 'ara' which means 'oblique'. Wazir had picked up the style from the kathak dancers of Rajputana who wore a very wide skirt above such trousers so that when they moved fast in the circular mode, the skirt billowed out, revealing the ara trousers and the shape of the body below the waist.

Over her trousers, Wazir wore a jamah, which was a sort of gown similar to, but wider and looser than the skirts of the kathak dancers. It could be as wide as thirty breadths, gathered closely together below the breasts and the sternum in innumerable tiny pleats. The jamah was generally made of cotton, but Wazir had chosen a fine, almost gossamer-thin silk fabric in violet. (This fabric too was called ara coincidentally.) On account of the translucency of the jamah, one could discern, if one was shameless enough to look that long, the shapeliness of the thighs and the calves, and also the colourfulness of the delicate, small print on the pants below.

On her body, that is, the breasts and immediately below them, Wazir had on a sleeveless tunic, very low, and made from the famous Dacca muslin, worked over with minute flowers in gold. Under the tunic was a bodice made of black velvet—this was again in the style of Rajputana—whose neckline in front and back, and the sleeves were heavily decorated with gold thread and filigree work. This time again she had on a dupatta of netting, but it was much heavier, made from sky-blue brocade. How the heavy wrap managed to stay on her torso was something even Wazir would have found impossible to explain; it covered her head and breasts like the blue halo which brightens evermore the luminosity of the moon.

The dupatta sat on her head with a studied elegance, not the least part of which was the effect of casualness with which she wore it. Her long, thick hair and the pearls strung in some of the longer braided tresses, and the netting that kept the long braids partly under discipline, could be well glimpsed under the dupatta. She was wearing on her forehead a gold crescent encrusted with small gemstones such as cat's eye, blue sapphire, pink ruby and white pearl. The lower eyelids and corners of her smiling, eloquent eyes were circled with a light thread of kajal. In jewellery, she wore long earrings glittering with diamond and blue sapphire, and a heavy nose pin worked with white pearl and dark-green emerald. A tiny red ruby hung by a small, delicate chain on her neck along with a seven-stringed pearl necklace. On her wrists she had solid gold bracelets whose ends were shaped like crocodiles; on both sides of the bracelets she had delicate glass bangles with a few fine gold lines worked upon them.

On her feet she wore silver anklets with tiny, subdued bells attached to them, and brocade slipper-like shoes which had no back to support the heels, the uppers of which were brief enough to reveal a hint of the hennaed patterns of lines, dots and tiny leaves painted on the feet. She had long, tapering fingers, and the right index finger and the left middle finger were adorned by gold rings of yellow diamond and yellow topaz. Her measured and balanced but unhurried walk suggested the delicateness of hands and feet, and the softness of an elegant, well-formed body.

In that agreeable, well-lighted hall, it seemed as if the soft lights were dancing around Wazir Khanam's body, and the dark blue of the cheerful night seemed to play upon her person, as if she was not just a woman, but an unearthly spirit. She was a little taller than the average Indian young woman, and her steps fell upon the thick pile of the carpet without a hint of uncertainty and with full self-confidence. Her walk had a pleasing flow, as if a neat budgerow were floating on the gentle wavelets of the river Jamna.

Suddenly, from the far side of the room, a Firangee woman began to say aloud something in English. Silence fell everywhere. Bearers and water carriers (those who served wines and spirits were also called water carriers) who were circulating respectfully in the great hall with wine or spirit bottles or carafes on trays loaded with condiments, or held aloft hookahs and their appurtenances, stopped in their tracks. Wazir listened attentively and found that the lady was saying a poem. The voice was clear and mellifluous, but lacked the resonant ring one associates with professional readers of poetry. Wazir had picked up a thin smattering of English in Blak sahib's company, but had no idea of English poetry and its beauties. The Englishwoman, leaving her seat, was coming up to her smiling, saying:

She walks in beauty, like the night
Of cloudless climes and starry skies;
And all that is best of dark and bright,
Meets in her aspect and her eyes.

Wazir, of course, could not have known that the lines were written by Lord Byron, the most famous English poet of the time, but she could certainly get the idea that the lines had been said by the lady in her praise. She felt bashful for a moment, and coloured slightly, but the moment the poem was over, the English applauded with loud clapping, and the Indians responded with 'Wah, Wah!', 'Indeed, only God is free from all blemish!', and she realized that her bashfulness must have been covered by the noisy response.

Wazir stepped a little faster towards the Englishwoman, and the woman herself came forward to greet her, speaking Hindi fluently and without any stiltedness at all: 'Come, please come, Wazir Khanam sahib. We were all looking forward to your coming. I'm Fanny Parkes, I live in Allahabad. I hope you did not mind my reciting the poem?'

'No . . . no. There is nothing to be unhappy about. I submit my salutations to you.'

Taking Wazir's hand in her own, Fanny Parkes led her to the divan where she had been sitting. 'Come, please sit with me here. Your walk was so ravishing that Byron sahib's poem came to my mind quite on its own . . . My heavens, your hands are so delicate, so pretty, and these floral patterns that you've made on your hands, there is some name for it? Am I right? It is a pretty name.'

'Yes, these are called nigar.'

'Yes, yes, nigar, what a lovely sounding word! And please, your clothes suit your forms so well! Our dresses make us feel like pigeons locked up in their coops. Really, I have on this skirt and hat quite under duress.'

Fanny Parkes was diminutive and a little plump, with dark-brown eyes, which were bright and reflected intelligence, a pleasant nature and a certain independence of spirit. Her dress was not too bad, considering the ungainly accoutrements of English ladies in general. Her frank and easy behaviour helped reduce Wazir's diffidence. The couch on which she and Fanny sat had an occupant from before: she was a comparatively old Firangee lady. She did not talk much, but Fanny and Wazir had a pleasant time talking to each other. Wazir learnt that Fanny's husband was the manager of the ice factory at Allahabad. Fanny memsahib was fond of travel and was enamoured of Indian customs and way of life. Leaving her husband behind in Allahabad, she had travelled to Agra by boat and having enjoyed the sights and monuments there, she had taken the same boat to Delhi and was staying with Fraser sahib.

Fanny did not ask Wazir anything about her and just went on talking about herself. For example, she made a comparison between the Mughal forts at Agra and Allahabad, describing the merits of each; she compared the Ganga and the Jamna, and told Wazir about the qualities of the two river waters. She profusely praised the people of Allahabad and said their speech and voice were both dulcet and soft. The servants there did not steal, and that the mangoes and melons—both watermelon and musk melon—of Allahabad—were extremely delicious.

Fanny Parkes and her husband lived in a big house on the Jamna's bank on a slight elevation and had a pleasant all-round view. She could see the green waters of the Jamna rising and falling in strong waves up to a fairly long distance. The river was alive with crocodiles, large fish-eating gharials, freshwater dolphins and huge turtles. And then, during the cold weather, the arrival of countless migratory birds and their nesting around the area of the confluence of the two rivers for months altogether was an unforgettable sight in terms of novelty, a sight that never turned stale; then there was the colour, noise, and movement. As for that strange bird, the crow pheasant, large, arboreal, half black and half red, and the stork, the peafowl: they were to be seen all the year round.

In the evenings, she went on to report, the Shahjahani Mosque would be brilliantly lit, and the musical call for prayer could be heard easily in the silence of the sunset. (Here it may be noted that this mosque was destroyed by the English after they retook Allahabad in September 1857.) Between the city proper and the Parkes residence, there were two villages called Kydganj and Mutthiganj. (The former is now known as Kitganj, and both are now among the most densely built-up parts of the city.) Thus, if one needed to go into the city, one had to organize the trip so that return was possible before the sun went down.

There was a sort of suburban neighbourhood called Alopibagh, the scene of great merrymaking and general bustle during its annual fair and also during the festival of Dasahra. During that time, night and day were hardly different from each other. Once or twice in the year, a suttee was performed in the open space in front of the temple at Alopibagh. The suttees were reported to have been willing participants in their own death by burning; though the Company was often successful in preventing it, sometimes the crush of the people became uncontrollable, and sometimes the widow—the Suttee Mother herself—insisted upon being immolated with her husband, rendering the Company soldiers powerless to prevent the horror.

Carried off by her own loquacity and her desire to communicate with

Wazir, Fanny Parkes went on in this mode, regardless of the others present there. Wazir found Fanny's account interesting; she was a good listener, but took an occasional opportunity to glance at the others, especially the Indians, who were among those present. Fraser sahib had left her to Fanny Parkes's care and was attending to other guests now.

During her animated account of Allahabad, Fanny would sometimes go suddenly off on a tangent to say a few admiring words about an item of Wazir's dress or jewels. Sometimes she would touch her face, enjoying the brilliance of her nose pin, and then return to her theme. An interesting and rather strange thing that she reported was that though there were greater security and less civic problems in Allahabad under the Company, those who lived on the far side of the Ganga and were subjects of the King of Avadh, did not like to cross over into Allahabad and preferred the King's rule over the Company's rule.

'Why? Why should this be so, Fanny memsahib?' Wazir asked.

Fanny Parkes was lost in thought for a little while, then she spoke softly: 'The fact of the matter is . . . that the city dwellers live in comfort under the Company's rule, but the village people have many problems. The Company has raised the rates of land revenue, the landowner and the peasant don't have good relations, local artisans are out of jobs . . . but let us not talk of such things, that is how the world is.'

Wazir wanted to inquire more into the matter. She also wanted to know if Fanny memsahib had any children, and if so, how many? And where was her Sahib now? Was he among the guests? But she knew that asking personal questions was bad manners and improper among the English. Wazir figured that it must have been the reason for Fanny memsahib's restraint in asking about her personal circumstances. Or, maybe she already knew everything. Certainly, she must have known about Blak sahib.

26

The greatest poet of the age, Mirza Asadullah Khan Ghalib, recites a poem at the august gathering

SHE WAS INVOLVED in these thoughts when there was an announcement at the door: 'The Presence, Dilawar-ul Mulk, Navab Shamsuddin Ahmad Khan Bahadur has arrived.'

Fraser went out immediately and returned with his hand on the shoulder of a supremely handsome, tall, powerfully built, and richly dressed young man. Most of those present stood up to greet him. Even those who did not rise welcomed him in Hindi or English. Shamsuddin Ahmad Khan's age at that time could not have exceeded twenty-one, or at most twenty-two, but his visage reflected the arrogance of wealth and nobility, and the maturity of experience.

Shamsuddin Ahmad Khan had on his head a tightly wrapped turban, jutting out a little, in the style favoured by Mughal nobility. Artfully woven around his turban, he had a sarpech—a brocade or silk band, about two and a half inches wide and three to three and a half yards long. He had departed from the general practice by having pinned to his sarpech a huge Badakhshani ruby, almost the size of a pigeon's egg and cut cabochon, highly polished, its brilliance winking at all the lights in that room.

Ignoring the cool weather, he wore a pure white kurta of tanzeb. Over it he had on a nima of heavily embroidered Kashmiri wool called jamavar. The cut of the kurta and that of the nima had provided for the latest fashion: a part of the right breast could be glimpsed from under the kurta. He had a pearl necklace of seven strings around his neck and wore a brocade sash around his waist; a dagger with gold-and-gemstone work on its sheath and haft was stuck in the sash.

His trousers made of brocade were narrow, but he wore no jamah over it, so the shape of the muscular thighs and calves could be discerned. His complexion was extremely fair and his large eyes were suggestive of his Transoxianian origins. His beard was cut in the Mughal style, not too long but pointed; the moustaches were not heavy, but prominent. The total impression created by his deportment, the composed, confident expression on his face—the attractiveness of his commanding male presence, and his walk and general bearing—was so assertive of power and dignity and nobility that everyone in that huge room where the minimum value of the jewellery worn by the guests would have exceeded a couple of million rupees, paled for a moment into insignificance. Even Fraser, who had regular dealings and contact with Shamsuddin Ahmad Khan, looked a little dazed and faded.

Behind the Navab, two staff-bearers had unhesitatingly entered the chamber, though the guests' attendants were not as a rule allowed inside. Now when Shamsuddin Ahmad Khan signalled to them briefly with his fingers, they performed three salaams and withdrew, walking backwards. William Fraser had just seated the Navab in a prominent place and was presenting with his own hands the silver mouthpiece of a hookah to him when the announcement was heard at the door: 'Navab Mirza Asadullah Khan Sahib!'

William Fraser went out at once and came back in a moment, hand in the hand with Navab Mirza Asadullah Khan Ghalib. From all sides came salutations and greetings:

'My submissions!'

'Honourable Navab sahib, your servant!'

'Please to come this side, you have made us wait a long time!'

Wazir noted that such profuse welcomes and greetings had not been the case at the entrance of Navab Shamsuddin Ahmad. Mirza sahib was tall, his forehead high, his eyes bright and smiling, his chest broad, his wrists wide and his neck upright. His walk exuded confidence and control, but was devoid of vanity or self-regard. His complexion was very fair, with a touch of gold in it—the technical name for this somewhat rare complexion was 'maidah shahab' ('finest ground flour kneaded with the juice of red safflower')—his face was void of a beard, but he wore moustaches, somewhat long and pointed in the style of the Turkmen. His brows were thick, his eyelashes long, and his delicately formed lips bore a natural, though not pronounced, smile. All these had gone into making his face so attractive and absorbing that one felt like gazing and going on gazing.

For a moment, even Wazir moved her eyes from Shamsuddin Ahmad to concentrate on Mirza Ghalib.

Seating Mirza Ghalib next to Muzaffar-ud Daulah Nasir-ul Mulk Mirza Saifuddin Haidar Khan Bahadur, Fraser said: 'Mirza sahib, I've ordered for you today a few bottles of your favourite French liqueur, but my condition is: Give us your newest ghazals, please.'

It will be recalled that Wazir Khanam and Saifuddin Haidar Khan were already acquainted, from his days as Shah Nasir's pupil. Saifuddin Haidar and Wazir Khanam had exchanged formal salaams and greetings when she had first entered.

Mirza Ghalib's brotherly friendship with Mirza Saifuddin Haidar Khan, eldest son of Mubariz-ud Daulah Mumtaz-ul Mulk Navab Husam-ud Din Haidar Khan Bahadur was well known all over Delhi. It was therefore quite appropriate for Ghalib to be seated next to him. It was said that Mirza Saifuddin Haidar Khan had been largely the cause of Mirza Ghalib veering away from Sunnism, the creed of his birth, and becoming strongly inclined toward Shi'ism, the creed of Mirza Saifuddin Haidar and his ancestors.

In those days the progeny of Navab Husam-ud Din Haidar was extremely influential at the Court in the Haveli. It was Saifuddin Haidar's love and loyalty to the King that caused him to die by an English bullet during the siege and destruction of Delhi after the English retook the city in September 1857. At the present moment, the Haidar family was regarded with favour by the Company Bahadur too, and a love for Persian poetry was common between Fraser and Saifuddin Haidar.

'I must boast at my good fortune for such princely measures to be undertaken for such a small fellow as I,' Ghalib smiled and said. 'For us, it is enough from the wine house of the Firang that there should be just the dregs from the bottle, and full liberty to sprinkle fire-wine on all. We poets do not demand more compensation than that.'

Mirza Ghalib's voice had a unique suppleness and musicality. With very clear enunciation, the voice carried easily, but was neither loud nor low, and his tone was filled with warmth and such friendliness that his immediate interlocutor felt as if they were the chief person of his interest.

Navab Shamsuddin Ahmad Khan drew on the long pipe of the hookah, and spoke in mild and measured tones, but a slight sting of satire could also be discerned somewhere deep in his utterance: 'Only God is free from all blemish! Our respected brother Mirza Naushah sahib, but truly, you roll pearls of poetry in your prose. Actually, we too are keen to enjoy your excellent poems.'

The subtext of the Navab's speech was that the foreigner, and a Firangee to boot, may well acquire the Persian language from elementary and well-known works of its literature and learn by rote the works of Persian grammar and syntax, but appreciation of poetry, and that too of high Persian poetry, was something beyond his capacity and ability. This art remains limited to us Transoxianians and Iranians. The signification of the blow from the spear of Shamsuddin Ahmad's sarcasm had not escaped William Fraser, but he was well aware that Mirza Ghalib would certainly come up with a well-judged and delightful repartee. And he was right. Mirza sahib smiled his extremely pleasing spontaneous smile, and looking Navab Shamsuddin Ahmad in the eye, observed: 'Your Command is perfectly true, Mian Navab Shamsuddin Ahmad Sahib. Yet the writing of poetry as well as the appreciation of poetry is like being cribbed by Firangee fetters, and there is nothing to be gained from labouring at them. Benefit in the presentation of art there is none. Indeed, I often think that I was rather unwise in giving up the profession of a hundred generations of my forebears.'

'Firangee fetters! A point well taken, respected brother Mirza Naushah sahib. Apparently, the land of your poetry seems eminently tillable. And that land is like God's own Earth: it has no end, no frontiers. Where is the question of prison houses there? Indeed, it is upon people like us that God's Earth seems to have become narrow and inhospitable.'

Here again, there was more to Shamsuddin Ahmad's words than was apparent. He was hinting at his apprehension of the State of Loharu being taken away from him, and was also implying that Mirza Ghalib's cultivation of poetry seemed to be flourishing profusely under English patronage. Ghalib laughed and said, 'Yet, Mian sahib, it is worth recalling what the Persian poet said:

Unless you sprinkle the seed of your tears on your tillage,
Oh Master!
All your labouring and husbandry will avail you nothing.

So that is how it is with us and maybe with you as well.'

Mirza Saifuddin Haidar perhaps felt that the exchange between the poet and the Navab might turn into a sharp debate, so he gestured with both hands, as if addressing the entire assembly, but in such a way that it seemed that the person he was really addressing was Wazir Khanam. 'Your Command is perfectly true, Mirza sahib, but we are gardeners and servers in the garden of love. Just hear what the Tongue of the Unseen has said:

Let us see when the tree of friendship bears fruit,
I have just gone and sown a seed.

Navab Yusuf Ali Khan raised his right hand in the traditional gesture of admiration and approbation: 'Only God is free from all blemish! Very well commanded, Saifuddin Ahmad Khan Bahadur. Again, in the words of Hafiz:

I have not read the sagas of Alexander and Darius,
Ask me nothing but narratives of love and fidelity.

Both these gentlemen were men of great discrimination; they could read the nuances of a situation as well as those of a literary text. The general population of Delhi was unaware of the crack that had developed in the friendly relations between Fraser and Shamsuddin Ahmad Khan, and as opposed to it, was also not much in the know of the growing closeness of relations between Fraser and Mirza Ghalib. The rancour in the heart of Shamsuddin Ahmad Khan against Ghalib originated not just in part from the fact that the latter had been complaining to Fraser against what Ghalib genuinely regarded as the iniquitous treatment meted out to him in the allocation of income from the State of Navab Shamsuddin Ahmad Khan's father, the late Navab Ahmad Bakhsh Khan. These complaints, coming on top of Ghalib's palpably growing friendship with Fraser, had ensured that there was no love lost between Ghalib and Navab Shamsuddin Ahmad Khan.

The names of both Ghalib and Fraser were known to every citizen of Delhi, though for different reasons: Ghalib as the major Persian poet of Delhi, and Fraser as its virtual ruler. Very few among the nobility and the powerful in Delhi were privy to the inner tensions and the accumulating bitterness between Navab Shamsuddin Ahmad Khan and William Fraser on the one hand, and between Mirza Ghalib and the Navab on the other. It was a puzzle that none among those present could solve to their satisfaction: Had Fraser brought together the poet and the Navab so as to effect a reconciliation between them? Or was there a subtle hint underneath to the effect that Shamsuddin Ahmad Khan might look upon himself, as much as he liked, as the autonomous ruler of a large state, but in the eyes of the Grand Sahib, the English Resident, he was a mere native chieftain? The Navab Resident Bahadur was free to give audience and invite to his palatial mansion whomever he wanted to; he was answerable to none.

Fraser might thus be sending out a subtle signal to Shamsuddin Ahmad Khan that he was free to take umbrage, but Mirza Ghalib would continue to be a visitor at the Resident's house, and if the Navab needed to, he must visit the Resident a hundred times or more, and also be a dinner guest in Ghalib's company. Or, maybe, Fraser had invited Shamsuddin Ahmad Khan to humiliate him in some other way?

The truth in this case was indeed hidden from everyone. The fact of the matter was that Fraser's womanizing instinct had been awakened when he heard about Wazir Khanam from Navab Yusuf Ali Khan. Thus the dinner and an evening of poetry with Mirza Ghalib were a nice enough excuse to invite Wazir to his house. The invitation to Shamsuddin Ahmad Khan was intended to be a gesture of conciliation towards the young Navab.

Still, Fraser may have been playing a deeper game: it was obvious to those who knew him that to the proud and haughty Shamsuddin Ahmad, with his quickness to take offence, accepting Fraser's dinner invitation—particularly when Ghalib was to be among the invitees and the near impossibility for the Navab of turning down Fraser's invitation—would have been gall and wormwood. On the other hand, Mirza Ghalib's consciousness of his own noble lineage and his keenness never to compromise his self-respect was second to none.

True, an older cousin of Navab Shamsuddin Ahmad Khan—a daughter of his uncle Navab Ilahi Bakhsh Khan Maruf—was married to Mirza Ghalib and thus Mirza Ghalib was the young Navab's brother-in-law. Navab Ahmad Bakhsh Khan was, doubtless, a Sayyid, and thus in terms of birth and progeny, he was immeasurably superior to Ghalib, but the woman with whom he had Shamsuddin Ahmad was of low caste and in no wise even distantly of the same or similar clan to make her eligible as Ahmad Bakhsh Khan's wife. Thus, in terms of status by birth, Ghalib regarded Shamsuddin Ahmad as his inferior. On the other hand, worldly status and wealth placed Navab Shamsuddin Ahmad superior not only to Ghalib but also to numerous other noblemen of Delhi. So Ghalib's pride and spirit always felt threatened where Shamsuddin Ahmad Khan was concerned.

Considering these subtleties, both the noblemen—Saifuddin Haidar Khan and Yusuf Ali Khan—made a conscious effort to prevent the exchange from turning into hostile channels, and began to display, artfully and covertly, their virtuosity in the area of love poetry and poems about the beloved's beauty. Some could get to the bottom of the almost coded conversation, some could not. But both Navab Shamsuddin Ahmad Khan and Mirza Ghalib immediately realized the undertow in the change of subject and welcomed it in their hearts. Thus, a soft smile played on the lips of Mirza Ghalib and travelling up to his eyes, it made his face look even more bright and attractive. Mirza Saifuddin Haidar's subtle gesture with his hands directed Ghalib's attention to Wazir Khanam. As for William Fraser, he had been stealing glances at Wazir's face and had been ecstatically marvelling in his heart: if there is to be a principal source of light at a soirée, it should be she, or one very much like her.

Shamsuddin Ahmad Khan now turned slightly to look at Wazir Khanam, and a thrill, almost palpable, he thought, ran through his whole body. Wazir's eyes at that moment were somewhere between Mirza Ghalib and Navab Shamsuddin Ahmad Khan. It seemed as if she was conscious of both, but only because of the fact that they were a part of the assembly, not because they claimed any special attention or respect from her. In point of fact, Wazir's eyes were taking account of Ghalib's broad wrists and his long, delicate and conical fingers, and her ears were tuned in to the conversation in general, but her secret attention was concentrated on Navab Shamsuddin Ahmad's handsome and impressive self, a personality strong and attractive enough to stop pedestrians in their tracks. She also intuited a bitterness, a restlessness, a sense of not belonging, somewhere deep in the Navab's soul.

On his part, when Shamsuddin Ahmad Khan cast a little more than a casual eye at Wazir Khanam, he had an inner sense of something happening between them: a strange flame was ignited, touching both of them. Or perhaps the truth was that an extremely eloquent but extremely intriguing sense of womanhood, a sort of magnetic wave, seemed to be emanating towards him in undulating, hypnotic waves from Wazir Khanam's body. He felt as if he was in a slim boat right in the middle of the Jamna where it was the deepest and the strongest, and the waves of the sacred river were rising and moving from the distant bank and obscure depths to touch his boat, to make it wet . . .

Was his body aquiver because of the cold spray of the river water, or because of the strange, chill wind that buffeted his tiny boat? He feared drowning; but he was also burning with the desire to go on being sprayed to full wetness. For a moment he was convinced that there was no one else in that chamber but himself and Wazir Khanam; and in the profundities of their beings, the foundations were shaking because of many fears, and whips and lashes from unknown ocean waves.

The wine had begun to circulate again, or rather, it had been lost and absorbed for a short while in the complex, attractive, but rather dark turns and twists of the magnetic personalities of the newer arrivals, and now it shook itself and opened its eyes. Fraser's chief wine server presented before Mirza Ghalib a sealed bottle on which the inscription was in the Firangee script and there were some decorative designs as well. The wine server had placed the bottle in a cut-glass vessel made to look like a swan, and the vessel was on an engraved and ornamented silver tray with a matching cup.

'Navab sahib, Bismillah,' Fraser said to Ghalib, smiling with the pleasure of a host who offers some rare delicacy to his guest.

Ghalib also smiled with pleasurable anticipation. He took the bottle in his hands, broke the seal, and said: 'The fact of the matter is that my mouth is watering, but I shall leave the bottle for a little while so that it may be touched by the air. Although, in Persian, by the term "touched by air" we mean a wine that is gone bad because of exposure to damp air; some of your wines, like this one, need to be touched by the air, so that they may breathe before they're drunk.'

'Well, truly Mirza Naushah, it is these very subtleties of yours for which I would be prepared to die!' Fraser laughed with pleasure. 'Men should learn the art of drinking from you! But Presence, may God preserve you, how did you get to know the term "to breathe" in regard to wines? This idiom is English and is used for some wines which are left open before drinking so that their vapours may dissipate.'

'Kind sir,' Ghalib partly quoted one of his Hindi verses, but not as if he was quoting poetry, '"It is these very ideas that come to us from the Unseen." Did you not hear the Arabic saying that "The poets . . .'

'Yes, surely,' Fraser hastened to supply the remaining part of the proverb, ". . . are God's pupils." But dear sir, how exactly you arrived at this rather peculiar idiom, let the curtain be raised upon the mystery!'

'Oh, I have some other friends who are good to me. You may have heard of Alec sahib, whose nom de plume is Azad, that is, Captain Alexander Heatherley. But let us quit these little matters,' he gestured lightly towards Wazir Khanam. 'You granted me the favour of being the neighbour of an everlasting wine house and put this bottle in my hand . . . You thus proved false one of my verses!'

'Mirza Naushah, your poem—as if it could prove false!' Mirza Saifuddin Haidar Khan patted Ghalib's shoulder. 'Anyway, let us hear it and decide for ourselves.'

'Yes, Mirza sahib, count me also among those who are keen on your poetry,' said Navab Yusuf Ali Khan, who was a poet but had not yet become the pupil of a master.

'Yes, in fact I'll submit yet another verse which goes well with that one,' saying this, Mirza Ghalib particularly addressed William Fraser: 'Be pleased to look at these, Honoured Mentor and Guide.'

Navab Shamsuddin Ahmad Khan felt extremely resentful that a Nazarene, and that too an Englishman, should be addressed with the honorific 'Mentor and Guide': Pir o Murshid. Until the time of Muhammad Raushan Akhtar Muhammad Shah Badshah Ghazi, now resting in Paradise, among worldly persons, only the King was addressed as 'Mentor and Guide', an honorific otherwise used only for a Sufi who was someone's spiritual master. After the passing of that Sovereign, sycophants of regional chieftains, maharajahs and navabs began also to address them in that fashion. But an infidel, and that too an Englishman, should be spoken of as 'Pir o Murshid' was a newfangled wrong.

'So now matters have come to such a pass that infidel Kristans are considered entitled to such words,' he spoke in a low voice to the man sitting next to him, but the pitch was not so low as to sound like a whisper. 'And this again is a funny thing, leaving the wine bottle open. Everything that these people do is upside down. They write from the left to the right, remove their hat if they want to show respect, eat with the left hand . . . and strut about the whole of Hind like Chinese pheasants.'

The person to whom Shamsuddin Ahmad Khan had addressed these words was from Lucknow. He wore a light cap of a white, embroidered cotton called chikan, the embroidery of which was delicate and also in white cotton. He wore the cap a little askew, as was the fashion in Lucknow then, and his hair, closely set in flat locks, could be clearly glimpsed bright beneath the cap. A little plump of body, he wore a kurta of the same cloth as that of his cap, and over it, he wore a nima of a light, woollen printed fabric called malinah, and a jamah of the same fabric.

The loose trousers he wore were in the style still fashionable in Delhi, but of a cotton and silk mixed cloth made only in Aurangabad, called mashru. The novelty in its design was that it had neither stripes nor a woven floral pattern, but very small sprigs embroidered on it in silk. The young man wore a long necklace of white pearls and gemstone rings in all five fingers of the left hand. His mixing of the styles of Delhi and Lucknow was eye-catching and attractive.

For some obscure reason, everyone addressed him as 'General sahib'. His name was Ashraf-ud Daulah Navab Ahmad Ali Khan Bahadur, son of Muntazim-ud Daulah Hakim Mahdi Ali Khan Bahadur, formerly Chief Minister of the kingdom of Avadh. He and his father were now residing in Fatehgarh. He was in Delhi for a few days to visit with Fraser. He nodded in agreement with Shamsuddin Ahmad Khan.

Wazir had not been able to clearly hear Shamsuddin Ahmad Khan, but since she was mostly concentrating on him, she understood the general purport of Shamsuddin Ahmad's remarks by his body's unconscious gestures and the few snatches of his words that reached her. Looking at the Navab, she nodded and smiled with a hint of intimate confidentiality, as if she was expressing agreement. In the context of Wazir's past life with Marston Blake, perhaps her smile of agreement held some meaning, or probably something even more than meaning.

Mirza Ghalib, who had been during this time gently puffing on the long pipe of the hookah, raised his head, cast a glance at the audience, and commanded: 'I present the opening verse. Then will come the verse I had promised.'

Voices came from everywhere in the hall:

'Please command, at your pleasure!'

'We wait for the privilege!'

'Sirs, be pleased to look,' he said and recited the opening verse of his Persian ghazal. His manner of saying poetry was just like his usual voice, flexible and sophisticated. It seemed as if this man would never need to raise his voice or speak up: his normal voice was as carrying as its rhythms were clear and refined.

It is one and the same: neither accepts separation from the other—
Your lustrous manifestation from the heart, and wine from
the wine glass.

Navab Yusuf Ali Khan immediately responded enthusiastically in Persian: 'Very correctly said, Mirza sahib! The lustre of the beloved's beauty in the lover's heart and the wave of wine in his cup are of the same level and the same rank!'

Gravely, Mirza Ghalib bent his head and salaamed in acknowledgement of the praise. He now sat up a little more alertly while there were accolades of 'Wah! Wah!' and similar expressions of appreciation from all sides. When the clamour subsided a little, Ashraf-ud Daulah spoke in a rather high but clear voice: 'Mirza sahib, I must admire your use of the rather rare word "guna" in the first line to mean "style", for a lesser poet would have said something trite like "tarz". Truly, it behoves you to use such a word.'

Fraser was about to make some comment of his own when Fanny Parkes, who had no Persian and was straining to get something out of Ghalib's verse, pricked up her ears when Ashraf-ud Daulah used the feminine gender for 'lafz', the Hindi for 'word'. She knew him well, so she felt no diffidence in asking him: 'General sahib, you used . . . oh, what is the Hindi word for "feminine gender"? It slips my mind.'

'Muannas,' Fraser promptly supplied the word.

'Oh, yes, many thanks, Colonel Fraser. So, General sahib, you have used the Hindi word lafz as if its gender was feminine, whereas I have always heard it as masculine. How is that? Or did I hear wrong?'

'No, Fanny memsahib, you did not hear wrong. You live in Allahabad where the word lafz is treated as masculine, but we of Lucknow are of a different persuasion. We use this word always as feminine. Perhaps Delhi observes a different rule. What do you say, dear Mirza sahib?'

'Your Command is perfectly correct. For us, the masculinity of the word lafz is fully established and universally preferred.'

'The matter regarding the gender of Hindi words is really confusing. Now take this word rath; it is used as feminine by some, some others use it as masculine,' said Fraser. 'Now, Mirza sahib, what would your verdict be on this case?'

Ghalib laughed. 'Oh well, that is not a hard one to determine. If a woman is riding it, rath is feminine, otherwise, it is masculine.'

This was greeted with loud guffaws. Since Wazir had travelled to the Resident sahib's house in a rath, she felt mildly embarrassed but laughed with the others all the same. Ghalib was smiling a tiny bit, as if enjoying the happy response to his witticism. His way was never to laugh at his own jokes, but to sit unconcerned as if he had said or done nothing.

The laughter had not yet quite died down when Fraser said, 'Now look, Mirza sahib, don't let the matter pass in jest. You still owe us another verse.'

'Yes, dear sir, without doubt. I present it now. Be pleased to give it a hearing.'

Saying this, Ghalib looked at Wazir, and said:

Ghalib, I am prepared to give you a place next to the tavern,
On condition that you be contented with the wine's bouquet alone.

There was a roar of admiration and appreciation from all. Ghalib gestured lightly towards Wazir and said: 'William Fraser Bahadur, you sat next to me an evergreen, mobile tavern, and on top of it, you placed upon my feeble lips this peri from the wine house of the Firang. In such circumstances, why shouldn't my verse be proved false? But having this bottle in my hands also called to my mind an old Hindi verse of mine.'

Then he recited, with the same aplomb as he had shown with the Persian poem:

The circulation of wine causes it perplexity and distraction:
Do it one time, place the whole vessel against my lips.

'Well, if it is not a whole vessel, at least it is a whole bottle. Same difference, so far as the effect is concerned,' Ghalib concluded.

Wazir Khanam felt her ear lobes redden. Overcome by shyness, she lowered her head, but looking sidelong at Shamsuddin Ahmad through the corner of her eye, she found him frowning a bit. Had he begun to harbour some real feelings for her, she wondered. As far as she could see, William Fraser desired her and was looking for a suitable moment to make his move, but was he now in a quandary because he sensed Shamsuddin Ahmad as a potential rival?

She would certainly throw a flat 'No' at Fraser, be what the consequences may. But what was the meaning of the way Shamsuddin Ahmad Khan seemed to regard her? And there were some whispers in her heart. From where did they come and what were they saying to her?

While she was engaged upon these reflections, she sensed a certain restlessness in Navab Shamsuddin Ahmad, as if he were in a hurry to leave, but was mindful of the etiquette, and also maybe of Wazir Khanam. Fraser, too, sensed the young Navab's slight restlessness and lack of equanimity and felt that it was expedient to work towards a bit of conciliation. Whatever devious purpose he had in putting Navab Shamsuddin Ahmad Khan and Mirza Ghalib together had also perhaps been achieved. He left his place and walked up to the Navab. Casting a casual glance at Wazir, he said, 'Dilawar-ul Mulk Bahadur, be pleased to come this way, sit next to me.'

During private visits, Shamsuddin Ahmad Khan addressed Fraser as 'Uncle', but such encounters had trickled into almost non-existence since the souring of their relations. On formal occasions, he addressed him as 'Navab Resident Bahadur' or 'Navab Senior Sahib Bahadur'. Fraser's formal address to him was 'Navab Shamsuddin Ahmad Khan Bahadur', and when he felt extra pleased with him, he would address him as 'Dilawar-ul Mulk'. Doubtless, Shamsuddin Ahmad Khan's father had the official title of 'Fakhr-ud Daulah Dilawar-ul Mulk' but that had not been ratified upon the son by the English. Thus, Fraser addressing Shamsuddin Ahmad Khan as 'Dilawar-ul Mulk' was a mark of special favour. Shamsuddin Ahmad Khan wanted to refuse Fraser's invitation, suspecting that it was a ploy to put him at some distance from Wazir. He was about to refuse when Fraser went on, 'Also, be pleased to command if we should eat my poor fare now, or should Mirza Naushah Sahib be troubled to recite his poetry first?'

This special attention helped cool the temper boiling up in Shamsuddin Ahmad Khan's heart, and he also welcomed this interlude as an opportunity to make some direct conversation with Wazir. Taking Fraser's hand in his, he said warmly, 'This servant has no special preference, Navab Resident Bahadur, whatever your exalted mind may desire. But . . . it may possibly delay Bi Wazir Khanam sahib.'

Hearing the Navab say her name, and that too in a context which suggested that her wishes carried some weight with him, Wazir smiled in spite of trying to keep a straight face. She rose, did three salaams, and said, 'This servant girl is here at your service with her eyes and her heart. The servants of the Exalted Sir may direct as they will. As for the apprehension of delay, it is of no matter.' She raised her eyes towards Yusuf Ali Khan and continued, 'I'll travel safe under the benevolent shade of the servants of the High Presence.'

Her soft voice tinkled and travelled down the ears just as the velvet taste of the choicest wine of the best year slips down the throat to the chest, enlivening palate, nose and tongue. Hot but gentle rays of woman-appeal seemed to shoot forth from her person, making her face glimmer with beauty's luminance. Yusuf Ali Khan was about to make a reply when Shamsuddin Ahmad Khan half turned towards Wazir and said, 'I am ready and available to be employed for this duty. And if permission from my brother of exalted lineage, Navab Yusuf Ali Khan Sahib, is needed, I hope it will be forthcoming.'

Yusuf Ali Khan said: 'Doubtless. And in any case, our and Dilawar-ul Mulk's routes are more or less the same. There will be no problem.'

He said this just for politeness' sake and so as not to disappoint Shamsuddin Ahmad Khan. For, in fact their destinations lay in different directions. One of Shamsuddin Ahmad Khan's mansions was in Ballimaran, behind Chandni Chowk and the other was in Daryaganj, near the Red Fort. Yusuf Ali Khan's mansion was close to the mosque in Pul Bangash, on the opposite side, near Tiraha Bairam Khan. Anyway, no one went into the details and the matter was settled amicably.

Fraser was a little piqued at the way Shamsuddin Ahmad Khan had directly netted Wazir's attention for himself. But it was no use fretting about this little thing. Fraser was confident that in pomp and power, honour and acclaim and authority, and above all, experience and political clout, he far exceeded Shamsuddin Ahmad. And it was just the beginning, the dawn of the first day. There was much time for him.

He turned towards Ghalib, and said, 'May I now request you, Mirza sahib, to unfold your poetry before us. All of us are eager to hear you.'

Voices of 'Bismillah!'; 'All of us are equally eager!'; 'Please give us your ghazal!' had not yet quite died down when Mirza sahib said: 'I present the opening verse.' Everyone fell silent. The servants stood rooted where they were. The burble of the long pipes of the hookahs stopped. Ghalib's voice now had a new depth, a new feeling, as if he was addressing some mysterious non-physical being. The opening verse of his Persian ghazal was:

The intensity of my longing for your sight,
Come, and take a look;

I am about to drop like a tear from the eyelash,
Come, and take a look.

In the midst of applauding voices—'Wah! Wah!' 'Good, very good!'—the voice of Saifuddin Haidar was heard, who spoke up: 'I take the name of God! What an opening verse indeed! I am about to drop like a tear from the eyelash, come, and take a look. Please bestow it upon us in your voice again!'

Fraser rose from his place impulsively and spoke in Persian: 'Mirza sahib! Please, do trouble yourself again! You spoke beautifully, I swear it!'

Ghalib did a salaam without rising, and ignoring all other applauders, said, 'Now the verse after the opening one', and went on to say the next one:

You used to avoid me: my crime was thrashing and
flailing about, restless;

Those among the audience who were near him repeated the line as required by convention. 'Only God is free from all blemish!' someone added. 'Good, how extremely good!' Another voice arose: 'How proper! You used to avoid me, and the "crime was thrashing and flailing about, restless", is truly beyond human praise.'

Ghalib now said the second line of the verse:

I am now dead and at rest, how well do I rest,
Come, and take a look.

It now seemed as if the ceiling, the glasses, bottles, chandeliers, jugs of wine, everything was shaking as in an earthquake. None was aware of the words in which their neighbour, or the others, were applauding. Mirza sahib, utterly oblivious of the clamour, with his head bent and his hand striking his side over and over again in slow rhythm, kept repeating to himself, as in a trance: 'I am now dead and at rest, how well do I rest, come, and take a look.' Sometimes he would just hum the words, or say them in an undertone, not enunciating all the words. Then suddenly, he raised his eyes, looked at the entire assembly and said in a low voice:

You used to avoid me, my crime was thrashing and
flailing about, restless;

I am now dead and at rest, how well do I rest,
Come, and take a look.

After the audience became comparatively quiet, Ghalib recited the next verse:

I envy the Other; I am undone by it; have some shame!
We are together, alone, yet I do not see myself,
Just take a look!

Before the din of applause could subside, Mirza sahib raised both hands in entreaty, appealing for the whole ghazal to be heard: 'How can I finish when each and every verse is given such prolonged acclaim?' Still, muted compliments of 'Excellent!' 'Praise be to God, what force, what freshness!' 'How unusual are the rhymes!' and repetition of individual lines by the audience continued while Mirza sahib recited:

I heard that you look at no one, but I am not without hope,
Well, I did hear about your looking at no one;
So how did I take it, come, and take a look.

The seed sprouted, grew up, became a home for nesting birds;
I, still hoping for the Phoenix, still spread my snare—
Just come, and take a look.

This verse too transported the audience into an ecstatic frenzy. Mirza sahib, in the style now becoming popular among poets and orators of Lucknow, folded his hands in a gesture of appreciation and humility, and said in Persian: 'I beg to be excused; the throat of this feeble servant is now dry. I have not the strength to say the verses over and over again.'

Still, the audience, quite lost in the effect of loss and hopeless hope created by the verse, kept repeating to themselves: *I, still hoping for the Phoenix, still spread my snare—Just come, and take a look.* 'Ah! The pain of it! The pity of it!' *The seed sprouted, grew up, became a home for nesting birds.* 'By the Truth of God, Mirza sahib, what a marvellous thing to say!'

Fanny Parkes looked, open-mouthed. This is also a way of listening to poetry and raining down showers of acclaim! In my country even

Shakespeare does not transport the audience of the theatre to such ecstasy. Indeed the very civilization of Hindustan rests upon its poetry.

When the voices of applause dimmed a little, Mirza Ghalib began again:

You have no idea how submissive are those who draw sighs
of hopeless desire for you,
Be my eyes to see how secretly I glance at you:
Come, take a look.

Should you be in the mood to enjoy the sights in a rose garden,
There is a world of colour in my thrashing about
and my bleeding wounds—
Come, and take a look!

The theme of writhing and flailing had already been used in an earlier, better verse of the ghazal. Thus there was not much chance for this verse to move the audience to any extraordinary applause. But there was in the verse a bit of what is called 'poetic craftiness', for the speaker was tricking the beloved to come and see him by saying that if you feel like enjoying the sight of a rose garden, here am I, roiled in my blood; for the beloved, the scene should be no less colourful than a rose garden, because it is the wounds inflicted by her upon the lover which have caused his blood to flow.

Wazir got the point of the verse immediately, but was too diffident to openly praise it; she just said, 'Very good,' in an undertone. Navab Shamsuddin Ahmad Khan had also caught the oblique meaning of the verse, but he did not prefer to applaud openly. He looked at Wazir, smiled, and said, 'You would surely know all about such tricks to summon the beloved, would you not?'

Wazir smiled shyly and bent her head, but now the Navab's observation made the indirect sense clear to the others too who were within hearing distance. Now, they also applauded.

Mirza Ghalib presented the next verse:

How cruel is the comb, to have broken off a hair from her tresses;
I bite the back of my hand in grief, making it look like a comb:
Come, and look.

This drew only mild praise, because most of the audience knew that Mirza sahib had used this theme many times in the past and it was nothing new.

Mirza Ghalib passed on to the next verse:

Be my springtime and see how I abound in bloom and blossom—
Let me into your audience chamber alone, to drink;
I will drink, and drink,
And you will look!

The phrase 'be my springtime' was much appreciated and the audience said it over and over again. Someone called out: 'Only God is free from all blemish, Mirza sahib! Mir Taqi sahib, our great master of the past, used the phrase "abounding in bloom and blossom" for the beloved, but you apply it to your own self in such a novel way. Good, very good indeed!'

Ghalib smiled with pleasure at the speaker's discernment and said, 'You hit the point nicely and well, Rai Pran Kishan sahib. The word "springtime" is also from the same source. Each of us finds his own morsel from that open feast.'

Rai Pran Kishan was among Delhi's wealthiest and most honoured nobles, and not only among the Hindus. Everybody acknowledged his rare ability to understand and appreciate the subtleties of poetry. Nearly everyone who was anyone in Delhi knew him also because of his expertise in music, especially in its pre-Mughal style, called the dhrupad. His friendship with Navab Zain-ul Abidin Khan, son of Sayyid Khvaja Farid, one-time Prime Minister of Emperor Akbar Shah II, was proverbial.

'Yes, sir, you are quite correct,' said Rai Pran Kishan and recited the Hindi verse of the Master Poet, Mir:

Wine has made her abound in bloom and blossom, just see;
Friends, let her have another sip, then see the true splendour of spring!

In a voice full of enthusiasm and the pleasure of appreciation, Rai Pran Kishan cried, 'How beautifully are new themes created, Mirza sahib! Only God is free from all blemish!'

These words were applicable to both the older poet and the younger one, and were appreciated as such. By a happy chance, Ghalib's next verse could be taken as a tribute to both the appreciation of his poetry and the appreciator.

You did not applaud me, did not deign to do justice to me
and the pain killed me off;
I applauded and did justice to your style of indifference,
And how, just take a look!

'By the truth of God, your search for new themes is admirable,' exclaimed Fraser. 'The indifference of one and the affective power of the other are of equal and opposite strength. But Mirza sahib, we did applaud and we did justice by you. You should have no complaint against us.'

The use of the Hindi first-person plural nicely covered everyone present, but was most probably deliberate on Fraser's part to suggest his own self. Ghalib's answer made it clear enough: 'Sir, without doubt! And this is precisely why I rub my forehead on your elevated porte.' Then he quickly presented the last verse, which was in its own way his comment on the soirée and its host. Its oblique meaning was that if you do not give me the value that I deserve, I am not the one to be found anywhere around you.

Ghalib, I do not bend unless the Other does, too:
I bend my head at the shadow of her sword where it is curved,
Just come and look!

Fraser, who was extremely good at probing subtleties, spoke at once. 'Mirza sahib, this verse mirrors your own self so well! How admirable is your self-respect, and how marvellous your concern for upholding your conventions and protecting your soul from the ungraciousness of others!'

Again, there was a clamour of praise and approval, but this time some of it was for Fraser at his eloquence. Yet, some of the Indians also realized that while the Navab Resident Bahadur got the point so well, he made no pledge to say that Mirza Ghalib's self-respect and pride would never suffer loss or harm. Wazir said to herself, these people have begun to behave like kings now.

William Fraser's chief wine server presented another glass to Mirza sahib; from his side, the hookah-bearer presented the silver mouthpiece of the hookah's pipe. Mirza sahib drained the glass in one long, enjoyable draught. A ghazal of eleven verses, and each verse having to be said again and again, and the prolonged voices of acclaim, all this took more than half an hour without anyone being conscious of it. The guests were clearly not sated yet and wanted more, but Mirza sahib had no energy left. The composing of the eleven verses would not have cost him so much energy as presenting them here in such an appreciative assembly.

To round off the poetry session, he presented a Persian rubai; gesturing towards the bottle and the glass of wine, he said:

So long as the dregs of the wine remain at the bottom of the glass,
I boast that the poppy flower's spring also remains:
For those who trust in God, worrying about the morrow equals infidelity,
Excellent wine, two years old, sufficient for a day, remains.

This rubai, so much suited to the occasion, elicited yet another clamour of acclaim. Obeying a hint from Fraser, his butler announced, using the English word, that dinner was served. Fraser requested each guest individually to please proceed to the dining room. The dining room, like the drawing room, was high-ceilinged and spacious. Wazir Khanam was a little surprised to see that though the dinner was taken at a table, with suitable cutlery and silverware, the fare was entirely Indian. Fraser was unmarried but had four, or maybe even six, bibis. None of them, however, was at the table.

27

Navab Shamsuddin Ahmad Khan pays a visit to Wazir Khanam

THE NIGHT HAD travelled through many watches when the carriages began coming out of the Fraser mansion. Navab Shamsuddin Ahmad Khan's closed carriage was accompanied by four armed riders, then two staff-bearers, behind them two torchbearers with closed lamps on their heads. Aside from these lights, the Navab's carriage was also lighted with blue globes fitted on either side of the buggy driver's box. Behind the Navab's buggy were the staff-bearers of Wazir Khanam, then her rath. The caravan slowly descended the slopes towards Bara Hindu Rao. Navab Shamsuddin Ahmad Khan keenly desired in his heart to put Wazir alongside himself in the buggy but desisted either because he stood in awe of her beauty or because he felt diffident; William Fraser was looking; on his part, he was mentally wringing his hands for letting Wazir go away without his having made any overt gesture to her.

Mist pervaded, oozing from light clouds; the roads and alleys were deserted. The shrine of Khvaja Baqi bi-Allah was still the scene of some activity, with visitors praying, and qavvali singers offering their last musical oblations for the day. The areas of the city which were under the King's direct administration were well lighted; especially in Chandni Chowk from the large Fatehpuri Mosque to the Haveli, there were bright lamps on both sides of Ali Mardan Khan's canal, better known in those days as Saadat Khan's canal. Having left Paharganj, they took a somewhat circuitous route, and rather than turn left towards Turkman Gate, they came up right behind the Fatehpuri Mosque. The route from this point was quite safe, but Shamsuddin Ahmad Khan and his entourage kept with Wazir until they reached Sirki Walan and the door of Wazir's modest house.

As Wazir prepared to come out of the rath and a staff-bearer knocked at her door, one of the Navab's outriders got down from his mount and approached her. Before her door could be opened to the knock, the rider made a low salaam and said, 'There is a message from the Presence, Navab sahib. May I submit, if not deemed impertinent?'

Wazir's heart knocked hard against her ribs. 'Please command,' she said.

'The Honourable Navab Dilawar-ul Mulk commands. Could it be possible to find a way for him to see you again over the next day or two?'

The underlying meaning of this inquiry was clear to Wazir. The Navab wanted to know if Wazir was formally attached to someone.

'I would be proud of my good fortune. At what time does the Honourable Sir have the notion to trouble his noble self?'

'Tomorrow, should it be possible?'

'About an hour and a half before sunset, if his Honourable Self has the leisure.'

'Very well. Information will reach you early tomorrow,' saying this, the rider salaamed and turned back, but not before Wazir's door had opened. She went straight to her bedroom, her heart full of imaginings of the possibilities in store for her.

*

The next morning, the first thing Wazir did was to get her house cleaned and spruced up a bit. Her next chore was to find out as much as she could about Navab Shamsuddin Ahmad Khan from different sources that she could muster.

It was the time when bitterness had fully permeated the relations between the Navab and William Fraser. The former had practically broken off with his two younger stepbrothers, Aminuddin Ahmad and Ziauddin Ahmad, even before the cracks developed between him and Fraser. He was somehow not happy with his two wives whom he had married in quick succession. He had no influence or even presence at the Royal Court, for his two states had not been bestowed upon him by the King, but by the English, and by the late Maharajah Bakhtawar Singh of Alwar. Thus, he was somewhat lonely in both the political and domestic realms of his existence. Above all, he was inclined to act hastily, on impulse, in the heat of the moment. He was naturally haughty, if not overbearing. This was the reason why he had never succeeded in establishing truly friendly relations with his peers. Yet, on the other hand, he was extremely popular with his subjects because of his generosity, willingness to reward good work, and personal valour.

Lord Lake had richly rewarded Navab Ahmad Bakhsh Khan in recognition of the latter's excellent services, desiring to acknowledge and enhance the Navab's worth. The territory awarded to the Navab was Firozepur Jhirka, in modern-day Haryana. It was equivalent to a full state in size and prosperity. Maharajah Bakhtawar Singh had already granted to Ahmad Bakhsh Khan the smaller but substantial territory of Loharu in modern-day Rajasthan. Above all, the Maharajah gave away to him a woman called Muddi, the sister of his favourite and well-loved concubine Musi. The Emperor Shah Alam II had conferred on his father the hereditary titles Fakhr-ud Daulah Rustam Jang; the Maharajah granted him the title Dilawar-ul Mulk. All this contributed to Navab Ahmad Bakhsh Khan's being counted among the highest nobility whose relationship with the English was almost on terms of friendship and equality.

Musi and Muddi were women of low caste and status. What religion they professed is not certain, except that they were most probably Hindu, for Musi was reputed to have committed suttee on the pyre of her noble lover. Clearly, both were without parallel in beauty, graceful deportment and good sense, and in their ability to win and keep the total devotion of their man.

Muddi gave birth, in quick succession, to Shamsuddin Ahmad Khan and Ibrahim Ali Khan, and then two daughters. Ibrahim Ali died in infancy. In the meantime, Ahmad Bakhsh Khan married a beautiful girl, Begam Jan, of a well-known Mughal family, belonging to the Turkish tribe called Barlas, who were from Central Asia like Ahmad Bakhsh Khan's father. Begam Jan gave birth to two sons, Aminuddin Ahmad and Ziauddin Ahmad, and five daughters.

Shamsuddin Ahmad was not only the eldest child, he was also handsome and charismatic like his father; extremely bright in his studies, incomparably quick to learn and master the art and science of governance, temperamentally well suited to the lifestyle of wealth and nobility, God had given him everything. In spite of all this, there was no possibility for him to succeed to his father's states: his mother not only came from a background entirely foreign and inferior, but was not even married to his father. The entire extended family was opposed to her. But Muddi, thanks to her natural ability to please and behave tactfully and wisely, and her untiring industry in making sure not to do anything that might be viewed with disfavour by Ahmad Bakhsh Khan, stopped the paths of all opposition. Navab Ahmad Bakhsh Khan made a proper Islamic marriage with her, named her Bahu Khanam and proclaimed her as his wife. At the same time, he appointed Shamsuddin Ahmad his successor to the Navabi of Firozepur Jhirka.

Thus it was that Shamsuddin Ahmad and his mother rose, in the twinkling of an eye, from the depths of the earth to the heights of the Pleiades. This naturally raised Begam Jan's and her progeny's choler by many degrees. In spite of the environment of opposition by Begam Jan, Ahmad Bakhsh Khan drew up, in February 1825, a formal will and had it witnessed by personages no less than General Ochterlony and Sir Charles Metcalfe. He appointed two successors: Shamsuddin Ahmad Khan to the seat of Firozepur Jhirka, and Aminuddin Ahmad Khan to the seat of Loharu.

Unfortunately, this disposition gave satisfaction to neither Shamsuddin Ahmad nor Begam Jan. The former believed that according to convention (or law) of primogeniture, he had the right to succeed to both the seats. On the other hand, Begam Jan and her sons held Shamsuddin Ahmad to be illegitimate because Ahmad Bakhsh Khan had married Muddi after he was born. Shamsuddin Ahmad was not only born of a woman who was of low caste and thoroughly alien to the traditions of the family, according to Begam Jan's side of the narrative, but he also attracted the mischief of an allegedly Islamic rule, according to which a child belonged to the woman on whose bed it was born; thus Shamsuddin Ahmad had no legitimacy whatsoever.

It was a different matter that according to the English law, primogeniture, not legitimacy, was paramount: the firstborn male child took it all. On the other hand, there was no law or even convention governing succession according to the Islamic or even Mughal practice.

Ahmad Bakhsh Khan was troubled by the thought, always recurring like the pricking of a little thorn lodged under a fingernail, that his haughty and self-willed older son would not let his stepbrothers live in peace, nor would they treat him with the fraternal respect and affection that he was entitled to by virtue of being the eldest among the children. He was still far from resolving the problem, trying to make sure that his sons' innate abilities, wealth and honour should somehow not be lost by their being embroiled in disputes about ownership and power, when news came to him of Sir David Ochterlony's death (July 1825). He was the one Englishman of whom Ahmad Bakhsh Khan was fully confident as the true well-wisher, patron and unselfish friend of his House.

This was a terrible shock, for although Ahmad Bakhsh Khan had good and pleasant relations with Charles Metcalfe as well, the Navab did not expect him to be a real replacement for Ochterlony. Ochterlony had, to employ the disparaging phrase later used by the British for the English individuals who adopted the Indian lifestyle, 'gone native'. He was fully acculturated to India; he could appreciate the nuances of the conduct and manners of the nobles, the rich and the learned men of Delhi. Charles Metcalfe, on the contrary, was from the 'new generation' of the English, the generation that were convinced that they had to rule India to ensure her welfare and development. Because of this disconnection between the temperaments of the old generation and the new, and the latter's belief in the Englishman's mission in India, there was hardly anyone in the new generation who could imagine that the Indian and the Firangee could coexist in some kind of relationship that betokened fraternity.

In spite of being of the new generation of English rulers, Fraser was different from them, probably because of his friendship with the much senior Ochterlony and the 'East Indian' James Skinner. Neither Charles Metcalfe nor William Fraser approved of each other; Metcalfe regarded Fraser as too native, Fraser described Metcalfe as 'boorish'.

Just as General Sir David Ochterlony became 'Akhtarloni sahib' on the Delhiites' tongues, Skinner became 'Sikandar sahib'. A person of what was then often described as 'half-caste', Skinner became very close to the English and commanded a battalion of irregulars known as 'Skinner's Horse' of which we have heard before. In spite of his origins, Skinner comfortably spanned the two worlds of the Indian (especially Muslim) and the English. His son, Alexander Skinner ('Alec sahib') was to become the husband of Wazir Khanam's daughter Sophia, but that event was far in the future at that time.

Originally described by the English as 'East Indian', persons like James Skinner soon came to be called 'Eurasian', then 'Indo-Anglian', and much later, 'Anglo-Indian'. The pejorative 'half-caste' was coming into use more and more among the new generation of the English at the time of the events narrated here.

So Fraser's way of life was partly due to the influence of Ochterlony and the friendship with Skinner, and certainly more due to his own temperament, akin to that of the Indian nobility and distant from the English ruling class of that time. Navab Ahmad Bakhsh Khan's children addressed him as Chacha jan (very dear Uncle), but Charles Metcalfe was a different kettle of fish. After Ochterlony's passing, Ahmad Bakhsh Khan's old fears grew stronger. He had little expectation that Shamsuddin Ahmad's ambitious temperament would let him deliver full justice to his siblings. Nor was Ahmad Bakhsh Khan fully confident that Charles Metcalfe, like David Ochterlony, would make his best efforts and be fully effective in ensuring the implementation of his intent and decision to dispose of his estates on the lines inscribed in his will. Ahmad Bakhsh Khan, therefore, during his last illness in October 1826, organized a banquet for Charles Metcalfe and other notables of the Residency in Delhi. He formally abdicated his seats and made over, in their presence, the Navabi of Firozepur Jhirka to Shamsuddin Ahmad, and that of Loharu and a smaller territory called Pahasu to Aminuddin Ahmad. He made Charles Metcalfe give his word that the dispensation would continue after the time of Navab Ahmad Bakhsh Khan.

Almost exactly one year after this covenant, Fakhr-ud Daulah Dilawar-ul Mulk Navab Ahmad Bakhsh Khan Rustam Jang left this House of Oppositions and Incompatibilities on his journey to the House of Retributions and Results. Shamsuddin Ahmad Khan observed the rules and etiquettes of mourning for his father as prescribed and was in mourning for some more time before he submitted a petition to the Honourable Company Bahadur. He stated that his father did not do right in dividing the State into two; in fact, he being the eldest son should inherit the entire territory ruled by his father. He cited the principle of primogeniture with the argument that since it prevailed among the ruler community, there was no reason for it not to be applied to the ruled as well. This argument was rejected out of hand.

Shamsuddin Ahmad Khan, in spite of the initial setback, continued petitioning the Company and also pursuing his cause on the level of personal appeals and contacts with the English. Finally, Francis Hawkins, the third Resident after Charles Metcalfe, supported Shamsuddin Ahmad and recommended to Calcutta that his petition be granted. Consequently, Aminuddin Ahmad was ousted from his domains, with Shamsuddin Ahmad becoming the sole ruler.

Aminuddin Ahmad Khan and his mother, in their turn, petitioned against the decision and continued to do so untiringly. Now when William Fraser became Resident, he, with his direct knowledge of all matters concerned, viewed Aminuddin Ahmad Khan's request favourably and submitted a report to Calcutta to the effect that the previous decision be reversed, restoring the staus quo ante. Shamsuddin Ahmad, on his part, had imagined that Fraser whom he called 'Uncle' was bound to support him. The result was obvious: relations between uncle and nephew became strained almost to the stretching point.

Mirza Ghalib had his own grouse against Ahmad Bakhsh Khan. It is a long story, and the gist of it is as follows. On instructions from the Company, Navab Ahmad Bakhsh Khan had allocated an annual pension of five thousand rupees from his State for Ghalib's extended family. Mirza Ghalib regarded this as too little. He claimed that out of this tiny amount, Navab Ahmad Bakhsh Khan had also endowed an annual share of two thousand rupees to an insignificant person called Khvajah Haji who according to Ghalib was no blood relation of his father or uncle; the relationship was marital and that too a very weak one. According to Ghalib, Khvajah Haji was a mere nobody. Ghalib's grandfather Mirza Quqan Beg's wife had a widowed sister; Khvajah Haji was that sister's grandson. According to Mirza Ghalib's narrative, a person of unknown parentage was employed in the stables of Navab Ahmad Bakhsh Khan as ostler and loader. Taking pity on the daughter of the widowed sister of his wife, Mirza Quqan Beg married off the fatherless girl to that obscure individual. Khvajah Haji was the result of that marriage.

The roots of Mirza Ghalib's resentment went deeper and the story in fact became even more curious as one went into its origins. Ghalib's father died young in a battle in the Company's service. His estates, including Pahasu, which had been awarded to him by the English in recognition of meritorious services, passed to his younger brother Nasrullah Beg Khan on condition that he would support the child Ghalib and his extended family in perpetuity in a manner appropriate for the Mughal nobility. Nasrullah Beg Khan died shortly afterwards in an accident. The English resumed the State of Pahasu and awarded it to Ahmad Bakhsh Khan on condition that he would grant, in perpetuity, a pension of ten thousand rupees annually to the survivors of the extended families of both brothers.

According to Mirza Ghalib, the villainous Khvajah Haji, immediately after the sudden, accidental death of Nasrullah Beg Khan in the field, plundered all his tents, horses, palanquins, carpets, tableware and other properties and rode post-haste to Navab Ahmad Bakhsh Khan and surrendered the entire property of the encampment to the Navab, and there lay the real root of iniquity. For Ahmad Bakhsh Khan, when it came to dividing the pension equally between the two brothers' families, decided that Khvajah Haji was in fact a member of Ghalib's family, and allocated to him the not insubstantial sum of two thousand rupees annually to be paid out of the five thousand rupees determined as the share of the survivors of Ghalib's father. In other words, Haji was granted a handsome pay-off for his treason.

Ghalib, aside from his eventful history as a child aristocrat, was also well connected by marriage. His late uncle Nasrullah Beg Khan had been married to a sister of Ahmad Bakhsh Khan. Ghalib's own wife was the daughter of Navab Ilahi Bakhsh Khan, younger brother of Ahmad Bakhsh Khan. His resentment against Ahmad Bakhsh Khan and later against Shamsuddin Ahmad Khan was fuelled by the fact that neither of them paid any regard to this close relationship which according to the custom of those times entitled a son-in-law to special consideration. He appealed, and appealed again to Calcutta, but had no success. In one of his petitions, he made many allegations against Shamsuddin Ahmad Khan as well.

Coldness and even animosity developed between the two families, especially between Shamsuddin Ahmad Khan, on his succession, and Ghalib. None from either side, or from Delhi's aristocracy, made any effort to mend the fences and untie the poison knot. Ghalib's persistent plaints to the English for restoration of his pension was not a matter to cause much concern to Shamsuddin Ahmad Khan, but the disagreement with Fraser about Loharu was something else altogether.

It was not the time for Shamsuddin Ahmad Khan to permit a sickness of the heart to distract him from weightier matters. But as the Persian poet said:

Love has done, and indeed does all the time,
much more than all this.

On her part, Wazir was lost in her own labyrinth of thoughts. Perhaps, on the chessboard of her life, a new prince was to rise like the sun; the name

Shams did mean 'the sun'. Marston Blake had left her but a lonely pawn on the board. To remain in her spot was impossible, equally impossible it was to move up. The thought of her children abraded her soul like a sharp steel file. How should I bring them up, how should I give them the necessary grounding in their own culture, so that they may not stray from the true path? Oh well, grow up as Firangees they will, but they must regard me as their true mother, know the scents and sights of their own land, so that even if they go to settle across the seven seas in The Country, they do not forget their origins.

And who knows? Does the Navab want me on a permanent basis, or is it just a bit of entertainment that he craves? No, but I will not agree to be a mere plaything of a few days.

None at that moment had the faintest notion of how Shamsuddin Ahmad Khan's life was to unfold and end. As of now, he was the sole master of Firozepur Jhirka and Loharu. Granted that he and the English Grand Sahib did not hit it off well, and the Grand Sahib had reported against him to Calcutta. But these were matters of state: things kept changing all the time in the realm of mastery and governance. After all, Colebrooke sahib wrote against the Navab, but what did it matter, finally? Everything was set right when Hawkins sahib came in his place. All right, let us accept that Fraser sahib has written adversely; but Fraser sahib is not going to be here forever. Maybe someone else will come and do the right thing again. And then . . . and then, there is the King here above us. Who knows, perhaps tomorrow or sometime soon the High Presence may regain his power everywhere with the assistance of the Marathas. There is nothing difficult for the Almighty; perhaps, finally, He will take pity on us.

Navab Shamsuddin Ahmad Khan's handsome, charismatic personality, his aristocratic bearing and deportment, his refined manners, had all made their mark on Chhoti Begam; was her heart too entangled there somewhere? She did not know. She did not know how deep her love for Blak sahib was. No doubt she wept, and wept again and again over him, but she did not weep for Marston Blake alone. Her evil fortune, her children, her home in Delhi which she could not now call home: she was mourning over all of these things.

Yet Blak sahib had been such a dear, such a darling. She somehow seemed to feel somewhat fearful of Shamsuddin Ahmad. She had never stood in any kind of awe at all of Blak sahib. True, the Navab sahib was of her own people, but for some reason that she could not understand, she felt a little intimidated by him. If I have to establish any sort of connection with him, I'll have to eject this awe from my heart, she told herself.

*

The next morning brought a mace-bearer from the Navab to say that Navab Shamsuddin Ahmad Khan sahib would be enhancing the elegance of her house after the afternoon prayer and it was hoped that Wazir Khanam sahib would have the leisure at that time to receive him. Wazir sent the reply that the Navab should bring his noble presence most assuredly; the eyes and heart of his servant girl were already spread for him like a welcoming carpet.

The mace-bearer salaamed and left, after having been adequately rewarded by Wazir. In spite of her resolve not to be overwhelmed by Shamsuddin Ahmad Khan's charisma, her heart began to palpitate with worry: How should I deal with him so that he does not feel slighted while I maintain my dignity too? Anyway, before the worry could harass her unduly, she busied herself in preparing for the visit and making her own toilette that she did not even notice how quickly the time had passed. She realized with a little regret that she could have picked Manjhli's brains to gather some useful points.

It must have been only a few minutes past the appointed time that cries of 'Move, move!' 'Give way!' were heard in Sirki Walan. The Navab rode in an English-style closed carriage pulled by four Arabians. The coachman, dressed in red-coloured, light woollen livery with appropriate insignia, sat erect on his box, obviously proud of the horses with their crests of peacock feathers bound in silver, their mouthpieces made of silk and their tail ornaments of golden thread. The coachman bore a delicate whip in one hand and held the reins of the horses in the other.

The coach was preceded and followed by four armed horsemen, and two staff-bearers walked at double speed alongside it. The Navab alighted in full dignity and was greeted at the main door by Wazir who bowed and salaamed and said words of welcome to him: that she was fortunate to have the Navab at her home. From a silver sprinkler, she lightly sprayed rose water over the Navab's dress. Placing a garland of roses round his neck, she said, 'Oh your coming here gladdens my heart!' This she said in Persian and followed it with Hindi, 'I am proud of my good luck that your feet reached this little shoebox-like house of mine! We, the lonely abiders, now have their slumbering fortune awake, at last. Bismillah, please ennoble this door.'

The Navab took off a pearl necklace from around his neck and wound it gently around Wazir's head. Then he smiled and said, 'By the same token, it truly pleases my heart to be here.'

Taking the Navab's hand in her own, she led him into her little divan khanah. The Navab cast a careful eye at the furnishings, as if judging their value and the taste and good management of the lady of the house. Wazir had no doubt inherited quite a few good items from Marston Blake, but she also had a knack for arranging and positioning them attractively. In this regard, she had certainly learnt from both Marston Blake and Aby memsahib, for prosperous, upper-middleclass English people generally excelled in furnishing and decorating their living quarters beautifully.

Everything in Wazir's house had an understated elegance, neatness and freedom from excess, whether of enthusiasm in collecting or eagerness in displaying. Most importantly, she organized her home in such a way that everything from a flower vase to a wall mirror or hanging, seemed to be made just for the space which it occupied. Some English ladies had, indeed, a weakness for collecting and cluttering up their homes with things that they fancied regardless of whether there was appropriate place for them in the house. Some Indian ladies and gentlemen, especially those of Lucknow, in imitating the English, seemed to make their houses look like a museum of miscellany. Ironically, it was the English who mocked at such houses in their hearts, little realizing that the taste for piling up bric-a-brac was acquired from them. Speaking of Ashraf-ud Daulah and his father Muntazim-ud Daulah, Fanny Parkes had mentioned to Wazir that their palatial mansion in Fatehgarh was so chock-full of things, and of such incompatible variety, that it was hard even to find room to stand. Anyway, Wazir's house reflected good management and good taste in all things.

This was how the house was constructed and organized: the front door opened towards a small hall. As one entered the house, there was a veranda on either side and a courtyard in front of it. At the end of the veranda was a room whose length was just a little more than its width. The room had wall-to-wall carpeting covered with dazzling white cloth, with a few smaller carpets at strategic places upon the white sheeting; there were four doors and two windows. Both windows and two of the doors faced the east. On each of them were delicate bamboo screens that let the light percolate quite well, but permitted no view of the inside.

A large cut-glass chandelier hung from the ceiling; there must have been floor globes at night, but they were not needed at that time of the day. The room was still bright, though the sun had begun westering some-time ago. At the western end of the room, that is, opposite the main door, was a low platform created by two thick quilts spread across the room's full width, over which were two Kashmiri carpets. Two large, cylindrical bolsters were set against the wall, with a silver spittoon in front, and and near it, a dome-shaped silver betel box with a conical top. A small silver tray held tiny cut-glass phials of attars, and on a larger tray were small silver cups full of dry fruits and nuts like almonds, walnuts, sultanas, chilghozah (the seed of a Central Asian pine), pistachios and cardamoms wrapped in silver foil. Rose garlands hung at suitable places on the western wall, and posies of fresh flowers adorned the alcoves.

Her hand still in the Navab's hand, Wazir led him into the divan khanah, placed him at the head of the room and stood before him, both her hands one upon the other, just below the sternum, in the classic silent gesture of submission and readiness to serve. In daylight, the Navab looked even more handsome and elegant than the previous night. The tension and the uneasiness betrayed by him almost all through the previous evening were gone.

He was dressed almost in the same way, but had a pistachio-coloured jamavar cloak over his nima. His face looked so fresh, so much expressive of the springtime that one was reminded of a mustard field with its butter-yellow flowers stretching to the far horizon and glowing under a November sunset. The pistachio-coloured flowery cloak also suited his fair face, at present lit up with a half smile.

The Navab spoke like a highly educated person; but his speech, always refined and often Persianized, was sometimes marred by what can be described as a 'prop word', that is, a word or expression which is uttered involuntarily, and though not devoid of meaning, it is often delivered quite fast. In the Navab's case, it was 'bhai wallah', which can be loosely translated as 'brother, by God, I say!' Such props are still quite common among modern-day Urdu speakers everywhere.

'Bhai wallah, Wazir Khanam, what a powerful test of the heart's attraction it was that drew me, rather pulled me, up to your door,' he said. He sat with his feet tucked beneath his thighs, as demanded by propriety. But his tone had no hint of submissiveness or supplication. Rather, there was an unspoken sense of closeness, even intimacy. The warmth wafting from Wazir's body was affecting him like a pleasant sense of inebriety. When Wazir took his hand in hers, he had the impulse to stop then and there to embrace her and take her in his arms, put her in his buggy and drive away. He desisted, for it would have been contrary to his own rules of decorum. He wanted, even now, to pull her by the hand and seat her next to him, but here again, it was Wazir who would have to take the first step.

'Navab sahib,' she said, 'the famous Persian line of verse—"The corner of the peasant's cap touched the sun"—must have been composed for just such occasions. I am wondering whether to believe my eyes that the noonday sun is illumining my door.'

'But it is your face which is the rising sun. Bhai wallah, your fine golden dupatta is around your face like a nimbus. How I wish that the cloud would disperse and the light of the sunrise point of your face and neck illumine my eyes.'

Wazir had never heard such eloquence, such appropriate phrases, so full of delightful wordplay, from Navab Yusuf Ali Khan even; while Marston Blake had been a far cry from such language anyway. And the Navab's voice did not carry the least hint of the raucous roughness so characteristic of the Mewati community to which his mother belonged. This was perhaps partly because his mother came from that part of Rajputana which is contiguous to the territory of the Braj language. In the Rajputani of that area, the colours of the much softer and mellifluous Braj glimmered like goldfish underneath the surface of a deep lake. The other reasons were the Navab's suckling maid and dai khilai: both were the daughters of genteel though poor Muslim families of Saharanpur and Muzaffarnagar, areas where only Braj and Hindi were spoken. When very small, they had been kidnapped by dacoits who had sold them off into Navab Ahmad Bakhsh Khan's establishment at very low prices.

'The Honourable Sir's acuity of the eye sees good things even where there are none. What name should I give to it, if not the Navab's wish to nurture his poor subjects well?'

'You illuminate the whole house like the moon. There is nothing like acuity of vision needed here. It would be a blind man indeed who would fail to see your excellent charms. If I could, I would wrap you around my body like the moonlight's chador and go to sleep.'

'Your Honour has called me the moon, indeed you have honoured me. But the Being of Exalted Honour is himself the brightest star of governance and the sunlight of power and prosperity. The Being of Exalted Honour must have heard the Arabic proverb, "The light of the moon is gained from the sun." The sun will pass on to its destination and the moon's chador will be left behind, folded up after use.'

Shamsuddin Ahmad Khan laughed with genuine pleasure. 'What beautiful phrases you use, bhai wallah! These aren't just phrases, you let them fly like bird bolts and arrows! I fear I may be forced to fly away!'

'Your Honour, I am but a blade of grass. I await the cool morning breeze of your compassion to pick me up and fly me to my destination.'

'But where is your destination? You never named it.'

'What destination could a blade of grass have? If it is green, it could be used to tie a bunch of flowers; if shrivelled by autumn, it will go into the furnace.'

'You are neither a blade of grass, nor something struck by autumn. In fact, full spring has not reached you yet.'

Wazir smiled a bashful smile. She lowered her eyes and spoke a verse of the Persian poet Talib Amuli:

Your marauding the garden for flowers
Does a kindness to the spring:
For the rose is longer in bloom in your hands,
Than on its native branch.

The Navab was delighted, in fact, ecstatic. And, of course, Wazir would not give a more open invitation; nor would the Navab have liked to accept it. Both had read each other's meaning quite well. The Navab removed a long pearl necklace from his own neck and extended it towards Wazir Khanam.

'Chhoti Begam, only God is free from all blemish! How subtle and how delicate was your answer. Come, please accept this from me.'

The Navab waited to see what Wazir would do or say in reply. By addressing her as 'Chhoti Begam', the Navab had extended a step towards intimacy. He was not sure if Wazir would get to the meaning coded in it.

If Wazir thought she should wait for the Navab to half rise and advance, she was in grave error. It was impossible for the Navab to make such a gesture. But if she was really waiting for this to happen, it meant rejection and abrogation of all that had passed between them that evening: it meant that Wazir had just been indulging in friendly banter and mild, kernel-less flirtation and she did not envisage anything like a lasting connection. If Wazir gestured that the necklace should be tossed up to her, it meant that she did not desire anything more than being the Navab's mistress, someone 'attached' to him for a time. If Wazir advanced towards the Navab and accepted the necklace, then it should mean that . . .

Before the Navab could resolve the last conundrum, Wazir went down on her knees, sat with her feet under her, bent low and took the necklace from the Navab's hand. She touched it to her eyes and put it around her neck. Now she was a little closer to the Navab than before, but it was clear that she was not going to move closer. The Navab looked at her intently; now it was his turn to try reading her meaning. It was a game of chess, delicately poised, with every move made after the fullest cogitation: yet both desired an endgame that suited them. But the slightest error in the signals, the least hint of needlessly prolonging the conversation, could spoil the game for both.

The Navab put out his hand and, touching Wazir gently on the shoulder, he said, 'Come here, come to my side. Let me see from close up how the necklace looks on you.'

'Your Honour, how can I come closer?' She quoted a Persian proverb: 'Respect is the water of life for love'. Without rising from her place, Wazir moved up a little. She was now just a couple of feet, or less, from the Navab, but the waves of the dusky red of desire were apparent on both their faces. The word in the Persian proverb, translated here as 'love', has many meanings; while one of its meanings is also 'intimate relationship', another of its meanings is 'swimming'. Thus the word in its main sense of 'love' had opened another door for Shamsuddin Ahmad. He touched Wazir gently, almost caressingly on her chin, then raised her face a little and said: 'Is not the word "swimming" an invitation to float in the ocean of love? Then where does the matter of "respect" arise?' He quoted a line of a Persian verse: '"The first condition to enable the first step is to be crazed like Majnun." And I believe in jumping into a whirlpool without giving it a thought.'

Then he spoke the following Persian verses:

If your beauty grows at this pace,
Everyone will practise nothing but the art of going crazy;
In the ocean of your sorrow, the boat of a hundred Noahs' wisdom
Will be upside down, like the bubbles.

'Now it is your decision, bhai wallah! Should I sink or swim?'

Wazir smiled, and quoted a wonderfully mysterious line from the Hindi poet Mir:

Such tumults, such restlessness, oh my God! Whose mystery does the ocean hold?

The Navab again touched her face and lips gently and said, 'It is all yours. You are the mystery and the one who holds the mystery is yours as well. For me, you're a mysterious river of secrets, Wazir Khanam. I rush on without a rudder, helpless in the river of my desire, hopeless in the river of your loveliness.' Then he quoted a Hindi verse:

Oh, I am being swept away in a river-flood
Which has no boat, no hillock, nor islet.

'Exalted and Honoured Sir, it is you who are both: the river, and also the island in it.'

'Well, in fact, the only space where I can be sure of not being lost is where you are.'

Shamsuddin Ahmad looked at Wazir so that his eyes were on her neck and the hint of her cleavage. From the neckline of the heavy bodice and extremely fine tunic could be glimpsed the soft-swelling breasts, rosy, flourishing like distantly seen hillocks of pink blooms in the season of verdure. In spite of having given birth twice, Wazir's body had not lost the tautness of its youthful muscles. Her hips and breasts had become a trifle bigger and heavier, but there was no loss of shape, and in the presence of the Navab, Wazir had shrunk her body in some such way as to suggest modesty but still let her look younger than her nineteen years. And the most distant glimpse of her cleavage and breasts was enough to slay even the most hardened gazer.

The meaning of the Navab's glance was not hidden from Wazir. She, too, felt the tug in her heart for the person of Shamsuddin Ahmad. But she was still uncertain: she felt that she needed more thought, more self-examination. The days of letting herself to be blown away by the winds of passion were over. Life with Marston Blake, and his sudden and brutal murder, had taught Wazir the lesson that life did not just comprise of taking a decision and putting it into immediate effect. Nor was decision-making as easy as it had seemed to her when she tied the knot in the thread of her life with Marston Blake. Nor was it the case that converting a potential decision into actual action was caused by some infallible wisdom or unfailing law as decreed by the Eternal Distributor of Fates, in the manner of morning invariably following night.

She also no longer believed that decisions once translated into practice from abstract thought ran a true course, a course whose turns and twists, even if not knowable and planned for in advance, could at least be surmised, and could possibly be provided for, however imperfectly, in the light of the surmise. The semi-starved dogs roaming the lanes and alleys of a big city; the birds, perching motionless for hours on the copings and parapets of houses and on tall, dense neem and peepul trees waiting for a morsel of food to keep death away; the sparrows, pigeons, doves and mynahs that came down warily on the ground enticed by a few grains, and then flew away in a whirr, thrilling to some real or imagined danger: perhaps these had more control over their life and more command over their state.

Wazir saw herself harbouring the notion that the decision was hers to make. But she also knew that it was just that: a mere notion. She knew that even if it were possible to envision and ponder all the possible results and implications of a decision, it would not necessarily lead to some positive advantage. Under the circumstances, she did not have the leisure to do any such examination of the possible outcome of her decision. Navab Shamsuddin Ahmad Khan's eyes betrayed lust, but perhaps his heart had the tiniest modicum of integrity and affection for her.

Was there any other option for her, should she reject the Navab? If so, what was it? Was it William Fraser? I beg forgiveness from God! Are my paths so blocked, is the earth so small and so narrow upon me? But I have to bring up two children, and have also to live. I cannot live by begging, after all . . .

'So where are you lost, Wazir Khanam?'

She started. The Navab's voice had pulled her out from her reverie. She saw that his eyes now had the light of something other than mere physical desire. If she wished, she could interpret it as the heart's inclination.

'Sir? Oh, nothing . . . Nothing at all. I . . . I was in fact lost in your search.'

'Looking for me? Just look at the young lady! Am I not right here, bhai wallah!' He laughed, trying to make light of the gravity of Wazir's reply.

'Yes, but . . . I was looking for you many stages ahead in life's journey to see if the name of this nameless one could be discerned somewhere.'

The Navab became silent. The radiance of eagerness and desire dimmed in his eyes, as if he had fallen in deep thought. He bent his head and said, after a moment's pause, 'Wazir Khanam, it is for no one to rein in or control the wave and flow of life. Who knows, my destination may be anterior to yours.'

'May the parents of this servant sacrifice their lives for you. Please do not utter such words.'

'Our keeping quiet about it cannot change that which must be, into that which must not be,' the Navab smiled. 'And that is the reason why, at my stage of life today, I behold but a dim trace of the road ahead and the stages to come. I do not extrapolate tomorrow from today, but I treat the joys of today as the peafowl's egg which conceals in its shell the potential for multi-hued birds, their colours glimmering in the penumbra of the future and their resonant calls capable of reaching far and wide. What will be is what must be. Still, one needs some trust somewhere, in some place and at some time, or life's ship will be taken by tempests in no time at all.'

'So Your Honour's command is that one should live from day to day? That one should imagine every night to be one's last and every morning to be one's first?'

'No, certainly not, bhai wallah! But let your breast be peopled with desire and hope, and regard every today as the beginning of the unfolding of a more gracious tomorrow.'

'Your Honour is of an illustrious house. You rule a sovereign state of your own; you have wealth and power. Above all, you are of noble birth and possess an authoritative personal elegance. Whatever piece the Exalted Servants may like to place on the chessboard of their life can advance to become the queen. But I am nothing more than a broken-legged pawn, left behind on the board and Time's Knight is impatient to crush it under its massive hoof.'

'Every pawn can become the queen, and just one pawn is enough to cut down the queen's legs and stab her in the breast with the dagger of dusty death. The Functionaries of Fate and Destiny have no need of anyone's help in order to manifest their Power.'

Wazir raised her head and the Navab saw that her eyes were bright with unshed tears and her face was red with the effort to stop them from flowing.

'Hey, what is this, bhai wallah! Did I say something which fell heavy on your gentle heart?' The Navab stepped up quickly and dried her tears with his own handkerchief.

'No doubt Your Honour heartens me quite much, but my arms lack strength, and my basket of earth becomes heavier by the moment. I beg forgiveness from the Presence. His generosity to the friendless poor is well known . . . '

Now she was sobbing and weeping openly, and it was with difficulty she checked her tears a bit and said: 'The rain of the pearls from Your Honour's clouds of compassion somehow called to my mind the Hindi verses of Khvajah Mir Dard sahib.'

With a voice somewhat choked with emotion, but in an extremely attractive manner of delivery, she said the following two verses of the eighteenth-century poet:

Why have my eyes burst their bounds and are flowing so,
I do not know.
Why did they break down, intent upon weeping,
I do not know.
My tearful eyes, tied like a boat to the thread of sight
Have broken the bonds and tears are erupting forth.

She then recited the following verse, and while doing so, the soft light of a gentle smile, as if from a little candle, appeared on her lips, and not only on the lips but also in her tear-filled eyes:

Whose glowing presence has so enriched my eyes
That like a river, they have run over my cultivation,
I do not know.

The Navab, who was warmly applauding every line with bent head, and occasionally with his eyes raised to Wazir's face, now quite lost his self-control and drew Wazir to himself and put her head against his chest. Caressing her head with his other hand, he declared, 'I can become the strength of your arms! I will stand with my being like the levee against the uncontrollable flood of tears which devastate your harvest of endurance and darken your life. Tears, after this night, will not visit your eyes, but will destroy the homes and possessions of your enemies.'

'You nourish me and cherish me by your generosity. God has made your chest wide and sky-kissing like the ramparts of the Haveli,' Wazir said, raising her head and drying her tears. The Navab made to take her face in his hands and kiss her, but Wazir slipped out of his arms and, controlling her own breathing and the waves of emotion buffeting into her breast, she said, 'Presence, it has been quite a time since the evening light disappeared from the horizon. At what time would you like to dine? If commanded, dinner may be served, or should your exalted mind be so inclined, we could have a ghazal or a performance of classical music.'

Her dupatta had slipped from her head, revealing even more of the swell underneath the bodice, but she did not apparently mind it.

'That is a very nice thought, bhai wallah! I feel like listening to a ghazal performance. But you will not sing, or will you?'

In the Navab's observation, there was the hint that he was aware of Wazir not being a nautch girl, and that he had had inquiries made about her.

'No, sir. But I made some arrangement, on the off chance that the Exalted Servants might like some music. She is a new singer, just recently arrived from Jalandhar.'

'Nice, very nice. Then let us not wait further.'

'Sir, she will present herself in a moment,' saying this, Wazir gestured to the maid who was fanning the Navab with a peacock fan. Within seconds, musical instruments and their players came in, made three salaams and took their seats. Nasim Jalandhari was the last to appear: good-looking in a plumpish way, she was past her youth, but her deportment and body movements had an easy grace. She made seven salaams, then stepped up to kiss the Navab's right hand and said, 'What should I submit to the Exalted Presence? Some Sufi poetry in Persian, or perhaps a ghazal in Hindi?'

'The Hindi poets of Delhi have lit the lamps of their names from here to Iran and the Deccan. I would like to hear something in Hindi.'

'Very good, sir. I am here to carry out whatever your exalted temperament desires. I present a ghazal of the Presence, Mir Hasan of Delhi, may God raise his station.'

Wazir breathed a sigh of relief. Her heart had been thumping wildly for fear that Nasim Jalandhari may choose a ghazal of Mirza Ghalib. She did warn her against it in advance, but who knows what goes on in the heads of these singing women?

Nasim Jalandhari set the taus in tune with the other instruments, and began to sing in the raga Charu Keshi, a comparatively rare raga, but beautifully suited to the deepening night.

She beckoned to me with her eyes, today,
Was that a dream? What did happen today?
Today, I could not properly look at you, at all;
Do not count this as a meeting, today.
I just said in my heart, Let there be
A round of wine, and it was so; truly
You made a miracle today.
Such words never did pass before
Between us; words that you said, today.
Hasan, doubtless you will see me there
Again tomorrow, if I could just live safely
Through the night, today.

Nasim Jalandhari sang with the fullest passion of her art, using the prescribed gestures and movements of her hands with sophistication and to the best advantage. It was as if she was presenting her own ghazal, and it was a happy chance or maybe her happy choice that each of the five verses could be interpreted as having some bearing upon the evening's occasion. After a little while, Wazir too was so affected by the singing (and perhaps also the words) that she was moved to gently keeping time by slapping upon her thigh; then she broke into song herself, though in a low voice, staying in perfect accompaniment with the more mature singer. Her voice still had the flexible lilt and tinkle of adolescence.

Wazir's spontaneously joining with Nasim created a rare mood that evening. They sang for quite some time. When the music stopped, the Navab made a brief gesture to his mace-bearer who stood respectfully at the door in front of him. The mace-bearer immediately presented to Wazir two bagfuls of one hundred rupees each which he had ready tied under his sash. Wazir placed the money before Nasim, who stood up, made seven salaams again, and left, but not before expressing profuse thanks to the Navab and praying for his perpetual good fortune and prosperity.

On being asked again about dinner, the Navab indicated that he was ready now. Wazir had the food served in another room. Life with Marston Blake had taught her many things, including the desirability of having the dining room separate from the meeting room. Yet, contrary to the Firangee custom, she did not sit at the tablecloth with the Navab. Although Shamsuddin Ahmad Khan seemed to hint that he would like Wazir to eat with him, she quietly ignored those hints, and the Navab did not put his desire in actual words either, for he had the feeling that Wazir might not like it. He knew, of course, that in all well-born or even genteel Hindu and Muslim households, women ate strictly segregated from the men.

The food was entirely Indian and had been cooked by expert cooks in the city. Everything but an English-style cake, made by Wazir herself, had been left to the efforts of the professionals; her cook had made the pickles and chutneys at home.. Wazir did not stand in front of the Navab while he ate; she stood a little behind him to his right and in addition to organizing the service from there, pressed the Navab to eat some more of everything. Contrary to her hope, the Navab ate frugally, but made it evident in different ways that the fare was to his liking, and if he was not eating much, it was just that he was a poor eater. There was no conversation, aside from the occasional comment or urging from Wazir for the Navab to taste a particular dish. Eating and talking did not go together according to the Indian etiquette.

Hookah and betel were proffered after the meal. Wazir had specially commissioned betel cones enriched with the best Jaipuri tobacco for chewing, each cone wrapped in gold leaf and pierced with a silver pin to keep the layers together. The Navab expressed delight at every little thing and rewarded the serving maids, peppering his conversation with harmless raillery. One of the maids who was a little bolder than the rest, said, 'His Honour ate very little of the repast but does not tire of giving us a taste of his words!'

'No, that is not the case, bhai wallah. I am a fast eater. Remember that we may have come recently from Turkestan, but are originally from Arabia really. The Arab eats speedily. Wazir Khanam, did you not hear the story of the Arab Bedouin and his soup?'

Wazir, emboldened a little by the Navab's playful conversation, smiled and said, 'Your Honour, what do we know of Iran or Turan, Arabia or Egypt? We are the home birds of the narrow alleys of Jahanabad, we sing in our own tunes, and that is all.'

'Yes, that is quite the case. And that is why the voice of your parrot birds is heard above everything else!'

All the maids and other women servants burst into giggles, but not too loudly.

'Your Honour, the story of the Arab's soup . . .' one of them spoke, but tentatively, being careful not to appear too free.

'Oh, yes. This is how it happened: An Iranian asked an Arab, "Hey, what is your word for cold soup?" The Arab replied . . .' the Navab paused a beat for effect, '"We don't let our soup grow cold, we drink it up instantly."'

The maids greeted this with open giggles. Even Wazir laughed softly from behind her wrap. The whole ambience seemed to be laughing with them.

The Navab's staff had all been fed but the Navab himself did not seem in the mood to wrap up the evening. Wazir was now seated in front of him, rather close, but to his right. The distance between them was not less than a foot or a foot and a half. The Navab glanced at Wazir's face a number of times and each time he looked away, as if he wished to say something, but was somehow deterred from opening his mouth.

In spite of all her show of humility, there was a kind of power, an almost awe-inspiring refulgence around Wazir's personality, and Shamsuddin Ahmad Khan could feel it like waves of energy even from that distance. He could also feel, he thought, a radiant heat travelling from her body to his. It was an experience, a confusion of both intellect and spirit that he had never encountered before.

Ordinarily, what should have happened was that he would speak to Wazir directly, or if there was a desire to observe full protocol, he would have had word sent to her through his steward or a senior woman servant that he would stay the night after dinner. Shamsuddin Ahmad Khan, for some reason not clear to him, had desisted from such an action not because he thought it was wrong or improper. He thought that once he was in her house, he would indicate his wish to Wazir through some subtle suggestion.

Yet, as the evening wore on into night, his sense of the power emanating from Wazir grew in proportion with the passing of the hours. Now his state of mind was that far from suggesting his intent to stay the night, it seemed necessary for him to seek Wazir's permission; but even such words refused, and kept refusing, to come to his lips. The hour was getting late. Now it was imperative to clinch the matter, or accept a betel-nut cone as a parting gift and leave.

Wazir was most possibly aware of the conflict in her guest's mind but she did not want to betray the tiniest bit of a soupçon of invitation, or willingness, from her side. In the first place, she was still unclear in her mind about what she expected from herself and what hopes she harboured in her heart from the Navab. She also feared that if there was even a faint suggestion of weakness in any kind of relationship that she desired with the Navab, he might interpret it as impatience or lack of self-respect and this could upset the delicate balance between them as it existed. But this apparently mutual consent to silence was out of place and, in fact, a cause for discomfort and confusion. They were not there, after all, just to look at each other.

'Should His Honour so desire, we could have a short second session of the new musical mode of khiyal,' she ultimately broke the silence with downcast eyes. 'Or would you like to have some coffee?' she smiled, more like a good hostess than a person with some special interest. A polite, formal evening, perhaps being drawn towards its close.

'N . . . No, Wazir Khanam, I should take your leave now.' He looked at Wazir a little intently; their eyes met for a beat, then Wazir's eye lowered first. She strongly felt that the Navab expected some sort of a first step from her side, however minute. And if she did do what he expected, they would have to travel again the distance that they had covered that evening.

'I take the name of God! When will that auspicious and fortunate moment arrive when this dark hovel will be illumined again with the dust of your feet?'

Wazir's smile at that time was her special smile: full of intimations of the first expression of the soul's inclination when a young girl looks at someone with a new kind of interest. It was as if she was entirely unschooled about the ups and downs on the path that was before her. Her smile spontaneously brightened her eyes and descended to her lips and her face, which shone now like beaten gold.

Navab Shamsuddin Ahmad Khan had a strong urge to say: 'I am not going away at all, did you not know? So there is nothing about revisiting between us.' But obviously, the time for this was past, if it ever was. He rose, touched Wazir's face gently and stepped forward towards the door. The girls who stood behind him moved to put his shoes on his feet, but Wazir sprang to it, and bent at the Navab's feet, his shoes in her hand.

Shamsuddin Ahmad Khan withdrew his feet at once and cried, 'No, Wazir Khanam. This can never happen! Don't put me to shame, bhai wallah!'

By that time the maid had come quickly forward to take the Navab's shoes from Wazir's hand. At the same moment, obeying some imperceptible gesture from the Navab, his staff-bearer appeared bearing a large tray, which had on it a double shawl made of jamavar, a bolt of brocade from Benaras, and several bags of rupees. Shamsuddin Ahmad Khan draped the shawl around Wazir's shoulders and looked at her with an inquiring eye about the bolt of silk and the money. Reading the hint in Wazir's eyes, a maid took the tray from the staff-bearer, put it on her head and went into some inner room.

Wazir wrapped the shawl around her head and shoulders, and drew its edge over her head and face the way Muslim women do when they say the prescribed prayer. The subtlety in expressing thanks and appreciation for his present was not lost on the Navab. He was about to say something when Wazir bent low in salaams and said: 'The Exalted Servants' renown for cherishing and nourishing their subjects reverberates through the whole of Hind; as long as we live, we will sing Your Honour's praises.' She smiled with just a hint of coquetry and invitation. 'But my question was rather different.'

Something like an ebullition seemed to rise in Shamsuddin Ahmad's loins, there was perhaps a tremor in his legs. He felt like spreading himself on the carpet in front of all and pleading, 'Chhoti Begam, I feel weary and exhausted. Please take the trouble to press my back awhile.' It was of course quite out of the question, given their temperaments; instead, he answered cordially, 'Soon, very soon, as God wills. We will meet again. And indeed, if you were ever to gladden my doorstep—whose destiny has been nothing but lonesomeness—with the rosy hue of union by visiting, how entirely splendid would that be!'

'Your servant girl could never be out of the pale of obedience. It is you who are the true spring. I am just the yellow leaf that your noble step has brought back to life. To become bound in allegiance to such a Messiah-patron is to reawaken my fortunes from deep slumber.'

Shamsuddin Ahmad Khan observed that behind the shawl's jutting edge, Wazir's face had a purity of charm and a clarity of grace that would be the pride and aspiration of a newly wedded bride. Her voice was well modulated, her enunciation clear and polished; it was like a master poet saying his poem.

'Very well, we shall meet again in the near future. But before I depart, I have the mind to recite a verse from Urfi, poet laureate to Emperor Akbar, as you must know.'

'Command, if you please. The maidservant is all ears.'

The Navab paused, cleared his throat, as if he was a little self-conscious about the verse. Then he said, 'I say this verse to you because I feel a special need to say it.'

'Let all such things be cast aside. Why should you ever have need for anything at all! But do please bestow the verse.'

The Navab spoke:

I am proud about Love, and I am proud about Beauty. Inebriate
they are with the wine cup
Of full concord, and yet blushful
Shyness does not leave them.

Before she could utter even a word in applause, the Navab continued, 'Chhoti Begam, quaff the wine cup of concord, quaff it yet more. Make Love also drink it yet. But . . . a curtain is still a curtain, even if made up by shyness. And it is also a way of coquetry . . . It is a delight to carry out coquetry's mandates, but—'

Now Wazir could not resist interrupting, she exclaimed, 'May God never let the day dawn when I be coquettish with you! Let there be numerous like me to be sacrificed at your feet. The brilliance of His Honour's daystar of love dazzles me. That is all. If shyness is a curtain, there is someone to raise the curtain too.'

Navab Shamsuddin Ahmad Khan now knew that his purpose had been understood. He smiled and said, 'Very good, indeed. Now please permit me to depart. Visiting with you has gladdened my heart.'

The Navab's shoes were put on his feet. An elderly maid appeared and drew her hands over his face before pressing them to the sides of her face: the traditional way of saying, 'May all your troubles be passed on to my head.' She said a prayer, and blew upon him. Wazir formed a vase with her two hands and presented a long-stemmed red rose to the Navab. He took both her hands in his and kissed each of her fingers separately and answered her through a Persian verse:

The tips of your hennaed fingers are places to kiss;
The floret became a full-blown flower
For it is proper for the flower to be culled by you.

'This gift of yours and its beauty says something to me,' he continued. 'My heart has vacated my breast and gone away to some place unknown. This gift of yours says not to open the door should the heart return home. It should be told that there is no one there.'

Wazir's eyed brimmed over. Restraining her sobs, she said: 'Your Honour's heart, wherever it may be, is still yours and in whichever land it is, that land is subject to your rule. Now you must go; and let me have sight of your face the way you turn your back today.'

The Navab wiped off Wazir's tears gently with his fingers, and placing his right hand upon his breast, he bowed. Raising his head, he passed his hand over Wazir's head, and spoke in the softest of voices: 'You're right,' then he quoted an Arabic proverb. 'All things are bound to the time of their happening.'

He turned, crossed the small hall quickly, and left.

28

Wazir Khanam has a consultation with Navab Yusuf Ali Khan

WAZIR DISMISSED, WITH suitable remuneration and tips, the servants whom she had hired from outside; she told her personal maid that they should eat and then close up the kitchen, for she had no appetite. She then went into her room with her head bowed as if with a burden, and laid herself down on the bed. Her body was tremulous, as if with fever, though it was not a cold night by any means. But she lay without a covering in spite of her shivers. Suddenly, her eyes began to flow, as if of their own accord. Then came the sobs. Ultimately, she sobbed herself to sleep.

It was very late in the night when she woke up, feeling cold and finding herself shivering still. She felt as if she were frozen, like ice. She pulled a light quilt anyhow over her body and stared at the ceiling with empty eyes. Sleep had deserted her now. The overpowering, handsome, magnetic Shamsuddin Ahmad Khan, his sophisticated speech, his refined accents: all this had generated in her heart a throbbing pain of desire, but in front of her eyes were the days and nights that she had spent with Marston Blake. Every time she thought of Blak sahib, grief welled up in her heart at his untimely and lonely death, but even more than that pain, the warm waves of her yearnings and successes and currents of love for him who was both Firangee and Hindustani began to overrun her inner self like a physical sensation, as if someone had thrown a pebble in a pond and the waves kept on spreading, ever widening in a gyre, as if driven by some unseen power.

A lover like Blak sahib—his zealous lovemaking, his never-ending enthusiasm for her, his amorous ambitions for Wazir, his awareness of the mysteries of her body as if his instincts had such empathy with her that all of him had permeated every vessel and every nerve in her body and her spirit—where would come such another? Could anyone else in the world be so lucky?

That night of our return from the Noble Village of Mehrauli, the storms, the fears and risks of the road, the bullock cart's curtain flurrying away in the wind . . . and someone's eyes—not on my body, but lost somewhere in the labyrinth of my life and my heart—who knew that one day I would make a home with him, and who knew that my home in Jaipur would become his burial ground? . . . You should have no fear, not at all, I will be absolutely secure in the Residency. I'll return very soon and we will repeople our home . . . It isn't necessary that I should desire the man who desires me. But the Navab?

Her eyes closed, as if of their own accord. She thought she had slept but a minute, yet when she looked outside she found the sun high in the sky. Sparrows were twittering away in the lime tree in her little courtyard. In a big cage, her amdavats, Indian waxbills brought from Jaipur, were whistling, warbling and talking among themselves animatedly. Black-eyed, dun red of body and dark red of head and breast, with small white dots sprinkled randomly all over, they were larger, but not much larger, than sunbirds. The recent rains had caused their red breast and head to become darker, almost like the black rose. Their whistles seemed about to lift the house up in the air and make it fly away with them.

Wazir had just finished cleaning her teeth in the water room and was now rinsing her face when she was told that a mace-bearer from Firozepur was at the door, awaiting her pleasure. He was asked to come into the hall, and Wazir, concluding her ablution quickly, dried her face with a soft cloth, rearranged her wrap and came out of the water room. The mace-bearer had a porter with him, with a large basket on his head.

Getting a fleeting glimpse of Wazir from behind the curtain, the mace-bearer bent low, made a respectful salaam and spoke up, 'Honourable Bibi sahib, I make my submissions to you. The Presence, Navab sahib, has sent a dali; the porter awaits your pleasure. The Presence has also written a note which is with me.'

'I'll order purdah in the house momently; let the porter come in,' said Wazir. The mace-bearer, who had hopes of getting himself a glimpse, was disappointed a bit, but answered, 'Very well, Honourable Bibi sahib,' and made over to the maid the Navab's missive which was contained in a small silk purse, its knot sealed with wax, imprinted with the Navab's personal signet, and instructed the porter, 'Hey, you lout, convey the basket inside quickly. Look sharp. The Honourable Navab will be annoyed if we tarry.'

'Right away, sir steward. I'll take it inside in no time!' Saying this, the porter accompanied one of the maids into the house and placing the basket on a wooden platform, turned back promptly. Wazir gave five rupees to the mace-bearer and one rupee to the porter, and with words of submissions and salaams for the Navab, permitted them to depart. She now looked at the presents that the morning had brought for her. The wicker basket was full of red Kashmiri apples of the ambari variety. The silk purse had a small cut-glass phial of the attar of saffron, and a message on fragrant notepaper of the same orange-yellow colour as the attar; such paper was used for formal communications. The following Persian verse was inscribed on it in the Shikastah script used for informal communications. The Navab's hand was neat and sophisticated:

The tree became full of flowerets, the flowerets
Became full blooms; the full blooms
Became ripe fruits. Please come, so that the labours
Of the orchard may not go to waste.

Wazir's whole being throbbed with delight. Such subtleties were way beyond Marston Blake's capacity. But the very next moment she trembled with fear. What is happening here? Where am I going? Am I going . . . or am I being taken?

The same evening she sent her maid to Manjhli Khanam for an appointment to visit with her. On the following day, with the sun fairly up in the sky, she presented herself at Navab Yusuf Ali Khan's mansion . After paying the usual respects, she narrated to Manjhli Begam what had passed between her and Navab Shamsuddin Ahmad Khan.

'Do you think it would be proper for me to consult with the Honourable Brother Navab Yusuf Ali Khan sahib in this matter?'

'Dear Little One, where is the question of proper or improper in this? Surely, you should ask. I will be with you, and if I feel the need for it, I will intervene in the conversation. Come, bismillah! You enjoy the betel cones while I request the Navab to step inside for a moment.'

Navab Yusuf Ali Khan arrived at the women's quarters in a short while. It was his first meeting with Wazir after the party at William Fraser's. Of course, his informants had made him aware of Navab Shamsuddin Ahmad Khan's visit with Chhoti Begam, but he considered it proper not to reveal it to Umdah Khanam so that she might not misunderstand him as spying on her sister.

'Everything is crystal clear before the Honourable Sir, but I have another worry too. Should I ask Bari Baji or Baba Jan what they think about these happenings? Or should I tell them anything at all?'

'Chhoti Begam, this concerns you entirely. It would be better for me not to open my mouth in this matter. But I seem to recall that you and Anwari Begam had a conversation when you returned from Jaipur. Am I right?'

'Yes, Your Honour, and I did tell her that I . . .'

'So, you've yourself closed that door upon you.' The Navab paused and pondered for a moment or two. 'So in the case under our advisement, I would say the decision rests with you. But I can also say with certitude that Navab Shamsuddin Ahmad Khan's terms with us are friendly and we would place reliance upon him.'

'But the Resident Bahadur . . . ?'

'Oh, don't worry about the Resident Bahadur! Is there any certainty about his posting here? Here today, elsewhere tomorrow, the Company sends them where it lists. Or he could return to The Country one of these days. These are people of small duration. The Navab and his subjects will endure much longer.'

'Your command is very true.'

'So, if Shamsuddin Ahmad's conditions are suitable to your state, and his conduct and deportment seem agreeable to you, then bismillah, give your consent.'

'May God elevate your fortunes. You have taken off a huge burden from this servant girl's heart.' Wazir rose and salaamed the Navab.

Manjhli Begam was well pleased and said with a smile: 'We, your maids, should be sacrificed for you for your excellent counsel! God has made your heart on the model of Jamshed's wine cup, which reflected everything in the world. Your heart can glimpse the truth in no time!'

Manjhli Begam's smile was made even brighter by her flawless complexion, her face above her delicate, well-proportioned neck suggesting the rising sun. Not only was the Navab warming his heart with her beauty: Wazir had half a mind to hug her and shower kisses all over her face. After a long time—she could not recall how long—she felt her body to be her own, her mood and her heart in her control. It was the first time she was feeling that she was not alone and friendless in making decisions about her life.

Having taken leave from Manjhli and Yusuf Ali Khan, she went straight back to her home. All through the journey in her palanquin, and then on reaching home, she did nothing all day but wander from one room to another, looking at herself. And when she tired of doing that, she let her mind dwell on the Navab's words. He had spoken of 'conditions', and that those conditions should be suitable to my state. So what did those words really mean?

Obviously, the Navab did not speak of marriage; he did not say: Accept him if Shamsuddin Ahmad Khan proposes marriage. The matter rested with her; if she wished, she could set a precondition of marriage. Or, if there was no suggestion of marriage from that side, she could convey her objective by suggesting that she was available for marriage alone. Or, if she did not want to bring in marital issues at once, even that was all right: living with him as his sole woman could also be mooted. In fact, she could even propose staying on in her little home but remaining loyal to the Navab alone. But what was she going to live by, then? Will she get to openly go into the Navab's dominions? Will there ever be any prospect of marriage, however formal? And there was that overbearing, hardy, moustachioed, ancient Firangee, Fraser Sahib—may death take him! He had God knows how many bibis and how many catamites tied to his tail in his lustful old age; funny that the English can marry only one woman, but can have as many permanent or temporary connections as they please. I would not let that bastard see his face reflected in my chamber pot even. But it is he who is Master, is he not? He must have numerous subordinates like Mattan Blak sahib. I understand he is highly regarded at the Court of the Great Lord sahib in Calcutta. Yet Navab Yusuf Ali Khan sahib is right, surely. What price is their friendship, and how long is it going to last? They will run off to their land soon, or will be driven away from here. Well, if not soon, surely that day will come. Let Mirza Naushah regard him as his true friend in a thousand, in a hundred thousand. He does not even belong to Delhi. So why should his heart ache for the King here? If he wishes to have the hem of his garment tied to the strings of the power and wealth of an alien, foreign Firangee Kristan, so let him. What interest could we Hindis have in such affairs? But it is true that he is a mighty poet: whoever is with him will have his name assured for all time. But no, that is not necessarily true. Whoever has heard of or asked about the wives or sweethearts of Khusrau or Hafiz? Did anyone want to know their names, or where they were born, and what lives they lived and how they died? The real world consists of men only: it is they who rule, it is they who run the business of the world. All that we can do is to somehow keep our hands on them and not let them slip away from us. The Navab and his subjects and his dominions: these are the things that will endure. These poets are also like the Firangee: flies that flit from one lump of sugar to another. They are not honeybees. They're like the fly that falls in the milk jug and drowns—it cannot swim to the other end, nor remain afloat at one end. But I have so many more issues that need sorting out. And what will happen to my children: Amir Mirza, a piece of my heart, Badshah Begam, the light of my eyes? Yes, they were with Aby memsahib, but it was she who was to defray the expenses for their upbringing . . . and no, she was not separate from them, not at all. Visits, casual meetings, all these must be there, even if rarely. How I wish Amir Mirza would learn quickly to read and write! Let it not be Persian, let it be Hindi he learns to write. Of what surpassing beauty are those words of Amir Khusrau: *He neither comes to me, nor does he write.* The beloved is not everything in life, certainly not! A woman lives by the face of her offspring. Man may be the vermilion for her forehead and the crown of her life, but there is no greater wealth than a young, strapping son. The young son can even make death his prey. Truly, it is the son who should be regarded as master of the house. These menfolk are so stupid and unreliable; they're short in wisdom, long in life. Their bodies also lose their tautness after a few years; pleasure distinctly diminishes. Oh, for my Amir Mirza! How comely, how heart-enticing a youth he will turn out to be! He will be a shade taller than even Mattan Blak sahib. But where and how will I see him? Where will I have the chance to gladden my heart in observing his growth? I will be homeless myself, so how and where to build a threshold and a door to welcome him? I can bear wandering like a homeless beggar from door to door, but those bits of my heart—may God preserve them—will need a home with a well-born family, if not a mansion or a fortress. Could they ever find a home better than that of Navab Shamsuddin Ahmad Khan? I should discuss and determine the conditions with him . . . or should I wait for him to make his proposal? Well, his heart is on fire, he should himself send word . . . What a marvellous line it was that Mir Muhammad Taqi sahib composed:

I will cut off my head, take it in my hand
And I will go there myself, on my own.

Oh, these poets, really! It is wondrous how they seek and find new themes, new talking points! What waters do they sound, what depths do they delve so as to uncover such pearls?

And this verse again is from him, so true about himself, and perhaps of other great poets too:

Indeed, how astonishing are the poets
I love their tribe;
In full assembly, fearless, they reveal
All mysteries, all secrets.

A thousand pities, that Nizam-ul Mulk—may death take him—enticed away Shah Nasir sahib, my dear ustad, to the Deccan, or I would address a poem to the Navab and send it after showing it to Shah sahib for correction. Perhaps the poem could prove to be the key to his intentions; or at least I could reveal something of mine to him. A pest on that wretched memsahib, she has not sent me news of my babies for many weeks now. I am so entirely lonely here without them and I cannot even aspire to go back to Jaipur. Now all that I can pray for is to be joined here to the dust of Delhi which gave birth to me.

Could someone describe her own looks, her own body? So how could I convey to a strange man that which is in my heart? But Mattan Blak sahib was a stranger too. In fact, he was the most alien among aliens: a Kristan with nothing to unite us, neither manners nor modes, neither community nor customs. Oh, but how can I speak of him? He was fashioned by the Maker with the earth of some special quality perhaps. How tightly kneaded, how bright, how splendid was his body! And now, as regards our Navab Shamsuddin Ahmad . . .

It was as if she was stopped short, suddenly confronted with a well, or the foot of a hill. Our Navab! By what right or duress do I think of him in this fashion? Has he had my heart ravished and placed by his side? Or am I giving it away to him of my own accord?

She recalled the Navab's words at parting: 'My heart has left my side to go away somewhere. Should it return and knock at the door, do not open the door; say there is no one at home.' But she also must have said something in response, did she not? Did not something take place between them? Was there not some kind of a knot tied by them? What else is a first step?

Should I write back in my own hand, or should I wait for something like a proper message from his side? But now what should be, what could be, the excuse or occasion for it? Should I have the Divan of Hafiz searched for an augury? Or should I do it myself? But did I not hear it said that the interested person shouldn't herself search for an augury? As opposed to this, the interested party should do the istikharah, the prayer which is performed to get a 'Yes' or 'No' reply for some act. So whom should I ask? Should I send out one of my trusted maids to find out if an augur lives somewhere nearby, and if he could visit?

She was exhausted and disheartened by the incessant turning over of the same questions and thoughts in her brain; but no solution came. The day passed, evening became night, but she just could not see a way that would lead to a resolution.

She ate rather sparsely, rinsed her mouth and was about to flop down on the bed when she thought of Pundit Nand Kishor. The Pundit was a person of an earlier age. Of undisputed renown, he was an augur, an astrologer, an interpreter of signs and dreams. He occasionally visited Chhoti Begam's maternal grandmother, but only after numerous requests and invitations. He must be very much older now, maybe even dead and gone. Well, I thought of something at least. Resolutions made during the night are not said to be advisable to put into effect. So I'll do nothing at present. Come morning, I will give it more thought. If it becomes necessary, I'll myself go to grandmother.

29

Wazir Khanam consults Pundit Nand Kishor, and the Divan of Khvajah Hafiz is read to resolve a troubling dilemma

SHE WAS IN luck. The next day, she was able to get to Pundit Nand Kishor with no difficulty at all. Actually, he had left Delhi years ago, to settle with his son in Hansi Hissar. His wife's death and his own chronic backache had left him greatly handicapped. Loneliness had ultimately driven him to give away his house in Khanam ka Bazaar to his daughter and son-in-law and settle in Hansi Hissar with his son and daughter-in-law in their house. He had no lack of means and his son too, by His Grace, was quite prosperous, but the Pundit was not prepared to impose even a trace of burden on anyone. The son practically went down on his knees to let him accept residence with them at no cost, but he was adamant. The son pleaded that Parameshwar had not put them in any kind of want, and after all, Babu ji's expenses would amount to hardly anything, but the Pundit looked after himself independently to the extent possible. He had his food cooked separately; he occupied the upper room and the terrace in his son's house, and though he paid no rent, he had constructed separate stairs leading to his room. The family would use the inner staircase whenever they wanted to meet or when he wished to see his son or grandson or daughter-in-law in their home.

It was the happiest of chances for Wazir that Pundit Nand Kishor was actually visiting his former home in Khanam ka Bazaar when Akbari Bai's messenger went there to ascertain his whereabouts. He cheerfully consented to visit Wazir the next morning, specifying that he needed no carriage or even a guide, and would find his way there with ease.

Wazir breathed a small sigh of relief. She immediately busied herself in suitably organizing a room where Pundit ji was to be received, and also in getting the house generally cleaned up. She chose the room where he would be seated and entertained; later, that room could be the venue for Pundit ji's purposes of divination. This room was immediately to the right of the entrance hall. She figured it to be the best as it was somewhat separate, and yet the servants would be easily within call. It had an air of solitude and would also save the venerable guest from walking up into the house.

But it occurred to her suddenly that Pundit ji might not like the isolated nature of the room and might even feel offended that he was palmed off with a small room, very nearly outside the house. So she now decided to receive him in the room where Navab Shamsuddin Ahmad Khan had been entertained. The room was thoroughly dusted, then swept, and then its floor was washed with rose water and dried quickly by assiduous fanning. Heavy cotton rugs were spread in it from wall to wall; the rugs were then covered with milk-white sheeting. The room was then fumigated by burning amber, frankincense and aloes wood in small burners made of fired clay. The room was then locked.

Next morning, well before Pundit Nand Kishor started from Khanam ka Bazaar, thick carpets were spread on the floor and a large bolster was placed at one end of them. The betel box and the hookah were set up, and the room closed again after spraying rose water everywhere.

The morning's light spread into the lanes and alleys, sprinkling them with its golden, perfumed particles of dust. The royal road-sweepers disseminated and mixed the dust they raised with the fragrant smoke rising up from the wood and charcoal stoves of the sweet-makers. The roseate waves of the light of the true dawn were like a sieve through which the hot, mouth-watering smell of sweets freshly fried in ghee was being strained to enrich the atmosphere with messages of friendliness to the nostrils, eyes and throats of those who were coming out of the mosques after offering their predawn prayers. In Wazir's alley, sellers of sweet milk whipped into froth thick slabs of cream which could be cut with a knife and eaten with a spoon, and vendors of milk, egg and chicken began to call and hawk their goods.

A new day started in Jahanabad, the city where even the environs were heavenly. The city that ceased to remember past sorrows in the shortest possible time, raised its head from out of the dark, proclaiming its undying youth and beauty through the proudly rising, heart-fulfilling, confidence-brimming and delicate head of the towering spire of Qutb Sahib; through the power and grandeur of Muhammad Tughlaq's mausoleum at Tughlaqabad; through the mellifluous sounds of the reciters of the Quran or the Primary Declaration of Faith in the ancient mosque attached to the meeting house at the effulgent mausoleum of Nizamuddin Auliya, Delhi's most loved saint; through the grey-blue pigeons roosting at the two-toned dome of Shahjahan's mosque, who then fly down to wet their beaks in the water flowing in the tank of ablution at the centre of the mosque's huge courtyard, and then coo in remembrance of some faraway wild, flowering shrub which was perhaps their home once; through the sudden starting up of the fountain in savan bhadon, the large six-sided tank in the Haveli; through the tremulous sounds of a variety of musical instruments and the reverberations of the complicated hand-and-finger strokes on the twin percussion instrument, the tabla.

In the midst of all this, there was a gentle rattle of the chain at Wazir's street door: Pundit Nand Kishor's noble presence had arrived. Wazir's maid sprang to open the door, and bending and salaaming, she led him to the chamber that was now redolent with the scent of roses. She seated him with full veneration against the bolster, offered the betel box to him, then the hookah, which was ready beforehand; the bouquet of the Faizabadi tobacco smouldering in the hookah had filled the whole house with its aroma. Placing the silver mouthpiece of the long hookah pipe in his hand, she submitted: 'Let the Presence enjoy the hookah for a moment or two; Bibi sahib has been looking forward to your coming. She will present herself in the twinkling of an eye.'

'It is perfectly all right,' said Pundit Nand Kishor with a kindly smile. 'Let her be comfortable and take her time. I am not running away anywhere.' His voice was low and heavy, but pleasant in a masculine way. There was very little fluctuation in the pitch, as if the speaker was in a state of full intellectual confidence and content of the heart, and nothing could frighten or surprise him. He was tall, thin and fair of complexion. His fingers, long and conical like those of painters and sculptors, had no rings except on the ring finger of the left hand. On that finger he wore a large cat's eye, green and grey, large as a sparrow's egg; it had two and a half lines of light in it. In the boat-shaped ring, the cat's eye was prominent like the sun rising on the sky of Venus. Its light lines shone like steel spears made in the Central Asian city of Khatt, which were famous over the centuries for being highly tensile and sharp.

As described above, the cat's eye scintillated with two and a half lines of light. Normally, a good cat's eye has one, or at best one and a half lines.

Two lines are rare, and a cat's eye with two and a half lines of light is valued as the tribute of a whole kingdom. Nobles and wealthy personages had viewed the cat's eye with longing eyes, but none dared asked Pundit Nand Kishor where and how that jewel of great price had fallen into his hands.

Pundit Nand Kishor was dressed entirely in white; even his turban, tied in the Brahminical style, was white though astrologers and officiators at ceremonies normally favoured a saffron-coloured turban. Pundit ji's old-style muslin cloak, rather wide, was indeed not devoid of colour, but it was pale yellow, almost cream white, so much so that the white trousers underneath had almost overcome the yellow of the cloak. His trousers were cut in the style of Delhi, very wide-bottomed, such that its edges often kissed or even impeded the slippers whose toes were slim and raised like a crest. The trousers were of a fabric called sangi which is a mix of silk and cotton, with very fine woven stripes and much white left between them. He usually favoured lengklat or even coarser cotton, but that day he wore sangi in honour of his visit to Wazir Khanam.

Pundit sahib's face was practically free of wrinkles. There were no palpable signs of aging, but his beard was long and entirely white and even his eyebrows were white. In his left hand he carried an ebony stick, twisted somewhat like a snake, and with a strong head to lean on. In his right hand he had a very long sandal rosary. A white kerchief or sash was loosely wound around his neck, and below it could be seen a necklace of the dried brown berries of the rudraksha considered as holy and health-giving by many Indians. The whole effect of his presence was like a cotton flower, delicate and soft.

He had just begun to smoke the hookah when Wazir drew aside the curtain and entered. Out of respect to Pundit sahib, she had not made any effort at dressing up and had avoided all such dress or jewellery as might give the impression of ostentation. Even then, her much-favoured dupatta of golden cotton netting looked exceedingly ravishing on her medium-breadth trousers of a striped, light silk called mahramat. She wore no jewellery in her nose, ears and wrists, and nothing on her neck except a small necklace with a sapphire pendant surrounded by very small diamonds. She bent low in salaam and said, 'Pundit ji, you have been so incredibly kind and bountiful to your insignificant servant girl . . .'

Pundit Nand Kishor raised his right hand, gesturing to her to stop, and said, 'Child, what is this talk of kindness and bountifulness? To whom am I being kind, except to my own dear child, and it is no kindness to serve one's own children. The sight of you makes my eyes feel cool with comfort. But tell me, how were you reminded of this old man who has been dwelling in seclusion for so long? Your dear grandmother was telling me that you were prepared to trouble your feet to come to me. But I said, no, dear Sister, I'm not for committing such a huge sin. I will go and visit with my dear little girl.'

'I take the name of God! You have stopped my tongue entirely! Now if I give thanks, you will be displeased; and if I do not, I will be like a culprit in my own eyes,' Wazir said. Her eyes were downcast but there was a slight smile on her lips.

'All right. So I hereby accept your thanks,' Pundit ji smiled in turn. 'Now reveal to me what suddenly brought me to your mind? . . . Or should I tell you?'

Pundit ji's strong but heart-warming voice was to Wazir's ears like some angel of God's Mercy inviting the weak and the sinful towards honour and security. She felt insignificant like a small child before Pundit sahib. She sat with her knees bent and her feet under her thighs, as if in prayer, and spoke in a low voice, with bowed head: 'Everything is open and clear before the Presence. I can say nothing but what is already mirrored in the heart of the Presence.'

Pundit ji smiled, 'So just name a flower, any flower.'

'White jasmine,' she said spontaneously.

Pundit Nand Kishor closed his eyes, counted something on his rosary, and then spoke in a moment. 'In the north-west of Delhi, not very far from here, there is a state ruled by a navab. The name of the ruler is . . .' he paused a beat, 'Shamsuddin Ahmad Khan.'

Wazir's face turned pink; she spoke again with bowed head, using a Persian proverb: 'Your Honour, for you, it is like "there is no need to describe that which is already apparent". But my heart is full of fear.'

'There is nothing to fear about. But what else do you desire to know? Are you worried about the end of it all?'

'No, sir. I am afraid to look into the future. I feel like someone lost, wandering to find the right way. May the Presence be so kind as to guide me.'

'Guide you towards what you should now do? Is it not so? You wait for the Navab to take the initiative?'

'Sir, that has already happened. But what should I do now? Should I wait longer, or should I move in step with him? My brain refuses to function.' Her eyes became wet in spite of herself as she said this.

'So what is there to worry about, little young lady? The answer is right here, in front of us. But come, let us consult the Khvajah sahib for your satisfaction.'

Wazir's face bloomed with joy. How did Pundit ji read my heart's desire? she asked herself.

'Sir, your words are extremely auspicious. Should I go and fetch his Divan?' she asked eagerly.

'Yes, do. But see, be sure that you have clean and pure hands, and put it on the bookstand used for holy books, do you follow me? Also bring a sheet of unpolluted paper, an inkpot with unpolluted ink, and a piece of new reed.'

The meaning of 'clean and pure hands' was not hidden from Wazir. 'Sir, I am bathed, and have also performed the ablutions necessary before prayers. I'll bring the Divan in a second.' She had already procured the kind of ink, paper and reed required for auguring from the Divan of Khvajah Hafiz. Thus there was no problem for her there. She went out and returned presently with a manuscript Divan of the poet calligraphed and decorated in black, gold and blue, placed on a walnut wood bookstand. Behind her was a maid, bringing paper and inkstand.

Wazir placed the book with the bookstand before Pundit Nand Kishor, but did not open it. The inkstand and paper were also placed near him, within easy reach. Now Pundit Nand Kishor turned his face to the west, that is, towards the Kabah in Mecca, as Muslims do before praying. He also sat in the same way as prescribed, with his feet tucked under his thighs. He spoke a few words under his breath and then he commanded: 'Let a bit of rose water be sprinkled again, and have a second, short round of fumigation with frankincense, aloes wood and bdellium. Although this room has been perfumed and purified already, yet it is necessary at this time too. Do you follow?'

During the time that rose water was sprinkled and the fumigation carried out through incense burners, Pundit Nand Kishor sat still, with his eyes closed. When this was over, he raised his hands and said some prayer that Wazir was unable to identify. After the prayer, he said 'Amen' aloud and asked Wazir also to do the same. 'Now have all doors and windows closed,' he directed. When the room was closed and secure, he commanded:

'Now you sit before me, so that the Divan is between the two of us and I can open the book with my right hand. You, sitting on the other side of me, should concentrate and imagine that the holy soul of Khvajah sahib is present among us. Do you follow?'

'Yes, sir. But . . . but I don't know how to concentrate and imagine . . .' Wazir said apprehensively.

'Oh, it is nothing. Just imagine that you're here, reading his Divan, and the Tongue of the Unseen has just walked in, casually, during one of his wanderings.'

'But did he not join with the Almighty centuries ago?' Wazir asked in fear and wonder.

'Yes, certainly. Yet he is still among us. He's present through his utterances. If you read his poetry, imagining that those words have just been uttered by him, and uttered for you alone, then the image of his person will establish itself in your mind without effort on your part. The poet never dies. He's present through his words: it is just that he speaks his words in a multiform existence. He talks to us in twig and branch, in garden, park and meadow, in the palace and the poorest alley, in castle and tent . . . Come, let us hurry. Otherwise, the auspicious moment will pass.'

Trembling, Wazir sat in front of Pundit Nand Kishor, closed her eyes tight and concentrated on the first verse of the Divan. Pundit ji's voice seemed to reverberate around her, and it also seemed to be coming from some distance.

'Light of my eyes, please note that there are many ways of divining from the utterances of the Tongue of the Unseen. But the first thing to do is to be ritually clean, and then perform the ablution necessary before the prayers. The next thing to do is to determine which pass of the day or night it is. You can see that the second pass of the day is about to start. We will begin our work after the second pass has begun. Still, before we commence, we must find out about Venus, the Dancing Girl of the Skies who is the Patron of All Poets. We must know in which station of the zodiac she is at present and for how long she will remain there. So I will tell you now that Venus at present is in the station of Mercury who is the Secretary and Writing Master of the Skies. Thus this time is even more suitable for our purposes. Do you follow?'

Wazir made no reply. Suddenly, she thought she saw a tall, extraordinarily distinguished person of powerful presence—with a turban of the style used by men of learning wound around his head, his eyes hypnotic yet somehow lost in thought—had just walked through a wall in the room and had passed in front of her with a proud gait. She could not know how he came in, and how he went out. Did he pass through a wall? Is there a gaping crack in the wall? Was it a shade? She trembled and felt cold for a moment, but Pundit Nand Kishor's voice had somehow converted itself into the warmth and ardour of organic life and the chastity of the Voice of the Unseen, and was flowing and rippling through the room, and in fact her entire abode, like long silk tassels and threads undulating in the air.

'Right, here we are now in the second pass. She who inspires the poets' dead words with life is still flirting with the Secretary of the Skies. We have sufficient time, in fact plenty of it, for our task. And here I have before me the ephemeris of the second pass of this day. I bow low before the Lady Venus and do pranam to her and open the Divan of Khvajah Hafiz. My purpose is to inquire from him what command he wishes to give in regard to Little Girl Wazir Khanam, daughter of Muhammad Yusuf, maker of plain gold ornaments, in the matter of Navab Shamsuddin Ahmad Khan. I put my finger arbitrarily on any box in the augury chart before me. I find that my finger is on the letter "dal", the tenth letter of the Persian alphabet.

'Bibi, open your eyes, take the pen and paper and write the letter "dal".'

Tremulously, she somehow wrote the letter dal, and looked at Pundit ji with her large eyes, dark and somehow golden, like the darkest hibiscus. Now he counted some figures and thought a bit, then he commanded, 'Now write the letter "ra", the twelfth letter of the alphabet. This gives us the word "dar". Do you follow?'

'Yes, Your Honour, I follow.'

Pundit sahib counted some figures again, thought some more and said, 'Now write; it is the twelfth letter "ra" again.'

'Yes, sir, I have written it.' She felt that the pen was in her hand; it was as if she was scribing her own fate.

In the meantime, Pundit Nand Kishor ordered, 'Now write "alif", the first letter of the alphabet. Did you write?'

'Yes, sir, I did.'

After a few moments, Pundit ji said, 'Now write the letter "ha", the last but one letter of the alphabet. So that gives us the word "rah", and we get the phrase: "dar rah"—"in the way". You follow me?'

Now Wazir's hand was trembling so that she dreaded she might let fall a drop of ink on the paper and spoil its purity or make the writing look mutilated. Pundit Nand Kishor immediately saw her anxiety and confusion and spoke encouragingly in the kindest of tones: 'Just write. Go on writing. Have no fear at all of the letters being ill formed. Now write the letter "ain". Do you follow? Write the letter "ain" which comes before "ghain".'

'Yes, sir, I have written it.' For no reason that she could fathom, she felt like weeping. She spoke haltingly: 'Presence, may I go and get myself a glass of water?'

'Water? Let water be brought here. Have a carafe full of it. Do not panic, everything is all right.'

Wazir clapped once with her hands. Her personal maid knocked and put her head inside and looked inquiringly for orders. Wazir gestured for water, which the maid brought in a pewter carafe with a drinking cup. Wazir Khanam drank the whole large cup without pausing for breath.

'Feeling better? There is nothing to be frightened about, little daughter. Right, now write the letter "shin", the one that follows "sin".'

'I have written it, sir.'

Pundit ji again paused for a few seconds, then he directed, 'Now write "qaf". Did you hear? Now write "qaf", the one that precedes "kaf".' His voice had a hint of a pleasurable smile. 'So now the whole phrase becomes "dar rah-e ishq", which means, as you must know, "in the path of love". You understand?'

'Yes, Your Honour. I understood.'

In this way, adding one letter after another, Pundit Nand Kishor constructed the following line of verse in about half an hour:

Dar rah-e ishq farq-e-ghani o faqir nist

(In the path of love there is no distinction between the wealthy and the beggar)

'By the grace of God, what a beautiful line of verse we brought out! Bibi, congratulations!'

'But I do not understand its real meaning.' Wazir's forehead was now moist with perspiration. 'Presence, what direction does it have for me?'

'Little daughter, you're so artless, so simple-minded! This is just one line, the first one of a two-line verse, my dear one. The Presence, the Tongue of the Unseen, should vouchsafe the next verse, only then will we be enlightened. At present it is the case of a line from another Shaikh of Shiraz: "The water of the Stream of Life lies deep in the dark." Yet certainly, the line that we constructed seems to be apposite. So let us now search for the second line. Pick up the pen and paper again and write as I tell you.'

After the labour of another half-hour or a bit more, they arrived at the following line of verse:

Ay badshah-e husn sukhan ba gada bigo
(O sovereign of beauty, speak to the beggar.)

Wazir's heart began to throb and thud against her ribs as if she was suffering from tachycardia. It rose and came up and fell many yards, it seemed to her. Impetuously, she wanted to rise and bend her head at Pundit sahib's feet. She was just about to do so when Pundit ji spoke: 'Only God is free from all blemish! We got the answer to our query. But let us make sure that the verse is really the property of the Tongue of the Unseen.' Saying this, he opened the Divan, went to the appropriate page and laughed with pleasure. 'Yes, yes! This ghazal is right there in the Divan. The Presence, the Khvajah has commanded the opening verse like this:

O messenger of the true and the righteous
Give us the news of our walking cypress,
Narrate to the bulbul, the singer of songs,
How it goes with the rose.

He slapped his thigh with pleasure and enjoyment. 'The Khvajah of Shiraz had determined you to be the Sovereign King of Beauty, and him he describes as the mendicant. It is not just that you should speak to him. It is that you speak as the kings of the world deign to speak to the supplicants who approach their portal for charity. You are not the seeker: you are the sought. Congratulations!'

He raised his hands in prayer. His prayer concluded, he passed his hand lovingly on Wazir's head and desired leave to depart. Quickly, Wazir presented him a bag of rupees, a large silk kerchief, a small parchment bottle of the attar of double jasmine from Jaunpur and a bolt of the cotton fabric bulbul chashm to be used for his turban. She prayed that he accept her insignificant offering. Pundit Nand Kishor refused to accept anything at all.

'When Allah the Most Exalted brings your wish to pass and makes you achieve your objective, you then remember me in your prayers. I consider it forbidden to take anything from my sons or daughters. Do you follow?'

'I take the name of God! God forbid, I was not offering any such objectionable thing like payment for services. I would not commit such disrespect even if I was out of my mind. I was just making an insignificant offering to be touched by the feet of Your Presence. But perhaps I can never be so fortunate.' Her voice was wet with tears.

'Oh! Look here! She's upset! My child, one does not lose heart at such minor matters. All right, I'll take this bottle of attar.' Saying this, he picked up the bottle, pulled out the wooden stopper and smelled the attar to enjoy the fragrance. He liked it, for he smiled, rubbed a couple of drops on his scarf and said, 'Here, are you happy now?' Before leaving, he quietly placed five Shah Alami silver rupees in an alcove in the hall for the servants, and saying, 'Be sure to remember me when the time comes,' he went out in the twinkling of an eye without any other formal leave-taking. It seemed to Wazir that the house had suddenly gone quiet, as if some object of great value and weight had been taken out from her house.

30

Poetry facilitates an exchange of love letters between Wazir Khanam and Shamsuddin Ahmad Khan

AFTER PUNDIT NAND Kishor's departure, Wazir was lost in thought for a long time, trying to recapture his conversation, his loving kindnesses and his effulgent visage. She was overcome with a wave of pleasure, a thrill of newly discovered knowledge, and it was giving to her body an unaccustomed warmth of life, and to her spirit, renewed freshness like the first shower of rain in summer.

It took quite a while for her mood to revert to normal and when her maid presented herself to inquire about the household affairs, she recalled that while Pundit ji advised her to take the initiative in writing to the Navab, she quite forgot to ask him about the words and the mode she should use for her missive. She was very angry at herself for being such a dolt, and now having realized that she did not ask the question, she was being such a weakling as to be unable to take her own decision in the matter. There is, indeed, nothing formidable about it. I'll put pen to paper and write my letter in a second.

But that whole day passed. She could not decide on the salutation even, not to speak of the contents of her letter. What should I say? Do I say that I miss you greatly? Oh, what folly, she thought sheepishly, how cheap, how thin would those words read on paper. Could I ever write like that? And if I did, somehow, what will he think of me? So then? Should I say, when can we meet again? Yes, that seems not inappropriate; but what words should I use? It shouldn't feel as if this fine lady is absolutely impatient. What was the phrase that Grandmother used on such occasions? Yes . . . this little strumpet walks about with it on the palm of her hand! The very thought made her go pink and hot all over. A thrill of shame ran through her body. I and Navab Shamsuddin Ahmad Khan . . . and I, shorn of the purdah, and an invitation, a seductiveness in my eyes? I beg forgiveness from Allah, I'm a girl of a good family. Or am I a daughter of Satan? To walk about with it on the palm . . . Oh my God, this is worse than even beckoning or speaking.

The body slim, svelte, like a fawn, a little above average height, the neck proud like a peacock's, the breasts and the hips heavy but not big, slender waist, large, deep-brown eyes with a hint of the kohl around them, salty, lickable relish raining everywhere on her face, each of her gestures and movements like those of a high-born begam, and yet, each of those actions—the whole of her body speaking the language of a fille de joie—every word charged . . . who is the person who looks and talks like this? Navab Shamsuddin Ahmad thought with surprise. He was unable to sleep, even though that night he had gone to bed sooner than usual. The girls on the duty of pressing and patting his body gently, or running their fingers softly through his thick hair and rubbing his temples, they were getting tired. But sleep eluded the Navab's eyes.

Wazir Khanam woke up with a big start, her brain in some kind of frenzy. What did I see or say just now? Where am I? Where was I? I do not know, and why should I be wondering about Navab Shamsuddin Ahmad's thoughts about me and about how I look in his imaginings? How am I concerned at all with all this?

But who are those people who are inebriate with the wine cup of full concord? And who said, let me have sight of your face the way you turn your back today? The neck and collar drenched with perspiration, the upper-body wrap almost dripping, the breath irregular and fast, body feeling scratchy as if ants were running all over it, biting away as they went. What am I doing to myself? I'll surely lose my mind in no time if I go on like this. If not mad, I'll become a maniac. I've heard that maniacs get fixated on something and they go on and on about it. What impelled Navab Shamsuddin Ahmad to connect with me, why did his eye fall on me who am wan with my own miseries? Why did he come here? Why did he disrupt my loneliness?

A smile suddenly suffused her lips and eyes, as if the horizon in the evening, long, dark with clouds, was unexpectedly pierced by a strong light, running across the expanse of it; light, or a semblance of it, pervaded the air, with strange rays of light sprouting from under the head-bowed leaves of plants and trees; bird and beast, terrorized by the advent of evening, again became active and quick. It seemed to her that Shamsuddin Ahmad had suddenly appeared from somewhere and clasped her in his arms and she, with her head resting upon his broad chest, was whispering to him in tones of loving complaint:

By visiting me for a few short moments,
You disrupted my taste for being alone.

Oh? my good God, did the heavenly Mir Hasan sahib compose it for me and for this occasion alone, or do such things also come to pass on others? How critical a moment and how wonderfully opportune it was for me to be reminded of this superb piece of poetry! Now I don't need to do anything else: just put this verse on paper and send it to him, and I'm through. No, should I send the bare verse? It seems like bad manners, as if I trundled a rock towards him. But what is there left to say? Still, I must put in something, a salutation, a submission of good wishes. Shouldn't there be a subject for a letter? Should I not let the person know what my purpose is in writing to him?

No, I am not going to say any more, just the poem. My God knows my intent, now let him guess at it. No, wait, I have a thought. It is only two lines, this verse. Maybe I could compose three more lines of my own, making a regular five-line stanza, give it a sense of completeness, and also perhaps make my intent clearer?

She had thought this thought for a fleeting second, when she composed a line spontaneously, fully metrical and taking the theme of the original verse of the eighteenth-century master a little further:

You changed the state of my house

No, that won't do. Changing the state of my house: it is somewhat inappropriate, if not meaningless. Why not say:

You changed the state of my heart

No, no, this is very prosaic. Oh, why not:

You changed the very state of my heart's affairs

This is most appropriate, she said to herself. Now let us try to expand upon this theme.

Her mood was now so elevated that almost in a paroxysm of joy, she composed the next two lines in almost no time:

You crushed and tore off my cover of self-possession
You trampled underfoot my narrow path of patience:
You changed the very state of my heart's affairs;
By visiting me for a few short moments,
You disrupted my taste for being alone.

Now is that not something! I produced a nice five-line stanza, all my lines meaningful and well connected with the older poet's original two. Now should I myself write it out on a notepaper, or should I employ a calligrapher? No, there is no occasion for getting someone else to write. I am not sending him a formal present like a fine example of a professional calligrapher's art; I'm bringing to the point of the pen that which is hidden in my heart. I must do the writing; well or ill, it must be I who am reflected in the words.

Having made the decision, she immediately sent for new writing reeds from Mina Bazaar at the eastern gate of the Jami Masjid. She pared one end of each neatly with a penknife and made three new pens: thin, medium and thick. She then sent them to the Maulavi sahib of the neighbouring mosque, with two rupees as a humble offering, and the request that he smooth and split their points and cut them at the proper angle. The Maulavi sahib kindly performed these tasks quickly, tested each pen to his satisfaction and sent them back with his good wishes and the assurance that the cuts would stay firm for quite some time.

It was afternoon by the time all this was done. Wazir was exhausted and somehow felt a little out of sorts. She said in her heart that she should practise her hand at night and send her letter the next day. She had ready the orange-saffron notepaper and a little brocade pouch. All that was to be done was to write and dispatch the letter.

During the night, she used up many sheets of paper before she felt satisfied. She wrote the poem with the medium pen in her best possible style, in the standard Nastaliq script, the preferred mode for formal communications. However, at the top of it, she used an ancient Arabic secretarial script to write one of the ninety-nine names of the Almighty: hu al Wadud ('He Is The Most Loving'). In the valediction, she wrote with the thin pen:

'Written and submitted by Wazir Khanam.

She awaits a reply. May her sins be forgiven.'

She rolled up the paper like a cylinder and wrapped it in wax cloth. She now placed the rolled-up letter in a lightly scented pouch, tied its strings and sealed it. It was late night before she finished, but she preferred to work late because then she had the night and morning still to ponder and review her decision and her action. It was only words so far, but once the letter left her house it was an arrow shot forth from the bow, never to be recalled. Thus let me give myself some more time over the night and morning to decide if the letter should go or not at all.

The noise of the birds awoke her before the dawn. As soon as she arose, the thought came to her that the letter must go, but it must be accompanied with some small present. But what should it be? I am not yet free enough with him to send something intimate like a handkerchief embroidered by me, or a phial of attar. As for valuable worldly goods, the Navab wants for nothing, the rarest of things would be in abundance in his houses. There can be nothing in the world that I could provide and which would not be already there. Actually, my best present would be something which though not necessarily costly, may not be common in this part of the world.

She recalled that some weeks ago a merchant from Garhwal, a hill-state in the north-east, had sold her a leather bottle full of mountain honey. Honey is nothing so fancy as to merit being sent as a present, but the peculiar thing about this honey was that its hive was located on a litchi tree and all the honey had apparently been gathered from litchi blossoms. Thus the honey had a delicate hint of the litchi fruit in it. That must indeed be something rare, for litchi was not grown anywhere near Delhi. She had the bottle brought out from the pantry, cleaned and dusted. She pulled out the wooden stopper. The litchi aroma was the same and the honey's colour was also unchanged: a pale yellow that was almost white and fine-grained like pure ghee clarified from cow's butter.

The bottle was sealed at the top, wrapped in wax paper, and then sealed again. Having done so much, she now made up her mind most firmly that she would rest only after she had dispatched the letter and the present. She immediately summoned a messenger through the guard of her neighbourhood and personally instructed him: 'Remember that Navab sahib has two mansions: one is in Ballimaran, not very far from here, but the other is in Daryaganj. You must first ascertain in which haveli Navab sahib has his auspicious Presence. Go there and nowhere else, and gain access to him, observing the full protocol of salaams; you should then bend your head, with your right hand just above your heart. Only then must you place these things at his feet.'

'I understand, Bibi sahib. I understand fully. I will carry out your instructions to the letter . . . and should I wait for an answer?' He made a respectful salaam and waited.

'No. Just inform His Honour that Wazir Khanam sahib sends her salaams and these two packets. Say that a reply is not needed.'

'Yes, your instructions are very good, very auspicious. God willing, all things will be as you have directed.'

'All right, now go. Come back quickly. I'll await your return and will richly reward you if you do your duty well.'

The messenger salaamed again and left. As against her outward calm and businesslike demeanour, her heart was in a veritable tumult. She felt sick and weak. She knew in her heart of hearts that by the consequence of this step hung the decision for her future life. If I do not get a desired reply, I will have to spread again the board of my life's game. This act of mine concerns the business of my heart and also my future days and nights. Did I do well, or did I do ill? But did I have any other choice? It is beneath my station to wait, but was it right for me to open my lips? Was it not the Navab himself who opened the conversation? I did nothing else but convey my reply to him. So what was wrong with it?

And even if there was some wrongdoing there, it was supported by Navab Yusuf Ali Khan's advice, encouragement from Pundit sahib, and above all, the positive sign from Khvajah sahib. Did not these things have some value?

Suddenly, her heart ached for Marston Blake. How I wish he had not gone away so soon . . . and how happily, how free of care, I had gone off with him! The displeasure of my parent held no fears for me; nor did I have regard for the laws and precepts of religion. Nor did I mind the possible criticism or disapproval of my peers or our neighbours. But at that time I understood so little and aimed so high. I was like the Holy River Jamna in full flood, heading up and rising to break my own path. No children, nothing to worry about or care for. But I now have two little lives to provide for, one way or another.

The thoughts coursing through her head made her feel dizzy and uneasy. This lonely house—a plague on it—feels as if it is going to bite me.

She summoned a palanquin and went straight to Manjhli Begam's house. She narrated a full account of the recent happenings and declared that she would stay as Manjhli's houseguest until there was some response from Shamsuddin Ahmad Khan.

*

The Navab was at that time at his haveli in Daryaganj. The moment he was informed about the arrival of a messenger from Wazir Khanam of Sirki Walan with the humble petition that he be allowed access to His Honour, he had him shown into the chamber that he used to meet friends in the afternoon. Although the chamber was meant only for persons close to him, Shamsuddin Ahmad was so eager, so ardent in his feelings for Wazir that he was impatient to see the messenger without delay. The messenger, walking respectfully behind the Navab's mace-bearer, removed his shoes at the door and having crossed the threshold, he bent low to salaam him seven times. Then he waited for permission to proceed. The mace-bearer bent in salaam and submitted: 'Wazir Khanam sahib's courier is present in the service of the Elevated Honourable Sir.'

The Navab gestured for the messenger to be permitted to advance. Approaching close, the messenger made one more salaam and said, 'May the fortunes of the Presence continue to rise, Wazir Khanam sahib has directed an offering to be submitted to the Exalted Servants. May I present it, if so desired?'

An involuntary smile was about to adorn the Navab's face, but he checked himself just in time and spoke gravely, 'Very well. How is the Begam sahib doing?'

'She is very well, Your Honour.'

Reading the tiny hint in the Navab's eye, the mace-bearer came forward. There was an occasional table nearby, carved from ivory. The mace-bearer removed the few things that were on it and beckoned to the messenger to place on it whatever he had to present to the Navab. The messenger loosened his sash and removed from under it the pouch containing the letter and the bag containing the honey bottle, and placed both objects upon the table. He then walked backward to the door, making the salaam. The mace-bearer again interpreted correctly a vague gesture from the Navab and going out of the chamber, returned within a few moments accompanied by the Navab's steward. The steward was also equally adept at interpreting the Navab's veiled hint and immediately gave five rupees to the messenger as reward.

The Navab now said, 'All right. I am pleased, bhai wallah. Convey my greetings and submissions to Begam sahib.'

'May Your Honour's fortune continue to rise and your star always be in the ascendant.' The messenger again made seven salaams and walked backward out of the chamber. The steward and the mace-bearer also left, seeing that there was nothing further for them to do. The Navab could hardly contain his patience and keenly desired to be alone so that he could look at his presents. The smaller pouch, he knew, must contain some written words. The bag must enclose a present, but he was not, for the moment, interested in it. As the steward went out, he saw from the corner of his eye the Navab's hand moving to pick up the pouch.

The hand is so neat, so well formed, just like strings of pearls. And how subtle, how meaningful was the poem. Shamsuddin Ahmad immediately saw that the last two lines were from Mir Hasan, and the preceding three had surely been composed by Wazir herself. Had she been here before me, I would kiss her hands . . . and why the hands alone, I would kiss much more! I would give a new kind of praise for each word.

And how pure this honey looks . . . Oh, it has a faint but distinct aroma of the litchi fruit! Litchi is not a fruit grown in our parts, so where could have its tree been found and how were the bees made to collect their honey from the tree's blossoms? Bhai wallah, one is compelled to admire such good taste and perfect selection. Now how can I answer in kind? But the greatest thing was that his hope was fulfilled: Chhoti Begam had taken the next step. That is, there was some inclination, some propensity on that side too. And surely, it is not a propensity to gain, to acquisition of wealth or pomp and a luxurious life, or power and honour in the world; or if such an attitude was there at all, it was of a minor nature. She would adopt other methods, did she desire those things. It is her own state of emotions that seems to be in turmoil, seeking to reach out to me.

So what should I say in reply? Should I say: Please come, oh, please come into my arms? Oh, how stupid and how vulgar! Then should I go there and say, come, I'll take you home in my arms? No, no, not at all. Such words are not to be used with professional girls even. My problem is to win Chhoti Begam's heart, and it is most important that I convey my eagerness and desire in the best possible style, and win her heart in such a way that there should be a hint in it of her own readiness to let it be won.

He recalled a line of verse: 'There is just one radiant presence, and that is you.' He called to mind the person who, just a day or two ago, was passing by his window, singing a ghazal of Mir Asar's; this was the verse that was on his lips:

She pays no heed at all to the state of my affairs;
She never even passes my way.

It had seemed to him as if the ghazal, or the singer, was saying just what his heart told him all the time. And now he had the Divan of Asar brought to him from his library. It was a very short Divan; he found the ghazal easily.

There is just one radiant presence, and that is you;
How sad, I had no knowledge, no clue.
She pays no heed at all to the state of my affairs;
She never even passes my way.
I should not give away my heart, nor lacerate my liver?
Well, I do not have that kind of heart, that kind of liver.
I should go away, leaving my heartache behind,
But where? There is no going out for me from here.
Your grief changed him into someone else:
When I saw him today, it was not the Asar of old.

Only God is free from all blemish! How neat and delectable is the poem! In fact, I don't need to say anything else; just these lines will be sufficient. What language could be superior to the miracle-working words of the Master, and what message could be subtler than what is contained in these words? All that I desire is expressed here, and without compromising my dignity and self-control. Shamsuddin Ahmad went into his library and wrote out the whole short ghazal in dark-black ink on a sheet of the standard orange-yellow paper. He inserted no salutation, but after some thought, he decided there should be at least something to indicate that it is a message, not just a ghazal. So he wrote the following words in Persian on top of his scribal effort:

'Ghazal of the Presence, Khvajah Mir Asar sahib, may God elevate his station, from Muhammad Shamsuddin Ahmad who pines for your sight.'

So far, so good. I wrote about the state of my heart. Now what? Do I say something about my physical condition now? Again, what words should be appropriate? Is there a way of saying that my eyes are sleepless, looking forward to your coming; my arms are impatient to clasp you; my mouth will not rest until it touches yours?

How delectable, how delicious those lips must be . . .
The mouth waters just by looking at them!

My bedchamber wears black, grieving, for it is deprived of the light from your face . . . But how to put all this on paper? And have I not said many of these things already during our last meeting? No, such words are not to be uttered over and over again. This is not an acrobatic display, to do somersaults as many times as the audience desires. How good it was not to inhabit the stage of expressing one's longing in words, written or spoken. She should have understood everything without my saying a word, or I would have burned away in silent passion. He recalled an Arabic proverb: One who loved and remained chaste and hid his love and died, he died the death of a martyr. How true is that apophthegm coined by our ancestors. And perhaps the Persian poet even went one better:

The moth flew in fast and burnt itself before the candle;
Poor thing, it did not know how pleasurable
It is, to burn secretly.

I grant all that. But we who worship appearances, we cannot see anything except when it is a tangible, touchable figure. How well did Amir Khusrau say:

If, even for the Haji, there has to be
A physical emblem of Grace like the Kabah,
Poor Khusrau, he adores the idols—
What else but the face and its beauty spot should fall to his share?

People like us can have no rest, no comfort, unless they touch and feel, and give adoration to the face and its beauty spot. So let me write a few more verses, imploring her to illumine my shoebox-like house with the rays of her beauty's sun.

After some thought, Shamsuddin Ahmad wrote on another sheet of notepaper a Persian quatrain from Qasim Beg Halati. It was one of his perennial favourites:

I am sick, but you are not of the mind to visit the sick;
Have no fear of keeping faith just one time,
It is not habit forming.
And it will not diminish your beauty if you visit me, a sick man. And remaining away from me
Will not enhance your beauty.

Well, I have inscribed the quatrain, and am done with it now: what next? How to word my personal petition for a meeting? It must not seem importunate and yet it should make clear that both my body and soul are burning with the fever of love. Oh, what is the need for these extravagances? By God, I should write plain words. I should say, please come now and let me hold you in my arms. Enough is enough. Really, is that what I should write? Of course, that is the undoubted truth, but should there not be an ostensible excuse for asking her to come and visit? Right, but the excuse should be such as to leave my true meaning in no doubt at all.

Taking a smaller notepaper, Shamsuddin Ahmad finally wrote a love letter, or rather a plea to her, to dine with him at his mansion the following evening. He made clear that no one else had been invited, but should her auspicious temperament so incline, invitations could be sent to those whose names she specified. A fully equipped carriage could be sent to her ever-fortunate door to drive her down, if she so commanded.

The following presents accompanied the letter and the poems: two double shawls from Kashmir; two packets of white betels from Mahoba in Bundelkhand; about a little more than half a pound of catechu from the forests of Najibabad, so pure as to be almost white (catechu is consumed along with betels, but if it is immersed in water for quite a while, it dissolves slowly and the water is reputed to become a mild intoxicant); and a large, copper betel box made in Murshidabad, its various inner containers filled with material relevant to betel chewing.

A mace-bearer, accompanied by a staff-bearer and a lancer, was ordered to proceed to Sirki Walan and submit the presents to Wazir Khanam. He was further commanded not to say a word about an answer, but if some reply was vouchsafed, he was to bring it back with full honour.

*

At Manjhli Begam's, Wazir was about to retire for rest after lunch when Bi Vafadar, her personal maid, arrived panting and out of breath due to having walked at the double all the way. She reported that a message had arrived from the Honourable House of Loharu with a variety of gifts.

'May God make it auspicious for you, Bibi,' said Umdah Khanam, passing her hand over Wazir's face and then touching the hands to her own head. 'It seems your arrow has found its mark. Just see, with what ease you brought down such big game!'

'Come, Manjhli Baji, go on with you! Take the name of God! Who shot any arrows and what was the target? I want nothing but two plain meals a day, but with honour. I don't want to live as someone's concubine or kept woman. Let your prayers and the Almighty's grace be with me always, I want nothing more.'

'I'll have the nalki brought at the main door. Take the name of God and get into it. Go to your home. God willing, you will become a Rani and rule like one.'

Umdah Khanam hugged and kissed Wazir and helped her to get into the nalki. It was not too far from Tiraha Bairam Khan to Sirki Walan; the nalki brought her back home in no time. Bi Vafadar got down first and had the door opened. In the hall sat Navab Shamsuddin Ahmad's mace-bearer, enjoying the short hookah, a glass of cool drink stood on a teapoy in front of him. Opposite stood the lance-bearer and the staff-bearer, with cups of cool drinks in their hands. A makeshift purdah was arranged by stretching a sheet across the hall. Accepting salaams from everyone, Wazir entered her home. The Navab's presents had already been sent inside, now his letter was conveyed with some ceremony. It was placed on a silver tray and Vafadar carried it in upon her head.

Wazir was enchanted. How well formed and proportionate was each letter of the writing, how loving and lovely were the message and the poems! She felt her heart softening to the core. But what was that about the dinner invitation? He says that it is to be only the two of them, unless I name some guests. So it is really a matter that has two sides: 'Yes' is risky, but 'No' is not less risky.

Go I must, she told herself, and after some cogitation she knew that she should prefer just the two of them to be present. She did not give herself more time: more time meant prevarication. She wrote a couple of lines saying 'Yes' and suggesting no other guest. She put her seal on the letter, gave five rupees to the mace-bearer and two rupees to each of the other servitors.

The Navab's servants departed at once with their reward and her reply. Wazir said to herself that before she became engaged and engrossed in preparing for tomorrow, she should write to Manjhli, giving her the news. As she sat down to write, she was unaware that Navab Yusuf Ali Khan's informant would submit the news to him in his evening report. She had also no knowledge of the spies of William Fraser reporting hourly to him on the goings-on at her house and at the Navab's mansion. Wazir Khanam could have no idea that the reports to be submitted to Fraser that night and the next day would trigger a series of events which, in the far future, would prove to be disastrous and almost tragic for her, and that her future was not as secure as she imagined it to be.

31

An exquisitely attired Wazir Khanam pays a visit to Navab Shamsuddin Ahmad Khan's imposing and splendid residence in Daryaganj

IF ANYONE HAD caught a glimpse of Wazir that night, they would have gone crazy and torn off their clothes; or they would have laid down at her doorstep, their head heavy with gratitude to the doorkeeper for letting them lie there. But that pearl of bright vision was on that night destined to adorn only the fortunate treasury of Shamsuddin Ahmad Khan. And he had prepared himself for it to a great extent. But the actual sight was beyond his expectations, even his dreams.

The moment he was informed that Wazir Khanam's carriage had entered his compound, he felt the impulse to come out running, escort the carriage to the main door of his residence, himself help her out of the carriage, and walk with her into the divan khanah. All this was impossible, obviously; still, it should be quite proper to come out of the chamber on to the veranda and welcome her there.

Navab Shamsuddin Ahmad Khan's mansion in Daryaganj was designed in the English style: a compound surrounded by a wall, which had just one entrance gate. The grounds were laid out like a small park with a part of it planted with roses and seasonal flowers. A wide passage, loosely packed with red gravel, led to the main door. The passage was wide enough to accommodate a large rath, a horse-drawn vehicle or an elephant. The path led to high steps, which rose to a wide veranda. The veranda was built around the haveli like the moat around ancient forts or palaces.

In the middle of the veranda was a massive main door; on two sides of it were two other doors, which perhaps opened on to the Navab's Secretariat and Court. The main door opened on to the divan khanah, the drawing room in English terms. On the whole, the haveli's facade resembled William Fraser's mansion, but Fraser's house was more impressive outwardly in terms of size, splendour and height. The servants' activity was also much less here, and in any case, in the absence of the attendants and carriages of other guests, the Navab's haveli looked comparatively deserted.

The moment you entered the meeting chamber, you instantly realized that you had left behind the English architecture, style of life, manners, everything that could remind you of an alien world. In the first place, the arched main door opened on to an inner door, also arched, except that it was designed like a half-dome, and was thus true to its technical name—tajdar darwazah, or crowned door—by which it was known to builders and engineers. On both sides, it had a seat for the doorkeeper, made of a rare turquoise-coloured stone, similar to marble. Its walls and door leaves were covered with dense relief and inlay work in the Mughal style. The door leaves had no supporting wood staves or bars. The inlays had such abundance of colours—green, azure, gold, white—that it seemed as if it was not the walls and leaves of a doorway; rather, it was a huge stone in one piece into which the colours had permeated through some miraculous process of nature.

Actually, the door leaves were of Indian rosewood and sandalwood, and their decorations consisted of pieces of ivory painted or relief-carved to resemble tiles. These 'tiles' had been set all over without the least gap or crack between any two of them. It was difficult to decide whose art and workmanship were greater: the ivory painters and relief carvers who made the ivory pieces look like tiles, or the joiners who had set the pieces of ivory on to the wall and doors with unimaginably delicate dexterity. The work was so marvellously neat that when closed, the door seemed part of the wall.

The threshold was quite elevated, and the door was tall and wide, but its walls and arch were even higher. That was the reason why, in spite of the density of the floral patterns on the tile work, the whole unit produced no impression of undue profusion or heavy ornamentation. The floor behind the door was a foot or so lower than the threshold, effectively creating the psychological image of a sublime porte. Thus it was only an alert and agile visitor who would not commit the faux pas of missing his step when entering the chamber. In front of the door was thick velvet on which was spread a reed mat, serving as a foot mat.

The first thing that attracted the visitor's attention on entering the divan khanah was a sense of diffused light. This was not only because it was lit by a large number of chandeliers and floor globes, but also because to the right and left, as one entered, were two tall windows on which were fine muslin curtains which rippled with the slightest breeze. There were no bars or wire gauze on the windows; they too had ornate door leaves echoing the leaves of the crowned door. There was yet another door right in front of the visitor as he came in. This door had been constructed by removing three walls that had been supported by arches. The arches had been left intact, but the space released by the demolished walls was filled in by trelliswork. The most interesting part was, however, not so much the trellises but the arches, for each arch had a different design. The central and the widest one was of the Shahjahani style; the one to the right had three smaller arches making up one big arch; the one to the left was of horseshoe design, but it had a slight tinge of the Hindu or Buddhist style to it.

The trelliswork in the arches was of the pattern of the popularly called Jali Masjid (actually, Sidi Said Mosque) of Ahmedabad. That is, though the patterns were carved from marble, they deceived the viewer into believing that they were wooden. There was such a proliferation in the design and pattern of the trelliswork that no two adjacent trellises were alike. It is not possible for a person who has not seen them to imagine their form from their names. Still, here are some of the names in translation: Turkish, Parallelogrammatic, Fish Scales, Infinite Series. Each of these had been made with exemplary neatness and dexterity. Behind the trellises could be seen glimpses of an interior garden, or chaman, not the park and garden seen without.

Although night had fallen, the interior garden was lit so that a sense could be gained of its extent and its charms. In fact, the trelliswork, aside from giving the visitor glimpses of the garden, enhanced its charm, for with the light and colour behind them, the trellises created the illusion of stained glass.

Within the big hall, in front of the central arch, was an oval fountain nearly equal to the arch in its length. Carved from pink marble, the fountain was modelled on a similar one in the Hall of Private Audience at the Red Fort of Agra. Shallow like the one in that hall, and carved like a flower petal with inlay work of flowers and leaves along its borders, again on the model of the Mughal Fort's fountain, its jet was low enough to prevent its spray from moistening the chamber floor. The fountain basin was carved differently in different places, that is, in both relief and bas-relief. It was kept clean most assiduously, so there was not the least trace of moss or lichen anywhere.

The hall floor was covered with carpets from Kashan, Turkey and Kashmir. A part of the floor in the north-west was slightly raised by a foot so as to be level with the threshold. On this raised part, there were carpets again, but soft quilts had been placed between two layers of carpets to give greater softness and a little more elevation. Bolsters, cased in velvet, were placed next to the wall behind the raised area. Some other parts of the hall had quilts too, but they were covered not with woollen carpets but rather with light, silky carpet-like sheets made in Mirzapur and Agra. There were no bolsters in such areas.

The ceiling of the hall was most probably wooden, for no stone could have been carved or inlaid or painted with the intricate and subtle artfulness displayed on it. There was no difference in the varieties of colours used on the walls and the ceiling, except that various methods—or crafty tricks—had been used to break the monotony. For example, about four feet below the actual ceiling, a four-inch-wide skirting of red sandstone with white inlay had been stuck along the entire length of the four walls; the stone strips had been inserted into the wall by carving out a half-inch-deep channel and inlaying the sandstone into it. Indian architects called it kangni, perhaps from kangan, a thick, ornamented bracelet-like bangle mostly made of gold, highly popular among the richer classes. There is no word in English either for kangni or kangan.

Not content with that highly decorative piece of variety, the architect had installed about six inches below the kangni yet another stone strip so painted as to simulate wood inlaid with ivory. Then, immediately below the ceiling, floral and ornamental designs of a different kind had been painted. Instead of tulips, poppy, wine glass and carafe, Hindu-style lotus buds and blooms had been painted in different colours, but only those colours which are colours of the lotus: red, pink, blue, white, purplish grey. Between the actual ceiling and the projecting stonework of the kangni ran a painted cornice but not so as to detract from the strong statement made by the kangni.

The monotony of the painted walls had been broken by dividing the surface into squares, rectangles and parallelograms, and each area had been painted differently, in terms of both colour and design. The dominant design in each area was a vault or arch, drawn into the square or the other area of the wall surface. The arches were again of different styles. Some of the parcels were painted to look like open windows within the vaulted design.

As noted above, the ceiling seemed to have been made of wood, but that again was simulation. It was actually mortar composed of shell-lime, Indian cement and coarse sand, plastered over with shell-lime again. Its technical name was gach, or rekhtah, and it was supported by low-vaulted arches without any pillars or spirals.

In spite of this superabundance of colours, figures and Euclidian shapes, the hall did not feel oppressive or heavy, partly because of its huge size and high ceiling, but mainly because of the architect's and the craftsmen's marvellous sense of proportion and homogeneity among the shapes and the colours. No colour, no drawing was mismatched with its neighbour.

Right in the middle of the hall was a patch of green; it was real green grass with a medium-sized pomegranate tree growing on it. Under the tree sat two black bucks in the style typical of such deer: all four legs tucked under their bodies, comfortably chewing the cud. Opposite the tree was a Chinese-style floor globe made of greenish jade in which twenty-four candles burned. The light given out by the large candles was so strong that the jade's green seemed to be mixed with some white and some crimson.

It was obvious that a new entrant to the chamber would be so dazed as to be unable to make up his mind if he should admire the hall or look for a place to sit. Navab Shamsuddin Ahmad Khan, and before him, Navab Ahmad Bakhsh Khan, would stand on the raised space in the north-west of the hall to welcome the guest. For special guests, he would get down from it and walk up a few paces in welcome. Honour more than that was not accorded to anyone at all, not to the Firangee officers or even the Navab Senior Sahib Bahadur. But on the night of Wazir Khanam's visit, Shamsuddin Ahmad Khan had made the crowned door his permanent station, and his heart was importuning him to go even beyond it.

*

Wazir Khanam was dressed in the Turkish style for the evening. Her feet were shod in Shirazi shoes—actually Siraji, for they were designed by a Delhi artist called Sirajuddin; Siraji became promoted to Shirazi on the tongue of fashion—of sky-blue Kashani velvet and white buckskin, with thin heels and long uppers, very low walls, and no support for the heel of the foot. The toes were long and pointed and slightly curved upward like the sunbird's beak, and decked out with feathers of the junglefowl in the red of velvet beetles. There was a slender lace at the edges of the shoes, encrusted with white and golden topaz.

The elegance and splendour of the shoes would stun the gazer, but in order to shift the gaze above the shoes, one needed the intrepidity of a tiger or the notorious audacity of a panther. The pants were made of extremely fine Dacca muslin, so fine that the roundness of the hips and the posterior, and the lines of the thighs were quite discernible. Had the gazer the determination or the opportunity to look some more, he could even descry occasionally the thin cleft between the two cheeks—aptly described by the Persians as 'a pair of black suns'—of the posterior.

But no, if the pants were so revealing, why could not the gazer from the front notice at least the glimmer of the tiny mound of the groin and the pubes, the soft elevation and slope of the Mount of Venus—lovingly described by the Persians as 'the sandal skirting around the well of fresh water'—but the front elevation appeared to be quite plain. Only the stomach—again dotingly named by the Persians as 'the velvet circle, or the sign of Aries' ('hamal' in Arabic and Persian, which can also mean 'pregnancy')—occasionally sent out a flash like an ambiguous hint of things hidden.

Clearly, it was possible only for a nine- or ten-year-old girl to have both her front and back so devoid of highs and lows. The fact of the matter was Wazir wore long underwear, flesh coloured, and so tight that it could almost have been painted on her body. But it was not so importunately daring as to suggest even a few, if not all, the contours of her body. The trousers that she wore over the underwear were a little higher and narrower, in the sense that they revealed the ankles and the feet, and above the ankles the trouser bottoms—made of velvet, very nearly flesh-coloured like her underwear—were tight like bandages. They were also embroidered like lace, thus enhancing the illusion of colourful bandages.

Above the lace, and reaching up to the thighs—the Persians had again a loving name for them, 'wine-red boughs'—the trousers were so loose and full of pleats that they could be compared to light, onion-shaped painted domes or balloons. In the middle, much above the knees, the pants had again been tightened with a wide, embroidered lace of the same pattern as the lace above the ankles but with the difference that the lace was now golden and brocaded, and its top and bottom were bordered with thick black-and-gold thread: so thick that it created the effect of gold bangles worked with black worn on the thighs.

The pants, now tight above the gold lace and the middle of the thighs, again began to loosen as they moved upward, so that by the time they reached the luxuriant, seemingly never-touched posterior—here again the narrator has to take recourse to the Persianist and describe the hips and the posterior as 'the storage of wild, brownish-purple eglantine' or 'a pair of the sorcerers' magic globes'—the effect was like magic. Because, the state described by the Persian poet as 'You show us glimpses and you also avoid us' was again evident, as there was no way of telling where the top of the pants ended; while the trouser strings inside the pants' top highlighted the waist like the thin line on the inside of a wineglass—which indicates the limit to which the glass should be filled; the tunic and the trousers were strictly of the same colour.

The muslin pants were light orange and wine red in colour, and the tunic was of a slightly heavier muslin, in a light shade of burnt orange. Just as the grass stalk used to tie a bunch of flowers is cunningly hidden among the leaves, so also the trouser strings and the hem of the tunic were hidden under a tight waistcoat of azure velvet. There was no bodice under the waistcoat, and it was so designed at the neck that while it was high and almost closed in front, it was so low at the back that the valley dividing the shoulders down to the back seemed like a furrow carved on a life-size chunk of purple-grey topaz.

The waistcoat was actually a part of the tunic, in the sense that both had been sewn together, and the tunic worked like the lining to the waistcoat. Thus the upper body had been hidden without any underwear, and the sleeves of the waistcoat were cut so short that they did not go above the shoulder joint. The neck, the cleavage and the upper back were therefore strongly suggested by this device, and the neck was kept free of any ornamentation so as to emphasize its shapely curve and height. The sleeves of the tunic were long and tapering towards the end, fully covering the arms and forearms and ending tight at the wrists. There was lace on the right sleeve, matching the one on the ankles and the thighs, but even more prominent and velvety. There was no discernible pattern or attempt at balance in the designs created by the lacework.

On the left sleeve, there was a long brocade lace with tiny floral designs embroidered on it in cotton. It ran from the bone of the wrist to the elbow. There was a slightly wider and heavier lace in the middle, to look like an armlet. It was encrusted with small square-cut garnets and dark-red

Himalayan topaz. Just below the point where the sleeve joined the shoulder, there were three narrow velvet bands in orange-red. The rest of the sleeve had tiny sprigs similar in colour to the muslin of the trousers. There were also small circlets enclosing the tiny red sprigs and three tiny dots within the sprigs in the circlets, creating a vague effect of a smiling human face.

The right sleeve, on the contrary, was devoid of any lace or band on the upper arm, but it had the same circlets, enclosing sprigs and dots described above. The forearm and the wrist, however, had bands of a new pattern, which had been designed by combining the pattern on the ankle lace and the lace on the left sleeve. Just below the elbow, where the series of bands began, hung a small coral necklace of three strands, wine red and yellow in colour, looking, to all intents and purposes, like a garland of unopened buds. It was hung so that one strand of it fell to the wrist and was tied just between the hand and the wrist. The wrists, as the neck, were devoid of ornaments.

On her right thumb Wazir wore a ring set with a light-pink, pea-sized star ruby from the Irawaddy River Valley (now part of Myanmar), recently conquered by the English. In the ring finger of the same hand, she wore two emerald rings, the emeralds cut rectangular with their bezels highly polished. Her nose was kept free of jewellery, but there were two long, many-stranded gold pendants on her ears, which looked like fragile tassels, each tassel of a different length, though there seemed to be no pattern to their length. It looked as if some master craftsman had jumbled them together with a seemingly artless artfulness.

Wazir had gathered her long hair together into a bun, but it was not prominent, for she wore a short turban of sky-blue velvet around her head that appeared to be loosely tied; one end of it fell upon her forehead and part of her face, giving the impression of a veil carelessly placed upon the face. In order to keep the loose turban in place, she had tied a wide silk lace-band upon its edge and the upper part of her forehead. The lace was somewhat, but not quite, similar to the one on her left sleeve.

A brief suggestion of the actual length of her tresses was provided by keeping the back of the head free of the turban, but the turban had an appendage, something like a hair net, tied around the back of the head with a narrow ribbon. Out of this rose a turban ornament of red-and-black feathers which had the effect of making the tallish girl look taller and more commanding.

In view of these elaborations, there was no need of a dupatta or a wrap for the upper body. Still, she had placed a cream-coloured narrow Kashmiri shawl, more like a sash, on one shoulder with apparent casualness, but in such a manner that its other end was touching the other shoulder, like a careless ripple. The front body, as we described above, bore no hint of nakedness. An unsheathed dagger, narrow and bright and slightly curved like a flash of lightning, hung at her waist, as if presaging the nakedness of the body underneath the plethora of habiliments.

32

Wazir Khanam and Shamsuddin Ahmad debate who among them is the alms-giver and who the beggar; Chhoti Begam is displeased with the Navab's proposition

WAZIR HAD AGAIN borrowed a carriage for the occasion: it was the personal buggy of Navab Yusuf Ali Khan. Made of teak wood imported from the Irrawady River Valley, it was pulled by two white horses. Its doors were painted light blue and in order to entirely eliminate any chance of breach of purdah, they were lined with thick brocade curtains and fully shut. The ceiling and the wheels were painted cream white. The horses wore plumes made of ostrich feathers and those of the colourful Himalayan pheasant called monal. They wore mouthpieces of golden silk netting, their tails had ornaments of golden silk tassels and their blinkers were made of white buckskin. Strips of rhinoceros hide, twisted to resemble a strong rope, were used for their reins.

On the coach box, Wazir had a staff-bearer travelling by the side of the coachman. When the buggy stopped at the stairs leading up to the outer veranda of the Navab's haveli, the staff-bearer vaulted down with alacrity and knocked softly on the buggy's door. As the door opened and the curtain moved, the staff-bearer promptly fixed wooden steps on to the door sill. Wazir descended, not deigning to look to her right or left, and set foot on the bottom step of the veranda. She climbed up, slowly and deliberately, with her eyes on the steps as if careful to be sure-footed. She had hardly put her foot on the third step when the Navab's doorkeeper spoke up in careful, measured tones: 'The Presence, Wazir Khanam sahib's noble feet are here.'

By now, Wazir had negotiated the last step. Navab Shamsuddin Ahmad Khan, too impatient to wait any longer, left the inside of the crowned door and opening the big outer door, opened his arms wide as if to embrace her. Wazir raised her eyes a little; a brief smile touched her mouth and face.

Stopping where she was, she bent and made a salaam. Then she looked at him full in the face with an effort of will, but spoke shyly: 'May God preserve the Navab sahib, and keep him always secure. Your Honour took so much trouble for me, who am nothing before you. I drip the sweat of shame.'

Having said this, she lowered her eyes again. Looking people in the face while you speak to them was an art that Marston Blake had taught her. After numerous misunderstandings and irritating exchanges of words, she learnt finally that among the Firangees, persons who do not look you in the face or who avert their eyes while talking to you are universally believed to be cheats or frauds. On the contrary, in her culture the rule was that when one talked to one's elders or close relatives or strangers, one must not look them in the face. Gradually, and after not a little distress of mind, she taught herself that looking someone in the face as you talked to them might not be something desirable, but looking straight in front was de rigueur in the Royal presence even. So there could be no real harm in occasionally raising one's eye to the interlocutor's face, especially when the subject is of some import and gravity.

Although the Navab realized that not keeping her eyes down was to Wazir a metaphor for her equality and independence, he in fact appreciated and somehow enjoyed her boldness and self-willed pride. The Navab saw in her a kind of confident sense of self-worth, and an aura of dignified indifference which stemmed not just from her pride of beauty or sense of desirability. It also indicated an uninvolvement with the world, an attitude which was somehow a little like that of a fakir's. He had a feeling that Wazir was not averse to loving. If she loved someone, she would not at all be miserly in giving from her beauty's riches. But the point was that if she loved someone, and he did not desire her (which, Shamsuddin Ahmad recognized, was well-nigh impossible), then she would not run after him like mad, nor would she ever go round him like a supplicant and seek the alms of his attentions.

It would indeed take some time to traverse the veranda, which was about twelve to fifteen feet wide. And this time, the Navab also realized that Wazir's gait was feather-light and full of elegance, and yet it seemed so commanding, sovereign-like, that the very ground seemed to spread before her in welcoming submission. By now, Shamsuddin Ahmad had fully quit his position near the outer door and, meeting her halfway, he put his arm around her waist and led her towards the crowned door.

'God must have sent down some angel to teach you how to walk,' he said. 'We ordinary mortals cannot walk with such grace. How well Nimat Khan Ali says:

The way she looks at things,
Her eye lays the foundation of gardens wherever she walks;
The impressions of her feet scatter
Fresh roses in her path.

'Navab Sahib, Presence, you drag me over thorns. Do please count me as no more than your serving maid. I'm gasping for breath in this place as it is. I take the name of God! I and this gracious and splendid palatial dwelling! How could I at all fit in here? This thought worries me to death.'

By now they had crossed over the threshold of the crowned door and were in the divan khanah, and like all newcomers, Wazir was marvelling at its state and its quality. She did not know where to put her feet. In her dazed condition, she was happy to let the Navab continue to keep his arm around her waist and lead her to the high seat. In her heart, she thanked God and the Navab for solving her difficulty. The Navab put her in the centre and sat himself in front of her, slightly to the right of her—a mirror arrangement of what she did at her home when the Navab had visited.

Wazir was perfectly conscious of the coded meaning of the way the Navab met her at the door and had seated her. She was going to say something when the Navab raised his right hand to stop her and said, 'Wazir Khanam, bhai wallah, I consider it my great good fortune for you to have troubled your feet to come here. I am ready and prepared to serve you in any way you desire for the hardship. Believe me, I will not stint at all.'

'There can be no service that one may ask from the Presence, the Treasury of Generosity. Nor is it my station. But indeed, I do yearn to travel down the road of my life to a few destinations of kindness and hospitality in your company.' Wazir looked at the Navab with a smile in her eyes.

'But if I am to be the caravan leader or even the camel driver, who is going to pay my wages?'

Wazir screwed up her courage and said, 'Ask, and you will be given.' She was a little fearful in her heart but was confident that the Navab would not say anything unseemly in reply.

Shamsuddin Ahmad recalled a verse from Mirza Naushah. Although he did not much care about him, the verse was so apposite that he was obliged to say it to Wazir. He spread out his right hand and palm in the special way of those who beg, and said:

Give the prescribed tithe of alms from your loveliness
O radiance for the sight, so that like the sun
It may illuminate the beggar's bowl
And light up his home.

In spite of her thousand resolutions to be in total control over her reactions, Wazir's face lit up with the roseate hue of a smile, only for the blush of humility and abashment to quickly overrun it. Yet this was not the time to give way to bashfulness, for then there was the possibility of her losing control over the conversation. So she looked at the Navab with a hint of flirtatiousness and said, 'That old adage must have reached the auspicious ears. "Three qualities the givers have: they may give, not give, take back after giving!"'

'Yes, but this destitute beggar asks for something which, once given, cannot be taken back.'

Wazir had no answer to this. In order to gain time, she changed the subject. 'Your honour has a great liking for the poems of Mirza Naushah?'

'No, bhai wallah, years ago I lost my heart to the poetry of Mir Taqi Mir sahib. Although beautiful women are immune to all entreaties, please listen to Mir sahib for a second.'

He then quoted:

The nargis flower looks like an eye, but has no
power of sight;
I too, like the nargis, went about begging for a glimpse,
With my eye an empty bowl, sightless.

'Doubtless, sir. But Your Honour's begging bowl is like God's Kingdom, endless, and with no beginning. But if one goes by the utterances of Mir Taqi Mir sahib, the best answer to the importunate beggar is an equally obdurate indifference.'

Wazir's reply had an oblique allusion to a famous verse of the poet. Now the Navab was left without an answer; he changed the subject. 'Is it not, according to the laws of our religion, obligatory upon those who have the capacity to give alms at the prescribed rate?'

'Your Command is absolutely right,' Wazir laughed with glee, for she was now losing her diffidence and gaining boldness. 'But what is the value of gazing in your religion? The Exalted Servants must have heard what Mirza Jalal Asir commanded:

It is proper if I extract tribute from the sun,
For I obtained from her a gaze upon her face
As alms.'

'Please, Wazir Khanam, do not palm us off with mere words. Is it really proper that the ocean of riches and wealth should be in the fullest flush of waves and the poor beggar should be shown mere excuses and pretences? Bhai wallah, our speech is the voice of the Bulbul of Shiraz. Please hear:

The riches of your beauty have touched
The apogee of eligibility for giving alms:
Please give, for I am utterly penniless.'

'Quite right, sir. But I, Your Honour, have learnt a different lesson:

The best alms for beauty is
To keep control over your eyes:
Remember these words from me.'

'Bhai wallah, God knows what a miserly, stingy fellow you had for a teacher! Did you not hear that the best quality for the miserly is to give up their actions, and the worst quality for the munificent is to give up their actions?'

'Indeed, sir, indeed! One must learn from you to speak ill of those from whom you have expectations.'

'Bhai wallah, I'm trying to persuade you to pay your debt to God. As for me, I have nothing to fear. It is you who will have to answer before Him. The sins of the deprived ones are forgiven anyway.'

'Sir, you are quite right.' Wazir laughed out aloud. 'So remain deprived.'

'No. No. I am not such a sinner either.'

'But you are my culprit, for sure.'

'So be it. This culprit is prepared to be awarded imprisonment for life.'

Wazir paused in mild surmise. Imprisonment for life? Or was it the story of Blak sahib over again? Several retorts came to her lips but she restrained herself. Perhaps this was not the occasion for such things. She pulled herself together and thought of turning the conversation again towards mildly flirtatious banter. But why—the thought suddenly came to her like an echo from afar—should I not be able to make a decision now? Do I lack the willpower to settle the issue and is that why I am losing my nerve to see the conversation take the turn that I desire? Or do I not desire to have the kind of relationship with the Navab which is his objective? But what is the Navab's objective? It is not really clear to me.

In her heart, she prayed to God for guidance, and called upon the holy spirit of Shaikh Abdul Qadir Jilani, venerated all over Asian Islam as the giver of support and succour in moments of crisis. She produced a smile on her lips somehow, lowered her eyes and was going to say something when the Navab spoke, perhaps divining her hesitancy. He gestured to her to say nothing and began to say: 'Chhoti Begam, there is no bargain that would remain sweet from the beginning till the end of time.'

He paused for a beat before continuing. 'Hard and soft, dry and wet, sweet and bitter, all this is encountered over a journey, any journey. People decide and determine after taking things as a whole. That is why I say: Try me for some time at least. Doubtless, I am not bound by your wishes, but I certainly do not find myself empowered enough to go outside your wishes either.'

Again, a wave of rebellion rose in Wazir's spirit. She strongly felt like asking: 'Yes, but for how long? What happens to me after that?'

Very soon, the waters of the sea of her thoughts changed their character from tumult to calmness, or if not true calmness, it was like those little wavelets that appear where the water is particularly deep. Now there was storm and flood at the bottom, and beaming, happily gambolling little chains of waves on the surface. It was not hidden from her that in their meeting that evening, the Navab was ardently desirous of matters to be decided on some sort of a stable, long-term basis. Perhaps he believed that Wazir had other suitors and he feared that if he did not get her quickly to his bedchamber, the road ahead could become subject to twists and turns and uncertainties. Who knows, Wazir's door could be opened for another, either under duress or with her consent.

Wazir found herself in a double bind. She was no longer the fourteen-year-old beauty of six years ago, unthinking and uncaring of the consequences, drunk with the desire of being loved and taken with the emotional wave of need: need for love and adventure. Nor was Shamsuddin Ahmad—in spite of all the physical and mental appeal that he had for Wazir, and all his manners promising to be the comfort for Wazir's heart—that strange, novel, mysterious ocean of love whose waves had drenched Wazir from the very first day in the form of the gestures and hints of the Firangee Marston Blake. Numerous highs and lows of living, coupling and pairing, owning a home and managing a family, had passed over her since she impulsively left home. Now, she was unwilling to plunge, with closed or even open eyes, into the sea of loving and love, however easy of approach and amenable to her feet it might have seemed to her before the actual deed.

But the burning question, the overwhelming question, was the very first that Wazir's heart had asked her: What did the words 'imprisonment for life' mean to Shamsuddin Ahmad?

The Navab was looking at her with patient and expectant eyes. During the past half-hour or so, the curtain on one of the doors had moved briefly once or twice. Perhaps the servants wanted to know how much time it would be before the command to serve dinner might be issued. But both of them, host and guest, were lost in a world of their own. Neither had any insight into how to get out of their prison. Wazir said to herself, 'Wazir, darling, do something towards your purpose; this is the world of each to herself.' The voice in her heart was so loud that she paled for a moment, fearful that the Navab might have heard her.

She reached a sudden decision, and rose. The Navab almost lost his cool and his power of reasoning for a heartbeat or two. What is this? What happened here? And then, a wave of displeasure, sharp and quick, ran through him. Would Chhoti Begam be so impertinent as to rise in this fashion, without taking permission or concluding their dialogue? He was about to shift from his place and rise, or say something, when Wazir Khanam folded her hands, in the manner of the people of Lucknow when they wish to be humble, and said, 'It was on that day, the very first day, that I accepted you in my heart as my master, my prince, my friend; but you stand in need of nothing and I am a beggar. It is your boundless generosity and your loving inclination towards me that you demand me from my own self, and that too by declaring me rich and extending the begging bowl in my direction. Despite being the giver of rewards you play the loving game of appearing before me in the disguise of one who asks for favours. This servant is already sold over to you at no price and is willing to live all her life, ever saying your name on her rosary but . . .'

The Navab now half rose from his place and cried, 'But? But what? What else do you demand from me, Wazir Khanam? Is there a let or hindrance in your heart about me? Do you doubt me in some way? If not, what should I understand you to mean by your declaration to live your whole life saying my name alone? And should you not think about how long one can live and how much can be the real duration of the few days of life that we are given?'

The Navab now rose to his full height, took a step nearer to Wazir Khanam, and gently put his right arm around her waist. Equally softly, he tried to pull her to his side and was about to kiss her when Wazir took a step backwards, folded her hands on her breasts and said, 'Your Honour, everything that I have is yours. Were I asked to sacrifice everything that I have, including my life for you, I would cross that river with a smile on my face and pleasure in my heart. I can be yours even if you and I were to live our lives alone and separately. I would boast about my good fortune if Your Honour desires to take me in his golden shade. Yet, if the Presence were to tarry a little and give some thought to the matter, I would regard that as the greatest favour.'

At that time the Navab saw a luminance, a sort of pride and self-control, that he was obliged to describe to himself as the power of her inner self, if not the power of her soul. He tried to look Wazir in the eye, but was unable to stand the incandescence radiating from her face. He lowered his eyes and said, 'Chhoti Begam, I'm not sure there is anything left now to consider. Still, please command. I am all ears.'

'My story and my present state are not hidden from His Honour. Once I was something, but . . . my Fate, or perhaps my heart, made something else of me, transported me somewhere, some place I did not know. In my own estimation, and my pride, I was something, and quite substantial in the eyes of others. But despite everything, the Executioner of the Skies cut off the head of my Sahib and threw it away in the Death-house of Rajputana and stole my children from me. Not due to your fault nor mine, but that is the way it was. My luck has now brought my caravan—fatigued and left behind on the road—to your exalted gates, so now it needs space for halting and staying.'

A slight smile of approval lit up the Navab's face; something like affection flashed in his eyes. He wanted again to advance a little and not fail this time in taking Wazir in his arms; but Wazir remained rooted to her place stolidly, in a manner that was clearly meant to discourage him. Still, he extended his arm and touched the hem of Wazir's garment and said, 'Dear lady, you described me as needing nothing and you as a beggar. Have you not heard the Persian poet say:

Master, you take pride in your silver and gold,
You are exceeding beggarly, in fact
Master is he who is not penurious in love
And fidelity.

God willing, you won't find me penurious in love and fidelity. Life and death are not things about which there could be certainty. I've said this before and I also know that . . . bhai wallah, you must be familiar with a great verse of Mir sahib's?'

Navab Shamsuddin Ahmad paused, as if expecting a reply. Wazir stood as before, her arms on her breasts, her eyes on the ground, but quite unconsciously, she had moved a mite nearer to him when the Navab had touched the hem of her garment. Now, both stood quite close to each other.

'Which verse of Mir sahib is it that His Honour inquires about? Even if I have heard it before, it would be something else again to hear it spoken by His Honour's auspicious tongue.'

This time, the Navab also brought up his hands to his chest and folded them there, as if in prayer. Then he recited in a sonorous voice which had just the slightest hint of a deep trill:

Mir, the world is a gaming house,
What is apparent here is actually unapparent;
Should you come here, lose your own self in the very first throw of the dice.

The Navab fell silent for a brief minute, as if in contemplation. 'Wazir Khanam, you made a throw of the dice and initially your pieces moved extremely well. So what if they became blocked and stood still at some stage? Please come and throw another dice in the Universal Gaming House. To use the Persian saying, "Take your turn at hitting the goal, for your piece now is in the penultimate house." God is the Most Dexterous Remover of problems.'

Wazir felt a wave of anger rising inside her, her throat seemed about to choke with sobs. So the Navab did not desire the permanency of marriage. He was a buyer of just the fruit, not the tree. But why such disappointment and annoyance at this? They are constant companions: hope and hopelessness. What the Navab was saying in his Arabicized and Persianized rhetoric was nothing different from what I knew. These matters were of buying and selling, not of giving oneself up or of true union.

Shamsuddin Ahmad took Wazir's silence to be consent. He imagined that Wazir now had no problem with the questions in hand. I have made my mind clear and Wazir has nothing more to say about it. Though it is not fully revealed before me yet if Wazir accepts my proposition, it should not cause me any anxiety. One can expect things to become clearer in due time. So there is no need, nor cause, to give more thought to it.

He looked up at Wazir and said, 'So, madam, should we have dinner served? At what time would you care to dine?'

Wazir felt some sort of a curtain drop between her and the Navab. But this did not surprise her. She well knew that between formal, if pleasant, acquaintanceship with the unity of body and soul fell many shadows, and many stages and degrees of alienness. It was proper to grieve, for grief is inalienable from life. But there was no occasion here for surprise, especially for women like her who always made their own decisions.

'Any time that Your Honour may like to give us food,' she said with a degree of sarcasm. 'I am just the beggar here.'

A wrinkle of displeasure appeared on the Navab's brow but dissolved almost at once. He clapped, and when the mace-bearer came in and made his salaams, he commanded for dinner to be served in the dining chamber.

33

Wazir Khanam tries to reconcile herself with her disappointment even as the Navab suggests that she stay the night

NEITHER WAZIR NOR Shamsuddin Ahmad could later recall what they had for dinner that night. Thanks to her training at the hands of Marston Blake, she had become fully au fait with the art of conversation, exchange of small jokes and friendly conversation during meals. She also knew well that according to Indian etiquette, respect for food demanded silence most of the time while eating, except occasional praise for the food.

Shamsuddin Ahmad would often look at her with eyes full of love and desire and press her to eat more of some of the choicest dishes. Perhaps he thought that there was nothing more to discuss now and consideration of matters relating to the night would come up sooner rather than later after dinner. So he concentrated on feeding her, but when he began to put on her plate large spoonfuls of saffron-coloured and saffron-scented pilaf garnished with shavings of a variety of nuts, she protested, 'Stop, please stop! Your Honour is perpetrating cruelty upon cruelty! How could I ever eat so much?'

'Bhai wallah, all the dishes are as they were served, practically untasted,' cried the Navab. 'I should say the food did not pass muster with you! You're pecking at the food like tiny birds. Granted that you are extremely slender, almost like the rice husk, but even you must hold dear the relationship of body and soul!'

'Any relationship that relates her to you is dear to your servant girl, be it her life. But how can I stand you rising from the tablecloth with an empty stomach and coercing me to eat more and yet more?'

'Oh well, mistress, how in the world could I coerce you? I can only request with a happy heart and pray in good faith.'

The subtext of the Navab's remark was not hidden from Wazir, but she replied pretending not to have appreciated his subtlety, quoting a Persian proverb, 'Yes, sir. All of us know that a happy-hearted labourer works more.' Shamsuddin Ahmad, in his turn, apparently ignored Wazir's hidden meaning and said, 'Madam, unlike you, I've not been bashful. Just the sight of you is like food for me, so I've been freely enjoying your looks and feeling that I'm having my fill of food.' He then quoted the eighteenth-century Persian poet Darab Beg Juya with great relish:

Your body, from head to foot, looks good to eat,
You can be tasted with the eye.

Wazir blushed, but the Navab did not stop. With a brief laugh, partly made up of shyness and partly of shameless banter, he went on, 'Though I have seen just a little glimpse of your face and hands and feet, something more was needed for us the perennially hungry ones. But . . . bhai wallah, as much as I have tasted, my belly is full, though I have no feeling of satiety.'

Wazir recalled an English saying that Aby memsahib was wont to use when the children demanded something more than their share at dinner or at other times. She translated the saying into her own Hindi and said with a smile, 'Your Honour's auspicious eyes have more capacity than your auspicious stomach.'

Shamsuddin Ahmad took a little moment to get to her meaning. He laughed in glee and retorted, 'Bhai wallah! That is a marvellous repartee! One feels like kissing your mouth.'

The bitterness of the evening had largely dissipated in Wazir's heart. During dinner, she had been educating her heart to accept what was being offered at the Navab's palace door. The golden if temporary shade of the Navab's umbrella of desire was at all times better than the longer shadows of growing old alone and friendless. Her heart was lightened when she reached the decision that wandering from house to house like the pachisi counter (here she was unconsciously quoting Ghalib) was in no wise preferable to a situation where all her counters (now she was echoing Mir) were in the vulnerable houses and the haven of home was far away. Her pieces may not be nearing their destination yet, but they were in the seventh house at least, and the possibility of hitting eleven or even seventeen did exist. It was not like falling into eighteen from seventeen and the game ending against her.

She looked at the Navab with an eye particularly charged with erotic indifference, and said, 'Your Honour, go wash your hands of this matter, it is not going to work.'

Shamsuddin Ahmad laughed, again with glee and pleasure. 'Friend, if I get you, I'll be certain that I bathed in the Ganga and all my troubles are now over.' Then, somewhat gravely, he continued, 'Right now I carry nothing but a pitcher full of the tears of longing on my head. The drops are splashing and washing my face and making my eyes wet.'

'Your Honour's name and state are perfectly in tune with each other. Your name is Shams, and the sun's eyes never water . . .' Here she was, perhaps intentionally, alluding to an Urdu verse by the eighteenth-century poet Khvajah Mir Dard. 'In fact, the truth is that if you were not there, there would be no rain. You own both the wet and the dry.'

'Bhai wallah! These exchanges of witty words are enjoyable—but they also excite. Should we be like this forever, laughing and talking, but dry of mouth?'

Before Wazir could answer, a servant entered and asked whether fruit, hookah and betels should be organized for His Honour and Khanam Sahib in the divan khanah, or should these be presented here in the dining chamber? Wazir found the occasion to postpone further talk on this point and said, 'The plate of the Exalted Servants has remained empty. It would be good if you were to enjoy at least some dessert and some fruit.'

'If my begging bowl were to be filled up I would pray for your welfare. Now as regards the issue about hookah and dessert, I should think we repair to the divan khanah. I'll have the curtains raised to add to the enjoyable occasion.'

Both returned to the high chamber. Trays of fresh and dry fruit and assorted types of dry halwa were brought in. A hookah-bearer presented the hookah to the Navab; another presented, in a silver tray, white betels from Benaras, rolled into cones and wrapped in gold leaf. The Navab refused the eatables, but began to enjoy the hookah with obvious pleasure.

Wazir refused the hookah, saying that she had no taste for it, but accepted a betel cone. When she was younger, she did not mind enjoying the hookah once in a while. But when she found out from Marston Blake that among the Sahibs of Exalted Glory, smoking the hookah by women was viewed with disfavour, she gave it up willingly and never desired it again. Shamsuddin Ahmad continued to pull at the hookah quietly. Indeed, both were silent for a while, but it was silence of the kind which denotes the quiet content of old friends who did not worry about keeping up appearances by talking on a given topic or even going for light banter, for they had no need to prove their mutual trust and affection.

Moisture was now permeating the night with constant fall of the dew; it was quite late and Wazir was unable to determine if it was time to take leave, or if she should wait for a suggestion from the Navab to leave. Or was there a way for her to indicate that she was willing to stay the night?

The silence was about to become uncomfortably long when the Navab broke it by clapping his hands loudly. A mace-bearer entered immediately and it seemed as if he knew the purpose of his summons. Without being bidden to do so, he approached the Navab, made a low salaam and whispered something in his ear.

The Navab dismissed the servant with a brief gesture and said to Wazir quietly: 'Your servants have all eaten.' He smiled his famous, charismatic smile. 'Should you desire to leave now, you have permission, but not from my heart. My heart tells me that it is now late in the night, and though you don't stay far from here, and my staff-bearers will certainly accompany you, yet why take the risk of going out at night when there is no real need to do so?'

Wazir was willing, but also unwilling to accept the invitation. The clouds of depression which had blocked her mood had now dispersed. She also knew that sooner or later and most probably sooner than later, she would have to face such an invitation from the Navab. But she hated having to put her foot inside the women's part of the haveli. She did not know the system and management inside the zenana. And if she was not to be wedded to the Navab, she considered it most desirable to stay off the premises.

The Navab perhaps read the meaning of the dubious look on her face; he said, 'Our guest house is entirely separate from the haveli. It is on its own grounds and is safe and secure in every way. It has all the comforts, and your staff shall be spending the night within call.'

Wazir did not make any reply. A sense of relief and comfort overran her face and that was reply enough. With full deliberation, she put her hand out to the betel box, took a cone, and putting it in her mouth, she said, 'This is excellent. Whatever your Exalted Temperament desires. So, bismillah.'

She rose; it was now the Navab who had to pause and ponder for a few heartbeats whether the phrase 'whatever your Exalted Temperament desires' could admit of two meanings. He decided that it could, but he did not let on. He clapped his hands to summon the mace-bearer and the torchbearer and directed that Khanam sahib be escorted to the guest house with full honour and security.

Wazir bent, made three salaams, and said, 'The star of this servant was ascendant today for her to be allowed to be present at today's dinner. May God vouchsafe to me such feasts and such company a million times.'

There was no indication from her of the hour of the next meeting, or of even the possibility of such an hour. With a grave mien, Shamsuddin Ahmad put his right hand on his left breast, bent his head just a little, and said, 'It was my heart that was gladdened.' Then he quoted a Persian proverb, 'May you have good times, for you gave me good times. God willing, we shall have more such meetings.'

This last sentence had a trace of the interrogative, and this time Wazir made her mind clear. With equal gravitas, she salaamed again, and said, 'His Honour enhances my value. Everything rests with you. I cannot go against your pleasure.'

After this, further clarifications and interpretations became redundant. Wazir Khanam walked a couple of steps backward, then she turned, and walking in the special, easy way that she had—as if walking with intense care, but so comfortably that she seemed to walk on water—she went towards the crowned door. Near the door, she turned again. Navab Shamsuddin Ahmad was looking at her with a certain absorption. When he saw Wazir turn, he put his right hand again on his left breast, and spoke up from where he was: 'I entrust you to God's care.'

34

Habib-un Nisa helps Wazir Khanam prepare for the night, and Navab Shamsuddin Ahmad Khan teaches all possible lessons of pride and restraint to his body and his soul

WAZIR ARRIVED AT the guest house in splendid style: two torchbearers with hand-held torches to her right and left, and a little in front of them a staff-bearer. Similarly, there was another staff-bearer behind her, a little to the left. All the servants made their salaams and left when they reached the door.

Though called a guest house, it was actually like a proper haveli, the only difference being that it was not enclosed within a boundary wall and there was no garden in front of it. There was just a fountain, well lit, and around it there were flower beds in star shapes, separated from each other with red sandstone borders. All the beds were in full colours with the flowers of the season and some perennials.

Light could be seen filtering out from inside, but the door of the guest house was closed. As Wazir's procession arrived, the door opened soundlessly, spilling out a good quantity of light on the doorstep and beyond. Wazir found a woman standing just within the door. Since the light was behind the woman, Wazir could not determine her facial features, but she was dressed in the style of genteel Muslim women and she looked somewhere between late youth and middle age. The woman took a step forward, bent before Wazir and making three salaams, said, 'Khanam sahib, you are most welcome, ahlan wa sahlan.' She used the formal Arabic phrase, popular all over the Muslim world even now; its literal sense being: 'You are like family to us; so feel easy and comfortable.' She went on, 'Please do bring in your Noble Presence. This servant is here to serve you.'

Wazir could not surmise what service could be needed or offered at such a late hour but she soon realized that it was an example of the Navab's fine understanding and management skill: he had deputed an intelligent, reliable and homey woman as her companion, so that Wazir would not feel bored or anxious in the new environment, and if she had any routines before retiring for the night, or if she needed something unexpectedly, she could frankly tell the woman about them. She accepted the salaams of the woman with a smile and followed her into the guest house. The bedroom Wazir was led to was well lit but not ostentatiously so. She now saw that the woman was of the type called mughlani: a general-purpose senior lady's maid or attendant. The mughlani wore narrow trousers of flowered silk, called gulbadan, and her kurta was long and simple, made of sangi, the fabric used by Pundit Naval Kishor for his trousers. Her dupatta was of light-green cotton. She wore a gold chain around her neck, devoid of gemstone or pendant, and gold circlets on her ears, again relentlessly plain. The palms of her hand and the soles of her shoeless feet were decorated with delicate floral patterns of dark-red henna. Two of her toes on each foot had silver rings whose ends were curled like the scorpion's sting—hence the name bichhua, from bichhu, meaning 'scorpion'—and the silver had a wondrous colourful effect against the dark red of the henna. Her lips had a similar dark-red shellac colour because of her habit of chewing betel; her teeth were tinged with the dark powder known as misi.

On the whole, the mughlani was quite a good-looking woman whose clothes suited her extremely well. Her face was gentle and sophisticated, suggesting good breeding. She must have been around forty, but nineteen-year-old Wazir's eyes saw her as quite ancient. 'Your slave girl is called Habib-un Nisa, but the begams call me Habiba. Call me by my full name, or call me Habiba, or give me some other nice name that you like. I am agreeable to everything.' Her voice was sophisticated and well modulated, with a tinge of Mewar, but also traces of the sweetness of Braj.

'Habiba is a nice name,' said Wazir. 'I will call you Habiba.'

Habiba gestured towards a large armchair and said, 'If you would care to sit here for a little while, I will remove your shoes and softly knead and pat the soles of your feet and the palms of your hands.'

Wazir felt uncertain for a moment. Patting and kneading someone's body to sleep or to induce a feeling of restfulness was practised at Jaipur too, but she had not employed a full-time servant for the job. And of course, there was none there to match Habiba's considerateness and gentility. Wazir suddenly realized that she was quite exhausted and her body felt rather slack. She recalled that the evening with the Navab, however agreeable it had been, was also much filled with inner tensions—at least for her—and the tensions had been both physical and mental. Now that the evening was over, a great quantity of tiredness and a sense of vapidity had overcome her like a falling wall.

She cast a glance at the room. It was a little above medium size. One end of it was taken up by a massive ebony bed whose thick legs were made of Indian rosewood and inlaid with light floral decorations in brass and silver. It had ebony poles at its four ends and shafts of the same wood as testers to convert the bed into a bedstead. By the ebony strips hung green silk curtains. The bed was higher than usual, having been designed in the Rajputani style. For climbing onto the bed, there was a small but wide stool, padded and covered with satin.

In the centre of the room, but placed against a wall, was the big sedan chair in which she had been invited to sit. It was designed in hybrid style, partly Indian and partly English. It had velvet cushions and its legs were heavy but plain. Its long arms were wide enough to accommodate a cup or glass or plate. The sitter could use the chair's arms to extend his or her legs on them. There was a spittoon and a washbowl on two low teapoys placed next to the chair.

The room had wall-to-wall blue-green carpeting and was lit with chandeliers and globes, all of whose shades were green; thus the light was cool and comforting to the eyes. A light scent of the attar of ambergris, normally used in hot weather, enhanced the soothing effect. It was the beginning of September and the weather was cooling down a bit. Still, one needed the fan for additional comfort. Two velvet fans were therefore hung from the ceiling in the centre of the room through its width, supported by heavy, stout wooden beams. The puller was aided by a wheel-and-pulley arrangement, which was set up outside the room.

On the other side of the bed was a long and low table. Some books, some cool drinks, a silver betel box and a silver candlestick sat on it. The candles were unlit, but there was a box of matches with the candlestick. Between the sedan chair and the bed was another table, which had another betel box, a small gilded tray with readymade betel cones covered with gold leaf. A long tray was also there, laden with fruits of the season, prominent among them a grey Kabuli musk melon. Next to the tray were some small silver bowls and a fruit knife with an English-style blade whose handle was decorated with gold inlay work. There was nothing more by way of furniture or furnishing except a couple of plain but good-looking chairs.

Wazir's upper body touched the chair's back the moment she sat on it. Quite without intending to, she flopped into the big chair and stretched her arms down its two wide arms. She looked like a life-sized doll in the huge sedan chair and her face had the same delicate softness. She now looked closely at Habiba and felt that waves, warm and pleasant, seemed to be emanating from her body. These waves contained a heady mixture of fragrances: respectful regard for Wazir, cordial welcome, rituals of honour, but also something like love and even ownership, as if in her eyes Wazir was not a stranger, a guest for the night or for a few nights. Rather, she was Habib-un Nisa's own daughter, brought up most lovingly and with dedication, and Wazir's elevation to her present status was causing Habiba extreme happiness. She was looking at Wazir with eyes whose every atom seemed to be lit with the fireflies of love, pride and a sense of oneness with her.

Why is it so? Wazir asked herself. I saw Habiba just today; I was not even aware of her existence before this evening. Maybe she had heard about me vaguely in the haveli sometime. And if the Navab wants to establish a temporary arrangement with me for a week or two, why did he depute a senior lady's maid to attend to me, a woman who looks at me with such affection as though I'm a near relation? Wazir suddenly felt unfocused, anxious. What is going on here? To what purpose have I persuaded myself to be here tonight?

Although the lines of worry and strain were faint on Wazir's forehead, Habiba apparently read her like a book. She laughed a short, bashful laugh, went forward, and dried with her light upper wrap the beads of perspiration on Wazir's face, ran her hands on both sides of her head, touched all her fingers to the sides of her own head and face, and said, 'My life for you. What is it that makes my Begam anxious? I would say it is nothing; you are very tired, that is all. I should think that if you chewed a betel cone with the essence of ambergris in it, your heart and mood would stabilize at once.'

Habiba took out a betel cone from the box and put it in Wazir's mouth, despite Wazir's resistance. Immediately as she began to chew the cold cone, she felt the cool scent of ambergris run through her body. She smiled involuntarily. Habiba came up and again did the customary gesture of passing her hands on Wazir's face, and cried, 'A spring tide of smiles overran that prettiest of faces at once! Oh, what a lovely visage! The moon can have some alloy, this one has none!'

Wazir's voice was naturally low and somewhat husky. She spoke shyly, almost in a whisper, 'Off with you, madam Habiba! You are making fun of me, aren't you? I, dark as the raven, have neither a comely nose nor long tresses. It is only the likes of you that could wax eloquent about me. As the saying goes: Who admires a one-eyed woman? Her husband.'

Habiba humbly folded her hands and said, 'I swear by Allah, with the Thirty Discourses between us. Did I ever see such a seductive, ravishing face!'

She went behind Wazir and began to run her fingers gently over her eyelids and forehead. The effect was of butterflies fluttering their mealy wings on them, or of the sunbird moving her tiny wings incredibly fast, hovering to drink the nectar of flowers. Wazir had a feeling of extraordinary comfort and relief. Her eyes began to close. Soon, she felt the same fluttering on her neck and shoulders.

She fell into a light slumber and did not know when Habiba's fingers did the same things to her waist, her thighs, went down to the soles of her feet and came back up through to her arms and fingers. After a while, she heard soft clicking sounds—the velvety jerks of her fingers being cracked—and she woke up.

Now the oppressive room seemed familiar as her own home, and Habiba's face was kind like that of a nurse, and considerate and professional like a dexterous matchmaker or an expert bride-dresser. Her smile was so homey, so like that of a confidante, and so heart-tugging, that Wazir impulsively put out her hand to drag her to her side and seat her on the chair with her. But the moment Habiba saw that Wazir had awakened, she disappeared somewhere behind a curtain. Wazir realized that attached to her chamber there must be a washroom and a toilet. Perhaps Habiba was there.

When Habiba returned after a few minutes, Wazir saw her surmise being confirmed: Habiba was carrying two wet, steaming hand towels. With practised ease, she rubbed Wazir's face, neck, shoulders and hands and feet with the lukewarm wet towels, taking away the lassitude of her muscles and removing any possible speck of dirt or mark of perspiration. Wazir sensed a faint whiff of the attar of bdellium in the towels. It felt a little heavy at first, but soon became light and invigorating. Her body found a renewed freshness.

'Behind that door is the washroom,' Habiba gestured. 'And attached to it is . . . the . . . toilet. Should you desire to use it, I could come rub your back. Your back is so delicate!'

Her life with Marston Blake had taught, or made her appreciate, certain things. For instance, sometimes he would knock and come into the bathroom when Wazir was there, taking her bath. On occasion, he would rub her hands and feet or back as she bathed and during such sessions, would inordinately praise her overall beauty or particularly select some limb for special praise. She knew that Firangee couples sometimes bathed together, but it was not generally an approved or desirable practice.

Indian women of the upper classes were assisted at their bath by their personal maid or bride-dresser. But Wazir did not adopt the manner of the begams in this regard. She bathed alone, and always wore some light garments, for instance a bodice of fine muslin on the upper body, and loose trousers or a wide Rajputani skirt on the lower limbs. To have someone go and put the ablution pot in the water room or even help wash her hands was anathema to her. And to have someone rub your back as you sat on the toilet . . . ugh! . . . My God! I never saw such practices even among the Firangees. Indeed, these elites of the Indian nobility have strange ways. In any case, Wazir did not need to go then or perhaps even later. Like all girls of good families in India, she had been rigorously trained to withhold such actions for long periods of time.

'No, no, Habiba, I'll wash my face. You do not need to worry at all.' Wazir's refusal was firm, but delivered with that famous smile of hers which had softened alike the hearts of Fanny Parkes, William Fraser and Mirza Ghalib. The smile was so enchanting that Habib-un Nisa almost dropped dead.

'All right, then please trouble your feet to the washroom. I'll hold the washing pot, you could then splash water with both hands on your face to your heart's content.'

'Dear Madam Habib-un Nisa, mind your words,' Wazir said with laughing eyes. 'If you go too far, the pot might slip from your hands and you may have to be chastised!'

'Bibi sahib commands special skills in the use of language, it seems. And why not? She commands special skills in the use of her heart-winning powers, like a queen.'

'A queen is she who has a country to rule, one who has a king by her side. A few tattered outfits and a couple of dark and narrow hovels are all I command.'

'I take the name of God! May your currency be honoured in country after country. Your treasury of words seems endless!'

Laughing, Wazir rose and delivered a light slap to Habiba's face, as if patting it affectionately. Somehow, Habiba did not look of any great age to her at this time. She rather seemed a girlfriend and playmate of Bari Begam's. The affectionate light on her face was quite like that of a well-wishing senior friend. She drew Wazir's hand to her breast and then exclaimed, 'Oh Almighty! I, and such temerity as to touch your hand to my breast! I beg to be forgiven.' As she said these words, she gently slapped her own face.

'Well, if you go on gabbing and spinning out strings of words thus, madam, you will be entitled to get more slaps! All right, I am off to clean my teeth and wash my face. I'll be right back.' Cleaning her teeth before retiring for the night was a habit she had acquired under the tutelage of Marston Blake.

Wazir had barely turned towards the bathroom when someone softly tugged the edge of her dupatta. She looked back to find Habiba's beseeching eyes on her face.

'So, what is it now?' She spoke sharply. She suspected that Habiba wished to accompany her into the washroom, and this was entirely unacceptable to Wazir.

'Khanam sahib,' she said submissively. 'Should I come help you change?'

Wazir was puzzled. Help me change? Living with Marston Blake had indeed taught her that among the Firangees, women wore a separate garment to sleep in. She knew it was called a 'nightgown' (she pronounced it 'nat gaun'). It was a long garment that often came down to the ankles and was made of wool or cotton, depending on the weather. It had, or sometimes did not have, buttons (she called them 'butam', a word common in the Hindi of those days, though she did not know that it was from the French, 'bouton'). Well, buttons or not, the nat gaun was open from the front. Sometimes it could be wrapped and tightened with a belt of the same material. Nothing was worn under the nat gaun. Wazir regarded the practice as thoroughly shameless, but had made herself accept it at Marston Blake's insistence.

In India, women of the upper classes wore the same garments through the day and night, except on special occasions like marriages, when specially made expensive clothes were worn and often changed for ordinary clothes for sleeping in. Ordinary, everyday wear was used for two or three days and then given for washing, mostly at home. Among the elite nobility, women wore their expensive dress over day and night for four or five or at most seven days. Every dress was worn new. Once discarded, it was given away to the servants. The Begam then put on another set of new clothes until it became 'worn' and eligible to be given away. Their clothes were never given out to a washerman or washerwoman for cleaning or washing.

Giving in to Marston Blake's repeated importunities, Wazir did indeed begin to wear a nightdress, but it was not a nightgown. She wore the usual Indian-style long tunic and pants, but looser than usual, and agreeably with the weather, they could be light or heavy, but she dispensed with the dupatta.

The extremely expensive and complicated dress that Wazir wore for the evening could not at all be slept in. One or more of the garments would be torn while turning in sleep, making it impossible for her to return home with her clothes ripped in places. But there was also no question of her bringing ordinary clothes to change into before she slept. Apart from open shamelessness, this could also demean her in the eyes of the Navab, for it would mean that she had planned to stay the night.

Now that the decision was to sleep in the guest house and most probably share the bed with the Navab, her clothes were at every kind of risk. She had therefore reluctantly made up her mind to sleep in her underclothes. Therefore, Wazir was somewhat startled to hear Habib-un Nisa talk about changing clothes. Was she going to give her own clothes for Wazir to wear, and did she know from before that Wazir was coming to stay the night? If she did not, it was certainly sagacious of her to have organized some sleeping garments for Wazir.

'Is there . . . is there any arrangement for change of clothes, then?' She came out of her silence to ask.

'Yes, madam. Should you care to trouble your feet to the bathroom, I will show you what choices of clothes are available.'

'Right, but I'll change on my own.'

'Very well, just as you command,' Habiba smiled briefly. She knew that the kind of complicated garments Wazir wore could not be removed and folded away safely without the assistance of a personal maid. She thought it was better to keep her counsel for the moment, and quietly followed Wazir into the washroom.

On one side of the room was a small, low, wooden platform for bathing, and fresh earthen pitchers, full of water, on a wooden stand. On a lower stand glistened and glittered newly scrubbed and shined brass pitchers, the light reflecting from them warmly. There was a large dipper made of metal alloy, and a smaller one, of chased and engraved silver.

Beside the wooden platform, on the floor, there was a large, somewhat shallow basin made of alloy metals, perhaps for hot water. There was a wide stool on which were placed a container of sandal powder, cakes made from powdered and roasted chickpeas, different kinds of herbal powders and soaps, as well as a few cakes of English soap. She also noticed some boxes—blast them—of English powders. Small, flat-bottomed leather bottles contained scented oils and attars. There were also bouquets of flowers in some of the wall alcoves. Separate from this was a small stone platform on which was a water pot, quite heavy, and a cake of soap made from powdered and roasted chickpeas in a little soap box of its own. These were to be used for formal ablutions.

At the far end, behind a screen, was perhaps the urinal, though there was no trace of smell, alkaline or other. Instead, there was a faint fragrance—perhaps of the attar of aloe vera—resonating through the environment of the room which was large enough to contain another wooden stand to accommodate two clay pitchers for drinking water, a table where stood bottles of syrups from which cool drinks could be made, silver drinking cups and English-style glasses; there was a large wooden box, much like a foot locker, in another corner. It stood on a wooden platform of its own to protect it and its contents from the damp.

In front of the big box were two Rajputani-style narrow chairs, somewhat higher than usual, for convenience in removing and putting on garments. On the wall opposite the box and chairs was a tall mirror, full size, with its wide margins decorated with paintings of flowers and birds and beautiful women and saki boys. The mirror was so large that it reflected a substantial portion of the room, and did not distort the viewer's image even the least bit.

It was impossible not to wet the clothes that Wazir was wearing, if she chose to wash her face with the dress on. The better choice was to remove all the upper garments and approach the water in just the undergarments.

Habib-un Nisa stepped up and opened the wooden box in the corner of the room. The first garment that she produced was a heavy dupatta of yellow-coloured silken muslin, its length going up to the whole extravagant six yards. The next thing she brought out was a pair of pants, loose and light violet in colour, made of plain Bhagalpuri silk. Wazir took the pants in her hands to find that they did not weigh any more than the long muslin dupatta. Last of all, she was presented a long, loose tunic of phulam, a flowerly cotton fabric with a bit of silk mixed in it. The flowers, in light yellow-green, were painted all over, though not densely, and the tunic had a high neck; it was open at the collar and had no buttons.

Wazir felt her mouth watering at the sight of the clothes. Who wouldn't love to sleep in such an outfit! Over and over again, she would pick up one of the items and put it against her body to see how well it suited her.

'Should you like me to present the undergarments too?' Habiba said.

On being told by Wazir that small clothes were not needed, Habiba looked at Wazir with meaningful eyes, inquiring if she could assist her in undressing. Or, Habiba hoped if Wazir needed to go behind the curtain, she needs must remove her clothes in front of her.

Wazir's hesitancy was quite clear, but she decided quickly. Seated on the chair, she said, 'So, where do we start?'

The decision was taken, but her face still revealed hints of her annoyance, not unmixed with a bit of a smile. It was clear that she did not approve of the idea of someone, even if it was Habiba, assisting her in activities like removing clothes, washing, bathing or sitting on the toilet.

With slow deliberation, Habiba removed all her upper garments, some of which she could fold with some difficulty and place in the footlocker. The rest could not be folded conveniently, perhaps they were not meant to be folded. These she handled with extreme care, and hung them on the brass pegs that were affixed to the walls. Then she washed Wazir's face and hands and feet, and dried them with a large, scented kerchief. Wazir's narrow waist, heavy hips and prominent breasts had now become more prominent. It seems as if the weight of the hips was supporting the breasts upwards, Habiba thought. Or this little darling would lose her balance when she walked. Somewhere deep in her psyche, Habiba felt the reverberations of some obscure desire. She checked herself sternly and did not let her face or subtle gestures reveal anything at all. She also felt that she might incur Wazir's displeasure if she stayed longer.

'I shall wait outside. Your Honour can call me when you need me,' she said.

A little knot of displeasure appeared for a moment on Wazir's brow. She did not say anything, but said in her heart that there could be no further business for Habib-un Nisa in the water room, so why was she hinting that she be readmitted? Anyway, she was smarter even than Habib-un Nisa in concealing her true feelings: if Habib-un Nisa learnt this during her career as a maid, Wazir had suffered all emotional environments—love and passion; occasions when she felt revolted against someone; and occasions of refusal—and had taught herself well to show what needed to be shown and lock up the rest inside.

She easily cast away her pique and responded briefly and matter-of-factly: 'Very well,' and directed her attention to her clothes for the night and the furnishings in the room.

The moment Habib-un Nisa left, Wazir removed all her underclothes and was intending to visit behind the screen when her eye fell on her reflection in the life-size mirror: exactly as she was, without the mediation of any kind of covering. She started, but then was arrested by her image. The mirror showed everything, even the slight elevation of the Mount of Venus and the suggestion of a little patch of darker sward on it. She could see everything clearly, as if rays of light were gently breaking forth from her body and were enhancing the bright reflectivity of the mirror.

There was no trace at all on her body of her having been a mother twice over. Her stomach did not show, as most women's do, those creases which are caused by the stretching and contraction of the skin and muscles during and after pregnancy. Her thighs, so well made and smooth as if a potter had just removed them from his wheel and had put them out to dry in the sun; the pink of the heels and soles of the feet reinforcing the beauty of the dark purplish henna, tinged with rosy pink, on the toes and the feet. Her stomach was flat as a board, and the graceful curve of the neck suggested strength and pride. The glinting of the reflection from the mirror in her large, deep-brown eyes was as if small goblets of clear glass, full of deep-red wine, were placed in front of candles and their flames reflected on them.

Suddenly, her throat became choked with tears. None except Blak sahib had ever seen her unclothed, and even he had perhaps not looked at her the way the mirror was seeing her now. And today . . . today someone else shall see her. He may be her heart's comfort in a thousand ways but he was not the first. Her eyes brimmed over. She felt as if all the energy and sense of security that Habib-un Nisa's care and attention had generated in her had been hauled down into the depths of a well. She flopped into the chair, as if she had no strength left, and put one leg on the other, pushing inwards her already flat stomach, the joining of the thighs creating a small, not quite shallow triangle with her pelvis forming the base of it.

She lowered her head. Now she was not looking into the mirror: she was looking at herself in her heart. She was looking at that inexperienced but headstrong girl, all the secrets of whose body—and some of her soul too—had been laid bare before her by someone who was an infidel, a Nazarene and a Firangee. He revealed those mysteries to her in such style as if they had been revealed to him through divine visitation, and then all her self had become for her the Truth of Seeing, as in the manner of seeing is believing. She wept for Marston Blake, for today she knew with iron-hard certainty that no life lives forever, and dead people never return. Tears started to fall from her eyes. She kept on weeping, her head bent, and her tears slipping down the slopes of her breasts accumulated in that small cup that was formed between her closed thighs and her pelvis.

⋆

Habib-un Nisa stood rooted close to the washroom door, worrying about the non-appearance of Wazir, and also apprehensive that she might displease her if she called out or went into the room. There was a door at the back of the urinal behind the screen. It opened on to the toilet (she called it sehhat khana—house of recovery—according to the practice among the elites of Delhi). Maybe she's in the toilet. I don't know if there is a light there . . . No matter, she can light the candle, surely. It is not proper to disturb her at present. How heart-tugging her person is! But she is very proud. If something annoys her, she will reprimand you promptly. No, she will probably not reprimand in words, but her brow will be clouded. That is enough to discourage the best of us.

With a little clack of bolts and chains, the washroom door opened and Wazir Khanam came out. She looked tired and forlorn. Habib-un Nisa sensed at once that something untoward had happened, but she could not make bold to ask. Wazir had put on the nightclothes which Habib-un Nisa had brought out of the box. In the greenish light of the bedchamber the clothes looked stunning on her, like an orange-yellow shade on a candle in a golden candlestick. Habib-un Nisa had often heard about 'sad beauties' or 'grieving damsels' in the oral romances, but she had never imagined that a sad beauty's visage could be so attractive, so proud, with her dark colour suggesting the dark of rose leaves mixed and kneaded with large orange-yellow hibiscus flowers, and emanating, for all she could see, the dusky light of a sun setting behind the clouds.

Habib-un Nisa came near her, softly touched her shoulder, and said, 'You must be tired. If you care to lie down, I will pat and lightly knead your body.' A sense of gratefulness awoke in Wazir's mind, but at the same time she felt a little vexed, if not nettled. Who is this woman, spreading herself like a mat before me at every possible occasion? She may be a senior ladies' maid or bride-dresser or whatever, but she's still a servant. Does she not have the sense to see that I feel out of sorts? . . . No, I do not feel out of sorts, actually, but somehow this chamber no longer seems as pleasant as before.

She approached the bed with tired legs, and making a conscious effort to plant her feet firmly on the footstool, she climbed up and sat listlessly on the bed. Habib-un Nisa immediately removed Wazir's shoes and gently, almost tenderly, she raised her legs onto the bed so that now Wazir was comfortably reclining in it.

'Please lie down, just for a few moments. I will put oil in your hair and comb it. The patting can follow.'

There were soft pillows and also some small, round velvety cushions to rest the face on. Everything smelled faintly of flowers and the attar of the small jasmine. Wazir pulled herself up against the bolster and closed her eyes.

'Which oil would you prefer? Flower oil from Jaunpur, almond oil from Kabul, coconut oil from Bangalah, which also has a little element of camphor and ginger, or . . .'

'Enough, dear madam, do you go around hauling an entire perfumer's box? All right, let it be the flower oil from Jaunpur.' Wazir was not peremptory, but rather indulgent.

Habiba hustled to the water room and came back in no time with a small leathern bottle of the oil. She poured a few drops on the palm of one hand, then rubbed the palms together and touched the fingers of the right hand to Wazir's head with slow, even movements. Instead of spreading the oil over her tresses, or combing them, she began to run her fingers through her dense locks. Wazir felt a rush of comfort; her eyes began to close. Not even ten minutes had elapsed when Wazir's inner tension began to dissolve, like the unravelling of a skein of twisted silk threads. She sobbed a sigh of pleasure and comfort and stretched her whole body on the bed.

She was very close to dropping off to sleep, when she woke herself up with a little jolt . . . How is it that I am here? Is this not the haveli of the Navabs of Loharu? It is not proper for me to fall asleep here in this fashion. She opened her sleepy eyes, looked at Habib-un Nisa and wanted to ask her: For how long have you been in employment here? Where did you come from? Surely, you cannot be the ladies' maid of one of the Navab's begams. You were perhaps in the service of his mother, and are still here because the Navab must trust and like you, and that is also why he deputed you to my service.

No, it is not proper to ask such questions in the very first meeting. If the connection here turns out to be lasting, I will get to know these things in due course. And if the connection does not last, my knowing or not knowing will be one and the same.

Habib-un Nisa noticed that Wazir's face now showed signs of composure, even of cheerfulness. She said, 'Should you now like to rest, then bismillah, I will beg your leave.' She paused for a brief moment, then continued, 'At what time would it be convenient for you to receive the Navab sahib? May I let him know?'

On hearing the question, a thrill, or rather a tingle, rose in Wazir's heart. It was a moment that she had been waiting for; she had not looked forward to it perhaps, but she had expected it. Though she had accepted the Navab's dinner invitation willingly, and did entertain some hopes in regard to Shamsuddin Ahmad, and truth to tell, she knew that her own heart inclined towards him, yet she had evaded to look in the eye the possibility of the moment of final choice.

Now all opportunities of evasion were over. She was silent for a few moments, then smiled, looked at Habiba full in the eye, and said, 'All times are convenient when he desires to visit. I am the guest here . . . and now my hand is caught under a heavy stone.'

The possibility of two meanings in Wazir's words was not hidden from Habib-un Nisa. She was unable to decide if Wazir was serious or if she was speaking in a lighter mode. She stopped a bit to consider what she should say and how to say it. Then she spoke clearly, taking full care to avoid all ambiguity, 'You are no guest. I see your rule extending all over the place. And the Navab, it appears to me, is preparing to surrender to you the proud riches of his heart so that you may buy him for free.'

'Habib-un Nisa, there you go again with your jokes and pleasantries!' Wazir said with sham annoyance. 'Granted, I may have bought him out like a slave. But here and now I feel as if I am bound with the Firangee's fetters.'

'Madam, take the name of God!' Habiba touched her ears to symbolize repentance. 'This is not a country of the English! No, not by any means!'

'Well, it may not be, but Habiba, nowadays my soul seems to be shaken and wan for no reason.' She stopped. It seemed that she wanted to go on, but was restrained by her pride or sense of judicious conduct. Habiba thought she understood Wazir's mood, or perhaps she did not. Again, she answered en clair, taking care not to give any impression of tergiversation: 'God is the Greater King, Khanam sahib. Put your trust in him always.' She advanced, and running her hands lightly over Wazir's face, then touching and cracking her fingers against her own, repeatedly performed the traditional act of taking upon oneself a loved one's adversities. 'This servant now craves permission to leave. I'll inform the Navab sahib. Goodbye.'

Habiba dexterously ran her fingers through Wazir's tresses. Her thick braid became free of its twists and her long hair spread free over her shoulders and back. A whiff of the flower oil touched Wazir's nostrils and a sense of lightness touched her heart. Bending, Habiba made two quick salaams and stepped backward.

Wazir wished in her heart to thank Habiba, as the English did among themselves. She knew that they never thanked their servants, and especially the native servants who were barely regarded as human beings. Among the Indians, the tradition was to honour and respect the older servants. Normally, such servants were addressed as 'Grandfather' or 'Uncle'; similarly, it was common to address them in the respectful second-person-plural 'aap', rather than the singular 'tum', but Wazir could neither place Habiba among old servants, nor among relatives. She doubted if it was proper for her, at the very first acquaintance, to thank Habiba. Still, she ignored all rules and principles and spoke up impulsively, 'Goodbye, Habiba. I am truly grateful to you.'

Habiba was walking up fast towards the water room; she stopped, as if in surprise. Her face betrayed disbelief. She turned and said, 'You, and grateful to us! May God preserve you, please do not say such things. We are eaters of your salt, we could not pay back your kindnesses even if we laid down our lives for you.'

'Well, now that I have done the deed,' Wazir said, attempting to be facetious, though her eyes were bright with unshed tears. 'You shouldn't forget this. I will not, certainly.'

Saying this, Wazir tucked her feet under her thighs, so that the curves of her upper body became a little hidden behind her loose clothing. But when she put her back against the bolstered pillow, the rebellious lines of her neck and breasts became prominent again. A few of the smaller tresses adorning her forehead; the darkness of the bright curls of a braid falling down in a gentle cascade from one shoulder; the deep-brown eyes hidden behind long eyelashes, though the light from the lamps filtered through the lashes and played hide-and-seek upon the surface of the eyes; one hand in her lap and the other extending towards the book placed on the nightstand; the throat and the wrists still shorn of all ornamentation, except for the ruby red of the ring on her right thumb and the grass green of the emeralds on her right index finger glinting and glittering against the yellow of her upper wrap and the light yellow green of her long tunic: the ceiling of the chamber would have rarely, if ever, seen such a pleasing, languid, rainbow spray of colours. It was absolutely out of the reckoning of anything experienced by Habib-un Nisa.

Stunned, Habib-un Nisa watched her, unblinking, for a long moment, as if she could not believe that the girl who occupied the bed in front of her was made of flesh and blood. Wazir once again said 'Goodbye' and devoted herself to the book. Habib-un Nisa made a low salaam again and walking backward a few steps, entered the washroom.

A door at the far end of the washroom opened on to a narrow corridor. Once you entered the corridor, you had, to your left, the back door of the toilet; to the right, the corridor ended at a veranda in front of which was a courtyard designed as a rather informal interior garden: it had the bigger trees such as a couple of neems, a few date palms, an ancient, flowering maulsari and sundry smaller flower plants and flowering shrubs. The servants' quarters of the main haveli could be reached from the veranda as well.

Wazir was unaware of these particulars, nor did she need to know them. She knew that the Navab, when he entered, would use the front door and would be announced by a mace-bearer. She was content, now that the night was more or less mapped out in her brain. The book, which she had picked from the nightstand, turned out to be the Divan of Hafiz. Bound in leather, the book was quite antique; the gold margin on its front and spine had faded. It was, however, clear that the book had been much used and handled, as many of the pages had their corners turned or dog-eared. She imagined that the Navab had it placed there for her reading. She opened the volume quite casually and found that the very first verse on the right-hand page was:

How can this broken heart manage
To extricate itself? Each curl in your tresses
Has no less than fifty snares.

'How nice!' She smiled to herself, though not without a sense of irony. Oh, well, perhaps that verse too concealed an augury, she thought, as she pushed back the curls that had strayed on to her forehead. She was about to open another page when she heard the knock of a heavy mace on the stone floor outside. She put the Divan back and covered her head with her wrap.

The door opened soundlessly; the Navab entered, unaccompanied by a servant or maid. The mace-bearer's knocks on the hard ground were obviously intended to warn the occupants of the guest house of the Navab's advent.

Wazir shrank her body a little more and kept her eyes on her knees. The Navab's personality looked even more attractive in the informal ambience of the bedroom. He wore the dress that he usually had on indoors: loose tunic of ultra-soft, white muslin, worked on the shoulders and neck with sky-blue lace, worn above wide Delhi-style trousers of the same fabric except that the muslin of the trousers had stripes, a fourth of an inch wide, of light green. He wore a green turban, somewhat in the Rajputani style but a little taller. On his feet he had heavy brocade shoes decorated with green lace, somewhat wider than usual, and featuring the fruit and sprig of grapes. He wore nothing symbolizing his status as an independent ruler except a five-stringed pearl necklace and a ring on his right index finger, the large ruby of which was carved to be used as his seal.

He moved up, but not too far inside, cleared his throat, and said, 'Good evening, Wazir Khanam.'

Now Wazir raised her eyes and looked at the Navab. She smiled her famous or notorious smile which no one had been able to resist loving. Shamsuddin Ahmad felt his knees weaken. In spite of Wazir having her breasts and her body below the pelvis well concealed, the Navab felt erotic invitations emanating from the entire person of the girl before him. He restrained himself when Wazir rose to salaam him and gently patting her face, he kissed her forehead, then her eyes and finally, her mouth.

Putting his arm around her waist, the Navab led her to the bed. Seating her there, he sat cross-legged before her on the bed. This time, she did not half recline against the bolster; she sat on her haunches but did not put her head upon her knees, instead, she wrapped both arms around her knees and thighs. The posture indicated a somewhat informal intimacy, but much of her body was fully protected.

She looked at the Navab with smiling eyes. He put one hand on her knee and the other around the shoulder. During this movement, Wazir's dupatta slipped from her head, revealing the gentle grace of her slim neck. The Navab ran the fingers of his right hand through her hair and was about to put his other hand under her trouser leg and, maybe, even enjoy what was there further up or down. Sprigs of desires began gently to sprout in Wazir's heart, but she was not about to expose herself as easily taken. Just at the moment the Navab pushed his hand up her leg and kissed her on the knee, intending to go further, Wazir stretched her legs, smoothed her trousers and said, 'Indeed, one did hear of bold ones going on to the wrists from caressing the fingers, but it is a new one on me, your desire to travel down from the height of the kneecap to the depths beyond.' She laughed. 'Your Honour, where did you learn the ways of the acrobats?'

Laugh she did, but she did not also want the Navab to imagine that she was mocking him. She clasped his hand to her breast and said: 'Just see now, what the state of my heart is, thanks to your depredations! It is beating so fast! I fear I'll go down in a faint.'

Trying to take her whole body in his arms, the Navab said, 'Well, here I am fainting already at your sight. If you faint, I will hold you up. After all, why did God create arms and hands?'

This time Wazir let herself come into the arms of the Navab and putting her head on his shoulder, she said, 'Oh! You smell so sweet, drunk on your redolence, anyone could stumble and fall.' She quoted the eighteenth-century Hindi poet Sauda: *Take the wine cup from my hands, for I am about to be gone!*

'You could never slip so that I would not be there to support you. Do lose your step a little. I am impatient to hold you!'

Saying this, he pulled aside Wazir's wrap and betook his hand to her collar in order to unbutton it and saw that she wore nothing under her tunic. Wazir sprang aside and said, 'Please. What is this that you are doing? All the lights are burning!'

'Don't you mind all that. If the candles are burning, why, let them burn.'

'No, no! I didn't mean that! There is nothing common between me and the splendour of the lights. What I meant was that in the light . . .'

'Yes, surely. In the very brightness of the lamps. Faced with the light of your beauty, the lamps will soon flicker and fade . . . Please. No more of your cruelty now. The night itself, drenched in my tears, is about to flicker and die.'

'Well, all right.' Wazir resumed her wrap covering her head and face as if she were veiling herself. 'Please. Remain at some distance,' she said, gently pushing the Navab's face away from her. 'Please do not look. And if your eyes were closed, so much the better.'

Before Shamsuddin Ahmad could think of a suitable retort, Wazir threw both her garments off, and put the wrap around her whole self like a chador. 'There. You can turn your face now. Now there is nothing to hide.'

Wazir's body could be discerned vaguely through the dupatta, but she wore it chador-style so artfully that she still did not seem without proper clothing. Yet her eyes, shy somewhat and brightly laughing somewhat, seemed to be knocking at the door of love.

The Navab understood the message well, but he had not expected Wazir herself to remove her clothes. A small whirlwind of revulsion rose in his heart. The company of the English has taken away her sense of shame. He must have taught her to remove her clothes by herself . . . But the very next moment, he was ashamed at his foul imaginings, for he recalled a line from Mir:

She removed her clothes and I pulled my head
under the shroud.

So what was proper two hundred years ago in Mir sahib's days must be also proper today. Gently, he drew aside her chador. She had gathered her body close, as before, but nakedness this time had defeated concealment on all fronts. He felt every nerve tingling and as the lights of desire woke up everywhere in his body, reflecting through his eyes, he recalled with a strange sense of enlightenment the whole of the verse from Mir:

I died a thousand deaths at the sight of her naked body:
She removed her clothes and I pulled my head
under the shroud.

This is exactly my state at this moment, or maybe even worse. His body seemed to be breaking all bounds of decorum. Gritting his mental teeth, he taught all possible lessons of pride and restraint to his body and his soul in an instant.

In his brief but busy life, Shamsuddin Ahmad had seen countless naked female bodies: of those who were of the streets; or who carried on the business of clandestine loving from their homes; begams driven by the erotic impulse, or loving desire, or sense of duty. Yet here it was a different world altogether. Wazir was taller than average, and still she was able to conceal her body so well that even when fully clothed, she looked extremely delicate—like the husk of a grain of rice or a betel leaf—and without anything on, she looked not only delicate and svelte, but also a storehouse of eroticism, even lust.

From the forehead to the eyes and the nose and the lips; from the chin to the neck; from the clavicle to the arms and forearms; from the palm of her hands to her fingers; from the shoulders to the breasts; from the belly to the navel; from below the navel to the hips; from the buttocks to the thighs and calves; from the ankles to the soles of the feet and the toes; from her tresses to the pubes and the soft, fragrant dark down on them; there was no part of her body which was not, according to its location, fully in proportion, or well shaped, or heavy, or slender, or narrow. And there was no fault or shortcoming in elegance either.

Shamsuddin Ahmad found that he was unable to breathe naturally. Or perhaps his world was in revolution, rotating and revolving so fast that every ligament in his body seemed about to be torn off. Wazir's body was like that of a statue, made of dark crystal, finished and preserved by a master sculptor in the hope that the power of the Omnipotent Breath may breathe life into it. And that was what had perhaps happened. Shamsuddin Ahmad Khan was afraid to touch it, and was also dying to do so.

Wazir put out her hand to unbutton the Navab's tunic. But he took both her hands, small and hennaed in floral patterns, in one of his, and kissed each of the ten fingers. Then he put his face upon her thighs and lay down with his eyes closed.

35

Wazir Khanam receives a loving message and a gift worthy of a princess

FOR MUCH OF the night, Wazir would wake up briefly and drop off to sleep almost at once when she saw Shamsuddin Ahmad lying by her side. She would touch him and every time she did so, a wave of comfort and thankfulness would run through her whole self. She did not doubt that the Navab would be ever-faithful to her. About her own heart, she was even more certain that her feelings for the Navab were not a function of a planned desire for materialistic gain. She greatly liked, if not actually loved, the Navab's person and his personal qualities of nobility and impeccable gentlemanliness. Over time, she would come to love him too; of this again she was quite certain.

She respected Shamsuddin Ahmad's intrepidity: being always ready to challenge a powerful and overbearing Firangee like Fraser was no easy matter. As for the art and ceremonies of love, Shamsuddin Ahmad was in no way inferior to Blak sahib. Like him, the Navab also did not believe in duress, or undue importunity, or not paying much heed to his lover's mood or readiness. Persuading and stimulating willingness and desire, giving equal satisfaction to the two of them: Blak sahib and the Navab were both equally strong and versed swimmers of those streams.

So, it was all well there. Yet Wazir was unable to sleep properly. It was true that after conversation with a man, women did not fall asleep, and certainly not quickly, even if they were exhausted by the labour of lovemaking. Whereas men usually dropped off to sleep immediately; or at best, they talked for a short minute, played with the woman's hand or body, maybe kissed her, and then swiftly dived into sleep. This was true of both Blak sahib and the Navab.

But there was another cause for Wazir's lack of sleep. Her heart was like a verdant field, swaying this way and that under the gusts of the breeze of thankfulness for the Navab's goodness to her. Yet despite her being sure of his love for her, she somehow felt insecure: Would the plant of her love in his heart grow and prosper still more over time, or would it fall and die quickly?

Only very late at night could she fall into real sleep. It must have been three o'clock or four. During the night, Shamsuddin Ahmad had woken once or twice and looked at her smilingly, as if judging whether the conversation should be resumed from where it had ended earlier in the night. But sleep was dominant over him and exhaustion on her.

Both of them woke up at the same time well before the dawn, and then they performed a reprise of the text of life with honeyed words and sweet smiles. Quite unexpectedly, Wazir now found herself sleepy and then dropping off into a deep slumber. The tedium, tension, uncertainty, states of hope and fear, confusion of the mind, incoherence of thought, which had begun when her carriage left for the Navab's haveli the previous night, now began to dissolve in the cool, darkling scent of the morning which was gradually pushing its head out of the dark-grey, smoky mist of the last watch of the night. All the bad things of the past several hours melted away, and became transformed into a sleep which was benign and exhilarating like the morning breeze.

Wazir was dreaming when the muezzin's call for predawn prayers rose from the minaret of the mosque of Zinat-un Nisa Begam, and birds began to sing and twitter in Navab Ahmad Bakhsh Khan's garden at the back of the mosque. I am in Jaipur; the children are with me and we are going to visit with Blak sahib who lives in Rajputana, but somewhere far from Jaipur. There is an album in my bedroom. The album contains portraits made after the Mughal imperial style. Each portrait is glowing, as if it was finished only minutes ago. A vast array of hues and tints: sky blue, lapis lazuli, azure, sea green, darkish leaf green and numerous other shades of green—rice green, pistachio, dark brownish, yellowish green, grape green. Lovely faces, delicate limbs, but no portrait is clear. A wind is blowing from God knows where, the pages of the album flutter so that the eye cannot stay on any one.

For a split second, the wind stopped, enabling her eye to observe . . . it was the portrait of banithani. Her eyes snapped open. Sleep had now disappeared like camphor in the sun. Still, she shut her eyes again. There is no hurry for me to rise, she said to herself. But what was that dream?

She tried to puzzle it out. Was there any meaning to it at all? She had heard that the dreams of early morning were always true. But Blak sahib is not in this world, so where am I going to visit him with my children? Does it mean that we will be united with him very soon in the Higher World? Has God written reunion in our fate? Or does it mean that Shamsuddin Ahmad is now for you what Blak sahib was before? Is it here that I will find the centre of my existence, my home and refuge? So will my darlings be returned to me? And what does banithani's portrait mean in this context? No one ever saw that lady, she is just a creation of the imagination, a Devi who is presumed to be human. People seek her, painters paint her picture, but she is not to be found anywhere.

Her eyes closed, Wazir was lost in her thoughts. The muezzin at Zinat-un Nisa Begam's mosque had an extremely good voice, open, unhurried and well balanced, without affectation or pressure. His call was hardly over when the muezzin at the mosque of Raushan-ud Daulah began to issue his call, a little deeper and heavier, like the deep notes of a late-night raga flowing upon the wings of a breeze, smoothly like the royal couriers. More muezzins began to send out their calls, like streamers of light through the dwindling darkness.

Wazir turned over to her other side, her eyes still shut. She put out her hand to feel for the Navab, as if trying to reassure herself that he was really there. But her fist caught nothing but air. Her heart thumping, she half rose, trying to rub the sleep from her eyes. She looked around, but Shamsuddin Ahmad was nowhere to be seen. Maybe he is in the bathroom? But how could I possibly spy into the bathroom? Should I call out for him? Hush, what a stupid thought that is! Dear little fool, will he not come out sometime if he is in there? Surely he's not going to be there for hours. Oh, maybe he has gone away for the predawn prayer? Chhoti Begam was not quite particular about offering the five daily prayers though she did not neglect any opportunity to go to the mausoleums of the saints and friends of God.

She had been informed that the Navab rarely missed the predawn prayer. So would he be offering it tonight as well? Well, why ever not? Those who have to do the prayer will do it, rain or shine, whether they slept in their usual bed or in a newer one. Great ones have great ways of doing things.

A surge of anxiety overtook her. So when will it be morning finally? When will my staff get ready for departure? I'm not sure that the Navab will return in the course of the day. But he is not here, so how can I know about the manner in which things will turn out?

There was a muffled click at the water-room door. Wazir Khanam started. Lord, the Navab is here. What will he think of me, awake and without a shred of clothing on me! Surely, he will think that I'm a shameless strumpet. Should I wrap myself well with the quilt and pretend that I am asleep? But he is no fool, he's a good judge of what is sham and what is not. So let him guess. I should at least do my bit.

It was a Jaipuri quilt, light and double-sized, with extremely fluffy cotton stuffed in high quality flowered silk sheets and neatly sewn all over. It was commodious enough when there were two persons, but a single individual, and one as lightweight as Wazir, had her work cut out to wrap it closely around her. She spread it over her somehow and made no effort to wrap it fully around her body, except that she half turned on her side, covering her head and face with the quilt; her open tresses spread all over her half-hidden shoulders and the edge of the quilt.

She felt the touch of a small, soft hand on her back, but not from underneath the quilt. She was undecided yet about how to interpret the touch and the owner of the hand when she found that her feet had been released from inside the folds of the quilt. The feather touch of the gentle little hand was now tickling the soles of her feet. The softness, the smallness of size and the faint warmth of the hand persuaded her that it could not be the Navab.

She turned, put out her forehead and peered from under the quilt. Her large eyes opened wide. A girl, fourteen or fifteen years of age, sat at the foot of the bed and was softly running her fingers on the soles of Wazir's feet. She was smiling a little by herself, as if she was hugely enjoying the job. The moment she felt Wazir's eyes on her, she jumped down with a sinuous motion, which was totally free from affectation or haste, and stood near the bed. With a smile which was even more delightful, she bent and salaamed Wazir and said, 'Good morning, Khanam sahib. I submit my obeisance.'

Her voice had a free, open timbre, capable of being heard clearly over the distance of the whole room, and the trill of a bulbul in late winter. Wazir, whose own voice was husky and sweet and subdued like a whisper, and had no capability for loudness or harshness, immediately lost her heart to the girl's voice, dulcet and so different from hers. Did she not apprehend revealing that she was unclothed, she would have risen from her supine position and made the girl sit by her side.

'I came as your wake-up call,' said the girl. 'But here you are, awake by yourself. I hope this slave girl did not disturb you. Did you sleep well?'

Wazir Khanam hugged the quilt some more and pulled it upward and rested her back against the head of the bed. Now she looked at her awakener attentively. She was just about fifteen, or a little less, neither tall nor short, her body slightly plump, suggesting puppy fat rather than heaviness of body. She was very fair of complexion, reminding Wazir of Mirza Ghalib in that aspect. Her nose was somewhat depressed, but not at all unpleasing, and she had a small mouth with delicate lips, naturally rose pink without the aid of betel juice, well formed and with an occasional flutter, suggesting a natural willingness to smile or share a joke, as if she was just about to laugh in merriment. Her eyes, black with a hint of kohl, were like big almonds, again with the hint of a smile not far from them. Her hair was thick and bright and black, the smaller locks in the front were twisted into little braids hanging down upon her forehead. The longer tresses were braided into two, one hanging behind on the back and one cascading in front from her shoulder.

She wore a long kurta of light blue mahmudi, a plain cotton cloth much favoured by the austere or the poorer classes, and above it she wore a violet waistcoat of plain velvet. Her pants were of the same colour but of satin, lightly worked over with golden and silver sprigs. In her ears were small gold circlets, each set with a small diamond, but her nose and neck were without any jewellery. On each of her wrists she wore a wide Hyderabadi bracelet, bright and good-looking but made of shellac and set with artificial gems. Her dupatta, two and a half yards in length, was of muslin, coloured at home in green stripes and crinkled to enhance the effect of the stripes. She wore light, plain shoes open at the heels. On the whole the impression given out by her person was friendly, genteel and homey. And her voice had already won Wazir over who smiled her own winning smile and said: 'No, you did not disturb me at all. But let us know something about you. Who are you, and how did you happen to stray in here so early in the morning?'

'Yes, madam,' she said shyly. 'I was deputed to waken you. I live right here in the haveli. Rahat Afza is my name.'

'Oh, what a lovely name it is!' said Wazir. She thought that the girl could not be a relative of the Navab, but she did not look like a servant either. She might take offence if I asked about her parents. Yet I should know more about her, so that I can find out about the Navab's whereabouts and when I should expect to leave. She spoke with deliberate care, 'So the Navab went off somewhere and left you to be taking care of me. Is that so?'

'No, madam. That is not how it was.' She approached nearer, sat on the bed and began to press Wazir's feet and calves. 'The matter is this . . .' she gave some stress on the word 'matter', 'Navab sahib left for inspection to Pahasu immediately after the prayer before dawn, commanding us mother and daughter to do certain duties. So we are here, discharging them.'

Wazir felt a small stab of pain, which at once became active annoyance. If he could not wait for me to wake up, he could have awakened me before going. Going away without talking to me even, as if I am a mere servant and no words of farewell need be said. But these are not things that I should say in front of this lovely little girl.

Then her annoyance was transformed into pain and deep grief. So the boat of my life will ever look for a captain and an anchor . . . She realized that Rahat Afza was speaking again. 'You are familiar with Habib-un Nisa, she is my mother. She recites many special prayers after the predawn prayer and on top of that she also reads from the Noble Discourse. So she told me, "Rahat Afza, you need not look at my ancient face after the prayer. Go straight to Khanam sahib's—"'

Before Rahat Afza could conclude, Wazir interrupted her impatiently and cried out almost involuntarily, 'But why did the Navab sahib go away like that? Why . . .?'

Rahat Afza realized that Wazir was somewhat perturbed in her heart about the Navab's absence. She decided not to hurry with her answer and continued to press Wazir's feet. Perhaps she was waiting for Wazir to complete her outburst, but Wazir also realized that silence was now preferable.

After a long pause, Rahat Afza said, 'Yes, madam, the fact of the matter is that the Navab sahib rose before the muezzin's call for prayer and took his noble presence to the men's quarters. A dromedary rider from Pahasu presented the news sheet and reported that a gang of dacoits had raided last night and when the Navab's soldiers chased them off, they took shelter in an old fortress in the forest a few miles from the town . . .'

'Oh! How horrible! I hope no lives were lost?'

'No, madam, no lives were lost so far as I know, but they plundered quite a large quantity of valuables, and in order to get the moneylenders to surrender their valuables, they even hurt them with red-hot irons and they also made off with one or two young girls.' Tears welled up in Rahat Afza's eyes and she lost colour. 'One of them was the local Judge's daughter. One of her legs is defective, but she is beautiful like the sun and the moon. Poor thing, she could not even run. One of the brutes caught her with his lasso and thrust her on his horse.'

Rahat Afza was trembling all over, her face pallid. Her voice choked with sobs. Wazir did not know how to comfort the stricken girl. Putting aside her own anxieties, she cried out, 'Oh Lord, oh Lord! How would that poor unfortunate one have survived? The savages did not spare that poor child even! Bibi sahib, do not lose heart. The Lord will be merciful. Navab sahib has gone out there with all possible speed. He will surely rescue that hapless one.'

Wazir caressed Rahat Afza's head and face and making a kissing sound to soothe her, she said: 'Go, have a drink of water, or something soothing. It will stabilize your heart. One does not weep on such occasions. One holds one's courage and prays.'

Rahat Afza dried her tears with her wrap and said, 'Water . . . no . . . The Navab sahib left a message and a present for you and commanded that these be presented to you once you have washed your face.'

Wazir's heart jumped and knocked against her ribs. So the Navab has left something for me! Not wanting to look eager, she spoke with feigned indifference, 'All right, but, Rahat Afza, you must go and have a drink of water. Let your spirits be high and your heart stout. All shall be well when Allah wills. I will rise now and wash my face and get ready. You may return in a short while, right?'

'Actually, I brought for you a cool beverage of almonds and honey. It is extremely beneficial at this time of the year if taken on an empty stomach.'

'All right, child, bring out your drink. In fact, I'm not used to eating or drinking anything immediately after waking up, but I will now, because you say so. But look, be sure to let my people have some milk with their breakfast.'

Quickly, Rahat Afza went into the water room and returned carrying a silver tray with a tall, engraved silver glass; the glass had a silk cover with a tassel of fine, colourful beads on it. She said, 'Here, please drink it up slowly, Khanam sahib. I do assure you, your heart and mind will brighten up no end, God willing. This drink has been prepared according to a prescription of Hakim Ahsanullah Khan sahib; he was personal physician to the Senior Navab sahib, who has his home in Paradise now.'

It was a fact that Wazir did not usually eat or drink anything immediately on waking up. She removed the cover somewhat uncertainly and found the drink to be hibiscus-red in colour with the pleasant suggestion of a whiff of musk and saffron. She took a tentative sip: it was not cold, or even chilled, just moderately cool but it was suggestive of a number of pleasant flavours, including some spices. She felt cheerful, almost exhilarated, as the liquid went down her throat. It seemed to have directly touched her heart, as if the rosy hue of the morning was coursing through her veins.

'It was a truly delightful drink, Rahat Afza, did you make it?'

'Oh no, madam. It was there, already in a bottle. I just took out a measure of it and dissolved it in fresh water. It is my good fortune if you happen to approve of it.'

'Then there must be some alchemy in your mixing of it, I'm sure. Right, now off you go. Please ask your mother to come in after a short while.'

'Should I not send her right now?' Rahat Afza asked a little doubtfully. 'She will help you wash your face and change your clothes.'

My God, again the same hassle! This is no point in arguing with this chit of a girl. I could rid myself of her mother only after so much effort and persuasion. 'All right, let her come whenever she desires.'

The moment Rahat Afza put her foot in the bathroom, Wazir rose quickly and put on her sleeping dress of the previous night. Then she smoothed out the bedsheet where it was crumpled and sat down demurely with the book, as if she had been studying all night.

All the lights in the bedroom were out when she had first woken up after the muezzins' calls. There was only a floor candlestick near the bathroom door, and an English-style candelabrum in one of the alcoves. The English called it 'lump' (lamp) and it burned mustard or sesame oil. Indians mixed one part of flower oil to nine parts of the main fuel so as to reduce the harsh smell of burning. Before she left, Rahat Afza had lit a few more lights so the bedroom was quite bright. The little sunlight that was coming in from the skylights suggested that the sun had moved up in the sky, lighting up the tops of the city's numerous havelis.

She had just opened the book when there was a faint knock at the door to the water room and Habib-un Nisa entered.

'Good morning, Khanam sahib. Did you sleep well?'

'Yes, the night passed well enough, but I am now worried about the Navab.'

'Khanam sahib, there is nothing to worry about, really. God willing, he will be here before the pre-sundown prayers. By that time all will be peace and quiet there, the robbers will have been hanged.'

'And that little girl whom . . . ?'

'Oh, dearest lady, are you heavy in your heart for her? My life be laid down for you, by now she must be back in the benign shade of her father and brothers. Bibi, victory is God's guerdon, none can command it, but our Navab has never been bested in any such campaign. May Allah preserve him; his musketeers were reported to have surrounded that fortress most efficiently. None of the blackguards could have got away.'

It must have been so; it must have certainly been so, Wazir thought sadly, but even an hour or much less is as long as Doomsday for a girl who is being tyrannized by men. It could have been all over for her by the time the Navab's cavalry arrived. In order to change the subject, and also to learn more about Habib-un Nisa, she said, 'Habiba, you never told me last night that you have such a lovely daughter!'

'May you be happy always, Khanam sahib, of what worth is a poor woman or her daughter? But the fact of the matter is that there was no occasion to narrate these details last night. Please take your noble self to the water room and let me help you wash your face and change your clothes. We will then submit for your inspection the present left for you by the Navab.'

Wazir felt like retorting: Why the precondition? Can the gift not be proffered before I have washed? Leastways, they could tell me what it is. There is so much talk bouncing back and forth but the real matter stays unrevealed. However, she knew that restraint and caution were important in such situations, so she suppressed her impatience—and also her curiosity—and quietly went through the lengthy procedures of toilette and change of clothes.

Conversation during the change of clothes gave Wazir the information that Habiba's husband, who was called Ghulam Nabi, came from the territory of Merath near Delhi and had been in the employ of Navab Ahmad Bakhsh Khan as a sepoy at his Court. He lost his life fighting in a campaign similar to the one in which Navab Shamsuddin Ahmad Khan was presently engaged. Habib-un Nisa was big with child at that time and was delivered of a daughter soon after. Navab Ahmad Bakhsh Khan of sacred memory bore the entire expenses of her delivery and confinement and later appointed Habiba to be the maid to Bahu Khanam, who was Shamsuddin Ahmad Khan's mother. Since then, mother and daughter had become permanent domestics at the Navab's haveli. Habiba was now senior maid and Rahat Afza her attendant.

There was no dearth of men in the haveli ready to have a fling with Habiba, or even make her a mistress or concubine. Some might not even have baulked at forcibly having their way with her, but everybody stood in such dire awe of the Navab that none dared raise an eye at her. May God preserve him, our present Navab was no less bountiful and generous in providing for his servants. Now the greatest desire of both mother and daughter was to be permanently given over in the employ of Khanam sahib. They did not even expect a regular salary: Habiba's pension for her husband's past services was still paid to her regularly and in addition were tips, rewards and dresses on appropriate occasions.

The time taken in toilette and dressing up passed comfortably as Habiba chatted away about herself. Fully dressed and made up, Wazir now sat in the large, easy chair that she had used the previous night when she first came in. Almost at once, Rahat Afza arrived with a small wooden box in her hand.

'Congratulations, and may you live long and secure, Khanam sahib,' said Rahat Afza, as she put the box on one of the wide arms of the chair. 'Let this present from our Revered Navab be auspicious!'

'And may it please God for you to gain always even better benefactions!' Habiba added her bit of good wishes. She saw that Wazir was demurring somewhat to open the box, so she urged her: 'Come, please open it. You shouldn't feel diffident. Open it and be done with it.'

She also wanted to say, 'Open, that we too may get to see your presents.' But she held her tongue. There was not enough familiarity between them for being somewhat playful, given her distance as a serving woman. It was for Wazir to take the first steps in this case.

The box, about eight inches long and four inches high, was of heavy Kashmiri walnut carved with Chinese patterns. Its interior was lined in velvet and at the centre of it sat a smaller silver box shaped like a dried-out peepul leaf, in filigree work so fine that the thinnest vein could be seen and the effect was that of the finest silver netting. The silver, being pure and antique, was tarnished, and strengthened the impression of a dried-up leaf. Wazir was not unfamiliar with the silver filigree work that came from Cuttack, but had never seen a work so finished and so delicate that one was afraid to even touch it.

A piece of folded paper and a ring could be seen clearly beneath the filigree netting of the box. Wazir was glad to see that it was not a trick box and could be opened in the normal way, or her ingenuity might have been put to the test. She took out the piece of paper first, and both Habiba and Rahat Afza immediately drew aside and became busy in other chores around the bedroom. Rahat Afza began to smooth the bedsheet and carefully fold the large quilt. Habiba began to scrape off the wax congealed in the candlesticks and the candleholders.

Wazir opened the message. Outwardly, it was folded in the usual four folds, but when opened, it became a small four-petalled flower. A delicate wave of the attar of henna, soft and warm, caressed her nostrils. Wazir felt as if she had come in from the cool outdoors and Shamsuddin Ahmad's fingers had touched her cheeks. It was a light-blue paper, on which was inscribed the following Persian verse in saffron-gold ink:

Last night, my beautiful, vivacious love drank with me, naked:
A chandelierful of candles, it seemed, was lit up right into my side.

Wazir felt the lobes of her ears, then her brow, then her cheeks blush hot. She could also not help enjoying the beauty and the appositeness of the verse. Quickly, she twisted the paper in a small pellet and pushed it under her collar, but there was still the possibility of the paper being glimpsed or slipping from under the thin bodice, so she pushed it into the safety of her cleavage and prayed in her heart for it to remain secure until she reached home.

'Please, Khanam sahib, do take a look at the ring as well!' said Rahat Afza, with boldness driven by a tiny coquettish impulse. 'All of us are dying to see how it looks.'

Wazir put her hand inside the box and was stunned and dazzled. Purest gold, almost malleable to the touch, at least five grams in weight; the first gemstone was a deep-green emerald carved in the shape of a grape leaf, at one end was a ruby the size of half a chickpea, carved like a bunch of grapes and supported by a small leaf of its own. Important details of the leaf and the fruit were distinct and it seemed that both came from one stone. The dark-green radiance of the emerald was lightly reflected upon the ruby and the rosy red of the ruby slightly toned down the greenness of the emerald. Below the emerald leaf and the ruby fruit were four small diamonds of the size of mustard seeds, but the diamonds were cut so that each bezel reflected light on its own, giving the impression of a tiny sparkler.

In their own nature, neither the ruby nor the emerald were overly bright gems, and an emerald, however costly, will have small blemishes. The value of these stones was in their rang (colour) and dhang (cutting), but what those stones lacked in lustre had been made up by the glow of pure yellow gold, and like gilding on the lily, by the brilliance of the diamonds.

'Oh my!' Rahat Afza involuntarily drew a sigh of pleasure. 'It must have cost two . . .'

She had wanted to say that the ring must have cost two or even two and a half thousand rupees, but Habib-un Nisa shut her up with a glare. It was not good manners to assess the price of a gift, especially in front of the masters. Rahat Afza finished lamely, 'It must have cost two or two and a half days' labour and taken two or three craftsmen, I am sure, to make it.'

'Undoubtedly,' Habiba said, 'this ring is to jewellery what our Khanam is to beauty and our Nawwab to the nobility.' She pronounced 'Navab' as 'Nawwab' in the Arabic way, for additional stress.

'There, Habiba, that is too much really! You are mashing my poor self with the Navab!' Wazir smiled. 'But the fact of the matter is that rings like these suit only princesses and the nobility.'

Before Habiba could say something in reply, there was a soft knock on the main door. Quickly, Rahat Afza went up, opened the door a little and looked out. A bit of the morning light, pleasant like a freshly washed sheet, slipped into the room along with the murmur of the fountain. She spoke in low tones with the person at the door and saw the expectant eyes of the women upon her when she turned after closing the door. Before they could say something, Rahat Afza spoke: 'Khanam sahib, your servants were asked if they would like to eat breakfast from the haveli's kitchen or if they would prefer to have provisions given to them for cooking on their own.'

She stopped for breath, and Wazir asked, 'Good. So then what did they prefer?'

'Madam, they submitted that kindling and pots and pans are all available in the servants' kitchen, so they would prefer to do their own cooking, should they be given their rations.' She stopped again, perhaps trying to recall what provisions exactly were issued. Then she spoke quickly as if reading out from a list: 'Wheat flour, one seer; chickpeas pulse or green-skinned chickpeas, quarter seer; suji, one-eighth of a seer; ghee, one-sixteenth of a seer; mustard oil, one-sixteenth of a seer; sugar, white, one-tenth of a seer, and sugar, black, one quarter of a seer; and cash, two royal paise. That is the daily ration given here to all servants who do not eat at His Honour's kitchen.'

'Good. Very good,' said Wazir. 'So are they done eating?'

'Please, yes, Khanam sahib . . . I am sorry, I forgot something. As per the command of the Exalted Khanam, each servant was also given a quart of buffalo's milk and two spoonfuls of brown sugar.'

'As Allah wills! Habiba, this young girl of yours is an extremely good manager. How well she performs all her duties!' Wazir looked at Rahat Afza with admiration and affection, and Rahat Afza's face turned pink with pleasure and bashful modesty.

'Daughter dear, you did not report if breakfast is over in the servants' quarters. And are you going to feed the Exalted Khanam sahib too, or will you starve her?' Habiba asked her.

'Khanam sahib's servants must have finished their breakfast. As for Khanam sahib, Amma ji has already organized everything. I await orders,' Rahat Afza answered quickly.

Wazir felt a little abashed, if not ashamed concerning the mother–daughter duo; they had been busy looking after her, running around everywhere like whirligigs. Better I save them from more duty. She also worried a little about the Navab's schedule. Lest he decide to visit me in Sirki Walan in the evening and I while away the time here undecided? And if the dinner is anything to go by, breakfast won't be over before it is midday.

Considering all this, she smiled pleasantly and said, 'My good Habiba, I should be truly grateful if you let me go now. Much better if you did not discommode yourself feeding me breakfast. There is no one there at my house; I shouldn't leave it empty any longer.'

'You command rightly, but Navab sahib will have me for breakfast if he gets to know that I let you go away with an empty stomach. Do please accede to my plea: eat just a tiny little bit, then go. I will be spared losing my nose and my head of hair.'

This argument was perhaps not entirely based on truth, but Wazir could see no way to reject such forceful pleading. She said, 'All right, let the tablecloth be spread. But I conjure you with the Big Bread between us, do not have the full breakfast laid for me.'

Despite the conjuration with the Quran, and despite Wazir's constant refusal to eat much, the sun was almost noon-high in the sky before breakfast could be done away with. Habib-un Nisa and Rahat Afza said tearful goodbyes and handed her into her carriage from the door of the guest house, rather than at the main gate used by her the previous night, thus assuring a certain anonymity for her.

There was not much distance to cover to Sirki Walan, and the horses and the attendants were all fresh and rested. They trotted away, reaching their destination in about half an hour. The multitude of buyers and sellers was growing in Chandni Chowk by the moment, and there was no dearth there of resplendent and yet more resplendent bullock carts, nalkis, tomjohns, palanquins and sedans hurrying away in all directions like shooting stars. In such an environment, a buggy, even if so splendid as the one in which Wazir rode, would not be noticed at all. Wazir thought that she was home and dry, safe from prying eyes and unnoticed by the throng.

She did not know that William Fraser's spies were all over the place. There were at least two servants at the haveli of Shamsuddin Ahmad Khan, who reported to the Navab Senior Sahib Bahadur independently. The advantage of having two spies in the same place was obvious: information purveyed by one could be checked against the other for lies, half-truths, intended or unintended omissions or exaggerations. The other point was that each one believed himself to be the only one spying on behalf of the Navab Resident Bahadur and was thus keen to prove his loyalty in the fullest possible measure.

That was how a full and explicit account of the previous night and that morning's doings had reached William Fraser even before Shamsuddin Ahmad Khan had returned from Pahasu. On the other side, the informants of Navab Yusuf Ali Khan had reported to him on the events of the previous night. Yusuf Ali Khan was quite content with the course of the events, but Fraser tied himself into myriad knots of displeasure at the news. It was as if gross curls of black smoke rose from the oven of his chest and broke through to the stove of his head. It was now extremely necessary for him to visit condign punishment on Shamsuddin Ahmad, and if possible, on Chhoti Begam as well.

36

Hakim Ahsanullah Khan meets William Fraser with reluctance and subsequently warns Navab Shamsuddin Ahmad Khan of Fraser's unsavoury intentions

WITHIN TWO OR three days of getting the news of the union of Wazir Khanam and Shamsuddin Ahmad Khan, Fraser made his preparations. First of all, he sent a report to Calcutta about the robbery in Pahasu, making only a brief mention of the speed and efficiency of Shamsuddin Ahmad Khan in dealing with the malefactors. The Navab had destroyed the gang, publicly hanged two of their ring leaders and had recovered the two abducted girls and most of the property looted by the dacoits. Fraser reported these as mainly rumours, and implied that the success, as it was, of the expedition against the marauders did not owe much to the strategy, leadership or personal valour of the Navab. In fact, he reported the event as proof of the weak grasp of the Navab on his territories.

Fraser reasserted his view that the previous Resident, Mr Hawkins, had erred in recognizing Shamsuddin Ahmad's undisputed right to the entire territory ruled by his father, Navab Ahmad Bakhsh Khan. He wrote:

> I therefore resubmit my recommendation to the Governor General in Council that the division of the State effected by Dilawar-ul Mulk Navab Ahmad Bakhsh Khan in the presence of Sir Charles Metcalfe be reinstated so that the other two fatherless children of the late Navab, namely, Aminuddin Ahmad and Ziauddin Ahmad, may get what is their rightful claim and also support their mother and sister in a manner suited to their status.

Fraser's use of the term 'Governor General in Council' was a calculated move. Though he did not expect that the Navab Governor General Lord

William Bentinck Bahadur would be amenable to decide in favour of Shamsuddin Ahmad Khan on consideration of some valuable and costly gifts, nor was the matter of such import as to deserve being placed before the Council, he hoped that his words might prompt the Political Department in the Writers' Building to submit it before the Council anyway. Should the case go before the Council, the Governor General would not take a decision as he pleased, even if he were inclined to support Shamsuddin Ahmad Khan. Further, the Council in those days was generally minded against the 'native' navabs and rajahs and was almost certain to uphold the actions of the officers of the Company, namely, Sir David Ochterlony and Sir Charles Metcalfe.

Fraser dispatched his report, thought for another day, and ordered that Hakim Ahsanullah Khan be summoned to the Residency.

Hakim Ahsanullah Khan was originally from Kashmir. He traced his descent to Abu Bakr Siddiq, the first Caliph of Islam. From the Pearl Scattering Court of Muizz-ud Duniya wa al-Din Abu Nasr Muin-ud Din Muhammad Akbar Shah II, he had been granted the grand title of Umdat-ul Mulk Haziq-uz Zaman. In the future, he was to be accorded the posts of Khan-e-Saman (Administrator General), Prime Minister and the Emperor's Personal Physician, and the even grander titles of Ihtiram-ud Daulah Umdat-ul Hukama Mutamad-ul Mulk Sabit Jang, from the Heaven Simulating Portal of Abu Zafar Muhammad Sirajuddin Bahadur Shah II.

At the time of writing, the entire city of Delhi was ringing with the hakim's name and fame as a man of learning and a physician of the greatest proficiency. He was routinely compared to Rhazes and Avicenna. It was also the common view that apart from his unique excellence as a physician, he was adept at the art and craft of statesmanship and was a man of extremely wide culture and learning.

The hakim was also, in keeping with the culture of that age, well versed in poetry and other literary arts. Hakim Momin Khan Momin, one of Delhi's leading poets in Persian and Hindi, expert physician, astrologer and master chess player, was his close cousin. Among his dear friends he counted such eminent poets and scholars as Mirza Asadullah Khan Ghalib, Shaikh Muhammad Ibrahim Zauq, Navab Muhammad Mustafa Khan Sheftah, the great polymath Fazl-e-Haq Khairabadi, Imam Bakhsh Sahbai and many others. This was the reason why the meeting chamber of his haveli at Chitli Qabr was the centre of attraction for not just the sick and the infirm, but also the nobility, poets and men of learning.

In those days, there were countless mansions, havelis, modest homes and poorer people's tenements spread around Chitli Qabr to what is now Delhi Gate. In this area were also to be found the mansion and madrasa of Shah Abdul Aziz, the great Sufi and man of Islamic learning, and the haveli of Dabir-ud Daulah Syed Farid Khan (grandfather of the man who was to become nationally famous as Syed Ahmad Khan), as well as that of Hakim Sanaullah Khan, poet and physician. From Chitli Qabr to Kucha Chelan was a whole different world of shops and workshops and homes of shoemakers, needle makers, and numerous other artisans. Hakim Ahsanullah Khan's huge haveli seemed to be the centre of that teeming complex.

The hakim owned a number of havelis in the city but he held his morning surgery at the haveli in Chitli Qabr. This was because the area was heavily populated, and as described above, the neighbourhood was home to a number of other distinguished men of learning and experts in law and religion. He took his place in the clinic after performing the late-morning prayer at about eight o'clock, and stayed until the afternoon prayer. Nothing, not even the most inclement weather or untoward happening, could upset this schedule. He had not yet purchased the huge and splendid haveli of Badal Beg in Sirki Walan which became a site to visit for tourists and others after he had effected many changes and improvements in it by his creativity in design and expertise in architecture and engineering.

Hakim Ahsanullah Khan was quite young when Navab Ahmad Bakhsh Khan Rustam Jang appointed him his personal physician and made available for his residence a substantial part of his own haveli in Ballimaran. As narrated above, Shamsuddin Ahmad (b. 1810) had attained adulthood when Navab Ahmad Bakhsh Khan died in 1827. His other two sons Aminuddin Ahmad (b. 1814) and Ziauddin Ahmad (b. 1821) were minors at that time. We also saw that Shamsuddin Ahmad had rejected the division of the State effected by his father and had taken possession of all three segments of their father's vast holdings, namely, Firozepur Jhirka, Loharu and Pahasu.

Shamsuddin Ahmad Khan had offered to retain Hakim Ahsanullah Khan as his personal physician, but the hakim's wise and shrewd judgement perhaps foresaw that Shamsuddin Ahmad, by depriving his brothers of their due share, had sowed the poison of discord in his House and the seed would later grow into a fiery tree of dissonance and dissension. He therefore politely refused the offer and shortly thereafter vacated the Navab's haveli in Ballimaran.

Soon enough, Navab Faiz Muhammad Khan of Jhajjar appointed Hakim Ahsanullah Khan to be his personal physician. Kalan Mahal, a well-known neighbourhood of Delhi, popularly known as Kala Mahal, was owned entirely by Faiz Muhammad Khan. He allotted to the hakim a haveli called Rang Mahal in that same neighbourhood for his residence. At that time, Hakim Imamuddin held the honour of being personal physician to the Shadow of God, the Presence, Akbar Shah II. Hakim Imamuddin was not only counted among the chiefest of Delhi's physicians, but was also held to be a true man of God. As chance would have it, the King Emperor developed a medical problem, which Hakim Imamuddin, for all his knowledge and experience, could not diagnose, far less treat successfully.

Hakim Ahsanullah Khan was then summoned for a second opinion and as Allah wills, he was able to treat and cure the Emperor within a short time. Aside from rewards and costly presents, the Shadow of God bestowed upon the hakim all three types of honours: Khan, Mulk and Zaman. Thus Hakim Ahsanullah was now proclaimed Umdat-ul Mulk Haziq-uz Zaman Hakim Ahsanullah Khan. A few weeks later, the Emperor permitted Hakim Imamuddin to quit his post and appointed Ahsanullah Khan in his place.

What with his extremely pleasing bedside manners, humility, soft speech, and excellence in both diagnosing and prescribing, Hakim Ahsanullah Khan was the pupil of Delhi's eyes. Nobleman and commoner, whether Hindu or Muslim, swore by him. The hakim was tall and well built but not heavy bodied, he had small but bright eyes and was brown of complexion with his face lightly pockmarked with the smallpox contracted in childhood. He had a full beard, thick black, but not too long, cut circular in the style of physicians and men of learning, and was always clad in white.

He held his clinic in the divan khanah: a very long and slightly less wide hall. Next to its eastern wall was a spacious wooden platform, covered with cushions over which was spread a snow-white sheet in the centre of which was placed a white, green and azure silk carpet. The hakim sat on it with his legs tucked under him, as if on a throne. On both sides of him on the platform sat a prescription writer. The patients sat on long benches or small chairs in front of the wooden platforms in two rows to the right and the left.

Beginning from the right and alternating to the left, Hakim sahib examined the patients one by one. Howsoever many patients he saw in a sitting, there was never any sign of strain in his demeanour, or a manner that suggested dullness of routine and impersonality. Indeed, it was rarely that the patient needed to describe his ailment or symptoms. Hakim sahib felt his right pulse and that was sufficient in most cases. Sometimes he felt the pulse on both wrists, especially when the patient reported some condition that the Hakim sahib had not expected. Usually, the pulse of the right wrist would reveal everything to him. Sometimes he would himself narrate some part of the patient's medical history: 'You married quite late, did you not?' Or, 'Mustard oil was used much in your family for cooking.' Or, 'There is inflammation in your right kidney. On the first occurrence, you must have had fever. Did you not consult a physician then?'

Once he had reached his diagnosis, Hakim sahib would dictate the prescription to the prescription writer on the appropriate side. He spoke fast, and in almost a whisper. The writer would then explain the regime to the patient who might ask, again in a near whisper, a question or two if clarification was needed. The consulting hall was almost always quiet; the ambience was of awe and majesty.

There was no consulting fee. There was an apothecary near the haveli who was the unofficial dispenser of medicines and charged the appropriate price for it. It was not necessary for the patient to buy the medication from the apothecary. Sometimes Hakim sahib would, for reasons that only he knew of, have a mysterious sign on the prescription to indicate that no price should be charged on this prescription, or it should be half the price.

A mace-bearer and a lance-bearer, deputed by William Fraser, entered the hakim's surgery when it was nearing midday. The newcomers were pointed to the vacant seats where they should sit and await their turn, but they pressed forward boldly and stopped in front of the hakim. The mace-bearer salaamed and said: 'Your Honour is remembered by the Senior Sahib Bahadur.'

Many of the waiting patients' brows clouded. One reason for their displeasure was that they did not believe the Resident to have the authority to summon a personal employee of the Emperor. Some were unhappy that the Hakim sahib would now rise and they would not get to consult him that day. Hakim Ahsanullah Khan inquired in his normal, cool voice, 'What is the matter? Is he feeling poorly?'

'We do not know anything, Your Honour. We were just commanded to go and convey the Grand Sahib's greetings to Hakim sahib and come back to the Residency along with him.'

'I'm seeing patients at present. I will rise a little before the afternoon prayer and will come with you after I'm through with the prayers.'

'But the Grand Sahib . . .'

Hakim sahib interrupted the mace-bearer firmly, but without a hint of unpleasantness or petulance. 'I cannot leave so many patients here who wait to be seen by me. If you wish, you can go back to the Navab Resident Bahadur and convey to him what I said.'

Obviously the two servants had no choice but to sit quietly in a corner and wait. Hakim Ahsanullah arose at his usual time, offered his prayers and proceeded to the Residency in his open palanquin. The two couriers walked fast alongside.

It was about four o'clock in the afternoon when the hakim's palanquin entered the gates of the Residency. The keeper of the time house stated that the Senior Sahib Bahadur must have risen, and Hakim sahib could go in, perhaps he might be given audience.

The conversation between Fraser and Hakim Ahsanullah Khan took place not in the large meeting chamber, but in Fraser's private office, known as the Darbar Room. Bookshelves containing Greek, Latin, English and Persian volumes adorned the walls up to the ceiling. At the centre was a large and impressive table, behind which sat William Fraser in full official dress. He looked quite impressive with a staff-bearer and a flywhisk-bearer behind him, a mace-bearer to his right, with a bundle of papers, and numerous papers spread on the table. Fraser's eyes were on the papers when the doorman-cum-mace-bearer called out: 'Umdat-ul Mulk Hakim Ahsanullah Khan Bahadur.'

Fraser looked up. Before he could gesture for Hakim sahib to sit, Hakim Ahsanullah raised his right hand in salutation and sat on a chair in front of the table. Fraser half rose to greet the hakim, waved to the servants to leave, and said, 'Umdat-ul Mulk, you brought your Noble Presence here, I am much indebted.'

Hakim sahib made no reply, except bending his head a little in acknowledgement, as if intimating to Fraser that here he was before him as summoned.

Fraser waited for a second, as if expecting some reply, but when he found that the hakim was not minded to spend time in routine conversation, he said, 'Umdat-ul Mulk, everyone acknowledges your statesman-like qualities and your wisdom.'

Now Hakim Ahsanullah Khan had no choice but to speak. He rose a little in his seat, offered another salute by raising his right hand, and said, 'It is nothing but Navab Resident Bahadur's diffusive benevolence and the enhancement of my value by him.'

Fraser smiled. 'Your wisdom is the reason why I have troubled you to come here.'

'I will not stint at all from any service that I can perform.' The hakim's tone was grave, but dry and devoid of effusiveness.

'Hakim sahib, taken as a whole, I have no complaints against Delhi or the people of Delhi. But I regret to see Navab Shamsuddin Ahmad's laxity and ineptness in matters of administration of his State. Some of his actions have pained me personally. I would like you to deliver an admonition to him and advise him to treat me as his elder and well-wisher as before and not do anything that may cause unhappiness to me and spell trouble for him.'

Fraser paused for a moment, as if weighing in his mind if he should disclose this fact or not, and then said, 'Shamsuddin Ahmad's activities could cause vexation to the Navab Governor General Bahadur as well.'

In his turn, Hakim Ahsanullah Khan remained silent for a few seconds. Fraser was entirely out of order and his tactics were devoid of statesmanship. If he had some rancour in his heart against the young Navab, it was his problem entirely, and it was he who should find a solution to his predicament.

'It must be quite clear to the brilliant intellect of the Senior Sahib Bahadur that I wield no influence on Navab Shamsuddin Ahmad khan, or in fact on any of the progeny of Navab Ahmad Bakhsh Khan.'

'But you have been personal physician to the late Navab. Shamsuddin Ahmad has played on your knees.'

'Quite true, sir. But now there is neither the Navab, nor my rank as his physician.'

A wave of displeasure ran across Fraser's countenance. These Indian Mussulmans are extremely churlish and proud. And this fellow does not seem to be regardful of his own well- or ill-being. Now Fraser spoke up somewhat forcefully, 'Hakim sahib, we are fully conversant with what goes on here. There is nothing in Delhi that is not transparent to me. You're most suited for the job that I've chosen you to perform.'

'Very well, I'll do all that I can. I won't be deficient at all.'

'You should warn Shamsuddin Ahmad that Chhoti Begam has been chosen by another's eye. So he should give up thoughts of wooing her. You may tell him in plain words: this is my message to him and you have been given this message without any intermediary.'

'I am grateful to the Senior Sahib Bahadur for the confidence that he reposes in me, but I can have no pressure or influence to bring on Shamsuddin Ahmad, nor is it my station to be the bearer of your message to him.'

'Why? Why is it not your station?' Fraser was now openly infuriated. 'Are you not loyal to the Honourable Company Bahadur?'

'I beg your pardon, but I do not imagine that this matter has any bearing on the question of one's loyalty to the Honourable Company,' Hakim Ahsanullah Khan answered coldly. 'And even if it had, I eat the King's salt, not the Company's salt.'

'And your King eats the Honourable Company's salt, Umdat-ul Mulk Hakim Ahsanullah Khan.'

'It is a matter of the point of view, Navab Resident Bahadur,' the hakim spoke even more drily, almost disdainfully. 'The Shadow of God and his ancestors have been ruling from the throne of Delhi for more than two hundred years now.'

'I have not summoned you here for a history lesson, Hakim sahib.'

'Yes, sir. Quite. Nor have you summoned me here to write a prescription for the juice of the viper's bugloss. And I know just these two things. I am sorry I proved worthless for you.'

Hakim Ahsanullah Khan rose from his chair, made his salaams with full dignity and gravity, and went out of the room. Leaving the Darbar Room without permission was direly insulting, but Fraser swallowed it quietly, for he knew that taxing the hakim would only lead to his own ridicule. But a quiet war began that day between the hakim and Fraser. In fact, not only Fraser, every Resident after Fraser seemed to bear some grudge against the hakim, or perhaps there was some confidential note in the records of the Residency to the effect that Hakim Ahsanullah Khan should not be shown any kindness or consideration. Once, during the reign of Bahadur Shah II, Hakim Ahsanullah Khan in fact sought the King's intercession to remove any adverse feelings against him in the Residency. The King's efforts availed nothing and Hakim Ahsanullah Khan remained under a shadow as far as the Residency was concerned.

*

William Fraser's mansion was at quite a distance from the Auspicious Haveli, and the hakim was apprehensive of missing the late-afternoon prayers before he arrived there. So he decided to do the prayer in the Jami Masjid at Fatehpuri before proceeding to Lahori Darwazah to seek audience with the King whose magnificence rivalled Jamshed's splendour. He considered it necessary to report the whole conversation to His Majesty for two reasons. One, it was his duty to convey to the King any information that came his way about Navab Shamsuddin Ahmad Khan or any Indian noble. Two, Fraser had committed a breach of protocol in summoning Hakim Ahsanullah Khan directly to the Residency. Fraser had no authority over the hakim. Did he wish to consult him for any reason, he should have obtained the King's consent to do so.

The evening Durbar had risen. The Shadow of God was about to proceed to dinner, but Hakim Ahsanullah Khan was permitted audience. The King heard Hakim Ahsanullah Khan's statement in silence. He, of course, did not at all like Fraser's audacity, but it was expedient to say nothing before the hakim. For, the displeasure of kings is not without consequences, and Akbar Shah II had no power of his own to take any effective step against the Resident. As the Hindi saying went: 'True might is your own might, or you burn bright.' Thus it was contrary to the Royal wisdom to give any kind of expression to his emotions.

A complaint could certainly be made to the Governor General, but even such action should be taken only when the time and occasion were appropriate. In any case, the result was a foregone conclusion. Although until the time of Akbar Shah II, the King could correspond directly with the Governor General (later even this privilege—if privilege it was—ceased to be), yet the Resident invariably got to know of the Royal communication and its contents. More often than not, the Royal Missive was transmitted to none other than the Resident himself for his report or for being deposited in the archives.

Having obtained permission to leave from the King whose pavilion rivals that of Mars, Hakim Ahsanullah Khan departed from the Divan-e Khas. The muezzin of Moti Masjid was calling for the evening prayers; he offered the prayers there and postponing the extra prayers that he was wont to do at that time, he proceeded to Shamsuddin Ahmad Khan's haveli in Daryaganj. Not finding the Nawab there, he instructed the officer at the gate that the Nawab be informed of his visit and requested that he come see him at his convenience.

The meeting with Fraser, and his uncalled-for and unreasonable demands had upset Hakim Ahsanullah Khan greatly, and the main reason for his feelings of distress was Fraser's arrogant belief that he was entitled to intervene in the private and domestic affairs of the nobility of Hindustan. This did not augur well for Indians and India. Granted that Fraser had some kind of claim on Shamsuddin Ahmad: the latter addressed him as 'uncle'; but that was purely a family matter. In fact, the nature of Fraser's relations with Shamsuddin Ahmad made it all the more imperative for him to ignore and turn a blind eye to affairs which had nothing to do with politics or governance.

But the Firangee mind was by nature haughty, tyrannical and overbearing. The Hakim was apprehensive that the haughtiness of the English and their disdainful attitude towards Indians would grow in proportion to the growth of their power. The riches of the wealthy, the distinguished ancestry of the high-born, the poor man's sense of honour: the crops of all would be cut down with the same scythe of scorn. And should these people become rulers of Hind, they would outdo the Pharaohs and the Nimrods in repression and bloodshed.

The next morning, Shamsuddin Ahmad called upon the hakim who gave him, in confidence, a full account of what had transpired with Fraser. He also told the Navab that he already had conveyed a similar report to the Presence's auspicious ears. Hakim sahib, however, did not evince any curiosity about Chhoti Begam, nor did he offer any counsel to the Navab about his future conduct. The Navab, quite unlike the King's sedate self-discipline, did not at all feel inhibited against expressing his displeasure and uttering various kinds of threats against Fraser.

Having done his duty by the young Navab, the hakim devoted his attention to his clinic where there was, for some reason, a greater throng of patients than usual. Shamsuddin Ahmad returned to his haveli in Ballimaran and immediately dispatched two energetic dromedary riders to Loharu with the instruction to return post-haste with a posse of eight stalwarts skilled in fighting with cudgels. Should they not find the required number or quality in the Fort, immediate enlistment should be effected from among the local populace. They must, under any circumstance, report to him in Delhi by the morning of the third day. He then instructed his steward to depute four of the fighters in Sirki Walan at Wazir Khanam sahib's residence by day and the other four at the same place by night. They should not leave their post even for a minute and if any of them was found guilty in this regard, they would have their arms and legs broken before they were dismissed back to Loharu. He further ordered that pending the arrival of the posse from Loharu, an equal number of reliable and resolute staff-bearers from the haveli should be drafted for the duty.

37

William Fraser pays a visit to Wazir Khanam at Sirki Walan, stirring up anxieties and fears

MANJHLI BEGAM'S HEART was all but lost in thoughts of Chhoti. What had transpired with Navab Shamsuddin Ahmad? She was anxious, and also worried. It had been nearly six months since Chhoti came back from Jaipur. It was now supremely important for some protector or support to be found for her: a person who should have her approval. If marriage was not possible immediately, so be it, but let some responsible and respectable person take her into his house in a long-term arrangement; even that would be something worth having. It often happened that many such connections grew and matured from mere erotic friendship or loverly entertainment into a relationship which rivalled or was even stronger than marriage. In any case, was there really a difference between marriage and a stable relationship? There were many men nowadays who divorced their wives without any thought or regard for the woman; and there were yet others who openly and freely maintained relationships with several women at the same time. And there were some who respected and honoured marriageless relationships far more and for far longer than ordinary people did their so-called legal spouses.

Indeed, luck or destiny seemed to play a much greater role in matters of human relations than was generally recognized. If the marriage bed and the status of mistress of the house were written for you, you must get it, sooner or later. Chhoti was of no considerable age really; in fact, she was still quite young. But the time was so evil that for numerous girls, youth and ageing came at the same time, or at best with a gap of merely a year or two. Apparently, Navab Shamsuddin Ahmad was romantically inclined towards Chhoti. Now should their union be destined to happen, the doors of good fortune would open for her. No diminution in romantic regard and considerateness, no lack of ordinary, respectable comforts, plenty of servants and domestic help . . . if such could be a woman's lot, she would go through life rendering thanks every day to the Almighty.

Honour was the most important thing in life. How well did our elders put it: 'Do honour and have honour done to you.' And the protective shade of some nobleman's fidelity was essential for living honourably. Should Navab Shamsuddin Ahmad Khan grasp Chhoti's arm and provide her with a corner in which she could live her life securely and with honour, Chhoti must accept the offer. But she was crazy, poor thing; she talked of love and courtly behaviour and romance in the daily course of life. Was it not artless innocence to seek tenderness and lasting adoration in this, the thirteenth, century? Ingenuous and still untutored in the ways of the world, she was dying for love, while the real thing was security, and honour.

What price love, and how long does it last? It is a butterfly of the springtime, extremely pleasing and colourful and romantic, but it falls and dies so fast! Well, anyway, a door seems to be opening for her now. After the passing of Blak sahib she had been left alone, with nowhere to go after she had rejected the conventional options proposed by Bari Baji.

*

The moment Umdah Khanam was informed of Wazir Khanam's safe and happy return, she ordered her carriage and had herself driven straight to Sirki Walan. The anxiety burning her heart cooled when she saw Wazir's bright—in fact, sparkling—visage. The sisters hugged each other for many minutes and before Umdah inquired about any gifts that the Navab may have given her, Wazir showed her the ring. She then narrated a brief account of her night.

'Little Lady, may Allah make it auspicious for you. You have been suitably rewarded for your uncomplaining forbearance. Now you will rule and govern like a princess! The Navab has immeasurable wealth, matches you in looks and age, and above all, he is mad about you. Now all manner of things will be well!'

Umdah Khanam had given no thought or significance to the question of William Fraser. Nor did Fraser ever suggest to Navab Yusuf Ali Khan that he desired something from Wazir Khanam. Umdah Khanam and Yusuf Ali Khan were both unaware that Fraser had designs on Wazir Khanam. Since

Fraser had not apparently taken any steps to invite her or visit her again, they understood this to indicate his lack of interest in Wazir, while in fact Fraser was actually watching the situation quite keenly.

He was quite put out when he was informed by his spies about Shamsuddin Ahmad visiting Chhoti Begam the very next day after his dinner party. Still, he led himself to believe that the Navab's attraction for her meant nothing more than a few days' fling, if that; his passion would cool off quickly and the fever of the affair would abate in no time. When his spies reported on the exchange of messages and gifts between them, he realized that matters were going far, or maybe had already progressed far enough. Before he could plan a suitable strategy to bring Wazir to him or go visit her, he was informed about Wazir's stay overnight at the Navab's guest house in the haveli at Daryaganj. Now he was well and truly mad, but Umdah Khanam and Navab Yusuf Ali Khan had no idea about these matters. Umdah was quite certain that there was nothing now to impede the course of the romance between Shamsuddin Ahmad Khan and Chhoti, and in fact, Wazir too had no perception at all of the danger that lurked from Fraser.

'Baji, it is only due to your earnest prayers and the ascendant fortune of Navab Yusuf Ali Khan sahib that my affairs have been pointed in the right direction. But . . . but I have one perplexity still.' Wazir spoke hesitantly.

'Perplexity, confusion? Why and what is it? Did the Navab say something or hint at something which has put you in doubt?'

'No, it is not that,' Wazir dragged out the 'no', as if she did not want to articulate what troubled her. She was silent for a few moments. Then, with her head bent, and wringing and twisting a corner of her dupatta, she said, 'No. There are no fears in my heart, really. But the Navab has not made things clear at all.'

'Look at the girl! She's now exercised about the clarity of things! Would someone give away such a costly ring for no reason at all? Would someone go to such lengths of surrender without cause?'

'That is all very well, Baji, but he only spoke in hints and vague suggestions. The main issues are unresolved. He does not make clear what exactly he wants from me.'

Manjhli was minded to ask, 'And what compacts and covenants did that Mattan Blak Firangee—well, he deserved his death—seal with you? If he took you away, sweeping you off your feet, he could have also married you!

All right, he could not enter into an Islamic wedlock, but what stopped him from registering and signing papers in a civil court? None, of course, have power over life and death. But alive or dead, that Nazarene made absolutely no provision for you!'

She could not say these things, obviously, but it also occurred to her that Chhoti's dilemma flowed from that very reality: Blak sahib went off, leaving an extremely vulnerable household behind him. Left all alone in the world, she was right in being scared of her own shadow. Her heart overflowed with a wave of affection for Chhoti, and a glimpse of her own true estate also flashed before her mind's eye. Doubtless, Navab Yusuf Ali Khan treated her with full solicitude and provided every possible comfort for her, but no word of marriage had ever passed his lips. She might be quite much in the world's eyes, but in the eyes of God, and in the real House of the Navab, she was nothing.

Tears pricked her eyes, but she kept a hold on herself and said, 'Looked at in one way, you are quite right, dear girl. But what other choice do we have? We should devote our lives and our whole selves in managing and living as best we can on what fate has willed for us. In it alone lies our righteousness.'

Wazir's eyes also welled up. She dried them with a corner of her wrap, and then plucked up courage to ask, 'Tell me, Baji, what thoughts were yours before you tied yourself to the hem of your own Navab sahib?'

Manjhli was stunned into speechlessness. She had been with Yusuf Ali Khan for about six years now. During this time, she did not even cast a meaningful eye at another man; thinking about another man was anathema to her. After all, she had not been with the Navab in the fulfilment of a business transaction: No, she had lived with him fully observing all mores of chastity and following all rules of modesty . . . So did she lose her heart to the Navab even before he made his proposal? Was that why she quickly responded to the Navab's hinted compliments and left her parents' home to make the Navab's haveli the final haven of her life?

She spoke slowly, giving full thought to each word, 'Truth to tell, Chhoti, it is so long ago now that I don't quite remember what thoughts were coursing in my head at that moment . . . Perhaps I did feel something for him, he was a regular visitor there . . . and that vague feeling became love or affection, whatever. But as God is my Judge, the Navab sahib never played false with me. He never raised my hopes with deceitful promises.'

'May Allah preserve you as each other's sweetheart,' said Wazir. 'There has been nothing to repine about thus far.'

'Well, yes and no,' Manjhli Begam drew a cold sigh. 'But I put this dress on my body, and the Tailor of Fate did not apparently sew any other for me. Now if this dress becomes my shroud, I will thank God for not putting me to shame by letting me be exposed to the world's ridicule.'

'Yes, for me too, it is none but Allah who can solve my difficulty—' Wazir was going to say something more, but Manjhli interrupted her. 'Take the name of God, Chhoti! What is your difficulty? In what dire straits are you caught? Do try feeling your heart. Is it tangled with Navab Shamsuddin Ahmad, or not?'

'I do not know.' Wazir's eyes again reddened with tears. 'That is what I do believe, so far as I can judge, but . . .'

'But what? If you believe what you do, and if the Navab is also inclined towards you, then you must start the business of living anew. Treat as a good omen what has happened up until now.'

'But . . .' She paused again. 'Baji, what you say sounds good, but my children . . .'

'Oh, just listen to the little one! Worrying about the children so early in the game! You will always find hairs to split everywhere.'

Wazir thought of retorting, 'Baji, you have no children. How can you at all understand the torment of having your children taken away from you?' But such words were not to be spoken, not to be thought of even. And she had a faint suspicion that Baji intentionally did not bear children . . . or maybe the Navab forbade her. She said in placating tones, 'No, Baji, please. I'm not in the business of splitting hairs. But did not the relatives of Blak sahib play foul with me?'

'Well. But consider, how could you have brought them up all alone, they being the offspring of alien blood? You think they are going to love you? Is there any love lost between the Nazarene and the Mussulman? And do you possess the riches of Croesus to finance their upbringing and education, and all else like marriage and further support? Now that there is hope from Navab Shamsuddin Ahmad, we will see how things go. You've sprinkled just the seed, and here you are dreaming already of reaping the crop!'

A faint glow of a smile appeared on Wazir's face. 'Baji, you know I have ever been the hurrying type!'

'And you know full well that the way of undue hurry is the Devil's way.

Just look, how many were the knots and involutions in your purposes, and how well, at the proper time, the Opener of All Knots and Tangles undid them for you! Don't you know that the tension of waiting turns even children into old hags mentally?'

Saying these words, Manjhli rose from her place, ran her hand again and again on Wazir's face, and repeatedly cracked her fingers against her own face. She then hugged her warmly and said, 'I should be going now, but do let me know at once if anything happens.'

'Baji, would you not stay for dinner?'

'Oh no. Of an evening, the Navab sahib often inquires after me and on occasion comes into the zenana for dinner. Be stout of heart, I'll report all the things to the Navab sahib too. As Allah wills, all will be well. I'm off now. I give you in Allah's Protection!'

Seeing Umdah Khanam rise to go, a maid produced a wide silk chador to cover her so that her body and a good part of her face were effectively hidden. The maid went out to have Umdah Khanam's palanquin brought at the door. Vafadar, and Mubarak Qadam, another of Wazir's maids, drew a large sheet in front in such a way that the palanquin was quite isolated from the alley. Before putting her feet into the carriage, Manjhli again drew her hands on Wazir's face and cracked her fingers against her own, and hugged her again. Chhoti, with her head bowed and her left hand on her right breast, kept saying over and again: 'Baji, Allah ma'akum; Baji, I make my submissions; Baji, may God preserve you.'

*

Fraser was unable to decide upon the strategy about Chhoti Begam: success should be assured, and there should be no loose talk in the city about the Resident's high-handedness. Otherwise, it was no problem to have her picked up from her house; or she could be invited for dinner and then detained regardless of her wishes. (As if he was confident that if invited, Chhoti Begam would not refuse the invitation.)

Fraser knew that many debauched or tyrannical rulers of the native states were wont to openly commit such deeds, and the honour of women, especially of the poorer and depressed sections of society, was never safe in their regimes. The Residency itself routinely employed a number of persons of dubious or criminal character, or those who had access to some tribes whose members traditionally led a life of crime. In fact, Fraser himself was reputed to be not above having girls and boys of the weaker communities kidnapped and brought to the Residency for his pleasure. This was perhaps not true, but not unthinkable either: women of the profession, or even women from private homes, could be forcibly taken, or abducted through professional male or female woman-stealers and used for the pleasure of the powerful.

The problem had assumed a different dimension after the intransigence of the hakim became apparent. Now Shamsuddin Ahmad Khan must have been made aware that the Resident Bahadur has an amorous eye for Chhoti Begam. It was therefore quite obvious that Shamsuddin Ahmad should have ordered preventive and defensive measures to be put in place, including appointing a round-the-clock security guard at Chhoti's door. There was also a possibility, even if remote, of the King expressing or indirectly conveying his unhappiness at the action of Fraser's as oppressive or arbitrary.

It was therefore inexpedient to employ force. It was, of course, feasible—even desirable—to mount a direct and peaceful offensive by paying a visit to Chhoti Begam, especially now when the Navab's security would not yet be in position. In fact, even if it was, no one could dare stop the advent of the Grand Sahib Bahadur. Fraser may have cogitated on the course of action for a time, but once his decision was made, there was no reason not to put it into effect without lingering further.

The time of his usual evening promenade in the city was approaching anyway, so it was quite proper for his favourite elephant Surat Sundar to be brought around for him to ride. With eight musketeers on another two elephants behind him, and four horsemen with carbines in front, he made for the city.

The practice of a promenade in the city every evening had been established by David Ochterlony. He was also the first to dare defy the time-honoured rule prohibiting all but the King Emperor to ride an elephant within the city limits. Over and above the pomp of riding an elephant, Ochterlony also used a golden howdah for himself and a brocade coat for his elephant. No one at all was permitted to use the canopy above the howdah; it was a privilege strictly reserved for the King Emperor. Even Mahada ji Sindhia—though he had the titles of Beloved Son, Absolute Plenipotentiary, Minister in Chief—and the traitor Ghulam Qadir Rohilla did not use the canopy. Ochterlony bent the rule by using not a canopy in the Royal style, but an English-style umbrella held over his head by a servant who stood behind the howdah.

The unauthorized innovations of Ochterlony became part of the conventions and privileges of the Residency, and the daily evening excursion on a caparisoned elephant complete with howdah and umbrella became a sort of unofficial substitute for the jharoka darshan, a practice—which became almost a ritual—introduced by Emperor Akbar. The Emperor would appear at a window every morning at a fixed time when the people gathered to view him as an act of virtue, and also to reassure themselves that the Emperor was alive and well.

Fraser knew that Muhyiuddin Aurangzeb Alamgir spent the second half of his long reign campaigning in the south, and five or six of those years were actually spent on active battlefronts or in military encampments. The jharoka darshan was impossible in such circumstances and Aurangzeb established a substitute for it by coming out from his Court Pavilion every day at a fixed time and going round the whole huge encampment, spread over many square miles, in an open palanquin, or a nalki, depending on the weather. The ride took an hour or two. Aurangzeb would have a book in his hands and he kept his eyes on it all the time, not looking up, or in any direction whatever.

Everyone stood, leaving whatever they were doing, as the Emperor's exalted suite passed. They made three salaams, bent low and remained so until the auspicious carriage was out of sight. Aurangzeb betrayed nothing by gesture or eye movement. He remained rigidly austere, unmoving, an effect of concentrated awe in his whole being, as if he were in a full Durbar, receiving an ambassador of a foreign prince.

The Emperor's lack of movement of body or eye was not just part of the etiquette of the Mughal Court: it also signified that the affairs of the State and the activities of the military went on smoothly and with alertness, regardless of whether he was looking or not. About eighty-six years old, dressed simply but expensively, tall and extremely thin, with the eyes of an eagle, a predatory, hooked nose and a wide, prominent forehead under the Royal turban topped by a brilliant ornament, with sunken cheeks that had no hint of frailty, a long and sharp face that seemed further lengthened by the longish, snow-white beard: Aurangzeb at such times indeed looked the part of Alamgir, the World Conqueror

William Fraser was quite enamoured of Aurangzeb's style and grace in creating a newer and perhaps more elegant form of jharoka darshan. And he believed himself to be Aurangzeb's equal if not in power, might and splendour, then certainly in knowledge and gravitas, and he believed that the Company's Abstract Being was shortly going to be elevated to the same rank which Aurangzeb had occupied for half a century. The way Aurangzeb had brought under his sway the whole of Hind, Kamarup and Bangalah, and then the entire depth of the Deccan, in the same manner, in Fraser's dreams, the Company Bahadur would one day consolidate its supremacy and command over the length and breadth of this seemingly immeasurable land.

The only difference in this narrative was that while Aurangzeb's subjects regarded him as the Shadow of God and a divine emblem, for Fraser, the body of the Exalted Presence, the Company Bahadur, was the Shadow of the King of England, and the Extended Shadow of the Ideal Existences of the Holy Trinity, who was lighting up and illuminating the English Kinghood with such refulgence and glory that the face of the entire earth, from Australia to China, and from Africa to America, was dazzlingly brilliant for all to see. The wealth and treasure of the whole world was hauling itself into England, and everlasting springs of knowledge—mathematics, philosophy and science, astronomy and medicine—were shooting up from the soil of England, washing over the four sides of the earth and illuminating and irrigating the entire surface of the planet.

Thus, according to his lights, Fraser was well entitled to go round the streets of Delhi with the pomp of an Aurangzeb in the field of battle, or in the Royal encampment, to provide his people with the evidence of his presence and puissance and his capability to govern and rule over them. During his elephant ride Fraser, too, kept an open book in his hand. Still, despite his best efforts, he had not so far succeeded in keeping his body still and his eyes on the book. Also, he told himself, what use was an outing when one did not constantly look around to observe what was going on? And while he did not yet have as many to render salaams to him as were readily available to Alamgir, there were still plenty of men to pay obeisance to him and he liked to acknowledge their submission. Giving full regard to a person's status, he would merely smile at some, say words of greeting to some—the words again commensurate with the person addressed—and to some very special Indians, he would say, 'Good evening, sir.' He wouldn't bare his head to anyone, except to white women of high rank.

On that evening, when Fraser's suite arrived at Sirki Walan, he was somewhat surprised to see that the main gate leading into the neighbourhood was closed and just the wicket gate was available for pedestrians. Carriages had to stop and be identified and their purpose ascertained before the gate could be opened. A cudgel-wielder would look out from behind the gate and open it wide only when he was satisfied about the bona fides of the newcomer.

The cudgel-wielder was in the process of shutting the gate after admitting a palanquin when he espied Fraser's party arriving at the gate. He did not close the gate, nor did he open it wide, making it clear that the newcomer too should state his business before he could be allowed in. Fraser's elephant and the rest of the party were obliged to stop. Casual strollers, shopkeepers and shoppers around the area were not yet quite clear about what was happening, or was going to happen, but the natural tendency of Delhiites to crane their necks and to foregather where something of even passing interest might happen was active as usual, and spectators began to collect within a few moments. This was Delhi, where even a massacre was a spectacle. How well the Hindi poet Hakim Momin Khan said, making use of the image of the throng for the beloved who kills scores of persons within no time:

You cast a glance, killing a whole world
With that one glance;
None could enjoy the spectacle
Of the other being slain!

And here was a marvellous spectacle, somewhat frightening too; so there were two thrills for the price of one. The Navab Resident Bahadur riding his favourite elephant in a colourful procession towards the gate of Sirki Walan behind which resided the celebrated Chhoti Khanam, with the redoubtable cudgel-wielders of the State of Loharu guarding the entrance: this was certainly going to be a spicy dish. Whose progress actually were the cudgel-bearers appointed to stop? It was a question not unmixed with the sensational and a bit of delectation. The Grand Sahib was reputed to be fluent in the language of Delhi, and that was another attraction; for most of those present had never clapped their eyes upon him, much less heard him talk.

So there was no dearth of onlookers: children, and even some purdah women's eyes could be seen looking or peeping from behind bamboo screens or makeshift curtains. Fraser's Indian dress, his Firangee looks, the mace-bearer sitting behind him on the elephant, carefully holding the hookah and its long pipe: each had its own novelty for the audience.

Fraser kept his self-possession when faced with the obstacle. He did not speak, but correctly reading his intent as he waved his hand briefly, a horse rider spurred his horse forward, with his carbine aimed at the half-open gate and growled at the cudgel-fighter: 'Hey, you! You pecker poker of your own mother! Have you lost your limbs? Do you dare not give way to the Senior Sahib Bahadur's elephant?'

The cudgel-bearer was a true Mewati, tall, muscular and hardened. He wore narrow trousers of white drill and a long, green tunic of the same cloth with a red sash tightly bound around his waist, by which was hung a long dagger. On his head he wore a short, black turban. He had a steel bangle on each of his wrists and held a heavy and strong cudgel, a little above six feet in length, made heavier and stronger by having been exposed to the rains for several years, then immersed in heavy mustard oil for many more years, resulting in an extraordinarily heavy, supple and strong killing instrument. In the hands of an expert, such a staff was even more lethal than a sword. One end had been thickened with sheets of brass wound on it, capped by iron. The other end was shaped to a thick point with an iron-mounted ferrule.

The cudgel-fighter extended the cudgel through the half-open gate and placing its point on the neck of the rider's mount, near its lungs, spoke in cold, measured tones, 'Telanga sahib, do put a bit of rein on your tongue, and also rein your ancient pony a bit. If you hustle it further even by a hand's length, the point of this staff will sink into its jaded liver.'

His voice and intonation were so hard that even a sword could not have marked it. The word 'Telanga' was a deliberate insult, for it was used for the comparatively short-statured, dark soldiers from the south who were reputed to be uncouth and somewhat cowardly. Fraser's outrider roared, 'You wretched tramp! Do I look like a Telanga to you? We are Pathans of the Baruzai tribe. Say another word and I will tear your tongue out!'

Apprehending that the matter might escalate, the other three cudgel-bearers also came forward, but took no part in the exchange. Fraser saw that it was inexpedient to let the heated conversation deteriorate into a dispute:

it would be a matter of levity for the onlookers and cause him loss of face. He said something softly in English to one of the riders on the elephant behind his own. The elephant rider quickly pressed his mount forward, putting the horseman behind him. He spoke gravely, 'Mian Khan, it is not advisable, not giving clear passage to the Senior Sahib Bahadur.'

The cudgel-bearer also became softer in tone and words, though his accent was still extremely hard. 'Why not? How could we not give passage? But where is he headed for? We should at least know that much.'

The elephant rider turned to look at Fraser with inquiring eyes. Fraser made some gesture, which his attendant interpreted correctly, and said, 'His Honour, the Pivot of Prosperity and Power, the Senior Sahib Bahadur commands that he wishes to honour Khanam sahib by paying her a visit.'

The four cudgel-wielders were in a quandary. Having been posted for sentry and security duty at Khanam sahib's door, they were plainly required to prevent entry of undesirable persons, and if it came to that, to protect and defend her. But the Senior Sahib Bahadur? They were, of course, unaware that the Navab had installed them there to pre-empt any move from the Senior Sahib Bahadur. Certainly, there could be no question of anyone else, not even the Resident Bahadur, taking an interest in Khanam sahib when it was known that Navab Shamsuddin Ahmad Khan sahib was inclined towards her. But . . . not permitting the Senior Sahib Bahadur could also lead to complications, could it not?

After some wordless consultations among them, one of the four staff-bearers, older in age and graver in outlook, came up and said, 'Very well. Perfectly understood, sir. But let me go and inquire if Khanam sahib will agree to receive the Senior Sahib Bahadur at this time.'

His voice was not only grave but also somewhat refined and urban; perhaps he was originally from Delhi. But his apparently reasonable request created a veritable dilemma for Fraser. This was unusual in itself: that the Resident should come to visit someone, and the person, instead of welcoming him with the greatest eagerness and honour, should think in terms of the suitability and the timing of the visit! Should Wazir Khanam refuse to see him, he would be not only be the laughing stock of the whole city, but the Company Bahadur's awe and majesty would also be seriously compromised.

Accepting the refusal implicit in the staff-bearer's reply and quietly going away would be as bad as forcing his way into Wazir Khanam's house. It was the first time in his life that Fraser had gone about something in such a blundering fashion. It would have been much better to have her summoned to the Residency. She would certainly have been filled with dread and dismay at the sight of the Company's full might and majesty in action. It would have been so much more feasible there: making her conscious of the vast difference in their station, putting the distinction of high and low fully in practice. Now, one had to make the best of a bargain already gone sour.

He gave the briefest of nods, and the elephant rider told the guards, 'All right. The Senior Sahib Bahadur deigns to stay here. Now go at once and inform Khanam sahib.'

Wazir, although surprised at the news of Fraser's advent, did not feel apprehensive or anxious. It was certainly an insult to her dignity that Fraser should inflict himself upon her without notice; for, it meant that in Fraser's eyes Wazir counted as a mere nautch girl, to be made available to an appropriate patron at any time of the day or night. Wazir was not unaware of the nuances involved here, but preferred to attribute Fraser's action to the characteristic arrogance of the English and their disdainful, tyrannical demeanour towards Indians. Still, she could not think of a suitable excuse to deny Fraser's request.

Certainly, in her heart she believed that she was tied to Shamsuddin Ahmad Khan, but did not believe that she was so strongly connected with the Navab as to justifiably refuse to receive Fraser in her own home. She did not quite know that a sort of rivalry for her had developed, or actually existed, between the Navab and Fraser. So she reasoned that good sense and wisdom demanded that she admit Fraser into her house and accord him the necessary dignity. In any case, Navab Shamsuddin Ahmad must have had to pay due deference to Fraser's wishes in administrative and official matters, so it was not advisable to thwart him.

'Fine,' she instructed the senior cudgel-bearer. 'Let the Senior Sahib Bahadur be escorted here with full honour and ceremony.' She then went into the water room to wash her face and comb her hair. She instructed Vafadar to open the room and have some perfume sprinkled in it. This was the room where she had received Navab Shamsuddin Ahmad Khan and Pundit Nand Kishor. The other maid, Mubarak Qadam, she dispatched to the kitchen to get some sweets and betels ready, and prepare tea.

In the water room, she quickly splashed water on her face, but made no other toilette, except that she exchanged her usual dupatta for one of six yards, made of aquamarine muslin and decorated with stars woven all over in thin gold thread.

Mubarak Qadam was ready with the sweets and the betel box when Wazir emerged from the water room. Vafadar, having welcomed Fraser, had seated him in the designated room, and stood behind him with a fly-whisk fan of peacock feathers. Fraser looked around the chamber and was extremely impressed by the simplicity and good taste, and the understated quality of the expensive furnishing. He was also not a little surprised, because he had always believed that Indian women did not maintain their homes in good style. Perhaps she learned all this in Marston Blake's company and due to his training, he mused.

Fraser was also surprised by the fact that he found nothing anywhere which could be associated with a nautch girl's profession, though that was what he had been told was Wazir's profession. No musical instruments, no one who looked like a professional musician, or woman attendant of the type one could expect in such an establishment. In spite of his vast experience and natural capacity for discerning subtleties, Fraser completely misjudged Wazir and did not appreciate that her own sense of self was that of a refined woman of good family, though of decidedly liberal views.

Wazir indicated to Mubarak Qadam that she proceed ahead with the plate of dry fruits and the betel box. She herself entered after Mubarak Qadam had placed the betel box and the plate of sweets on a small occasional table to the right of Fraser and now stood behind him after doing a salaam. Wazir bent low, performed an elaborate salaam and forcing a welcoming smile on her face, she spoke with feigned pleasure: 'Your maid submits her salaams. How exceedingly fortunate I am that the doorstep of my destitute home has kissed the feet of the Senior Sahib Bahadur!'

Certainly, Wazir's words and tone of voice were somewhat ingratiating, but her face betrayed nothing like obsequiousness, far less a sense of being overwhelmed by the occasion. Fraser looked up, and for the first time saw her fully as she was. He was almost taken aback: Wazir did not look quite like what he had imagined. She was even better looking, and had a stronger presence. Her body was demurely covered in the copious wrap, but the delicate beauty and appeal of the female body seemed to glow behind her apparel like a candle flame.

'Chhoti Begam, I was quite keen really to be better acquainted with you. At the dinner in my house, you made a good impression on all the guests.'

Fraser's Hindi was normally quite fluent and in accordance with Delhi's refined accents, but the effect of Wazir's beauty or perhaps the extra effort in adopting a patronizing tone made him sound stilted and Anglicized.

Wazir came deeper into the room and stopped. She wanted to sit at some distance from Fraser, with her feet tucked in under her thighs, but Fraser half rose from his place and extended his hand, perhaps desiring to get hold of her arm and gently pull her next to him. With admirable agility, but without apparent effort, Wazir chose a spot at some distance. She did not at all like Fraser's attempt at such liberty but decided not to pursue the matter.

Tea was brought in, with some more snacks and sweets. Tea was becoming popular among Indians, especially among those who were inclined to ape the English lifestyle, and among Christians, particularly those one of whose parents was English. Indians, though, made tea in their own way, full of milk and Indian cream, and some gave it a dash of saffron too. Among the English, tea was served in cups without milk or sugar. Some drank it with a little sugar or a little milk—never both at the same time. Fraser was gratified to see the tea served at Wazir's was just according to his taste.

Wazir was unable to think of a topic of conversation; nor was she able to get to the real reason for Fraser's visit. This much she could deduce easily: Fraser took her to be just a nautch girl, if somewhat superior to a common courtesan, and one easily available to a fancier. It was therefore clear to her that Fraser must have felt a little awkward, if not disappointed, to see a different order of things at Wazir's house. What she did not discern was Fraser's hot sense of rivalry, and over and above it, his wounded pride which, like a guttering torch that produced more smoke than light, had singed and blackened his entire inner self.

'Chhoti Begam, you organized the tea very well indeed.' Fraser, somewhat irked and at a loss to see Wazir not saying anything, found himself speaking just for the sake of making a conversation.

'His Honour enhances my value,' Wazir smiled. 'But . . .'

She wished to say, 'But you have not troubled to visit here for the pleasure of my tea.' She held her tongue at the last moment. It was not improper among the English to straightaway inquire the purpose of one's visit, but it was extremely objectionable, and in fact a gross insult among the Indians. The other point was that if the Senior Sahib Bahadur was here for the purpose of opening negotiations about Wazir and coming to an arrangement, the etiquette among the community of women of the profession was for the man to state his purpose first and then make an offer if the response from the woman permitted such an offer to be made.

Inwardly, she was worried and uncertain. She must find a way not to let the situation get out of hand; but how should she respond if the Sahib did make a proposition? She therefore wanted to have some sort of control on the direction of the conversation. Fraser, however, was clever and eager enough. He pounced upon Wazir's hesitation. He said, 'Yes, but what? Should I understand that you're not pleased at my being here? Actually, I was rather keen to meet you, converse with you and gain propinquity with you.'

The word that Fraser used for 'propinquity' was harmless enough in its original Arabic sense, but in Hindi it was rarely used, except in the sense of 'sexual congress'. It was unlikely that Fraser was just being pompous and was unaware of the specialized sense of the word in the Indian literary culture. Anyway, Wazir was certainly not so naive as to fail to read the real meaning of both 'converse' and 'propinquity'. She did not know that in English 'conversation' also implied 'the act of sex', but she certainly knew that in Hindi, one of the meanings of 'to talk' was 'to have sex'.

So she could well see the drift that Fraser's words could take, and suddenly she felt a passion of rage rise up in her, whirling like a wheel of fire, but even at such a moment she could see that she was furious also at her kind, at the world she lived in, and was sad that her world insisted on seeing her as a commodity. And who is this abominable Englishman—let death take him—to have expectations from me? Do I owe him money or am I his subject? And what kind of civilized conduct is this? Why should anyone from the bazaars, or wherever, feel empowered to push his claim over a woman and the woman be not permitted to open her mouth even in protest? Are women goats and sheep to be driven wherever one listeth?

So far, she had had her head meekly bowed, but now she raised her head and sitting erect and looking Fraser in the eye, she spoke in cold, hard tones without raising her voice, 'Navab Resident Bahadur, please do not try to play those ragas for which you do not possess the requisite instruments.'

Fraser could not quite gather the sense of Wazir's words. He was about to make a casual reply when suddenly Wazir's real meaning flashed upon him and he bristled, as if stung by a bee. He pursed his lips tight for a moment before responding sarcastically: 'These high flights of fancy are indeed laudable, but I am familiar with the art of tying up a highflyer's wings and plucking her feathers to make her fly at an ordinary pitch.'

'Flying is of no interest to birds whose feet are already bound with a thread, Navab Resident Bahadur. But we also believe in what Hafiz said about every word having an occasion and every point having a station.' She paused for a moment, and then said: 'But you are perhaps minded to deny and deviate from your ability for recognition of value?'

This again was too subtle for Fraser and he had to pause and ponder before answering. And this need to ponder made him even more inflamed, and ashamed as well. But he knew that he would compromise his credibility and gravitas even further if he gave vent to his displeasure at that moment. He saw that he needed to tread most cautiously. 'I value you greatly, Chhoti Begam. Perhaps it is you who are no connoisseur of gemstones.'

Making an oblique reference to a Persian proverb—Only a King or a lapidary can know the worth of a gem—Wazir replied with deliberate false modesty, 'People like us are far from being King or lapidary. The expectations of the Navab Resident Bahadur could scarcely be satisfied by the destitute and the indigent like us.'

'I don't believe in expectation,' Fraser smiled a crooked smile. 'I believe in the fullest unity between the intent and the result.'

Wazir moved back a little, as if intending to rise, but she changed her mind and said, 'Yes, sir. If you are such a firm believer in the fullest unity . . . then you might not even be looking in the mirror. It would have been better for you if you did.'

Fraser, according to his lights, had said something profound and unanswerable. But he had never dealt with a girl like Wazir. Nor had he ever seen an Indian girl so quick to take offence and whose mood could change so quickly from soft to hard, even when she faced an Englishman. He was flabbergasted. The veneer of Indian sophistication, of oblique speech, of refinement, all this was wiped away from his face as if destroyed by acid. He struck his fist on the occasional table, upsetting the table and what was on it. He stood up, erect and rigid, as if inspecting a parade.

'Chhoti Begam, this bargain will cost you dear.'

'There is no bargain between me and you. I do not believe in cheap bargains anyway. I assay and judge the buyer's seal and stamp of temperament in the first place.' Wazir drew herself to her full height, waved towards the door, and said, 'There is the door, Senior Sahib Bahadur.'

She then bent low, made the salaam with correct formality, then smiled a proud and derisive smile. Fraser stood motionless, his colour darkening and then paling and then reddening like red-hot copper. He clenched his jaws so hard that the cheekbones became exceedingly prominent.

Seeing that both guest and host were completely upset, Mubarak Qadam quietly went out and beckoned to the senior cudgel-wielder and another one to come inside. Both stood alert and at the ready in Wazir Khanam's hall. Fraser's staff had been kept engaged by the other cudgel-wielders in idle chat and exchange of news, so they were not at Fraser's immediate call.

Fraser's dilemma grew by the second. If he could, he would chew up his own body or bring the roof down with shouts and harangues and threats. Within a few moments, the temperature of hospitality inside the house had plummeted from cosy warmth to very near freezing. Vafadar had stopped plying the fan and was looking at Wazir intently, as if expecting some unusual order. Fraser made up his mind and took a couple of steps forward and stood at the edge of the carpet. In spite of what had happened between him and Wazir a minute ago, he still expected some maid to come forward and help him put on his shoes. But there was not the slightest movement from any of those present.

Mubarak Qadam, when she saw the upsetting of the table and its contents, promptly opened the door which led to the hall. Thus the two cudgel-fighters were clearly visible, and Mubarak Qadam had her eyes on them, as if she was heedless of what was happening in front of her and unaware about Fraser's impending departure.

Having no choice, Fraser had to put on his shoes unaided. There was nothing like a chair or wooden platform in the room. So he must needs sit on his haunches and push his feet into the shoes, or just somehow shove them into the shoes without bothering about his heels fitting into them, and walk out, almost limping. Fortunately, he was wearing patent leather pumps and could manage to insert his feet into them more or less successfully without having to bend or go down on his haunches. He came out of Wazir's house, thanking God that he got out with his dignity reasonably intact.

The moment Fraser's suite quit Sirki Walan, Wazir deputed the senior cudgel-wielder, whose name was Amir Ghulam, to go look for Navab Shamsuddin Ahmad Khan wherever he was to be found at that time, and request him to come immediately to Sirki Walan, and look into a matter that had cropped up there, or failing which, he permit her, Wazir Khanam, to go where he was at that time so that she could report the event to him. Wazir did not know exactly why the Navab's men were deputed to her house, so she did not relate Fraser's visit to any danger perceived by the Navab, but still, she considered it necessary to apprise him of Fraser's visit and his unfriendly, in fact ungentlemanly, conduct.

Wazir waited for the Navab's answer most anxiously; she prayed that he would take the trouble to come and give solace to her heart. She did not still think that she had substantive cause to fear any harm from Fraser, but in her heart she did feel uncomfortable, and in fact somewhat ashamed that Fraser believed her to be just another woman of the street, or someone who was a clandestine prostitute, working from her home. She also feared that Navab Shamsuddin Ahmad might form an unfavourable impression about Wazir; worse still, he might feel so disgusted at the episode as to veer away from her and leave her in the lurch.

Even after dispatching Amir Ghulam, Wazir continued to feel restless and unhappy: What more or what else could I have done? To whom should I unburden my heart? Fraser's coming here could certainly cause her opprobrium, even if she had done nothing to earn it. But did anyone ever stop the tongues from wagging? No one in the world is ashamed of making a mountain out of a molehill or proving that a good person was in fact evil.

She thought of requesting Manjhli to come, or of going off to meet her. But there were problems with that: she would have to reduce yet another security guard, or at least one maid, and she could not countenance that; for, even if she did not perceive any danger, she certainly had cause for disquiet. In fact, she had a strong urge to have her main door locked and strongly barred and then lock herself up in the farthest room in the house. Even if she did not do so, she surely wanted to have familiar faces, and if not familiar, dependable faces around her. The other problem was that if she did go away to Manjhli's, and the Navab arrived during her absence, he would justifiably be upset to find that having urged him to come to Sirki Walan, Wazir had disappeared from there. As for consulting Bari Baji or their father, that was not an option at all.

Evening fell, bringing darkness quickly in its wake. In Wazir's inner courtyard, her pet birds had finished their songs of the evening, and little robins, sparrows and grassbirds, having done their travels and wanderings in search of food, were now back to roost in the two yellow jasmine shrubs and the pomegranate tree that adorned the courtyard. In the Sirki Walan market, and from then on to Chitli Qabr, the bright lights, the throngs of shoppers, the press of pedestrians, the water-sellers clinking and clanking their cups to attract the thirsty, the hordes of carefree, jobless youth and the active craftsmen, all enjoying the sights and sounds in Bazaar Sitaram and Kucha Chelan, had created a festive air all around. But Wazir's heart grew heavier with each passing moment. It was not that much time had passed since she sent out her messenger, but it was just like the Arabic proverb: To wait is harder than death.

At long last, Amir Ghulam returned from his mission, but his report was not encouraging at all: the Navab was not at either of his havelis. He was in Qutb Sahib to visit the holy tomb of the Presence, Qutbuddin Bakhtiar Sahib Kaki and proposed to spend the night there. Amir Ghulam had instructed the keepers of the gates at both havelis in clear and elaborate language that the Navab must be informed of the events at Sirki Walan immediately as he returned, and Khanam sahib's message must be conveyed to him at the same time. The confusion and anxiety in Wazir's mind was now greater, and she had no choice but to wait. It was quite late also to visit Manjhli. She directed the four security men to stay alert and awake the whole night and not permit any suspicious person to enter her alley.

Like a traveller lost in a trackless desert, Wazir spent that night in ever-increasing fear and uncertainty. She was feeling nearly half dead when the sun rose and brought good tidings for her. Those who had stayed in the nearby mosque to perform the after-sunrise prayer were still at their task when Navab Shamsuddin Ahmad Khan entered the alley of Sirki Walan with the crackle of horse and equipment.

Four female Abyssinian attendants, taut of body and tall of stature, led him on four chestnut Marwari horses. Their jet Abyssinian bodies were glossy with health; they held a spear in their left hand and had pistols on both sides of their waist. A turban of the tie-dye fabric of Rajputana on the erect head, with a light turban ornament and the red-and-black plumes of the wild junglefowl. They each carried a sword of Indian steel inserted fast in a lacquered sheath of gold and blue, the golden sword handle glittering in the rising sun. Their breasts were high and prominent, though fully covered with a heavy tunic; their waists were narrow, their hips heavy but firm and well shaped, their necks proud; and the purple-black of their complexion seemed to be boiling with the health of their blood. Their faces intent with concentration of valour, each seemed capable of getting the better of fifty, if not a hundred, Telanga or Baksaria soldiers. Courage and boldness of spirit emanated from their stance as if the sun's rays were piercing through the dark of the dense clouds of an evening.

Behind the Abyssinian women were two male riders on Gujarati horses, with their carbines held ready to fire, their mounts trotting comfortably, keeping just the right distance from the Navab's horse so that the Navab should have freedom of movement and also protection from both sides. Behind the Navab, two musketeers rode on an elephant, with their muskets trained to the right and the left. The last item of this procession was a palanquin with gold work on its frame and curtains in heavy brocade. Two staff-bearers walked to the right and the left, crying, 'Beware!', 'Give way!', 'No gawking please!'

The entry of Shamsuddin Ahmad Khan's suite inside the gate of Sirki Walan signalled a total silence and the disappearance or dispersal of all kinds of people who had so far been swarming everywhere. Although everyone knew that they stood in no danger from the Navab's force, and all knew well the reason for his appearance with his entourage there at the somewhat unusual hour, yet the awe of the suite impelled everyone, pedestrian or rider, to stop in their tracks and give the Navab's convoy the widest possible berth. Even the labourers, out in their droves to earn their daily bread, sought the safety of quiet nooks and corners behind shop doors. The hawkers and vendors of the goods of the morning—butter, solid cream, milk, sweet foam of whipped cream and milk in different colours, heavy pancakes much preferred for breakfast, kebabs, roasted liver of goat, almost the whole of the breakfast table—forgot to call out their goods, and lurked, biding their time. Shopkeepers stopped admonishing their shop boys to sweep and dust efficiently, and quietly sat on their seats.

The Navab's phalanx, oblivious of the sensation it was causing, passed in no time; and in even lesser time, the Navab dismounted and crossed into the narrow hall of Wazir Khanam's house. The door was locked from inside the moment he entered.

Wazir, who had been waiting most ardently for the Navab, concentrating her whole life and soul on the glorious moment when he would arrive, was now overtaken by new dreads and torments. She trembled to face him for fear that the Navab might disapprove of her conduct in some way. No doubt, I was not to blame, but was it not something dire that an outsider, and an Englishman to boot, was allowed to cross my door? Everybody hastens to blame women in such matters, and here am I, pronouncing myself guilty . . . Oh, am I the Chief of Police to impose a curfew on all comers and goers? But the world is not a just place. Everybody is concerned about his own self. Does anyone care for the truth? There is no one to utter the truth of God, everybody bends to the desires of the powerful . . . even an ant will bite if pressed too much, but women . . . women have no strength, no daring.

Shamsuddin Ahmad was installed in the same room where Wazir had received him upon his last visit. Mubarak Qadam stood behind, fanning him. Vafadar prepared betel cones hurriedly, presented the box to the Navab and stood hugging the door, saying that Khanam sahib would be in attendance in a moment or two: she had in fact been looking forward through the night to His Honour's coming.

Shamsuddin Ahmad had his own anxieties: Why is Wazir Khanam not appearing? Is she annoyed with me, or is she not feeling quite well? But the maids have reported nothing about her being out of sorts, and since Vafadar has informed me that Khanam sahib will come out soon, it will be bad manners for me to feel around further. But why this remoteness?

Shamsuddin Ahmad was convinced that yesterday's events must have greatly upset Wazir's temper and he should now go and personally mollify her. This procedure might or might not be quite proper, but there was nothing to be gained by sitting here alone, waiting for her.

'Bhai wallah,' he said, 'if Khanam sahib is not inclined to trouble her feet and come here, it is no matter. If she's angry with me, I'll go and placate her.'

He rose; Mubarak Qadam sprang to help him put on his shoes and saying, 'Your Honour, please ennoble us by your steps,' she went a step ahead of him, indicating with her hand the way for him to proceed. Vafadar practically ran into Wazir's room and said, breathlessly, 'Khanam ji . . . Navab sahib . . . he is about to enter your room!'

Wazir had been lying curled up on the bed like a foetus, hugging herself, her head buried under a pillow. She sprang from the bed, in a flurry of confusion. Hai Allah! What a disaster! What will he say, seeing me in this state? With my face swollen, my hair all disarrayed, I lie here as if in mourning. I've not washed my face, nor cleaned my teeth. Quickly, she took a couple of cardamoms from her betel box and put them in her mouth, crunching them down instantly so as to release the sharp and pleasant smelling oil. She then took a drop of the attar of rose from her perfume box and rubbed it on her collarbone, and was applying another drop to her dupatta when she heard Vafadar's voice: 'Your Presence, His Honour of Exalted Highness has come!'

Wazir came down from the bed and ran to the door barefooted. By this time, the Navab too had crossed the inner courtyard and had stepped onto the veranda. Winding her wrap carefully around her upper body, Wazir came out to greet him. Apprehension, confusion, shame, exhilaration, all were competing in her soul for supremacy and expression, causing her to totter and almost sway on her feet. They met halfway in the veranda. Shamsuddin Ahmad stepped up to her with a grave smile, but Wazir nearly ran to him and catching hold of the hem of his garment, spoke in a choked voice: 'Your slave girl makes her submissions . . . Your Honour, you are extremely . . .' She could not finish the sentence and gave way to open sobs.

Shamsuddin Ahmad understood her to mean that he was 'extremely late'. Putting his arm around her waist, he pulled her tenderly to his side. With her head against his breast, and running his fingers lovingly through her hastily combed hair, he said: 'No, I thought I was not all that late. I came running the moment your message reached me.' The mellifluous notes of Rajputani Braj were prominent above the hard tone of Mewati Hindi in his voice.

A weak smile glowed on Wazir's wan face. 'Your Honour, my life be sacrificed for you! Did I ever say that you delayed?'

Walking with small, gentle steps, they entered the room together. Drawing the curtain shut, Shamsuddin Ahmad imprinted copious kisses on Wazir's eyes and mouth, and said: 'Let's set the complaints aside for now. First you tell me why you were avoiding to come out and meet me.' He teased. 'Or did you wish me to come here, into your own room?'

Wazir blushed to the roots of her hair. Playing with the fingers of Shamsuddin Ahmad's right hand, she said with bowed head, 'I am greatly ashamed, Your Honour.'

'Ashamed? Ashamed why and for what? Bhai wallah, it is certainly to be regretted, and the occasion is for me to regret that you had to suffer such hardship but I was not here by your side!'

'A man, a shameless impudent stranger at that, should barge into my home and I should fail to slap him with my shoe and kick him out . . . I was drenched with the perspiration of shame. What will His Honour think . . . God forbid, he might believe me to be one of those accursed fortune-hunting professional women . . .' Wazir was trying to be serious and also a little playful, but her colour was pale and it seemed that she would burst into tears.

'Hey, Wazir Khanam! Bhai wallah from what I was given to understand, it seemed that though you did not hit that fornicator's son with your shoes, you dealt him something even worse. Now he should learn that one does not make eyes at women who are outsiders, nor does one invade their privacy like uncouth mercenaries from the Deccan.'

Shamsuddin Ahmad put his index finger on Wazir's chin, raised her face a little, and smilingly nipped her cheek with the same index finger and thumb. Then he said, 'Please. Now you must give up your displeasure; laugh a little; talk to me. You have nothing to worry about, and none to fear. I used to address Fraser as "uncle". All such relations cease to exist from today. I will bury him too one of these days like those relations.'

'No, no. Please do not say such things. Your Father of sacred memory counted him among his friends. You should ignore his malfeasance. What is past is past. My worry was that you might blame your servant girl for what happened.'

'Bhai wallah! What did the dear servant girl do to believe that she was deserving of admonition? As regards that fellow Fraser, he was not a relative; we had friendly relations. How could I treat him as friend when he did not observe the rules of friendship?'

Wazir made no reply. The Navab put his hand on her shoulder in a gesture of love and kindness, and said, 'All right, let us leave these matters. It seems that you did not sleep the night. Come on now, rise and be happy. Should you wish to change, please do. If not, come sit with me in the meeting room. I have some important things to tell you.'

Saying this, he rose and headed for the door.

At that time, Wazir's mien was like a rose garden in springtime. She had scarcely slept, and had many times shed tears through the night. This had caused some of the most delicate capillaries of her eyes to appear pink, as with the effect of intoxication. The onlooker would be stricken, but also pray—though the prayer would be unfair—that those great, expressive eyes should always seem so reddened as to be like delicate crystalline goblets full of red wine. Shamsuddin Ahmad was tempted to clasp her in his arms and bolt the door from inside. But he knew that such conduct would be insulting to Wazir and improper for him, and it might even demean him in Wazir's eyes.

'Please, Navab sahib, you must be counting me one slovenly shameless woman for appearing before you with my head looking like an untrimmed tree and my mouth open like that of a harridan!' Wazir said as she tried to cover her upper body properly with her dupatta.

'No, not at all! The way you illumine this chamber, even the greatest painters like Mani and Bahzad would lose their heart to you.' Shamsuddin Ahmad cast a casual but lusting glance at the hem of her wrap, which was still not quite covering her breasts, and her loose tunic with its top buttons undone. 'It seems to me that the lady has no disposition to look at herself in a mirror. For the truth is,' he recited a Persian verse:

Your open collar reflects the bounties of your body;
Because of your body, your garment overflows
With the delights of spring.

Wazir pulled up her light duvet and covering her body completely, she turned her face away and said, 'Enough! Please, enough. Let us have no more of poetry and poeticism!'

'Little Lady, not to talk of us humans, plants and trees, rocks and stones would become poets if they could have eyes and could look at you.' He then said another Persian verse:

Wherever I look, nothing is empty of your presence:
The grass is bold and verdant; and the rose is fair.

'Oh my! Would that I have a tongue like yours and a memory like yours! And even if I had those, shame and bashfulness would prevent me from opening my lips.'

Wazir keenly wished for the pleasing banter and romantic talk to go on, but she was also anxious for the Navab to leave the room so that she might do minimum toilette and make herself presentable like a normal human being. The Navab stood at the door, leaning against the frame, and behind him Wazir could see Mubarak Qadam who stood with a tray of sweets and condiments. Wazir found a good excuse to retire: 'Your Honour must not have breakfasted. Mubarak Qadam is anxious to serve sweets and cool drinks, and whatever else your noble temper may desire. You just need to command: tea, coffee, kebabs, heavy pancakes, all are available right here.'

Shamsuddin Ahmad laughed. 'Bhai wallah! My good fortune came when I came here. But my appetite ran away! You take your time. I will enjoy the cool drink, take pleasure in betel cones, and divert myself with the Divan of Hafiz.'

'Most proper. Your servant girl will return in the twinkling of an eye.'

The Navab left the room and turned towards the outer part of the house. As Mubarak Qadam followed him, another maid sprang to move the curtain of the meeting room, and when the Navab came in, stood behind him with a fan. Vafadar, entering Wazir's room, closed the door from inside and opened her mistress's footlocker to help Wazir choose and put on a suitable dress.

It took Wazir barely a quarter of an hour to complete her toilette, but when she came out of her room, it would have been no wonder for the twittering waxbills and the cooing doves which peopled her courtyard to have praised Allah in their hearts at the vision of unrivalled grace and elegance that she presented before them. There were traces still on her face of the previous night's exhaustion and the continual pricking of the thorn of anxiety, but like a full rose just before it wilts, her visage had a melancholy charm which more than compensated for mere freshness of mien. Her eyes bereft of kohl and her lips devoid of artificial gloss; on her neck she wore only one gold chain with a large lapis lazuli as pendant, and on each of her wrists she wore two slim gold bangles which had little golden orbs attached to them. On her nose she wore a plain diamond pin, and delicate but jewelled drops in her ears. Elegant simplicity seemed to rain down on her entire person.

She looked like a simple young girl who had suddenly become a woman, but who was not quite aware of that marvellous phenomenon. Her body, svelte and a miracle of perfection in proportion, did not at all have that heavenly ripeness which is characteristic of fully beautiful young women who have been loved and who have borne the fruit of that love. All the contours of Wazir's body, all the curves and promontories, were prominent without being openly inviting, but it was not at all the case that the balance and the pure eloquence of her body did not give intimation of those hidden mysteries.

Shamsuddin Ahmad was, as before, staggered speechless at the sight of Wazir when she came out. He just gazed, and quite forgot the immediate reason of his visit and the things that he intended to say to her. Wazir entered, bowed in salaam, and sat in front of him, a little to the right, as she had before. Shamsuddin Ahmad found that he was breathing hard; he controlled himself with some effort. Also, but with greater effort, he reined in his impulse to pull Wazir to his side, wave to the servants to close the door, and enjoy her in privacy.

She who had opened herself to him in delicate but tantalizing stages when he visited her in the guest house of his haveli in Daryaganj, and then had opened the arms of desire to him with such an impetuous flow of spontaneity that Shamsuddin Ahmad had felt as if he was being tossed and heaved about in an ocean of beauty, and as far as his own desire went, her body seemed to go with it, the swell of kisses and embraces rising like tumultuous waves: that very girl now seemed to him the embodiment of dignified bashfulness. Shamsuddin Ahmad felt his mouth going dry for want of appropriate words.

Wazir cast a shy but affectionate glance at the Navab and said, 'Your Honour is thinking some thoughts?'

Trying to find the most appropriate words, Shamsuddin Ahmad said, 'What am I thinking?' He paused. 'Actually, I was looking for the real Wazir. From where did you acquire it or were you given such bashfulness? And how does it happen for that very bashfulness to fly away on strong wings somewhere very, very far? I also want to understand what you would be if you were not such a rare combination of impetuosity and bashfulness. Would you be the same Wazir Khanam as you now are? . . . Bhai wallah, such an appropriate verse has come to my mind! It would seem as if the poet composed it for just this occasion.'

He then recited a verse from the Persian poet Mirza Rafi Vaiz:

If coquetry, and indifference, and quickness of gait,
And playfulness, and dignified self-control
Are one assembly, the Being that heads
That assembly is bashfulness.

'It is nothing but the loving and kind eye of His Honour that makes him see me as modest and bashful. I really do not see any merit in me. Maybe this bashfulness is what makes His Honour like this slave's face. I can only be proud of the ascendancy of my fortune.'

'Oh, so it is nothing but the elevation of your stars that I happen to desire you? But even so, there is substance in what you say. If your person, your personality, your body from head to foot, all of these are so charged with the quality of belovedness, one reason for it must be that you make the most proper use of modesty.'

He then quoted another verse of the same poet, saying that it must surely have been written for someone like Wazir:

Vaiz, you have eyes for her stature, her face,
Her hair; these for you are the attributes of beauty.
For me, beauty's attribute is bashfulness.

'The truth is, bhai wallah, that I cannot really enumerate your qualities of beauty which have slain me truly.'

A little black thorn of annoyance pricked in Wazir's heart. There has been nothing but words, words, so far. Will there be anything more? Or less? And when? As for me, I have already given him my body and my heart.

Shamsuddin Ahmad sensed that Wazir's silence was not because of her usual reticence. He asked, 'Wazir Khanam, why did you fall silent? Did my words displease in some way?'

Wazir raised her eyes; she smiled wanly, but spoke with careful deliberation, 'Flowers and their petals fall from Your Honour's lips as you speak. I just listen, speechless and unable to reply. But . . . I also believe that the fruit appears after the flowers fall.'

The Navab was quick to understand Wazir's meaning. He said, 'A flower-laden branch bends. Should you put out your hand, why then the flowers are yours, and the fruit too.'

Wazir laughed. 'For the destitute, your sweet words are the greatest treasure. I would say, if not flowers, let there be just a few petals for us who lie forlorn by the flower beds in your garden, with the hem of their garment spread like a beggar's tattered mantle.'

'So come. Fill the hem of your garment to capacity. Don't pull the mantle back.'

'Your Honour, I do not follow.'

Now the Navab spoke in grave, measured tones; his mood of light levity had suddenly disappeared. 'A three-storeyed house in Khanam ka Bazaar, Chandni Chowk. Two upper storeys for your residence, four shops on the ground floor, their rent to accrue to you in perpetuity. So what do you say to this?'

A light crimson glow appeared on Wazir's face, but her dark-brown eyes were not without thoughtful questioning. She looked at the Navab with those questioning eyes, but the Navab went on: 'Papers and transfer deeds for the house can be ready by this evening. You can ennoble the house with your auspicious feet immediately, or tomorrow, as you may desire. Packing, removing and reinstalling all the appurtenances of this house to the house in Khanam ka Bazaar by tonight is my responsibility. Through your lifelong, the house is your property, then it passes to your descendants.' The Navab laughed lightly, perhaps a little self-consciously before concluding, 'I have just one condition: I should have free run of the house and no one else but me should be allowed in.'

'His Honour puts his maid to shame. When there is no one but you in my heart, there can be no question of anyone else entering inside my house. If that house is mine, it is also yours, for I am yours. The door will always be open for you.'

'And you?' the Navab asked meaningfully.

Wazir parried the question deftly. 'Your Honour, I count for nothing. Put thy head at the beloved's feet, put thy brow at his footprints, is all the art that I know. I would be happy enough to be placed beside your doormat.'

'Hush! One never utters such self-debasing words! Bhai wallah, I will come to you with steps light as a secret entering one's breast. I shall not be a burden on your heart, or your soul, or body. Of course, if you kept me close as the necklace around your lovely neck, I would happily make the hem and collar of your garment my secure house and my permanent habitation.'

'I accept this service. I accept every service!'

'Your household expenditure and your servants' salaries will be taken care of by me. Towards expenses for your betel box and miscellaneous minor outgos, a sum of five hundred rupees will be presented to you every month. In earnest of a year's payments, six bags of a thousand rupees each await your pleasure.'

Wazir was astounded, unable even to gasp in astonishment. So much, and with such free generosity! Could anyone ever give even a fraction of it to her, or indeed, to anyone else? And I give nothing in return, except to lord it over in his house and be his woman! Nothing could be easier . . . but that one question? If I do not ask it now, the matter remains unresolved . . . No. There are hardly any words for me now to put my question . . .

'Elevated Presence, you favour me much more than I could claim or expect or hope. Even ancient kings of legend and fable could not have been so bounteous. I, a valueless particle of dust, have turned into the lamplight of a whole house and the flambeau of a bedchamber with just one glance from the heavenly orb of your love. I have no words, and even the greatest masters would have found their tongues halting for want of words at such moments.'

The Navab smiled a wry smile. 'So, that is all there is? Just largesse and bounty?'

'Your Honour, I can understand it to be nothing but largesse when you see beauty in my unbeautiful self and count that worthy which is of no worth. May Allah preserve you up until the end of time. What else is it, if not bountifulness of mind that sees good where there is no good and brightness where there is the dark of stain?'

'In former times, they termed it love, not bounty.' The Navab again smiled a dry smile. 'Well, let it go at that. If you were to practise a little magnanimity with me, I might get some return on my labours.'

'I lost everything. I lost all to you. There is nothing here, only you in the secret chambers of my body and soul.'

Shamsuddin Ahmad could not fail to detect the trace of tiredness and loss in Wazir's tone of voice, but he preferred not to pursue it. After a little pause, he went on: 'For the purpose of managing and efficiently supervising the affairs of your illustrious portal, there will always be at your service the mughlani Habib-un Nisa, and to keep you diverted, there will be Rahat Afza, more in fact your playmate than maid. I believe these arrangements will suffice for complete fulfilment of the desire for a life of comfort?'

'It is sufficient, My Lord, for my complete fulfilment of the desire for a life of comfort, to find a small place beneath your feet.'

Wazir again smiled, a little cryptically, but her meaning was not hidden from the Navab. Again, he decided not to go there. In his heart, he was certainly somewhat disappointed to find that Wazir too, like ordinary women, hankered after marriage, and maybe the rank and position that marriage would have conferred on her. Indeed, my mother was better, he said to himself. She was unable to read or write, and obviously, was quite ignorant of the graces and sophistications of the high-born begams; she wanted nothing but to please my father, may he rest in Paradise. Later she became his married wife, his Navab Begam, Mistress of his House, and everything else, but she lived only for her husband and her children. She cared not at all for property or glory or power.

Wazir noted that Shamsuddin Ahmad was now not as forthcoming as before. She, too, perceived immediately that the message coded in her last speech had been received and understood, and had proved somewhat irksome. But she did not do anything to make amends. She knew that the Navab did not believe her to be desirous of marriage because she considered marriage to be the threshold of power and authority, but that she had other, deeper reasons. Still, though she could see that the Navab was reading more into her utterances than she intended, she did not care to elaborate her meaning. Perhaps it was too abstruse even for her to put it in words. In any case, she knew that matters of integrity, fidelity and love were not resolved by mere conversation or negotiation.

The silence between them was about to become heavy. Wazir wished to break it before it could be interpreted as discord. So she spoke in reaffirmation, 'There is no worth in one who lies below, at the base. Yet I should be quite happy to lie beneath your feet, and will always be happy there. You give much more, so how can I contain within me the pride and joy of your ennobling kindness? Indeed, I would be unfortunate not to be overjoyed.'

A wave of relief and a smile of pleasure brightened the Navab's mien. 'Right. Now I have to settle some important tasks concerning the State,' he said as he rose. 'A team of packers and movers will be here shortly for your move from here to Chandni Chowk, or as and when you command.'

'My heart desires that I fly and arrive at my home just at this moment, but I think it will be convenient for all to move bag and baggage tomorrow,' Wazir replied with open happiness. 'But why is Your Honour going away at this time? It is almost lunchtime. You must eat before you go. Our fare will certainly not be anything like it should have been for you, but let us have a Barmecide feast today, as in the Alf Lailah!'

These happy words did please Shamsuddin Ahmad, but he really had some important business to conclude. He took a step forward, gave a loving pat on Wazir's cheek, kissed her on the forehead, and said, 'Thank you, Wazir Khanam. But not today. As Allah wills, you will soon have set up your house in Chandni Chowk. I would then feast there with you most pleasurably . . . And look, these security men will stay here, but you will have them even in Chandni Chowk, where there is full safety anyway.'

By the time Shamsuddin Ahmad reached the end of the carpet, Wazir, in spite of the Navab's protest, quickly picked up his shoes and helped him put them on. Shamsuddin Ahmad's attention, however, was not on putting on the shoes properly. Wazir Khanam's long tresses had slipped out of her wrap and were now adorning her neck and shoulder. The glory of her slender neck and the curve of her back now looked twice as alluring.

38

Wazir Khanam moves to a house in the colourful and pleasant locality of Chandni Chowk; a dark, beautiful boy is born to her and Navab Shamsuddin Ahmad Khan

EARLY OCTOBER 1830: In these times, homes, even stately homes, could be established as easily as they could be destroyed. The city of Delhi in particular had always seen sky-kissing mansions erected and peopled with dwellers in months, if not in weeks. The three-storey house in Chandni Chowk had shops on the ground floor; the two floors above each had a spacious courtyard, three verandas, three large rooms, a storeroom, a garments room, a water room and a toilet. Kitchen, pantry, provision room, servants' rooms, often shared, were on the lower floor. Habib-un Nisa had two small rooms to herself: one on the upper and the other on the lower floor. The largest room on the upper floor was used as a bedroom, but it also had, among other furniture, two cabinets full of books. Some of the books were Wazir's favourites and many others were those that Shamsuddin Ahmad liked to read when he had the time. There were a few books in English too, but they were rarely opened.

In the courtyards on both the upper floors a small fountain in marble played at the centre; there were flower beds with a couple of flowering shrubs at the farther end of the courtyard, facing the street. The upper floor had, in addition to a pigeon coop, a large wire-gauze cage for Wazir's pet birds. The house and its furnishings and appurtenances took barely three days to be set up and started as a going concern.

Downstairs in the Chowk and the smaller bazaars, the hum and bustle of life, beginning from almost sunup, only ceased very late at night. Besides the shoppers, sightseers and spectators, numerous pleasure-loving or idle young men—and quite a few older ones too—were to be found sauntering and enjoying the lights and flowering shrubs on both sides of Saadat Khan's canal and through the length of the Chowk, making use of the occasion to indulge in poetry and gossip and to keep an eye out for a glimpse of a lover or a well-known beauty. There were quite a few among the strollers who would these days be picked out as gay, but were then a part of the seamless whole.

Given the situation, it would have taken more audacity than could be within the capability of a brazen rascal to even think of making an adversarial play for Wazir or her house. Even so, the Navab put in place several procedures for her security. Two sepoys roamed the immediate area from start of the Chowk day until past midnight. Their duty was to remain on the alert against any suspicious person or activity near the house.

There was no approach to the upper floors from the shopfronts. Strangers would have to ask, and would thus betray themselves. The way upstairs was from the alley behind the shops. Just inside the door on the ground level was a narrow hall, occupied round the clock by three hefty and battle-hardened staff-bearers, each of them working an eight-hour shift. The first-floor landing was more spacious, walled from three sides, and with a heavy door on the fourth. The door, stout and well made of Indian plane wood, was decorated and strengthened with brass plates in floral designs, with a strong brass chain to be clanked by the visitor. The landing had a small wooden platform and its floor was covered with a carpet.

When a stranger rattled the chain, a tall, powerful Central Asian Turk woman, fully armed and in male battledress, would appear and inquire elaborate details about the visitor's name and business. It was obvious that no one, barring acquaintances or known persons, could reach the stage of being interviewed by the armed woman. Occasional tradesmen or women, and watchers of processions during the days of Muharram, Ram Lila or Basant were admitted only when they bore some introduction. From among the inner circle, Umdah Khanam and her attendants were the most frequent visitors. Wazir Khanam rarely went out; her most important destinations on outings were Manjhli's mansion, the mausoleums of the saints, especially The Elevated Presence, Nizam-ud Din Auliya, just outside the city, and The Elevated Presence, Khvajah Qutbuddin Bakhtiar Kaki at Mehrauli—the village was called Khvajah Sahib, rather than Mehrauli. These trips were invariably in a closed vehicle, and in the company of Shamsuddin Ahmad. During the times when Shamsuddin Ahmad stayed at his haveli in Ballimaran behind Chandni Chowk, there were frequent visits from the officers of the State, and their faces became familiar to the guardswomen; still, they were allowed entry only after all necessary inquiry.

Most of the women who were, in those days, employed as security guards or bodyguards, hailed from the territories of Sind and Kathiawar, independent states not yet annexed by the English. With their bodies extremely well knit, with powerful backs and arms like those of wild ponies, these women were expert at knife-throwing and knife-fighting in general combat, and tracking runaway horses, absconding criminals and prisoners with the help of natural and man-made clues.

Some havelis employed women of Turkic origin as was the case in Wazir's establishment. Those who wore female apparel were called urdabegni; qulmaqinis wore male dress. Both did the same kind of duty: security and bodyguarding. Very tall and brawny without even an ounce of flab on them, with pink complexion, their hair black or golden, and with smiling, almond-shaped eyes, these women were as ferocious and bloodthirsty as they were brave. It was reputed that one of these women could easily overcome ten men, and they never took prisoners: once they had disarmed or disabled their victim, they butchered him.

Shamsuddin Ahmad's grandfather Arif Jan, when he came to India in the eighteenth century from what is now Uzbekistan, had brought along with him a platoon of Uzbek fighter women as personal guards. These women married only among Uzbeks and Cossacks; that was why, even after many generations, they retained their looks and native character. The women with Wazir were the offspring of the original Uzbeks.

The elaborate security arrangements were mainly to discourage Fraser or his agents. Fraser apparently lost interest in Wazir Khanam quickly: partly because of the formidable security, but mainly because towards the end of October 1830, his spies reported an unusually high number of midwives visiting Wazir's house. Apparently, Wazir was pregnant. This was soon confirmed by one of his female informers. Now Fraser's hopes were dashed. An early break-up, or even a break-up at all, between Shamsuddin Ahmad and Wazir Khanam was now unlikely. Further, it was not expedient for Fraser to try to befriend a pregnant woman; he did not also have the patience to wait for Wazir to get through her pregnancy and then the confinement period before he could think of taking steps towards restarting action.

The Navab was now such a frequent visitor to the Chandni Chowk residence that his two havelis in Daryaganj and Ballimaran remained practically unused by him. Often, returning from his estates, he would stop at the Chandni Chowk residence instead of going to one of the havelis. Affection, easy familiarity and very nearly a meeting of the minds between him and Wazir seemed almost to grow every day, so much that Wazir quite forgot, or at least suppressed, the pain of being only a mistress and not the Begam. She made Shamsuddin Ahmad's pleasures, his likes and dislikes, the very pivot of her life. On his part, Shamsuddin Ahmad was always keen to shower gifts and presents on her, and not only in the physical sense, but also in terms of genuine words of sweet love and gestures expressive of value.

Habib-un Nisa was wont to observe that the unity between the two reminded her of the love stories of legend and romance, something which she did not ever expect to see in real life. They were like a pair of swans, famed in stories as being ever inseparable, once they chose each other as mate. One did not feel content without the other; if one of them felt even the least bit unwell, the other unfailingly intuited it.

It so happened once that Shamsuddin Ahmad was away in Firozepur Jhirka and did not make an appearance for a full fortnight. It took six days for a round trip from Delhi to Firozepur Jhirka. For Loharu, the round trip took five days; thus a stay of just four days at either place entailed an absence of nine or ten days. Wazir had become so attuned to the ten days' regime of absence that by the ninth day she began to feel restless. This time, when the Navab did not return after the customary number of days and sent no message either, Wazir became so distracted and worried that Rahat Afza and Habiba, when they looked at her, could barely maintain their own equanimity.

Rahat Afza and Wazir were now so friendly and familiar with each other's ways that during the Navab's absence, Rahat Afza slept in Wazir's bedroom, and during the Navab's absence, hers was the first face that Wazir saw in the morning. And even when the Navab spent the night there, Rahat Afza was always the second person whom Wazir saw in the morning.

Customarily, Shamsuddin Ahmad woke well before the crack of dawn every day. On getting up, he would leave Wazir sleeping, get bathed and dressed and go down to the meeting room on the lower floor to study his State papers, or decide on important issues. A small durbar would become active within a short time. By the time of breakfast, Shamsuddin Ahmad would have taken care of most official matters that had needed his attention.

By then, it would be time for Wazir to rise. Rahat Afza would carry to her a small basket of flowers of the season and a little tray of cool drinks. She would tiptoe in, and as she had done on that first morning in the guest house in the haveli, gently tickle the soles of Wazir's feet, and when Wazir opened her eyes, she would smile in the same old heart-winning way and said, 'Good morning, Khanam sahib.' Rahat Afza assisted Wazir at all the routines of the morning, from waking up to putting on her day clothes.

Despite so much friendliness, affability and near equality in age, Rahat Afza was unable to do anything to lighten Wazir's black humours during Shamsuddin Ahmad's unusually long absence. Wazir was tormented by fears that Fraser might do some mischief to the Navab, or have him waylaid and assassinated. Rahat Afza did her best to convince her of the impossibility of such an eventuality, but Wazir would not be consoled.

Finally, it was the evening of the sixteenth day, when dusk had fully fallen, that Shamsuddin Ahmad's arrival was announced. Wazir ran down to the landing, took his hand in her two hands fast as if she feared he might disappear suddenly. Without making her usual inquiries about how the journey passed and whether Shamsuddin Ahmad would like some cool drink or to freshen up, she began to speak without pausing for breath: 'Navab sahib, please, where have you been all this while? You know that I have life only when I look at you. If I do not see you for even an hour, I feel suffocated. If you come here with such huge gaps between visits, I should have expended my life soon enough!' It was the first time ever that Wazir had used words of such open ebullience and such fiery emotions to express her love for Shamsuddin Ahmad—or anyone for that matter—and that too in the presence of others. It was usual in their cultural tradition to overstate things, especially protestations of love; ordinary friendship usually merited extremely warm and effusive—in fact, almost romantic—language in that culture. But both parties in such transactions well knew also which words and tones of voice were merely formal—though not entirely bereft of the truth—and which words and intonations expressed the true feelings of the heart.

The truth of her feelings was clear and hotly bright on that occasion. It seemed to everyone present that the white heat of the passion of love, and the fear of loss, had become a conflagration of words, ready to burn away Wazir's customary reticence and modesty.

The Navab, though he knew well Wazir's various moods of surrender and conquest, was taken aback. He took Wazir's hand in his, pressed it tenderly, kissed it and spoke in a low voice, 'Bahu Khanam, I too have my life only when I can look at you. My breath seems to falter and stop if I do not see you for some time. But, sometimes . . . it is the world, after all. If Mir did not come, he must have had something important to do.'

Having recited a line and a half from Mir, Shamsuddin Ahmad permitted a pale smile to come to his lips, as if conveying apology and shame. Wazir took her hand out of Shamsuddin Ahmad's and began to dry her eyes. It was the first time that he had addressed her as 'Bahu Khanam'. Indeed, that was the title that Ahmad Bakhsh Khan—may he dwell in Paradise—had conferred on Shamsuddin Ahmad's mother after he married her. One reason for Wazir's tearfulness was the Navab addressing her as 'Bahu Khanam', and that too in front of witnesses. There might have been some meaning coded in there, or there might not, but no one doubted from that moment that the pair of lovers could ever be separated.

*

Although it was Wazir's third conception, and her general health was extremely good, and all the midwives were fully agreed that Khanam sahib would have a fully safe and easy delivery and the baby would be born without delay or not too early either, and would be quite healthy, Wazir's heart was besieged by a variety of fears. As the weather cooled, the wave of fear in her heart became colder and more frightening . . . One of her most dreadful thoughts was that she might give birth to a girl, and the Navab might not like it, for he already had two or three daughters. Moreover, despite her good health and the prognosis being bright, she was anguished at the possibility of miscarrying the baby.

Wazir had some vague notion that the Navab wished devoutly for a son. She had also learnt—more by way of gossip than by way of information—that the Navab's second wife was unable to conceive because of some medical problem. She was called Husaini Begam and was given the title of Amir Bahu on marriage. Her father was Vali Muhammad Khan, a minor nobleman of Delhi. With the senior wife Afzal-un Nisa Begam, who was commonly called Jani Begam, Shamsuddin Ahmad already had two daughters. Married to Shamsuddin Ahmad in 1828, she was the daughter of Mirza Mughal Beg Khan, a member of Delhi's senior nobility.

Wazir Khanam did not know it at that time, but Shamsuddin Ahmad had yet another daughter by a concubine from the poorer classes. Her name was Champa, and the daughter was called Rahmat-un Nisa. The daughters that he had with Afzal-un Nisa Begam were called Ahmad-un Nisa Begam and Shams-un Nisa Begam. A male heir could be seen as an important and even urgent need for Shamsuddin Khan, given the unstable nature of the times and the dispute with his stepbrothers and their families. The fact that he named his legitimate daughters Ahmad-un Nisa Begam and Shams-un Nisa Begam would seem to suggest Shamsuddin Ahmad's keenness for the name of his ancestors to survive.

. . . And if it is a son, but stillborn, or with some congenital defect? Granted that I'm quite whole and hale in body, and the Navab's person is often cited in society for both beauty and strength of body . . . but who knows? No hakim or vaid or midwife could ever probe the depths of these mysteries. Perfectly proportioned and healthy parents are known to have defective offspring. And if the baby has some deformity, it is invariably the mother who gets the blame.

All her attending physicians had confirmed repeatedly that Wazir stood in no need of extra medications or overages by way of 'strengthening' food. They affirmed that the normal diet and precautions were just perfect. The pregnant mother's pulse, urine and all other signs clearly suggested a healthy baby and an easy, normal delivery. Still, Wazir had, unbeknownst to the physicians and even, or rather especially, Shamsuddin Ahmad, used Habiba's good offices, or using her as a go-between, secretly obtained all possible charms, amulets and 'spiritually advised' medicines. One by one, she visited the shrines of the twenty-two leading Sufi saints of history buried in Delhi—these shrines gave Delhi the universal sobriquet of Bais Khvajah ki Chaukhat ('Portal of Twenty-two Sufi Masters')—and prayed for their intercession with Allah that she may give birth to a healthy and defect-free son.

She had been extremely fond of bathing in cool, if not actually cold, water. But the moment the early winter inaugurated pleasantly chill mornings and evenings, she took to drinking water that was half cool and half warm, while bathing in warm water, followed shortly thereafter in hot water lest she catch cold and the cold affect the foetus. Her dilemma about foods was that she was scared of eating those things which the Graeco-Islamic system of medicine pronounced 'dry and hot'—the fear was that the foetus's brain might be affected by the hot and dry humours.

The problem was that as the winter marched ahead, things described as 'hot and wet' by the hakims and also some vaids, became more and more scarce in the bazaars. She gave up all kinds of meat because all red meat was 'dry and hot'. She was very fond of venison when her life used to be normal and less anxious; but venison was not risk-free, because it was meat, after all. Still, she sometimes drank a venison soup or thin broth with some actual meat in it. She never did like any of the waterfowls, but since waterfowls by nature were 'hot and wet', a roast duck was put on the tablecloth on some days.

As for fish, alas, nearly all of them were 'cold and wet', so they were clearly prohibited. Prawns, especially the tiny ones found in Indian rivers, were admissible in spite of their strong fish smell, because all prawns were designated as 'hot and wet'. Wazir gave up rice, because there were two theories about it—according to one of them, all rice was 'hot and dry'. She was fond of lettuce and all kinds of greens. The problem was that spinach and purslane were both 'cold and wet', and chaulai (*Amaranthus polygamous*) was 'cold and dry'. So all the greens lost out in the culinary stakes. Khirni (*Mimosups kauki*), the slim, bright yellow, rather sweet but somewhat astringent berry, and carrot were desirable, being 'hot and wet', but they were not always available.

The most desired edibles were almonds, grapes and sweet potatoes: all were 'hot and wet' and also preventive of many medical conditions. Spices—like turmeric, black pepper (both large and small), mint, cumin seed—being 'hot and dry' were practically out of bounds, even if that meant her table was bland and somewhat odd for want of spices and seasonable foods. Among the pulses, she began to favour the urad (*Delichos pilosus*); though it was costive, it was 'hot and wet'.

For fear of catching a cold and transmitting it to her baby, she gave up on cool drinks, especially in the morning, and took to coffee and, occasionally, tea. She used these beverages sparingly and unwillingly, more like medicines, and mainly because tea ('hot and dry') was supposed to be an aid to digestion and coffee a stimulant and a cure for headache.

Another condition, which must always be taken into account before choosing any food, was to make sure that it was astrologically compatible. All eatables, she knew, are governed by or have their qualities influenced by one or more of the planets, and their position in the zodiac. She had no horoscope of her own, nor was one ever drawn for Shamsuddin Ahmad either. So she could not be certain whether, for instance, almonds would suit her and her baby. She knew almonds were 'hot and wet', and were good in almost every way. She found out that almonds were ruled by Jupiter! Well, then, nothing could be better, because Jupiter was the most powerful planet. Similarly, waterfowls were governed by the Moon and their flesh was 'hot and wet', so nothing better, because Moon and Jupiter were close friends.

Thus Wazir's pregnancy made her a sort of amateur and, in fact, also quite a naive dietician for pregnant woman. Shamsuddin Ahmad smiled inwardly, but said nothing. Habib-un Nisa and Rahat Afza were of course most ardent compradors in pursuit of Wazir's dietetic philosophy. In other ways too, Rahat Afza was a true source of comfort. She was fond of poetry, and though she had no musical training, she had a good singing voice, and she had become quite adept at singing, having taken part, since she was small, in singing parties during marriages or religious occasions where poems, and sometimes poems of a very high order, were recited or sung.

Rahat Afza, during those days, sometimes hummed or sang snatches of such Hindi and Persian poetry as were Wazir's favourites. She often sang solo, though once in a while she took a small tanpura as drone accompaniment. A ghazal by Emperor Akbar's Poet Laureate Faizi was Wazir's abiding love. She had Rahat Afza sing it to her as often as feasible:

O amour-provoking, coquettish Turkic beauty
Who are here in the assembly with us;
You pierced my eyes deep and have settled
In my heart.

Because Shamsuddin Ahmad was of Turkish origin, Wazir was particularly fond of this verse with which the ghazal began. The words 'Turk-e ghamza zan', here translated inadequately as 'amour-provoking, coquettish Turkic beauty' sometimes reduced her to tears. She loved the other verses of the ghazal too. Moreover, Wazir saw in this ghazal a true picture of her love and her absorption in Shamsuddin Ahmad.

A pity that I, whose blood was fated to be shed
Am not today; while you are seated

In the assembly, dagger in hand and sword
Hanging by your neck.

All the beauties stand abashed,
Their colour is flown:
For it is you, everywhere, bright like the sun.

There were days when she felt that the love for the Prophet of God was overflowing in her heart. Perhaps she identified the Prophet as the ideal of all existence; perhaps she sought to blow away her deep-seated uncertainties by calling upon her love for the Prophet. At such moments it was the verses of the fifteenth-century Persian poet Shaikh Jami singing his love for the Prophet and celebrating the uniqueness and universal sweep of the Prophet's spirit that filled her with power, almost ecstatic in its intensity:

And may there be salutations from God
For the Light from which were created
More lights. The earth, unmoving in the intensity
Of his love; the ever-wandering heavens
Crazed for the love of him.

Praise for his
Kohl-beautified eyes, like the nargis flower,
Described by God as 'unswerving',
Praise for his
Scented tresses, like 'night when it conceals (the world)'.

Jami, about the mysteries in his breast, read:
'Have we not expanded for thee thy breast?'
What praise could one give for his Ascension,
But the Quran: 'Glory to Allah, Who did take
His servant for a Journey from the Sacred
To the farthest Mosque.'

This poem by Jami spoke to Wazir as the very essence and distillation of the Prophet's status as the beloved of all believers. It seemed to her that the whole world, all the mysteries and causes of its creation, the moons and stars, the Milky Way, the woods and hills and rivers, men and djinns: all were lovers, feeble lovers and servants of her Master, her Lord. She was convinced that whoever or whatever loved him truly would acquire the same quality and glory of belovedness.

She was quite certain that all the nine skies, all the eighteen thousand worlds, loved her Prophet, and whatever there was in the world to entice the heart and ravish the senses were the flowers of that very love with which the Garden of Reality was permitted to light up the world of possibility. She made Rahat Afza sing the verses again and yet again, and even then, she persuaded herself that she had not heard them to her heart's content, and she would sing or recite the poem, and her eyes would mist over with tears. She prayed that her son's fortune be of the brightest—she was convinced that she would have a son—fortune by the grace of the dust clinging to the sandals of that Lord of the two worlds and the luminance of the poet's blessed words. She prayed to God to let the boy be so fortunate as to be given his share of personal valour—the courage of being unworldly with a Mirza's style and flair—and the gift of winning the hearts and opinions of the people.

As we reported earlier, Wazir had some smattering of music in her and had a good singing voice, and while Rahat Afza had no musical knowledge, she did have an excellent, if unformed, singing voice. Wazir's relaxed relationship with Rahat Afza and her love for Shamsuddin Ahmad had created such an ecstatic thrill in Wazir that she began to put some heart into her singing. We just mentioned Jami's poem on the Prophet, but in addition to Persian poems, Wazir knew by heart many songs of Mira Bai, the sixteenth-century Hindu saint and Krishna devotee. Similarly, she had learnt many love songs to Krishna attributed to the legendary blind poet Surdas.

Now, with so many stimuli working for a revival of music and devotion in her spirit, Wazir had called to her immediate memory many of those songs, and she sang them often with Rahat Afza as her vocal accompanist. She now made a practice, also, of having women professional singers over to her home and have them sing for her Amir Khusrau's qavvalis.

In those days, Chandni Chowk started just where Chowk Sadullah Khan ended. To the west of the Chowk was Khas Bazaar, to the south was Kashmiri Katra, to the east, the Neighbourhood of the Boatmen and the haveli of Asad Ali Hazari. As one entered the Chowk from the north, the first building at its very mouth was the Jain Temple, also called the Lal

Mandir (Red Temple), which went back to the time before the founding of the city of Shahjahanabad by Shahjahan who had donated lands in trust for the temple in perpetuity. The trust was still functional and supported the temple. As you went past the temple, you were within the main Chowk, and here the first notable building was the Gauri Shankar Mandir, reputed to have been constructed with grants from Emperor Aurangzeb, the Dweller in Paradise. Just a little beyond the Gauri Shankar Mandir was the tall building of Gurdwara Sisganj, holy to the Sikhs.

All three houses of worship always had a throng of visitors and worshippers, as they do today; except that now the throngs are many times greater and much more motley in character. In the times that we are writing about, Hindu and Sikh and Jain songs of devotion and prayer began to be sung at dawn and continued unabated up until the closing of the Chowk, well past midnight. These voices not only added to the liveliness and excitement of the Chowk but also created a prayerful mood very nearly throughout that almost frenetic place.

A little beyond the Sikh Gurdwara, on the right as one entered from Chowk Sadullah Khan, had been a place called Fav-varah, later called Fountain, but nothing of it survived in Wazir Khanam's time. To the right, there were shops whose upper floors were residential. In front of the shops was that famous mosque called Sunahri (Golden) Masjid. It was in the courtyard of this mosque that Nadir Shah drew his sword, signalling the dreadful massacre and sack of Delhi in 1739. Conservative estimates put the number of dead at thirty thousand, within the space of a few hours.

Wazir's house was situated at a point from which the North Gate of the Red Fort would have been visible but for a myriad houses and Khanam ka Bazaar blocking the view. The agreeable noise and bustle of Khanam ka Bazaar melded and poured into the colourful, pleasant and vehement world of Chandni Chowk. Those who knew Ilahabas (as Akbar sometimes called it, otherwise Ilahabad, and then Allahabad as the English called it) would appreciate this better, for it was in that Holy City that the light, wide and sluggish waters of the holy Ganga hugged and embraced the deep, swift and greener waters of the holy Jamna.

Immediately opposite Wazir's house was a mosque, again called Sunahri. This mosque had a very high plinth and Wazir could see, from the upper floor of her house, its arches and its balcony. Built in 1747 by Javed Khan Khvaja the Eunuch, whose official title was Navab Bahadur Khan, this mosque was distinguished among the numerous others in Delhi because it was made of a stone called 'sang-i-basi'. A red sandstone with a tinge of black, it was not generally used for large and heavy structures, but had been used with great finesse in the construction of this mosque.

It was said that when Aminuddin Ahmad Khan, who was very young at that time, was once riding with his father Ahmad Bakhsh Khan in a buggy, an extremely large musth elephant attacked their carriage. The horse and the coachmen died on the spot and the buggy was smashed to pieces. When Ahmad Bakhsh Khan and Aminuddin Ahmad Khan were ejected from the carriage, Ahmad Bakhsh Khan instantly picked up his son and observing that the high staircase of the Sunahri Mosque was in front, he leaped for the stairs, unreachable by the elephant, and thus found safety inside the mosque. It was often said that Allah gave them back their lives in return for the Navab's unselfish service to His house.

The building in which Wazir now lived was bought by Navab Ahmad Bakhsh Khan around 1816. From that time, he also assumed the responsibility of the mosque's maintenance, necessary repairs and lighting, while also giving out salaries to its staff. Shamsuddin Ahmad Khan now discharged that duty.

*

It was now February in the year 1831, and the holy month of Ramadan for the Muslims. The weather was marvellously pleasant, the sky entirely devoid of clouds and the air free of dust, and voices travelled far in the clean atmosphere: if Wazir was a little attentive of an evening, she could hear the prayer leader in the Sunahri Mosque reciting long chunks of the Quran during the special Ramadan prayers in his flowing, musical voice. These prayers were called taravih and as a rule, the whole of the Quran was recited at least once during these prayers performed through the month of Ramadan. Wazir took particular care to avoid noises or loud, idle talk during the time that the taravih prayers were being said. Maybe not everybody else did so, but Wazir certainly took pains to keep her ear attuned to the voice of the taravih leader as he recited the Quran. Mian Jafar Husain was renowned all over Delhi for his clear voice, his grave and balanced enunciation, observing in full the rules of pronouncing the Quranic Arabic, carefully avoiding any affectation. There were many in

Wazir's house who kept the fast; even those who did not (like Wazir), gave full respect to the sanctity of the month.

The month of Ramadan passed like a continuing festival. Just before the festival of Id, signifying the end of the days of fasting, Wazir and her baby-to-be-born were regaled with gifts: garments, ornaments, toys, money. Special sweets were cooked for visitors of whom there were many, but two special visitors were Navab Yusuf Ali Khan and Umdah Khanam. More interesting and pleasant a surprise were Shamsuddin Ahmad's sisters, Navab Begam and Jahangirah Begam, who visited a few days after the day of Id. The Navab's two wives, naturally, gave Wazir the coldest of shoulders.

Navab Begam and Jahangirah Begam stayed quite a while. They were not only remarkably friendly but also remarkably graceful. Good breeding and the sense of a grand lifestyle oozed from every word and gesture of theirs. Both were taller than average, fair-complexioned, with delicate bodies, long, almond-shaped greenish eyes, and long, golden hair. There had been many proposals of marriage for Navab Begam, but nothing had been settled yet. They became friends and sisters with Wazir in no time.

*

It was about two in the afternoon of the 12th of Zil-Hijjah, 1246 (25 May 1831), when a son was born to Wazir Khanam. The voices of women singers proficient at singing songs of joy at the birth of a son, various other visitors, and of Habib-un Nisa and Rahat Afza, filled Wazir's house with words of felicitation.

It was the third and last day of Id-al Azha, the feast to commemorate the Prophet Abraham's sacrifice. As was his wont, Shamsuddin Ahmad Khan spent the actual day of the feast in Firozepur Jhirka, and departed for Loharu the next day. The first destination was Tijari, only eight miles away, but there was no real road to it. The entire route consisted of narrow foot trails and forests of palash, wild berry and some flowering but thorny shrubs. The Navab's suite, entirely on camels, negotiated the difficult journey with no difficulty but with little speed. From Tijari to Loharu the road was full of all kinds of traffic, and was therefore well maintained. A couple of miles past Tijari a branch led to Loharu, and the main road went on to Delhi passing through Faridabad and Sohna.

Shamsuddin Ahmad Khan entered the Fort at Loharu before sundown.

Ritual sacrifices were performed on his arrival; a substantial portion of the sacrificed animals' meat was distributed among the poor. Relations and the employees of the State were given rewards and presents of money and goods. For some reason, perhaps intuitively, Shamsuddin Ahmad Khan suddenly decided to formally present himself before his stepmother Begam Jan and submit his greetings. He gave to his stepbrothers a thousand rupees each as Id gift; his five sisters received new expensive outfits and one hundred and a quarter rupees each. To the dowager mother, he presented a five-stringed pearl necklace. He partook of the special Id delicacies and took his seat in the divan khanah, which was the formal drawing room and also his court room. Receiving presents from his subjects and giving gifts in return kept him busy through the day, but his heart was not really in the business of the State; his mind kept on wandering towards Delhi and the expected news of birth.

There was no information about the childbirth up until the evening of the 12th of Zil-Hijjah. Shamsuddin Ahmad Khan left for Delhi early in the morning the next day and reached Delhi on the 15th of Zil-Hijjah (28 May). Happy tidings awaited him there. The courier dispatched by Habiba from Delhi had left on 26 May, and it was quite by chance that the Navab's party did not meet him during one of the numerous stoppages.

When she saw her baby for the first time, Wazir Khanam felt that her heart was going to stop: the experience was so shocking. The baby was quite healthy, giving promise of a good height as he grew up, the bones of its face were noble, its nose and mouth well proportioned, but its colour was dark . . . No, it was not just dark. The baby was jet dark, almost an Abyssinian. Although, as we have noted a number of times, Wazir's colour could not be described as anything but light brown, the fact that she could have given birth to a baby of such dark hue quite passed the imagination. The newborn gentleman was not only very dark, his hair too was quite black, dense and curly already; it was not at all like Wazir's fine and shiny tresses.

Careful examination with the view of determining the infant's favourable points, and lifting and putting him back in the cradle a number of times to inspect him from all sides, revealed the following: Quite contrary to the Abyssinians, the baby's nose was straight and prominent, so much that in spite of its chubby cheeks, the nose was the first thing that one noticed on the face; then, his forehead was quite high, and his eyes were exceptionally large with long lashes falling upon them like delicate screens; last of all, his fingers were long and pointed, his wrists wide and strong, and even his toes were well formed and somewhat longer than usual.

The baby looked alert and seemed to take an interest in his environment by raising his wrinkled little neck and looking around. Quite unlike other newborns, the child, within a few hours of coming out from the mother's womb, showed a tendency to open its eyes and look at the person who tried to lift it from the cradle or the bed and lay it on his or her lap, as if it were examining the reasons for the disturbance. Held lovingly close to the breast, its dark complexion actually began to look attractive, because there was, on its baby face, an unusual liveliness, almost a magnetic pull. It was also easily consoled and preferred to play with its toys rather than cry. Habib-un Nisa instantly lost her heart to him; she always proclaimed that it was the truest child of Khanam sahib and took after her in every important respect. She did not tire of cooing to the baby, singing to it, kissing it and declaring that he would grow into a young man as beautiful as his mother, but in a manly mode.

Wazir hoped ardently for her father and Bari Begam to come even for the briefest of moments and see her, maybe pray for her and give a protective amulet or charm or two before she went into confinement. But repeated messages and requests had no effect. Wazir's father did not deign to visit even though it was his first Muslim grandchild from Wazir. Wazir was understandably sad, but she could rationalize by telling herself that as neither she nor Umdah had anything to show by way of acts of honour or conduct suited to girls of good family, it was not unnatural for her people to shun them.

Wazir invited a muezzin who knew the Quran by heart to come and say the call to prayer in the infant's right ear and the Affirmation of Faith in its left. They waited for the Navab before the baby could be named. For the present, by some consensus, everyone called it Bacche Mian ('the honourable baby'): 'The honourable baby is hungry', 'The honourable baby is awake' and so on. They always spoke about him and of him in the respectful second- or third-person plural as if he was not an infant, but a senior person to be revered. This practice was to remain permanently in place.

When the 'honourable baby sahib' was not asleep in his cradle, he was invariably to be found in someone's arms, looking intently at whoever was there in front of him. Somewhat understandably, within just two or three days of giving birth, Wazir declared in her heart that Bacche Mian was the sweetest, cuddliest and the most beautiful baby in the world. Though she did hire a dai pilai (maid-to-suckle), she would surreptitiously give her own nipple to him even at the risk of overfeeding him, and offered all kinds of prayer so that the milk would not upset the poor thing. Finally, the Navab arrived in Delhi on the 15th of Zil-Hijjah and alighted straight at the house in Khanam ka Bazaar. Quite forgetting that her own colour was not of the fairest, and that the Navab's own mother could not have been fair by any means, Wazir trembled in her heart, fearful that the Turkestani family (and Shamsuddin Ahmad Khan, above all), all pink and rosy like the apples of their land, might reject her Bacche Mian for being too dark.

Navab Shamsuddin Ahmad was extremely and truly happy to see his first son. Quite contrary to Wazir's fears, the Navab did not say a word about the boy's complexion. Instead, he observed that he took after Bahu Khanam in good looks. He promptly had a sum of 2100 rupees circled around Wazir's bed, and then had the money distributed to the poor and the needy. After this ceremony, he gave away handfuls of rupees to all the midwives, servants and to anyone who was attached to the establishment at Khanam ka Bazaar in any way, regular or casual. He again said the call for prayer in the baby's ears and said, 'I name this my first son after my dear brother Ibrahim Ali Khan who died in infancy; for his informal name I give him the name Navab Mirza, because I see in him the elegance and style of both a navab and a Mirza.'

The name Navab Mirza became so well loved and popular that everyone soon forgot Ibrahim Ali Khan and Navab Mirza became the true name of the newborn.

39

A couple of blissful years pass by, a wedding is celebrated in Navab Shamsuddin Ahmad's family, but storm clouds gather on the horizon

TWO YEARS PASSED. Those were the two best years in the life of Shamsuddin Ahmad Khan. His control over his State was firmer than ever before. Crops had been good; tradesmen visited his territories in larger numbers. Under his strong and just rule his lands became free of thugs, highwaymen and dacoits. The annual revenue, between three and five hundred thousand rupees in his father's time, rose and became seven hundred thousand to a million rupees. His love for Wazir Khanam grew apace. Navab Mirza's intelligence, quickness of wit and comprehension, and cheerful playfulness won the hearts not only of his parents but also of all those who saw him. By the time he was eleven months old, Navab Mirza had begun to talk and comprehend the conversation around him. By the age of two, he knew many verses and small songs by heart. His sense of rhythm and notes was so strong that he could sing simple songs keeping to the rhythm and the tune.

As a child of three, he was able to pick up enough Persian through his father's conversations, and understand the language when it was delivered slowly. Soon after, he was able to talk in Persian, if haltingly. His physical beauty grew as fast as his faculty of speech. He could be distinguished among his peers not only for his good looks and sweet temper, but also for his well-developed, well-proportioned and bigger-than-average body. Everyone now believed that very soon Shamsuddin Ahmad would marry his beloved Bahu Khanam and have Navab Mirza's succession approved by the durbars at Alwar and Calcutta.

During this time, the wedding ceremonies of Shamsuddin Ahmad Khan's sister Navab Begam were performed with great pomp and circumstance. The actual wedding took place at Firozepur Jhirka, but food was given to the poor of Delhi for seven days, and huge trays of food, called torah, were sent over to all friends' and relatives' houses.

The bridegroom was Zain-ul Abidin Khan Arif, a nineteen-year-old aristocrat and poet; extremely handsome, but somewhat wan and pale of face, he was later diagnosed with phthisis. His father, Sharaf-ud Daulah Navab Ghulam Husain Khan Masrur, was the son of Sharaf-ud Daulah Navab Faizullah Khan Bahadur Suhrab Jang, a close relative of Shamsuddin Ahmad Khan. Navab Ghulam Husain Khan's wife and the bridegroom's mother, Buniyadi Begam, were the daughters of Navab Ilahi Bakhsh Maruf, younger brother of Navab Ahmad Bakhsh Khan. Thus, Buniyadi Begam was first cousin to Shamsuddin Ahmad Khan, and her son, the bridegroom, was his nephew.

There was also another older connection between the two families: Arif's great-grandfather was Qasim Jan. Gali Qasim Jan, a street named after him, still exists in Delhi. The title Sharaf-ud Daulah was conferred upon him by the Mughal Prince Ali Gauhar in recognition of his gallantry in a battle in the Province of Bihar. Ali Gauhar, affectionately known as Lal Mian, and also as Mirza Bulaqi, became King Emperor—Shah Alam Bahadur Shah II—in 1759 and commanded that the title Sharaf-ud Daulah should continue as hereditary in Qasim Jan's family. The younger brother of Qasim Jan was Arif Jan, whose son was Ahmad Bakhsh Khan, Shamsuddin Ahmad Khan's father.

Unfortunately, despite his noble birth and eminent ancestry, Arif was not financially strong. Ahmad Bakhsh Khan had settled upon him a monthly pension of two hundred and fifty rupees; it was continued by Shamsuddin Ahmad, and that was the bridegroom's main source of sustenance. The wedding dinner, customarily given by the bridegroom's family, had actually been paid for by Shamsuddin Ahmad Khan. Sharaf-ud Daulah had kept up appearances by arriving at the dinner well in advance, as if he was in charge. William Fraser was invited to the marriage and the dinner, but he did not come. Wazir Khanam was given no part in the celebrations, though the bride and groom paid personal respects to her in Khanam ka Bazaar a few days after the marriage.

Buniyadi Begam had separated from Sharaf-ud Daulah Navab Ghulam Husain Khan on grounds of incompatibility. On separation, her husband had assigned to Buniyadi Begam some property; she was also given custody of their son. Due to his stressful boyhood and lack of the best of means,

Zain-ul Abidin Khan Arif grew up to be a sickly youth with unsystematic education. He was extremely able by nature and therefore was able to acquire a great deal of Persian and adequate Arabic, Astronomy, Philosophy and History, mostly through his own diligence. Commemorating his ancestor, he took Arif for his nom de plume.

It might be worth mentioning here that Buniyadi Begam's younger sister, Umrao Begam, was married to the aristocrat-poet Mirza Asadullah Khan Ghalib. It was through the intercession of his aunt Umrao Begam, that Arif became a pupil of Mirza Ghalib in poetry. Umrao Begam was so close to Arif that after Arif's untimely death she took in and brought up his two children as her own.

The marriage had been arranged, thus, more on the basis of the family connections between the two Houses rather than on any individual rank and affluence to which Arif might have had a claim. It was expected that he would, after marriage in the House of Shamsuddin Ahmad, get some more assets and support from him, over and above the pension granted by Ahmad Bakhsh Khan. He had, after all, a wife to support, and probably soon children too, and was expected to live in a style commensurate with his new connection.

*

Navab Mirza was now three years old (May 1834), and his birthday was celebrated most lovingly and splendidly. Yet the birthday also seemed to signal a new phase in the lives of Wazir Khanam and Shamsuddin Ahmad Khan. Unexpected disorders, tumults and conflicts raised their ugly head everywhere. In the beginning, everyone thought that it was one of those phases that invariably happen over a lifetime and then go away quickly, leaving no trace and not causing permanent harm. But everything seemed to develop fast into ugly tumours, eating at the very roots of the couple's physical and mental well-being.

At first, it was nothing much: Navab Begam fell ill. Though nothing was apparently wrong, she did not get better in spite of the best medical care. She had become pregnant during the second month of marriage, but the midwives saw nothing untoward or alarming in it. Many weeks passed before she could be diagnosed with a consumptive abdomen. Now it was feared that the foetus might be lost, or if it survived, it might be affected prenatally by the consumption, or it might be born with some serious physical handicap. Another and more urgent fear was that the disease had caused Navab Begam's pelvic bones to become brittle and hollow. Childbirth could cause death for both mother and the baby.

In the event, Navab Begam's race was run sooner than the maturity of the foetus. She was about to conclude her seventh month when she went into labour and began to bleed copiously. It took no more than a day and night of pain and bleeding for the flame of both lives to expire. The mother was barely eighteen at that time.

40

Resident Sahib William Fraser visits humiliation upon Navab Shamsuddin Ahmad Khan in public

GRIEVING FOR ONE sister, Shamsuddin Ahmad Khan now became even more anxious to do his duty of getting his surviving sister married expeditiously. There were many proposals, but none appealed to him. Busy in sending out women who were professional bride-dressers and marriage negotiators to Houses of repute, in his heart praying to God for his sister to quickly find a husband who suited her status, he was a little less mindful of other affairs.

Shamsuddin Ahmad Khan did not expect Fraser not to feed his grudge against him and not pursue any plans that he could hatch to do harm to him. Because Fraser was, in addition to being Resident at the Delhi Court, Commissioner of the vast area designated as 'Delhi' by the Company, and numerous occasions and excuses were available to the Company Bahadur to interfere in Navab Shamsuddin Ahmad's administration and keep him under critical observation. Fraser had four kinds of power: political, judicial, criminal and civil. There was thus no lack of opportunity for Fraser to assert his authority on the 'Native States', and Navab Shamsuddin Ahmad was but a small potentate in the Indian scheme of things at that time.

They met, of course, on social occasions if such meeting was unavoidable, though Shamsuddin Ahmad managed to stay away often from parties where Fraser could be expected. He duly presented, or rather submitted, the mandatory dali of presents on the English Great Day, though the return gift from Fraser was invariably paltry. Shamsuddin Ahmad was obliged to pocket the implicit slight.

Suddenly one day, information reached him that having become impatient at the delay from the Great Lord Sahib Bahadur's Court at Calcutta in conveying a decision on the issue of the succession to the territories of Firozepur Jhirka and Loharu, the Navab Resident Bahadur had now dispatched a personal but official letter to Sir Charles Metcalfe, the Excellent Acting Navab Governor General Sahib Bahadur, reiterating the recommendation to dispossess Shamsuddin Ahmad Khan of Loharu and restore the distribution of the State according to the last Will and Testament of Fakhr-ud Daulah Dilawar-ul Mulk Navab Ahmad Bakhsh Khan Rustam Jang, which had been witnessed by Sir Charles Metcalfe Sahib Bahadur himself.

Immediately following this intelligence was another report to the effect that the Senior Sahib Bahadur, not content with writing the missive as above, had prevailed upon Navab Aminuddin Ahmad Khan Bahadur, who had now attained adulthood, to go to Calcutta with copies of all the papers to plead his case personally and to make efforts for a quick decision on the matter.

A few days later another report reached him. It was stated therein that Navab Mirza Asadullah Khan Bahadur Ghalib had sent a number of letters to important friends and acquaintances in Calcutta advising and urging them to use their influence in having the matter of succession decided in favour of Navab Aminuddin Ahmad Khan. Shamsuddin Ahmad was much hurt that Mirza Ghalib had not paid any regard to his relationship with the family of his father—Ghalib was, after all, married to the daughter of Shamsuddin Ahmad's uncle—and had represented as enmity what was essentially a family dispute, thus choosing to wash the family's dirty linen in public.

Shamsuddin Ahmad felt that since the matter of Mirza Ghalib's pension had been settled personally by his Paradise-dwelling father—who was, after all, father of Aminuddin Ahmad and Ziauddin Ahmad too—Mirza Ghalib had as much cause to cavil against those two as he had against Shamsuddin Ahmad. In fact, Aminuddin Ahmad had never given the slightest hint of admitting Mirza Ghalib's claim for higher pension in case Loharu was restored to him and his younger brother. Mirza Ghalib too had once taken his noble presence to Calcutta to plead for his case and returned empty-handed.

Now, thought Shamsuddin Ahmad, only he could reveal what gain he expected by opposing me and abetting and supporting the two brothers against me.

But there was nothing to be gained by taking his unhappiness to Mirza sahib; in fact, there would be nothing but loss of face for Shamsuddin Ahmad if he opened his mouth. And Mirza sahib had shot his bolt anyway.

It was quite possible that the news about Fraser's latest dispatch to Calcutta and then Aminuddin Ahmad going to Calcutta—supported and coached by the Navab Resident Bahadur—to press his plaint had been leaked by Fraser with the view of delivering an indirect public affront to Shamsuddin Ahmad. This conjecture was strengthened by the fact that a rumour was at that time making the rounds in the city, especially among the roué and the rakes, that the Senior Sahib Bahadur had sent a proposal for his marriage with Jahangirah Begam, and had hinted that should the marriage materialize as he wished, the Company Bahadur might favourably consider Shamsuddin Ahmad's position in regard to his full succession.

Obviously these rumours were galling Shamsuddin Ahmad to the very depths of his spirit. He could do nothing to scotch them or to thwart Fraser, for it could never be proved that the leak and the rumour had originated from Fraser. Leaving Delhi and going away to Firozepur Jhirka was no solution; that again entailed loss of face. It was quite feasible for Shamsuddin Ahmad to humiliate Fraser somewhere in public and openly heap abuse on him. This would give him moral victory of a kind, and also cool his burning rage a little. But that was no long-term solution, in fact not even a short-term one. It could cause a bit of a sensation and provide Delhi's idle youth a juicy theme for more gossip and tittle at their watering holes: coffee houses, cockpits and quail-pits, and gaming dens. There was also the possibility that Fraser, smarting under the insult and aggression, might put his own trusty guards into action and have Shamsuddin Ahmad shot or attacked with swords.

Another incident during the hot currency of rumours drew a curtain of fire and blood before Shamsuddin Ahmad's eyes, very nearly provoking him to draw his own sword against Fraser.

It was the middle of July 1834. The rains had been profuse and lavish that season. The whole city seemed aflutter with green ribbons and streamers and balloons waving in the wet gusts on the rooftops, hilltops and ancient buildings. The alleys and lanes, and paths and doorways were full of plants, small or large, in flowerpots and large planters. It was just as Mirza Ghalib had said in a Hindi ghazal of his early youth:

What a season, this season of the rains!
It would be no cause of wonder

If the wave of life converted into
The wave of wine.

The mood of the season is the same everywhere:
Storming, leaping, organic;
From the newly sprung grass swaying in the wind,
To the wave of wine.

William Fraser's excursion procession wended its way through Ballimaran to Gali Qasim Jan. Maybe it was not a chance wending: perhaps it was by design, possibly Fraser had some such episode with Shamsuddin Ahmad Khan in mind because he knew that Shamsuddin Ahmad Khan was in Delhi, staying in his Ballimaran haveli. Anyway, when Fraser's elephant was opposite the massive gate of Husamuddin Haidar's haveli in Gali Qasim Jan, Navab Shamsuddin Ahmad had just exited the haveli, hand in hand with his friend Muzaffar-ud Daulah Mirza Saifuddin Haidar Khan Saif Jang, second son of Navab Husamuddin Haidar Khan, and was just about to summon his carriage, parked at some distance.

Fraser's elephant, three and a half yards tall, with a one-and-a-half-yard-high howdah on top, seemed to lowly pedestrians like a piece of the sky come down in their midst, with Fraser riding in the company of the high heavens. Shamsuddin Ahmad was quite tall, Saifuddin Haidar was even taller; still, both of them looked like pygmies before the elephant. Even in ordinary circumstances, one feels inadequate standing in front of someone who is seated.

Having ordered his elephant to halt, Fraser spoke with affected warmth and friendliness, 'Muzaffar-ud Daulah, Dilawar-ul Mulk. I present my greetings.'

Addressing Muzaffar-ud Daulah before acknowledging Shamsuddin Ahmad Khan was a veiled insult, for though Muzaffar-ud Daulah ranked superior in terms of the antiquity of his lineage and the avowed 'purity' of the descent of both his parents from the Prophet's immediate family, Shamsuddin Ahmad's father too was from the same prophetic stock; moreover, Shamsuddin Ahmad ruled a large state situated in three locations while Muzaffar-ud Daulah's fortune now consisted of some land in the country and some shops in the city.

Shamsuddin Ahmad swallowed, as if he was swallowing a mouthful of blood, made a formal salaam and replied coldly, 'Navab Resident Bahadur, may Allah preserve you. I present my submission.'

Fraser's countenance still bore its artificial smile, but his accent was not standard and clear as before, it was heavy with Englishness. He said, 'So, Dilawar-ul Mulk, how is Jahangirah Begam now? I heard—may it be the fate of her enemies—she has been feeling poorly of late. Swings and other play objects can be set up in Nur Bagh in no time. She can take her noble presence there. Doubtless, she will feel diverted.'

It seemed as if the whole world was listening with bated breath. Navab Shamsuddin Ahmad's eyes were raining fire, but his whole body felt paralysed, as if no blood would flow if he were to be cut.

A few miles out from Delhi to the west, the park-cum-orchard called Nur Bagh was at one time the property of Navab Ahmad Bakhsh Khan. During those days, a struggle was going on between two groups of nobles, one led by Vinay Singh and the other by Balwant Singh, on the issue of succession to the State of Alwar. Ahmad Bakhsh Khan was supporting Balwant Singh. Suspecting that Ahmad Bakhsh Khan's power and prestige may tilt the balance in favour of Balwant Singh, supporters of Vinay Singh planned to remove Ahmad Bakhsh Khan by assassination.

Some Mewati mercenaries were deputed by Vinay Singh to kill Ahmad Bakhsh Khan. The probable assassins traced him to Nur Bagh where Ahmad Bakhsh Khan had retired quietly for a few days. One of the assassins scaled the wall of the park in the quiet of an afternoon and attacked the Navab while he was resting. Fortunately, the first blow was just a glancing blow, removing a pinkie from the Navab's hand as his bodyguards overpowered the attacker and his companions.

The incident made Ahmad Khan so unhappy and he felt such repulsion for the garden that he sold it off to David Ochterlony for less than a fraction of its real price. After Ochterlony's death, his 'Mussulman Begam' Mubarakunnisa Begam sold it to Simon Fraser, a cousin of William Fraser's, for an even lower price. Simon Fraser was now City Magistrate of Delhi and a trusted lieutenant of William Fraser.

To take Jahangirah's name with such familiarity, and that too in public, was an insult which could cause swords to be drawn to avenge the slight. It was considered extremely offensive for the name of a purdah woman of a high-born family to be taken by a male who was not a close relation: it was, in fact, a mortal insult to her and to her entire family, for it implied some intimacy between the girl and the one who brought her name up. Even if the implication of intimacy was not there, it was against the norms of civilized behaviour and an affront to the dignity of the girl and her family to have her name bandied about. For a stranger, and that too a Firangee of Fraser's evil reputation when it came to women, to mention a girl's name was almost an occasion for her guardian or father to commit suicide. It was dire to even inquire about Shamsuddin Ahmad Khan's sister; mentioning her name was even worse.

The invitation for Jahangirah Begam to come to Nur Bagh for diversion and rest implied multiple barbs and humiliations in itself, not to mention the impudent style in which the invitation was delivered: it was as if it was quite routine for Jahangirah or other women of Shamsuddin Ahmad's family to go there and enjoy themselves. Asking the girl to visit Nur Bagh especially was a not-too-hidden poisonous thorn stabbed into Shamsuddin Ahmad's status and dignity: Fraser was saying that Nur Bagh may have been your father's property sometime in the past; now it is we, the Firangees, who own it; you and your people can only go there by our sufferance. The place where her father was the target of a murderous attack was now a place where Jahangirah Begam was being invited to be skittishly sportive and have a good romp generally. Perhaps another hint was that women of families like Shamsuddin's had no place in the city or the Fort for excursion and recreation. If they were so minded, they could clandestinely visit a Firangee's garden.

Shamsuddin Ahmad Khan's countenance changed colour every second: from angry red to thundering black to blue for shortness of breath. He stepped up towards Fraser's elephant, hand on his sword's hilt. Saifuddin Haider gripped his elbow hard and spoke under his breath, 'Stop! Don't be a fool.'

Shamsuddin Ahmad drew a deep breath, exhaled slowly, letting out a sound like a muffled sob. He turned his back with slow deliberation and began to climb the high steps of the huge gate of the haveli of Husamuddin Haidar, as if Fraser, his suite, his inquiry about Jahangirah, all of these did not exist at all. This deliberate showing of back to Fraser was a rude act, but it weighed for nothing against the dishonour handed out to Shamsuddin Ahmad Khan. Fraser smiled a thin and vitriolic smile. Dropping his Firangee accent entirely, he spoke in clear Delhi accent: 'Muzaffar-ud Daulah is a person of great tact and practical wisdom, as Allah wills. I present my submissions.' He made a small gesture for his train to return the way it had come. The moment they vacated Gali Qasim Jan, a nearly palpable sigh of relief seemed to be collectively emitted by not only the captive though avid audience, but also the walls and doors, the tall buildings and terraces, and the alleyway. Shamsuddin Ahmad desired his carriage to be brought around and ordered the coachman to proceed to Khanam ka Bazaar.

The hot and burning face of Shamsuddin Ahmad and the slight tremors in his body clearly indicated to Wazir that something untoward had happened. It was her intuitive understanding that she judged Fraser to be involved.

'Is everything all right?' She took the Navab's right hand into her hands. 'Did something happen with the Resident Sahib?' She rubbed the Navab's hand gently. 'I invoke Allah's mercy! Your hands are ice cold! So why should you take these little things to heart? Please. Let bygones be bygones.'

'How can I? I am on fire inside; I strongly wish to go just this minute and take off the head of the bastard!'

Wazir was now palpably upset. 'Oh, please! What is the matter? Do please tell me. It is not good to be so enraged. Cool down, please. Navab Mirza is out with the playing maid. I'll have him recalled this very moment. Divert yourself by talking and playing with him.'

'These little entertainments are not going to work, Chhoti Begam. I will not rest until I have put paid to this sordid affair.'

'Goodness, will you tell me what happened to put you out so much? Come, take a cool drink.'

She ordered Rahat Afza to serve a glass of pomegranate juice mixed with other refreshing ingredients.

'Let me fan you a while. Please stretch your legs comfortably on the large easy chair. Let me remove your shoes and loosen the buttons of your coat.'

Wazir raised her head to look at the Navab as she spoke and was aghast to see his eyes misting over with tears. She was quite stupefied, not knowing how to comfort him. When Shamsuddin Ahmad leaned back against the chair, Wazir quickly wiped his face with the hem of her wrap, thus concealing the action of drying the Navab's tears. She made him take a few sips of the cool drink, and said, 'Now tell me, what is the matter?'

'Nothing is the matter,' he heaved a deep sigh of despair, 'my stars are now moving against me, as if they have lost their way. That bastard of a pimp dishonoured me tonight in the teeming bazaar!'

'May God preserve you! How could that be! I am sure he could not dare do any such thing.'

'Well, it did happen. Did I not say that my stars are wandering from their true path? When that happens, even good things produce a bad result. This evening I went visiting with Saifuddin Haidar, for I heard that he was sick. Fortunately he was better. Giving his hand into mine, he walked me to the gate of his haveli when the incident happened.'

Shamsuddin Ahmad narrated the whole story in a dull voice and concluded by saying, 'You remember I once told you that I would bury him the same way as I now bury our nominal relationship as uncle and nephew? It now seems to me that the day has come. I will not let this matter drop before I execute him.'

'Your Honour. I beseech you in the name of God and his Prophet, do not say such words! Do not think such thoughts. Please, first of all, give thought to the matter that lies at the root of today's incident.'

'What do you mean? Could there be anything at the root except the mean, base nature of that low-born cur?'

'Your Honour is quite right. But this slave girl must point out to you that the matter of Jahangirah Bibi is of prime importance. The protection of her honour is above everything.'

Shamsuddin Ahmad frowned. 'So? What do you mean to say?'

'My submission is that you must find some suitable groom and solemnize her marriage. Do it soonest. If possible, let that auspicious event take place this month. Please appreciate the fact that everything actually emanated from Jahangirah's marital situation. Had she been in her own home today, do you think that pig-eater, that fit-for-death burly dog could have uttered any such thing? The whole world knows that even angels swear by the chastity and purity of our Jahangirah. And once she gets married, all innuendoes will be silenced for all time.'

The Navab thought for a minute or two and replied in a tone heavy with worry, 'There is something in what you say, but where are the marriage proposals?'

'Oh, well, as if there can be a dearth of proposals for a girl as beautiful as she, who is like the sun and the moon! You need only look carefully.'

'Yes, I see what you mean. I'll very soon organize something for Jahangirah. But before I do that, I must go punish that wastrel. I am off to the Residency right now.'

Saying this, Shamsuddin Ahmad Khan put on his shoes, buttoned his coat, and clattered down the stairs. Wazir kept on calling, 'Do not go there. I appeal to you in the name of God and His Prophet. Please do not go there. Do not go for your children's sake.' But the Navab recked not, and soon the sound of his steps stopped reaching her ears.

41

A misadventure at William Fraser's mansion: Shamsuddin Khan suffers another humiliation

HE ORDERED THE coachman, 'Residency. Now!'

The coachman hesitated, 'Exalted Presence, should we take a few staff-bearers?' He spoke haltingly. 'We can collect them from Ballimaran in no time.'

Shamsuddin Ahmad felt like snatching the horsewhip from the coachman, striking him with it and saying that his duty was to drive the carriage, not give advice. But he stayed his hand, for he was not the kind of aristocrat who hit his servants. Reason prevailed over fury. He said nothing for some moments, then, 'All right, but hurry. The time is short.'

Ill fortune seemed to be raining down upon Shamsuddin Ahmad. He was a tent from which the canvas had been ripped away. As the Arabic proverb says, when it is time for the writ to come to pass, the earth becomes narrow. The space of Delhi was about to shrink for him. Even if he had not gone to the Residency at that time, the end wouldn't have been different. By going there he just took a step forward to hasten the conclusion.

Within about half an hour, Shamsuddin Ahmad Khan arrived at the Residency; two armed riders in the vanguard and two lance-bearers each to his right and left made up his train. They found the gate closed. In his naiveté, Shamsuddin Ahmad Khan still believed that he could pass through the open gate without let or hindrance, and if the gate was closed, he could have it opened by berating the guards or by sheer force of personality. But Fraser was much wilier than the hot-headed young man had reckoned. He had known Shamsuddin Ahmad since the latter's boyhood; he well knew that Shamsuddin Ahmad was as impulsive, obstinate and precipitate in action as he was brave and full of practical daring and courage in warfare. He would therefore not be surprised if Shamsuddin Ahmad suddenly appeared at the Residency and challenged Fraser in some way.

As soon as he returned to the Residency, Fraser put in place the necessary steps designed to prevent any mischief from Shamsuddin Ahmad and also, if need be, work to humiliate Shamsuddin Ahmad even more. So Shamsuddin Ahmad found two musketeers with double-barrelled guns behind the seven-barred gate; the gate was closed, and the guardsmen were accompanied by four Baksariya soldiers armed with French carbines. Thus the six soldiers spanned the whole width of the gate. Now, even if the gate was opened by force, the visitor had to go past the six soldiers.

One of the armed outriders of the Navab came forward and spoke in a firm but polite tone, 'What is the matter? Why is the gate not being opened? Do you not see that His Honour has come to pay a visit?'

All the six had been fully coached before being posted at the gate. One of them smiled a meaningful smile and said, 'Not open the gate? How could we dare not open the gate? But the Senior Sahib Bahadur is in comfort.'

'To be in comfort' or 'sukh kar jana' meant 'to have retired to bed'; the idiom was only used for the King and in fact the phrase was not in use outside the Exalted Fort at all. Used for the Firangee, it was like acid poured into the ears of Shamsuddin Ahmad Khan. The halfpenny-worth Firangee of obscure family dares to have the phrase used for himself! They were already robbing our country, now they were grabbing our special words and usages for their own use. But it was no occasion to pick quarrels of this sort, or any sort at all.

'Shahbaz Khan, ask this man to go inside and report that we are here.'

'Yes, sir.'

Shahbaz Khan conveyed to the sentry guard the desire of his Lord Benefactor for his arrival to be announced, and have the gate opened for him.

The Baksaria again smiled a knowing smile, as if he was privy to a secret of which none else, far less the newly arrived guest, was aware. Saying, 'Yes, very well', he walked along the drive with deliberate, comfortable steps and disappeared from view as the driveway curved towards the main building. He returned momently and informed Shahbaz Khan, 'Kan Sab, the Exalted Sahib has commanded that Navab sahib can come alone, and on foot.'

Acting again as intermediary, Shahbaz Khan haltingly, and in softer words, conveyed the information to Shamsuddin Ahmad Khan who thought for a moment or two and said in a loud voice so that the Baksaria could hear him, 'Navab Resident may be informed that I agree to be on foot, but I do not go anywhere without a minimum number of guards. Two lance-bearers will accompany me.'

The sentry guard went back, again returning in no time. 'All right. Navab sahib can come in with two lance-bearers.'

He waved to the commander of the guards for the gate to be opened. The Navab alighted and entered the driveway with quick, firm steps. The guards and the soldiers bent low in salaam and divided into two groups so as to give ample space to him. One of his lance-bearers, to his right, had a naked spear in one hand and a torch in the other. The other lance-bearer had a naked spear in each hand.

There was no risk of the Navab being ambushed by Fraser's men, or some unknown, untraceable mercenaries taking advantage of the dark, clouded sky, the advancing night and the green-black of the dense shrubbery and trees on both sides of the driveway. Still, the Navab's lance-bearers were taking no chances. They walked very close to the Navab, almost touching him, the torchbearer just a few inches ahead of him to the right, and the other, a few inches behind him to the left. The torchbearer tilted the torch so that the Navab was in comparative darkness and the torch illumined the road ahead.

Shamsuddin Ahmad Khan walked along, his head held high and his chest jutting out. Though the first round had been to Fraser, the Navab was not dismayed. He believed that he still had at his command many other, and winning, tactics. As he walked up to the house, he was giving thought to how he should open the conversation when he and Fraser came face to face.

Now they were at the outer, high veranda of the Residency, with its many and somewhat steep leading steps. There were no lamps lit, nor was any servant there who could be asked to announce the Navab. The question of Fraser, or at least his steward, being present for welcoming the Navab, did not apparently arise in the circumstances.

The lance-bearer with the torch climbed the steps ahead of the Navab, intending to knock at the large main door. The other lance-bearer was now alone, below the veranda and under the dark, open sky, made darker by the absence of stars. Suddenly, two tall and powerful Mewatis appeared from nowhere and grasped him from behind, one putting the armlock on him and the other immobilizing his legs by coiling one of his own legs around them. The lance-bearer tried hard to stay on the ground, but his opponents were too strong for any such move. They broke his leg hold and lifted him a few inches above the ground; one of them said in a cold, flat voice, 'Kan Sab, now walk quietly with us to the main gate, if you value your life.'

The Navab and his torchbearer looked back, startled. Before either could react, another Mewati sprang at the torchbearer, and using a blow from the repertoire of unarmed combat, struck him with his staff at the elbows, paralysing them. An involuntary sob escaped the torchbearer's lips, as he tried to massage his injured limbs, dropping the lance and the lamp with a clatter in the process. Helplessly, he tried to flex his fingers, but found no strength in them. The big front door opened and two Telangas appeared, immobilizing him with ease. The glass shade of the handheld torch broke into numerous pieces; a slight gust extinguished the torch.

The Navab was now alone and very nearly helpless in the darkened, hostile space. His lance-bearers were being half pushed, half dragged towards the main gate like animals brought down in a chase. They knew that it was no use making even a token effort at resistance. They tried to avert their faces from the Navab, their eyes closed in shame.

Shamsuddin Ahmad now realized that all the moves in the dismal scenario in which he found himself had been choreographed nicely by Fraser. The idea behind his being deprived of his carriage and forced to be on foot was to disarm him and make him helpless. It was then easy to do whatever else was planned next. He could even be shot. Fraser's men could pretend that they believed they were under attack from armed intruders or dacoits.

The Navab's bodyguards, who were being dragged and pushed, cried out 'Help! Help!' once or twice, hoping that their voice might be heard by the Navab's outriders and the other two bodyguards waiting outside the gate. But it was an exercise in futility: their hoarse, muffled voices could not reach that far, and even if they did, the Navab's men had to get past the six armed guards who had instantly closed the gate, anticipating precisely such a move.

Shamsuddin Ahmad Khan drew his sword, stationed himself before one of the massive pillars of the veranda to protect his rear, and waited for the worst to happen. When the sound of the Navab's men being dragged away could not be heard any longer, the lights went on in the big drawing room. Its door opened noisily and Fraser appeared in his dressing gown.

'Nephew, it is you! With a drawn sword and in the dark veranda! Now if I fired at you, believing you to be a thief or a dacoit? . . . No, I would not fire, but my damn sentries are all stupid in the extreme.' He barked a short laugh. 'But how do you happen to be here at this time of the night?'

He used the informal *tum*, instead of the formal *aap* as was the standard practice in polite society even for a younger person.

Shamsuddin Ahmad smiled. 'Do I need to make an appointment to call on Uncle William Fraser?'

'Why? Was not our meeting in the evening sufficient?'

'I came to conclude the reckoning of that meeting.' Shamsuddin Ahmad Khan said, advancing with his drawn sword now pointing towards Fraser.

Fraser clapped his hands. Six armed soldiers appeared who had apparently been waiting for the signal. Two sprang forward to take a firm hold of the Navab's arms. Two placed themselves in front of and behind the Navab, boxing him in. One of the Telangas extended his arm, 'Navab sahib, please deliver your sword to this slave.'

In spite of the restraining arms, Shamsuddin Ahmad Khan turned on his heels, raised his sword hand with lightning swiftness and brought it down on the Telanga's shoulder. Exhibiting rare dexterity and fine judgement in swordsmanship, he checked his blow just at the last moment, so that instead of sinking at least two inches deep into the Telanga's shoulder, the sword just alighted on it like a butterfly. The razor-sharp edge of the sword cut through the Telanga's tunic, leaving a thin line of blood.

'Another such affront and I will tear your tongue out, chop it to pieces and stuff it in your throat,' the Navab said with cold fury. The Telanga quailed and retreated a step. Folding his hands in submission, he bent his head and quavered, 'Your Honour is the Master.'

'Very nice, young fellow!' Fraser guffawed. 'And why not? You are a progeny of Dilawar-ul Mulk Rustam Jang, after all.' Now his tone became dry and deadly serious. 'But this game becomes uninteresting by the minute. The correct course was to have you ejected by a couple of my guards with their arms tight on your neck and shoulders, but I am peace-loving by nature and I also give due consideration to past histories. Hence, my guards will throw a protective but armed ring around you and walk you to the gate. The other guards there will grasp your arms and help you into your carriage. And that is the maximum civility that I can observe with you. Now get out.'

Fraser turned his back upon him. The sepoys moved closer to

Shamsuddin Ahmad, so that they were within an arm's distance of him from all sides.

As Fraser was about to resume to the drawing room, Shamsuddin Ahmad Khan roared, 'Stay!'

Fraser waved a hand pretending disgust and indifference, but he turned and sneered, 'Well? So you still want something?'

'William Fraser, you insulted me twice today. I have put my sword back into its sheath for today but soon your body will be its sheath and your blood will be its bridal dress.'

Fraser, unperturbed, laughed out loud. 'As for the bridal dress, I fancy Jahangirah Begam . . . '

Shamsuddin Ahmad Khan snarled like a leopard. He brandished his blazing sword and scattered the men who encircled him. His next blow would have felled or wounded Fraser, but the latter was prepared for any such eventuality. Running back into the room, Fraser shouted from inside, 'Help! Help! Murder! This man is going to kill me! Don't just stand and look, you miserable fellows! Kick him out of my house now!'

A number of musketeers and staff-bearers, clearly waiting for such a call, appeared from all sides like a swarm of bees and clung to the Navab like ants. He tried to move back a little, so as to create space for himself to wield his sword but to no effect. Still, he wounded one of the assailants and was about to play his sword blindly into the crowd when a staff-bearer expertly struck the Navab's sword arm. His fist opened involuntarily and the sword fell at his feet. There was no time or space to bend and pick up the sword with the left hand.

Shamsuddin Ahmad Khan was immediately deprived of his dagger, and the assailants, clutching different parts of his body, began to drag him away. In the melee, one of his sleeves was ripped in two or three places, and he lost one of his shoes. Half carried and half dragged and buffeted all the way to the main gate, Shamsuddin Ahmad Khan was pushed out of Fraser's mansion.

42

They desire joy, but sorrow awaits: Wazir Khanam is caught in the dread grip of fear and the Navab makes a vow

SHAMSUDDIN AHMAD DID not at all know when his journey ended and how he was brought to Wazir Khanam's house. He did not remember if it was he who had ordered the carriage to Chandni Chowk, or the decision had been taken by the commander of his guards.

His body was rigid like a board, his eyes seemed to be blind, as if made of stone; his neck was slack and had rolled to one side. Wazir struck her brow in consternation and shock when she saw him. She did not know what to do and could not think of any way at all to bring him back to consciousness. Asking a hakim, even Hakim Ahsanullah Khan, to come and treat him was not the best thing to do, for then the news—or rumours—would only disseminate quicker and farther, even though the hakim would certainly not reveal anything to anyone.

It was clear that the Navab had not suffered any wound, nor was his pulse weak or sinking. Something inimical to his temperament must have happened at the Residency, then matters must have got out of hand, raising his temper, and something dire must then have shocked him into unconsciousness. The need, therefore, was to lessen and diminish the effect of that shock from his heart.

Somehow Wazir, assisted by Habiba and Vafadar, managed to carry Shamsuddin Ahmad to his bed. They removed his headgear and coat, and cleaned his hands, feet and face. Soft muslin kerchiefs were soaked in mildly warm water and the exposed parts of his body were sponged gently. Vafadar and Mubarak Qadam began to tenderly massage his soles and palms. Wazir, with the help of another housemaid, forced open his tightly clenched jaws a bit and poured a restorative cool drink into his mouth slowly, drop by drop.

When the tension in Shamsuddin Ahmad's body diminished somewhat, and his eyes became normal—though still shut—they pulled his legs to the edge of the bed and laved his feet slowly and for a long time with warm water. After this, his feet were covered in a soft but somewhat heavy sheet to help them retain the warmth for some time.

Gradually, Shamsuddin Ahmad slipped into a state between sleep and unconsciousness. Some more time passed before his body relaxed and it was clear that he was now comfortably asleep. The whole house was wrapped in a heavy shroud of silence, as if some calamity was about to descend from above, and everyone was busy concentrating in their hearts to find a way to ward it off, or say some efficacious prayers to avert the impending doom.

After having put Navab Mirza to bed, Habiba sat on the prayer mat and continuously told her beads and said the prayers learnt from childhood for such occasions. Rahat Afza recited over and over again the Arabic words for the Salutations of Allah to the Prophet Muhammad, for it was believed that it could somehow help in such situations. Vafadar and Mubarak Qadam, who were literate enough to read the Quran, even if haltingly, placed their copy of the Holy Book on a wooden stand and sat before it, head and body fully covered with their wraps, and read, word after separate word, from the famous chapter of the Quran, the fifty-fifth, called Al-Rahman (The Most Gracious), considered to be one of the most mellifluous and eloquent chapters of the Book and whose recitation is believed to help bring peace and grace upon the house:

All that is on earth will perish:
But will (forever) abide
The Face of thy Lord, full of Majesty, Bounty and Honour.

One of the senior maids, a Hindu called Kunwar Rani, performed the traditional Hindu ceremony, a magical formula much favoured by the Muslims too, to take away the influence of the evil eye, or any kind of evil, including black magic: she took some red chillies in her hand, ran the hand slowly in a circle three times above the Navab's head, and threw the chillies into the fire. She then took a few grains of black lentil in her hand and performed the same action. She gazed intently at the pungent smelling smoke as if the evildoer's figure could be glimpsed spiralling in it for a split moment of time.

Another maid who, because of her fair complexion—with a touch of yellowish gold in it—almond eyes and a small flat nose, looked vaguely like a Central Asian, though her height was less than average and her body somewhat plump, and who was very popular because of her friendly nature and artless ways, sought a corner of a room, gathered her body in as small a bundle as she could, and began recalling the names of her river goddesses, tree-dwelling spirits and wild, godlike, mountain-dwelling supernatural beings, and prayed to them constantly. She came from a remote part of Kamrup and belonged to a tribe called Angami. Her name was Vanisi; she had been abducted by a professional kidnapper of women and girls from somewhere in Calcutta when she was a little girl. The kidnapper then brought her to Delhi for sale. It was just after Navab Mirza's birth and a young, attractive woman was needed to look after the baby when he was not with his mother. Shamsuddin Ahmad Khan's steward purchased her at a good price and she had been settled in Wazir's household since then.

Wazir sat forlorn and silent near the Navab's bed, trying to dissipate the fears in her own heart by reciting a well-known Arabic prayer—popular among the Shia community, but also not unknown among the Sunnis—which calls upon Ali, the Prophet's son-in-law, to come to the caller's succour. She was quite certain that the Navab would get well. But a fear sat in her heart with its claws dug deep into her being that his recovery would not end the evil that was upon them; rather, there would ensue changes that would revolutionize both their lives. She did not doubt that the Navab would remain ever faithful to her; nor did she dread that Fraser would do something heinous to them. But something had happened somewhere, which was going to eat away the wall of their security as easily and persistently as the white ants ate away doors and windows. All the power and pelf, all the beauty and elegance, all the give and take of love, all the hopes and all the exultations of ambitious desire would go away forever within a few days.

She thought of Marston Blake, that marvellous young man. He also took his leave from her in almost the same way: confident that he would come back soon; no harm is ever going to touch you; I go with full security in place for you. She had had no premonitions then, no fears, no frightful imaginings. Then Blak sahib was cut off from me and from life, and what a savage cutting off it was. Then my children . . . and now—may God preserve him—I have Navab Mirza with me. I have very nearly wept away two of my babies. I did get occasional news of them, but I could see that there was no vacant space in their hearts for their mother. Nor did their present guardians ever desire that they should visit their mother, at least once in six months or so, if not more frequently.

And I? Do I have the same longing, the same anguished urgency for their sight as I have for Navab Mirza? May God preserve him. Is it because they are of alien blood, they are Kristan, they are Firangee? But then Blak sahib was all those things, yet I still remember him. I remember him like a wound which has healed but whose scar remains as the sad memorial for the hurt that it caused, and also as a heart-ravishing token of him who is no more.

I know nothing like the special prayers, the silent or vocal chants, which one could invoke for unwriting something that is written . . . Pundit Nand Kishor . . . yes, Pundit Nand Kishor, I could seek succour from him, should he be in the city now . . . But I hear that he is very sick and frail, and unable to move about. He acknowledged my message, reporting my success, but had not been heard from since then. That bastard of a Firangee! My Navab did wrong in buying honour at the expense of the Firangee's friendship. But what could he do, being what he is? It is not just me; it is much more important, it is his own sister, his and her family's honour. I am nothing more than a puny, valueless ant, of no station whatever, and these people are like hurricanes drunk on power, not suffering anyone or anything to stand in their path.

Who knows, perhaps the Elder Begam sahib, the widow of the Paradise-dwelling Navab Ahmad Bakhsh Khan sahib, or those who are influential around her, are having some special prayers read, some white or black magic practised so as to bring about the downfall of my Navab sahib, so that they may rise when he falls. I know that those who reside in the Fort at Loharu look down upon my Navab as of inferior stock,' and regard themselves of pure stock. The Senior Navab sahib had apportioned their share before he left for Paradise. I wish my Navab sahib had not chosen to repudiate his father's Will . . .

Can the writ of Fate be erased or changed? I think that if the present situation had not cropped up, some other, similar one would have arisen. If my home is fated to be pulled down and taken apart; if my protector, my legatee, is to be torn away from my side; if my body is to travel alone to the grave, something else would surely make it happen. These things are above the might of the likes of William Fraser or those who are residents of the Fort at Loharu. If I did not have my looks . . . but for how many days or weeks will my looks stay? And the phenomenon of good looks is actually a phenomenon of the beholder's eye . . . In fact, that is the crux of the matter and there lies the rub. Men? What else do they want but toys to play with, to break and shatter, to abandon, to forget and forsake? And also, they must have maids, serving women, doers of their bidding around the house.

But I have nowhere to fall back to. If I face the truth, I will know that I do not now belong anywhere. But am I not being stupid in going round and round in long and complicated mazes of imaginings just because something has happened, something which must be very small really? At this time, I do not even know what exactly transpired between my Navab and the Resident. It is not necessary that it was a total falling out with Fraser sahib; it could be something smaller, or something else entirely.

She recited the 'Calling Ali' prayer slowly, haltingly, over and over again. Sometimes she would take to repeatedly reciting two of the shortest Quranic chapters—the recitation of which, and their being blown upon the afflicted person, was reputed among the pious to be a most potent prayer to ward off or take away the effects of Evil. One of them, in full, was:

Say: I seek refuge
With the Lord of the Dawn,
From the mischief
Of created things,
From the mischief
Of darkness as it overspreads;
From the mischief
Of those who blow on knots;
From the mischief
Of the envious one
As he practises envy.

Sometimes a horrible thought occurred to her: Perhaps Fraser was on his way here with armed soldiers to assault her home and make off with the Navab? Clearly, this was an absurdity, and her home was quite secure anyway.

The men who had formed the Navab's suite had left, perhaps for Ballimaran, but the spies of the Navab must be there and they would give adequate early warning. Anyway, though the men of the Navab's suite had said nothing, their faces were pale and drawn; two of them seemed to have been disarmed. Even so, had something untoward happened at the Residency, none of them would ever say a word even if they were beaten and hung upside down. But what could be that untoward event? The Navab had lost none of his jewellery, or his sword, and he bore no apparent injury. It was just not possible for him to have been attacked by dacoits, or by Fraser's sepoys.

But was it not possible for Fraser to have uttered some improper words about Jahangirah to the Navab's face? After all, he had gone there precisely because of Jahangirah; and Fraser might have had him set upon by his hirelings. Certainly, that is possible, but it does not follow that Fraser's men or the Company's sepoys will storm my house. And even if such a thing happens, does anyone conceive that we will let the Navab, or ourselves, be taken cheaply? I do not know how to take life, but I do know how to give my life. And my guardswomen well know how to fight not only with sword and pistol, but also with their hands, legs and heads.

. . . Navab Mirza? Would it not be wise to have him removed from this place? But where? I can send him to Manjhli Baji's, but who will escort him? And who knows, the streets out there may not be danger-free . . . I could depute a guardswoman and a senior maid as escort, but that would mean reduction in the defensive power here. Oh dear, am I not being foolish, to think of sending him out with comparative strangers from a secure home, making them wander in the streets and bazaars? And what answer could I give to the Navab when he recovers consciousness and inquires about his son? May Allah make my legatee, my inheritor, my protector, better very soon and save him from further calamity. Everything can be achieved if he remains here . . . Even those things will happen which are not happening . . .

She realized the possible underlying meaning of this last thought and reddened. She looked at Shamsuddin Ahmad with loving eyes. He now lay on his left side, one hand stretched upon the pillow, as if he was looking for something. Wazir began to gently rub with a soft cloth the palm of the extended hand, pushed aside her vexing thoughts and recommenced reciting the 'Calling Ali' prayer.

No one knew how long it took for the night to pass; perhaps Wazir also had nodded off. Certainly, Rahat Afza, clinging to the Navab's bed frame as she recited the Divine Salutations to the Prophet, had dropped off to sleep flopped down where she was. Habiba and the other Quran-reading women were now sleeping, foetus style, on their prayer mats. Kunwar Rani, Vanisi and the female guards had not slept at all.

Wazir woke up with a start when the sound of the muezzin rose from the Sunahri Mosque and the other nearby mosques. The Jain Temple, the Gauri Shankar Temple and the Sikh Gurdwara began to reverberate with the sounds of bells, conch shells, drums and cymbals. Light was spreading slowly in the house. In the courtyard, amdavads, stonechats and brown robins began to whistle and warble. Cautious doves and turtle doves, on the copings of the courtyard walls, billed and cooed before coming down. Even before the arrival of these feathered guests, the sparrows, hoopoes, mynahs, babblers and pigeons had become alert to the opening of the free kitchen in the courtyards. Most of them alighted silently, some of them chattering, especially the babblers, creating a large fraternal club. Some crows and a few brown kites began to circle the sky above the courtyard.

With so many lovable and lively creatures making their presence felt, the lights that had burnt through the night and had not yet been put out began to glimmer and pale, but their paleness did not seem melancholic. It seemed to Wazir, and in fact, to all those who dwelt in that house, that the evil shadow that had enveloped them the previous night had now dissipated.

The house seemed to take on a new lease of life as the bazaar downstairs woke up with the sounds of water carriers, hawkers, itinerant sellers of kebobs and small, hot pancakes stuffed with the sharpest of spices, and purveyors of butter and thick cream. It seemed that the entire city was awake. Breezes began to blow and frolic on Saadat Khan's canal, and shadows of the flowering shrubs swayed upon the water. At that time, the city air seemed to exude a comfortable sense of content, an energy, a puissance such as to create the illusion that the city was still under the rule of Muhyiuddin Aurangzeb, Emperor of India and the Deccan, and his resplendent suite had just arrived from Aurangabad in the Deccan, and having passed under the massive Delhi Gate, was now about to enhance the beauty and the luminance of the Auspicious Haveli. This ambient light, this peace, this quiet happiness, this bustle and glitter was all because Mahabali's Shadow was shining over the entire world. The Maratha, the marauding Pathans of the Durrani and the Abdali, the Firangee: none could be discerned even dimly in the far distance. Delhi was still the heart of India and the life of the world, as Mirza Ghalib said in a Persian verse:

I asked: Tell me now what is Delhi?
My guide said: It is the soul, and the world,
Its body.

Shamsuddin Ahmad Khan woke up to find Wazir Khanam bending over him, tenderly wiping his face with a soft, moist handkerchief. She had a small leather bottle containing rose water in her other hand. Her large eyes had been clouded with worry just a few seconds ago; now although her face betrayed exhaustion, a small light of happiness shone on her features when she saw Shamsuddin Ahmad open his eyes.

'I submit my salaams. A thousand thanks to Allah that you opened your eyes, at long last.'

The Navab drew a brief yawn and sat up. Quickly, Rahat Afza placed two overstuffed pillows against his back, bent low in salaam, and removed herself from their presence.

'Why?' he asked. 'Was there anything to worry about?'

Wazir Khanam fell into a small flurry of uncertainty: The Navab had entirely forgotten the night's incidents, or he wanted it to seem as if nothing had happened.

'Sir, no, nothing special really. It is just that you seemed rather worn out when you came in. You did not partake of dinner even, and immediately fell asleep.'

'Yes . . . yes . . .' Shamsuddin paused a moment, then went on, 'Yes, I felt rather dilapidated yesterday.' He smiled his attractive smile. 'That is why I came here straight, for it is here that the comfort for my soul is to be found.'

'Go to, Navab sahib, you and your extravagant words! You really shook me up inside entirely. You arrived, and just fell into bed . . . Habiba inquired a number of times about dinner, but you spoke not a word.'

'All right, let the dinner go. I'll eat a hearty breakfast now; all your complaints will vanish. And yes, where is our Navab Mirza? He must be asleep yet?'

It must be remembered that everybody continued to use the second-person plural or the third-person plural when speaking of Navab Mirza.

'Sir, I'll awaken him at once. He will bloom like a flower when he sees you.'

'No, let him sleep until his wonted hour.' The Navab looked lovingly at Wazir and said, 'And you too. You must sleep now. It is still quite early, and you seem quite weary, somehow. Actually, it is time for me to rise, otherwise I . . .'

Wazir cut in quickly, 'But I'm up already. Sleep is not going to come to me now. You just have your legs and back patted and pressed, then take your bath. I shall organize breakfast in the meantime.'

The Navab tried to get hold of the edge of her wrap. 'Hey, listen, just you listen!' But Wazir exited, a bashful smile on her face and in her eyes.

The Navab enjoyed the patting and kneading of his body so much that he fell off to sleep, a sleep of pleasure and mild intoxication. When he awoke for the second time, the sun was quite high in the sky; down below, life in the bazaar was in full flow, with its familiar noises and conversations and hawkers' cries. Shamsuddin Ahmad found himself generally recuperated: the painful knots of the previous night more or less unravelled, his heart comparatively stable and peaceful.

Having got through bath, breakfast and dressing up, Shamsuddin Ahmad found plenty of time to play with Navab Mirza whose baby prattle regaled his heart. Actually, Navab Mirza could now articulate short sentences and poems, though he still could not pronounce the harder consonants and some combining phrases, so his talk was even more enjoyable. Wazir thought again and again to ask the Navab about his plans for Jahangirah. But the Navab kept up with jokes and laughter and banter and managed never to be alone with her so that she could speak to him freely.

Wazir had recently taught Navab Mirza to recite a couple of verses of Mian Mushafi, the recently dead Hindi poet of great reputation. Shamsuddin Ahmad Khan would make the child recite the verses again and again, and would also reward him over and over; sometimes he also ordered sweets or fruits to be brought in and distributed among those present. The verses were about loving and love, but their gentle playfulness, and the faint cloud of sadness that pervaded the mood of the poem went extremely well with Navab Mirza's innocent child face and voice, and produced a rare joy among the listeners:

Beset by troubles and tears
I hew through my days and nights in her lane
Like travellers in the season of rains
On muddy, slippery roads.

I cut through my life under the sword,
Like the candle, whose head is cut
Many times by the snuffer before morning comes.

Navab Mirza enunciated each word most correctly, all the pauses were observed perfectly and all the four lines spoken with full regard to the metre; his voice occasionally halting but free from childish mumble. This capability of the little soul of three years made Shamsuddin Ahmad Khan and Wazir Khanam brighten up joyfully like the moonlit night. Time and time again, Habib-un Nisa made the prescribed gestures to take away misfortune and calamity from the child. Other maids, in order to protect him from the evil of the eye, would circle a few drops of mustard oil and black lentil around his head, then throw them into the flames. Sometimes they would spread wide their upper wraps upon their hands and pray for Allah to save their Bacche Mian from the evil of the eye and vouchsafe a long life to him.

All this took up the whole morning, and even after lunch, Shamsuddin Ahmad Khan carried on with his fun and entertainment, not letting Wazir or Navab Mirza out of his sight. It was late afternoon when Navab Mirza fell asleep in the arms of his maid-for-play, fully tired but fully content, and the servants were through with their own lunch. Shamsuddin Ahmad now commanded privacy. Taking Wazir to the bedchamber, he shut the door. Wazir protested over and over again: broad daylight is no occasion for such flourishes and dalliances; but the Navab paid no heed at all. In fact, Wazir was not at heart averse to his attentions at that time.

Shamsuddin Ahmad clasped her in his arms and showered hot kisses on her face, her lips, her eyes, her breasts, so that her whole being dissolved in the rain of kisses and permeated each and every vein and artery of Shamsuddin Ahmad.

Much later, when the shadows of the evening began to peep through the cracks and crevices of the doors and windows and the bedchamber became almost dark, Shamsuddin Ahmad awoke. Wazir's head was on his breast, and one of her arms was pressed under his side. During the whole time that Shamsuddin Ahmad slept, she had not slept nor moved, nor tried to ease the pressure on her arm. Her eyes were drinking in the fair and shapely warmth of his shoulder, and breast, and neck. She was fully in command of her senses, but she still felt mildly inebrious. When Shamsuddin Ahmad awoke, he touched her face and spoke in surprise, 'Oh, you have been awake all the time!' He sat up. 'I am so sorry. Your arm lay underneath mine. Bhai wallah! It must have hurt frightfully. Why did you not say something?'

'What should have I said? I was perfectly comfortable.'

'Bhai wallah! You are something remarkable indeed! I was of course quite beside myself . . . but you could have done a bit of nudging and pushing.'

Wazir put her arms around Shamsuddin Ahmad's neck, and averting her face a little, spoke in a bashful but firm tone, 'Why, have you not heard?' She recited a Persian verse, but in a conversational tone:

Happy the night when I should hold you in my arms
Until it is dawn; and pressed under your side,
My arm should go to sleep.

Shamsuddin Ahmad leapt up from his place in joyful agitation and cried, 'Oh! You cruel, wonderful lady! This verse deserved to be spoken by me, and it was my lips that suited it best! Bhai wallah! One feels like kissing the lips that spoke those words!'

Keeping her face averted as before, Wazir replied, 'But it takes two hands to clap.' Her voice was almost devoid of abashment or discomfiture, as if she was passing a judgement.

'You reduce your station. It is I who am the seeker. You are the sought.'

She now turned her face towards him and smoothed her disarranged clothes. 'Why shouldn't the seeker and the sought be equal in rank? Why should I be determined to be the sought? Is it not that sometimes the sought can also be determined to be the seeker?'

'How so?'

Wazir rose from the bed, folded her hands on her breasts, bent her head and said the following Persian verse:

Happy the time when the beautiful ones
Go on a rampage in the city;
You lay hold of me and declare:
This is my prisoner!

Her voice choked a little as she finished saying the verse. She wiped her tears with her thumb and index finger, extremely gently, as if wiping perspiration's moisture. Shamsuddin Ahmad was moved to say something, but Wazir took herself in hand somewhat and continued, 'Now do you not see? The sought is also the seeker. The prisoner is the same as the one who takes prisoner.' She laughed gently, but there was a bit of the water of tears splashing over her words.

Shamsuddin Ahmad was tremulous all over. He knew the verse of Shahidi Qumi quoted by Wazir, but had never looked at it or thought about it from that angle. 'Wazir Khanam, I was always helpless before you. But I imagined that it was my powerlessness, for it was I who was questing.'

'Your Honour's powerlessness must have flowed from some strength. But perhaps I was powerless too.'

'Now perhaps it is so that neither I can release you, nor can you release me . . .' Shamsuddin Ahmad's voice had a tremor.

Before he could finish, Wazir Khanam drew a faint sigh and said, 'And releasing yourself is now beyond your power. I cannot free myself from my fetters either, nor perhaps can Your Honour . . .'

'No, no. It is not a matter of "perhaps". It is so doubtless, without question. Bahu Khanam, I could not release myself from you even if I wished.'

Wazir passed her hands on her face, in the manner of one who finishes a prayer. She went close to the Navab and made the gesture of taking his misfortunes upon her own self. Then, making for the door, she said, 'Let me have the candles lit now; it is quite dark.'

'Let the candles be,' said Shamsuddin Ahmad. 'The light of your face is pleasing to the eye in the darkness.'

'Please. You really are a master at hilarious talk! Is it not unfair that I should not see your radiant face and you should see the pink of dawn in my colour which otherwise is dark as the evening?'

'Whatever. But please come, sit beside me.' His face suddenly clouded.

Wazir's heart missed a beat but she spoke with good humour, 'To hear is to obey. Please command.'

She came back from the door and sat on the bed, close to Shamsuddin Ahmad whose face was still clouded over. Perhaps it was nothing, just the shadows of the night as they descended; or was it that last night was still with us and its ominous feet were still at my doorstep? A wave of fear passed over Wazir's heart, but she said nothing, gazing at Shamsuddin Ahmad's face with loving eyes. He put his arm around her and pulled her so close that they were almost touching each other, almost in each other's embrace, actually.

'Bahu Khanam.'

'Sir, please command.'

'I have made some decisions and I want to submit them to your ears too.'

'Very good, sir. I am ready to carry out whatever service is within my capability.'

'Your service . . .' He stopped, not finishing the sentence, then resumed after a beat. 'Right now, you must lend your ears to my submissions, and take the best care of Navab Mirza in the days to come.'

Wazir was taken aback. 'I do not follow. What is it that His Honour commands?'

'Nothing. You just listen. I will spend tonight in Ballimaran. Very early tomorrow, I will leave for Firozepur. What you say about Jahangirah is perfectly solid and true. A marriage proposal for her has come to my mind. I will have it investigated further and if I can, I will perform the duties of her wedding and formal farewell from Firozepur just after the rains, and with the wonted ceremonious etiquette.'

'Your Honour's words are extremely proper. May Allah vouchsafe auspicious prosperity to your plans and may all your tasks be completed with excellence and elegance.'

'Madam. As Allah wills. And after that . . . we will see what Allah makes us see.'

Confusion again prevailed upon Wazir's thoughts. 'Please, I don't understand. His Honour will surely return to Delhi after the marriage and the bride's farewell? When will I cool my eyes with your sight?'

Shamsuddin Ahmad was silent for some time; Wazir could not muster up the courage to make him break his silence or ask for an answer to her query. Fearfully, she raised her eyes to the Navab. The chamber was more or less fully dark now. The grey-green wisps of light that seeped through the tiny cracks in the doors and windows seemed to cast a wan and unhealthy hue on his face. His cheeks looked sunken; his cheekbones seemed somehow more prominent than ever; the straight, well-formed nose looked longer and thinner. The proud neck was still straight, but it seemed to be tense, such that a few veins seemed to stand out against the gaunt face. Wazir looked surreptitiously at the Navab's body. She could not see his legs, covered as they were under the light coverlet, but his hands were visible above it: his fists were clenched.

Wazir broke into a cold perspiration. A line of the Hindi poet Momin crept into her brain: *What is this wind that blows to send a thrill of fear into my heart?* Has that night come again . . . ? She wanted to shake Shamsuddin Ahmad by the shoulder, but again her courage failed her. Should I go out and call one of the outside guards? No, that will be even more impertinent. Quite involuntarily, she wrapped her arm around Shamsuddin Ahmad's neck and touched her cheek to his. Apparently, the warmth of her feeling, more than the warmth of her touch, helped to unwind the tension in Shamsuddin Ahmad's body. He raised Wazir's chin lovingly, smiled, and said, 'Sorry for this long silence . . . Anyway, I'll make all things clear now. Having performed my duty by Jahangirah, I will settle my account with Fraser.'

Wazir impulsively tried to interrupt, but the Navab shushed her, putting his hand on her mouth. 'Please, just listen. Do not interrupt. I cannot at present say how that account will be settled. But he must certainly be punished for his excessive haughtiness and rude arrogance.'

'But . . . but what punishment will His Honour mete out to him? And is there only His Honour on whom this duty devolves? There are other nobles, other chieftains, after all; and then there is His Majesty, God preserve him.'

He snorted. 'Well, I've had dealings with them all. Everybody is interested solely in their comfort, their bedstead, their meat and drink, their lusts and passions. Everybody looks at life, and their life's capital, with their own eyes. We should have no concern with others.'

'Then when will I see you?' She wailed. Big tears began to drip fast from her eyes to her face, but she did not know it.

'I do not know. We will meet when the Joiner of the Separated joins us. I don't even know if my ambition will prosper. Please be patient. The world may not move as we will it to, but we can move ourselves as we will.'

Shamsuddin Ahmad rose, straightened his clothes, put on his cloak and, opening the door a crack, clapped softly. When Habiba entered, he ordered the lamps to be lit in the bedchamber; lights were already burning everywhere else in the house, preparations for serving dinner were afoot. Shamsuddin Ahmad had Navab Mirza brought to him. Again, he spent quite some time in play and jokes with Wazir and Navab Mirza.

It was now bedtime for Navab Mirza and nearly time for the night prayer. Shamsuddin Ahmad took Navab Mirza in his arms, kissed him profusely, ran his hand tenderly upon Wazir's head, and pronouncing the benediction, 'In the Protection of the Almighty', he went down the stairs. His back was straight and his steps were firm and measured. As the Navab turned his back to her, Wazir arranged her prayer mat, and spreading the hem of her wrap on her arms, she prayed for a long time with tearful eyes, trembling hands and choked whispers. None knew or dared to ask what she was praying for. Nor could they open their lips to remind her that the dinner was growing cold.

BOOK 5

43

At Firozepur Jhirka, Navab Shamsuddin Ahmad Khan accepts a proposal from Akbarabad for the hand of his sister Jahangirah Begam; but he receives shocking news on another front

THE THREE-DAY JOURNEY to Firozepur Jhirka was uneventful and comfortable. The rainy season had clogged all roads with mud and had filled to overflowing all dry watercourses, but the Navab's elephants and camels were well trained. One set of tents and other equipment went ahead of his caravan, while one accompanied the Navab. Thus if it became necessary to camp somewhere before a scheduled stage, the Navab's men could set up tent and pavilion at some suitable spot. The equipment that went ahead was properly defended with carabineers on horses and gunners on camels. Each camel carried two pieces of portable cannon called zamburak, their shot and shell kept safely dry under tarpaulins. The zamburaks were mounted one on each side of the gunner, called zamburakchee; the guns were so designed that they could be fired simultaneously by one gunner. There was no better weapon of defence in a small battle area. The zamburakchee were mostly from the Deccan and were reputed for their steadiness in the face of enemy fusillade.

Before the time of Dilawar-ul Mulk Ahmad Bakhsh Khan, Firozepur did not boast of a proper fort; it had only a garhi—that is, a fortified residence—used by the Imperial Faujdar up until the end of the administration of Navab Najib-ud Daulah. Delhi's authority on the area waned after Najib-ud Daulah's death in 1770, so much that when Lord Lake was appointed Absolute Plenipotentiary by Shah Alam Bahadur Shah II in 1803, a huge territory up to and including Hansi-Hissar fell under the sway of the English. The political and military importance of Firozepur Jhirka suffered an eclipse when an English Revenue Collector and Magistrate was headquartered in Hansi, and because the Resident was also the English Commissioner for the vast region loosely called Delhi, the writ of the English ran throughout the area in the north-west of Delhi up to Hansi-Hissar.

Once Ahmad Bakhsh Khan won the independent chieftainship of Firozepur, he devoted much energy to renovating, extending and fortifying the garhi into a proper fort within one year. The older portion of the building housed his office, drawing and court room, and was also the male sleeping quarters. Two new havelis ran adjacent to and inseparable from the old structure and were designated the haram sara—forbidden quarters, for the exclusive use of the females of the Fort. A secure zone, called kucha-e salamat ('secure alley') both joined and separated the two parts of the new Fort.

A park and garden, protected by a lightly fortified boundary wall, surrounded the entire construction. This was in addition to an interior, more secure garden, which connected the two parts of the Fort at the back. A canal meandered around the entire enclosed area, providing water to the Fort and all its inhabitants. Many fountains were set alongside formal pavilions inside the grounds. The park and garden were designed on the pattern of the garden built by Emperor Jahangir near Sirhind in the 1620s; the main characteristic of this garden was that it was an ornamental park and also an orchard.

Firozepur Jhirka began to gain in prosperity and population after Ahmad Bakhsh Khan became its ruler. Very soon, it was no longer a small country town but a bustling provincial city, which had all the requisites of urban life. Two fee-less hospitals, a number of inns, public gardens, permanent bazaars for each major profession with their residential neighbourhoods, many secondary-level schools, open to both Hindus and Muslims, one Jami Masjid and many smaller mosques, one Karbala, used by the Shia community for the mourning month of Muharram, a Ram Lila Ground for Dasehra and other Hindu festivals, many Hindu temples, a Sikh Gurdwara, and even a Methodist Church sprung up, the latter constructed by the English with the Emperor's permission in the last year of his reign.

The bazaars of Firozepur were bursting with merchandise and shoppers. The grain merchants' godowns were full of edible oils, oilseeds, grain, sugar, ghee, coarse sugar and treacle. Tradesmen from faraway places were establishing their factories there apace. Bigger markets of the adjoining areas were exporting their goods, especially grain and cattle, to Firozepur Jhirka in a continual stream. Shamsuddin Ahmad had worked to further raise and improve the city's prosperity and business levels. In fact, now some Englishmen in high positions had begun to regret that an area so prosperous and productive should be ruled by a native potentate.

Within a few days of his arrival in Firozepur, Shamsuddin Ahmad Khan reviewed all the extant marriage proposals for Jahangirah. He did have a reasonably attractive proposal from one of the many distinguished families of the Mirzas resident in Akbarabad (Agra). But he was looking for not just an attractive proposal: he desired something even better, if not the best. He knew that the good is the enemy of the best. He had therefore not conveyed his acceptance; but had not rejected it either.

Now he had his Agent in Akbarabad inquire deeper into the matter. The Agent reported that the family, Iranian in origin, Sayyid by ancestry, were of the Sunni faith—that is, of the Navab's own faith—and that their immediate ancestor Agha Mirza Muhammad Ahsan Ali came from Shiraz in Central Asia in the 1750s. Ahsan Ali had two sons; one married in a Shia family of Rampur and who had become Shia. Now all in that family were Shia and a prominent member of that family was called Agha Mirza Turab Ali, a young man of good manners, excellent education and sophisticated speech. He was the Manager of the Horse and Elephant Stable and Tent Equipment to the Navab of Rampur.

The Akbarabadi branch of the family continued to be Sunni. The other son of Agha Muhammad Ahsan Ali was Librarian at the Red Fort in Akbarabad during the reign of Shah Alam Bahadur Shah II who now rests in Paradise. He had been conferred the titles of Itibar-ul Mulk and Khan, and was known officially as Itibar-ul Mulk Agha Mirza Amjad Ali Khan. The position of Librarian was abolished when the English obtained control of the Fort. Considering any other employment inferior to his dignity after serving the King Emperor, Itibar-ul Mulk settled permanently in his haveli at Mewa Katra and managed his properties and holdings. Occasionally, in his free time, he gave lessons in Philosophy and Logic to the sons of some of his aristocratic friends.

Mirza Quqan Beg, grandfather of the poet Asadullah Khan Ghalib, came from Transoxiana around the same time as Agha Mirza Muhammad Ahsan Ali. The havelis of these two men were situated close to each other. Gradually, friendship developed between the young people of the two families, and one of the young men was Itibar-ul Mulk's son, Mirza Muhammad Muazzam Ali Khan, whose younger brother Mirza Muhammad

Azam Ali Khan was the prospective bridegroom for Jahangirah Begam. The proposal had been received through Mirza Ilahi Bakhsh Khan Maruf, Ghalib's father-in-law and younger brother to Navab Ahmad Bakhsh Khan.

Shamsuddin Ahmad Khan's Agent reported that Mirza Azam Ali Khan was seventeen or eighteen years of age, handsome and well educated. They were firmly of the Sunni persuasion of the Hanafi School, but were so close to Iran spiritually and culturally that Persian, not Hindi, was the language spoken in the house, though Mirza Quqan Beg's family had adopted Hindi in their second generation.

These people were not rich in the accepted, worldly meaning of the term, but everybody swore by the purity of their stock and their learning; and the piety, chastity, beauty and good household management abilities of their women were well known among the local aristocracy. They were prosperous, not wealthy. An addition to the honour of the family had transpired recently when Mirza Azam Ali Khan was appointed to the station of Naib Meer Moonshie (Assistant Chief Secretary) at the Commissariat of the Navab Laftain (Lieutenant) Governor Bahadur of the Province of Agra.

After much thought, Navab Shamsuddin Ahmad Khan conveyed his acceptance to the proposal. On 12 September 1834, after the Friday Prayer, Jahangirah Begam was tied in the nuptial knot with Mirza Muhammad Azam Ali Khan. The bridegroom and his party travelled from Akbarabad to Firozepur Jhirka; the actual marriage was pronounced and executed on the third day of the party's arrival—a manifestly Hindu practice, but common among the Muslim elites of that area. The ceremony of bidding the bride farewell took place on the seventh day. The marriage settlement on the bride was one hundred thousand Mughal rupees; as per the marriage contract, one-fourth of the sum was payable at once; this was done well before the party left for Akbarabad.

The entire expenses of the bridegroom's party—travel, wedding equipment, formal dresses for the groom, and for everyone in his party and his immediate family, commonly known as ghore jore ka kharch ('horse and dress expense')—were borne by Navab Shamsuddin Ahmad Khan. Again a manifestly Hindu practice, but prevalent among the Muslim upper classes of Delhi as well. This was in addition to the bride's actual dowry. It must be recorded that the groom's family outdid themselves in bringing expensive dresses and jewellery for the bride and formal presents for members of her family.

The whole city of Firozepur Jhirka ate at the Navab's kitchen or table on all seven days and nights until the groom's party left for home.

Jahangirah Begam was received with open arms in the groom's family. Very soon, her physical beauty, aristocratic sophistication, elegance and dignity won all hearts. She was given the title of Jahangir Dulhan (World-conquering Bride). Mixing with ease and effortless comfort with her new family, Jahangirah Begam began her life in Akbarabad in quiet happiness, and gradually attained contentment, that surpassing wealth that many seek but very few find. When Shamsuddin Ahmad Khan learnt of his sister's good fortune in her new home, he gave thanks to God and hoped for better days to come in his own fortunes. He was proud to hear that his sister's husband was respected all over Akbarabad for his nobility of conduct and loving treatment of his young wife. Now it was only the matter of William Fraser that needed his attention. It seemed to him that the day was not far when he would succeed in untying the one knot that constricted his heart after his dear sister had tied her own nuptial knot so well. But he did not know that special plans were already being spun for him:

Time does not loosen one single knot
In my heart before it has borrowed the nail
From a panther's claw to do the job.

*

4 October 1834: The day was Saturday; the weather had become pleasant. Cool winds had begun to blow from the north and the refractory hot winds of untrammelled pride, blowing from Rajputana in the west, had slackened. The park in the Firozepur Jhirka Fort was resonating with the sharp, persistent calls of partridge and quail. Even the dark, elusive shama, sometimes called the Indian nightingale, could be heard of an evening. Flocks of large and small parakeets could be heard all the time chattering in the sky or in the trees.

Shamsuddin Ahmad Khan was more than usually pleased with life today. Jahangirah's letter had come from Akbarabad along with a gift from her father-in-law: a large consignment of fresh vegetables grown on the banks of the river Jamna. The Navab, as a rule, ate lunch on Saturday with the ladies in the haram sara. Dismissing the morning durbar, he gave himself the pleasure of reading Jahangirah's letter once more; he gave instructions for the stay, board and hospitality of the messengers from Akbarabad, left the Durbar Hall and was about to go into the secure zone when there was some sound at the principal gate of the Fort, as if someone were seeking permission to enter.

The Navab paused where he was; two staff-bearers from the guardhouse came running to report that a dromedary rider-courier from Delhi prayed for permission to enter upon His Honour's presence, but had been stopped at the guardhouse because His Honour had risen from the Durbar. The Navab thought for a second, and then commanded that the courier be permitted to enter.

The dromedary rider, whose name was Aniya, was commonly known as Aniya Mewati. He had long been in the Navab's establishment as dromedary rider and was famed for speed, stamina and endurance of hardship on the road. Leaving his dromedary at the gate, he came running, and halting before the Navab, made seven salaams and submitted: 'His Exalted Honour's Mukhtar-e Kar (Chief Authorized Representative) Bahadur has sent his petition.'

The thought immediately crossed the Navab's mind that something untoward had happened, although there had been no hint or rumour of such an event from any side.

'You've made very good time and come in hot haste,' he said by way of expressing his approval. 'Let us see what you have brought. Is there anything special?'

'His Exalted Honour can know best. I was summoned last night by the Divan sahib who ordered that this servant should depart at break of day and submit this petition to the Presence before lunchtime tomorrow.'

'Very good. So you traversed these eighty or so miles quite quickly, Bhai wallah.' He gestured for the letter to be presented to him. Aniya unwound his turban, and from between the twists and folds of it, produced a sealed silk pouch, placed it upon the palms of his hands, advanced a step, and extended his hands towards the Navab. One of the musketeers, who stood slightly behind and to the right of Shamsuddin Ahmad, put out his right hand and took the pouch. Reading his master's extremely faint signal correctly, he broke the seal and produced a piece of thick paper rolled like a cylinder. The musketeer placed the rolled paper in his hands and presented it to the Navab.

The moment the paper touched Shamsuddin Ahmad's hands, it seemed to him that it was heavy with some very bad news. He would have had it thrown into the fire or the river, had that act been meaningful, but such an act would have availed him nothing: the information that the letter contained would become public knowledge, whether he willed it or not.

Unrolling the paper carefully, the Navab cast a cursory eye over it and felt as if someone had hurled a heavy chopper, such as the one used for cutting fodder, at his legs, shearing both his legs and forcing him to the ground. He swayed, as if he was before a gust of wind, and thought of grasping the musketeer's shoulder for support; but he quickly recovered without letting anyone know of the shock that had struck him. He went over the letter again, meticulously, as if he had missed something in the first reading.

The Quranic phrase used universally among Muslims at the news of someone's death or some severe loss, escaped his lips: *'Inna li'Allahi wa inna ilaihi raji'un'* (Surely to God we belong and to Him we return). Without saying another word, he went back into the main drawing room and sat quietly in his favourite easy chair. He gestured for a glass of water to be brought to him, and read the letter for the third time as he drank from the glass. It was written in the standard official Persian, which was developed in the eighteenth century. It contained much officialese and Indian expressions not to be found in the Persian of earlier ages. It was also somewhat stilted and extremely prone to protocol-oriented expressions.

Though it is impossible to convey in English the flavour of the kind of Persian we are talking about, appended below is a possible near-literal translation of it in early nineteenth-century English. While the Quran had been rigorously and meticulously punctuated for a little above one thousand years, punctuation was not introduced in Indian languages and in the Persian written in India until very much later. The only concession to easy comprehensibility—vaguely practised since the beginning of the nineteenth century—was to mark the paragraphs by making a small sign above the word with which a new paragraph was supposed to begin. A similar symbol, borrowed from modern Arabic (though used there for another purpose), has been employed here to mark the paragraphs; the unpunctuated text has also been lightly punctuated:

Exalted Presence, Lord-Benefactor, May You be Secure Always: after respectful Salutations it is submittedے Intelligence has been to hand to the effect that Verdict in the matter of the Case pertaining to the Presence has been pronounced from the Exalted Portal of Navab Governor General Bahadur, and a Certified Copy thereof was transmitted to the Residency and it reached there early this morning and expectations and apprehensions are that in two, three days, the Navab Resident Bahadur shall issue the Command to execute the Verdict and translate the same into practice. This servant feels great sorrow and pain in penning this petition: the Verdict does not conform to the purpose of the Nourisher—May He be always Secure—of this servant. The Navab Governor General Bahadur has decreed that the Territory of Loharu and other Lands attached thereto shall be sequestered from the care and charge of the Exalted Presence, and Governance of all the above Country shall be transferred to Aminuddin Ahmad Khan Bahadurے It has been further commanded that compliance to the Judgment aforesaid be made without loss of time. The Divan of Loharu and functionaries subordinate to the Officiary aforesaid, are desired to present themselves post-haste before His Honour the Exalted Presence and take possession of all Documents, Instruments, Financial Papers and Books of Account pertaining to the Administration of Loharu in the name of Aminuddin Ahmad Khan Bahadur. Of the havelis in the City of Delhi, the one situated in Ballimaran Gali Qasim Jan Shall and Will be the Property of Aminuddin Ahmad Khan Bahadur and the other haveli which stands in Darya Ganj Shall and Will be in the Ownership of the Exalted Presence, and Firozepur Jhirka and all the Sub Divisions and Country and Places and Wards included thereunder Shall and Will continue to be under the Rule of the Luminarious Presence as beforeے Determining that the submission of instant Petition was Necessary, I dispatched this Extended Missive. Submissively presented by Divan Abdullah Khanے Inscribed on Paper on Date the Twenty-seventh Jumad-al Avval, 1250, on the day of Friday, corresponding to Thirtieth September 1834 at the time of Sunset Prayer in the City of ShahjahanabadXII.

The numeral 'XII' represents, according to the numerological system called the Jumal, the value of the Arabic word 'hadd'; also used in Persian and Hindi—the language now called Urdu—this word means 'limit', 'extreme', 'boundary line'. It was very often put at the end of a communication to indicate that the communication was now concluded. It may also have been a device to ensure that nothing could later be interpolated in it.

It is clear that the communication had nothing that was obscure or ambiguous; so if Shamsuddin Ahmad read it over and over again, it was because he found himself unable to take a decision about it. It was also perhaps the case that he was still unable to believe his eyes and he read the letter again, and then again, to make sure that he had read it correctly and that there was nothing in it that was even vaguely favourable to him.

With each reading, the purport of the letter became clear and yet more clear to Shamsuddin Ahmad, and with each reading, his displeasure, anger and sorrow became greater, and also his sense of helplessness, for what was there, after all, that he could do about it? He was naked, powerless and without resource to resist the Governor General's decision. Nor could the Maharajah of Alwar be of any help to him. The Presence, the Shadow of God on Earth, could do still less.

The fire was lit by Fraser and the Navab's burning desire for revenge could only be doused by Fraser's blood. Some recompense could then be also possible for the calumny and ignominy that the damned, hog-like Nazarene had poured over his head . . . But it would not bring Loharu back to me. And I do not possess the power and the wealth to take the Firangee to court and fight on till I got back what is mine by rights. Taking up arms against him was not an option by any means. The Governor General Bahadur is in Calcutta. There is no way that I can lead an insurrection against him from here: I have lost territory, I'll also lose my life. No, I am ready to lose my life if it is possible and practicable to rise up against him . . .

. . . But I must punish that arrogant lecher. Let everyone else—cowards all—remain tongue-tied and hand-tied; I will do what I must. I will demonstrate to the world that I am his executioner, giving him punishment condign to his maliciousness, giving him a taste of his own medicine for his impudence against me and my honour. The haughty arrogance of the Firangee is like a rising river, a gathering storm. It is bent upon uprooting and destroying everything that stands in its way . . . How I would that our own Sovereign was not so ineffectual . . . No matter, I surely can do my petty mite, come what may.

With every passing moment, the pain and rage in Shamsuddin Ahmad's heart became more conflagrant. The letter had fallen from his hand. His eyes were hot and turned up, glaring mindlessly at the ceiling, as if he had been awake the whole night and had become disoriented. Faint tremors had invaded his body, he was trying to control them by clenching his jaws and fists and by making his back rigid; his breath came quick and shallow, his brow knitted as if he was in great pain. Had a hakim seen him in that state, he would have been alarmed and would have suggested that he was about to go down with meningitis, or that he had suffered an attack of tetanus.

Aniya Mewati, the musketeers, the doormen and staff-bearers on duty at the Durbar Chamber, all stood, full of fear, unmoving, as if turned to stone.

When the Navab failed to arrive in the haram sara, the Senior Begam, Afzal-un Nisa, deputed her personal maid Subh Daulat who was much liked both by her and the Navab to go and find out why His Honour was delayed. Traversing the interior garden at the back, she reached a secure doorway that let her into a rarely used corridor, which terminated at the Durbar Hall.

One brief look at the Navab from behind the heavy curtain terrified her; she turned and immediately ran back to the chamber of Afzal-un Nisa. She reported that—May God not desire it—apparently His Exalted Honour has been stricken by some shock, or—May it be far from him—something untoward has happened in the State. His Honour sits in the chamber, quite silent and lost. His face is reddening and darkening with displeasure; his body is quite rigid and unmoving.

Afzal-un Nisa almost decided to go and find out personally what was wrong and if possible, bring the Navab round, or immediately organize some therapeutic regime. But she had never stepped into the men's part of the Fort; she had been brought up so that she had full freedom to move around and pursue her mode of life, including pleasure and education, inside the walls of the haveli's haram sara and the interior garden, but no alien man could hear her voice or even footfall. All areas where even the shadow of an alien man could be suspected were out of bounds for her. It was also horribly against protocol for her to go out to the men's quarters. Having no choice, she postponed the lunch and ordered Subh Daulat to keep her ears trained to the happenings outside and determine exactly what had affected the Navab so severely, and whether a hakim or a vaid, that is, a Brahman practising the Hindu style of medicine, or a siyana, a practitioner of shamanic arts, had been summoned.

Having given these instructions, Afzal-un Nisa sat on her prayer mat, rosary in hand, and began to quietly recite the prayers that she had been taught in childhood as efficacious for such occasions. The maids-to-play of her two daughters took them into their chamber, trying to soothe them and make them eat some food. Both the children were disappointed and full of complaints at their father for depriving them of his company and his loving and entertaining conversation. Shamsuddin Ahmad Khan always spent the whole day every day and most nights in the male quarters of the haveli. Thus his weekly luncheon visits were greatly valued and much talked about by the little girls.

Within a short while, Amir Bahu, the Junior Begam, and Champa, the Navab's concubine, also came to know of the Navab's unhappy condition. Now the entire haram sara was enveloped in a chador of shock and silence. Only Rahmat-un Nisa, the Navab's daughter from Champa, just about two and a half years old, would fret or cry demanding why her Nab Shab had not come. Imitating her mother, she would try to say 'Navab sahib' but her prattling mouth could only enunciate 'Nab Shab'. This name, or title, pleased Shamsuddin Ahmad no end: every time he saw her, he induced her to say 'Nab Shab' as often as possible, and every time he rewarded her with something the child could cherish.

44

Karim Khan, the Chief of the Hunt, meets his Lord Benefactor Navab Shamsuddin Ahmad Khan

THE SOUND OF a horse's hoofs was heard outside the main gate of the Fort at the male haveli. The newcomer handed the rein of the horse to a staff-bearer manning the guardhouse, straightened the pistol that hung by his tight sash, and removing a muslin kerchief from the bag at the pommel of his saddle, he carefully wiped his face, dusted his shoes, smiled at the keepers of the guardhouse and said, 'Dear Mian sahibs, keep an eye on my horse.'

'Be careful as you go in, Bharmaru ji,' said one of the staff-bearers.

'Why? What's the matter?' He turned and looked closely at the guardsmen. They seemed to lack their usual verve and colour.

'His Honour is . . . is smouldering a bit.'

'But why? Was the luncheon not to his liking?'

'Kan ji, I swear that not even a morsel has passed his mouth. In fact, he has not yet taken his Noble Presence inside the haram sara. He's sprawled in the divan khanah, quiet and unmoving like a crocodile on a sandbank.'

The newcomer's brow clouded with concern. Saying, 'All right, just let me go and look', he strode towards the inner gate of the Fort, but his body movements did not express the same spruce confidence. He was a very tall, muscular young man, broad and strong of chest. Even the air around him seemed to have an aura of force. He had keen, black eyes and long shining hair that fell in thick locks up to his shoulder. His slightly heavy moustache and beard trimmed very short in the Rajputi manner looked handsome on his young, energetic face. He wore a turban of the Rajputi style, and riding breeches and boots in the English style.

About twenty-four years old, with a back that was ramrod straight, he had a taut and powerful body; his stomach, abdomen and thighs did not have an ounce of extra muscle, not to speak of any fat anywhere else on his body. This was Karim Khan, Chief of the Hunt to Shamsuddin Ahmad Khan; with his fluid gait and deportment, his masculine beauty, light but firm steps and confident eyes, he strongly called to mind a cheetah, brimming with power and youth, stepping proudly in the thicket of a dense green forest. It was said that he could track and follow game on foot even as far as thirty miles without stopping. He was unparalleled in tracking and chasing: even the dimmest and faintest of marks made by the animals as they moved or stayed, the state of the grass or shrub where they passed and the time since they had passed, the calls of the birds, the different kinds of ungulates, monkeys, carnivores, were as mother tongue to him.

He was a never-failing marksman and sniper, equally at home with different kinds of guns, and equally comfortable in firing on foot or from the height of a horse or elephant or a machan (a raised and camouflaged platform from which one watches for the sight of the animal being hunted). He never missed his shot, regardless of the state of the light or the speed of his game animal, or his own speed on a horse. These qualities had earned him the nickname of Bharmaru.

As the name suggests, a bharmar ('stuff and shoot') was a muzzle-loading gun. Such guns were also called toredar and topidar. The difference between modern guns and traditional guns was that the latter's nipple had a small space underneath, which was stuffed with superfine gunpowder. The gun was fired by touching a burning match or fuse, called a shitaba, to the gunpowder, which took instant fire, producing a high-temperature flame. The flame whooshed into the gun muzzle through a pinhole chamber called kothi in Hindi, and the gun fired instantly. In the modern version, there was no shitaba; instead, a hammer in the gun's lock struck the nipple with great force, igniting the gunpowder inside by creating pressure. Because of the hammer and lock, such guns were also called topidar ('capped'). The latest version of this gun was called patthar kulah ('stone cap') or flintlock because it used a small piece of flint instead of the gunpowder in the gun's nipple.

All these guns were loaded through the muzzle; the English called them ML for 'muzzle loading'. Indian MLs were mostly single barrelled, but the English had also made popular a double-barrelled gun called a DBML (double-barrelled muzzle loading). Other than being an expert in the use of all kinds of muzzle-loading guns, Karim Khan was well versed in the qarabin, and the bedharmi. The qarabin was indeed the French carbine, used by both the French and the English. Shorter barrelled than the bharmar, the carbine was longer barrelled than a pistol and was therefore much favoured by the cavalry. Its mouth was a little wider than the barrel, permitting a satisfactory scatter of shot. Sometimes double barrelled as used in India, it had a small rectangular space between the butt and the barrel called tosdan and the shot was inserted into the gun through the tosdan.

The qarabin was much liked by Indian troops for face-to-face fighting and for defensive purposes, because though its range was comparatively short, it was light and its smaller barrel permitted quick and frequent fire from horseback or camelback. It used a heavier shot than other guns and not needing a nipple or fuse, it permitted easier shooting than most conventional guns.

A qarabin that could fire more than one shot with successive pulling of the trigger was known as chand zarbi (multi-shot), though most qarabin fired only one shot at a time. The qarabin and the bedharmi used hammer and trigger for firing and were therefore much more efficient. All such guns were called SBBL or single-barrelled breech-loading guns by the English. In such guns, ammunition was stuffed not through the end of the barrel, but through the top of the barrel. These guns had a supporting stock, called palki in Hindi, and a pin called maghz kil; the stock separated from the barrel once the pin was removed, revealing the top of the barrel; munition could then be inserted in the gun from the top and the stock replaced after the operation was complete. Such guns, if they had two barrels, were called DBBL (double-barrelled breech loading). In Hindi, they were known as do nali qarabin (two-barrelled carbine) or dugara (double).

In spite of their greater efficiency, none of the breach-loading guns were much liked by Indians. The bedharmi was a long-range, single-barrelled rifle invented and much used by the English. It was because of their English origin that they were called 'bedharmi', or 'godless'. During the time when Karim Khan was acquiring expertise in these guns, the word 'bedharmi' was falling into desuetude, the word 'rifal' (for rifle) rapidly taking its place, as we can see in this verse by the Hindi poet Atash of Lucknow, composed around 1830:

In the hunting ground of the world
I have but one desire:
I should be in your sights and
Your rifal should fire.

In spite of his dexterity with the rifle—the Navab's armoury and his own collection had quite a few of them—Karim Khan never used it to hunt. He always said that concealing oneself in a hide at a distance of a hundred, hundred and fifty yards or shooting from the elevation of an elephant was against the rules of chivalry. A patthar kulah or a bharmar by its very nature gave too much superiority and advantage to the hunter, not to speak of a rifle, which was a coward's weapon. He even said that the best hunter was he who hunted on foot with only sword or spear, and confronted the tiger or even the elephant face to face.

Karim Khan was born and brought up in the Fort at Firozepur. Younger to Shamsuddin Ahmad by two or three years, he grew up as playmate and later friend to Shamsuddin Ahmad. They learnt the arts of combat, armed and unarmed, together from the same master. For Arabic and Persian too, they had the same tutor for the first few years. On account of his good looks, sense of humour and elegance of speech, he was welcome wherever he went. Delhi's young men about town had nicknamed him Gul-e Surkh (Red Rose). In spite of good proposals for marriage from many homes, Karim Khan consistently refused to marry, saying that the flowering shrubs in the jungle are my ranis, and the tall, dense trees my marriage procession, so why should I ever think of marrying anyone else?

Karim Khan noticed that musketeers were stationed at the main door of the Durbar Chamber. He lifted an eyebrow inquiringly; the musketeers gestured to him to go in, but not without the hint of some diffidence, if not fear, in the unconscious gestures of their bodies. It was as if they were hinting that Karim Khan must enter at his own risk, and should not blame them if his reception was adverse.

Stepping through the main portal, Karim Khan entered the expansive courtyard before the chamber. The courtyard was green and gold and red with flowering shrubs and flower plants of the season. Between small patches of greensward were walkways in Kotah stone, and a little stream ran burbling around them. At the far end was a raised platform with a small canopy above it. Where the courtyard was not covered by grass and plant beds, the walkways were paved in white marble. At the end of the courtyard, and also on its left side, were wide verandas, again paved in marble. The Durbar Chamber was situated at the far western end of the courtyard.

Karim Khan was proceeding towards the Durbar Chamber when there was a movement behind the curtains on one of the doors in the left veranda. Someone was beckoning to him. Karim Khan raised his eyes to find that it was Subh Daulat who had again come out to inquire about the Navab's condition, but not having plucked up courage to enter the chamber, she was on her way to the servants' apartments to seek the help of a senior male. Subh Daulat and Karim Khan were well acquainted with each other, and occasionally, Subh Daulat cast a glance at him in some special way, though Karim Khan was not interested. This time too, he imagined that the little hussy wished to talk to him, taking advantage of the seclusion. He frowned, but spoke in a near whisper, using the familiar tu, 'What is the matter? Why are you mincing about here in the male quarters?'

'Please, Karim Khan ji, did you not hear? His Exalted Honour has had some kind of a fit! All the begam sahibs are running around, vexed and worried to craziness. Everyone is at their wits' end. No one knows what to do.'

'That is certainly a matter of real concern. Is he unconscious? But what are you doing here?'

'Senior Begam sahib is inquiring all the time: "What is happening? Has the Hakim sahib come?" But no one is sending any news inside to say how His Honour is doing now.'

'Well, I'm on my way to His Honour's service anyway. You scoot from here. I'll find out all that is there to find out and devise a way to improve matters. I'll also have a report submitted inside.'

Saying this, Karim Khan walked quickly inside. Subh Daulat stayed back, feeling stranded, and hoping that Karim Khan might look back.

In the chamber, the Navab's condition was slowly moving towards normalcy. He still lay half sprawled on his long chair, but his body was no longer convulsed; he was perspiring in spite of the cool weather. A personal attendant was drying his brow with a soft kerchief; two others stood some way behind and were slowly waving large fans, each made of a single palm leaf. A mace-bearer stood with a cool drink in a tall, engraved glass on a matching tray. The Navab apparently paid no heed to any of them; his eyes were still vacant, fixed upon the ceiling. A woman attendant was tenderly rubbing the soles of his feet with her muslin orhni.

Karim Khan stepped into the chamber gingerly; he gestured to the mace-bearer to ask if a hakim or a vaid had seen the Navab. The reply being in the negative, he sat down at the feet of the Navab and softly touching his knees, he spoke in the sweetest, most cajoling of tones, 'What happened to my King? Who annoyed him? Who has been so insolent?'

The Navab moved his eyes from the ceiling and looked at Karim Khan with the same vacant gaze. His face would always open like a flower when he saw Karim Khan, but this time around it remained dead, expressionless.

'Please, do say something, my Lord,' Karim Khan now shook the Navab's knee gently, as if trying to wake him up. 'It is for you to command. Everybody is here, willing and ready to give their life for you. You only have to say the word; it will be carried out.'

Now the Navab looked at Karim Khan with wonder in his eyes, as if it was only now that he had become aware of his coming.

'Karim Khan, there is nothing else now,' he said in a hoarse voice. 'Now is the time to kill and be killed.'

Karim Khan emitted a short laugh, but there was a hint of menace in his attempt at gallows humour: 'His Honour should at least command whose time it is to be killed. I am here to kill them!'

'Loharu is lost, expropriated. It is due to the machinations of that procurer, that pimp! I should have made short work of him on that very day.'

'His Honour speaks in riddles,' said Karim Khan in the manner of an old friend.

Shamsuddin Ahmad Khan pointed to the paper that was still where he had dropped it. 'Why don't you pick that up and read it? Everything is narrated there.'

All facts became mirror-clear to Karim Khan as he read the paper through. Clouds of pain and regret passed over his face but were soon replaced by gravity and firm determination to act.

'I await His Honour's command. Should I go to Delhi or to Calcutta? Will the appeal now lie with the Firangee King?'

'What appeal and what petition?' Shamsuddin Ahmad spoke almost in a whisper. 'Nothing can be changed now. It is God who will exact revenge from them. He is the Most Weighty, and the Greatest Avenger.'

'Your Honour. We can also take revenge.'

Navab Shamsuddin Ahmad Khan brought his fist down with a dull thud on the armrest of his chair and cried out, 'Is there no one to put paid to Fraser, that unworthy infidel, so that my heart could at least be consoled somewhat?'

A silence seemed to fall on everything. After a noticeable pause, Karim

Khan spoke, 'Your Honour has not yet partaken of his lunch. There is much anxiety and confusion in the interior of the haveli. Please, how long will you keep them and the little children waiting?'

Shamsuddin Ahmad Khan looked at Karim Khan with some surprise. There must be some reason for this sudden change of subject? But what could the reason be? He wanted to say something but Karim Khan spoke in pre-emption, 'Actually, I came to take permission from the Lord Benefactor, the Pivot of Prosperity,' he paused, as if he was speaking about something mundane and routine, not needing any emphasis or hurry in its utterance, and then continued, 'I have something urgent to attend to and am about to leave for Delhi presently. The Exalted Presence should partake of the midday repast. He is feeling poorly, it seems. Let him rest a while, then this slave will submit some measures for consideration.'

He touched the Navab's knee again, rose and bent seven times in salaam.

The Navab spoke almost in an undertone, 'Go. I entrust you to God's care.'

Karim Khan sedately walked backwards and quit the chamber. There was silence again for a few minutes. The mace-bearer again offered the glass of the cool drink to the Navab; he again declined it. Again, there was no activity or movement for some time. Shamsuddin Ahmad Khan, however, seemed in greater control of himself now; he sat up presently and desired that fresh water and washbasin be brought to him for washing his face. After the Navab had washed and dried his face, an attendant sprinkled on his face and hands and feet some water lightly scented with the attar of roses. The Navab now looked around the chamber and saw Subh Daulat, who had sneaked in when she saw Karim Khan go out, standing in a corner, her body gathered up demurely in her chador. Shamsuddin Ahmad asked her in kindly tones but using the familiar tu, 'So, Subh Daulat, how are you present here at this time? Is everything all right?'

Subh Daulat again made three quick salaams and said, 'How is His Honour of Exalted Highness feeling now? The Grand Begam sahib inquires if opinion did not favour summoning the Hakim sahib. Does His Honour feel better now?'

Shamsuddin Ahmad Khan drew a deep, wintry sigh and, partly addressing himself, partly addressing those present, said a verse by the Iranian poet Saidi Tehrani:

The world has nothing to do with me,
Except to burn me down;
Like the candle, the ears of my corn
Bear no grain other than tears.

Trying to regain a normal tone of voice, he spoke kindly to Subh Daulat, 'There is no need for a hakim. I'm all right. Go back in and have the luncheon laid. I will be there presently.'

Making three salaams, Subh Daulat walked backwards out of the chamber. The Navab commanded for a light, open sedan to be made ready for him so that he could take the air briefly before he proceeded to the haram sara.

*

It was late Tuesday evening, the seventh day of October 1834, when Karim Khan and Aniya Mewati arrived in Gurgaon, twelve miles from Delhi, and stayed the night in a local hostelry. By midday next day they were in Delhi, staying at the Daryaganj Haveli. Since they were frequent visitors there, no one was surprised and no one even asked why they were there. Since the Navab went out on tours of inspection in his territories during these months, no one inquired when and if the Navab was expected there.

Karim Khan quickly found out that Fraser was not in Delhi at that time, for he too was out on his winter inspections. The territory of 'Delhi' controlled by the English was immense in its own right, but it had assumed special importance in those times because the Firangee sahibs had their covetous eyes on the Panjab; so areas contiguous to the Panjab and therefore farthest from Delhi always had priority in the inspection programmes of the Sahibs of Exalted Glory. Fraser returned to Delhi in those days, but rarely. His taking the evening air stood discontinued; and he spent most of his time inside the Residency. A few days later, news came that on account of some disturbance to the peace in that part of the country, the Senior Sahib Bahadur had declared Karnal to be his camp headquarters and he would be returning to Delhi later rather than sooner.

It was now almost three months since Karim Khan had been cooling his heels in Delhi. During this time he barely glimpsed Fraser once or twice, not to speak of coming face to face with him. His trusted informants and spies, deputed to keep watch over Fraser through day and night, had been drawing salaries on a paid holiday, as it were. November had drawn into mid-December now. The camps and mansions of the Sahibs of Exalted Glory began to buzz and hum with preparations for the Great Day.

Karim Khan learnt that William Fraser was about to return to Delhi to celebrate the Great Day and the Firangee New Year's Day. He now nurtured strong hopes that it was no more than a week or ten days when his shot would pierce Fraser's breast. He strongly instructed his team to be more than usually vigilant to ensure that he was kept informed of Fraser's movements from hour to hour, if not at lesser intervals.

Before news of Fraser's return to Delhi could reach him, a courier delivered to him a letter from Shamsuddin Ahmad Khan. Written in Persian, but less formal and convoluted than the official Persian of those days, the letter is literally translated below:

> The Khan of weighty value and the symbol of valour, Chief of the Hunt, Muhammad Karim Khan Bharmaru: may he be safe and secure ∠ The reason for inscribing this: You have been staying for more or less three months in the Capital City of Auspicious Foundation but have not still concluded the important business of buying the hunting hounds and have even not submitted a report or information sheet on this matter. Thus the thought crosses my mind that you are entirely incapable of discharging important duties such as purchase of hounds for hunting. Hence, and therefore, you must, immediately on sight of this Direction to Act, return to the Fort. Delay is not at all proper∠ Written on the fifteenth of Shaban of the current year, on Tuesday, at the time of late morningXII.

The missive was written in the informal Shikastah script by Shamsuddin Ahmad Khan in his extremely pleasing hand. It was unsigned, though, nor did it bear the Navab's seal, or in fact any seal at all. The paper on which it was written was not the high quality thick paper used in the Navab's Chancery. Karim Khan did not doubt that the author of the Direction to Act was none other than his master. The following morning, he packed his bags for Firozepur Jhirka. As he was setting out, the thought came to him that it was against good judgement to leave the Direction to Act in the haveli; in fact, good judgement demanded that it should be destroyed by fire. His conscience, or temperament, did not bear to rip or burn a paper that had his Navab's handwriting, so after some thought he dropped the paper in a well situated in front of the haveli at Daryaganj.

Travelling at double speed, Karim Khan arrived at the Fort in Firozepur on the afternoon of the second day. It was after the pre-sunset prayer that he was granted audience with the Navab who had just sat down to dinner with some senior advisers and companions. The Navab gestured to Karim Khan to join them. There was no conversation during dinner except formal greetings and salutations, but it was clear that the Navab's mien did not have its usual sunny aspect. During the after-dinner round of the hookah, Karim Khan responded to some casual remark of an adviser by declaring that should his Master and Safe Haven and True Home face any kind of hurt from an enemy, he would not stay put and would breathe the breath of rest only when he had sent that enemy to his final resting place.

'Doubtless,' said the Navab with a brief smile. 'That is how pamperers of their belly spin out their long yarns.'

Karim Khan needed no explication or interpretive effort; it was clear that he was the object of the barb. It hurt all the more because it was not devoid of justice. Because Shamsuddin Ahmad Khan and Karim Khan had been friends from childhood, the Navab's observation pierced Karim Khan's heart like the twist of a long needle, but silence was the best policy at that time. After some reasonable gap, he took permission to leave.

When he reached his apartment in a remote corner of the Fort, he was told that some 'native' accountants—then called mootsuddy, and now called clerk—from the Residency, as well as the Chief Treasurer of the State and the Divan of Loharu had been camping for the last two months, preparing papers for Loharu's separation from the main State. No revenues from Loharu had been remitted to the State's Chief Treasurer for the last two months. Many years ago, when the dispute had arisen over succession, the Firangee had ruled that Loharu would be common property between Aminuddin Ahmad Khan and Ziauddin Ahmad Khan. Loharu yielded an annual revenue of 25,000 royal rupees at that time. The Firangee further decided that the sum of 15,000 rupees would be docked from the revenues to defray the cost of administering the State, and the sum of 10,000 rupees would be divided equally between the two brothers with the stipulation that because Ziauddin Ahmad Khan was in his nonage at that time, his expenses would be the responsibility of Aminuddin Ahmad Khan until the former came of age, and his share should be deposited every month in the English Treasury at Hissar.

When that arrangement was nulled, the surplus revenue of Loharu began to be submitted to the main Treasury at Firozepur, and payment to both the younger siblings was made from there. Now the position had been reversed in favour of the status quo ante. The Residency's mootsuddies were hot upon the trail of each paisa to see if the Loharu revenue had been misspent in any way at all. Adding insult to injury, the two siblings were demanding a share in the cash assets and jewellery left by their father, and also in the furnishings, glassware, carpets, so forth, at the Firozepur Fort. Thus all the valuables inside the Firozepur Fort were being inventoried so that the siblings' share could be made over to them under acquittance.

For Karim Khan, Loharu was as much home as Firozepur; the forts at both cities were coloured with his memories of childhood. Now the true reality of the sequestration of Loharu and the brutal division of goods, hit him like a blow to his abdomen. He felt that his own home was not only being divided, but it was somehow being desolated as well. His intent to avenge what he regarded as injustice became stronger if that could be possible; now it was also mixed with the sense and perspiration of shame.

He thought he should return at once to the haveli, beg admittance to the Navab and apologize most abjectly and promise that he would carry out his pledge most certainly and expeditiously. But it occurred to him that to discuss such a subject where they could be overheard was against good sense. He kept his patience, waiting for a suitable occasion.

A couple of days later, when he accompanied the Navab on a hunting expedition, he managed to find himself alone with him, and said, 'I am ashamed before the Excellency.'

'I'm ashamed in my own eyes, Karim Khan.'

'I am not a pamperer of my belly; I idealize and idolize my Master.'

'And I am not a self-willed tyrant. But I expect serious effort, and good results from the effort.'

'There will never be any curtailment of effort. There has never been any curtailment. I have eaten His Honour's salt and will always be doing so. I am a Rohilla, not a distiller or seller of wine. The word given by a true man is a living word.'

'Does it take long for a true man to turn into an abject fox?'

Karim Khan pulled out his hunting knife from his waistband and piercing the skin of his throat with its point, he said, 'It is you who say this to me?'

The Navab put out his hand and gently removed the knife from Karim Khan's neck. Putting the knife at the base of his own throat, the Navab said, 'There is no one who knows your value and valour more than I. You have been my comrade since childhood. You too should know me well.'

'I know well what lies in the depth of your heart. I will not sleep contented before I've done what your heart desires. I have had just that one hunger, hurting me like a pain, from the very first day.'

The Navab stepped up to Karim Khan and patted him on the shoulder. 'I have full faith in you.'

Both seemed lost in their own thoughts, for Karim Khan made no reply. After a couple of minutes, the Navab said quietly, as if to himself, 'The conditions might be better in March.'

'Sir, most appropriate. I will go to Delhi in early March.'

No further conversation took place between them on the topic, then or ever. A large flock of blackbucks was reported to have entered the cultivated fields just outside the city, causing much damage. The two hunters went out to kill one or two and frighten off the rest. However, in spite of riding over a large circumference, there were no blackbucks to be found. Neither hunter was very keen to hurt the blackbuck anyway, so they came back to the Fort, satisfied that there was no apparent danger from the animals.

45

The rumour mills of Delhi shift to high speed and Navab Shamsuddin Ahmad Khan comes under suspicion

JANUARY PASSED, THEN February, as if in the twinkle of an eye. The day was Monday, and the date was 3rd of March, when Karim Khan and Aniya Mewati were in Delhi again, and were greeted by the news that Fraser sahib was in Delhi. Karim Khan immediately set his spies on their previous job. Not content with the regulars, he enlisted Aniya as well and they began keeping an eye on Fraser's Haveli on the Hill, and the Commissioner's Court in Ludlow Castle, Alipore Road.

They soon found out all about Fraser's schedule, but the information was not helpful. Fraser rarely went out unescorted during the day, nor were his wonted routes such that they would be reasonably free from traffic and remain so for at least fifteen minutes. Fraser's visits were mostly confined to meeting Thomas Metcalfe, or his distant relative Simon, and to a lesser extent, Sikandar sahib (that is, James Skinner). Metcalfe's mansion, then as now called Metcalfe House (Matka Kothi for most natives in those times), was situated at the very end of Alipore Road. Simon Fraser and James Skinner resided in Civil Lines, just a little past Kashmiri Gate. Only Metcalfe House was at some substantial distance from Fraser's mansion; the other two were within a couple of miles from it.

In the evening, Fraser invariably returned home a good two hours before sundown, and the streets through which he passed even at a late hour were always well lit and reasonably busy. In order to go to his house, one had to leave the main road and enter his private road on the Hill. This road was quiet and movement-free at nearly all times and was thus not suited for hiding in ambuscade. Strategy demanded that Fraser should be located somewhere alone and dispatched there.

It has been often stated that Fraser's mansion was situated in Bara

Hindu Rao. This is not quite accurate. The mansion certainly was in the neighbourhood of modern Delhi, which is called Bara Hindu Rao; actually, Bara Hindu Rao did not exist at that time. Between Kishan Ganj and the Hill, there was nothing then but stray shops and petty homes; the rest was densely covered with thorny shrubs and small flowering trees. The land was gravelly and stony. A road joined Kishan Ganj with the shops and homes mentioned previously. The ascent to the Hill began where the road ended; as mentioned earlier, it was Fraser's private road, narrow, and covered with red gravel and pea-sized white stones. Fraser had cleared a small area on both sides of his road and had it planted with evergreen or seasonally flowering shrubs and plants, and some fruit-bearing trees.

As one proceeded up the road, the first gate of Fraser's mansion was encountered. Beyond it, the road meandered up, bordered on both sides by the same kinds of plants and trees. Thus while the road presented a somewhat pleasant sight, the rest of the land and the Hill looked quite forbidding and dark on account of the dense foliage everywhere. As narrated earlier, there was no name to the forested area, except that the Hill was just called 'Pahari' in Hindi and the neighbourhood went by the name of Fraser Sahib's Kothi. At the sale of Fraser's effects after his death, a rich landowner called Hindu Rao bought the whole lot of land and the mansion, and hence the name Bara Hindu Rao which persists even today. Much of the Fraser mansion is now an uninhabited ruin, having been subjected to heavy shelling by English troops during 1857, because it was an important tactical headquarter of the rebel troops. Only a small part, which is now a segment of the Hindu Rao Hospital, remains of that once-proud pile.

*

It was unusually late for Fraser on 22 March 1835 when his buggy left Kishan Ganj. He was a guest at a dinner party hosted by Kalyan Singh, the Rajah of Kishangarh (not to be confused with Kishangarh, Rajputana). Song-and-dance shows and drinking sessions lasted very long after the dinner and Fraser somehow drank much more than he normally did. Nearly unconscious, he had been helped along by his guards and Kalyan Singh's servants to his carriage. A rider rode in front with a lantern and four others followed the buggy. All the five had fully enjoyed the Rajah's conviviality resulting in an appreciable slowing down of their reflexes. And even though the road was lonely, it was considered as absolutely no risk.

Delhi had had an unusually cold winter; even March was extremely cold, and the environment was misty dim because of the dense vegetation and fall of dew. It was so dark that visibility was reduced to about ten steps or so. There was no light except what was emitted by the lamps mounted on Fraser's carriage. They were coach lamps of English design; quite ornamental, they sported blue or green shades. Fraser's advance rider did have a powerful lantern on the pommel of his horse, but his light was not visible: the lantern was either out, or the rider was so far ahead as to leave Fraser's carriage out of range of this light. He was clad in black and rode a huge black Arabian that was surefooted and fluid in his gait on the familiar road: both horse and rider seemed to have melded with the dark.

Fraser was in full court dress: tight woollen pants; white shirt of the best quality muslin whose sleeves and neck were embroidered in silk; a black brocade waistcoat over the shirt, the waistcoat showing a gold watch chain; a short coat over the waistcoat, very tight at the waist and with tight but short sleeves so as to show off the embroidery and tassels; a flowery silk cravat around his neck; a long, heavy coat called a topcoat; and a high, black, hard silk hat called a 'top hat' which had just come into fashion, completed his couture. He was only half conscious, his eyes shut, his neck slack and slumped to one side. He was snoring but occasionally fell silent with a start.

The buggy's roof was made of leather and canvas and was stretched tight, supported by iron springs and stays. It had a half-door on each side, closable from the outside or inside. Fraser, sprawling on the back seat, was easily visible in the light of the coach lamps.

The carriage was now at the bend leading into Fraser's private road. The air was so dark that the rider on the musk-black horse—actually of a deep and dark red-brown colour that looked musk-black in the dark—could miss the bend with the slightest lack of vigilance. The rider expertly and comfortably turned his musk-black into the bend, followed a few minutes later by Fraser's buggy. His front rider was nowhere to be seen, or maybe the coachman mistook the musk-black to be the front rider. As the buggy turned deeper into the bend, the four rearguard riders became unsighted for many moments.

Suddenly the rider of the musk-black slowed. The distance between him and the buggy began to shorten; the musk-black's rider slowed yet more, but the coachman whose intoxication the cold night air had deepened, took no notice. Now the musk-black and the carriage were parallel on the narrow road. Leaving his mount to its own control, the rider hefted the gun resting on the bow of his saddle. Fraser's right side was just where it should have been.

Three shots were fired with almost no gap between them. The first shot hit Fraser in the abdomen. Passing through his lungs, the bullet seared his liver and exited, smashing two of his ribs. The next exploded a hole in his heart and was stuck between two ribs on the left side. The third hit the sternum, travelled downward, tore open the stomach and buried itself in the spleen. Fraser's death was instantaneous: the first shot itself had finished him.

The coachman did not at all understand what had happened. The musk-black rider spurred his horse and with lightning quickness, turned towards Kishan Ganj, his speed and the dark night helping him disappear before the rearguards could notice him. On hearing the shots, they went up very fast to see if the buggy and its rider were safe. In the meantime, the musk-black rider had left the narrow road, seeking the additional concealment of the scrubby bushes and trees. By the time the rear riders came up to the coachman, he had realized that the dark rider who disappeared so fast was not Fraser's front rider, but someone else, and perhaps it was he who had fired the shots. He began to wail and call for help, beating his breast. One of the four rear riders went on without stopping, overtaking the real front rider, and they raced to the mansion to seek help and bring out more lights. The other three stopped at the buggy, amazed and clueless.

Within minutes, a medley of Fraser's men appeared, their torches and their bayonets and spears creating a small forest of lights that reflected off the naked steel. Fraser slept the sleep of death, oblivious to the sensation and the dread created by the mystery rider. His mouth had fallen open and his face was slack; his yellow teeth seemed dirtier and more yellow in the pale, almost penumbrous light.

Thomas Metcalfe, Fraser's deputy, and Simon Fraser, the City Magistrate, appeared shortly, their faces tired and shocked. They were still in their nightdress, but had a posse of their own soldiery. The coachman and all five of Fraser's outriders were immediately arrested, put in irons and marched off to Alipore Jail, secured and surrounded by a platoon of soldiers. The Company's surgeon, Dr MacNaughton, and his assistant, Dr Chaman Lal, had arrived a few minutes earlier and had nearly finished their necessarily brief examination of the corpse by the time Thomas Metcalfe and Simon Fraser arrived. The body, however, remained in the surgeons' custody who escorted it with due honour to Fraser's mansion.

Preparation for public viewing and burial started immediately. Before dawn, the news had spread all over Delhi and nearby towns. Delhi, always known as the rumour factory, began to manufacture rumours before the predawn prayers had been said.

The body was prepared and placed in the main drawing room for viewing at 10 a.m. the next day. The Company Bahadur issued a proclamation and had it disseminated by an army of criers through the whole city well before the time of viewing. The proclamation was in Hindi; a literal translation is given below:

> The Land is of the Shadow of God, the Commandment is of the English Company Bahadur. Everyone, Noble or Plebeian, is hereby informed that today, at the half hour past 3 p.m., at the Gora Graveyard in Alipore near Ludlow Castle and the Court and Secretariat of Navab Resident Bahadur, burial will take place of the Navab of High Portal, who has the Rank of Governing and Chieftainship, Muazzam-ud Daulah [Most Respected of the Empire], Amin-ul Mulk [Trusted Custodian of the Country], William Fraser Senior Sahib Bahadur, Martyr, upon whom is the Mercy of God, and who has received Allah's Forgiveness. Whoever among the subjects in the City wishes to come for Sacred Viewing and Condolence, should present themselves at the mansion of Muazzam-ud Daulah Amin-ul Mulk, the Senior Sahib Bahadur, Martyr.

Well before the proclamation was cried out, a multitude of sightseers and condolatories had begun to assemble at the Fraser mansion and the crime scene.

*

Among the rumours making the rounds of the city, two were the strongest. The weaker of the two purported to say that William Fraser was responsible for the removal of Loharu from the rule of Shamsuddin Ahmad Khan;

further, he had used improper and insulting language for Jahangirah Begam. The theory was that Shamsuddin Ahmad Khan exacted revenge upon Fraser for these offences by having him killed. The stronger talk was that a woman or a young boy (professional or otherwise) was behind the murder. It appeared that Fraser sahib had abducted some woman he fancied; the current lover of the woman had organized the murder by way of revenge. The loiterers and carefree of the populace, most of whom were homosexual, and who thronged the various Delhi gardens between Kabuli Gate and Shalimar Garden—like Raushan Ara Bagh, Bagh Mahaldar Khan, Bagh Patni Mal—held the theory that it was not a woman but a boy who was at the bottom of the incident: it was even possible that the boy himself, his sense of honour aroused by some improper conduct or act of Fraser's, had had him assassinated.

The English were fully aware of these and other rumours: their spies were everywhere in the city, trying also to pick up the tiniest whiff of information about the killer. It was not just the rife rumours that were taxing the English mind, but also the possibility that the assassination was the opening move in a conspiracy of insurgency and had a political or at least an administrative angle to it.

Memories of the events in Bareilly, an important city formerly under the Rohillas, were fresh in the minds of the veterans among the Company's administrators. It was just about a dozen years since Navab Mustafa Khan, a grandson of the legendary Rohilla chieftain Hafiz-ul Mulk Hafiz Rahmat Khan, joined hands with Mufti Muhammad Ewaz, chief arbiter in questions of Islamic law at Bareilly, and led an armed insurgency against the English rule there. The uprising was short and bloody, but till the time it lasted, it shook the pillars of the Company's Government from Delhi to Calcutta. It was the presence of mind and strength of purpose exhibited by Edward Colebrooke, the Commissioner, and Francis Lowe, the Collector, that finally carried the day against the rebel forces, which were crushed mercilessly. Rebels, who had held Bareilly for two weeks, were rounded up after their defeat and given the most brutal punishments.

Had such an event taken place in Delhi, its effects could have reached not only far, but could have also been lasting. Flustered at the possibility of similar trouble irrupting in Delhi, Metcalfe and Simon Fraser decided upon an early, simple burial in the Gora Graveyard near the Residency with full police and military presence, not as guard of honour, but to prevent any undesirable incident. Fraser was to be quietly buried in an unmarked grave at present. Later, after the investigations led to the apprehension of the murderer and the unravelling of the conspiracy, if any, a full, formal funeral would be mounted for him.

Among the first to appear for Sacred Viewing and Condolence at the mansion were Mirza Asadullah Khan Ghalib and Fathullah Beg Khan, a blood relation of Shamsuddin Ahmad Khan. Fathullah Beg's grandfather, Arif Jan, and Shamsuddin Ahmad's grandfather, Qasim Jan, were brothers. Fathullah Beg Khan's haveli was also in Ballimaran, in front of the Katra and the mosque of Adinah Beg Khan. The cousins were once close friends, but a minor, jocular dispute between them about a horse led to great bitterness and enmity between the two.

That morning, when Mirza Ghalib and Mirza Fathullah Beg reached the Fraser mansion, they found a long line of carriages and people on foot from the ascent to the Hill to the inner gate of the haveli. The protocol for the viewing was that Fraser's coffin was placed in the large drawing room, with the body in full court regalia with all medals, personal weapons and honours showing; the stone coffin was laid on a wooden platform to resemble a catafalque. Four English soldiers of the Company's army, in full dress and arms, were arrayed unmoving at the head of the catafalque, and their commanding English sergeant stood to attention at the foot, facing the soldiers. Viewers and condolatory visitors were required to enter, go round the catafalque once, and then go out from another door. No one was allowed to stay. Thus the viewing chamber was always full of people.

As Mirza Ghalib and Mirza Fathullah Beg entered the chamber, the latter broke the line and vaulted over to the catafalque. He emitted a howl of mourning, fell on the coffin, and cried, apparently beside himself: 'Woe! Woe! Shamsuddin did not spare thee!'

An Englishman grasped him by the shoulder and shook him, and unceremoniously pushed him out of the chamber. Mirza Ghalib was ashamed at Fathullah Beg putting up the silly, meaningless spectacle. Indeed, Fathullah Beg had needlessly drawn the attention not only of the Indians present to the possibility of Shamsuddin Ahmad's implication in the matter, Englishmen like Simon Fraser took instant notice of the allegation.

John Lawrence, Panipat's Magistrate and close friend of William Fraser, travelling non-stop over fifty-odd miles, had just arrived at Fraser's mansion when he was informed of Fathullah Beg's dramatics; he found that Thomas

Metcalfe was inclined not to give much importance to the incident. Metcalfe believed that it was nothing but a cheap show and its main motivation was Fathullah Beg using the occasion to publicly express his grudge against Shamsuddin Ahmad and, if possible, humiliate him. But Lawrence and Simon Fraser were quite clear that the matter needed investigation. Simon Fraser ultimately won the debate.

The first thing that Simon Fraser did on the following day was to summon Fathullah Beg Khan to the district court and rigorously examine him. Clearly, Fathullah Beg knew nothing at all, and had been feeling angry and ashamed at himself. Now he could only say that he was sorry, he knew nothing. The long and stern questioning by the two Englishmen was fruitless. Even so, the English rulers arrested not only Fathullah Beg Khan, but also Shamsuddin Ahmad Khan's father-in-law, Mirza Mughal Beg Khan, merely on the ground that he lived in the haveli of Shadul Khan, close to where Fathullah Beg lived.

In the English circles, Mirza Mughal Beg was considered to be a guileful and cunning person whose loyalty to the Company Bahadur was suspect. Thomas Bacon, author of a contemporary account of these events, has in fact clearly imputed to Mirza Mughal Beg knowledge of and involvement in the case from the very beginning.

The fact, however, is that Mirza Mughal Beg had not the least inkling of Shamsuddin Ahmad Khan's encounter with Fraser in July at Ballimaran. Mirza Mughal and Shamsuddin Ahmad Khan had not met since long before the news of the alienation of Loharu from the main State became public knowledge. Thus, the arrest of Mirza Mughal Beg turned out to be as fruitless as the arrest of Fathullah Beg Khan. But it did damage the position of Shamsuddin Ahmad Khan, because the rumour mills came out with another titbit: Shamsuddin Ahmad Khan was somehow involved in the case.

Mirza Ghalib was also questioned, but not much. This produced yet another rumour: Mirza Naushah (Ghalib's popular name) had already done all the informing on the very first day; there was nothing more to inquire from him now. It is true that Mirza Ghalib, in those days, had become very friendly with a Firangee officer called Theodore Prescott. But that apart, throughout his long relationship and marriage kinship with the family of Navab Ahmad Bakhsh Khan, not a single word had dropped from the admittedly eloquent pen of the aristocrat-poet in favour of Shamsuddin Ahmad Khan. This was surprising, given his liberal ways and manner of life, his love for peaceful relations with all: Hindu, Muslim or Nazarene. When Shamsuddin Ahmad Khan had succeeded to the State, Ghalib wrote in Persian a letter to the effect that now the ignoble and the vile would have the upper hand, and persons of petty mentalities would rule the roost.

Ghalib's unhappiness with Shamsuddin Ahmad Khan had been the talk of the town ever since the death of Navab Ahmad Bakhsh Khan, and after Fraser's assassination, the gossip in the city was that it was Mirza Ghalib, and not Fathullah Beg Khan, who was the informer against Shamsuddin Ahmad Khan. This 'news' became so popular that Mirza Ghalib was obliged, in many of his letters at that time, to assert his innocence. He said that he was only guilty of having friendly relations with Prescott sahib.

Still, the aristocrat-poet's grudge and rancour against Shamsuddin Ahmad drips from many of his letters that he wrote in those days. For instance, in a letter in Persian to the famous Hindi poet Shaikh Nasikh of Lucknow, Mirza Ghalib described Shamsuddin Ahmad as 'ungrateful for favours received, and murderer of the Just'. In another letter to the same correspondent, Mirza Ghalib cursed Fraser's murderer, praying to God that that 'cruel, un-God-fearing fellow may be seized in eternal torment'. Shortly after the demise of Fraser, he wrote a Persian ghazal of which the concluding verse ran as follows:

Ghalib, just see, what oppression, what injustice!
That a person like William Fraser should die
Because of the bold arrogance of his enemies.

Certainly, this does not prove, or even suggest, that Mirza Ghalib was informing the English against Shamsuddin Ahmad Khan. Another well-known poet in Delhi at that time was Ghanshyam Lal Asi. He wrote two Persian chronograms commemorating the event. One of them was:

The Angel spoke, with face full of pain and sorrow:
Alas! For the murder of William Fraser!

Mirza Ghalib may or may not have been active against Shamsuddin Ahmad—and the strong likelihood is that he was not—regardless of his frequent hate-fuelled fulminations against the younger man. But the environment of suspicion at that time made sure that some tiny spots of suspicion stuck to the garment of Delhi's greatest contemporary poet and a well-known aristocrat. It is, of course, quite likely that Mirza Ghalib harboured suspicions against Shamsuddin Ahmad Khan in the murder case, but it is also quite clear that he did nothing to give words to his suspicion.

Disregarding the event involving Fathullah Beg, and discounting suspicions against Mirza Ghalib—and disregard them we must—no evidence at all was forthcoming to point the finger of suspicion at Shamsuddin Ahmad Khan. The hoof marks left by the musk-black at the scene of the crime were extremely confusing. Investigators had been unable to determine even the route taken by the mystery rider on his way to Fraser's carriage and on his way back from there.

Still, the fire of revenge burnt hot in the breast of Simon Fraser, and perhaps raged even more strongly in John Lawrence's heart. Simon Fraser was strongly suspicious of Shamsuddin Ahmad Khan; there were two motives, not one. And Simon had been fully posted about both. He also believed that the rumour mills of Delhi very often spun a fabric which at least had a colour of the truth. Naturally, the two officers quite ignored the fact that it was their own actions—the arrests of Fathullah Khan and Mirza Mughal Beg—which had stoked the fires of suspicion so much that the smoke was now touching the sky.

They argued, and examined the meagre facts that they had. It must be said they did not take any decision precipitately. Fully three days had passed before Simon Fraser and John Lawrence could persuade Thomas Metcalfe that Shamsuddin Ahmad's haveli in Daryaganj should be raided on the following day at 4 a.m. All exits should first be blocked, then each and every nook and corner should be searched thoroughly, though it was not clear what was to be found. Should the raid there be fruitless, the haveli at Ballimaran should be subjected to the same treatment. But mounting a surprise assault on the latter did have the complication of disturbing, even destroying, the sanctity of the haram sara. It was decided they would cross that bridge when they came to it.

None of the Indian staff was made privy to these decisions.

46

The news of William Fraser's assassination reaches Navab Shamsuddin Ahmad Khan

AS SOON AS he got the news of the assassination, Simon Fraser had ordered all the exits from the city to be closed, and when he was informed that a black-clad rider was seen galloping away towards Daryaganj from around Kashmiri Gate, he further ordered that any rider out anywhere in the city should be immediately stopped, his identity ascertained and he be asked to account for his movements. The Company's policemen, cavalry and irregulars spread over the whole city and made this order the occasion for harassing innocent citizens abroad, even if they were pedestrians. But Aniya was too canny and too experienced a runner to let himself be captured by those lazy, city-bound functionaries. He disappeared in the warren of lanes and bylanes behind the vast Id Mosque in Pahar Ganj and running through comparatively darker and less densely inhabited neighbourhoods, arrived near Bulbuli Khana. It was then easy to jump the high threshold of Turkman Gate and run into the graveyard in Menhdian, which was close, though rather dimly lit.

He circled the graveyard, approaching the Kotla of Firoze Shah, and groping through the dilapidated buildings surrounding the Iron Obelisk, and taking advantage of the lights and shadows in Abd-un Nabi's mosque and the Khair-ul Manazil Mosque, he found himself at the shrine of the great twelfth-century woman saint Bibi Fatimah Sam. Fortunately, there was a crowd of visitors assembled there from far and wide on the occasion of her annual Urs. Aniya easily mingled among them and slept in anonymity under a marquee erected for the pilgrims.

He rose before dawn and speeding unnoticed towards Firozepur Jhirka, he was under the ramparts of the Fort early in the morning of 24 March

1835. Navab Shamsuddin Ahmad Khan had not risen yet, but in view of his standing instructions that Karim Khan or Aniya, whenever they reported at the Fort, should be admitted inside and allowed to present themselves before the Navab, his personal mace-bearer at the door had information sent in that Aniya Mewati was at the gate, awaiting permission to make his submissions. The Navab came out of his bedchamber and received him standing in the interior garden. The moment Aniya's eye fell on the Navab, he cried in high glee, 'Let the fortunes of the Exalted Highness be always High!'

Then he ran up, touched the Navab's feet and before he could say anything, the Navab asked, 'So what brings you here? Is everything all right?'

'Our purpose is achieved, by His Honour's ascendant fortune!' Aniya bent low in salaam and said. 'The road has been cleared of the enemy.'

'Oh? Very good! Did you see with your own eyes?'

'No, Your Honour. But I heard with my own ears the sound of three shots fired from a qarabin. There was noise and shouting everywhere soon after. The news that the Senior Sahib Bahadur is no more spread through the city at the speed of lightning.'

'And Karim Khan?'

'Excellency, I have no information. Karim Kan sahib was out in pursuit of the enemy. I immediately took off when I heard the reports of the gun, so that I may be the first to bring the good news to my Honourable Master. His Honour knows that Kan sab's aim never misses. So there was no room at all for doubt.'

A new surge of life seemed to course through Shamsuddin Ahmad Khan's blood vessels. But he kept full control over himself, not betraying any excitement or pleasure. He clapped for the mace-bearer and commanded that ten gold mohurs be awarded to Aniya at once. Then he said, 'Aniya, you remain at Firozepur. I am very pleased with you, bhai wallah, and there is much more destined for you yet.'

The promise implied in the Navab's words was that Aniya would be given much more by way of rewards, but it would be against good sense to single him out for some special treatment at that time. Aniya understood the Navab's meaning but imperfectly; he hesitated, and somewhat uncertainly removed himself from the Navab's presence after doing seven salaams. Perhaps the Navab descried a glimpse of unreliability in Aniya's eyes, for immediately after Aniya left, the Navab summoned the Chief of Police and instructed that Aniya should be watched secretly and should not be allowed to leave the city.

Aniya was no novice at pursuit and secret shadowing; he was acknowledged everywhere as an expert courier and runner and knew all about ambush and secret watching and the quiet pursuit of a subject. Or perhaps the spies deputed by the Chief of Police were not up to the job, for Aniya very soon espied the spies. Quite naturally, he believed that since he was privy to a great secret of the Navab's, it was not impossible for the Navab to desire his removal so that the secret may be buried with him. The next day, Aniya's suspicions hardened into certainty.

Early in the morning, he was out in the jungle to relieve himself and chose a stony hillock to squat behind. Just as he was about to squat, a large stone came hurtling down the hillock and very nearly crushed his legs, if not his whole body. Aniya convinced himself that the stone was intended really to flatten him and it was merely a small miscalculation on the part of the would-be murderer that he had escaped. He ran up the hillock to look for footprints or traces of the enemy, but found nothing. This merely served to strengthen his fears: the enemy was highly experienced in such matters; staying here in Firozepur now was to court certain death. He did not appreciate the fact that the Police Chief did not need to use such crude and chancy methods to liquidate an undesirable person.

It is said that some people were heard saying that while Aniya was coming out of the haveli, he heard that the Navab had been advised to get rid of Aniya, a low-born individual, who was in possession of such a deadly secret. Now when he realized that he was being stalked by spies, he was quite convinced that he did not have many days of life left with him.

Aniya confided in his older brother and persuaded him that his best course to save his life now was to assume a disguise and disappear. Since there was greater hope of security in the Company's dominions, Aniya struck out on the road to Agra in the dark of night the same day. Since he was a seasoned and proficient runner, the night did not present any problems for him. The Chief of Police suppressed the information and kept the Navab uninformed, for obvious reasons, of Aniya's disappearance. He was not aware of Aniya's significance anyway, so he thought that his slip from duty was but venial.

The news of Fraser's murder became common knowledge in Firozepur on the fourth day of Aniya's disappearance. It was also rumoured that the Firangee sahibs, after the most strenuous investigation, had arrived at the conclusion that Karim Khan Bharmaru, our Navab's Chief of the Hunt, was responsible for the crime and so had clapped him in jail, to be tried as a criminal in an English court. Most of the subjects of the Navab were dumbfounded, silent, and unable to decide what role, if any, the people of Firozepur must play in this situation. Should we congratulate the Navab because his enemy had been killed? Or should we condole with him for his chief servant being arrested and accused of the murder? As for Shamsuddin Ahmad Khan, he seemed quite unaffected. Perhaps he believed that there was no danger for him. As a responsible ruler, he kept discharging his office as he normally did.

*

Much before the morning drums and bells began to toll on the 28th day of March 1835, the main road and alleyways of Daryaganj began to resound and reverberate with the sound of horses' hoofs, the commands of English officers, and the thump of soldiers' and policemen's boots. These people and their numerous lights created the illusion of day even in the darkest lanes, as if it was the wedding procession of some grandee's only son. Led by Simon Fraser and John Lawrence, a large force of the Company Bahadur surrounded Shamsuddin Ahmad Khan's haveli in Daryaganj. The moment Fraser, Lawrence and other Firangee officers entered the haveli, all its doors and gates were locked from inside. They had obviously no cause to fear resistance. Simon Fraser went straight into the divan khanah; John Lawrence began to search the outbuildings, like the horse and elephant stables, and the armoury, and met with success almost at once.

In the very large stable, a tall, powerful stallion of deep, dark red-brown—a colour called teliyan (that is, red-brown like mustard oil) —stood alone in a corner, its head bent and eyes somewhat dim. On inquiry, he was informed that it had been ill for some days and was not eating. Out of simple curiosity, Lawrence had a basket of the horse's favourite food placed near its mouth. No sooner had the food basket touched its mouth than it began eating like a normal horse.

Lawrence was wondering why an apparently pointless untruth was stated about the stallion when his eyes fell on the elegant brown-black's hoofs and the shoes on them. They seemed odd, somehow. He asked a syce to lift one of the horse's feet for closer inspection. When the foot was raised for him to inspect, a thrill ran through his body. The shoe had been put on backwards. Hurriedly, he examined the other three hoofs and found them too shod in the same manner. His heart thumped against his ribs, almost aloud. Bull's eye! He said to himself. It was natural for the Company's men to have failed in making head or tail of the hoof prints at the scene of the crime when the horse's shoes were all wrong.

Suddenly another revelation flashed into his brain. He remembered stories about Dick Turpin, a brigand famous in his country in the last century. His modus operandi was the same: his horses were shod backwards, and he was thus able, for a long time, to confuse and elude his pursuers. He recalled that Dick Turpin was finally hunted down in the north, and hanged. Lawrence was convinced that he had found his man's murderer, and he would make sure that he got his just deserts and was hanged.

Investigation and search in the interior of the haveli yielded nothing, though Simon Fraser, driven by his investigative zeal, had some parts of it dug up in the hope of recovering documents or weapons. Anyway, another breakthrough was achieved when many horseshoe prints at the scene of the crime were proved by measurement to agree with the shoe-size of the suspect horse. The steward of the stable and all the syces were put under arrest.

It now seemed that Karim Khan's ill luck walked alongside him, or in fact, walked ahead to lead the investigators to him. Even before Aniya could arrive to report on the developments, Shamsuddin Ahmad Khan, beleaguered by anxious thoughts, deputed Wasil Khan to Delhi to ascertain the news. Wasil Khan was married to a sister of Karim Khan and since both were quite friendly with each other, Karim Khan could be expected not to evade giving information to Wasil Khan. Now this Wasil Khan, travelling in the normal way, reached Delhi on the night before the raid on the haveli. When questioned, he freely admitted to being a brother-in-law to Karim Khan, but could not give a convincing reason for being in Delhi at that juncture. Wasil Khan too was put under arrest.

No one knows for certain what finally happened to Wasil Khan. An English writer has speculated that Wasil Khan—whose name he gives as Wasail Khan—was fully involved in the case and was perhaps the real murderer. Anyway, Wasil Khan disappears from the historical record since that time. It is not unlikely that he languished in jail without trial for many years and finally died a prisoner against whom evidence was still being gathered.

The Company's spies reported that Karim Khan was often seen riding the same teliyan stallion which was suspected to have been used to commit the crime. In view of his universally high reputation and expertise at firearms, Karim Khan immediately became a person of interest. Another spy reported that Karim Khan was seen at the house of Mr William Macpherson, a well-known arms dealer in Delhi. Simon Fraser immediately went to Macpherson's house with a posse of policemen and was gratified to find Karim Khan there, negotiating about the sale of the teliyan horse to Macpherson. Simon Fraser, determining that the negotiations justified action, promptly put Karim Khan under arrest.

Karim Khan was taken to a secure interrogation room in Ludlow Castle and was subjected to extended and intensive questioning. But the interrogators had nothing on which to base their questions, or any evidence implicating Karim Khan, far less Navab Shamsuddin Ahmad Khan. All that they had was the suspiciously shod horse and the rumours. Karim Khan continuously denied that it was he who had the horse shod in that peculiar way. He admitted to riding the stallion off and on, but its shoes were perfect whenever he rode it.

'So when did you have the horse's shoes reversed?'

'Excellency, only the owner of the horse can tell you this. What can I, a lowly employee, say about it?'

'Why not? Are you not Chief of the Hunt to the Navab?'

'Your Honour, I am not the steward of the stable, am I?' Karim Khan smiled.

'So how is that a laughing matter? Speak respectfully, or this sahib,' he gestured towards John Lawrence, 'will speak to you with his shoes.'

'The Presences are the Masters. Larren sahib and Saimon sahib both know me very well. How could I do anything against the Sahibs of Exalted—'

Lawrence cut him short. 'This smooth talk you may keep for your tarts and petticoats. You Indians only understand the language of staffs and staves. You will be whipped so much that you will cry for your mother.'

Simon Fraser whispered to John Lawrence, 'Lawrence, be a bit careful. You know the Company's orders: the natives can be beaten up, but with some care. Their bones are brittle and their bodies frail. Do nothing such that the prisoner may die. We shall earn a bad name and lose evidence too. Strike him, but be sure not to break his bones.'

John Lawrence smiled. 'Don't worry. I'll break this evil Negro's spirits, not his bones.'

'Better starve him in a dark cell for a few days.'

John Lawrence considered this for some moments and then agreed, 'Yes, that's a good idea, Fraser.'

The cell in which Karim Khan was incarcerated had nothing but a fragile cot, the charpoy, woven with rough ropes of rush. The cot was removed and the window and door of the cell were shut and covered with black canvas sheets. Four native sepoys overpowered Karim Khan and tore away all his clothes. He was pushed into a corner of the cell, having been kicked all the way. One of them warned, 'Beware and do not move from here. If you do, you will be hit with staves.'

After many hours, the door opened. Though it was late evening, no light was allowed in. John Lawrence entered and found Karim Khan shivering from the cold in a corner, wet with his own urine. Lawrence struck him with full force repeatedly on his calves and the soles of his feet. He failed to make Karim Khan draw a sob or even a sigh. Finally, Lawrence was obliged to ask, 'Where were you at the time of the murder? What were you doing at that time?'

'Your Honour, how can I say anything when I don't know the time the murder happened?'

Lawrence waved to a native jamadar (corporal) who stepped up resolutely and repeatedly hit Karim Khan on his neck, head and back with a stout, supple staff at two-second intervals. Karim Khan's torso became drenched in blood. Lawrence said coldly, 'Bastard dog of a fornicator, don't be insolent, or we will do worse than this to you. Where were you from the late evening of 22nd March up until morning the next day?'

'I was asleep in my little cell, Your Honour.'

'Did anyone see you there? Do you have a witness?'

'Presence, a very high fever had done me down. I wrapped myself well and kept to my bed. I did not eat even.'

'You lie! On that night you were seen near the Senior Sahib Bahadur's mansion.'

'Not possible, sir.'

The jamadar again hit Karim Khan with his staff. He snarled, using the insulting tu: 'Motherfucker, is the Sahib Bahadur telling a lie, then? Base fellow, why don't you reveal the truth?'

'Jamadar ji, you can say what you like. I can say only what—'

Lawrence did not let Karim Khan finish the sentence. He strode up to him and delivered a few hefty strokes on his stomach and the soles of his feet.

'Right, now you tell me. When was the last time you rode that horse?'

Karim Khan kept quiet for a minute or so, as if trying to recall something. Then he said, 'I do not remember, Your Honour.' Then he smiled briefly. 'I do not maintain a journal, Your Honour.'

Karim Khan's smile was derisive, or perhaps it was not. Lawrence certainly felt that the petty, low-paid native flunkey was making fun of him. He pointed towards the sepoys. A dozen strokes of the staff were again given to Karim Khan. Lawrence found another tack. 'So did you not think it suspicious that you were negotiating the sale of that very horse which is involved in the murder?'

'Yes sir, Presence, it certainly is suspicious . . . Has the murderer confessed using—'

Lawrence shook Karim Khan savagely and pulled out a handful of hair from his moustache. Then he kicked him with his heavy boot and screamed, 'You are the murderer!'

Karim Khan passed his hand over his face, then shook his hand, as if dusting something away. He said, 'His Honour is the Master.' His voice carried no hint at all of humility. He spoke as if he was soothing an angry child.

'Why did you want to sell that horse, and especially try to sell it now?'

'Presence, I was carrying out the orders of my Navab sahib. His command was to alienate that horse for it was obstinate and did not obey commands.'

'What is the proof of this?' Lawrence roared.

'Your Honour can inquire from the steward of the stable.'

'That we will do when we want to. Right now it is you who are here, bastard. You son of Satan, you tell me! Was it not improperly shod when you last rode it?'

'The shoes were perfectly all right, Exalted Highness. I can swear to it.'

'Why didn't you go to a hakim if you were sick?'

'Sir, paupers like us, and a hakim? We get well,' he said, smiling, 'just like that, writhing and groaning.'

It seemed to Lawrence that a furious flame had shot through his whole body. He sprang at Karim Khan and delivered a savage blow on his face. Blood spurted from his forehead, drawing a thick red line down to his chin.

'Fucking filthy cock of a swine,' Lawrence muttered, and gestured to the policemen who began to rain down their cudgels on Karim Khan; no sound escaped him, but he put his head between his knees. After a few minutes of the beating, Lawrence kicked him in the ribs and shouted, 'Bloody nigger, raise your head and talk!'

Karim Khan raised his head. One of his eyes was dull red like a garnet, the other was swollen shut.

'When did you get the horse shod with reversed shoes?'

'I never got that horse shod. Believe me, Your Honour. I never lie.'

'Cheating bastard! Why did you decide now to sell that horse?'

'Presence, Macpherson sahib was out of town. He returned only the day before.'

John Lawrence smarted inside; it was a fact that Macpherson had been out of town.

'So who got those shoes affixed? Were you not the rider of that horse?'

'Presence, I am not the steward of the stable.' He cleared his throat and spat out a gob of bloody phlegm in such a way that it fell near Lawrence. 'It is true that I have been guilty of riding that horse a time or two. But my sahib knows of it. He never punished me.'

'Treasonous wretch! Where were you at the time of the murder?'

'Excellency, I do not know the time of the murder.'

'You lie, you villain. You were seen near Fraser sahib's mansion on the night of the murder. It is no use lying. We know it all.'

Karim Khan stretched and tautened his body, as if he were yawning. 'I was not there, Your Honour. But even if I was there, it doesn't mean that I committed the murder.'

Lawrence wished to crush the recalcitrant native dog's head under his boot. But he recalled Fraser's advice and desisted. He paused to regain some calm, then spoke in a cool, conversational tone, 'So when did you last see the Senior Sahib Bahadur?'

Karim Khan too was silent for a few seconds, as if trying to recall the occasion. 'I cannot remember now, Presence. It has been a long time . . . and we natives generally avoid appearing before the Firangee sahibs as it is.' As he spoke, he urinated calmly, with insouciance, as if he were relieving his bladder in a secluded place. Lawrence and all the others present heard the sound of the stream falling in front of them. Lawrence could say nothing, for it was he who had ordered Karim Khan to be deprived of his clothes and locked in dark seclusion. He covered his embarrassment by shouting in a voice more peremptory than before, 'Hit him some more, and yet more.'

This order was carried out with gusto. Karim Khan did not make a sound. Lawrence asked coldly, 'You will tell the truth now. Where were you on the night of the murder?'

'In the haveli in Daryaganj, Your Honour.'

Lawrence gnashed his teeth mentally and recommenced asking the same questions. This went on through the night. Lawrence did not rest for a moment, nor did his men. He repeated his questions with metronomic regularity, but would often punctuate the series by putting in an irrelevant or unexpected question. Sometimes he cut short Karim Khan's reply and asked something nearly meaningless. His effort was to somehow find or trap Karim Khan in a contradiction. But Karim Khan's answers were always the same: short and to the point. His voice became low and hoarse; continuous and severe punishment, resulting in loss of energy and body heat, and plain exhaustion took their toll upon him. Still, his head bent and voice becoming fainter, he gave the same answers. He was almost semi-conscious now. Lawrence was bleary-eyed and hoarse.

Ultimately, the questioning was stopped just before dawn. Lawrence was desperate for a bath and some rest followed by a good breakfast. He ordered for two or three pitchers of cold water to be poured on the prisoner; Karim Khan should then be clad in a cheap cotton tunic and pants, and be transferred to another cell. He should be fed sparingly, and not allowed to sleep. Lawrence left, saying that he would return in the evening.

In the event, it was night when Lawrence returned, but this delay in fact spelt more evil for the prisoner than he expected (if he expected something at all). A piece of evidence had been found during the day which convinced all the Firangee superior officers and high-ranking Englishmen involved in the investigation that now they were in the possession of means which would put in their clutches not only Karim Khan, but the Navab himself.

Sometime during the day of the raid, someone lost his leather bucket in the well in front of the haveli in Daryaganj. A diver went down to recover the bucket. When he came up with the bucket, he also brought up a stone-cap gun which had a sawn-off barrel. Over and above that, he found a piece of paper stuck to the bottom of the bucket, which had been caught in a muddy corner of the well. When he had exerted some force to pull the bucket, he had found an official-looking paper sticking to its bottom. He submitted both objects to the policeman on duty at the haveli who immediately sent them with a report to Thomas Metcalfe Sahib Bahadur.

Metcalfe ordered both objects to be confiscated in favour of the Honourable Company Bahadur; he then had the paper sent to Simon Fraser to be deciphered, and the sawn-off gun to John Lawrence to trace and question its owner.

The paper had been reduced almost to pulp, and the text inscribed on it had become very faint. However, when some chemicals were applied to it after drying, it became clear that the text was a letter written to Karim Khan by Navab Shamsuddin Ahmad Khan about the purchase of hunting dogs. The letter had no seal or signature, but witnesses were forthcoming to testify strongly that it seemed to have been written by the Navab himself. There was no date or day on the letter, but it did say that Karim Khan had been in Delhi for three months for the purpose of purchasing hunting hounds. Simple investigations about Karim Khan's stay in Delhi made it obvious that the letter was written in 1834 or 1835, and the words 'the business of buying hunting hounds' were read as code for killing William Fraser.

But the Company's officers were unable to prove that the real purpose of Karim Khan's being in Delhi from October 1834 was to murder Fraser. The spies and informers appointed by Karim Khan to watch and report on the movements of Fraser were fully loyal to Karim Khan and none came forward to testify; nor could the Company's informers identify those men. But this lacuna in the evidence—such as it was—was comfortably filled in the investigators' eyes by the evidence of the gun.

Simon Fraser's men were able to find, within a few hours of searching, an ironsmith who identified the gun and said that he had sawn off its barrel at the behest of Karim Khan. John Lawrence and Simon Fraser were now prepared to testify on oath that the crime of murder had been proven not only on Karim Khan, but also on Shamsuddin Ahmad Khan. They were so certain in this conclusion that they even suggested to Metcalfe that there was no need to keep Fathullah Beg and Mirza Mughal in custody any longer. But Metcalfe was a more sedate, careful and experienced official.

He did not agree to the suggestion on the ground that Shamsuddin Ahmad Khan would continue to be under pressure so long as Mirza Mughal was in jail; as for Fathullah Beg Khan, it did not matter if a small fry like him was in or not in jail. Thus both of them remained in the Alipore Jail, as did the steward of Shamsuddin Ahmad Khan's stable, his syces and William Fraser's coachman.

After thus sewing up the case—to their satisfaction at least—Lawrence and Fraser arrived at the Alipore Jail when night had fallen. This time, instead of visiting Karim Khan in his cell, Lawrence ordered that the prisoner be tied to a chair in the jail courtyard and be stripped off his clothes. Strong torches were lit in front of him so as to blind his sight. Simon Fraser waved the paper which had been recovered from the well, and asked Karim Khan, 'Do you recognize this paper?'

'Excellency, how can I see anything from such distance? Were the paper in my hand, I could see it better and make my submission.'

There was no question of passing the paper to Karim Khan; Fraser read it haltingly, as far as it was legible, then ordered a tall and burly policeman to bring the paper close to Karim Khan's eyes without giving him the chance to touch it.

'So? You heard, and you saw. Now tell me.'

'Your Honour, what can I tell you? I never saw this letter, nor can I say who wrote it.'

'You base fellow! Do you not know your own Navab's handwriting?'

'I do know, Presence, but this paper does not have my Master's seal or his signature.'

Simon Fraser gave up the pretence of formal interrogation and switched over to tu. 'Is not the handwriting his? Why don't you clearly say who wrote it?'

'Excellency, how could I know who wrote it? Someone must have done some forgery or fraud.'

Fraser spoke with obvious force and conviction, 'I say it was written by Shamsuddin Ahmad and purchase of hunting dogs means the murder of William Fraser. I say you carried out this task under the orders of the Navab.'

'Sir, you are the masters and rulers, you can say whatever you like. But I never got this letter, nor do I admit that Navab Shamsuddin Ahmad Khan Bahadur—'

Fraser did not let him finish the sentence. He almost pounced upon

Karim Khan, and kicking him in the stomach, he shouted, 'You describe the marauding villain and killer as Navab and Khan Bahadur! I have you and your ingrate of a navab at the toe of my boots!'

But Karim Khan calmly finished his sentence as if he had not been interrupted. '. . . could have penned such a letter.'

'The enmity between the Senior Sahib Bahadur and your bandit of a navab is no secret.'

'Highness,' Karim Khan again smiled the same smile which seemed evil and vitriolic to his interrogators, 'matters of the great can only be understood by the great. I am only a lowly servant, worse than an insect in your eyes.'

Fraser did his best to contain himself. 'Did you not grow up and thrive with Shamsuddin Ahmad?'

'Your Honour's dog also grew up with Your Honour's babas and babies (male and female children).' Karim Khan spoke in an apparently humble and submissive tone, but was rewarded with another half a dozen staves.

'You will die a death worse than that of a mad dog.' This time it was Simon Fraser who smiled a vitriolic smile. 'I will have you sewn up in a boar's hide and have the parcel thrown into the Jamna.'

'Let His Honour have these ropes removed and a sword placed in my hands.'

'I will kill you in such a way that you will drive the sword into your own breast,' Fraser growled. 'Why don't you tell the truth about this letter?'

'Exalted Presence, the paper is much affected by water. Was it found in water somewhere?'

'We are asking the questions. Do not try to be too clever. Answer the question.'

'Presence, if this letter was written by my own sahib, and if it did come to my hand, do you think I would have thrown it away in water?' Karim Khan looked at the Firangee sahibs as if he pitied their intelligence.

*

More than half the night passed; the interrogators could achieve nothing: repeating the questions, getting frustrating answers or denials, humiliating Karim Khan; the cycle went on, unavailing. Finally, Fraser looked at Lawrence, then at the gun that was kept hidden in a corner. Lawrence beckoned to a policeman who came forward and put a gun before Karim Khan who could see that its barrel had been sawn off. The gun was clearly visible in the light of the torches. For a second, he was shocked into immobility.

'Karim Khan, do you recognize this gun?'

'How can I, Your Honour? From this distance, I can only say that it is a gun.'

'This gun belongs to you!'

'Excellency, I really do not know,' he paused, as if considering a possibility, then he said innocently, 'Does it have my name on it?'

'You whoreson of a whore, you are still at your old wiles? I want to know if the gun is yours!'

'His Honour knows best.'

A policeman who stood behind Karim Khan hit him on the face with his shoe. 'Sisterfucker, no more of your loud-mouthed, shameless talk,' he snarled. Because he was hit with a shoe, a faint crease of pain and disgust showed on Karim Khan's face, but he remained silent.

'Confess, or you will lose your life,' said Lawrence in a conversational tone, as if he was talking about the weather.

Karim Khan drew a cold sigh, obviously fake, and said, 'Your Honour, I am nothing short of being dead anyway.' This resulted in another blow to his neck and yet another to his head. The blows were so powerful that Karim Khan's head drooped to one side, but he did not say anything else. After a pause, Lawrence asked softly, almost in a half whisper, 'Karim Khan, are you acquainted with Juma Deen, the ironsmith?'

Karim Khan's pinched and sunken face betrayed a few furrows of concentration and thought. 'Is it the Juma Deen whose shop is in Kucha Bulaqi Begam, behind the haveli of Lala Puran Mall?'

'You may suppose what you like,' said Lawrence, apparently uncaring.

'Your Honour, if it is really that Juma Deen, then I do know him.'

Lawrence and Fraser smiled victorious smiles. Lawrence said, 'This Juma Deen has stated on oath that the gun is yours, and he sawed off its barrel at your behest.'

Karim Khan again fell into thought. Eventually he spoke slowly, as if not certain of what he was saying. 'Juma Deen, if he said so, must be telling the truth. It must be my gun and I must have had its barrel sawn off.'

Excited, Lawrence was about to say something, but Karim Khan continued: 'But if it is that same gun, then it has not been with me for some time. I lost it a while ago.'

'You did not lose the gun. You are lying again, you son of a leprous camel. But why did you have its barrel sawn off?'

'To kill the pigs, Presence.' He pronounced the word 'pigs' as if he was saying something humorous.

A Muslim jamadar, who stood near Karim Khan, spat on him and cried, 'You wretch, you are a Mussulman and you hunt pigs!'

'I do not hunt them, Jamadar ji. I just make short work of them.'

Lawrence could not restrain himself this time. Using the common Hindi expletive for 'motherfucker', he shouted, 'Why do you talk in riddles? Why don't you speak plainly?'

'Your Excellency knows about guns,' he began, as if teaching a class of students. 'The advantage of having the barrel shortened is that although its range is reduced, the shot does not scatter, but falls in a cluster, more or less. Thus a sawn-off shotgun is a weapon of close combat. If such a gun is fired at someone from a few steps, why, then . . .' he smiled the same smile which the Firangees detested, '. . . he will break into two, thus!'

He brought two of his fingers together and snapped them, looking at Simon Fraser with meaningful eyes. It seemed to Fraser that a cold shiver was running down his spine. Seeing that Karim Khaṇ had fallen silent, Lawrence prompted him, 'So, then?'

'So then, as His Honour is aware, there are numerous herds of wild pigs on the way to Khvajah Sahib after Arab Sarai. Once they attacked the palanquin in which my sahib was travelling. Fortunately the lance-bearers accompanying him were alert, otherwise there would have been a disaster. So I had this gun prepared, for it could be easily borne in a palanquin and my Sahib could use it in a second, if needed.'

'You therefore confess that the gun was yours and was in your use.'

'Without doubt, Presence . . . but I lost it a long time ago. Once during a hunt I took it off my shoulder and put it near a stream on a rock. But I forgot to pick it back when I left that place.'

'You reported this to Shamsuddin Ahmad?'

'Navab Sahib Bahadur was right there in the hunt, Presence. He was very displeased with me.'

'When did this happen?'

Karim Khan counted on his fingers, considered his calculation and replied, 'It will be nine months at the next moon, sir.'

'How did the gun get to the well in front of the haveli in Daryaganj? Did you not lose it in a forest somewhere?'

'Your Honour, may I ask a question?'

'We are asking the questions, sisterfucker. Your job is to answer.'

'Excellency, Juma Deen would surely have revealed in his statement when I had the gun barrel—'

'Answer our questions. Don't bark like the dogs.'

'It must be obvious upon the luminant opinions of the Masters of Exalted Highness that a gun that uses shot is useless for shooting from a distance. The shot scatters far and wide. Only one or two of them can reach the target, if at all. And if its barrel is shortened, its range is reduced even more. Please be kind so as to—'

'You dirty swine! Barking and yelping again like a mad dog!' Lawrence said with extreme conviction in his voice. 'The bullets recovered from the scene of the crime were shot from this gun. This gun will hang you.'

There were two major holes in the case as prepared on the basis of available evidence. First, Juma Deen was just not prepared to state that the event of the barrel being sawn off was recent. Extended and intense questioning had failed to make him change his story that it had happened quite a while ago but he could not recall the date or the month. Second, it was clear that the shots must have been fired from a rifle or at least a stone-cap gun. Grapnel-like shot recovered from the scene of the crime were being studied to determine if the shot recovered from the victim's body was identical with those found at the crime scene. Since stone-cap guns had no rifling or spiralled grooves on the inside of their barrels, there was no way to find a satisfactory answer to the question of whether the shots had been fired from the same gun.

Thus, while their case was obviously weak, Lawrence and Fraser hated the thought that an answer of Karim Khan's could damage the case further. So they were obliged to tread most carefully in questioning him.

Another night passed. In the dim whiteness of the false dawn, Karim Khan's face looked nearly black, sunken and shrivelled. His mouth was slack and his face and body bore many stains of his own and his questioners' spittle. His eyes had disappeared behind the blue-black swelling around them. The night-long torture, the cold and the exposure to the night air, had made his body rigid and twisted. When the chill air of end-March began to blow from the north and the growing light of the day began to pale the brightness of the torches and sundry kind of lamps in the questioning area, the Firangee sahibs, who had begun to look wan and squeezed to the last drop of their energy, made one last-ditch effort. Fraser spoke up authoritatively, 'Karim Khan, do you hear?'

When Karim Khan failed to answer, one of the native sepoys strode forward and shaking him violently by the shoulder, shouted, 'Don't you hear, you motherfucker? Our Sahib Bahadur is commanding something.'

Karim Khan straightened his neck, looked around, and pulled a clearly fake yawn. 'Sir, Your Honour, I am present.'

'Karim Khan, the crime is fully proven against you. You will surely hang . . . But if you reveal the truth, and state clearly that you did the deed at Shamsuddin Ahmad's urging, you will be made the Company's evidence. Thus you will save your life . . . and the Navab will be punished for his crime.'

Karim Khan raised his head, looked at Fraser with glazed eyes and spoke in a hollow, weak-chested voice, 'Your Honour. Better die than lie.'

Lawrence and Fraser looked at each other in near desperation. Lawrence said, 'It is no use subjecting this man to more hardship. We must remember that he is to be tried in open court . . . This fornicator's son will doubtless hang, but we must find more evidence against Shamsuddin.'

'Not to worry,' said Lawrence grimly. 'It will be my task to bring that hybrid mongrel of a nabob to the gallows.'

*

When Navab Shamsuddin Ahmad Khan received reports of the arrest and the subsequent constancy of Karim Khan in spite of severe hardship, and of the possibility that he too could be arrested in the case, he sent two petitions—dated 11 April and 27 April 1835—to the Governor General at Calcutta. He protested the arrest of his blameless servant from the house of Mr Macpherson. He further alleged that all mischief was wrought by Fathullah Beg Khan who, though a kinsman, bore a severe grudge against him. It was he who, wishing to bring disgrace to Shamsuddin Ahmad, had informed against him and laid a false charge against his servant Karim Khan.

Shamsuddin Ahmad Khan further said:

> I have come to know that Fathullah Beg has announced a reward of 16,000 rupees for those who would provide evidence against me and Karim Khan. As regards the matter of Mr Fraser's sad death, be it brought to the notice of the Honourable Navab Governor General Bahadur, that I, Shamsuddin Ahmad Khan, have announced a reward of 2000 rupees to anyone who can help find the murderer of my dear and respected Uncle, William Fraser Sahib Bahadur. The blessed Senior Sahib Bahadur was my benefactor and among the close friends of my father, Fakhr-ud Daulah Dilawar-ul Mulk Navab Ahmad Bakhsh Khan Rustam Jang, upon whom be the Mercy of God, and may he receive Allah's Forgiveness. The question, therefore, does not arise of my taking any step at all to cause any kind of harm to him.

Shamsuddin Ahmad Khan concluded:

> Since my life, my State, my honour, all owe their existence to the English Company's Government, I send this petition so that my state may become evident to the Excellent Navab, the Governor General Bahadur who is the Home of Benevolence.

It is difficult to state if these petitions were honoured with submission to the Governor General. All that we know is that these and other papers submitted by Shamsuddin Ahmad Khan on this matter are not filed in the Law Department of the Company's administration; they are filed in the Political Department. This suggests that from its very inception, the Company looked at the case not from the angles of law and justice, but from a political point of view.

Preparations went apace to try Karim Khan for murder. On Thursday, 30 April 1835, the Police Chief of Delhi filed charges against Karim Khan and Shamsuddin Ahmad Khan in the Court of Simon Fraser, City Magistrate of Delhi. There was not a shred of evidence, far less proof, against Shamsuddin Ahmad Khan. But John Lawrence argued before Metcalfe that a relationship of master and servant existed between Shamsuddin Ahmad Khan and Karim Khan, so according to the English law, the master could be held responsible for the acts of his servant. His other argument was that once the news of charges being framed against the Navab became known, new evidence, or witnesses, could come forth against him. It was also likely that many, finding the Navab in dire straits against the Company, might desert his cause and even give evidence against him.

This second argument was proved partly right. When the news of charges filed against Karim Khan became public, a number of persons were heard saying that Karim Khan was not the sole culprit: his companion and chief courier to the Navab was also a partner in the crime.

This was the first time that Aniya Mewati's name had surfaced in the case. The Company's spies promptly conveyed the news to Fraser. Other than this, none of the elites of Delhi, not even Aminuddin Ahmad Khan, was prepared to say a word against Shamsuddin Ahmad Khan. All that the English had was Mirza Ghalib, but his hostility to Shamsuddin Ahmad was no secret. The English author Thomas Bacon has written that many of the city's elites were well-wishers and friends of Shamsuddin Ahmad Khan.

John Lawrence began investigating Aniya Mewati, and was almost at once rewarded with the information that over his last two visits to Delhi, Aniya had accompanied Karim Khan; and that no one had seen Aniya after the night of the murder. Karim Khan was again subjected to rigorous questioning to explain why he and Aniya together visited Delhi on two successive occasions. As usual, Karim Khan gave answers which did not at all satisfy. Lawrence could do nothing more than tear his hair out in frustration.

The impasse would have continued, but Karim Khan's ill fortune was, as usual, leading his enemies and showing them the way to score against him. Investigation into Aniya's movements grew more and more fruitful: a spy sent to Firozepur to look into Aniya's past and present, returned soon to report that Aniya had come to Firozepur on the day after the murder, but had soon disappeared, and was now reported to be in Bareilly.

On the prosecution side, examination of the evidence and the charge sheets in light of the English law of criminal procedure established the fact that the case against the accused Shamsuddin Ahmad Khan and Karim Khan was fit for committal to a judge of the Circuit Court. In the former days, the English Court of Sessions was called Circuit Court. Later, when the district administration passed fully into the hands of the Company Bahadur, and yet later when it was finally taken over by Her Majesty the Queen of England and Empress of India, the Circuit Court was named Sessions Court, and still later, the District and Sessions Court. Simon Fraser was just a magistrate, and was thus not competent to hear a case committed to the Sessions Court. Within a few days Thomas Metcalfe appointed John Alexander Colvin, a senior and experienced Englishman, to function as Special Judge and Commissioner and try the two cases. It was the first of May 1835.

It is said that when news of the prosecution of the Navab and Karim Khan, and its likely outcome became known—the news was most assiduously disseminated far and wide by the Company Bahadur's well-wishers—Aniya sent his brother Dhanney Khan and another friend to John Lawrence with the offer to reveal the whole secret if the Company Bahadur undertook to have him fully pardoned. Another version of the events is that Lawrence had the whereabouts of Aniya traced in Bareilly through his own efforts. He then threatened him with hanging and also held out to him the inducement of pardon if he toed the Firangee line. Aniya duly appeared before Lawrence and was promptly put in jail.

Aniya was questioned over many days, but he could not by any means show that he had some direct or even primary evidence to inculpate either of the accused. He could not claim to have been present at either of the two crucial conversations between the Navab and Karim Khan. And he himself, on being permitted to enter upon the presence of the Navab, and then reporting the news of the murder, did not have anything by way of the Navab's words or actions to directly implicate the Navab in the case. About the letter recovered from the well, he did say that the order to act emanated from the Navab, but he admitted that he was illiterate and could only recognize the Navab's seal. But there was no seal on the letter, so his evidence was valueless. His evidence about the gun was even more devoid of worth, for he could not state which gun, if any, was in Karim Khan's possession on the night of the murder.

Aniya's evidence against Karim Khan was weightier in regard to the horse's shoes. He declared that it was in his presence that Karim Khan drove the shoes backwards into the horse's hoofs. Later, both went out together on the job of killing William Fraser. Aniya did not see the actual shooting, but it had been decided between them earlier that it would be Aniya who would run away to Firozepur with all possible dispatch with the news of the killing. Aniya stated that he heard the shots being fired, then saw a rider on a dark horse speeding away from there, and concluded that William Fraser was dead. He stated on oath that the rider on the musk-black was Karim Khan, though he did not see him from close, and the rider was clothed in black from head to foot anyway, and the night was dark, not to mention the gloaming of the forest.

Aniya's revelations made the case against Karim Khan somewhat stronger, but there was nothing substantive to nail his master. An informal council, consisting of Metcalfe as Chair and the other two key English officers as members, met to review the case and came to the conclusion that the case against both the accused should be considered complete. Now it was the job of the Prosecutor and the investigative officers to convince the Court of the truth of their case. It was therefore expedient to arrest the Navab at once and subject him to questioning in full detail. It was eminently possible that the Navab, stupid as he was, would reveal something unwittingly which would strengthen the case against him. The Council was unanimously of the view that further delay in arresting the Navab and putting him on trial was likely to hurt the Company's interests and create misunderstandings, leading to loss of face—the natives would believe that the Firangee was powerless against the murderer of so senior and important an officer of the Company as the Navab Resident.

It was noted that Shamsuddin Ahmad was in Firozepur, and was effectively beyond the authority of the policemen of the Company. There was also the risk of civil disturbances and armed protests against the Company's functionaries: they might be surrounded by a rebellious mob and put under restraint or even murdered. A letter was therefore dispatched to the Navab on 2 May 1835, from the Agent to the Governor General Bahadur and Commissioner of Delhi. Written, as usual, in the formal court Persian of those times, it is literally translated here below in the English of the early nineteenth century. The letter, as usual, was unpunctuated and not divided into paragraphs. In the translation, the paragraphs have been marked with the sign used earlier, and very light punctuation has been allowed.

> Of High Station and Special Friend of the English Government Bahadur, and Close to the Heart of Navab the Excellent Sir Charles Metcalfe Governor General Bahadur, Dilawar-ul Mulk Navab Shamsuddin Ahmad Khan Bahadur, Chieftain of Firozepur Jhirka may, after Prayers for his well-being, be pleased to observe∠ Whereas a servant of the Exalted Highness whose name is Karim Khan is under arrest and being prosecuted for the Crime of the Murder of the Senior Sahib

Bahadur, upon whom is the Mercy of God, and who has received Allah's Forgiveness and who has been Purified by God, and another servant of that same Person of Great Value is also under suspicion in that same Case and the statements of the Two above named do make it appear that some Matters of Importance relating to that Calamitous Event are possibly within the Knowledge of the Person of Exalted Highness mentioned aboveے Hence, and therefore, we Respectfully request you that, in order to aid the Investigators and the Prosecutors in this Matter, should return to Delhi as soon as this Petition reaches your Hand. That is allے With Salutation and Prayer for Your Security, the Petitioner Ikhtisas Yar Khan [(His Majesty's) Friend of Special Value] Thomas Theophilus Metcalfe Firoze Jang [Victorious in Battle], Acting Agent to the Governor General Bahadur and Plenipotentiary in Matters concerning the Government of the Pivot of Prosperity and Power, the Company Bahadur, and Acting Commissioner Sahib Bahadur of the Capital Region of Shahjahanabad and Delhiے Inscribed in the City of Delhi on Thursday the 2nd of May 1835 in the Year of Our Lord, corresponding to the 5th of Muharram, 1251 the Year of the HegiraXII.

Two trusted couriers of the Company, who also doubled as spies, presented the letter to Navab Shamsuddin Ahmad Khan on 3 May 1835.

47

Night descends on Firozepur Jhirka as the Navab meets the ladies of the haram sara and bids them farewell

VERY SOON, THE news spread throughout the city: our Navab has been summoned to Delhi in the matter of Fraser's murder. The same evening, a further rumour became hot: Company Bahadur has issued a threat to the Navab in clear words that should he not present himself at the Residency in Delhi as summoned, Firozepur will soon be facing military invasion by the Company. Many of the braver spirits and the unemployed youth of the city began immediately to mount defensive measures. Groups of villagers from around the city began to collect in the marketplace, openly threatening that if the Company's troops appear in our city, they will be cut to pieces like vegetables. They declared: We will shed the last drop of our blood before the Company's forces can carry off our Navab.

By the morning, not only villagers, but also functionaries of the State and landowners from surrounding areas appeared before Shamsuddin Ahmad in groups of twos and threes, with assurance of their resistance and armed struggle against the Company, if need be. Malkhan Singh, the Chief Divan of Shamsuddin Ahmad Khan's total estates, repeatedly submitted advice against the Navab's going to Delhi; there seemed to be some deceit or duplicity going on there. He said, 'Presence, do not go to Delhi, please. Be here. We assure you that we will force the Company's army to withdraw. The enemy, however powerful, can never beat the force of the people.'

An astrologer sought permission to appear and was allowed to enter. He advised the Navab to stay in Firozepur for at least two months; this much time is needed for the Moon to free itself from Scorpio, the Eighth Sign, he said. All manner of things will be well once the Moon leaves Scorpio.

Shamsuddin Ahmad Khan did not pay the slightest heed to any of these urgings. His first reaction on receipt of the Company's letter was to ignore the summons and stay put in Firozepur. On second thoughts, he changed his mind. Orders were soon issued for immediate arrangements to be put in place for a formal trip to Delhi. To his people and the visiting landlords, he said that there is nothing to worry about, far less be afraid of. I shall return whenever I wish to; the English cannot stop me, far less do me any kind of harm. The same astrologer who advised against the trip, was now commanded to determine the best day to start. He made most careful calculations and stated that on Sunday, the day after tomorrow, after the passing of the most inauspicious hour, called the rahu kalam, the movement of the stars would be somewhat less adverse, so if at all a journey to Delhi was to be undertaken, it should begin on Sunday, between the hours of eleven and twelve.

On the following day, an ancient Sikh arrived at the gate of the Fort, seeking an audience with the Navab. Giving his name as Ujagar Singh, formerly chief courier to Navab Ahmad Bakhsh Khan, he said that he retired on pension to his native village sometime before the Navab journeyed to Paradise. He came to the Fort in hot haste when he heard of the developments.

'May the fortune of His Honour be always in the ascendant,' he said. 'My dromedary will not stop for rest before a run of at least a couple of hundred miles. I beg you, Exalted Highness, to put on a Sikh dress for a very short while and leave tonight with me for the Sikh Kingdom. I swear by the Holiest of our Holies, Your Honour will be received with open arms by the people of my community at the border and you will be escorted with full honour into the Fort at Lahore.'

Navab Shamsuddin Ahmad appreciated the suggestion, but said, 'Sardar Ujagar Singh, I don't want to be seen as a fugitive by the Maharajah, the Lion of Punjab, and look small in the eyes of the Maharajah, his own peers, and most of all, my own people.' Most earnestly, Ujagar Singh assured the Navab that the Maharajah, the Lion of Punjab, would treat him as a dear brother: the enemy of the Firangee is his dear friend too. Shamsuddin Ahmad remained unmoved; he thanked Ujagar Singh, gave him a reward of ten gold mohurs, and dismissed him with the respect due to his years and his loyalty.

The next day was Saturday; at about midday, as the Navab was dictating some letters after giving some instructions to his Chief Clerk in the

Chancery, a mace-bearer appeared and submitted that Subh Daulat was at the gate of the Chancery, petitioning to be given audience.

'I know the purpose of her visit,' said the Navab. 'Information may be sent that I will come to the haram sara in a short while and will eat lunch there.'

*

A large tablecloth was spread in the portion of the haram sara occupied by Afzal-un Nisa Begam. Some foods were placed on it already. Maids were going around, looking busy, but there were no signs yet of a full lunch being served or eaten shortly. The Begam's main chamber, the aiwan, was large and spacious, and had wall-to-wall carpets: Kashmiri, Turkish and Indian, these latter having been woven mostly at Bhadohi, six hundred and more miles to the east in an area where some families of carpet weavers and designers had been settled by Emperor Akbar in the sixteenth century.

The chamber was in semi-darkness to reduce the effect of the heat. Only four floor lamps with white shades burnt at the four corners. Some pale green light filtered through screens made of the roots of the uniquely cool-smelling grass called 'khas' (pronounced and spelt 'cuss' or 'cuss-cuss' by the English in those days). Thick screens of cuss cuss, supported by light bamboo staves, were fixed to doors and windows facing any open space. Kept constantly wet, they cooled the area and also produced a light, summery scent. Sometimes fans were plied inside the enclosed space. This inventive strategy to beat the summer is also ascribed to Emperor Akbar.

The total effect of the scented coolth combined with the semi-darkness, was that of comfort and peace. But the faces of the three women in the chamber showed nothing but tension, anxiety and confusion. Close to the far wall, on a carpet-covered wooden platform, sat Afzal-un Nisa Begam; her two daughters Ahmad-un Nisa and Shams-un Nisa sat on small chairs close by. All three were silent; the little girls' posture was taut and their unconscious gestures and body movements showed that they were uncomfortable in the tension-charged atmosphere. Nearby was a fair-sized padded armchair, occupied by Husaini Begam, the Junior Begam. A little away from the chair sat Champa, the Navab's concubine; Rahmat-un Nisa, her daughter, who was the smallest of the three children there, sat in her lap but frequently tried to go to the other two girls, trying without success to make them interested in playing with her.

The cuss-cuss screens were being kept moist by constant spraying of water. A servant from outside pulled two large ceiling fans, made of silk and brocade, through a pulley. The scent of the cuss-cuss mingled pleasantly with the fragrance of the two hookahs in front of the begams who, for the sake of doing something, were trying to draw a puff or two. Another hookah awaited the Navab's arrival.

No maid except Subh Daulat was inside the chamber. As the Navab entered, all rose and made salaams. Subh Daulat presented seven salaams; the begams, three, Champa, five; and the children made two salaams as best they could. The Navab answered all by making one salaam and then putting his right hand on the left side of the breast, near the heart. The standard way of offering salaam was to bend slightly, place the right hand, palm up, on the ground, then rise and place the hand on the head. Speaking during a salaam was forbidden. As opposed to the salaam, the kurnish was presented only to the King. The way to do the kurnish was to raise the right hand to the forehead, then bend the head. This was always in addition to the salaams.

The Navab, his head decorously bent, advanced into the chamber and sat cross-legged on the platform, near Afzal-un Nisa Begam, so that he could see and be seen by Champa and the little girl who at once jumped up joyfully and went to sit in the Navab's lap. Shams-un Nisa, older to Ahmad-un Nisa, rose and made salaams again, and came and sat at the Navab's feet, clutching one of his legs. The Navab kissed both of them, and affectionately combing their heads with his fingers, smiled and said, 'Well, ladies, why has the Supreme Court convened? Have I offended all the judges in some way? And why is Little Lady Ahmad-un Nisa sitting aloof? Does she not wish to be near her Bilaval?'

Contrary to practice, Afzal-un Nisa did not address the Navab as 'Navab sahib' or 'Mirza sahib'; she addressed him as 'Dilawar-ul Mulk'. Imitating her mother, little Ahmad-un Nisa wanted to do the same, but her prattling tongue could only produce Bilaval and that became her mode of calling or addressing her father. She was just five years of age, Shams-un Nisa was eighteen months older, while Rahmat-un Nisa was just about two and a half years old. Afzal-un Nisa delivered a light pat on Ahmad-un Nisa's head and spoke in gentle chastisement, using the familiar 'tu' in the manner of the people in Delhi. 'So why don't you now go to your Bilaval? You! Right this minute you were whining and murmuring asking what was holding him up.'

Bashfully, doing more salaams to the Navab, Ahmad-un Nisa rose and came to sit near the Navab's knee. Tenderly putting his hands under her chin, he raised her face to kiss her and he felt as if he had been stabbed in the chest; her huge, green jade eyes were brimming. He bent, kissed her eyes, picked her up and hugging her close, he cried out in Persian: 'There! There! Bhai wallah, Jani Begam. What mystery is this? The eyes of the light of my eyes are moist! God forbid, is she not well? Did you summon the Hakim sahib?'

'Dilawar-ul Mulk, your darling child is not at all unwell,' Afzal-un Nisa answered in Persian. She normally spoke to the Navab in Persian; he generally spoke to her in Hindi, but sometimes tension or pressure of some emotion induced him to commence speaking in Persian. 'Your darling is sad that you are leaving her when the times are so bad; you go to Delhi, depriving her of your company.'

Shamsuddin Ahmad made no reply for a moment or two. He seemed lost in thought. He had been aware of the gravity of the situation in the haram sara, but did not think it would be so bad. Everybody was quiet. Shamsuddin Ahmad put the girl on his shoulder, and patted and caressed her neck and back. The women's eyes were on him. The other girls, as if aware of some dramatic situation inside the aiwan, had become still.

'Jani Begam, please listen, and listen carefully,' said the Navab. 'And Amir Bahu, you too hear what I have to say . . . Champa, it's good that you're here. You also hear me out. What I say is a matter of some benefit to you all.'

Transferring Ahmad-un Nisa to his lap, he straightened his shoulders, and spoke with some authority, 'I am a soldier. A soldier's foot, if it advances not, is fit to be chopped off . . . I go by my will; I will return at my will. But if I do not return, God is the Master and Nurturer of all.'

Her head submissively bent, Champa heard the Navab's words. She wanted to ask, a soldier is the guard and protector of his honour, but who will guard the soldier's honour left behind in his house? But she knew that it was not her station to argue or even ask. There was no need even to understand.

'Sir, Your Honour,' she spoke in a tiny voice without raising her head.

Shamsuddin Ahmad expected a little more from his begams. He looked at them and said with a half-smile, 'Bhai wallah, you have greater understanding and higher wisdom. Please use your power of speech and command.'

Amir Bahu's face revealed a carnival of colours: anger, anxiety, shock. It was clear that she did not like the Navab's method: he had made the decision on his own and now desired its ratification from our tongues. Trying to control herself, she made no reply for a beat or two. When she spoke, her voice was either choked with anger or hoarse due to anxiety. 'The soldier's world does not extend beyond the point of his sword. We, who live behind the purdah, have no world at all. We have only paths to be taken, willingly or no. If there is none to guard the purdah, the path becomes the hangman's noose. You leave us here to suffocate and die by inches.'

Amir Bahu was svelte and petite, her colour golden brown like the champak flower. Her beauty was so wild and seemed so untouched by man that the effect of her presence was gazelle-like, rather than merely feminine: just look and admire. Her breasts and hips were heavy but so well made that even in the loose, light summer dress, full youthfulness seemed to flow out of her body. She was a little waspish of temper, perhaps because she was proud of her beauty, but her words at that time seemed appropriate: in the sense that the other begam must also have felt like her, but it required not a little boldness to say what she did.

A small shadow, a little cloud of displeasure passed upon Shamsuddin Ahmad's face. He answered coldly, 'All of us are pieces on the chessboard of Heaven. Someone becomes a fil (bishop), another becomes an asp (knight), yet another a mere piyadah (pawn). None knows what the player intends. All have to assent to the conclusion, when the time comes.'

A silence descended upon the room. Ahmad-un Nisa looked towards her father, as if she wished to say something. The Navab understood, and said, 'Ahmadi Begam, you wished to say something?' Unlike Afzal-un Nisa Begam, the Navab always spoke to his children with the respectful aap, the second-person plural.

Feeling her father's eyes upon her, Ahmad-un Nisa became even more bashful. Hiding her face behind her small hands, she said haltingly, 'N. . . No, nothing at all. But I just wanted to say . . .' She stopped.

'Come on, speak up. You said "but" and stopped. So what was it after the "but"?'

'Sir, that . . . that is really nothing . . . But did you not tell us that chess is not something good?'

'Yes, that's quite true. One who's addicted to chess becomes quite useless for other things.'

'So, Bilaval, why are you and all of us pieces in some game of chess?'

A wan smile played upon Shamsuddin Ahmad's face. He tried to laugh the child's question off, but could not. Instead, he went elsewhere, 'The snake charmer's child plays with snakes. We are children of soldiers, we play with death. You are our children: the boat of the children of Kings and Chieftains faces the risk of a typhoon all the time.'

This was not quite within the apprehension of the little girl. She was about to ask another question when Afzal-un Nisa Begam interjected impulsively. She spoke in Persian as usual. It is impossible to convey in English the sharp crispness of her utterance: 'A boat whose boatman was, like you, the child of a soldier would undoubtedly suffer the slaps of a turbulent, stormy sea.'

Signs of displeasure and annoyance again appeared on Shamsuddin Ahmad's face. He considered what he should say in reply; then answered in Hindi, using the standard mode of second-person plural. His voice was subdued, all hint of annoyance leached out of it. 'Perhaps you did not fully appreciate the implications. Even if I go somewhere else, you'll still be at the mercy of the Firangee. There is a diabolical shadow over this entire Paradise-rivalling land of India. The shadow will continue to envelop me wherever I go. If I remain here, the marauding Firangee will invade us sooner rather than later. He has already wrested Loharu; Firozepur will resist him, but for how long? It will have to capitulate ultimately. I won't be with you on that day, and you won't get even that treatment which was meted out to the family of the martyred Tipu Sultan.'

Afzal-un Nisa could think of nothing to say. But Amir Bahu spoke out again, in an accusatory reply, 'Did you ever try to imagine what will happen to you if you go to Delhi?'

'I don't expect any harm from anyone at all, but I am also aware that things can happen otherwise. I go, but I have made adequate arrangements for all of you, be assured.'

'Of what use will those arrangements be if—God forbid—you are not . . .'

Before Shamsuddin Ahmad could say something in reply, Champa looked up towards Afzal-un Nisa who turned to her. Champa quietly moved a little nearer and spoke to her in a whisper, with delicate gestures of her hand. Afzal-un Nisa nodded, and addressed Shamsuddin Ahmad in a pleading voice, 'Your Honour, the proposal about the Maharajah . . .'

'Please put that notion out of your mind, Jani Begam.' Now it was the turn of Shamsuddin Ahmad to plead. 'To place myself under someone's obligation and leave you here, what else can it be if not entirely unacceptable? And I am not a Rajput or a Pathan to tie my shroud around my head, put my family to the sword and come out fighting.'

He paused, trying to collect his emotion, then said, 'Also, you must consider: for how much longer in this world is the Maharajah's rule? The Firangee's tooth and claw will surely be dyed in Sikh blood one day.'

Tears welled up and began to flow down Afzal-un Nisa's face. Little Shams-un Nisa went quickly over to her mother and tried to dry her tears with her muslin orhni, hugging her and making sounds of kissing, as if Afzal-un Nisa was the baby and she the mother.

A leaden silence ensued. Shamsuddin Ahmad cleared his throat and spoke, still in the conciliatory mode, 'There is no substituting the act of living, Amir Bahu. Each of us lives our own life and dies our own death. This is Allah's command, do you recall? No bearer of burdens will bear the burden of the other. You should have good hopes and think good thoughts. Be of strong mind and stout heart. We'll have lost everything if arrangements for tomorrow are not made today.'

He clapped his hands to summon a mace-bearer and instructed for the money bags to be obtained from the Treasurer.

In a minute, a large metal tray loaded with bags made of strong, coarse cotton was brought in. Shamsuddin Ahmad said, 'Amir Bahu, your dowry was determined at two hundred and fifty gold mohurs. One third was payable at once, which I duly paid, did I not?'

All of Amir Bahu's tartness of tongue and sharpness of temper had evaporated. Her throat clogged with tears of grief welling up from the heart, and she said, 'Sir, quite right.'

'So now, I repay what was already paid, and submit to you the entire two hundred and fifty gold mohurs. Please accept.'

Amir Bahu was now openly weeping copious tears which she did not even have the strength to dry.

'Your Honour, I absolve you, I fully absolve you.'

'Madam, your absolution avails nothing. In fact, you don't have the power to pardon this debt. Please, come and receive your due.'

Shamsuddin Ahmad rose to his full height. Taking the tray in his two hands, he extended his arms, as if making a formal offering. Amir Bahu covered her head with her upper wrap, came up to her husband with head bowed, made a salaam, and accepted the tray. Shamsuddin Ahmad placed his hand upon her head as if in benediction and made her sit next to him. She sat with her body gathered up as small as she could; she was still sobbing quietly.

'Please don't lose heart,' he said. 'Nothing is lost yet. Whatever I do is just normal caution, or pre-emption in such circumstances as prescribed by Islam. I have transferred some houses to you; their ownership papers will be in your hands tomorrow.'

Amir Bahu was now wailing, unashamed. Shamsuddin Ahmad did not consider it proper to interfere at that moment. So he turned towards Afzal-un Nisa Begam and said, 'Jani Begam, your dowry was agreed to be a quarter of a million rupees in the Shah Alami coin. I have not paid it so far. But he who lives now in Paradise had loaned to the Firangee Company an equal amount in perpetuity at an interest of one and a half per cent per annum. It was contracted at the time of our marriage that the loan documents, duly ratified and sealed, will be presented to you as your dowry. This action has not been taken so far, but the papers were not in my hands either. They were in safe deposit in the State's treasury, bearing your name as lender and beneficiary of interest.'

Afzal-un Nisa Begam made to say something, but Shamsuddin Ahmad raised his hand to stop her.

'Pardon me, I am not yet done. Please hear me out. I was submitting that the loan document which is in safe custody in the treasury, was reassigned to you and your assignees in perpetuity with witness borne by the Court Registrar and two independent witnesses.'

He clapped for a servant and when the mace-bearer appeared, he desired that the Treasurer may be requested to present himself with the loan papers before the Grand Begam sahib. Within a minute, Lala Prag Narain, the Head Treasurer, appeared with a bundle of papers wrapped in cloth, like a portfolio. Shamsuddin Ahmad took a sealed bag from the bundle, broke the seal, took out the papers and, rising, put them at the feet of Afzal-un Nisa Begam.

'Afzal-un Nisa Begam, please do me the honour of accepting what has been due to you.' Suddenly he hesitated, and spoke in a strangled voice, 'A hundred regrets; I could not be capable of more.'

Afzal-un Nisa Begam dried her tears; taking her husband's hand in hers, she spoke beseechingly, 'Please, for God's sake, Navab sahib, do not put your maid to more shame.'

It was impossible, in ordinary circumstances, for Afzal-un Nisa Begam to hold her husband by the hand, or even touch him, in the presence of others. But, today none had power over their words, emotions and actions. She instinctively knew that it was better to hold her husband's hand for a moment than start weeping bitterly like a common woman. Even so, the Navab was initially struck dumb at such a show of intimacy, but soon realized the symbolism of it. He placed his hand most gently and lovingly on Afzal-un Nisa Begam, as if she were a seeker of blessing and he a venerable saint, and spoke tenderly, 'Allah protects and supports all. There is no shelter greater than Allah's shelter.'

His implied meaning was that even if my protection is taken away from you, you have God's protection always. Speaking in more measured tones, he resumed his conversation about settlement.

'For the two daughters as well, I have put arrangements in place. The Treasurer will explain all to you tomorrow. Should this haveli become the property of my brothers, I think you should still be able to live here in comfort.' Making a feeble attempt at humour, he added, looking at Afzal-un Nisa Begam and Amir Bahu: 'If nothing else, you can live here as rent-paying tenants.'

Both the begams stood, heads bent, and tongues bereft of the power of speech. Champa wanted to break out in gushing tears and loud weeping, but even this was denied her in the begams' presence. She would occasionally raise her head and look at the Navab with tear-filled eyes. Suddenly, she heard the Navab speak to her. She felt as if someone had thrust a needle in her side.

'And Champa Bi!'

'Sir! Your Honour.'

'I have sent word to the house in Chandni Chowk. They will take care of you. You may stay there as long as you wish. Should you so desire, you may set up your own kitchen there. I have provided for that too . . . Hey, Rahmat-un Nisa! Will you not gain some reward from your Nab Shab today?' While he addressed Champa with the familiar second-person singular 'tum', but in a kind, friendly tone of voice, he used the more familiar, but affectionate tu with Rahmat-un Nisa as one sometimes did with small children.

He picked up Rahmat-un Nisa again, put her on his lap and said, 'All right, even if you say nothing, I'll reward you, but the reward this time will go to your mother in your name.'

He beckoned briefly to Champa who came forth with stumbling steps, trying to render salaams while trying not to weep. Her face was flushed with the effort of keeping a hold on herself. She approached slowly, made two salaams again, bent forward to take the girl away from the Navab's lap, and said, 'Let this petty little girl be sacrificed at His Honour's feet. Please let me have her. You must be tired, having held her for so long.' She was trying again to smile, as if it was a normal domestic situation, but losing all her restraint, she hid her face in her dupatta and began to sob loudly. Shamsuddin Ahmad did not let go of the child, but spoke to Champa with feigned sternness, 'Enough! That's enough. No more weeping and crying. For sure, I am not going to die!'

He then ordered for Lala Prag Narain to enter again and present Champa Bi's money bag to her. The Lala parted the curtain at the main door and beckoned to the mace-bearer who stood there waiting. The mace-bearer came in with money bags made of stout red cloth in a large canvas bag and stood aside after doing the salaams. The Lala counted out the bags in two heaps, five at a time, and gestured to Champa to accept them. She spread out her upper wrap, intending to somehow take the load, but the Navab said, 'No, not like this. Let a maid be summoned. She will take the bags to Champa Bi's quarters.'

Champa wanted to say something, but Shamsuddin Ahmad gestured for silence, then addressed them all, 'I entrust you to Allah's protection. Please keep praying for me. Remember, I am not a snake or a scorpion to spend my life hiding in holes or obscure corners and sting suddenly at the opportune moment. We are the followers of the Prophet who remained strong and constant even under threat to his life . . . If I were to go in hiding for fear of the godless Firangee, what face will I show to my Master? And you will see, none shall be able to harm me. After all, I am the Ruler of Firozepur Jhirka.'

He then hugged the children one by one, kissed them, then made salaams to each of the women severally. Afazl-un Nisa and Amir Bahu quickly tied amulets of protection on his right arm. Afzal-un Nisa then made a circle around the Navab's head with a cup of water, drank a little from it, and sobbingly spoke in Hindi, 'Let me see your face just as you show me your back today. I give you in the Protection of the Eighth Imam,

Guarantor of us all.' She paused, tried to fetch a smile to her face, and then resumed, in Persian, 'Thousands of lives like mine may be sacrificed at your feet; I pray to God for your fortune to be more and more in the ascendant with each step that you take. Amen, oh Lord of All the Worlds, for the sake of the Glory of the Prince of all Prophets.'

Everyone present echoed 'Amen!' aloud. Each then came forward, said whatever prayers and benedictions they could and blew over the Navab's face and head. Just as Shamsuddin Khan turned his back to go, Afzal-un Nisa crashed on the wooden platform in a faint. Amir Bahu began to pray aloud to God, her words interspersed by chest-racking sobs. Then the children's voices rose higher than those of the rest in weeping and wailing. Finally, even Champa gathered her courage to wail and pray aloud to God.

*

It was the sixth day of Muharram, the Muslim month of mourning for the martyrdom of the Imam, Husain, son of Ali, at Karbala on the 10th of that month in the year 61 of the Hegira, which corresponds to 10 October 680 of the English year. The sixth was a special day of mourning, for Qasim, a youthful son of Husain, was reported to have been married and then martyred on the following day. Sounds of weeping, of declamations of speakers and religious leaders from the pulpits, and of recitations of mourning songs arose from the streets and lanes and homes of the city and began to dissolve in the evening sky like the cries of travellers lost in the dense, penumbrous forest of the night:

Woe! Woe! The thirsty throat which the Prophet was wont to kiss,
Cruel Shimr ran his dagger through it
Oh Imam! Oh Imam!
Woe, my friend, woe!

Before your eyes, they were killed
By the heartless army of the Kufans
Your two sons, Ali Akbar and Ali Asghar!
Oh Imam! Oh Imam!
Woe, my friend, woe!

The fire of grief burnt down the firmament,
The stars and starlets glow like embers,
Oh Imam! Oh Imam!
Woe, my friend, woe!

When the day dawned, the mourning for the pre-marriage and marriage ceremonies of Qasim, and the lamentations and dirges for his widow pounded the hot rising sun in the face. The susurration of the warm breeze blowing from the west turned into sobs. Dirge-reciting ladies of the purdah, whose houses were connected by windows pierced in the walls that divided their homes, gathered in ones and twos at the house of an aged lady, reputed to be a descendant of the martyred Imam. As the sun went up, the courtyard in the lady's house and the sky above echoed with subdued and choked voices formally speaking or reciting the nauha, or the dirge:

Come back, oh come back, from the killing field!
My master, my man, support me in my youthful widowhood;
I have no hope of my parents' home; no modesty I feel in front of my in-laws,
I cry:
Tell me—where should I go to live, where
Is my resting place?

As evening descended on the city, the city's Imam Barah was the scene for more lamentation and ritual recitation of dirges:

At that time the Bride, Oh! Oh! The Bride
Weeps and says to the women: Woe is me!
He goes alone to face the cruel people,
Alack, we are not to meet again in this world.
Qasim goes away, making the day
Dark, like the evening.
Woe, my friend, woe!

The whole world weeps for you, in pain and sorrow,
The birds, the animals, the genies, all.
Said the poet: None is devoid of lamentation,
Alack! Oh, woe! Woe! Qasim, forever Qasim!
Woe, my friend, woe!

Once the assembly was over, all the boys, young people and some old men too formed a procession, and ritually reciting the nauhas, they went, through circuitous routes, to the Karbala just outside the city. They returned to the city by another route and reassembled before the Jami Masjid. They dispersed slowly after weeping and reciting the dirges for a long time.

Qasim's marriage
The Sovereign solemnized
On a day when no power
Was left in his hands.

As night fell, the bazaars of Firozepur Jhirka were deserted. It was as if the whole city had gone in exile to some wilderness.

48

An arrest and a trial: the Navab is caught in a web of betrayal and conspiracy

SUNDAY, 6 MAY 1835, corresponding to the 7th of Muharram 1251 from the Hegira of the Prophet: Navab Shamsuddin Ahmad Khan set out on his journey to Delhi at 11 a.m. Loud and subdued sounds of mourning continued to be heard from the city and the villages on the road as he passed. His entourage consisted of ten armed riders, six lance-bearers and twelve palanquin-bearers to carry the palanquin in two-hour shifts. Whenever he passed a town or a substantial village, landlords and people of good family as well as ordinary peasants, thronged the road at suitable points and welcomed him, treating him to betel cone, cool drinks and flower garlands. He was then sent off with the prayers and good wishes of the populace. Indeed, it was more like a progress in state, rather than the journey of an alleged suspect to his trial judgment.

He travelled fast, but not post-haste, not permitting any idle resting or entertainment on the way. On the afternoon of 8 May 1835, he was in the village Palam on the outskirts of the city of Delhi. He camped in the old and desolate but serviceable Fort at Palam where arrangements were in place for his welcome and rest. He promptly dispatched two riders to Thomas Metcalfe in Delhi, reporting his arrival. The riders were admitted to Metcalfe's presence at about sundown. They were ordered to await further orders at the haveli in Daryaganj.

The Company was, of course, receiving regular news of the Navab's progress. Fraser and Lawrence gnashed their teeth at the cordial welcome and send-off accorded to the Navab by the populace everywhere. They knew that this was one sphere where they were powerless. But they had no need to do anything anyway, for their target was entering their range of his own accord. In order to allay misgivings, if any, on the part of Shamsuddin

Ahmad Khan, Metcalfe dismissed all charges against Mirza Mughal Beg and ordered that he be released from jail. The moment he learnt of Shamsuddin Ahmad Khan's arrival in Palam, Metcalfe had immediately summoned Fraser and Lawrence for consultations about further tactics. The first point that Lawrence made was that Captain James Skinner, known among the natives as Sikandar sahib, should be brought on the informal committee of consultations. Skinner was not of 'pure blood', but his main quality was that as a 'half-caste' Englishman, he was pretty au fait with the ways of native thinking, especially of the Mussulmans. His other merit was that since he had been a close friend of Navab Ahmad Bakhsh Khan, he was fully acquainted with Shamsuddin Ahmad Khan's temperament and enjoyed the confidence of the young Navab.

By virtue of some outstanding successes on behalf of the Honourable Company—his irregular regiment was called 'Skinner's Horse' by the English, and 'The Savars of Sikandar sahib' by the Indians—Skinner was well thought of in the Company's circles, though he was not treated with any kind of equality with the Europeans. A self-styled Lt Colonel, he was granted the rank of Acting Captain in the Company's military establishment, but not before much hesitation on the part of the Company and much petitioning by Skinner himself. Even that much was a mark of extraordinary favour in the eyes of both the Company and the Indians. At that time, no European of 'mixed blood', far less a native, could hold an officer's rank in the Company's armed forces. Those who died were native, those who commanded were English.

Even so, it was an unusual step: The inclusion of a 'half-caste' individual in the secret confabulations of a matter bristling with many dimensions was perhaps the greatest preferment that the Company could have bestowed upon Skinner. And the favour brought good results.

Skinner's huge haveli was not too far from the Residency; so he reached there within half an hour of being summoned. Tall, with a powerful but slim body, and extremely agile, Skinner looked much younger than his sixty years. His colour was quite dark, in fact, black; his black hair, generously sprinkled with grey, was cut en brosse to hide its curliness as much as possible. His eyes were light brown and bright, and suggested an intelligent and perhaps clever and quick-thinking brain. But for his colour and to some extent his hair, everything about him was English: lifestyle, speech, attitude to religion, dress and deportment, attitude toward the natives. In fact, he was perhaps more English than most of the army-type Englishmen of those times. Welcomed warmly by those present, he was given a chair next to Metcalfe at the committee.

The matter under discussion at the time of his arrival was whether Shamsuddin Ahmad Khan should immediately be jailed in the English part of the city, or if he should be incarcerated at a haveli in Shahjahanabad. Metcalfe apprehended civil unrest, even disturbances, in Delhi if the Navab was put under arrest, so it was better, he thought, as a pro tem measure to put him under house arrest in his haveli. The accused was of course to be hanged promptly after the quickest possible trial. The locale for the hanging, he suggested, should be some place outside Delhi. He thought that an inn of the Mughal times, now not in use and situated a few miles out of Panipat, about fifty miles from Delhi, was the best place for the purpose. Gibbets should be quickly installed inside the inn, and burial of both the hanged criminals should also be carried out there. Since John Lawrence was Magistrate at Panipat and knew that area particularly well, he supported the proposal.

The passion for revenge was blazing in Simon Fraser's heart; but he also saw in his cousin's murder, politically and administratively, an occasion for sending a strong message to all the natives, including the King. The message was to be a warning: taking the life of an English officer was not something to be attempted lightly. He was firmly of the belief that the existence and continuance of English power in India was based on tyranny and fear. Should the least opportunity be allowed to the natives by softening our rule of fear and showing the smallest indulgence to the subject populace, they would scratch and tear at us and would swallow us.

He used his parable of the bear and the bees to illustrate his point. The Himalayan bear, scratching and clawing at the beehive, demolishes the hive, throws away the wax, and gobbles up the honey. The bees, furious and frenzied, swarm upon the bear, dancing, gyrating in a fever around him, but they cannot do a thing to the bear. His hairs are far more numerous than the largest swarm of bees. In our case, the slightest relaxation in our strictness, and the natives will rise against our meagre numbers; the handful of our cantonments, factories, arsenals, storehouses and courts of law, our policemen and informers, all will be trounced in no time, trampled to dust under the bare feet of innumerable natives, far more in number than the hair on a bear's body.

He shuddered at the thought: our women will prostitute themselves for the savage blackamoor, or will be in concubinage to fat, ugly and lecherous landlords and wealthy merchants. In the land of Hindustan, and even in the Deccan, there were many regions where there was no more than just one English officer over hundreds of square miles: just one English home, and the rule of the master of that home kissed the skies in prestige and power by virtue of his practical wisdom, his devious methods of ruling over a motley group of subjects, his ascendant fortune, and the awe in his governance.

Simon Fraser saw that John Lawrence was hot and fervent in the investigation of the crime and in the building up of the case against its perpetrators. He therefore thought that Lawrence would be equally keen and fervid about maintaining and even enhancing the awe and magnificence of the Honourable Company Bahadur. He was disappointed when Lawrence advised that the hanging and burial of the malefactors be in a secluded location far from Delhi. Yet he also believed that the meeting was not the occasion for expressing his discontent; for his compatriots and worse still, the semi-English Captain Skinner would understand by his protest that he, Fraser, was placing revenge for his cousin's blood above considerations of administration and State. He therefore spoke in an extremely reasonable tone, weighing his words carefully: 'I feel that the accused should be arrested here in Delhi, and both the culprits should be hanged nowhere else but in Delhi. Were we to evince the least bit of leniency, the desi riff-raff—and very nearly all of the natives are no better—will construe our indulgence as a sign of weakness. My experience of these people tells me that they are inordinately prone to spreading rumours against their superiors. They roar like lions when it suits them; keep them on a strong leash, they are wet cats or dogs roiled in the mud.'

Metcalfe asked, 'What do you then advise, Mr Fraser?'

'The intelligence reaching me indicates that the locals are sympathetically inclined towards Shamsuddin Ahmad and Karim Khan. Word is abroad that . . .' He cleared his throat, '. . . that two daredevils took the torch to the Firangee's face. Under the circumstances, it is all the more incumbent upon us to take the severest punitive action, and take it openly.'

'So you think that there will be no repercussions? The events of Bareilly, do they not provide a precedent?'

'We should forget the events of Bareilly,' said Fraser calmly. 'The luxury-loving and loose-living Mirzas of Delhi, and retaliation?' he laughed derisively. 'If we exhibit our true power and strength of mind at suitable times and in suitable places, none would dream of retaliation now and here, or on any other occasion and at any other place. The nobles of Delhi now die for beautiful boys and wily courtesans, not for honour.' Fraser laughed again. This time his laughter was charged with the sour intoxication of scorn.

'But the King will have to be brought around, won't he?' Metcalfe observed. 'Also, some of the chief mullahs, I believe. They can do mischief.'

'Don't worry about the mullahs. There is none after the Sufi Shah Abdul Aziz who would even let out a squeak. The mullahs will do nothing without the King's say-so anyway, and the King won't stand even a suggestion from us.'

Skinner, who had been an attentive listener so far, now spoke, 'I agree with Mr Fraser. The most important point is that we are not arresting Shamsuddin on some political grounds. We are arresting him on the charge of wilful murder. The native subjects admire and wonder at our policy and practice of not doing anything without the support of the law.'

Lawrence asked, 'Captain Skinner, so you advise putting Shamsuddin under arrest and sending him to jail the moment he enters Delhi?'

'No, sir.' Skinner thought for a moment before continuing. 'We must use some practical wisdom. I know these fellows well. They're very particular about keeping up appearances, following established customs and maintaining intact the conventions of their forefathers.'

'So?' Metcalfe asked a little impatiently.

'I wish to make a proposal for your consideration.'

Lawrence made to interrupt, but Metcalfe flicked his eye to indicate that he desist. James Skinner looked Metcalfe full in the face and spoke with precision and deliberation: 'Shamsuddin Ahmad should be arrested before he enters the city. The way to do it is for me to meet him in Palam and disarm him without arousing his suspicions. Immediately thereafter, a posse of the Company's armed forces, led by Magistrate Fraser, should arrive on the scene and put him under arrest. He should not be handcuffed, nor put in fetters. He should travel in his closed palanquin, surrounded by our men.'

He paused to gauge the reaction of the rest of the committee. Everyone was listening attentively. Skinner continued, 'Shamsuddin Ahmad trusts me. He will readily agree to see me and remove his arms at my request.

The natives will have no occasion for complaint, for the arrest will have taken place outside Delhi; by voluntarily disarming himself, Shamsuddin Ahmad will be seen to have surrendered voluntarily. He will be allowed to travel to the city in his closed palanquin. There will thus be no ostensible insult to him on any count.'

Metcalfe, and also the others, were clearly impressed. Metcalfe hit the table with his fist and cried, 'That's indeed a fine set of suggestions, Captain Skinner. Quite like eating one's cake and having it too!'

Though Metcalfe approved of Skinner's suggestion in its entirety, there were some voices later among the sahibs that it ill behooved the Glorious Firangee sahibs to arrest Shamsuddin Ahmad by guile.

Skinner cast a glance of triumph at those present. The details of the action were then worked out within minutes. In a brief while, Skinner could be seen riding out, apparently alone, on his horse. Fraser and his soldiers followed at a discreet hundred paces. Having arrived at Palam Fort, Fraser and his men entered through the massive door in the battlement, but stayed outside the main gate that led to the residential area. Skinner went in alone and had his name sent in through one of the guards.

As expected, Shamsuddin Ahmad came out immediately in welcome and on seeing Skinner, he spoke a well-known Persian line used to welcome dear friends: 'Oh, your coming is the cause of my heart's happiness!' 'Bhai wallah, Sikandar sahib, what an unexpected pleasure! So how are you doing?' Saying this, he took Skinner's hand into his and led him inside the Fort where Shamsuddin occupied a large chamber, originally designed perhaps as the Hall of Public Audience. It occurred to Shamsuddin Ahmad that Sikandar sahib might have brought some message from the Residency and might like some privacy. Seating him at the head of the carpeted floor, he said, 'Please place your noble self here and cast a glance at this cool drink. The hookah will be presented momently before you.'

He looked around to make sure that there was no one else present and looked at James Skinner with expectant eyes.

'Dilawar-ul Mulk, I won't lie to you or mislead you,' Skinner spoke with downcast eyes. 'But you are in dire trouble.'

'Sir, I understand. But the Glorious Sahibs have some misunderstanding about me. They have no proof, no evidence against me at all, I swear. But of course, if it's a case of "I was killed because I was innocent", as the poet says, then I don't know what to plead in extenuation.'

'Dilawar-ul Mulk, you are still very young and inexperienced. Matters of State have many kinds of complications, numerous subtleties . . . None can say who can be held as an accused, and when.'

Shamsuddin Ahmad lost colour. 'Sir, I could not follow your drift.'

'My advice is that you should surrender yourself to the protection of Mr Metcalfe. Make over your sword and sidearms to me. I will go side by side with you.'

Skinner's face showed nothing but total gravity and commitment, as if he was quite sure that Shamsuddin Ahmad's future was fully secure in his hands. He said 'Mr Metcalfe' advisedly, maintaining the ambiguity between Thomas and Charles Metcalfe, the latter (Thomas's elder brother) being the Acting Governor General at that time. This was a small way out for him, should things take a turn not according to his scheme, or should Shamsuddin Ahmad accuse him of duplicity.

Shamsuddin Ahmad recalled his childhood when both William Fraser and James Skinner were frequent visitors at his father's house. James Skinner, in particular, was held in such affection by the late Navab Ahmad Bakhsh Khan that when he built his new haveli in Ballimaran, he had the marble plaque at the top of the main gate inscribed with Skinner's, and not his name. The plaque, in standard Persian calligraphy, clearly read:

Haveli James Skinner Sahib

The plaque was still there for all to see.

Shamsuddin Ahmad said to himself in his heart: I am, in effect, under siege by the English. Rather than be ignominiously arrested and put under English fetters, I should surrender my arms now and go quietly with Sikandar sahib. We'll see how the future unfolds. As the Persian verse says: *Happen what may; I put my boat in the waters.* I should be better off if I accept the present situation. At least a further charge of resistance or rebellion cannot be laid against me.

Shamsuddin Ahmad removed his Ispahani sword with its hilt worked in gold and his name showing on it in clear gold letters, his Bidari dagger with bejewelled hilt and his silver-plated French pistol. Making them over to Skinner, he said, 'Take these, they are yours in trust. I am your servant.'

Skinner rose at once. 'I'll have them placed in safe custody with some reliable nobleman. In the meantime, you organize your departure for

Delhi.' With these words, he quit the chamber. Fraser and his men observed Skinner come out with his armload of weapons, and promptly marched into the chamber unheeding of the protests of the Navab's guards. Shamsuddin Ahmad, taken by surprise, was trying to get to the bottom of the new turn of events when Fraser advanced, pistol in hand, and said coldly, 'Navab Shamsuddin Ahmad, you are an accused in the crime of Mr William Fraser's murder. I take you in custody in the name of the Company Bahadur.'

Shamsuddin Ahmad couldn't believe his ears or his eyes. 'Sikandar sahib!' he called out, as if crying out to him to come to his aid, or perhaps he wanted to say, 'Sikandar sahib, you cheated me.' In the wink of an eye, the Company's soldiers made a circle around him. Doubtless, Skinner did not wait a moment as he came out from the Fort and galloped fast on the road to Delhi; there was no question of his answering the young Navab, even if he had been within earshot. Hearing Shamsuddin Ahmad call out to Skinner, Shamsuddin Ahmad's men came running, but it was too late. Permitting Fraser to enter with an armed company had turned fatal. Still, they made an attempt at resisting and even attacking, but Shamsuddin Ahmad ordered them to do nothing. He then spoke to his Sikh Commander of Horse, 'Gurinder Singh, there is no need to stay here now. We will go to Delhi. Organize the departure at once.'

Gurinder Singh was about to go out, saying, 'As you command', but Fraser harshly ordered him to stay. 'No! I have asked the palanquin to be brought round here. You shouldn't move from here.'

Shamsuddin Ahmad smiled a pale smile, 'Saimon sahib, you remind me much of your late brother, upon whom be the mercy of God. May Allah grant him Paradise, he was always most specially kind to me.'

Simon Fraser was inwardly puzzled: was this genuine condolence, or was there some sarcasm, or some other meaning hidden there? He was still considering what to say, when the Navab strode to Fraser, put his hand on his shoulder, and spoke in a faintly patronizing tone, 'So why delay now, if the palanquin is ready?'

Shamsuddin Ahmad Khan's voice and visage at that time were so dignified and superior, and his body's gestures so brimming with self-confidence, that Simon Fraser involuntarily stepped back. Trying to regain control, he smiled a vicious smile and said, 'There's no delay at all. The end is very near now, my dear Navab.'

Shamsuddin Ahmad laughed out aloud and quoted a line from the poet Mir: 'I can see my home from a hundred miles away. So let's start. There's nothing to do here. I have already seen my end in the mirror of my kneecap!'

Fraser was confused even more; he did not know or understand the purport of Mir's line, and was quite at sea to get to the bottom of the 'mirror' and the 'kneecap'. In fact, 'mirror' is a metaphor for the 'kneecap'. When in deep thought, one sits with the chin on the kneecap, which is round like a mirror, and sitting in that posture indicates that one is contemplating one's ultimate end.

Fraser managed to reply with cold hauteur, 'You will always be encircled by my soldiery. Now go. Enough, get a move on.'

Navab Shamsuddin Ahmad travelled in his own palanquin, its curtains on both sides drawn; no one saw him enter the city. Mirza Mughal Beg was informed late in the evening by his men that his senior son-in-law was in the Company's custody in Ludlow Castle. Mirza Mughal Beg, whose own imprisonment had already left him feeling depressed and defeated, found himself prey to a new uncertainty. What action, if any, could he take to achieve at least temporary short-term relief, when permanent long-term relief seemed to be something far below the horizon?

After much cogitation, he summoned Mirza Isfandiar Beg, who was a sort of agent-adviser (pairokar) for the State of Firozepur Jhirka and Loharu in legal and administrative matters concerning the Company's offices. He sent him to the Residency to ascertain Shamsuddin Ahmad Khan's status and when he could be visited. Isfandiar Beg went off immediately but could return only after many hours with the information that Shamsuddin Ahmad was under guard in the Castle; his personal status was not compromised: he was being given due honour, consideration and comforts. Legally, he was a prisoner, an accused, or rather a criminal. As for the possibility of a meeting with him, the criminal court had long closed at that time. Between 10 and 11 a.m. the next day, a formal application should be made before the Magistrate so that the matter might be considered by the powers that be.

Mirza Mughal Beg Khan signed a power of attorney in favour of Isfandiar Beg and instructed him to do everything possible to secure a meeting the next day, stipulating that Beg himself be present at the meeting as the legal adviser to Navab Shamsuddin Ahmad Khan.

The next day was the 10th of Muharram, the chief day of mourning.

Isfandiar Beg spent the entire day running between the Residency, the English Office and the Magistrate's Court. He submitted an application asking for a meeting between Shamsuddin Ahmad Khan and his legal representatives; he also asked for a copy of the charge sheet filed against the Navab with the Magistrate. In addition, he submitted an original application to the Sudder Dewauny Adawlut (Chief Civil Court) at Allahabad: Delhi, even the King at Delhi, at that time being in the civil and administrative jurisdiction of the NWP (North Western Province). He gave a brief summary of the case against Navab Shamsuddin Ahmad Khan and stated that while he was shortly proceeding to Calcutta to ascertain the position of Navab Shamsuddin Ahmad Khan's petitions to the Navab Governor General Bahadur, he felt it was necessary that the Chief Civil Judge should also hear the matter from the civil rights' point of view. It was therefore petitioned that the august Chief Civil Court depute some representative at once to Delhi to record the Navab's statement. Such a statement, the petitioner believed, would be immensely helpful in uncovering many important points related with the case.

An informal meeting between Navab Shamsuddin Ahmad Khan and Mirza Mughal Beg Khan could have become possible late on the night of the 10th of Muharram, but the Sudder Dewauny Adawlut at Allahabad did not find it feasible to consider Mirza Isfandiar Beg's petition for the curious reason of 'holidays on account of Moharram'.

In fact, none of the petitions submitted by Isfandiar Beg to the Governor General on the matter of Shamsuddin Ahmad Khan was subjected to any examination. As reported above, all papers relating to the case were filed in the Political Department, and none of them bears any indication of being seen by a senior officer of the Company Bahadur, far less the life-giving eye of the Navab Governor General Bahadur.

No formal order was passed on Mirza Isfandiar Beg's application demanding his and Mirza Mughal Beg's formal access to the prisoner. He was advised orally to be present at the Court of Saimon Sahib Bahadur at 12 noon on 8 May 1835. In the Court, Isfandiar Beg and Mirza Mughal Beg found the Navab tired and deprived of sleep, though in formal Navabi dress. All that he said to his father-in-law and Isfandiar Beg was that he had already authorized the latter to represent his case at all levels. For the women in Firozepur Fort, his message was that they should not worry; there was no case against him, and he would soon be set free.

John Lawrence, as the prosecutor in the Magistrate's Court, delivered an eloquent speech and asserted that the crime of murder was fully proven against the accused and his servant. The latter was already committed to the Sessions Court and was standing trial in the Court of John Colvin, Special Judge and Judge of the Sessions. He therefore prayed that the case against the present accused be also committed to that Court so that he might be given a full and fair trial. Shamsuddin Ahmad made no statement, nor was he cross-examined. He was only asked if he pleaded guilty or not.

'Not guilty,' Shamsuddin Ahmad averred in a clear, unhesitant voice. 'The allegation against me is false and is the product of a conspiracy against me.'

Isfandiar Beg was not allowed to plead, except to say that since his petition in the matter, already submitted, was due to be considered by the Sudder Dewauny Adawlut, no hearing could take place before that august Court delivered its opinion. In the absence of any direction from that august Court, the Magistrate refused to entertain Isfandiar Beg's urging. Two hours later, Simon Fraser committed the case to the Sessions Judge after observing the usual formalities.

The accused was delivered back to his makeshift prison in Ludlow Castle, none except Isfandiar Beg being allowed to meet him. Isfandiar Beg left for Allahabad by a specially commissioned fast boat before nightfall on 8 May 1835. Leaving the river at Farrukhabad, he proceeded on the rest of his 150-mile journey by fast horse and ox cart. Stopping at Allahabad for just a few hours in order to urge early hearing of his petition, he left for Calcutta by the fastest Dawk Sowarree (Mail Carriage), often exchanging it for a horse or an ox cart when the overland route became too difficult.

Isfandiar Beg arrived at Calcutta on the midnight of 11 May 1835. He immediately called on Stanford Thackeray, the English Advocate, already chosen by the Navab, to pursue his case. A petition, dated 11 May 1835, was prepared in Persian on behalf of Shamsuddin Ahmad in the small hours of the morning and filed with the Secretary to the Governor General by 8 a.m. on 12 May1835.

In Delhi, restrictions and hardships on Shamsuddin Ahmad began to harden. Initially, it was the Navab's own men who were put on guard duty. But late on the night of 11 May, they were removed summarily because Shamsuddin Ahmad happened to ask one of them if it was midnight already. Or perhaps he desired to know the time that was to pass before midnight.

Perhaps the English feared that it was some kind of code through which the prisoner hoped to establish communication with his supporters with a view to mounting a conspiracy. Anyway, Shamsuddin Ahmad was instantly deprived of his familiar guards and private servants, and an announcement was made through the city to the effect that if a relative or friend of Shamsuddin Ahmad was found at large in the city at any time, and for any reason whatever, he would instantly be arrested and clapped in jail. This proclamation had the desired result: soon it seemed as if Shamsuddin Ahmad had no supporter or relative left in Delhi.

In the Court of John Alexander Colvin, the prosecution case against Shamsuddin Ahmad stood entirely on Aniya's evidence. John Lawrence used every possible trick of drama and oratory in presenting that evidence before the Court. Yet, in spite of going over the evidence over and over again, and cross-examining Aniya within an inch of his life, Lawrence was unable to put Aniya on the scene of the crime. He did not also succeed in getting Aniya to confess that he had ever heard the Navab ordering Fraser's execution; or that the Navab, in Aniya's presence or within his hearing, had given an instruction to Karim Khan or anyone else, which could constructively mean that the Navab intended or desired for William Fraser to be killed; or that the Navab had instructed him to report to him the event of Fraser's death the moment it occurred. All that he would say was that he ran as fast as possible to report the incident of Fraser's death to the Navab.

The prosecution made much of the fact that Aniya took only one day to cover a journey that normally took three days, and this was because the Navab had commanded him to report the incident of murder within the shortest possible time. He repeated his story—which, incidentally, was quite true—that he had Karim Khan's strict instruction to follow him, and to run away to Firozepur the moment he heard the sound of gunfire, and to report to the Navab that Fraser Sahib was no more.

Since Karim Khan was not examined at that time, and the Navab refused to be examined by the defence or cross-examined by the prosecution, all that the Navab's advocates could urge and emphasize upon was that Fraser's death was no ordinary matter, and Fraser himself was very close to the accused, so it was not at all unusual for him to wish to be informed most urgently of any event concerning William Fraser.

The Court tried to put some questions to Shamsuddin Ahmad Khan. But there was no way to place him in Delhi on the night of the murder, far less anywhere near the scene of the crime. The ownership of the gun, of which much was made by the prosecution, could not be traced to Shamsuddin Ahmad. The evidence of the horse's shoes being backwards was certainly suggestive and significant. But no one could prove or even suggest that the horse found in the Navab's stable was the one ridden by the murderer when he perpetrated the crime. No evidence was there to show that Karim Khan ever said that he would murder William Fraser, or he would do the deed at the behest of the Navab.

The prosecution's technical case against the Navab boiled down to this: The statements of Karim Khan and the evidence of Aniya provide proof positive of Karim Khan's guilt. Karim Khan admitted being an employee of the Navab. According to the English law, the master was held responsible for his servant's actions. This was known, in English law, as the 'Master and Servant' theory. Thus, when the crime was proved against the servant, ipso facto it was proved against the master too. There was much background evidence to prove Shamsuddin Ahmad's chronic enmity towards the victim. The newest proof of this was the cry of Fathullah Beg Khan when he viewed the victim's body. Thus there was nothing more to be proved. Both master and servant were fully culpable.

There was some circumstantial evidence from which the prosecution tried to squeeze out as much as possible. The main item here was the water-affected piece of paper which was purported to be a letter from Shamsuddin Ahmad to Karim Khan, reprimanding the latter for not having till then carried out his task of buying 'hunting hounds'. But the paper, or letter, did not have either the Navab's signature or his seal. Then, the letter was undated in the sense that the year of its writing was not mentioned anywhere. There was just a suspicion—much flogged by the prosecution—that the letter was written in 1835, but there was no proof at all of this. Karim Khan, of course, in spite of all persuasion did not confess that the author of the letter was the Navab, or that it had anything to with the murder.

The prosecution produced many witnesses testifying that they were familiar with the handwriting of the accused and that there seemed no indication to deduce that the writer of the letter was someone other than the accused. The Navab refused to provide a sample of his writing. His advocate's argument was that the entire proceedings were illegal according to Islamic law, and also Mughal law. Thus there was no question of the accused presenting any evidence, or refuting any evidence admitted against him.

This last point about the legality of the proceedings under Islamic or Mughal law caused a bit of concern to the prosecution. Finally, it was decided to fight fire with fire: a maulavi from a madrasa at Khari Baoli was introduced as witness for the prosecution. It was sought to prove, through his expert evidence, that under Islamic law, and also Mughal law as established by Emperor Aurangzeb Alamgir in the *Fatawa-e Alamgiri*, William Fraser had the status of a dhimmi, and Islamic law mandated punishment for the murder of a dhimmi. Thus Shamsuddin Ahmad and his servant Karim Khan could be held culpable for Fraser's murder, which already stood proved.

This did not elicit derisive laughter from those in attendance, for everyone loves their life, but subdued sniggers and giggles could be heard around the Court. Colvin banged his gavel angrily, but one of the defence lawyers sought permission to cross-examine. Colvin had no choice but to accord permission. The lawyer asked, 'Mullah ji, when was the last time the victim paid the jizia to enable him to maintain his dhimmi status?'

Since the maulavi was unable to answer the question, the defence asked him further, 'Mullah ji, if the victim by virtue of paying the jizia was eligible for State protection as a dhimmi, then which would be the Court—mandated by Allah and authorized by the ruler competent—to try the case of his murder?'

Because there were no replies forthcoming, the witness was excused and the Court ordered that the hearing be continued.

The trial lasted seven days, with the Court sitting late on many days. The accused were represented by Mirza Isfandiar Beg, his assistant Mirza Bhacchu, and Shamsuddin Ahmad Khan's Mukhtar-e Kar (Chief Authorized Representative), Divan Abdullah Khan. The latter two were not empowered to cross-examine a witness; their right was limited to frame issues, if any, on the evidence of a witness, ask for clarification on those issues, and make a formal statement thereon. No one from the general public had permission to watch the proceedings; the Company's functionaries, both native and English, could attend by permission.

Unlike Shamsuddin Ahmad Khan, Karim Khan quite willingly agreed to give evidence as a witness: not for the prosecution, but for the defence. He wholeheartedly consented to be cross-examined again and again by the prosecution. In his examination in chief, he merely stated the known facts and denied everything else. He was, in any case, not permitted to say anything in the Navab's defence; even the purview of the examination in chief was limited strictly to the witness's personal knowledge. During his rigorous cross-examination by the prosecution, he denied all knowledge of the events as narrated by the prosecution; he denied that the Navab gave him any instruction to assassinate Fraser; he denied that the suspicious gun, or the horse, were used by him to kill Fraser; he denied the receipt of a letter from his master about the purchase of hounds, although it was usual for him to buy hounds.

Finally, and in exasperation, the Court asked him if he would carry out an order by the Navab to kill someone. He answered, 'Take the name of God, Sahib, and beg His pardon. To take an innocent life! No, Your Honour, it is entirely contrary to my faith.'

Aniya's evidence was presented again through a redirect examination. But nothing could be distilled from it above what he had already confessed to. That said, the case and its trial were no longer issues of law, or imposition of order and discipline, or visiting retribution upon the guilty. As if by its own force, it had moved into a different territory. It was now stuck deep and firm like an iron rod in the realm of governance and enforcement of power, and not many years would pass when its point would have been driven into the heart of the Indian Empire.

On the eighth day, Colvin read out his fifty-page judgment in open court. The accused, Shamsuddin Ahmad Khan and Karim Khan, were found guilty of wilful murder. According to the English Penal Code, both deserved to be hanged till they were dead. The Court further directed that they might be hanged publicly as soon as possible. The date of the judgment was 8 August 1835.

Metcalfe immediately convened his informal committee to consider the question as to whether the guilty should be permitted to move the Governor General Bahadur in appeal. It was brought to the notice of the committee that there was no provision in the extant laws of the Honourable Company Bahadur which enabled a convicted criminal to file an appeal with the Governor General Bahadur. John Colvin was appointed Special Judge expressly for hearing the two cases. There was no court above his Court, for the purposes of the two prosecutions, to which appeals could be made. True, there was a Supreme Court established by the Company

Bahadur in Calcutta, but its jurisdiction did not extend to matters arising within the boundaries of the NWP (whose headquarters were at Agra) and the Commissionerate of Delhi.

There was, indeed, the Sudder Dewauny Adawlut at Allahabad whose presiding officer ranked above the Special Judge, but his Court had no jurisdiction over criminal matters. Even that Court had been unable, for technical reasons, to record the statement of Shamsuddin Ahmad Khan. A Sudder Ameen, deputed by the Sudder Dewauny Adawlut, Allahabad, arrived in Delhi on 14 June 1835, to record the statement of the accused Shamsuddin Ahmad. He was advised by the Commissioner of Delhi that charges were filed against the accused some time ago. There was, thus, no need to record his statement now.

The committee decided unanimously that the convicts should not be allowed to appeal. In any case, the committee noted, no appeal had yet been received from either of the two convicts. And should such an appeal be received at some future date before the punishment was carried out, the Special Judge would be within his power to turn it down, there being no appellate authority above him in the case.

At this time, a member of the committee, perhaps it was Prescott, or Metcalfe himself, raised the question whether ratification or upholding of the conviction and punishment of Shamsuddin Ahmad should be obtained from the Governor General Bahadur, because the person in question was Shamsuddin Ahmad, an independent ruler of a native state and who had also been decorated by the Company with formal titles. Simon Fraser and John Lawrence strongly opposed the suggestion. When the argumentation became rather hot, Metcalfe silenced everyone by asking Fraser the question: 'Mr Fraser, do you think the punishment will not be ratified by His Excellency?'

Simon Fraser cried out, 'No! It will be ratified! By God, it must be ratified.'

'Mr Fraser, what is the occasion for swearing?' Metcalfe said somewhat testily. 'It's the duty of all white officers of the Company to observe decorum and restraint at all times.'

Fraser at once realized his mistake. His face became what the English describe as 'beetroot red'. He wiped his face with his kerchief, swallowed, and said in a subdued voice, 'Sorry, I got carried away. Shan't happen again, I'm sure.'

Prescott tried to douse the heat by observing, 'Perhaps Mr Fraser feels that the decision from Calcutta might take some time,' he smiled. 'First, there's no real possibility of it; second, the convict Shamsuddin is young and energetic. Surely, he's not going to die in four or six weeks.'

'Right,' John Lawrence said, 'but his guards report that when he learnt about his punishment of death, he repeatedly struck his head against the walls of his cell, as if he were trying to kill himself,'

A crease of vexation appeared on Metcalfe's brow. 'But, Mr Lawrence, you are well aware that the guards took immediate steps to prevent his doing it again. And now, in fact, even his food is prepared under the supervision of an English sergeant, so as to obviate the chance of death by poison.'

'So, it appears that he can die only when we kill him,' Prescott smiled, attempting some humour. This had the desired effect. The air of bonhomie returned to the committee. It was ultimately decided by consensus that a full report of the case and a copy of the judgment be submitted to the Excellent Navab Governor General Bahadur through a special and reliable courier for ratification of the punishment to Shamsuddin Ahmad. Arrangements for the hanging of Karim Khan should go ahead apace. It was further decided by consensus that Karim Khan should be hanged publicly at twelve o'clock on the 26th of August 1835, in the open meidaun in front of the Jami Masjid of Fatehpuri at the western end of Chandni Chowk.

At the time Karim Khan was brought to the gallows, a large multitude, apparently silent, gathered in the meidaun; they were watched with hawk eyes by four hundred armed Telangas. There was no Englishman present, except the doctor. When asked to state his last wish, Karim Khan said in a composed voice, but loudly enough to be heard by those who were closest: 'I have no wish. All I ask for is that the people of Hind pray for me.'

The life's flower of the Red Rose wilted and withered in no time on the murderous bough of the gallows. In the afternoon prayers, and then in early evening prayers, the Mussulmans of Delhi everywhere prayed for his soul. In the evening, devotional music was played and sung in the ancient Hindu temples of Kalkaji and Jog Maya Debi. Prayers and devotional songs were organized at the Lal Mandir of the Jains, and the Sikh Gurdwara at Sisganj.

Karim Khan's body was delivered to his brother-in-law Wasail Khan who was still in jail. He was instructed not to observe any of the Indo-Islamic ceremonies before and after the burial which was to be in an unmarked grave. There was no funeral procession, no prayers, no mourning. No trace can be found of his grave today, but the presumed place of burial still became a pilgrimage spot for the people of Delhi, regardless of religion. Flowers were presented and lamps were lit on his grave. For many years, in fact, a fair of his Urs (date of his death, or his marriage to the Eternal Truth) was held punctually on the date of his hanging. Qavvalis were sung on the usual devotional themes, but also about his goodness, piety and bravery.

The convict Shamsuddin Ahmad was not informed of his file being sent to Calcutta for ratification. His people, who were following his case, could not ascertain the cause of delay in executing the judgment. This gave occasion to the rumour merchants of Delhi for circulating, as was their wont, the most fantastic rumours. It was said, for instance, that the King of the Firangees had held a council in London where he had decreed that Navab Shamsuddin Ahmad Khan should be accorded a full pardon. Another story was that the Prophet's son-in-law Ali, the Lion of God, who attacked repeatedly and never retreated, had appeared in the English King's dream and warned him against any action against the Navab. He told him that from his father's side, Shamsuddin Ahmad Khan was his progeny; and so should any harm come to him, the King's bones shall be pounded to powder. The English King, thoroughly intimidated, had issued orders forthwith for Shamsuddin Ahmad's pardon.

The Residency's spies reported to Metcalfe that an air of celebration was blowing through the city: the people believed that Navab Shamsuddin Ahmad Khan would soon be returning to Firozepur a free man. In view of these rumours, the Firangee rulers decided to have the information spread through the city by official criers that the case of the condemned criminal had been submitted to Navab Governor General Bahadur for ratification. Moreover, an Official Gazette was published on 4 September 1835, giving the same news.

Mirza Isfandiar Beg, on learning about the Gazette notification, prepared a petition to the Governor General in which he referred to the notification as the first official information about the status of his case:

> I, therefore, depute Mirza Isfandiar Beg, who holds my Power of Attorney, to your Sacred Service. His submissions, written and oral, will make it crystal clear to your Luminous Intellect that the Court in Delhi paid no heed at all to my Objections, Statements, and the clear Evidences in the Case. I have been Ensnared and Inveigled as a culprit

through a clear Conspiracy. I therefore most humbly and fervently Pray that my Attorney may be accorded a Sympathetic and Attentive hearing, and the Papers submitted by him may be kindly Perused with Due Diligence. In this wide World, I see none but Your Excellent Self who can give me redressal; nor do I have any concern with anyone else.

Mirza Isfandiar Beg filed this petition in the Office of the Governor General on 10 September 1835, through Mr Thackeray. He submitted a similar petition on 28 September 1835. After hot and persistent efforts, he and Thackeray were able to obtain an audience with the Secretary to the Governor General. The meeting remained barren of result. The ratification of the judgment of hanging the accused was passed by the Governor General in Council and it was received in the Residency at Delhi on 7 October 1835. Considering further delay to be inexpedient, the decision was taken to execute the punishment on the very next day, 8 October 1835, in the meidaun in front of Kashmiri Gate at nine o'clock in the morning.

A stout gibbet was erected under torchlight late on the evening of 7 October. It was secured against intrusion and disturbance by installing tall and strong poles and palings of teak wood. Military regiments from Meerut and Kaul (modern Aligarh) were already in position. A force of one thousand two hundred—one hundred of whom were English—guards, commanded by experienced English officers, was deployed from a late hour of the night of 7th October to prevent any disturbance or public demonstration.

Mirza Isfandiar Beg was so ashamed and grieved at his unsuccess that he gave up wearing a turban: instead, for the whole of his remaining life, he wore a large, rough kerchief or an informal and humble headgear called a phenta, something like a poor man's bandana, around his head. He became known everywhere as Mirza Phente Baz. His outstanding abilities, however, took him from preferment to preferment: he became Assistant Divan, and then the fully fledged Divan of the large native State of Alwar, before dying in 1862.

Simon Fraser's informers reported to him late in the evening of 7 October that there was a possibility of one or more rescue attempts being mounted over the night, or even very early in the morning of the next day. Metcalfe therefore decided to shift the prisoner from Ludlow Castle to the Gora Barracks near Kashmiri Gate. This would mean reduction of distance and time for the condemned prisoner's palanquin transit to the gibbet—Kashmiri Gate being much nearer to the place of execution than the Ludlow Castle. The shorter distance would correspondingly reduce the risk of disturbance or agitation by the natives.

Shamsuddin Ahmad had retired for the night; he was asleep when he was aroused by the Brigadier in charge of his guard and asked to ride in the palanquin to Kashmiri Gate. The Navab protested, saying that he should be allowed to sleep in peace on his last night upon this earth, but was powerless. He was moved to a dormitory of English officers in the Gora Barracks at Kashmiri Gate.

Lieutenant Thomas Bacon, an English officer, was sharing the dormitory with many others when Shamsuddin Ahmad arrived. Bacon and his friends were sleeping in the dormitory overnight so as to obtain good seats as close as possible to the site of the execution. Bacon writes that he and his friends offered to vacate the dormitory to afford full privacy to the Navab, but he politely refused, saying that he could quite conveniently have his bed placed in a corner. Shortly thereafter, the Navab's servants arrived with his heavy bed. The Navab asked Thomas Bacon if he might put on the green dress that the navabs usually wore at night. Bacon apologized, saying that only Metcalfe could say anything on the matter.

Shamsuddin Ahmad lay down in his street clothes, his back to the English officers. His servants quietly began to mildly knead and pat his body to induce sleep. Thomas Bacon reports that Shamsuddin Ahmad, who was to sleep the eternal sleep the next morning on the gallows, soon fell into a profound slumber. Bacon says that sleep did not come to him that night after the Navab's advent in his Barracks.

Shamsuddin Ahmad rose very early and offered the predawn prayer. A short while later, a maulavi arrived who opened the Quran and had Shamsuddin Ahmad read the Ya-Sin with him: the thirty-sixth chapter of the Quran which is recited to ease the agony of death. The maulavi himself now recited the chapter and blew on Shamsuddin Ahmad's head and face. Thomas Bacon has described the maulavi as 'padre', and wrote that the padre recited some prayers and had them said by Shamsuddin Ahmad.

The Navab's personal barber arrived to trim his beard, moustaches and hair. While the barber attended to him, Shamsuddin Ahmad looked at his face in the mirror again and again and asked Bacon if permission would be forthcoming for him to wear green during his last moments on earth. Bacon could only maintain a helpless silence.

Thomas Metcalfe arrived with two officers and twenty armed horsemen to escort the Navab to the gallows at about half an hour past 8 a.m. and found the Navab perfectly ready and prepared. He was in a white dress. In the slightly chilly morning of early October, the Navab's tall and princely personality, with his face slightly pale but not sickly, rather rutilant, looked extremely attractive and handsome. His barber had also done a superb job: each hair of his beard and moustaches trimmed just so, like the bezel of a gemstone. A resplendent turban in green Benarasi silk, embroidered with small, pink rose buds in gold; a long tunic of the same fabric; a short upper coat in green muslin, its sleeves cut from above, leaving them hanging, and thus revealing the gold threadwork on the ends of the tunic's sleeves; trousers in light-green mashru from Aurangabad; light shirazi shoes in dark-green leather: this was the ensemble that waited to be put on by the Navab at his execution. He asked Metcalfe in Hindi, 'Senior Sahib Bahadur, I do not want to meet my Maker in the ordinary outfit that I am wearing now. Will you let me put on these green garments?'

Metcalfe looked at Shamsuddin Ahmad, intently, somewhat surprised. He was trying to fathom the point, or the hidden meaning, behind the colour of the dress. Report had reached him in the night that the condemned criminal was importuning to be allowed to wear green. Suddenly, it occurred to him that Mussulmans identified themselves with the colour green . . . perhaps it had some religious significance too. He apprehended that the Mussulmans might feel offended or provoked if the Navab was hanged wearing green: there could even be disturbance to the peace. He answered in Persian, 'Shamsuddin Ahmad, the colour does not appear suitable to your station and for one about to be visited with the punishment of death. I would suggest you wear some other colour.'

Shamsuddin Ahmad had a thought: Let me refuse; what can this clown do, after all? I am to die anyway. But a moment's thought suggested a better tack to him.

'We were always told that a condemned criminal's last wish is invariably granted,' he smiled a tight, cold smile. 'But if the Company Bahadur, not content with my tree of life being squeezed of all its greenery, is unable to tolerate my wearing the green dress of a fakir, so be it. I'll put on a white dress, treating it as my shroud. My turban will be green.'

Shamsuddin Ahmad Khan spoke in formal, metaphorically charged Persian; Metcalfe got the drift of it, but could not decide why the turban was favoured to be green. He had won his small, tactical victory and was content with it. Shamsuddin Ahmad Khan promptly gave away in charity all the green garments except the turban; he also gave away the turban and the sash that he was wearing at that time. He proceeded to the place of his execution in his usual palanquin; an English officer rode with him. Four armed horsemen of the Madras Regiment accompanied on each side of the palanquin. Metcalfe was on his own steed, leading the procession; four mounted English military officers accompanied him on each side. Two horsemen followed the palanquin.

Neither Shamsuddin Ahmad Khan's speech nor his deportment revealed any strain or tension. On the way to the Kashmiri Gate meidaun, he noticed a village fruit seller vending kaseru, the root of the plant *Cyperus tuberosus*. Shaped like a medium-sized berry, its skin black and somewhat prickly, the root was popular as fruit because of its crunchy snow-white flesh and pleasantly sweet taste. The Navab had the palanquin stopped and bought a quantity of it. He peeled the berries and ate them with obvious relish; the peelings he threw away, on both sides of the palanquin, as if playfully teasing the pedestrians, like one who had not a care in the world. He offered to share the fruit with the Englishman.

'Come on, young sahib, eat some of these, shouldn't you enjoy a morning treat?' He laughed a short, pleasant laugh. The young man declined, unable to meet the Navab's eye.

It wasn't much of a distance from the Barracks to the gallows ground; somehow, the sure-footed bearers faltered in one or two places. The Navab delivered an affected reprimand to them: 'Hey, fellows! Move fleetly and smoothly. Don't stumble like drunks!'

*

Navab Shamsuddin Ahmad Khan was hanged on the gallows at 9 a.m. on Thursday, the 8th of October 1835. For the English, in their native land, it was common for a hanging to be an occasion for going out to watch—if not enjoy—the spectacle. The English therefore expected that the hanging of Shamsuddin Ahmad Khan would be a similar spectacular occasion, though there was a possibility of protests, even violent protests. With the view of preventing such happenings, a vast military force, consisting of both Goras and Natives, was in position from very early in the morning. It was expected that the navabs and rajahs of nearby states would be present, and they would have their own force with them.

In the event, very few commoners and noblemen from Delhi turned up. Prominent among the visitors-spectators from outside were Rajah Hindu Rao and the maharajahs of Gwalior, Alwar, Nabh and Patiala.

Having arrived at the gibbet, with Shamsuddin Ahmad just behind, surrounded by English officers, Metcalfe stopped, had the Navab nudged forward, and spoke in a loud, ringing voice in Hindi: 'Convict Shamsuddin Ahmad, the crime of murdering Mr William Fraser, Senior Sahib Bahadur, is proved against you. Do you confess your crime?'

Shamsuddin Ahmad answered with his back straight and his head high, 'I committed no crime. I confess nothing.'

Metcalfe gestured for the hangmen, two in number, to come forward. Before putting his foot on the platform on which the gibbet was erected, Shamsuddin Ahmad Khan first recited aloud the Muslim declaration of Faith, and then the Affirmation of and Witness to the Faith. A pale smile appeared on his face as he put his foot forward on the wooden stairs. Before going up further, he turned and whispered a query to the two hangmen. Perhaps he was inquiring about their faith or caste. He was answered in the same timbre of undertone. He then paused and spoke a little loudly, but as if he were talking half to himself, and half for the benefit of the doctor who stood close by, the two hangmen, and others like Metcalfe who were within hearing, 'I know not if my clay will be fortunate enough to be granted a Muslim burial. So let me recite my own prayer for the dead.'

He bent his head, and recited in a firm and strong voice the Arabic prayer, 'In the Name of God, and for God, and upon the Path of Muhammad, the Prophet of God; May there be Divine Salutations and Security upon Him and His progeny.'

He then recited the formal salutation to the Prophet, his progeny, his companions and his wives, and smiled at his hangmen. 'Let's go, dear friends, I am ready.'

As Shamsuddin Ahmad reached the top of the gibbet, one of the hangmen made to put the noose around his neck. Shamsuddin Ahmad put out his hand, took the noose and placed it around his neck. The second hangman came forward to put the hangman's cap—somehow red rather than black—on Shamsuddin Ahmad Khan's head. He took the cap too and put it on his head; the cap came up to his chin. He was at that time twenty-six years and some months old.

The hangman's jerk and the breaking of the neck were practically simultaneous. His body did not convulse or thrash around even for a second. Even his shoes, laceless as Mughal shoes were, did not fall from his feet. His face turned towards the Kabah, apparently of its own accord. It was like, as has been said by the eighteenth-century Hindi poet Mir Hasan, celebrating the martyrdom of Mansur-e Hallaj, the ninth-century Sufi mystic, poet and, according to some, revolutionary writer:

Mansur, be grateful to Love whose power
Pulled you up from your lowly station
To the height of the gallows.

Many of the English were struck by Shamsuddin Ahmad Khan's dignity, restraint, and lack of emotion, as well as his rather carefree air in the face of death—that too a death by hanging. Thomas Bacon reports that the English army officer who stood next to him, exclaimed, 'By Jove, the villain takes it so coolly as if he is accustomed to walking to the gallows every morning of his life!' The body remained hanging for full one hour and was brought down only when the Firangee doctor was convinced that the cageling of life had flown its cage of clay.

That Shamsuddin Ahmad Khan's face turned towards the Kabah persuaded even the doubters that the Navab died a martyr. A vibrant hum of lamentation rose and enveloped the entire city like clouds at the height of the rainy season. The hanged man's body was wrapped in black cloth and delivered to his father-in-law, Mirza Mughal Beg. Still apprehensive that some ugly situation could arise, Simon Fraser strongly suggested to Mirza Mughal Beg all possible haste in the burial.

The body, still draped in black, was placed in a wooden box, open at the top—symbolically enough, the box was and is still called a gahvarah, that is, a cradle—and was conveyed to the haveli in Daryaganj. Male and female relatives—Wazir not included—were already assembled there to mourn and prepare the body for burial. The body was ceremonially washed in Shamsuddin Ahmad Khan's bedchamber. Special pure white muslin was used for the shroud. Prayers were read, including the Quranic chapter called

Ya-Sin, incense was burnt and sandalwood fragrance sprinkled on the body.

The funeral procession started in early afternoon and the body was taken to the Noble Footprint. The funeral prayer was led by Shah Muhammad Ishaq, Delhi's most respected Sufi and Islamic scholar. Contemporary estimates put the attendance at eight thousand.

*

The Noble Footprint has no basis in history, actually. The people of Delhi believed it to be a true, sacred relic of the Prophet Muhammad. According to an account, written a few years before the events herein narrated, it was believed that the great Sufi, known as the Presence, the Served one, the World Wanderer, Hazrat Makhdum Jahanian Jahan Gasht, brought it to Delhi from Medina five hundred years ago. The story went as follows:

When Hazrat Makhdum desired to enter the tomb of the Holy Prophet, he was stopped by those who stood guard. They said that the door could be opened only for the true progeny of the Prophet. 'You should first prove that you are the Prophet's progeny.'

Hazrat Makhdum said, 'Let all the holy men, pious men, learned men, true fearers of God who are here, assemble before the tomb so that I may request for the door to be opened.'

So everyone assembled, and in his turn, each said in Arabic: 'Salutations and security be to You, O Prophet of God!'

No reply came for anyone. When it was the turn of Hazrat Makhdum, he also called out: 'Salutations and security be to You, O Prophet of God!'

Upon this, the answer came from the grave: 'Salutations and security be to thee, O best of my children!'

The lock unlocked itself, and the door opened of its own accord. Everyone present was speechless in wonderment at such eloquent proof of Hazrat Makhdum's high rank and the regard that the Prophet of God had for him. The Chief Keeper, some say Caliph, took him also to view the Auspicious Footprint of the Prophet. As commanded by the Prophet, Hazrat Makhdum obtained the Footprint from the Caliph, and clasping it to his breast, brought it to India.

At that time, Firoze Shah Khalji was Delhi's Sultan. He commanded that the Noble Footprint may be kept in the Firozabad Fort, and when the time came, it should be placed on his breast before he was buried.

Now it so happened that that good fortune was writ not for the Sultan, but for his grandson, Fath Khan, when the latter died after a short illness. Fath Khan had been brought up by the Sultan after the death of the boy's father. Out of love for the young man, the Sultan had the Noble Footprint placed on his breast, and even had some other holy relics placed in his grave.

The Sultan built a mosque on the site of Fath Khan's grave, established a madrasa there, and had a well dug upon the premises. He possessed a few cans of the water of the Zam Zam, the Holy Well at Mecca. All the cans were poured into that well to sanctify its water even more. Water was drawn every day from that well, ten maunds (about 800 pounds) of sugar candy would be mixed in it, and the sharbat distributed free, along with food, to the pilgrims. The Sultan endowed some land for the whole complex, calling it Zarih-e Khas (Special Sepulchre).

At the time of our story, the complex consisted of Fath Khan's grave wherein reposed the Noble Footprint, the well, a few ancient graves, and another tomb above which a tamarind tree spread its shade. Women prayed at this tomb, took the vow that if their prayer was answered favourably, a present would be made at the tomb of a special rice preparation and some glass bangles—the quantity of both was determined by the woman according to her capacity—and by way of token for the promise made, the woman hung one of her bangles on a branch of the tamarind tree. There was an ornamental pond in the courtyard of the complex, which went by the name of Qadam Sharif (Noble Footprint); the pond was always filled with a mixture of milk, sugar and water. Visitors drank the water as a source of benediction.

Whatever the historical truth, people everywhere believed the story to be true, and the Noble Footprint to be an authentic Relic of the Prophet. Men of high families or of great wealth aspired to be buried in the complex and took advance action to obtain a spot there for their burial. Thus, the Company officials did not like it one bit when the people of Delhi declared to their satisfaction that Shamsuddin Ahmad Khan had died a martyr, and should therefore be buried at the Noble Footprint. Also, the worry again raised its head that the Navab's tomb might become a sort of rallying point for civil disturbance. Judging the mood of the people, they decided to turn a blind eye.

A few years later, Emily Bayley, one of Metcalfe's daughters, wrote that the sanctity of Qadam Sharif was at that time compromised so much that murderers and scoundrels like Shamsuddin Ahmad were now being buried there.

The sanctity of Qadam Sharif may well have plummeted in Emily Bayley's estimation, but the Navab's tomb remained, for a very long time, a place of pilgrimage for large numbers of blessing seekers. The yearly Urs was held there regularly at the appointed time. Even on other days, visitors of all persuasions—from Hindu to Sunni Muslim to Shia Muslim to Nanak Panthi—regarded it their holy duty to visit and offer prayers for the martyred Navab's soul according to their faith.

BOOK 6

49

Disquieting rumours make Wazir Khanam's fear for the life of Navab Mirza; like a flood, from all sides, communications of Fate pour in

WAZIR KHANAM NEVER went to Shamsuddin Ahmad Khan's grave during the days of his annual Urs. On other days, she visited almost daily, after sunset. Accompanied by Habib-un Nisa or Rahat Afza, or both, she swept the grave and the small tomb that enclosed it, lit candles on the grave and sat in meditation for an hour or two. No one knew what was the subject, or object, of her meditation. Perhaps she wished somehow to regain some contact with her dead love. In her heart she often said a verse from the sixteenth-century woman Persian poet, Bicha Mahsiti, whose pen name was Mah (Moon):

The star of my fortune, which lighted the heavens
Look, oh moon, it now lies below the ground
By the action of my separation from you.

In order to make the similitude more perfect so as to accord with the name Shams (Sun), she altered the second line to read:

Look, oh sun, it now lies below the ground

Above all, a ghazal from her old favourite Hafiz Shirazi often came to her lips. What she could not say in her own words, the words of the Lisanul Ghaib (Tongue of the Unseen), as Hafiz was often called, said for her with thousandfold eloquence:

I did not taste even a little of the sweet taste
of his ruby lips

And he went away.
I did not look enough at his moon-like face
And he went away.
It was as if he was tired and bored with my company,
He packed his bags; I could not catch even the dust of his feet
And he went away.
They cheated me; they said, he will pass by me.
So did you see? I was fooled
And he went away.
He walked, proud and swaying this way and that
In the garden of beauty, and elegance and grace,
I did not get to walk in the garden of union with him
And he went away.
Like Hafiz, all nightlong I wept and lamented:
Woe, oh woe is me! I could not attain union with him
And he went away.

Aside from visiting the tomb of her Navab, she did not go out anywhere; she did not visit even Manjhli. Bari Begam, and then her father, came and spoke words of condolence. The memory of those words was as dear to her as the memory of Shamsuddin Ahmad. She got even greater consolation by the fact that both her eldest sister and her father lost their heart to Navab Mirza, his childlike playfulness, his little pranks and mischiefs. This did not induce them to visit frequently, but Muhammad Yusuf often sent small presents for him; sometimes he had him taken to his house for a day-long stay, returning him to his mother with an unwilling heart and the promise that he would soon be having him over again for the day.

At the time of her leaving after the condolence visit, Bari Begam hugged Chhoti Begam; her eyes dimmed with tears when she said that her heart wept tears of blood to see her youth and her home laid waste. 'How I wish I could do something for you,' she said as the tears swept over her face. Seeing that Chhoti preferred to remain silent, Bari Begam chose to draw apart with apparent unconcern, as she had done in the past. Manjhli, on the other hand, maintained the earlier relations; in fact, she intensified her links with Wazir. Navab Mirza was another factor in the stronger bonding. She loved the boy like her own son, and being childless herself, she could freely lavish her motherly instincts upon him.

Financially, Wazir Khanam was not as strong as before, but was not poor either. Indeed, she could be described as being better off than the other women who had been in Shamsuddin Ahmad's life.

After the Navab's death, the Firangee lost no time in taking possession of the Fort at Firozepur. Afzal-un Nisa and Husaini Begam were obliged to leave without even completing the statutory period prescribed for widows to remain confined to the home immediately after the death of their husband. Further, the Firangee claimed many hundreds of thousands of rupees' worth of dues outstanding against Shamsuddin Ahmad. They promptly auctioned the Daryaganj haveli, its extensive and myriad appurtenances—even curtains, bedsheets, kitchen utensils—for a fraction of their value. In spite of this, the Sahibs of Exalted Glory claimed that the debt was not yet fully paid.

In order to 'compensate' for the dues still remaining unadjusted, the Company started proceedings to confiscate the papers pledging the interest on the loan of a quarter of a million rupees to Afzal-un Nisa Begam in perpetuity. The Company also made efforts to seize Wazir's house and eject her from there. Since she possessed perfect and complete papers proving her ownership, that enterprise did not succeed. But the Company had issued unilateral orders of confiscation anyway, so Wazir had to move the court, and bribe the policemen and other civilian functionaries before the danger could finally be averted. Afzal-un Nisa Begam also moved the courts. The suit was decided ultimately in her favour, but not before many years had passed. During this period, she was forced to stay with her father, almost like a poor relation.

Husaini Begam became, at the insistent urging of Jahangirah Begam, her permanent house guest in Akbarabad. Several years of widowhood and frugal, dependent living did not affect her beauty or her pride. She was finally persuaded to remarry. And with her remarriage, she disappeared from the pages of history into respectable obscurity.

Champa and Rahmat-un Nisa came to live with Wazir Khanam, as directed by the Navab. Wazir did not permit Champa to eat or live at her own expense: she treated her as a minor member of her household. She organized, with Champa's consent, her marriage to Muhammad Ali, a widower who was the son of an old and respected personal servant of the Navab of Jhajjhar. Champa thus found a safe home for herself and her daughter. One does not know how severely she felt the shock of her great fall and her being torn asunder from her roots.

Afzal-un Nisa Begam filed a suit against the Company. She asserted that Shamsuddin Ahmad Khan had paid for his crime as he deserved, but his two little daughters Shams-un Nisa and Ahmad-un Nisa were innocent and should therefore inherit the State as their father's legitimate and sinless children. Mr Thomas Metcalfe, the Sahib Commissioner Bahadur, dismissed the suit summarily without permitting anyone to lead evidence or present arguments.

Now another rumour started to fly everywhere in the city: Higher officers and decision-makers in the Company have resolved to make sure that none was left alive from the offspring of Shamsuddin Ahmad who might one day claim to succeed to his State or sue the Company for adequate compensation for the Navab's surcease. It was further rumoured that although Navab Mirza was not a legitimate child of Shamsuddin Ahmad Khan and, therefore, could have no claim on his father's estates according to Islamic law, among the Firangees, the law provided for the succession of a male child even if he was born to a mistress of the decedent, if there was no other legitimate successor. Under the English law, the offspring from a mistress was described as 'natural son', and his mother as 'common law wife'.

The secret resolve of the Company Bahadur, therefore, the rumours went, was to have Navab Mirza poisoned somehow; in the event of such a plan not meeting with quick success, a professional child kidnapper would be hired to take the child away to some remote native State where he would be entrusted to a loyal servant who would bring him up as his own son.

Clearly, these rumours had no basis in fact. Wazir did not know this, but she did know Delhi and its expertise in manufacturing rumours. Still, she persuaded herself of the truth of the rumour that the Firangee was seriously planning the murder or kidnapping of her son. She was half dead with worry, cogitating all the time to find some place totally secure where she could take Navab Mirza.

She was still trying to resolve the question of Navab Mirza's security and safety from what she thought was certain death or kidnapping when a letter arrived from Jaipur. Written in Persian and signed by the Tyndales, the letter informed her that the name of Wazir Khanam, also known as Chhoti Begam, had become notorious as the concubine of a criminal convicted of murder. Under the circumstances, they did not like that the names of the biological offspring of a noble and high-ranking Englishman might be linked with that of a fallen woman like Chhoti Begam. The two children were, as from the date of writing, formally received in the Protestant Church. From now on, they will not have permission to have anything to do with Chhoti Begam. For the present, they will be nurtured in the Faith of our Lord, Jesus Christ, and will be brought up exclusively in the Firangee way. When the time comes, they will marry by their own choice, but with our permission. They are, in any case, now fully persuaded that the English sahibs are superior to the Indians by numerous degrees. Lastly, since all links between Chhoti Begam and the two children are fully and finally severed, Chhoti Begam need not continue to send money for their upkeep.

Wazir was thunderstruck. For a long time, she sat, stunned and shocked, in almost a catatonic trance, anger, pain and protest boiling in her but not finding expression. Fortunately, her inner dam burst suddenly and she wept and wailed aloud. Did God write all sorrows and all disappointments in the book of my life, she cried, and wept and wailed again. Habib-un Nisa and Rahat Afza did their best to minister to her and console her. After some hours, when she felt somewhat better, Wazir had a strong urge to immediately go to Jaipur and file a suit against the Tyndales and follow it up with a visit to their home, to quarrel with them, to try to make them see reason, take back her children, the pieces of her heart, from them by force if necessary.

Within minutes, as she cooled down a bit, she realized that none of it was possible or even feasible. She saw the Tyndales sitting secure behind the law, and behind their own power as the ruling class. She remembered that soon after Mattan Blak sahib's passing, when she talked the whole matter over with the Tyndales—Allah, it feels as if a whole age has passed over her since then—they had made it clear to her that their legal position was impregnable: Chhoti Begam had no status in the eyes of the Honourable Company's law. They told her that she was not going to get anything by suing them. She thought bitterly: Yes, why should this not be so? Above all, it is the Firangee who rules her, the might of the military is his, the policemen are his; it is he who makes the laws and it is he who benefits by them. Everything is his, I am alone, pitted against him who wields a mighty force. I am not going to achieve anything. She could see that she did not have the capability to untie the knot of the whirlpool and break out of it.

Still, she was not going to give up without a struggle. The next day, when she found that she was somewhat in control of herself, she requested Mirza

Isfandiar Beg to come for consultation. Mirza Isfandiar, smarting under his experience of the bitter defeat in Shamsuddin Ahmad Khan's case, and feeling ashamed and somehow responsible for it, came readily, but he did not have the heart to discourage Wazir in clear words. He had observed at first-hand in Calcutta the power and the awful might of the Company's rule. He knew that the Firangee did not wish to exceed the limit of the law by one inch even, but the law was in any case weighed in his favour. He also saw that the Firangee felt no remorse, no compunction at administering the law, particularly if it suited him. He also saw that heartless and full of malice was the Firangee's rule when he dealt with the native.

He knew well that Wazir had no case anyway. He saw no wisdom in hurling one's head against a wall that was not going to collapse even if it was breached. He therefore advised Wazir to bide her time and wait for things to get better, or to see if the Tyndales attempted to carry off the two children to The Country.

The rumours, although totally without foundation, of the schemes of the English about Navab Mirza, continued to endlessly oppress and agitate Wazir. Now that Isfandiar Beg's advice extinguished her already feeble hope of recovering, or at least regaining some contact with her firstborn daughter and son, Wazir decided to do whatever it took to keep Navab Mirza from falling into the clutches of the Company's functionaries. After many days of cogitation and furiously ransacking her brain, she decided, most unwillingly and with a feeling of betrayal and defeat, that the only way to secure Navab Mirza's life and future development was to entrust him to the protection and care of Manjhli Begam and her Navab, Yusuf Ali Khan.

Her decision made, she did not delay its implementation for fear that she might change her mind. When the proposal was placed before the Navab through Manjhli Begam, he jumped at it, as if he had been hoping and waiting for such a proposal. The details were worked out over the next few days, in the most cordial of atmospheres.

It was decided that Habib-un Nisa should accompany Navab Mirza as his chief caregiver and attendant. Navab Mirza would be brought up and educated in the manner befitting the children of noblemen and families of distinction. His position would clearly be of a nephew of Umdah Khanam as the son of her sister, Wazir Khanam. He would not be made the adoptive son of either Navab Yusuf Ali Khan or Umdah Khanam. He would always be known as the son of the martyred Navab Shamsuddin Ahmad Khan and Wazir Khanam. And the latter would have full access to Navab Mirza at all times.

These decisions were taken and implemented in the month of February 1836. Keeping her tears in check, Wazir hugged her son, prayed for his security and welfare, and had a number of protective amulets tied to his right arm. After being hugged a number of more times by everyone in the house, the young gentleman was taken downstairs one night and put in Navab Yusuf Ali Khan's well-guarded rath, sent specially for the purpose of taking him to the Navab's house. All the items of his wardrobe, his toys, his Persian primer, his wooden slate and his counting beads were packed most lovingly in boxes. Rahat Afza put oil in the boy's head and kohl in his eyes. Wazir put a black spot in a corner of his left temple as a protection against the evil or jealous eye.

The little boy's age was just short of five years, but he had been separated from his father for a long enough time. During that entire period, the child never missed or called upon his father, as children do when they suffer some injury, or feel unwell, or are bullied by stronger or older playmates.

The reason for this was that during the initial weeks of Shamsuddin Ahmad Khan's absence, everybody pretended in the presence of Navab Mirza that his father was touring his State or camping in Firozepur. Sometimes Habiba told him: Your father was here last night; he came when you were in bed, and left very early when you were asleep. We didn't want to disturb your sleep and wake you up. Sometimes she gave him some small present—a toy or a songbird or a box of sweets—and told him that his father had left it for him as a present.

Obviously, such subterfuges could not be continued over a long period of time. Once, when on the occasion of some feast or festival, Navab Mirza sulked and wept obstinately to be taken to his father, Rahat Afza made up a new story: Bacche Mian, your father is not well. He's being treated by a very important Hakim sahib. In fact, he was wounded in a battle and is under treatment at the Hakim sahib's hospital outside the city.

'So why does he not come back? When does he sleep? And where does he sleep?'

Rahat Afza turned away, dried her tears surreptitiously with her wrap, and said, 'Bacche Mian, there's nothing at all that your dear father can lack.

He is quite comfortable there. If you don't believe me, ask your auntie or your Amma Jan.'

From then on, if someone was thoughtless enough to ask Navab Mirza about his father, he readily answered gravely, and with a trace of some unspecific hope, in his prattling speech, 'He sleeps in Qammam Sharif. Hakim Zi gives him medicines there to drink.'

It did not occur to the questioner to ask how the little one was so certain about his father being at Qadam Sharif. No one in the house had heard him mention Qadam Sharif, so no one realized that the child had some intuition about his father.

Several weeks after the conversation between Rahat Afza and Navab Mirza, when it had been many months since Shamsuddin Ahmad Khan's tree of life was struck by the lightning of death, and he had been sleeping the sleep of eternity under a maulsari tree for quite a length of time, Wazir thought of going one night to the grave to embrace it and put her head on it in memory of that night of July 1834, a night that was full of the secrets of love and full of its own intoxications when she and the comfort of her soul were in each other's embrace for the first time. Quite unusually, Navab Mirza importuned her with unwonted recalcitrance: late hour or not, he would accompany his Amma Jan where she was going. Wazir was obliged to give way and they, accompanied by Habiba, rode a closed palanquin to Qadam Sharif.

They had scarcely alighted when suddenly, Navab Mirza said, 'Amma Jan, where is the Hakim Zi who attends my father?'

Wazir was stunned. What could be the occasion for the child to ask for his father's attending physician? She then realized that Navab Mirza, through occasional mention of Qadam Sharif by her and others in the house, had been unconsciously absorbing the knowledge of Qadam Sharif as the place where his father was to be found. He already knew from Rahat Afza and others that his father was unwell. He thus put two and two together with his artless logic.

She checked her sob and said with apparent conviction, 'Both of them are right here, my dear little child, underneath this grave. There is a fine room there where your father rests.'

'I will also go . . . go there now, Amma Jan!' The tone of obstinacy was back in his voice.

Wazir was flustered; diverting her son's mind from the issue was a tough task, but her Indo-Muslim mind was quick to read bad auguries in the child's desire to join his father. She knew that bad things, when spoken aloud, even if innocently or in jest, have a tendency to come true.

'Hush! Don't say such things, darling. Allah Mian will be annoyed with you. Hakim sahib will send your father back home when he gets well.'

She could not know the extent to which she had been able to persuade the child of the truth of her words, nor to what extent the child's imagination drew a picture in his mind and before his eyes about the reality of his father. Navab Mirza, for years afterwards, used to say that his father was staying with a hakim in Qadam Sharif. Very gradually, this belief—or hope—faded from his heart. When he was grown up, quite unconsciously he put the image of Mirza Fathul Mulk Bahadur in the niche of his heart previously occupied by his father. Yet, in many difficult situations and moments in his later life, his mind conjured up without it willing to do so, the image of a handsome, grave, upright, commanding presence, about whom he felt sure that it was the Hakim sahib of Qadam Sharif, come to give him news of his father.

*

It was now someday in February 1836, and the son happily left his mother's side, in glad anticipation of being coddled and pampered even more than he was in the Khanam ka Bazaar house. As evening fell, Wazir felt feverish and was soon laid up with delirious fever. She would call Rahat Afza to her side and demand that she go at once to Tiraha Bairam Khan and snatch her child back from his aunt and uncle. Sometimes she cried out for Amir Mirza or Badshah Begam to come look after her or at least clasp her in their embrace. Yet she never let herself bring the name of Marston Blake or Shamsuddin Ahmad Khan to her lips.

Throughout her illness, when they often despaired for her life, she was tended to by Rahat Afza and Vanisi. Manjhli, alone or along with Yusuf Ali Khan, visited every alternate day. Both of them held her hand, caressed her forehead, spoke words of comfort to her. But it was enteric fever; it had to run its relentless, destructive course. On the thirteenth day, tiny raised dots and a rash of redness appeared on Wazir's chest and abdomen—hence moti jhara ('rain of pearls'), the Hindi name of the fever—lowering her temperature by two or three degrees, but she was weakened even more.

For a long time, both eastern and western systems of medicine were agreed on the point that fevers—especially enteric fevers—should be starved. In the Graeco-Islamic system, the patient was given just medicinal juices. Through the duration of the pyrexia, Wazir was fed, for instance, the juice of sweet fennel and the diluted juice of ginger, and a week or ten days after the commencement of the fever, the sweetened juice of pomegranate.

Finally, the fever left Wazir on the morning of the twenty-second day. She was kept on a weak, liquid diet for another ten days before graduating to soft food. Her illness and full recovery took the best part of two months. This, and her little boy's going away, her still pinching anxiety about his safety, the change in her state: all of it made her irritable and melancholy, and she could see no way out of the wasting sickness of her spirit and her life.

By the time it was December 1835, the English were finally convinced that there was no chance of disturbance of the peace or violent demonstrations to protest Shamsuddin Ahmad Khan's hanging. The spies' reported consistently that the people still remembered him with sorrow, but they were also reconciled to the machinations of Fate and the Almighty's Will.

The feeling generally persisted that Shamsuddin Ahmad Khan might or might not have been involved in Fraser's murder, but it was just his ill luck that many vital clues were uncovered pointing towards his guilt. As for Aniya, his conduct was clearly wicked and traitorous. It was also often said that the shot was not fired by the hand of Shamsuddin Ahmad Khan; so how could he be considered guilty and deserving of the maximum penalty? In faraway Allahabad, Fanny Parkes wrote in her diary that in that city, the general feeling was that even if the hanging of Karim Khan could be justified, there was no cause to punish the master for the crime of the servant.

Anyway, with the English mind now set at rest, Metcalfe consulted his informal committee about the burial and erection of a tomb on Fraser's grave. It was determined that while it had been proper for him to be buried quietly in an unmarked grave at that time, it was now time for a funeral procession to be taken out with the same pomp and show of power and authority which was his when he was alive. A suitable tomb must be built on his grave. James Skinner proposed that the body be exhumed and reinterred at a suitable spot in the yard of his church, St James', in Kashmiri Gate. He also offered to finance the construction of a suitable mausoleum over the grave. Both the proposals were gratefully accepted.

James Skinner did not stint on money. He constructed an octagonal tomb in marble, clearly Firangee in style, but also an attempt to replicate the Mughal practice of enhancing the beauty of the marble with floral inlay work in many colours. Recalling the ancient Greeks, the building was established on eight Doric columns in marble, but the platform on which the structure stood, which also functioned as its plinth, was in plain red sandstone. In order to provide greater support to the roof, the columns flared at the top, with a plain marble cornice providing a further platform to the roof. The marble just below had a band of inlaid black marble. The most prominent feature of the building was its high, heavy and rounded spire which topped a large, low dome. Both the spire and the dome were of marble; they were carved in a vaguely Hindu style, somewhat like a lotus flower. The overall effect was of a massive crown.

Skinner had the following text inscribed on the gravestone:

THE REMAINS
INTERRED BENEATH THIS MONUMENT
WERE ONCE ANIMATED
BY AS BRAVE AND SINCERE
A SOUL
AS WAS EVER VOUCHSAFED TO A MAN
BY HIS
CREATOR.
A BROTHER IN FRIENDSHIP
HAS CAUSED IT TO BE ERECTED
THAT WHEN HIS OWN FRAME IS DUST
IT MAY REMAIN
AS A
MEMORIAL
FOR THOSE WHO CAN PARTICIPATE IN LAMENTING
THE SUDDEN AND MELANCHOLY LOSS
OF ONE
DEAR TO HIM AS LIFE
WILLIAM FRASER
DIED 22ND MARCH 1835

There is no doubt that the words were most dignified, heart affecting, and appropriately immersed in grief. At the same time, the words ensured that no doubt could ever arise in the visitor's mind about the probity of Fraser's character and about his universal popularity as a man of impeccable—almost ideal—character. No hint was given of his murder. Skinner did not put his name anywhere, but by implication described that he was like Fraser's brother because he was an extremely close friend. It was also implied that while he would surely mourn for his friend all his life, there would be other mourners too after him, and the building was in fact a memorial for future generations.

The author of the text made sure to emphasize grief; and more than grief, the text emphasized the racial pride of the English; above all, it was an indirect paean to the glory of English power: a power that was most certainly destined to be everlasting. But History did not hide its secret lessons and future meanings for too long. Even a quarter century did not pass before rebellious fighters shed their blood like water to defend against the Company's forces each and every brick and stone of the Kashmiri Gate area. Fraser's tomb also became a victim of the street-to-street fighting: St James' Church and Fraser's epitaph remained standing, but the symbolic crown that was the domed structure above Fraser's tomb was razed to the ground.

50

A pen name is found for Navab Mirza, the budding poet, from the Divan of Khvajah Mir Dard sahib

VERY SLOWLY, WAZIR'S grief abated. Correspondingly, her visits to Qadam Sharif became fewer. Now her routine was limited to visiting a day before the Urs: she would weep a few tears, give alms in the name of the Navab, and return home before sunset. The burden of Navab Mirza's upbringing and upkeep was no longer hers, but still, she did not have enough means to live comfortably. One required costly jewellery, expensive clothes, at least one carriage and quite a few servants for living like a well-born lady. Despite the reduction of all supernumerary expenditure, her permanent income could not suffice for these things. She began to sell quietly—and especially not letting Manjhli know about it—some of her more fancy jewellery and clothes which had heavy gold or silver work on them.

Her expeditions out of her home were more infrequent than before: now she visited even Manjhli only once in six or eight weeks, or on festival days, and that too for a short while. Thanks to Manjhli's visiting much oftener, she wasn't starved of the sight of Navab Mirza. There was no other core to her existence aside from her love for the boy. She taught herself, not without anguish, that the thread that held her life together was the grief for Shamsuddin Ahmad. Were she able to concentrate that grief in her heart, she should manage to live the rest of her days, not with equanimity, but with strength of mind, supported by a heart which was well acquainted with sorrow, and a sense of universal loss on the human earth.

She told herself firmly: I am not going anywhere now; I am not going to do a thing but love Navab Mirza and cherish those who are closest to me. Lying curled up in her semi-darkened bedroom, she would often think of a verse from the seventeenth-century Persian poet Saidi of Tehran, and hoped to make her life a living commentary on it. The poet said:

Without love, the pieces of a broken heart
Become scattered;
His love worked as the thread that bound together
The pages of my story of sorrow.

She did not know that the functionaries of the Court of Fate and Decision had perhaps drawn the map of her fortune with a pencil (qalam-e surma), and that its lines could easily be rearranged, erased or drawn anew.

*

Ahmad Ali Khan, Navab of Rampur, died on 20 July 1840. His surviving offspring was a daughter, Shamsa Khatun. The Rohillas did not like to be ruled by a woman. The impasse was resolved quickly by the Governor General who invited Navab Muhammad Said Khan, the son of a previous Navab, to take over the State. Muhammad Said Khan was at that moment working as Deputy Collector in Pilibhit, a nearby district in Avadh. He agreed readily and was installed as Navab of Rampur on 26 August 1840. He immediately summoned his only son Navab Yusuf Ali Khan to Rampur and appointed him heir apparent. He also renamed Rampur as Mustafabad, but the new name never caught on.

Thus began the end of Navab Yusuf Ali Khan's life as a nobleman at large in Delhi, and the beginning of his star's ascendance in the firmament of power, influence and wealth. For Wazir, the immediate repercussion was the departure of Umdah Khan, and therefore Navab Mirza, to Rampur. Umdah Khanam promised to be a visitor to Shahjahanabad as frequently as possible, with Navab Mirza in tow.

Things were rather different in the small and busy city of Rampur. Yusuf Ali Khan quickly became involved in the affairs of the State. Because Rampur was much smaller than Delhi, the ruler and his chief men could be easily viewed by the subject populace and their presence noted; their absence was noticed as easily. As for Navab Mirza, who was very nearly ten years old now, he needed to be educated formally and intensively if he was to grow up in the tradition of the Indo-Muslim elite. He was therefore placed under the charge of Maulavi Ghiasuddin Izzat Rampuri, polyglot, expert in all traditional subjects, both religious and secular, lexicographer and poet. Navab Yusuf Ali Khan's only son, Navab Kalb-e Ali Khan, was also placed with the same Maulavi Ghiasuddin Rampuri; they thus became playmates and classmates. Navab Yusuf Ali Khan was busy with matters of the State, Umdah Khanam with routine and ceremonial matters inside their sprawling haveli, and Navab Mirza with his education: none had the time or opportunity to frequently undertake the short but somewhat hazardous journey to Delhi.

Another result of Navab Yusuf Ali Khan's departure for Rampur was that the new bridge of love and affection between Muhammad Yusuf and his daughter Chhoti Begam—Navab Mirza—was ripped off its foundation. This might have hastened his end. He had always had a weakness for spicy foods. Living alone, and without his wife to monitor and regulate his diet, he became nearly addicted to the foods against which his physician repeatedly warned him. His liver was weak (overheated, as in the parlance of the Graeco-Islamic system of medicine) and his stomach's linings were all corroded by the acidic and acidity-promoting foods that he was never able to resist. He liked all kinds of deep-fried foods, sour foods, savouries and sheep's flesh cooked in plenty of mustard oil or ghee.

At the time that we are writing about, Shah Alam's edict against the slaughter of 'horned animals' (read 'cows') was still honoured in Delhi, at least in public. Mutton—that is, the flesh of sheep and goat—was plentiful. Goat was the preferred meat. Sheep was not favoured by the rich and those of 'delicate' temperament, because it was regarded as tasteless, smelly, acidic, fibrous, and 'hot and wet'. Quite by chance, during those days, there was an exchange of poems between Mirza Ghalib and Mirza Alauddin Ahmad Khan, oldest son of Aminuddin Ahmad Khan, the current ruler of Loharu, about meats and vegetables, and mangoes. Ghalib wrote:

The rainy season is here, bringing the joy
Of drinking fine wine and eating mangoes.
Am I blind, that in the beginning of the season
I should leave Delhi and go to Loharu?
There is nothing there but grain, though it sustains life:
No grapes, nor mangoes to be found there.
The cooks were commanded: go and ask, what is cooking for tomorrow?
Where could they find tamarind blossoms?

And the bitterest of bitter gourds?
There's nothing in Loharu, but the fibrous meat
Of the lamb; say, what pleasure could it bring me?

Mirza Alauddin Ahmad Khan, who was a poet himself, wrote in reply the following poem in the same metre and form:

How nice it would be for the Presence
To quit Delhi and come to Loharu at the beginning of the season!
Green Saraoli mangoes, and grapes, arrive here
By the post-carriage every evening.
Let him command the cooks: Hey, you fellows!
Cook everything most quickly.
Pluck from the orchard the tamarind blossoms, and
Get the bitterest of bitter gourds from the jungle.
And the soft, fresh, fibreless flesh of the goat:
Oh! How much we should enjoy eating it!

Muhammad Yusuf knew that his weak stomach could ill digest the hard, fibrous flesh of lamb. This and his love of fried and sour foods eroded his liver, causing loss of appetite, excess of the wind and frequent vomiting. His weight diminished to about a hundred pounds; he had dark circles around his sunken eyes, showing lack of iron and other elements which enhance the quality and quantity of blood in the body. So long as he was in touch with Wazir Khanam through Navab Mirza, his dietary habits were much monitored by Wazir. Now he was back to his childish ways.

It was the last day of November 1840, when Muhammad Yusuf suddenly vomited a copious quantity of blood. He knew that his time in the world was over. He managed to clean and wash himself, put on fresh clothes, and offer a small prayer for his soul and for his children. He remained on the prayer mat, reading the Quran. But before he started reading the Quran, he sent one of the street urchins to Bari Begam's house, asking her to come at once and organize his last rites. Bari Begam came quickly, but not before stopping a minute by Chhoti's house and giving her the bad news. She went on to her father's house and found him on the prayer mat, head bent, and the Quran barely held in his hands, doing his best to protect the sacred pages from the blood that he spat continuously.

Just as Bari came in, Hakim Ghulam Najaf Khan arrived; he felt the patient's pulse and found it extremely weak, almost non-existent: dudi ('crawling like a worm') in the lexicon of the hakims. He hung his head in sympathy and honour of the dying soul, and told Bari, 'Nothing can be done now, I am sorry. Lay him down facing the Kabah, read the chapter of Ya-Sin from the Holy Quran, and make the arrangements for his last rites.'

Wazir met him in the hall as he was going out. She cried tearfully, 'How is my father? Please, Hakim sahib, please save him for God's sake!'

'Bibi, everything is in Allah's hands now. We are helpless here.'

Chhoti Begam ran into the house, weeping and stumbling, trembling with fear and sorrow. She approached her father's bed. Bari Begam was gently rubbing one of his hands. Her face wet with tears, she had the same copy of the Quran before him from which Muhammad Yusuf had been reading. Bari Begam's husband was reciting the chapter of Ya-Sin. Muhammad Yusuf's eyes were open, but they seemed sightless, turned inwards. Chhoti Begam somehow imagined that a small ray of dying light could still be dimly descried in them. She ran to put her head on Muhammad Yusuf's feet and sobbed, 'Abba ji, please just look at me for a moment and say that you forgive me.'

The dying man's other hand quivered, as if he was trying to raise it in solace and benediction. Wazir almost snatched his hand into hers. Bari said, 'Say the Affirmation of Faith and Witness to Faith. Chhoti, say it now. Don't weep.'

The words had barely left her lips when Muhammad Yusuf gave a loud hiccup, and a spray of blood spewed from his mouth. The girls extended their hands to stop the spray, but it was no longer possible to stop Muhammad Yusuf's caravan of life from journeying into the Unknown.

When Manjhli heard about the event of her father, she came as quickly as possible, and let herself weeping and keening into the house, which she had quit an age ago. She could not be present at the pre-burial viewing of her father's body, but the event bound the sisters in the bond of love and sisterly companionship once more. Forgetting the reservations and mutual unhappinesses and a lifetime's estrangements, they became as they were before, in intuitive knowledge of what the other wished to do or say.

After the fortieth-day rites and prayers and distribution of food to the poor, they sat down to talk about the disposition of what was left of their ancestral home. Anwari Khanam, being the eldest, opened the discussion and immediately proposed that the two older sisters surrender their claims in favour of Chhoti: Everything, the house and what was in it, should pass to Chhoti. Umdah Khanam agreed at once, but Chhoti did not agree at all. She declared that she appreciated the suggestion, and was grateful, for it was made with nothing but love in the older ones' hearts. But they also perhaps acted thus, in some measure, because of her having been left alone in the world.

She firmly suggested that all their father's effects, including the house, be sold and the proceeds given away to the Rahimia Madrasa in Fatehpuri as perpetual charity for use of that school. Everybody fell in with the suggestion which was then carried out quickly through the good offices of Maulavi Nazir Ahmad, Bari Begam's husband.

About a couple of weeks later, the sisters were able to resume their wonted lives: Anwari with her husband and small girl in Phatak Habash Khan, Umdah in her haveli in Rampur, Wazir Khanam in her house in Chandni Chowk.

*

One whole year rolled by quietly. Navab Mirza had already been quite well up in Persian while he was in Delhi. In Arabic, he was well past the first few books of elementary grammar and syntax. He was no sluggard in other disciplines: Mathematics, Logic, Prosody, Rhetoric and Poetics. Above all, he had a good ear for words and a good taste for language. In Rampur, his progress was satisfactory in all subjects. Often, he missed his mother's presence, sometimes with a poignant nostalgia, but he had now begun to enjoy conversations with his peers and elders even. He began to feel grown up, and to be conscious of the fact that his real world consisted of his mother, himself and a few other women. He also appreciated that his aunt loved him dearly; she would go along with him to Delhi to visit with his mother whenever feasible. His fretting about lack of frequent visits to Delhi was not something that his aunt was likely to appreciate.

It was May 1842 now. Navab Mirza was just short of eleven, but according to the Islamic lunar calendar, he was now eleven and a quarter years old. He had begun to sprout very fine down on his upper lip, though it was barely discernible against its dark background. Umdah Khanam drew up plans for large-scale celebrations to welcome the down and to pray for the longevity and prosperity of the boy who was just about to start his journey into adulthood. Wazir firmly blocked all proposals for an open celebration: she still wasn't sure of the English, and also feared Time's—or Time's Children's—evil eye.

Umdah Khanam was persistent, though she curtailed her plans drastically to allay Wazir's misgivings: let there be no nautch girls presenting dances; let there be no professional women singers to sing songs suitable to the occasion, that is, a boy's expected entry into adulthood; let there be no prayers by the mullahs; let there be no feasting even. But there must be the traditional ceremony: cooking of special foods which would then be placed in medium-sized earthen pots especially favoured for the occasion, followed by family prayers and distribution of food.

After a prolonged exchange of letters on the subject, Wazir agreed to the ceremony being conducted on an even more reduced scale. She arrived in Rampur in the last week of July 1842 and was housed in a medium-sized residence near the haveli of Navab Yusuf Ali Khan. Umdah Khanam had the house specially furnished and provided with all necessary creature comforts. Within an hour of her arrival, Navab Mirza also came to stay for the duration his mother was to be there.

Wazir looked at Navab Mirza's tall form from head to toe, hugged him, and made the symbolic gesture of taking away his troubles on her own self. She spoke, her eyes pricking with tears, 'Allah, Navab Mirza, may God preserve you! You have so quickly grown into a fine young man!'

Before Navab Mirza could say something in reply, Rahat Afza interjected, 'Yes! Yes! And let all evil things be far from him, he is quite like the Senior Navab sahib. His colour is just a shade darker, but his face . . . it seems that the Senior Navab sahib. . .' She broke off, in confusion, realizing her crassitude and youthful gush.

She looked at Wazir Khanam and said to herself, 'How I wish my tongue were cut off before I opened my mouth!' Colours of pain, sorrow, anguish and anger were passing on Wazir's face with rapidity. Her jaw clenched, her head drooping, it seemed that she was just about to burst into tears and was using all her strength of body and will to keep her throat closed. In earlier days, it was not difficult for Navab Mirza in such a situation to put both his arms around his mother's neck, and sway and swing a little, nuzzle into her neck or chest, purring like a favourite cat, and take away her unhappiness in an instant. But now he found himself under some unexplainable restraint, restriction even. It was not just the distance created by their living in two different and distant places for a year or more. Navab Mirza was now a tall, strapping boy, almost a man by the standards of the times. His mother had always been slender like a sylph and hardly looked the mother of three children. Now that she had had nothing to do with a man for half a dozen years or more, her youthful and delicate person looked almost virginal. She was now thirty-one years old, but the way she moved, the way her clothes sat on her, the way she seemed inexpert in keeping her dupatta in place, all this seemed to give off the subtle fragrance of early youth. This was especially true of her voice, which had not lost its bell-like clarity and the mild resonance of bangles and ankle bells.

Navab Mirza moved forward impulsively, wishing to put his head in his mother's lap, take her face in his hands, make kissing and cheeping sounds as if it was she who was the child and it was he who was the mother—just as things had once been between them. But he knew intuitively that many things were now different, many new experiences and feelings obstructed; a replay of old scenes was not possible.

For one thing, Navab Mirza had never seen his mother lamenting for his father openly and with tears. More important, now the image of Shamsuddin Ahmad Khan in his heart carried a sadness as before, but it also seemed to be dissolving momently in some kind of past which was like a mist in its own self. The fragrance and the warmth of that image was still redolent in his inner being, but now it was more like a dream one had in childhood, remembered but not quite remembered in later years. It now seemed to him that it was not Shamsuddin Ahmad so much as his mother from whom radiated the constituent particles of his inner being. Similarly, he was sure that his outer being, expressing itself in his attractive person, in the delineation and coloration of his social and creative abilities in the form of his refined and eloquent power of speech, his ability to quickly compose poems, the attraction in his heart for beautiful and stylish things: all this, and much more, came to him from Wazir Khanam alone. He believed that in beauty, in sophistication, in poise, he was less than what was contained in her littlest finger even, but he was at least a tiny emanation of her.

He was not acquainted with anyone at all from his father's House. Truth to tell, there was none in that House who could give him some perspective. No uncle, no cousin, against whom he could imagine his father in terms of lovability, popularity, personal temper and manner of living; these parameters did not exist for him. He did have one aunt alive: Jahangirah Begam. But she was a mere woman, married off well before he could be sensible of relatives and perspectives. Navab Begam he never saw; Jahangirah Begam did come a few times as a visitor and as a relative living in some faraway place. In his mind, Jahangirah Begam's image was one of the several agreeable images of persons existing away from the centre of his existence, persons not relevant really.

By the time he passed his tenth year, he had gathered some basic facts about babies, how they were made, how they came into the world. Many friends, who were close to him, were also the source of such information. By the time he was nearly eleven, he himself could experience in his body and his inward being, changes that were mysterious and pleasurable. Now he could appreciate, with greater clarity, the changing colours of his body and its humours, his imaginings and the new way in which he now looked at the world.

Up until the age of seven or eight, Navab Mirza not only believed that he was fatherless: he was fully certain that he was his mother's child, with no contribution from his father. Now when he learnt about the close resemblance between him and his father in personal appearance and even the way he moved and behaved, and found his mother in such anguish when the resemblance was openly mentioned, he found himself at a loss to understand what he should do to mitigate his mother's pain.

Having been born on the 25th of May 1831, Navab Mirza was a few weeks past eleven years according to the English calculation. But he looked at least fourteen, if not actually fifteen. Tall, slightly shy of his tall mother, with strong muscular arms and broad wrists. He was black of complexion, with a soft and handsome face. His large, deep-brown-black eyes were a replica of his mother's, but his long, thin and slightly crooked Turkic nose and high brow came from his father. A tiny flare of the nostrils indicated strength of will and perhaps a short fuse, though it had never been in evidence so far.

He wore a fine muslin tunic in sky blue, over which he had a smart cloak of phulam, a stylish flowery fabric in cotton with a bit of silk mixed in it. His upper short coat was again in cotton, very light blue with darker blue stripes, its sleeves cut away from above in the high fashion of the day. His trousers were wide bottomed in the Delhi fashion, made of the silk and cotton fabric mashru, in pale pink. Instead of a hard and tall black velvet cap in the Rampuri manner, he wore a high, five-pointed black cap in velvet, its edges worked over in gold. This was again after the fashion in Delhi, except that the gold work distinguished it from similar caps favoured by learned professors and Sufis. The high cap sat lightly on his head, letting the shining black, long and thick locks of hair show as they descended from the head to his shoulders. Worn somewhat askew, the cap identified him as a nobleman's son with an artistic and pleasure-loving temperament.

The gravity of youth and the boyish attractiveness of his dark, sculpted face met in Navab Mirza's person such that he always tugged at people's hearts and compelled attention. His mother, aunt and all the women servants felt always like talking to him, laughing with him, pampering him. But the delicateness of the present moment needed some mode of conduct, that should allay the mother's grief and also let the boy express his unqualified love for her. It was Navab Mirza's brilliant intuitiveness and natural flair at pleasing all those with whom he interacted that he did what was just right for the occasion. He took a small step forward, sat at his mother's feet, tenderly pulled them, shoes and all, towards his lap and said, 'Amma Jan, I'm here, right here at your service. Please ignore these little girlies and their nonsense talk,' he smiled. 'Rahat Afza regards me as a prancing young colt, so what is she then? A filly that's just cutting her milk teeth, eh? I am your son, no more and no less!'

'A filly, whose mouth is toothless, rather,' Umdah Khanam delivered a light, affectionate pat on Rahat Afza's pinkish cheek. 'The filly may not have cut her teeth yet, but she has a long tongue. But Navab Mirza, you should please rise, don't be sitting on the ground, moving your arms like a dancer!'

Umdah Khanam laughed her special laughter, a low, sweet gurgle, suggesting a taste of friendship between them, as if Navab Mirza now deserved a certain parity in the mother and son equation, and hinting to the mother that the son was nearly a young man: you should forget his father and embrace the son.

'Khala Jan, you command me to rise, so I rise most quickly, like the flowering champak which is said to rise from the earth in no time. But Amma Jan isn't prepared to talk to me even.' Navab Mirza tried to raise his mother's drooping head. 'Dearest Amma Jan, just look at me! Or at least just listen, I'll give you a beautiful verse from Mian Nazir Akbarabadi.' Then he recited:

I was nothing, but like the cherry bomb
Or the moonlight cracker,
When a spark touched me,
A spectacle sprung from me.

'And here's my dear Khala Jan, she's determined to make me a spectacle and also its director!'

Perhaps, in quoting the eighteenth-century Hindi poet Nazir Akbarabadi, Navab Mirza was unconsciously asserting his own potential as a poet and as a man, or perhaps he was creating a diversion, knowing as he did his mother's taste for poetry. He achieved the desired result.

Wazir swallowed her tears, made the action of taking away her son's perils and cried, 'Oh! Navab Mirza! Please rise, it is so inauspicious for my feet to be in your lap! Placing you on my eyes or putting you inside my heart would still be nothing compared to what you are worth to me. Please. Rise now. Look, I am smiling, aren't I?'

She drew away her feet, took Navab Mirza's hands in hers and tried to pull upwards to make the boy rise. Navab Mirza said, 'No, no. That won't do at all.'

'Bacche Mian sahib, don't shame me more,' Wazir pleaded.

'There's nothing of shame here. It's just that for no reason you made everyone cry, and on top of that, when I gave you such a beautiful verse on the theme of "spectacle" you didn't even applaud. Thus you must be mulcted on two counts, madam. First, you must promise that you will not weep so long as I am in this world.'

'Hey, Navab Mirza sahib, aren't you being tyrannical? Did anyone ever have command over weeping with the eyes or in one's own heart?'

'Granted. But you must concede this much: those who are left behind have rights no less than those who are gone.'

Wazir was speechless. There was a loving authoritativeness here, which she had not experienced before from Navab Mirza. There was also a kind of worldliness. It was the first time that Navab Mirza had openly acknowledged the reality of his father's death, and that too in such a way that the mother's being seemed to be more meaningful and significant than the father's non-being. Wazir collected her thoughts and spoke with care, 'Surely, justice is on your side.'

'So all right then. My claim on you is that you must always be happy. Now we come to the other matter.'

'Oh, so there's something still to be resolved? Please, first bring your tallness up from the ground, only then we'll hear your claims and plaints.'

'Here I am, I rise as you command,' Navab Mirza smiled. 'But I will still extract my restitution. Please be good enough to pay a fine for not applauding Mian Nazir's lines. So let's have a sparkling verse on "spectacle"; let the world know about your proficiency in poetry.'

This time, Wazir pulled Navab Mirza to her with somewhat greater force. Both loosened their hold and Navab Mirza stood up with his arm around his mother's shoulder.

'Only God is untouched by blemish! It's Navab Mirza who reads with the renowned Mullah Ghiasuddin of Rampur and it is a poor servant girl who should be tested!' Wazir was smiling, but was inwardly anxious. 'Please play such games of capping verses with your Mullah sahib.'

'Fine, but you aren't going to be excused this time. You made me learn heaps and heaps of poems when I was small. Now it's your turn. Let's have Persian, if you can't recall Hindi.'

'Oh dear, oh dear, I am a crazed old woman, now how can I recall verses for the satisfaction of my Bacche Mian?' Wazir paused, pretended to be annoyed. 'So here's a decrepit one from Nadim, an old poet from Lahij in Iran. Don't blame me if it doesn't pass muster with you.'

'Very good, indeed. Please command,' Navab Mirza said.

Wazir spoke the verse in a plain, but charming manner:

I have been witness to many engagements
In this ancient place, but
The sport of children is yet another spectacle.

'Only God is untouched by blemish! Amma Jan, what an excellent verse! It affects me almost like an intoxicant.'

Navab Mirza gave wholehearted praise, but he also noted a subtext there: Amma Jan is hinting at my inexperience; she sees quite much of a child in me. Navab Mirza, who fancied himself now as a fully grown man, smiled inwardly at the artlessness of his mother. A wave of affection ran through his heart: poor little Amma Jan, how simple a soul she is! He retorted, 'But

Amma Jan, "the sport of children" is not fair. Just listen to Mirza Bedil.' He recited with obvious relish and in a vibrating voice:

Another spring is here; the world is out, enjoying
Excursions in the gardens; but our crazy mode
Of life and action has its own spectacle.

'Oh, what a fine verse! And what a nice idea, "but our crazy mode of life and action has its own spectacle".' Both Umdah and Wazir cried in unison. Navab Mirza bent low in salaams, as if it was his own poem and it was he who deserved the accolades.

'I acknowledge, Navab Mirza, you are no longer in the playground of children. Please accept my congratulations.' Wazir took Navab Mirza's hand in her hand again. 'But do you intend to be a poet yourself? Will you compose in Persian or in Hindi?'

'I want to be a poet. In fact, I desire it strongly,' Navab Mirza spoke somewhat diffidently. 'If ever I write poetry, it'll be in Rekhtah, as Hindi is sometimes called. At present, I have no pen name, no mentor.'

'Once you make a strong resolve, a pen name and a mentor will both be found with no trouble,' said Wazir.

'I should think so, but our Mullah ji may not approve. He says that poetry writing is the profession of the idle.' He smiled his boyish smile. The next moment, his smile became even more ravishing because it had genuine shyness in it.

'Amma Jan, why should I not become your disciple? Were you to suggest to me a nice pen name, I'd really become distinguished among my schoolmates.'

'Who, me? Really, dear son, it is ages since I wrote even one line of poetry. May he be granted Paradise, had my Shah sahib been alive, I would have gladly taken you to him and sat you at his feet. I too would have learnt some more from him. Allah! Allah! Whence comes another such mentor? But he was enamoured of the Deccan, may death take it. And that land, like a rival wife, enveloped him into her arms forever.'

Sensing that memory of her mentor had perhaps saddened Wazir, Navab Mirza importuned her like a child, 'No! No! I am not going to take that! Tell me, for how long will you hide yourself in the minaret of the past? The world has changed; the people in the world have changed.'

Umdah Khanam cast a meaningful glance at Navab Mirza, as if gratefully conceding that the boy had said what she, an elder, had balked at saying. Rahat Afza, however, jumped to defend her beloved mistress and spoke half in jest and half in displeasure, 'Hey, Navab Mirza sahib, your tongue is indeed running away with you! Be on your guard, you might leave it behind.' She put her arm around Wazir's neck and called Ram Jiai, the second maid, to bring a glass of pomegranate juice for her mistress.

But Navab Mirza was no longer a boy: he was approaching adulthood. He could clearly gauge the meaning of Umdah Khanam's glance. His awareness of the transition from boyhood to near adulthood, and the somewhat upsetting experience of the footfalls of approaching youth prevented him from putting his head in his mother's lap, teasing and tickling her, taking her hand in his and nuzzling her. Equally, his consciousness of a new authority developing in him had made him freer with his tongue. Somewhat sharply, he said, 'And Bi Rahat Afza, should you not first look to yourself? Your tongue is getting long and sharp enough to make a hole in the sky and then even patch it up! Why should it be my dear Amma Jan alone left to wander grieving in the narrow alleys of the past?' He smiled, robbing his words of any hurtful intent. 'Amma Jan, I think you must give me a nice pen name. Please. By and by, we'll find a mentor.'

'All right, Mian, I'll do what you demand. Manjhli Baji, is there a copy of Hafiz anywhere about?' Wazir was a little miffed at being given the extra trouble, but she was easy and conversational in tone. 'We shall seek succour from the Tongue of the Unseen. Let's see what transpires from the Realm of the Unseen.'

'I'm sorry, Chhoti, but I don't have a copy of the Divan of Hafiz handy; I do have a fine copy of the Divan of Khvajah Mir Dard. Someone presented it yesterday to Navab sahib. I began to look into it and brought it here with me.'

'No one actually consults Mir Dard for augury or clues. But no matter, if Hafiz was the Shaikh of Shiraz, Mir Dard sahib was the Shaikh of Jahanabad. So why not him?' Wazir said.

Mir Dard was a great Hindi and Persian poet of the last century. He was also revered as a prominent Sufi. Before someone could be sent to fetch the Divan of Mir Dard sahib, a fakir came wandering. As he reached Wazir's home, he was heard playing a ghazal from the seventeenth-century Indian Persian poet Nisbati Thanesari on a sih tar:

One heart and a horde of desires:
To which purpose should I devote my heart?
My whole body is nothing now but scars:
Where should I put the soothing balm?

His voice and enunciation were clear and resonant, with underlying scents of pain. Manjhli Begam said, 'Bacche Mian sahib, what excellence is here, just see, "My whole body is nothing now but scars".'

Someone brought out the Divan of Khvajah Mir Dard sahib. Wazir recalled the time when she had Pundit Nand Kishor come over to her house to consult the Divan of Khvajah Hafiz hoping to get some guidance about her future. The entire sequence of the scenes, and more than the scenes, her fears and anxieties, her hopes and imaginings flashed before her inward eye like a stab of ultra-brilliant light, painful to the eyes. She trembled and was about to drop the slim volume on the floor but pulled herself together, took a draught of the cool drink and said, 'Please listen, you ladies and Navab Mirza, none of us knows the art of divination. That is a job for pundits and mullahs. All I can do is to simply recite bismillah and open the volume at random, and turn the pages. The verse on which my eye stops, contains the augury. Do you agree?'

'Madam, extremely proper,' said Navab Mirza. Wazir touched the little book to her eyes, said bismillah and found the following verse when she opened the book:

I am scarred by my own fortune:
Breath of Jesus, I am a lamp,
You blow on me, and I die.

'What a marvel of a verse!' Manjhli exclaimed. 'Though not quite appropriate for the occasion, it's not improper either. For, what does a poet do, but burn in pain because of the intensity of emotion? My Navab sahib says that none can be a poet without a heart brimming with the sense of pain. Is it not the sense of pain which makes the poetry of Mir Dard sahib popular even today?'

'Yes,' said Wazir, 'and the word "pain" (dard) has a congruity with "scar" or "sorrow" (dagh). We've just had a beautiful verse on the theme of dagh. It could be a sort of augury too. So why not "Dagh" as Navab Mirza's pen name?'

'Yes, Amma Jan. And the theme of "chiragh" (lamp) conjoined with the "Breath of Jesus" (nafas-e Isavi) is supported by the Songbird of India, the Presence, Amir Khusrau, may God raise his station. The Amir says:

The lamp dies when it is breathed on,
Even if it was the Breath of Jesus.'

'So from today, Allah preserve you, you are the Presence, Navab Mirza Dagh, of Delhi, and subsequently, of Rampur. We'll decide the question of pupilage in a day or two. The ustad Shaikh Ibrahim Zauq's name is on everyone's lips in Delhi. There is Ghanshyam Lal Asi, another reputed pupil of my Shah sahib. As for Lucknow, Shaikh Imam Bakhsh Nasikh is no more, but he left behind a number of renowned pupils. Then, we have Navab Sayyid Muhammad Khan Rind.'

'All these are auspicious names. But, Amma Jan, I'm not going to be known as Rampuri. I am a true and honest son of Delhi. The whole of Hind reverberates with our speech. The word "Rampuri" lacks vitality and verve.'

Manjhli Begam was alarmed for a moment at this forthright comment on Rampur. Should the word reach my Navab sahib . . . These Navab types do not see; they only hear. Then she thought, it's just boyish banter, quite harmless. No one ever took such things amiss. She smiled, her face blooming with pleasure: 'Agreed, Navab Mirza, you are a smooth rock rolling in the streets of Delhi; we are the rough, gritty sand from the bank of Ram Ganga. Delhi's maestro, be happy ever with Delhi!'

'I hear, and obey,' said Navab Mirza. 'Amma Jan, let us compose a few verses. After all, I am the owner of a fine pen name. Give me now a line by way of a paradigm; then you'll see my search for new themes.'

'Well, "spectacle" was talked about recently. So here is a line from Mir Taqi Mir sahib about "spectacle". It's from the opening verse. You must now make an opening verse of your own.'

In her sweet, formal voice and engaging style, Wazir spoke the line:

When I looked hard, I saw that the world is a droll spectacle!

'Oh, Amma Jan! Now that is a bit much! You test me with a line from a master of masters, and that too a line which is so utterly full. I should wring my hands in despair. Could anyone ever do a matching line and make an opening verse of it?'

Manjhli Begam laughed. 'No facile excuses, no silver-tongued oratory, please! You can make a line even as you make excuses.'

'Be sure to make an opening verse, Bacche Mian.' Wazir was playfully peremptory.

'Madam, very well,' Navab Mirza mumbled. Almost in the same instant, he presented the full two-line verse:

The polite ones here view the spectacle of the impolite,
When I looked hard, I saw that the world is a droll spectacle!

'Excellent!', 'As Allah wills!' and 'Only God is untouched by blemish!' were the exclamations that greeted Navab Mirza. Wazir kissed him on the forehead, and spreading her wrap wide, as if she was begging, prayed: 'Allah, let the name of my child shine bright. Let the world call him "The World's Maestro".'

All said 'Amen' to this. Manjhli Bagam instantly had sweets brought in which she distributed to everyone in the house, including the servants.

'Bacche Mian, indeed you pleased us all with your extemporized line. Now if we could have a vibrant line added to this new one here, I would declare you a perfect pupil, beyond the need for a maestro,' Wazir said, smiling, and extemporized a line of her own making:

There is not a single human being in the assembly of the Milky Way

Wazir had just finished when Navab Mirza came out with his own line of verse:

A meaningless spectacle this, got up by the sky.

Again, there were noises of applause. A beaming Navab Mirza gave salaams and said, 'I don't think I have any need of a maestro. I will put my best efforts in my poetry and will occasionally consult Amma Jan, but I have to finish my studies first. I hope to God that Amma Jan's prayers will be heard.'

Another round of 'Amens' followed. It was almost dinner time now. The tablecloth was spread. The dinner had come in large containers from Manjhli Begam's kitchen.

51

Navab Mirza is consulted; a proposal is made: springtime arrives once again in Wazir Khanam's courtyard

AFTER DINNER, BEFORE she went back to her haveli, Manjhli Begam again cast an apparently more-than-casual glance at Navab Mirza.

'Navab Mirza, our new haveli is not too far from your madrasa. It would be nice if you could stop by in the evening.'

Navab Mirza did not quite get her purpose. Clearly, she wanted to say something special to him. His heart fluttering with suspense and not a little anxiety, he said, 'Yes, surely, Manjhli Khala. It's no problem at all. I will come kiss your feet tomorrow evening.'

'Very good. In God's care, till then.'

Manjhli Begam rode off in her palanquin. Navab Mirza and Wazir retired to their rooms for the night. The next evening, at Manjhli Khala's house, he was a little surprised to find a well-decorated, sumptuous bullock cart at the main door and the bustle of some new servants at the hall. Because he was still regarded as young enough not to require purdah being observed for him, he went straight into the house, without sending in his name.

As he crossed the hall, Umdah Khanam's senior maid met him and said that Begam sahib desired his presence in the divan khanah. Navab Mirza halted at the door when he saw an unfamiliar lady there. Umdah Khanam used the well-known Persian phrase in greeting and called out to him, 'Come, please come. You brighten our eyes and gladden our hearts! Do you know this lady?'

Now when Navab Mirza looked carefully, he thought that the face looked familiar, but could not recall the name. Tall, youthful body fully fleshed out, straight nose, but with a small curve in the middle, bright eyes that were long, somewhat like almonds, delicate pink lips; she had rings on three fingers of each hand: diamond, amethyst and ruby. Her dress was fashionably plain but expensive. Her whole personality dripped the confidence of beauty, youth and excellent health. She smiled, rose a little from her seat, and said, 'Oh, my! Navab Mirza, you didn't recognize me, but I recognized you at once from just one glance at your tall stature!'

'Aha! It's you, Phupi Jahangirah! Only God is free from all blemish . . . Now I can recall you very well. You haven't changed at all.'

Navab Mirza put out his hand and walked up to Jahangirah who was quick to notice the boy's complete resemblance to his father in his gait and his voice. Her eyes misted and her first impulse was to pull him to her and warmly hug him, the memorial of her martyred brother. But she desisted, intuiting a little something of hesitancy in Navab Mirza. He salaamed the two ladies and sat by their feet on the thick carpet.

'No, no! Not there, Navab Mirza. You should be here, next to me.' Umdah Khanam took his arm and gently pulled him next to her on the wooden platform.

'Tell us, how are your studies going, Navab Mirza?' Jahangirah inquired. 'What are the books that you are reading specially?'

Navab Mirza grimaced inwardly. It was clear that the purpose of having him over was not to make small talk about his academic attainments. Jahangirah phupi's presence here was not without some ulterior motive. What is it that she wants to speak to me about? The sooner the puzzle was solved, the better.

With a slightly bored air, he briefly listed out a few of the books and subjects which he was being taught, and asked, 'When did you come from Akbarabad? Is Uncle well? I hope all is well?'

'Everything is perfect, by the grace of God. How's your mother doing? I must see her before I go back. Let her send for me whenever she's free, I will come at once.'

'Yes, madam. Very good. You can come whenever you wish. How about tomorrow? Will you stay in Rampur for some days?'

'Yes . . . yes, I need to stay a few more days. You must know my husband's elder brother? I have some small business with him.'

'Yes, madam. You mean Agha Mirza Turab Ali? I do know him by his illustrious name, but haven't had the opportunity to meet him.'

'He's a man from a good family, pure Iranian stock. They have been here for some generations, but converse among themselves only in Persian.'

Navab Mirza felt bewildered, if not truly miffed. Why am I being burdened with this useless information? What use could I possibly make of it? Out of respect for the older relatives, he held his tongue, and mumbled, 'Yes, madam. Very good.'

'He is the Steward of the Honourable Navab Sahib's Horse and Elephant Stable, and also of his Camp equipment. As Allah wills, he holds a fairly important position, and draws a good salary. Our Navab sahib regards him highly.'

Navab Mirza made no response. Umdah Khanam and Jahangirah Begam exchanged looks. Navab Mirza was puzzled even more. What exactly is going on here? Does this Agha sahib have a marriageable daughter to whom these ladies are proposing to betroth me? He maintained a rigid silence; the pause lengthened. Finally, Jahangirah broke the silence: 'Your mother must be quite lonely, I thought. Especially now that you too have left Delhi for Rampur. I hear that even in Delhi she doesn't go out much?'

'Yes, madam. Lonely she is. My heart pines for her. But . . . I'd very much like her to come to Rampur and live with me. But she doesn't want to, not at all. In fact, my view is that the past is not a place to spend one's life . . . ' Navab Mirza checked himself from saying more. What did I say, about not living in the past? Jahangirah phupi may not like the way I put it. She's blood sister to my father—may God award him the highest position in Paradise—she must miss him terribly, too.

'Yes, how nice that would be . . . ' Jahangirah spoke slowly, as if weighing every word. 'Listen, a situation is developing . . . Who knows, it may have the potential for the good of all of us.' She looked at Umdah Khanam, as if appealing to her to take the conversation further from there. Umdah Khanam cleared her throat, placed her wrap carefully on her head and sat up, as if she was going to say something of great import: 'Listen, Navab Mirza. My strongest desire is for some suitable pattern of life to emerge for my little sister . . . I . . . wish I could again see her settled happily and securely, so that her loneliness may go away . . . her sorrow may abate somewhat.'

Umdah had been speaking with her eyes on the floor, her head bent, as if she was unable to face Navab Mirza. Now she raised her head and looked keenly at him, trying to gauge the effect of her words on him. Perhaps he was upset and was unhappy at what Umdah Khanam was clearly going to propose? But Navab Mirza, whose puzzlement was diminishing, was now silent, his own head bent.

'I consulted Jahangirah Begam and was delighted to find her of the same opinion. Navab Mirza, are you listening?'

'Yes, Manjhli Khala. Please go ahead.'

'So the matter now stands like this: There is a message for your mother from Agha Mirza Turab Ali, brother-in-law to your Jahangirah phupi . . .'

'Sorry. What did you say? I don't understand.'

'Nothing . . . except that Agha sahib wishes to tie the knot of marriage with your mother.'

'Is he not married yet?'

'No,' Jahangirah intervened now. 'His poor wife was called to the Almighty sometime ago. They had no children. Agha sahib's big haveli looks and feels quite desolate . . . He heard praises of your mother in many quarters . . . he ascertained further details and had me over specially from Akbarabad so that I could broach the matter with your people.'

'Then, then why are you talking to me about it?' Navab Mirza was clearly piqued, and also perhaps annoyed. He thought he was not the person to decide. How should he view the entry of a stranger into his mother's life: this was something about which he believed that he had no right to have any thought or have anything to say.

His father's death, which he always saw as martyrdom, was not a direct memory for him. But the details and the circumstances of that event were now in his memory as a part of his real-life experience, thanks to the conversations, accounts and narratives that he had heard at home and outside. The narrative was now a part of both his conscious and unconscious mind. Sometimes he woke up in his bed, groping to touch his father beside him because that was how he had just dreamed of him: he dreamt that he was waking up from sleep in his father's arms. His father was someone who protected him from bad dreams, from the hostile world. He had never considered the possibility of his mother's remarriage, or the need for a protector or patron. It was quite proper, he thought, to feel the want of a father at the spiritual or abstract level whenever he took a new step in life. But to feel the need of another man in his mother's bed, or in her normal existence as a woman, was altogether something else. Truth to tell, Navab Mirza regarded himself as a complete person, not needing any outside being to be his guardian or his guarantor in public life. It never occurred to him that his and his mother's way of life could sustain another, newer way of life, far less be in need of it. Although the faint intimations of the arrival of adulthood had made him aware of the changes about to occur in his physical and mental being, he had not ever given thought to the necessity or need for converting the new physical demands of his body into actual execution, or that there could be the need for a woman for him in the house, or a beloved in his heart. Right now, he enjoyed agonistic contests with his friends, schoolmates and other growing boys in matters of games and sports, reciting prose or poetry, competing about who could show better feats of memory. Sometimes he enjoyed teasing or indulging in soft erotic banter with a good-looking schoolboy friend. These things he considered as the essence, the vital blood of his external life. As for his inner life, the undisputed rulers there were his father and mother. Awake or asleep, it was they and no one else—even though he could not recall how his father looked, or spoke. His imagination sometimes placed his mother, sometimes his father's tomb in Qadam Sharif, sometimes the tall, imposing figure whom he took to be his father's hakim, wearing a formal dress, brimming with health and exuding power, just like a curer and restorer of health should be. There was no question of any other person replacing the image of his dead father. But his Amma Jan's loneliness and near helplessness in this big, strange world . . . what about it? How to deal with it? Children generally regard even their youthful parents as quite old, far older than they really are; especially when the children start growing up, they look at their parents as not only old-fashioned, but also ancient, and somehow outworn, even if the feeling that the parents are old doesn't necessarily mean that the children are critical of the parents. However, in Navab Mirza's mind, the image of his father and also of his mother had become fixed at one point of time, regardless of their ageing, or the natural effect of the flow of time over their lives. It seemed to Navab Mirza that his mother was very young, if not actually unmarried. Whenever he thought of his mother, his heart welled up with the desire to somehow protect her from the long, cruel hand of Time and the injustice that the world seemed always to wreak upon her. His love for his mother was somehow fatherly, always imagining her as needing his protection and defence. This notion—of being a knight in shining armour, ever ready to save her from any possible distress—prevailed over every other emotion that he might have had for her. It never occurred to him that he would have to marry when he grew up: he would then have his own children; a domesticity of household life in which his mother would scarcely find a place. He could not imagine a future in which he lived his life separate from his mother, even when she was dead. But his mother's essential loneliness, without a man in her life . . .? He did occasionally think of it, but he never stopped to consider its implications and its meaning in the larger scheme of things. Perhaps the thought lurked in his unconscious mind that Amma Jan should make him the pivot and axis of her spiritual and intellectual life, that she should somehow transfer his father's place to him in spirit, and our lives may thus go on with light-footed ease, in even tenor. He never paused to think that lives are not lived the way he imagined. Even if the day came when he was married and had a family of his own which could somehow coexist happily with his mother, another day would surely come when his mother was not in this world and she would perforce have to vacate the position that she held in the centre of his life now.

Now, when Jahangirah Begam and Umdah Khanam placed before him the possibility, even desirability, of his mother living like a housewife, and also like a married woman, he experienced a sense of pain and restlessness. Though he himself said that living in the past was not good for his mother, now when a practical suggestion was mooted to bring his mother into the present from the past, he balked at it; he felt a sadness, an anxiety, or perhaps an indefinable displeasure. Who needs this rigmarole after all? Why upset their smooth lives, especially when the benefits of the change were unclear?

Jahangirah Begam interrupted the flow of his thoughts. 'We are talking to you first because . . .' she paused, 'we don't want to do anything that you may not approve of.'

'My approval? Who am I in this transaction to give or not give my approval? If Amma Jan doesn't agree, then?' A feeble smile crept into his heart, though not his voice.

'I'll talk to Chhoti,' Umdah Khanam said. 'Obviously, nothing can happen against her wishes . . . But . . . man is a woman's greatest support and strength. Life's sun blazes harder with our ageing. If there be no shade on a woman's head as she grows old, all of her life could be scorched away; she might lose everything.'

'Manjhli Khala, that is all very well,' Navab Mirza spoke in a reasoning tone. 'But I cannot speak to Amma Jan on this matter.'

'I beg Allah's pardon!' cried out Umdah Khanam. 'No one is suggesting that you talk to Chhoti. All that we mean to say is that we'll take the next step only when we're certain that you like the proposal.'

Navab Mirza almost lost his cool, and his nerve. 'Like the proposal? How does liking enter here, and that too, my like or dislike? I already said that the decision rests with Amma Jan, not with me.'

Umdah Khanam wished to argue further, but Jahangirah Begam sensed that Navab Mirza was labouring under an emotional and mental burden that already seemed heavy enough. It was clear that he was not violently opposed to the idea, or even the proposal under discussion; it was perhaps not possible at present to persuade him to go further. She hinted to Umdah Khanam with a flicker of the eye to desist. She then changed the subject.

Smouldering and seething inwardly, Navab Mirza aimlessly roamed the bazaars for some time before he returned home. Umdah Khanam was already there, having ridden in her palanquin to Wazir's dwelling almost immediately after Navab Mirza left her. She broached the subject of Wazir's remarriage without much ado and laid before her the details of Jahangirah's embassy and Agha Mirza Turab Ali's proposal of marriage.

'Look, Bibi, there's nothing here to be annoyed or sad about, but it's a lifetime's transaction. You need to consider it from all angles. It's perfectly all right if you don't like the idea, we'll . . .'

A sad, bitter smile touched Wazir's face. 'I made a lifetime's transaction, even my whole life's transaction, numerous times, Baji. Now how many times more do I need to go through the fiery ordeal?'

'The Scribe of Fates has a pen in hand, a sword in the other. Whatever the pen writes may be cut out by the sword. The fates of some of us are inscribed many times and are cancelled many times. Our games are played and lost or won time and time again.'

'Of what use is the victory when the game is to be played over and over again?'

'If you don't want to play, someone else will make the moves for you. There lies the difference between dead and living pieces.'

'Why? Why should an alien hand make my moves? And who will play my game?' Wazir's voice was somehow an amalgamation of anger, sorrow and protest. 'What price our lives and our games, our losses and gains? Are they no more than a mischievous old man's puppet shows? Manjhli Baji, you have no right to make such speeches!'

'What am I saying? What am I saying?' Umdah Khanam cried out in some desperation, some pleading. 'But you tell me: Why should someone be alone in the world when a hand is extended to her in love?'

'In love, or in self-interest?' Wazir was seething.

'Love also is a kind of self-interest, perhaps the most tyrannical and the most oppressive. Why don't you talk some sense, Chhoti? I and Jahangirah are not your enemies.'

Wazir made no reply for a long minute, then said in a tired voice, 'All right, I'll give it a thought,' and went into her bedroom, without giving another look towards Umdah Khanam. Umdah waited, hoping that Wazir might come out, or Navab Mirza might come by. Nothing happened for many minutes; she rode back to her haveli.

That night, Wazir could not sleep at all. But was there anyone to whom she could pour her heart out? There was Manjhli, keen to cut off some of the old skeins of her thread of life and reshape the rest into other, equally convoluted knots. Navab Mirza is my son; but how can I discuss this matter with him? He's himself an immature youth, almost a boy . . . and if there were someone else to broach the subject with him? What would he say then? Would he not think that Amma Jan, in her dotage, is trying to recover the lost ground of her youth? . . . More important, he might be hurt. He would die to preserve his father's memory intact . . . And I? What am I? What about my own memories of his father? Were someone to open my heart, they would see that it is a desolate, lonely tomb where my Navab sahib's memory glimmers like a lamp. But for that weak little light, my life would sink in the dark, traceless forever. So where are Blak sahib and my babies? Blak sahib was pulled away from me, then my babies too torn away from my side without a thought spared for me. Yet, yet . . . Allah, how could I have managed to nurture them, to take care of them? No, why not? I surely would have, just as I have been watering and keeping the tree of my Navab's memory green with my tears. But if Amir Mirza and Badshah Begam had been living with me, would I still have attracted the heart of my Navab as I did? Everyone looks askance at others' children. Those favoured are one's own children and the wives of others. That is the rule.

And who is this gentleman? This Agha sahib? What does he want from me? I hear he is a Shia. So what does he want? A short-term contractual marriage, as is common among them? Or will he enter into a proper marriage with me? And what happens then to my child, and to the babies who were taken away from me? I cannot hope for them to come back. But who knows? They could come back; anything is possible in this world. But if they desired to return, how would this Agha sahib react?

Two days passed over Wazir in unravelling and ravelling, in asking and answering. Jahangirah was now in some hurry to return; but she was equally keen to see her proposal bear fruit before she left Rampur. By now, she could make a fair assessment of Wazir's temperament: she was unlikely to be swayed by anyone. Wazir had become aware of her enchanting looks even as she was growing up; she well knew that she possessed some power, which could win hearts for her—any heart at all—almost without her making an effort. Then, the experience of being an actual beloved for so many years gave her a pride, almost an arrogance, which was attractive and even desirable in the eyes of anyone who had anything to do with her. The proud, arrogant, unheeding beauty was after all one of the most popular tropes in the Indo-Muslim love poetry system. Her experience of life helped her grow the power to discriminate—between what could be and not be good for her—and also develop the knack of being naturally distant and proud with all possible suitors. The absence of a man left no gap in her personality: she knew that she was a complete person in herself. What she did desire was an affirmation of her being, and her personality, through a man. She believed that if there was love anywhere in the world, it was for the woman who was the giver of that gift. She said that men do not love: they are given over to the feeling of being loved; if they start enjoying passionately the state of being loved, then that is their loving, or their substitute for loving someone. She thought that only a woman is capable of real love. But the woman might have to pay a very heavy price if she did not love wisely, or if she let herself be deceived by her vanity. Still, she thought, even that heavy price was acceptable if she could create in the man an overpowering emotion of being loved: she could thus see her own image mirrored in the man's image.

One night Wazir started and woke up from a state between dreaming and waking, and found herself saying that women perhaps are fated to wander through life looking for love. It was not a conclusion arrived at in despair, but a kind of self-realization. In the morning, she had a palanquin summoned and rode straight to Manjhli Begam's house.

Without her usual warm greetings or going about it in a circuitous way, she put a direct question to Manjhli: 'Baji, tell me plainly, what benefit do you see for me in this proposal?'

Umdah Khanam laughed affectionately. 'Little girlie, are you out of your mind? Do I now need to explain that man is the chador on a woman's body, the roof on her head, her refuge in youth and her support in old age?'

'Really, Manjhli Baji, you should have been chief priest or prayer leader in a mosque!'

'Chhoti Begam, don't please laugh these matters away; it is the time and place for you to stop and consider.'

Wazir was provoked into a sharp reply. 'What support have I had from men so far that I'll get it now?'

'Try to think with a cool head. Navab Mirza—I take the name of God—is about to enter the stage of youth. He's bound to have a household, a family. Who knows where he would choose to live? Perhaps he goes off to Delhi, perhaps elsewhere. Nowadays, young people prefer to live away from the parental home, especially when there is no father on their head.'

'No, I am sure my Navab Mirza will never do that!'

Manjhli wanted to retort, 'Like Badshah Begam and Amir Mirza, that is?' She desisted, not wishing to hurt her younger sister. She desired with the full depth of her heart for Wazir's boat to reach a salubrious shore.

'Granted. But what will you feed him? And how will you feed yourself? You spent a large part of your life in comfort, if not in luxury. You had servants, maids, guards, gatekeepers, palanquin, nalki and all the rest of it. You brought up Navab Mirza giving him everything, even pampering him. Don't I see that your finances are now weakening every day?'

Wazir, who had been ready to argue the matter out with Manjhli, fell silent suddenly. She hated for someone, even her loving sister, to comment on the poverty which was staring her in the face. She felt her lips and tongue go dry. She wished to answer back, but could find no appropriate language. Manjhli Begam anxiously called for Chandni, her maid, to bring in an iced glass of the juice of bed mishk, a medicinal drink suitable for anxiety, dismay or perplexity. Then she spoke to Chhoti in the kindest of tones, 'Look, Chhoti, I certainly am not the one to force something on you. You are the decision-maker, it's you who will decide, ultimately. Nor do I urge that you should approve my proposal. Give it full thought. You can even meet him face to face, should you like. Accept the proposal if you wish; if not, say a polite no without causing offence to anyone . . . And look, one advantage in this proposal is that you won't be separated from Navab Mirza.'

'Who is this person, Baji? I just have no knowledge about him. How did he happen to hear of me? Or if he saw me somewhere, how did that happen? Why did he choose me, of all people?'

Wazir seemed genuinely bewildered, although she knew of the Jahangirah connection. Umdah Khanam, who had been perfectly familiar with instances of throngs of Wazir's admirers outside the door in their narrow lane, smiled her famous smile. 'Indeed! The young lady now needs to be informed that her accomplishments and her youth and beauty are being talked about everywhere! In fact, Chhoti, you look quite unmarried even now.'

'Manjhli Baji, please don't act funny with me. Give me a full and truthful account so that I could give some thought to the question.'

'Well, there is nothing more to be narrated. He is the elder brother of Jahangirah's husband. He heard of you from Jahangirah . . . And, in fact . . . there's none who did not hear of you anyway after the Navab's martyrdom. Now, when you came to Rampur and the begams here saw you and talked to you in person, you exceeded all their expectations. Agha Sahib's first wife passed away a little more than a year ago. So he asked Jahangirah if you could possibly be interested.'

'So he wants a proper marriage?'

'What else, girl? Jahangirah is in the middle, is she not?'

'No, I thought maybe he wants one of those temporary marriages that are permissible among the Shias.'

'I beg Allah's pardon! Doubtless, Rampur has a Shia ruler, but his family was Sunni originally. People in Rampur don't think well of such practices.'

'And would my children by him, if there are any at all, be brought up as Shia?'

'Bibi, do we really need to look that far? We'll deal with the question when the occasion arises.'

'No, I want this to be clearly understood. If there are any babies, they will be brought up in our creed.'

'All right, I'll talk to Jahangirah. Anything else?'

Wazir Khanam again fell into thought. 'I haven't even seen this Agha sahib. What kind of a person is he? What is his normal way of life? Is he severe and harsh in his dealings? I hope he will stint on nothing in loving my Navab Mirza.'

'Had there been the slightest slur on his character or his ancestry or nobility of temperament, Jahangirah would never have dreamt of making this proposal. Nor would I. You can see him and talk to him, if you like.'

'No, no. Not at all. But . . . I have never made a blind connection. I feel fearful and anxious.'

Now it was Umdah Khanam's turn to become thoughtful. 'Agha sahib is a gentleman of the old school. I'm not sure how he'll react.'

'There should be nothing to cavil at. The Shariah permits it.'

'Dear girl, custom and convention are more important in such things, the Shariah comes second. Anyway, you stay the night with me. I will visit Jahangirah later in the day and have every point aired and discussed. If there is to be a next step in this, let it be from here. I will consult with my Navab sahib too.'

*

Agha Mirza Turab Ali seemed to have his heart on fire with the desire to gain Wazir's favour. Not much time had passed since the conversation between Umdah and Wazir when a staff-bearer and two porters appeared at Umdah Khanam's door with the message that they were from Agha sahib. He has sent some presents, they reported. There were four large pitchers of Moradabad brassware full of dry fruits. There was also a delicately fashioned wooden box in Indian rosewood. The key to the locked box was in a small, sealed pouch. Umdah Khanam allowed the staff-bearer and the porters to leave after offering them suitable rewards, and had the brass pitchers sent to the storeroom. She put the wooden box in Wazir's hands as something personal to her, to be opened by her. Wazir blushed and took the box into her room, unable to decide what it could possibly contain. She was clear about not accepting anything valuable, but the decision could be made only after opening the box. She broke the seal, but the key kept slipping from her almost nerveless fingers.

Finally, she opened the box and found that it had two rolls of thick paper, tied separately with gold thread. I thank you, God, it is not something of value, she breathed. Unrolling one of the papers, she found a ghazal by the great Persian poet Sadi, inscribed in the attractive but somewhat casual calligraphic style called Shafiah after the Iranian master Mirza Shafi, its designer. It was clear that the scribe had taken no special pains, but his hand was so firm, so neat and so balanced that he would not have needed to take pains. She perused the ghazal with rising admiration not only for the poetry, but also for the choice of it:

To write the account of love,
Rolls of paper
Do not suffice.
For love's narrative,
Discourses
Do not suffice.
Love's music
Intoxicates the crazed ones;
For hearing it,
Wise men's ears
Do not suffice.
I cannot praise you
As you really are,
For the length and breadth
Of my song, a whole bazaar
Does not suffice.
I will not give
My heart to any other
Face in Creation;
Compared to you,
Painted figures
On the wall
Do not suffice.
I look at you
With my heart's eye;
For the lightning-flame
Of your vision,
The eye in my head
Does not suffice.

Wazir was enchanted, stunned. It seemed as if the poet had written the poem just for her, and just for this occasion. The depths of meaning hidden in each verse proclaimed to her: Here are all your answers! Do you have any more questions?

As Wazir's wonder and pleasure abated somewhat, her eyes began to mist with unshed tears. It used to be just like this with Shamsuddin Ahmad. They used to exchange poetry in letters and conversations. Oh for the tender grace of those days and nights, now trampled into shapelessness and buried by the world. The world never looks back; the cycles of days never run backwards, or even stop for the blink of an eye. Even now, Navab Shamsuddin Ahmad Khan's image was not at all dimmed in her heart, but somehow his image in her mind's eye had begun to resemble Amir Mirza, and Navab Mirza, and even her own father.

Life had forced the realization on her that however independent, self-willed, headstrong she might be, nothing exists alone, nothing is self-existent. Navab Mirza's being had altered something of the image of Shamsuddin Ahmad Khan in her mind. Though Amir Mirza and Badshah Begam were now severed from her, Marston Blake to some extent still lived in her blood through them. So now . . . this new wave is out to water and overrun the shore of my life, and its effects and remnants will be found in others in the future; I won't be the only one affected. So am I ready for this?

She cast a glance at her body. She was certainly broken and churned up inside, but her external appearance was more or less as it was at the time when the martyred Navab left her to go to Firozepur for the last time. Will not those lacerations in my soul emerge someday soon and occupy my body? Will not all this beauty, virtue and grace, all this lack of style and make-up, so comely in its absence, all this lack of embellishment, so ravishing in its absence, shrink and be crushed like so much paper and become the food for wrinkles and creases all over the body?

She recalled Manjhli's words: It is only a matter of time before Navab Mirza gets married and sets up his own house. You will live all alone then, she had declared. It will be you and your frail old age . . . There is certainly an advantage in the proposal: I will live in Rampur; Navab Mirza will be here. I will be spared the growling silences of Jahanabad, a wasteland of love for me anyway. And I will gain new strength to live as I see my son grow up into a strapping youth. Am I fated always to give birth and then forcibly be removed away from my darlings, the pieces of my heart? My side to be torn open and my heart and liver tormented away from it, is that all I am made for?

. . . Oh, I quite forgot to unroll the other paper! She collected her thoughts, and unrolled and straightened the paper and saw that it was a full-face portrait. Flashes of lights and colours danced before her eyes, slowing her down. A handsome, but somewhat aged male, about forty to forty-five years old, of fair complexion, and with lively, bright eyes and a noble brow. His head was covered with a short, stylish turban worn somewhat rakishly. The turban was mango green, with fine yellow stripes lending it a distinctive style. His beard, short, very thin, was cut in the Iranian style; the moustaches were somewhat more prominent. He wore a long tunic of light, flowered muslin; over the tunic he had a short, Mughal-style half-sleeved coat. Each and every line, each and every dot of the painting oozed an absence of pomposity which had not to do with the painting alone, but also the sitter: friendly, good-natured, sympathetic.

Wazir gazed, and gazed again. Many minutes passed. She collected herself, as if waking from a short, light slumber. She looked again, putting the picture at some distance from her, in better light: the picture was the same, equally friendly, not smiling, but suggesting a readiness to break into a pleasant smile.

Suddenly, she was furious; it was a fury of helplessness, of a child who is burning with rage but cannot find the words to let them out. Was I not determined to have my wish, my preference, prevail over everything? Why is this happening, then? Manjhli Baji, Jahangirah, this attractive, highly literate stranger who calls himself Agha Something . . . They are relentlessly in pursuit of their goal to bend me to their design. What right do they have to draw the map of someone's life? We cannot live as we like, but can we not at least die as we like?

. . . The decision has to be mine. . . . Manjhli Baji and Jahangirah may not have worked to a plan, but it does seem like a plan. And Navab Mirza? He must have also played a part. If he doesn't want me to remarry, I won't remarry. But I am no longer a free agent. These people will keep putting pressure on me.

She came out of her room, looked for Manjhli and found her in the veranda, cutting some betel nuts, as if there was no issue, no problem before her.

'Manjhli Baji, did you . . . did you talk to Navab Mirza?'

'Yes, certainly. Be assured, little one; I and Jahangirah talked to him at length.'

'So what did he say? I hope he wasn't offended?'

'Oh dear, my dear. Why should he be offended? He said that it was for Amma Jan to decide. But he did seem to favour the idea of ending your isolation and loneliness.'

'I am not lonely!' She said sharply. 'I am content to be what I am.'

'Bibi, no one is not lonely. But no one can live alone either. There is a world; there is Time which compels us in myriad ways. You were never one to let pass a good opportunity. You know that most things do not happen twice; some do, especially the bad ones.'

Wazir flounced back into her room and broke down into tears. Manjhli sensed her mood and went in without asking and put her hand on her head, caressing and soothing her, forcing a sip of water on her. When Wazir's tears stopped, she drew a deep sigh and said, 'All right. So I make my play again with my life.' She spoke the famous line of a Persian verse: *Happen what may; I cast my boat upon the water.* She dried her tears, returned to Agha sahib's papers, took her pen and wrote, underneath the ghazal of Sadi, the following verse from Mirza Saib, the great Persian poet of the seventeenth century:

Before now, I hid my treasure in a wilderness;
Now, I hide the wilderness inside a treasure.

*

Wazir Khanam and Agha Mirza Maulavi Turab Ali were married on the first Thursday of the following month, 11 August 1842. The wedding was first performed according to the Sunni method, followed by another, somewhat more elaborate, ceremony according to the Shia way. The dowry was fixed at two hundred and fifty gold mohurs, so called because they bore the stamp, or muhr of a Mughal mint. Most of the gold mohurs then in circulation were struck in the 1760s by Shah Alam II; their gold was considered superior to the English gold by five shillings in the ounce, that is, a little above 6 per cent.

Half of the dower was paid immediately as per the marriage contract. Wazir Khanam did not return to Delhi; her formal 'bride's farewell' took place from Umdah Khanam's haveli. Anwari Khanam and her husband came from Delhi with great gusto and pleasure, laden with gifts for the bride and the groom. Anwari's heart was set at rest, for her wayward sister had finally found a proper and stable haven, away from sinfulness and closer to redemption. Navab Yusuf Ali Khan took upon himself all the expenses and ensured that all ceremonies and procedures bore the stamp of opulence and good taste. Navab Muhammad Said Khan Bahadur sent sweets, dresses and jewelled rings for the newly-weds.

Wazir kept possession of her house in Delhi; she entrusted its keys to Anwari Khanam so that she might air the rooms occasionally, or carry out the necessary maintenance. Wazir moved into Agha Mirza Turab Ali's haveli after the fourth-day ceremonies. Her husband stinted on nothing in making her feel desired, and secure, and in her own home. It was a lifetime since Wazir had last experienced the protective moons of peace and safety; now the distance from distress surrounded her like many haloes: the hideous dark of the world outside now should never cross her threshold and never pollute her or her son.

By virtue of his learning, Agha Mirza Turab Ali was also known as Maulavi, but his was not the bookish, humourless, rigid personality one associates with that of a Maulavi's. Nor was he much given to grand notions about the Iranian nobles who were his remote ancestors; there was no question of his regarding Chhoti Begam as his inferior in birth. His temperament was truly poetic and loverly. He treated Wazir with a tenderness that was coloured with a light hue of respect. For example, he never addressed her as Chhoti Begam, nor did he call her Wazir Khanam. Instead, he always spoke to her and of her as Wazir Begam. He habitually spoke Persian, but with Wazir he was careful to talk in chaste Urdu-e-Muallah, or Hindi, the name by which the language was better known.

Agha Mirza Turab Ali also made efforts towards Wazir reviving her forgotten interest in writing poetry. He insisted—though lovingly and with a clear indication of his own genuine interest—that Wazir Khanam, poet, with the pen name of Zuhrah Dihlavi, should search her memory and pull out whatever verses of hers she found there. If she had an old notebook or pieces of paper on which she had jotted down her poems as a promising young poet, she must make the most diligent search for it. 'I wish to prove to the people of Rampur,' he said, 'that I am not enamoured of just the physical beauties of Wazir Begam: I also love her for her poetry. Let them know that I haven't merely found a gorgeously painted partridge; I have found in her the sweetest of sweet singing shama bird as well! (The point that the shama is dark brown of plumage and that sham means 'black', was not lost on Wazir.)

Wazir retorted, 'Enough, Agha sahib, enough is enough! Please let me be happy in my skin. Should you go on in this strain, I fear people would believe that the famous proverb applies to you of the vain fellow getting hold of a painted partridge, and worrying himself to death if he should display it or hide it.'

Agha Mirza Turab Ali burst into a peal of delighted laughter. 'Do you know, Wazir Begam, that the chess piece we call Wazir or Vizier is known in English as Queen? Thus I am in clover both ways: You are Queen and you are Vizier. So where arises the question of your being clad in a mere skin?'

'I beg Allah's pardon! Please be serious. Domestic life or poetry, these aren't games of chess or pachisi. Look at me, the scent of your hookah fills me with nausea; I am just not able to breathe evenly, and here you are lost in talk of the breath of music and poetry!'

Agha Turab Ali laughed again. 'Well, the Greek philosophers thought that the revolutions of the heavenly spheres produce the music which is the breath of all life.'

'To hell with those crafty failsuf types!' Wazir's voice was full of unsaid blandishments. 'You couldn't even get me a handful of fresh green baby mangoes from Rataul or Gangoh.'

'Oh, thanks for reminding me, I quite forgot to tell you. Just yesterday I dispatched two riders, one to Muzaffarnagar and Rataul, and the other to Saharanpur and Gangoh. You'll see that before tomorrow evening there will be so much green of mangoes before you that the crimson dusk will die of jealousy.'

Wazir became pregnant shortly. This time she had no anxiety like the way she had had during her last pregnancy. Still, Habib-un Nisa took extra care of her because of the long gap between the two pregnancies. Hakims and midwives were in constant consultation. Agha Mirza Turab Ali was considerate and attentive as usual, rather more than usual. The fruit of all this effort appeared in the form of a son, born on the 28th of June 1843. The newborn was good-looking, strong of frame and fair-complexioned like his father. At Wazir's suggestion, the baby was named Shah Muhammad Agha Mirza. Like all his siblings, he grew up to be a poet. He wrote in both Hindi and Persian; with the pen name Shaiq in Persian and Shaghil in Hindi, he gained a wide reputation as a master poet.

The rains came early and by the time Wazir was through with the ceremonies of the sixth day, the thirtieth day, and the ceremonial shaving of the baby's head, the season of rains was at its peak. The drier parts of

Mirza Turab Ali's courtyard garden and interior garden, which were so thoroughly parched by the blistering western wind through the seemingly endless days of summer, and looked so pallid and subdued as if they never saw a drop of rain in their apparently miserable lives, woke up almost overnight, and gleaming with new leaf and branch, celebrated a new lease of life. The streets, lanes, gardens, open spaces—wherever there was any possibility of growth in the city of Rampur—became alive with nature and also with human artifice, loquacious among themselves, reaching out to each other symbolically and physically, as if they were friends whispering among themselves, with heads close to each other, as the great poet Mir said. The clusters of large and small mangoes almost hid the leaves and branches of the trees on which they were ripening with sweet delight. The river Kosi, on whose banks sat the city of Rampur, came almost into flood.

Swings were erected in gardens and orchards, on garden-green and colourful open land. Seasonal foods, spicy, hot, deep fried, spread their scent everywhere; the environment became a royal kitchen. The sharp, powerful, long, penetrating call of the peacock, the koel's koock-coo . . . oou . . . the call of the peewit, shouting the arrival of rain, and asking for more of it, looking for her newly hatched babies whom, with her usual absent-mindedness, she had left alone and uncared for, and remembered much later, frantically telling them, 'Here! Here I am!' All this made Rampur truly Darus Surur (House of Rejoicing). There was springtime in Wazir's courtyard and also her home. Her arms luxuriously heavy with a strong, bright infant; her bed full of the presence of a loving, loverly man; her heart free from fear; her loving son Navab Mirza growing apace both as a handsome young man and a promising poet; now what more could she have asked for? Days were like the day of Id for her, nights were like the night of Shab-e-barat when there are prayers and expensive foods and brilliant lighting and firecrackers everywhere in the world.

It was therefore quite appropriate that Wazir's heart should lurch and roll with the desire of revival in the season of revivals of all life: she should again try her hand at poetry. Maulavi Turab Ali had been assiduous as usual in trying to persuade her to make that return. In the city, the poets, recovering from the hot weather, began to foregather in literary assemblies for organized or impromptu mushairahs.

With Navab Muhammad Said Khan's advent, Rampur, already an important centre of learning, began to establish itself as a salubrious city for poetry. Navab Yusuf Ali Khan was himself a poet, and not just an occasional one. His pen name was Yusuf; he was a pupil of the formidable poet, astrologer and chess player Hakim Momin Khan Momin. Momin died in 1852, so when Yusuf Ali Khan became the ruler in 1855, he became a pupil of Mirza Ghalib. The new mentor gave him a new pen name, Nazim, and that is the name by which he is known today. Among the cousins of Navab Yusuf Ali Khan, there were many like Abbas Ali Khan Betab, Inayat Ali Khan Inayat, Hidayat Ali Khan Ghurbat and Abdul Wahhab Khan Sarosh, who became Momin's pupils. All of them were now settled in Rampur.

Among those who came from Delhi to Rampur in the wake of Navab Yusuf Ali Khan, were Mujid Rampuri, Mir Taskin Dihlavi and his son Mir Ghamgin Dihlavi. The last two were summoned by Navab Yusuf Ali Khan who established a monthly mushairah when he came to Rampur in 1840. Mir Ahmad Ali Rasa, pupil of the famed Ali Bakhsh Bimar, was noted in those days for new themes and new phraseology. One of these poets, or maybe Yusuf Ali Khan himself, happened upon the poetry of Siraj Aurangabadi, the great early eighteenth-century poet from the Deccan. He became an instant success; his poems were imitated; new ghazals were attempted following the rhymes and end-rhymes used by him. For one of the mushairahs, Yusuf Ali Khan set the following line from Siraj as the 'model' line. Ghazals were to be written in the same metre and the same rhyme pattern as this model:

My beloved's tresses, and links in a chain, are alike
Exactly.

The line was so full of the power of spontaneity and had such a strong rhythmic effect that it attracted numerous poets to compete and outdo the old master. Agha Mirza Turab Ali was so enthused by the interest evoked by the line that he insisted that Wazir compose at least one verse or a line to complete the model line; better still, she should try writing a whole ghazal. On his way back home that evening, Agha sahib had stopped at the State Library to copy the full ghazal of Siraj Aurangabadi. He now said it to Wazir:

My beloved's tresses, and links in a chain, are alike
Exactly.

Her eyebrow like the bow, her eyelashes like arrows,
Exactly.
On the page of my heart, the wounds of separation
Are inscribed like golden-blood writing,
Exactly.
All the Indian bulbuls agree:
Your street is like the Garden of Kashmir,
Exactly.
I looked at my beloved's face. It was like
The Quran, writ by the Scribe of Fate,
Exactly.
To trim the hot ember-tears from the candle of the
Eye, oh Siraj, your eyelashes are like candle-trimmers,
Exactly.

As Agha sahib recited line after line, Wazir was struck more and more by the tight versification and the fully effective agreement of the rhyme word with the repeating end-rhyme. As he finished the ghazal, Wazir exclaimed, 'Wah, wah! Only God is untouched by blemish! This is not poetry. It's miracle-working in words.'

'Well, Wazir Begam, you now must compose your ghazal in this pattern. I pleased you with Siraj; you now please me with your poem!'

'No, no! You coerce me too much, Agha sahib. I am not a crazy fool to try to move my limbs in this territory.'

The more strongly did Wazir resist, the more urgently did Agha sahib importune. In the middle of this friendly give and take of repartee, Wazir paused for a moment and cried out:

The eyebrow is like a bow, the glances are arrows,
Exactly.

Agha Turab Ali opened his mouth to applaud the flowing effect of the line, but Wazir checked him and said, 'No. That won't do. There is too much of the master's line in it. Your friends will blame me for plagiarism,' she smiled. 'Let me try again.'

Within a minute or two, she spoke up, 'Well, now there's something here:

Her glance has the effect of magic,
Exactly.'

'Very nice, very proper!' said Agha Turab Ali. 'The word "effect" is a new word here.'

'Oh, don't take me for a fool, please,' Wazir laughed. 'It's nothing close to the master, but could just do as a completing line for the model line:

Her glance has the effect of magic,
Exactly.
My beloved's tresses, and links in a chain, are alike
Exactly.'

'No, there's subtlety of thought here: first, the eye's magic will enchant to madness; then the mad lover will be chained in the tresses. Very nice.'

'At least you made me compose an opening verse! Delhi was not shamed.'

'Sorry, Delhi's ladies can't get off so lightly. Was it not Mushafi who said:

Oh Mushafi, never fall in love with them!
Baneful and full cruel are the women of Delhi.

Now that you are in Rampur, you'll be fined in lieu of all those bad ladies. You must give a full ghazal!'

'All right, all right! Let my mood become somewhat amenable to the task. You will get your ghazal by and by.'

The next evening, when Agha Turab Ali came into the zenana for dinner, Wazir was prepared, primed with her new ghazal. But instead of reciting it to him, she handed the paper over to him shyly. She promptly disappeared, excusing herself to tend to the baby. Agha sahib unfolded the paper and found the ghazal, written in Wazir's clear but somewhat unformed hand:

Her glance has the effect of magic,
Exactly.
My beloved's tresses, and links in a chain, are alike
Exactly.

On the white book of her face, the rays of morning light
Are like the flow of colour from the white manna of the forest,
Exactly.
In that little lane, where I left my heart,
Is a house, like Paradise,
Exactly.
As I breathe my last, I feel the warmth of my
Beloved's candle-face at the pillow:
My reality is like my dream,
Exactly.
Lost in the wilderness of the night: a tiny stream
Is the portrait of my slumbering fortune,
Exactly.
In the garden of the morning, who
Could have the power of sight? Her beauty is
Like the growing light of the sun,
Exactly.
It is not the stain left by a crushed rose petal
On her marble foot: It is like golden lettering
On a Royal Proclamation,
Exactly.

Agha Turab Ali was so transported by the poetry that he called out aloud to Wazir, even though it was rather improper to cry out to the lady of the house in this fashion, 'Hey, Wazir Begam! Where are you? Please come here!'

Wazir entrusted the baby to its suckling maid, rearranged her clothes and walked over somewhat hurriedly.

'Please command,' she smiled. 'You terrorized me really, yelling out so loud. Is everything all right? You didn't like my ghazal?'

'Like? Please. Wazir Begam, it is a marvellous poem! By Allah, your search for new ideas is unrivalled. Only Shaikh Nasikh or your master, Shah Nasir, can do justice to your effort!'

Wazir reddened with pleasure; trying to be appropriately modest, she said, 'Take the name of God! What is it that you say? They are the undisputed Sovereigns of poetry's land; I am a mere maid at best.'

'Well, they may be the Sovereigns, but you are Vizier too, and not only in name!'

'This is just like the Persian proverb: "The Abyssinian is called Mr Camphor!" But you liked my effort and that's enough for me.'

There was, of course, no question of Wazir herself presenting the ghazal at Yusuf Ali Khan's next mushairah, or even have it presented by someone else. Agha Turab Ali showed it privately to the Navab who did not lag behind Mirza Turab Ali in admiring the ghazal. Indeed, he made a perceptive point: 'Although there is no distinction of gender as far as the speaker in the ghazal is concerned—even women poets use a male voice—yet you should appreciate, Mirza Turab, that the thought of a tiny stream lost in the night's wilderness could only have occurred to a woman. Very good, as Allah wills. Indeed, only God is untouched by blemish!'

The ghazal's high level of artistry, then the Navab's praise of it, and his subtlety in appreciating the 'tiny stream' theme, soon put Wazir's ghazal on the tongues of all poetry lovers of Rampur. When Navab Mirza heard the ghazal, and the Navab's point about the woman poet, he noticed that in not a single verse had the poet used a word specific to masculine gender. Respect and love for his mother swelled in his heart evermore.

Shah Muhammad Agha seemed to be growing up quite on the lines of his far older stepbrother. Friendly and playful, he began trying to stutter a meaningful sound or two even at five or six months of age. The sound of his joyful shrieks and screams filled the whole haveli until he was put to bed, or dropped off to sleep, exhausted with laughter and play. In the past, Agha Mirza Turab Ali's normal practice was to enter the zenana only once in the day, preferably for dinner. Now he began to visit much more frequently and his young son became so familiar with him that he rarely left his father's bosom, even trying to sleep with his pudgy, short arms around the father's neck.

52

Agha Turab Ali sets out for the great annual cattle fair in Sonepur on the banks of the mighty Gandak

IT WAS THE beginning of November 1843, when Agha Mirza Turab Ali decided to travel to Sonepur, in Bihar, for the purchase of horses and elephants for the Navab's stable. Sonepur was far away, but it was the site of the biggest annual cattle fair in the whole of Hindustan, or perhaps both the Hind and the Deccan. This fair was held—is in fact still held—from the 3rd of Pus until the Great Bathing Day of Makar Sankranti, in the middle of Magh. In additions to horses, elephants, draught animals and pack animals, the fair—held on the bank of the small but mighty river Gandak on whose bank the city of Sonepur spreads in a north–south direction—attracted dealers in exotic birds and unusual animals. A few freaks also were shown, if possible, though not sold. Games, competitions, dances, dance dramas, plays, acrobatics, wrestling shows and competitions, religious displays: everything was provided.

The purchasing journey to Sonepur was undertaken at the suggestion of the Navab, Muhammad Said Khan, and with his permission, Agha Turab Ali set out on 9 December 1843. He kissed Shah Muhammad Agha profusely, hugged Navab Mirza many times, and in the seclusion of the bedroom, he kissed and hugged Wazir to his heart's content. He then took leave from his two female relatives who lived with him. Habiba, Rahat Afza, Manjhli Begam and Wazir tied upon Agha Turab Ali's right arm separate amulets of protection dedicated to Imam Musa Kazim, the Eighth Imam, known as the Protector and Guarantor. Similar amulets were tied by Agha sahib's female relatives. Wazir Khanam circulated a cup of water around Agha Turab Ali's head, took a sip from it and said a prayer for him. All the women said in one voice, 'Go, please, and show us your face soon just as you show your back today.'

Agha Turab Ali entrusted all to the protection of Allah, and saying a prayer for their safety, blew on his sons' heads and faces. He left immediately through the eastern gate of the city, his first stage being Moradabad, twenty miles away. Travelling through the whole of Rohilkhand and Avadh over land, and over water from Allahabad in the Company Bahadur's territory, he reached Sonepur late in the day on 29 December 1843. His train consisted of four personal servants, twelve spear-wielders, four syces and two mahouts. The journey had lasted twenty days.

Judging from the proliferation of animals in the fair, Agha Turab Ali determined that it would be a week before he could be through selecting, bargaining and paying for the animals that he desired. He also wished to make his departure as many days before Makar Sankranti as feasible, because traders and visitors from outside began normally to break camp in large numbers immediately after that Great Bathing Day, resulting in overcrowding at all the stopping places and inns and saddlers' establishments which were often unable to cope with the extra demand. While it was good for the roads to become busier, the dearth of stopping places made for hardship, especially for a large entourage like his.

The purchasing party from Rampur were nearly through with their task by the end of the fifth day. Some more dealers in elephants were expected the next day from the foothills of Nepal; the final decision about the elephants to buy would be taken after examining what they had on offer. Thus, when Agha Turab Ali took stock of his purchases on 11 January1844, he had six elephants and eight horses. The total price, including the salaries of some extra syces and mahouts to be employed over the journey—but who hoped to be taken in the Navab's establishment on a long-term basis when they reached Rampur—came to 52,500 John Company rupees. There was no problem of payment, for Agha Turab Ali possessed the Navab's pay-on-demand paper for one hundred thousand rupees payable by any money-dealer who had dealings with the State of Rampur's chief money manager.

Agha Turab Ali and his crowded entourage left for home on 12 January 1842. On account of the large number of animals in the caravan, Agha Turab Ali preferred to avoid the river route as much as possible, except where there was no road or where passage was difficult because of the density of the forest. Since there was no real urgency, and the river Ganga was wide and quite placid from Allahabad, from thereon Agha Turab Ali ordered the animals to be transported up to Fatehgarh by the river. This would be slow, but the animals would not be subjected to hardship, and in fact there was greater security too on the river, except for the very unlikely event of a boat foundering in the shallows against a riverine hillock. River robbers or pirates were unknown in those days.

On 20 January 1842, the road caravan left the river train at Phaphamau, six miles north of Allahabad; led by Agha Turab Ali, the road travellers turned towards Kara Manikpur. He had four horses, two syces, two spear-wielders and four pony-riding personal servants. Their road would take them to Cawnpore—Kampu in common parlance at that time, while Cawnpore is now Kanpur—through Kara Manikpur and Bindki. The riverine party would also arrive later at Cawnpore through Kara Manikpur. Although there was another land route to Cawnpore, Agha Turab Ali determined his choice to be safer, for it was always busy during the day. Travelling by night was something to be avoided anyway.

A seasoned syce, well acquainted with the roads in that part of Hind, tried to warn Agha Turab Ali in subdued tones about the possibility of encountering the thugs on the route chosen by him. But Agha Turab Ali scoffed at him.

'The Company Bahadur has broken the thugs' backs. They are rotting in jails or have been drawn and hanged. Where are the thugs now, Munir Khan? Have you lost your mind?' He smiled, to rob his words of offence.

'The Presence knows best. But we have heard that the thugs are like venomous snakes. So long as their head is not cut off, there is always the danger of their striking back.'

53

Agha Turab Ali's journey back home is riddled with sinister perils and diabolical betrayals

AGHA MIRZA TURAB Ali's temperament had more than its share of firmness, even obstinacy. Life with the hot-headed Pathans of Rampur had done nothing to mitigate his inflexibility. He was now quite determined to prosecute his journey by road, and by his chosen route. Though he spoke with a smile, everybody knew that Agha sahib was never going to change his mind. He knew quite well that the thugs of Hind spent the whole month of Agahan worshipping at their Devi's temple in Vindhyachal not too far from Benaras. They spread far and wide as Agahan concluded, and the main season for thuggee, their chosen profession, came into full swing with the Bathing Day of Makar Sankranti.

The high-sounding and loud proclamations of the Company Bahadur and its favour seekers regardless, it was not a fact that the thugs had disappeared from the face of the earth. Agha Turab Ali had heard that on account of the continuous pressure exerted by the Firangee authorities, many of the thug families had moved into the contiguous country of Avadh. Thus the regions which straddled the English and the Avadh King's domain—like the one through which he was proposing to travel—were particularly dangerous because the thugs often committed the crime in one territory and promptly crossed over to the other.

Agha Turab Ali did not know this, but there were many points near Cawnpore which the thugs had established as their chosen spots—'bel' in their secret language—that is, places which they had determined to be particularly suited for committing their atrocities. Since these places were safe and secret, the thugs used them over and over again. At the time of which we are writing, there was a village spot named Chakatiya between Fatehpur and Cawnpore, and another called Chaparghata just near Cawnpore which were reputed to be notorious as bel.

Even if Agha Turab Ali had known about these places, it was not likely that his obstinately erect neck would soften and flex itself. Observing the tightness of displeasure in his eyes, the servants preferred to hold their tongue on the matter of thugs and thuggee. The journey to Kara Manikpur and then to Fatehpur by the Royal Road of Sher Shah, was quite comfortable and safe, and at good speed. The road was wide and well kept, with plenty of stopping places. There was no shortage of water on the road, which was often shaded by big trees on both sides. Once they even had the chance to stop for the night at the English Dawk Bungalow (Post House, Rest House) whose cleanness and good management, and the politeness of its manager, won their hearts.

The scene was quite changed by the time they reached Bindki, beyond Fatehpur. Most of the region was uncultivated and desolate. The road on both sides was overhung by low hillocks and dunes made of ancient, decomposed rocks. Occasionally the roadside was one long ravine. Much of the land was arid, alkaline and overgrown with wild jujube, blackthorn, acacia and henna. In some places it was a veritable forest, trackless and dry. Mirza Turab Ali's experienced travellers and mounts negotiated the desolate path comfortably, but did not try to stop anywhere, for the environment somehow suggested the existence of the lairs of robbers and hideouts of thieves. At every turn, they expected to encounter some mysterious jogi or unfamiliar apparition to block their progress.

They had travelled quite a distance beyond Bindki, and Cawnpore was apparently only about five or six miles away, when they sighted their first considerable group of travellers. They were just ahead of them, a group of pedestrians, walking with dejected steps and drooping heads as if they were extremely worn out. Agha Turab Ali's train overtook them quickly: about twelve or fifteen men—no women or children—middle aged or older, apparently they were Hindus of different castes; they were clad in plain, inexpensive clothes, somewhat grubby, but free from rips or patches. On closer examination, Mirza Turab Ali determined one or two of them to be from the better castes; the rest of them were petty farmers, agricultural labourers and shepherds of good character and law-abiding ways, earning their bread through honest labour.

The elder of the pedestrians waved to the rest of his people to make way for the riders, but when Agha Turab Ali's horse approached him, he went down on his knees, practically blocking the road, and made his submissions to Agha Turab Ali, 'Salaams, Mai-baap! May Your Honour's fortune be ascendant always!'

His tone was grave, without a hint of the rustic, and extremely polite and submissive, suggesting that he often had occasion to greet persons of superior or even noble station. The meekness of the old man affected Agha Turab Ali's heart a trifle, but he preferred to respond harshly, even disdainfully, and spoke in a loud, somewhat threatening voice, 'Who are you fellows? Why do you block our way?'

'Blocking your way! Your Honour, we couldn't dare be so disrespectful. We are pilgrims, going to Kannauj for Sight of our Devi there.'

'So go!' Agha Mirza Turab Ali growled. 'Don't block our path. Move!'

Now the old man became even more meek and pitiful. He spoke beseechingly, 'Presence, we are alone. There is no policeman or soldier to protect us if we are waylaid here.'

Now another old man, clearly more rustic and also more decrepit, approached near. Outdoing his companion in talking softly and deferentially, he said, 'Yes, Your Excellency, some of us are also feeble and sick. Were we so lucky as to get under the Exalted Honour's protective umbrella, the safety of our pilgrimage would be assured.'

Agha Turab Ali looked closely at the two old men, their eyes on the ground, their bodies gathered tight to seem smaller—they were the very image of helpless humility. But he also realized that during the time the conversation was in progress, the companions of the old men had somehow crept closer among themselves and also closer to him, such that there seemed to be a loose ring of men around him. A sharp tremor thrilled his body. 'Are they the thugs?' The question burnt through his consciousness like a drop of acid. 'No, how could they be the thugs? They are quite harmless.' But the ring of men was now perhaps closer still?

He looked towards Munir Khan whose eyes were anxious and perhaps full of doubt. 'No. It's just my imagination; Munir Khan doesn't seem suspicious of these puny fellows.' But then he noticed something at the extreme edge of his vision on the left: a sturdy young man, not shrinking in his body like the others. His eyes had a cruel brightness which was also full of expectancy, like a serpent who has espied a dozing, hapless rabbit.

Agha Turab Ali was filled with fear, a fear that he had never experienced before. He wanted to say something when a crow flew raucously cawing over them. He noticed that though the pilgrims were seemingly looking humbly at their feet, they were actually full of curiosity to see if the crow flew away or alighted at a nearby branch. Munir Khan cleared his throat delicately, as if he had plucked up his courage to open his mouth. Before he could say anything, the crow flew far away, calling as before.

A grey disappointment seemed to overrun the pilgrims' faces when the crow flew away over them. Perhaps they had somehow lost hope that the protection of the travelling nobleman would extend to them; we should now go on to our destination alone. Or does this disappointment mean something quite different? The thought suddenly occurred to Agha Mirza Turab Ali. Are these ruffians really the thugs? And now they realize that I am wise to them and cannot become a prey to these carrion-eaters? The circle around him seemingly loosened somewhat, though none of the pilgrims seemed to be of the mind to budge from where he was.

'Your Honour,' Munir Khan spoke in a tight, strangled whisper. 'Your Honour, let us clear out now.'

Munir Khan's voice struck Agha Turab Ali's heart like the bell of a departing caravan. His face cleared, and he spoke in a hoarse voice, 'Eh? Yes, let us.' He swallowed to clear his throat and bellowed at the two old men, 'Out! Out of my sight, now!'

He was unable to read in the gloaming the enigmatic expression on the faces of the two old men, but it was obvious that they were not in much of a hurry to give way. Agha Turab Ali backed his horse a step; he raised his whip and struck the air with a menacing crack; pressing his thighs hard to the horse's sides, he cried out, 'Come, son, let fly!' The powerful mount raised his heavy neck and bared his teeth, his dark grey-black mane flew against the wind; he brought up his forelegs hard against his stomach and pushed with his front muscles and back at full power. His rear legs now under his waist, forelegs stuck under the chest, he vaulted several yards and came down upon the earth lightly, like a big leaf in the wind. The old men in front were not able even to appreciate the happening fully before the violent blast and the whirling sound made by the steed's passing forced them to the ground. The rest of the pilgrims scattered like so many matchsticks. Within seconds, Agha Turab Ali and his train had disappeared down the desolate road.

Having run full blast for some miles, they stopped at a well to water the animals. Munir Khan spoke in a low voice, 'Your Honour. They were the thugs . . . Better not to stop here for too long.'

Agha Turab Ali's perverse obstinacy returned. 'Why?' he asked querulously. 'What is the problem in stopping at this place? Are there any thugs around now at all?'

'Sir, these people choose their prey from well before, and stalk him by dispersing into two or three small bands and do surveillance from both front and back, and attack where the ground favours them best.'

'I say, Munir Khan, are you a Pathan or a shepherd or grass-cutter, man? You fear where there is nothing to fear, and die before your death.'

'Sir,' an old spear-wielder spoke with his hand on his breast, 'I have travelled these roads in the past. Right there in front of Your Honour is the river Pandu. I have often heard that the scoundrel thugs hide in the river's defile and after committing their atrocity hide in the nearby village. The village is not even a mile from here.'

'Well,' Agha Turab Ali conceded, 'I had no intention of spending the night here anyway. Let's go ahead.'

The wintertime evening was quite upon them when they entered the city of Cawnpore without further incident. Not finding a large enough inn to accommodate all of his people, Agha Turab Ali was obliged to travel at double speed, arriving at Bilhaur through the sleepy village of Bithur. Both the places, almost unknown then, were fated to become famous during the armed struggle of 1857 as scenes of fierce fighting and resistance.

They made their night halt at Bilhaur, sleeping late and cooling their eyes with the misty manna of the morning when the sun rose trying to peer through the mist. The cold humours of the morning, rising from the river Ganga nearby, made for a wondrous cold, bracing and daunting at the same time. They left as soon as they could organize themselves. Still, their progress was slow; evening began to fall rapidly. Kannauj was barely six miles away, but they preferred to spend the night in a convenient inn and make a leisurely start the next morning.

They had travelled just about a mile on the road to Kannauj when they overtook a group of twenty or twenty-two travellers. They were Muslim, obviously, because they wore four- or five-cornered coarse cloth caps much favoured by Muslims of the poorer classes. Some had beards of the style and cut prescribed by the Shariah: beards longer than 'a fist's length', upper lips shaven almost clean. Their trousers were short, showing the ankles, as again prescribed in the books. There were no women or children in the group. One of the travellers stopped on the road, somewhat like the old man on the road to Cawnpore a couple of days ago. He salaamed in the style prescribed by the Shariah: no gesture of hand or head, just the words, 'As-salamu alaikum, Excellency. Where is the Presence bound for?'

Mirza Turab Ali, much impressed by the calm, grave demeanour of the man, his coarse but clean clothes, the grey scar on his forehead, sure sign of regular prostration in prayer, looked at just the man, without appreciating that the rest of the travellers were arranged on the road in some significant way. But his naturally elitist temperament did not permit him to stop on the wayside and converse with a man who was clearly from the artisan classes.

'People of good family do not stop and talk on the road. Get a move on. Don't stay here.'

'Excellency, we are poor Muslim artisans. We have no wealth, no power to command guards and protectors. And this route is fraught with risks. We have been waiting and hoping for so long for Allah to send to us a valiant gentleman like you. We should attach ourselves to the hem of your noble garment and make the difficult road in safety.'

Mirza Turab Ali had a vague sense that Munir Khan and his senior companions were under some sort of tension and their bodies betrayed the tension in spite of themselves. He grimaced inwardly: these wretched fellows are dying of a fear that has no cause or source. He was about to reprimand them when he noticed with an inward thrill an uncanny but undefined resemblance between the Muslim artisan types before him and the Hindu pilgrims on Cawnpore Road. He put his hand on the pistol in his belted waist and said coldly, 'So you think you can use me as your guard? Where is your leader? Let me talk to him.'

The middle-aged traveller instantly noticed the threatening gesture; he touched the ground in abject submission and stepped back. He spoke in a tearful voice, 'Your Honour, we serve John Company Bahadur in Kampu. Fortunately we were given a few days' leave to go to our homes in Kannauj. We are artisans, not petty thieves or low-caste labourers.'

He spoke with such misery-charged humility that Agha Turab Ali felt himself melting with pity. But then he recalled the words of his senior spear-wielder: the thugs often broke into small groups to hunt their prey. Some go ahead of the intended victim while some pursue him from behind. But no, those thugs—if thugs they were—on Cawnpore Road could not have so wide a beat. Still, care and discretion were important.

'All right, you may be what you say. But you cannot be in our company. Get out of my way, or I will shoot.'

In a low, defeated voice dripping with sad hopelessness, the man said, 'As the Master wills', and moving away from Agha Turab Ali, he joined his fellows. When they were out of sight and sound of those travellers, Mirza Turab Ali's companions spoke with one voice, 'Let's be sacrificed for His Honour's wisdom and sagacity! You saved us from the thugs!'

Agha Turab Ali pulled a face. 'Thugs, what thugs? You fellows slander those poor Muslim artisans.'

None had the heart or fortitude to answer back. In their hearts each one thanked God for deliverance, whatever way it came. Inwardly, Agha Turab Ali himself felt shaken: a smoky cloud of apprehension and, in fact, terror and anxiety, seemed to hang upon his heart. But it was broad daylight: the sun was warm, the sky was clear, and the road was easy and smooth. They made very good time, halting a couple of stages beyond Kannauj; Fatehgarh was nearly next door, just about two or three miles away.

They put up at a spacious inn. The bustle of activity, the noise of mounts and carriages—camels, horses, mules—and their attendants, the welcome woodsmoke rising from the cooking stoves in the big kitchen, the gleeful calls of children at play in the open ground around the inn, the familiar, reassuring sounds of temple bells and the muezzin's call to prayer: all this uplifted Agha Turab Ali's heart. He ordered full rest for the day. They would start the next morning, after a hot bath and a full breakfast.

Morning came, misty; but the sun and a nice breeze were fast eating up the mist and the sweet smoke of the kitchen fire and the fire lit to heat cauldrons of water. Agha Mirza Turab was dressed for breakfast when Munir Khan appeared and did a low salaam. He spoke a little haltingly, a little shyly, 'Your Honour, I have to make a submission.'

'Yes, what is it, Munir Khan?'

It occurred to Agha Turab Ali that Munir Khan had the same abject, hangdog expression on his face, which was characteristic of the travellers on the road the previous day. But what he had to say was something quite different: 'Your Honour, this man is from my family, the son of my mother's brother.' He paused, then said, as if in reinforcement, 'Yes, sir. He is my cousin from my mother's side. His name is Sadiq Khan.' Saying this, he turned and gestured to someone who was apparently waiting just outside the door. It was a thirty or thirty-five-year-old man, wiry of body, short of stature. He wore a small chintz turban on his head; his tunic was long and green, of the coarse cotton fabric known as guzzy; his narrow trousers were of the same cloth, very clean, free from rips or patches. Clearly, he was of a poor but good family.

'I make my submissions, Your Honour.' He bent low in two salaams, and then stood to one side, his body closely shrunk, as if trying to take the smallest possible space. His eyes were firmly on his feet.

'What is your name? Where are you coming from?'

'This slave is called Sadiq Khan, Your Honour. We are on our way from Kampu.'

'So you are not alone?'

'No . . . no, Your Highness.'

A brief chill ran down Agha Turab Ali's spine. 'How many of you are there?'

'We are fifteen, twenty people, Your Honour.'

'Women and children?'

'None, sir. We are returning home from our service station. Our women are there, in the village.'

Mirza Turab Ali was silent for an appreciable moment. Then he spoke coldly, 'Munir Khan.'

'Yes, sir, Your Honour.'

'This man is a son of your mother's full brother?'

'Sir, no. No, sir, a relation by marriage, Your Honour.'

'Have you known him from before?'

At this, the newcomer scrunched his body even more, as if trying to disappear; still, he was brazen enough to open his mouth, wanting to say something.

'Munir Khan,' Agha Turab Ali spoke sternly, 'I asked you.'

Now the faces of both Munir Khan and Sadiq Khan betrayed confusion and fright. Sadiq Khan tried to convey something to Munir Khan with a flicker of his eye, but Agha Turab Ali was not having any more of their play-acting.

'You keep your dirty mouth shut. Munir Khan, it seems that you are now prepared to do a bit of treason.' He picked up the pistol that lay upon the occasional table. The newcomer jerked back and made himself scarce like a rat down a tunnel. Mirza Turab Ali made to go out in pursuit, and then realized that a more important matter was at hand. He thrust his pistol against Munir Khan's chest and roared, 'Bastard, you were to keep me alert against the thugs, but you sold your loyalty to those very murderers!' His body was shaking in fury and also not a little out of fright. 'You gave no thought to my suckling baby even!'

Munir Khan thrust his chest out, his neck hard and erect. 'Doubtless, the Presence must shoot me dead; I pray you to kill me. You are my master and I am the eater of your salt. My loyalty and faith have been pawned to your Presence since the first day. I am guilty. I erred greatly in judging that man.'

'Satan's offspring! No more of your smooth talk! I'll break all the bones in your body and cripple you for life.'

'Excellency, I am ready to die. It is the just punishment for my blunder. But I am no traitor. I can swear with the Word of God on my head.'

'So you call it blunder? The world has only one name for it and that is treason. You introduced a stranger as your first cousin and set me up for him so that he could take my life.'

'Your Honour, I did not knowingly introduce the stranger as my cousin. I was deceived into accepting him.'

'Bastard, you could have made at least a rudimentary investigation.'

'Excellency, it was as if they had worked some magic spell on my head using an owl's bones . . . I had no notion at all that I was being cheated.' Munir Khan's eyes were now dimming, his erect neck no longer so. The tension in Mirza Turab Ali's gun arm was now lessening; he almost lowered his gun, but he clenched his teeth and kept the gun aimed fast at Munir Khan's chest. He was also somewhat curious to know how a total stranger was able to convince an experienced and mentally alert man like Munir Khan that he was his close cousin, or at least a cousin. Munir Khan apparently divined what was going on in Mirza Turab Ali's mind. He said, his eyes lowered and full of unspoken apologies, 'Your Honour, that man, and one or two companions of his, talked so glibly and knowingly . . . I can't tell how glibly they talked. They concocted relationships and kinship from all kinds of places and angles so convincingly that I thought I had known this man Sadiq Khan from long before . . . I now pray with folded hands . . . Please. Let your bullet go down into my heart. I will die happy before Allah and the world, having washed my sin with my blood.'

'And thus I should be guilty of your murder? Is that what you want?

How will I answer your family, your people? Will not the evil that attaches to your name bury them alive? Now get out of my sight. Go. I pardon your error. As for the truth of your heart, only Allah can know.'

Agha Turab Ali felt sad and heavy at heart. Escaping death by so narrow a margin, the regret at dismissing Munir Khan, so trusted a servant who had grown old in his service, and dismissing him in such inauspicious and hurtful circumstances, knowing that he had no choice but to dismiss him: he lost his appetite and his enthusiasm for the journey. He ate nothing, rested but little, and started for the next stage. He had only seven servants left now: three personal attendants, two spear-wielders and two syces, effectively a defence force of three. Munir Khan, with his experience and sagacity, would have outweighed the rest. If he could be duped, there could be no telling about anyone else.

Lost in these thoughts, looking to his right and left every now and then, keeping some of his train in front and one servant on each side of him, with two on his back, they travelled rather slowly. Their aim was to pass through Qaim Ganj and reach Kakralah by sundown. From then on, they were in Rohilla territory. They travelled through the ancient city of Badaon, passing by Aonla and Shahabad; Kakralah was a mere seventy-two miles away from Rampur: just four and a half days' journey at normal pace. But their speed of travel, at least at present, was much reduced because of the precautions they were observing.

The travellers by boat were to leave the river Ganga at Fatehgarh and travel twenty miles overland to Qaim Ganj, then reach Kakralah. Mirza Turab Ali had the idea that slowing down their speed might in fact be good, for they could then hope to meet with the boat contingent somewhere between Badaon and Aonla. The addition to their strength would be very welcome. But Agha Turab Ali was not prepared to break the journey in the hope of joining with the river travellers. He thought, and perhaps rightly, that stopping for more than the barely necessary time and waiting for the riverine party outside the Rohilla territory was unacceptable. His slow pace was not desirable, not by his choice. He could not delay himself further for anything else now.

He started, and looked at the environment. Without quite realizing it, they had done some fair distance, perhaps because they had not stopped for a water break anywhere. The sun was high; since they were moving from the east to the north-west, the winter sun's transparent might was behind them, lengthening their shadows to monstrous sizes and warming their bodies to near discomfort. Not having stopped on the way, they could not be sure exactly how many miles separated them from Qaim Ganj. On all sides, they saw arid fields spreading into the far distance, dozing, and the road was seemingly slowed down by the heat of the sun. The plains seemed endlessly lonely, featureless and devoid of life, except in the air. Looking at their long shadows crawling along the naked road, Agha Turab Ali now prayed in his heart for some travellers, an ox cart, horsemen, anything to break the oppressive monotony. He recalled a line of Hindi poetry: 'How desolate is the jungle; one wishes to encounter something, even a wolf.' It was a stupid line, really. One needs security, not thrills.

Or perhaps the road was not so frightening: it was his fevered imagination, the terror in his heart which ran in front like an evil spirit of the jungle, dragging him along; sometimes she turned to look at him, making horrible faces. Mirza Turab Ali looked hard in front of him; he could descry nothing. But actually, the road ahead bent sharply, making it impossible to see what lay beyond the bend. Perhaps there is a band of thugs waiting to ambush us on the other side of the bend? Mirza Turab Ali's heart lurched up to his throat. How should we deal with the satanic pack? He had heard that two or even three thugs joined in attacking a horseman, like wild dogs. One would hold the reins so powerfully that the horse was immobilized; the other would grab the rider by the waist and pull him down; as the rider fell, the third thug would bring up their favourite weapon—a white-and-yellow striped cloth band like a muffler, which the thugs called 'rumal' ('handkerchief', spelt 'ruhmal' by the English)—to strangle and suffocate the victim within seconds. The victim does not even get to struggle, or even writhe in his death throes . . . Agha Turab Ali noticed darkness or some shadows down the road. Perhaps a spinney, and perhaps an ambush . . . ?

'La haula wa la quwwata illa billah!' Agha Turab Ali uttered in his heart the traditional phrase used by the Indo-Muslims to express disapproval or disgust, and also—when the occasion demanded—to beg God's succour and support: There is no Power and there is no Strength except God. But I am being foolish and superstitious like an illiterate woman! He jerked and wrenched his fearful imaginings from his heart. Even then, the thought would invade him again and again. He did not want his party to fathom his jitters; he pulled himself together and began in his heart to recite the prayer which calls upon Ali, the First Imam, to come to the aid of the distressed:

I cry out to Ali . . . He finished the prayer, and began again. He then resolved in his heart that if . . . when he reached Rampur safely, he would, at the first possible opportunity, present himself at the holy mausoleum of Shah Jamalullah, gift a ceremonial sheet for his grave and provide a feast for everyone present there. Later, he would go to Amroha and make submissions at the holy tomb of the Presence, Makhdum Shah-e Vilayat.

His heart found some rest and solace after the prayers and the resolutions; he realized that the clump of shadow down the road, which spread right to the middle of the road, was no spinney, and thus no ambush. It was actually a group of travellers, eight or ten in number; one of them slept by the side of the road, covered with a sheet. Someone injured, or perhaps ill, he thought. Two or three men sat at his head and foot, talking quietly; perhaps they were saying some prayers. The rest of them, three or four, stood in the middle of the road, their heads drooping, their shoulders bent: a picture of hopelessness and despair. One of them raised his head and looked at Agha Turab Ali's train with eyes brimming with fear and hope.

54

Agha Turab Ali's party is persuaded to stop and help a group of travellers

THE FRONT RIDERS of Agha Turab Ali gestured to the pedestrians to stay where they were. One of Agha sahib's riders went forward and carefully inspected the party. They were seven or eight in number. They were in soldiers' clothing, but were unarmed and meek in appearance. The three or four who were at the head and foot of the person who was lying on the ground looked sad and mournful. They did not rise, but continued to say their prayers in undertones. The rider could not hear them clearly, but the words sounded like Arabic prayers used by all Muslims everywhere. Four men stood by the roadside; their miens dark and dusty with sorrow and pain, their shoulders drooping, their bodies loose, as if they had travelled past the last stages of exhaustion, having been always meek in life, overtaken by their peers in their journey to success. They were dark of complexion; their faces showed them to be from Avadh and not from some exotic land like the Deccan. They too were unarmed; their luggage seemed to be contained in four or five large, shapeless bundles on the roadside: their size suggested they contained arms such as matchlocks or SBBL guns.

They looked at the rider with expectant eyes. One of them bent low in supplication and spoke in a voice almost dead with hopelessness and pain, 'Kamidan sahib, how lucky that you came this way! We had in fact lost all hope . . .'

The other riders approached near, and one of them cut the stranger short and barked, 'Yes? What's the matter? Who are you, mean fellows, and why do you stand here?'

The meek man, who seemed to be middle aged, his rather unkempt head of hair and beard shot with grey, his neck somewhat thin and wrinkled, made to take a step towards the riders, but the rider snubbed him harshly,

'No! Don't take a single step forward. Stay where you are and say what you have to say.'

'Kamidan ji, my name is Karimuddin. We are soldiers of the Navab sahib of Chandpur. We are Mussulmans; we had been on leave in Kakralah. We are on our way back to duty.'

Despite his riders' request to the contrary, Agha sahib had approached so near the group that he could hear the dialogue between them and his riders. He noted that they were soldiers, undoubtedly, and were most certainly Muslims too. They wore short and narrow trousers of guzzy, and a tight, short tunic of blue susi or mahmudi—both cotton fabrics, coarse and hardy, much favoured by the soldiery—with a medium length coat of flowered long cloth over the tunic. The left side of the open coat wrapped over the right side, in the style of Muslims. Their turban was again small, but like the Muslim formal headgear, with one end dropping down their neck and upper back. They wore a strong cotton sash around their waist, but no dagger or sidearm hung by it. They wore low-heeled shoes with high back and uppers, making them suitable for long or rapid marching.

From head to foot, they seemed to be tired, or rather defeated, soldiers. There was nothing obvious of arms or ammunition anywhere near them. Finding that they had Agha sahib's attention, the meek man with the pepper-and-salt beard, who called himself Karimuddin, raised a shout of gladness and called out, 'Thanks, and again thanks, ya Allah! The Navab sahib has himself arrived! It is not His Honour, but the angel of God's mercy!' He prostrated on the ground as he spoke, while the other three bent low in salaams and cried out, 'Allah preserve His Honour! Now our dead will gain life!'

'Don't kick up a row,' Agha Turab Ali said gruffly, though not unkindly. 'What is the matter? What is this about some dead man gaining life?'

The four who were at the head and foot of the covered man, could now be heard: they were reciting the first and the last but two chapters from the Quran in accents that clearly were those of illiterate men. Karimuddin, who was still prostrate, now raised his head and spoke in a tear-stained voice, 'Exalted and Honourable Sir, the man who lies there on the ground is our brother. This morning he went out on the plain to answer the call of nature. He was bitten by a snake.' He began to wail aloud, 'Hai hai! He died young, so young. He died within a minute!'

Karimuddin now rose and removed the sheet from the body to reveal a young man: his face had turned bluish and he had been frothing a sort of green froth at the mouth. Karimuddin resumed his tale of woe. 'Since then, Your Honour, we have been stuck here, waiting for some learned or at least well-born, educated Muslim to lead the prayer which is read for the dead before burial. We could then bury him like a proper Muslim. We are Mussulman, sir, but we know only a bit of the five prescribed prayers . . . We know nothing about leading, or even offering the prayer for the dead.'

'I see. So how do you happen to be here at all?'

The soldier who stood next to Karimuddin again salaamed and said in a small, thin voice, 'Your Honour, we are from Kakralah, we are going to Chandpur where we are in the service of the Navab sahib. We had been on leave to our homes in Kakralah.'

Mirza Turab Ali knew that there was, indeed, a small native State called Chandpur; it lay between Bilhaur and Kannauj. He did not know the Navab, but was familiar with his name.

He asked, 'What is the name of your Navab?'

'Azim-ud Daulah Navab Mustaqim-ud Din Khan Bahadur, Your Honour.'

Hearing the traveller pronounce the Navab's name accurately and correctly, Agha Mirza Turab Ali felt a little reassured. 'All right, we will go off at double speed and send a good maulavi from the next village to lead the prayer for your dead,' he said.

'Excellency, there is no village nearby. There is only a small hamlet, inhabited only by skinners of dead leather and removers of carrion. There is not even a high-caste Hindu there.' Karimuddin paused, as if considering whether he should say what he wished to say. 'Your Honour. There is a possibility of the body going stale if we delay more. Could you . . .'

'Yes, sir, Your Honour Bahadur,' said one of the men who was reading the Quranic lines at the head of the body. 'Should you be so kind to us strangers, should you lead the prayer, we will pray good prayers for seven generations of your noble house. Allah will reward you besides.'

Mirza Turab Ali was undecided, and aware of it. 'Are you Sunni?' He inquired.

'Your Honour, all of us are Sunni.'

'But I am Shia. Will it be proper for you if I led the prayer?'

They fell into thought. Then Karimuddin spoke slowly, 'May His Honour Bahadur's fortune be always in the ascendant! Your and our Allah and

Prophet are the same. So your prayer is also Allah's prayer. We just want that our brother should get a Muslim burial. He should not be consigned to a fiery pit like a non-believer.'

Agha Turab Ali turned to look at his companions. Their faces mirrored their inward perplexity and unhappiness. Clearly, they did not want to stay a minute longer, let alone say the prayer for the dead. Agha sahib's obstinacy and contrariness came into play at once. I will not leave without saying the funeral prayer, he resolved. It is against all humanity to abandon the poor fellow without a shroud and burial.

'Sabir Bakhsh,' he ordered, 'let me have some water for ablutions. All of you men should also do the ablutions; if there's not enough water, you can do the ritual cleansing on a lump of clay.'

He began to remove his weapons. 'You should also remove your weapons.' His tone was peremptory. 'Hurry, don't you see we have quite far to go yet?'

With clouded brow and obvious reluctance, Sabir Bakhsh and the others removed their weapons. They washed their faces, hands and feet, and stood in one horizontal line, with the dead man's covered body in front, leaving some space for the leader between them and the body. The traveller-soldiers already stood in a similar line. By way of security for their baggage, Agha Turab Ali's men made sure to stand in front of the line made by the traveller-soldiers, one of whom stood apart, for some reason. Pointing to him, Karimuddin said, 'Honourable Navab sahib's weapons and baggage will be quite safe. Our own weapons are in these bundles. This man, Sar Buland Khan, will stand on guard. Presence, Navab sahib, please lead the prayer.'

The moment the name Sar Buland Khan was mentioned, it seemed to Agha Mirza Turab Ali that something like a quiver of lightning ran among the traveller-soldiers and revitalized them. They seemed to shed their looseness of body; their drooping heads and shoulders apparently straightened—they seemed to be ready and prepared for something. Agha Mirza Turab Ali's heart did a somersault and thudded against his ribs, as if someone had thumped his chest, delivering a hard blow . . . No, it's nothing; perhaps the effect of the sun. The winter sun is deceptive; it seems pleasant, but can be awfully hot, he said to himself. He stepped up to the spot where a small sheet had been spread for him to stand on.

Agha Turab Ali called out 'Allahu Akbar' and commenced the prayer, his hands free in the Shia fashion. The rest folded their hands on their chests, Sunni fashion.

Barely a few seconds had passed when someone spoke in a mild, conversational tone, 'Chew this tobacco.'

The words had scarcely dissolved into the atmosphere when the dead man who lay in front, sprang like a panther and caught hold of Agha Turab Ali's hands in an iron grip. Behind him, Karimuddin produced from behind his collar a piece of coarse cotton cloth, narrow, with yellow and white stripes, and about three quarters of a yard long. There was a knot at one end of it. With a speed that was quicker than the strike of a mongoose or a lynx, he threw the rumal around Agha Turab Ali's neck and gave a savage tug. Agha Turab Ali was rendered helpless and suffocated. He tried to open his mouth to breathe, but his mouth remained tightly shut. For a brief moment he experienced exquisite pain, and then he fell to the ground. His larynx was crushed and driven into the upper part of his cervical spine, breaking it like a piece of dried twig. He died within a minute or less, without a struggle or uttering a cry, not even aware of the cessation of pain and breath in his body.

In the meantime, the other travellers had dealt with the rest of Agha sahib's party in identical fashion. The thugs worked with practised ease, like a set of movements choreographed and carried out a thousand times. It took less than a minute for each victim to die. The whole operation, precise and with the utmost economy of movement, took six minutes.

The thugs removed all the valuables from the bodies more or less simultaneously with the acts of murder, paying no heed to the mechanical, uncoordinated convulsions of some of the muscles of the dying or the dead. The loot was rolled into a shapeless bundle. Just as they were finishing this part of their operation, they noticed the dirty brown shadows of vultures forming on the treetops. Karimuddin commanded tersely but still in conversational tones, 'Bring out the mattock.'

One of the thugs unfolded a bundle and produced, with the greatest care and reverence, a mattock, rolled in a white cotton sheet. The thugs took turns to widen and deepen a grave-like pit below the camber of the road. The pit had been dug in advance in a place where it would not be observable by a passing traveller unless he stopped at that exact place. Within ten or twelve minutes the pit had been deepened and elongated, capable of receiving its grisly load. The eight bodies were stuffed into the pit—one head touching one pair of feet, the other pair of feet touching the other head—like shoes in a box.

Within minutes, the pit-grave was filled and packed with loose earth and rocks and gently thumped down. On the almost level surface, they spread scrub and scree and shale, thorns, lumps of dirt; a few plants which could take root even without much water were uprooted from some distance in the scrubland and planted on the levelled grave in a haphazard fashion so as to imitate nature's unruly growth. Nothing now remained for the scavengers or carrion-eating carnivores to dig up, or any possible search party to find.

They washed the mattock carefully, but near the pit-grave, sprinkling some water on it. It was again wrapped in the white cloth with the same care and reverence as when it had been unwrapped. Then they turned their faces to the west, and cried, 'Victory to Our Mother Devi!'

The packet containing the mattock was most lovingly kissed and placed in a bundle of luggage. The saddlery and other impedimenta on the mounts were removed with the usual efficiency. The horses and the ponies were let loose, to run away and become feral, or become food for the panther, the cheetah, the wild dog or whichever other beast of prey could get the better of them. They were nine men in all; picking up their loads with ease, they walked fast, though apparently at a sedate pace and within minutes, disappeared from view.

INTERLUDE

Mahakali's devotees and the John Company's role and motives in eradicating them

THIS IS A story of the days when the World was young and the gods and goddesses, genies and peris, giants and giantesses, demons and devils, infernal spirits of the South Pole and fiends, ghouls and evil spirits freely walked the Earth and sometimes became visible to humans.

Among the goddesses was Bhavani, wife to Siva and most often called just Devi. Once it happened that the denizens of Earth faced a great calamity: a huge demon was born in some subterranean region and appearing on Earth, he overcame all human powers and forces and all living beings became his subjects. He ate up all human babies as they were born, with the result that the population of humans began to diminish on Earth; animals began to thrive and increase.

This produced another dire situation: once the number of carnivores became greater than their food available on Earth, the carnivores shifted their attention to humans, creating thus a situation where the demon ate up human babies and the carnivores rent the bodies and shed the blood of human adults. Within a few days, the desolate places, then the villages, then the bigger population centres and the cities, and even the palaces of the kings were overflowing with tigers, lions, panthers, cheetahs, wolves, lynxes, hyenas and jackals.

People began to come out in droves and army formations to lay the demon low. In some places, elephants, hippopotami and wild buffaloes were harnessed for the purpose. But all was in vain. All efforts to kill the demon were unsuccessful. He was so tall that even the deepest ocean barely touched his midriff. Men or animals, they lost consciousness when they confronted him, making it even easier for him to grab them and swallow them one at a time.

There is another version of the story which says that it was not a demon, but an infernal fiend called Rakat Bej.

When the entire World began to wail and shriek in sorrow and pain, then the Goddess Bhavani, who is also called just Devi, or Mother Durga, or Mother Kali, took pity on the humans. She bared the golden sword that hangs by her sacred waist and cut off the demon's head. A fountain of blood issued from his neck as it was slashed, and began to fall like rain. And with each drop of blood that fell on Earth, another fiend, or demon, sprang up, exactly a replica of the original. Now Bhavani was truly angry. She began to wield her sword with both hands and began slaying the demons as they sprang. The entire plain, charged with the roar and trumpet of the dying demons, became choked and saturated with their huge carcasses.

As she cut and killed, cut and killed, her arms grew tired and perspiration wet her whole body, from the head to the toe.

She then dried her sweaty arms and let fall two drops of her perspiration on the battleground. No sooner had the drops fallen on Earth than the Earth became soft, like pummelled clay. Two valiant and intrepid fighters rose from that clay. Mother Bhavani tore off two strips from the hem of her yellow-and-white-striped sari and gave one to each intrepid fighter. She commanded, 'Strangle these worthless and wicked ones one by one. Beware, not a single drop of blood to be shed!'

The intrepid warriors made short work of the demons in almost no time. Bhavani was pleased, and she vouchsafed the two strips of cloth to the warriors and said, 'This will be your dharma from now. Kill humans with this strip, but shed no blood. I will eat those whom you kill, but do not look back after you have killed. Since the human killed by you will die by my command, he shall not become a ghost; nor will there be any reckoning of the deeds of the dead man: He will go straight to Paradise and he will never, never see the face of Hell.'

Another version is that the Mother herself strangulated and killed Rakat Bej with her kerchief. And then she gave away that kerchief in charity to a petty beggar of the Kachni caste. She granted to him the boon that he could use the kerchief to kill travellers, and thus earn his bread. 'It will be my job to bury those whom thou killest; it will also be my job to protect thee and thy tribe,' she declared.

She also imposed some restrictions and made some exceptions. For example:

Do not kill women

Do not kill a relative

Never kill if there is no expectation of material benefit
Give full mind to the sata

But the chiefest condition was: The killing weapon should be the strip of cloth (or kerchief) that I give to you; or use another piece of cloth like it; kill by strangulation, and never look behind after you kill.

The worshippers of Bhavani spread throughout the the World and began to hunt and kill human beings without fear. Bhavani gulped down the victim in no time; nobody could ever unravel the mystery of the missing person.

Many thousands of years passed and nothing untoward happened. But the child of man is not known as a fool for no reason. Once it occurred to an audacious one to look back and see how the Mother disposed of his victim. So he killed a pedestrian and ran away. As he ran, he looked back and saw that the Mother was swallowing up the dead man with great gusto and dispatch. Another tradition says that when the audacious one looked back, he saw the Devi, quite naked and in her real form. She was herself loading the body on her rath.

Yet another tradition says that the Devi was miraculously lifting the body up with her toes and tossing it into her jaws.

There is yet another version: the Devi picked up the body so easily as if it was a dry leaf. She then hurled it into the air and made it disappear in an instant.

When the Devi noticed the impudent observer, she was furious. She said, 'From now I will have nothing to do with the removal of the bodies. You may do what you wish. I don't care.' She and her rath then disappeared. From then on, it has been the duty of the Devi's worshippers to manufacture mattocks, dig a burial pit and bury those whom they kill.

Another version is that when the impudent one wept and begged the Devi's pardon most abjectly, she took pity on him. She said, 'I am not going to pick up your killed ones any more.' But she pulled out one of her teeth and threw it before him and commanded, 'Take it, and make a digging instrument out of it and call that instrument kassi (mattock). So long as thou honoureth and worshipeth thy kassi, it will be thy friend and helper. It will show thee the way to do thy duty; it will save thee from error. With it, thou shouldst dig the pit-grave in very little time. Once it hath done thy job, throw it away down a well. Later, whenever thou goest forth to do thy work, which will be called jitai, and the actual strangulation which will be called bhanauti, thou must needst go to that selfsame well and summon the kassi in my name: it will come up to thy hand by itself.'

*

Major General William Henry Sleeman was knighted as Commander of the Bath (KCB) towards the end of his long life in recognition of two memorable and outstanding achievements in the service of the Company Bahadur. He writes in his memoirs that many thugs described to him on oath the phenomenon of a Jamadar (Group Leader) of a band of thugs visiting a well and requiring, in Mother Kali's name, for his kassi to rise up to the rim of the well, and the kassi obeying his command. One of the thugs even averred that if more than one kassi reposed in the well, the jamadar's own kassi came up without error.

An interesting though little-known titbit of the British Army's history in India is that seven or eight decades after the rout of the thugs and the uprooting of thuggee, Colonel James Sleeman, the grandson of the famed Sir William Henry Sleeman, thought of designing, for the Indian Army, an efficient implement for cutting and digging earth. The final mattock design that he came up with bore an uncanny resemblance to the kassi of the thugs, though Colonel James Sleeman had never before seen such a kassi.

When a group leader of the thugs wishes to prepare a kassi, he chooses an auspicious and favourable day and goes to the ironsmith. He makes sure that the ironsmith does not do other work while the work on the kassi is going on. Nor should any stranger or alien be allowed to be present at that time. When the kassi is being made, an auspicious day is chosen for it to be exposed to the sun, so that it may imbibe affection, abundance and prosperity. Then, if the thugs are not travelling, they shut themselves in the house and organize a gathering of their people. If they are travelling, they organize the assembly in some secret and safe place. The exception is that such assembly cannot be organized on a Saturday or a Sunday.

A clean, square piece of ground is then chosen and plastered with cow dung and mud. It is a square, large enough for one man to squat or sit comfortably. A thug, well-versed in the rituals of the homa (or havan) occupies the square and makes the other thugs sit close. Then the kassi is washed in clean water contained in a shallow, handheld tub. The wash water is allowed to run off into a small hole, dug in advance. The kassi is then again washed or bathed in a mixture of water and a lump of molasses, making sure that the run-off goes straight into the hole. After this, the kassi is washed in curdled milk or dahi; lastly, the mattock is washed with some local wine or spirituous liquor, and the wash is again collected in the hole. Now, while the mattock is still wet, seven dots of a powdered mixture of red lead and vermilion—everywhere in India regarded as auspicious and the symbol of a woman's marital status—are applied on the kassi from the edge of the handle to the edge of the cutting blade.

The head of the kassi is placed on the lip of the shallow basin in which it had been bathed. In another shallow basin are now placed a coconut, five or six leaves of betel, a few cloves, pieces of bitter, blue gum, some seeds of the sparrow's tongue, white sesame and a lump of molasses. In a small cup, some ghee is poured. A fire is then lit with dried cow dung. For good fortune and benediction, a little mango wood and jujube wood are burned too.

When the fire is in full blaze, the knowledgeable thug throws, one by one, the contents of the shallow basin except the coconut into the fire. With each throw, the fire flares up yet more. Each time this happens, the kassi is passed seven times over the fire. The officiator removes the hairy husk from the coconut, then obtains permission from all present, and hits the bared nut hard with the head of the kassi where there is a hole to fit the handle. The strike is so hard that the coconut shell shatters with just one stroke. Now all thugs, Hindu or Muslim, cry in unison: 'Victory to Our Mother Devi!'

A little of the coconut's kernel, all its skin and husk are then thrown into the fire. Now all the thugs prostrate themselves with their face towards the west and eat up the coconut kernel.

None except a jamadar is entitled to have a kassi made. It is strictly prohibited to touch a kassi in a state of ritual unseemliness, like—immediately after sex or while attending to nature's call. Even in an ordinary state, it is an act of severe lese-majesty to jump or step over a kassi. The thugs believe that once a resolve is made to go out, the kassi should be buried in the ground, facing the direction in which they intend to travel. Should that direction be not favourable, the kassi changes its direction to indicate the auspicious and desired way.

When they are out on their beat and the opportune time to hit the prey is near, the jamadar or some other senior person will give a coded warning to all members of his group. Using some plausible excuse, the name Sar Buland Khan or Dillar Khan or Sar Mast Khan is taken. Now the thugs become alert for the jhirni, which is the actual command. The jhirni is an apparently innocuous word or phrase, spoken in soft tones, but is actually the command to start the kill. The words of the jhirni are of the most banal character, For example:

tamakhu khalo (chew tobacco)
surti khalo (eat a bit of tobacco granules)
huqqa pi lo (smoke the hookah)
tabak lao (bring some tobacco)
pan do (give me/him a betel)
kabit parh lo (read/say some poetry)
aye ho to gahre chalo (now that you are here, finish him)

The moment such words are pronounced, the designated thug, called a bhanot, does his job in no time.

In addition to the practice of having certain fixed days, and certain exceptional categories, all groups of thugs pay full heed to the sata. The sata are the seven days before the day determined for going out to do their duty, which is called jitai. During these seven days the thug, and even the members of his household, strictly avoid certain things, such as giving alms. This avoidance is so severe that they take care against even a cat or a dog making away with a piece of bread. During the sata, they eat no meat but fish, they do not get their head shaved and do not give their clothes for washing. During the days a thug is on jitai, the members of another thug household, if their own thug is also out on jitai, are not received in the house, or even permitted to cross the host's threshold.

Some of the individuals and groups of people to whom the rule of killing is not applicable are: a guest; a blind man; one whose ears have been cut off, or are not there by birth; an itinerant singer; an oilman; a Saivite mendicant with long, matted hair; a snake charmer; a remover of carrion skin; a washerman; a goldsmith; a woman; a beggar; a pimp; a member of the Kayastha caste (superior, but neither Brahman nor Kshatriya); a professional singer; a destitute; a leper; a lame person; a cripple; a Nanak

Panthi (a Sikh who does not worship the likeness of Guru Nanak, but believes in the Invisible God); and a nose-clipt.

Now about the Itab. It is a set of prohibitions, as described below. The following days are Itab:

When a thug's wife is delivered of a child, or his wife or daughter has flowers for the first time; or if a thug's daughter is getting married; or if his son is circumcised: He must not travel for twelve days from the event; if he is travelling already, he must return at once.

If a death occurs in a thug's home, the same restriction applies, but the duration is ten days.

The same restriction (ten days) applies if a thug's horse or mare dies.

In the event of a thug's cow or another four-legged animal dying, the restriction is seven days.

If a thug's wife has flowers in the routine way, or his goat, bitch or cat has been delivered of young ones, the restriction is three days.

It is not that the Itab applies to only the specific thug in such cases. No. If a thug hears about an Itab-attracting event happening at another thug's place at a distance of twenty-four miles, the Itab will apply to that thug too.

The Itab also comes into play if a thug under Itab touches another thug, or even if his garment touches another thug; the Itab will apply to the touched thug too.

North Indian thugs say Itak, not Itab.

People have claimed that the community of thugs, which had different names in different parts of the Land of Hind and Deccan, were simple, well-behaved, soft-spoken, kind-hearted and charitable followers of their faith in ordinary days. It has also been said that Sleeman sahib had cleaned up just the upper surface. Thug groups and families still exist secretly in abundance and pursue their real calling.

It is also said that the thugs are much active in the Land of the Deccan. The reason is that the territory from Aurangabad to Daulatabad has been their favoured stamping ground since antiquity. One thug even stated to Sleeman sahib that others may or may not see, but different minor or small sculptures in the caves at Ellora near Aurangabad carefully describe the entire procedure of thuggee from two thugs overpowering their victim by immobilizing his hands and feet, strangling with the rumal, using the mattock, and then burying the victim.

There is even a tradition that the wicked thugs are still to be found in London and America and there they use their special secret language Ram-asi (the English spelt it Ramasee) to communicate with each other.

Another, and generally oral account is that Sleeman sahib overstressed the thug menace: both their numbers and their cruel atrocities. For, thuggee was not as common as supposed. In fact, there were only some unfortunate sinners, thieves and confidence tricksters who habitually strangulated their victim. They were members of sundry criminal tribes, called 'thug' in some areas. It was just another ploy of John Company Bahadur to spread the good news of the blessings of the Company Raj and the peace brought by it to the country. On the excuse of establishing peace, thousands of individuals were arrested under the 'Thug' rubric. Many hundreds were hanged; many more hundreds were condemned to be transported across the brine. Some turned King's evidence; countless were imprisoned to rot in the jails at Shahjahanpur, Indore, Saugor, Jubbulpore and Lucknow.

Before the commencement of Sleeman sahib's operations, the law required that the punishment of death could be carried out against an accused only when the Qazi of the city issued a fatwa supporting the penalty. In order to facilitate the execution of the thugs, John Company passed a law whereunder the Qazi's ratification of a death penalty was dispensed with: the penalty of death awarded by an English court was enough. All the anti-thuggee campaign, its hype, its flurry of arrests, accusations, trials, penalties and hangings was mainly to brighten the John Company's good name.

Allah knows best.

55

Expert trackers retrace the steps of Agha Turab Ali's party;
the mourning caravan finally reaches Rampur

ON THE SEVENTH day after the murders, the riverine party of Agha Mirza Turab Ali disembarked at Fatehgarh and left immediately for its final destination. Inquiries at Fatehgarh and elsewhere on the way gave them no information about the land travellers. They imagined that Agha sahib and his horses and the rest of his train must, by now, have reached Rampur.

They heard a disturbing rumour at Qaim Ganj about a Rampuri nobleman's servant who found his master's horse or some other mount wandering riderless and unharnessed. It was said that he even succeeded in capturing the runaway beast. Now the river travellers were confused and anxious. Full of disquiet, their intuition for danger fully aroused, they decided to look into the matter, first by tracing the elusive servant, and then by hiring some expert trackers who knew the area. Such persons were mostly from Kathiawad and were Abyssinian by descent; their ancestors had settled there many centuries ago to work as soldiers, bodyguards and trackers. Being Abyssinian, they were all called Sidi; the word was a corruption of the Arabic 'sayyidi' ('my master') and was often used by them to address others as well.

By virtue of their profession as trackers, they were known as 'khojia'. Their long service at the Court and under Court officials of the sultans of Gujarat and the Mughal governors had enhanced their natural tracking abilities, which they had virtually refined to a fine art. They could identify footprints, however dim or scuffed; they could see the minute signs left in the forest or on the plains by the most cautious of animals or humans; they had a powerful sense of smell. All this, besides their naturally sharp senses and instincts, had made them exemplary in looking for lost property, fugitive criminals, escaping political prisoners and in recovering kidnapped women and children. Over the centuries, their reputation and area of operations spread far into the north and east, even as far as Rohilkhand and Avadh where they were called Shaidi.

They came to India speaking Swahili, which was their mother tongue. They still spoke Swahili at home, but with others they spoke a free mixture of Gujri and Gujarati, Gujri being the name of early Hindi in Gujarat. Some of them were Muslim when they arrived on Indian shores. Gradually, they all converted to Islam. Their Muslim religious leaders developed a genre of their own for religious songs and ceremonies. The genre was called Zikr (Remembrance) and its language was a mixture of Swahili, Gujarati and Hindi. These Zikr songs are still common among the Sidis of Gujarat; they are often sung to the accompaniment of a dance, but the dance bears no resemblance to a Gujarati dance. Here is a brief Zikr:

Who brought the Immortal to the mortal world?
Who saw the Immortal in the mortal world?
Immortal is Allah's name in the mortal world,
The Prophet brought the Immortal Name.

At the time that we are writing about, the number of the Sidis was declining, but a couple of them could always be found in important cities. Fatehgarh, if not Qaim Ganj, would surely show a couple of them. Thus Shah Nur Khan sent one man to Qaim Ganj and another to Farrukhabad to find and hire a Sidi. Success met them at both places and they soon had the services of two experienced Sidis, Sidi Ikram and Sidi Munim, at their disposal. They began investigation immediately; their first task was to find out the true details of the putative nobleman from Rampur and his runaway horse, and discover the whereabouts of the servant, if he existed; their next target was to obtain verified and verifiable information about Agha Mirza Turab Ali and his party and their present location. At that time, no one suspected their death, nor was anyone willing even to consider that possibility.

Sidi Ikram left immediately for Fatehgarh. Within a couple of days of inquiry, Sidi Munim succeeded in discovering that the unknown Rampuri nobleman's fugitive servant was nowhere else but in Qaim Ganj, or nearby. He was finally able to run him to earth at a dancing girl's, where he was hiding like an escaped convict. He admitted to his name being Munir Khan, and also admitted to have in his possession his master's horse which he had captured quite by chance, having found him grazing in an open plane. Because his master was displeased with him and had dismissed him from the service during the journey home, he felt ashamed and humiliated, unable to face the possibility of returning home, especially after he found his master's horse astray. He suspected that his master had met with an unhappy end.

'And now . . . now there is even greater ignominy and risk for me,' he almost wept as he spoke. 'What face do I have to return to Rampur and be the bearer of the inauspicious news? I had no choice but to hide here, waiting for some positive news of my master with which I could gain some courage to return. If that does not happen soon enough, I will kill myself, or go off into the mountains and live there like an unknown hermit.'

The Sidi spoke gently and in a reasoning tone. 'The first thing,' said he, 'is to get news of your master. Killing yourself or going off to live like a hermit, all this comes later. You should come with me. As of now, no one has more information than you about your master. Your former companions are putting up at the inn maintained by Daroga Himayat.'

'No! No! I am not willing to accompany you on just your say-so,' Munir Khan said, despairingly. 'I don't know you. If you are really from those people who came recently by boat from Ilahabad, show me a sign.'

Sidi Munim untied his turban and produced from its folds a yellowish paper, like the paper made by the English in one of their factories in Bangalah. On the paper was written a laissez passer in Hindi by Shah Nur Khan, below his own seal, to the effect that the bearer is 'on our establishment', appointed to discharge some duty on behalf of His Honour the Navab Sahib of Rampur, may his shadow lengthen upon the world.

With extreme unwillingness and a heart halted with sorrow, his spirit lame, but with a faint glimmer of hope of success and rehabilitation, Munir Khan accompanied the quaint-looking stranger. He fainted immediately as he came face to face with Shah Nur Khan. He and his companions believed him to be faking, but when Munir Khan did not regain consciousness even when water was profusely sprinkled on him, and one or two of the persons present pinched him hard, they were obliged to believe that it was no pretence. They had a vaid and a practitioner of shamanism come over to see him and advise on further course of action. Both were of the view that it was nothing supernatural, or even a pathological affliction; it was just that the patient's heart was under severe stress.

Munir Khan regained his senses after restoratives were applied and prayers were said by the shamanic practitioner, but he was extremely weak and pale. His eyes were full of tears and his cheeks were sunken, as if he had lost all his teeth. Shah Nur Khan considered it proper to speak to Munir Khan softly and deal with him gently; reprimand or punishment could be counterproductive at that time.

After a great deal of quiet, relaxed, unstressful questioning, Shah Nur Khan was able to extract the full story from Munir Khan. The most important aspect of Munir Khan's state of mind was his fear that though he and his alleged cousin had been strongly rebuffed by Agha sahib, there was every possibility of another attempt by the thugs against Agha sahib and his train; the thought that he would not be on hand to support and defend him at such a dire time of the journey was intolerably heavy for him to bear.

While it was impossible for him now to present himself before Agha Mirza Turab Ali after his dismissal—entirely just to his mind—he thought best to travel behind him, on foot perforce, but making sure that he did not lag much behind and thus remain unable to be of any use to Agha sahib's party. He thus walked as fast as possible, his heart heavy and his feet unwilling to overtake Agha sahib.

He did not know how far behind he was from Agha sahib's party, but as he reached the outskirts of Qaim Ganj, he felt extreme unease and terror in his heart. He could not have been too far behind them, he knew, but there was no sign of a big party of riders or travellers having passed there recently. In fact, he had a strong sense of some persons, he could not say how many, walking a few yards behind him. He clenched his teeth in strong resolve and looked back: there was nothing at all. Still, he almost ran to Qaim Ganj. The sun was just about to go down when he began to run.

He reached Qaim Ganj without incident. The sun had set and the small main street was about to close. He did not look for a suitable inn to stay; instead, he began inquiring from the traders, shopkeepers and stable-keepers if they had heard anything about Agha sahib or his party. He drew a blank; his heart turned to blood, while his resolve to go on searching weakened; he asked about the riverine group that was to debark at Fatehgarh at about the same time. There was no information about them either.

The failure of Shah Nur Khan's group to reach Fatehgarh so far was no immediate occasion for anxiety. But the non-appearance of Agha sahib and his men was something else altogether. Munir Khan also appreciated that a stranger making searching inquiries about a group of travellers might be considered suspicious and invite hostility from the local innkeepers and tradesmen. And night was not the time for him to retrace his steps. He slept at a small roadside inn and woke up very early to be on his way back to retraverse the road. He travelled back as far as Bilhaur, with no results to show for his labour. Here again, he stayed just the night and commenced the long trek back to Qaim Ganj to make more inquiries, and wait out the arrival of Shah Nur Khan.

He was just a few miles from Qaim Ganj when he again sensed the same terror and unease which he had experienced two nights before. He felt that he should stop and investigate with some vigour the source of his unease and terror. But his courage failed him. After a few minutes of cursory looking around, he forced himself to drag his feet back towards Qaim Ganj.

He had walked just about a mile when he descried some shadows waving and undulating on the far plain to the left of him. His heart sank to his ankles: they must be thugs, or more probably, ghouls or other evil spirits. He wanted to make a mad sprint . . . anywhere, in any direction but where the shadows were. But his legs refused to move, not even backwards.

He sat down on the road, said whatever prayers he remembered so as to combat or ward off evil things, and called upon the great Muslim Iranian-Iraqi Sufi saint Abdul Qadir Jilani (1078–1166) who is believed to come to the faithful's succour when called upon to do so. Perhaps the prayer did its work, for he finally came to the conclusion that there were no ghosts or evil spirits, male or female, in Islam. They could be genies . . . they could not be thieves, because the plain was not smooth, it was strewn with rocks and pebbles and shallow or deeper cuts and cracks.

He said again the Quranic verse of The Chair, which praises Allah, Who encircles all things, and again called upon the Shaikh of Baghdad to give him power to stay firm. He now noticed that the shadows were moving, coming nearer to him where he stood on the roadside . . .

Oh God! My God! He recognized them as animals, and animals from his master's train! There were two horses and a pony, sporting deep scratches, almost gashes, all over the neck and body, as if they had been battling against dense thorny shrubs . . . or perhaps they had been attacked by some wild carnivores? Munir Khan's hair stood on end. Perhaps the wild beasts are right here, in ambush somewhere? But there are no tigers in these parts, and the cheetah does not have claws. It could be the panther, he realized. The panther, the most malicious, sneaky and patient of animals: it could lie motionless under a tree for a whole night, waiting for the poor monkey on the tree to lose strength or patience and come tumbling down.

Well, it was still quite light. The animals too were at some distance. Let me wait here, motionless. Should they come anywhere within practical distance, I could try to catch them, or perhaps call to them; they might recognize my voice. But had Mirza sahib's party been attacked by wild animals, they could not have got the better of the whole party. How many panthers would there have been, after all? Maybe they were attacked by dhole, the feared Indian wild dog? They hunt in groups. But Mirza sahib's men had firearms: double-barrelled guns, and also two spear-wielders. If it was an attack of wild beasts, there would have been some signs of disturbed earth, some blood, perhaps a few animal carcasses. No. It must have been those bastards, those thugs.

The animals were quite close now, and Munir Khan recognized one of them to be Agha Turab Ali's personal mount. The other horse, and one of the ponies, had been bought in Sonepur; the pony was a few years old, but was skittish, difficult to control. Munir Khan stepped up cautiously, trying to bring them within the grasp of his arms. But the new pony shied and jumped away; the old horse did the same, even faster. Within no time, the two had galloped off a few hundred yards from Munir Khan. Mirza sahib's horse recognized Munir Khan; he approached him unhesitatingly and began to nuzzle against him affectionately. Munir Khan caressed him on the head, made loving noises, and talked to him as if he was human; he took out a lump of molasses from his bag and gave it to the horse to savour. To Munir Khan the horse's state clearly indicated that he had been wandering for at least two days. Allah knows the truth, if it is not the doing of the thugs, then it must be some evil genie's mischief, he thought.

Munir Khan walked the horse to Qaim Ganj. His immediate fear was that if, God forbid, Mirza sahib's party had become victims of the thugs, his possession of Mirza sahib's horse, read with the circumstances of his dismissal and apparent survival, would be very strong evidence against him. The first thing to do, therefore, was to place the horse with some reliable person where he would be taken care of, and find for himself another safe haven. After some searching and inquiry, he found a rather obscure stable-keeper, much in need of money. Munir Khan told him that the horse had shied and run away from his master, having been frightened by a snake, apparently.

'I recovered the horse after diligent search, but my master is out hunting. He'll return in a few days. Please take care of the animal until his return. You'll be adequately rewarded.' He said, and left, but not before he gave instructions and money for the feeding and care of the horse.

For his own self, Munir Khan found an ideal hiding place in the establishment of a nautch girl whom he had known from before. No one at that place would expect him to go out, or mix with other visitors.

Shah Nur Khan heard this narrative in full detail, interspersed with his own questions, in the presence of the two experienced Sidis. They concluded that Munir Khan was telling the truth; the fact that he had willingly and of his own accord produced the horse also worked in his favour.

'If the Presence Sahib has been murdered by the thugs, and if he is buried in the area where the horse was found, I assure you, sir, that we'll find his grave in two, at best three days,' Sidi Munim and Sidi Ikram declared with full conviction.

Shah Nur Khan said, 'But it is reputed that they bury their victim with such devilishly clever art that they leave no trace at all of the grave, or of the place where they committed their crime.'

'That is quite so, Janab ji. But we are also something proficient in our job. You will see.'

A suitable remuneration was decided upon; half was paid in advance, and the Sidis got on with the task immediately, Shah Nur Khan accompanying them. The Sidis walked, neither needing nor caring for a mount or carriage. Shah Nur Khan had no difficulty in keeping with their slow pace. He was surprised—in fact, shocked—to observe that roads, plains, trees, shrubs, half-eaten pods or seeds, even the droppings of animals and birds, to which no traveller paid any heed, were like a children's primer to the Sidis, where every page was devoted to a huge A, then B, and so on. They could read all the contours, the tiniest roughness and edges of each line, each circle and each angle with ridiculous ease. They were narrating the events of the past few days as if those were a part of a well-practised story.

Their first journey from Qaim Ganj to Bilhaur was covered at a comparatively quicker pace. Even so, wherever they suspected that the spot merited further inspection, they installed a piece of red cloth as a marker attached to a strong stake. On the return journey, they stopped for a considerable time at each such marked spot, examining foot marks, or drag marks, or marks of carriage wheels, or bird droppings, which were quite invisible or unimportant to Shah Nur Khan. They thus were able to determine two spots where Mirza Turab Ali and his train had stopped for short durations.

'But how can you say that?' Shah Nur Khan cried out, trying to keep his exasperation in check, but without success in hiding his deep scepticism.

'Mian ji, swear to it we cannot, obviously,' Sidi Munim replied calmly. 'But our philosophy tells us that a party of men and animals stopped here sometime ago: there were eight men, four ponies and four horses in it.'

'Oh come now, how could you at all distinguish man from beast and horse from pony?'

'Everything has its own odour, and its own aura. Everything has its own way of moving, sitting, or doing something. Look, there are pony hoof marks here, much obliterated, but visible still. The ponies stood here for a short while. There is no superposed footprint or hoof mark. It's our good fortune that the earth is soft and accepts marks without difficulty.'

Shah Nur Khan looked closely. There really were some marks, much scuffed, but they were there. Or was it his imagination? He could not very well deny that there was something to see. Now a small hope lit up in his heart. Perhaps these two will trace my master, somehow. But what will they trace him to? He thought with a sinking heart: a graveyard of strangers?

Qaim Ganj was just about six miles away when they reached their last stake, or rather stakes, for there were quite a few, scattered over a relatively small area. Here, the Sidis drew a square on a large piece of land. They then subdivided the square into many equal squares. Now, with one Sidi on one side, and the other on the opposite side, they went down on their stomachs and began to examine, smell and observe with the utmost care each sub-square one by one. Flat on their stomachs like scent hounds trying to smell a prey underground, they moved with painful slowness. They occasionally scratched the ground with a short, sharp stake, but most of the time they made use of their eyes and nose, their bodies taut and quivering with concentration, their brows knitted hard. Sometimes they remained immobile for minutes on end, as if trying to imbibe the spirit of whatever lay underneath the unspeaking, uncaring earth.

It was two and a half hours, or a little more, when they stopped in front of each other at a distance of a few feet and cried out loudly: 'Got them! Khan sahib, let the digging start here!'

Shah Nur Khan and his companions began to dig with their spears and swords. It did not take more than half an hour for the pit-grave to become apparent. One or more bodies could be also discerned. 'Ya Allah!' they cried out, their gorge rising. They stumbled back, like blind men, and soon their retching became a stream of vomit, ruining their upper garments. The Sidis remained at their grisly job and they soon uncovered eight bodies, all of them almost naked, bereft of all outer clothes. Poor Agha Mirza Turab Ali lay eighth in the order. The duration of rigor mortis was long over; the bodies were now slack, but there was profuse post-mortem bruising because of the lack of space and ante-mortem and post-mortem convulsions. The jaws of some were crooked and distorted, not having regained their original slackness after rigor. The backs of some were arched and crooked; the hands and feet of yet others were twisted. Almost all of them had black tongues hanging out in a horrid reminder of the Goddess in whose name they were done to death. Some had bled from the nose, some from the ears, but the burial pit was deep enough not to let the smell of gore abroad. Almost all of them had, at some time or the other, lost control of their bladder and sphincter.

Some of the blood, mixing with body excretions, had begun to spoil. Otherwise, the bodies were not in danger of starting to decompose immediately. Still, the smell—of the extrusions, the gases, the blood—was intolerable in a diameter of many yards. Almost out of his mind with worry and grief, Shah Nur Khan decided to close the pit-grave with its gruesome contents and hide it with a strong tarpaulin or heavy cloth. But the Sidis advised against this, not by saying anything, but by looking at him expectantly for proper orders about transporting and burying the bodies in a suitable place. He asked Sidi Munim, the older of the two, for advice.

'Should we dig proper graves and bury the poor martyrs here?'

Munim shook his head in dissent. 'Sidi Jamadar ji, the bodies are unspoilt yet. But now that they have been touched by the air, they will start to deteriorate fast. Burying them here will entail a great deal of trouble for you: many large tankards of water, many bolts of shroud, more than one gravedigger, a person competent to read and lead the prayer for the dead. Organizing so many things will take hours. The bodies will certainly go bad.'

'So what should I do? Should I roll them up strongly and take them to Rampur as they are?'

'No, no, this is not at all what I mean to say. If you try to take them to Rampur, what arrives there will not be whole bodies, but decomposed pieces. You should send someone to Qaim Ganj now. Order many bolts of unused long cloth and at least five palanquins to be procured and brought here in double quick time. Simultaneously, someone should go separately to Qaim Ganj to find a proper graveyard, organize the digging of graves and proper washing of the bodies. By the time the graves are nearly ready, your man should go find a maulavi for the prayer. Here, you should have the bodies rolled in many layers of long cloth and have them placed in palanquins and taken to Qaim Ganj.'

One of Shah Nur's companions agreed that all this could be done by sunset, as Allah wills.

*

So far, Shah Nur Khan and his fellow travellers had kept a hold on themselves, but they wept uncontrollably as the bodies were lowered into the graves. They wept for the helplessness of their compatriots in death, for their cruel, lonely and untimely deaths in a strange land, and their burial in graves that were far from their home, in an alien land, in a graveyard they had never before visited. Shah Nur Khan was thankful that by Maula's grace, a Shia gentleman could be found for Agha Mirza Turab Ali who provided the paper with the prescribed prayers on it, to be buried with the body. He also recited whatever prayers he knew for the occasion. Munir Khan wept loudly and torrentially when the time came for a last glimpse of the dead before burial.

Shah Nur Khan left for Rampur the very next day. He had with him Agha Mirza Turab Ali's horse and the animals that Agha sahib had bought in Sonepur. Munir Khan brought up a discreet rear. Before departure, Shah Nur Khan reported the full facts to the Chief of Police in Qaim Ganj and had detailed statements recorded from Munir Khan and the two Sidis. He made a formal request for investigation and for tracing the murderers of their master and his servants; he appealed that when caught, they should be hanged publicly. Shah Nur Khan also said that the stolen property, if recovered, may be distributed among the brave policemen who discovered and arrested the wicked murderers.

The Chief of Police did promise to act as best he could, but his eyes betrayed a lack of conviction. In fact, had the Sidis not been men of impeccable reputation, he might even have considered the possibility of arresting Shah Nur Khan, Munir Khan and the rest of them on suspicion of being thugs.

Some areas of Badaon and Aonla were at that time still under the nominal control of the King of Avadh, some others were under the nominal rule of the Emperor at Delhi. The reality on the ground was that the English power held sway everywhere, and the Commissioner at Bareilly was the de facto ruler. The English sahibs' police posts dotted the countryside. At one such post, Shah Nur Khan had his report recorded again with the same request: John Company Bahadur was beseeched to arrest the criminals at the earliest and have them hanged. Whoever among the members of the English police force was successful in catching the murderers would be handsomely rewarded by the Navab Sahib Bahadur of Rampur.

On the fifth day, the mourning caravan reached Rampur. Wails and lamentation rose from many houses until late that night in Rampur; no one slept. Wazir Khanam also kept her eyes stuck at the door, vaguely hoping that her Agha sahib would appear soon. She did not know when her bangles were smashed and when a white dupatta was draped around her drooping head and shoulders.

56

Wazir Khanam and Navab Mirza debate the beliefs of men; the ill-bred malice of her in-laws compels Wazir to make a decision

1844, THE CITY of Rampur. Those were the days, marked by good omens and heavenly fortune, of the rule of Navab Muhammad Said Khan Bahadur. In its sophisticated decorativeness, in its burgeoning businesses and marketplaces, in its bustle and agreeable noises of the alleys and the streets, in its assemblies of spiritual men, in its schools of learning and thought, in its private circles of teaching and schooling, in its refined and beautiful assemblages of poets, in its profuse narrators of the oral romance of Amir Hamzah, Rampur was just about to become the envy of Delhi and Lucknow. As regards density of urban population, Lucknow was certainly far ahead, while Delhi had no match near and far in the large number of its magnificent and beautiful buildings.

Through the eighteenth century, some buildings, especially the Fort at Najibabad built by Najib-ud Daulah, then some others built by Hafiz Rahmat Khan, and lately by Navab Faizullah Khan in the cities and towns of Bareilly, Badaon, Bijnor, Miranpur Katra and Sahaswan—many of them fallen into disrepair now—told the visitor of their bygone splendour. Even so, none of these historic piles could really compare with the unbelievable grandeur, grace and charm of historic Delhi even when many of its edifices had fallen on evil days in the nineteenth century.

Still, the way Rampur was developing and growing, none of the much older, bigger cities like Moradabad, Bareilly, Sambhal and Amroha could match it in wealth and peace, order in society and brilliance in the quality of life. From the times of Navab Faizullah Khan (1774–94), Rampur had assumed the character of a City of Peace and a City of Learning. It had begun to attract experts of different disciplines, arts and crafts from distant climes and places. They made Rampur their home and soon acquired the famed characteristics of the Pathans of Rampur.

Munnu Lal, an early historian of Rampur, tells us that during Navab Faizullah Khan's rule, Rampur could boast of at least five hundred men of learning, Sufis and scholars who were paid substantial stipends by the Navab but had no duty, except to be there in Rampur. They were free to teach in the schools established by the Government, or set up their own circles of teaching and education at home.

Among the eminent Sufis who came from outside and settled permanently were Hafiz Jamalullah, Shah Dargahi, Shah Baghdadi and Shah Jamaluddin; they made Rampur an auspicious city by the touch of their holy feet. The library and the madrasa established by the Navab whose Abode is now at the Highest Level, became renowned everywhere and are even now important centres of wisdom and learning. The library became known later as Riza Library, and the madrasa was named Madrasa-e Aliya. Navab Faizullah Khan invited the formidable scholar Mullah Abdul Ali and the lesser-known Mullah Muhammad Hasan Firangi Mahli from Lucknow and appointed them Head and Deputy Head of the madrasa respectively. Soon, the madrasa began to attract students from abroad; Rampur came to be spoken of as the Bukhara of India.

Navab Faizullah Khan did not have much inclination for poetry and the arts, but this shortcoming was compensated for by his younger brother, Navab Muhammad Yar Khan, at his small but prosperous Court at Tandah. For a short time, Hindi poets of quality, even greatness, like Qaim Chandpuri, Mushafi, Qudratullah Shauq, Fidvi Lahori and Kabir Ali Kabir had foregathered there.

The sack and destruction of Tandah and Aonla at the hands of Emperor Shah Alam II scattered the illustrious members of Muhammad Yar Khan's Court like so many leaves struck by the autumn. Muhammad Yar Khan settled in Rampur at the invitation of the Heaven-abiding Navab. With him migrated many stars from the skies of Tandah and Aonla to enhance the glitter of Rampur. Among them were Qaim Chandpuri and Kabir Ali Kabir. The arrival of these luminaries gave the much-needed fillip to the establishment of a literary culture in Rampur. The long rule of Navab Ahmad Ali Khan continued the wave of literary activity, and in fact extended and strengthened it. By virtue of his long residence in Avadh, the present Navab, Muhammad Said Khan, was a follower of the Shia faith practised by the Navabs and kings there, but instead of making Rampur an appendix of Lucknow, he actively encouraged the Rampuri version of literary culture. This culture reflected the formal glory, and the power and strong-mindedness of Delhi, rather than the religious preoccupations and the love of delicateness and subtlety for which Lucknow was becoming known all over the land of Hindustan.

All this, yes, and much more, was there in Rampur. But she who wailed at the untimely death of Agha Mirza Turab Ali, she who loved him as the bulbul loves the rose, she, the flower of the garden of loveliness, she whose fragrance scented the bedchamber of Love, she whose sweet scents were the perfumes of the garden of lovingness and loverliness, was not in Rampur. Agha Turab Ali's haveli, his official residence as a high functionary of the State, had been resumed by the State after Agha sahib's death. Among Agha Turab Ali's close relatives were a sister and an aunt, both widowed. Wazir followed them with her baby to Agha sahib's old house. Navab Mirza was insistent that he also move in with her, but looking at the small house, Wazir sent him back to Manjhli Begam's haveli.

It was an old-style house, mostly of thin brick and plaster typical of historic buildings all over Avadh and Farrukhabad. A small hall opened on to a courtyard adjoined by two rooms on each side. There was a veranda at the end of the courtyard, and behind it was a larger veranda which could be used, when need arose, as a large room. The front hall was flanked by a kitchen and a water room and lavatory. That was all that the house offered. There was no interior garden or artificial pond, no formal platform on which to enjoy the sun or the breeze. A water carrier supplied water two times a day from the river Kosi.

Wazir's life changed its colours and tenor in no time. The wonted crowd of maids, servants, palanquins and bullock carts was no longer there. The stream of visitors was reduced to a trickle, except for the religious assemblies associated with the third, the tenth and the fortieth days of mourning. Had she not had the support and love of Habiba and Rahat Afza, Wazir might have ended her life by jumping into a well. It seemed too much: the burden of grief over Agha sahib's death—and what a death it was, as if the killers had no God, as if death could never touch them—the trouble and responsibility of caring for a little baby for whom she could no longer afford a maid; the not very covert hints from her in-laws, Agha sahib's aunt and sister, both widows and full of the bitterness and frustration of lonely lives—hints to the effect that Chhoti Begam did not have the status of Agha sahib's contractual, temporary wife even, not to speak of a properly married one. Life as a young widow was hard enough for Wazir, and these new burdens seemed too much to bear.

The aunt and the sister-in-law sometimes granted, grudgingly, that there had been a marriage between Chhoti Begam and Agha sahib, but as the aunt never missed an opportunity to point out, formal marriage and marriage vows and bonds meant nothing to women like Chhoti Begam. And daughter-in-law Chhoti Begam was in her own class among unstable women—women of the type who adorned the bedchambers of the rich debauchees—and was inauspicious to boot: whoever grasped her hand ended soon enough with the Angel of Death grasping his own hand in turn.

Wazir could see clearly that she was not long for Rampur now. She could also see that she could not further postpone her own separation from Rahat Afza. In fact, judging from the standards of well-born girls, Rahat Afza was well over the age of marriage, and therefore of marriageability. As a junior or senior maid, or even as a lady's maid, she was very nearly past the best age for marriage. In fact, in a couple of years, she might not be considered suitable as a mistress even, despite her good looks and desirable qualities. Habib-un Nisa, out of love and consideration for Wazir, did not ever bring up the subject of her daughter's marriage; but now, when Wazir was herself almost homeless, it was necessary, and urgent, for a good husband to be found for her.

It was quite feasible to find a good man for Rahat Afza. The first condition, of course, was Rahat Afza's consent and Habiba's acceptance of the proposal. The next thing was to organize a good living space and household effects for the newly-wed couple. Wazir knew that given her regard for her mistress, Habiba would never take the initiative to moot the subject of Rahat Afza's marriage. She therefore informed Habiba that soon after the statutory period of her seclusion as a widow was over, she would start looking for a good husband for Rahat Afza.

'If it was in my power,' she said, 'I would never let Rahat Afza go away from my side. I would have her husband stay with us as our home's own son-in-law. But . . .'

'Khanam sahib,' Habib-un Nisa dried her tears and spoke in a hoarse, heavy voice, 'from our first day with you, you have been father, mother,

Angel of Mercy, everything, for Rahat Afza. How I wish your fate was not written with a crooked pen . . . Still, I will always be with you and spend my days clinging to your feet . . . But, but how will I stand Rahat Afza going away from us in my old age?' She was now weeping large tears, not bothering to dry them.

'Be courageous, Habiba,' Wazir said mournfully, but with a hidden strength in her voice. 'Had the conditions of our lives been normal, Rahat Afza would have become a bride long ago. It's not proper to delay things any more. And you observe the temper and the mood here, don't you?'

'It is the thirteenth century, Khanam sahib, there's nothing that cannot happen in this day and age.'

'At present I am like a prisoner in the house. I can't move before my unhappy days are over. One doesn't know what these gentle ladies will do to me once I am allowed to move about.'

'Allah knows best, but I am convinced that the evil in the eyes of these grand dames consumed our poor Agha sahib.'

'Repent, Habiba, please repent! Why should one give the evil eye to one's own supporter and survivor, he who will inherit all that they would leave in this world? In the whole wide world there was no one else to hold them aloft in the river of life.'

'True. But if they had affection for Agha sahib, why should they be disaffected with you? You weren't separate from him, after all.'

'I was not, but I was.' Wazir drew a cold sigh. 'In the first place, I am not of the same clan; then there is the difference of faith. To top it all, I am not from Rampur, and have a reputation too!'

'Murky reputation or a bright good name, what are these things, Khanam sahib? I would happily sacrifice these ladies for one paring of our Navab Shamsuddin Ahmad Khan's toenail! May the eyes of those who look askance at you be torn from their sockets! One's good name or evil name is from one's deeds. And these women! They are like the saying, "I'm good for nothing, but the bridegroom is my nephew"!'

Wazir laughed, in spite of herself. 'Oh, let's quit these tales of Turan and Iran. First things should always be first! Do you have some husband in mind for Rahat Afza?'

Habib-un Nisa fell into thought. She sat quietly for some minutes, then rose and stole to the door, closed it firmly from inside, returned and sat with her side nearly touching Wazir Khanam.

'What is it, Habiba?' she whispered.

'Nothing,' Habiba whispered back. 'It just seemed to me that your revered auntie-in-law was somewhere close, her ear to the door.'

'I ask Allah's pardon, Habiba! You really are full of fond superstitions, like the Hindus who see the shadow of a baram or a rakshas in every shady tree! Anyway, tell me, do you have something in mind?'

'Yes, madam. You remember Shah Nur Khan? He was the one who brought back from Sonepur the animals bought by our dear, Paradise-abiding Agha sahib.'

'Yes, then?'

'He is connected with my departed. He comes from Merath; he doesn't belong here.'

'Which means that they are reliable people. That's good. So is there a proposal or a hint from their side?'

'Yes, his aunt came once, dropped some hints. But those were different days. So I too hinted my refusal to her.'

'We should reopen that conversation. Is that what you desire? And what about Rahat Afza?'

'I beg Allah's pardon! What's the need to talk to her? What you approve, what I desire, is what matters!'

'No. It is essential to have her consent!'

A thin crease contracted Habiba's brow, but disappeared immediately. She changed the subject quietly.

'A few days ago I happened to meet a sister of Shah Nur Khan at Umdah Khanam sahib's haveli. She said that her aunt was looking for a good bride for him. It occurred to me that she must have had something in mind again.'

'Yes, I think it's quite likely. So did you inquire some more?'

'No, I couldn't dare do anything without your approval.'

'Well, all right. But don't delay any more. Find out all you can. I'll talk to Manjhli Baji. She'll help in ascertaining all that there's to know.'

All the details were gathered within the next ten days, with Umdah Khanam's help. It transpired that the family of Shah Nur Khan, the prospective bridegroom, were Pathans of upright reputation. The groom's parents were not alive; he supported an old cousin from his father's side and her blind son. From an earlier marriage, which ended in divorce, Shah Nur Khan had a daughter, about twelve to fifteen years of age, who lived with him. The reason for divorcing the first wife was her evil temper and sharp tongue. It appeared that she was particularly harsh on the widowed cousin and her blind son: she hated them as idle ne'er-do-wells.

Shah Nur Khan, it was reported, was a little shy of forty years and had been serving in the Presence, Navab Sahib Bahadur's elephant stable for the last two decades, or a little more. He drew a good salary and was well thought of among his peers.

Considering everything, the connection seemed reasonable, or even desirable. Apart from family and good pay, the absence of any relatives on the groom's side was a bonus: there would be no mother-in-law to tyrannize the young wife. The two relatives that were there, lived with him as poor relations and could not present any problems or cause any conflicts.

'The real nature of a man can only be known by living and dealing with him on a day-to-day basis,' Umdah Khanam told Wazir. 'As the saying goes, "Man is known by essay, gold is known by assay." All apparent indications are favourable. The rest is in God's hands.'

Marriage negotiations and proposals are like defects of character: however much effort one may make at their concealment, they will be out. And news, or even rumours of a marriage proposal, surely reaches those who are, for whatever reason, hostile to one or both of the parties. That was exactly what happened in the case of poor Rahat Afza's proposal. Almost simultaneous with the arrival of a formal declaration of interest from the side of Shah Nur Khan, the information reached Amir-un Nisa and Nur Fatimah, Mirza Turab Ali's widowed aunt and sister, de facto mother-in-law and sister-in-law to Wazir. Amir-un Nisa promptly summoned Wazir to her room and began, without any courtesies. 'Look, Chhoti Begam, you are still within the statutory period of restraint. It's not proper for you to start talks about betrothal and marriage.'

Wazir flushed to her ear lobes. She answered sharply, 'I don't understand. What betrothal and whose marriage do you have these wild notions about?'

'That girl, Rahat Afza . . .' Amir-un Nisa was quick to interrupt.

Wazir also was not to be stopped so easily. She cried out: 'This kind of talk doesn't behove you, Aunt Amir-un Nisa. To have a few holy words pronounced and let a fatherless girl be provided a safe sojourn . . . I'm sure it should be a meritorious deed in your religion too.'

'Let matters of merit or demerit be decided by the mullah or the scholar.

I just say: Look to your own self! How are you going to go through your time of restriction and your life of widowhood?'

'God forbid. Am I doing something about my remarriage and a new home for me? What's wrong with you?' In spite of herself, Wazir's voice betrayed her nearness to tears.

'Allah save me from untruth! Are you not well versed in those matters and well travelled down those paths?' This was Nur Fatima, the only sister of Agha Turab Ali, and much pampered by him when he lived. She had been extremely unhappy when her brother brought a new wife into the house.

Wazir rose and made to go out. 'You have no manners, no good sense.'

Amir-un Nisa raised her voice, wanting to stop Wazir from leaving. 'Well, we who stay at home cannot have the sophistication of wanderers like you! But Chhoti Begam, you must understand this: At this door there never has been a marriage party from a petty elephant driver, nor will it ever be.'

Wazir retorted, 'Is this door not mine, too?'

'Ah! Only God is untouched by blemish! Did you ever look at your face in a pot of water, dear madam? The offspring of the child of my mother, the seed of pure, undiluted Sayyids from both parents, you must have bewitched him with a packet of some petty magic. Poor little soul, he lost his senses for a while. My nephew brought you into his home, so now you pretend to be the embodiment of chastity. You and this threshold! Really!'

'Yes, madam, very well. But I was brought here through a proper marriage. And the son of your darling nephew was born from my belly. Were it not for him, all your tall claims to high birth would have been consigned to the archives. If the name of your ancestors is to survive, it will survive through him alone.'

'We will sort that out on some other occasion. First you must go through your period of immobility as a widow. We will turn Habib-un Nisa out of here, bag and baggage. Let her not delude herself that her daughter's marriage palanquin will leave from this door.'

'You don't need to trouble your head or your tongue in the matter of Habib-un Nisa and her daughter. I have homes in both Delhi and Rampur. The offspring of your mother's son could bring me to this door only after he had made hundreds of plaints and the humblest of entreaties to me. Otherwise, even the meanest of my slippers would not deign to come here.'

Wazir was trembling with rage. 'And you! I would not suffer for the likes of you to even bring the washing pot in my lavatory! May God have mercy upon you! One whose own perch is on a broken bough should threaten another with homelessness! Now listen, you two. Rahat Afza's marriage party will come, and will come here, nowhere else.'

Wazir was burning hot with the passion of fury. She tied her dupatta tight around her waist, as if preparing for battle, her face full of the same energy, the same iconic puissance, which had depressed the wilfulness of the likes of Navab Shamsuddin Ahmad Khan. Wazir left the room, yet for a long time the two women felt it to be overflowing with her.

Directly after quitting Amir-un Nisa, she sent a note to Manjhli, requesting her to come see her soonest. When Manjhli came, she narrated all that had happened between her and Amir-un Nisa, and then she went on to say, 'There is nothing firmed up about Rahat Afza yet, but some decision must be taken, and sooner rather than later. I am not at all willing to let these two frustrated widows pour the bitterness of their barren lives on that poor girl. I cannot permit them to insult and demean her and put me to shame too.'

Unlike her usual cool, collected and nearly dispassionate way of talking, Wazir spoke with a suppressed frenzy, as one who was determined to avenge herself for the contumely in which the two women held her and hers. She declared, 'The marriage I will perform at this house. It's my house too. But I am not going to live here a minute after the ceremonies are over!'

'That's all right, Chhoti. The moment you finish your time of constraint, you move into my house.'

'No, Manjhli Baji, I'll go back to Delhi. I have a shelter there, after all. Be it ever so devastated and desolate, but it's a dwelling. For a fakir, a coarse blanket is a cashmere shawl. But all that will be later. The first thing is that I need your support, the support of your Navab, and the protection of the Exalted Servants.'

'Without doubt, I and my Navab sahib are your supporters and backers, as before. I can't vouch for the Exalted Presence, but there will be no lack of effort. I will mention all this to my Navab sahib right this day.'

Nothing happened over the next few days, except that negotiations for Rahat Afza's marriage to Shah Nur Khan were pretty much finalized. All that was now needed was the date, the amount of dower, the number of persons in the bridegroom's party and similar details. Amir-un Nisa and Nur Fatimah totally sequestered themselves from Wazir, going to the extent of establishing a separate kitchen and not using even the pots and pans of the regular kitchen. It was a small house, so it was quite unavoidable for them not to get under each other's feet. But Wazir maintained a studiously polite and sweet demeanour; she behaved as a proper daughter-in-law should behave in the house of her in-laws.

Amir-un Nisa, on the contrary, missed no opportunity to rub it in: Wazir's existence was unacceptable to her. Were a snake to bite Wazir, or lightning to strike, burning Wazir to cinder, Amir-un Nisa would have lamps of celebration lit with expensive ghee as their fuel and not plain mustard or sesame oil. The two—mother-in-law and sister-in-law—made no bones about it: Rahat Afza's bridegroom's party could very well be welcomed on God's own Throne, or be entertained in public at the crossroads. They could not care less, so long as the party did not defile their house.

Wazir's statutory days of restriction came to an end; the date of Rahat Afza's marriage was settled; arrangements for the various ceremonies began to near their conclusion. All this was as it should be, but invitations to the wedding could not be distributed. Umdah Khanam did confirm that Navab Yusuf Ali Khan had stated forcibly that the marriage should take place from Mirza Turab Ali's house. He was quite clear that Wazir's right to that house was as great, if not greater, than her relatives-in-laws. She was, after all, the legitimate daughter-in-law of that house. But the Luminous Presence, the Exalted Servants did not still make their intent apparent in the matter. At least, there had been no expression of his intent either way.

Despite this, Wazir was steadfast in her resolve for the marriage to happen at Agha Turab Ali's house: her house, in effect. And the marriage would be not according to Habib-un Nisa's status, but according to Wazir Khanam's status. How her resolve would be translated into practice was something not at all clear in her mind. Still, she was somehow quite satisfied in her mind that her will would prevail over that of her adversaries. She decided that if there was no indication or command from the Exalted Porte until just a week before the determined date, she and Manjhli Baji should present themselves at the official residence of Navab Yusuf Ali Khan, and should try, through him, to gain access to the Sacred Service of the Presence.

It was just ten days before the date of the marriage. In spite of her strong resolve, Wazir began to feel anxious. She even considered the idea of sending for a score or more of bold and venturesome young men from Firozepur Jhirka: the State may well be under English rule, but there must be countless men and women who remembered the martyred Navab with affection and respect. She could appeal to them to come help her organize the events and deal with any untoward situation that might arise. But on second thoughts, she rejected the idea. Though not impractical, it was not a proposal to be viewed with favour by a sagacious eye. True, they would come, and come willingly, and make sure that everything happened as it should. But should a report reach the Exalted Presence about stave-wielding young men from a foreign state being installed as managers for the occasion, it was most likely that he would not be pleased. Living in a river and earning the malice of the crocodile was not what wise people do. And where was the fun in a wedding ceremony which needed guards and strongmen from outside to ensure that the wedding did happen?

Wazir had just finished her early afternoon prayer and was preparing to order a palanquin for going to Manjhli's haveli, when there was a vague disturbance or subdued noise at her main door. She was informed in a moment or two that the Illustrious Presence was desirous of her attendance at the Sublime Porte; a palanquin was at the door to convey here there. In place were two staff-bearers and a front rider to escort and protect the palanquin to the gate of the Fort.

Wazir was taken aback. She expected some indication from the Sublime Porte to the effect that Amir-un Nisa Begam would be given some proper instructions. At the most, a few cavalrymen might be positioned in her alley at the time of the arrival of the bridegroom's party and stay until the end of the ceremonies. But summons . . . ? Allah, how should I face him? What is the protocol for women there? What is the prescribed method of doing the salaams? Will I be given a seat or will I be expected to remain on my legs? And my widow's weeds . . . I changed into fresh clothes just today, but these are the plainest possible. Of course, there is no question of doing some make-up or even combing my hair in a formal style. Let me just splash a couple of handfuls of water on my face, rearrange my unruly hair and put my dupatta over my head so as to conceal the face. That should be enough.

It was after many weeks that she was looking at herself in the mirror. There was no freshness, no colour, but apparently there were no wrinkles, either. The hair, and the hands and feet were dry, devoid of sheen, uncared for; but there wasn't a single grey hair in her head, and no shrinkage in the muscle to suggest the onset of old age.

She was just finishing combing her still-luxurious hair when Habiba came to report that the outrider suggested that they better hurry, because Navab Sahib Bahadur was ready to receive her.

'Say bismillah before you go, Khanam sahib,' said Habiba. 'It's an extremely opportune moment to decide all difficult issues. While you are being conveyed to the Fort, go in saying the darud—Allah and His slaves' salutations to the Prophet—and also say Allah's holy name Ya Wadud calling upon Him in His Quality of Being Full of Love, and blow on yourself. And when you are before the Presence, don't forget to say in your heart Allah's Names betokening His All Mercifulness and Universal Benignity.'

Wazir hurriedly finished doing her hair, straightened the wrinkles in her clothes as much as she could, wrapped herself in a plain white chador and stepped into the palanquin. She did not have much of an idea of the roads and paths, nor could she see anything much from inside the palanquin. She could just make guesses from the sounds on the way that she was perhaps passing a busy market. She could not judge the distance covered; the palanquin-bearers and the staff-bearers stepped smoothly, noiselessly; occasionally she could hear the rhythmic tap, tap, of the outrider's horse.

Rampur was not a big city; the distance must not have been great, but to Wazir it sometimes felt very much; sometimes she felt that she must be at the Fort any minute now.

The palanquin slowed for a few seconds, then stopped. She heard an authoritative voice call out: 'Screens on both sides of the palanquin, now!'

Wazir tried to judge the exact spot where she should be, so that she would not stumble or not be sure-footed when she alighted. Within less than a minute she heard the same voice, now softer and deferential: 'Screens are in place. Your Honour may now trouble her noble presence to alight.'

Wazir, fearful of stumbling, put out one foot, then the other, then her legs, with what seemed to be agonizing slowness. She was fully covered in her chador; only a small part of her forehead was visible, but there was no one to watch. She pulled down her chador's edge a little more, like a mantle-veil. She could see, but was invisible in effect.

She was a little surprised to find that she was not at the main gate, or even at a side gate, of the Fort. She was in a sort of walled alley, like a security zone. Her palanquin was screened on both sides. The outrider, the staff-bearers and the four palanquin-bearers were all behind the screen. She saw a high portal. She was not sure what she should do and how she should enter. There were four women guards, fully armed, who stood at the threshold, clearly expecting her to proceed. Wazir saw that the guardswomen preferred to stay at their posts. Seeing her hesitate, one of them advanced just a step towards her, salaamed and said, 'Please come. Have no misgivings at all. His Worshipful Excellence awaits you inside.'

Wazir breathed a sigh of relief in her heart; she made a gesture of greeting and thanks towards the guardswomen and entered the door. She had taken just a couple of steps forward when she saw one of Navab Yusuf Ali Khan's senior maids who salaamed her and said, 'Please let me have your chador, Khanam sahib, and enter the Great Hall. The Navab sahib will grant audience to you there.'

The moment she removed the chador, Wazir felt her body and soul blossom like a flower in the first rosy light of dawn. From the moment she had entered the palanquin, she had been subject to numerous emotions of uncertainty and confusion. She had felt the tension affecting her body so much that even her normal movements seemed artificial and affected to her. Now that her environment felt lighter and less constricted, an unconscious, automatic spray of rising spirits made her blood circulate freely and more comfortably. Her soul, already much bruised by her widowhood, and now under the extra burden imposed upon it by the unreasonable recalcitrance of her husband's relatives, had been cribbed, confined and constricted, but now the pressures seemed lesser, her inner light less dim, at least for the time being.

She kept her eyes strictly on her feet, and walking comfortably behind the maid, entered the Great Hall. It had a high ceiling that was almost plastered with chandeliers and candelabra, but only one huge candelabrum was lit, with at least three hundred lamps burning; Turkish and Kashmiri carpets covered the floor from end to end, but a small area was carpet-free at the centre; a tulip-shaped red-veined marble fountain played silently in it. Big bolster-like pillows were placed along the walls, with small occasional tables in front of each; the tables had silver plates heaped with dry fruits. A most delicate breeze, slightly scented, seemed to blow across the Hall where unostentatious good taste and understated elegance seemed to rule. The Hall was really large; she walked demurely but steadily and there seemed to be no end to the Hall and its carpeted floor.

The maid walked with her, also quite steadily, a little to Wazir's right but in front of her. So she was confident that she would know where to stop. She noticed a huge curtain in brocade, at what seemed to be the far end of the Hall. The curtain hung from ceiling to floor. Approaching the curtain, the maid gestured Wazir to sit.

She had just taken her seat against a bolster, but was sitting erect and somewhat tense again, when the curtain parted a few inches from the middle. The maid whispered to her, 'The Exalted Presence has arrived. Please do your salaams.'

Wazir stood up, a little ill at ease, fearful of committing some breach of protocol. She bent low in three salaams, facing the parting in the curtain, though she could see nothing.

'His Honour's fortunes may always be high; may the shadow of the Huma bird of felicity always rest on his auspicious head.'

From behind the curtain she heard an extremely refined, grave and almost awe-inspiring voice, 'Wazir Khanam, Agha Mirza Turab Ali was a faithful servant. All of us grieve at his martyrdom, but the Will of the Supreme Master is Superior to everything.'

'This slave woman constantly wears black in his grief and lives with his memorial clasped to her bosom.'

'I am quite certain that he attained the high station of a Martyr of God.'

It seemed to Wazir that the observation contained the hint that while the departed was in the Highest of High Heavens, she should now look to her own present and future. She was trying to frame a suitable reply when the voice came again, 'And I am also desirous of your safety and welfare.'

'May the Prosperity and Fortune of the Presence rise ever higher day by day. Your Honour's regard and concern for the nurture of your subjects is reputed throughout the four directions.'

'You are not merely our subject; you are our daughter-in-law as well. I would never like that you should not be accorded the comforts and considerations of home at the hand of your in-laws.'

Wazir now clearly understood the Navab's intent: Amir-un Nisa and her cohorts will not at all have their way. Wazir should organize for the reception of the bridegroom's party, the marriage ceremony and all other customary rites of marriage precisely as she felt necessary. None will dare interfere or cause any impediment.

She still could not distinguish any physical presence behind the curtain, but now she could at least see the carved legs of an ebony chair. She had remained standing throughout; now, with her eyes firmly on her feet, she answered, 'This slave woman will never be able to repay in the least measure the kindness and generosity of the Presence. May Allah cause your rule to last till the Last Trumpet and keep your land ever happy and populous.'

Wazir made three salaams, and thought of starting to walk backward when she again heard the Navab's voice, 'You may regard Navab Yusuf Ali Khan Bahadur, may Allah preserve him, as your own patron. Whenever you have any submissions to make, you may freely do so through his embassy. You may go now. God protect you and aid you.'

'Each and every particle of this slave's body will pray for you always. This humble handmaiden will sing your praises to her last breath. May the Blessings of Janab Bibi Fatimah and the Twelve Sinless Ones be always part of your State.'

On her way back from the Auspicious Fort, it occurred to her that she should petition through Navab Yusuf Ali Khan for the temporary restoration to her of Agha sahib's haveli. On a little consideration, she decided against making it: Had the Navab sahib been so minded, he would have passed the order without her request. In fact, what has been bestowed on me is quite much, she told herself.

*

Rahat Afza's wedding was celebrated on the appointed date with colourfulness and display of riches, and gathering of guests appropriate to the status of Wazir Khanam. A posse of horsemen in formal dress was present from the Navabi Court. Navab Yusuf Ali Khan sent presents consisting of expensive dresses for the bride and the groom. As a part of the bride's dower, he sent many sets of brass and copper pots and pans. The Exalted Presence, Sovereign of Rampur, sent ten gold mohurs to be included in the 'Greeting Present' to the bridegroom. He also sent dresses for all the groom's close relatives. Amir-un Nisa and Nur Fatimah were present, though with ill-concealed reluctance.

The day after the solemnization of the wedding rites, Rahat Afza was accorded her formal 'bride's farewell'. She was full of the tears and unwillingness customary for the bride before she departs for her husband's home for the first time. Navab Mirza tied the sihra—formal marriage garland of flowers and also brocade and silver tassels and threads—around a weeping Rahat Afza's head, for it was his duty and right as the bride's brother. Not only did he perform this formal act, but also in the rukhsati—a farewell poem to the bride—that he wrote for Rahat Afza, he spoke of her as his sister. His poem was full of grief over his sister's separation, loving acknowledgement of her kindnesses, her affection and her willingness to fulfil his every wish so long as it was in her power, and of the rosy pink-violet light of fond memories, for he practically grew up in Rahat Afza's arms. Habib-un Nisa and Wazir Khanam were unweeping, so as not to intensify the departing daughter's sorrow. They wished they could weep and wail loudly and long, but were obliged to be silent, like pictures painted on a wall. They were managers and problem solvers and could ill afford to show any emotion.

Fourth-day ceremonies, and others after those, came and went with lightning swiftness. Amir-un Nisa and Nur Fatimah remained sullen and full of silent disapproval, as before. They were not on speaking terms with Wazir, but now they began more and more to make Shah Muhammad Agha the centre of their attentions and ministrations. He was now a little above a year old and was beginning to articulate meaningful sounds. He could understand simple words and phrases and could recognize the people whom he saw frequently. Nur Fatimah had him over to her room with a thousand excuses and kept him by her side for whole livelong days. She fed him, washed him, changed his clothes, and sang him to sleep, trying her best to wean him off his mother in more ways than one.

Wazir Khanam's milk had been rather scanty at this birth. She avoided breastfeeding, anyway. Now when she could not afford a suckling maid of good antecedents, she breastfed Shah Muhammad Agha to the extent that she had milk, but it did not suffice for the growing, robust baby. She was therefore obliged to supplement her milk with soft, palatable and light foods by the time Shah Muhammad Agha was a month or two short of one year. Obviously, there was nothing secretive about it, but it gave Amir-un Nisa and Nur Fatimah a perfect excuse for getting the baby to learn to enjoy outside foods and thus reduce his dependency on his mother. They believed that this might dilute his need for his mother and thus help create a distance between mother and child.

Wazir knew all this well enough, but she did not want open warfare with her relatives-in-law while she shared a residence with them. Rahat Afza's marriage was quite a different matter. She considered it beneath her, and also somewhat impertinent for her, to seek the Navab's support in resolving an apparently petty matter, not involving custody or adoption of the child.

She waited for the opportune time. It was not at all a problem for her to get out of Rampur for good, and settle herself back in Delhi, but she felt apprehensive about Shah Muhammad Agha's closeness to his grandmother and aunt. Sudden separation from them might affect the baby's well-being. It was certainly likely that Shah Muhammad Agha would miss them in Delhi for quite a few months. She also feared that with Rahat Afza's caregiving no longer available, she might fail to do justice to the task of bringing up the baby.

Navab Mirza was not unaware of these things. He knew that his mother's inner life was teeming with problems and multiple complexities; no one saw them, but he knew that her uneasinesses and disquietude were like dragons spewing their venomous vapours into her brain. His mother's face no longer had the bloom of fulfilled youth which spread its roseate vigour over her just before Shah Muhammad Agha's birth, and the general feeling of wellness which Agha Mirza Turab Ali's attentions, solicitations and unfailing, polite gallantry had produced in her personality.

Navab Mirza could see, and sense more than see, that his mother, who always looked young for her age, now looked old for her age. Not that she was becoming old, or the paleness of morning was beginning to pervade her beauty's bedchamber, but it was certainly the case that the anxieties which were eating at her spirit made her feel tired and spent at all times.

Navab Mirza spent not a little time and thought on how to make his mother feel stronger, better. One thing seemed quite obvious to him: Life in Rampur could not give back to his mother the peace of mind which the last six months or so had taken away from her. Peace of mind was in fact a far cry; she could not even have the feeling of elementary security and emotional strength in the city of Rampur now. But, obviously—at least it seemed obvious to him—his mother was in no mind to overcome or solve her problems. True, once she did say that she wanted to leave Rampur, but that was apparently a momentary mood; she did not broach that subject again.

After some thought, Navab Mirza decided to talk the matter over with Manjhli Khala, keeping Amma Jan out of it initially. He went to his mother's house to ascertain the latest mood there, only to find that the state of affairs was direr than before: His mother had not eaten since lunch yesterday;

Muhammad Agha had come nowhere near her since last night, his auntie had fed him, sang songs to him and had him sleep next to her, without ever mentioning his mother. Nor had Muhammad Agha asked even once to be taken to his mother. Wazir did not shed tears in front of Navab Mirza, but the redness of her eyes and the wanness of her face clearly indicated that she had been weeping.

'Amma Jan, these people plan to take Muhammad Agha from you.'

Wazir's eyes misted with tears. 'It seems I am fated to bear children and have them promptly taken away from me.'

'No. Amma Jan, please. I too came from you, did I not? No one can ever separate me from you.'

Wazir closed her eyes tightly, trying to keep the tears from running down her face, but the tears still came. She wrapped her face in her dupatta and said, 'Mother's Life and Soul, those were other times. Because everyone was in fear of the Firangee, none dared to take you. It was said that the officials of the Company wanted to put you to death. As regards the people of Loharu, they didn't like to hear of you, ever.'

'All right, I grant you all that. But still, there's no gainsaying this: I am yours, and will ever, ever, be yours. So long as your benign shadow is on my head, I will achieve things and will show myself before the world as one who didn't let the blood of the martyr Navab Shamsuddin Ahmad Khan go waste in him. I will be like the Great Wall of China between you and whatever calamity the world may throw at you. You should fear none, worry about nothing.'

It was the first time that Navab Mirza had spoken to his mother with such candour and confidence. Her spirits soared and her breast swelled with pride. A brief candle of thanks and comfort lit up in her soul, but his last few words flashed into her inner self like a beacon. She raised her head with pride, but looked at her son with something like entreaty. 'I want nothing from the legacy of the martyred Agha sahib. But his memorial, which I nurtured in my womb, and brought out of my womb, and of which I took care like it was a newly blossomed rose: why should I give it up, and how should I find the heart to do so? Navab Mirza, what is it that you want from me?'

Navab Mirza realized that he may have hurried a little in uttering his decisive words. 'Nothing, I want nothing, Amma Jan.' He spoke with diffidence, not with the certainty that he had employed a minute ago. 'I want your peace of mind. That's all. I cannot see you sad and grieving.'

Wazir sighed. 'It seems Allah Mian made me at a moment when only the unfortunate and the unlucky ones were being made.'

'Everything has two sides, madam,' Navab Mirza made an attempt at some levity, and loving impertinence. 'Good luck you did not get, but you were given wisdom and beauty as bonus!'

'Better be a cretin than have such wisdom, and let such beauty go to hell!' Her mild smile robbed her words of passion and intensity, but Navab Mirza could see that she meant every word. 'That I shouldn't be able to clasp the pieces of my heart to my bosom; that I should be deprived of the support of one who valued me. Navab Mirza, you take me for a child, don't you?'

Navab Mirza had no reply to this. After a moment's silence, he tried another tack. 'I was just going to present myself before Manjhli Khala. Amma Jan, why don't you come too? In fact, she was remembering you. Shall I get a palanquin now?'

'So what else will be new there? Muhammad Agha is here; should I leave him behind?'

'There is no harm—in fact, it might do you a power of good, getting away from the narrow environment here.'

'He who went away left me to live here.' Wazir was bitter, as if it was Agha Mirza Turab Ali who had caused his own death.

'But you are not in a prison,' Navab Mirza responded a little sharply.

Wazir said nothing, but looked at him in somewhat enigmatic reproach, as if saying but not saying that it was not for everyone to understand everything. Navab Mirza was shaken from inside. He was trying to find some suitable words when Wazir said dryly, 'You are welcome to speak to Manjhli Baji, but you need not expect me to be bound to accept what you or Manjhli Baji may prefer to believe or prescribe.'

Navab Mirza reeled inwardly in confusion. Has Amma Jan fathomed my thoughts? Does she somehow know what I want her to do? But I must come out in the open sometime soon. So why not now? But I should first consult with Khala Jan. Or Amma Jan should at least leave this house and come live with us at Khala Jan's? She did mention it once . . . But will Amma Jan consent to leaving our little brother behind? I think the present crisis in her mind is just because of the baby. The grandmother and the aunt wish to charm the little one into choosing to become their child.

He was lost in his thoughts when Wazir interrupted him in a voice that was nearly breaking with tears and reproach. 'Navab Mirza, you know I place everything that you say on my head and my eyes. But please don't imagine that you can understand a mother's feelings for her child and her pain when she fears losing it.'

'God forbid! I could never be so presumptuous.'

It was as if Wazir did not hear him. 'You are a piece of my heart, but you are a male, first and last. The community of males believes that all the mysteries of the world, all the secret corners of all hearts are accessible to the male. And even if some are not, the male believes that he has the power to decide on behalf of everyone and everything. Men believe that women are just as they believe them to be in temperament, in preferences and hates, and they know that their beliefs about women are founded on their own better understanding and superior faculty to solve problems.'

She was silent for a beat, as if aware that she was no longer in the conversational mode. She went on: 'And if women are not what they believe or want them to be, the fault lies at women's doors. She should have been as the male believes her to be.'

Navab Mirza now plucked up courage to interrupt. He spoke in a low but clear voice: 'Amma Jan, I was made a man by God; the Shariah and custom taught me certain things. Yet, opposed to them all, I always understood, and believed, that my mother's words, my mother's beliefs, my mother's decisions, always outranked all men. Whenever Manjhli Khala, or Jahangirah auntie spoke to me about you . . . I mean your . . . Agha sahib's proposal, I maintained that my mother's decision, whatever it was, was right by definition.'

'It is your auspicious love for me, Bacche Mian, that you are of this view, but custom, and the Shariah, or its wrong interpretation, and men acting with unshakeable firmness and thoughtlessness according to those wrong interpretations, are everywhere among us. Please don't be offended; you too are not entirely free from such notions. After all—'

'I beg your pardon,' Navab Mirza broke in, somewhat urgently. 'I should not interrupt you, Amma Jan . . .'

'No! I interrupt you and ask you: How did you conclude that it was your duty to solve my difficulties for me?'

Navab Mirza was now utterly stupefied; his thoughts in disarray, he was at a loss for words. He opened his mouth to speak, but no words came. He dried the perspiration on his palms, then on his brow. Then he spoke, haltingly, 'Well . . . actually . . . I . . . well, I am sorry I must not have understood you correctly. Do I understand you to say that it's not the duty of a son, or a sister to help their mother or sister at the time of need?'

'No, that's not the point. Why should the son assume the mother to be incapable? Why should it be held that since she is a woman, only a man is entitled to help her when she is in need of help?'

Navab Mirza was almost shocked. He never saw the matter in this light, never considered that there could be a problem here. After all, what is a son expected to do? Who but a son should hold his mother's hand when her life is in trouble?

Wazir must have read his mind. She certainly saw his confusion at this unexpected angle. She spoke with deliberation, like a teacher trying to elucidate a difficult theorem to a bright pupil. 'Now look at the problem this way. Were it your father, and not your mother, in some dire straits, would you instinctively reach out to help, believing that it was your duty to hold your father's hand if he stumbled?'

His reaction was entirely a reflex, driven by his innate beliefs. 'No, not at all. A man is quite competent . . . competent to deal . . .'

His voice trailed off. He shut his mouth tightly, almost clenching his jaw. May God forgive me, what is it that I say? Has not Amma Jan been making this very point? Men believe in a natural hierarchy, placing themselves above women. Men believe that the world's business is run by them, and them alone.

'So you saw, Bacche Mian,' Wazir said sadly. 'Fired by love, you declare me competent and even superior. But your reason tells you differently.'

'But . . . but that's what the Shariah also teaches.' Navab Mirza felt at a loss to justify his contradictory stand. 'That's what our books say. That's what our elders teach us.'

'Who wrote those books, if not men? Your qazis, your muftis, your elders, who are they, if not men? I don't know what the Shariah may say, but I do remember what Baba Farid said about Bibi Fatimah Sam who is buried not too far from Baba Nizamuddin's shrine in Delhi. Baba Farid was asked by someone why he venerated Bibi Fatimah Sam so much, was she not a mere woman? Baba Sahib said, "When a tiger appears in the jungle, no one asks if it's a male or female." I ask you, was not the great Sufi Rabia Basri a mere woman?'

'But she was a wali-Allah, an acknowledged friend of God.'

'Yes, and I am a godless woman of the world; each hair in my head is loaded with sin.'

'Amma Jan, please. For God's sake do not distort my words and my meanings thus, I pray you.' Navab Mirza sounded shocked and tearful.

The mother in Wazir was instantly aroused. She stood, with tears of remorse in her eyes, and did the wonted action of taking upon herself all the misfortune that might befall her son, and cried, 'Navab Mirza, I am really and truly sorry. I did not at all mean to score a point. I would rather die before I let you feel offended with me.'

Navab Mirza's eyes pricked with tears. 'Amma Jan, I would gladly die to give you the smallest happiness.'

'Please don't be sad. All things will be well in just a few days. Now you go back to your Manjhli Khala; tell her I will soon come and see her.'

*

Navab Mirza rose from his mother's presence most unwillingly, subject to numerous doubts and uncertainties. On her side, Wazir carefully washed her face and rubbed it hard to bring back some colour, and rearranged her hair. She put on a clean, white outfit, wore diamond earrings and a couple of rings on her fingers. In short, she made a conscious effort to look presentable for the first time after she became a widow. She then dispatched Habiba to inform her aunt-in-law that Khanam sahib was coming to visit.

Amir-un Nisa, not expecting Wazir to take the initiative, lost her nerve for a few seconds. She now knew that Wazir wielded considerable influence in the Exalted Fort. In the early days of Wazir's widowhood, she was apprehensive that she might use her influence to the detriment of her relatives-in-law; if nothing else, she might take strong steps to assert her right on Shah Muhammad Agha. Amir-un Nisa and Nur Fatimah, on their part, were determined not to let go of the child. They were making every effort to divert to their own selves Muhammad Agha's affection and dependency on his mother. They were also trying to have some women of the Fort inform the Navab sahib that Wazir was incapable of bringing up the child in the true Shia faith. There were some vague indications of their message being viewed favourably. They were sure that success would be theirs, ultimately.

Wazir entered Amir-un Nisa's room to find that her little son and Nur Fatimah had apparently been at play together; Nur Fatimah, trying to pretend that Muhammad Agha had just drifted out of sleep, was gently patting his back, his head in her lap. But the child, still intent on play, tried again and again to make a bid for the toys scattered around him. Wazir immediately made to go and pick him up; he gave out a cackle of pleasure, but did nothing to rise, far less try to leap into his mother's arms. His interest was in the toys, not the women. Nur Fatimah continued to pat his back.

'Shah sahib, please. Why don't you sleep a tiny bit more? Just look, the sun is not far up in the sky, and Li'l Lady Sleep sits in your eyes; she says, "Oh, should these lovely lids close for a little while, I too would rest a tiny moment".'

Wazir noted that the baby was paying no heed to Nur Fatimah's syrupy words and was trying to go for the toys again and again. 'Great! I like your earnest efforts to entice and seduce the little one!'

Nur Fatimah retorted, 'Yes, sure. There are some who seduce and entice the hulking male; there are some who try to keep a little baby diverted.'

'Doubtless, some bibis use up a lifetime weaving webs of hope to entice someone. But no one comes by.'

'Yes, those who love their honour, devote themselves to the Lord. Those who love goods and property, their youth flourishes in platefuls of delicacies.'

'Chastity is tested when the lady has no chador to cover her body,' Wazir quoted a famous Persian saying. 'There's a world outside your little dark cell, Nur Fatimah. Your outworn feminine blandishments won't work there. But aside from those things, if you are done with casting your spells on my baby, give him back to me so that the poor child may know that there is something called "mother" too.'

Now Amir-un Nisa strode forward, placed her hand on the little boy's head and cried out, 'God save us from this woman's tongue! It spins words like the widow's spinning wheel spins threads. Listen, you. You may be this child's mother, but it's we who have charge of him. We are his caregivers and nurturers. He is our heir and survivor.'

'Indeed! Only God is untouched by blemish. To this day, we were taught that a child's parents have charge of the child, and the child inherits from the parents. Now we have a new phenomenon: a decrepit crone presumes to have the dignity of the Prophet's wife and claims that she has charge of all fatherless children! She who has nothing to eat and nothing to wear hopes to snatch my baby whom I brought into this world and nurtured with my blood. Haven't you heard, madam: The elephant goes from town to town but is known by his owner's renown?'

'Chhoti, learn to speak with humility. This is not Delhi; this is Rampur. It won't take a moment to unwind your tight curls.'

'My key lies with my Allah, and in my Navab's hands.'

'Oh really? Dear woman, how is he your Navab? You, a woman of the wrong faith, the wrong community, whoever clinked a few coins before you, you promptly gave yourself to him.'

'Sticks and stones, dear Auntie. With a flick of my tongue I'll convert them into flocks of cotton and blow them away. Your vulgar, dirty language won't give custody of my child to you.'

'So I should leave him to your tender mercies so that you may take him from his ancestral faith and ruin him in both worlds. That's what you desire, don't you?'

'A mother's faith is only her maternal love for her baby. And the just ruler's faith is to do justice by his subjects. Don't be deluded; you think since the Exalted Navab Sahib is of the Shia faith, he will force separation between mother and child, just because the child's father professed the same faith? You didn't learn from the experience of Rahat Afza.'

Shah Muhammad Agha, upset by the raised voices, lost interest in both sleep and play. He was trying to crawl down to his mother. Wazir cried out impulsively, 'Oh, take care! Shah sahib might stumble and fall!' She lifted the baby to her bosom and said, 'I know well your real motivation. You want this house, and all the rest of my martyred husband's property. It's not much, but it is a whole kingdom in the eyes of charity cases like you. My Paradise-dwelling husband bore all your burdens.'

'And what do you have, Chhoti Begam? Are you not another pauper, wholly dependent on his legacy?'

'I have nothing. But I hold dear my honour and I value my dignity.'

'This then is your dignity? You'll live here and be a continuous pain for us?'

Wazir smiled sarcastically and spoke with the sense of her own superiority. 'So now your secret is out! You are a case of "The mother-in-law is gone visiting, the starveling daughter-in-law to her fill must be eating."'

Nur Fatimah rose and tried to take the baby from Wazir's arms. 'Be quiet. Our sole concern is with this innocent one.'

Wazir clasped Muhammad Agha even more tightly to her bosom; she then smiled and said, 'Sister-in-law, perhaps you weren't paying attention. Your dear auntie is concerned solely about me. She wants nothing but that I entrust my house to her and go live like a hermit in a jungle.'

Cut to the quick, Nur Fatimah hissed, 'Chhoti Begam, your heart is a cesspool of evil things, just as your name is a name of thoroughly ill fame.'

'Nur Bibi, open your ears and hear the facts of life. The old harridan's luck smiled upon her when her nephew was called to Paradise by the Almighty. She's now dreaming to become the sole owner of the poor man's legacy, even if it should mean depriving his wife or his widowed sister.'

'You want to sow the seed of discord between us. That is not going to happen. Nur Fatimah is well aware of your mentality and your social capacity.'

'But, she, poor thing, is not aware of your mentality and your social capacity.' Wazir said scornfully. 'Anyway, let that be. Talk business. It is now quite clear that you have no real interest in Muhammad Agha.'

'Why not? Should we deprive him of the traditions and beliefs of his ancestors and thus be sinners in the eyes of God?'

'The beliefs are the same. Is not Islam our faith, too?'

Nur Fatimah tried to butt in again. 'But . . .'

'Have some patience, Nur Fatimah. Let me finish,' Wazir said gravely. 'I say, it's the same religion. It is just a matter of ways and paths. So I declare and make this vow and invoke Imam Jafar Sadiq, the Exalted Imam who was your lawgiver, as my witness: Shah sahib will be brought up in the ways and paths of his father.'

Aunt and grandmother were shocked into speechlessness. After a moment, Amir-un Nisa produced the loser's argument, 'And should you renege on your vow?'

'Repent, please. Don't say such words! I should go back upon my word after making the Exalted Imam—peace be upon him—my witness? Do I want to become a log for the fires of Hell?'

'No, we desire some more, something above a word.' Amir-un Nisa was thoughtful. 'And what do you say about . . . that other matter?'

'Speak candidly, say what is really in your heart.' Wazir smiled. 'All right, I won't expose you. Now listen: I won't live here any more. I'll go settle in Jahanabad, in my other house. This little house, its appurtenances, everything is yours.'

Aunt-in-law and sister-in-law both opened their mouths to speak, to make some objection, perhaps. But no words came. They stared at each other, crestfallen. Wazir used the silence to make baby talk with Muhammad Agha, make kissing and caressing noises at him. Finally Nur Fatimah stirred, as if waking up.

'And Shah Muhammad Agha . . . ?'

'He will be brought up in the Shia faith. He will learn everything that a Shia gentleman should. I will sign an agreement. The property here will be yours, on condition that he inherits all of it when he comes of age. This paper will be witnessed by you both. Do you hear?'

'Yes, we heard.' The two women articulated the words with some difficulty. But Wazir did not wait. Saying, 'Fine, so I'll leave you now', she went out, clasping her son as before.

BOOK 7

57

A luminant new star rises on the firmament of poets and poetry in the Heavenly City of Delhi: Dagh makes an impression

ABU ZAFAR MUHAMMAD Sirajuddin Bahadur Shah II had been on the throne in the Red Haveli for seven years now: years of 'English Peace' as the English and their chroniclers liked to describe it. The lights of beauty and love, learning and spiritual grace, astronomy and engineering, logic and mathematics, astrology and geomancy, poetry and literature, piety and Sufism, glittered in every street and neighbourhood, making Delhi the envy of Baghdad and Cordoba. Experts in martial and recreational sports, masters of music and dance, culinary arts, pharmacology, leaders in every trade, every craft that needed manual skill and dexterity, designers and makers of jewelled or plain silver and gold ornaments: the Heavenly City of Delhi, Hazrat-e Delhi ('Delhi, the Presence'), teemed with these and all kinds of people of sophistication. You go looking for one and return with four in tow. Barring military campaigns and warfare, establishing one's sovereignty by force or diplomacy, there was nothing whose masters were unknown in Delhi.

Among civilian disciplines, including statecraft, Haziq-uz Zaman Umdat-ul Hukama Hakim Muhammad Ahsanullah Khan had a status and a portfolio of intellectual attainments such that had his unfortunate King been really King, and his Vizierate really a Vizierate, the days of Bahadur Shah I, if not those of Jahangir or Shahjahan, could easily have been the reality of Delhi's contemporary life; Delhi's evil fortunes could have been reversed. But Delhi was fated not just to be ravaged and savaged: it must be widowed, its master driven off to Cawnpore, then to Allahabad, from there to Calcutta and finally to Rangoon in something like a slave ship.

Anyway, that vile and ominous day was twenty years into the dark dust of the future when Bahadur Shah II assumed his place in history. At that time, no one imagined that the might of Hindustan was already on an irreversibly downward slope. Delhi had seen worse, and had recovered stronger. Surely, this time it would not be different. Delhi had had scores of bloodbaths, dozens of transfers of power in its ancient life. The times changed, but the order of things, the rules of the times, never changed. The sciences and the arts, crafts and manual or mental disciplines: these were always there to be acquired and practised. For such things were proof that man was a spirit; such things were as inevitable for man as breathing.

Delhi was still ahead of everyone—or so Delhi believed—in the arts and the crafts, in the learned and noble disciplines of Philosophy, Mathematics, Astrology. And new lights had begun also to glimmer in her ancient chandeliers and floor lamps; the flame of even the humble, oil-burning little earthen lamps seemed capable of absorbing or at least incorporating the light from the English lanterns. People who read the Firangee's books in the original English, or those who designed their lives on the pattern and in the style of the Firangee; those who could devise and operate iron implements and engines and power them with hot vapour: the heart of Delhi had begun to boast of even such people. Sikandar sahib's church near Kashmiri Gate seriously seemed to rival the mosques that were built many scores of years ago.

Everybody apparently was quite convinced that the Presence, Delhi, was still the same old melting pot: gold, silver, copper, iron, every imaginable ore came to the boil in it, melted and seamlessly melded with those already simmering and bubbling with vitality, was refined and became a new ore, stronger but sharing the qualities of all its contents, even if much of those had been thrown into it by chance or warfare. None imagined that the blood that would rain down on Delhi in a mere score of years would break and burn all crucibles, all melting pots. The red colour of the Red Haveli would be almost the first to be washed white in that rain.

When he was born to Shah Alam II's eldest son Mirza Muinuddin and his Hindu wife Lal Bai on 30 October 1775, none knew, far less Mirza Bulaqi himself, as Shah Alam II was affectionately known, the ultimate destiny of Mirza Sirajuddin, the newly born grandson, affectionately known as Mirza Ibban. Shah Alam II was crowned King Emperor in 1759, far away from Delhi, and had been under English 'protection' at Allahabad after his defeat at the hands of the English in 1764. Although Muinuddin was his eldest son, the governance of the Empire and the management of the Red Fort and other personal properties of the Sovereign were in the hands of Shah Alam's second son, Mirza Sulaiman Shikoh. None could predict, therefore, who would succeed as Emperor after Shah Alam II.

In the event, the Emperor returned to Delhi in early 1771 and assumed the throne in the Red Haveli. Enterprising and able ministers—like Mirza Ghulam Najaf Khan, then Najibuddaulah, and lastly Mahada ji Sindhia—ran the administration, until finally, Lord Lake sahib became the 'protector' of the Emperor in 1803. (Some of this we narrated long ago, in earlier pages.) Officials of the John Company ensured the smooth transition of Muinuddin to the throne. Under the supervision of the English Resident, he was crowned King as Muizz-ud Duniya wa al-Din Abu Nasr Muinuddin Muhammad Akbar Shah II in 1806 after the death of Shah Alam II.

Although Sirajuddin was the eldest, the Emperor's eye of favour was on his second son, Mirza Jahangir Bakht. The Heavenly Throne-abiding One made long and serious efforts in promoting the case of Mirza Jahangir Bakht. But he was a cavalier young man, brilliant and erratic; his dislike for the Firangee was well known. He was also very nearly addicted to the bottle. The English therefore sent him off to Benaras which meant that he was practically in exile. He lived a turbulent life and died young, in 1821, at Benaras. His body was brought to Delhi for burial in the courtyard of the Sultan-ul Auliya Hazrat Nizamuddin sahib's mosque outside the city of Delhi.

Officials of the Company Bahadur promptly declared Sirajuddin to be the heir apparent. Thus Sirajuddin, poet in four languages, Sufi, scholar, commentator on Sadi Shirazi, marksman, archer, swordsman and rider of commanding renown, became King Emperor on 28/29 September 1837. He assumed the titles of the Presence, Shadow of the Blemishless, Caliph to the All Merciful, King with the Grandeur of Jamshed, Commander of the Army of Angels, Ruler and Shadow of Allah, Shelterer and Protector of the Path of Muhammad, Choicest Offspring of the House of the Lord of the Auspicious Conjunction, Emperor of Magnificence, Great King of all Kings of Kings, Emperor, son of Emperor, Sultan, son of Sultan, Lord of Honours and Holy Wars, Truest Nurturer Lord, Metaphor for the Divinity, Abu al-Muzaffar Siraj-ud Duniya wa al-Din Muhammad Bahadur Shah Ghazi, May God perpetuate His Land and His Law, May His Bounty and Good Deeds benefit the Worlds, thus enhancing the brightness of the Royal Seat.

Maulavi Imam Bakhsh Sahbai, who had been one of the men of learning in the newly crowned Prince's Court, composed a Persian chronogram of three verses in the somewhat unusual metre of the rubai:

At Bahadur Shah's succession to Empire
Intoxication of pleasure
Filled the wine glass of Delhi.
He sat on the throne
Of everincreasing felicity; because of him
Fragrance increased in the garden of Delhi.
On Reason's lips came the date of ascension
On the throne of that King of Exalted Value:
The Light of Delhi.

The value of the two words, chiragh-e dihli ('Light of Delhi) adds up to 1253, the date, according to the Hijra calendar, of the King's ascension.

Historians later interpreted it as one of the blessings of the English power; some described it as the last flicker of Delhi's flame. Some saw it as the magical effect of the everlasting flame of India's Indo-Islamic culture. The fact remains that the Delhi of Bahadur Shah II had everything that was difficult to find in one city at that time, great as a city might have been. Above all, the city was teeming with people; its subjects were happy; the rich, drunk on their prosperity, the beggar, happy in his rough animal skin. Delhi was, in the truest sense, the heart that is full of Divine Illuminations.

But Wazir had her heart full of sorrow. Come she did to Delhi, with Navab Mirza and Shah Muhammad Agha, hoping to be the mistress of her own peace, but she found that her home in Delhi and in fact the whole of the city seemed to pinch her and bite her. Old memories of parents, the worry-free days and nights of childhood; the time of her growing up, bringing with it a huge train of an unending, ever-increasing and ever-blooming springtime of youth; her own coquetries, merciless on the drove of admirers, and her enjoyment of their discomfiture, and her own indifference to them; and after the passing of Mattan Blak sahib, Shamsuddin Ahmad Khan's submission of his body and soul to her, her own restless coveting of his love and the slow but sure ebullience of her desire for him; then the Navab's martyrdom and her spiritual homelessness and physical loneliness: there was so much, so many portraits and landscapes, like the bright pages of an album of words and pictures. They filled her heart to overflowing with the tangy, coppery taste of blood that flows from failure, and pricked her soul with nostalgia: for what was and what could have been. She had never thought that happy memories could come accompanied with so much regret, so much pain, so much repining and discontent. If you plucked a rose without due care, its thorn pricked you to protest the thoughtlessness and the inconsiderateness which you displayed in taking away its crowning glory. Here, it was nothing else but the rose which was the thorn: its each and every petal was saturated with the scents of the past but it stung like the scorpion plant. But was it possible not to touch those memories? For their scents travelled in and out of your being like breath, and their colours were inside every blink of your eye.

She did not want to live in Delhi; but was Rampur any better? How much burden could she expect Manjhli Baji to bear on her behalf? Her own self was not a little burden, and there were the growing minds and bodies of the two children: they were like delicate plants destined to grow to the state of powerful and shady trees, but right now both needed their own kind of care, watering, watching, pruning. In any case, were the memories of Rampur different from those of Delhi? Not so deep rooted and so densely foliated, but the memory tree of Rampur had strong enough roots, and its fruit was both bitter and sweet. When she left Rampur, she was like a living, breathing, dense plant suddenly pulled out of its planter and deprived of water and shade. But the shade of that plant also housed homes of snakes; snakes which missed no opportunity to bite and sting.

Was it not yet a proof of the Might of the Almighty? That an arboretum that seemed immune to the yellow leaf should be targeted by the yellow-grey eyes of the sere over and over again, turning its air to poison? The breezes, on whose shoulders the song of the bulbul, impulsive or playful like a baby's movement towards its mother, travelled free from one end of the garden to the other . . . that those breezes should now become the breath of laments and of sighs! Double-coloured rose; jasmine, purple or white; the tiny, early musk rose, whose subtle and delicate play and sway in the breeze made the water spout beat its head upon the stone, and made the wavelets in the garden's rivulets and streams move ever restlessly, full of desire; that those flowers should now droop their heads and grieve over the sad fact of being. Were these not the workings of the Almighty?

Wazir had long given up looking at herself in the glass, or doing up her hair in style. Most thirty, thirty-two-year-old women, especially those who had borne children, looked and felt like old women. But Wazir's body was still taut, with no hint of looseness of muscle or decline of softness. Her face had still the gentle, inexperienced look one associates with virgins. There was not a single crease on her face or neck. Though she had breast-fed all her babies, not overmuch, but certainly for a few months in each case, and more than that in the case of Muhammad Agha, her breasts were not flabby or overlarge: there was no droop, no hint of use. But now she hated her good looks, tremendous as they still were: it was her looks which caused the barge of her young life to founder and beat against shoals; and she had no hope now for her looks to tug the barge of her life to some safe haven after all.

She recalled the verses of Mir sahib who wrote many decades ago:

Beauty and concealment can never
Go together. There was none whose beauty
Did not achieve its purpose: to become apparent.
From Jacob's son to the rose,
From the rose to the candle;
There is none whose beauty failed to find
Its way to the marketplace.

Oh, well. What did Mir sahib know about the fate of things and how they change? These poets care for nothing; they just go on searching for new things, and new ways of saying them. True, I did not want concealment; but I never, ever, desired to be saleable merchandise in the marketplace of Fate. Really, I would not let even my slippers to go to the marketplace! But I became exposed without ever visiting the marketplace which only men rule. Perhaps the dénouement is ever the same. Blak sahib once told me that a very great poet of his language said something like 'before the gods, human beings are like butterflies before thoughtless children'. There were some more words, something like they kill us for sport. They catch them for their own fun, pull their colourful wings, killing them in the process. I told him that we Muslims do not believe in such rubbish. We have no gods and goddesses . . .

But now I have a thought: the Hindus have gods and goddesses, don't they? Perhaps they mean Destiny and Fate when they say 'God' or

'Goddess'? Did I not try all my life to find my own way? Do I not aspire still to discover my own light? No, I should now live for these two children of mine. That is the straightest path and the truest bliss.

The thought of paths and ways pulled from the memory yet another utterance of Mir:

Son of Adam, to be crushed underfoot
By death; it's your first step.
What will happen to you, by and by, until the end?
Who knows?

God, my hair stands on end just to say those words! Perhaps he was writing an answer to the verses about Beauty and the Purposes of Beauty? But what would be the residue, once we are inexorably trampled under Death's paws? So what is there left to discuss about the conclusion? Perhaps another name or the only name for going through life is to live and die each minute of your existence? Perhaps being born is worse than being dead. For, you are not really born; you are dead, in fact. But does not that dead life offer so much pleasure, so much comfort as well?

She heard a baby crying. Perhaps it was Shah Muhammad Agha, waking up from his mid-noon sleep. She hurried into the bedroom. The baby was in deep sleep. Perhaps she heard someone else's baby . . . or perhaps it was just her imagination. Habib-un Nisa was curled up asleep on a small cot nearby. Wazir had just one maid nowadays. A boy worked part-time, to do the necessary outdoor duties in the morning and evening. She recalled the days when her house seemed crowded with servants. She did not so much miss the luxuries, the comfortable pace of life, as the flying away of the thrills and the near intoxication that she had experienced in the love of Shamsuddin Ahmad. Then there was the bustling merriment, the air of festivity. The rising sun every day seemed like the first chapter of a new experience of pleasure and hope. How soon her race of joy was run. How quickly did the women and men of her household scatter, never to reassemble.

Did she have hopes of Navab Mirza for healing her lonely existence, of being her support in her old age? And Shah Muhammad Agha? I'll surely be dead by the time he grows up. She heard a voice rising from her heart: Whatever is today has been breathed into life by Navab Mirza; whatever will be in the future, will again be by him or because of him . . . Now what else is there left for me, or for anything else of mine, to grow into, or become? Does something remain from life for me? Should I still have some expectations from life and its transactions of loving, or winning in love? How well Hakim Momin sahib said in one of his recent ghazals:

There are those who long for love, for loving;
And here am I, immeasurably repentant that I loved.

No, no, again no. Was all that that happened in the past nothing but a maze that I saw in a dream and under whose spell I still remain? How could all that be a maze of loving and of being loved? Pictures began to flash before her eyes, full, life-size paintings, brilliant in colour and vibrant in rhythm: the dark, stormy night of our return from Khvajah Sahib, the fearful thrill of being overtaken by the dust storm; it was the first time I saw Mattan Blak sahib. It seemed to her that she was a child, bending over what was known as a magic lantern when she was small. Only once had she the pleasure and the thrill of looking through its large glass eye: the device was introduced by the Firangee and was viewed with much suspicion by the natives. You looked through an eyepiece; the operator cranked the handle of the box, and an enlarged picture in colour appeared, showing the King and Queen of England, or the Taj Mahal, and similar fascinating things. The operator intoned in a special kind of sing-song voice as he presented picture after picture.

Today, the enlarged eyepiece was producing pictures of different kinds, painted with the vivid hues of sorrow and regret and joy . . . He did not, I am sure, mean to look me in the eye. In fact, he was not even looking in my direction. It was I who was peeking at him from behind my chador. But the saucy operator cranked the handle again, exposing me; my chador was blown away. I looked up in confusion and saw for a fraction of a moment his eyes on me. Allah, how wilful and confident those eyes were! It was at that time that I understood: a man's eye can remain fixed at one spot and can still, like a whirling flame, circumambulate a woman's body, as if drawing a wall around it. I then knew that a man's eye could at the same time seem indifferent and yet ask a personal question. Inquisitive for what else could be unveiled, and ask the question: how much of what lay exposed, or could be exposed, could belong to the man who saw? My own body seemed hot, as if he didn't merely see me, but he also touched me. I had never known, though I had heard often in stories, that desire for man, and desire for a particular man, could be born in a woman at one and the same time.

Actually, at that time, I had no thoughts about how I should spend my life. What I said to Bari Baji was just one of those things, just to end the altercation. Still, I was quite sure in my mind that none could put the handcuffs and fetters of marriage on me against my wishes . . . Perhaps I did not even want to marry, ever. So what did I want? Did I have a scheme for my life?

I don't know, she answered her own question with some pique. Or maybe I was just bored? Is it necessary for everything to happen according to a plan? But I do know: Becoming a man's plaything or maid, or mistress, these are just forms of the hateful thing called 'selling one's honour'. But did I not believe that I came into this world to save women's honour if I could, and certainly be vigilant of my own honour? Then why did Blak sahib's one single glance destroy me as if by fire? Is it, perhaps, that my reason taught me things in which I had full faith, but when it came to action, I acted just like those dull-witted women, cheap and vulgar of mind, women who prefer to regard everything as inferior to nightly pleasures in bed and starvation rations by the day? As the saying goes, I found myself a husband, for enjoying life, not for starving myself.

No, I was something else, and I wanted to be something other than those women. Can I say that Blak sahib seduced me? I don't think so, at least not then. I fell for him with both eyes open. Or maybe what happened between us was a product of a sense of gratefulness? For, it's quite true: all of us were bound for dire ends, had he not found us that night. Girls of my age, should they fall into the hands of robbers or dacoits are serially raped first, and then sold off to a madam for a pittance. And if you ask me, those who are sold off in some whorehouse are better off than those whom the evil dacoits keep for their own pleasure. True, they would treat them worse than the lowliest maid, and the moment the poor girl's body slackened a bit or she lost her appeal, she would be driven off like a useless buffalo or cow. Her 'man' would of course be angling for another 'maid', and then yet another. There are many proverbs like 'She's twenty: She's shrivelled. A sixty-year-old male: He's a young blade!' Such proverbs are made by men, who else?

True, I and my father had every reason to be grateful. Yet, it was disproportionate, really. To so heedlessly drop into the bag of a stranger, a muscle-bound Firangee, my dignity and good name, my religion, my customs and traditions, it was certainly out of all proportion. Well, all that may be true, but I was determined to go with Blak sahib. And what other way was there for me to notify my father and Bari Baji forcibly that I was not a mechanical doll? That I was the mistress of my own wishes?

And the plain truth is that I liked him very much. At any rate, I was not the first Mussulman girl who went with a Firangee male. Do people not remember Faiz-un Nisa Begam? The Exalted Presence, Ali Gauhar Shah, Alam Bahadur Shah who now rests in Paradise, had proclaimed her his daughter. The Begam married the English General Palmer. What a beauty she was, how awesome her personal grace—she really looked like an Emperor's daughter. Then there was that Begam from the Deccan, let me recall her name . . . yes, Khair-un Nisa Begam. It is said that she became big with the Firangee's child without marriage. The Firangee was Resident at the Court of Nizam-ul Mulk. So what could the mother and grandmother do, except to approve a marriage?

True, the Firangee treated her with exceptional tenderness, but he made Kristans of the children, sent them to The Country, and promptly died, leaving the poor mother high and dry. Boy and girl became strangers to everything, their origins, their religion, their culture.

Then there was another daughter of the Emperor, married into the Royal family of Lucknow. She was treated there with such cruelty that she ran away with a son of Colonel Gardner sahib, and her second marriage was solemnized without annulment of the first one.

She remembered that she had made similar arguments before. In fact, she made them almost always when she introspected about life. So how many examples should one cite? Did I not do the same as those grand ladies? And there's another thing: For those begams the axis of their lives was just that—marriage with a suitably high-born or powerful husband, followed by life imprisonment in the Palace, haveli, wherever. Imprisoned so rigorously that not only their face and voice, even their shadow remained wrapped in a chador.

Wazir, were you not like a high-spirited filly, unwilling to be owned and broken in? But didn't you end up doing the same? Did you not let your neck be enclosed in a man's collar at the very first opportunity? No! I deny this! I wore no man's collar on my neck!

But what's the use of all this talk, all this soul-searching? Why ever not, silly girl? Are there not just two questions for the world to ponder: What status does the male have in our world? What is the female doing here? I need answers to just these two questions. Are both bipeds pretending to be quadrupeds? Or are they really quadrupeds, though they are cleverer than the rest in creation? In their book, is the meaning, therefore, of living not more than stuffing their stomachs and trying to make as many reproductions of their own selves as they can?

But why should these questions concern me? I can only speak for myself. Let others cry, or sing, or take a vow of lifelong silence. But I do know that whatever a human does, those acts are his and his alone. And it is none but the human who should make decisions and choices.

I know just this much: I am full of discontent at having been created a woman . . . I have heard there are medications, or if not medications, there are words of power which, if pronounced properly, could ensure the birth of male children. There was a local prayer leader in my neighbourhood, and it was said about him that he knows some such words of power, and by virtue of reciting those words, he always ensured the birth of a male child to his wife. I say, why didn't my Abba ji learn those words, mantras or whatever? I would have one less cause for discontent, a big one at that, in my life. I heard the Maulavi sahib never revealed those words to anyone at all. Perhaps, but there must be other words, other acts to achieve the same objective. Or perhaps my father was extremely fond of girls; that's why he produced three girl children, one immediately after another, and was so happy when we were born. Amma often said to me that Abba ji was so pleased at my birth that he broke into peal after peal of laughter.

All right, be that as it may, but I for one am not willing to put up with a state of affairs where half the world's population, and that too the dominant population, should regard keeping the other half under its heels as its birthright. She called to mind the proverb, 'The cultivation preserves the fencing; the fencing preserves the cultivation,' and snorted mentally. Ha, these are mere words, not a plan or course of action. But what use is this hot cogitation, what result will come of cutting and slashing my own liver? A thousand regrets, this last was one favourite phrase of Blak sahib. Whenever I was upset with something, or when something saddened me and I lay myself down on the bed in the bedroom, and Blak sahib got to know of it, he would come to console and soothe me. He would say, 'Do not chew on your liver, Chhoti Begam, I am here, I am yours.'

It now seems to me that Blak sahib was not being true; they were mere words. He might have thought that he had a lifetime to make a permanent settlement and endowment for his children and for me. And that lifetime did not even run up to one day . . . But why blame poor Blak sahib alone? My dear, my loving Navab sahib, what did he do for me and his own son, before he went away? So why should he deserve from me a whole life of being in the widow's weeds, with his memories clasped close to my bosom? Still, there was Agha sahib. He sprinkled love at me as a fountain sprinkles water. And why should he not, was I not his wife of old age and son to his child born in the same old age? It would seem as if it was I who proved unpropitious and ill-omened for his life which had been smooth and perhaps even happy enough without me.

I liked him; genuinely, I liked him, and that liking increased daily because he cared so much; he couldn't see me upset or thwarted in the least in my wishes. Even so, all his accepting, even pampering, of my contrarinesses could not wash away the memory of my martyred Navab. True, I do remember and miss Blak sahib, and more than him, I miss my darlings . . . But my Navab was something else altogether. God knows how many magical actions and how many words of magic he knew to use on my emotions. Each and every thing that he said or did lives in me like the hurting of a tiny thorn under a fingernail. Were he to cut me up into pieces, every nerve of my body and every drop of my blood would still call out his name. And it was not because he was so young, so handsome, so sinned against, so rich and so powerful. There was another kind of meeting of the hearts there, unexplainable and perhaps more unbreakable precisely because its nature could not be understood.

But look, a moment ago I declared myself to be extremely strict and practically ruthless in judging these matters. I said, should a man like me, I should first determine if I liked him. If such is my belief, how can I, in the same breath, declare that if the Navab sahib cut me to pieces, every nerve of my body would . . . ?

*

The flow of thoughts took her to many shores and shoals, and did not stop at all, and in some way helped her to pass the days. Or perhaps all these thoughts and introspections occurred over only one day. Wazir's diurnal routines had changed; sometimes she did not know about the time. Often, she forgot to eat, even when reminded by Habiba. The food would grow cold, sometimes for reheating, more often for giving away. Feeding Navab Mirza was no problem. He did not eat tiffin at home, and had no fixed time for dinner. He asked for food when he felt like it. He was not unconscious of his mother's pain and nostalgia. But he did not know what he could do about it. Most fourteen-year-old boys were married, in fact would have been married for a year or a year and a half. But Navab Mirza did not drop the least hint, by word or gesture, that he was even slightly minded to marry.

Wazir did give thought to Navab Mirza's marriage because he was old enough to set up a house on his own. But she somehow found herself unable to broach the subject with him. At the age that he was, and the age in which they were, the doors of marriage were always open for him, given his good looks and refined ways. There were numerous possibilities of love—with man or woman—in that culture. And Navab Mirza's great-grandmother's household was there anyway, for casual dalliances, or more. He did go there once in a long while, but only by way of duty. Wazir had not been there in months, even years, perhaps. Akbari Bai, her grandmother, had been dead many years.

Navab Mirza's education was, nevertheless, suspended. This was partly because of the excellent education he had received in Rampur at the hands of Mullah Ghiasuddin, and partly because of his own untiring labour; he had been much ahead of his classmates in Persian, History and Philosophy. He did not care much for other subjects. He was quite sure that he could be a very good poet, and could attain the level of ustad (master) soon enough. He enjoyed the act of writing poetry, and enjoyed even more the act of reciting poetry before others. His memory was remarkable. Because of the countless Persian and Hindi or Rekhta verses at the tip of his tongue, he was envied by his peers. Apart from a magnificent memory in the abstract, he was remarkable for his active memory of verses. It sometimes happened that a phrase or construction used by him in a verse was challenged as unrecognized in standard speech and unsupported by the usage of some past master. Navab Mirza was always able to cite, from memory, its usage by an acknowledged ustad; the person who had raised the objection was then obliged to accept that he was in error.

One of Navab Mirza's verses was much quoted and discussed among men of letters in those days:

I have my eyes on my loved one's
Many-storeyed house; and why not? The royal falcon
Never chooses lowly places for his nest.

The verse became popular because of its own merit; but there was another reason too. During the days that Navab Mirza's verse was making the rounds in Delhi's literary circles, there arrived in Delhi from Badaon a young man of a notable Sayyid family, a person of refinement and with Sufi tendencies, and also a budding poet like Navab Mirza. His name was Sayyid Dildar Ali and his pen name was Mazaq. Immediately on arrival, he became a pupil of the great maestro Shaikh Ibrahim Zauq who had also the honour of being the King's instructor in poetry. Dildar Ali was a staunch admirer and lover of Zauq's works, and though they had never met before Dildar Ali came to Delhi, it was in imitation and appreciation of Zauq's poetry that he chose the pen name Mazaq: both come from the same Arabic root and both mean almost the same thing. So he presented himself before Zauq with the request to be accepted as a pupil and composed the following verse extempore:

I chose the pen name Mazaq because
Of my keen zauq *to be your pupil.*

This for the nonce composition was much appreciated. The Presence, Khaqani-e Hind, was pleased and at once accepted Mazaq as a pupil. A news item appeared in the *Dihli Urdu Akhbar* of 15 December 1844:

> A traveller poet arrived here some days ago. We happened to make his acquaintance too. Extremely intelligent, sharp of intellect, he has sufficient expertise in the art of poetry. The poetic temperament granted to him by the Generous Nature is very similar to that of Khaqani-e Hind Shaikh Muhammad Ibrahim Zauq. Having arrived in this city, he obtained the relationship of pupilage with the Shaikh and was greatly delighted. His name is Maulavi Dildar sahib; he comes from Badaon, which is also the birthplace of the Presence, Sultan Ji Sahib, May his grave be hallowed always. The fact is that the earth of that place is fertile in respect of the birth of [admirable] people: Many persons, having the heart of love and true feeling, are reported to have been

> born there. He is a closely related descendant of Zahurullah Khan Nava, who was a renowned poet, contemporaneous to Mirza Sahib [Sauda], peace be upon him, and the author of a Divan in Hindi, and another in Persian. We met him three, four times. At the request of those present, he composed some verses extemporaneously and recited them in the assembly. In short, one with such quick temperament and temperate, right-minded brain has been observed but rarely.

It so chanced that Navab Mirza was present at one of the assemblies mentioned in the story above. He was well known because of being the son of the martyred Navab Shamsuddin Ahmad Khan, and his relationship with the House of Loharu. The literati in the city also knew that although a newcomer to the land of poetry, Navab Mirza was quite well versed with the twists and turns of its ways. After Mazaq sahib had finished reciting his compositions, poets of Delhi were requested to produce their poems. Navab Mirza's turn came right at the end. When Navab Mirza said his verse that we quoted above, he noticed that someone among the audience had shifted his posture. This was a signal indicating doubt or uncertainty about something in the verse recited. He was, Navab Mirza ascertained later, Hakim Ghulam Maula Qalaq Merathi, a pupil of Hakim Momin Khan sahib Momin; he was fond of Persianate constructions in Hindi like Momin, and this fondness had been further intensified by virtue of his being a pupil of Maulavi Imam Bakhsh Sahbai in Persian.

When the assembly concluded, Navab Mirza approached Hakim Ghulam Maula sahib, made a salaam and asked in his dulcet Hindi, to which just a little piquancy was added by a Rampuri Pathani style of speech, 'This servant noticed the worshipful reverence shift his posture a bit. If some defect was noted in one of this servant's verses, I beseech that I may be informed of his error.'

Hakim Ghulam Maula sahib was extremely shy by nature; that was why he had not challenged Dagh in the open assembly. Now when Dagh addressed him directly, he was quiet for a beat or two, and then spoke in his measured tone, 'No, sir. I wasn't aware of a defect. Indeed, I just found something that I couldn't quite follow.'

This promised to be a juicy interlocution. Those who were leaving, or about to leave, stopped to listen.

'Sir, please command. I am all ears.'

The expression on Hakim sahib's face clearly revealed that he repined raising the question. He said to himself that he should have denied that there was something the 'matter' with Dagh's verse; that should have been the end of it. But now he had no choice but to continue, 'Mian sahib, my problem is just this much: You did well in constructing the phrase or the image of the royal falcon's nest. But I understand that it said about the royal falcon that it never has a nest. This I found a little . . .' Hakim sahib was so diffident now that he did not complete his sentence.

'It is the Presence's liberal kindness to pay so much attention. But actually, the phrase "falcon's nest" has been used by Kalim Hamadani.' He now folded his hands on his chest and recited, in a clear and mellifluous voice, the verse from the great seventeenth-century Persian poet:

He recks naught, spilling the blood of innocents:
The feathers of the sparrow line the floor of the royal falcon's nest.

It was partly the excellence of the verse and partly the quickness with which Dagh produced a most appropriate certification for his usage, that the assembly broke into a long and loud applause. Hakim Ghulam Maula Qalaq rose and embraced Navab Mirza. 'Only God is untouched by blemish! May you be ever happy, young man. How appropriate was the certification, and how beautiful was the verse itself! I will mention you in the ustad's assembly too. Do keep it up; you'll soon be the honour and pride of Delhi, Allah willing.'

Hakim sahib left, humming the words of Kalim Hamadani to himself. Dildar Ali Mazaq patted Navab Mirza on the back and said, 'Before I leave for Badaon, I would love to meet with you one more time at least.' He also told himself that he should introduce the young fellow to his ustad right away, lest Hakim Ghulam Maula Qalaq mention him to his own ustad, Hakim Momin sahib, and induce him to accept Navab Mirza in his circle of pupils. Such a bright young man, he must be made a pupil of my ustad, he said to himself.

The rising of a hot, luminant new star in the firmament of poets and poetry warmed the hearts of those who worked in the world of poetry. Senior poets were keen to see if the newly fledged sparrow would become a simurgh: the legendary griffin. The younger ones all agreed that such genius at his age was a rarity. Adept as Dagh was in remembering and recalling other poets' verses, he was equally felicitous at composing extempore. Now his friends and acquaintances played chess with him in coffee houses and the wager was that if he lost, he must compose a ghazal extempore in a prescribed rhyme pattern and metre.

It soon became a common sight: people foregathering to watch Dagh play, and to advise his opponent on the best moves. Light banter would be exchanged all the time; sometimes Dagh's opponent became confused with the plethora of advice, thus improving the game for Dagh. The idea, of course, was to hand out a defeat to Dagh and then invite him to compose, then and there, a seven-verse ghazal in some particularly hard rhyme and metre. However, since Navab Mirza was a good player, his opponents found it difficult to beat him despite advice and instruction from the watchers of the game.

'Ho, Yaar Hamid! Your horse (knight) is no better than a donkey at present. My brother, move it from there and put it behind the farzin (queen).'

'No, no, not at all, Hamid, my brother! This Mian Khan's wits have eaten a lot of hay. Hamid Mian sahib, you move the queen pawn up against Navab Mirza, and then see how your game hots up! That's how to play the game!'

'Really! Really, what friends are these, they move against their own side; they are worse than enemies. Ho, dear elder brother, don't you see? If the pawn moves up, Navab Mirza's horse will become free to move.'

'Yaar, you fellows are worse than mules tied to the halters of horses and asses. Don't you see? Navab Mirza is mating in five! Take my advice, withdraw your king behind the entrenchment. This front becomes dangerous for him by the minute!'

Thus confused by the gratuitous advisers, one of the two would be checkmated quickly. If it was Navab Mirza, the poets in the gathering were invited to propose a sample line. 'But see, the end-ryhme must be ringing and clanging like a bell, and galloping fast like the horse. Let this young Mian sahib appreciate a bit how one goes to Delhi from Rampur, trotting away and unstopping!'

This was greeted with loud mirthfulness, Navab Mirza's laughter being heard above the others. Then he spoke, addressing one of the more obstreperous among the audience, 'Hey, friend! Just take care of this unchained elephant. He's roaring away in great passion. Watch him, lest he begin to assault his own lines!'

There was even more laughter now, and many among those present recalled a somewhat obscene proverb about an elephant who marches up against his own army lines.

Thus, during the exchange of banter and suggestions and counter-suggestions regarding the line to be proposed to Navab Mirza for composing a ghazal, a line would be approved by consensus:

None ever saw death approach that house

Before the line was even properly spoken out, Navab Mirza exclaimed:

Lord, is my enemy's dwelling a paradise?
None ever saw death approach that house!

Before the applause had died down, Navab Mirza spoke out two more verses:

Kind counsellor, just tell me this much:
The face of that moon-faced beauty,
Did you, or did you not, ever see?
A pity, the pages of the story of true lovers, carefully
You never did see.

'No! Not at all! You fellows threw the contest! No one ever can compose so fast and so well.'

This was Mir Baqir Ali; his pen name was Jafari. He was a younger brother and pupil of the Pride of all Poets, Mir Nizamuddin Mamnun, dead these few months, and in whose mourning, Jafari still wore a black sash on his waist. He was barely finished speaking when Navab Mirza said the concluding verse:

I always found Dagh in some idol-house or another;
What a godly fellow, him in his own house
I never did see!

The ceiling of the coffee house almost came down with the clamour of applause, but Mir Baqir Ali was not through with Dagh. He raised his voice over the others, and pronounced judgement, 'All right, I grant that the words are colourful, each word is properly connected to the meaning, but where is the opening verse here? Navab Mirza has failed to give us the opening verse.'

Some of the audience glared at him. But there was among the audience the distinguished young poet Mir Muhammad Ali Tishnah. His days of inebriety and perhaps a little madness or 'absorption' were just beginning. He went about very nearly unclothed, and often came to assemblies of poets or coffee houses, but rarely took part in any discussion. His wits were entirely sharp and his brain fully active. He smiled a slightly derisive smile. 'So why should not the Presence utter something? There seems no need to make the boy answer every demand.'

Navab Mirza understood the hint at once. He rose, made a salaam, and touching Mir sahib's feet, he said, 'Your Honour, the Exalted Presence need not be troubled. I submit an opening verse for your consideration.'

My beloved idol, who robs my senses,
If there is any who did not see her,
Then it is a fact that God Himself
He did not see!

Mir Muhammad Ali Tishnah was silent, swaying quietly through the applause that rained down on Navab Mirza. He spoke when the noise abated, 'Only God is untouched by blemish! Dear young man, the day is not far when you will quench the thirst of all of us who have a craving for poetry. There is just one thing: were you to say "The seer did not see" instead of "He did not see", your poem would become perfect like a true gemstone.'

Navab Mirza again touched Tishnah sahib's feet. 'The ustad's place is vacant.' He meant that there would always be room for masters like Mir sahib. Tishnah sahib replied, 'Oh, I am no ustad, no assayer of poetry's bullion. You should, in fact, go knock at Mian Ibrahim's door.'

'Very well, sir. I will soon find some way to approach him.'

*

A similar assembly took place at the house of a friend where Ghanshyam Lal Asi, one of Delhi's leading poets, was present. He was a pupil of Shah

Nasir's, like Zauq, but relations between the two ustad-brothers were strained. There were many who accorded him the same rank as his late ustad, Shah Nasir. He was fully adept at composing ghazals which had extremely difficult long rhymes and end-rhymes. Renowned for the creation of new themes, immensely learned, an expert swimmer and calligrapher and musician, it was as if all such art and artistry ran in his veins like blood. He never set foot outside Delhi, and rightly considered himself to be the model and custodian of Delhi's literary and social culture. Navab Mirza's name had reached him, especially his ability at quickly composing poems extempore.

Asi sahib was not overly fond of Zauq, nor of the King Emperor, but not due to any rivalry as poets. When a big debate was going on about a particular ghazal of Shah sahib's, Asi sahib naturally supported Shah sahib; by his own strong compositions, he crushed into silence all who were critical of the ghazal in question. Zauq, being the Heir Apparent's mentor, was opposing Shah sahib. The Heir Apparent was supporting Zauq, and it was alleged that the Heir Apparent had written to someone called Maulavi Rashiduddin to the effect that he should not praise the 'Hindu infidel'. This putative letter was read out in open assembly. All the poets present declared the directive to be unfair and also revealing of the anti-Hindu bias of the Heir Apparent. They also pronounced Asi sahib's ghazal to be immeasurably superior to that of Zauq.

The story of the letter seems apocryphal, seeing as how Abu Zafar Sirajuddin Bahadur Shah was well known for his love of amity and peace between Hindus and Muslims, and for his selfless fondness for all his subjects. He would certainly have wished for his mentor Zauq to outdo Asi sahib, but he was not stupid or narrow-minded, certainly not to the extent of writing such a direction to an unknown person. Anyway, there had been since then a knot of displeasure lodged in Asi sahib's heart against Abu Zafar Sirajuddin Bahadur Shah, and his relations were consequently strained with Zauq as well. He perhaps came to know from somewhere that Tishnah sahib was suggesting to Dagh that he should become a pupil of Zauq. So he was doubly keen to test the newly arrived star-to-be on Delhi's literary horizon. Thus, in that assembly, he had someone open the gambit against Dagh.

'Dear young sir,' he said, 'we are quite keen to hear you. You have a reputation for extempore composition.'

'Sir, I am at your service. Please command.'

'Right, here's an opening verse from Mian Jurat, the great maestro from the last century. We would like you to compose according to its pattern.' He recited the verse:

One would sacrifice oneself
For her voice, and die to hear her speak;
One would sacrifice oneself
For her coquetry, and die to hear her speak.

Munshi Ghanshyam Lal Asi was not too pleased, apparently, with the challenge verse. But he preferred to keep quiet. Navab Mirza promptly replied, with a little hint of derision, 'Presence, that's not much of a test pattern. I can produce verses after it in no time. It's actually a trick: you need to change just one word or two, and your verse is ready. For example, please observe this opening verse from Jurat sahib again.'

He recited:

It raises a tumult of wonder, and admiration
When you come here, laughing;
And your smile: It raises a tumult of wonder, and admiration!

'So you can see, sir, you just need to find one word, and your verse is done. Now please hear.' Navab Mirza, without even a moment's pause, went on to recite:

One would sacrifice oneself
For a friend, and die to hear him speak;
One would sacrifice oneself
For a confidant, and die to hear him speak.
The music, which burns with passion,
The conversation, which causes tumult:
One would sacrifice oneself
For such music, and die to hear such conversation.

Then he paused for a breath or two, and went on to recite:

It raises a tumult of wonder and admiration
When you come here at night;

It raises the clamour of the Doom, when you leave.
Just for a moment, like the new moon of Id,
Your coming here thus,
It raises the clamour of the Doom.

The person who had set the test was looking open-mouthed at the verses flowing out in plenitude like the coming of the springtide. But Ghanshyam Lal Asi was not going to give away his praises so easily. There was a faint smile on his lips when he said, 'Mian Navab Mirza, you are perfectly right. It's easy to compose such verses for a ghazal. It is clear that your taste is sound, and your temperament commands the art of poetry. But a rubai, that's something else again.'

'Yes, sir, for one has to produce four lines which are interlinked, and not just two.'

'Very good. Very right.'

A clever smile radiated from Navab Mirza's countenance. Quite by chance, he had composed a rubai, just the day before, in the pattern where the end-rhyme was very long. He was imitating a great Persian master from the twelfth century.

'So, Presence, I could present a rubai, if you so desire.'

'You mean now, just this minute?'

'The Presence may look at it whichever way he pleases. I can certainly present a rubai right now.' Navab Mirza advisedly kept his words somewhat vague.

'So why not here and now,' Asi said. 'All of us are eager for your poetry.'

'Very well, sir, to hear is to obey.' Navab Mirza spoke the following lines in a conversational flow and without the least pause. No one could imagine that he was not extemporizing:

None could understand, what is the nature
Of the world;
None do say, what is the nature
Of the world.

Ghanshyam Lal Asi practically jumped up with pleasure. He raised both his hands and cried out, 'God, oh my God! This cruel boy can produce such marvellous lines! Let me now see how he manages the third line. Sir, please recite, please go on reciting!'

Navab Mirza half rose from his seat, did a salaam, and began again:

None could understand, what is the nature
Of the world;
None do say, what is the nature
Of the world.

'Now, sir, I present the third line,' he said:

The heavens went on presenting riddle after riddle;

Even before he could finish speaking the third line, a venerable gentleman half rose from his place and cried out: '"None could solve the riddle: what is the nature of the world." Only God is untouched by blemish! One wishes to kiss the lips from which such a line came! Mian Dagh, may Allah brighten you even more!' This was yet another pupil of Shah Nasir; his name was Mirza Fida Husain and his pen name was Fida. He was a grandson of Navab Hatim Khan. The beauty of this speech was in his intuiting the whole of the fourth line, and also in that 'dagh', which means 'scar' (of a wound or a burn), is supposed to be bright.

Looking to Dagh's soft, youthful face, many among the audience smiled inwardly at the observation, 'One wishes to kiss the lips from which such a line came!' There was no let-up in the applause; Dagh went on reciting the rubai over and over again with full absorption amid approving sounds of 'Wah!', 'Only God is untouched by blemish!' and 'True, very true!'

None could understand, what is the nature
Of the world;
None do say, what is the nature
Of the world.
The heavens went on presenting riddle after riddle;
None could solve the riddle: what is the nature of the world?

When the clamour of applause abated, Ghanshyam Lal Asi went up to Dagh, caressed his head with affection and in benediction, and said,

'By Allah, had our Shah sahib, may Allah raise his Station, been here today, I would take you to his service, for such a rare jewel suited his treasury best.'

Navab Mirza bent low in salaams, took his leave from Asi and the host, and went directly to his mother. Wazir was disturbed and upset to see her son's flushed face.

'Please, Navab Mirza, you are not unwell, are you? Why is your face so hot?'

'No, Amma Jan,' he said with a tired smile, 'It's just that I think . . . '

He then realized that if he uttered even a word about his mother's loneliness or her apparently insoluble problems, she would take serious offence at what she would regard as his presumptuousness. She was particularly sensitive to patronization, imagined or real. But Navab Mirza could see clearly that loneliness and straitened circumstances were now fated for his mother's remaining days. The life of comfort, often of opulence and luxury, to which she had become accustomed, was no longer possible now. Reducing her expenses as much as could be possible, she had got rid of the servants and began to assist Habiba in household chores. Wazir's social life had been narrowed down anyway after Manjhli left for Rampur. Now that Wazir was back in Delhi, whenever Manjhli came to Delhi from Rampur, she herself visited Khanam ka Bazaar, rather than put Wazir to the trouble of coming to her haveli in Tiraha Bairam Khan, thus incurring the expense of carriage hire, fine clothing and hostess gifts. Wazir's visits to the mausoleum of the martyred Navab were also much curtailed now; the expense of going and the distribution of charity to the beggars there were commitments which she found she could no longer afford.

On the other side of the picture, there was Navab Mirza, quite convinced that he must make poetry his life's passion and also his profession. Being of practical service and support to his mother could be possible only when he got himself a job: that of a court poet in some prosperous native State. But that destination was quite far, in spite of Navab Mirza's present brilliance and promise: he was too young to be appointed Court poet, or be attached to a Court as poet-employee. His options were limited: he could give up his life of poetry and secure employment with some nobleman on some mundane, non-literary duty; or, he could live with his mother, thus adding to her burden rather than reducing it. Yet even such worldly, 'practical' jobs were hard to come by. There was no one from his father's side who had some affection for him and his mother, or who had at least a sense of blood affinity strong enough to regard them worthy of help or succour.

Afzal-un Nisa Begam, Navab Mirza's senior stepmother, in fact preferred to be in denial of his existence. She knew that, according to English law—though not enforced in India, yet being in existence nevertheless—even a natural son, if firstborn, was entitled to inherit from the father. She imagined, or apprehended at any rate, that once Wazir Khanam gained some opportunity to establish a footing in the world, the day would not be far when they could claim a share in the Navabi of Loharu. She saw them as gold-diggers, adventurers at best, devoid of family traditions, personal prosperity or inherited wealth. Such people, she believed, could do anything for gain.

Furthermore, Navab Mirza realized, they were in Delhi—a Delhi where the English had the upper hand in everything. He remembered his mother telling him once that during the detention and trial of his father, the English were so tyrannous that they practically debarred everyone of Navab Shamsuddin Khan's family or retinue from coming out anywhere in the city. Since then, the stern and awful might of the English upon the natives had grown many times over. There could be no person of any consequence who would dare employ Navab Mirza in a lucrative capacity. He was, after all, an illegitimate son of a recalcitrant native Navab who had caused the murder of an extremely powerful English official.

All things considered, the best option for Navab Mirza seemed to be that he should as quickly as possible establish his reputation and seniority as a poet and obtain employment as one at some native court where the ruler could pay him enough to live in comfort and provide full support to his mother.

'Where are you, Navab Mirza, lost in thoughts? You were saying something?'

His mother's soft words brought him back out of the maze of thoughts, but he said nothing; he just looked forlornly at his mother.

'Out with it, boy! What is it that troubles you? You gaze at me, open-mouthed like a witless fellow! Say something, Bacche Mian sahib, what is it that bothers you?'

She called out, 'Habiba, what are you doing down there, Bibi? Aren't you going to organize dinner for Bacche Mian?'

'Yes, everything is ready, Khanam sahib. I just sent Jani Ram to get some fresh chapattis from the baker's. Just let him come back, dinner will be served in no time. But what's the matter, is Mian sahib somewhat peckish this afternoon?'

Like most middle-level homes in Delhi, especially Muslim homes, chapattis or other breads, like the Afghan nan, were procured fresh from the baker's; only meat or stew was made at home.

'So, madam,' Navab Mirza said with a pleasant laugh, 'you want us not to eat?'

'Young sir,' Habiba smiled back, somewhat teasing. 'The fact of the matter is that you are a poet, and a master poet at that. Appetites run away at the sight of poets.' Both senses of the joke were clear to Navab Mirza. Poets are indigent types, they do not get much to eat; the other sense was laudatory: everybody wants to hear the poets, rather than indulge in mundane things like eating.

Wazir smiled. 'Hey, what's that, Habiba? Do you mean to tell us that poets don't need to eat?'

The subject of poets' appetite, or lack of it, gave the opening to Navab Mirza that he was looking for. 'Amma Jan, the fact of the matter is that I should be a poet; I should do nothing else but earn my daily bread by poetry and serve you and look after you. In fact,' he used a Persian phrase, 'I can't do anything else.'

A weak smile appeared on Wazir's face, not reaching her eyes, though. Her big, deep-brown eyes clearly reflected thoughtfulness, if not worry. She was quiet, for a heartbeat, then she spoke slowly, careful not to use a sneering tone, 'Aha, a soldier's son, and poetry? Very good, very good indeed! So what else is there to say? There exists something as the sword-blade of poetry, is there not?'

'Is Mirza Ghalib not a soldier's son, Amma Jan? And does he not call himself a poet?'

'Oh, him!' Wazir spoke somewhat dismissively. 'He also describes himself as the son of a navab.'

'Then, am I not the son of a navab, too?'

Wazir wished to say: But the sun that shone in the firmament of your life sank many years ago. Your second father was also taken away by the Highwayman of Death. Now depending on whose backing could you claim for yourself the luxuries of life?

She did not dare speak her mind as she looked at her son's face with anxious eyes. She saw a well-formed oval face, incandescent like a hot, black flame. Turkish nose, long, but slightly curled. The cheekbones prominent, also like his father's, the complexion even darker than his mother's; eyes replicas of his mother's: large, dark brown with a hint of delicate red lines. A strong and straight neck, a high forehead. A tall and balanced body, whose language dripped with his father's self-assurance. The beginnings of a light, regular beard, rather than a youthful down, casually growing on his face. He looked so alluringly beautiful that one wished to do nothing but sit and stare.

He had a dense head of hair worn in the latest fashion in Delhi: slightly less than shoulder length, bright, somewhat curly locks, combed carefully but not styled. He wore a four-cornered black hat whose corners and rim were heavily worked in gold. His trousers were of the flowered silk fabric called gulbadan. They were long and loose, again in the approved fashion. The dress became him so well that he seemed like a resplendent chrysanthemum. Such a charismatic young man should be king somewhere, Wazir said to herself. What a pity, my darling son lacks for two square meals a day suitable to his station and a night of comfortable sleep, let alone commanding all kingly luxuries.

To top it all, he hankers after poetry; he wishes to make his poetry his means of earning his daily bread. Budding poets need to run all over the place, attach themselves to the hem of some major, prominent poet, sit at his feet for years, then at long last they can claim the rank of Master for themselves; that too when the master declares that the pupil is now a master in his own right, not needing further practice and instruction. It is no joke to become a major poet. One has to work himself to the bone, like the miller who grinds for a whole day and picks up only a thimbleful in the evening. Even so, success is more a matter of luck than merit.

She looked at her son's face, somewhat more intently, as if trying to understand him better. The expression on Navab Mirza's face was an amalgamation of colours: self-confidence, stubbornness, a spoilt child's obduracy in claiming all as his own. Wazir said to herself: Well, perhaps it's a child's obstinacy, no more. Let me counsel him, explain to him what he is really bargaining for, or avoid bringing the matter to a head. Possibly, he will change his mind in due course. I am in no hurry, certainly.

A sudden thought came to her: Navab Mirza might not be really serious about poetry as a profession; she should find another way to gauge the strength of his mind on this. She smiled, and recited a rubai of Mushafi's in her dulcet, mellifluous voice:

I really have nothing, but a craze for poetry;
I can do nothing else: nothing mundane, nothing sacred.
Mushafi, those who know the tricks of money-making
Can make bread from stones, too!

She looked at her son with a slightly inquiring, slightly teasing eye, as if asking if he could think of an effective counter to the older poet's wisdom. Navab Mirza's face betrayed some helplessness: Could he really answer such a beautiful and such a telling poem? Or could he produce an apophthegm of his own to counter the thesis of the poem? A reply occurred to him, though not in verse. He laughed and said, 'But Amma Jan, bread from stone could also choke, or become its own kind of noose!'

Wazir smiled, for she could immediately delve into the hidden depths of her son's meaning. 'Very true, for a mad desire for bread can indeed suffocate our purity of heart.' She paused. 'But I should have thought that one could hold the craze for bread in check, so as not to let foul fat and blood dominate the heart.'

Navab Mirza was piqued. So what does this Begam sahib want? We are not talking about what the Persian poet said:

You desire God, and also the base world?
It's an empty thought, impossible. It's madness!

We are talking about rational existence. I don't say that I should rend my collar and go mad forever and run around like Majnun, driven by the power of the madness, which sometimes poetry generates in a poet for brief moments. I just maintain that a man can make his place in the world and also earn his bread on the strength of his poetry.

He repressed his pique, and in fact spoke humbly, 'Amma Jan, I think Mushafi means to say that he'd retain his craze for poetry and also use his reason to earn his bread?'

'Sorry, I don't see that meaning here. Clearly, he's saying that one who's crazy after poetry is of no use in this world, or in the other.'

A wave of hot displeasure touched Navab Mirza's heart, but he kept his cool. 'We extract our desired or desirable meanings from poetic texts. Just tell me, what is it that you want?'

'I want nothing,' Wazir said gravely. 'I want to understand, that's all.'

'What is it?' Navab Mirza said, his tone deliberately short, though not curt.

'Nothing special, just that the gush and ardour for poetry . . .' She stopped herself just in time. She wanted to say that a life in poetry is for those who are flush with cash, who eat their bellyful without worrying about the next meal. She changed tack. '. . . the gush and ardour for poetry, where is it going to take you?'

'Why, Amma Jan! That's not really a question to be asked,' he looked his mother straight in the eye. 'Will poetry not open paths for me towards earning steadily, and will it not create the joy and bustle of life in my . . . spiritual . . . intellectual and emotional life?'

'That is just what I fear,' Wazir began to say, and it was one of the very few times in their lives when Navab Mirza cut her short. He said sharply, 'By Allah, Amma Jan, you don't have even this much faith in me that I can be a poet and my heart aches to see you well cared for and in comfort! Success or unsuccess is not in our hands, but one can at least try.'

Wazir's tongue faltered for the first time before her son. 'All I want . . . to say is that . . . you are still quite young.'

Navab Mirza snorted, a sharp and bitter sound. 'I, and still young! That's rich indeed! I have been educated to the level possible for us. Don't you see? Had there been a guardian for us today, he would have married me off quite a while ago, making me a husbandman, the head of a family. Many much younger than I are shoved into the oven of life; they gain something, or even perhaps lose something, but go through the fire they do. They have no choice.'

He paused for breath, with his mother looking at him in stupefaction. Was this the little child whom I wanted close to my bosom all my life? But Navab Mirza's fusillade was not going to stop any time soon. He continued, hotly as before, 'Do you see what our estate is at present? Your face is a portrait of lifelessness; your home a picture of desolate discomfort. The kind of life that you deserve, the kind of life that is your birthright, is for me like a silver candlestick, hung far up somewhere, something even farther than the sky of all skies. Should these days and nights continue some more, your life will have become a story, forgotten by all; your tree of life will be cut down even before it fully came into flower and fruit. You have just me, man, boy, whatever, who can go out in the world, do something. But you believe that I still need Habiba's lullabies and the warmth of your arms! For how long will you nurture me in a secure underground chamber?'

Navab Mirza's throat began to choke. Wazir sat quietly, her eyes suffused with tears, seeking somewhere to hide her wet face. Habiba stood silently, supporting herself against a wall. She was more conscious than Wazir of the dilemma and worry of Navab Mirza, but she had not dared open her lips so far. Now she picked up her courage. 'Khanam sahib,' said she, almost in a whisper, drying her tears with her dupatta. 'Truth to tell, Bacche Mian has the right on his side. The world is very big; our lives are too puny. There is no refuge for the likes of us without approaching the wide world. May Allah preserve him, Bacche Mian is the man in the house. He's quite right to worry about us, about running the house.'

'Did I ever say that I should clasp him to my bosom all my life?' Wazir spoke in a tired, defeated voice. 'Don't I understand these things? But no man from my house has ever returned after he went out. How can I find the heart to remove a piece of my heart from my side?'

'Pardon my impertinence,' Habiba spoke haltingly. 'Khanam sahib is quite right. But it's a world out there, it will be what it is. Were our Navab sahib alive today . . .'

'Habiba, don't take his name! It is like a dagger into my heart. May Allah grant him Paradise eternal. It is due to his generosity that we have a roof over our head and we can light our stoves twice a day.'

Wazir was silent, lost in her memories. No one spoke. Then, she drew a cold sigh and began again, 'I hear the Firangee dispossessed many like him, on false excuses, or took their lives unrightly. Yes, it is the thirteenth century, anything can happen . . . What you say is the truth, Habiba. I have heard our elders say that one must live in the world like a wire in a piece of soap, to be pulled out smoothly at any time. But it's easy to get involved, much harder to be uninvolved. So long as there is life, there are its traps and snares as well.'

Navab Mirza now sat cross-legged near his mother's feet. 'Right, Amma Jan, let's close this debate here. I too have the right to face the world, and the calling of a poet is not without honour, and it suits my temperament very well . . . Forget your wrath, and your pain too. Let's eat; I am hungry, really.'

Wazir now noticed that it was late afternoon; dinner time was long past. 'Lord!' She cried out. 'I got so involved in my wailings that I didn't notice the time! Habiba, please, ask for new chapattis; those old ones will now taste like earth.'

'No need really to get into the hassle of going to the baker's, Khanam Sahib. I'll make a few new chapattis in no time. Our Bacche Mian and Khanam Sahib will eat in less than a quarter-hour.'

Habiba went into the kitchen, and Wazir moved off to the water room, ostensibly to wash her face. But Navab Mirza was ashamed in his heart: he knew that washing her hands and face was nothing but an excuse to dry her tears and remove the tear stains. An almost unbearably strong yearning raged in his heart. Somehow, even if he could sell himself into slavery for it, he should be able to get so much wealth for his mother that she would eat after feeding four, five hungry stomachs with the best food. And . . . she should have to fear nothing about him and his life.

Suddenly, the image of Qadam Sharif, and his father's tomb in it, lit up before the eye of his mind. Is there a sign there for me, he wondered. Perhaps not, but it has been quite long since I made the pilgrimage to his sacred grave. I will surely visit there tomorrow.

58

Navab Mirza chances upon the greatest poet of the time, Mirza Ghalib, and has an unexpected encounter with his father's stepbrother

HE COULD NOT go the next day, but organized himself for a visit to Qadam Sharif on or the fourth day after. Whereas there was mental pressure on the son caused by his long discussion or disputation, with the mother, the mother was also equally under tension. She, however, managed to push the matter to the back of her mind and diverted herself by getting busier in organizing the daily hospitalities for the son. Navab Mirza was not so strong-minded: he caught a severe chill and was laid up with fever for a couple of days.

He went to Qadam Sharif on the fourth day, but did not tell his mother: he knew that Wazir's visits were now few and far between, due to lack of adequate means. He felt that if he told his mother about the visit, she would certainly like to go, but would be hard put to find the money for it, and would grieve even more.

He first went into the shrine at Qadam Sharif and meditated for a while. He then offered the necessary prayers for his father at his tomb. He also said a general prayer for all who were buried there, and was about to go out of the premises when he heard a little commotion at the main gate. It appeared that some mace-bearers were calling out: 'Clear the way!'; 'Move, gentlemen!'; 'Keep going!' He then noticed a resplendent, open palanquin at the main gate, surrounded by servants in red broadcloth, green-turbaned mace-bearers and white-clad lance-bearers.

The person who rode in the palanquin was extremely handsome, with a fine deportment and noble presence. Navab Mirza had never set eyes on the King, but copies of his coronation portraits were freely available; because of the portraits, Navab Mirza could describe himself as one who could recognize the King if he saw him. The occupant of the palanquin put him in a slight doubt: Is it the Shadow of God himself? But his doubt was dispelled immediately, for had it been the King, he would have been riding on his personal elephant, surrounded by a large equipage of princes and officials. But the person who was visiting must at least be a Prince of the Realm.

With his gaze respectfully straight and towards the front, he tried to carefully observe the distinguished visitor. He was about thirty or thirty-five, tall and spare of body, but obviously a body that was strong and kept trim with gymnastics and athletics. His face was fully oval, with high cheekbones, the nose long and straight, the neck high and erect. His eyes were jet black, bright with the refulgence of a sharp and well-informed mind; his complexion was light brown, and his face covered with a longish, but pointed beard, not too dense, reminiscent of his ancestor, the Emperor Babur. Beautifully trimmed, prominent moustaches hung on both sides of the face like silken tassels, but were very spare on the upper lip.

He wore a loose, long pair of green silk trousers, worked in bullion; a long, well-fitting tunic in green Dacca muslin, above it he wore the char qub made of a heavily embroidered Kashmiri woollen cloth known as 'jamah var', the char qub being a special waistcoat worn only by the King and Princes of the Realm. He wore a four-cornered black velvet hat worked in heavy brocade and a light-green sash of Benarasi silk, called pote. A jewel-encrusted dagger hung on one side in his sash; on the other side was a bejewelled silver pistol. A pearl necklace of seven strings hung around his neck, but he wore no ornament on his hat. On two fingers of each hand he had brilliant rings of diamond, ruby and emerald. He had a slim book in his hands, perhaps a collection of prayers. On all sides of the palanquin, people were doing salaams; he responded with a smile, placing his right hand on the left side of his chest, speaking no word.

Someone whispered: 'It's Mirza Fathul Mulk Bahadur! As Allah wills, what a princely person, and how well all dresses sit on his body! He is a true picture of our King, may Allah preserve him.'

Navab Mirza's steps, apparently of their own accord, kept moving towards the Prince. It occurred to him that it might be counted impertinence, his moving up so freely towards the august personage. But there was a sort of magnetism at work somewhere. He felt himself drawn, almost against his wish. When he reached close, he made the kurnish, the formal Mughal salaam, and was about to go out of the gate to the main road, when a mace-bearer, perhaps on a slight gesture of the Prince, put his hand lightly on his shoulder, and said, 'Your Excellency is remembered by Sahib-e Alam wa Alamiyan, the Master of the World and of those who are in it.'

He remembers me? No, there was some mistake somewhere. How would Sahib-e Alam know me? Navab Mirza, not a little confused, was about to refuse or protest, when the bearers placed the Prince's palanquin on the ground, and the mace-bearer, his hand still on the young man's shoulder, presented him before the Prince. Navab Mirza made a salaam apprehensively, his eyes firmly on his shoes. He then stayed where he was.

'May you live long,' someone said in an extremely refined and sophisticated voice. The voice was clear, like that of a practised musician, like the ringing, vibrant sound of a heavy brass plate when it is struck gently.

'We were pleased with your respectful deportment. What is your name, and who is your father?'

'Your Honour . . . I . . . am the son of . . . of Navab Shamsuddin Ahmad Khan. I am called Navab Mirza.'

'So! You are the offspring of Navab Shamsuddin Ahmad Khan, ruler of Firozepur Jhirka and Loharu?'

'Your Honour spoke correctly.'

'Bhai, subhan Allah! He was a person of truly noble temperament. Is he not buried right here? And how is it now with you and your people?'

'Exalted Highness, your domestic slave and his mother live under your benign shadow in Khanam ka Bazaar.'

'I see. Your m . . .' The Prince paused, perhaps remembering that it was improper to talk of women in public. 'Good, convey our greetings.' He enunciated the last remark almost in an undertone, and made some invisible gesture to the palanquin-bearers. They understood immediately and lifted the palanquin in a smooth, almost poetic motion.

'The Presence nurtures us,' Navab Mirza made three salaams and stood rooted to the spot until the passing of the procession.

*

During his journey back, Navab Mirza cogitated upon the question of Sahib-e Alam wa Alamiyan choosing to show interest in him, but he did not tell his mother about it. He made casual-sounding, tentative inquiries with his friends if there could be anything special about him or his mother which may have aroused the Prince's interest, but with no useful result. All that he could find out was that the Prince was a pious, gentle-hearted being, and that he wrote poetry under the pen name of Ramz, and Shaikh Zauq was his mentor in Rekhta poetry. Navab Mirza believed that he would learn more by keeping more social relations with the notable people in the city. It was already in his mind to make the acquaintance of the master poets in Delhi. He thought he should begin with Mirza Ghalib. He informed Wazir in the evening, 'Amma Jan, tomorrow I'll go calling on Mirza Ghalib sahib.'

Wazir was caught between anxiety, and uncertainty about the wisdom of the move. 'About Mirza Ghalib sahib . . . I trust you know . . . know about him?'

'Yes, surely. He is a truly great master in Persian; his rank as a poet in Hindi is also second to none.'

'But about your Paradise-abiding father . . . I mean, he did not have good thoughts for him, you know?'

'Yes, madam, I did hear reports. But that was another time.'

'You must remember that Ghalib sahib is still very thick with the people of Loharu; he's married there. And the Loharu people, they may not be your active enemies, but are not among your friends either.'

'But Amma Jan, it's the poets' world. The state of that world is different.'

Wazir spoke sharply, despite not wanting to do so. 'Oh, you force me to open my lips! I want to know, why should you choose to have social ties with those who were sworn enemies of your father? Does it at all become you?'

'Amma Jan,' Navab Mirza said in his cool, collected mode, 'haven't I always said that the best policy is to let bygones be bygones, and bury the past somewhere in the archives of memory?'

'Please, you'll teach me wisdom! You father's murderers will be pleased no end to see that the son has forgiven and forgotten all.' Wazir's eyes were misting with tears.

Navab Mirza beat a hasty retreat. 'Please don't be upset, Amma Jan. Things will be just as you please. I just said something practical about the realm of poets and poetry. Poets are from a different order of things. And Mirza Ghalib had nothing to do directly with . . . with that matter. If I set up as a poet, I'll have to interact with these very people. Some will be my mentors, someone else will be my ustad. Some of them can even become my comrades and friends.' He smiled, trying to distil any possible offence from his speech. 'And I too have to become an ustad, soon enough.'

Wazir too changed tack: It was impossible for her to be upset with her son. She said, 'Dear son, my advice was for your own good. Look before and after, and then set foot in the hurly-burly. The city is teeming with master poets.'

'Yes, madam. Quite true. Please have no anxiety at all.'

*

Navab Mirza gave up the idea of visiting Ghalib. In fact he did not go anywhere at all, yet his name was on the lips of everybody who counted in the world of poetry. Rather than his knocking at Ghalib sahib's door, Ghalib sahib was himself keen to have the young man over and encourage his pursuits in the field of letters.

Khvajah Haidar Ali Atash, Lucknow's leading poet, had been blind for many years now. He had the temperament of a true dervish, uncaring for money or recognition. He did not have a social life; not going anywhere to socialize, he even discouraged visitors. Still, the moment he finished a ghazal, his pupils and numerous admirers published it everywhere in no time by word of mouth. After the demise of Shaikh Nasikh (1838), Khvajah sahib was the only poet from the eastern climes to be remembered and mentioned with respect, if not awe. He was not very old, but was frail, and the general feeling was that he was not too long for this world. Thus even a glimpse of him, and whatever poetry came from him, were valued greatly. Who knows, he might not be among us tomorrow?

A new ghazal from Khvajah sahib was like a small event, to be celebrated and enjoyed. A new ghazal from him was indeed making the rounds in Delhi in those days; many poets were trying their hand at imitating or outdoing the old master. The opening verse of Khvajah sahib's ghazal was:

It seems that she has learnt the tricks of intoxication from
the nargis flower,
For when her eyes roll like the wine glass,
Lines and lines of drinkers lose their senses, and fall.

In many assemblies, the first line of the opening verse was set as the model; numerous poets of Delhi tried their hand at it. Dagh, too, composed a ghazal on the pattern; his opening verse was not much to speak of:

Dwellers of Kabah, how well do I remember
The House of Idols!
The inebriate roll around freely,
The crazed ones come and go.

Some other verses of his ghazal, however, became almost proverbial. It was said about one of them that the indirect description of the beloved's face, the description of her mood and deportment, the colourfulness of the theme, had never been heard of, far less composed so well in a two-ine verse:

Placing a lamp before her radiant face,
She says, now let's see:
Where does the moth make for? For the lamp, or for my face?

Some more verses of the ghazal were sung by people of all callings in the marketplace as they went about their business, just as it once used to happen with the brilliant verses of the great Mir Taqi Mir:

It reached my heart, but stumbled at a hundred places:
Was it the arrow of your glance, or
Was it someone drunk?

*

Cheating, coquetry, mischief, impudence,
Spreading unrest all round;
Drunk on your power, do you know anything else,
My beloved eyes, drunk like the nargis flower?

Two young men who roamed the city with Navab Mirza, reciting their new poems whenever an occasion arose, were Qamaruddin Raqim, son of Khvajah Aman, and Sayyid Zahiruddin Husain, son of the famous calligraphist Sayyid Jalaluddin Haidar Murassa Raqam Khan Bahadur Yaqut Raqam Secondus. Raqim was just about twelve or thirteen, and had begun composing poetry just recently. He was formally a pupil of Mirza Ghalib's, to whom he was distantly related. Obviously he could not be much of a poet at that age, but he was welcomed and valued everywhere because of a connection with the Haveli. He took lessons in archery from the Presence, the Shadow of God, and wrote poetry in his free moments. Zahiruddin was eighteen or nineteen, yet unmarried, so he felt closer to young boys like Navab Mirza and Raqim than to persons in his age group.

Zahir too was a pupil of Mirza Ghalib's in poetry; he also took occasional lessons in calligraphy from the Exalted King. Actually, his father had trained the King Emperor in calligraphy, so he claimed a special kind of relationship with the Haveli. Zahir was the unofficial chief of the trio, but could be pretty free and informal with them when occasion demanded. The three had already been noticed in the city as promising, clean-living and sober young men. Two of them were connected with Mirza Ghalib anyway, and Ghalib's own interest in Dagh was also exercising its pull on the young man. It was thus inevitable that Ghalib and Dagh would meet, sooner rather than later.

Dagh's ghazal, and in particular the 'lamp and face' verse in it, reached Mirza sahib's ears a few days before the moment arrived for their meeting. Mirza sahib happened to espy them from the upper balcony of his house. Flower garlands around their wrists; fashionable, curled toe slippers on their feet; loose, flapping trousers on their legs; caps worked in gold; a very slight but discernible line of kohl below the eyes: seemingly without a care in the world, three young men sauntering in the bazaar like casual tourists in the city.

Mirza sahib called out impulsively from the height of the balcony, 'Hey young fellows, gentlemen at large, where are you going? Come here, come to me!'

The three looked up, startled, and saw Mirza Ghalib sahib's face, radiant with goodwill and high intelligence, handsome beyond measure, looking at them avidly. If they were a little shy and confused at having been addressed so precipitately by such a grand personality, they recovered quickly, and calling out, 'Yes, sir, very well, sir', managed to trundle up the stairs to the balcony. Mirza sahib, back in his chamber, was smiling with satisfaction as the three came up, made three salaams each, and stood at the door. Zahir and Raqim needed no introduction; Navab Mirza's mind was in a whirl. He well remembered how his mother felt about Ghalib and the House of Loharu and was quite unsure how he should behave with Mirza sahib, and how Mirza sahib would treat him. Inwardly saying, 'Well, what's to happen, let it happen,' he set foot on the doorstep and made one more salaam.

'Presence, I make my submissions.'

Mirza sahib looked at Navab Mirza from head to toe—his handsome face and well-proportioned, youthful body. The boy's body might have betrayed his uncertainty of mind, but he stood with the same self-confident posture which was his father's, and looked Mirza sahib in the eye. Navab Mirza's tall frame quite filled the door, leaving the others behind. Mirza sahib spread his arms in affectionate welcome and said, 'Aha! So it's you! My brother Shamsuddin Ahmad Khan's own son!' He patted Navab Mirza on the cheek and continued: 'Come in, I have been looking for you all these days.' Waving his hand towards Navab Mirza, he gently pulled Raqim by his ear and said, 'Come in, my dear scoundrel! Come and sit comfortably cross-legged.' He then touched Zahir's shoulder and said, 'Come in, Mian Zahir, come on in. Don't stand there like strangers!'

Thus, with immense tact and good sense, Ghalib sahib made the three young men feel welcome and comfortable. He organized their seating with the same tact: Navab Mirza to his right, a little in front, more or less facing him; Zahir sat straight to Ghalib's right; Raqim on his left. All this he managed with such facility that it seemed to happen by itself. Ghalib sahib now looked at Navab Mirza with admiring eyes, 'Young man, what an opportune time it was, that you passed by my home. The whole of Delhi is agog about you, and the one person who could not get to know you all these days was just me.' He recited a famous Persian verse in a clear, strong and mellow voice:

The fire of disunion with you burnt all hearts
Like the kebab; the flood of your desire
Devastated and desolated all souls.

'Young fellow, I'll oblige you today to say to us the selfsame ghazal which has earned you such a reputation . . . Such maturity and so young a poet! It's true what they say, it is Allah's gift . . . But tell me, what will you young blades eat?' He made a small dramatic pause, smiled a mischievous smile, 'And what will you drink?'

The youthful guests were weighing the matter in their hearts: should we, with all humility, excuse ourselves, saying that we have no appetite, when an old but wiry man of middle height entered. He was clothed in a clean cotton outfit, had a colourful kerchief on his shoulder folded in a triangle, a necklet made of silver beads around his neck, and a turquoise ring set in silver on his right index finger. He brought in a spacious metal tray, loaded with a variety of dry fruits.

'Oh, here is Mian Kalyan himself,' Ghalib sahib smiled. 'His tray is loaded with goodies.' He smiled a little more broadly. 'He knows the visitors to be the children of men of substance: they'll only eat things that strengthen the mind and body.'

Mirza sahib lightly clasped Qamaruddin Raqim by the neck, and bending the young man's head to the plate of dry fruits, cried out jovially, 'Little fellow, grab the fruit with your teeth, stuff your jaws, so that all may know that you are a tiger cub. What's this daintiness of yours, picking them up in ones and two, like a chicken pecking at the earth?'

Mirza sahib kept his gentle pressure on Qamaruddin's neck, making sure that he did as bidden. Good humour and jocundity oozed from Ghalib sahib's actions and voice all the time. 'Navab Mirza, do you know, or I suppose you do,' he said with affectionate grace, 'this young squire's father is my nephew. So I am his grandfather, but also his grand lover!'

Mirza sahib's laughter was gentle, not boisterous, but infectious all the same. Everyone burst out laughing at the pun in 'grandfather' and 'grand lover', and Mirza sahib's playfulness in speaking thus. Navab Mirza said to himself, I was worrying for no reason, really. Anyway, no one else but Mirza Naushah sahib could carry off this feat of diplomacy and use delightful words appropriate to the time and circumstance.

Navab Mirza knew the history between Ghalib sahib and Raqim and his grandfather Khvajah Haji, who had apparently no right to any share in the pension settled upon Mirza sahib and his people by the Company. According to Mirza sahib—and perhaps some others of his family—this Khvajah Haji, a feckless fellow, and no relation to his family, had villainously inveigled Navab Ahmad Bakhsh Khan into allocating one half of that pension to him and his progeny. Mirza sahib had appealed and appealed, but the decision remained unchanged. Now, the pension was shared by Khvajah Haji's two surviving sons: Shamsuddin, nicknamed Khvajah Jan, and Badruddin nicknamed Khvajah Aman; the latter was Raqim''s father. Mirza sahib seemed to have relegated the past disputes to the dunghill of bad memories. When the laughter ceased and everybody regained their gravitas, Ghalib sahib had Navab Mirza recite his ghazal with the 'lamp and face' verse in it. After praising the ghazal highly, he turned to Zahir. 'Well, Mian Zahir, have you composed something recently?'

Zahir cleared his throat in abashment. 'May the Presence be always with us, but I am sorry, I have written nothing new recently.'

'Why is that?' Mirza sahib spoke sharply.

'Sir, there are some indications of a job at the Exalted Fort . . . '

'Job, what does that mean? Did not I understand that you have been employed there for quite some time?'

'The Exalted Presence is quite right. This insignificant person was appointed Steward and Manager of the arsenal at the age of twelve. That was nearly six, seven years ago. Now there are signs of my promotion and elevation as Keeper of the Royal Procession's Appurtenances, and of the Royal Standard of the God Fish. Thus I am summoned to the Presence many times a day. It's like being hanged on the gallows of suspense all the time.'

'Good, my congratulations. Maula willing, all things will be right very soon.'

The word 'Maula' was used often for God, or Ali, the Prophet's son-in-law. People of Shia persuasion generally meant Ali, Sunnis occasionally meant either one, or both. Ghalib was not Shia, but he leaned towards Shi'ism somewhat openly.

'I beg for Your Honour's prayers in my favour. But as regards poetry, Mian Navab Mirza's temperament is shining brilliantly these days.'

'Yes, sure. Even those who presume to compete with him would be obliged to throw in the towel before the ghazal he just recited. Mian Navab Mirza, do drop in whenever convenient; and look, this time I want from you a ghazal in the pattern of Shaikh Jurat's ghazal.'

Mirza sahib now recited the opening verse of Jurat's ghazal:

My restless heart and its tossing about in pain
Were never separate;
I don't care that I lost my life:
Now at least I am free from the torment.

Mirza sahib spoke the verse again amid sounds of applause, and said, 'Note the flow of the line: "My restless heart and its tossing about in pain were never separate." Ha, such a beautiful way of concluding the utterance: My restless heart's tossing and turning in pain left me only when I died. See, the state of giving up the ghost is itself a state of tossing and turning and writhing. Wah! Only God is untouched by blemish!'

'I don't have the capacity or ability to write after Shaikh Jurat,' said Navab Mirza with appropriate humbleness. 'But I'll scratch my heart and liver as much as I can, and carry out your command.'

'Very good,' said Mirza Ghalib. 'And look, Mian Zahir, you too must try your wits in imitation of Jurat.'

He paused for a moment, then went on: 'God forbid, I have no intention at all to create a competition between you two. It's just that the rhyme and end-rhyme patterns are good, and Mian Zahir is also a poet endowed with the power of imagination.'

'The Presence is most kind,' replied Zahir. 'I too will pull and struggle a bit.'

The three young guests now rose, did three salaams, and saying, 'Please grant us permission', they walked backwards to the door. They put on their shoes and came down into the alley.

'Phew! What a narrow escape for me,' Raqim breathed when they were well clear. 'Mirza sahib did not command me to compose!'

'Heh, that's not because of your green years, fellow.' Zahir snorted. 'Actually, Mirza sahib doesn't wish for Delhi's gamblers to start a cycle of betting.'

'Cycle of betting?' Raqim wondered. 'And what's that, pray?'

'You dolt, the whole city knows that Mirza sahib is inordinately fond of gaming. Now if he sets no less than three novices to write in one and the same pattern, everyone will assume that there's some sort of a wager going here. Soon enough, all punters in the city will start putting money on you fellows.'

'May Allah save us!' Dagh and Raqim cried out with one voice. 'Is this a city or a gaming house? As if Delhi's population has nothing else to do!'

'What else, dear son?' Zahir chortled. 'An addiction to gaming is not plain addiction: it's a disease of the mind. Delhi's population bet on the most trivial things. In fact, they bet even more on things which are less than trivial!'

*

Navab Mirza composed his ghazal within two days and presented himself before Mirza Ghalib at a suitable time on the third day.

'Well, indeed, you carried out the chore soon enough!' Mirza sahib clearly showed his enthusiasm for the young man's calibre in poetry. 'Allah save you from the evil eye! Let's now hear what you have.'

The growing young poet had a ghazal of no less than twenty-two verses; perhaps the excess was also a kind of answer to the world. Dagh in those days was truly fluent in composition. Ideas and themes seemed to stand before him, their hands on their chests, awaiting his call. Dagh's opening verse used azab (torment) as Jurat's did, and if Justice were asked to make judgement, the thirteen-year-old was way ahead of Jurat, a major ustad, who had extensively been in the company of such greats as Mir and Sauda:

When did Love ever become separated
From my ravaged and savaged heart?
Even in Paradise,
I could not be rid of Love's torment.

Some more of Dagh's verses that received Mirza sahib's approval were as follows:

Her inebriate eye made me drunk:
I was rid of wine; wine was rid of me.

⋆

Why shouldn't I be envious
Of such joinings:
Colour did not leave the rose,
Intoxication did not leave the wine.

⋆

How could Dagh depict his qualities in full?
The King who's called Bu Turab left no merit
For others.

Ghalib, with his Shi'i bent of mind, was particularly pleased with this last verse; for, Bu Turab is one of the most popular appellatives of Ali, venerated by those of the Shi'i faith as the First and the Greatest Imam. The maestro was so well pleased that he presented his own hookah to Dagh to smoke. Dagh refused bashfully; Mirza sahib ordered a glass of a cool drink based on the hibiscus flower to be brought for the boy poet and followed it up with a betel cone. Perhaps he would have liked to suggest a change or two in the verses by Dagh, but he preferred to say nothing, lest someone imagine that by offering correction or improvement in that one ghazal, he was preparing the ground for taking Dagh into his circle of pupils.

The fact of the matter was that though Ghalib greatly admired Dagh's untiring creativity and inventiveness, there was a bit of boyish boisterousness in Dagh which did not really dovetail with his own sombre, intellectual and abstraction-loving genius. Dagh was more given to sleek and polished writing, creating effects from ready use of idioms and nearly colloquial speech, and depicting matters relating to the amorous verbal transactions between the lover and the beloved.

Navab Mirza wanted to leave now: he feared that he might be overstaying his welcome, but Ghalib would not hear of his going. Dagh deeply longed for Ghalib to offer to say some of his poetry to him; many times, as he remained in Mirza sahib's chamber as a desired guest apparently, he even thought of requesting Mirza sahib to recite some of his poems. He knew that such a request from him could be construed as an impertinence. Now, when Navab Mirza was saying for the third or the fourth time, 'Presence, you must be tired now. Please grant me leave to go,' Kalyan came upstairs to announce the arrival of Navab Ziauddin Ahmad Khan Bahadur.

It was as if Ghalib blossomed up for a second time that day. He exclaimed, 'Bhai wah, wah! Only God is untouched by blemish! Mian Nayyar is very welcome!' He gestured towards the door and said to Navab Mirza, 'Come, I'll introduce you to a relative of yours, and a very promising poet.'

In the meantime, Navab Ziauddin Ahmad Khan had arrived, and making a proper salaam to Mirza sahib, took his seat to the right, very close to Mirza sahib. Navab Mirza stood up to his full height, made two salaams, and again indicated that he should now go. But Ghalib waved to him again, to indicate that Navab Mirza should resume his place.

Navab Mirza had been subject to doubt and anxiety over facing Ziauddin Ahmad Khan Bahadur: How will Mirza sahib introduce me to him? How will Ziauddin Ahmad Khan Bahadur react to my presence here? Again, his anxieties proved to be without foundation. With his usual tact and good sense, Mirza sahib talked to them both as if the events and tensions of the past were firmly buried in the past. And this was true, more or less.

Delhi had not forgotten Navab Shamsuddin Ahmad Khan, but he was no longer a subject of conversation. The annual fair at his mausoleum had been suspended for many years now. Of course, pilgrims to Qadam Sharif rarely omitted to say a brief prayer at the Navab's grave too. In fact, a section of the nobility of Delhi appeared to be of the view that the State of Loharu could very well settle a small pension on Wazir Khanam. Among others, Navab Ziauddin Ahmad Khan Bahadur was of that view. One reason for his thinking in this way could have been his own somewhat strained relations with his elder brother Aminuddin Ahmad Khan Bahadur who held the title of Navab but actually was required to share the revenues of the State equally with his younger brother. Ziauddin Ahmad Khan had been alleging that his elder brother's treatment of him was not fully just, or fully in keeping with the protocol. He even alleged that he was paid somewhat less than half the revenues of the State to which he was entitled.

There was a considerable gap between their ages: Aminuddin Ahmad Khan Bahadur was born in 1814 and Ziauddin Ahmad Khan in 1821. His complaint was that the big gap between their ages should have caused the elder brother to behave with him with fatherly tenderness and consideration; this was not happening. A number of times, Ziauddin Ahmad Khan petitioned to the Firangee, asking that the State be divided into two, declaring each of them independent potentates. This was not approved. Now he was asking that his share of the revenues be computed by the Company's officers and paid to him from one of the Company's treasuries. This petition was under consideration in Calcutta at the Court of the Navab Governor General Bahadur.

Unlike many of the younger nobility of his times, it was in order to acquire wide learning that Ziauddin Ahmad Khan put to use his wealth and freedom from the need to earn an income. He was fully au fait in Persian, Arabic and Chaghatai Turkish, the language of his remote ancestors and of the early Mughal Emperors. He was fully learned in Literature, Court Correspondence, History, Family Trees, Quranic Exegesis, Hadith, Astrology and Astronomy. He was no stranger to English, either. Beginning very early in life, he had accumulated a large library.

Gossip had it that Ziauddin Ahmad Khan had some interest in Chhoti Begam, but nothing was known for sure. Today, perhaps, that interest, if interest it was, was up for reactivation. He cast a casual eye on Navab Mirza. In the young man's deportment and the way he talked and spoke, Ziauddin Ahmad Khan could see glimpses of his stepbrother. Both Aminuddin Ahmad Khan and Ziauddin Ahmad Khan were brought up hating and abominating their eldest brother. Yet, if the truth were to be told, Shamsuddin Ahmad Khan had always behaved towards his step-siblings with impeccable kindness and generosity. Today, the dead person of Shamsuddin Ahmad Khan, as embodied in his son Navab Mirza, recreated in Ziauddin Ahmad Khan's mind the long-dead tumult and memories of imagined slights and injustices.

Should my elder brother's woman—he, a stepbrother and in adverse possession of our rightful estate—were such a brother's woman to come to my hand . . . But Brother Shamsuddin Ahmad had always treated me kindly . . . I was not sorry when died—I was very young at that time—but now, when I look at his son, I feel a little sad somehow. Every atom of his body exuded the same confidence, the same quiet arrogance . . . the same high, straight neck . . . looking at the boy, no one can judge that they are fallen upon hard times. There isn't the least hint of clouding in the eyes, the brow absolutely clear of passive acceptance. He is surely going to be a man of ascendant fortune . . . and how arrestingly beautiful the mother would be, when the son is so compellingly beautiful! But should I . . . ? Were my late brother alive today . . . he would most possibly have left her by this time, Ziauddin Ahmad Khan told himself. He had not married her, after all. And even if he had married her, it wouldn't have been much of a hindrance . . . I wonder what Brother Aminuddin Ahmad would think of my making overtures to her . . . But it's no concern of his.

In the meantime, Navab Mirza took stealthy glances at Ziauddin Ahmad Khan. He saw a tall, slim young man, twenty-two or twenty-three years of age, broad-chested and strong-shouldered. His beard was not fully dense yet, but was cut square, suggesting the Rajput style; moustaches too were not very heavy yet, but curled upwards, again in the Rajputani manner. His upper garments were all made of Dacca's milk-white muslin. Below, he wore trousers of striped Benarasi silk called ara. His each and every gesture revealed nobility of lineage and of the mind.

'The dear boy Navab Mirza, his pen name is Dagh, he is the living relict of your Paradise-abiding brother.' Mirza sahib told Ziauddin Ahmad Khan in a free and easy manner, as if he were making the introduction at some routine gathering, as if there was never anything, any history, any tension, between the younger stepbrother and Shamsuddin Ahmad Khan.

'So this is that young man, Navab Mirza. Very nice,' Ziauddin Ahmad Khan spoke drily, successfully concealing his private thoughts. 'Just recently, Ghanshyam Lal Asi sahib was mentioning him in an assembly.'

'Yes, Mian Ziauddin Ahmad, we have great expectations from him. After your generation, there hadn't been a worthwhile young poet in Delhi.' Mirza sahib continued. 'You must have heard that verse of his . . . did you not, with the theme of the lamp and face?'

'Yes, sir, quite right,' he quoted effortlessly:

Where does the moth make for? For the lamp, or for my face?

'That was indeed an admirable theme,' he concluded.

'Yes, I wanted him to know you. It's good that it has happened. Nice conjunction, was it not?' He turned towards Navab Mirza, 'Tell me, who awarded you the pen name Dagh?'

'Sir, my mother suggested it.'

'Yes, nice pen name, that . . . Oh, is she herself not a poet?' Mirza sahib asked. 'To whom does she submit her poetry?'

'Sir, she used to consult the late Shah Nasir sahib; but that connection is no longer extant. She is not a practising poet now.'

Ziauddin Ahmad Khan shifted in his seat suddenly, and observed, 'But one of her ghazals from Rampur became rather popular, was it not so? And what was its pattern . . .' He paused for a brief moment. 'Yes, "chain, alike exactly; arrows, alike exactly".'

Navab Mirza knew about Ziauddin Ahmad Khan's phenomenal memory; still, he was somewhat surprised to see that Ziauddin Ahmad Khan's interest in his mother was strong enough for him to remember an odd ghazal of hers. This was not the time to ask, or show curiosity. He recalled the pleasant face of Agha Mirza Turab Ali, paid him a brief tribute of sadness, was silent for a beat, as if trying to recall his mother's ghazal. Then he spoke the opening verse of it:

Her glance has the effect of magic,
Exactly.

My beloved's tresses, and links in a chain, are alike
Exactly.

Both Mirza Sahib and Ziauddin Ahmad Khan praised the verse. Navab Mirza bent low in salaam, and was now able to obtain leave to depart after a few more minutes of casual conversation.

*

As he walked back home—Ghalib's place, in Ballimaran, was not too far from his own dwelling in Khanam ka Bazaar—Navab Mirza was simmering, if not seething. No prospect of meliorism in their mental and mundane life made itself apparent while new disputes or complications raised their heads. First, it was Mirza Fathul Mulk Bahadur; now it was Ziauddin Ahmad Khan. What concern could they have about my mother? Why should they be interested in her? And was it a sincere pull of the hearts, or was it a mere passing lust for novelty? Was it that they were clothed in the nakedness of shameless desire, obliged by their own basenesses to run about like headless chickens? Can we not claim even two moments of peace for our own?

For Navab Mirza, those days were days of questioning: questioning the tangled knots of fate, dexterous fingernails unravelling, or failing to unravel, those knots; destiny that could be postponed or avoided; destiny that could not be avoided or evaded; auspicious moments when a prayer was always granted by the Almighty; talismans, magic drawings and pentacles, words of power; prayers or intonations which were sure to be effective if carried out for a long enough time in the prescribed manner. What are these things? He knew that no human being could escape the unbreakable bonds of doubt. Or perhaps life was free of doubt for the Friends of God, or those who had God with them? But to give tongue to doubts, or try to find rational solutions for them, or to live a life concentrated on doubts: all these proceedings were dangerous.

No, perhaps they were not full of hazards, but they certainly were the enemy of the peace of one's mind; in fact, they were quite as much one's enemies as the frustrations, the complaints and the experience of the failure of one's proposals and schemes, and the cruelties of the irony of fate. Further, these things could grow stronger quickly and soon their lines would begin to merge into the boundaries of rejection, of kufr, of denial of God and man's destiny and God's Eternal Will. Then, God help him who bruits these matters openly: the mullahs and the maulavis would lose no time in condemning the poor doubter as kafir, a denier, as one who strayed out of the sphere of Islam. His marriage is automatically annulled, they would declare, and pronounce social boycott of the victim. You could expect anything, anything at all, at their hands.

Whatever is written in one's destiny . . . but what is written there, and why? Navab Mirza sometimes found himself despising himself, despising the whole sorry crooked timber of humanity, from which nothing straight could ever be fashioned. We do not know the answers to the questions; nor do the birds of the air and the beasts of the jungle. So tell me, who is better off: they or we? No fear of the King; no authority of the Censor; no Police Chief shouting, 'Stop thief!' No unchecked horde of questions, no disputations about the answers.

We poets are cleverer, anyway. Sometimes we put the blame vaguely on the Sky or the Heaven; sometimes we implicate Fate and Determination, pretending that they are separate from the Reality of God; sometimes we blame the Pious Preacher, or describe the beloved as beautiful, but with a heart of stone, like the idols and statues worshipped by the Hindu. Sometimes we just speak of 'They' or 'S/he', being careful not to specify the identity of 'They', or 'S/he'. But for these subterfuges, we poets would be condemned every day as godless and kafir.

For some time now, Navab Mirza had been trying to get out of the thorny brake of questions. It was during this time that he composed a piquant, rather mysterious verse:

They are oppressive; they are wrathful,
They have the same haughty pride, the same vanity:
The idol-beloveds are God, except that
They don't do Justice, as the True God does.

Did he mean to say that God is indeed Just, but Oppression and Wrath and Haughty Pride and Vanity are His attributes? Or did he mean to say that the idol-beloveds should be declared God, once they start doing Justice? Or perhaps he was suggesting that there are two Gods, but only one Estate: one God in the Heaven, and the other at the apogee of the Sky of Injustice?

Do both have the power to intervene in the world, or at least in the world of lovers?

But is that not something worse than active denial of the Kingdom of God? No, perhaps he was really feeling oppressed; perhaps his meaning was that to complain against the oppressive rule of the idol-beloved was just a fig leaf. Truth to tell, in the Kingdom of God Himself, there was oppression and wrath and everything else besides. Well, he told himself, one can understand a God who is Wrathful, but for all that wrathfulness, someday soon His Attributes of All Mercifulness and All Forgiveness must come into play. If the Knower knows everything, He would certainly see that we humans are oppressed more than oppressing.

It was lucky for Dagh that he had been born in an age which was liberal, and which could forgive a poet, even when it did not understand his meaning.

59

Ziauddin Ahmad Khan pays a visit to the house at Khanam ka Bazaar;
Dagh experiences the turbulence of love

NAVAB MIRZA DID not mention to his mother his encounter with Mirza Fathul Mulk Bahadur. In the same fashion, he made no mention of his becoming acquainted with Navab Ziauddin Ahmad Khan. Still, he had a sort of curiosity, even anxiety, to know if there was anything at all in the interest revealed—perhaps unconsciously—by them in his mother. And if there was something there, how should he respond to it? No, he should first make some hint to Amma Jan, so that she would not be taken by surprise if she got to know about it from some other source. The sudden surprise could be unpleasant, and could affect her well-being. But how should he broach the subject before his mother? Whatever he said could easily be construed as impertinent and spoken out of turn. Even so, it seemed to him that putting off telling his mother about the two men showing some hazy interest in her might not be advisable. The Sahib-e Alam would perhaps open some cautious dialogue, and not behave precipitately, but Ziauddin Ahmad Khan was a relative of sorts. He might throw protocol to the winds and come visiting whenever he pleased.

What do these gentlemen take my mother for? he asked himself angrily. But a moment's consideration provided the answer: The world out there made its own rules. It abased itself before those who wielded any kind of power, but never forgave the weak, especially women. He appreciated that his mother was one of those women who had their own history, their own past. The world always looked at such women with suspicion and fear; with fear came expectation of easy pickings, and it was not a new belief either: the woman had strayed, and every man had the right to hold her by the hand.

So Navab Mirza gave a full account of his two encounters, and his thoughts about the underlying meaning of the veiled words of the Prince and the Navab. Wazir Khanam heard him out without interruption. She knew that she did not need a man; she needed a support. But she also knew that in the world's marketplace, they meant the same. Perhaps she had not loved Agha Mirza Turab Ali; she had liked him, certainly. And . . . was that not her chief condition that she would look and observe and then decide to accept? But how long could this go on?

As if on cue, within two or three of days of the conversation, a weather-beaten but powerful-looking mace-bearer appeared at the street door of Wazir Khanam's house and called out, 'Navab Ziauddin Ahmad Khan Bahadur has come!'

Habiba promptly informed Wazir. By a happy chance, Navab Mirza was present at the time. He quickly went downstairs and made sure that the divan khanah was clean and fit to receive the visitor. The room was practically in disuse now: it was opened on the rare occasion when a friend of Navab Mirza's visited. He dusted it quickly as best he could and instructed Jani Ram to have the guest handed out from the palanquin with the maximum honour and respect, and taken into the divan khanah where he should be seated in the most prominent place. Jani Ram was then to offer him the hookah and betel cones, and inform him that Navab Mirza sahib would be presenting himself very soon.

Ziauddin Ahmad Khan was in white, as usual, but was apparently dressed with greater care. Instead of a hat, he wore a formal-looking silk turban in white, adorned with a crest of two red-and-blue feathers of the junglefowl. On his arms he had a wide jewelled ornament vaguely designed to look like a piece of a coat of mail. He wore a broad silk sash worked in gold and silver; on one side of the waist he sported a silver-plated pistol. His white buck shoes were open at the end in the Mughal style. Tiny golden topazes were encrusted on the white silk lace neatly sewn on to the uppers of the shoes.

He somehow looked even slimmer and younger than what Navab Mirza remembered. Youth and good grace and sophisticated breeding were apparent from his whole personality. Following him, there was another mace-bearer, holding a large, covered copper tray. Handing the tray to Jani Ram, the mace-bearer went down the steps quickly. Just as the mace-bearer was going down into the alley, Ziauddin Ahmad Khan noticed Navab Mirza come down from the uppermost storey. Seeing him enter, Ziauddin

Ahmad Khan rose slightly from his place. The arms of both rose almost in unison in greeting.

'I submit my greetings. I am so happy that you could come.' Saying this, Navab Mirza seated himself in front of his guest, both feet under his thighs. 'Please take a look at the hookah. Should you so desire, some cool drink could be served just this minute.'

'No, no. Please don't take the trouble at all, young sir. Getting together, meeting is all that matters.'

There ensued a silence for a few seconds. Navab Mirza did not have anything to say; Ziauddin Ahmad Khan seemed to be searching his heart for appropriate words. Finally, he spoke, 'Navab Mirza, your poetry is brightening up day by day. Your name is often mentioned among literary personages nowadays.'

'It is the Excellency's generosity and his enhancement of my value. Truly, your servant is no more than a beginner in a primary school. Indeed, your servant hopes to become something, should he be regarded with favour by the perfectly accomplished like you.'

He spoke with the purely formal intent of being polite. But having spoken, he realized that his words could be taken to have an oblique hint or desire to be accepted in Ziauddin Ahmad Khan's circle. He hated himself for his inexperience and foolishness. Had he been older, or been through the cool and heat of life, or was familiar with the finer shades of philosophical and logical discourse, he would never have said such rash and foolish things. But the words had left his lips, there was no taking them back; the best course was not to say anything else. On his part, Ziauddin Ahmad Khan was unable to decide if Navab Mirza's words were on account of his naivety, or there was more to them. He decided not to pursue the matter, unless Navab Mirza made things clearer, if at all.

'No doubt,' Ziauddin Ahmad Khan observed, 'the journey on the road of poetry becomes easier if one has the guidance of an accomplished ustad. Do you consult anyone for your poetry?'

'Sir, I haven't yet shown my work to anyone at all. The fact of the matter is that I don't regard myself worth the training and trouble of a major ustad.'

'Why? Why is that?' Ziauddin Ahmad Khan smiled. 'As far as I can see, any of the leading ustad poets will accept you gladly.'

Having said this, Ziauddin Ahmad Khan realized that he was guilty of the same kind of faux pas as the young Navab Mirza. There was a clear hint in his words, if someone wished to find it, that the young Navab desired the brilliant young boy to enlist as his own pupil, if not as Mirza Ghalib's. Ziauddin Ahmad Khan was Mirza sahib's successor, as Mirza sahib himself proclaimed once, and though Ziauddin Ahmad Khan had no pupil of his own so far, he could always accept pupils any time he liked.

Ziauddin Ahmad Khan kicked himself inwardly. When one is unable to get down to business, the conversation was bound to be idle, and even deleterious to the real purpose. He put the hookah's mouthpiece to his mouth; the tobacco was finely scented and fresh, but the hookah itself seemed to have been dusted in a hurry. Apparently there was no one fond of the smoke in that house. He thought of articulating a few careful words in praise of the tobacco, but realized that it was yet another ploy—bound to result in yet further idle and potentially harmful talk. No result could be obtained from such conversation. It was better to be silent; and it was Navab Mirza's turn to speak anyway.

'It is the Excellency's generosity to regard me worthy. Undoubtedly, I will benefit greatly from a kind and helpful mentor. Delhi today is full of unlimited potential for newly fledged poets. The Presence, Mirza Ghalib, heads the list of the great masters here.'

'Doubtless. The alchemic glance of Excellency the Mirza Sahib has metamorphosed the raw copper of countless aspirants into beaten gold.'

Ziauddin Ahmad Khan's brow had begun to cloud a little by now. For how long should our conversation be ravelled in the threads of polite, meaningless talk? For how long was it advisable to lengthen this kind of exchange, devoid of enjoyment, if not of sense? A small spark of displeasure against Chhoti Begam was igniting his mood. Was it hospitable or even civilized to keep me hanging about like a suppliant? Navab Mirza was also becoming impatient on his side: I should say a tactful goodbye to him and send him on his way, or ask him flatly why he is desirous of meeting Amma Jan. But, both courses were impossible at present. Both parties had to behave as if Ziauddin Ahmad Khan's visit was nothing out of the ordinary; it was just one of those brotherly visits that oiled the axle of the heavy wain of day-to-day life.

'I will certainly present myself soon in the service of Ustad Zauq,' Navab Mirza said a little lamely, a little desperately. Fortunately, footfalls coming down from the upper storey were heard even before he finished speaking. The door from the landing into the room opened and Wazir Khanam spoke from the threshold in an extremely mellifluous, sophisticated voice from which the last atom of greeting or welcome had been distilled away. 'I submit my respects, Navab sahib. How lucky that I am able to welcome you here!'

Both the men rose quite involuntarily and Ziauddin Ahmad responded in a voice which even sounded somewhat forced to him, lacking the natural flow of language. 'Actually, it's my fortune that's on the rise, so that I could make my pilgrimage to your abode . . . Be pleased to come in, give your feet the trouble to enter.'

But for a black chador, Wazir was clad entirely in white. She wore the chador in the approved Iranian-Central Asian style. It was wrapped firmly around her whole upper body so that her head was tightly covered but her face was partly visible: a portion of the brow, above the brow a quiet, bright glimpse of jet black hair, eyes, well-formed nose and delicate mouth if the observer viewed her from the front; otherwise, a perfect profile of a clean-cut face. Her large, profound eyes prevailed upon all else if the gazer was close in front. She came in and took her seat upon the carpet in front of the visitor, but not quite four-square: there was more than a hint of a turned back in her posture.

Navab Mirza made some excuse and left them alone, drawing the curtain and pulling the door ajar as he went out. Ever since she entered, Wazir had been taking stealthy looks at Ziauddin Ahmad Khan. Much of his aspect reminded her of Shamsuddin Ahmad Khan. The younger brother now was the same age as the dead Navab when she had first set eyes on him. The more she glanced at him, the more her heart ached; each memory of what was bygone—her joys, ecstasies and pains—seemed to brand her heart like a soldering iron. Some part of her seemed to like Ziauddin Ahmad Khan for what he was: a relic of her beloved lover. In the same instant, she seemed to hate him for being alive when someone who was much better than he was not allowed his due share of days. And it was due to these very cursed ones that my Navab lost his life; it was they who conspired with the Firangee to dispossess him and finally led him to his death. So what has he come here for? Has he come to jeer and dance in joy to see me in my present state? But I too will not be Wazir Khanam if I do not foil them in their designs.

'I have been very keen to visit with you,' Ziauddin Ahmad Khan's words interrupted and scattered her imaginings. She was also quite conscious of the implications of 'visiting' her, but she was not about to give him an opening.

'Fate and the Angel of Death pulled us apart, or meeting and being united was not impossible.' She spoke dryly, without a hint of recrimination or self-pity. But the tiny suggestion of failure on his family's part did not escape Ziauddin Ahmad. However, this was not the time for debate or entering into caveats.

'Yes, madam. We human beings look at ourselves as proud, our necks held high and higher all the time. But on the vast map of the Divine Utterance, "Be"! we count for no more than a broken blade of a shrivelled-up piece of hay.'

He then recited a verse from the great Persian poet Saib in a sombre voice:

Whoever arrived in this Sorrowtown, this world;
Tasted the dust, danced on his own axis
For a length of time, like a whirlwind,
And disappeared.

'Yes, sir,' Wazir was somewhat ironical. 'But what caused us to arrive in Sorrowtown in the first place?'

Ziauddin Ahmad Khan found himself at a loss for an appropriate reply. He smiled weakly and said eventually, 'This question was best put to Omar Khayyam. But the truth is, Wazir Khanam, those who are given, always long for more, and those who are not, they go on seeking to find more.'

Ziauddin Ahmad Khan had, according to his lights, answered both of Wazir's points and also stated his desire. But Wazir was not to be placated so easily. She retorted acidly, 'The Navab sahib perhaps did not consider a situation where relinquishment of all desires should be of the same order as fulfilment of all desires.'

'Is that so? How?' Ziauddin Ahmad Khan was obviously being deliberately obtuse.

Wazir replied with a verse from Kalim Hamadani, another great Persian poet of the seventeenth century:

One who has ceased to hope, doesn't desire
The pleasures of the world:
A lopped-off bough has no eye for the spring.

'God forbid!' Ziauddin Ahmad Khan spoke with some passion. 'Why should you be a bough that has been lopped off? I should say that the mysteries of countless leaves and fruits are hidden yet in your arbour of desires.'

'I thank you for your attempt to lead me into error about my own self. But the state of the dwelling is best known to the dweller. Further, not every keeper and tender of a garden knows the ways of bringing every tree of life into fruition. The Persian saying "For every tree, there is a watcher and tender" must have reached His Honour's auspicious ears?'

Wazir had, in her own view, made everything clear: Navab Ziauddin Ahmad Khan should not hope to enjoy the fruit of her garden. The problem was, given all his learning and sharpness of mind, Ziauddin Ahmad Khan was a child of his times. No women, according to him, could have anything to do with matters of choice and preference. It was the male who chose, who liked or disapproved. Or perhaps Ziauddin Ahmad Khan was lacking in a sense of humour: he was unable to visualize the possibility of a woman twitting him with subtle sarcasm and even enjoying it. Finally, he still failed to appreciate that his coming to her house was entirely devoid of any kind of attraction for her.

Ziauddin Ahmad Khan was learned in History and well versed in Philosophy and Logic. The city of Delhi, which in those times seemed overcrowded with perfections and overachievements in almost all disciplines, would be hard put to find his equal. But he was also a younger brother, not only of Aminuddin Ahmad Khan, ruler of Loharu, but also of Shamsuddin Ahmad Khan, ruler of Loharu and Firozepur Jhirka. Younger brothers have long been unhappy with the older—especially the inheriting—brother. Practically since birth, Ziauddin Ahmad Khan had been fed stories of Shamsuddin Ahmad's enviable good looks, his sense of dress and deportment, and also his vile temper, his avarice and rapine in claiming even that which was not his, and his unjust treatment of his younger brothers. Ziauddin Ahmad Khan was quite clear in his mind that Shamsuddin Ahmad, in being hanged by the Firangee, got nothing more than his just deserts.

Mirza Ghalib was the literary guru of both the brothers, but Ziauddin Ahmad had also imbibed the maestro's avowed dislike of Shamsuddin Ahmad Khan. Thus, quite unbeknownst to almost anyone, Shamsuddin Ahmad Khan became an object of hatred to the two brothers, and especially to the younger one, who somehow resented the eldest sibling's conquest of Wazir Khanam, a celebrated beauty, a woman of a tempestuous reputation whose charm was nothing short of miraculous. In addition to resentment, Ziauddin Ahmad Khan occasionally felt also an undefinable twinge of jealousy against the eldest brother's successes. Yet all that was very much in the realm of vague thought, or at best, in the realm of remote possibility. In his daily, practical life, he had never considered the matter at all. Now, when Shamsuddin Ahmad Khan was long dead, Aminuddin Ahmad Khan was also a different kind of thorn that pricked him: Aminuddin Ahmad Khan was in control of the Fort and the Durbar at Loharu, dispossessing him in practically the same way as Shamsuddin Ahmad Khan had done.

Thus, if Ziauddin Ahmad Khan was inclining towards Chhoti Begam, it was as no more than compensation for previous losses and hurts. It would have been appropriate for Chhoti Begam to participate in this process of compensation. By refusing him, she was being doubly unjust and was causing hurt to his male pride. He could not imagine that Chhoti Begam could also have some complaints against the world, or Fate. He spoke in a low voice, almost as if in soliloquy. 'Why should the tree of a life which regularly obtains a caregiver and a tender and attendant complain of ill fortune?'

'Every caregiver does some pruning, some barbering and some reduction. He doesn't just bestow; he also takes away quite much. It is a kind of symbiosis. So, if the caregiver's own tree of life be destroyed by sere, the poisonous tongue of autumn starts to eat into the tree which the caregiver was tending to. You are still . . .' She wanted to say, 'You are still young', but she checked herself in time. 'You are still . . . to examine this fact, Navab sahib: just as lack of a smooth run is inevitable for the course of a man's life, so also is he slave to his own fickle nature. Sometimes, he hates and rejects the soft bed; at other times, hot ashes feel like a mother's loving arms to him.'

'Such hair-splitting subtleties are well within my ability too, Chhoti Begam,' Ziauddin Ahmad Khan's tone of voice was cold, if not testy.

'This is exactly what this maidservant is submitting before you. This servant is Chhoti Khanam for some; for some, she is Wazir Khanam.'

This was transparent enough, even for the humourless young scholar-aristocrat. He smarted inwardly, but did not like to admit defeat. He was a Sayyid, but also a Mirza, after all.

'Well, I was quite keen to have a friendly meeting with you. That longing remains unfulfilled.' His smile was bitter, his words halting. 'Do I have permission to rub my forehead again on this threshold?'

'Navab sahib, this door is open to none. But you are not alien. You are not to be treated like another.'

She turned, so that her full face was now before Ziauddin Ahmad Khan. He gazed earnestly, trying to discern some hint of an encouraging smile, or some mild radiance of even a little personal inclination. But that superbly lovely face seemed somewhat stern, somewhat set. Ziauddin Ahmad Khan arose with a feigned air of indifference. After he had pushed his feet into his shoes, he stayed a moment and spoke a verse from Zuhuri, the sixteenth-century Persian poet whom Ghalib greatly admired:

So long as the breath holds
The thread of conversation,
One could go on weaving desires.

He bent in the style of the formal Mughal salaam, placed his right hand on his chest above his heart, and said, 'Do I have the permission to say: There are hundreds of accounts yet to be settled between us?'

Wazir did not rise from her place, but the tension in her body was as evident as the tension on her face. She clapped for Jani Ram with her back almost towards the young visitor. As she waited for the servant to appear, she laughed briefly and said, 'Only God is untouched by blemish! As if there's anything here that still remains to square the accounts.' She quoted a line of a Persian verse:

I washed my hands of the two worlds and settled all accounts.

Never had Ziauddin Ahmad Khan heard such a soft, musical and sad laughter. Something stirred in his inner self and ran down towards his loins. But the laughing girl had softly laughed her young lover's destiny out of her house.

*

The futility of that visit rankled Ziauddin Ahmad Khan for quite some time, but did not prevent his paying another two or three visits over the next two months. The series came to an end only when Wazir told him in clear words that the huge gap between their ages made it impossible in her eyes to consider any kind of liaison between them. Navab Mirza had, characteristically, shown no interest, or felt any real curiosity about how the relationship, if that it was, would develop. He was quite sure that his mother was the wisest and the most reliable of judges, and the most perfect of parents. No decision of hers needed any scrutiny or justification. But he worried about that most mundane of things: a comfortable life for his mother. Should she decide to develop some arrangement with Ziauddin Ahmad Khan, it was clear that it would include Shah Muhammad Agha as well. And in that case, Navab Mirza could contemplate going back to Rampur and obtaining some minor employment at the Court there. If, in the unlikely event of his mother having to sequester Shah Muhammad Agha, Manjhli Khala was always there to take him in, and Navab Mirza's salary in Rampur would be enough to supplement Manjhli Khala's material investment in the little boy.

He also had another plan in his mind about himself and his half-brother. On returning to Delhi, he visited his Bari Khala out of familial regard, and also because Bari Khala had a soft corner in her heart for him. This was partly because her Paradise-dwelling father had greatly loved Navab Mirza, and partly because she herself inclined to him on account of his good looks and courteous, respectful behaviour. There was also some transference or compensation: the love that she could not shower on her youngest sister had been shifted to her son without her even being conscious of it. Bari Khala did not invite Chhoti to visit, but told Navab Mirza in no uncertain terms that he and Shah Muhammad Agha were always welcome to her house. In fact, she hinted, should Chhoti make a suitable marriage but be unable to take care of the two sons, they were welcome to move in with her.

There was yet another attraction for Navab Mirza at Bari Khala's. It was her daughter: his cousin Fatimah. She was just about thirteen, extremely beautiful, quite like her mother in looks, deportment, domestic skills, observance of religious rituals and willingness to be helpful to her elders. In addition to knowing a bit of Arithmetic and Islamic History, she was literate in Hindi and Persian. She had a very good voice, and used it to good effect in singing poems in praise of the Prophet, and similar quasi-religious poetry on appropriate occasions. Navab Mirza's heart was instantly attracted to the lively but essentially artless young beauty. It was not yet clear if Fatimah, whom Navab Mirza named Pari Bano (Fairy Lady) partly to tease her, and partly by way of genuine tribute to her beauty, had some reciprocity for her decidedly good-looking cousin who was fast becoming popular as a poet; but love for Pari Bano very quickly made its home in Navab Mirza's heart.

It should be obvious that because of the numerous marts and houses of love in Delhi, and because of no particular blame attached to young men visiting them, Navab Mirza, like other young men of his age and class, was no stranger to the affairs of the bedchamber. In those days, a popular line of poetry was:

It is the lovers' honour
To be given beatings, and abuses.

The conventional interpretation was that it was the boys who mouthed abuses, and the nautch girls who delivered beatings. Navab Mirza was certainly of that impressionable age when every good-looking face made the heart long for it. Yet Fatimah was something else all over. Navab Mirza gave her the nickname Pari Bano not for his own, formal reasons: he really looked at her as some preternatural being, from outside this world. Sometimes he feared if delicate, slim, sweet as milk-and-sugar beloveds like Fatimah were made for physical love at all. For him at that time, those things seemed remote, unattainable and even impossible to happen anyway.

Navab Mirza's first problem was that though Bari Khala loved him inordinately, she was not too happy with his mother, and would therefore not even start to consider him as a prospective son-in-law. Like anyone inexperienced in a world driven by need and self-satisfaction, he did not know that in such matters, the girls' people looked at the son-in-law, not his parents. And Chhoti was, after all, her youngest sister, and the boy was, after all, not just a jobless poet: he was also the son of a powerful Navab, even if the father was dead; the fact of Navab Mirza's noble parentage remained, and would always remain.

In Navab Mirza's early poetry, traces and suggestions of personal experience and feelings can be discerned, but the interesting thing is that it has very little by way of the beloved's physical, bodily, female presence. Perhaps it was because he left those things out on purpose, and out of a sense of delicacy: his beloved was really a young girl who observed the purdah and who was his cousin as well. Let's look at some of his verses of those days in which the youthful lover boasts of his love's power, and also observes restraint and rectitude in giving words to his longings.

Judge for yourself: Was there such style, such composition of physical beauty before?
No. It was my love that refashioned you
In a new mould.

★

How can I do the impossible?
Explain to you the meaning of the word 'longing'?
It's just a word; I breathed it into your ears.

Self-appointed critics of poetry and morals of a later date have pronounced Dagh's poetry to be the favourite of singing and dancing girls. Perhaps it was how they saw things, but the transparent, youthful gravity, sophistication and restraint in the two verses quoted above do not at all seem to be of the nature of the erotic, easily accessible sentiments which should perhaps have met with the approval of those classes. Certainly, Navab Mirza's temperament had its share of gaiety and youthful abandon, but it was allowed entry into his poetry only rarely. The stage in his life that we are talking about was a trying time for him where his present seemed fraught with crisis and the future could not be descried even in imagination. His verses like the following ones date from that time:

The moth is close to the candle-flame,
The bulbul-lover is close to the beloved-rose;
Here am I, with you, but stung by seclusion.

★

Newly arisen desires, do not tease and tempt me;
My eager feet and longing hands,
Both are now lopped off.

A young man of fifteen or sixteen years would compose such poetry only when he was trying to do something other than creating themes in the abstract, as was the rule in those days. Verses like the following would result when the poet tried to come to terms with the beloved on a familiar, homey level:

So what would you have to do with the news of
Those whose wits are scattered?
Go on, take your time collecting and arranging
Your tresses.

The following verse is also part of the same ghazal. No wonder, a master so highbrow and full of gravitas as Sahbai rose from his place in an open mushairah and hugged Dagh when he spoke it:

What has happened, Dagh? You are mournful
And a silence has befallen you.
Dear luckless boy, do tell me some of your story.

Now look at this verse—it is the same tune of love, sung with a new theme; such poetry cannot be composed by the use of the power of reason, or just by artifice:

Simplicity, elegance, indifference, mischief, sauciness:
You've been given gifts of manners whose power
Only the loving heart can fathom but never express.

The great Persian poet Urfi narrated this theme in the sixteenth century in the intellectual and complex manner that was uniquely his:

At all times, every moment, I am taken
By a new unhappiness, for none of your styles
Is acquainted with the other.

Doubtless, Urfi's depiction of the theme of a beloved who has a thousand styles and manners of behaviour is subtle, and has greater possibilities of meaning than the comparatively simple utterance of Dagh, but the young poet's language has a simplicity and idiomatic flow which enables him to say much in less than a handful of words. Easy flow and a simple elegance which defies imitation, these were later recognized as the characteristic qualities of Dagh's works, but actually, they had always been present in his poetry. Possibly, it was his love for Fatimah which persuaded the newly blossomed plant and flower of the garden of poetry to narrate his love to his beloved in an affective, informal language not made complex by metaphor. Here, we may sample a few:

Death is better than the night of separation:
I can at least sleep well.

⋆

Dagh, the round will come to me surely, sometime;
Like the going round of days and nights.

⋆

She lets me have no rest, ever:
When I say, I die of love, she says:
Live you must!

⋆

That cruel one, when she heard my plight, said:
Better that he die than live like this.

⋆

You face is certainly radiant
Like the candle-flame; but what do you know
Of the pleasure of melting, and burning?

⋆

Well, it irks you to hear me praise your loveliness.
Right, far be the evil eye! My Beauty is superior!

⋆

No, no. Don't repent! Do not give up your cruelties!
Don't worry at all, Dagh is not dying yet.

No doubt, in regard to theme, these poems are not from a realm other than the convention-driven poems about imagined, amorous transactions between the lover and the beloved. But their tone seems to have a truth-based urgency of desire and appeal; the more we enjoy them as verbal artefacts, the more we are persuaded of their authenticity as personal utterances. Winning Fatimah's approval; making myriads of plans to bring a smile to her lips; feeling stricken for hours and hours on Fatimah's slightest gesture of neglect, imagined or real: the essence of all such states seems to permeate much of his early poetry. Making sure to go to Bari Khala's once or twice daily on one pretext or the other; offering his services for buying groceries; if, by any chance, Fatimah was not home, then nurturing a thousand complaints in his heart till he finally saw Fatimah face to face and she smilingly asked where he had been all that long: these things became the daily routine of his life.

On the other side, there was Fatimah: offering a betel cone or a glass of cool drink to Navab Mirza, a light rosy wave of bashfulness suffusing her face as she tries, with one hand, to keep her dupatta properly cover her upper body, while she balances the tray and glass or betel box with the other. Without making it obvious, she makes sure that the best food on the tablecloth should be first offered to Navab Mirza; she intuitively recognizes the rhythm of Navab Mirza's knock at the door; involuntarily raising her eyes towards the main door again and again if on any day she does not hear that knock even when the day was many hours old. What did all this signify, if not an entanglement of the heart?

With typical male self-regard, Navab Mirza did not know these things. But even he could see that there was an alacrity with which the honeyed voice responded to his knock: an alacrity which had a tint of bashfulness; a voice which had the delicateness and colour and warmth of the Marvel of Peru, the flower that blows just before midday, not bothered by the hot sunlight; a voice vibrant with life as it called out, 'Please come in. There is no purdah.' Navab Mirza clearly understood that the girl asking him to enter was not just being formally hospitable: she seemed to be saying, in unspoken words, a Hindi verse from the great eighteenth-century Persian poet, Bedil:

When, at the heart's door, Love arrived
And called; the Beloved called out from behind
The curtain: There's no one here called Bedil!

Navab Mirza's heart was burdened at that time with two problems, not one: to provide for his mother the wherewithal of a comfortable, peaceful life, and to make Fatimah his bride. Neither goal seemed achievable in the short term, or even in the medium one. Certainly, his reputation as a poet was growing, but he was not able to find a way to use that reputation for earning a respectable livelihood. He considered requesting Zahir to intercede on his behalf at the Red Haveli. But the fact of the matter was that he had no interest in an office job, or a station as quartermaster. He believed, in fact it was his faith, that poetry was sufficient for a poet. Vocation, avocation, a means of idling away the days: poetry should suffice for all purposes. The trouble was, his poetry at that time presented a living picture of Mushafi's rubai: his poetry was good for no purpose—mundane or sacred. The needs of living, the demands of duty; he was attaining full youth, and his longings and desires for the pleasures of love and pairing were also growing to full youth in his heart: all this was knocking away at the doors of his conscience and his consciousness. Navab Mirza was quite persuaded that no one in the whole city of Delhi was more frustrated, more dogged by ill luck than his poor self.

*

Navab Mirza was quite aware that his mother, if she was so minded, could easily make an arrangement—with or without marriage, with someone of her choice. But he also saw that his mother was on her way to becoming old, not only in her body and her visage, but also in her soul. As if, after losing so much, she no longer had the heart to lose more. It was also true that her mother had admirers other than poor Ziauddin Ahmad. Even the Sahib-e Alam wa Alamiyan Mirza Fathul Mulk Bahadur seemed to be still and in fact actively interested in her. Zahir Dihlavi told him once, after a session at the Fort, that the Sahib-e Alam wa Alamiyan had summoned Delhi's most famous painter Ustad Ghulam Ali Khan and desired him to find a portrait of Chhoti Begam.

Ustad Ghulam Ali Khan was now very old, and retired from the profession. But he ran an atelier which had many talented painters and cartographers. Despite his having retired, the old maestro was connected with the Fort, in the sense that the Shadow of God always accorded him a position of honour at the Court. Besides painting, he was adept at calligraphy, was extremely good in the social graces, and was a wonderful raconteur. His father, Ustad Mazhar Ali Khan, was a distinguished painter during the blessed and auspicious reign of the Presence, Emperor Akbar Shah II. Mazhar Ali Khan sahib was expert at sketching pictures of buildings in full, minute detail. His younger son was Ustad Faiz Ali Khan; this son, who was thus younger brother to Ustad Ghulam Ali Khan, gave up portrait painting many years ago and sketched pictures of buildings alone. It was partly in observance of the Shariah interdiction on sketching pictures of living beings and partly out of the desire to keep up his father's tradition. Zahir told Navab Mirza that Ustad Ghulam Ali Khan was promised by the Sahib-e Alam any reward that Khan sahib fancied, should he produce a portrait of Wazir Khanam.

Navab Mirza fell into thought. Should he tell his mother about this development? From where could Mian Ghulam Ali Khan obtain a picture of his mother? Asking his mother entailed revealing all. He was still cogitating upon the problem when quite by chance he learnt at Bari Khala's that a portrait of his mother had been painted when she was in the bloom of her youth and it was now owned by some nobleman. Bari Khala gave him the information with not a little disapproval. The occasion for the matter coming up was a discussion about making likenesses in stone, or even on paper. She said that the Prophet of God specifically banned it because it led to the violation of the purdah. Navab Mirza longed in his heart somewhere to have a portrait of Fatimah made by some master and keep it clasped to his breast all his life. The discussion in fact began with his tentative thoughts about having portraits of one's loved ones as remembrance. He did not succeed much in obtaining his purpose, but ended with at least this miscellaneous information about his mother.

*

Mian Ghulam Ali Khan was the acknowledged Master Painter of the day; he also knew much about paintings and their history and provenance. He had little difficulty in finding out that while the original had been sold off to an

Englishman, an imperfect copy of it existed with a dealer in old paintings. Mian Ghulam Ali Khan had the picture bought through a pupil for the sum of twenty rupees and gave it to the brighter ones in his atelier to make a better copy with a few years added to the sitter's age. The portrait was ready within a few days; the ustad then gave it his characteristic finishing touches and added refinements.

Ustad Ghulam Ali Khan's main instruction to the atelier painters was to draw the portrait—contrary to the standard, traditional practice—as if the sitter was aware of the painter, or the gazer; this was in accordance with the Company School of painting, and in keeping with the preference of Sahib-e Alam wa Alamiyan, who inclined towards modernity. The ancient ustad himself was taken aback when he looked at the finished picture. He sent salutations to the Prophet in his heart . . . his hands trembled for a moment: the picture seemed more alive than a living human being. Did Wazir Khanam's spirit somehow float in and energize the portrait to life for a heartbeat?

The maestro was all aquiver, inwardly. But no, certainly not. Flesh and bone could never attain such appropriation of the laws of God. And the Bibi who sits here could not have the smallest inkling of her portrait being drawn, here or elsewhere. But what mystery is this? It seems as if the sitter was just about to quit the portrait and step out . . . This is not inscribing a picture: this is inscribing magic, and the magic is nowhere else but in the sitter; he who made the drawing could never have imagined the finished picture could plunder the old painter's senses and art both at the same time.

With his old, trembling hands, the ustad wrapped the painting in a silk portfolio and presented himself at the Fort at the time when the Sahib-e Alam wa Alamiyan's Court usually assembled. The Prince glanced at the painting, locked it in his private box and had two hundred rupees awarded to Ustad Ghulam Ali Khan.

Mirza Fathul Mulk Bahadur was in a hurry to wrap up his Court, but he did everything according to his wonted practice and in keeping with his own rules. He was conscious, more than any other Prince or Princess of the Realm, or other hundreds of Royal descendants who lived in the Fort, of the qualitative change in the structure of politics and power of his land. Perhaps the Exalted King was more acutely aware, but there was none else who was certain that the Empire's sun would never rise again. This was not just because of the many weaknesses of the Empire that emerged a century ago. It was also because of an alien presence in their midst. That alien presence was impinging not just on economics, trade and money: it had become the most effective presence on the chequerboard of political power, methods of governance, and military strategy. The Firangee's impact changed the values that had been attached to art, poetry, social conventions; it changed the myths and narratives of the main communities on the political and social stage, history and legend. They were increasingly successful in teaching the Hindustani that the values that he loved, the lights which he hoped to lead him into worldly success and Heavenly favour, were false, or at best outdated.

The Third Heir Apparent believed that the change in the circumstances of a people contained a hidden message for the wise: since circumstances change, they can also be made to change, or can be moulded to suit those who had the requisite will and knowledge; or we can ourselves develop new capabilities to enable us to take advantage of the changed circumstances. He employed an English tutor to teach him English, maintained a sizeable library, and was also meticulous in observing the mandates of the Shariah without being bigoted about them. Kingship would of course go to the First Heir Apparent, Mirza Dara Bakht, but the Third Heir Apparent loved the history and the traditions of his illustrious ancestors more than the Royal Throne of Delhi. He had fashioned his lifestyle and conduct much on the pattern which, according to him, his status as a Prince of the Realm demanded. Anyone may be King; kingship is not everything; what matters is the standard of conduct of the princes whose forebears were Babur and Akbar.

The Court concluded, and Mirza Ghulam Fakhruddin Fathul Mulk Bahadur rose to proceed to his private chamber; his principal mace-bearer was immediately behind, with the Prince's private box, while two mace-bearers were in front. Once he reached his chamber, he made the gesture for all to leave. He took out the portrait from the box.

The eyes reflected such a powerful consciousness of youth and sexuality that Prince Mirza Ghulam Fakhruddin Fathul Mulk Bahadur almost dropped the painting from his weakening grasp. It seemed as if the portrait was just about to make some gesture—a flicker of her eyes, a lifting of her eyebrows—but the gesture was absolutely devoid of invitation or vulgarity. The delicate, well-formed face was almost dominated by large eyes overhung with long eyelashes, but the eyes were not demurely lowered.

They were dark brown with subtle hints of red streaks in the whites; the face exuded a desirable coolness, something like a bunch of freshly bloomed wild roses. The long, proud neck was like that of a deer's, on which was a necklace of emeralds, stretching from near the collarbone to the delicately but clearly hinted cleavage. The stones were all of equal size—half of a chickpea—their greenness cool, attracting the viewer's eyes just like how a border of green grass around a flower bed would. The head was not covered with the hem of the dupatta, but it was clear that the sitter was not overly concerned about her bared head.

Her age, just like mine, give or take a year or two at best. But who cared about the concord or discord in the number of years? The important thing was that the face, the neck, the shoulders, the arms, seemed to have been energized into life by the magic of some powerful urge—the urge to be alive in a world that would surely look dead without her. It was not a painting: it was a running, lively stream of life, flowing with the lifeblood of the sitter; a stream in which one had a compelling desire to immerse oneself.

*

Mirza Muhammad Sultan Ghulam Fakhruddin Fathul Mulk Shah Bahadur, affectionately known everywhere as Mirza Fakhru, was at that time thirty-four years old. Someone truly brilliant at devising chronograms used the numerical value of the Quranic verse *Inna fatahna laka fathan mubinan* ('Without doubt, We made thee victorious with an extremely open victory') to make the chronogram of the date of his birth AH 1254, to equal 1812 according to the English calendar. Its beauty and appropriateness should become clear when we consider his name: Fathul Mulk (Victory of the Land). He was the fourth son of Abu Zafar Muhammad Sirajuddin Bahadur Shah, who adorned the Throne of the Empire on 29 September 1837. At the time of his coronation, Muhammad Dara Bakht Bahadur, affectionately known as Miran Shah, was the eldest son. Immediately after the assumption of the throne by Bahadur Shah, Thomas Metcalfe proclaimed Muhammad Dara Bakht Bahadur Heir Apparent, presenting him five gold mohurs as nazr: the formal, ceremonial present.

The son next to Miran Shah Bahadur was Mirza Muhammad Shah Rukh Bahadur: he was proclaimed Prime Minister and General Plenipotentiary. The third son, Mirza Kayumars Bahadur, was appointed Second Heir

Apparent. Mirza Muhammad Sultan Fathul Mulk Shah Bahadur, the fourth son, was proclaimed Third Heir Apparent. It is not clear why in spite of his being appointed to the most powerful posts of Prime Minister and General Plenipotentiary—we might recall that Mahada ji Sindhia was graced with similar titles by Shah Alam Bahadur Shah II, Absolute Plenipotentiary and Minister in Chief—Mirza Muhammad Shah Rukh Bahadur was not declared Second Heir Apparent and why he was given no place in the order of succession.

Possibly, Mirza Muhammad Shah Rukh Bahadur was not much liked by the Emperor. It was popularly believed that Mirza Kayumars Bahadur considered himself most suited for appointment as First Heir Apparent by virtue of his personal ability, though some said that it was ambition more than anything else. The Mughal State had never had a post or rank of Heir Apparent. The successor to the Sovereign was determined after his death by plain bloodshed, or civil war. The English, with their typical ways of interventionism and desire to fashion things Indian in their own image, imposed the rule of primogeniture and decided, during the reign of Akbar Shah II, that the eldest son of the Sovereign should be the Heir Apparent. Hence the Proclamation, simultaneously with the coronation of Bahadur Shah, of Mirza Dara Bakht as Heir Apparent. This did not actually shut the door on other princes that they stopped trying, or scheming, or machinating to succeed the ruling Sovereign.

Mirza Fakhru was highly educated, like almost all Princes of the Realm of that age. He was master of many calligraphic styles, and had the rank of supreme master in music and dance. He was also an expert rider and archer. He knew English reasonably well. He was a substantial poet in Hindi, or Rekhta. His pen name was Ramz; and he was the pupil of Shaikh Zauq in that discipline. He did not compose in Persian, but was an avid student of its prose and poetry, and was the pupil of Sahbai in Persian. As we have seen above, he was almost the perfect image of his father. Unlike other Princes of the Realm, Mirza Fakhru rode into the city on occasion, and had friendly intercourse with some distinguished natives and also Firangees.

In spite of, or perhaps because of, his outstanding qualities, Mirza Fakhru was not very popular at Court. He certainly had a clear head on his shoulders: he was conscious of the change that was overtaking society and state everywhere in the vast empire that had been ruled by his ancestors. He believed it necessary for the Sovereign and his Government to resist, or to adapt to the change. He wished himself to be a man of the thirteenth century, equipped with new weapons to face and overcome the adverse circumstances. Perhaps the Shadow of God was suspicious of change and adaptation, and Mirza Fakhru represented just those things. He was determined to follow his own path.

Contrary to most Timurid princes, the love life of Mirza Fakhru was not marked by oversexuality. His first and truly beloved wife was his cousin Fazilat-un Nisa Begam, daughter of the cavalier, jaunty, handsome Prince Mirza Jahangir Bakht, known for his rebelliousness against the English, and younger brother of the King. As we narrated earlier, he was exiled by the Firangee and died in 1821, during his second exile. The daughter was as much renowned for her beauty throughout the Red Haveli and the Timurid clan as her father had been reputed for his good looks. Fazilat-un Nisa Begam, too, did not live long. She was the mother, with Mirza Fakhru, of Mirza Abu Bakr. The young son earned renown, along with his uncle Mirza Zahiruddin, better known as Mirza Mughal, during the rising of 1857 against the Firangee and then during the defence of Delhi. Mirza Abu Bakr, Mirza Mughal and Mirza Khizr Sultan were among the princes murdered by Hodson in cold blood after the retaking of Delhi in September 1857.

Mirza Fathul Mulk Bahadur remarried only after the death of Fazilat-un Nisa Begam. His second wife was Hatim Zamani Begam, daughter of Mirza Hidayat Afza, better known as Mirza Ilahi Bakhsh. A daughter was born from this marriage. The King Emperor showed great favour to the daughter-in-law, or perhaps to Mirza Ilahi Bakhsh, by being present at the music and dance shows organized at the weaning ceremony of that daughter and bestowing rewards and gifts to all who were present. This Mirza Ilahi Bakhsh is the same who was reputed to be a secret enemy of the King Emperor and was suspected to be spying against the Haveli for the English. The Firangee honoured him greatly at the cessation of fighting and restoration of English rule after they took Delhi in September 1857. They even proclaimed him head of the Royal family. There were indications that relations between Mirza Fakhru and Hatim Zamani Begam were not too cordial.

*

Mirza Muhammad Sultan Fathul Mulk Bahadur put the portrait down, but kept it in front of him. He had had occasion to see Navab Mirza on many other occasions, besides the brief meeting at Qadam Sharif. He could now appreciate the reason why the young man was so outstandingly good-looking, and still so very dark of aspect. He thought of putting the painting away in his secure box, so that the eyes of someone undesirable might not fall upon it. But he feared that if he took it in his hands again, he would be hard put to prevent himself from putting it inside his tunic, near his heart. Indeed, Mian Ghulam Ali Khan was an incredible master.

But how should he go about meeting her, or approaching her? Should he propose marriage, or just an arrangement to live with him? But if she refused to be my concubine, or to live separately but bound to him alone? He had heard some vague report of Ziauddin Ahmad Khan making overtures to her, but did not know of the outcome of it. If Wazir Khanam was a woman who really possessed depth of thought and feeling, and dignity and self-control, as she seemed to in portrait, it was more than possible that she could spurn him from her door as a callow young man . . . How should I open a conversation with her? True, I have social relations with the notables in the city, both with those from our side and from the Firangee's, but meeting her at one of those formal, constrained occasions is one thing, and my going to knock at her door is something else again. It will be a huge loss of face for me if she refuses . . . And how can I bear to live without her?

Very gently, a mace-bearer pulled the curtain apart by a few inches and spoke timidly, 'Your Honour Sahib-e Alam, the ustad has arrived and seeks permission to enter.'

Mirza Ghulam Fakhruddin started a bit and quickly placed Wazir's portrait in his secure box. He rubbed his face and eyes, as if just woken from sleep.

'The ustad's noble presence is here? Very good. He may be permitted to enter.'

'Sir. Noble Presence,' saying this, the mace-bearer briefly beckoned to Ustad Zauq who stood just behind him. Zauq drew the curtain aside and entered, speaking with a voice full of eagerness, as if meeting the Sahib-e Alam was what he had desired most in life.

'I make my submissions, Sahib-e Alam. How is His Honour feeling today?'

'Welcome, you are very welcome. Come in, Presence; take your seat near me.' Mirza Fathul Mulk rose to his full height and spoke with genuine pleasure.

Shaikh Muhammad Ibrahim was about sixty years of age, of average height, with a well-proportioned body. He was a good-looking man; his beard a little longer than the minimum prescribed by the Shariah, pepper and salt, not too dense, pointed, and trimmed with care. His moustaches were not dense, but not close cropped either, just as were considered desirable by the Shariah. He had on a four-cornered black velvet cap with a wide bullion lace around the edge. His tunic was of pale- green muslin, and against the fashion, the muslin was not so fine as to permit a vague glimpse of the chest underneath. Over the tunic he had the short, white, half-sleeved coat called the nima, made from the Aurangabadi fabric mashru; above the nima, he had a light-coloured caftan in chintz. His trousers were of the thin striped cotton called sangi; the bottoms were so wide that they would have covered his shoes, if he had had his shoes on. He had removed his shoes before entering the chamber, as required by protocol. His complexion was quite dark, while his brow was high and his nose straight, giving the impression of a lively temperament. Although heavily pockmarked, his face reflected alertness and intelligence, very nearly cancelling out the uncomeliness of the pocks. His eyes were large and bright, with a glance that was sharp and interested. His carriage and bearing bespoke his mental acuity and self-confidence.

Ustad Zauq moved up the large chamber, sure-footed, his eyes strictly in front. He embraced the Prince with unaffected warmth; Mirza Fathul Mulk kissed his right hand, and giving him place next to himself, he opened a small box in gold filigree and took out a few silver-coated cardamoms and a few small pieces of betel nuts treated with scented tobacco and appropriate spices. Placing the condiments on his right palm, he offered them to the ustad and said, 'Take a look at these, if you please. The hookah will be ready in a minute.'

'Sir, it is the Sahib-e Alam's great kindness, but I would deem it an act of nurturing your subject if I was not vouchsafed the hookah at this time.' He picked up a couple of cardamoms and salaamed.

Not accepting the tokens of hospitality from a Prince of the Realm would be regarded as almost lese-majesty in the case of others. But Zauq was the Prince's ustad, and was permitted such familiarities. Mirza Fakhru smiled.

'Indeed, you are a master of subtle points. It should be regarded as the nurturing of our people if something of ours did not reach you.'

Shaikh Zauq sensed a faint tint of reprimand in the Prince's words. Perhaps he did not view with favour his ustad's not accepting the offer of the hookah. The ustad hastened to make amends: 'The Sahib-e Alam's nurture of his subjects is clearer and brighter than the sun. All of us indeed take our bread from your tablecloth.' Zauq smiled disarmingly. 'Being bestowed the hookah from your porte is my good fortune, plain and simple. Sir, I am afflicted with a racking cough these past three days. Sleep has become a forbidden commodity for me. The instruction from Umdat-ul Hukama is that I must entirely eschew everything which has smoke, or dark vapour.'

The long apologia restored the Prince's good humour. He said, 'No, not at all. How could I be the cause of a lack of comfort for you? Do not engage yourself with the hookah, if you do not feel like it.'

In the meantime, a mace-bearer had entered, bearing a silver tray on which there were two smaller silver plates, loaded with dry fruits. The ustad bent low from the waist, picked two almonds from a tray, put them in his mouth and submitted with a smile, 'Your Honour. On these almonds someone should sacrifice their eyes!'

'Yes, sir,' Fathul Mulk replied with a smile. 'Oh look, here is a metrical line: "The hint is that you must take your eyes out and make me a present of them."' He then looked expectantly at his ustad, as if he desired a line to cap his line, thus making, perhaps, an opening verse. Well, themes used to stand before Zauq, their hands folded submissively, waiting to be noticed. It was just like the great Arab poet Imraul Qais, who once wrote that rhyme words were before him like a locust swarm before a boy: by the time he caught two, four had eluded his grasp.

The ustad folded his hands on his chest and submitted, 'I do not have the worth to open my mouth in front of a son of my Mentor and Guide. I just submit an opening verse in compliance to the command.'

'Very good, Ustad. Please command.'

With his hands still folded on his chest, Zauq recited the opening verse:

She sent me a couple of almonds in a little purse;
The hint is that I must take my eyes out and make her a present of them.

'Oh my dear Ustad! You are a rare jewel of the age! By Allah, it is an opening verse to beat all opening verses. One would love to kiss your hands for it!' Mirza Fathul Mulk Bahadur was ecstatic.

Zauq half rose from his place, made a salaam, and said, 'It is nothing of my own, Presence. It is just a generous wavelet from your House. But Sahib-e Alam must surely have composed something recently. Will you send us, who are thirsty for the Water of Life of your poetry, back home, crying: "We are burning"?'

Mirza Ghulam Fakhruddin's face betrayed some abashment, some confusion even. He was silent for a few seconds, and then said, 'Ustad, I don't know what calamity or adversity overtook me last night. I could not sleep a wink; the entire night passed but I could do no more than change from one side to the other and pray for sleep to come soon. And you know that famous ghazal of Shaikh Nasikh's, from Lucknow:

I cannot forget her, wherever I go.
I am at my wits' end: What should I do?
Where should I go?

'That was exactly my state last night. I said this verse to myself over and over again. The maids on duty to pat and knead my body to sleep recited the Quranic Verse of The Chair and blew it on me a number of times, but sleep did not come, it just did not come. Finally, it was your own last verse from your famous poem that accurately portrayed my state:

Welcome to amplitude, O Muezzin, you called
Quite on time. May your voice carry
To Mecca, and Medina!

'The muezzin at Zinat-un Nisa Begam's mosque called out for the pre-dawn prayer. I sprang from the bed, made the ablutions, said the prayers somehow and went back to my bed. I dozed off, when, I don't know. But when I woke up, I had again that very verse of the Presence, Shaikh Nasikh, on my tongue.'

Ustad Zauq pricked up his ears, and continued to do so as the Prince's narrative proceeded. It was the Fort, after all: new rumours became current here every day. By the time one rumour had lived out its life, or one was proven wrong, two new ones of a similar type gained circulation within no time. Like all good courtiers, Zauq also kept himself informed of all news, gossip, rumours and frivolities that made the rounds of the Haveli at all times and in all seasons. Thus the news that the Prince had summoned Ustad Ghulam Ali Khan and commissioned him for a portrait of Chhoti Begam reached him as soon as it left the Fort. Now, when he heard the Sahib-e Alam's narrative of his sleepless night, and his calling to mind Nasikh's opening verse on the theme of separation, he at once sounded the depth of the rumours: doubtless, the Sahib-e Alam is stricken; his heart is now entangled somewhere. May God have mercy upon him and upon us; he seems to be smitten badly.

There was, of course, no question of asking him about it. He just listened to the Prince's speech with full attention, exhibiting sympathy and anxiety on his face. Now when Sahib-e Alam recited Zauq's own verse, and paused for a few seconds, Ustad Zauq submitted, 'I am quite certain; the sleeplessness must have spurred the steed of His Honour's poetic temperament. How could a poetic genius, which is full to overflowing with thoughts, desist and stay?'

The Prince smiled a brief smile. 'Sir, I did compose a verse or two on the pattern of Shaikh Nasikh's ghazal. By and by, I might complete a ghazal. At present I bring before the Presence a few verses, hoping to be favoured with correction.'

'Ah! Very good, indeed. Only God is untouched by blemish! Please do command.'

The Prince folded his hands on his chest and said the opening verse:

I find no trace of her wherever I go;
Now where should I go with my eager heart?

'Only God is untouched by blemish! Sahib-e Alam, it's a very good opening verse.' The ustad spoke spontaneously. 'Even the Shaikh's soul must be ecstatic in the Higher Realm!'

'Presence, you drag me over thorns!' Mirza Fakhru smiled in pleasure. 'Now listen to the next; it should be worth something, I hope.' The Prince recited:

Should your sorrow not hold me back,
I should leave this world
And go to the next world.

He looked at Zauq with expectant eyes. The ustad did not also stint—he gave rapturous praise. He was about to say something more when the Prince said, 'Ustad, let this one too reach your auspicious ears.'

'Certainly, most certainly. Let's see if you could find a theme better than the previous one! Nowadays the flow of Sahib-e Alam's poetic inspiration would outdo the flow of the Ganga and Jamna.'

The Prince said:

I am the apparent; she, the spirit of the unapparent;
I should go where I am not.

Ustad Zauq struck his side in a state of exuberant appreciation. 'Doubtless, now Sahib-e Alam has attained the rank of ustad. Let there be no doubt about it! Who else could compose such a poem? May Allah increase, and increase again, your capabilities.'

A hint of moisture seemed to touch Mirza Ghulam Fakhruddin Bahadur's expressive eyes. He half rose and made a salaam to his ustad. In his heart, he said: 'Our grasp in the human world is now about zero; the heart's state, too, is a world, both hellish and paradisal. Would that we had some power over that world at least!' Before his mind's eye, he saw the mysterious smile of Wazir Khanam, a smile which was farthest from being flirtatious, but which also seemed to declare that should there be someone deserving in quality, someone whom she could choose, the smile then could open for him the door to the blossoming of the heart's desires, a whole world of gladness that only poets and lovers can know. In every bower of the garden of the spirit, it can let bloom new boughs of the pleasures of life and death. The upraised and proud neck exuding the haughty pride of beauty and the self-assurance of being desired; the neck which no one could bend, but which promised, or held out the possibility of bending double in pain, should one whom she loved be pricked even by the tiniest thorn. I am dense, visible, polluted by the apparent world, and she, subtle and soft and delicate like the unapparent world. How could I ever go there, how could I ever reach her?

Ustad Shaikh Muhammad Ibrahim Zauq was well acquainted with his King, and with each of his patrons in the Auspicious Fort, their temperaments and their preferences. He had a fairly good notion of the meaning and significance of his Sahib-e Alam's absorption, the mood of his recent poems. It occurred to him that a door seemed to be opening for Chhoti Begam. But what do I have to do with that? The business of the Sultanate was not any longer there; now the conquests of hearts and the running of writs over them were all that were there to be termed conquests and establishing sway over new territories. May she prove auspicious for the Prince. Chhoti Begam was a diamond, but whoever had her as an ornament for his turban soon ended up on a dunghill.

Sahib-e Alam wa Alamiyan Mirza Muhammad Sultan Fathul Mulk Bahadur raised his head and even a hardened courtier like Ustad Zauq was shaken inwardly to see that the Prince's visage and person revealed a dignity, a haughty presence, occupying a largeness of space that he had never seen before: it was if what was before him was not an old and frail moth-eaten banyan tree from the decrepit garden of the present century, but a proud, dense, shady plane tree in the wide, wild meadows spreading out into the vast opennesses of Samarqand and Khiva, raising its head in hauteur and spreading its bosom in generosity, giving benefit to persons and beings from near and far. And . . .

'Ustad, we are truly obliged.' The Prince's voice broke into his thoughts. Zauq knew that the giving of thanks was a signal for him to take his leave. He rose, made three salaams. The Prince, already lost in his waking reverie, did not move from his place; he just brought his right hand over his left breast, and said, 'In Allah's protection', and bent his head again. He did not know when the mace-bearer pulled the curtain aside, when the ustad set foot outside the chamber, or when the shoe-bearer put his shoes on his feet.

The ustad walked behind a female bodyguard, eyes in front; his steps measured and grave, he went past the ornamental pond and marble seats called savan bhadon—the Indian names of the two rainiest months—through the walkways around the flower beds until he arrived at the deep well where another female bodyguard took charge of him and escorted him up to the passage leading to the massive Lahori Gate. Two shield-bearers took over from there and led him up to the guardhouse of Lahori Gate where they salaamed and left him.

The Sahib-e Alam, the moment Ustad Zauq's went out of the chamber, walking backwards, opened the box and took out the portrait.

60

Scholar and creator of riddles, Maulavi Imam Bakhsh Sahbai attempts to solve the Prince's dilemma

THAT WHOLE NIGHT was very hard on Mirza Fakhru: to drag its darkness up to the dawn of day. Getting to know Wazir Khanam and establishing relations with her—not just relations, but a lifetime of fellowship—had quickly become the greatest need of his being. Had he regarded Wazir as a woman of the profession, of however restricted a social life and however many conditions she imposed to grant her favours, but a professional woman nevertheless, the matter would not have been difficult at all. But his heart refused to regard her as a sex object, as a saleable or exchangeable commodity. It was not that he did not know of Wazir's past history. In fact, the whole of Delhi knew of her history. And everyone knew that after Nur Bai a century and more ago, if there was a woman from outside the class of the begams, or a woman of the marketplace—you could take your pick—whose name, whose qualities of beauty and the power in taking men's hearts, were the talk of the town, it was Wazir Khanam. It would not be far wrong to say that a whole age was her lover, sight unseen. There was something else too: Not everyone could dream of having access to her doorstep. The story of what had happened with Navab Ziauddin Ahmad Khan had now become well known as news, or rumour, or gossip among those citizens of Delhi who regarded enjoying the air of the lanes and bylanes of sex and love as a necessity of life; or if not a necessity of life, they found a desirable and enjoyable pastime in keeping themselves in the picture about the goings-on in those streets.

Mirza Fathul Mulk Bahadur was not a man of appetites. Unlike his father, he had no interest in marrying frequently and fathering children on his wives. His interest in the 'mistresses of joy' and in matters of losing or winning hearts was not at all greater than what was then routine with the rich and the noble. In Wazir Khanam, he was looking not for a bedmate, but a mate for life. He sought her not just because of her beauty's renown, which reached him from many sources, and had just been verified as true by her portrait. To have the heart engaged with someone was an important purpose of life for him; but having the heart engaged and having the heart diverted were two different things in his lexicon.

Quite late at night, Mirza Fakhru thought of Imam Bakhsh Sahbai, his teacher and friend who had been his instructor in Persian for years. Well known in the city as a scholar, poet and expert creator of some of the most puzzling word riddles that fell to the misfortune of anyone to solve, he was not much older than Mirza Fakhru. He soon became more a companion than ustad, or even courtier to the Prince. Because he had a fine sense of humour, he almost always succeeded in improving the Prince's mood when he was out of sorts or upset for any reason. Consulting with Sahbai had an added advantage: by virtue of his good relations with the religious and Sufi elite of the city, he could easily be the negotiator or go-between for approaching Wazir Khanam.

⋆

The next morning, Maulavi Sahbai was just through with his late morning prayer when a mace-bearer arrived from Sahib-e Alam wa Alamiyan with the gift of a medium-sized clay drinking pot full of cold milk, another but somewhat larger pot containing hot gulab jamun—the dark, soft and extremely rich sweet much favoured by both the rich and poor in Delhi—as well as another, similar pot containing mal pua, a deep-fried, heavily sugared pancake, much favoured for breakfast by the elites of Delhi. He also brought the message that the Sahib-e Alam wa Alamiyan has sent breakfast and has desired Maulavi sahib's presence at the Auspicious Haveli, in the special chamber of the Third Heir Apparent. The mace-bearer was dismissed, but not before he was suitably rewarded. Something like three-quarters of an hour later, Maulavi sahib rode away to the Red Haveli with reasonable haste.

Sahbai was a little shy of forty at that time—he was slim, almost thin, and his facial features were soft; thus he looked nearer thirty than forty. His beard was in the Mughal style, not heavy, and thinner in the upper part of the face above the chin. He wore a white pair of trousers, unfashionably narrow-bottomed, and a four-cornered cloth cap, again white, picked with a light blue and golden lace at the edge. His hair was shoulder length, in the approved fashion, very black, bright and neatly combed. His long cotton tunic was in very light blue, and his short coat over it was of a shade deeper blue. Over it all, he used to wear a plain caftan, light or heavy, according to the weather. In short, Sahbai was a good-looking and frugally dressed man, but the dress suited his thin form very well. His sunny temperament was reflected in his smiling visage.

In Persian language and literature, he was second to none in Delhi, except Mirza Ghalib, and perhaps Hakim Momin Khan Momin. In Arabic, he was outdone by none throughout the land of Hind, except Maulana Fazl-e Haq Khairabadi. From his father's side, he traced his lineage back to Umar, Islam's second Caliph; from his mother's side, he was a Sayyid, tracing his genealogy to the great Sufi saint, the Presence, Abdul Qadir Jilani of the twelfth century in Iraq. He did not come from a prosperous family, and had to subsist on the fixed pay he drew from Delhi College. The pay was not meagre according to the standard of living in those days, but there has always been a social gap between one who lived on unearned income and one who had to earn his living. Aristocratic poets like Mirza Ghalib did not regard him as their equal, his great erudition notwithstanding. Another point was that Sahbai was the youngest among the prominent men of learning contemporaneous to him in Delhi.

Nevertheless, Sahbai's facility and expertise at creating riddles and in Prosody and Rhetoric made him a much-sought-after maestro in Delhi. It was said that he would compose a two-line verse by way of a riddle, which concealed hundreds of proper names. Many who were interested, or some who thought they were clever enough to solve the riddles, were obliged to accept defeat and knock at his learned door to find the solution.

Rekhta Prosody will always owe Sahbai a debt of gratitude for his translation, in Hindi, of the eighteenth-century Persian tract on the subject. Called *Hadaiq-al Balaghah* and composed by Shamsuddin Faqir, it is regarded as the most authoritative text on Persian Prosody written in India. Sahbai's innovation was that in his translation he replaced the original Arabic and Persian examples with Hindi ones, thus making the text more accessible to the students and practitioners of Hindi literature. During the days we are telling you about, his riddles made on God's ninety-nine names had become a challenge to the students; they could not really be understood properly in spite of the author's own explication. Many of them eluded even Hakim Momin Khan Momin who had some aptitude for riddles. Sahbai's tract on composing riddles, called *Ganjinah-e Rumuz* (Treasury of Riddles) was the talk of the city's literati in those days.

It was the Prince's practice to first ask Sahbai on every meeting, 'Ustad, do you have a new riddle for me?' Then Sahbai would say his riddle and the Prince would rack his brains to break it; he often failed, but the unwritten rule was that if Mirza Fakhru solved the riddle, the ustad would reward him with a quarter-rupee coin (almost pure silver then). If the Prince accepted defeat, he paid a fine of one rupee to the maestro.

The day we are talking about, Mirza Fakhru opened the conversation with his usual, 'Ustad, some new riddle?'

Maulana Sahbai placed his hand above his heart. 'Sir, riddles I could compose by the thousand. Our being is itself a riddle. But this riddle is a strange, headless and legless thing; if we place the head where the foot is, and place the foot where the head is, then its existence will become common. Then what price my riddle, Sahib-e Alam?'

Obviously, Sahbai's speech was in the mode of a riddle. The Sahib-e Alam fell into thought: he must arrive at the solution and give a suitable riddle-like reply to the ustad in the same idiom, or he would cut a truly sorry figure. Suddenly, he heard a maid passing by in the corridor, muttering something about 'khassi' ('castrated') goats whose meat the Sahib-e Alam did not like. By association, the word 'khass' ('special') flashed before his mind's eye; from 'khass', he jumped to 'akhass' ('most special'); he then immediately made the transition to its antonym 'aamm' ('most common, most ordinary'). Now it was easy: all of it played on the various Arabic roots. In Arabic and Hindi, 'riddle' is the same as the Arabic 'muamma'. Cut off its head, you get 'amma'. Cut off the foot, 'amm' results. Now transpose head and feet and you get 'amam', pronounced 'aamm'. But pronunciation-wise, the word suggested 'ama', which in Arabic, and sometimes in Rekhta or Hindi, means 'blind'.

So he said: 'Ustad should be good enough to say something about the ama.' His was hinting that he had solved 'aamm' and was teasing him with 'ama', which was from a different root altogether, but created the illusion of a commonality of root.

'Who wouldn't admire the long reach of the Sahib-e Alam's reasoning power?' he said gravely. 'But if you were to cut off "muamma's" head yet another time and join it to his feet, then—God forbid—will you regard your honourable uncle as "blind"?'

Sahbai's expression was deadly grave, like a man of learning giving an examination. No one could imagine that he was still playing in the riddle mode. But Mirza Fakhru was well versed in his mentor's ways; he knew that he was being challenged to another riddle. He thought, cut off the head of 'muamma' and you get 'amma' which can be read as plain 'ama' because in the Hindi style of writing, the doubling of the sound was not explicitly shown. Now this 'ama' clearly sounds similar to 'ama' ('blind') which we encountered earlier. Now if we detach the foot of 'muamma', that is, 'a', and join it to 'ama' . . . no, no, we should join it to the foot of 'ama': we get 'amam', and we know that it is the plural of 'amm', meaning 'uncle'.

'No, Presence. Never,' the Prince answered. 'We believe in "kulla amin". How could we think ill of anyone, far less of our revered uncles?'

Now this was a clever thing to say. For 'am', which generally means 'common', also means 'year' in Arabic. In those days, as now, the Arabic phrase of greeting *kulla amin wa antum bikhair* ('the whole year, all of you may be well') was quite popular.

Sahbai smiled with pleasure. So my pupil is bright, and has learnt well from me. But clearly, he could not have summoned me so urgently for solving riddles. Anyway, he must wait for the Prince to open the conversation. Just as he was suggesting to Sahib-e Alam that he try his riddle-solving skills on one of his verses which was considered well-nigh unsolvable by all aficionados of riddle making and solving, when quite unexpectedly, the mace-bearer announced the arrival of Prince Mirza Qadir Bakhsh Sabir, another poet and pupil of Maulavi Sahbai. On hearing about Sahbai's visit, he had come to pay his regards. It was rumoured (God save us from the rumour mills of the Haveli!) that Sabir's voluminous account of Hindi poets, called *Gulistan-e Sukhan* (Garden of Poetry) had not been merely gone over by the learned ustad, he had actually dictated it to his pupil. Mirza Sabir was only a couple of years older than Mirza Fathul Mulk Bahadur, and was nowhere in the line of succession, but was respected greatly by all the princes because of his lineage: his father, Mirza Mukarram Bakht, was a direct descendant of Emperor Aurangzeb.

They talked for some time about Sahbai's riddle mentioned above but to no avail. Finally, Sahbai produced the incredibly complicated solution and fully defeated Mirza Fathul Mulk Bahadur's boast that he was going to 'hit the ustad for a quarter-rupee today'. By the time Sabir left, the sun was quite high in the sky, and Sahbai began to consider in his heart some suitable way of bringing the Prince to his real purpose. Suddenly, Mirza Fathul Mulk Bahadur asked the ustad in a casual, conversational tone, 'Ustad, there's something to say.'

'Yes, surely, Sahib-e Alam. I am all ears.'

'You've heard of Chhoti Begam?'

'Sir, do you mean the lady who was connected with Navab Shamsuddin Ahmad Khan? I have not seen her, but . . .'

Fathul Mulk Bahadur finished the sentence for him, 'have heard about her legendary beauty!'

'Sir, quite so.'

'The custom of our House was, or rather still is, that the Shadow of God suggested someone . . . or the Exalted Presence the Queen made a proposal.' Fathul Mulk Bahadur was silent for a few moments, then resumed. 'If ever a formal proposal was made, it was always within the House. The bridegroom's party proceeded and was greeted within the Haveli, from one house to another. If the bride was an outsider, her ceremonial palanquin and equipage formally arrived in the Haveli at the agreed time. No one ever went out.'

The point was instantly clear to Sahbai. In fact, he did not really need the Prince to elaborate so much upon the matter. He knew about the centuries' old practices at the Exalted Fort. 'Precisely,' he said. 'The main point is that just one person spoke to both the parties about the matter. Or at most, one meeting between the two parties was enough to conclude the negotiations.'

'As you can see, Ustad, the position is somewhat novel. We do not take the initiative; we do not make proposals to marry outside. The consent of the Shadow of God will be forthcoming only if all overtures are from the other side, and even for the other side's overtures to begin, it's essential to have His Majesty the Mahabali's tacit or implied permission.'

'Chhoti Begam has an elder sister . . .' said Sahbai.

'Yes, yes, quite. But then . . . ?'

Sahbai was quick to respond. 'Then there is no problem, Sahib-e Alam. Ihtiram-ud Daulah Hakim Ahsanullah Khan sahib should drop a word in Mahabali's ears. I will take care of the rest.'

'But . . . Mahabali's eye . . . well, it never falls too kindly on me . . .' Mirza Fakhru spoke haltingly, unwillingly. This aspect of Court politics was hidden from none, still the Prince, and everybody in his circle, preferred not to talk about it.

Sahbai did not share Zauq's interest in the politics of the Exalted Haveli, but he was certainly aware of its basics, and the most important things connected with it. So, using his natural tact and good sense, he observed, 'Sir, there is undoubtedly the question of the Exalted Temperament of the Queen of the Age, Navab Zinat Mahal sahib, may her Advancing Fortunes be Perpetual and may her Days be Everlasting. She might have some apprehensions about the possibility of the First Heir Apparentship of Mirza Javan Bakht . . .'

The Prince smiled with pleasure. 'Hush, even walls have ears! I am glad Ustad got to the essence of the matter so well.'

'Offspring of the World's and the People of the World's Guide and Mentor,' Sahbai began formally. 'Allah has already bestowed one son upon you. May the Lord of the World keep safe and secure the Exalted Presence, Miran Shah sahib; at the present time the question of someone else becoming First Heir Apparent is purely hypothetical; it's not even academic. The Exalted Presence, the Queen's notions, if she has any in this regard, are bound at present to be futile. I fully believe that the Presence, the Shadow of God, May his Bounties be Perpetual, will not give even the least attention to the Exalted Highness the Queen's suggestions on this subject. My limited intelligence tells me that all matters should be placed before the Shadow of God through Ihtiram-ud Daulah. As regards Khanam sahib, her elder sister can be taken into confidence.'

The Prince was extremely pleased; he spoke with a new bloom in his face. 'As Allah wills! Ustad, we are extremely pleased with your wishing us well and the sharpness of your reason. I think I will trouble Ihtiram-ud Daulah on this matter very soon, perhaps tomorrow itself.'

'Most auspicious. As Allah wills, I will make my best efforts to bring the matter to a happy conclusion through Khanam sahib's elder sister.'

'May God bring you success.' Unexpectedly, the Prince drew a cold sigh and quoted an Arabic proverb: 'There is no difference between death and disunion.'

'Please, Sahib-e Alam, do not utter such words. He is Maker, Creator, Beneficent. He is the Ocean of Bounty. Did you not hear the Arabic wisdom:

"The Ocean has no fear from the thieves"? And we are begging, not thieving. He will give; surely, He will give.'

'That may be. I can only quote the great Khan-e Khanan of Emperor Akbar, "My heart is very, very, full of longing."'

'Sahib-e Alam, I am well aware,' Sahbai quoted another line from the same ghazal: 'It is a thousand leagues from love to patience. But love, in a single leap, can blow away the longest distance.'

In spite of Sahbai's pleasant and hope-filled conversation, Mirza Fathul Mulk Bahadur's temperament now seemed to give way to melancholy. Sahbai thought that it was inexpedient to stay any more, and was trying to find some stratagem to be given leave to go, when a mace-bearer came and reported, 'The Exalted Honour perhaps summoned Ustad Mir Nasir Ahmad sahib, Binkar. He petitions for permission to present himself.'

'Oh, yes. Good that you reminded me. Let him be presented. Perhaps he could sing something to suit the hour. It might divert me.'

This provided a natural opportunity for Sahbai to beg leave for departure. He stood, made three salaams, and petitioned that he be allowed to depart. Mirza Fakhru half rose, made a salaam, and said, 'Do remember your task, ustad.'

'Exalted sir, it is engraved on the agate of my heart with a diamond pen. As Allah wills, good results will be forthcoming soon.'

'Go. Go with God,' Mirza Fakhru spoke in a grave, leaden voice.

Immediately as the Maulana exited, a mace-bearer entered, made a salaam, and announced in a low tone, 'May the Sahib-e Alam's fortunes be always ascendant, Ustad Mir Nasir Ahmad sahib awaits permission to enter.'

The Prince beckoned with a finger and the mace-bearer, going to the door, announced, 'Fix your gaze! Please submit salaam with due respect; Sahib-e Alam Third Heir Apparent Bahadur, may he be safe and secure!'

Ustad Mir Nasir Ahmad sahib was not only the acknowledged master of bina—the standard musical instrument, and also of a style of playing it—in those days, he was also a direct descendant of Khvajah Mir Dard, the great eighteenth-century Hindi and Persian poet, Sufi and master musicologist. The whole city looked at Nasir Ahmad sahib with awe and reverence. He did not visit anywhere, as a rule, but always obeyed the invitation from Mirza Fathul Mulk Bahadur. Making seven salaams, he entered along with Ustad Nizam Khan, master of the vocal style dhrupad, and Ustad Mukkhu, master of the percussion instrument pakhawaj, as well as four other musicians.

Everyone in Delhi was well aware of Mirza Fathul Mulk Bahadur's knowledge and expertise in music. Performing before him was a sort of trial and test. Even Mir Nasir Ahmad sahib felt a flutter of uncertainty in his heart, praying to God that his performance be the most perfect ever and the Prince have no occasion to withhold his wholehearted approval.

Immediately as he sat on the carpet before the Prince, Nasir Ahmad sahib began to tune his bina; the other accompanists started on the qanun, the tanpura, and two small percussion instruments resembling the Middle-Eastern daf. Mukkhu, expert of pakhawaj, and chief of all pupils of the Paradise-dwelling Ustad Gulab Singh ji, did not do anything with his musical instrument; he just waited for the signal to commence. When all instruments were set and all sounds synchronized, Mir Nasir Ahmad sahib began the introductory notes, the alap in the raga Jaunpuri, without a percussion accompaniment. After about half an hour of alap, the two daf players began their gentle, almost tentative accompaniment. Just as the alap was coming to an end, Ustad Mukkhu went with the deep, but flexible sound of the pakhawaj. Now, Nizam Mian began his alap in the gentlest of notes. The instruments went along with the singing for some time, then began to withdraw, gradually became dim, and then all but disappeared, but for the drone of the qanun and the tanpura. Still more gradually, the drones became like a slowly flowing stream, down a very easy slope. The bina became the sobs and sighs of a lovestruck woman lamenting for her fickle beloved.

Against this environment, the words of the Persian poet Khalil Sharvani slowly reverberated around the big chamber; it was like the remote call of the papiha bird, coming nearer, *pi . . . pi . . . pi kahan* . . . my beloved, my beloved, where? Where? The call coming near, as if emerging from all four walls of the heavily curtained chamber:

Woe, woe for the one whose lover you are,
And I am that one;
Woe, woe for the one whose companion is crazed with love for you,
And I am that one;
Beloved, nothing's better for me than your sorrow
Should be the companion and lover of someone,
And I am that one.

Mirza Fathul Mulk Bahadur was stunned. What is it that's being sung? Are these people aware of my inner state? Did they conspire to sing this poem before me? Or do they want to soften me to extract from me rewards more than usual? But within a few moments the music, the poem and the voice permeated his music-loving soul and his heart. Forgetting everything, he began to keep time on his thigh, swaying to the sound and rhythm. After about an hour, the speed of the bina and the rhythm of the singer became fast, then faster, then so fast and high that it seemed no distinction would now remain between the bina's voice and the human voice. Mirza Fathul Mulk began openly to weep. Within minutes, his handkerchief became soggy with tears, his head drooped on his knees, and it seemed that he was just about to collapse, senseless.

Seeing the Prince's deteriorating state, all instruments slowed down, and stopped; the singer also slowed down and stopped with a soft, dying fall. Nizam Mian began to mop his brow and neck with his large handkerchief; he was not even aware that the perspiration had reached his armpits and chest. Sometimes, it was said, even his fingertips would begin to drip with perspiration.

Mirza Fakhru's water-bearer appeared with a restorative in a small chinaware cup; his mace-bearer softly dried his face and neck with a broad kerchief made of muslin. The mace-bearer smoothed his clothes; everybody now sat alert and respectful in their places. Mirza Fakhru resumed his normal stance. When the Prince seemed to be better, Nizam Mian sahib, without waiting for a cue from Mir Nasir Ahmad sahib, began the introductory notes of the alap in the raga Jai Jaiwanti. He began a rubai from Kamal Ismail; this time the poem was not of frenzy and agony. The theme this time was ecstasy: ecstasy of the true, physical union with the beloved. The manner of composition was the same, a very long end-rhyme:

I put my lips on yours,
Is it I, or it is not I?
Tonight I am with you,
Is it I, or it is not I?
Wine on our lips, lips open, the door closed,
Lord, tell me please
Is it I, or it is not I?

Mirza Fakhru heard the sounds and the voice, spellbound, taken aback. The raga, the timing, the words: as if God himself had sent them down from on High for my solace, for the strength of my heart. And then, the voice of Mian Nizam, not deep, not bass, but tenor tending towards the baritone, charged with practised ease, slightly thin, but not without the power to reverberate; it was a voice just suited to express the depths of a heart which was full of a thousand desires—or perhaps just one desire—and all of it took form and shape in the notes of the raga Jai Jaiwanti and became a stream, drenching and saturating Mirza Fathul Mulk Bahadur's veins and sinews.

Looking at the Sahib-e Alam's absorption, his profound silence in place of the turmoil that had shook his soul when the first poem was sung, the magical silence which seemed to envelop every living being in a wonder that was like a waking dream, Mir Nasir sahib thought of prolonging the session, but the Prince's chief mace-bearer beckoned to him to be quiet. Then, without asking the musicians, he whispered in the Prince's ears, 'Sahib-e Alam, Mir Nasir sahib, Mian Nizam Khan sahib, and the players beg to leave.'

It was as if Mirza Fakhru had woken up from sleep. It was long past midday. Candles and floor lamps had been lit quietly. 'Oh, it's so late now!' He spoke, as if to himself. Then loudly: 'Bhai, one could sacrifice oneself for our maestros and artists of music. Within no time they transported us from here to some faraway land!'

Both the ustads bent low in salaams. Mir sahib said, 'Your Honour, our throats were choking and our hands were shaking on our instruments. To commence even an alap in front of the Presence is impertinence, far less singing a whole dhrupad. Allah saved our honour.'

Mirza Fakhru ordered that suitable rewards and formal court dress of three pieces may be presented to all the members of the troupe. Before they left, he praised them again, saying that there was no question of their being out of turn. He whose throat has the notes and he whose fingers have the thrill of the raga, will by himself become a prisoner of sound and the rhythm and the ups and downs of voices. He concluded with a Persian verse:

Every thread of the lampshade is like a net;
The moth's impudence is not because of
Its wings. The moth cannot stop itself.

61

The King Emperor summons Mirza Fakhru to the Royal Hammam

AS FAR AS appointments go, Umdat-ul Hukama Ihtiram-ud Daulah Hakim Muhammad Ahsanullah Khan Bahadur was merely Chief Quartermaster and always held office in the Quartermaster's building and was never seen in the Prime Minister's office or in the Chief Paymaster's building. The reality on the ground was that he wielded more influence in matters of governance than the First Heir Apparent or the Prime Minister. This was partly because he was the Sovereign's personal physician, and partly because the advice that he gave was always acceptable to the Shadow of God, for he was no sycophant, but a disinterested and statesman-like adviser.

The only other person who wielded comparable power within the administration was the King's Personal Holder of the Power of Attorney and Chief Eunuch Mahbub Ali Khan. Inside the Red Haveli, however, there was no one even close to Malika-e Dauran Navab Zinat Mahal in having influence over the Emperor. The main point is that as far as the people were concerned, none among the Court elite was more respected and popular than Hakim Muhammad Ahsanullah Khan Bahadur.

It was an established practice of the Mughal Sovereigns that aside from formal banquets, the King ate in the company of none except his closest relatives. The Royal women always ate in total seclusion. In spite of these standing embargoes, the occasion for a royal meal was a time for bustle, a frenzied but enjoyable activity with a bit of humour and banter, even jealousy. After the meal, the King would sometimes have a high official or a noble who was close to the throne as guest to 'share the betel cone'. He also used the opportunity to discuss some weighty matter of State, or hear some petition.

In spite of the fact that he was hard up, at least when viewed from the perspective of rulers and kings generally, and his needs were very large,

Abu Zafar Sirajuddin Muhammad Bahadur Shah Secondus retained, albeit on a smaller scale, all the elements of the lifestyle of his great ancestors. So that was how it happened that day. When the Emperor concluded the day's business at Court, and rose to leave, his chief female crier and runner—from the regiment of Jasolnis—knew from the infinitesimal movement of the Emperor's brow that he desired to go to his main residential chambers, called Tasbih Khanah.

A Jasolni ranked below a Qulmaqni and above an Urdabegni. The latter mostly stayed at the gate or at the doors of the chambers inside the Palace. The Jasolni was lightly armed and had a free run everywhere inside the Fort, including the zenana, and was therefore considered most suitable as runner and messenger inside the Palace. The Jasolnis came from a village in the south of Delhi called Jasola. The Qulmaqnis were generally Central Asian or Abyssinian in origin. They were fully armed and were expected to participate in firefighting, if necessary.

The Jasolni cried out, 'Beware! Mentor and Guide! Exalted Presence! His Majesty, may he be always secure! May he live long!'

The Emperor's steps came down from the throne, and instantaneously the Jasolni stepped out smartly and fast, proclaiming in a hard, loud voice at every step, 'Refuge of the World! Mahabali! His Majesty!'

'Take care!

'Mentor and Guide! Exalted Presence! His Majesty! May he live long!

'Refuge of all Worlds! His Majesty! Mahabali! May he live long! Salaam him with full honour!'

All the imperatives were spoken in the second-person singular; the respectful second-person plural was avoided. In the zenana, all the ladies stood straight, doing the salaam; the Emperor took his place upon the throne behind which a richly clad eunuch was waving a heavy fan made of peacock feathers. All ladies came forward in order of rank and did the salaam again. By the time the ladies had finished paying their respects, the maids of the tablecloth spread a leather tablecloth, seven yards long and three yards wide. On it, they spread a snow-white cotton cloth. Exactly at the centre of the cloth, they placed a low table, two yards long, one and a half yards wide, and six inches in height. On the low table, they again spread a leather tablecloth, and a cotton one over it. The moment the cloths had been laid, senior maids sprang forward, sealed metal containers of food in their hand. The containers were also covered with silk cloth, worked lightly in bullion. All the foods were covered in gold or silver leaf, shimmering like the lights of a spring night. Very light sprays of water mixed with musk, saffron, ambergris, rose and the flowers of keora were being played behind the throne.

A maid, appointed for the job, said bismillah, broke off a piece of food, and put it in the Emperor's mouth. Just as she raised the morsel, a mace-bearer called out aloud, 'Auspicious Dinner!'

The moment this salutation was heard, the covers from the large cooking pots and containers of food were removed and food began to be distributed to the usual diners and anyone else who happened to be around: the destitute, the needy, the traveller with nowhere to eat. After the dinner, they were regaled to their heart's content with a cool drink made of the fruit of the season.

Just as the Emperor finished, everyone among the eaters outside cried out in prayer, 'May our Mahabali live long! May the Shadow of the Mentor and Guide be there always; may Allah preserve the protection on our heads of our Emperor with Jamshed's Honour!'

The maid in charge of the betel box presented to Mahabali silver boxes containing cones of the best leaves: each cone was wrapped in gold leaf; in order to keep the folds of the leaf in place, a thin silver needle was pierced through each cone. The Emperor bestowed the silver needle on the betel-serving maid as he picked up a cone. Just as he was almost finished with the betel cones, the maid in charge of the hookah presented it to him. The flat-bottomed water container—placed firmly in a deep and large silver basin—was made of brass and chased in gold and silver; it had been freshly washed, polished and filled with rose water. Embers of acacia wood charcoals glowed bright with low flames trying to emerge out of the silver-filigreed hookah cup with a brass cover that had small holes; the holes were not big enough to let the sparks escape. The four-yard-long hookah tube of coloured silk was strengthened with gold and silver wires wound upon it, thick at the end and tapering as it joined the gold mouthpiece encrusted with rubies. The tube had been soaked in rose water and the scent of the rose and the fragrance of the sweet and bitter tobacco enriched with fermented apples was making the chamber glow with warm wafts of perfumes and bouquets. While the Refuge of the World slowly drew upon the hookah, the servants on fanning duty stood a little away from the throne, lest an unwary blast permit some foolish spark to be bold enough to spring out of its place. Navab Zinat Mahal had her own hookah brought in. None except Navab Zinat Mahal was permitted to enjoy the hookah in the King's presence. She was hoping to glean a few moments of time with the Refuge of the World after he was through with the hookah but before he took his noble feet to the Hammam, also known as Ghusl Khanah, for his siesta. She wanted to make some submissions about the fifth birthday celebrations of her son Mirza Javan Bakht, favourite of the Emperor as well.

Both Hammam and Ghusl Khanah mean 'bathroom'. The names have misled quite a few historians. At the time of the events that we are narrating before you, the name Hammam had almost fully replaced the name Ghusl Khanah. It was a sizeable building, standing in its own grounds. It was kept warm during the winter and cool during the summer. The chamber in which the Emperor rested was in the middle, surrounded by two water channels which ran with hot or cold water all the year round. There were also ornamental ponds, full of fragrant water, again hot or cold according to the season. All its walls were pierced with ornamental trelliswork or little windows whose marble leaves were also trellised. The walls, windows and apertures were designed with great ingenuity: a fresh breeze always ran through the building, even if the weather was muggy or airless. The building had two floors: one which faced the river Jamna was called the Cool Hammam and the one which faced the Pearl Mosque inside the Exalted Haveli was called the Hot Hammam.

The Hammam was actually a most exclusive locale for rare audiences granted to the most favoured or honoured by the Sovereign. Shivaji's audience with Aurangzeb was in the Hammam. Other than such audiences, it was used by the Emperor for prayer, or concentrating on some thought, or meditation, or having a quiet uninterrupted rest before preparing himself for his next duty. Unexpectedly that day, the King finished enjoying the hookah sooner than usual. Navab Zinat Mahal was caught unawares, and didn't get the opportunity to broach her intended subject. The Refuge of the World rose; the Jasolni sprang forward and cried out, 'Beware! Salaam him with full honour! Mentor and Guide, His Majesty the King!'

By now the Jasolni and other maids could judge that the Mahabali was making for the Hammam. Voices rose in near unison, 'May the Hammam be auspicious! May the Mahabali enjoy comforts of the cool and the warm!'

The Emperor stepped out of the Divan-e Khas; the mace-bearer, whose duty was to be always in front of the Presence, made three salaams and awaited orders. This was because the Emperor did occasionally summon some high official of the State or some Prince of the Realm into the Hammam. The Emperor stopped for a moment, and commanded in an extremely soft, sophisticated voice, 'Ihtiram-ud Daulah had petitioned for a grant of audience. Is he present in the Nishast?'

The building which housed the office of the Chief Quartermaster (Khan-e Saman) was known to the common people as Khan-e Samani. People of the Exalted Haveli, for some reason, called it Nishast (Sitting-chamber). The mace-bearer placed his hand on his breast and submitted, 'He is all ears for the summons from the Presence.'

'Please make a request to the Third Heir Apparent Bahadur to trouble his feet to the Hammam and speak to us.'

As we have narrated above, his numerous qualities as a Prince of the Realm and as poet and intellectual notwithstanding, Mirza Fathul Mulk Bahadur was not looked upon with much favour by the King. Mirza Javan Bakht was the all-time favourite not just because he was the youngest offspring, and was born of Navab Zinat Mahal, the youngest and most loved of the queens. Next to them, the Emperor's eye of favour was on Mirza Dara Bakht, the First Heir Apparent, and then on Mirza Kayumars Bahadur, the Second Heir Apparent. Even so, the King of Exalted Honour acknowledged Mirza Fathul Mulk Bahadur's acuity of mind and intellectual attainments. Further, Mirza Fathul Mulk Bahadur greatly resembled the King, the Refuge of the World. In fact, some jealous persons went to the extent of hinting that the Prince had made himself look like the Shadow of God so that the people might regard him as the Emperor's Vicegerent.

The fact of the matter is that practically every Prince, whether he was in the line of succession or not, nurtured longings for the Crown and Throne. Each one imagined that the dice might fall at any moment in his favour. True, the Firangee Bahadur had declared Mirza Dara Bakht the Heir Apparent on the very day of the King's Coronation; but no one could really claim the throne just by virtue of being the Heir Apparent. The Mughals did not recognize that institution. After all, Shahjahan declared Dara Shikoh his Heir Apparent, but he ended up on the scaffold, not the throne. Now, the entrance of Navab Zinat Mahal upon this confused and uncertain world of kingship and succession introduced a new and novel element.

In 1840, Abu Zafar Sirajuddin Muhammad Bahadur Shah Secondus married the beautiful daughter of an Afghan nobleman, and made her his

Chief Queen with the title of Navab Zinat Mahal. The King was sixty-five; the Queen was nineteen, though some alleged she was sixteen. Ghanshyam Lal Asi, whom we met some while ago, was not much enamoured of the Shadow of God. He wrote a poem to 'commemorate' the marriage and included in it a chronogram to signify the date. It was no commemoration; it was barbs and bolts at the King who had no power nor the inclination to chastise the delinquent. Anyway, the poem described the Emperor as seventy years old, as against the eleven years of the bride.

The Emperor had the last laugh. Not a full year had passed when the King whose majesty was like that of the legendary Faridun, filled Navab Zinat Mahal's arms with a son whose beauty rivalled that of the moon. The ill-wishers were amazed and confused. But the birth of the new Prince and the ambitions of Zinat Mahal brought their own problems. She began to dream of her son as the First Heir Apparent, then Emperor of Hindustan. There was no conceivable prospect of this, given that Mirza Dara Bakht, affectionately called Mirza Shabbu, was the declared and recognized Heir Apparent. The Presence, who Commands the Destinies, would never agree to the change anyway. Still, Zinat Mahal clandestinely began trying to bring round the Grand Sahib Bahadur to her point of view. Apart from sending him expensive gifts, she also began to open social relations with the John Company's high officials. So far, these efforts had borne no fruit; but Zinat Mahal knew how to wait, and there was the vast plain of years before her: she and her son were the youngest in the fray.

The Emperor proceeded to the Hammam with measured steps. In the meantime, Mirza Fathul Mulk Bahadur was informed that the Mahabali had remembered him. His haveli was beyond the open space in front of the Divan-e Am. So it was just about twelve minutes or less from his house to the Hammam. In accordance with the practice of all Timurid princes, and contrary to the fashion prevalent among the princes of Lucknow, Mirza Fathul Mulk Bahadur rose early and did not doff his full court dress until he retired for the night, regardless of whether his attendance was desired at Court or not. Thus he did not have to make any special preparations for appearing before His Majesty. A mace-bearer waited for him at the door. He took the Prince into the Hammam without delay.

After the bright sunlit park and its open air, Mirza Fathul Mulk found the air inside somewhat dim, but cool and pleasurable. He had been summoned to the Hammam often, so he did not feel nervous, or unable to find his way into the Royal Chamber. He was slightly uneasy, but certainly curious about the reasons for being called there at that time. There was nothing to suggest the nature of the matter on which the Luminous Presence desired his advice or consultation. But he also knew that the Luminous Presence, who Commands the Destinies, had summoned Ihtiram-ud Daulah's attendance as well. This suggested that it could not be something to worry about too much.

The Hammam's upper storey was a medium-sized chamber, surrounded by corridors in which ran water channels. The chamber itself was lighted with small lamps and a chandelier, all with green shades. In the middle of the chamber was a water channel with a small fountain whose water was scented with cloves and cinnamon. The marble floor, chequered like a chessboard, was bare of carpets. On one side, there was a heavy platform in ebony wood, with a prayer mat spread on it and a large copy of the Quran in its traditional stand, made of silver. The Quran was bound in gilded leather. Next to the Quran was the Exalted Presence's caftan in jamavar, and his four-cornered hat, heavily worked in gold. On the opposite side of the platform was a large bedstead, its frame worked in brass and silver; its legs were of solid silver and its curtain rods of brass. Leaning against two overstuffed brocade pillows, the Emperor rested, his eyes closed, telling some sacred words on an emerald rosary, his fingers softly moving up and down. He knew the Prince by his light, cautious footsteps, and so he opened his eyes and spoke in affectionate welcome, with the famous line of a Persian verse: 'Oh, your coming causes delight to my heart! Come, Mirza Fakhru, come sit.'

Since no one was allowed to sit in the Emperor's presence, there was nothing of the kind of a chair or even a stool, in the chamber. Begams and Princes of the Realm, when commanded to sit, waited for a flicker of the Emperor's eye and chose the platform or the bedstead accordingly. Here, the Prince saw that he was required to sit on the bed. So he gingerly sat on the edge of the frame. It was eight or nine inches wide, covered with soft bedding, so there was no problem with that. Mirza Fakhru began to press his father's legs, his eyes bent, not daring to look the Presence in the face.

'Ama Mirza Fakhru,' the Presence, Knowledgeable of the whole World, broke the silence suddenly. 'So what are your views and what is your practice about sending a proposal of marriage somewhere?'

Mirza Fakhru was struck dumb. How did the Presence come to know?

I entrusted this duty to Ihtiram-ud Daulah. But if I ignore the query and reply vaguely, the Exalted Emperor might not like my prevarication. At least he began with 'Ama', a friendly way of address, much like the 'Hey' of English, as he knew from his English tutor. In return, he explained to his tutor that Ama was composed of two words rolled into one: 'ay' and 'mian'. The 'ma' was fully nasalized.

After a suitable pause, he answered, 'Up until now, all such matters were resolved and concluded under the benign Shadow of the Presence and in accord with his wise guidance and instruction.' He paused again. 'The other thing is that traditionally, in the Timurid House, proposals of marriage are never sent out, especially outside of this Illustrious House.'

'Correct,' the King said gravely. 'Petitions are received for our daughters; such petitions are granted or rejected. Or sometimes, the Head of the Chaghatai clan, who is the Ruling Sovereign, chooses a bridegroom for a girl of the House.'

'The Mentor and Guide is quite right. It has happened that absent a suitable groom, our chaste and purdah-nashin virgins have preferred a lifelong state of celibacy.'

'For our princes, if our eye of favour falls on some chaste virgin from without the House, we perform the marriage ceremony here and bring the lady in with proper respect.'

Now Mirza Fathul Mulk Bahadur understood the drift of His Majesty's words. But bashfulness and propriety did not let him open his mouth. Where is Ihtiram-ud Daulah? He asked himself in vexation.

'The mother of Mirza Abu Bakr, may God preserve him, left this servant most lonely when she went away to the World of Eternity.'

'We know that Hatim Zamani could not win your heart.' The Emperor spoke with slow emphasis: 'But Mirza Ilahi Bakhsh has our confidence.'

'It is clear to the Exalted Reason of the Mentor and Guide that I do nothing not sanctioned by the Shariah.' The Prince spoke dryly. 'Nor do I want to sequester anyone attached to me.'

A ray of satisfaction played on the face of the King, the Protector of the Faith. Before he could continue the conversation, the mace-bearer announced as if on cue, in his curiously upper register but dulcet and gentle tone, 'Ihtiram-ud Daulah Hakim Muhammad Ahsanullah Khan Bahadur!'

The King clapped lightly; immediately, the curtain was drawn a few inches. Hakim Ahsanullah Khan entered and performed the formal kurnish. Then he made three salaams, folded his hands just below the midriff and stood erect, his eyes in front, but not on the Presence.

'Ihtiram-ud Daulah Bahadur,' the Presence spoke in a light, genial tone. 'Ama, you come at a good time. And perhaps the business which you wish to place before us has just been the subject of our conversation.'

Hakim Ahsanullah Khan knew at once what the business must have been. The Exalted Presence was au fait with all that transpired in the Haveli. Perhaps even the secret diurnal reporter had mentioned something to the effect that the Third Heir Apparent was interested in a certain Begam sahib. It was natural for the Sovereign to be informed of all the facts. With his eyes in front as usual, he said, 'The Mentor and Guide is fully aware of all that is in his subjects' hearts.'

'So you are soliciting permission to send out a marriage proposal?' The King spoke sharply.

Mirza Fathul Mulk started and was about to say something, but he checked himself. The Luminous Presence was speaking to the hakim. If he intervened, he would be speaking far out of turn. He looked at the hakim with expectant eyes.

'Were we to exceed even by a hair's breadth the practice established by the hallowed ancestors of the Shadow of God, we should be deserving of death.' He spoke with full respect, and firmly.

'State your meaning clearly. Don't talk in riddles.' The King's tone was still rather sharp.

'Refuge of the World, should I be considered guilty of a little impertinence, I beg to be forgiven. But the full state of the affair is that the chaste and purdah-nashin begam on whom the eye of the Sahib-e Alam wa Alamiyan's selection has fallen, is a widow. Her husband was a man of good family and substantial means. The marauding hand of the thugs dragged him to the grave. Now this good Bibi is back in Delhi, which is the place of her nativity.'

'We are sensible of her estate. We hope that she will now never put her foot out of the strong ramparts of fidelity and chastity.'

The Emperor was hinting at the early life of Wazir Khanam. Though he didn't agree with the King's view—Mirza Fathul Mulk believed that Wazir had always been chaste and faithful—he held his tongue.

'The elder sister of this Bibi is married here in Delhi to Maulavi

Muhammad Nazir Rifai. The Maulavi sahib will manage all things. Maulavi Sahbai will function as the intermediary.'

'And the actual rites of marriage?'

'The words and the contract will be pronounced in the city. No one from the Auspicious Fort will be troubled. The older sister will escort the bride's ceremonial palanquin into the Auspicious Haveli.'

'Well, if this is what Mirza Fathul Mulk desires, then let all things be carried out agreeably with the status of this Haveli.' The Emperor commanded after a brief silence.

Mirza Fakhru looked towards his father with grateful eyes. Ihtiram-ud Daulah judged that his own audience was over. He performed the wonted kurnish, then made three salaams and walking backwards, quit the chamber.

The Emperor briefly patted the Prince's shoulder in approval, and said, 'Very good. Allah be with you.' This last phrase of blessing was in Arabic.

Mirza Fakhru stood, performed the kurnish, then again took his place at the edge of the bed frame and began gently to press his father's legs. The King fell asleep in a few minutes; Mirza Fakhru then left the chamber, walking backwards, even though the Sovereign was asleep.

62

Anwari Khanam and Maulavi Muhammad Nazir receive a marriage proposal for Chhoti Begam

MAULAVI MUHAMMAD NAZIR called himself Rifai and also Mujaddidi because of his connection with two Sufi silsilahs, or chains, which is how Sufi schools are designated. The Rifais traced their spiritual lineage to Shaikh Ahmad al-Rifai, and the Mujaddidis so called themselves because their original master was Shaikh Ahmad Sirhindi Mujaddid-e Alf-e Sani. The harmony and affinity among the Sufi silsilahs is demonstrated by the fact that one person could attach himself to one or more lineages.

Muhammad Nazir was not originally from Delhi. He was a descendant of Umar, Islam's second Caliph; he was born in Baroda, a famous city of Gujarat. His father Shaikh Din Muhammad was a follower of the Presence, Sayyid Nuruddin Saifullah al-Rifai. He stayed in or near his Guide's monastery for many years and spent his time in meditation and prayers, acting as the Guide's personal attendant, and also carrying out social services as commanded by his Guide.

The Rifai silsilah was originated by Shaikh Ahmad al-Rifai (1106–82). He was an Arab but spent a long part of his life in a small village called Bataih in the wetlands of southern Iraq. He himself was of the Qadiriah silsilah, but his maternal uncle, Shaikh Mansur al-Bataihi, appointed him Shaikh of a silsilah founded by him and called it Bataihia and Rifaiah. But the name by which the silsilah was known in history was just al-Rifai. Very soon, it became popular far and wide. Ibn Khaldun spoke of Shaikh Ahmad al-Rifai in his History. The silsilah's followers spread to Maldives, Ceylon (now Sri Lanka), Lakshdip and then the Deccan in the fourteenth century. It soon spread through the whole of the Deccan and Hind.

The Rifai Sufis first appeared in Gujarat in the sixteenth century. They were soon established in Baroda, Surat and many other cities. The Presence,

Sayyid Nuruddin Saifullah al-Rifai was one the most illustrious Gujarati Sufis in the eighteenth century. Shaikh Din Muhammad was an extremely devoted and loyal follower of his Guide, but he had no interest in the rather bizarre and outré practices of a certain, and the most populous, group of the Shaikh's followers. The practice was called 'ratib' (firm practice) and its practitioners were called 'ratibdar' (holder of the firm practice).

The ratibdars were noted for their addiction to pain and violence. As they performed their ecstatic dance, they inflicted knife or sword wounds upon their bodies. Hitting an iron or bronze mace on their head was another favourite practice. Some ratibdars actually pierced their cheek, thigh, stomach, even the tongue with a sharp weapon. Some drew their breath violently, held it there, then shut and choked their nose, mouth and ears, and blew out so hard that an eye would pop out and hang on their face. The common name for such deeds was 'khel' (game) and 'khelna' (to play a game); but since these words were also used for the acts of maddened frenzy performed by women (and sometimes men) under the influence of a genie or spirit, it is possible that the ratibdar, when he behaved thus, believed that he was under some preternatural influence.

Some ratibdars of old were reputed to swallow a live snake, or walk on burning coals without any ill effect. It was also said that no ratibdar was ever actually wounded as he mutilated himself: not a drop of blood was spilt from the wound. Before commencing the khel, the ratibdar obtained the blessing of the Presence, Sayyid Nuruddin Saifullah al-Rifai or his designated deputy. The saint said some prayers or holy words and blew upon their weapon. It was said that sometimes the ratibdar presented himself before the saint and pulled out his weapon from his tongue or thigh in his presence. On such occasions, the saint applied his saliva to the wound and the mark of the cut disappeared instantly.

The ratibdars were extremely popular because of their dramatic and bizarre practices, but Shaikh Din Muhammad looked upon such things with disfavour, if not clear disapproval. He believed that acts which caused hurt to the body, or smacked of acrobatics or jugglery, or seemed to be performed to gain name and attention, should not be elevated to the status of religious observances. Such things were clearly against the teachings of the Prophet and his Shariah. Shaikh Din Muhammad viewed with disapproval such practices which were not just condoned, but apparently encouraged by his Shaikh. It proved his love for the Shaikh, and not to the contrary. During the special season for these activities, which were undesirable in his view, Din Muhammad stayed at home, not even making his daily submissions before his Mentor and Guide. Colourful streamers and bunting were brought out, on which Shaikh Nuruddin Saifullah al-Rifai blew his blessings; similarly, he blew his blessings on the swords, knives, iron nails and daggers that were to be used in the khel. The parties would then go out into the city, displaying their macabre skills and earning the praise and faith-inspired love of the citizenry.

Many years passed like this; Din Muhammad practically separated himself from his Mentor and Guide during the days of these undesirable activities. Once, just before the khel season was to start, Shaikh Nuruddin Saifullah al-Rifai summoned Shaikh Din Muhammad to his private chamber and spoke thus: 'Din Muhammad, we can see that you make all efforts at all times to advance on the Path and achieve one advanced stage after another. There is no difference at all in what you do and what you say. This is a sure sign of the Grace upon you of Allah, Lord of the Worlds, and the spiritual attention of our great predecessors, the Friends of God.'

Din Muhammad folded his hands and with bent head and trembling voice replied, 'This worthless one is nothing at all. It is one radiant ray of the Sun-like dust of your portal that has touched me and made this worthless particle to shine.'

Shaikh Nuruddin al-Rifai was silent for a moment. Then he commanded, 'But I have observed for quite some time that your progress is apparently halted.'

Shaikh Din Muhammad's eyes welled up. He was unable to understand if the Mentor was issuing some sort of a warning, or was offering some way out of what he saw as an impasse. He weighed the possibilities and after a brief silence, he submitted fearfully, 'It is you who are my destination. You are my Guide as well. So where can I go, leaving your sublime threshold?'

'Some practices and some rites prevalent here are in your view objectionable, indeed contrary to the Shariah. And you are right, if one looks at those things from a strictly theological standpoint.'

Din Muhammad was quite at his wits' end. Could it be possible for the Mentor to put a stop to those acts and practices just for my sake? And if such a result did come to pass, what face would I have to show before his pupils and numerous followers and admirers? And am I at all capable or empowered to test my Mentor's word or deed on the imperfect anvil of my Reason? If my heart does not feel content here, it is up to me to let go of the hem of his garment and search for some other Person of Perfection and seek blessings from him.

'Exactly.' The Presence, Nuruddin Saifullah al-Rifai commanded, as if he had read Din Muhammad's thoughts like an open book. 'This is exactly the commandment of the Friends of God, and also of the Mentor of all Mentors, Shaikh Abdul Qadir Jilani: If the flower of your heart does not blossom and bloom under the care and attention of one Guide, go to another.'

'Is the Presence spurning me from his portal?' Shaikh Din Muhammad was trembling all over.

'No. We will be with you, wherever you go. In times forgotten our forebears and predecessors introduced the things that are repellent to you. I, or anyone else, cannot give up those practices, for such an act could lead to confusion and despondency among the people of our Prophet who have love and faith in their hearts for the illustrious ones of our silsilah who are now part of the history of the Sufi world. Since your heart is not here, therefore your progress also has come to a halt.'

Shaikh Din Muhammad impulsively moved closer to his master and bent to touch his feet. As the tears flowed down his face, he spoke in a voice broken by entreaty, 'Your Honour, let me die here at your feet, heartless and ignorant as I am. Do not let me be separated from yourself.'

The Presence, Sayyid Nuruddin Saifullah al-Rifai smiled. It was a smile to turn a stone to water. He commanded, 'I and you will never be separate, as Allah wills. But your Shariah-loving temperament will gain more by travelling on the Path in the company of those for whom the Shariah and the Path coalesce, such that they become indistinguishable. Now, go. I give you in God's trust.'

The Presence, Shaikh Nuruddin Saifullah al-Rifai ripped off a strip of cloth from his tunic and put it around the neck of Din Muhammad, like the necklace of threads worn by fakirs and homeless wanderers in search of God.

Then the master recited the prayer, in Arabic, which was recited by the great twelfth–thirteenth century Sufi Saint Shaikh Fariduddin, also known as Ganjshakar (Treasury of Sugar) and often lovingly called Baba Farid. The occasion was his granting permission to the Presence, Shaikh Nizamuddin Auliya of Delhi to leave him and go out in the world: 'May Allah grant thee auspicious felicity and endow thee with knowledge that is beneficial and actions that are worthy to receive His acceptance.'

*

It was January 1790 when Shaikh Din Muhammad went fearfully out of the wonted protection of his Master. He spent many months travelling in Punjab and further north-west, visiting Sufi shrines and saints. He spent some considerable time in Sirhind, at the shrine of Shaikh Ahmad Sirhindi Naqshbandi, the sixteenth–seventeenth century Sufi who was known for being at odds with Authority, for his assertion that there was no Sufism without the Shariah, and whose own silsilah came to be called Mujaddidiya, because his popular image was that of the Mujaddid-e Alf-e Sani (Renewer [of the Faith] in the Second [Islamic] Millennium). He was much attracted to Shaikh Ahmad's teachings, particularly his insistence on the strict observance of the Shariah. Shaikh Din Muhammad began to look for and inquire about a living Sufi of the silsilah to learn more from him and perhaps become his pupil.

He was lucky. He found out that Shah Ghulam Ali Naqshbandi Mujaddidi of Delhi, a major disciple and successor to the Sufi saint and poet Mirza Mazhar Jan-e Janan Naqshbandi Mujaddidi of Delhi, was then staying at Sirhind. He immediately sought and obtained permission to visit the master, and his heart was instantaneously enticed and ensnared by the charismatic saint. He tied the game of his heart to the saddle straps of Shah Ghulam Ali's Spiritual Courser. He was particularly attracted to the teachings of the Exalted Presence, Mirza Mazhar Jan-e Janan, who held that the Vedas were Holy Scriptures revealed by God, and Shri Krishna and Shri Rama were Prophets sent by God; thus he privileged the Hindus too as the People of the Book.

Shaikh Din Muhammad followed his new Mentor and Guide to Delhi by his permission. As commanded by his Mentor, Din Muhammad accepted the post of a teacher at the madrasa attached to the mosque built by Princess Zinat-un Nisa Begam. Again, following the behest of his Mentor and Guide, he married a poor widow and began to lead the life of a quietly useful member of the community. He also received permission to call himself Rifai and Mujaddidi. By the time of the passing of the Presence, Shah Ghulam Ali (1824), Din Muhammad was a respectable person in both worldly and spiritual terms. The Presence, Shah Ghulam Ali did not pronounce him his successor, but made him happy beyond measure one day; that day, the Mentor's mood was easy and expansive, and he observed, 'Mian Din Muhammad, both you and your past Mentor are with us.'

Shaikh Din Muhammad had his son Muhammad Nazir educated adequately, in fact better than most of his station. He initiated him in the Rifai and Mujaddidi silsilahs. Muhammad Nazir's social and spiritual circle widened and diversified after his father's death. Among his new acquaintances there were some who were regular visitors with Muhammad Yusuf sadahkar, and also with Akbari Bai Farrukhabadi. Muhammad Nazir was now of a marriageable age; he was also well-to-do, if not rich. Some well-wishers became the go-betweens, and Muhammad Yusuf's eldest daughter Anwari Khanam, lovingly called Bari Begam, was married to Muhammad Nazir with appropriate pomp and ceremony. It was many years before a child—a most beautiful daughter—was born unto them. She was named Amat-ul Fatimah and was brought up with the greatest possible pampering and loving. As she grew up, she was educated up to a level above what was usual for well-born middle-class Muslim or Hindu girl children. She also acquired the standard household skills.

*

Navab Mirza was present at his aunt's house, paying one of his daily, or twice daily visits. Light-hearted banter, but without any kind of sexual innuendo, was being exchanged between him and Fatimah. He was also, as usual, gratuitously offering his services to do their household chores.

'Bari Khala, are you out of ghee, by any chance? I happened to be near Qadam Sharif this morning. I saw dozens of Mewatis there with jars full of high quality ghee. Should you so desire, I could go and get you adequate quantities of the best quality ghee, in no time.'

'Go, get on with you, you naughty brat! Do we have no one but you to have his clothes spotted with grease in the ghee market? Don't I have servants?'

'All right. Did you know that in the fruit market of Azadpur there have arrived dozens of carts full of melons from Kabul? Huh, I could go right now before they are sold out. I'll bring back such fruit . . . such fruit that my Uncle and Fatimah would just love them!'

'May Allah grant you some sense!' Bari Begam said with genial affection. 'Should your uncle get to know that I sent off Chhoti's darling son to Azadpur to fetch and carry! Really, God knows how he'll deal with me then!'

'Please, Navab Bhai,' said Fatimah with a shy smile and mischievous looks. 'You send all kinds of kites flying in the sky!' She laughed lightly, her dupatta on her mouth. 'Really, we don't lack for anything here.'

'Dear madam,' came back Navab Mirza's characteristic mild double entendre, 'but I find something lacking in everything.'

Fatimah reddened; she knew what her cousin meant, but did not know what to say in reply. She was saved further abashment when a call was heard from outside, 'Submissions, Your Honour. Please order purdah. Maulana Sahbai sahib and his begam have arrived.'

Bari Begam rose, a little flustered. Maulana Sahbai sahib's begam was a rare visitor, anywhere. Something special must have brought them here. She asked Navab Mirza to receive the Maulana in the divan khanah with the greatest courtesy and keep him suitably engaged until his uncle who had stepped out to visit a friend came back home.

'Now you scoot from here, so that I may have his begam come in. I'll shortly be sending betel cones and hookah for the guest.'

Navab Mirza, straightening his cap and tunic, hurried outside to welcome the learned visitor and take him to the meeting room. In the meantime, word was sent that purdah prevailed in the house now and Begam sahib may please come in. The palanquin was placed immediately contiguous to the main door; sheets were employed as curtains to effect complete purdah. Bari Begam welcomed her guest in the hall, behind a curtain. She took her through the veranda and inner courtyard into her chamber. It was, of course, highly impertinent to inquire the purpose of the visit. The guest and host were to pretend at all times that it was just a social visit, with no business to discuss.

Sahbai's wife was about thirty or thirty-five, but silver shone rather much in her hair, perhaps because she was a chronic patient of cold and catarrh: in those days, that ailment was regarded as the main cause of prematurely grey hair. She was short and plump, and her complexion was of the colour of wheat, light brown, lighter than café au lait, and much prized in Indian society. Her face was lively, revealing a sweet-tempered, sunny disposition, while her eyes reflected good sense and a sharp mind. In short, she was an extremely attractive person. Her husband was a staunch Delhiite, but she came from Panipat, and her voice had just a little of the hard ring of the Haryanvi speech.

Maulavi Sahbai was expecting to find Maulavi Muhammad Nazir home at this time, and was a little disconcerted to be greeted by Navab Mirza instead: it was not desirable to open discussions with Navab Mirza, or in fact with anyone else but Muhammad Nazir. He, of course, was acquainted with Navab Mirza as an up-and-coming poet. You will recall that it was Sahbai who had, in the mushairah held in Zinat Bari, spontaneously and most enthusiastically applauded Navab Mirza on one of his verses that he presented there. He decided to wait for Muhammad Nazir sahib's arrival. For the present, he made casual conversation with Navab Mirza about—what else?—his poetry.

'So, Navab Mirza, good to see you here. As Allah wills, the talk about your poetry and your prowess as poet is now spreading everywhere in the city. Some days ago, a three-part ghazal of Shaikh Nasikh attracted much discussion. The first line of the first ghazal was: *The centre point of the ocean of beauty, her waist/How supple and sweetly rolling!* In fact, the whole three-part ghazal has become extremely popular.'

'Yes, sir. That poem is being talked about everywhere even now, Presence.' Navab Mirza returned. 'That very first verse is truly explosive.' He then recited the full verse, of which Sahbai had just said the first line:

The centre point of the ocean of beauty, her waist,
How supple and sweetly rolling!
Say, could a water-wave ever have such suppleness, such roll?

'Only God is untouched by blemish!' Sahbai exclaimed in admiration. 'Even Mirza Ghalib has composed a two-part ghazal in the pattern. And indeed, Mian, the reach of the Mirza's imagination is astounding.' He smiled, 'And young man, it would be great for you to test your power of thought on this pattern; let people see how well you can write about love's transactions.'

Navab Mirza smiled; it was a somewhat wily smile, as if he was laughing inwardly at some joke of which Sahbai had no idea. But not for nothing was Sahbai known for his appreciation of nuances; he immediately divined that there was something behind the young man's smile, though he thought it best to behave as if he did not notice the meaningful smile at that time.

'Yes, sir. But Shaikh sahib, whom God has accepted, did not use the rhyme javab (reply). Perhaps because he thought it was too trite?'

'Oh, none of us ever perceived that omission!'

'Sir, and Mirza Naushah sahib probably imagined that the Shaikh—on whom be Blessings from God—left that rhyme for him so that he could make the best possible use of it. So, Mirza sahib commanded:

Let me do another letter by the time my messenger returns . . .

Maulavi sahib completed the verse instantly:

I well know what she'll write in reply!

He went on, 'Ha! What a thrilling line came to him to complete the verse! Only God is untouched by blemish!' He then repeated the whole verse and said, 'It is a wonder: the creation of such a theme, and the use of it to compose on such a delicate transaction of love!'

By now Navab Mirza's smile had become somewhat expansive, though he said nothing; Sahbai now clearly understood the meaning of the smile. He observed, 'So! That is the lie of the land, Navab Mirza! You already have composed a verse on that pattern, using the rhyme javab! Come, out with it!'

Navab Mirza recited triumphantly, but without the least hint of crowing at his success:

I cheated my heart hundreds of times in my restless impatience:

'So you made an opening verse? Good. That's a fairly good line. Now let us have the whole verse.'

Navab Mirza, without raising his head, said the full verse with a marvellous, natural flow:

I cheated my heart hundreds of times in my restless impatience:
I wrote letters upon letters to myself by way of her reply.

It was if Sahbai was shocked into a trance. He put a hand on his heart, and swayed, and repeated over and over again the phrase, 'I wrote letters upon letters to myself', in an undertone, as if he was talking to himself. Navab

Mirza was bewildered, not knowing what to do. He grabbed the box of perfumes, took out a phial, applied a few drops to his handkerchief and gently chafed Maulavi Sahbai's wrists and palms with it. He took out from the betel box a betel cone wrapped in gold leaf, offered it to him and spoke extremely softly, 'Presence, taste this little cone at least.'

'Eh? What was it that you said? A betel cone. But, Mian, "I wrote letters upon letters to myself" . . . Only God is untouched by blemish! Wah, wah! Transactions of love narrated with such spontaneity and absorption in the beloved! May Allah enhance you, and enhance you again.' He repeated the whole line with the same fervour, and then said, 'All right, Mian, let's have some more verses from this ghazal of yours. In fact, I wish that such ghazals should be presented in the service of the Refuge of the World, the Shadow of God!'

Before Navab Mirza could reply, Maulavi Muhammad Nazir Rifai Mujaddidi entered, with an apology on his lips. Navab Mirza thought it a good time to make himself scarce, but Sahbai said, 'Dear boy, let's have that verse again. Maulavi sahib, please observe; this young gentleman, your nephew, has a temperament simply bubbling with poetry! What freshness of theme, and what language, flowing and idiomatic!'

Navab Mirza was mortally afraid of his uncle, though that gentleman always treated him with affectionate gentleness. He somehow had a terror of his piety and gravitas; he ever went in fear that he might say or do something disagreeable to his uncle's temperament: he was sure to be annoyed with him then. He did his best to avoid having to say his poems where his uncle was present. But now he had no choice. He mustered up his courage and spoke in a firm and clear voice, 'I present the opening verse.'

He spoke the verse again:

I cheated my heart hundreds of times in my restless impatience:
I wrote letters upon letters to myself by way of her reply.

Maulavi Sahbai was rapturous, as before; even Maulavi Muhammad Nazir could not prevent himself from an involuntary 'Wah, wah! Only God is untouched by blemish! Say that verse again!'

Navab Mirza salaamed and said the verse again. Then, while both men of learning were still applauding, he folded his hands in humbleness and said, 'The next two or three are rather playful, if not impudent. I beg the forgiveness of the venerable gentlemen.'

'Yes, yes, go on,' said Sahbai. 'These things are poetry's salt.'

Navab Mirza began:

Pious people, it is not too far from the Glorious Forgiveness
That the winebibbers' sins drown and are lost in wine!

Rather than not being happy with it, Maulana Sahbai liked the verse. As he used words of effusive praise, Maulavi Muhammad Nazir smiled quietly. Now Navab Mirza was emboldened even more. He said, 'Presence, I have expressed another aspect of this theme.' He recited:

Oh Shaikh, he who forbids the wine of love,
Such a one should be hit, and hit again
With a shoe soaked in wine!

Now even Maulavi Muhammad Nazir sprang up from his seat. 'Oh, what a subtle justification, and quite in accord with the Shariah!'

'And saying "soaked in wine" instead of "soaked in water", which is the standard usage, creates a piquancy of its own,' Sahbai observed astutely.

Navab Mirza said the next verse:

I always took care not to disappoint
The Old Man of the wine house.
I was deserving of merit
Even before I gave up drinking.

'How interesting!' Sahbai cried. 'This verse, indeed, is in the true manner of Hakim Momin sahib, it's so oblique. And true as well, because not to disappoint someone is an act deserving of merit.'

'I present the concluding verse,' said Navab Mirza, and recited:

Dagh, there could be no greater sinner than I:
My sins are a cause of torment to hell itself.

This won praise from both Sahbai and Muhammad Nazir. Sahbai said to himself: 'The boy has a marvellous temperament for poetry. Should the proposal that I have come with come to fruition, the superior cultural environment and education of the Haveli will become freely available to him, leading his talent to even greater brilliance . . . True, there are no Faizi and Todar Mall today, but this Court too knows the value of its jewels. The King, may he remain always secure, would gladden the poets and the learned men of his Court with bounties of ruby and pearl, if he just could.'

Navab Mirza sensed that the two older men would need privacy for Maulana Sahbai to state his purpose before Maulavi Nazir and for both to talk it over. He made salaams and took his leave. His heart was eager for at least a glimpse of Fatimah, if not an exchange of a few words with her, but far from permitting a glimpse even, the purdah was absolutely strict there: no question of even a strange bird being allowed to fly over, he said bitterly to himself. He paused, spoke in a loving whisper to the closed door, 'God protect you; will meet tomorrow', and left.

In the zenana haveli, the ladies talked about everything possible except the reason for Begam Sahbai's visit. The subject of Fatimah's marriageable age came up with apparent casualness; Navab Mirza was mentioned most obliquely as a possible bridegroom. When every possible subject was exhausted, Begam Sahbai said, 'Sister, I have been sitting here for hours now, wasting your time. May Allah preserve your house, you must have much to do. I don't know if Maulavi Nazir sahib has come back at all from his visit. I should take your permission to leave, once he and my Maulana ji have had their little talk.'

'No, no. I won't hear of that. You just came, and now that you have come, you should partake of our frugal lunch before you go. As for my Maulavi sahib, he came in quite a while ago. He has been treated to betel cones and cool drinks. Mian Navab Mirza has been regaling them with his poetry and is being profusely applauded.' Bari Begam spoke of her nephew's poetic prowess with obvious pride.

'Yes, truly! What a promising and pleasing young man he is! Allah preserve him.' Sahbai Bibi paused for effect, bent close to Bari Begam, and very nearly whispered in her ear, 'Akbari Khanam, there is something important. Listen carefully!'

'Yes. Tell me, please. I am listening.'

Sahbai Bibi pushed herself even closer, and spoke in a furtive manner. 'We have a marriage proposal for Chhoti in view.'

Akbari Khanam could not believe her ears. It was her most cordial desire for Chhoti's boat to arrive at some salubrious shore. But Chhoti did not even let the matter be mentioned before her. And a proposal for her to come from quite outside their immediate circle, and that too, it should be Maulana Sahbai as the go-between! Was she dreaming? And how was Chhoti going to react? Most probably, she will say a resounding 'No!' Bari Begam was inwardly perplexed; not just perplexed, she was anxious. She spoke with made-up elation after a few seconds, 'Wah, wah! It's just like the saying: "My heart and the Brahman's book say the same!" What greater fortune for Chhoti that you should bring a proposal for her!'

'It's not I who is the source of this proposal, Bibi,' Sahbai Bibi's voice was still quite low. Her voice sank lower. 'Word has come from the Haveli. We are mere couriers.'

Bari did not believe her ears and could not keep her voice down. 'Haveli? Which haveli? Who are those people?'

'Hey, Bibi, there is only one Haveli in the city. They do not send proposals of marriage. They just inquire the other party's willingness. Once that is done, other matters take their natural course.'

'You mean . . . ? You mean from the Shadow of God's threshold, it is from the family of . . . of some earlier Sovereign . . . or some minor Prince of the Realm?'

'Well, you may take that to be the case.' Now she too gave up her whispering mode. 'The only difference is: it is the Sahib-e Alam wa Alamiyan, Mirza Fakhru Bahadur, the Third Heir Apparent, who is desirous of your youngest sister.'

Mirza Fakhru Bahadur, the Third Heir Apparent! She remembered what Chhoti had once said—it seemed ages ago: If there's a prince in my destiny, he will come, sure and certain. I am not one to encourage inferior persons. And now those words seemed to be coming true!

'Hey, Sister mine, why do you stare at me open-mouthed? Please to say something!'

Sahbai Begam's own heart was fast aflutter. Should she be handed a rejection, they would be left with no face in front of the Sahib-e Alamiyan. My husband would also be chagrined.

'Bibi, the proposal is acceptable to me with all my heart and soul. But I am no one to give the word until I have Chhoti's consent. She doesn't seem to be inclined to these things nowadays. You know how much suffering she saw with her previous . . . '

Seeing that Bari Begam was not objecting in principle, Sahbai Bibi struck again while the iron seemed hot. 'Right. Now you must have her understand that her sorrows are over. She will lord it over in the Fort as the Third Heir Apparent's wedded wife. And who knows about the revolutions of the times? Who knows the Third Heir Apparent may be King some day tomorrow, Allah preserve him.' She laughed in glee. 'Then your sister will be known as the Queen of Hindustan!'

'I am ready in every way, dear Sister. I will ride down to Chhoti's immediately. And I should also ask my husband what he thinks of the proposal.'

'Do ask him,' said Sahbai Begam. 'But you are her true guardian, and the matter directly concerns your little sibling. You must tell her that she must—in fact, it is her bounden duty to herself and her children—look for her own good. This is the world, heartless and blind. She must consider favourably on this: Even princesses wouldn't be so lucky as to find a husband of such quality.'

Purdah was organized to enable Maulavi Muhammad Nazir to enter the zenana. He conferred quietly with his wife in a separate room. He came out a short time later, a smile on his face. He spoke to his wife, loudly enough for Sahbai Begam also to hear, 'All right, madam, I will convey your views to Maulana Sahbai. The rest is in God's hands.'

'Yes, please. You should request Maulavi Sahbai ji from our side to pray for a good outcome.'

'As Allah wills, we will all pray. Be assured.'

Immediately after Maulavi Muhammad Nazir quit the zenana, Sahbai's begam rose from her place and stood at the prayer mat with her upper wrap spread on her arms, like a beggar. She prayed aloud, 'Ya Allah, in the name of Thy beloved Prophet, let this matter be concluded satisfactorily. Let our word and honour be safe. Let Chhoti Begam prosper and be happy in her new connection.'

Tears began to prick Bari Begam's eyes. She dried them with her upper wrap, said 'Amen' aloud, and taking a pinch of sandalwood powder, she sprinkled it like gold dust on the centre parting of Sahbai Begam's hair.

'Dear Sister, God will reward you with higher than the highest reward for this good deed.' Her eyes misted over again. 'I will acknowledge your act of altruism towards me and my sister as long as I live. Should the auspicious hands of you and yours become the rudder for the boat of my sister's life, she will never have fear of tempests and shipwreck.'

'Bibi, what we are doing is no more than a common human action. There is no altruism here. Just let us pray that all things may reach their proper end as soon as possible. Jealousies abound these days.' Then she looked right and left, and spoke in a whisper again. 'And look, word should never, never reach Navab Zinat Mahal's ears.'

Bari Begam returned, sotto voce, 'Oh Sister, we are far, far below them. Who is there among us to convey the news to that high portal?'

'Hush! Even walls have ears! I should be on my way now. Your husband must have tired of offering hospitalities to mine!'

'No, there's nothing of the sort. He's always welcome. I will ride a palanquin to Chhoti's this very evening.'

'So, let everything be settled within the next one or two days. Good deeds mustn't be delayed.'

'There will be no delay. Chhoti's consent is all that is needed.'

'Yes, certainly that's the most important thing. We know quite well that her heart has been slashed and lacerated more than perhaps anyone else's. But Bibi, you must make her understand this clearly: Allah Mian is minded to give a new turn to her days. She must not be guilty of rejecting His Gracious Beneficence.'

Sahbai Begam wrapped the chador carefully around her body, hugged Bari Begam, did a salaam and turned towards the door where purdah was fully in place. Her husband rode in an open palanquin, called havadar; she entered her palanquin in security. Both left for home.

On her part, Bari Begam went on the prayer mat and took out her rosary. Before she started telling some prayers on the rosary, she instructed that a palanquin be organized for her to go to Chhoti Begam's.

63

Chhoti Begam hears from Anwari Khanam, and consults Bai Ji sahib for a solution to her dilemma

She was a woman: a Person of Perfection. She spent her entire life just outside the city of Shahjahanabad under a thatched roof near the old Id Mosque. No one knew her real name, but people called her Bai Ji. During conversation, she often recited verses from the Quran, especially the [one hundred and eighth] Chapter [of just three verses] called al-Kausar. It was often observed that when someone went to her for a solution of their difficulty, or answer to a query, she separated seventy cowries from whatever [money] was brought to her as offering. Then she picked up that handful of cowries seventy times, each time putting it back on the ground. As she did this, she also recited the selfsame Chapter. After this, she said whatever her heart was inspired to say in answer to the seeker's query or by way of solution to his problem. And now observe the power of Divine Destiny: whatever she uttered at that time, came to pass exactly as she spoke. It is about a year now that she departed this transitory world.*

BARI BEGAM WAS hoping to arrive at Chhoti's before the sunset prayers. As it happened, one of her palanquin-bearers suddenly complained of severe stomach ache just before they reached Khanam ka Bazaar. He left the palanquin at the edge of the road and bent double, retching and trying to throw up. But those who earn their bread through physical labour can rarely overeat. So all his efforts to empty out of his stomach whatever was

* Javad-ud Daulah Syed Ahmad Khan Bahadur, from *Maqalat-e Sir Syed*, vol. 16, ed. Maulana Muhammad Ismail Panipati. 1847

troubling him were in vain. Someone from a nearby shop tried to help him by getting some medication from an apothecary. This had some effect and he actually felt better within a few minutes, but he could not find the strength in him to help lift the palanquin. The three palanquin-bearers could not handle the heavy palanquin on their own, apart, of course, from the extreme difficulty of balancing it with only three bearers. So he went off to his home, promising in a weak voice to send a replacement soon.

Bari Begam remained in the palanquin, guarded by the three bearers, but chafing at the delay, apprehensive that she might miss the sunset prayers. She was also anxious and upset, for she feared that the unexpected interruption could be a bad omen. It was not often that she ventured out of the safety of her home with the purpose of doing something which could truly be described as an expedition: something, which, if done well and successfully, could brighten again the star of her unfortunate younger sibling. She hated being stranded in the busy market, virtually locked in a narrow space. But there was no choice but to wait.

Finally, in about half an hour, a new bearer came running. The four bearers went off at a quick trot and reached her to Chhoti's house in practically no time. She was at her sister's door when the muezzins everywhere were calling for the sunset prayer; Wazir was in the water room, doing her ablutions. She came out at once when she heard of Bari's arrival: her sleeves rolled up, the delicate, smooth length of her wrists and forearms radiant, like purple flames, in spite of being wet; drops of the clear water on her forehead and chin took on the colour of her person and gave the illusion of a tasty cool drink made from the falsa fruit; a few droplets were trembling on her long eyelashes, as if peeking at the rose garden of her face through the lattice of the eyelashes.

Whenever Akbari Khanam saw Wazir, she had to make herself believe anew that it was the same Chhoti Begam who became a mother before she was sixteen and the garden of whose bosom had since been adorned with not one, but four roses, may Allah preserve them and her. And this was not just because Bari was older by a few years and she saw Wazir as the small girl that she was when they were growing up in their parents' house. In fact, the gap of years between them was not so great. It certainly was a gap; and the culture and society of those days attached very great importance to the difference in ages however minor, and Wazir always respected that difference, as far as she could. But why was the bloom of

Wazir's garden always unchanged? Bari had no reply to this. So she was obliged to accept it as a wonder among the wonders of God's Power. And on top of her youthful looks was the sense of dignity and iconic energy that seemed to envelop her being; it was such that she dazzled even a hardened and hard-bitten womanizer like William Fraser. Akbari Khanam knew no other woman on whom dignity and consciousness of the self, and modesty and sense of self-respect seemed to rain down like a cool spray of a light shower on a hot afternoon. It was obvious that this was no ordinary, run-of-the-mill beauty: she was to be cowed down or intimidated by no man; her self-sufficiency and feminine consciousness were like a lead-filled wall. There was no room for uncertainty or defensiveness.

On that evening too, Akbari Khanam impulsively called out salutations to the Prophet in her heart: the greatest tribute that could be paid to a beautiful person or thing. On her part, when Wazir saw Bari Baji at her doorstep, whose kindness and affection she had always craved for, she was overwhelmed with joy. Throwing all restraints to the winds, she hugged her hard, looked at her with infinite affection and regard, and cried out, 'Hai Allah, Bari Baji! How did you happen to stray to my humble door? It's a great good fortune for me, but you could have asked me to come! You don't normally go out anywhere, especially at a time when night and day are coming together.'

'There, there, enough! Pipe down, little one. Look first at your own sweet face.' Bari performed the action to prevent misfortunes overtaking Wazir and went on, 'Who would not like to look at such a sweet-tasting face? Come on now, let's do the prayer, then we'll have time to jabber.'

'But how come you are here . . . so suddenly? Is everything all right? Is your husband, or Fatimah . . . ? Are they well?'

'Woman, you cackle away, nineteen to the dozen! All's well, dearie. Let me first perform the ablutions and do the prayer, time is getting on.'

Habib-un Nisa hurried in with a spouted large brass waterpot full of water. She salaamed and said that Bari Begam need not go into the water room, she could make the ablutions in the courtyard and do the prayer in the veranda where everything was ready for her.

'Do your prayer here, Begam sahib, in the meantime, I'll be ready with a cool drink.'

'We'll see about the cool drink, Habiba,' Bari Begam said, smiling, 'but yes, let me do the ablutions and the prayer here.'

Wazir, just as she finished doing her prayer, was about to call Habiba to organize tea and other things, when Bari Begam, with a flick of her eye, asked her to desist and signalled to her to go into the bedroom. Bari Begam followed her in a minute, and she closed and bolted the door the moment she went in.

'Please, is all well, Bari Baji? You . . .'

'Hush!' Bari Begam said in a fierce whisper, pulling Wazir close to her. 'Now pay attention. And don't tell anyone yet!'

Wazir's big, deep-brown eyes were full of perplexity. But she obediently sat side by side with her elder sister. Bari Begam was silent for a few moments, as if trying to catch her breath. She then narrated the whole story to Wazir. Her narration did not have her usual note of confidence and flow; it was slow and careful, just like someone reading the Quran aloud to herself. She was worried about Chhoti not accepting the marriage proposal and at best, perhaps agreeing to an arrangement similar to what she had had with Navab Shamsuddin Ahmad. She did not know that Wazir had been willing to have Shamsuddin Ahmad on any terms, and she did desire marriage with him. Akbari Khanam's other dread was that Wazir might refuse not only marriage, but also any kind of possible connection with the Third Heir Apparent. She could very well say that her heart was supped full of such things and she was having no more.

On the other side, Wazir was lost in her own thoughts. This caused more fears to arise in Bari's heart. God knows what sort of hour it was, auspicious or otherwise, when she agreed to undertake the project. Actually, Wazir was full of concern for her sons: the marriage proposal did not stipulate anything about their fate. She was unable to decide if she should raise the question of the sons before, or after accepting the proposal for marriage. The circumstance that at her age—middle age by the standards of those times—she could still attract a serious lover, and the lover should be the Third Heir Apparent, was not the cause of any satisfaction or pride to her. She was quite clear in her mind about her desirability, and was aware that her beauty was not under the constraint of months and days. She also knew that beauty was not just a proportionately fashioned body and a pretty face.

'Bibi, say something. Don't you like the house, or the family?' Bari tried to inject a bit of humour to the situation.

Finally, Wazir broke the seal of silence, 'Bari Baji, I cannot repay you for the good deeds that you've done for me . . .'

Bari Begam was now truly disquieted. This seemed to be a prelude to refusal. She wanted to interrupt, but Chhoti raised her hand to stop her and went on, 'Who would not accept such a proposal? It is my good fortune and your love and concern that you think me worthy of it. But I need some time to consider. My heart seems to sink on receipt of such momentous good news.'

'What's this about sinking hearts, dear little Sister? You have a whole, vast and lonely life before you. Now someone desires to hold your hand as you walk those ravine-riddled roads. And who should be that someone? A Prince of the Realm of Hindustan, who could be King even. So do take your time to think and ponder, but it is certainly no occasion for fear or losing heart.'

Wazir drew a deep sigh and quoted Hakim Momin Khan's line of verse:

Here am I, no end repentant

She went on, 'Who knows what else is written for me, how many joinings and breakings.'

'Only Allah knows what will happen down the corridor. All we can say is that what we have before us is obviously full of hopes for a good future.'

'Yes, but all my rosy hues turned out to be painted with soot when the critical time came. Well, these are complaints best made to God, and these are not just about one moment, but for all my life. You could be right. This jointure could have some good hidden in it. God! Oh my God! What should I do?'

She was almost in tears. If Bari was expecting for Wazir to be jubilant at the possibility of becoming the wedded wife of the Third Heir Apparent, she was in error. She was not a little chagrined at Wazir's response and her state of mind. But while she was chagrined and disappointed, she had also the real fear that Wazir's past—full of near successes and the bitter drops of failure poured down her throat just when she thought she was on the brink of achievement—might prevent her from agreeing to undertake another adventure of life. She wanted to make some measured reply when Wazir interrupted her and asked in a mournful voice, 'Bari Baji, what happens to my children? Should I fill my home with the noise and bustle of marital life and turn my back on my children, and leave them desolate? How could I do that?'

'We'll think upon all that. They have made no conditions about the children. But even if they do, so what? Navab Mirza, may Allah save him, will be married soon enough and be in his own house. As for Shah Muhammad Agha, I could take him in gladly and bring him up.'

'No. Is it my destiny or part of my function in life to forsake my children always? You yourself say that Navab Mirza is now of a marriageable age. So how does it behove me, an aged crone, to have a young unmarried son in my house and I should be celebrating my own nuptials?'

'You are not an old crone, child. Nor are you celebrating a marriage with prothalamions being composed about it and a procession with drums and cymbals accompanying it. Do you think an Heir to the Kingdom would desire you if you were an old crone? And making a merry marriage, with you riding the palanquin in the shadow of the Quran and being formally sent off in tearful farewell while sad marriage songs of separation from hearth and home, and lilting, playful songs of union with your man are sung in the background: these are not for you. It is just that God is opening up a new path for you, a path which takes you straight through the Lahori Gate into the Haveli.'

'Even so, I'll need to talk to Navab Mirza.'

'Do talk to him. No action of yours, no new step that you may take, can be worthy of you if it wants of the agreement of Navab Mirza. Now, as regards that other thing . . .' Bari Begam seemed to pull herself short.

'What's that other thing, Bari Baji?' Wazir prompted her, seeing the older woman's silence.

Akbari Khanam was extremely fond of Navab Mirza. She had a fair sense also of Fatimah liking him, and it was quite clear to her that Navab Mirza passionately loved Fatimah. Perhaps Chhoti was not unaware of the state of Navab Mirza's heart either. Still, Bari Begam could not herself initiate any steps in the direction of the boy and the girl being joined in marriage. Proposals for marriage always emanated from the prospective bridegroom's side. In most good families, the girl's parents would prefer death for themselves and perpetual spinsterhood for their daughter rather than choosing a bridegroom and initiating a marriage proposal, far less negotiations of such a kind. Here was a somewhat unusual problem: It was important for Bari Begam to make Chhoti agree to Mirza Fakhru marrying her; at this juncture, it was therefore even more difficult for Bari Begam to say something about Navab Mirza as a prospective son-in-law for her, though this could effectively remove one of the major problems that seemed to inhibit Wazir from accepting the marriage proposal. She felt a little irked; what was the constraint in Chhoti's mind, what sense of alienness was preventing Chhoti from saying even a word here about the possibility of Navab Mirza becoming Fatimah's husband?

In a tentative, hesitant tone, she said, 'Oh, nothing else, really. I was just thinking about Navab Mirza. It's now the time for his marriage party to be organized so that he can enjoy a settled and responsible life on his own.'

Now it was Wazir's turn to become tentative. After a moment's silence, she said, 'In fact, my heart is much in it. I often think about it, but . . . I just feel that I should wait for Navab Mirza to obtain some suitable employment before I broach the subject with you about Fatimah.'

Now Bari Begam felt as if she had been given a new life. She had now a suitable opening to pursue the matter further. 'Well, I believe in looking for good family, good conduct and loving nature in the prospective bridegroom. As regards the means of livelihood, God has given more than enough for all of us.'

Wazir brightened perceptibly. 'So you think it's not essential for my son to be earning a living before he marries?'

'I already told you what we want, Bibi. Navab Mirza is as much our son as yours, and Fatimah is as much your daughter as ours. There'll be no change of homes, no alteration in the hearts. All I need is to talk to my Maulavi sahib. It'll be no trouble to bring him round!' Now, at last, Bari Begam laughed her special laughter, a laughter that can be imagined only by those who have heard the burble of wine being poured from a long-necked carafe. She went on, 'But there should at least be a call from you. We'll respond, and accept without loss of time!'

'Yes, Bari Baji, without doubt. I hold Fatimah dearer than my own life. And I feel that Navab Mirza will also be very pleased. It's just that I could not pick up the courage. May Allah keep you safe, you have taken a huge burden off my heart.'

Akbari Khanam repeated the gesture of taking away any misfortunes of Wazir's, and spoke with great feeling, 'My child, may God grant you happiness forever. May whatever you say or do come true like the bloom of spring, and its goodness be felt far and wide like the scent of champak flowers. As Allah wills, the idea of both marriages will become reality very soon.'

'But Bari Baji, I still need some time to think and to talk to Navab Mirza.'

'So who's asking you to have the marriage contract solemnized right this minute, silly? Do collect your emotions and satisfy your heart to the extent such things are possible. I'll come by again in a day or two.'

'And Bari Baji . . .'

'Yes, tell me all else that is there. Let all your doubts be removed.'

'I will not leave Shah Muhammad Agha and Navab Mirza behind.'

'I think it's premature to worry about that. All your conditions will be faithfully conveyed to the Haveli. But you should first make your heart firm and intention clear.'

'Quite true. And I know you will always do the best for me.'

*

Akbari Khanam rode back home in her palanquin. Wazir asked Habiba to come to her bedroom. When she came in, Wazir spoke in a questioning tone, without a preamble, 'Sahib-e Alam Mirza Fathul Mulk Bahadur? What about him?'

'You mean Mirza Fakhru? Yes, Khanam sahib. Everyone knows about him. It is said that in his looks and behaviour he is quite like the Shadow of God . . .' Habiba laughed softly and a little shyly. 'But not in one thing.'

'So what could that be?' Wazir was somewhat alarmed.

Habiba laughed more openly this time. 'Oh, it's just that the Shadow of God is very fond of making marriages. On the contrary, Fathul Mulk Bahadur had just one wife, and he remarried only after she died. It is rumoured that he's not too pleased with this second wife, but even then, he has no eyes for elsewhere. He has some taste for poetry and a lot of it for music. I heard he has written some entirely new songs for the khiyal singers.'

'Is he . . . is he, I mean, does he like the company of . . . boys?' Wazir was blushing.

'Uhi Allah! Take the name of God, Khanam sahib. He is extremely pious. He doesn't miss any of the five daily prayers and also organizes at Tis Hazari a facility for free water and cool drinks during the mourning days in the month of Muharram. He's certainly not one of those who throw in their lot with the people of Lot!'

'Well, I hear the dwellers in the Fort have nothing to do but fly kites, organize quail fights and game with cowries, or play pachisi.'

'Khanam sahib, it is one House, one Clan, after all. It's like chapattis from the same griddle: some are thicker, some are thinner. What should they do when they have now no kingdom to govern? God did not make the five fingers equal. I hear that Fathul Mulk Bahadur never starts anything before saying salutations to the Prophet and reading the fatiha from the Quran.'

'How do you know all this, Habiba?'

'Oh, these are no secrets, Khanam sahib. Everyone in Delhi knows this much. Fathul Mulk Bahadur visits the people in the city much more than other princes. He is on visiting terms with the Firangees even: death take them! But why do you want to know about him, Khanam sahib?'

'I . . . I am in dire trouble, Habiba.'

Habiba's heart lurched and lodged in her throat. What could this be? How does it concern the Third Heir Apparent? Every moment of Wazir's life was open to her. Wazir had had nothing to do with anyone at all. Connection or arrangement was a far cry; she was not even acquainted with any notable in the city, except perhaps Ziauddin Ahmad Khan, if he could be termed an acquaintance. Is it that Ziauddin Ahmad Khan is bringing pressure on her through Mirza Fathul Mulk Bahadur? Habiba's anxiety went up a notch or two when she saw that Wazir was looking down and seemed not willing to face her. Perhaps it was something to do with her honour? . . . God forbid! Let it be distant, as distant as something across the Water! Or does she believe that she, Habiba, could not possibly be of any service to her in the matter? She spoke thoughtfully and with care and deliberation: 'Let my life be sacrificed for you. Khanam sahib, please be strong of heart. Remember Maula Ali, the Solver of all difficulties. Maula Ali will make all things easy. If there is something that I can do, your word is my command.'

Wazir realized that perhaps her words and mode of delivery both were rather sensational, or at least sudden and unexpected. Unintentionally, she seemed to have put a fright into Habiba, though actually it was she who had been shaken by an unknown and unexplainable fear. She decided to come clean, 'No . . . it's nothing really dire, Habiba. It's just that I am not able to find the way to the best answer. Actually . . . Mirza Fathul Mulk Bahadur, I mean Sahib-e Alam Mirza Fathul Mulk Bahadur, he has expressed . . . the desire to marry me.'

A thrill ran through Habiba's body. She swayed and would have collapsed had she not put out her hands on Wazir's bedstead for support. Sahib-e Alam

Mirza Fathul Mulk Bahadur! This is what the waking up of one's sleeping fortunes means! Enhancement in honour and value; emancipation from anxieties and sorrows; days and nights of peace in the very heart of the land of Hind! What they say is true: When God chooses to give, he even rends open one's thatched roof to rain down gold and silver.

A panorama opened up before the eye of her mind: huge foreheads of mountain-bodied elephants painted in saffron and ochre, and sparkling with silver dots; their bodies resplendent with sashes and head stalls of billon, made heavier by additional gold and silver threads; tassels of silver and gold hanging down from silk coats covering the elephants' massive bodies; silver howdahs on their wide backs; each elephant with a mahout holding a gold or silver goad, driving his elephant expertly; the elephants in the front carrying princes in glittering dress, followed by elephants carrying the nobles and high officials of the kingdom; ahead of all, the tallest of elephants, his tusks decorated with heavy, solid gold bracelets, a big silver bell hanging from his neck; in the most resplendent howdah on his back, under a silver shade which itself was under the shadow of a large, brocaded canopy, sat the King whose pavilion was high as the sky; facing the King in the howdah, the Imam of the Jami Masjid Sayyid Muhammad Shah Bukhari; and standing behind the Emperor on the howdah, two fan-bearers with heavy fans of peacock feathers; a vanguard of singers of battle songs clad in red broadcloth, spears or staves in hand, reciting poems of bravery in a thunderous voice. Coming behind them were lines upon lines of fully armed cavalry. Just behind, and slightly out of line with the King, the Protector of the Faith, another elephant, loaded with baskets full of gold and silver rings to be scattered among the onlookers and the poor; just a little behind the King with the Glory of Jamshed, an elephant, wearing a brilliant blue brocade coat; riding that elephant is the Prince bridegroom; his dress sumptuous, his jewels lustrous, almost incandescent; he has a heavy formal garland of marriage, the sihra, over his head; it covers his neck and front, and cascades down almost to his feet; he is decked with long strings of red roses intertwined with gold and silver thread, and a string of pearls. Is this the marriage procession of Sahib-e Alam Mirza Muhammad Sultan Ghulam Fakhruddin Fathul Mulk Bahadur Third Heir Apparent, and is it wending its way to the doorstep of my Khanam sahib?

'What happened? Where are you lost, Habib-un Nisa?' Wazir's voice came into Habib-un Nisa's ears as if she had been asleep and someone was calling her from afar. 'It's I who am gasping for air, but it's you who are holding your breath!' There was a soft hint of laughter in Wazir's voice.

'I beg your pardon, and God's forgiveness too,' said Habib-un Nisa, abashed. 'I seem to have lost my whole self. First you frightened me, and then you gave such glad tidings that I was plain stupefied!'

'Go, get on with you!' returned Wazir, a little piqued. 'You have no reason to be stupefied. It's I who am nearly at my wits' end.'

'Why should you feel upset, Khanam sahib?' Habiba hesitantly dared to come closer to Wazir and perform the action to signify taking upon herself whatever trouble could happen. 'A husband is falling to your lot who would be the envy of the whole of Delhi, and the most honoured princesses would be jealous. May Allah preserve you, your lot is now going to change, and change so that you will lack for nothing until Doomsday, as Allah wills.'

Wazir was now visibly upset. 'Habib-un Nisa Begam, you see nothing but green everywhere, like one who went blind in the season of rains. Were you to look with someone else's eyes, then you would see the real colour of things!'

Habib-un Nisa was now in real bafflement. She pulled a long face and inquired gravely, 'My life for you. I did not understand.'

'Oh, you dimwit! Am I now of the age to acquire a mate for myself, or rather to bring home a moon-like beauty as Navab Mirza's bride?'

'Please. You are not all that old! Why, you have your flowers even every m—'

'Stop, stop that!' Wazir very nearly blushed. 'I don't like such talk . . . Just think, what will the world say? And these princely types are known to be fickle. Who knows, he may bring in another woman someday soon . . . And I will not leave my Muhammad Agha behind! Let the Haveli go to hell. I am happy enough in my thatched hut!'

'Without doubt, one's own home outweighs all others. But Mirza Fathul Mulk Bahadur . . . everyone knows him to be a serious, gentle and mild Prince. If he brought you in, he will certainly take the best care of you.'

'How do you know?' Wazir replied a little acidly.

'Oh, did you not hear it said from all the past ages, "I did not marry, but I have seen the marriage processions!" All know his clean conduct. He is not the kind of nobleman who fools around with bits of stale meat and bazaar mutton.' She laughed, but not without embarrassment at having to use such expressions.

Wazir pretended not to hear and pursued her own theme: 'And Navab Mirza and Muhammad Agha?'

'What's there to worry about on those matters, Khanam sahib? May God protect him, Navab Mirza well knows that should a great man like the Third Heir Apparent grasp his mother's hand, tears will be wiped off from both his and your eyes to the extent possible. In any case, you must first tell Navab Mirza and ascertain his reaction.'

'But if the people at the Fort do not consent to accept the boys?'

Habiba considered for a minute. 'As far as my limited judgement can determine, Navab Mirza, as Allah wills, is the son of a great man, is promising and is sure to brighten the name and fame of his forebears. Society will accept him with open arms. As for the little one, there may be some problem initially; so I am here; in any event, I will gladly keep him with me.'

'No, I will take you with me . . . but that poor little mite will miss me and may even sicken.'

'You aren't going to Kabul or the Deccan, Khanam sahib. You'll be right here.'

'Bari Baji will take him, she told me.'

'So, there is no complication then; all is well.'

'I fear Bari Baji already gave them word; she did not think of the problems of my situation.'

'No madam, she would never do that. Anyone who knows you, also knows that you don't bend to another's will in these matters. Though undoubtedly she must be keenly wishing for you to become the King's daughter-in-law.'

Wazir sat quiet, her head drooping perhaps in despondency, perhaps due to irresolution. Two little tears shone on her eyelashes, dropped silently and were absorbed in her collar. Habiba took her hand in both of hers and began to chafe them gently, almost lovingly, as one does with a baby. Many minutes passed, Habiba kept carefully quiet. At last, Wazir raised her head, dried her eyes and drew a sad sigh.

'Habiba, my heart does not now incline to these things. And I have fears as well. It has happened with me over and over again; my few days of happiness are inevitably followed by ages of weeping.'

With a near sob, she spoke a Hindi verse of Jurat, the eighteenth-century master:

Jurat, the humpbacked sky occasionally
Gives me a smile, like a new wound;
The wound then makes me cry big tears
Of pain for a long time.

'Khanam sahib, it is not necessary that such should be the case every time. As they say: "Sometimes the days are long; sometimes it's the nights that are long."'

Wazir smiled a bitter smile. 'Don't they also say: "The days become long when the poor man keeps the fast?"'

'Now who can win against you in word battles and capping verses, Khanam sahib!' Habiba giggled. 'You are, after all, a pupil of Shah Nasir sahib. But I have a suggestion for you to consider.'

'What is it?'

'Ask Bai Ji. Do as she says.'

'Bai Ji sahib?' Wazir considered for a moment. 'But what should I ask her, and how should I frame my question?'

'Leave all that to me. Tomorrow is a good day too; it's the first Thursday of the new moon. And from there, you might go to Qadam Sharif, if you were so minded.'

'So will it be suitable to go there just after the predawn prayers?'

'That is the best time, Khanam sahib. The multitude there grows very large by the time the sun is high.'

'At what time does Bai Ji Sahib arise in the morning?'

'Arise? Oh, I hear that she doesn't sleep a wink. Perhaps she just naps a little after the midday prayer. Some say that she sleeps not at all. And indeed, her eyes are always blazing red.'

'All right, organize some cowries. I understand she looks with favour at an offering of cowries.'

'Very good. I shall be sending out Jani Ram shortly to buy chapattis. I'll ask him to get cowries as well. They are a little high these days, at five thousand to the rupee.'

'Whatever, get two rupees' worth.'

Habib-un Nisa busied herself in household chores. But the remembrance of Qadam Sharif had awoken Wazir like a thorn that pricks suddenly and unexpectedly. Her visits there were few and far between now. Even so, whenever she did visit, she visited with due ceremony. And now, when there was the possibility of a new man entering her life, the remembrance created chaos in her heart. Would she visit the graves of Marston Blake or Agha Mirza Turab Ali with the same regularity, the same emotional charge, if they were buried in Delhi?

She looked, and again looked into her heart, but instead of getting the answer to the question, hypothetical though it was, she went into one of her usual introspective reveries. She did love Blak sahib most dearly; and even now, sometimes in the night, memories of their embraces seemed to do something to her heart. She did not know what it was in Blak sahib that made her give away her heart to him so quickly. Was it his charismatic person, his handsome body and self-confident deportment? But even the English acknowledged that Navab Shamsuddin Ahmad Khan was an extremely handsome young man, with a strong presence . . . so . . . was it Blak sahib's smiling, humorous mien, his numerous jokes and sallies? No, he was not all that extraordinary there. It is of course true that there was never a dull moment with him. He was not overly self-regarding, and then his expertise in matters of love and lovemaking . . .

Wazir flushed; and suddenly becoming conscious of her arousal, her flush changed into the blush of shame, and she shrank, as if trying to make herself smaller, wrapping her dupatta tightly around her upper body, as if trying to hide . . . But, no, there was something else; she felt perennially attracted to Blak sahib because of his physical magnetism and numerous worldly charms. But she had not realized that if there were men who demanded, even extorted, love from the women because of their overwhelming physical presence, there were other men, too, who could also command both love and respect by virtue of their sophistication, dignity and natural nobility. This she knew only when Shamsuddin Ahmad Khan entered her life. She also knew that even though the Firangee Fraser had his own prejudices against the Navab, officials of the Company in general held in high regard Navab Shamsuddin Ahmad Khan's administrative ability and the successful governance of his State.

A memory of the past surfaced in her mind. During the days when the Company's officials were investigating Fraser's murder, its spies reported an incident which could be used against the hapless Shamsuddin Ahmad Khan. It so happened that a grain dealer in the Navab's State had been murdered in mysterious circumstances. The Company pressured the Navab to find the murderer soonest and surrender him to the Company. Shamsuddin

Ahmad Khan flatly refused, saying that the murderer was guilty against the laws of his State and none but he could have him captured and given the punishment that was condign in every way. The English officials began to openly accuse Shamsuddin Ahmad Khan of inefficiency and weakness in matters of administration. But Shamsuddin Ahmad Khan bravely refused to be intimidated by the mighty John Company. He had the murderer captured within a short time and hanged in the bazaar of Firozepur Jhirka.

Wazir never saw such strength of mind, such firmness of resolve in anybody else. And on top of that, there was the Navab's good taste—his taste for poetry, his choice of clothes, his speech, his way of life—which was evident in everything; he seemed superior to his peers in all things. Though not in so many words, the Company officials did send out broad hints suggesting that if Navab Shamsuddin Ahmad caught the murderer quickly and surrendered him to the Glorious Sahibs, the investigation into Fraser's murder could change course. The Navab paid no mind to these ignoble hints. Wazir looked into her heart again. Blak sahib's amorous ways, his apparently genuine passion for her, the ascendancy of his fortune, wealth and power—and none of it was of any avail to him—all this she granted, yet it seemed obvious to her that her Navab was the living embodiment of the great Amir Khusrau's famous line:

What the entire cohort of the beautiful ones possess,
You possess alone.

She thought of Agha Mirza Turab Ali, that beautiful, gentle man, so much older than she and high-born, but friendly and loving. Wazir thought that she did repay the great value that Mirza Turab Ali had placed on her as a woman by doing all her spousal duties cheerfully and to her best ability and capacity. She was sure that Agha sahib did not die unhappy with her. She was also certain that looking at the times, and the prevailing masculine temperament and culture, he was a very good husband indeed.

So? Was it that now her life should be about nothing but mourning for the three who had been taken away? Was it that she should always be scratching the face of her heart with the fingernails of pain, saturate her being with the bitter, vitriolic poison of disunion, and not let a drop of the blood and water of life reach near her inner being? No. I cannot do that. Her heart shuddered and grew cold at the possibilities of the unknown.

But what other choice? Grieving for Shamsuddin Ahmad Khan she could renounce the world, become a fakir; she could make the floor of his tomb the roof over her head and live there like a recluse; she could live unknown and alone. But could she really do that? She again remembered Mir Taqi Mir's dread-inspiring truth:

There is none whom beauty failed to draw
To the marketplace.

But could I find some place, somehow, for a newcomer in my heart, in my life? In my life, perhaps. This great Prince, Mirza Fathul Mulk Bahadur, everyone praises him. But I don't know how he looks even. The truth is that however weighty the female might regard herself, the male always tipped the scale when weighed against her. If I could get Navab Mirza married, his bride would be a great source of comfort to me. But there's no telling about boys. They prefer to make their own home. Surely, he is not going to watch over his mother and his mother's home for any length of time. As for Shah Muhammad Agha, I am both parents for him. Bari Baji . . .

She did not know when she fell asleep, but her sleep was so deep that she did not respond to Habiba's repeated entreaties to wake up and eat. She finally awoke when it was about a couple of hours to dawn, and could not sleep for the rest of the night though she tried her best, by whatever means she could recall, to reclaim her sleep. Finally, the off-white thread of the false dawn ran across the dark eastern sky, and a few minutes later the muezzins began calling for the predawn prayer, and she rose to offer it.

*

Habib-un Nisa had, while getting the cowries the previous night, also ordered a palanquin for the next morning. When Wazir Khanam's palanquin arrived at the slope rising up to the old Id Mosque, there had already foregathered a largish crowd inside the mosque's tall and wide gate, and in front of a decrepit thatched hutment that stood in a corner in the open area of the mosque. It was just one middle-sized room, fronted by a long veranda on three sides. The door of the hut was closed and there was no one in the veranda. Wazir and Habiba alighted from the palanquin, wrapped in black chadors, only their faces and hands visible. They walked up to the veranda with hesitant steps, followed by a palanquin-bearer holding two sacks of cowries. The veranda had a very low plinth, and one shallow step was enough to go up to it. Looking at their begam-like deportment and expensive chadors, the throng gave way. But one woman grabbed the hem of Wazir's chador and prayed, 'Bi sahib, the door is not open yet. Be pleased to wait here. But when you are granted leave to enter, please have me summoned to her presence too.'

Wazir stopped, gestured to the palanquin-bearer to stay where he was. She had not said anything yet, when the door opened suddenly and a middle-aged woman, who was clearly well born and had soft, attractive features—but seemed to function as a lady's attendant—appeared at the doorstep. She called out in a conversational, cultured tone which was curiously carrying: 'Who is the lady from Khanam ka Bazaar? Bai Ji sahib is kindly remembering her.' Her Hindi revealed her Deccani origins, musical and more flexible than was normally heard in Delhi.

Wazir and Habiba looked around, and then at each other in wild surmise. They saw no one rising from her place. How could she have been identified? She had never been there before. She looked at Habiba again, who seemed bewildered and somewhat frightened. The attendant lady looked back through the open room. Some further instructions were given to her, in a very low voice, not heard by the people around them. The attendant lady turned to the multitude, and in a somewhat louder, more deliberate tone, called out, 'Honourables, I say again. Who is the venerable lady from Khanam ka Bazaar who has troubled her steps to be here from opposite the Sang-i Basi Mosque? Delay not, please. Bai Ji sahib does not have much time today.'

Now Wazir had no choice but to rise and make for the door. She beckoned to Habiba to go with her, and put out her hand to take the cowrie bags from the palanquin-bearer. The woman who had requested Wazir to intercede for her, sprang forward and said, 'My life for you, don't you take the trouble. Please give the bags to me.'

Bai Ji's attendant glared at her. The woman shrank back in terror, but did not give ground. The attendant spoke, half in reprimand, and half in a light, cheerful voice.

'Nakko, sahib. It's not your turn. Be patient a while, my Sister. And these bags, we are here for them!'

She took the two bags in her hands and gestured to Wazir and Habiba to enter. The door was shut the moment they went in. They did not know it, but this was unusual, for the door, once opened for visitors, was not closed before the day's audience was over. Stepping cautiously, Wazir and Habiba found themselves in a nearly dark chamber. There was no light, except what trickled in from two or three cracks in the walls. A spacious reed mat was spread in the centre of the room. Bai Ji sat on it, her feet under her thighs, and without the support of a pillow or bolster. The mat apparently did duty for both prayer and rest, for there was nothing like a bed or a wooden platform to be seen. In a corner was a new earthen pitcher on a low wooden stand, its mouth covered by a clean and carefully rubbed and shined drinking bowl. To the right there was a niche on which the Quran stood upon an elaborately carved wooden stand. That was all. There was no sign of a water room or a water closet. Perhaps these things were in another hutment, behind the main one. There were no eatables, or pots and pans, to be seen. In front of Bai Ji, there was a heap of cowries, beyond it, a worn-out cotton carpet for visitors.

The attendant poured the contents of the two bags in the heap that was already there and stood behind Bai Ji, her hands folded on her chest. Wazir raised her eyes fearfully and tried to look Bai Ji full in the face. She was quite thin, and seemed taller than average. Her face was a fine oval with very large eyes, but she was looking down, as if she never raised them, and was in meditation. Purple black rings around her eyes suggested long nights and little sleep. Apart from her face and hands, her upper body was covered with a Multani chintz chador in very light jasmine yellow, printed with small light-blue sprigs. Her trousers were of snow-white muslin, with wide bottoms, as was fashionable in Delhi some years ago. Neither her face nor hands revealed anything of her age, or ageing: no wrinkles, no looseness of muscle. Her hair was covered with the chador, but a few locks that seemed to have strayed out by themselves were jet black and had the shine of youth.

No one knew how old she was. Some said she was above seventy; someone quoted her grandfather to say that she was just as she is today when the grandfather was a mere boy. Some even went to the extent of saying that she came to Delhi from Kashmir in the year of the death of Muhammad Shah Ghazi (1748), who now rests in Paradise. By that reckoning, she should be more than a hundred now. Anyway, whatever her real age, she was certainly not young. In fact, she could be said to be in late middle age.

Although her eyes were lowered, from her face, or rather her whole presence, emanated such dignity, such control, sanctity and power that Wazir was obliged to blink and look away, again and again, and she dreaded the moment when Bai Ji would raise her eyes to her. She gathered up her body even more, wrapped the chador around her as tightly as she could, and placed herself gingerly in a corner of the carpet, more on its edge than on it. Habiba sat close, but a little behind her, more on the naked floor than on the carpet. Now Bai Ji raised her eyes and looked at Wazir. Oh God, what eyes they were! Deep black, with the whites showing extremely delicate red bloodshot capillaries—but a red that did not suggest any vitality, or the rosy tint of life. It seemed as if every wish, every longing, every need, every feeling of pleasure or pain, every hope had departed those eyes. Profound like a black unreflective ocean in which every scene, every emotion would drown without a trace.

In a supremely sweet and heart-affecting voice, Bai Ji recited the bismillah, then the three verses of the al-Kausar, the 108th chapter of the Quran. The recitation obviously took hardly any time. When she finished reciting, she picked up a handful of the cowries in front of her and put them aside. This process she repeated seventy times. Wazir seemed to be quite unable to do anything but try to absorb in her being the mellifluous voice reciting the verses. Later, Habiba told her that Bai Ji did not apparently do anything to keep count of the recitations; perhaps she knew by intuition, or perhaps the maid who stood behind made some sign. Allah knows best.

Bai Ji now addressed the visitors. 'Tell me please, what is your need?'

Her voice had the same music as her Quranic recitation.

'Everything is like a mirror before Bai Ji,' Wazir replied haltingly, swallowing once or twice.

'Navab Shamsuddin Ahmad will have to be abandoned.'

Hai Allah! What is it that Bai Ji is commanding! Wazir's heart was filled with fear and foreboding. She wanted to put something in her ears, not hear more.

'The begams of the Fort do not visit the tombs openly,' Bai Ji spoke patiently, as if explaining things to a child. 'The regime of the purdah is very strict there.'

'But . . . but, my children? What . . . will happen . . . happen with . . . with my children?'

'Something. Something good will surely happen.'

'So Bai Ji sahib commands that I should accept the proposal from the Fort?'

'We command nothing, baba. These events must happen.'

'And . . . and then all my sorrows will be over, Bai Ji sahib?'

'Joy and sorrow are like sun and shade. Everything is changeable. The days of the Kingdom at the Fort will also be over someday.'

Saying this, Bai Ji closed her eyes. The maid signed to Wazir from behind Bai Ji Sahib that the audience had ended. Wazir and Habiba rose, made three salaams and were about to withdraw, walking backwards, when Bai Ji half opened her eyes and said, 'The one who was offering to carry your sacks, tell her that her child will not come back now. But she should be patient. She will get something in replacement.'

Saying, 'Yes, madam, very good', they left the chamber. As soon as they came out, the missing child's mother, who stood right there, put out her hands impulsively towards them, and cried out, 'Oh Bibi ji! Let my life be sacrificed for you! Have I been summoned?'

'No, summon you she does not, Bibi; she stated that you might not get your child back, but Allah will give you something in its place.'

'Hai Allah!' The woman sobbed. 'Bai Ji has destroyed everything in my world!'

At that very moment, Bai Ji's maid appeared at the door and reprimanded the woman, 'Shush! Don't say sinful things! Bai Ji Sahib will be annoyed. Now go from here.' She then called out, 'All the ladies may please come in!'

The throng began to enter hurriedly, but not in a disorderly manner. Seeing that Wazir was now coming out, the palanquin-bearers put down the palanquin close to the veranda steps; and once Wazir and Habiba stepped inside, they proceeded to Khanam ka Bazaar.

64

Wazir Khanam becomes Shaukat Mahal

BY THE TIME Wazir Khanam's palanquin reached Khanam ka Bazaar, the elegant bustle and brightness of the morning's activities in Chandni Chowk were in flow. The establishments of confectioners, bakers and vendors of fresh milk were now alive with expert cooks, their young attendants and the throng and press of clients. Among them there were many who ate their breakfast right there, sitting on small stools or makeshift benches. Others preferred to take home what they bought: halwa; deep-fried pancakes of several varieties; jalebis; thick, cuttable cream, looking, for all intents and purposes, like smooth packets of milk-white paper folded and layered, of the size of half a palm of the hand, with or without ice; fish kebabs; kebabs made from goat liver and lamb liver; the special, rich oven-baked saffron bread called shirmal, its appetizing fragrance affecting even those who were not hungry; the spicy and rich broth of goat's meat, called nihari, made richer with bone marrow, pieces of brain and big dollops of ghee, eaten with hot, triangular or circular crusty bread hot from the oven. For those who preferred vegetarian food, there were many kinds of spicy and deep-fried vegetables, cooked to within an inch of their life: okra—the word was unknown then—stewed or stuffed with tongue-twisting spices made into a paste; bitter gourd, shredded and fried, or again stuffed with the hottest spices ground into a paste; and many others too complicated to describe here. The entire area presented a marvellous combination of sweet, saffrony, spicy scents. Itinerant sellers of marigold garlands, jasmine bouquets, and regular florists were now appearing on the scene, to cater to the temple-goers.

> The colour of the eastern horizon grows vermilion red apace. The tablet of the moon has reached the lowest level of the sky's turrets and

> now looks ugly like a copper tray . . . From the drum-houses, the gentle taps on the drums form the background to the heart-attracting and emotion-arousing graceful notes of the raga Bhairavi on the shahnai. From the Lahori Gate to Nigambodh Ghat flows a river of loveliness. The main road of the Chandni Chowk has taken on the aspect of the Milky Way. Thousands of pieces of the moon pass before the onlookers, glittering like the stars . . . The River Jamna, full of flower-bodied beauties bathing in it, looks like a huge bed of flowers. A thousand of the stars of the Heaven of Beauty, clad in fine silk saris, stand up to the waist in the water . . . A peri-faced beauty, having performed the holy bath in the holy River Jamna, is twisting, squeezing out excess water from her long, shiny tresses. Another one, clad in a dry sari, is twisting and squeezing out her wet sari.
>
> *The coral fingers squeezed out*
> *Pearls from the dark cloud;*
> *The weeping moon appeared*
> *From the dark collar of the night.**

In Wazir's house, Mian Navab Mirza woke up betimes, performed the morning ablutions and waited, alert and expectant for his mother's return so that some breakfast could be rustled up, or should Jani Ram report for work, he could be sent out to get some breakfast items. Navab Mirza had no idea about his mother's thoughts or doings, except that she had proposed to go out somewhere very early that morning. Perhaps her destination was Qadam Sharif, and that was nothing unusual. But when she returned and alighted from the palanquin, he was quite alarmed to see that her mien was unusually grave and thoughtful. He made the salaam and asked urgently, 'Amma Jan, is everything all right? Where were you visiting so early in the morning? Why do I see your face so wan and careworn? Are you unwell? Did you consult a hakim . . . ?'

Raising her hand, Wazir cut off his shower of questions and in an attempt to check her affectionate mirth at the boy's innocent anxiety, she

---

* Raqim-ud Daulah Zahir Dihlavi, from *Dastan-e Ghadr*, being his autobiography and first-person account of the events of 1857 in Delhi. 1910

said, 'Hey, young fellow! Be a little patient! Keep your equanimity. Let's first have some breakfast, then I'll tell you all.'

'Amma Jan, please be truthful. Is anything the matter?'

'Oh dear, oh dear! What could be the matter? You can see I am perfectly all right. Eat some breakfast; you have been starving since morning. I'll tell you my story in a minute!'

Having done with breakfast, and after Wazir gave the necessary instructions for the day's domestic chores, mother and son both withdrew to Wazir's bedroom. She narrated the whole story to Navab Mirza, including a full account of her visit to Bai Ji. For fear that it might prejudice Navab Mirza in favour of the proposal from the Fort, she omitted telling him that she and Bari Baji had more or less agreed about his marriage to Fatimah. Instead, she revealed to him all her fears and uncertainties about her possible move to the Fort as wife to the Third Heir Apparent.

Navab Mirza listened with full attention, and remained silent for some time after his mother finished speaking. Quickly, he weighed the matter in his heart as best as he could, then he said, 'Amma Jan, I think you should not worry at all about me and Shah Muhammad Agha. For I can easily look after myself, and Bari Khala will be most happy to take Shah Muhammad Agha and bring him up like her own son.'

Shadows of sorrow, mixed with annoyance and despondency crossed over her heart's horizon. So the young Lordship is sure that I will accept the invitation from the Haveli, as if it is quite right and proper for me to do so. As if there is no love at all in my heart for my children and I should be perfectly willing to leave my children behind. Well, Shah Muhammad Agha is still so tiny that he will only weep a few days and will be quickly diverted by toys and affectionate care. But my Bacche Mian is young, as Allah wills. He has more sense, more understanding. Will he not miss me? Will he persuade himself that he has delivered me over into a grave, not into the Haveli, and so he need not look back? If he had a sister, would he dispatch and bury her in an alien home so easily and with such good cheer? He perhaps believes that once Amma is out of the way, the field will be clear for him to marry Fatimah and take off somewhere . . . perhaps the Deccan. Did not Shah Nasir sahib go to the Deccan, never to come back? Is the journey to the Deccan something like going to Shahdarah? You hire a place in a bullock cart, cross the river and lo!—you are there. I understand the journey to Agra takes eight days. Is not the Deccan thousands of miles farther?

'What are you cogitating about so furiously, Amma Jan? You seem quite lost.'

'No, there is nothing of the sort,' Wazir a little flustered, replied quickly. 'I was just thinking that I am long past the age of marrying and merrymaking. I was hoping to spend the rest of my days supported and backed by you two, my dear sons. How good it would be for you to find some employment!'

'Amma Jan, you must have no anxiety about me finding a job. I will find something, somewhere. You are quite young, and if you take good care of yourself, you will look even younger, as Allah wills . . . and in fact, the great thing is . . .' He paused, then resumed somewhat haltingly, 'Fate never gave you a chance to settle . . . I mean really settle somewhere in comfort and free from day-to-day hassles. Now, it seems that something is happening . . . something that you truly deserve. I mean, others may come and go, but the Exalted Fort is not going away anywhere.'

Wazir felt less vexatious, now that she understood that Navab Mirza spoke out of love for her, not out of self-love. Even so, how did he countenance the possibility of our being separated?

Navab Mirza perhaps intuited what his mother was thinking. So he spoke in a firm, deliberate tone, 'Look, Amma Jan, separated from you, none of us can really survive. I, certainly, cannot. But we must also appreciate that our continued existence is fully dependent on yours. Were you to live in comfort, free from the carking cares entailed in organizing a life alone, would you not live longer then? And will you not be then able to do even better for us?'

'I should leave you two behind and live elsewhere comfortably? I cannot accept that.'

'Who said anything about your leaving us behind? It's possible that we two, or at least one of us, may after all be asked to live with you in the Fort. You won't be requiring either of your sons to go far away somewhere anyway.'

Wazir interrupted impatiently, her voice on the verge of breaking, 'No, but if you get employed somewhere like in the Deccan, or even Rampur, where will I find you then?'

'How could I be getting employment elsewhere when I won't have made an application for a position?' Navab Mirza tried to laugh her fears away. 'And this house, will you sell it off?'

'Far be it from me, farther than across the farthest river! Never should you say any such word, ever! Your father's memorial, a nook of security for us, should I ever let go of it?'

'Then be of good cheer. You will live in the Haveli in royal splendour; we'll live here, proudly wrapped in our animal skin of poverty!'

'Go, get on with you! You are always so facetious! At your Bari Khala's, you . . .' Wazir checked herself just in time.

Navab Mirza ignored his mother's slip of the tongue, or did not notice it, though he got to her meaning somewhat, and was keenly desirous for the matter to be brought out into the open. Wazir still thought that the least hint of Navab Mirza's marriage with Fatimah would surely colour his vision even more strongly in favour of his views about the Haveli proposal. Navab Mirza deliberately twisted her sentence to an innocuous conclusion.

'Yes, Amma Jan, there is always Bari Khala: she will give her best care to Agha sahib, and I will sojourn here, free of all care.' In his beautiful voice he said a verse from the eighteenth-century Persian poet Sukh Raj Sabqat:

He involves Himself in caring for me
And I am carefree:
Being God's slave has its own kind of Godhood!

'You must agree, Amma Jan, what a nice point it is, and how well he puts it! Not for nothing was he a pupil of Bedil. I can see that your state is something similar: You wear yourself out for care for us, and we roam around, happy and carefree.'

'Yes, sure,' said Wazir with playful asperity. 'If it shouldn't be I who was wearing myself out caring for you two, then it should be those of Loharu, right?'

Despite the apparent playfulness, a greyness of anxiety could clearly be felt in her words. This was confirmed by what she said next, 'Please think and answer, dear son, my dear Young Lord. Won't you regret my going away?'

'Hey, sahib, God forbid, are you going away to someplace far? It's only the Haveli. You can see it from here if you step out.' Navab Mirza hugged his mother. 'The Haveli is no jail! We'll miss you all the time.' His eyes now threatened to flow. 'But should there not be some space in your life for peace, comfort and freedom from care?'

'Is there peace for her who is separated from her children?' This time Wazir's asperity was genuine.

'Oh, you embellish and exaggerate so much, Amma Jan!' Navab Mirza teased her. 'We'll be nowhere else but at your feet virtually, if not in reality.'

Finally, Wazir was convinced that there was no lack of love for her in his heart, nor was he annoyed at the prospect of her marriage into the Fort; he desired that his mother should choose to start her life anew, in which her two children would apparently have not much of a role. If Navab Mirza is agreeable that I marry the Third Heir Apparent, it is not for want of love or empathetic regard for me, but fully because of his sincere love for me. Yes—Wazir told her heart—Navab Mirza's agreeability is all right as far as it goes, but I too must weigh and consider fully. These are not matters of amorous flirtation and romance, which could induce a girl to take a blind jump—as I did, once. I am older, more mature now. My steps should now be measured.

As a first step, she now decided to speak to Navab Mirza about his own marriage. She said, 'There is another matter about which I think it is now necessary to talk to you.'

'Yes, Amma Jan.' Navab Mirza came up close to her. 'I am all attention.' He bent towards her, his head almost near her bosom, as it used to be when he was small.

'Well, the matter in fact is . . .' She paused. 'The matter is that you are of marriageable age now. The invitation from the Fort may or may not bring some result for me; regardless of it, my great desire is for this house to be lit up with a daughter-in-law's auspicious steps.'

Navab Mirza was genuinely astonished. 'Marriage? You mean my marriage? But Amma Jan, I still am dependent on you for living from day to day!'

'That's what I also considered. Bringing in someone's daughter . . .'

The phrase 'someone's daughter' was extremely unsettling for Navab Mirza. Whose daughter could she mean? He quickly interrupted her, 'But, Amma Jan—'

Wazir cut him off. 'Dear boy, first let me finish; you must understand what I say. Against what security and on whose guarantee should I bring into my home someone else's daughter? That's what troubled me. But Bari Baji has different ideas, apparently.'

Now Navab Mirza could not contain himself. In great agitation, he rose from his seat and very nearly cried, 'So what did Bari Khala say, Amma Jan? Did she say something about me?'

Wazir smiled. She well knew the reason for her son's agitation. She said, 'Bari Baji was waiting for me to ask for Fatimah as your bride. Since I had not broached the subject with her at any time, she was obliged to keep her thought to herself and not open her mouth. Now while we were discussing the matter about the Fort, the question of your future also came up, and she hinted broadly that she would accept you as a son-in-law who lived in her house.'

Navab Mirza changed colour a little. He longed for Fatimah with all possible intensity of desire, but to be a son-in-law living in Bari Khala's house was a thought quite far from his mind. He began to say, 'Amma Jan, this house, whatever its worth, is mine, and also Fatimah's . . .'

'Oh, my dear boy, those are matters that can come later. The most important thing is that Bari Baji will be happy, most cordially happy if you were to marry Fatimah. And obviously, this is just what my heart desires, as well. So I told her, "Just as Fatimah is my daughter, so is Navab Mirza your son. We accept from the depths of our heart."'

'By Allah, Amma Jan, you breathe new life into my dead body!' Navab Mirza again hugged his mother, this time with even greater ardour. 'You have been kind to me thousands of times, but this one kindness is above all others! Each and every hair in my body was in slavery to you even before and I don't know what I should offer you now in thanks. I will pray for you as long as I live. May Allah keep your shade over me forever.'

Navab Mirza hugged his mother over and over again; he kissed her hands; he laughed; he said words of prayer for her with a choked throat. Wazir was weeping copious tears. Again and again, she did the action of taking away his ills and said, 'Bacche Mian, my dear child, don't pray for my long life. My prayer always is that my own years may be added to yours. What must come to you may come and take me first and I should depart this life when I have seen you two happy and flourishing.'

When the tumult in their hearts subsided a little, Navab Mirza said, 'Amma Jan, please don't ever imagine that if I suggest that you accept the message from the Fort, it's because there has been, or is going to be, a conversation between you and Bari Khala about me and Fatimah.'

'No, I have no doubt now, at all. I had none before, but honesty demanded that I should not disclose to you my conversation with Bari Baji on the subject, so that your opinion should be entirely disinterested.'

'Yes, madam, and I may also be permitted to make it clear that to my mind, those are two separate issues: your entry into the Auspicious Fort is another matter, and whatever is between you two sisters is something else. I do not see one as contingent on the other.'

'Navab Mirza, I expected nothing else from your auspicious and loving nature. These matters I will convey in full to Bari Baji, but be sure that I shall make my own conditions to the people at the Fort.'

'But Amma Jan, please, for heaven's sake don't make your acceptance of their invitation subject to their agreeing to your conditions.'

'Bhai . . . Navab Mirza, truly, you talk like a lawyer!' Wazir smiled.

'Amma Jan, this is not a matter for light talk, please!'

'Master, let me first put forward my conditions; then we shall see.'

'Did not Bai Ji affirm that everything would be all right with your children?'

'But she also said that the days of Kingdom at the Fort will also come to an end sometime.'

'Oh, that was just a general statement, as you can surely see. Why should we go beyond her actual words?'

'Well, all right. Let's see.' Wazir sighed. 'I'll go to Bari's tomorrow and tell her. After that, Allah is the Master of us all.'

'Be sure to give a hint to Habiba, please. Some minimum preparations will have to be made. And we should send word to Manjhli Khala well in advance. She will need to make travel arrangements, and take the Navab sahib's permission.'

Wazir hesitated in her heart. Bari Baji was not overly fond of Manjhli. She did not at all look kindly on her being attached to Navab Yusuf Ali Khan without marriage and continuing with that nefarious arrangement. Granted that they had entered upon a contract for temporary marriage valid according to the Shia theology, but such a contract has no meaning in our theology. . . . Oh well, be that as it may, Chhoti Begam shrugged her shoulders (this was one of the things she'd learnt from Marston Blake, but she never did it when there were others present). Manjhli Baji is also my sister. And I am beholden to her for the numerous good things that she has done for me. So I'll just inform Bari Baji that I am inviting Manjhli Baji; I don't need to ask her permission. And I am sure she will be happy, if anything, to have Manjhli Baji present at the ceremony. As regards Maulavi Muhammad Nazir sahib, well, nowadays it was routine for practically all men, including the pious and the orthodox, to openly have one or two extramarital connections. Perhaps Nazir sahib did not have a connection of that type, but he wouldn't mind Manjhli's temporary marriage.

'Yes, quite right,' Wazir said. Navab Mirza had been wondering why his mother seemed to demur. 'I will send a letter to her by the Dawk, as soon as matters are firmed up.'

*

All issues were thrashed out over the next five or seven days. Mirza Fakhru Bahadur's view about the children was that Navab Mirza would be taken into the Fort a short while after the marriage; he would be brought up and educated as the Third Heir Apparent's own son at the Third Heir Apparent's expense. He would live with his mother at the Third Heir Apparent's apartment. About Shah Muhammad Agha, the verdict was that since he was very small, it would not be possible to give him due care and nurture at the Auspicious Haveli. A monthly pension would be granted for him, but Wazir would have to make her own arrangements for raising him and giving him adequate foster care. Wazir well understood that the real reason must be quite different. Doubtless, Shah Muhammad Agha was weaned; but he was still very small and would need quite a great deal of the mother's personal attention if he accompanied her into the Fort. In that case she would not be able to devote herself all the time, and wholeheartedly, to Fathul Mulk Bahadur, Wazir thought bitterly to herself. But when she looked at the matter coolly, the Fort's view could be seen as just. Having Navab Mirza accepted into the Fort should itself be considered a singular success for Wazir, and also—Allah preserve and protect him—a measure of the young man's value in the eyes of those who had discernment, and great hopes from him in the future.

The dower was suggested as one hundred thousand rupees Shah Alami, and one hundred gold mohurs, again Shah Alami. Nothing of it, however, was payable immediately: future payment of all the sums was firmly promised as a part of the marriage contract. In return, it was proposed that the bride's side need not offer any wedding presents to the bridegroom or his family, or make any other expenses at all; nor the groom give dowry to the bride. One or two maids could accompany the bride as dowry. The Emperor and the bridegroom each would present a full bridal dress to the bride. Anything that the bride got by way of 'gifts for unveiling her face' from the family and friends of the bridegroom would belong to her exclusively. There would be a marriage contract drawn up according to the Shariah which would be signed by the Qazi who pronounced the nuptiale rites, as well as by the bridegroom and the bride. After the marriage was solemnized, a nalki, accompanied by two outriders and four mace-bearers, would issue forth from the Auspicious Fort and would bring the bride into the Fort with due honour.

All conditions were acceptable to Wazir, except the separation from Shah Muhammad Agha. Sometimes a wild impulse would arise in her, to say 'No'! To declare that if the child was not part of the deal, she was not, either. Then she called to mind Bai Ji sahib's foretelling that all would be well with her children, and that these events must happen. On the other hand, when she gave thought to her future, and Navab Mirza's future, nothing seemed more attractive than a life inside the Fort. It occurred to her that she might revisit Bai Ji sahib and ask for further instruction; but she desisted, for it would surely be impertinence.

Finally, she found a solution, a sort of halfway house: She would organize some reliable caregiver for Shah Muhammad Agha; but when he grew up, he should be permitted to be educated in the Fort; and so long as he was small, she would have the right to have him brought to her once in a while, and especially when he was poorly.

The Third Heir Apparent Bahadur accepted this, though grudgingly. An auspicious date was determined in consultation with the Astrologer Royal. A night before that date, Wazir Khanam shifted to Bari's house so that a proper, though brief, 'bridal farewell ceremony' could be effected. At the appointed time, Maulavi Imam Bakhsh Sahbai appeared at Bari's, and from behind a curtain, sought Wazir's permission to pronounce her marriage rites with Sahib-e Alam wa Alamiyan Mirza Muhammad Sultan Ghulam Fakhruddin Fathul Mulk Bahadur, Third Heir Apparent to the Emperor of Hindustan, in exchange for one hundred thousand rupees and one hundred gold mohurs, both Shah Alami; Maulavi Muhammad Nazir Rifai Mujaddidi and Ihtiram-ud Daulah Umdat-ul Hukama Hakim Muhammad Ahsanullah Khan Bahadur stood as witnesses. After hearing Wazir's word of acceptance clearly enunciated, Maulavi Muhammad Nazir and Maulavi Sahbai rode into the Fort where a small and select gathering was assembled for the pronouncement of marriage, with all present hearing the groom's word of consent. Maulana Sahbai, and the bridegroom and the witnesses signed the marriage contract. A great din of congratulations arose, and Mirza Fathul Mulk Bahadur was seen to be grinning broadly, as if it was his first marriage, charged with all youthful desire and hopes for marital happiness. Sweets were distributed generously, but there was no dinner.

Mirza Fathul Mulk Bahadur sent, with the Emperor's permission, the Royal nalki for the bride. Earlier in the day, he had sent the elegant and sumptuous marriage dress of his first wife for Wazir. Significantly, Mirza Fatḥul Mulk Bahadur had not given it away to anyone, including his second wife, after Fazilat-un Nisa Begam, his first wife, died. Manjhli Begam, well versed in the customs and practices of the ruling elites, suggested that nothing should be sent back with the bride, apart from whatever came from the Fort by way of escort or bridal gifts. Wazir, who had been silently observing the proceedings so far, refused to accept this and insisted that Habiba, and whatever other things like dresses and jewellery that her eldest sister wished, must accompany her. If the people of the Fort did not agree, let them go to hell.

'Hey, what is it that you say, girl!' said Umdah Khanam, alarmed. 'Should someone get to hear, it'll immediately become the gossip of the day!'

'You are right, Manjhli Baji,' replied Wazir, 'but would it be appropriate for me to get there almost naked? Why, it'll be like the proverb: "Her head is her litter, and her feet are her litter-bearers; here comes the lady whose name is New Spring!" It seems so immodest, really.'

'Actually, custom-wise, Manjhli is right,' said Bari Begam. 'But Chhoti is not an ordinary bride; she has specially been asked for, or in fact invited. I should think that she may take with her some of her more valuable jewellery and dresses from the Navab's time.'

It was a cold, but agreeable evening on 24 January 1845: an evening, somewhat hazy, wrapped in the mysterious, sweet and profoundly affecting woodsmoke from the hearths, when Umdah Khanam, Navab Mirza, Amat-ul Fatimah and Maulavi Muhammad Nazir effected Wazir's formal 'bridal farewell' with their hearts full of hope and prayer; she was walked under the shadow of the Quran to Bari's main door and into the nalki. Akbari rode in it with Wazir, followed by another palanquin bearing Habib-un Nisa carrying with her Wazir's jewel box and footlocker containing her best clothes. Shah Muhammad Agha was disconsolate, demanding to accompany his mother, but Bari Begam's senior maid diverted his attention by sending him to the bazaar to enjoy the sights and to buy toys.

Travelling with Wazir in the nalki, Bari Begam was weeping a flood of tears, which were not slaked in spite of Wazir's entreaties. These are tears of joy, she said. Allah granted her the bliss of dressing and bedecking her little sister with her own hands and accompanying her to a new abode. There were no girls singing songs to give words to the mute bride as she left her father's protective, loving threshold, but I am sad, and also marvellously happy. How happy would our father be if he was here today to see Chhoti compensating, in the fullest measure of gladness, for the unhappiness that she had caused him. How profuse would be his prayers and blessings for me and for Chhoti! May Allah give security and permanence to the couple and give me the strength to care for Shah Muhammad Agha in the best possible way. It has been so long, she smiled a pale smile, since I did the duty of changing nappies. May Allah save my honour.

Inside the Exalted Fort, the stone-paved path leading to the Royal Apartment was teeming with an army of Qulmaqnis, Urdabegnis, and Turkestani as well as Abyssinian women bodyguards and numerous others. They promptly surrounded the nalki like a horde of sightseers. Some of the bolder and more pert ones approached close and opening the nalki's door a few inches, peeped in and stepped quickly back, loudly calling salutations upon the Prophet, the standard mode of admiring and praising a beautiful face. Another one was even saucier—she laughed with pleasure and said to the woman who stood next to her, 'Ha! Only God is untouched by blemish! I have heard about hazy winter moons, but this is the moon of sarad punam, which appears at the beginning of winter! Look at it and your heart will be filled with gladness.'

'Yes, biwi, burning hot and dark like the black rose!'

'Hey, you wretches! Don't linger. Send a Jasolni quickly to the Mahabali's Palace with the report that his daughter-in-law—bright and sweet like the sun and the moon—has brought her noble presence into the Fort!'

It was the Mahabali's practice to retire for comfort rather late at night, and he did not normally permit anyone to present themselves before him after the sunset prayers. For today, his command was that he should be informed if the arrival of the bride was not much delayed, for he would like the bride to receive her 'gifts for unveiling her face' from him before she took her noble presence to her Palace. Accordingly, a Jasolni sped to the Tasbih Khanah, the Emperor's main residential apartment, with the glad tidings. The nalki-bearers stood patiently waiting for further commands.

Those among the welcoming party who spied for Zinat Mahal mentally noted carefully the names of those who were rather more ebullient than the rest in welcoming the bride; those who showed no particular interest also came in for being remarked.

Within a few minutes, Fathul Mulk Bahadur could be seen approaching, followed by a Jasolni. She conveyed the order that the Mahabali of Good Fortune and Prosperity is remembering the bride. The train now moved forward and arrived at the main door of the Tasbih Khanah; the bearers placed the nalki upon a marble platform in front of the Exalted Portal. Mirza Fakhru advanced a step, intending to open the nalki's door and take the bride in his arms and thus help her inside the portal without her feet touching the ground. In the same instant, two colossal Abyssinian women bodyguards, extremely powerful-looking, though well past their youth, laughed out aloud and cried out in a free and friendly manner, 'Hey, hey, Sahib-e Alam, Heir Apparent Bahadur! Not so fast! It is our job to help the bride alight from the nalki! And aren't you going to loosen the purse strings for us, the destitute and the penniless? If not, well, your dear little begam will remain cooped up in her nalki!'

This was greeted with hilarious guffaws. But Mirza Fakhru was not going to withdraw so easily. He chortled, 'Yaqut-un Nisa, you have helped God knows how many brides cross the river. Would that you gave me a chance sometime!'

'Your Honour, you have all the chances in the world. It is us poor folk who don't always get to palm a bit of pure gold.'

The exchange was received with meaningful smiles, because Yaqut-un Nisa and her partner Zaitun were reputed to have a relationship.

'Well, Sister, we are Turk, you must know. We don't let others lay a hand on our property.'

'We beg to submit to the Son of the World's Guide and Mentor: It will be your property only after we pick it up and pass it on to you.'

'Biwi, it is the Almighty's own gift. It's not a ripe fruit that should fall from the branch for you to pick up and give it to me.'

'Your Honour, I can swear by the Thirty Discourses. I just peeked into the nalki and was dazzled! The ripe fruit falling doesn't touch it. It seemed to me as if God the Most Sacred had caused lightning to be packed in a basket and hung in there. Then, by the Power of the Lord the breeze of union blew . . .'

'And the basket's string broke and the basket plopped into your sacred hands,' Zaitun completed the sentence.

This was again greeted with a burst of laughter. Mirza Fakhru's laughter was the loudest. When the laughter abated somewhat, the Prince said, 'Now Lady Kitty may lick her chops, but the basket reached where it was destined for.'

During these pleasantries, Fathul Mulk Bahadur's Urdabegni had been distributing thin gold or silver rings, according to rank and seniority, to those who were present. Now a Qulmaqni pulled the curtain of the Emperor's audience chamber and announced, 'The Exalted Presence summons the bridegroom and the bride!'

Yaqut and Zaitun sprang to the nalki, opened its door and gently brought out in their arms the magnificently clothed Wazir, who had been sitting shrunk in a corner of the spacious conveyance. There were calls of 'Bismillah!' 'Let the Quran be the Guarantor!' 'Bring the chador!' Four women stretched a large brocade cloth above her as Wazir, held carefully and like a parcel by Yaqut and Zaitun in their arms, was brought in a slow procession towards the chamber. Bari Begam remained in the nalki while Habib-un Nisa's palanquin was escorted by two Urdabegnis to the Third Heir Apparent's apartment.

Just as they crossed the threshold of the audience chamber, the two Abyssinian women let Wazir softly down on the floor and signed to her to go forward. As the hem of her heavy dupatta hung in front of her face like a veil, Wazir could see almost nothing, but the Abyssinian bodyguards held her arms and guided her gently.

The rest of the bodyguards and the welcoming maids stayed outside. Mirza Fathul Mulk Bahadur, stepping confidently and with slow deliberation, led the bride into the chamber, which was aglitter with lights so powerful that Wazir could feel her eyes almost dazzled behind her upper wrap. Allah, it seems that all the city's lamps are burning here, she said to herself.

'Be aware!'

'Allah and His Prophet, be aware!'

'Do obeisance with full respect! Refuge of the World, the Mahabali, may he be ever secure! First station of audience!'

'Attention! Do obeisance with all respect! Second station of audience!'

'Refuge of the World, the King, may he be ever secure!'

'Look in front! Third station of audience!'

The first station of audience was the chief threshold of the chamber; the second station was a heavy curtain of red broadcloth which was drawn on pulleys; the third station was after the curtain, the point where the visitor stopped and from where the Emperor could be seen. At this stage, a visitor made the salaam for the third time, folded his hands just below the midriff and stood erect, with his gaze immediately in front, but not directly at the King.

'Be pleased to accept the obeisance of Navab Dulhan sahib!'

'Bismillah al Rahman al Rahim. Grace and Mercy of God and His Prophet! Let the enemy be crushed underfoot! Let the calamities be turned back! Dulhan sahib submits her salaams!'

The entire floor was covered with costly carpets. There were silk and golden curtains on all sides and the Emperor's seat right at the centre, with the Emperor seated in a formal posture. The energy and dignity of the Royal blood of many centuries coursing through him; the body fully erect, the neck high and full of self-confidence, it was as if the spirit of Jalaluddin Muhammad Akbar was embodied in that frail frame. Wazir somehow made the formal Mughal kurnish, made one more salaam, bewildered about what she should do next. But then she heard the Emperor's voice, sophisticated and strong, brimming with the sense of power, as if signalling that even though there was no Kinghood, he was still King, and even now could take up arms, if necessary.

'Only God is untouched by blemish! We acknowledge the excellence of Mirza Fakhru's taste. May Allah give protection against the evil eye.'

Yaqut-un Nisa quietly nudged Wazir to advance a step or two. Wazir, much awed by the occasion, felt incapable of putting even one foot forward. Slowly, her head bent, she took one step after the other and approached the Presence. The Refuge of the World made a brief sign to the Qulmaqni who stood with a gold-inlaid ebony box in her hands; she opened the box and brought out a pearl necklace; on another sign from the King, she hung the necklace around Wazir's neck. Wazir made three salaams and stood again in a quandary about what she should do next. Again, the Refuge of the World commanded, 'We name you Shaukat Mahal. It is our heart's desire for you both to be bestowed with the attainment of all your purposes in this world and the next, and may all the joys of marriage form a protective ring around you two.'

'Amen! May God and His Prophet's protection be always there! May the groom's and the bride's hearts be always joined together! Congratulations to Shaukat Mahal sahib on her title!'

As these voices subsided, the Court Crier called out, 'Pearl of the Crown of Empire, Aigrette of the Diadem of Caliphate, Third Heir Apparent, Ghulam Fakhruddin Fathul Mulk Mirza Muhammad Sultan Bahadur!'

Yaqut beckoned Wazir with a small gesture to withdraw. Wazir somehow walked three steps backwards and stood to one side while Mirza Fakhru made the salaams from the third obeisance station, stepped forward four steps and presented his nazr, the formal offering, to the Mahabali. The Emperor touched the offering with two fingers; the Receiver of Offerings took the nazr, put it on his head, and did the salaam to the Third Heir Apparent Bahadur who now walked back to the obeisance station. Then, before the ceremonial robe, or khilat, was bestowed on the Prince, His Majesty spoke suddenly, 'Ama Mirza Fakhru Bahadur!'

'At your service, my Mentor and Guide.'

'Isn't there a young fellow, the memorial of Shamsuddin Ahmad Khan? A nice poet.'

'Very true, my Mentor and Guide.'

'He is not in evidence here . . . what's his name, a somewhat nice name?'

'Sir, Exalted Highness, he is called Navab Mirza.'

'Ah, yes. Navab Mirza Khan. So what is his state?'

'It was a grievous lapse of memory on my part, Exalted Highness. I did not seek permission from the Noble Servants to have him presented at this Lofty Pavilion.'

'Keep him under your shade. Orders will issue for bestowal on him of a monthly stipend.'

'It is the miracle-working Mentor and Guide's nurture of his subjects and his far-reaching generosity. Orders of the Honourable Foundation of the State will be carried out forthwith.'

'Most proper.'

'On behalf of the fortunate Navab Mirza Khan and his mother, this servant expresses gratefulness and bends his brow at the Portal of the Emperor's Lofty Pavilion for the young person being awarded and ennobled with the title Khan.'

Now a parchment-bearer appeared with the ceremonial robe on a large silver tray. The Prince made three salaams, took the main outer garment from the bearer and put it on. He stepped up to the King, the Protector of Faith, and did the kurnish for a second time. His Majesty, as a mark of special favour to his servant, personally tied around the Prince's turban the brocaded ribbon with a gem fitted at the front—the sar pech—and followed this up with the jewelled pin worn upon it—the jighah. He hung the long ornament called the goshvarah on both sides of the Prince's turban, and wound up the dress part of the ceremony with a pearl necklace around the Prince's neck. He then tied a shield upon the Prince's back by means of a leather-and-iron thong wound around the shoulders, and finally, the Presence hung a sword on the front of the Prince's body with a thick brocade thread passed through a hole in its gripe. The Prince submitted another nazr in token of gratefulness for the ceremonial robe. The Presence touched it with his two fingers, as usual; the Receiver of Offerings then took it and put it away. The Emperor raised his hands to say a brief prayer. The moment the prayer was over and everyone cried out 'Amen', the Court Announcer called out in a powerful voice, 'The Court is dismissed!'

His Majesty slackened his posture, put down his feet. Before his feet could touch the floor, the shoe-bearer unrolled a silk and silver cloth, produced a pair of Mughal shoes whose uppers were so heavily worked in bullion that they looked as if they were painted with the stuff. He put the shoes on the King's auspicious feet and His Majesty sedately took his noble presence into the inner palace. Those present moved from their places only after the cries were heard to the effect that the Presence had troubled his feet to enter the palace. The nalki was stationed outside on the marble platform and Wazir was helped into it with the usual ceremony. The bearers pronounced the verse of bismillah and proceeded to the haveli of Mirza Fathul Mulk Bahadur.

65

Lust circles that silvery one's body like a tiger

NO SOONER HAD she arrived at Mirza Fakhru's haveli than Habiba took charge of the arrangements of bedecking the bride and organizing everything for the bridal chamber. Bari Begam departed after performing the usual action of taking upon her own self any adversity that might befall Wazir.

'I entrust you to the protection of God and his beloved Prophet,' she said as she dried her tears. 'I pray to God that you may now be granted nothing but happiness and freedom from care all your life.'

Wazir hugged her sister and whispered, 'Please, Bari Baji, you must pray for me at all times.'

Habiba quickly carried out the necessary and urgent beautifications on Wazir and led her into the bridal chamber. Inevitably, Wazir remembered that night of so long ago when Habiba had so lovingly cared for her. Her heart welled up with blood. Will I never be able to forget my martyred Navab? Not even at this moment, when my life is being rewritten? Habiba knew at once that those were not tears of joy, but of grief. Or, looked at another way, not even of grief: just the dew of past remembrances, anxious to be absorbed and lost in the land of the ever-fresh flowers of the heart's scars. Habiba dried her tears with a soft, light green muslin handkerchief and said, 'Khanam sahib, please take a hold on yourself. The Prince must be coming. The memory of those days will always be green, but this is the time for letting the new flowers bloom. Please.'

Sobbing, Wazir nodded in agreement, and whispered, 'Habiba, you are quite right. But my heart swells in a flood, for no reason really. But you are quite right, I must contain myself. Let me have some water, please.'

'Here, drink from this cup. I take leave now, but I beg you, on my life, efface these signs of grief from your face.'

Blue and green floor lamps and chandeliers softly and evenly lighted the bridal chamber. The light, low but clear, was everywhere in the room. The bedstead was fully decorated with flowers and gold lace. It was quite high, needing steps for setting foot upon it. There were wooden steps, heavy and well decorated; the tread wide enough to preclude any chance of a step being missed. Habiba sat Wazir at the head of the bed; a true bride she looked: her knees pressed to her bosom, her head resting on the knees; the veil-like hem of the extremely heavy, almost stiff brocade dupatta entirely hiding the head and the face; both hands in her lap, but hidden under the dupatta. There was tension in Wazir's mind, so much that a slight tremor shook her hands and knees. After Habiba went out, Wazir closed her eyes demurely, though she also felt a little incongruous in adopting the manner of a newly-wed young and inexperienced bride.

Habiba was just quitting the antechamber of the bedroom when Mirza Fathul Mulk Bahadur arrived, two torchbearers leading him and two staff-bearers bringing up the rear. A Qulmaqni announced, 'The Third Heir Apparent Bahadur, may he always be secure!'

Accepting the salutations of the servants, Mirza Fakhru proceeded inside. He started a little when his eyes fell on Habiba. He saw an unfamiliar woman, at the threshold of old age, good-looking, dressed like someone of good family. Habiba rose, advanced a step, made three salaams and spoke in her best voice, 'This maidservant presents her submissions before the son of the World's Mentor and Guide. I am known by the name of Habib-un Nisa. I am appointed to be in the service of Her Honour the Dulhan Begam sahib.'

Mirza Fakhru found himself approving of Habib-un Nisa and enjoying her sophisticated words and good manners. He looked at her kindly and said: 'Your coming has made my heart happy, madam, but do not say "Dulhan Begam sahib". Say "Navab Shaukat Mahal sahib", for that is the title bestowed on her from the Royal Pavilion.'

'Only God is untouched by blemish! Indeed, what a suitable and appropriate title. May Allah make it auspicious for both your Noble Presences! Be pleased to step in. The bridal chamber awaits you.'

'Bismillah.'

Habib-un Nisa walked the Prince to the door of the bedchamber, salaamed, and walked out backwards.

The son of the World's Mentor and Guide entered; his steps were confident and measured, but his heart was beating faster than usual. When he saw Wazir in the form and posture of a new bride, he had a sudden impulse to forget the protocol of good manners and fill his arms with Wazir's enticing body. But he desisted, as desist he must. His action could be construed as an exhibition of bad manners, or at least an undesirable and unnecessary hastiness. He kept advancing sedately, and Wazir, as she sensed his footfalls, wished to rise and do the salaam, but Mirza Fakhru had already arrived at the bed.

'I make my respectful submissions,' said he, and held out his hand to stop Wazir from rising. 'Please do not trouble yourself,' he smiled. 'I am here already! No amount of thanks to the Almighty will really suffice for this auspicious moment.' He approached close, put his right hand gently on Wazir's head, almost in benediction, and recited a Persian verse:

All praise to God, everything that my heart
Desired, finally made itself apparent from
Behind the curtain of Destiny!

He climbed the steps and intended to perch just on the edge of the bed, but Wazir made a little space next to her and spoke in a husky, somewhat tremulous voice, worrying at heart if she was doing the right thing, 'Be pleased to bring your Noble Presence here; there is enough room.'

'It would mean something for me if there were room in your heart, madam. You may or may not remain seated on the bed but I have seated you firmly in my heart.'

By now Wazir had got back some of her nerve, and said, 'Ahlan wa sahlan.' She used the Arabic phrase used long ago by Habiba for her: you are like family to us; so feel easy and comfortable. Perhaps there was unconscious symbolism here, for Wazir went on to quote a Hindi line from the great Mir Dard, suggesting perhaps her loneliness and her need for a man in her life:

The glass has been waiting a whole lifetime,
Eager for the stone.

'By Allah, what a line of verse you brought out, madam! But eagerness is the daily regimen of life of the likes of us . . .' Mirza Fakhru breathed a deep sigh of regret and quoted an Arabic line from an Arabic-Persian ghazal from Hafiz:

My disunion with you was a long and hard time,
Like the Doomsday.

Wazir had no Arabic, but Mirza Fakhru Bahadur apparently believed that she did; or perhaps he thought that she surely must be familiar with the Arabic lines in that ghazal from the celebrated Hafiz Shirazi. As it was, Wazir had been scared nearly witless by the splendour and the elaborate protocol of the Imperial Court. On top of that was the teeming multitude of memories from her halcyon days. Such a state was scarcely conducive for her to recall Persian poetry, especially one mixed with Arabic. It was just the Grace of God that she could recall an appropriate verse from the same ghazal:

My eyes bear hundreds of signs of our disunion:
Are not my tears a true sign of the lovers?

Mirza Fakhru was enchanted. 'My God, what readiness of wit, what power of memory! Should we hope also for being imprisoned in your prison house of memory, such that we should have no possibility of release?'

Wazir's mental jitters all but evaporated before the Prince's obvious admiration for her ready wit. Her power of recall also became fully functional now. She revealed her full face and said a verse, again from the same ghazal:

The morning breeze suddenly blew off
The veil from my hidden state,
Like the sun revealing itself from behind the clouds
Late in the morning.

Mirza Fakhru raised Wazir's face by her chin, kissed her forehead, and cried out, 'Truly, my heart's desire is for you to be seated in front of me as you are now, and for me to listen to you saying verse after verse from our great masters. But I, or should I say we, have other, more urgent and interesting tasks ahead of us. For the present, please hear the Shirazi

Khvajah yet another time.' He continued with the closing verse of that same ghazal:

Now that Hafiz is here, begging for a bowl of wine,
Give it to him, let him taste from it,
Most generously, and take his life in return.

Wazir whispered in reply, 'The son of the World's Mentor and Guide has everything that anyone could desire. I am a miserable pauper. How could I even dream of possessing something worthy of you?'

'I swear, madam, this feigned and deliberate ignorance murders me! Perhaps you wish to indicate that my life is not so valuable as to be worth a kiss, or even a sight of your face. I agree entirely. But sometimes a little regard for the buyer's avid temperament may also be allowed. Has not the Persian poet Baba Fughani already answered on behalf of all the desired ones?'

'Sir, you are clever and learned enough to be fully aware of the arguments that could support you. But to me, Baba sahib's words seem sheer affectation.' She followed it up by saying the Fughani verse to which Mirza Fakhru had just alluded:

'You, who are surprised at me for buying
A bowl of wine with my life, go and ask the Saqi
The reason why the wine is selling at a bargain price.

'I have sold nothing yet, Sahib-e Alam. There's nothing on show.'

'Oh, cruel maid, what is this? I was under the illusion that the power of love in my heart has drawn you here. It seems things are quite to the contrary! Madam, you need not lower the price of anything at all, or give anything away, but you must confer a little privilege upon us lovers, pay some regard to our feelings. Don't you recall the words of the divine Khusrau?' He recited:

You price yourself at the two worlds;
Raise the price some more, you are low-priced still!

'Presence, Sahib-e Alam, pardon me, but you misapprehend.' Wazir let her dupatta fall from her face and neck, revealing the full beauty of the soft curves and the miracle of symmetry that was her face. She looked at the Prince boldly in the face. 'Only those can raise the rate who were cheaply on show at some time or the other. You must have heard:

'The self-aware are their own guards:
The poppy flower is both the candle and the chandelier.

'You should not look for me in the marketplace, not even in that marketplace, where lovers and beloveds are bought and sold.'

'Please. You talk in riddles! Are you not my desired one, my longed-for one?'

'Actually, Sahib-e Alam, I came here begging for you and seeking you, prepared to be your slave without being bought. Thus, there can be nothing like raising or reducing any kind of price. But . . .'

'But what? What is it? Tell me, please!' Mirza Fakhru was much perturbed, in fact anxious and upset. He wanted to put his arms around Wazir's neck, but she anticipated him and took his hand in hers, pulling the Prince's arm around her neck. She drew close to him and said in a low voice, 'I do not seek worship. I am looking for stability, and endurance. Like you, I speak through the Tongue of the Unseen, who conjured his lover:

'Do not go away from me, for you are the light
Of my eyes.

'I ask you not to leave me alone, in the dark.'

Fathul Mulk Bahadur kissed both of Wazir's hands, looked long at her face and spoke in a gentle, loving voice, 'My lady, there are some separations which none can control or govern. Apart from those, there can be none others obliging us to part.' He recited Hafiz again:

Hafiz, be happy; tell the enemy to die trying
To harm thee. When I have your warmth,
Why should I fear the enemy's cold breath?

'I pray to the Almighty to create a state of unity between us forever, and nothing else.'

'Wazir Khanam, man is good for as much unity as is humanly possible.

We beg the Almighty for the unity that is humanly possible between us. This is the best world that can be, for God created no better. Perhaps maximum randomness is the key to human existence. Once dead, we can be conjoined again. Look at the Hindus, they burn their dead, consigning dust to dust, scattering the ashes. But the Almighty has the power to bring everything back, as he says in the Quran: "Surely Allah is able to bring him back to life!" That will be the time when all will be brought together forever.'

'What does unity mean when man's mould is stuffed with forgetfulness and self-seeking? You are the son of the World's Mentor and Guide, Sahib-e Alam, and you should give me the answer.'

'Madam, can you demand from man something other than that he be human? The reality will not change, even if someone were ever to solve your conundrums. We should be content with our truth. That is our station. That is what becomes us best . . . But Wazir Khanam, why do you ask these questions? Why, are our evening and night for proposing and analysing major and minor premises in a lesson in logic? Or are all these but an excuse for our fire to be stoked up even hotter? Bibi, do you not hear an ocean in tumult within our being? Do you have no thought for the wind of desire storming through my soul?'

He paused for a couple of beats or more. Perhaps he was exhausted, having delivered his long, passionate speech? No. He was taking a breather for another assault. He took both of Wazir's hands in one of his, implanted a light kiss on her lips, and said, 'Do you not know the celebrated verse from Muhammad Quli Salim?'

Wazir looked at him inquiringly, not quite comprehending. Mirza Fakhru smiled and recited in the sweetest voice, full of enticement and also almost brazen flirtation:

Lust circles that silvery one's body like a tiger,
For it has glimpsed the hoof print of a deer
Under her skirt.

Mirza Fakhru reddened slightly as he finished saying the verse. Indeed, he felt almost ashamed to say such an openly suggestive—not to say aggressive—verse to her in their very first meeting. But truth to tell, he found no choice, for he was getting bored, if not irritated by Wazir's intellectual question-and-answer session. He now wanted to draw Wazir into his arms, close to his breast, preparatory to entering fresh fields and pastures new. On her part, Wazir not only reddened, she experienced the heat of immodest desire run through her body, and also a sense of shame at the awakening of such a desire. Such a flirtatious, voluptuous verse even women would never think of saying and enjoying among themselves when there were no men anywhere near.

So far, there had been nothing more for the Prince in Wazir's heart than that he was her husband, and she owed him nothing above the faithful discharge of wifely duties, with proper feminine grace and flair. Doubtless, he was good-natured, pleasant and handsome, and the Third Heir Apparent. She had chosen him for these reasons. But up until now, those who occupied the inner space of her heart were other people, from other times. She was perfectly ready to treat her partnership with the Sahib-e Alam wa Alamiyan as a pleasant duty, but she did not see herself accepting him as a lover, or beloved, or even as a friend.

Now, hearing him recite Salim's verse with such obvious but powerful invitation, a change seemed to occur in her psyche; she was somewhat fearful of it, but there it was. It was as if the Sahib-e Alam wa Alamiyan had spelt some mantra around her, and spoke not just an openly erotic but sophisticated verse by a long-dead Persian poet. The fragile, formal thread that she believed to be the connecting link between her and the Prince, a thread spun by religious convention and public belief, like the cotton threads that people wore around their wrists or necks because someone blew on them to make them auspicious or efficacious, that thread was now cut and pulled away from Wazir's heart like the flimsiest of spider webs. It was not just a marriage between them now, a cold, barren, though honest transaction. A new tightness of energy, a new power, began to speed and flow like a flood through the so far dead arteries of her body. She felt her breasts fill and tighten. Where no impudent being ever raised its head these many years, two proud and purple points became evident, as if some magic was bringing down there the reflection from the dark, deep brown of her eyes. Because her breasts swelled and rose, the reflection of her impudent eyes falling upon them, she remembered a Persian verse long lost from her brain. Her body began to thrill to a new warmth. Below the whirlpool of the water of life and creation, the water of eternity began to spring and spray itself into the cave of the water of life. Within no time, that place became a place for slipping and losing one's footing, even for those hardened and pious. That one, whose eyes are so saucy, she now seems to have arrived at the level of enjoyment. There is moisture on her skin, like a ripened fruit. The imprint of the deer's foot became hot and bright at the edge of the rose's petals and began to open slowly, like a wound in the lover's inmost heart. Beneath the horizon of the morning of the lover's hopes, secret signs of a crack in the moon began to appear. What had so far been the picture of لا (la, 'no') began to morph itself into بلا (bala, 'yes'). The two crescents, which had been stuck fast to each other so far, began to drift slowly apart, watered by the salt of life.

Wazir had not ever expected for the dark purple lock to be opened again. She had, in fact, like the Hindi poet Insha'allah Khan of the previous century, 'wept away such things once and for all'. But the Sahib-e Alam wa Alamiyan wielded some enchantment, or wore some puissant amulet, or his love for Wazir bound and encircled his spirit and body so strongly that even Wazir's spirit and body could find no means to get away from its magnetic field. Gently, fondly, Mirza Fakhru rubbed the soles of her feet, kissed her toes, then tried to investigate the calves, sweet smelling like violets and smooth like two slim branches of the sandalwood tree. He hoped to go on to the thighs, the two flagons full of the wine of love, suck the wine and go on farther. Wazir was almost beside herself the moment his fingers began to play on her calves. She pulled him towards her, drew up her trousers, revealing the sculpted smoothness of her lower limbs as far up as the trouser bottoms could go. She crushed her breasts under his hands, moaned and mumbled something like: how nice it would be for the tunic, the bodice and the trousers to be dragged away. The wayward deer wants, and does not want, to run away. The hound of lust pursues her.

Mirza Fathul Mulk Bahadur was thrilled to the core. He recalled Mirza Ghalib's Hindi verse:

When benevolently she permits
Boldness, and impudence:
There is no fault, except
To be ashamed of the fault.

But was not there something more going on here? Was not she suggesting, asking, and even demanding? What was that about the hound of lust and the . . . wayward deer? He thought of Salim's tiger, and . . . and the deer's hoof print. A verse of the Hindi poet Mushafi exploded in his mind and almost in his body:

That wayward deer, were I to find her
In a dark night,
I would become a hunting hound:
I would bite, and tear, and mangle.

Oh God, my God! How utterly, delightfully, brassy! What temerity, what headstrong vivacity! Do not the pundits say that your woman should be a friend and caregiver, even a mother, outside the bedroom, but in the bed, she should be a strumpet?

He nuzzled even closer, and mumbled tenderly, 'Chhoti Begam, you should not be an errant deer. Your destination is the bower of my love. I will guard you, and serve you . . . and why should these artificial curtains remain between us any longer?'

He pulled away her heavy dupatta, undid the string of her trousers and unbuttoned his own tunic. Wazir held out her hands and felt his broad chest, as if writing something on it. As their bodies met, the lights in the chamber bedimmed, but they weren't looking really.

⋆

Wazir, as we know, was an early riser. She had taken to rising even earlier lately. She had been awake most of the night, which was apparently now in its last watch. It was not just keeping awake: almost all her waking hours last night were consumed by passion, and arousal, and ebb and flow. The loving but taxing tenderness of Mirza Fathul Mulk's desire had left each joint and muscle of her body aching, but the ache was as pleasurable as an inebriation, an ache that refused to go away and which she was not keen to say goodbye to. She had slept for barely a half-hour, but when she woke up, it was later than her wonted hour. The Sahib-e Alam wa Alamiyan was still fast asleep, and it seemed he would sleep very late.

The muezzin of the Pearl Mosque was yet to issue his call for the predawn prayer. She sensed that it was still very dark outside. Where would Habib-un Nisa be sleeping, she wondered. Habiba did say that she did not need a room: she would sleep hugging Wazir's doorstep. But it was so cold;

she must have been given a room to share with another senior maid or perhaps to herself exclusively. She was not going to be somewhere close anyway. Wazir thought of turning and going to sleep, but sleep was now far from her.

She had seen that men, after a short or long session of lovemaking, tried to talk and keep awake for some time, but inevitably succumbed to sleep sooner rather than later. Their talk would be romantic, or playful, or mostly devoted to domestic matters. As they spoke, they would turn their back to the woman, often in mid-sentence even, and quietly slip into deep slumber.

She often wondered why it should be so. Was it not the male's duty to keep guard, for it was his seed that had been reposed in the woman's body? Perhaps the male believed that the woman has his protection always? That is, so long as he slept by her side, no harm could come to the woman? Sometimes she said to herself, not without bitterness, that all that the male required was the satisfaction of desire: once he had obtained it, he did not care to inquire after the state of the woman who shared his bed . . . Or as she had heard some old and experienced women say, it was a little death for the male: after emptying his reservoir he needed relief and recuperation. Well, Wazir snorted mentally, as if what he did in bed was not relief! Or perhaps the turning of the back and slipping into slumber betokened his confidence and faith in his partner's fidelity. But this seemed far-fetched. She recalled a Hindi verse by Mirza Ghalib:

Should you have a doubt in your heart:
Whether desire would wane, and cease, in union?
Look at the wave, struggling to survive in the main;
That's how it is.

Wazir felt sure that sleep would not return for her that night. Better to get up, take a bath and refresh oneself. Sahib-e Alam wa Alamiyan, she noted with amusement, was apparently more spent than she was: there seemed no possibility of his getting up soon, and when he did get up, he might want to take her to bed again. Wazir wasn't very fond of eating breakfast anyway. So the best choice was a bath, and a change of clothes.

She rose, stretched herself a bit, and immediately felt the cold, for she had no clothes on. She wrapped a heavy shawl tightly around her body and stole into the water room. She found it equipped with every necessity, and many luxuries: English soap, scented chickpea powder, cakes of Multani earth used for washing the hair, other spicy powders and cakes for the same purpose; small and large flat-bottomed leathern phials and bottles of attars and scented oils; English sponges and pumice stones, loofahs for rubbing the body clean of dead epidermis; several pairs of small scissors and Indian nail-parers; a number of large, soft and heavy towels for drying the body; a low, wooden platform to be used as bath mat: you could stand on it, or sit in a comfortable posture to bathe; and many large, man-size mirrors in glass and metal; the metallic ones having complicated paintings around them for frames, while the glass ones had heavy, ornate wooden frames. There was a tall ebony cabinet for storing clothes and towels and handkerchiefs. Wazir opened it to find her everyday clothes, which she had brought with her, and a few other outfits placed in it in neat stacks.

A new thing that Wazir found there consisted of water pipes and taps made out of strong, well-seasoned, highly polished bamboo poles, brought down from somewhere through appropriate apertures in the roof. Wazir had heard that both hot and cold water was available round the clock through bamboo or clay pipes in some of the bathrooms and water rooms of the Exalted Fort. She was unable to credit these reports; but in fact she had also heard about similar systems installed over the years in the houses of some Company officials, and some of the richer citizens of Delhi. She had not had the occasion to enter a haveli of Shamsuddin Ahmad Khan, but she had seen no such arrangement in the water room of the Navab's guest house where she spent her first night. There were two large ewer-like pitchers under each of the water taps and there was a bronze pot with a handle, called mashrabah, for taking out the water from the pitchers. Wazir tested the taps and was delighted and surprised to find that hot and cold water was indeed flowing from them.

She discarded her shawl; in spite of the cold, she first splashed cold water on her face; then she splashed and sprayed warm water all around her, like a child enjoying her first bath in a tub. She then mixed hot and cold water to her desired temperature, and poured it over her body with the mashrabah to her heart's content. The warmth of the bed, the short, deep, excited breaths, the feeling of being taken away from herself, the sense of complete surrender: all of it was something to be remembered. But the permeating warmth of the water, the taking away of the pleasant aches and pains of the body, the washing off of the last and the least particles of sleep from her eyes: these were something else again, and they had their own intoxication. For the first time in many years, she felt like bursting into song. But no, she could not take the risk of Mirza Fathul Mulk Bahadur waking up and discovering her here in the water room. She began to hum to herself the ghazal of Hafiz whose lines they had said to each other last night in something like a session of capping verses:

> *My disunion with you was a long and hard time,*
> *Like the Doomsday*

She experienced such a pleasant drowning in the music and flow and delectability of the poet who was justly called the Tongue of the Unseen that the water grew cold as she hummed the lines and verses that affected her most. When she noticed that the water was no longer comfortable, she rose and rubbed and dried herself vigorously with a silk-soft towel, trying to speed up the circulation of blood in her quickly cooling body. Quite without intending it, her glance fell on her body reflected in a life-size mirror, just as it had happened in the Navab's guest house. Her still-youthful body, showing all its enchanting mysteries, made her entirely forget the words of Hafiz and catapulted her into that night when Habiba, trying her best to do the action of taking away her young guest's ill fortunes, had prepared her for the Navab's visit. She recalled her first love and how she lost it for no fault of his or hers. Unbeknownst to Habiba, she had been at that time not so keen on her being prepared, as she was prey to a nagging uncertainty: will today's event be no more than a flash in the pan, or was it a foundation on which she could build a life of her own? Was she reading a page separated from other pages of her life, though written in the brightest and the most pleasing colours? *If it were to last, its life will be one night; it won't last to the next*, she recalled a famous line of a Persian verse. But . . . last night was surely a page from a book with a much stronger binding. Last night her heart had felt the satisfaction of reaching the final destination, of reaching the last page of the story, a story that was ending happily, while a new story was beginning over which she had perhaps more control.

Or is the story of my life to be only a story of loss and search? A cold fear stabbed her heart. She had heard about certain kind of people: they could begin well, but could not finish. Am I, then, one of those? But are we capable of ever bringing something to a conclusion? In fact, the truth seemed to be that we were not capable of even beginning something, far less ending it. *You do what you will, and it is we who get a bad name for no reason*, she recalled a famous line from Mir Taqi Mir. No, that is not justice. The paths of destiny must surely be amenable to change, by action or by strategy, or by prayer, if all else fails. And if man reconciles himself to his fate, accepts it, that too will perhaps be a sort of change in his destiny, for then man won't fret and cavil against his ill fortune; and when there is acceptance, there is no sorrow, no pain, perhaps.

She recalled a Quranic prayer that her mother had taught her when she was growing up:

> *Our Lord! Condemn us not if we forget or fall into error; our Lord! Lay not on us a burden like that which Thou didst lay on those before us; Our Lord! Lay not on us a burden greater than we have strength to bear.*

So why this prayer? Or perhaps this prayer can, if granted, change the destiny of the one who prays? But then, why do they say that what is written in our fates is unalterable, even unpostponable; is it like a line engraved on stone? But was not there a most inspiring, most hopeful Hindi verse they taught us when I was little? Were water to fall uninterrupted on stone, without doubt, the stone will become worn. What does that mean, if not that He who wrote can also cancel, as water cancels stone? Or, He can be happy, even though in want? There was that Persian verse from some ancient poet: *No fears if I don't have the capacity to give; I at least have the capacity not to accept, for which all praise to God.*

She realized suddenly that she was cold. Lost in her thoughts, she forgot to note the time and the microclimate in the bathroom. She shivered. Why not take another, though shorter, warm bath and immediately put on fresh clothes? No, that's not a good idea. I don't know how much time I have been here. Who knows, Fathul Mulk Bahadur is awake and is looking for me? She thought of opening the cabinet to inspect the clothes that were there. A footfall at the door of the water room . . . was someone coming? She remembered that she had not locked the door from inside! Perhaps Habiba . . . no, it was a heavier footfall, and now Mirza Fathul Mulk Bahadur called in a low, musical voice, 'Wazir Khanam, are you there? Is everything all right, and can I come in?'

Before she could answer, Mirza Fathul Mulk Bahadur had opened the door, and in he walked. He wore a long, loose cloak-like nightdress, and looked quite awake. Wazir tried to snatch up the shawl and wrap it around her, but in her haste, she let it fall from her grasp and she bent to retrieve it. Fathul Mulk Bahadur stood rooted to the spot. Well-shaped, graceful, tight buttocks; thighs as if moulded from a master potter's mould; waist narrow like the cheetah's; the stomach smooth and flat as a carefully planed wooden board—there was no question of extra flesh there, not to speak of fattiness; breasts drooping towards the floor because of the bent waist and back, but without any hint of sagging; the nipples prominent and hard due to the cold air and also surely because of the presence of her man; a black fall of long, shiny tresses, falling down the face and a shoulder almost to the ground; soft and graceful neck and throat devoid of any hint of a wrinkle; the whole body aglitter even in the absence of jewellery, except for a gold chain and the Emperor's pearl necklace, which she had not bothered to remove.

Having spent the best part of the night in investigating, gazing at and enjoying the secrets of her body, the Prince should not have been overtaken by wonder, but he was, obviously. He felt like a stranger suddenly transported to a foreign place where a flourishing garden of love and desire was opening its doors to him without his asking even. He now realized that he had acquired no real idea so far of the excellent proportion of each of her body parts, her alluring height, the golden spray on her delicate body of the light of youthful virginity, the effect of evergreenness that ran from her toenails to her dense tresses.

For a long moment, Mirza Fathul Mulk Bahadur remained immobile, caught in the spell of her dark beauty. In the meantime, Wazir managed to pick up the shawl and hide herself effectively from his gaze. Except that what was left open to view seemed even more attractive to him. Wazir moved a step forward so that she might not have to raise her voice as she spoke, but found herself immobile and tongue-tied. She made a vague gesture to the Prince for him to leave, but he was not having any. He stood still, Wazir's beauty surrounding his heart like a garland of dark roses. Finally, trying not to speak in a tone above a husky entreaty, Wazir said, 'Please, I beg your pardon. I had no idea that you would look for me . . .' She wished to say, '. . . and barge into the water room and see me naked.' Obviously, she could not say those things; nor was it necessary to say them, really. What she needed to do was to say a few words, open some sort of conversation, and come out free from that web-like moment of shyness. Her words broke the spell for Mirza Fathul Mulk too, and he stepped close to her, 'What is there to forgive? A minute ago this morning you did such a good deed for me that I could not repay you, even if I endeavoured all my life!'

Mirza Fakhru came closer, grasped her firmly in his arms, pulled away her shawl and began kissing her hard on her head, her face and her breasts. Wazir attempted again and again to ask him to stop; that it was cold here in the water room; that they should go back into the bedroom, but Fathul Mulk Bahadur was unrelenting. He either stopped her with a kiss, or closed her mouth firmly with his hand.

'Please, Sahib-e Alam, I came away from your bed, but is it such a crime as to deserve such and so much punishment?' Wazir laughed between her gasps.

Mirza Fakhru picked up the shawl easily, without bending much, put it on his shoulder, and lifted Wazir with effortless ease. Only then he wrapped the shawl over her, carefully, as if she were a little child, needing cuddling and closeness. He carried her towards the bedroom, saying, 'Madam, you deserve much more punishment, but let's go into the bedchamber, then we'll decide your case.'

Mirza Fathul Mulk Bahadur put Wazir at the head of the bed, placed a number of pillows behind her back, covered her lower body with an ermine-and-gold-bordered blue velvet comforter, as if it was just the time for the bride dresser to arrive and start making her up again. Wazir tried to get out of Mirza Fakhru's hold by making her body as small as she could, but he was strong and sinewy, and was not going to let go. She drew up her knees to her chest, tried to hide her breasts and waist with her hands. Mirza Fakhru cajoled and also commanded in genial tones, 'No, no, Chhoti Begam, not like this! Stretch out your legs, recline against the bolster. If you keep your knees stuck to your chest, God forbid, then I won't at all get the opportunity to tire you out, and refresh you over again.'

'I beg pardon from God! You want to tire me out even more! There's nothing more left in your maidservant, Fathul Mulk Bahadur.'

'Possibly, but please be comfortable for now. Come, if you agree to my demand, I will sing something for you.'

Wazir pricked up her ears. Mirza Fathul Mulk, she knew, was a master musician, such that the most prominent and respected of singers and instrumentalists of the day touched their ears in a token of humility when his name was mentioned. But he never sang or played; at least that is what she had heard. He should sing something for his wife? That was unheard of; it had probably never happened.

'How lucky I am!' Wazir spoke with genuine and undisguised enthusiasm. 'Your Honour's David-like voice should be Paradise for my ears.' She smiled with a bit of coquetry. 'Please command. What service should I perform to earn the reward of being allowed to hear your eternally beautiful singing?'

'Service? Oh, nothing.' Mirza Fakhru smiled a wily smile. 'Nothing, madam, just recline as you are, with your legs stretched. Let me cool my sight with the vision of your calves and the branches of the Lote tree of Paradise, and a little above them.'

'Oh, Sahib-e Alam, would you leave me quite naked?' Wazir became rosy pink. 'Will you leave me entirely without a covering?'

'Well, I should have thought that no curtains or screens existed between us.' Mirza Fakhru laughed pleasantly. 'All right, here we are. Please hear this, and enjoy. Luckily, I just recalled an extremely appropriate ghazal from—' he smiled meaningfully, 'the last night's culprit, Muhammad Quli Salim.'

'Your maidservant's entire body has become her ears.'

Mirza Fakhru hummed for a minute or less, keeping time on his thighs, then began to sing. The raga was Nat Bhairav, a raga most suited for passion early in the morning. His voice was polished, indicating enormous talent and hundreds of hours of practice. It was a very soft voice, but low, something like bass in the lower register:

I have a beloved, from the land of colour and scent,
And she is naked;
A tall, straight, sarv tree, and like a stream of water,
Naked.
Her body naked, like the branch of blue lily;
Her arms are two branches of the wild hyacinth,
And she is naked.
The wild quail, so that he may pass
In her bright-as-water presence, has made
Both his legs up to the thighs,
Bare, and naked.
She is a child of an Indian, coursing everywhere

Like a flame, and naked.
Because of love for her, the blazing fire sits
Like a yogi, among the ashes,
Naked.
Salim, pull from thy heart the thorns
Of longing, for thy beloved is here,
She is barefooted
And naked.

The voice, the scene, the mood, the poem: Wazir could not imagine anything more enchanting. And the appropriateness of the poem was such that Wazir's dark body was also brought in most relevantly. It was as if Salim, two centuries ago, had a dream of a dark beauty called Wazir Khanam and painted his dream on paper in the form of a thrilling poem, leaving it behind for his dream to become reality. When Mirza Fakhru rose to the main body of the raga, Wazir exclaimed, 'Wah, wah! How absolutely perfect! Truly, only God is untouched by blemish!' But after that moment, it seemed as if she was struck dumb. Her heart swelled and heaved and surged with the swelling of the music. As the music, all billowy bosomed like a cloud, showered itself upon her ears, and on her whole being, in wave upon powerful wave, she lost all sense of where she was or who she was; she just wanted to empty her heart, so full of the music, into the heart of the singer, her husband, whom she had chosen, and who had chosen her. The voice was low and yet twanging sharp like the trill of the sarangi. It was not opened up to the full, for the singer did not desire to disturb those who still slept. And yet, with a near-human, bell-like pealing of the flute when the flautist was at the peak of the rendition of the raga, the voice charged her with the same near-mystic absorption with which the singer was expressing and exemplifying the raga.

The rising light of the morning was mixing with the waning light of the candles. Wazir's heart and eyes were both full. The passion of her soul mingled with the passion of Nat Bhairav. There was nothing more to say.

66

Life and times at the Auspicious Fort under the shade of the Mentor and Guide, Abu Zafar Bahadur Shah II

A WHOLE YEAR passed in the twinkling of an eye. Towards the end of the tenth month of the marriage, in October 1845, Wazir gave birth to a male child: a child which was truly a parcel of the moon. Rosy pink and fair, with large eyes and dark curly hair, the baby's beauty became proverbial as it grew up. Everybody said that the hair and the eyes were like his mother's, but the rest of him seemed like the Presence Akbar Shah II, who now rests in the highest Paradise. The Shadow of God Abu Zafar Bahadur Shah was of a quite dark complexion, and Mirza Fathul Mulk Bahadur was like his father. The Presence, Akbar Shah II was rosy pink and fair, very much like his Turkestani ancestors.

The child's chronogrammatic name, as also his official name, was determined to be Khurshid Alam; the numerical value of the letters of the two words total up to 1261, corresponding to 1845. In the Royal Records, the name was entered as Mirza Khurshid Alam, popularly known as Khurshid Mirza. The happiness of Fathul Mulk Bahadur knew no bounds, for God had bestowed upon him not one, but two sons in that one year. While Khurshid Mirza was some time in coming, Navab Mirza was commanded to present himself at the Auspicious Fort within a couple of weeks of Wazir Khanam's marriage to the Third Heir Apparent. With the title 'Khan' already conferred on him, he became Navab Mirza Khan for everyone who knew him. The word 'Navab' became part of his personality, so much so that people later came to believe that it was not his name, but his rank and title.

His nom de plume Dagh was already on everybody's lips in Delhi; he now became Navab Mirza Khan Dagh, up-and-coming master poet, and was addressed as 'son' by Mirza Fathul Mulk Bahadur. A sum of five rupees per month was approved for him from the Royal Portal. Having no expensive habits, Navab Mirza spent just about half of his pay in a month. The rest he submitted to his mother who put it away in a box dedicated for him, and for occasional charities. The Third Heir Apparent paid for Navab Mirza's education and training.

Mir Ghulam Husain Shikeba was a pupil of Mir Taqi Mir and had been ustad to His Majesty during his early career as poet. Mir Shikeba's son Maulavi Ahmad Husain was appointed tutor to Navab Mirza in Arabic and Persian. Sayyid Muhammad Amir, Master Calligrapher and much else besides, gave him advanced lessons in Calligraphy, Fist Wrestling and in two kinds of unarmed combat: Bank and Binote. The first one used a small, curved and pointed stick; the other used nothing but the body. Panja Kash (Hand Wrestler) became an unalienable part of Muhammad Amir's name, but he was expert at many disciplines besides: Wrestling, special kind of ornamental Calligraphy, Unarmed Combat of many types, Drawing, Painting, Calligraphy for title pages and ornamental headings, Page Preparing (for painting or calligraphy), Book Binding, and Gold Lace Making.

Besides, within a short time of Navab Mirza's arrival at the Fort, Mirza Fakhru had him formally enlisted as a pupil of Shaikh Muhammad Ibrahim Zauq. The kind maestro advised him to retain the pen name Dagh and even observed that if he continued his intensive practice and study, he should soon be able to dispense with the need for mentoring and correction, and even could set up as an ustad himself. Dagh began to be a regular presence at poets' private assemblies with other princes within the Fort; he also often participated in important mushairahs in the city. His not being a child of the Haveli gave him the advantage of being able to go out with just Mirza Fakhru's permission. This advantage gave him the opportunities to improve his poetry by sitting with other masters like Ghalib, and also the freedom to visit Bari Begam's as much as he liked, and gladden his heart by seeing and talking to Fatimah. He often thought of asking his mother about his proposed marriage with Fatimah, but was never able to pick up the courage. He knew that his mother had already mentioned the matter to Sahib-e Alam wa Alamiyan and obtained his consent; that should be enough for the time being, he consoled himself. After all, his mother had been big with child for nine months, and was now feeding and caring for the infant Khurshid Mirza. This was not the time for him to raise the issue of his own marriage. He had much to do and learn and many means of using his time profitably in the Fort anyway.

Because of his friendship with Zahir Dihlavi and Qamaruddin Raqim, Navab Mirza was generally conversant with the affairs of the Court, but he did not have the faintest notion of the Exalted Fort as almost an administrative State, and a whole cultural world of tradition, convention and Royal protocol in its own right. Among the sixteen sons of the Shadow of God, those who were active in matters of administration were: Mirza Muhammad Dara Bakht Bahadur, First Heir Apparent; Mirza Shah Rukh, Prime Minister and General Plenipotentiary; Mirza Kayumars Bahadur, Second Heir Apparent; and Mirza Muhammad Sultan Ghulam Fakhruddin Bahadur, Third Heir Apparent. These were the most prominent at that time. In later days, the sixth son, Mirza Zahiruddin Bahadur, popularly known as Mirza Mughal, gained much power and influence over all matters. All these princes held their own courts on the pattern of the Royal Court, though on a much reduced scale.

Even if the Court of the Shadow of God was a mere attenuated reflection of the courts of Aurangzeb, Shahjahan or even Muhammad Shah Badshah Ghazi, now resting in Paradise, this is how Munshi Faizuddin, a contemporary author, describes the Bahadur Shahi Court on the occasion of some celebration:

> Now look, all the nobles alight from their mounts at the gate of the Drum House [at the main Lahori Gate access to the Fort], proceed to the Divan-e Am on foot. This is the first station of audience, and observe: an iron chain, thick and hefty, hangs diagonally at the gate of the Divan-e Am; it functions as a barrier. No one can walk erect under it. Everybody bends low to get under the chain. This is the second station of audience. See now! A large, red, broadcloth curtain at the gate of Divan-e Khas: it is called Red Curtain. Chain-keepers, Foot soldiers, Gatekeepers, Armed soldiers and Tribunes stand holding red staves. Should an outsider or unauthorized person seem to want to go in, the Tribunes employ their hooked staves, pull the intruder by neck with the hook, and drag him out . . . After making salaams at the Red Curtain, which is the third station of audience, authorized visitors enter; arrived in front of the throne, they make a low salaam, and occupy their designated positions.
>
> An octagonal platform in marble, right at the centre of Divan-e Khas: on it stands the Peacock Throne. In front of the Throne stands a heavy front-screen [serving as a stop point, low enough to permit the

Emperor to be visible] . . . designed like arches; each screen having three arches; the screens are on all four sides, then, a wooden baluster runs around the Throne; the Throne has a bolster at its back; there are three steps in front of the Throne. The Throne has a canopy, designed like a dome, which is supported by arches and the ceiling strengthened by four layers, in the Bengali style. The dome has gold pinnacles; in the front arch, two peacocks, facing each other and each holding a pearl rosary in its beak . . . Two Fan-bearers, with fans made of peacock feathers, stand on both sides of the Throne. A prayer mat is spread behind the Throne.

Mutabar-ud-Daulah Itibarul Mulk Bahadur Prime Minister; Umdat-ul Hukama Haziq-e Zaman Ihtiram-ud Daulah Bahadur . . . Rajah Mirza Bahadur, Rajah Bahadur . . . Mir Adl Bahadur, Munshi-e Dar-ul Insha-e Sultani, Mir Tuzuk, and others; all stand to the right and left at their designated spots, keeping both hands on their staffs . . .

In the courtyard of Divan-e Khas: steeds of the Emperor's personal mount stand on one side, their accoutrements in silver; on the other side, his personal elephants: Maula Bakhsh, Khurshid Ganj, Chand Murat, and others. Painted foreheads protected by armoured shields, their decorative marks in gold, festoons and ribbons of bullion and silk hang from their ears; their silk coats are heavily worked in bullion. There is, on another side, the Exalted Insignia of the Fish prominently displayed; then the Ceremonial Canopy, and the Banners. Musicians and Drummers, Flag-bearers, Shield-bearers, all stand firmly rooted to their spots. Abyssinians, Tribunes with staffs, their silver heads designed like tiger's jaws; Chief Accoutrement Bearers armed with guns stand right below the wooden baluster.

His Majesty appears [at the gate of his private apartment]. Criers and Staff-bearers call: 'Bismillah al Rahman al Rahim. Grace and Mercy of God and His Prophet! Let the friends be overjoyed! Let the enemies be crushed underfoot! Let the calamities be turned back!' Outdoor-bearers of the havadar [open palanquin, like a sedan chair] spring to take charge of it from the Havadar-bearers of the Palace. The Emperor first goes behind the Throne and performs a prayer, standing on the prayer mat; having sought benedictions from God, he again seats himself in the havadar [for the short distance that separates the prayer mat from the Throne]. The Bearers park the havadar hard by

> the Throne. The Emperor alights, placing his Luminous Self on the Throne. Flags are waved; cannons are fired. The infantry fires muskets in salute. Congratulatory music is played. Pearl of the Crown of the State, the Eldest Son of the Caliphate, Heir Apparent Bahadur, stands to the left of the Throne. Other Princes of High Rank, Lights of the Eyes of the Caliphate, Moons on the Forehead of the State, stand to the right. Nobles and courtiers stand in front.

The number of residents in the Fort who depended on the Mahabali exceeded two thousand; there were a few who lived outside, with permission. All of them drew monthly pay from the Royal Treasury. Then there were the salaries of the ministers, clerks, other office holders, soldiers and menial workers. Additional grants on festival or celebration days; marriages; tonsure of babies; circumcision; birth; death; proceeding on a journey, or returning from one: all these were over and above the wonted salaries.

As we stated above, the convention of addressing or referring to the Emperor as Mentor and Guide arose during Shahjahan's reign. Bahadur Shah II was a practising Sufi himself, and possessed formal permission from Kale Sahib, one of contemporary Delhi's prominent Sufis, to make his own disciples. Thus, one of his important diurnal engagements was to honour his present or prospective disciples by meeting them, concentrating on their souls individually or collectively as a part of the grace granted to his disciples by a Sufi master. He also listened to his disciples' accounts of their spiritual difficulties, and prescribed spiritual remedies for them. He accepted no offering from his old disciples except the lowest amount—two rupees—as established by convention. He also bestowed a reward of the same amount upon the new disciples.

Apparently, the Emperor's total regular expenditure far exceeded his known income. But there were other, non-regular expenses too. Bahadur Shah II, more than any of the later Mughal Emperors—that is, those of the hundred years before him—was fond of building new edifices and properly maintaining those that he had inherited as Emperor. And imagine the cost of maintaining, even in a reasonable shape, the mountain-like pile known—with admirable simplicity—as just 'the Haveli'. Granted that the Haveli, thanks to the depredations of vandals and the ravages of time, was now in a much worse shape than a century ago; still, it was a 'working' edifice.

Its interior gardens and bowers and flower beds still looked verdant, even almost new. The Divan-e Am, Divan-e Khas, Pearl Mosque, Hammam, the chief apartments, many of the water channels and ornamental ponds, the massive gates: all these looked more or less as they had looked in the 1740s. We must remember that what we see in the Red Haveli today is much less than what it had then. The triumphant English destroyed almost the whole of the residential quarter, the Secretariat, the Archives, the Library, as also many of the interior avenues and vistas during and after September 1857.

Quite a lot of the main Mughal buildings outside the Haveli, like Humayun's Tomb, all the historic gardens, most of the chief inns—where the traveller was charged nominally or nothing whatever—many of the important mosques and schools, and above all the legendary Chandni Chowk and the equally legendary canal that ran through its length all the way, were maintained in good shape. The Emperor also built new gardens and a few palaces, or added to some of the existing ones; all were reminiscent, in quality and style, of Shahjahan and the ustads Ahmad and Hamid, his architects of genius.

Where did the money come from to do all this? This is a puzzle that has remained unsolvable. Shah Alam Bahadur Shah II (d. 1806), who now rests in Paradise, was a great economizer and collector of treasure. Nearly all of it was expended during the reign of the Presence, Akbar Shah II (d. 1837). Much augmentation of staff and dependents took place during his auspicious rule, and again during the rule of the Presence, Abu Zafar Bahadur Shah II. Things came to such a pass that it began to be proposed, and not only in jest, that barring the seventy direct descendants of Akbar Shah II and Bahadur Shah II, everyone residing in the Haveli should be ejected and the Emperor should cease to support them, since most of them were not useful members of the Haveli's community anyway. That did not take place, but the fact that such an idea could be countenanced is symbolic, to say the least.

So how did the Emperor meet his expenses? The English paid him a stipend of a hundred thousand rupees a month. It was not increased in spite of numerous representations, though the case for enhancement was supported by facts. A small source of extra income was the nazr submitted to the Emperor by the English Sahib Navab Governor General Bahadur and the Sahib Navab Commander-in-Chief Bahadur, on the two Id days, the Iranian New Year's Day and the Emperor's Birthday. The observance of this historic convention was given up by the John Company shortly after the accession to the throne of Bahadur Shah II. The reason, apparently, was that the Emperor had an octagonal throne in gold, silver and gemstones constructed for himself on the occasion of his coronation. (Some have stated its name to be the Peacock Throne, though actually it was called Takht-e Huma.) The Governor General and the Commander-in-Chief had not been permitted to be seated during the ceremony. The angry and affronted Governor General forbade the Emperor to use the throne in the future. Thus, since there was no assumption of throne, there was no need for the Governor General and the Commander-in-Chief to be present and submit the nazr.

After many years of pleading, correspondence and diplomatic activity, the English agreed to raise the Emperor's stipend to three hundred thousand rupees per mensem. This came into effect in April 1849, twelve years after his assumption of the Crown, and no arrears were paid. It has been estimated that the octroi receipts from the city of Delhi alone were 4.7 million rupees annually. The Glorious Sahibs did not permit even the smallest cowrie shell of this to reach the Emperor. His receipts from his own lands and gardens were about twenty-five thousand rupees per annum. Zakaullah, a contemporary and pro-Company historian, places it even lower.

Zahir Dihlavi writes:

> Delhi's Emperor did not have the means equal to that of the smallest Indian State. As [the eighteenth-century poet] Mirza Sauda wrote:
>
> *Well, there was one who was the Master*
> *Of twenty-two provinces;*
> *He doesn't now command even the tiny Fort*
> *Of Aligarh.*
>
> He received just a hundred thousand per mensem from the Honourable English. There was a tiny amount received from his personal lands, gardens, shop rents and market fees. We should imagine all this to amount to a hundred and twenty-five thousand. Yet, looking at the pomp, the grandeur, the dignity, the elaborate Court protocol and Imperial convention, the glittering arrangements at the Processions

> and Royal Assumption of the Throne: all this suggested that Yes, this glorious House, at sometime in the past, must have deserved to rule the Paradise-exemplifying land of Hindustan. Yet, in spite of the decline, and want of riches, and scarcity of means of livelihood, two things, wonder-arousing and astonishing, I have observed personally, and they still keep me in the whirlpool of wonder. First, God, Lord and Master of the Worlds bestowed such ease and expansiveness on those hundred thousand rupees, that I did not observe . . . in the States which were worth [revenues] of scores of millions of rupees:
>
> *If a noble becomes enfeebled, do not imagine*
> *That his exalted portal will also be feeble.*
>
> A sepoy earns four rupees a month, but he is prosperous; and one who earns a big salary, he is also in riches. I did not see anyone complaining against the revolutions of the time. This is the fruit of the [ruler's] chaste intentions, and the consequence of elevated generosity. Second, the indications and suggestions of the Court of [the true] Sultanate, and the majesty and authority of sovereignty that I observed in the Royal Court, I did not find in any State. The intellect is struck with wonder looking at the Royal expenditures and the outgo of cash. Lord my God! How and wherefrom came the expansiveness and abundance in the Royal Treasury so as to suffice for such expenditure?

Navab Mirza, as he observed the apparent abundance, felt as if he was losing his mind. The more he examined and observed the offices and institutions of the Royal Administration, the more he found novel entities, fold upon fold of facts about newer and yet newer offices and departments. Not to speak of the contractors and servants active outside the Fort, there were functioning in the Auspicious Fort the following 'workshops', or 'offices' in today's language: Chief of Big Personal Kitchen, Chief of Small Personal Kitchen, Water Department, Fabrics and Dresses Department, Gemstone House, Armoury, Chief Quartermaster's Office, Elephant House, Stable, Carriage Department, Department of Cannon and Guns, Camel House, Rath House, Office of the Assumption of the Throne, and Procession, Department of the Exalted Insignia of the Fish, and Canopy, and Banner, Chief Paymaster of the Army, Hospital, Library, Pigeon House, Superintendent of the Office of the Ceremonial Presents, Department of Carpets and Furnishings, Palanquin House, Superintendent of the Palanquin-bearers, Superintendent of the Soldiery of the Vanguard, Supervisor of the Children, and Navab Nazir (Chief of the Department of the Eunuchs).

Should someone feel that these were just formal designations, with no reality or personnel attaching to them, Zahir Dihlavi says that he is 'omitting to give the names of the officials to avoid prolixity'. We know the names of some of the Hindu nobles in charge of some of the departments, especially those concerning Finance and the Armed Forces. For example: Rajah Zoravar Chand, Rai Bahadur Genda Mal, Kunwar Debi Singh and Rajah Sukh Rai are the names that come immediately to mind.

It took Navab Mirza many weeks to ascertain the details of the sections and branches of the aforementioned departments. For example, the Armed Forces, which had not fired a shot in anger since the death of the Paradise-residing Shah Alam II, had the following sections or paltans: Black Paltan, Grey Paltan, Youngsters' Paltan, Soldiers of the Vanguard, and Battalion Leaders' Paltan. Although derived from the English word 'platoon', a 'paltan' was in fact more like a regiment; the word 'battalion' is a loose translation of 'risalah': a force of eight hundred to a thousand men.

There was a separate list of the nobles and the elites of the Court. Insertion of a name in the list was a matter of great honour. An official's name was struck off the list if he was dismissed from his job for bribery or inefficiency. Expulsion from the list was a stigma greater than the honour that had accrued on inclusion in it. Zahir Dihlavi informed Dagh that the list generally consisted of the following types of notables: princes, ministers, maestros of a discipline, men of learning, physicians, Chief of the eunuchs, Chief Paymaster of the Armed Forces, commandants, masters of any art or craft, superintendents of the offices, and petition-presenters before the Presence.

Obtaining funds for payment of the salaries, and their disbursement, was in itself a major activity; there were many departments devoted to it. Zahir Dihlavi gives a list of grantees as follows: Begams and Princes, Officials of the Previous Administrations [perhaps pensioners], Officials of the Armed Forces, Department of Daily Payments or Day Workers, Department of the Eunuchs and those connected with it, and Sepoys.

Any salary from the Fort, even as low as two rupees per month, was a signal honour, to be cherished for generations. Aside from these, there were monthly stipends payable to the princes who resided outside the Fort, and to miscellaneous employees, like tutors in various disciplines, poets, astrologers, and watchers and facilitators in official matters outside the Court.

Additionally, there were special expenses, though they happened so often that they should indeed be described as regular expenses. The Presence, Dispenser of Destinies, often ennobled the visitors from outside, and also the Fort dwellers, by bestowal upon them of ceremonial robes or gifts of money. Once, when Prince Mirza Shah Rukh expressed the intention to visit the Kumbh Fair at Hardwar, he was granted a ceremonial robe and travel grant from the Royal Portal. Similarly, grants, or gifts or ceremonial robes were sanctioned and awarded on the occasions of marriage, death, birth, excursion, the hunt, and the Haj pilgrimage.

The Presence, Protector of the Caliphate, was much given to marrying, and his offspring were myriad. Each of his queens had her own monthly salary, designated apartment, servants, all provided from the Royal Exchequer. Naturally, expense involving Royal marriages became a regular, though unbudgeted, outgo. Moreover, as His Majesty was expert at numerous martial arts, outdoor sports, and artistic disciplines—calligraphy, horsemanship, archery, marksmanship with firearms, and many others—he appointed, on suitable salary, instructors and sparring partners for each of them.

Zahir Dihlavi told Dagh that his father had been an eyewitness to instances of the Presence's marksmanship with firearms. Often, when the Presence observed a bird on the wing, he would pick up a gun that was in its rack in the havadar and fire, apparently without taking aim, and the bird, rolling over and over, would fall near the palanquin. In archery, the Emperor had as an instructor an archer of great renown, a Sikh called Apa Singh. During the time he was Heir Apparent, the Emperor had a 'block-and-tackle' system installed in the Divan-e Khas. A sack, full of chickpeas weighing three maunds (approximately two hundred and fifty pounds) was hung with a chain from the tackle. The Exalted Prince routinely pulled it down with the grip of his right hand's index finger and thumb. In spear-throwing, fencing and playing with clubs, the Presence was instructed by Mir Hamid Ali, the noted maestro of those arts in those times. The Presence, when young, was such an adept at unarmed combat that he practised against as many as eight fighters at one time, defending against or fending off their blows with ease.

Navab Mirza was told about His Majesty's exceptional prowess as a horseman. Everybody said that there were only two and a half truly proficient riders in the whole of Hindustan, the Deccan included. One was Mirza Abu Zafar Bahadur; the other was his brother of Exalted Station, Mirza Jahangir Bakht who had won a bet with the English when he galloped and cleared the moat of the Fort at Allahabad. The third was reported to be a Maratha. That this was not just routine exaggeration by His Majesty's admirers is proved by an entry in the Journal of Fanny Parkes where she says that she was personally acquainted with a woman rider in the entourage of the deposed Rani of Gwalior who was living in Allahabad in self-imposed exile. The woman rider, says Fanny Parkes, could come out unharmed, by virtue of her skill at horsemanship, even when a force of a thousand horsemen hemmed her in.

Such hobbies and pastimes needed leisure, of which there was plenty, and money, which was apparently scarce. The gap between the revenue and the expenditure must have equalled the revenue itself, which meant that the Emperor needed one hundred per cent more than what he had just to make both ends meet. So how were the expenses of the Pearl Scattering Court managed? Navab Mirza did not find a satisfactory answer or explanation, though he spared no efforts in seeking it. It was, of course, no secret that the Exalted Presence borrowed money. The Company Bahadur was moved many times in the past to assist the Emperor in the repayment of his debts. There was no success. Navab Mirza also heard on reliable testimony that many among the richer noblemen at the Court did not let the Emperor know the extent of their wealth, or their acquired riches. There were two reasons for this secretiveness: the individual could be ordered to account for his wealth; or, the Emperor might want to borrow from the rich man. Even if this was true, Navab Mirza said to himself, how much could His Majesty garner by such dubious means? The gap was too large to fill. He must surely have some secret, unrevealed source of liquidity.

Sometimes, Navab Mirza became aware of occasions when the Court made new appointments or conferred titles. The candidates presented substantial nazr when they sought some appointment. He was told that there could sometimes develop an auction-like situation, when the rivals tried to outbid each other to gain favour. So, that is yet another source of money, Navab Mirza told himself, but also asked himself: how many such occasions arose in a year, and how much could the Exalted Court gain thereby? Surely it could not exceed a score or more thousands, whereas money seemed to flow out from the Auspicious Haveli like the water from its drains.

Some people believed, and believed earnestly, that the Emperor possessed a piece of the Philosopher's Stone, which could instantly convert any base metal to gold. But, thought Navab Mirza, if the Royal Treasury really had such a Philosopher's Stone, the Emperor should be spending even more lavishly and bountifully. Some people held, with equal force of conviction, that His Majesty had what the Sufis called dast-e ghaib ('The Hand of the Occult'). One who was blessed with it, the Sufis believed, could find from the Occult, and with no effort, as much money as he desired. Another view was that His Exalted Majesty had many genies subservient to him. A genie, it was believed, could bring anything for his master from anywhere.

The same objection applies to all other such theories. If such was the case, there should have been even more splendour; nothing should have been stinted. At least the vandalized silver and gold and gemstones should have been restored. The situation on the ground was that the Exalted Presence found himself unable to even replace a gold-plated copper spire stolen from one of the turrets of the Haveli in his own times.

Sometimes, two or three of the older rumours were resurrected with renewed force: there was a secret treasure within the Fort, going back to the reign of the Paradise-abiding Lord of the Auspicious Conjunction, the Presence, Shihabuddin Shahjahan. Needless to say, only His Majesty had access to it; he drew from it the minimum that he needed to run his affairs. Another story was of a secret tunnel connecting the Red Fort of Shahjahanabad to the Red Fort of Agra. Only the ruling monarch knew its secret entrances and exits at both ends. And the Mahabali used the tunnel for secretly getting out some of the treasure hidden in the Fort at Agra.

'Ama Mian sahib, this is the Presence, the Exalted City of Dilli,' Zahir Dihalvi replied to Navab Mirza, using the city's popular name, when Navab Mirza quizzed and probed somewhat intensively about the reports of the Agra tunnel. 'We are past masters in fashioning rumours, making and exchanging news, flying every kind of kite in every kind of weather. Further, whatever we invent, disseminates itself to all four corners in an instant. It doesn't take half an hour even!'

'But there must be some basis, a grain of truth in all this. What is the power that makes this stupendous administration function like clockwork?'

'Dear boy, did anyone ever plumb the secrets of the divine and the miraculous? There's no paymaster, no commandant, no steward, no military outfit, but everything happens in the skies at the proper moment: the sun rises, then it sets; the season of rains follows that of the dust and heat . . . so Mian, you can make your inference from it.' He now spoke in the accents of the artisan of Delhi. 'Son, Allah is a very great king!'

Dagh was not satisfied. Nor could he ever solve the riddle of the smooth management of the Royal Administration. Anyway, what does that matter to me? He told himself. The Shadow of God regards me with a benevolent eye; Mirza Fakhru Sahib Bahadur's affectionate kindnesses on me are so many that only now I have come to understand what strength and what benediction a father can be for his son. And Mian Navab Mirza, he told himself a little arrogantly though not without equal ruefulness, whoever saw the morrow before it happened? Submit your thanks to Allah for today, and about what is to follow, and say as Khvajah Mir Dard sahib said long ago:

Oh Saqi, there's a crowd of drinkers
Leaving here at every moment:
Let the wine glass pass as long as it can!

Oh Lord, my God, please keep safe my dear Amma Jan, my darling Fatimah, Mirza Fakhru Bahadur, and my two aunts, for it is their breath that lights my world. And as for the glow and bustle of life's marketplace and factory here in the Haveli, I was within earshot when a number of times I heard the Shadow of God say there isn't going be the Fort and the Kinghood after him. How funny that there should be unity on the surface among the princes, but division and distance under it. Everyone harbours dreams and longings of being King. No one pays the least heed to the necessity of improving the state of affairs here.

Within the first four or six months of his sojourn in the Fort, Navab Mirza became conscious of the pulls and struggles within the Haveli. There was not much affection between Mirza Dara Bakht Bahadur, First Heir Apparent, and Mirza Fakhru Bahadur. If the reports he heard were to be relied upon, the First Heir Apparent was always trying to poison the Emperor's ears against Mirza Fakhru Bahadur. His Exalted Presence might or might not be convinced, but Mirza Fakhru Bahadur's faults and transgressions, real or imagined, were constantly hinted at before the Exalted Presence. It was not a very hard task, for the Exalted Presence, for some unknown reason, did not look upon Mirza Fakhru Bahadur with much approbation. Then there was the third son, Mirza Kayumars Bahadur, who was the Second Heir Apparent. He was reported to be extremely ambitious and was convinced that he alone was the true inheritor of the Timurid legacy. This fact he took care to convey to the auspicious ears of the Glorious Sahibs a number of times. Mirza Shah Rukh Bahadur was more interested in hunting and excursions. He was a harmless, gentle and generally uncaring and unambitious Prince. Apparently, he had no crow to pluck with anyone at the fact that although he was Prime Minister and General Plenipotentiary, the position of Second Heir Apparent was held by Mirza Kayumars, who was younger than he. Mirza Shah Rukh's mother, though, prayed in her heart that if, God forbid, something bad happened to Mirza Dara Bakht Bahadur, it was her son who should be considered for being declared Heir Apparent.

Mirza Shah Rukh's mother was the daughter of a mere Navab; so she had no influence over anyone. On the contrary, the Emperor's favourite, Navab Zinat Mahal, never tired of pointing out that besides being the most favoured wife, she was from an illustrious family, for her father Navab Ahmad Quli Khan was directly descended from the Iranian King and invader of Delhi, Ahmad Shah Abdali. Zinat Mahal was reputed to boast that Mirza Shah Rukh or even Mirza Dara Bakht were nothing before her son Mirza Javan Bakht who fully merited to be the Heir Apparent and then King. The Exalted Presence, in spite of his wisdom and dignity, never opposed Zinat Mahal in whatever she claimed; he merely said, 'We will see when the time comes. It is meaningless to write anything about it to Navab Governor General Bahadur at this time. Javan Bakht is barely five years old, and Mirza Shabbu—I take the name of God—is young and healthy, and there is no certainty about the Kingship, either.' Despite these commandments, Zinat Mahal kept on trying, assiduously and relentlessly, to promote the case of her son at the English Court. When she heard that Thomas Metcalfe, Grand Sahib Bahadur, was not keen on Javan Bakht, she became his sworn enemy and roundly cursed him, day in and day out.

*

If Navab Mirza could not get to the truth, or the mystery, behind the Fort's costly management, he also could not plumb the depths of the kindnesses and affectionate attention that the King of Exalted Station freely vouchsafed on the young man. The Presence, Protector of the Caliphate, chose Navab Mirza to be his pupil in horsemanship, archery and unarmed combat. He spared no pains in making sure that he got the best education possible. As a poet, Navab Mirza was formally a pupil of Zauq's, but the Emperor showed special interest in Dagh by sometimes inviting him to recite his new poems and occasionally honouring him with a correction, or suggestion for improvement. Dagh, of course, gratefully and happily accepted the Emperor's kind words. The participation of Dagh in literary sittings and formal or informal assemblies in the Fort and also in the city, especially at the haveli of Navab Mustafa Khan Shefta, came to be regarded as essential for an assembly's success. The reason was not just the Emperor's indulgent eye on the young man, it was also the excellence of his performance as a poet. It was not just a chance that the first formal mushairah where Dagh had the opportunity to recite his poems before a comparatively large audience after moving to the Exalted Fort was held in the haveli of Navab Mustafa Khan Shefta, sometime in the first quarter of 1845. Dagh's opening verse at that mushairah was much acclaimed and soon became popular everywhere in the city:

It's not a flying spark, nor lightning,
Nor flame, nor quicksilver;
Then why is it that my restless heart
Refuses to abide and wait?

There was not much in the actual theme, but the flow of the lines and the chaste language were remarkable. A growing reputation and youthful charm: nothing more was needed to launch the young poet. If Zauq and Mirza Fathul Mulk Bahadur were pleased with the situation, it was quite par for the course. But other ustads like Ghalib and Momin also praised and approved of Dagh. They could see that a new rose plant was raising its head in the garden of Hindi poetry, and its flowers were already competing with the older roses, and looking at them with a knowing wink. Let us see how far his prodigious courage would take him. These ustads, who often regretted that there seemed to be none ready and able to water the field of poetry after them, looked to Dagh with pleasure and anticipation as a possible, and worthy, successor.

As his popularity and reputation grew, so also did Navab Mirza's respect among his peers. As we know, Munshi Ghanshyam Lal Asi always deplored the absence and then the death of his beloved master, Shah Nasir; Dagh deserved an ustad like him—he would have gotten the best instruction from Shah Nasir, and would also have been a proud jewel in the old master's treasury. Once Dagh moved into the Exalted Fort, everyone knew that he was a Royal Falcon, not destined to be trapped by ordinary mortals. Occasionally, someone in the audience, or an envious peer, would, in an assembly, point to some flaw or shortcoming in a verse presented by Dagh. At such times, Dagh was well able to defend himself, as his ustad, Zauq, could in the past. Sometimes the ustad openly encouraged him to produce his own defence, saying that while he was always there to come to the young poet's aid, it was the poet himself who should have the knowledge, and the gumption, to offer his own vindications.

Once Dagh presented a ghazal in an assembly somewhere in the city. Its opening verse was:

Well, beloved, out of regard, or to save your face
I do accept your excuses;
But did you not lose your Faith
By swearing a false oath?

There was an instant murmur of applause. Literary culture had been starved of this kind of poetry, full of light-hearted banter, yet serious; the words smoothly flowing; the language highly polished; the tone conversational; and the theme, an original variation of an overused, almost trite, item in Hindi ghazal. Dagh followed up with verses that were unique in the same way:

It was certainly abject, demeaning,
To confess my love to her;
But I did tell her; leastwise, I made her aware.

*

She took my heart for free, and now
She says, it's worth nothing;
So I wasted my good deed, and earned
Nothing but complaints!

Absorbed in the mood of his verses, Dagh carried on, not fully mindful of the applause that was being showered on him. He arrived at the concluding verse:

Dagh, my senses, my wits, my energy, my strength:
They're all gone. Now it's the time for me
To depart; my baggage has already gone ahead.

When the applause subsided a little, a respected old man in the audience said, 'Wah, wah! My dear young sir, only God is untouched by blemish! So young, and such a theme!'

Now there was another admiring comment from the audience: 'My young gentleman, I take the name of God, you are yet far from the maturity of youth even, not to mention old age. How did you find this theme at this time of your life?'

'Sir, may I submit?' A middle-aged man, who looked like a primary school teacher, rose from the far end of the chamber.

'Yes, yes, Maulavi sahib, do command!' There were voices from the audience.

The Maulavi sahib cleared his throat and announced, 'Actually, this theme comes from the Presence, Lord of poetry, Mir Muhammad Taqi Mir sahib; may God raise his station.' He folded his hands on his chest, and spoke in a carrying voice:

Comprehension? Sagacity? Keenness to see, to hear?
Wits, energy, strength? Well, all have departed.
You see, I was bound ultimately for the destination
Of death; so I sent my baggage ahead of me.

Silence all around for a few moments; then Navab Mustafa Khan Shefta commanded, 'Bhai, it's undoubted that Mir sahib has used this theme much before. But Mian Dagh has achieved a spontaneity, a flow, which make his verse extremely pleasing.'

'Your Honour,' Dagh rose to say, 'the interruption may be pardoned, but this servant does not at all remember when he had read these verses from the Lord of Poetry, or if he had read them at all.'

'Well, even if not plagiarism,' said the Maulavi sahib acidly, 'but there is doubtless a parallelism here.'

'Without doubt there has been parallelism here,' answered Dagh with a little, perhaps clever, smile. 'The servant is prepared to accept the charge of plagiarism even. But I will now recite two verses: one is by Mir Muhammad Taqi Mir sahib, Lord of Poetry, while the other is by Mir Muizzi, a Persian poet who was much before. Let the Maulavi sahib hear them and adjudicate who committed plagiarism, or was there a parallelism?'

Maulavi sahib rejoined with some heat, 'Let the discussion be confined to your own verses!'

Some voices from the audience: 'No, sir. Let's hear those other verses too.'

Dagh said, 'Very good, sir. I shall present the two verses.' He first spoke Mir Muizzi's Persian verse:

You say: there's unity between us;
Yes, you cruel one, say:
We believe!

After the applause was over, Dagh recited Mir Taqi's Hindi verse:

You say: there's unity between us;
Yes, sure. Do say:
We believe!

Silence again for a few moments. Then, someone said, 'If Muizzi is anterior, then our Mir sahib surely is guilty of plagiarism.'

The matter now fell into another realm: the history of Persian poetry. Some of the audience looked at Navab Mustafa Khan; some others looked at Maualvi Sahbai, who commanded, 'Amir-ul Shuara Mir Muizzi is of the Saljuqi period. Sultan Sanjar Saljuqi conferred upon him the title Amir-ul Shuara. He died in Hijri 520, that is, seven hundred years before Mir Muhammad Taqi Mir sahib who died in Hijri 1225.'

'Thus it should be a case of plagiarism by our Mir sahib,' came a voice from the audience.

'No, the theory of plagiarism and parallelism is quite complicated,' observed Sahbai. 'The great theorist Jurjani, of the fifth Hijri century, practically denies the possibility of plagiarism.'

'This humble one submits, sirs, that plagiarism or parallelism, it can happen with anyone,' said Dagh, who still stood in his place. He then quoted a famous line of the great Sadi:

It's a sin committed in your city too.

Sahbai said, 'Possibly, Mir sahib was translating from Muizzi. Translating or incorporating bits of others' poetry into yours is also recognized as art.'

'True,' said Navab Shefta, 'but as the Arabic proverb says: "He who came before, is superior."'

'Yes, sir. The servant accordingly accepts the superiority of poetry's Lord wholeheartedly and without reservation,' Dagh said, and bent low in salaam.

The event became a subject of discussion everywhere. The general opinion was that even if Dagh did plagiarize, he did it with great élan, and he had made a nice point in his counterargument.

67

Death in Delhi: Like a decayed tooth in the mouth of Time, extracted at the flimsiest excuse

TWO MORE YEARS passed; the most notable event during these years was Navab Mirza's marriage to Amat-ul Fatimah. Mirza Fathul Mulk Bahadur did not accompany the bridegroom's procession, but he was present when Dagh rode out to the city at the head of it, and on the following day, he welcomed the newly wedded young people into the Fort. Although it was Umdah Khanam who had borne the greater burden in Navab Mirza's upbringing, she expressed her solidarity with the elder sister by declaring that she was from the 'bride's side' and was active in all matters of the wedding from Akbari Khanam's house. Fatimah stayed in the Haveli for a few days; with everyone's agreement she then moved into Wazir's house at Khanam ka Bazaar. She was free to visit the Haveli as and when she liked. Likewise, Navab Mirza was free to visit Khanam ka Bazaar at his leisure, or pleasure. Rahat Afza and her husband, who had a baby now, consented to come help the new bride set up her domestic system, and live with Fatimah for a while. As the days passed, the much younger Fatimah found herself liking and admiring Rahat Afza more and more. Navab Mirza, of course, was Rahat Afza's old friend, and a surrogate brother to her.

The love between Mirza Fathul Mulk and Wazir Khanam grew with each day and night that passed. Khurshid Mirza was now crawling on all fours and almost walking with support. He tried to articulate words, and was able to manage some nearly comprehensible sounds. The parents confidently expected the boy to grow up into a fine, strapping young man, devoted to his parents and proficient in the arts and martial disciplines as became a Prince of the Realm. Wazir was quite persuaded in her heart that the happy days and nights were here for life. After losing so much, and suffering so much, she thought she was now at the stage of her life where she could speak in the tongue of the great Jalaluddin Rumi:

> *Man's Essence takes the sea and land,*
> *The pied ones: slaughtered on the Day of Offering!*

She could now confidently say that what she lost in days gone by was less than a trifle before the wealth that she had now. What had been taken away from her was no more than the pied ones she sacrificed.

*

A strong outcry arose one day: the Shadow of God was unwell. Although the indisposition of Kings and Rulers is kept most secret, this time the matter became evident very early on. For, the Emperor did not hold Court for two or three days consecutively; he was not visible even in his private meeting-chamber. Moreover, it was noticed that Hakim Ahsanullah Khan Bahadur was spending as many as eighteen to twenty hours in the Haveli every day. Now the rumour factory began to work overtime, and the hottest one was that Mirza Kayumars Bahadur, Second Heir Apparent, has had poison administered to His Majesty so that his royal road to the throne could become free of obstruction.

This did not seem at all probable, or even possible. For, Miran Shah Mirza Dara Bakht Bahadur, First Heir Apparent, was very much among the living—may Allah preserve him—and after the Refuge of the World would join with his Maker, the Throne and the Crown would naturally go to him and not to Mirza Kayumars, who was only the Second Heir Apparent. But just as the lie had no legs to stand upon, the rumour had a hundred mouths to propagate its falsehood. In his *Glimpses of the Exalted Fort*, Arsh Taimuri reports the rumoured details:

> The [Emperor's] offspring, Prince Kayumars Bahadur Heir Apparent, corrupted by bad company, and falling prey to greed, had a hair from the tiger's whiskers fed to the Emperor in a betel cone, hoping that he would get the Throne if his father died . . . Anyway, when the Presence's condition deteriorated alarmingly, the physicians began to give him emetics in large doses. The Emperor now began to throw up blood in such quantities that washbasin after washbasin filled up with his blood

> in no time. Finally, the whisker also came out with the blood. The matter was investigated . . . It was revealed that the deed was done by Prince Kayumars Bahadur. When the Presence, the Emperor, regained his health, he summoned Prince Kayumars, and had ready in front of him, a bowl full of poisoned drink. The self-willed Prince came, terrified, his head bent low. He salaamed and stood waiting for his father's command. The Emperor took the poison chalice in his hand, beckoned to the Prince, and commanded, 'Son, just as you fed me the tiger's hair, now you must perform the retribution. Drink this cup of poison, this very moment.'
>
> Mirza Kayumars folded his hands, wanted to say something, but the Emperor roared, 'Noxious wretch! Do you also wish to be unworthy of your ancestors?'
>
> With folded hands, Mirza Kayumars approached close to the Station of Audience, and said, 'Very good', and gulped down the poison chalice in one breath. Within a few moments, he fell at his father's feet, cold in death.

No doubt, the narrative is dramatic and powerful; but it has no truth at all. Arsh Taimuri was not a contemporary, and no contemporary source mentions the incident. Plainly, it could not have happened. Medically speaking, there is no toxicity in the tiger's whiskers, nor can they induce their swallower to vomit blood. If the event dates to before 1847, the First Heir Apparent Mirza Dara Bakht Bahadur and the Prime Minister Mirza Shah Rukh Bahadur were both alive at that time, so there were two princes between Mirza Kayumars and the Emperor. If the event occurred after January 1849 when Mirza Dara Bakht died, actions were already being taken by the Emperor to promote the case of Mirza Javan Bakht, and by Mirza Fakhru to urge his claim for being declared Heir to the Throne. There could thus be no opportunity for Mirza Kayumars to machinate for himself, if he was living at that time, that is.

It is true that His Majesty had, at one time, a severe and painful affliction of the stomach, but that was much later. Stomach ailments were common in those days; the English sahibs often fell to them. It is true that sometime in 1847, or thereabouts, Mirza Kayumars became a traveller on the Road to Nothingness. The exact date of his death is not known, but it is extremely probable that it occurred, suddenly, sometime in early 1847. Sudden deaths in those days often ignited the rumour of poisoning. A short while after his death, Mirza Shah Rukh Bahadur, Second Heir Apparent, also joined those whom the gods love. The date was April 1847.

These deaths did not create any kind of immediate crack in the Royal Administration: Mirza Dara Bakht Bahadur, First Heir Apparent, was among the living, in good health, and popular among the elites and commoners alike. Unfortunately, he too travelled on to the Land of Eternity, on 11 January 1849. A few days before his passing, he complained of common cold and was found to have low fever. His physician, diagnosing a 'phlegmatic' temperament, prescribed medicines for ejection of the phlegm. Within a matter of two days, he developed a high fever, causing oedema of the lungs—pneumonia in modern parlance—leading to loss of consciousness. Having been ill for just four days, he died on the evening of 11 January, mourned by His Majesty and the entire Fort. There was no Court for three days and the sounds of weeping and lamentation kept crashing against the Haveli's ramparts for many more days. The shocked and grief-stricken Emperor composed a Persian chronogram to record the date:

The Heir Apparent, called Dara Bakht,
When he departed this mean world,
The souls of the people became scarred with grief;
The year of his death became The Soul's Grief.
1265=1849

The Flower Ceremony was held on the third day—a Hindu custom adopted by the Mughals—prayers were recited, then flowers on small trays were circulated and distributed among those present. Small sweets, made of pure white sugar, fashioned like a five-pointed star—called 'ilaichi danas' ('cardamom seeds') for some reason—were placed before the mourners. The First Affirmation of Faith was recited seventy thousand times over each ilaichi dana. The sweets were then distributed among those present after a prayer had been said to the effect that the merit of the recitations may go to the deceased. Food, garments and shawls were given away in charity in the name of the deceased, on whom be God's Mercy.

After the ceremony, His Majesty returned to his private apartment. To the sons, daughters, sons-in-law and daughters-in-law, he bestowed new shawls to be worn to mark the end of the three days of mourning. To the wives of the deceased, he bestowed widows' weeds. Loud noises of wailing and lamentation echoed through the Palace. His Majesty also wept, and said to the women, 'Amma, do not weep. Have the patience to endure your loss. None can dare breathe a sigh against the Divine Will.'

Prayers were again said on the ninth, nineteenth and the fortieth days. A new ceremonial sheet of flowers and silk was placed on the dead Prince's grave. Special pellets of sweets, called ilaichi danas, were distributed among all to signal the Conclusion of mourning.

If there was one person not grieving for Mirza Dara Bakht, it was Zinat Mahal. In her eyes, the quick removal of three major thorns from her son's path to succession was a clear signal of approval from the Almighty to her ambition. She immediately redoubled her efforts to have Javan Bakht proclaimed First Heir Apparent. She pressured His Majesty even more than before; she also commenced efforts to soften up the senior officials of the Company, especially Thomas Metcalfe Grand Sahib Bahadur, and his assistant Simon Fraser Sahib Bahadur, bombarding them with costly presents and forceful petitions. She also made numerous visits to the tombs of all the important Sufis and men of God buried in Delhi, and appealed to them to intercede on her son's behalf. She vowed, with the saint's soul as witness, that if her prayer was granted, she would perform specified good deeds, like feeding a certain number of the poor, presenting a costly silk and flower sheet for his grave, so forth.

There were two thoughts that were foremost in the Emperor's brain at that time: the astrologers had been predicting for many years now that there would be no King after Bahadur Shah Secondus. Further, even if the Firangee agreed to proclaim Javan Bakht First Heir Apparent, and later perhaps King even, Javan Bakht possessed no means to repay the Royal debt. Whereas Mirza Fakhru asserted on numerous occasions that when he would become First Heir Apparent, he would clear off the entire Royal debt even if he was obliged to sell himself to do so.

The Firangee Sahib Bahadur, on his side, was busy making his devious moves. It was clear to the Court at Calcutta that it was a unique opportunity to erase forever the Mughal Kingship, and to blow away the smoke of sovereignty from the heads of the Timurid clan. Largely ignoring the Emperor (Zinat Mahal did not count for much anyway), the Firangee thus opened direct negotiations with Mirza Fathul Mulk Bahadur. In fact, if credence be given to the (essentially unreliable) narrative of Arsh Taimuri,

Mirza Khurshid Alam informed him that his father, Mirza Fathul Mulk Bahadur, had begun talking to the English for his succession even before Mirza Dara Bakht became a traveller to the Land of Eternity. While this does not seem probable, there can be no doubt that Fathul Mulk Bahadur had begun conversations with the English, and after everything was wrapped up in his favour, he sent no less than three petitions to the Protector of the Caliphate in one single day—3 September 1852—protesting his loyalty to him and promising, in the event of being appointed First Heir Apparent, his everlasting slavery and subservience to the King whose Glory was like the Sky. In the second petition, the Prince promised to pay off the entire Royal debt. In the third petition, he promised never to go against the wishes of Navab Zinat Mahal and affirmed that all her privileges and those of Mirza Javan Bakht would continue as before.

It is probable that the Emperor, once he got wind of the agreement between Fathul Mulk Bahadur and the English, had put moral pressure on Fathul Mulk Bahadur to write those petitions as declarations of his loyalty and good faith to the Emperor and his two most favourite people in the world.

There are indications that the English, immediately after having been given news of the death of the First Heir Apparent, had decided unilaterally to make Mirza Fathul Mulk the First Heir Apparent, and to abolish the institution of King and Empire after the death of Abu Zafar Muhammad Sirajuddin Bahadur Shah II. They approved Mirza Fathul Mulk's candidature after many years of tortuous conversations. It was but a pyrrhic victory for the Prince: There would be no Kingship after the death of the Presence, Dispenser of Destinies, the True Mentor and Guide; the Haveli would be vacated; all signs and symbols of Mughal Sovereignty and Autonomy would be erased forever. There would be no Ceremonial Elephant Canopy, no Insignia of the Fish, no Ceremonial Drum. Coins had long before ceased being struck in the name of the Emperor. The Royal mints at Allahabad and Gwalior minted coins from the dies cut in the days of Shah Alam II. They were legal tender, but coins struck by the John Company were more and more in circulation. The Company Bahadur struck coins in the King's name at the Royal mints in Arcot, Surat and Murshidabad. This was discontinued in 1835 when the English King's name and effigy began to appear on the coins. Queen Victoria appeared on the John Company's coins in 1840.

All that remained of the Sign of Sovereignty throughout the land of

Hind, and much of the Deccan too, was the mention of the King's name, and prayers for his security in the formal oration before the Friday Prayer, performed at the Chief Mosque and all prominent mosques in a city or town. The John Company decided that since there would be no King, there could be no mention of the King, or any prayer for his well-being. Mirza Fakhru would be recognized as Head of the Timurid Clan, but he must live somewhere in village Mehrauli, building his own house there. He would accord chairs of equality to the Navab Governor General Bahadur and the Navab Lieutenant Governor Bahadur of the Northeastern Province. He would be paid no compensation for his vacating of the Haveli.

On 3 September 1852, Mirza Fakhru was installed as Heir Apparent with the titles of Sahib-e Alam wa Alamiyan, Son of the Mentor of all the World, Mirza Muhammad Sultan Ghulam Fakhruddin Fathul Mulk Shah Bahadur, may his Train and his Fortune remain forever. There were no celebrations in any quarter. Fathul Mulk Bahadur was sad that he became the extinguisher of the lamp of the Royalty of the Progeny of Chaghata. But, he consoled himself, now the Kingship was only in name anyway; its survival or non-survival was immaterial. Its life, or lifelessness, made no difference. I at least saved the name of my House.

The apartment of Zinat Mahal presented a scene of desolation and inconsolable mourning. The Queen of the Age was cursing Metcalfe sahib aloud, both hands raised towards heaven in dramatic exhortation. She was crying out aloud that the Grand Sahib Bahadur shall surely be punished for his dishonesty and injustice. Some say that she declared, 'Grand Sahib Bahadur and his Lady will both be compelled to take poison and will die vomiting blood.' She promptly had a petition prepared and dispatched to the Most Superior Queen Victoria, demanding justice. But there was none there to open the door to her petition. Dwellers in the Fort and people in the city were generally pleased for Mirza Fathul Mulk Bahadur being appointed Heir Apparent. He was a gentle Prince, of spotless character, learned, and truly deserving of the honour.

It was only a few months after Mirza Fathul Mulk Bahadur had been declared Heir Apparent that Thomas Metcalfe, Grand Sahib Bahadur, complained of cramps in the stomach. Convulsions of the stomach muscles, vomiting, loose motions and constant low fever quickly weakened him, laying him quite low. The English physicians having all failed, recourse was taken of the Graeco-Islamic practitioners of medicine, then of the

Ayurvedic practitioners, and finally even sorcerers and exorcists. Instead of receding, his illness intensified, almost by the hour. Metcalfe declared again and again that he had been poisoned, and would not survive. English physicians, Mussulman adepts in preparing charms and amulets, sorcerers and all kinds of yogis declared with equal certainty that His Honour had not been poisoned, in body or in spirit. Metcalfe was not convinced; and how could he be convinced? Much of what he swallowed by way of medication or food was being rejected by his system through vomit and expectoration.

Now this was a God-granted opportunity for the rumour manufacturers of Delhi. The most popular version was that Zinat Mahal, Queen of the Age, had had the Grand Sahib Bahadur poisoned, for she was highly displeased with him for depriving her son of the Heir Apparentship. The Emperor himself repeatedly issued formal denials, but who could really withsay the rumour when the Grand Sahib Bahadur himself affirmed that he had been poisoned?

Thomas Metcalfe Sahib Bahadur stated that he could not recover so long as he was breathing the poisoned, dust-laden air of Delhi. He demanded that he be taken to the hills; away from Delhi, there would also be no opportunity for his enemies to poison him. In accordance with his command, the entire staff of the Residency, his private attendants, much of his office and officials left for Simla in raths, ox carts and palanquins. Up to Ambala, it was the Sher Shahi highway, broad and well maintained. Soon after, they encountered narrow, potholed roads. The ascent to the hills began soon after; the narrow road became circuitous and in fact dangerous for the sick man. They persisted for another day before some of the advance runners returned with the report of a landslide a few miles ahead, snows all around on the upper slopes, and heavy forestry beyond. The road ahead, if not impassable, was certainly very hard. Senior members of Metcalfe's party did not want to risk his health and life further, and the whole train backtracked to Delhi, arriving there towards the end of October 1853, amid Metcalfe's repeated declarations that he was a victim of poisoning. His weight diminished, and dehydration increased day after day.

Finally, on 3 November 1853, exactly fourteen months after the proclamation of Mirza Fakhru as Heir Apparent, His Majesty's Specially Devoted Servant, Noble and Illustrious Son of the Sultanate, Muazzam-ud Daulah Amin-ul Mulk Ikhtisas Yar Khan Thomas Theophilus Metcalfe Firoze Jang Sahib Bahadur, Agent to Navab Governor General Bahadur and Plenipotentiary in Matters concerning the Government of the Pivot of Prosperity and Power, the English Company Bahadur, and Commissioner Sahib Bahadur of the Capital Region of Shahjahanabad and Delhi, submitted his soul to the Creator of Souls. He was buried the next day in the graveyard attached to Sikandar sahib's Church. It was the same graveyard where, eighteen years ago, the remains of William Fraser Sahib Bahadur had been consigned to dust:

I saw someone at the portal
Of the legendary King Faridun,
He rattled the door chain, and called:
Is there anybody there?

Reports still circulate in English circles that Metcalfe was poisoned, and that Navab Zinat Mahal had caused it. No investigation into the matter was made by the Exalted Porte of Navab Governor General Sahib Bahadur in Calcutta. Nor is there any comment or information on the matter in the Company's papers.

*

The English New Year dawned. The dwellers of the Fort, particularly His Majesty, the Dispenser of Destinies, Mirza Fathul Mulk Bahadur and Wazir Khanam, all hoped and prayed that the days that were now left to them would pass peacefully, with no new shocks. But before the year ended, the Sultan of the Poets, Khaqani-e Hind Shaikh Muhammad Ibrahim Zauq, His Majesty's mentor in poetry, departed to reside in the House of Permanent Residence, on 16 November 1854. On 14 May 1852, Hakim Momin Khan Momin, another of Delhi's master poets, had already left for the Court of the Hakim of Absolute Power. Now Delhi had only Mirza Asadullah Khan Ghalib to boast of, as the memorial of the ustads of the past and as the bulbul of a thousand songs singing in the garden of Persian and Rekhta poetry, who prevailed over all others in the field.

After the rank of Mentor in poetry to the Presence was bestowed upon Mirza Ghalib from the Threshold of the Caliphate, Mirza Fathul Mulk Shah Bahadur also enlisted himself as Ghalib's pupil. Yet, although Mirza Ghalib's eye of favour and approval continued to be on Dagh as before, the latter did not somehow choose to enter the circle of Mirza Ghalib's pupils. It is possible that he believed that his mother would still not like him to become formally close to Ghalib. Or perhaps the brilliant instruction of Zauq had made him perfect in all respects and he did not feel the necessity of another ustad. Dagh's relations with Ghalib remained pleasant and friendly, and in fact he was of some service to Ghalib in matters relating to his pension: From 1855, Ghalib drew a pension from the State of Rampur where Dagh had some influence on account of his Manjhli Khala whose fortunes in Rampur continued to be bright.

On 1 April 1855, Navab Muhammad Said Khan Bahadur, Ruler of Rampur, afflicted by pleurisy, became a traveller to Paradise. His Heir Apparent, Navab Yusuf Ali Khan Bahadur enhanced the glory of the Navabi Chair. In view of the relations between the new Navab and Umdah Khanam, some friends suggested to Navab Mirza that he should move to Rampur. But Dagh did not like to leave his mother's shade and the connection with Fathul Mulk Bahadur, and that was what Wazir desired, though she took care not to articulate her desire before Navab Mirza. She hoped that like Khurshid Mirza, her other son and daughter-in-law should live in Delhi, the city of security and peace. Navab Mirza got along quite well with his older half-brother, Mirza Abu Bakr Bahadur. Mirza Khurshid Alam was just nudging ten; Shah Muhammad Agha was in his fifteenth year. Though they were half- or stepbrothers, there was complete unity and friendship among them, as if they were full brothers. Mirza Abu Bakr was not interested in poetry, but Shah Muhammad Agha's temperament was getting practice and polish in Delhi's air, so favourable to literature. He adopted the pen name Shaiq, but was more interested in Persian than Rekhta; perhaps this was the influence of his Iranian origins. Mirza Khurshid also adopted the pen name Khurshid and began to do a bit of practice in poetry. Mirza Fathul Mulk Bahadur observed to Wazir that it was surely her influence that the sons born to her were poets; by himself, he surely could not have produced an offspring who wrote poetry. Wazir answered, 'May Allah keep you secure with your miraculous temperament; you are more than any poets that I could give birth to.' But Mirza Fathul Mulk Bahadur sometimes thought sadly: would that I was plain Ghulam Fakhruddin.

Reports of the implacable Firangee intransigence and appropriation of Indian states kept coming from all over. The direst event of 1856 occurred almost at the very beginning of the year. Firangee troops entered Lucknow on 7 February 1856, and the King of Avadh was forcibly transported to Allahabad, then Calcutta under armed guard. The hapless King described his suffering and humiliation en route in his long narrative poem Huzn-e Akhtar (Akhtar's Sorrows). The Firangee issued a Blue Book containing the English account of what was described as the misgovernment, incompetence and heartlessness of the King, thus justifying their patently unwarranted military intervention and deposition of him. The King replied by preparing a detailed refutation of all the accusations against his Government. This answer to the Blue Book was published in Persian, English and Hindi, and also transmitted to London via the King's embassy. However, the King's answer and his embassy achieved nothing.

Reverberations of the events in Avadh reached Delhi soon, causing shock and consternation. Before Avadh, the Firangee had dispossessed the nineteen-year-old Rani Lakshmi Bai of her State of Jhansi when her husband died childless. The Shadow of God was much perturbed at these events, especially the ouster of the King of Avadh, for the Royalty there was the offspring of Delhi's own nobles who had separated from Delhi's hegemony in the eighteenth century. Lucknow's rulers initially described themselves as Navab Wazir and they accepted titles from the Imperial Court; they offered the nazr to the Emperor on appropriate occasions and observed all protocols in dealing with the princes from Delhi. The English, in 1819, granted the status of King to the ruler of Avadh. Delhi always believed that the rival kingdom was an artificial construct. Relatives of the Emperor, who settled in Lucknow for one reason or the other, were paid their monthly stipend from Delhi's Royal Treasury and were regarded as Delhi's subjects, even if in name.

The loss of Avadh was politically and emotionally shocking; viewing the rape of Lucknow as a part of the pattern seen all over India, the Emperor expressed his grief and unhappiness with the political decline of India in a verse about Tipu Sultan of Mysore where the Sultanate of Mysore became a symbol of India's disintegration:

Zafar, what faith should I repose in my strength,
In my fortitude?
Did the army of Hindustan keep faith
With Tipu?

By saying Hindustan, a term not always used for the far south, the Shadow of God was clearly speaking of a larger, wider reality. Some idea can be had of the shock caused by the events in Avadh to the people of Delhi in a letter that Mirza Ghalib wrote a couple of weeks after the termination of the Kingdom of Avadh. He wrote to a friend, Qadr Bilgrami, on 23 February 1856:

> The destruction of the State of Avadh saddened my heart too, though I have nothing to do with Avadh. In fact, I hold most cruel and unjust those of Hind who were not saddened. Allah, it is Allah everywhere now.

The summer of 1856 was unusually hot in Delhi. Delhi was normally spared the torment of the hot, dry westerly winds, known as lu, which blow on most of north India for anything up to twelve hours a day. Somehow, it was not the case in 1856: strong, westerly winds, more like whirlwinds dancing the terrible Tandav dance of Shiva, Lord of Annihilation, invaded Delhi from Rajputana and eastern Haryana every day through the month of May and the first half of June. From Alipur to Delhi Gate, scores of women, children, labourers and domestic maids fell victim to sunstroke and died in great pain. The palms of their hands and the soles of their feet burning as if rubbed in live coals, a thirst that burned fiercely and yet more fiercely when the patient drank water: what little water there was in the wells or in the river Jamna which were dry and sandy for miles. The dehydrated body soon developed high fever, sometimes followed by delirium tremens. Some people died because, nearly insane with thirst, they quaffed a large quantity of water without waiting for the body to cool. Since the inner organism had become incapable of handling such massive and sudden demand to treat and absorb the water, the intake caused the patient to vomit copiously and fall into a coma from which recovery was a rare event.

Then the rains descended on the parched city in the second fortnight of June. The river rose, and rose, until it began to play and scoff at the walls of Emperor Humayun's tomb and the shrine of Hazrat Nizamuddin. The low-lying villages between Delhi Gate and Hazrat Nizamuddin were swept off the map. But then, the harsh sun came out again, though without the hot, westerly wind. Hundreds of homes, weakened by the rains and the flood, now dried too fast, and cracked and collapsed. The hot week or ten days were followed by another rainy invasion. Wood, earth, mud, uprooted trees, dead bodies of cattle, all began to rot and decompose, producing not only an evil, intolerable smell, but also hazards from pollution on the surface and contamination of water under it. Cholera, the scourge of the hot, wet, muggy weather, took the city like another horde of the Mongols.

Officials of the Company Bahadur began quickly to evacuate the city, going to safer places as much as they could afford and dare. The rich practically locked themselves in. The poor, left to their own devices, and failing to obtain relief by traditional methods, began to die. Sanitation workers became scarce, then practically non-existent. There was no one to clear the backed-up drainage, to remove the rotting bodies and carcasses, and to clean the open or closed latrines. Shahjahanabad, built on high ground, was safe from the flood, but not from the rains. Almost the entire city built by the English, or their subordinates and camp followers, was on a low ground to the north. Soon, cholera infected nearly half the population of the city, and not just Shahjahanabad.

On the morning of the 9th of July 1856, Sahib-e Alam wa Alamiyan, son of the Guide to the World, Mirza Fathul Mulk Bahadur complained of queasiness which soon developed into nausea, vomiting and low-grade fever. He also complained of a slight feeling of emptiness in the stomach, as if he had not eaten for some time. His personal physician, Hakim Muhammad Naqi Khan, was summoned at once. He diagnosed, looking at the bilious temperament of the patient, his general weakness and the feeling of emptiness in his stomach, that it was nothing but an onrush of bile. He prescribed light food and plain soup, and took his leave, assuring all that the Prince would be better soon. Shortly after being given the prescribed foods, the Prince began to retch, and he ejected all that he had been fed. The vomiting continued for an hour; the patient then seemed to have lapsed into a coma, or he had fainted due to debility. Hakim Ahsanullah Khan was consulted in the evening. He examined the patient carefully and diagnosed blockage of the large intestine, for which he prescribed a warm enema. This was to no visible effect; the Prince turned to his other side, and his coma became a deep unconsciousness. All efforts to revive him failed. By about six o'clock in the morning, he died, without regaining consciousness.

The whole of the Haveli shook with shock and lamentation and loud cries of amazement and consternation. Everybody was bewildered; people, as they wept, also cried out aloud, 'What happened? How did it happen?'

The rumour manufactory went into overdrive as soon as the Prince became unconscious. The main story was that Zinat Mahal had bribed Hakim Muhammad Naqi Khan to poison the Prince. The secondary story was that His Majesty, not satisfied with the current treatment, had summoned the English doctor to come and diagnose and prescribe. But the rumours were false, as rumours almost always are. The eighty-one-year-old Emperor had not the strength of will, or body, to treat the illness as the result of a conspiracy.

There is no doubt that the symptoms of the Heir Apparent's illness had almost nothing in common with those of cholera. Yet there is no evidence, not even a whiff of whisper in any of the reliable accounts, that Fathul Mulk Bahadur died an unnatural death. True, cholera works in many ways, and the city was undoubtedly stricken with it at that time. Wazir stared intensely at everyone, like one not in her senses, and whispered urgently, 'Please feel his pulse again. My Sahib-e Alam is unconscious. He is not dead.' Zinat Mahal was the only one laughing. She cried out gleefully, 'There! He is down! No one can now stop my son from being the Heir Apparent!'

When His Majesty felt slightly capable of dealing with mundane affairs, he sent condolences to Wazir through his personal maid. To the appropriate officials, he gave the command for organizing the burial. The weather was hot and humid; it was desirable not to delay the burial. Immediate steps were taken to prepare the body and have the grave dug in accordance with the Emperor's instructions. Wazir was beating her head, writhing and collapsing on the floor as she wept. Mirza Abu Bakr, Navab Mirza and Khurshid Mirza, in trying to console and quieten her, fell to weeping again and yet again. Although she was the dispossessed wife, and regarded Wazir as an interloper, Hatim Zamani Begam came into Wazir's apartment, weeping, her hair untied. She tried to console Wazir and went round the dead husband's body seven times in a symbolic gesture of being willing to give her life for his. Some of those present thought that it was too late for such gestures, empty of content as they were.

Akbari Khanam, Maulavi Muhammad Nazir and Shah Muhammad Agha arrived from the city; Maulavi Muhammad Nazir, despite his dignified deportment and deeply religious nature, was unable to stop his tears when he saw Wazir's deteriorated condition. He and Shah Muhammad Agha joined many others in the men's apartment in reading or reciting from the Quran. Akbari Khanam hugged Wazir, kissed her many times on her forehead, and said, 'Bibi, have patience. You must have patience. None can withstand the Will of the Almighty.'

As Bari hugged Wazir, trying to support her to the bed, Wazir fainted and was unconscious while her Sahib-e Alam was washed, shrouded with full ceremony and honour, even as Habiba and others tried to bring her back to consciousness by sprinkling rose water on her face and holding medicinal herbs under her nose. The four sons placed the Prince in the coffin, then helped place the coffin in a nalki.

Munshi Faizuddin, in his *Bazm-e Akhir*, describes the Heir Apparent's funeral:

> Blue silk in brocade was draped over the nalki. Sons, nephews, the chief nobles, handkerchief hiding their mouth and half their face, shedding copious tears, walked with the nalki, overwhelmed by grief. The bystanders found their hearts shaken to the core; they felt as if their hearts were going to leave their bodies. In front, the cavalry of the Emperor's vanguard with their guns reversed, the large and small drums held upside down; behind them, the elephants, loaded with milk-and-saffron bread and coins of various denominations, which were to be given in charity; the whole city had come flooding to watch the funeral procession; men, women weeping loudly and long. The cortege arrived at the Jama Masjid; the nalki with the coffin was placed near the ablution pond at the centre of the courtyard. Thousands of people gathered there. The funeral prayer was done; then the nalki proceeded for burial outside the city, only the chief mourners accompanying. The burial took place in the shrine of Khvajah Qutb Sahib, in Mehrauli. Coins of small and large denominations were distributed to the poor. Cash presents were made to the attendants of the shrine. Prayer for the dead was offered; a shawl was draped around the grave. A hafiz was appointed to recite the Quran; a guard was appointed to guard the grave. Everybody departed. The Emperor commanded the usual post-funeral food to be sent [to the house of mourning].

Sahib-e Alam wa Alamiyan, son of the Guide to the World, Mirza Muhammad Sultan Ghulam Fakhruddin Fathul Mulk Shah Bahadur was buried on the evening of 10 July 1856, in Khvajah Qutb sahib's shrine, close to the grave of Shah Alam Bahadur Shah I. Navab Mirza Khan Dagh composed a chronogram in Persian:

The grief for Sultan Fathul Mulk was an
Affliction of the soul; so the Bountiful
Forgiver gave him a place in Paradise.
When the afflicted heart inquired about
The year of his death, Dagh drew
A sigh of pain two hundred and twelve times.

212 x 6 = 1272 = 1856

While not brilliant, it was a fairly competent chronogram: The word for 'sigh' is 'ah' and its numerical value is 6; multiply it with 212 and you get 1272, the date when Mirza Fakhru departed for the Eternal World.

68

The Queen of the Age commands Wazir Khanam to her Court

ZINAT MAHAL LOST no time, after the fortieth-day mourning ceremonies and the official mourning at the Court came to an end, in putting pressure on His Majesty to initiate formal communication with the Honourable Company Bahadur on the matter of Javan Bakht being proclaimed the Heir Apparent. His Majesty was not very keen on the idea, partly because he was too old to open new fronts, partly because he was not in the best of health and spirits, and partly because he was convinced that there would be no King in the Haveli after him. In fact, the deal struck by the Company Bahadur with Fathul Mulk Bahadur had left no room for doubt on this score. On the other hand, his love for Zinat Mahal would not let him ignore the question.

It must be recorded that Zinat Mahal did love the Emperor in her own way, and her love for him was not just a function of the formal tie of marriage, or fuelled by selfish motives. Sixteen years ago, when she learnt that she was being married to the Emperor, whose glory rivalled that of the legendary Jamshed, she felt a thrill, which was more mental than physical: was it not truly sensational, her being married to the greatest personage in the whole of the land? But she also felt irked, if not disappointed: her husband-to-be was the King, but in name alone, and was just about to conclude the seventh decade of his life. What pleasures of the world or of the body could she then expect from him? But when she saw the pomp and splendour of life at the Fort, and the gentle, loving, sophisticated conduct of the King towards her, and above all, when she found her husband capable of doing his marital duty with complete success and even élan and flair, her heart gradually softened towards him. In due course, the soft corner became the site of love for her graceful and dignified husband. Thus the equation between the Emperor and Zinat Mahal was not just that of a husband in his dotage being constantly encroached upon by irresponsible youth and beauty. There was genuine love there; it was thus impossible for the Emperor to ignore the demand of his favourite wife.

After full consideration, the Presence of the Exalted Dignity had an Imperial Missive dispatched to the Resident. Simon Fraser temporarily held the station. Simon Fraser was on friendly terms with the Emperor, mainly because as the Heir Apparent he had remained neutral during the notorious arrest, trial and, finally, execution of Dilawar-ul Mulk Navab Shamsuddin Ahmad Khan. Not only that, he had advised his father, the Paradise-residing Emperor Akbar Shah II, to take no position on the matter. Thus the Shadow of God felt no discomfort in sending his representative to Simon Fraser with the proposal about Javan Bakht.

The communications that the Emperor sent to the Governor General about Mirza Javan Bakht placed particular stress on his distinguished pedigree, and also that he was highly educated and knew many languages. On her side, Zinat Mahal, or perhaps also Javan Bakht, had a paper signed by many of the princes to the effect that they were agreed on Javan Bakht being declared the Heir Apparent. Two of the Emperor's sons, Mirza Quvaish Bahadur and Mirza Zahiruddin Bahadur, popularly known as Mirza Mughal, did not sign the paper, declaring that their right to succeed was better than that of Javan Bakht. But the decision had already been taken where it mattered: The Company Bahadur was determined to abolish both Empire and Emperor after Bahadur Shah Zafar. The agreement signed with Mirza Fathul Mulk Bahadur was a first step towards it.

The Company Bahadur took no notice of the papers sent by the Emperor or by the princes in support of Mirza Javan Bakht. The Imperial communications and the petitions submitted by the princes were received at the Residency, but were forwarded, not to the Governor General, but to the Lieutenant Governor Bahadur at Agra, where they were deposited in the Records Room.

The Emperor fixed the date for the fortieth-day mourning ceremonies for Mirza Fathul Mulk Bahadur. Notices, written on white paper, were distributed to everybody in the Fort. The Chief Architect broke open a corner of the grave—an earthen mound up until then—and poured small quantities of rose water, keora water and attar into it. He then had masonry work done on it, and designed and constructed a tombstone in white marble; a miniature grave in marble, called 'tawiz' was made and placed on top; he designed and constructed a low trelliswork in marble around the grave. Finally, he had the area immediately around the grave paved in white marble, thus completing the work of the tomb.

On the thirty-ninth night after the Prince's passing, all the close relatives assembled at the dead Prince's Haveli. On the exact spot where the son of the whole World's Guide breathed his last, the following things were placed: large platters full of food; a complete outfit of new clothes; a shawl; a prayer mat; a set of rosary beads; a new pair of shoes; a comb; a neem twig, to be used as toothbrush. These were in seven large trays. Further, there was a full dinner service in china and copper; spoons and other silverware; a silver tray; a large tablecloth for covering the food trays; a water pot for ablutions; a washbasin. Two large, red and green candles, each burning 1¼ maunds (approximately 105 pounds) of refined lard and wax, stood at the head of the dead Prince's bed where they burned all night long as the air in the chamber, heavy with the smoke of bdellium sticks and frankincense, echoed with lamentations and sobs. In the morning, all the male relatives took their noble presence to the grave on which a canopy in brocade was strung on four silver pillars. Now a heavy curtain of flowers was erected around the noble grave on testers. The grave itself was then covered with a grave-cover in brocade; on the cover were placed strings of flowers to look like another smaller sheet over the brocade. The food, the dinner service, and other items were placed at the head of the grave; the shoes were placed at the foot. The men then vacated the area; screens were erected for the ladies of the zenana who came weeping, their hair undone. They wept and wailed. In the men's area, the last prayer of mourning was performed; handfuls of ilaichi danas were distributed to all present. Qavvalis were sung, followed by food for all, especially for the poor. In the third part of the day, the last prayer of mourning was offered for a second time. The food trays, the food that they contained, the clothes and all other items were then distributed among the attendants of Khvajah sahib's holy shrine. All the princes and begams then returned to the Exalted Fort.

Wazir's eyes were swollen due to constant weeping. Since the time her Sahib-e Alam breathed his last, she hadn't slept on a bed; nor had she eaten two square meals a day. It was now her wont to sleep on the floor and sparingly eat some coarse food only one time a day. While the Son of the Mentor of all the World lived, she had been so happy, so lost in his love that in spite of her title of Shaukat Mahal, she had rarely taken part in the activities and ceremonies at the Fort. The only exception she had made was when Mirza Muhammad Dara Bakht Bahadur, First Heir Apparent, died. She was present while he was being prepared for the grave, then at the second day's mourning, the third day's mourning, and on to the sixth month's mourning.

It must be an irony of fate that she felt curiously happy and content to see how elaborate those ceremonies were, and the genuine emotional outbursts of love and grief in the Fort and even outside the Fort for the departed Prince. Among other things, these formal and heartfelt displays were for her the expression of the solidarity that the community of numerous individualistic persons at the Fort felt for each other. She had always sought permanence and continuity; and she had always wanted to live as the desired one, rather than as the desirer who, at least in the literary culture of the Indo-Islamic world, was always fated to die unsung, without attaining her desire. She seemed to have found both in the Auspicious Haveli: permanence and the status of the truly desired one.

It therefore afforded her a kind of happiness, if that is the word, to see the long, elaborate, ceremonial, and emotion-and-convention-charged rites and rituals for the Prince whose life and death did not really matter to anyone except his near and dear ones.

*

On the third day after the fortieth-day mourning ceremonies, Wazir was informed that the Queen of the Age was remembering her, and she must immediately present herself at her Court. Wazir suspected that there was something the matter, for she had never been summoned thus by the Queen of the Age. Perhaps she desired to condole with her, Wazir tried to persuade herself. In fact, ever since the appointment of her Sahib-e Alam as the Heir Apparent, Navab Zinat Mahal had scarcely spoken a word to Wazir or her children, including Mirza Abu Bakr. Perhaps she feels a moiety of grief for me now, Wazir tried to reassure herself. She splashed a little water on her face, combed her hair with her fingers, put on a plain, white outfit in cotton, and proceeded alone to Navab Zinat Mahal's haveli. She was received with plain, cold courtesy and seated in front of the Queen. After a few moments' silence, the Exalted Queen stated, 'Chhoti Begam, we are sad at your widowhood.' She paused. Wazir was about to say a few words of gratefulness, but Navab Zinat Mahal resumed quickly: 'But you are quite used to such dire happenings, are you not? You will weather this one too. A woman who has had many men is stout of heart, they say.'

Some of the favourites among the Queen's companions pretended to hide their smirks by pulling a corner of their upper wrap on to their mouths. But some others bore expressions which revealed their discomfort. Wazir clearly saw that the intent behind these insulting words was to provoke her into saying something impertinent, or do something disrespectful, which could be used against her. She kept her head down, and said meekly, 'Queen of the Age, it is said that sleep overtakes man even on the gallows. However hard and dire the incident, even of death, one has to bear it somehow. I always do no more than pray before God for your and the Shadow of God's continued prosperity, health and long life and elevation of fortune. The shade of you two Patrons is more than enough for me.'

Zinat Mahal, not expecting a reply of such rectitude, was silent for a few moments. Then she changed tack. 'How much did the Heir Apparent leave you, Chhoti Begam?'

Now Wazir raised her head and spoke with her back and neck erect, looking the Queen in the face. 'The status and state of the Heir Apparent Bahadur is clearer before you and the Shadow of God than before me.'

'You will have to vacate his apartments.'

'Perhaps the Queen of the Age forgets. I am not just Chhoti Begam, I am Shaukat Mahal as well.'

'You were Shaukat Mahal,' Zinat Mahal enunciated every word with brutal stress. 'Now you are not.'

'That is for Him to decide Who conferred the title.'

'Chhoti Begam, don't suffer under any delusions. You seduced our guileless and gentle Mirza Fakhru Bahadur to gain a footing in the Royal Fort. You hoped that you would thus be counted a Princess of the House of Timur. Then, by the greatest good luck, the poor cat got to swallow the canary. And you, instead of being content with being the wife of the Third Heir Apparent, began getting drunk on the possibility of becoming the Queen of Hindustan. Women like you have chewed up marble palaces to dust. But remember, there is something like the Almighty's Power . . .'

Wazir, unable to keep herself in check, now broke protocol and interrupted the Queen in a low but firm voice. 'The circumstances in which I arrived into the Fort are fully clear to the Queen of the World. I cannot equal even the dust under the feet of my Sahib-e Alam wa Alamiyan. I was somehow getting through my widow's life in my dark dungeon. It was he who raised me from the earth to the sky.'

'Yes, but now he who raised you from the earth to the sky is himself under the dust,' Zinat Mahal said cuttingly. 'Now you are again the valueless dust mote that you were before you arrived here.'

'But, Your Exalted Honour.' Wazir did not raise her voice, but her sarcasm could not have been lost on anyone there, 'I will always be known as the widow of the First Heir Apparent of Hindustan. Let there be Heirs Apparent, let there be Kings after me, but none can remove that canopy from over my insignificant head.'

'Why not?' Zinat Mahal retorted hotly. 'We can, and we will!'

'Queen of the Age, you may have proclamations made over the drum by the criers within your Exalted Fort, but you cannot muffle the voice of the people, which is the Voice of the God's Crier,' Wazir said gravely and stiffly. 'But please command, what service do you desire from your maid? She is fully ready and prepared.'

'It's not just a matter of our Fort. We are still the Queen of Hindustan. On our head shines the diadem that adorned the heads of Nur Jahan and Arjumand Bano. The fact that our dear son Mirza Fakhru turned his face away from this world is a divine signal. Allah does not desire that some alien should inherit the Throne and the Crown after him.'

'Let the Crown and the Throne be yours forever. I am not interested in such things.'

'But it has been reported to us that you and Mirza Mughal are conspiring for Mirza Mughal to be King, and Khurshid Mirza proclaimed as the Heir Apparent.'

Wazir was shocked. She tried not to let it show, but she could feel that she had lost colour. Clearly, there was a conspiracy against her and against Fathul Mulk Bahadur's offspring. Or perhaps someone who hated her had fed Zinat Mahal's ears with false tales? The cause mattered little; the result was the same anyway. She drew a deep sigh, tried to control her breathing and slacken her heart rate. She spoke deferentially but in a clear, unwavering voice, 'Exalted Queen, shouldn't you have given thought to a simple fact? What assistance or aid could Mirza Mughal Bahadur get in such an immense project from a weak and useless widow like me? Then, what chance could my poor son Khurshid Mirza have when Mirza Abu Bakr Bahadur is among us? May God preserve him.'

'These are exactly your machinations, we are informed. Poor and motherless, Mirza Abu Bakr is now fatherless too. You are plotting to seduce the guileless boy somehow or the other into acquiescing to your scheme.'

'May Allah preserve him; Mirza Abu Bakr is a young man of ability. He is strong-minded, and well educated.'

'Chhoti Begam, we don't need you to extol our children in our presence. I am fully sensible of the qualities of Mirza Abu Bakr. But his close friendship with Mirza Mughal is no secret.'

'Your Honour has the power, and the last word, but I should be permitted to present my case before the Mahabali, to prove to him my innocence.'

'All is apparent before the Luminous Presence. It is his decision that you must vacate the Haveli within two days,' Zinat Mahal spoke with cold finality. 'You may take Khurshid Mirza with you, and also Mirza Abu Bakr, should he so desire.'

Once again, Wazir was stunned. She had not expected Zinat Mahal to dismiss her so cheaply and so suddenly. The worst that she had expected was that she would be asked to vacate the Third Heir Apparent's Haveli and go into some narrow, airless rooms as suited her position as an alien widow; Navab Mirza would lose his allowance, and her own allowance would be reduced; Khurshid Mirza's education, being imparted to him as to any Prince of the Realm, would cease. But not even in her worst nightmares did she imagine expulsion from the Haveli.

For the first time in many years, perhaps in her whole life, Wazir found herself at a loss for words, unable to process the news of the new calamity, which was upon her like Doomsday. It was clear that she must not oppose or struggle against Zinat Mahal so long as the Queen held over her the threat of successfully accusing her of conspiring against her or the Emperor. In fact, her resistance could make matters worse for her. It was impossible to gain admittance to the Emperor's Court; but even if she could do so, it was she, alien, widow, with a history behind her, posited against Zinat Mahal, the Mahabali's most favourite person, including even Hakim Ahsanullah Khan and Chief Eunuch Mahbub Ali Khan. So she had very small chance of success and every chance of humiliation, and defeat. His Majesty might not quite be a lump of wet clay in the Queen's hands, but he was past the age of eighty. He was by no means senile, but preferred to leave matters inside the Haveli to Zinat Mahal. He lacked the physical and mental energy to deal with such matters. It was futile to expect him to restitch what Zinat Mahal had torn.

A few seconds' quiet consideration was sufficient for her to say what she now said, 'I place the Exalted Queen's command on my eyes and my head. But I must remind her of the Day when no King or Authority shall have the power to command. There will only be God and the Scales of His Justice. If you know your Quran, you must recall the Almighty's pronouncement: "On that day, Command will be Allah's Prerogative alone." Allah knows the innermost states and secrets of the hearts. This maid does not know who sowed the seeds of poison in the Exalted Queen's heart against me. But I know the state of my heart and say that there is nothing but love and respect for my blessed departed Sahib-e Alam, for my King, the Shadow of God, and the Queen of the Age.'

'That is all as may be,' Zinat Mahal smiled a dry, somewhat triumphant smile. 'But the commands of the Shadow of God must be implemented without delay.'

'Very well, that's how it will be,' Wazir said as she rose from her place. She did not request permission to rise or to await her dismissal from the Presence. 'I never disappointed the Queen in the past, and I am not going to start now. If there is no space for us under your prosperous shadow, we will go to another habitation and there we shall claim our portion from God. The People belong to God, and so does the Land. I make my submissions.'

Instead of walking backwards from Zinat Mahal's presence, Wazir turned her back to her and headed out of Zinat Mahal's haveli, outwardly strong but inwardly shattered. By the time she had walked the distance to her own haveli, she found herself tottering, with black dots dancing before her eyes. She felt dizzy, worn of heart and lame of spirit. As she entered her room, she was no longer able to hold herself straight and fell onto her bed like a bough snapped off from its tree.

Quite by chance, the three sons were there in the haveli, two of them playing chess, and Khurshid Mirza, the youngest, advising both his older siblings. The three abandoned everything and crowded around their mother with cries of 'Amma Jan, is all well? How are you feeling?' But Wazir's jaw was clenched, her face pale and her eyes shut. Mirza Abu Bakr immediately dispatched a staff-bearer to summon Hakim Muhammad Naqi Khan. Habiba and others sprinkled rose water on her face, placed smelling salts under her nose and gently chafed the soles of her feet, fanning her with a herbal fan. Wazir had regained consciousness by the time the hakim arrived. Her face was still pale and devoid of expression, like a death mask. The hakim examined her pulse from behind the purdah, examined her fingernails and concluded that there was no systemic failure: it was just shock and grief. He prescribed some mood elevators, had a dose of a special medicine of his own creation given to her in his presence, advised full bed rest for three days, and left after assuring everyone that there was nothing to worry about.

The three sons were extremely indignant and upset when they heard the whole story from Wazir. Navab Mirza and Khurshid Mirza declared heatedly that they would shake the dust of the Haveli from the hems of their garments and the soles of their shoes and leave the Fort just that minute with their mother. Amma Jan should go where she wills. We are with her. If nothing else, she still has the house in Chandni Chowk. We are quite prepared to follow her to any jungle, any desert. We will hew wood, eat wild fruits, but will not set our eyes on the Fort again.

Mirza Abu Bakr took a more sober view. 'Ama, don't do anything in haste,' he said. 'I'll go to the nishast right now and look for Hakim Ahsanullah Khan. I will talk to him and make him intercede with the Shadow of God. He will not easily reject the advice of Hakim Ahsanullah Khan.'

'Sahib-e Alam, please give some more thought to the matter.' Wazir clutched Mirza Abu Bakr's sleeve earnestly. 'Even if the Chief Quartermaster consents to take the matter in hand—though I doubt it—and Navab Zinat Mahal is obliged to eat her words, how long is this going to last? You think she is ever going to give up? And the Satan of Conspiracy that she has concocted, or about whose existence some others have persuaded her, will keep raising its ugly head. Our lives will become even more hellish than now.'

'So what is it that you desire, Amma Jan?' Mirza Abu Bakr was a trifle waspish. 'We should let her do what she wills, without let or hindrance?'

'Sahib-e Alam, it's not at all like letting her have her wish unhindered. She *can* do what she wishes, unhindered. Is she not the favourite Begam of the Luminous Presence? You know that Navab Zinat Mahal has harboured malice against your late blessed father from the day your father—may Allah give him Paradise—became the First Heir Apparent and her own designs were foiled. Now my first priority is to protect my children from harm and hardship.'

Mirza Abu Bakr fell into thought, then said, 'Should I not at least consult with Uncle Mirza Mughal in this matter?'

'Why should you, Sahib-e Alam? Is she not already burning red hot with envy about him and Mirza Quvaish Bahadur? Why should we involve Mirza Mughal Bahadur in another matter now?'

Mirza Abu Bakr was a little peeved. 'Should you not fight for your right?'

'What is "my right", Sahib-e Alam?' Wazir smiled a bitter, grim smile. 'Have I been looking for anything other than "my right" all my life? Perhaps it can be found dwelling in underground caves of the mountains. It was never seen under the skies.'

Mirza Abu Bakr was silenced and somewhat intimidated. It was the first time that he had seen such vehemence and bitterness in Wazir's words. He was wondering how he should proceed with his theme when Navab Mirza spoke, 'Sahib-e Alam, if you would, please consider my suggestion: You should come out with us. It seems to me that the Auspicious Fort is not going to be auspicious and secure for much longer now.' His words mirrored the anxiety and stress on his face, and it was not just his mother for whom he feared.

'What do you mean, Navab Mirza? Why should I quit the Fort?' Mirza Abu Bakr and Navab Mirza were practically the same age—twenty-five—and were quite free and friendly with each other. Mirza Abu Bakr seemed to cool down a bit, but then he bent close to Navab Mirza and spoke in a low but measured tone: 'We, that is I and Mirza Mughal Bahadur and some others, are thinking . . . Well, we feel that should an opportune moment come, these Firangee Kristans should be thrown out of our land!'

Navab Mirza found himself ambivalent, and worried. He thought for quite a while as everybody else looked at him and Mirza Abu Bakr with wary eyes. Then he said, 'Brother, it is true that there is some unrest among the subjects, and especially among the Company's native soldiery, against the Nazarene Rulers. To the east, in Lucknow, there is someone called Maulavi Ahmadullah Shah who is reputed to be a true man of God, a Sufi in fact. He is commonly known as Danka Pir (The Mentor with Drums) because drumbeaters precede him wherever he goes. He openly tells the people that the Firangee is a sworn enemy of the dharma of the Hindu and of the True Path of the Muslim. He says that both Hindus and Muslims will be destroyed and effaced from the surface of the earth if the Firangee continues here. But I think . . . I wonder . . . can a single champion win a whole war?'

'It is just that kind of thinking, brother, which has deprived us of the will to act!' Mirza Abu Bakr retorted acidly.

Navab Mirza smiled somewhat defensively. 'Sahib-e Alam, you are the offspring of Zahiruddin Muhammad Babur. He came out, in the teeth of the world's opposition and conquered Bukhara. He was barely sixteen then. Soon, he and a handful of self-sacrificing men took Kabul, then the land of Hind from Kabul to the briny water. But it must be clear before your brilliant temperament that according to Imam Abu Hanifa, rebellion against a tyrant is permissible only when there is a chance of success.'

Mirza Abu Bakr snorted. 'Rebellion is miles away yet, dear brother Navab Mirza. But did you not yourself say that there is great discontent among the subjects?'

'True. But Brother Zahiruddin Husain told me that according to his father-in-law, there would be clash of swords and unthinkable slaughter in the city. Brother Zahiruddin Husain asked him, "Is the army of the land of Rus [Russia] about to come?" He replied, "That is known to God."'

'Please, do not speak about swords and guns,' Wazir entreated. 'God knows who is listening and what construction he may put on it. I want to know just this: I would be very happy for Mirza Abu Bakr Bahadur to come with us. But he is used to the Royal way of life, and we . . .'

'Pardon my interruption, Amma Jan, but it is not a matter of the Royal way of life. It is a question of principle, and of inheritance. My home is here in the Haveli. And the Haveli is not the property of Navab Zinat Mahal. So why should *I* go out from here?'

'Sahib-e Alam, I fear there is danger for you here.' Wazir looked at him with pleading eyes. 'And now what Raqim-ud Daulah sahib has told Navab Mirza makes matters even more disquieting.'

'Raqim-ud Daulah sahib was in fact telling me,' said Navab Mirza, 'that a majzub who is ever absorbed in God had told him, "Hey, what are you doing here, wasting your time in Delhi? You are a worldly man, go and travel in the states!"'

'Ama Navab Mirza!' Mirza Abu Bakr cried out, clearly at the end of the tether of his patience. 'I did not know that you and Raqim-ud Daulah are a pair of superstitious old women! Anyway, let the matter rest here, and I will do the same.'

Wazir could not do more to persuade the haughty young Prince to leave the Fort. She did not know that the danger to him was not within the Fort, but outside of it. The Grim Reaper had chosen him for himself. The great armed tumult against the English that was to arise within a few months, and the series of bloody conflicts that were to ensue during and after the siege of Delhi were to see both Mirza Mughal and Mirza Abu Bakr battling it out against the English. After the taking of Delhi by the English, both uncle and nephew were to be disarmed and shot dead by a junior officer of the Company Bahadur. Death had fettered the Prince's feet. He could not have left the Haveli even if he had wanted to.

'The Queen of the Age has indicated that I cannot take away from the Haveli anything which your blessed late father the Sahib-e Alam wa Alamiyan may have bestowed upon me or my children,' Wazir said in a firm voice; she was now recovering her strength of mind. 'You, Navab Mirza and Khurshid Mirza, will please organize bullock carts, labourers and foot workers today. We will leave here tomorrow after having all our property inventoried in the presence of Navab Nazir Mahbub Ali Khan. We will have the loading of our baggage on the bullock carts supervised by Navab Nazir and leave the Fort well before nightfall tomorrow.'

'But where should we go?' asked Khurshid Mirza.

Wazir thought for a while. 'I have the house in Chandni Chowk, so we will go there for the time being. But I am no longer inclined to stay in Delhi. I will decide after consulting with Bari Baji.'

'May I submit something?' Navab Mirza said in a tentative voice.

'Yes, sure. If there is any other suggestion in your mind, let us have it,' said Mirza Abu Bakr.

'Madam, I mean to say . . . Rampur could be an option; there is Manhjli Khala Jan there. We shall be quite safe in Rampur.' Perhaps Navab Mirza gave more credence to Raqim-ud Daulah than he was letting on.

Everyone fell silent, lost in thought. The thought of leaving Delhi was like sandpaper on their hearts.

'All right,' Wazir said. 'I should first speak to Manjhli Baji. And what about the house here if we should go to Rampur?'

Mirza Abu Bakr replied promptly, 'No, you mustn't give it up. I will arrange for it to be taken care of when you go away.'

*

The next day, after the sunset prayers, a short train appeared at the Lahori Gate of the Auspicious Fort. Wazir rode in a palanquin; a large bullock cart contained her total effects with Habib-un Nisa in it to keep guard. To the right and left of the palanquin rode Navab Mirza Khan and Prince Khurshid Mirza, their heads held high and their backs erect. The soldiers at the guardhouse made a gesture for them to stop, but they rode on, unheeding. They scattered fistfuls of silver and copper coins as they passed, their faces set, as if in stone. With her head bent and her body fully wrapped in a chador behind the palanquin's heavy drapery, Wazir Khanam could see nothing.

ACKNOWLEDGEMENTS

IT MAY NOT perhaps be necessary to say that the author of a book like *The Mirror of Beauty* has his shoulders bent with the debt of thankfulness to numerous writers, friends and kind strangers who contributed something or the other that went into the book in its original shape, or was digested into something different but essentially the same.

It is not possible to give even an abridged list of the books which I read, not necessarily with the view of using their contents for the novel, and in fact even long before the idea of this novel came into existence. The process was that of imbibing and absorbing matters of literature, politics, history and culture over a lifetime; much of my work over the last four decades is essentially a function of the love that I have for that literature and culture, some of the glimpses of which can perhaps be seen in this book. It is a history and literary culture that is sadly not accessible—that is even non-existent—for most of us today.

Under the circumstances, I think I could do worse than listing out the names of friends and family who made concrete contribution to the making of this book in some way or the other.

Afghanullah, late professor of Urdu at the University of Gorakhpur, whose untimely death I shall always deplore, who gifted me a copy of the rare first edition of Zahir Dihlavi's autobiography.

The outstanding modern poet and my dear friend Ahmad Mushtaq, now of Houston, Texas, one of whose lines of verse I appropriated as title for the Urdu and the Hindi versions of this novel.

Famous Urdu fiction writer and critic Asif Farrukhi, who never tired of reminding me to finish the Urdu version of the novel as soon as possible, and who published it from Scheherazade, his publishing house in Karachi.

Senior Pakistani scholar, essayist and poet of great renown, Aslam Farrukhi, who provided important information about Salim Jafar.

My younger daughter Baran Farooqi of the Department of English at Jamia Millia University, New Delhi, who read substantial portions of the Urdu manuscript and in fact made me rewrite the first fifty or so pages. She also read a couple of chapters of the Urdu as textual lessons with her older daughter Naisan Fatimah. Baran and her older sibling Mehr are the two who should also bear the most responsibility for leading me into the temptation of preparing the English version.

Bashir Unwan of Mirpur Khas, Pakistan, who provided much useful information about Salim Jafar and corrected my errors about his biography; Karan Singh of Mirpur Khas, Pakistan, who provided valuable information and corrected my errors about Salim Jafar.

Distinguished historian and my friend William Dalrymple, from whose conversations I gained much. I must also thank him for sending me pages from the extremely rare *First Impressions* by Thomas Bacon which gave a first-hand account of Shamsuddin Ahmad Khan's hanging.

Jamila, who read a substantial portion of the Urdu, made helpful comments, and provided information about fabrics and jewellery; it was in her incomparable singing voice that I first heard the nauha recited in the presence of Yahya Badgami; she also furnished copies of many old nauhas about the marriage ceremonies of Qasim, son of Imam Husain, at Karbala. As usual, she took the greatest care of me. Wife, caregiver and friend, she made life easy for me and never complained against my sometimes too-long hours composing the novel. That she did not live to see the Hindi and the English versions will be one of my everlasting regrets.

The award-winning modern Urdu poet and painter, and my friend, Jayant Parmar of Ahmedabad, who gave me valuable information about the Sidis of Gujarat and let me have a copy of one of their zikrs.

My young friend Kranti Kumar Shukla, Hindi writer and political activist, who went over the Hindi version (published by Penguin in 2010) with me, word by word and from cover to cover, and gave incomparable assistance in perfecting it.

Well-known Hindi critic, and my friend, Krishna Mohan of Banaras Hindu University gave valuable advice and even read the last proof of the Hindi version.

Dastan reciter, historian, film-maker, Rhodes Scholar and much else besides, my nephew Mahmood Farooqui introduced the Urdu version to Ravi Singh and was often my intermediary with Ravi Singh and Chiki Sarkar.

My older daughter Mehr Farooqi of the University of Charlottesville, Virginia, who read much of the initial Urdu draft, made suggestions, and most importantly, kept at me for doing the English version.

Prominent Urdu fiction writer and critic Mubin Mirza, to whom an apology is owed as well. I promised to let him publish the Urdu version from his publishing house, Academy Bazyaft, Karachi, but in a fit of absent-mindedness, I made the same promise to Asif. Mubin Mirza graciously withdrew.

Naimur Rahman Farooqi, my younger brother and major historian of medieval India, for letting me in on many obscure details of history.

Noted Urdu–Hindi translator and journalist Naresh Nadeem, for preparing the Hindi translation of the original Urdu in nearly record time.

Nasim Ahmad, Professor of Urdu at Banaras Hindu University, who researched the old Gazetteers of Rajasthan and ascertained the correct name and spelling of Colonel Alves.

Urdu's major fiction writer Naiyer Masud, major modern Urdu poet Irfan Siddiqi, noted bibliophile Aslam Mahmud, my dear friends all, who never forgot to inquire on the phone or in person whenever we met, about the progress of the Urdu manuscript. It's a pity that Irfan could not live to see its publication.

My long-time friend, collaborator and informal pupil Frances Pritchett of Columbia University, who read the entire English version and cleaned up my English and made valuable suggestions about the art of translation.

My cousin Qazi Nurus Salam, of Kanpur, who never had the smallest doubt about my successfully completing the Urdu version, and now its English avatar. He was quite certain that the novel would succeed. The Urdu and the Hindi ones did succeed, to a very large measure. One can have similar hopes about the current version, going by his assurances.

Ravi Singh, my first Publisher at Penguin Books India, New Delhi, and Naved Akbar, my first editor and an enthusiastic and informed reader. The support that I had from Ravi throughout the preparation and production of the Urdu and the Hindi versions was incredible. Chiki Sarkar, my present Publisher at Penguin, has been a model Chief Editor, Publisher and promoter, and a sympathetic listener. My current English editor R. Sivapriya is the kind of editor that most authors dream for, but rarely get. This novel owes much to her. Over the months and years that we have worked together, we have developed a kind of symbiosis: she and I have felt and imagined the novel as existing in a common universe created by both of us. For the stunning cover design, its idea and execution, I must thank Gavin Morris, Art Director at Penguin. I don't know who discovered that human-angelic beauty, the mysterious avatar of Wazir Khanam, who goes by the (equally heart-catching) name of Arshya Chhabra Singh (I've never met her), but I think I owe thanks, again, to Chiki Sarkar for finding the appropriate dress and jewellery for her. And I must thank Briana Blasko for photographing Arshya in the most imaginative of poses: uncoy, aware and utterly self-sufficient, something like one of the many woman-portraits whose verbal descriptions adorn (I hope), the text of the novel. I am glad that Arshya appears on the covers of all the three ensuing versions of the book—Urdu, Hindi and English. Total and comprehensive thanks again to Gavin and his team for getting up the ensemble.

Not liking to risk an overlong paragraph, I insert a break here to thank my editors, Shanuj V.C., Ambar Sahil Chatterjee, Renu Agal and Reyazul Haque. I always believed that copy editors must hate the texts which they have to spruce up with the greatest of pains, picking even the most infinitesimal nits. But Shanuj tells me that he has actually enjoyed working on this book; wonders will never cease, as someone said. Renu and Reyaz were prompt to prepare and publish the new Urdu and Hindi editions. Then I have Alankrita Shrivastava and Priyanka Sabharwal to thank for their efforts to make the book known everywhere, and especially among the circles that count.

Riyaz Ahmad Katib, for the Urdu page-making and correction of typos, and Amin Akhtar for managing my paper files and generally assisting me cheerfully.

My friend, and modern Urdu poet Shafaq Sopori, of Kashmir, who provided valuable information about talim, and let me have a page of an antique talim.

My friend, and modern Urdu writer Syed Irshad Haidar, of Allahabad, who spared no pains in proofreading the Urdu version.

Tanveer Aijaz, of Ahmedabad, Urdu poet and English journalist, who furnished essential information about the Sidi Said Mosque of Ahmedabad.

At Yatra Books, my thanks go to Neeta Gupta and Namita Gokhale who played major and helpful roles in the production of the Urdu and the Hindi versions.

My friend Zulfaqar Ahmad Tabish, Pakistani poet and painter of great renown, who made a beautiful painting for the cover; it was used by Asif Farrukhi for his Urdu editions (2006, 2011) and by Penguin for their first Urdu edition (2006).

A NOTE ON THE TYPE

DANTE WAS FIRST created as a metal typefont in the mid-1950s the result of a collaboration between printer, book designer and typeface artist Giovanni Mardersteig and Charles Malin, one of the great punch-cutters of the twentieth century. The two worked closely to develop an elegant typeface that was distinctive, legible and attractive. Special care was taken with the design of the serifs and top curves of the lowercase to create a subtle horizontal stress, which helps the eye move smoothly across the page.